THE FAR PAVILIONS

Unforgettable in the fire of its pomp and pageantry, jealousy and treachery, bloody battle and forbidden passion—a story that haunts like a dream, and helps us remember just what it is we want most from a novel.

JULI • A princess pledged to live and die for the royal husband she never loved—a woman daring to risk her life for even an hour in the arms of her English-born lover.

ASH • A son of England and the Himalayas, who valiantly gave his heart to both as the blazing events of a quarter century tore East and West apart and threatened to tear him from Juli—forever.

THE FAR PAVILIONS

"PULSATING, HEARTBREAKING . . .
A narrative thoroughbred sired by *Shōgun,* out of *The Thorn Birds* . . . Other than *Gone With the Wind,* I can think of no other historical novel with such stunning narrative tempo."
—**Philadelphia Inquirer**

"PEOPLED WITH VITALLY REALIZED CHARACTERS . . .
The immense scope of *The Far Pavilions* makes it an enthralling book."
—**Wall Street Journal**

"A GLEAMING TAPESTRY . . .
Historic drama interwoven with high romance . . . gives the reader a sense of being caught up in the fabric of another time, with the bonus of having an informed insider's viewpoint . . . This novel, with its unabashed vigor, has genuine power."
—**Washington Post Book World**

THE FAR PAVILIONS

"THIS NOVEL PRESENTS A WORLD . . .
A world of brilliant color and dark shadows, a world of valor and treachery, a world of good and evil . . . You will miss a tremendous experience if you fail to read it. This is a colossal novel, not just in length but in breadth and depth. It is one of the true Big Ones."

—**Cleveland Plain Dealer**

"A SPLENDID ACHIEVEMENT—that rare and desirable combination of storytelling and totally absorbing research . . . One of the finest novels I have read in years."

—**Helen Van Slyke**

"FABULOUS, ENCHANTING, ACTION-PACKED . . .
Like Scheherezade's tales of a thousand and one nights, one wishes it would never end . . . filled with beauty, horror, sorrow and great excitement."

—**St. Louis Post-Dispatch**

Home Box Office Premiere Films Presents
a Geoffrey Reeve Production for Goldcrest Ltd.

THE FAR PAVILIONS starring
Ben Cross   Amy Irving   John Gielgud
Omar Sharif   Rossano Brazzi   and   Christopher Lee

Director of Photography
Jack Cardiff

Written by
Julian Bond

Based on the novel by M. M. Kaye

Directed by Peter Duffell

Produced by Geoffrey Reeve

Executive Producer
John Peverall

THE FAR PAVILIONS

M. M. KAYE

BANTAM BOOKS
TORONTO • NEW YORK • LONDON • SYDNEY • AUCKLAND

*This edition contains the complete text
of the original hardcover edition.*
NOT ONE WORD HAS BEEN OMITTED.

THE FAR PAVILIONS
*A Bantam Book / published by arrangement with
St. Martin's Press, Inc.*

PRINTING HISTORY
St. Martin's edition published July 1978
Literary Guild of America edition published October 1978
Doubleday Book Club edition published March 1979
Serialized in Good Housekeeping *magazine, July 1979*
Bantam edition / August 1979

2nd printing .... August 1979	8th printing ... October 1980
3rd printing .... August 1979	9th printing .. February 1981
4th printing .. September 1979	10th printing .... April 1982
5th printing ... October 1979	11th printing .... March 1983
6th printing ... November 1979	12th printing .... March 1984
7th printing ... February 1980	13th printing ... August 1988

Cover photographs by David James.

Plan of Kabul Residency drawn by Reginald Piggott.

Map drawn by David Perry.

ISBN 0-553-27735-9

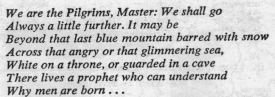

We are the Pilgrims, Master: We shall go
Always a little further. It may be
Beyond that last blue mountain barred with snow
Across that angry or that glimmering sea,
White on a throne, or guarded in a cave
There lives a prophet who can understand
Why men are born . . .

JAMES ELROY FLECKER

T'is not too late to seek a newer world.

TENNYSON

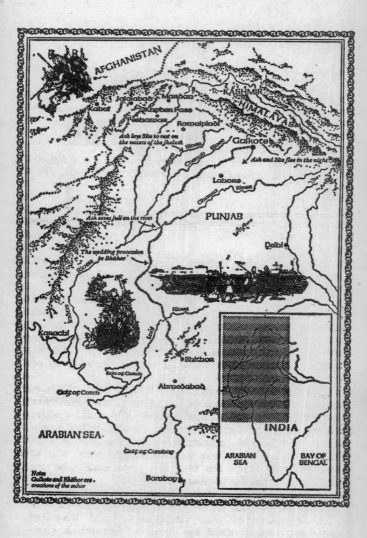

AFGHANISTAN

KASHMIR

HIMALAYAS

Kabul Jalalabad Mardan

Khyber Pass

Peshawar Rawalpindi

Gulkote

Ash lays Sita to rest on
the waters of the Jhelum

Jhelum River

Chenab River

Ash and Sita flee in the night

Ash saves Juli on the river

Lahore

Ravee River

PUNJAB

Delhi

The wedding procession
to Bhithor

Indus River

Ravee River

Luni River

Karachi

Rann of Cutch

Bhithor

Gulf of Cutch

Ahmedabad

ARABIAN SEA

Gulf of Cambay

Bombay

INDIA

ARABIAN
SEA

BAY OF
BENGAL

Note:
Gulkote and Bhithor are
creations of the author

BOOK ONE

The Twig is Bent

1

Ashton Hilary Akbar Pelham-Martyn was born in a camp near the crest of a pass in the Himalayas, and subsequently christened in a patent canvas bucket.

His first cry competed manfully with the snarling call of a leopard on the hillside below, and his first breath had been a lungful of the cold air that blew down from the far rampart of the mountains, bringing with it a clean scent of snow and pine-needles to thin the reek of hot lamp-oil, the smell of blood and sweat, and the pungent odour of pack-ponies.

Isobel had shivered as the icy draught lifted the tent-flap and swayed the flame in the smoke-grimed hurricane lamp, and listening to her son's lusty cries had said weakly: "He doesn't sound like a premature baby, does he? I suppose I—I must have—miscalculated . . ."

She had: and it was a miscalculation that was to cost her dear. There are few of us, after all, who are called upon to pay for such errors with our lives.

By the standards of the day, which were those of Victoria and her Albert, Isobel Ashton was held to be a shockingly unconventional young woman, and there had been a number of raised eyebrows and censorious com-

1

ments when she had arrived in the cantonment of Peshawar, on the North-West Frontier of India, in the year of the Great Exhibition, orphaned, unmarried and twenty-one, with the avowed intention of keeping house for her only remaining relative, her bachelor brother William, who had recently been appointed to the newly raised Corps of Guides.

The eyebrows had risen even further when a year later she had married Professor Hilary Pelham-Martyn, the well-known linguist, ethnologist and botanist, and departed with him on a leisurely, planless exploration of the plains and foothills of Hindustan, unaccompanied by so much as a single female attendant.

Hilary was middle-aged and eccentric, and no one—least of all himself—was ever able to decide why he should suddenly have elected to marry a portionless, though admittedly pretty girl, less than half his age and quite unacquainted with the East; or, having remained a bachelor for so many years, married at all. Isobel's reasons, in the opinion of Peshawar society, were more easily explained: Hilary was rich enough to live as he pleased, and his published works had already made his name known in scholarly circles throughout the civilized world. Miss Ashton, they decided, had done very well for herself.

But Isobel had not married for the sake of money or ambition. Despite her forthright manner she was both impetuous and intensely romantic, and Hilary's mode of life struck her as being the very epitome of Romance. What could be more entrancing than a carefree nomadic existence camping, moving, exploring strange places and the ruins of forgotten empires, sleeping under canvas or the open sky, and giving no thought to the conventions and restriction of the modern world? There was also another, and perhaps more compelling consideration: the need to escape from an intolerable situation.

It had been frustrating in the extreme to arrive unheralded in India only to discover that her brother, far from being pleased to see her, was not only appalled by the prospect of having his sister on his hands, but quite incapable of offering her so much as a roof over her head. The Guides at that time were almost continuously in action against the Frontier tribes and seldom able to live peaceably in their cantonment at Mardan, and both William and the Regiment had been dismayed by Isobel's arrival. Between them they had managed to arrange temporary accommodation for her in the house of a Colonel and Mrs. Pemberthy in Peshawar. But this had not been a success.

The Pemberthys were well-meaning but unbearably dull. Moreover, they had made no secret of their disapproval of Miss Ashton's conduct in travelling to the East, unchaperoned, and had done their best by advice and example to erase the unfortunate impression created by her arrival. Isobel soon discovered that she was expected to behave with stultifying decorum. She must not do this and it was inadvisable to do that . . . That list of prohibitions seemed endless.

Edith Pemberthy took no interest in the country where she and her husband had spent the greater part of their lives, and looked upon its people as uncivilized heathens who by the exercise of patience and strictness might be trained to become admirable servants. She could not conceive of there being any real communication with them on any level, and could neither understand nor sympathize with Isobel's eagerness to explore the bazaars and the native city, to ride out into the open country that stretched south of the Indus and the Kabul River or northward to the wild hills of the Khyber.

"There is nothing to see," said Mrs. Pemberthy, "and the tribesmen are murderous savages—entirely untrustworthy." Her husband had fully endorsed this view, and eight months under their roof began to feel like eight years to poor Isobel.

She had made no friends, for unfortunately the ladies of the garrison, discussing her over the tea cups, had decided that Miss Ashton was "fast" and that the most likely motive for her journey to India was the desire to snare herself a husband. A verdict that from constant repetition came to be generally accepted by the station's bachelors, who, much as they might admire her looks, her unaffected manners and her excellent seat on a horse, had no wish to figure as gullible victims of a husband-hunter, and consequently fought shy of her. It is therefore hardly surprising that Isobel should have been heartily sick of Peshawar by the time Professor Pelham-Martyn appeared in the station, accompanied by his long-time friend and travelling companion Sirdar Bahadur Akbar Khan, a motley crew of servants and camp-followers, and four

3

locked *yakdans* containing botanical specimens, the manuscript of a treatise on the origins of Sanskrit and a detailed report, in code, of a variety of official, semi-official and unofficial happenings in the dominions of the East India Company . . .

Hilary Pelham-Martyn bore a strong resemblance to that amiable and equally eccentric gentleman, the late Mr. Ashton, and Isobel had adored her father. Possibly this may have had something to do with her immediate interest in the Professor, and the comfortable feeling of security and ease that his company gave her. Everything about him—his mode of life, his intense interest in India and its people, his grizzled, crippled friend Akbar Khan, and his total disregard of the rules that governed the conduct and outlook of such people as the Pemberthys—appealed strongly to Isobel. Paradoxically, he represented both escape and safety, and she had embarked on matrimony as buoyantly, and with as little regard as to the hazreds of the future, as she had embarked on the S.S. *Gordon Castle* at Tilbury for the long voyage to India. And this time she had not been disappointed.

Hilary, it is true, treated her more as a favourite daughter than a wife, but this was pleasantly familiar and provided a comfortable leavening of stability and continuity to the haphazard camp life that was to be her portion for the next two years. And, having never previously fallen in love, she had no yardstick by which to measure the affection she felt for her vague, easy-going and unconventional husband, and was as completely content as any human being has a right to be. Hilary permitted her to ride astride, and for two happy years they travelled up and down India, exploring the foothills of the Himalayas and following the Emperor Akbar's road to Kashmir, and returning to spend the winters in the plains among the ruined tombs and palaces of lost cities. For most of that time Isobel had been without any feminine companionship and had not felt the lack of it. There were always books to read or Hilary's botanical specimens to be pressed and catalogued, and she would occupy her evenings with these while her husband and Akbar Khan played chess or argued hotly on involved questions of politics, religion, predestination and race.

Sirdar Bahadur Akbar Khan was a grizzled, crippled ex-officer of a famous cavalry regiment, who had been

4

wounded at the Battle of Mianee and had retired to his ancestral acres on the banks of the Ravi River to spend the remainder of his days in such peaceful pursuits as cultivation and the study of the Koran. The two men had met when Hilary was camping near Akbar Khan's home village, and had taken an instant liking to each other. They were, in many ways, very similar in character and outlook, and Akbar Khan had become restless and dissatisfied at the prospect of remaining in one place until he died.

"I am an old man, wifeless now; and childless too, for my sons are dead in the service of the Company and my daughter is married. What is there to keep me? Let us travel together," said Akbar Khan. "A tent is better than the four walls of a house to one who has had his day."

They had travelled together ever since and become boon companions. But it had not taken Akbar Khan long to discover that his friend's interest in botany, ruins and the dialects of the country provided an admirable cover for another activity: the compiling of reports on the administration of the East India Company, for the benefit of certain members of Her Majesty's Government who had reason to suspect that all was not as well with India as official sources would have them believe. It was work of which Akbar Khan approved, and to which he had given invaluable assistance, as his knowledge of his fellow countrymen enabled him to weigh the worth of verbal evidence with more accuracy than Hilary. Between them, over the years, they had compiled and sent home folio after folio of fact and warning, much of which was published in the British press and used in debate in both Houses of Parliament—though for all the good it did they might as well have confined themselves to botany, for the public, it seemed, preferred to believe that which disturbed it least and to ignore troublesome information. Which is a failing common to all nations.

The Professor and his friend had worked and travelled together for five years when Hilary unexpectedly added a wife to the caravan, and Akbar Khan had accepted her presence with a placid matter-of-factness that recognized her place in the scheme of things, without considering it particularly important one way or another. He had been the only one of the three who was not disagreeably surprised by the discovery that Isobel was pregnant.

5

It was, after all, the duty of women to produce children, and of course it must be a son.

"We will make him an officer of the Guides, like his uncle," said Akbar Khan, brooding over the chess board, "or the Governor of a Province."

Isobel, like most of her generation, was abysmally ignorant of the processes of birth. She had not discovered her state for some considerable time and then had been startled and more than a little annoyed—it had never occurred to her to be frightened. A baby was going to be a distinct complication in the camp; it would need constant attention, and a nurse and special food and . . . Really, it was too annoying.

Hilary, equally surprised, suggested hopefully that she might be mistaken as to her condition, but being assured she was not, inquired when the child would be born. Isobel had no idea, but she attempted to cast her mind back over the past few months, and having counted on her fingers, frowned and counted again, she ventured an opinion that proved to be wholly inaccurate.

"We'd better make for Peshawar," decided Hilary. "There'll be a doctor there. And other women. I suppose it will be all right if we get there a month ahead? Better make it six weeks to be on the safe side."

Which is how his son came to be born in the middle of nowhere and without the aid of doctor, nurse or such medicines as science possessed.

Apart from one or two sweeper's wives and several veiled and anonymous female relatives of the camp-followers, there was only one other woman in the camp who could be called upon to help: Sita, wife of Hilary's head syce (groom) Daya Ram, a hill-woman from Kangan way who had doubly disgraced herself by bearing and losing five daughters in the past five years—the last of whom had died the previous week, having lived less than three days.

"It seems she cannot bear sons," said Daya Ram disgustedly. "But the gods know she should at least have come by enough knowledge to help one into the world."

So it was poor, shy, bereaved Sita, the groom's wife, who had acted as midwife at Isobel's lying-in. And she had indeed known enough to bring a man-child into the world.

It was not her fault that Isobel died. It was the wind that killed Isobel: that cold wind off the far, high snows beyond the passes. It stirred up the dust and the dead pine-needles and sent them swirling through the tent where the lamp guttered to the draught, and there was dirt in that dust: germs and infection and uncleanness from the camp outside, and from other camps. Dirt that would not have been found in a bedroom in Peshawar cantonment, with an English doctor to care for the young mother.

Three days later a passing missionary, trekking across the mountains on his way to the Punjab, stopped by the camp and was requested to baptize the baby. He had done so in a collapsible canvas bucket, naming him, by his father's wish, Ashton Hilary Akbar, and had left without seeing the child's mother who was said to be feeling "poorly"—a piece of information that hardly surprised him, since the unfortunate lady could have received no proper attention in such a camp.

Had he been able to delay his departure for another two days he would have been able to officiate at Mrs. Pelham-Martyn's funeral, for Isobel died twenty-four hours after her son's christening, and was buried by her husband and her husband's friend on the summit of the pass overlooking their tents, the entire camp attending the ceremony with every evidence of grief.

Hilary too had been grief-stricken. But he had also been aggrieved. What in the name of heaven was he to do with a baby now that Isobel had gone? He knew nothing about babies—apart from the fact that they were given to howling and had to be fed at all hours of the day and night. "What on earth are we to do with it?" inquired Hilary of Akbar Khan, staring resentfully at his son.

Akbar Khan prodded the infant with a bony finger, and laughed when the baby clung to it. "Ah, he is a strong, bold boy. He shall be a soldier—a captain of many sabres. Do not trouble yourself on his account, my friend. Daya Ram's wife will feed him as she has done from the day of his birth, having lost her own child, which was surely arranged by Allah who orders all things."

"But we can't keep him in camp," objected Hilary. "We shall have to find someone who is going on leave and get them to take him home. I expect the Pemberthys would know of someone. Or young William. Yes, that's what we'd better do: I've got a brother in England whose wife can take care of him until I get back myself."

That matter being decided he had taken Akbar

7

Khan's advice and ceased to worry. And as the baby throve and was seldom heard to cry, they came to the conclusion that there was no hurry about going to Peshawar after all, and having cut Isobel's name on a boulder above her grave, they struck camp and headed east towards Garwal.

Hilary never returned to Peshawar; and being deplorably absent-minded, he failed to notify either his brother-in-law William Ashton, or any of his relatives in England, that he was now a father—and a widower. The occasional letter (there were not many) that still arrived addressed to his wife would from time to time remind him of his obligations. But as he was always too occupied to give them his immediate attention, they were put aside to be dealt with at some later date and invariably forgotten; as he came to forget Isobel—and even, on occasions, the fact that he had a son.

"Ash-Baba,"* as the baby was known to his foster-mother Sita, and to the entire camp, spent the first eighteen months of his life among the high mountains, and took his first steps on a slippery grass hillside within sight of the towering peak of Nanda Devi and the long range of her attendant snows. Seeing him toddling about the camp you would have taken him to be Sita's own child, for Isobel had been a brown beauty, honey-skinned, black-haired and grey-eyed; and her son had inherited her colouring. He had also inherited a considerable proportion of her good looks and would, said Akbar Khan approvingly, make a handsome man one day.

The camp never remained long in one place, Hilary being engaged in studying hill dialects and collecting wild flowers. But sterner matters eventually called him from this work, and leaving the hills behind them the camp turned southward and came at last, by way of Jhansi and Sattara, to the lush greenery and long white beaches of the Coromandel Coast.

The heat of the plains and the humidity of the south did not suit Ash-Baba as the cool air of the hills had done, and Sita, herself a hill-woman, longed for the mountains and would tell him stories of her home in the north among the great ranges of the Hindu Kush. Tales of glaciers and avalanches, of hidden valleys where the rivers

---

*baby; child

8

teemed with snow trout and the ground was carpeted with flowers; and where fruit blossom scented the air in spring and apples and walnuts ripened in the lazy golden summers. In time these became his favourite stories, and Sita invented a valley which was to be theirs alone and where, one day, they would build a house of mud and pine-wood, with a flat roof on which they could spread corn and red peppers to dry, and a garden in which they would grow almond and peach trees and keep a goat and a puppy and a kitten.

Neither she nor any other member of the camp spoke English, and Ash reached the age of four without realizing that the language in which his father occasionally addressed him was, or should have been, his native tongue. But having inherited Hilary's ear for dialects, he picked up a number of tongues in the polyglot camp: Pushtu from Swab Gul, Hindi from Ram Chand, and Tamil, Gujerati and Telegu from the southerners. Though he used, for choice, the Punjabi spoken by Akbar Khan, Sita and Sita's husband Daya Ram. He rarely wore European clothes, since Hilary seldom stayed in places where such things were obtainable. And in any case such garments would have been entirely unsuited to the climate and camp life. He was therefore dressed either in Hindu or Mussulman garb—the difference of opinion between Akbar Khan and Sita as to which he should wear having been settled by compromise: Mussulman one week, Hindu the next. But always the former on a Friday.*

They had spent the autumn of 1855 in the Seeoni hills, ostensibly studying the dialect of the Gonds. And it was here that Hilary had written a report on the events that followed the annexation (he had called it "theft") by the East India Company of the Princely States of Nagpur, Jhansi and Tanjore. His tale of the Company's dismissal of the unfortunate Commissioner and former Resident of Nagpur, Mr. Mansel, who had been ill-advised enough to suggest a more generous settlement with the late Rajah's family (and rash enough to protest against the harshness of the action taken) had lost nothing in the telling.

The whole policy of Annexation and Lapse—the taking-over by the Company of any native state where there was no direct heir, in defiance of a centuries-old tradition

---

*the Mohammedan Sabbath

that permitted a childless man to adopt an heir from among his relations—was, declared Hilary, nothing more than a hypocritical term for an ugly and indefensible act: barefaced robbery and the defrauding of widows and orphans. The rulers in question—and he would point out that Nagpur, Jhansi and Tanjore were only three of the states to fall victims to this iniquitous policy—had been loyal supporters of the Company; yet their loyalty had not prevented their widows and womenfolk being deprived by that same Company of their hereditary rights, together with their jewels and other family heirlooms. In the case of the titular principality of Tanjore, absorbed by right of Lapse on the death of the Rajah, there had been a daughter, though no son; and with commendable courage (considering the treatment meted out to the hapless Mr. Mansel) the President, a Mr. Forbes, had pleaded the cause of the princess, urging that by the terms of Tanjore's treaty with the Company, the succession had been promised to "heirs" in general and not specifically to heirs male. But his pleas had been ignored. A strong force of sepoys* had been marched suddenly into the palace and the whole of the property, real or personal, seized; the Company's seals had been put upon all jewels and valuables, the late Rajah's troops disarmed, and his mother's estate sequestered.

There was worse, wrote Hilary, to follow, for it affected the lives and livelihood of many people. Throughout the district, the occupier of every piece of land that had at any time belonged to any previous Rajah of Tanjore was turned out of his possession and ordered to come before the British Commissioner to establish a title, and all those who had depended on the expenditure of the state revenue were panic-stricken at the prospect of being left without employment. Within a week Tanjore, from being the most contented area in the Company's dominions, had been transformed into a hot-bed of disaffection. Its people had venerated their ruling house and were infuriated by its suppression—the very sepoys refusing to receive their pensions. In Jhansi, too, there had been a child of the royal house—a distant cousin only, but one formally adopted by the late Rajah—and Lakshmi Bai, the Rajah's lovely widow, had pleaded her husband's long record of

*Indian infantrymen

10

loyalty to the Company; but to no avail. Jhansi was declared "Lapsed to the British Government" and placed under the jurisdiction of the Governor of the North-Western Provinces, its institutions abolished, the establishments of the Rajah's government suspended, and all troops in the service of the state immediately paid off and discharged.

"Nothing," wrote Hilary, "could be more calculated to arouse hatred, bitterness and resentment than this brazen and ruthless system of robbery." But the Great British Public had other matters to think of. The war in the Crimea was proving a costly and harrowing business, and India was far away, out of sight and out of mind. Those few who clicked their tongues disapprovingly over the reports forgot about them a few days later, while the Senior Councillors of the Honourable the East India Company pronounced the writer to be "a misguided crank" and attempted to discover his identity and prevent his making use of the mails.

They had not succeeded in either task, for Hilary's reports were sent home by unorthodox routes. And though there were officials who regarded his proceedings with suspicion—in particular his close friendship with "a native"—they lacked evidence. Suspicion was not proof. Hilary continued to move freely about India and took pains to impress upon his son that the greatest sin that man could commit was injustice, and that it must always be fought against, tooth and nail—even when there seemed to be no hope of winning.

"Never forget that, Ashton. Whatever else you are, be just. 'Do as you would be done by.' That means you must never be unfair. *Never*. Not under any circumstances. Not to anyone. Do you understand?"

Of course he did not, for he was as yet too young. But the lesson was repeated daily until gradually it became borne in upon him what the "Burra-Sahib"* (he never thought of his father by any other name) meant, for Uncle Akbar too would talk to him of this, telling him stories and quoting from the holy book to illustrate the theme that "A man is greater than Kings"; and that when he grew up and became a man he would find that this was true. Therefore he must try always to be just in all his

---

*great man

11

dealings, because at this time there were many and terrible injustices being done in the land by men who held power and had become drunk with it.

"Why do the people put up with it?" demanded Hilary of Akbar Khan. "There are millions of them to a handful of the Company. Why don't they do something?—stand up for themselves?"

"They will. One day," said Akbar Khan placidly.

"Then the sooner the better," retorted Hilary, adding that, to be fair, there were any number of good Sahibs in the country: Lawrence, Nicholson and Burns; men like Mansel and Forbes, and young Randall in Lunjore, and a hundred others, and that it was ones in Simla and Calcutta who needed weeding out—the pompous, greedy and pigheaded old gentlemen with one foot in the grave and heads that had become addled by sun and snobbery and an inflated sense of their own importance. As for the army, there was hardly a senior British officer in India under the age of seventy. "I am not," insisted Hilary, "an unpatriotic man. But I cannot see anything admirable in stupidity, injustice and sheer incompetence in high places, and there is too much of all three in the present administration."

"I will not quarrel with you over that," said Akbar Khan. "But it will pass; and your children's children will forget the guilt and remember only the glory, while ours will remember the oppression and deny you the good. Yet there is much good."

"I know, I know." Hilary's smile was more than a little wry. "Perhaps I myself am a pompous and conceited old fool. And perhaps if these fools I complain of were French or Dutch or German I would not mind so much, because then I could say 'what else can you expect?' and feel superior. It is because they are men of my own race that I would have them all good."

"Only God is that," said Akbar Khan dryly. "We, his creatures, are all evil and imperfect, whatever the colour of our skins. But some of us strive for righteousness—and in that there is hope."

Hilary wrote no more reports on the administrative activities of the East India Company and the Governor-General and Council, but turned instead to those subjects that had always claimed the lion's share of his interest. The resulting manuscripts, unlike his coded reports, were dispatched through the normal channel of the mails, where they were opened and examined, and served to confirm the authorities in their opinion that Professor Pelham-Martyn was, after all, merely an erudite eccentric and entirely above suspicion.

Once again the camp struck its tents, and turning its back upon the palms and temples of the south, moved slowly northward. Ashton Hilary Akbar celebrated his fourth birthday in the capital of the Moguls, the walled city of Delhi, where Hilary had come to complete, correct and dispatch the manuscript of his latest, and last, book. Uncle Akbar marked the occasion by arraying Ash in the finest of Mussulman dress and taking him to pray at the Juma Masjid, the magnificent mosque that the Emperor Shah Jehan had built facing the walls of the *Lal Kila*, the great "Red Fort" on the banks of the Jumna River.

The mosque had been crowded, for it was a Friday. So crowded that many people who had been unable to find places in the courtyard had climbed to the top of the gateway, and two had fallen because of the press and been killed. "It was ordained," said Uncle Akbar, and went on with his prayers. Ash had bowed, knelt and risen in imitation of the other worshippers, and afterwards Uncle Akbar had taught him Shah Jehan's prayer, the *Khutpa*, which begins *"Oh Lord! Do thou great honour to the faith of Islam, and to the professors of that faith, through the perpetual power and majesty of thy slave the Sultan, the son of the Sultan, the Emperor, the son of the Emperor, the Ruler of the two Continents and the Master of the two seas, the Warrior in the cause of God, the Emperor Abdul Muzaffar Shahabuddin Muhammad Shah Jahan Ghazi . . ."*

What, demanded Ash, was a sea? And why only two seas?—and who had ordained that those two people should fall off the gateway?

Sita had countered by dressing her foster-son as a Hindu and taking him to a temple in the city, where in exchange for a few coins a priest in yellow robes had marked his forehead with a small smear of red paste, and he had watched Daya Ram do *pujah* (worship) to an ancient, shapeless shaft of stone, the symbol of the God Shiva.

Akbar Khan had many friends in Delhi, and normally he would have wished to linger there. But this year he

13

was aware of odd and uneasy undercurrents, and the conversation of his friends disturbed him. The city was full of strange rumours and there was a tension and an ominous sense of suppressed excitement in the narrow, noisy streets and crowded bazaars. It gave him a sharp feeling of apprehension and an awareness of impending evil.

"There is some mischief afoot. One can smell it in the very air," said Akbar Khan. "It bodes no good for men of your blood, my friend, and I would not have our boy come to any harm. Let us go away from here, to somewhere where the air is cleaner. I do not like cities. They breed foulness as a dunghill breeds flies and maggots, and there is something breeding here that is worse than either."

"You mean revolt?" said Hilary, undisturbed. "That is true of half India. And in my opinion the sooner it comes the better: we need an explosion to clear the air and blow those lethargic blockheads in Calcutta and Simla out of their complacency."

"True. But explosions can kill, and I would not have my boy pay for the errors of his countrymen."

"You mean *my* boy," corrected Hilary with a shade of asperity.

"Ours, then. Though he is fonder of me than of you."

"Only because you spoil him."

"Not so. It is because I love him, and he knows it. He is the son of your body but of my heart; and I would not have him harmed when the storm breaks—as it will. Have you warned your English friends in the cantonment?"

Hilary said that he had done so many times, but that they did not want to believe it: and the trouble was that not only men in high places, the Members of Council in Calcutta and the civil servants in Simla, knew too little of the minds of those whom they governed, but many army officers were equally ignorant.

"It was not so in the old days," said Akbar Khan regretfully. "But the generals are now old and fat and tired, and their officers are moved so frequently that they do not know the customs of their men, or notice that their sepoys are becoming restless. I do not like that tale from Barrackpore. It is true that only one sepoy rebelled, but when he shot down his officer and threatened to shoot the General-Sahib himself, his fellow sepoys watched in silence and did nothing to prevent it. Yet I think it was

14

unwise to disband that regiment after they had hanged the offender, because now there are three hundred more masterless men to add to the disaffection of many others. Trouble will come of it, and I think very soon."

"I too. And when it does, my countrymen will be both shocked and enraged at such disloyalty and ingratitude. You will see."

"Perhaps—if we live through it," said Akbar Khan. "Wherefore I say, let us go to the hills."

Hilary packed his boxes and left a number of them in the house of an acquaintance in the cantonment behind the Ridge. He had intended, before leaving Delhi, to write several letters that should have been written years ago. But once again he postponed doing so, for Akbar Khan was impatient to be gone and there would be plenty of time for such tedious business when they reached the peace and quiet of the hills. Besides, having neglected his correspondence for so long, a month or two would make no difference. Consoled by this thought, he shovelled a pile of unanswered letters, including half-a-dozen addressed to his late wife, into a cardboard box marked "Urgent," and turned to more interesting tasks.

There is a book, published in the spring of 1856 (*Unfamiliar Dialects of Hindustan,* Vol. I, by Prof. H. F. Pelham-Martyn, B.A., D.S.C., F.R.G.S., F.S.A., etc.), that is dedicated *"To the dear memory of my wife Isobel."* The second volume of this work was not published until the autumn of the following year and bore a longer inscription: *"For Ashton Hilary Akbar, hoping it may arouse his interest in a subject that has given endless pleasure to the author—H.F.P.-M."* But by that time both Hilary and Akbar Khan had been six months in their graves, and no one had troubled to inquire who Ashton Hilary Akbar might be.

The camp had moved northward in the direction of the Terai and the foothills of the Doon, and it was here, in early April when the temperature had begun to rise and the nights were no longer cool, that disaster overtook them.

A small party of pilgrims from Hardwar, who had been offered hospitality for a night, brought cholera with them. One of them died in the dark hour before dawn, and his companions fled, abandoning the body which was found by the servants the next morning. By evening three

15

of Hilary's men had taken the disease, and so swiftly did the cholera do its ugly work that none lived to see the dawn. The camp succumbed to panic and many snatched their chattels and vanished, not waiting for their pay. And on the following day Akbar Khan had sickened.

"Go away," whispered Akbar Khan to Hilary. "Take the boy and go quickly, lest you too die. Do not grieve for me. I am an old man and a cripple, wifeless and childless. Why should I fear to die? But you have the boy . . . and a son has need of a father."

"You have been a better father to him than I," said Hilary, holding his friend's hand.

Akbar Khan smiled. "That I know, for he has my heart, and I would have taught him—I would have taught him . . . It is too late. Leave quickly."

"There is nowhere to go," said Hilary. "How can one out-distance the black cholera? If we go it will go with us, and I have heard that more than a thousand are dying daily at Hardwar. We are better off here than in the towns, and soon you will be well—you are strong and will recover."

But Akbar Khan had died.

Hilary wept for his friend as he had not wept for his wife. And when he had buried him he went to his tent where he wrote a letter to his brother in England and another to his lawyer, and enclosing both with certain other papers and daguerreotypes in his possession, made a small packet of the whole and wrapped it carefully in a square of oiled silk. That done and the packet sealed with wax, he picked up his pen again and began a third letter—that long-overdue letter to Isobel's brother, William Ashton, that he had meant to write years ago and somehow never written. But he had left it too late. The cholera that had killed his friend reached out a bony hand and touched him on the shoulder, and his pen faltered and fell to the floor.

An hour later, rousing himself from a bout of agony, Hilary folded the unfinished page and having slowly and painfully traced an address on it, called for his bearer, Karim Bux. But Karim Bux too was dying, and it was, at long last, Daya Ram's wife, Sita, who came hastening nervously through the dusk of the stricken camp, bringing a hurricane lamp and food for the "Burra-Sahib." For the cook and his assistants had run away hours before.

The child had come with her, but when she saw how

16

it was with his father she pushed him outside the reeking tent and would not let him enter.

"That's right," gasped Hilary, approving the action. "You're a sensible woman—always said so. Look after him, Sita. Take him to his own people. Don't let him—" He found that he could not finish the sentence and groping weakly for the single sheet of paper and the sealed packet, thrust it at her. "Money in that tin box—take it. That's right. Should be enough to get you to . . ."

Another convulsion shook him, and Sita, hiding money and papers in the folds of her sari, backed away, and grasping the child's hand hurried him to his own tent and put him to bed—for once, and to his indignation, without the songs and fairy tales that were the normal accompaniments of bedtime.

Hilary died that night, and by mid-afternoon on the following day the cholera had claimed four more lives. Among them, Daya Ram's. Those who remained—by now a mere handful—looted the empty tents of anything of value, and taking the horses and camels, fled southward into the Terai, leaving behind them the newly widowed Sita, for fear that she might have taken the infection from her dead husband, and with her the four-year-old orphan, Ash-Baba.

Years afterwards, when he had forgotten much else, Ash could still remember that night. The heat and the moonlight, the ugly sound of jackals and hyenas quarrelling and snarling within a stone's throw of the little tent where Sita crouched beside him, listening and trembling and patting his shoulder in a vain attempt to soothe his fears and send him to sleep. The flap and croak of gorged vultures roosting in the *sal* trees, the sickening stench of corruption and the dreadful, dragging sense of bewildered desolation at a situation that he could not understand and that no one had explained to him.

He had not been frightened, because he had never yet had cause to be afraid of anything, and Uncle Akbar had taught him that a man must never show fear. Also he was, by temperament, an abnormally courageous child, and life in a camp that moved through jungles, deserts and unexplored mountain ranges had accustomed him to the ways of the wild animals. But he did not know why Sita wept and shivered and why she had not let him approach the "Burra-Sahib," or understand what had hap-

pened to Uncle Akbar and the others. He knew that they
were dead, for he had seen death before: tigers that he had
been allowed to sit up for in a *machan* with Uncle Akbar
and had seen shot. Kills that they had waited above;
goats or young buffaloes that a tiger had struck down and
partially eaten on the previous day. Black-buck and duck
and partridge shot for the pot. These creatures had been
dead. But surely Uncle Akbar could not be dead as they
were dead? There must be something indestructible—
something that remained of men who had walked and
talked with one and told one stories, men whom one had
loved and looked up to. But where had it gone? It was all
very puzzling, and he did not understand.

Sita had dragged thorn branches from the *boma* that
had once protected the camp, and piled them in a circle
about his tent, heaping them high. And it was as well that
she had, for towards midnight a pair of leopards had driv-
en off the jackals and the hyenas to lay claim to the feast,
and before dawn a tiger roared in the jungle beyond the
sal trees, and daylight showed the print of his pugs within
a yard of their flimsy barrier of thorn.

There had been no milk that morning, and little
food. But Sita had given the child the remains of a chuppatti—the unleavened bread of India—and afterwards she
made a bundle of their few belongings, and taking him by
the hand led him away from the horror and desolation of
the camp.

2

Sita could not have been more than twenty-five years old.
But she looked twice that age, for hard work and yearly
pregnancies, the bearing of five children and the bitter
grief and disappointment of their loss, had combined to age
her prematurely. She could neither read nor write and she
was not clever, but she possessed courage, loyalty and a
loving heart, and it never occurred to her to keep for herself the money Hilary had given her, or to disobey his orders. She had loved Hilary's son from the hour of his birth,

18

and now Hilary had given the boy into her keeping and told her to take him back to his own people. There was no one else to care for Ash-Baba now but herself: he was her responsibility and she would not fail him.

She had no idea who his own people were, or how to find them, but this did not worry her over-much, for she remembered the number of the house in Delhi cantonment where Ash-Baba's father had left the greater part of his luggage, and also the name of the Colonel-Sahib who lived there. She would take the child to Delhi, to Abuthnot Sahib and his Memsahib, who would arrange everything, and as they would certainly need an *ayah* for the boy she, Sita, need not be parted from him. Delhi lay far to the southward but she never doubted that they would reach it in safety, though because the money she had taken from the tin box was more than she had ever seen in her life, she became afraid of attracting undue attention on the road, and dressed Ash in the oldest garments he possessed, warning him that he must on no account talk to strangers.

It was May before they came within sight of the city of the Moguls, for Ash was too heavy for her to carry except for short distances, and though he was a sturdy child he could not cover more than a few miles in one day. The weather too, though usually cool for that season of the year, was getting hotter, and the long, burning days made for slow travel. Ash had accepted their journey without question, for he had never known anything else and a constant change of scene was nothing new. The only stability his life had possessed had been the presence of the same people: Sita, Uncle Akbar and the "Burra-Sahib"; Daya Ram and Kartar Singh, Swab Gul, Tara Chand, Dunno and a score of others; and though all of them had now gone except Sita, she at least was still here—together with all India and the familiar Indian scene.

They travelled slowly, buying their food in villages by the way and sleeping for preference in the open in order to avoid questions, and they were both very tired by the time the walls and domes and minarets of Delhi showed on the horizon, wraithlike in a dusty, golden evening. Sita had hoped to reach the city before dark, having planned to spend the night with a distant connection of Daya Ram's who kept a grain shop in a side street of the Chandi Chowk, where she could clean and press the En-

19

glish clothes that she had secreted in her bundle, and dress Ash-Baba correctly before taking him to the cantonment. But they had covered nearly six miles that day, and though the walls of Delhi seemed no great distance away, the sun went down while they were still a quarter of a mile short of the bridge of boats by which they must cross the Jumna.

A further half mile separated them from the shop in the city, and soon it would be too dark to see. But they had sufficient food and drink for an evening meal, and as the child was too tired and too sleepy to go further, Sita led him a little way off the road to where a *peepul* tree leaned above a clutter of fallen masonry, and having fed him, spread a blanket among the tree roots and sang him to sleep with an old, old nursery-rhyme of the Punjab, *"Arré Ko-ko, Jarré Ko-ko,"* and that best-beloved of lullabies that says—

> *"Nini baba, nini,*
> *Muckan, roti, cheeni,*
> *Roti muckan hogya,*
> *Hamara baba sogya!"**

The night was warm and windless and full of stars, and from where she lay with her arm about the child's small body, Sita could see the lights of Delhi twinkling across the plain, a spangle of gold on the velvet darkness. Jackals howled among the scattered ruins of other and older Delhis, bats and harsh-voiced night birds swooped and called among the branches overhead, and once a hyena laughed hideously from a patch of elephant grass a few yards away, and a mongoose chittered angrily among the shadows. But these were all familiar sounds, as familiar as the tom-toms that beat in the distant city and the shrill hum of the cicadas; and presently Sita drew the end of her *cuddah* over her face and slept.

She awoke in the first flush of dawn, aroused abruptly from sleep by a less familiar sound: a sharp urgent clatter of galloping hooves, the crack of firearms and men's voices, shouting. There were horsemen on the road, approaching from the direction of Meerut and riding like

---

*Sleep baby sleep, Butter, bread, sugar, The bread and butter are finished, My baby is asleep.

20

men possessed, or pursued, the dust of their headlong progress streaming out behind them like a trail of white smoke across the dawn-lit plain. They thundered past within a stone's throw of the *peepul* tree, firing wildly into the air and shouting as men shout in a race, and Sita could see their staring eyes and frenzied faces, and the clotted foam that flew from the straining necks and flanks of the galloping horses. They were sowars (troopers) wearing the uniform of one of the Bengal Army's cavalry regiments. Sowars from Meerut. But their uniforms were torn and dusty and disfigured by the dark, unmistakable stains of blood.

A stray bullet ripped through the boughs of the *peepul* tree and Sita cowered down, clutching Ash, who had been woken by the noise. The next moment the riders were past and the dust that whirled up behind them blotted them out in a choking cloud that filled her lungs, making her cough and gasp and cover her face in the folds of her sari. By the time it had blown clear and she could see again, they had reached the river and she heard, faint but clear in the quiet dawn, the hollow thunder of hooves crossing the bridge of boats.

The impression of desperate men who fled in fear of pursuit had been so vivid that Sita snatched up the child, and running with him to the shelter of the elephant grass, crouched there, listening for the hue and cry that must surely follow.

She stayed there for the best part of an hour, hushing the bewildered boy and begging him in whispers to stay still and make no noise; but though she heard no more hoof-beats on the Meerut road, the stillness of the morning lent clarity to a distant crackle of firing and the voices of men shouting under the walls of Delhi. Presently these too ceased or were absorbed into the work-a-day sounds of the awaking city and the normal noises of an Indian morning: the creak of a well-wheel, partridges calling out on the plains and sarus cranes by the river; the harsh cry of a peacock from the standing crops, and the chatter and chirrup of tree-rats, *saht-bai* and weaver-birds. A troop of brown monkeys settled in the branches of the *peepul* tree, and a faint breeze off the river stirred the tall elephant grass and made a dry monotonous rustling that blotted out all other sounds.

"Is it a tiger?" whispered Ash, who had sat up over more than one kill with Uncle Akbar and knew about tigers.

"No—but we must not talk. We must be quiet," urged Sita. She could not have explained the panic that the yelling horsemen had aroused in her, or what exactly she was afraid of. But her heart was still beating at twice its normal speed and she knew that not even the cholera, or the terrible hours of their last night in camp, had frightened her as the sight of those men had done. Cholera, after all, she knew; and sickness and death and the ways of wild animals. But this was something else. Something inexplicable and terrifying . . .

A country cart drawn by a pair of lethargic bullocks jolted slowly down the road, and the homely, unhurried sound of its passing reassured her. The sun lipped the rim of the far horizon and suddenly it was day, and Sita's breathing slowed and steadied. She stood up cautiously, and peering through the parched grasses saw that the road lay empty in the bright sunlight. Nothing moved upon it—which was in itself unusual, for the Meerut road was normally a busy one and carried the main traffic from Rohilkund and Oude to Delhi. But Sita was unaware of this, and the silence encouraged her, though she was not anxious to follow too closely on the heels of those wild-eyed horsemen, and it seemed wiser to wait awhile. There was still a little food left, but they had finished the milk on the previous night and were both becoming increasingly thirsty.

"Wait here," she told Ash. "I will go to the river to fetch water, and I shall not be long. Do not move from here, my heart. Stay still and you will be safe."

Ash had obeyed her, for he had caught the infection of her panic and for the first time in his life had been frightened. Though he, like Sita, could not have told what he was afraid of.

It had been a long wait, for Sita made a detour and reached the river bank some way above the spot where the road ran on to the bridge of boats, which would have been the shortest way to the water. From here she could see across the sand bars and the wandering channels of the Jumna to the Calcutta Gate and the long line of the wall that stretched away past the Arsenal to the Water Bastion; and also hear, more clearly now, the noise of the city, which sounded from that distance like the hum of an overturned hive of angry bees, magnified a thousand times.

Mixed with that sound were the sharper ones of shots, now a lone one, now a staccato crackle of firing; and the sky above the roof tops was alive with birds—hawks, cawing flocks of crows, and startled pigeons, wheeling and swooping and rising sharply again as though disturbed by something in the streets below. Yes, there was something gravely wrong with Delhi that morning, and it would be better to keep away and not attempt to enter the city until she had some knowledge of what was happening there. It was a pity that there was so little food left, but there would be enough for the child. And at least they would have water.

Sita filled her brass *lotah* in the shallows and stole back to the safety of the elephant grass by the Meerut road, keeping as far as possible to the sparse shelter of *kikar* trees, rocks and clumps of pampas in order to avoid being seen. They would remain here until the evening, she decided, and then cross the bridge after dark, and by passing the city, make straight for the cantonments. It would be a long walk for Ash-Baba, but if he rested all day . . . She trod out a more comfortable space for him in the heart of the grass patch, and though it had been dusty, airless and intolerably hot, and Ash, having forgotten his fear, had become bored and restless, the heat and the enforced idleness had eventually made him drowsy, and shortly after midday he had fallen asleep.

Sita too had dozed fitfully, soothed by the slow creak of bullock-drawn country carts plodding along the dusty road and the occasional jingle of the passing *ekka*.* Both sounds seemed to betoken the resumption of normal traffic on the Meerut road, so perhaps the danger—if there had been danger—had passed, and what she had witnessed had been no more than messengers hastening to Bahadur Shah, the Mogul, with news of some great event that had aroused the city to excitement and celebration; the news, perhaps, of a victory won by the Company's Bengal Army on some faraway battle field; or the birth of a son to some fellow monarch—perchance to the *Padishah* Victoria in *Belait* (England)?

---

*light two-wheeled trap

These and other comforting conjectures served to blunt the sharp edge of panic, and she could no longer hear the tumult of the city, for though the faint current of air that blew off the wet sand and the winding reaches of the Jumna River was not strong enough to raise the dust that lay thick on the highroad, it was still sufficient to stir the tops of the elephant grass and fill her ears with a soft, murmurous rustling. "We shall leave when the child awakes," thought Sita. But even as she thought it the illusion of peace was shattered. A savage tremor swept across the plain like an invisible wave, shuddering through the grass and rocking the very earth beneath her, and on its heels came an appalling crash of sound that split the murmurous silence of the hot afternoon as a thunderbolt will split a pine tree.

The violence of that sound jerked Ash from sleep and brought Sita to her feet, rigid with shock, and peering through the shivering grasses they saw a vast column of smoke rising up above the distant walls of Delhi: an awesome, writhing pillar, mushroom-topped and terrifying in the blaze of the afternoon sunlight. They had no idea what it meant, and never knew that what they had seen was the explosion of the Delhi magazine, blown up by a handful of defenders to prevent it falling into the hands of a rioting mob.

Hours later the smoke still hung there, rose-coloured now in the golden sunset; and when at last Sita and the child ventured out of their hiding place the first rays of the low moon had touched its fading outline with silver.

To turn back now, when they were almost within reach of their goal, was out of the question; though had there been any other way of reaching the cantonments, Sita would have taken it. But she did not dare attempt to ford the Jumna, and there was no other bridge for many miles. They would have to cross by the bridge of boats, and they had done so, hurrying across it in the grey starlight in the wake of a wedding party, to be challenged and halted by armed men on the far side. A lone woman and child being of little account, they had been allowed to pass while the sentries interrogated the wedding guests; and it was from the babble of questions and answers that Sita gained her first information as to the events of the day.

Hilary had been right. And so had Akbar Khan.

24

There had been too many grievances that had been disregarded, too many injustices that had not been recognized and put right, and men would not endure such things for ever. The breaking point had been a petty one: a matter of greased cartridges that had been issued to the Bengal Army for use in the new rifles, of which the grease was suspected of being a mixture of cow and pig fat—the touch of the first destroying the caste of a Hindu and the latter defiling a Mohammedan. But it was an excuse only.

Ever since the day, half a century earlier, when mutiny and bloodshed had followed the Company's attempt to enforce the wearing of a leather stock and a new form of headdress on the troops at Vellore in Madras, the sepoys had suspected a plot aimed at depriving them of caste—that most cherished of all Hindu institutions. The mutiny of Vellore had been put down with swiftness and ferocity, as had other and similar insurrections in the years that followed. But the Company had failed to read the writing on the wall, and were indignant at the outcry against the greased cartridges.

In Barrackpore an angry sepoy, Mangal Pandy of the 34th Native Infantry, having urged his comrades to revolt, had fired at and wounded the British Adjutant. He had subsequently been hanged, while his fellow sepoys who had watched in silence had been deprived of their arms. The regiment itself had been disbanded, and faced with further dissatisfaction the Governor-General had at last issued an order withdrawing the new cartridge. But by that time it was too late, for the sepoys looked upon the order as proof that their suspicions had been correct, and far from easing the tension, it increased it to danger-point. Outbreaks of arson were reported from all over India, but in spite of the explosiveness of the situation and the fact that knowledgeable men were only too well aware of impending disaster, the Commanding Officer of the 3rd Cavalry, stationed at Meerut, had elected to teach his regiment a lesson by insisting that they use the disputed cartridges. Eighty-five of his sowars* having firmly, though courteously, refused to do so, they had been arrested, court-martialled and sentenced to hard-labour for life.

General Hewitt, obese, lethargic and rising seventy, had reluctantly ordered a parade of the entire Meerut

---

*sowars = cavalry soldiers; sepoys = infantry

Brigade at which the sentences were read aloud, and the eighty-five men publicly stripped of their uniforms and fitted with iron leg-shackles before being led away to life imprisonment. But that long-drawn, inglorious parade proved to be an even greater mistake than the harshness of the sentences, for the sympathy of the watching crowd had been aroused by the sight of the manacled sowars, and all that night men in the barracks and bazaars of Meerut seethed with shame and rage and plotted revenge. With the morning the storm that had threatened for so long broke at last: a mob of furious sepoys attacked the gaol, released the prisoners and turned on the British, and after a day of riot, murder and violence the sowars of the 3rd Cavalry had fired the looted bungalows and ridden to Delhi to raise the standard of revolt and place their sabres at the service of Bahadur Shah, titular King of Delhi and last of the Moguls. It was these men whom Sita had seen in the dawn, and recognized, with terror and foreboding, as the messengers of disaster.

The Mogul, it seemed, had not at first believed them, for there were many British regiments in Meerut, and he had hourly expected to see them hastening in pursuit of the mutineers. Only when none appeared did he become convinced that the troopers of the 3rd Cavalry had spoken no more than the truth when they asserted that all the Sahib-log in Meerut were dead; and this being so, word had gone out for a similar massacre of all Europeans in Delhi. Some of the Sahibs had shut themselves into the magazine, and when it became clear that they could no longer hold it, they had blown it up, and themselves with it. Others had been slaughtered by their troops, or by the mobs which had risen in support of the heroes of Meerut and were still hunting down stray Europeans in the streets of the city ...

Listening to this tale of the day's doings, Sita had snatched the child away from the light of the flaring torches and dragged him into the shadows, terrified that he might be recognized as *Angrezi* (English) and cut down by the swords of the bridge guard. The roar of the mob and the crash and crackle of burning buildings carried a clearer warning than any words of the dangers to be encountered in the city, and turning from the Calcutta Gate she scurried away into the darkness in the direction of the Water Bastion, keeping to the narrow strip of waste ground that lay between the river and the walls of Delhi.

The ground was rough and strewn with rocks and other pitfalls, and Ash's short legs, trotting beside her, tired early. But by now the moon was up, and the reflected glare of burning houses filled the night with a sunset brightness. They had covered less than half a mile when they came across a strayed donkey wandering aimlessly among the boulders and the rubbish dumps, and appropriated it. Its owner was probably a *dhobi* or a grass-cutter who had tied it insecurely or, hastening to the city to take part in the looting of European-owned shops and houses, had temporarily forgotten it. But to Sita it was a gift from the gods and she accepted it as such. The little creature stood patiently while she placed Ash on its back and mounted behind him, and it had obviously been accustomed to far heavier loads, for at the touch of her heel it trotted briskly forward, keeping to some unseen track that wound between the rocks and scrub and rubbish on the glacis beyond the city ditch.

The donkey's hooves made very little noise on the sandy ground, and Sita's wine-coloured cotton sari was lost among the shadows; but there were men on the walls that night who were suspicious of any sound or movement, and twice harsh voices challenged them and shots ricochetted off the stones at their feet or whined viciously overhead to splash into the river. Then at last they were past the Water Bastion and the Counter-Scarp, and picking their way across the short stretch of open ground that separated the Kashmir Gate from the dark, friendly thickets of the Kudsia Bagh.

A final spatter of shots followed but did not harm them, and ten minutes later they were among trees, with Delhi left behind them—a black, uneven fringe of walls and battlements, rooftops and trees, spiked with the slim minarets of mosques and thrown into sharp silhouette by the glow of the fires. To the right lay the river, while ahead and to the left loomed the long dark line of the Ridge, a natural barrier of rock that lay between the cantonments and the city.

There were always lights in the cantonments, in bungalows, barracks and messes, and the quarters of the camp-followers. The glow they made in the night sky was a familiar sight, but tonight it was much brighter and less constant, waxing and waning as though there were fires

27

there too. The Sahib-log, thought Sita, must have caused bonfires to be lighted around the cantonment area to prevent any attack being launched under cover of darkness, which seemed to her a sensible idea; though it was going to make her own progress more hazardous, for there were armed men on the road that linked the city to the Ridge and the cantonments, hurrying figures on foot and on horseback whom she suspected of being mutineers or looters. The sooner she got the child and herself to the safety of Abuthnot-Sahib's bungalow the better, but it might be wiser to wait here where the trees and thickets offered a hiding place, until there was less activity on the cantonment road.

The donkey jibbed suddenly, almost unseating her. It stood still, blowing loud snuffing breaths of alarm, and when she urged it forward with her heel, it backed instead, so that she was forced to dismount.

"Dekho!" (Look!) said Ash, whose eyesight in the dark was almost as good as the donkey's. "There is someone there in the bushes."

His voice was interested rather than alarmed, and if he had not spoken before it was only because he had never been much given to talking, except, on occasions, to Akbar Khan. The shots and the shouting had excited him, but no more than that, for Uncle Akbar had taken him out shooting before he could walk, and the only alarming thing about the present situation was Sita's fear; and the fact that she either would not or could not explain their altered circumstances and why everyone he had known in all his short life, everyone but herself, had suddenly deserted him. But like most children the world over, he was resigned to the curious behaviour of grown-ups and accepted it as part of the scheme of things. He knew now that Sita was once again afraid, and this time of the person in the bushes: the donkey was too, and Ash patted the little animal's quivering back and said consolingly: *"Daro mut,"* (Do not fear), "it is only a memsahib who is asleep."

The woman in the bushes lay in a curious attitude, as though she had crawled through the tangled undergrowth on hands and knees and had fallen asleep, exhausted. The red light of burning buildings, glinting through the leaves, showed her to be an excessively stout lady wearing a whalebone crinoline and a number of petti-

28

coats under a voluminous dress of grey and white striped bombazine which made her appear even stouter. But she was not asleep. She was dead. She must, thought Sita, shrinking back from that vast, silent shape, be one of the Sahib-log who had attempted to escape the massacre in the city and had died of terror or heart-failure, for she bore no sign of any wound. Perhaps she too had been trying to reach the cantonments, and perhaps there were other English fugitives hiding in the shadows—or mutineers, hunting them down.

The latter thought was an alarming one, but a moment's consideration convinced Sita that any sounds of pursuit would be clearly audible among the thickets of the ruined garden, and that no search would be undertaken without torches to light the way. The night was quiet and the only movements she could hear came from the direction of the road. They could safely wait here.

Tethering the donkey so that it could not wander away, she made a nest among the grasses for the child, and having fed him with the last hoarded fragments of a chuppatti, lulled him to sleep with the whispered story of the valley among the mountains where they would one day live in that flat-roofed house among the fruit trees, and keep a goat and a cow, a puppy and a kitten . . . "And the donkey," said Ash drowsily. "We must take the donkey."

"Assuredly we will take the donkey, he shall help us carry water jars from the river; and wood for our fire, for when night falls it is cool in the high valleys—cool and pleasant, and the wind that blows through the forests smells of pine-cones and snow and makes a sound that says 'Hush—Hush—Hush' . . ." Ash sighed happily and was asleep.

Sita waited patiently hour after hour until the glow in the sky died down and the stars began to pale, and then smelling the approach of dawn, she roused the sleeping child and stole out of the Kudsia Bagh to complete the last lap of their long journey to the cantonments of Delhi.

There was no one on the road now. It lay grey and empty and deep in dust, and though the air was cool from the river and the long reaches of wet sand, it was tainted with the smell of smoke and a faint reek of corruption, while the silence magnified every small sound: the snap of a dead twig underfoot, the click of a stone struck by

29

the donkey's hooves and Sita's own short uneven breathing. It seemed to her that their progress must be audible a mile away, and she began to urge the donkey to greater speed, kicking its furry sides with her bare heels and exhorting it in a breathless whisper to hurry—hurry.

The last time she and the child had come this way they had driven in a carriage and the distance between the Kashmir Gate and the cantonments had seemed a very short one; but now it seemed endless, and long before they reached the crest of the ridge the sky was grey with the first hint of morning, and the black, shapeless masses to the left and right of the road had resolved themselves into rocks and stunted thorn trees. It was easier once the road began to descend; they made better time on the downward slope, and the silence reassured Sita. If the inhabitants of the cantonment could sleep so peacefully there could be nothing wrong and the trouble must be over —or else it had never reached here.

There were no lights at this hour, and roads, bungalows and gardens lay quiet in the dawn. But the smell of burning was suddenly stronger, and it was not the familiar smell of charcoal or dung fires, but the harsher smell of smouldering beams and thatch, of scorched earth and brickwork.

It was still too dark to make out more than the outline of trees and bungalows, and though the tripping tap of the donkey's hooves was now clearly audible on the harder surface of a made road, no one challenged them, and it seemed that the sentries too were asleep.

The Abuthnots' bungalow lay on the near side of the cantonment in a quiet, tree-shaded road, and Sita found it without much difficulty. Dismounting at the gate she lifted the boy down and began to pull at the knots of her bundle.

"What are you doing?" inquired Ash, interested. He hoped that she meant to produce something for him to eat, for he was hungry. But Sita was unpacking the sailor suit that she had meant to put on him in the house of Daya Ram's cousin, the grain merchant. It was not fitting that the "Burra-Sahib's" son should be presented to his father's people in the dusty, travel-stained garments of a street-arab, and at least she would see that he was properly clothed. The suit would be crumpled but it was clean, and

30

the shoes well polished; and surely the Memsahib would understand and forgive the lack of pressing?

Ash sighed resignedly and allowed himself to be hurried into the hated sailor suit without protest. He seemed to have grown a lot since he last wore it, for it was uncomfortably tight, and when it came to putting on the strapped European shoes he found it impossible to force his feet into them.

"You are not trying, *piara* (dear)," scolded Sita, almost in tears between weariness and vexation. "Push hard—harder."

But it was no use, and she had to let him tread down the heels and wear them as though they had been slippers. The white sailor hat with its wide blue ribbon had not been improved by its long sojourn in the bundle, but she straightened it with an anxious hand and carefully adjusted the elastic band under his chin.

"Now you are altogether a Sahib, Heart-of-my-heart," whispered Sita, kissing him. She wiped away a tear with the corner of her sari, and tying up his discarded clothing in her bundle, came to her feet and led him up the drive towards the house.

The garden was already silver-grey in the first pale wash of the dawn, and the Abuthnots' bungalow stood out clear-cut and distinct—and quiet. So quiet that as they approached it they heard a quick patter of paws on matting as a dark shape appeared out of the blackness of an open doorway, and scuttling down the verandah, loped away across the lawn. It was not a Sahib's dog, or even one of the pariah-dogs that haunted the cantonment bazaars, but a hyena, its high, humped shoulders and grotesquely stunted hind-quarters unmistakable in the growing light . . .

Sita stood still, her heart once again racing in panic. She could hear the receding rustle of leaves as the hyena vanished among the bushes, and the steady munching of the donkey by the gate. But there was still no sound from the house, or from the servants' quarters behind it, where surely someone should be awake and stirring. Where was the *chowkidar*, the night watchman who should have been guarding the bungalow? Her eye was caught by a small white object that lay on the gravel almost at her feet, and she stooped slowly and picked it up. It was a

31

high-heeled satin shoe such as she had seen the memsahibs wear in the evenings for balls or *burra khanas*,* an incongruous object to find lying discarded on the front drive at that hour—or any hour.

Sita's frightened gaze darted over the lawns and flower-beds and she saw for the first time that there were other objects littering the garden: books, pieces of broken china, torn fragments of clothing, a stocking . . . She dropped the satin slipper, and turning, ran back to the gate dragging Ash with her, and thrust him into the shadows of the pepper tree.

"Stay there, *piara*," ordered Sita in a voice that Ash had never heard her use before. "Get back—get down into the shadows and do not make a noise. I will see first who is in the bungalow, and then I will come back for you. As you love me, make no sound."

"Will you bring something to eat?" asked Ash, anxiously, adding with a sigh: "I'm *so* hungry."

"Yes, yes. I will find something. I promise you. Only stay quiet."

Leaving him, she went across the garden, and gathering all her courage, stole up the verandah steps and into the silent house. There was no one there. The dark, empty rooms were littered with broken furniture and the debris left by men who had looted anything of value and wantonly destroyed anything and everything else. The servants' quarters too were deserted, and there had evidently been an attempt to set fire to the bungalow, but the flames had not caught, and behind the broken door of the larder there was still a quantity of food that no one had bothered to steal, perhaps because the caste of the looters prevented them from touching such stuff.

Under other circumstances Sita might have had similar qualms. But now she filled the torn half of a tablecloth with as much as she could conveniently carry. There was bread and cold curry, a bowl of *dal* and the remains of a rice pudding, some boiled potatoes and a quantity of fresh fruit, a jam tart and half a plum cake as well as several varieties of biscuits. There was also milk, but it was sour, and various tinned foods that were too heavy to carry. But among a welter of broken wine bottles was one that had escaped destruction, and though it was empty

---

*big dinner-parties

there were plenty of corks, and she filled it with cold water from an earthenware *chatti* outside the kitchen and hurried back to Ash.

The sky was growing lighter every minute and soon yesterday's looters, the *budmarshes** from the bazaars, would wake after their night's rioting and come back to see if there was anything they had overlooked. It was unsafe to remain here a moment longer, but first she must strip off that betraying sailor suit; and she did so with hands that trembled with anxiety and haste.

Ash did not understand why she had taken all the trouble to dress him in it only to take it off again, but he was thankful to be out of it, and relieved to see that he would not have to wear it again, for Sita left it lying under the pepper tree. He ate his way solidly through a lump of cold rice pudding while Sita filled her brass *lotah* from a little well among the trampled oleander bushes and drew water in a leather bucket for the donkey, and when that was done they mounted again and set off in the pearl-grey light of a new day towards the Grand Trunk Road that stretches northward towards Kurnal and the Punjab.

The donkey would have kept to the level roads of the cantonment, but now that the sky was brighter Sita could see that most of the bungalows had been gutted by fire, and that smoke from a score of smouldering ruins still rose in ghostly columns above the scorched trees. It was a sight that increased her fears, and rather than cross the cantonment area she turned towards the Ridge and the dark bulk of the Flagstaff Tower, where the Delhi road ran northward to join the Grand Trunk.

Looking back from the crest of the Ridge it was difficult to believe that the once busy cantonment that lay below them was now a desolate shell, for the trees provided a kindly screen and the lazy smoke that drifted up to form a haze above it might have been the smoke of kitchen fires, cooking breakfast for the vanished garrison. On the far side of the Ridge the ground sloped down to merge into the level plain through which the silver ribbon of the Jumna wandered between white sandbanks and a wide belt of croplands, while a mile and a half away— a shadow of the shadowy plain—lay the domes and walls of Delhi, afloat on the morning mists that were rising off

---

*bad characters; riff-raff

33

the river. A long white road, straight as a sword blade, led from the Flagstaff Tower to the Kashmir Gate, but at that hour nothing moved on it, not even the wind. The air was still and the world so quiet that Sita could hear, from far, far away, the crowing of a cock in some village beyond the Najafgarh canal.

The Ridge too was deserted, though even here the mute evidence of panic littered the ground: a child's shoe, a doll, a woman's rose-trimmed and beribboned bonnet hanging on a thorn bush, toys, books, bundles and boxes lost in the darkness or discarded in the frenzy of flight, and a dog-cart lying on its side in the ditch with a broken wheel and smashed shafts. The night dew lay thick on everything, bejewelling the wreckage and dipping the grasses in a film of silver; but the first hot breath of the coming day was already drying the dew, and birds had begun to chirp and twitter among the thorn-scrub.

There was no one in the Flagstaff Tower, but here the debris lay thicker, and around it the trampled ground bore signs that a small army of women and children, officers, servants and horse-drawn vehicles had camped there for hours and left only recently; for there were carriage-lamps on the dog-cart, and one of them was still burning. The marks of wheels, hoof-prints and foot-marks showed that those who had been there had fled northwards towards Kurnal, and Sita would have followed them, but for one thing . . .

Fifty yards beyond the tower, on the road that led north past the Sudder Bazaar to the cut where it turns right-handed onto the Grand Trunk Road, stood an abandoned cart loaded with what at first sight appeared to be women's clothes. And once again, as on the previous night, the donkey jibbed and would not pass it. It was this that made Sita look closer, and now she saw that there were bodies in the cart: the dead bodies of four Sahibs dressed in scarlet uniforms and hideously mutilated, over which someone had hurriedly thrown a woman's flowered muslin dress and a frilled petticoat in a vain attempt at concealment. The flowers on the dress were forget-me-nots and rosebuds and the petticoat had once been white; but both were now blotched with dark brown stains, for the gay scarlet uniforms had been slashed with sword cuts and were stiff with dried blood.

A single hand, lacking a thumb but still wearing a signet ring that no one had thought to remove, protruded stiffly from among the muslin folds, and staring at it, flinching away, like the animal she rode, from the smell of death, Sita abandoned any idea of following in the wake of the British.

The stories of the men on the bridge, the sight of the dead memsahib in the Kudsia Bagh and even the desolation of the cantonments, had not succeeded in bringing home to her the reality of the situation. It was a rising; riot, arson and *gurrh-burrh*.* She had heard of such outbreaks often enough, though she had never been involved in them. But the Sahib-log had always put them down, and once they were over those who had caused them were hanged or transported, and the Sahib-log were still there, with their power and their numbers greater than before. But the dead men in the cart had been Sahibs—officers of the Company's army—and their fellow Sahibs had been in such fear and haste that they had not even paused to bury their comrades before they fled. They had merely flung some memsahib's clothes onto the cart to hide the faces of the dead and then run away, leaving the bodies to the mercy of crows and vultures and any passing ruffian who might choose to strip them of their uniforms. There could be no safety any longer with the Sahib-log, and she must take Ash-Baba away, somewhere far away from both Delhi and the British . . .

They turned and went back down the road they had just come by and crossed the ruined cantonments, past blackened roofless bungalows, trampled gardens, the gutted barracks and bells of arms, and the quiet cemetery where the British dead lay in neat rows under the alien soil. The donkey's small hooves sounded a hollow, tripping tattoo on the bridge over the Najafgarh canal, and a flight of parrots that had been drinking from a puddle in the dry cut flew up in a green, screaming explosion of sound. But they were clear of the cantonment now and out in the open country; and suddenly the world was no longer grey and still, but yellow with dawn and noisy with birdsong and the chatter of squirrels.

Beyond the canal the path narrowed to a track between sugar cane and tall grass, and presently it met the broad level of the Grand Trunk Road. But instead of turn-

---

*uproar, tumult

35

ing down it, they crossed over it and followed a field path towards the little village of Dahipur. Without the donkey they could not have gone far, but once out of sight of the highroad, Sita dismounted and walked, and in this way they put several miles between themselves and Delhi before the sun became too hot. Their progress had been slower than it might have been, for Sita was still actively aware of danger and made constant detours in order to avoid villages and casual wayfarers. It was true that Ash-Baba had inherited his mother's black hair and that the open-air life of the camp had burned his already brown skin as dark as any Indian's, but his eyes were agate-grey, and who was to say that some suspicious passer-by would not recognize him as a white child and kill him for the sake of blood-money? One could also never be certain what a child would say or do, and she would not feel safe until Delhi and the mutineers from Meerut were many days' march behind her.

The crops as yet provided little cover, but the plain was seamed and scored with dry gullies, and there were thickets of thorn and elephant grass that offered adequate hiding-places even for the donkey. Yet here too the English had passed, for a buzzing cloud of flies betrayed the body of an elderly Eurasian, probably a clerk from one of the Government offices, hidden in a patch of grass by the side of the path. He too, like the fat woman in the Kudsia Bagh, had crawled into the grass and died there; but unlike her he had been so sorely wounded that it was astonishing that he should have been able to drag himself so far.

It disturbed Sita to find that others too had attempted to escape across country instead of taking the road to Kurnal. The sight of such wretched fugitives would only serve to bring news of the rising to previously peaceful villages, and kindle scorn of the *feringhis* (foreigners) and support for the rebellious sepoys, and she had hoped by taking this route to out-distance the news from Delhi. Now it seemed as though she had set herself an impossible task, for the man who had died in the grass had quite obviously been there since the previous day, and it looked as though someone must have helped him to get that far —the same person who had carefully spread a handkerchief over his face before leaving him to the flies and the eaters of carrion. Sita dragged the reluctant donkey past, and distracted Ash's attention and her own anguished thoughts by embarking on his favourite story of the secret valley, and of how they would find it someday and live happily ever after.

Towards nightfall they were well off the beaten track, and she judged it safe enough to stop at a village whose twinkling lights promised a bazaar and the prospect of hot food and fresh milk. Ash-Baba was tired and sleepy and therefore less likely to talk, while the donkey too needed food and water, and she herself was very weary. They slept that night in a lean-to shed belonging to a hospitable cultivator, which they shared with the donkey and the cultivator's cow, Sita representing herself as the wife of a blacksmith from Jullunder way, returning from Agra with an orphaned nephew, the son of her husband's brother. She bought hot food and buffalo-milk in the bazaar, where she heard a variety of frightening rumours—each one worse than the last—and later, when Ash was asleep, she joined a group of gossiping villagers on the edge of the threshing-ground.

Sitting well back among the shadows, she listened to stories of the rising, the tale having reached here that morning, brought by a party of Gujars and confirmed in the late afternoon by five sepoys of the 54th Native Infantry, who had joined the mutineers at the Kashmir Gate on the previous day, and were now on their way to Sirdana and Mazafnagar to carry the news that the Company's power was broken at last, and that once again a Mogul ruled as King in Delhi. The tale had lost nothing in the telling; and hearing it retold by the elders of the village, after all she herself had seen since the men of the 3rd Cavalry galloped past her on the Meerut road, Sita believed it.

All the English in Meerut had been put to the sword, said the elders, confirming the words of the sowars on the bridge of boats, and in Delhi too all had been slain—both in the city and the cantonments. And not only in Delhi and Meerut, either, for the regiments had risen throughout Hind, and soon there would be no *feringhis* left alive in all the land—not so much as a single child. Those who had tried to save themselves by flight were being hunted down and killed, while any who thought to hide themselves in the jungles would be slain by wild beasts—if they did not first perish from hunger and thirst and exposure. Their day was done. They were gone like dust before the wind,

37

and not one would be left to carry the tale of their going. The shame of Plassey* was avenged and the hundred years of subjection at an end—and now there was no need to pay the taxes.

"Is Esh-mitt Sahib also dead, then?" asked an awe-struck voice, presumably referring to a local District Officer who was, in all probability, the only white man whom the villagers had ever seen.

"Assuredly. For on Friday—so Durga Dass says—he rode to Delhi to see the Commissioner-Sahib, and did not the sepoy with the pock-marked face say that all the *Angrezi-log* in Delhi were slain? It is certain that he is dead. He and all others of his accursed race."

Sita listened and believed, and stealing away into the darkness she returned hastily to the bazaar, where she bought a small earthenware bowl and the ingredients for making a brown dye that was equally effective and hard-wearing on the human skin as on cotton cloth. Soaked overnight it had been ready by morning, and long before the village was awake she roused Ash, and leading him out into the dim light of dawn, crouched behind a cactus hedge where she stripped him and applied the dye with a cotton rag, working by touch as much as sight and whispering urgently that he was to tell no one, and to remember that from now on his name was Ashok: "You will not forget, Heart-of-my-heart? Ashok—promise me you will not forget?"

"Is it a game?" asked Ash, intrigued.

"Yes, yes, a game. We will play that your name is Ashok and that you are my son. My true son: your father being dead—which the gods know is true. What is your name, son?"

"Ashok."

Sita kissed him passionately, and adjuring him again not to answer questions, took him back to the shed. After eating a frugal meal and paying for their night's lodging, they set out across the fields, and by mid-day the village was far behind them and Delhi and the Meerut road only an ugly memory. "We will go north. Perhaps to Mardan," said Sita. "We shall be safe in the north."

---

*The battle that gained India for Clive and the East India Company in 1757. (There was a legend that the rule of the Company would only last a hundred years from that date.)

"In the valley?" asked Ash. "Are we going to our valley?"

"Not yet, my King. One day surely. But that too lies in the north, so we will go northward."

It was as well for them that they did so, for behind them the land was ablaze with violence and terror. In Agra and Alipore, Neemuch, Nusserabad and Lucknow, throughout Rohilkhand, Central India and Bundelkhand, in cities and cantonments up and down the country, men rose against the British.

At Cawnpore the Nana, the adopted son of the late Peshwa, whom the authorities had refused to recognize, turned on his oppressors and besieged them in their tragically inadequate entrenchments; and when after twenty days the survivors accepted his offer of safe conduct, and were herded onto river boats that they were told would take them to Allahabad, the boats were set alight and fired upon from the bank. Those who managed to struggle to shore were taken prisoner, the men shot, while some two hundred women and children—all who remained of a garrison that at the beginning of the siege had numbered a thousand—were penned up in a small building, the *Bibi-gurh* (women's house), where they were later hacked to death on the orders of the Nana, and their bodies thrown into a near-by well, the dying with the dead.

In Jhansi that same royal widow whose wrongs Hilary had written of in his last report—Lakshmi-Bai, the beautiful childless Rani who had been refused the right to adopt a son and disinherited by the East India Company —avenged herself for those wrongs by massacring another British garrison unwise enough to surrender to her on her promise of safe conduct.

"Why do the people put up with it?" Hilary had asked Akbar Khan. "Why don't they do something?" Lakshmi-Bai, the unforgiving, had done something. She had repaid the bitter injustice dealt her by the Governor-General and Council of the Honourable The East India Company with a deed no less unjust. For not only the men, but the wives and children of those who had accepted her offer of safe conduct had been roped together and publicly butchered: children, women and men, in that order . . .

"John Company" had sown the wind. But many who must reap the whirlwind were as blameless and bewildered

39

as Sita and Ash-Baba, blown helplessly before the gale like two small and insignificant sparrows on a wild day of storm.

3

It was October and the leaves were turning gold when they came to Gulkote, a tiny principality near the northern borders of the Punjab, where the plains lose themselves in the foothills that fringe the Pir Panjal.

They had come slowly, and for the most part on foot, for the donkey had been commandeered by a party of sepoys in the last days of May, and the hot weather had made travelling impossible except in the cool of the morning before the sun rose, or after it had set.

The sepoys had been men of the 38th Native Infantry, a regiment that had disintegrated on the day that the sowars of the 3rd Cavalry rode in from Meerut. They had been returning to their homes laden with loot, and were full of tales of the rising, among them the story of how the last of the *feringhis* in Delhi, the two men and fifty women and children who had been imprisoned in the King's palace, had met their end:

"It is necessary to rid the land of all foreigners," explained the speaker, "but we of the army refused to turn butcher and slaughter women and babes who were half dead already from fear and hunger and many days of confinement in the dark. Some of the King's household also spoke out against it, saying that it was contrary to the tenets of the Muslim faith to slay women and children or other prisoners of war; but when Miza Majhli tried to save them, the mob cried for his blood, and in the end the King's servants took swords and slew them all."

"All?" faltered Sita. "But—but what harm would children have done? Could they not at least have spared the little ones?"

"Bah! It is foolish to spare the young of a serpent," scoffed the sepoy; and Sita quaked anew for Ash-Baba, that embryo serpent playing happily in the dust only a yard or two away.

"That is true," agreed one of his comrades, "for they grow up and breed more of their kind. It was well done to rid ourselves of so many who would in their turn have become thieves and oppressors." Whereupon he commandeered the donkey, and when Sita protested, struck her down with the butt of his musket while a second man picked up Ash, who had rushed to her defence like a small tiger-cat, and flung him into a patch of thorn-scrub. Ash had been severely scratched, and when he crawled out at last bruised, torn and sobbing, it was to find Sita lying unconscious by the roadside and sepoys and donkey already small in the distance.

That had been a black day. But at least the men had not taken Sita's bundle, and there was some consolation in that. Possibly it never occurred to them that the humble possessions of a ragged child and a lone woman could include anything worth taking, and they were not to know that at least half of the coins that Hilary had kept in a tin box under his bed were in a wash-leather bag at the bottom of the bundle. Sita had removed it as soon as she recovered consciousness and could think clearly again, and added it to the other half that she kept in a fold of cloth tied about her waist under her sari. It made a heavy and uncomfortable belt, but was probably safer there than in the bundle; and now that the donkey had been taken, she would in any case have to carry both.

The theft of the donkey had been a grievous blow; as much on sentimental grounds as practical ones, for Ash had grown fond of the little animal and mourned its loss long after even the worst of the scratches had healed and been forgotten. But that incident, and the sepoys' stories, served to underline the dangers of using the roadways that ran between towns and the larger villages, and the wisdom of keeping instead to the cattle tracks of the Mofussil and the little lost villages where life pursued a slow, centuries-old course, and news from the outside world seldom penetrated.

Now and again a ripple from the far-off storm would lap against even such remote fastnesses as these, and they would hear stories of wounded and starving Sahib-log hiding in the jungle or among the rocks, and creeping out

41

to beg food from the meanest passer-by. Once, following a rumour of successful risings throughout Oude and Rohilkund, there had been a tale of mutiny and massacre in Ferozepore and far-off Sialkot, and it was this last that made Sita finally abandon a nebulous plan that she had briefly entertained, of taking Ash-Baba to Mardan where his mother's brother would be stationed with the Guides. For if the regiments in Ferozepore and Sialkot had also mutinied, then what hope would there be for the British in any cantonment town anywhere? If there were still any left alive (which seemed doubtful) they would all soon be dead: all except Ash-Baba, who was now her son Ashok.

Sita never again referred to him as anything but "my son," and Ash accepted the relationship without question. Within a week he had forgotten that it had begun as a game, or that he had ever called her anything but "mother."

As they journeyed further north, skirting the folds of the Sawaliks, the rumours of rising and unrest became fewer, and the talk was only of crops and the harvest and the local problems and gossip of small rural communities whose horizons are bounded by their own fields. The blazing days of June ended in a torrential downpour of rain as the monsoon swept across the parched plains of India, turning the fields to bogs and every ditch and nullah into a river, and reducing each day's journey to a minimum. It was no longer possible to sleep out in the open and shelter had to be found—and paid for.

Sita begrudged the money, for it was a sacred charge and not to be expended lightly. It belonged to Ash-Baba and must be kept for him until he was grown. There was also the danger of appearing too affluent and thereby inviting attack and robbery, so it must be spent in the smallest coins only and to the accompaniment of hard bargaining. She bought, too, a yard of coarse, country-made *puttoo* (tweed) to keep the rain from Ash, though she was well aware that he would have preferred to dispense with this protection and go bare-headed as well as unshod. Ash's paternal grandmother had been a Scotswoman from the west coast of Argyll, and possibly it was her blood in his veins that made him take a particular pleasure in the feel of rain on his face, though it may well have been no more than any child's partiality for splashing through mud and puddles.

Constant exposure to the monsoon had succeeded in washing away most of the dye from his skin, and he was once again a colour that would have been familiar to Hilary and Akbar Khan. But though Sita was aware of this she did not renew the dye, since by now they were close to the foothills of the Himalayas, and hill-folk being fairer-skinned than the men of the south (many of them having light-coloured eyes, blue, grey or hazel, and hair that is as often red or brown as black), her son Ashok aroused no comment and was, indeed, somewhat swarthier than many of the pale-skinned Hindu children with whom he played in the villages by the way. Her fears for his safety were gradually diminishing and she no longer lived in terror that he might betray himself by some unguarded mention of the "Burra-Sahib" and the old days, because he appeared to have forgotten them.

But Ash had not forgotten: it was just that he did not wish to think or speak of the past. He was, in many ways, a precocious child, for children ripen early in the East, being reckoned men and women at an age when their brothers and sisters in the West are still in the junior forms at school. No one had ever treated him as anything but an equal or kept him immured in a nursery atmosphere. He had had the run of his father's camp from the moment he could crawl, and lived his short life among adults who had, by and large, treated him as an adult—though a privileged one, because they loved him. Had it not been for Hilary and Akbar Khan, he would probably have been spoiled. But though their methods had differed, they had both taken pains to prevent his becoming a pampered brat, Hilary because he could not have endured whining or tantrums and preferred his son to behave from the first as an intelligent human being, and Akbar Khan because he intended the boy to be a commander of armies, a man whom men would one day follow to the death, and such are not the products of a spoilt and over-indulged childhood.

Sita had been the only one who ever spoke to him in baby-talk or sang him childish songs, for Akbar Khan had early impressed it upon him that he was a man and must not allow himself to be molly-coddled. So the songs and

43

the baby-talk had been a secret between Ash and his foster-mother, and it was partly because they shared that secret that he accepted the necessity of keeping other things secret, and had not betrayed them both at the start of their ill-fated journey to Delhi. Sita had told him that he must not talk of the "Burra-Sahib" and Uncle Akbar, or the camp and all the things they were leaving behind them, and he had obeyed her, but as much from shock and bewilderment as obedience to her wishes. The swiftness with which his world had dissolved, and the incomprehensible manner of its going, was a black pool of shadow into which he would not look for fear of seeing things he did not want to remember: dreadful things, like Uncle Akbar being thrust into a hole in the ground and the earth piled over him; and the almost worse shock of seeing the "Burra-Sahib" weeping over that rough mound, when how many times had both he and Uncle Akbar said that tears were only for women?

It was better to turn one's back on such things and refuse to recall them; and Ash had done just that. Sita's urgings had been unnecessary, for even had she wished him to speak of the past it is unlikely that she could, under any circumstances, have persuaded him to do so. As it was, she imagined that he had forgotten it, and was grateful for the shortness of a child's memory.

Her chief anxiety now was the quest for some peaceful backwater, sufficiently remote from the bustling cities and the highroads of Hind to remain ignorant of such matters as the rise or fall of the Company. A place small enough to escape the eyes of those who would now be in authority, yet large enough to absorb a woman and a child without their arrival attracting attention or arousing curiosity. Somewhere where she could find work and they could settle down and begin life again, and find peace and contentment and freedom from fear. Her own home village did not fall into this category, because there she would be known and her return lead to endless speculation and questioning by her own and her husband's family; and inevitably, the truth would leak out. For the boy's sake she could not risk that: and for her own also. She could hardly conceal Daya Ram's death from his parents, and once that was known, she would be forced to conduct herself as a widow, a childless widow, should; and there were few worse fates in India, for such women

44

were considered to be responsible for their husbands' death, it being believed that some misconduct in a previous life had brought misfortune on their men.

A widow must never wear colours or jewellery, but shave her head and dress only in white. She could not marry again, but must end her days as an unpaid drudge in her husband's family, despised on account of her sex and resented as the bringer of bad luck. It was not surprising that in the days before the law of the Company had forbidden it, many widows had preferred to become suttees and burn themselves alive on their husband's funeral pyres rather than face the bitterness of long years of servitude and humiliation. But a stranger in a strange town could adopt any identity she chose, and who was to know that Sita was a widow—or care? She could pretend that her husband had taken work in the south, or run off and left her. What did it matter? She could hold up her head as the mother of a son, and wear gay colours and glass bangles and her few modest pieces of jewellery. And when she found work she would be working for the boy and herself, and not as an unpaid slave for Daya Ram's family.

Several times during the months that followed their escape from Delhi, Sita thought she had discovered the right place: the haven where they could end their wanderings and find work and safety. But each time there had been something that drove her on: the arrival of an armed band of sepoys from some regiment that had risen against its officers, and who were roaming the country in search of English fugitives; the sight of a family of starving *feringhis,* who had been given shelter by a kindly villager, being dragged out of hiding and put to death by a jeering mob; a passing traveller flaunting a murdered officer's uniform, or half a dozen sowars galloping through the crops . . .

"Aren't we ever going to stop *anywhere?*" inquired Ash wistfully.

June gave place to July, and July to August. And now the crop-lands were behind them and there was only jungle ahead. But Sita and Ash were both used to jungles. The silence and the hot, wet thickets held fewer terrors for them than the villages, and the jungle provided them with edible roots and berries, water and fuel, and shade from the heat as well as shelter from the rain.

45

Once, walking down a game-track through high grass, they had come face to face with a tiger. But the great beast was full fed and peaceably disposed, and after exchanging a long, surprised stare with the intruders, it had turned aside without haste and vanished into the grass. Sita had not moved for five long minutes, until the scolding chatter of a jungle-cock some thirty yards to their right told her the direction in which the tiger had gone; and then she had turned back and made a detour that took them away from the grass. It was astonishing that they had not lost themselves in those trackless miles of trees and thickets, elephant grass, bamboos, rocks and creepers. But here Sita's unerring sense of direction helped them, and as they were heading for no particular goal, but merely moving hopefully northward, it did not matter very much which path they chose.

By the end of August they had won free of the jungle and were in open country once more, and with September the monsoon slackened. The sun was once again cruelly hot and clouds of mosquitoes rose each evening from the flooded *jheels* and brimming ponds and ditches. But at the edge of the plain and beyond the foothills the high ridges of the Himalayas rose clear and blue above the heat-haze, and the night air held a hint of coolness. Here, in the scattered hamlets, they heard no rumours of strife and insurrection, for now there were few footpaths and no roads, and the land was sparsely populated; the villages consisting of no more than a huddle of huts and a few acres of cultivation, surrounded by miles of rock-strewn grazing ground that was bounded on the one side by jungles and on the other by foothills.

Always, on clear days, they could see the snow peaks, and the sight of them was a constant reminder to Sita that time was running out and that the winter was coming, and that it was necessary for them to find a roof to live under before the cold weather set in. But there was little chance of employment for herself or a hopeful future for Ashok in such country as this, and though she was tired and footsore and desperately weary of travelling she was not tempted to linger in it. They had come a long way since the April morning when they had turned their backs on Hilary's silent camp and set out for Delhi, and they were both sorely in need of rest. And then, in October, when the leaves were turning gold, they came to Gulkote, and Sita realized that here at last was the spot she had been looking for. A place where they could hide and be safe.

The independent State of Gulkote had been too small, too difficult of access and above all too poor to interest the Governor-General and the officials of the East India Company. And as its standing army consisted of less than a hundred soldiers—the majority elderly grey-beards equipped with tulwars and rusty jezails—and its ruler appeared to be popular with his subjects and displayed no disposition to be hostile, the Company had left him in peace.

The capital city, from which the state took its name, stood some five thousand feet above sea-level, at the apex of a great triangular plateau among the foothills. It had once been a fortified town and it was still surrounded by a massive wall that enclosed a rabbit warren of houses, a single main street that bisected these from the Lahori Gate on the south to the *Lal Dawaza*, the "Red Gate," on the north, three temples, a mosque and a maze of narrow alleyways. The whole was overlooked by the Rajah's rambling fortress-palace, the Hawa Mahal—the "Palace of the Winds" that crowned a towering outcrop of rock some thousand yards beyond the city wall.

The ruling house traced its descent from a Rajput chieftain who had come north in the reign of Sikander Lodi, and stayed to carve out a kingdom for himself and his followers. The kingdom had shrunk with the centuries, until by the time the Punjab fell to the Sikhs under Ranjit Singh, it had been reduced to no more than a handful of villages in a territory that a man on horse-back could traverse in a single day. That it had survived at all was probably due to the fact that its present frontiers were bounded on one side by an unbridged river, on another by a dense track of forest and on the third by a waste of rock-strewn country scored by deep ravines, whose ruler was related to the Rajah; while at its back the wrinkled, wooded foothills swept upwards to meet the white peaks of the Dur Khaima and the great snow-capped range that protects Gulkote from the north. It would have been difficult to move an army against such a strategically placed spot, and as there had never been a sufficiently urgent reason to do so, it had escaped the attentions of the Moguls,

47

Mahrattas, Sikhs and the East India Company, and lived serenely remote from the changing world of the nineteenth century.

The ramshackle town had been in a festive mood on the day that Ash and Sita reached it, there having been a distribution of largess from the palace in the form of food and sweetmeats for the poor, in celebration of the birth of a child to the Senior Rani. It had been a modest celebration, for the child was a daughter, but the citizens were disposed to use it as an excuse for a holiday: feasting, making merry and decorating their houses with garlands and paper flags. Little boys threw *patarkars*—home-made squibs—among the feet of the passers-by in the crowded bazaars, and after dark the thin fire of rockets soared into the night sky to blossom above the rooftops where the women-folk clustered like flocks of chattering birds.

To Sita and Ash, accustomed through long months to silence and solitude—or at best the humble society of small villages—the colour and noise of the jostling, lighthearted crowds were exhilarating beyond words, and they ate of the Rajah's bounty and admired the fireworks, and found lodgings for themselves in the house of a fruit-seller in an alley off the Chandi Bazaar.

"Can we stay here?" asked Ash sleepily, surfeited with sweetmeats and excitement. "I like it here."

"I too, little son. Yes, we shall stay here. I will find work and we shall stay and be happy. Yet I wish . . ." Sita stopped on a sigh and did not finish the sentence. Her conscience troubled her, because she had not obeyed the Burra-Sahib's order to return his son to his own people. But she did not know what else she could have done. Perhaps one day, when her boy was a man . . . But for the present they were both weary of wandering, and here they would at least be among the mountains—and safe. An hour or so in the town had convinced her of that last, for in all the talk in the bazaars and the gossip of the loitering, chattering crowds, there had been no word of the troubles that were shaking India, or any mention of mutineers or Sahib-log.

Gulkote was only interested in its own affairs and the latest scandals of the palace. It paid little or no attention to the doings of the world beyond its borders, and at the moment its main topic of conversation (apart from the perennial one of crops and taxes) was the eclipse of the

48

Senior Rani by the concubine, Janoo, a *Nautch*-girl (dancer) from Kashmir, who had acquired such a hold over the jaded monarch that she had recently succeeded in persuading him to marry her.

Janoo-Bai was suspected of practising magic and the black arts. How else could a common dancing-girl have raised herself to the rank of Rani, and ousted from favour the mother of the baby princess, who had reigned undisputed for at least three years? She was known to be both beautiful and ruthless, and the sex of the new baby at the palace was taken as further proof of her malignant powers. "She is a witch," said Gulkote. "Assuredly she is a witch. They at the palace say that it was by her orders that food and sweetmeats were distributed to the hungry to mark the birth of this child, for she rejoices that it is not a son, and would have her rival know it. Now if she herself were to bear a son . . . !"

Sita listened to the talk and was reassured by it; there was nothing here that spelt danger to Ashok, son of Daya Ram, syce, who (so she informed the fruit-seller's wife) had run off with a shameless gipsy woman, leaving her to fend for herself and the child.

Her story had not been questioned, and later she had found work in a shop in Khanna Lal's Gully behind the temple of Ganesh, helping to fashion the gaudy paper and tinsel flowers that are used in garlands and for decorations at weddings and festivals. The work was ill paid, but it sufficed for their needs; and as she had always been quick with her fingers, it was not uncongenial. She was also able to earn a little extra by weaving baskets for the fruit-seller and occasionally helping in the shop.

As soon as they had settled in, Sita dug a hole in the mud floor of their little room and buried the money that Hilary had given her, stamping down the earth and smoothing cow-dung over the whole surface so that no one could tell where it had been disturbed. There remained only the small pocket of letters and papers in its oiled-silk wrapping, and this she would have liked to burn. For though she could not read them, she was aware that they must constitute proof of Ash's parentage, and both fear and jealousy urged her to destroy them. If they were found they might lead to his being killed, as the children of the Sahib-log had been killed at Delhi and Jhansi and Cawnpore and a score of other cities, and her own life might well be forfeit for having tried to save him. Even if he escaped that penalty, they still proved that he was not her son; and by now she could not bear the thought of this. Yet she could not bring herself to destroy them, for they too were a sacred trust: the "Burra-Sahib" had given them into her hand, and were she to burn them his ghost or his God might be angry with her and take revenge for the act. It was better to keep them; but they must never be seen by any other eyes, and if the white ants destroyed them it would not be her fault.

Sita scraped a shallow cavity low down in the wall in the darkest corner of the room, and thrusting the packet into it, covered its hiding place, as she had covered the money, with clay and cow-dung; and having done so, felt that a crushing weight had been lifted off her shoulders and that Ashok was now truly hers.

The boy's grey eyes and ruddy complexion caused no comment in Gulkote, for many of the Rajah's subjects had come from Kashmir, Kulu and the Hindu Kush, and Sita herself was a hill-woman. Ash fraternized with their sons and grandsons and was soon indistinguishable, except to the eye of love, from a hundred other bad little bazaar boys who shouted, frolicked and fought in the streets of Gulkote; and Sita was content. She still believed what the sepoys had told her: that all the English were dead and the rule of the Company broken for ever. Delhi was far away, and beyond the borders of Gulkote lay the Punjab, which had remained relatively quiet; and though an occasional rumour of troubles would drift through the bazaars, these were always vague, garbled and months out of date, and mostly concerned with disasters to the British . . .

None told of the army that had been hurriedly assembled at Ambala. Of the long march of the Guides—five hundred eighty miles in twenty-two days of high summer from Mardan to Delhi—to take part in the siege of that city, the death of Nicholson, or the surrender of the last Mogul and the slaying of his sons by William Hodson of Hodson's Horse; or that Lucknow was still besieged, and that the great rising that had begun with the revolt of the 3rd Cavalry in Meerut was by no means over.

The *Shaitan-ke-Hawa*—the "Devil's Wind"—was still blowing strongly through India, but while thousands died, here in sheltered Gulkote the days were slow and peaceful.

50

Ash had been five years old that October, and it was not until the autumn of the following year of 1858 that Sita learned, through a wandering *sadhu,** something of what had been happening in the outside world. Delhi and Lucknow re-captured, the Nana Sahib a fugitive, and the valiant Rani of Jhansi killed in battle, dressed as a man and fighting to the last. The Company's rule had been broken, but the *feringhis,* said the *sadhu,* were back in power, stronger than ever and engaged in brutal reprisals against those who had fought them in the great rising. And though the Company was no more, its rule had been replaced by that of the white Rani—Victoria—and all Hind was now a possession of the British Crown, with a British Viceroy and British troops governing the land.

Sita had tried to persuade herself that the man was mistaken, or lying. For if his story was true, she would have to take Ashok back to his people, which by now was a prospect she could no longer face. It *could* not be true . . . or it might not be. She would wait, and do nothing until she was sure. There was no need to do anything yet . . .

She had waited all winter, and in spring there had been news that confirmed everything the *sadhu* had said; but still Sita took no action. Ashok was hers, and she would not, could not, give him up. There had been a time when she could have done so, but that was before she had begun to look on him as her son by right, and see him accepted as such. Besides, it was not as though she were depriving a mother or father of their right: he had lost both, and if anyone had a right to him, surely it was herself? Had she not loved him and cared for him from his birth? Taken him from his mother's womb and fed him at her own breast? He knew no other mother and believed himself to be her child, and she would be robbing no one —*no one*. He was no longer Ash-Baba, but her son, Ashok, and she would burn the papers that lay hidden in the wall and say nothing, and no one would ever know.

So they remained in Gulkote and were happy. But Sita did not burn Hilary's papers, for when it came to the point her fear of what the "Burra-Sahib's" ghost might do was greater than her fear of what the papers could prove.

Once again there had been feasting and fireworks in the city. But this time it had been in celebration of the

----
*Hindu holy man

birth of a boy to Janoo-Bai the Rani—sometime dancing-girl, and now virtual ruler of Gulkote, in that she ruled the Rajah to the point where her smallest wish must be gratified.

The Rajah's subjects had been commanded to celebrate and they had done so, though without much enthusiasm; the *Nautch*-girl was not popular with the citizens, and the prospect of a prince of her breeding was displeasing to them. Not that he was the heir, for the Rajah's first wife, who had died in child-birth, had left her lord a son: Lalji, "the beloved"—the eight-year-old Yuveraj, apple of his father's eye and pride of all Gulkote. But life was uncertain in India and who could say if the boy would live to be a man? His mother, in fifteen years of marriage, had given birth to no less than nine children, all of whom, with the exception of Lalji (and the last—a still-born daughter), had died in infancy. She herself had not survived that last confinement, and her husband had soon married again, taking as his wife the daughter of a foreign mercenary, a young and lovely girl who became known in Gulkote as the *"Feringhi-*Rani"— the foreign queen.

The *Feringhi*-Rani's father had been a Russian adventurer who had taken service in the armies of various warring Indian princes. Under the last of these, Ranjit Singh, the "Lion of the Punjab," he had risen to considerable heights; and on the "Lion's" death, had prudently retired to end his days in the remote and sovereign state of Gulkote. It was rumoured that he had once been an officer of the Cossacks who had been sentenced to life imprisonment for some misdemeanour, but had escaped from his gaolers and found his way to India through the passes of the north. He had certainly shown no desire to return to his native land when Ranjit's death had put an end to his employment in the Punjab, but had lived in comfortable retirement on the accumulated riches of ten years of power, together with a bevy of concubines and his Indian wife, Kumaridevi, the daughter of a Rajput prince whom he had defeated in battle, and whom he had demanded of her father as part of a conqueror's loot—they having seen each other in the sack of the city, and straightway fallen in love.

The *Feringhi*-Rani was this lady's last and only surviving child; born at the cost of her mother's life, since by then the once beautiful princess had been middle-aged and worn out by miscarriages and still-births that were due, in a large part, to the rigours of following her husband on many campaigns. Her daughter had been brought up with a brood of illegitimate half-brothers and sisters, all of whom had considered it a triumph when reports of her beauty had reached the ears of the Rajah of Gulkote, and he had asked for her hand in marriage, knowing that no lesser alliance would have been considered, as on her mother's side her lineage was more royal than his own.

For a time the *Feringhi*-Rani had been happy; none of her half-brothers and sisters or their various mothers had been particularly kind to her, and she had been glad to leave her home for the raffish splendours of the "Palace of the Winds." The enmity of the women in the Hawa Mahal had not troubled her over-much, for she was used to the intrigues in Zenanas, and the Rajah was infatuated with her and could refuse her nothing. Nor was she unduly grieved when her father died a year after her marriage, for he had never paid much attention to his numerous offspring. If she had any regrets they were solely on account of her childlessness, though she did not desire children with the single-minded fervour of purely Eastern women, and was in any case sure that it was only a matter of time before they appeared. But the avid interest, jealousy and triumph of the other women over this sore subject (together with their gloating hints that she—"the half-caste"—was barren) piqued her, and she began to worry over it and be impatient for the day when she too should bear a child—a son. Because of course it must be a son.

So far, of all the Rajah's women, only his first wife had borne him sons, and of these only one had lived. But one son was no good to a man; he should have many, so that whatever happened, the succession was secure. It was therefore her duty as chief lady of the palace, and his heart, to produce those sons for him, and she was delighted when she at last became pregnant. But perhaps it was her foreign blood that made her react to pregnancy less happily than other women appeared to do, for instead of blooming into further beauty, as they did, she became subject to incessant attacks of vomiting, with the result that she became sallow and haggard, and in a matter of weeks had lost both her beauty and spirits.

The Rajah was genuinely fond of her, but like most men, he did not feel comfortable in the presence of illness and invalids, and preferred to keep out of her way and hope that she would soon recover. It was doubly unfortunate for her that at this juncture, one of his ministers should have given a banquet in his honour at which a troupe of dancing-girls entertained the guests: for among the dancers was the Kashmiri girl, Janoo. An alluring, golden-skinned, dark-eyed witch, as beautiful, and as predatory, as a black panther.

The top of Janoo's head reached no higher than a man's heart, for she was a little woman, and would probably, one day, be a dumpy one. But now she was young, and to the men who watched her swaying to the music of drums and sitars she seemed a living, breathing replica of those voluptuous goddesses who smile from the frescoes of Ajanta or posture in stone on the Black Temple at Konarak. She possessed in abundance that indefinable quality that a generation as yet unborn was to call "sex-appeal," and she had brains as well as beauty: three invaluable assets that she now used to such good purpose that twenty-four hours later she was installed in the palace, and within a week it was plain to all that the star of the *"Feringhi-Rani"* was setting, and that there was a new favourite to be flattered and propitiated by those who desired favours.

Even then it had never occurred to anyone that this was more than a passing infatuation that would burn itself out as quickly as others had done, for they had not taken the measure of the *Nautch*-girl. But Janoo was ambitious, and she had been instructed from childhood in the art of pleasing and amusing men. She was no longer content with a handful of coins and an occasional trinket; she saw the chance of a throne, played her cards skilfully, and won. The Rajah had married her.

Two weeks later the *Feringhi*-Rani had been brought to bed, but instead of the son who might have restored to her some of her lost prestige, she had borne a small, plain, pallid daughter.

"It is all she is fit for," said Janoo-Bai scornfully. "One has only to look at her to see that such a milk-blooded weakling will never be the mother of sons. Now when *my* son is born . . ."

Janoo never doubted for a moment that her first

54

child would be a son. And a son it had been: a strong and lusty boy of whom any father could be proud. Rockets streamed up into the night sky to shower the city with stars while conches blared and gongs boomed in the temples, and the poor fed sumptuously in honour of the new prince; among them young Ashok and his mother Sita, whose clever fingers had fashioned many of the tin-selled garlands that decorated the streets that day.

The six-year-old son of Hilary and Isobel had stuffed himself with *halwa* and *jellabies,* shouted and thrown *patarkars* with his friends, and wished that a son could be born to the Rajah every day. He had no complaints against life, but there was no denying that the fare provided by Sita was plain and not overabundant, and the few sweetmeats that came his way were more often than not filched from some stall in the bazaar at the risk of capture and a beating by the incensed owner. He was a strong and well-grown child, tall for his age and as agile as a monkey. The spartan diet of the poor had kept him lean, and the games of tag that he and his friends played in the streets and across the rooftops of the city—not to mention the snatching of sweets and fruit and the headlong flights from pursuit—had hardened his muscles and helped to develop a natural fleetness of foot.

On the other side of the world, in the comfortable upper and middle-class nurseries of Victorian England, children of five and six were still regarded as too young to do more than learn their alphabet with the aid of coloured bricks, and bowl hoops under the careful eye of nurse-maids: but in mines and factories and on farms, the children of the poor toiled beside their parents, and in far-off Gulkote, Ash too became a wage-earner.

He was barely six-and-a-half when he went to work as a horse-boy in the stables of Duni Chand, a rich land-owner who had a house near the temple of Vishnu and several farms in the country beyond the city limits.

Duni Chand kept a string of horses on which he visited his fields and rode out hawking on the bad-lands by the river, and it was Ash's duty to carry grain and draw water, attend to the harness and lend a hand with anything from cutting grass to curry-combing. The work was arduous and the wages light, but having spent his infancy among horses—his supposed father, Daya Ram, had introduced him to them at an early age—he had never had

55

the least fear of them. It not only pleased him to work with them, but the few annas thus earned gave him an enormous sense of importance. He was a man and a wage-earner and could now, if he so wished, afford to buy *halwa* from the sweetmeat-seller instead of stealing it. This was a step up in the world, and he informed Sita that he had decided to become a syce and earn enough money for the day when they would set out to find their valley. Mo-hammed Sherif, the head-syce, was reported to earn as much as twelve rupees a month, a vast sum that did not include *dustori*—the one anna on each rupee that he levied on every item of food or equipment purchased for use in the stables, and which more than doubled his salary.

"When I am head-syce," said Ash grandly, "we will move to a big house and have a servant to do the cooking, and you will never have to do any more work, Mata-ji."

It is just possible that he might have carried out his plan and spent his days attached to the stable of some pet-ty nobleman. For as soon as it became apparent that he could ride anything on four legs, Mohammed Sherif, rec-ognizing a born horseman, had permitted him to exercise his charges and taught him many valuable secrets of horsemanship, so that the year he spent in Duni Chand's stables had been a very happy one. But fate, with a cer-tain amount of human assistance, had other plans for Ash; and the fall of a weather-worn slab of sandstone was to change the whole course of his life.

It happened on an April morning, almost three years to the day from the morning when Sita had led him away from the terrible vulture-filled camp in the Terai, and started out on the long road to Delhi. The young crown-prince, Lalji, Yuveraj of Gulkote, rode through the city to make offerings at the Temple of Vishnu. And as he passed under the arch of the ancient Charbagh Gate that stands at the junction of the Chandni Bazaar and the Street of the Coppersmiths, a slab of coping-stone slid from its place and fell into the roadway.

Ash had been standing in the forefront of the crowd, having wriggled his way, eel-like, between the close-packed legs of his elders, and his eye had been caught by a movement overhead. He had seen the slab shift and slip just as the head of the Yuveraj's horse emerged from the shadow of the arch, and almost without thinking (for there had not been time for conscious thought) he leapt at the bridle, and clutching it, checked the startled animal as the heavy slab of sandstone crashed into the street and exploded into a hundred sharp-edged fragments under the prancing hooves. Ash and the horse, together with several spectators, had been gashed by the flying splinters, and there was blood everywhere: on the hot white dust, the gay garments of the crowd and the ceremonial trappings of the horse.

The spectators had screamed and swayed and struggled, and the horse, maddened by pain and noise, would have bolted had not Ash held its head and talked to it and soothed it until the stunned escort, spurring forward, caught the reins from him, and closing up around their prince, shouldered him aside. There followed an interval of surging chaos filled with a clamour of questions and answers while the escort beat back the crowd and stared at the broken coping overhead, and a white-bearded horseman flung Ash a coin—a gold mohur, no less—and said "*Shabash* (Bravo), little one! That was well done indeed."

The crowd, seeing that no one had suffered any serious hurt, yelled their approval, and the procession continued on its way to the accompaniment of frenzied cheers, the Yuveraj sitting straight-backed in the saddle and clutching the reins with hands that were noticeably unsteady. He had kept his seat on the plunging animal with creditable skill, and his future subjects were proud of him. But the small face under the jewelled turban was strained and colourless as he looked back over his shoulder, searching the sea of faces for the boy who had leapt so providentially at his horse's head.

A stranger in the crowd had hoisted Ash up on his shoulder so that he might see the procession depart, and for a brief moment the two children stared at each other, the black frightened eyes of the little prince meeting the interested grey ones of Duni Chand's stable-boy. Then the crowd surged between them, and half a minute later the procession reached the end of the Street of the Coppersmiths and turning it, was lost to sight.

Sita had been gratifyingly impressed by the gold piece, and even more by the tale of the morning's doings. After much discussion, they had decided to take the coin to Burgwan Lal, the jeweller, who was known to be an honest man, and exchange it for a suitable quantity of silver ornaments which Sita could wear until such time as they were in need of ready money. They had neither of them expected to hear any more of the affair—apart from the inevitable comments and congratulations of interested neighbours—but the following morning a stout and supercilious palace official, accompanied by two elderly retainers, knocked on the door of Duni Chand's house. His Highness the Yuveraj, explained the official loftily, desired the immediate attendance of this insignificant brat at the palace, where he would be given living quarters and some minor post in His Highness's household.

"But I can't do that," protested Ash, dismayed. "My mother would not like to live alone, and I could not leave her. She would not want—" He was brusquely interrupted:

"What she wants is of no consequence. It is the order of His Highness that you work for him, and you had best make haste and clean yourself. You cannot come in those rags."

There had been nothing for it but to obey, and Ash had been escorted back to the fruit-seller's shop, where he hurriedly changed into the only other garment he possessed, and comforted the distracted Sita, urging her not to worry for he would be back soon. Very soon—

"Do not cry, mother. There is nothing to cry for. I shall tell the Yuveraj that I would much rather stay here, and because I saved him from injury he will let me return. You will see. Besides, they cannot keep me there against my will."

Secure in this belief, he hugged her reassuringly and followed the Yuveraj's servants through the city gate and up to the Hawa Mahal—the fortress palace of the Rajahs of Gulkote.

4

The Palace of the Winds was approached by a steep causeway paved with slabs of granite that had been worn into ruts and hollows by the passing of generations of men,

58

elephants and horses. The stone felt cold to Ash's bare feet as he trudged up it in the wake of the Yuveraj's servants, and looking up at the towering walls of rock, he was suddenly afraid.

He did not want to live and work in a fortress. He wanted to stay in the city where his friends lived, and tend Duni Chand's horses and learn wisdom from Mohammed Sherif the head groom. The Hawa Mahal looked a grim and unfriendly place, and the *Badshahi Darwaza*, the King's Gate, by which one entered it, did nothing to mitigate that impression. The great iron-studded doors yawned onto darkness, and there were guards armed with tulwars and jezails lounging in the shadows beyond the stone lintel. The causeway passed under a fretted balcony from where the mouths of cannon gaped down at them, and the sunlight was cut off as though by a sword as they entered a long tunnel, honeycombed on either side by niches, guardrooms and galleries that sloped upwards through the heart of the rock.

The transition from warm sunlight to cold shadow, and the eerie echo under the black vault of the roof, served to intensify Ash's unease, and glancing back over his shoulder to where the great gateway framed a view of the city basking comfortably in the heat haze, he was tempted to run. It seemed to him, suddenly, as though he was entering a prison from which he would never be able to escape, and that if he did not run away now, at once, he would lose freedom and friends and happiness and spend his days penned up behind bars like the talking minah that hung in a cage outside the potter's shop. It was a new and troubling thought, and he shivered as though with cold. But it would obviously be no easy task to dodge past so many guards, and it would be humiliating to be caught and dragged into the palace by force. Besides, he was curious to see the inside of the Hawa Mahal: no one he knew had ever been inside it, and it would be something to boast about to his friends. But as for staying there and working for the Yuveraj, he would not even consider it, and if they thought that they could make him they were wrong. He would escape over the walls and go back to the city, and if they followed him, then he and his mother would both run away. The world was wide, and somewhere among the mountains lay their own valley— that safe place where they could live as they pleased.

The tunnel took a sharp turn to the right and came out into a small open courtyard where there were more guards and more ancient bronze cannon. On the far side of it another gateway led into a vast quadrangle where two of the Rajah's elephants rocked at their pickets in the shade of a *chenar* tree, and a dozen chattering women washed clothes in the green water of a stone tank. Beyond this lay the main bulk of the palace. A fantastic jumble of walls, battlements and wooden balconies, fretted windows, airy turrets and carved galleries—the larger part of it screened from the city below by the outer bastion.

No one knew how old the original fortress was, though legend said that it had defied the armies of Sikundar Dulkhan (Alexander the Great) when that young conqueror swooped down into India from the passes of the north. But a substantial part of the present citadel had been built in the early years of the fifteenth century, by a robber chieftain who required an impregnable stronghold from which he and his followers could sally out to raid the fertile lands beyond the river, and retreat to in time of trouble. In those days it had been known as the *Kala Kila*, the "Black Fort," not on account of its colour—for it had been built of the same harsh grey stone that formed the towering outcrop of rock upon which it stood—but in reference to its reputation, which was of the darkest. Later, when the territory had fallen to a Rajput adventurer, it had been considerably enlarged, and his son, who built the walled city on the plain below and became the first Rajah of Gulkote, had transformed the *Kala Kila* into a vast, ornately decorated royal residence which on account of its lofty position he re-named the Hawa Mahal— the "Palace of the Winds."

It was here that the present Rajah lived in dilapidated splendour in a maze of rooms furnished with Persian carpets, dusty hangings shimmering with gold embroidery, and ornaments of jade or beaten silver, set with rubies and raw turquoise. Here too, in the Queen's rooms of the Zenana Quarters beyond the pierced wooden screens that separated the Hall of Audience from a garden full of fruit trees and roses, lived Janoo-Bai the Rani—her rival, the *Feringhi*-Rani, having died of a fever (though some said of poison) during the previous summer. And in a rabbit-warren of rooms that took up a whole wing of the palace, the little Yuveraj, known more familiarly by his "milk-name" of Lalji, spent his days among the crowd of attendants, petty officials and hangers-on who had been assigned to his service by his father.

Led into his presence through a bewildering number of passages and antechambers, Ash found the heir of Gulkote seated cross-legged on a velvet cushion and engaged in teasing a ruffled cockatoo who looked to be as sour and out of temper as its tormentor. The glittering ceremonial dress of the previous day had been exchanged for tight muslin trousers and a plain linen *achkan*,* and in it he looked a good deal younger than he had appeared when mounted on a white stallion in the midst of the procession. Then, he had seemed every inch a prince—and the inches had been considerably increased by a sky-blue turban adorned by a tall aigrette and a flashing clasp of diamonds. But now he was only a small boy. A plump, pasty-faced child who could easily have been taken for two years younger than Ash instead of two years older, and who was not so much cross as frightened.

It was this last that dispelled Ash's awe and put him at his ease, because he too had on occasions taken refuge from fear in a show of ill-temper, and therefore recognized an emotion that was probably hidden from any of the bored adults in the room. It gave him a sudden fellow-feeling for this boy who would one day be Rajah of Gulkote. And an equally sudden urge to take his part against these undiscerning grown-ups who bowed so deferentially and spoke so soothingly in false, flattering voices, while their faces remained cold and sly.

They were not, thought Ash, eyeing them warily, a friendly-looking lot. They were all too fat and sleek and too pleased with themselves, and one of them, a richly dressed young dandy with a handsome dissolute face, who wore a single diamond earring dangling from one ear, was ostentatiously holding a scented handkerchief to his nose as though he feared that this brat from the city might have brought an odour of poverty and the stables with him. Ash looked away and made his bow before royalty, bending low with both hands to his forehead as the custom demanded, but now his gaze was both friendly and interested, and seeing this, the face of the Yuveraj lost some of its ill-temper.

---

*tight-fitting three-quarter-length coat

"Go away. All of you," commanded the Yuveraj, imperiously dismissing his attendants with a wave of the royal hand. "I wish to speak to this boy alone."

The dandy with the diamond earring leaned down to catch his arm and whisper urgently in his ear, but the Yuveraj pulled away and said loudly and angrily: "That is fool's talk, Biju Ram. Why should he do me an injury when he has already saved my life? Besides, he is not armed. Go away and don't be so stupid."

The young man stepped back and bowed with a submissiveness that was sharply at variance with the sudden ugliness of his expression, and Ash was startled to receive a scowl of concentrated venom that seemed out of all proportion to the occasion. Evidently this Biju Ram did not relish being rebuked, and blamed him for being the cause of it; which was manifestly unfair considering he had not said a word—and had never wanted to come here in the first place.

The Yuveraj gestured impatiently and the men withdrew, leaving the two boys to take stock of each other. But Ash still did not speak, and it was the Yuveraj who broke the brief spell of silence that followed. He said abruptly: "I told my father how you saved my life, and he has said that I may have you for my servant. You will be well paid and I . . . I have no one to play with here. Only women and grown-ups. Will you stay?"

Ash had fully intended to refuse, but now he hesitated and said uncertainly: "There is my mother . . . I cannot leave her, and I do not think she . . ."

"That is easily arranged. She can live here too and be a waiting-woman to my little sister, the princess. Are you fond of her, then?"

"Of course," said Ash, astonished. "She is my mother."

"So. You are fortunate. I have no mother. She was the Rani, you know. The true Queen. But she died when I was born, so I do not remember her. Perhaps if she had not died . . . My sister Anjuli's mother died too, and they said that it was sorcery, or poison; but then she was a *feringhi,* and always sickly, so perhaps *That One* had no need to use spells or poison or to—" He broke off, looking quickly over his shoulder and then rose abruptly and said "Come. Let us go out into the garden. There are too many ears here."

He put the cockatoo back onto its perch and went out through a curtained doorway and past half-a-dozen salaaming retainers into a garden set about with walnut trees and fountains, where a little pavilion reflected itself in a pool full of lily pads and golden carp; Ash following at his heels. At the far side of the garden only a low stone parapet lay between the grass and a sheer drop of two hundred feet onto the floor of the plateau below, while on the other three sides rose the palace: tier upon tier of carved and fretted wood and stone, where a hundred windows looked down upon tree tops and city, and out towards the far horizon.

Lalji sat down on the rim of the pool and began to throw pebbles at the carp, and presently he said: "Did you see who pushed the stone?"

"What stone?" asked Ash, surprised.

"The one that would have fallen on me had you not checked my horse."

"Oh that. No one pushed it. It just fell."

"It was pushed," insisted Lalji in a harsh whisper. "Dunmaya, who is—who was my nurse, has always said that if *That One* bore a son she would find some way to make him the heir. And I—I am—" He closed his lips together on the unspoken word, refusing to admit, even to another child, that he was afraid. But the word spoke itself in the quiver of his voice and the unsteadiness of the hands that flung pebbles into the quiet water, and Ash frowned, recalling the movement that had caught his eye before the coping stone slipped, and wondering for the first time why it should have slipped just then, and if it had indeed been a hand that thrust it down.

"Biju Ram says that I am imagining things," confessed the Yuveraj in a small voice. "He says that no one would dare. Even *That One* would not. But when the stone fell I remembered what my nurse had said, and I thought ... Dunmaya says that I must trust no one, but you saved me from the stone, and if you will stay with me perhaps I shall be safe."

"I don't understand," said Ash, puzzled. "Safe from what? You are the Yuveraj and you have servants and guards, and one day you will be Rajah."

Lalji gave a short, mirthless laugh. "That was true a little while ago. But now my father has another son. The child of *That One*—that *Nautch*-girl. Dunmaya says

63

she will not rest until she has put him in my place, for she desires the *gadi* (throne) for her own son, and she holds my father in the hollow of her hand—so." He clenched his fist until the knuckles showed white, and relaxing it, stared down at the pebble that he held, his small face drawn into harsh unchildlike lines. "I am his son. His eldest son. But he would do anything to please her, and—"

His voice trailed away and was lost in the soft splashing of the fountains. And quite suddenly Ash remembered another voice, someone he had almost forgotten, who had said to him long, long ago in another life and another tongue: "The worst thing in the world is injustice. That means being unfair." This was unfair, and so it must not be allowed. Something should be done about it.

"All right. I'll stay," said Ash, heroically abandoning his happy-go-lucky life in the city and the pleasant future he had planned for himself as head-syce in charge of Duni Chand's horses. The careless years were over.

That evening he sent a message to Sita, who dug up the money and the small sealed packet she had hidden in their room, and tying their scanty possessions into a bundle, set out for the Hawa Mahal; and on the following morning Ash was told to consider himself a member of the Yuveraj's household with a salary of no less than five silver rupees a month, while Sita had been given employment as an extra waiting-woman to the dead *Feringhi*-Rani's little daughter, the Princess Anjuli.

By palace standards, the living quarters allotted to them were humble ones: three small and windowless rooms, one of which was a kitchen. But compared with their single room in the city it seemed to them the height of luxury, and the absence of windows was more than compensated for by the fact that all three doors opened onto a small private courtyard that was protected by an eight-foot wall and shaded by a pine tree. Sita was delighted with it and soon began to look upon it as home, though it grieved her that Ashok could not sleep there. But Ash's duties, which in the main consisted of being in attendance on the Yuveraj for a few hours each day, also required him to sleep in an ante-chamber adjoining the royal bedroom at night.

No one could have described such work as arduous, yet Ash soon came to regard it as irksome to a degree. This was partly due to the temper and vagaries of his

64

youthful master, but mostly on account of the young dandy, Biju Ram, who for some reason had taken a strong dislike to him. Lalji's nickname for Biju Ram was *"Bichchhu"* (scorpion) or more familiarly, *"Bichchhu-ji,"* though it was a name that no one else dared use to his face, for it was all too apt—the dandy being a venomous creature who could turn and sting at the slightest provocation.

In Ash's case no provocation seemed necessary, since Biju Ram appeared to take a positive delight in baiting him. His attentions soon became the bane of the boy's existence, for he lost no opportunity of holding him up to ridicule by making him the butt of endless practical jokes that seemed solely designed to inflict pain and humiliation; and as these tricks were usually lewd as well as cruel, Lalji would snigger at them, and the watching courtiers would break into peals of sycophantic laughter.

Lalji's moods were often ugly and always unpredictable—understandably so, for until the coming of the *Nautch*-girl he had been the spoiled darling of the palace, petted and indulged by his doting father and the adoring Zenana women, and flattered by courtiers and servants alike. His first step-mother, the charming, gentle *Feringhi*-Rani, had grieved for the motherless child, and taking him to her heart, had loved him as though he were her own son. But as neither she nor anyone else had ever attempted to discipline him, it was hardly surprising that the chubby, lovable baby should have grown into a spoilt and overbearing boy, totally unfitted to deal with the changed atmosphere in the palace when the new favourite bore a son and the *Feringhi*-Rani died. For now the little Yuveraj was suddenly of less importance; and even his servants became noticeably less servile, while courtiers who had once flattered and fawned on him hastened to ingratiate themselves with the new power behind the throne.

His rooms and his retinue began to look shabby and neglected, not all his imperious orders were now obeyed, and the continual warnings of his devoted nurse—old Dunmaya, who had been his mother's nurse also and accompanied the Senior Rani to Gulkote when that lady came there as a bride—did nothing to soothe his distress or improve the situation. Dunmaya would have laid down her life for the boy, and her fears for him were probably justified; but the voicing of them, and her constant criticism of his father's growing neglect, only served to increase his unhappiness, and drove him at times to near hysteria. He could not understand what was happening, and it made him frightened rather than angry. But because pride prevented him from showing fear, he took refuge in rage, and those who served him suffered accordingly.

Young as Ash was, something of all this was still apparent to him. But though understanding might help him to excuse much of Lalji's behaviour, it did not make it any easier to bear. Also he did not take kindly to the subservience that the Yuveraj, who had been used to it all his short life, expected from every member of his household; even from those who were elderly grey-beards and grandfathers. Ash had at first been properly impressed by the importance of the heir to the throne, and also with his own duties as this potentate's page, which, in the manner of childhood, he took half seriously and half as a game. Unfortunately, familiarity soon bred contempt and later boredom, and there were times when he hated Lalji and would have run away if it had not been for Sita. But he knew that Sita was happy here, and if he ran away she would have to come with him, not only because he could not leave her behind, but because he suspected the Lalji might treat her unkindly in revenge for his defection. Yet, it was, paradoxically, sympathy for Lalji as much as love for Sita that prevented him from running away.

The two boys had little in common and there were many factors that prevented them from becoming friends: caste, upbringing and environment; heredity and the social gulf that yawned between the heir to a throne and the son of a serving-woman. They were separated, too, by a wide difference in character and temperament; and to a certain extent by the difference in their ages, though this mattered less, for although Lalji was the senior by two years, Ash often felt himself to be the elder by years, and on that account bound to help and protect the weaker vessel from the forces of evil that even the most insensitive must feel stirring in the huge, rambling, ramshackle palace.

Ash had never been insensitive, and though at first he had dismissed Dunmaya's warnings as the babbling of a silly old woman, it had not taken him long to change his mind. The idle, aimless days might drift placidly by, but under that smooth surface ran hidden undercurrents of plot and counterplot, and the wind was not the only thing that whispered in the endless corridors and alcoves of the Hawa Mahal.

Bribery, intrigue and ambition haunted the dusty rooms and lurked behind every door, and even a child could not fail to become aware of it. Yet Ash had taken none of this very seriously until the day when a plate of the Yuveraj's favourite cakes had been found in the little pavilion by the pool in the Yuveraj's private garden . . .

Lalji had been chasing the tame gazelle, and it was Ash who had found them and idly crumbled one into the pool, where the fat carp gobbled it greedily. A few minutes later the fish were floating belly upwards among the lily pads, and Ash, staring at them with shocked, incredulous eyes, realized that they were dead—and what it was that had killed them.

Lalji had an official "taster" and he normally ate nothing that his taster had not sampled first; but had he found those tempting cakes in the pavilion he would have grabbed and gobbled one as greedily as the carp. Ash snatched them up and carrying them quickly to the parapet at the far side of the garden, dropped them over, plate and all, into the void below. And as the cakes fell, wheeling down in the evening light, a crow swooped and caught one in his beak; and a moment later it too was falling into the gulf, a limp black bundle of feathers.

Ash had told no one of this incident, for though it might have seemed the natural thing to run with it to anyone who would listen, a too early acquaintance with danger had taught him caution, and he felt sure that this was something he had better keep to himself. If he told Lalji it would only add to the boy's fears and send old Dunmaya into a further frenzy of anxiety, and if any inquiries were made it was fairly certain that the real culprit would not be found, and equally certain that some innocent scapegoat would be made to suffer. Ash's experience of life in the palace had already taught him that justice was unlikely to be done if Janoo-Bai had anything to do with it, particularly since her position had recently been further strengthened by the birth of a second son.

It never once occurred to him that the scapegoat

67

might have been himself, or that the cakes in the pavilion could have been intended for him and not, as he supposed, for the Yuveraj.

Ash therefore held his peace; for children can only take the world as they find it, and accept the fact that their elders are all-powerful, if not all-wise. He pushed the incident of the cakes into the back of his mind, and accepting servitude in the Hawa Mahal as a necessary evil that could not at present be avoided, resigned himself to enduring it until such time as the Yuveraj came of age and had no further use for his services. At least he now had plenty to eat and clean clothes to wear; though the promised pay had not materialized, owing to the rapaciousness of the *Nautch*-girl having reduced the Rajah's exchequer to a dangerously low ebb. But it proved a tedious existence, until the coming of Tuku, a little mongoose that had haunted Sita's courtyard and that Ash, in search of distraction, had tamed and trained.

Tuku was the first living thing that was wholly his own, for though he knew that he possessed every scrap of Sita's heart, he could not command her presence when he chose. She had her own duties and was only available at certain hours of the day; but Tuku followed at his heels or rode on his shoulder, slept curled up under his chin at night and came when he called, and Ash loved the graceful, fearless little creature, and felt that Tuku knew it and returned his love. It was a deeply satisfactory comradeship, and it had lasted for over half a year, until a black day when Lalji, feeling tired and cross, had insisted on having Tuku to play with, and having teased him unmercifully, was repaid with a sharp nip. The next two minutes had been a nightmare that haunted Ash for many months and that he was never entirely to forget.

Lalji, his finger dripping blood, had yelled with fright and pain and shrieked to a servant to kill the mongoose at once—at once. It had been done before Ash could intervene. A single slashing blow from a scabbarded sword had broken Tuku's back, and he had twitched and whimpered for a moment, and then the life had gone out of him and there was only a limp little scrap of fur in Ash's hands.

It did not seem possible that Tuku was dead: only a minute ago he had been fluffing his tail and chattering crossly at Lalji's impertinences, and now—

Lalji said furiously: "Don't look at me like that! What does it matter? It was only an animal—a savage, bad-tempered animal. See where he bit me?"

"You were teasing him," said Ash in a whisper. "It is you who are the savage, bad-tempered animal." He wanted to cry—to scream and shriek. Fury welled up in him and he dropped Tuku's small body and sprang at Lalji.

It had been a scuffle rather than a fight. A degrading scuffle in which Lalji spat and kicked and shrieked, until rescued by a dozen servants who had converged upon the room from every direction and dragged the boys apart.

"I'm going," panted Ash, gripped by a brace of horrified retainers, and glaring defiance. "I won't stay with you or work for you another minute. I shall go now, and I shall never come back."

"And I say you shall not go!" screamed Lalji, beside himself with rage. "You shan't leave without my permission, and if you try to, you'll find you can't. I shall see to that."

Biju Ram, who as a token gesture towards defending the Yuveraj had picked up a long-barrelled pistol—fortunately unloaded—waved the weapon negligently at Ash and said languidly: "Your Highness should have the horse-boy branded as one does horses—or mutinous slaves. Then if he should by any chance escape, he would be speedily recognized as your property and returned."

It is possible that the suggestion was not intended to be taken seriously; but then Lalji was far too angry to think clearly and, blinded by rage, he had seized on it. There had been no one to protest, for by ill luck the only member of his household who might have done so with any chance of success was confined to his bed with a fever. The thing had been done there and then, and by Biju Ram himself. There had been a charcoal brazier in the room, for it was mid-winter and the palace was very cold; and Biju Ram had laughed his giggling laugh and thrust the muzzle of the pistol among the glowing coals. Ash was barely eight years old, but it had taken four men to hold him down, for he was strong and wiry and when he realized what was to happen he fought like a wild-cat, biting and clawing until not one of the four remained unmarked, though it was a useless battle, for the end was never in doubt.

Biju Ram had intended to brand him on the forehead, which could possibly have killed him. But Lalji, for all his fury, still retained a measure of caution, and it occurred to him that as his father might not altogether approve of such proceedings, it might be wiser to mark Ashok in a place less likely to catch the Rajah's eye. Biju Ram was therefore forced to content himself with pressing the mouth of the pistol to the victim's bared breast. There had been an odd sizzling sound and a smell of burnt flesh, and though Ash had resolved that he would die rather than give *Bichchhu* the satisfaction of hearing him cry out, he had been unable to stop himself. His scream of pain had drawn another giggling laugh from the dandy, but its effect upon Lalji was unexpected. It had aroused his better nature, and he had thrown himself at Biju Ram, dragging him back and crying wildly that it was all his own fault and that Ashok was not to blame. At which point Ash had fainted.

"He's dying," shrieked Lalji, overcome by remorse. "You've killed him, *Bichchhu*. Do something, one of you. Send for a hakim* . . . fetch Dunmaya. Oh, Ashok, don't die. Please don't die."

Ash was nowhere near dying, and he had recovered soon enough. The ugly burn had healed cleanly, thanks to the skilful ministrations of Sita and Dunmaya and his own good health, though the scar it left was to last as long as he lived; not as a circle, but as a crescent, for he had flinched sideways as he felt the heat, so that the muzzle had not pressed evenly and Lalji had pulled Biju Ram away before he could rectify this error. "I would have marked you with the sun," said Biju Ram, "but it seems that would have been to do you too much honour, and it is only right that by your cringing you should turn the sun into a mere moon instead"—but he was careful not to say that in front of Lalji, who did not care to be reminded of the episode.

Strangely enough, the two boys had been better friends after that, for Ash was well aware of the heinousness of his offence and knew that in former days he would have been strangled, or trampled to death by the Rajah's elephants. The least he had expected even now was the loss of a limb or an eye, for it was no light crime to lay violent hands on the heir to the throne, and grown men

---

*doctor

had paid with their lives for lesser offences; so he was relieved that his punishment had been no worse, and astonished that the Yuveraj should have intervened to stop it. The fact that he had not only done so, but publicly admitted himself to be in the wrong, had impressed Ash a great deal, as he was aware what that admission must have cost the Yuveraj.

He missed Tuku unbearably, but he did not attempt to tame another mongoose. Nor did he make any more pets, for he knew that he could never trust Lalji again, and that to let himself become fond of some other creature might only mean providing a useful weapon to be used against him the next time the Yuveraj was out of temper or wished to punish him. Yet despite this (and certainly from no wish of his own) he was to acquire an unexpected substitute for Tuku. Not an animal this time, but a very small human being: Anjuli-Bai, the shy, neglected baby daughter of the unfortunate *Feringhi*-Rani.

It was one of Lalji's good qualities—he had many, and given the right circumstances they might well have outweighed the bad ones—that he was unfailingly kind to his little half-sister. The child was frequently to be found in his apartments, for being as yet far too young to be confined to the Zenana Quarters, she came and went as she pleased. She was a thin little creature who appeared to be half-starved and was dressed with a shabbiness that would have been considered disgraceful by many a peasant family—a state of affairs that was directly traceable to the enmity of the *Nautch*-girl, who saw no reason why money or deference should be wasted on the daughter of her dead rival.

Janoo-Bai could not be sure that the child might not develop some of the beauty and charm that had once so captivated the Rajah, and she had no intention of letting him become either fond or proud of his daughter if she could help it; to which end she saw to it that the baby was banished to a distant wing of the palace and cared for by a handful of slovenly unpaid servants who pocketed the meagre household funds for their own use.

The Rajah seldom inquired after his daughter, and in time almost forgot that he had one. Janoo-Bai had assured him that the child was well cared for, and had added some disparaging comments on its lack of good looks, saying that it would make the arranging of a good marriage a difficult matter. "Such a small, sour-looking little thing,"

71

sighed Janoo-Bai with feigned sympathy, and she had nicknamed the child "Kairi"—that being a small, unripe mango—and laughed with delight when the name was adopted
by the palace.

"Kairi-Bai" preferred her half-brother's apartments
to her own; they were brighter and better furnished, and
besides he sometimes gave her sweets and let her play with
his monkeys or the cockatoo and the tame gazelle. His
servants too were less impatient with her than her own
women, and she had taken a strong fancy to the youngest
of them, Ashok, who had found her sobbing quietly in a
corner of her brother's garden one day, having been bitten
by one of the monkeys, whose tail she had pulled. Ash
had taken her to Sita to be soothed and petted, and Sita
had bandaged the wound, and having given her a piece of
sugar-cane, told her the story of Rama, whose beautiful
wife had been stolen by the Demon King of Lanka and
rescued with the help of Hanuman, the Monkey God: "So
you see, you must never pull a monkey's tail, because it
not only hurts his feelings, but Hanuman would not like it.
And now we will pick some marigolds and make a little
wreath—see I will show you how—for you to take to his
shrine to show you are sorry. My son Ashok will take
you there."

The story and the construction of the wreath had
successfully distracted the child's attention from her hurts,
and she had gone off happily with Ash, holding confidingly
to his hand, to make her apologies to Hanuman at the
shrine near the elephant lines, where a plaster figure of the
Monkey God danced in the gloom. After this she was often to be found in Sita's quarters, though it was not Sita
but Ash to whom she attached herself, trotting about after
him like some small persistent pariah puppy who has chosen its owner and cannot be snubbed or driven away. In
fact, Ash did not try very hard to do either, for Sita told
him that he must be especially kind to the forlorn little
girl, not because she was a princess, or because she was
motherless and neglected, but because she had been born
on a day that was doubly auspicious for him: the anni-
versary of his own birth and the day of their arrival in
Gulkote.

It was this more than anything else that made him
feel in some way responsible for Kairi, and he reigned
himself to being the object of her devotion and was the

72

only person who did not address her by her nickname. He either called her "Juli" (which was her own version of her given name, for she was still unable to get her tongue round all three syllables) or on rare occasions "Larla," which means darling, and in general treated her with the tolerant affection he would have accorded to an importunate kitten, protecting her to the best of his ability from the teasing or insolence of the palace servants.

The Yuveraj's attendants had retaliated by jeering at him for being a nursemaid and calling him "Ayah-ji," until Lalji unexpectedly came to his assistance and turned on them, saying angrily that they would please to remember that the Anjuli-Bai was his sister. After that they had accepted the situation, and in time became so used to it that it was doubtful if anyone noticed it any more; the baby was, in any case, of no importance and would probably not live to grow up, being a scrawny little thing, unlikely to survive the normal ailments of childhood, while as for the boy Ashok, he was of no importance to anyone; not even, it would seem, to the Yuveraj.

But in this last they were wrong. Lalji still trusted him (though he would have found it hard to explain why) and he had no intention of letting him go. The fate of Tuku and the violence that followed it were never referred to again, but Ash soon discovered that Lalji's threat to prevent his leaving the palace had not been an idle one. There was only one gate into the palace, the *Badshai Darwaza:* and after that day he could no longer go through it alone but only, on occasions, in the company of selected servants or officials, who saw to it that he did not stray off on his own or fail to return with them.

"There is an order," said the sentries blandly, and turned him back. It was the same the next day and every day, and when Ash questioned Lalji, the boy had countered by saying: "Why should you wish to leave? Are you not comfortable here? If there is anything you lack you have only to tell Ram Dass, and he will send out for it. There is no need for you to go to the bazaars."

"But I only wish to see my friends," protested Ash.

"Am I not your friend?" asked the Yuveraj.

There was no answer to that, and Ash never knew who had given the order that he was not to be allowed to leave: the Rajah, or Lalji himself (who said he had not, but was not to be trusted), or perhaps Janoo-Bai, for reasons of her own? But whoever it was, the order was never rescinded, and he was always aware of it. He was a prisoner in the fortress, though he was allowed to go more or less where he chose inside the walls, and as the Hawa Mahal covered a very large area, he could hardly be considered as closely confined. Nor was he friendless, for he had made two good friends in the palace that year, and found at least one ally among the members of Lalji's suite.

Nevertheless, he felt the loss of his liberty keenly, for from the walls and half-ruined towers and wooden pavilions that crowned them, he could see the world laid out before him like a coloured map, beckoning towards freedom and the far horizons. To the south-west lay the city, with beyond it the wide stretch of the plateau— its far rim sloping steeply down to the river and the rich land of the Punjab, so that sometimes, on clear days, one could even see the plains. But he seldom faced that way, for northward lay the foothills, and behind them, spanning the horizon from east to west, were the true hills and the vast, serrated massif of the Dur Khaima, beautiful and mysterious, robed in forests of rhododendron and deodar and crowned with snow.

Ash did not know that he had been born within sight of those snows, or that he had spent his earliest years among the high Himalayas, falling asleep to the sight of them rose-dyed by the sunset or silver under the moon, and waking to see them turn from apricot and amber to dazzling white in the full blaze of the morning. They were part of his subconscious mind, because once, long ago, he had known them by heart as other children know the frieze painted on a nursery wall. But looking at them now, he felt sure that somewhere in the folds of those mountains lay the valley that Sita used to speak of at bedtime: their own valley. That safe hidden place that they would one day reach by long marches over hill-roads and through passes where the wind shrieked between black rocks and green glaciers, and the cold glare of snowfields blinded the eyes.

Sita seldom spoke of their valley now; she was too busy during the daytime, and Ash slept in the Yuveraj's quarters at night. But the old bedtime story of his childhood still retained its grip on his imagination, and by now he had forgotten—or perhaps he had never realized—

74

that it was not a real place. It was real to him, and morning and evening, whenever he could steal away from his duties—or, more often, during the long, idle mid-day hours when all the palace dozed and the sun lay hot on the battlements—he would climb up to a little covered balcony that jutted out from the wall of the *Mor Minar*—the "Peacock Tower"—and lying on the warm stone gaze out towards the mountains and think of it. And make plans.

The existence of that balcony was a secret shared only by Kairi, and its discovery had been a happy accident, for it could not be seen from inside the fortress, being hidden from view by the curves of the *Mor Minar*. The *Mor Minar* had been part of the original fort, a guard tower and a look-out, facing the foothills. But both roof and stairway had fallen long ago, and the entrance become blocked by rubble. The balcony was of a later date and had probably been built for the pleasure of some long-dead Rani, for it was no more than a folly, an elegant little pavilion of marble and red sandstone, pierced and carved into the semblance of frozen lace and topped by a humpbacked Hindu dome.

Fragments of wood still adhered to the rusty iron hinges that had once held a door, but the fragile-seeming screens still stood, except where there had once been a window cut in the marble tracery, from which the Rani and her ladies could look out towards the mountains. Here, on the front of the balcony, between the slender arches, there was now only open space and fragments of broken carving, below which the wall dropped for forty feet to meet the scrub and the steep rock faces, that in turn plunged downwards for more than four times that distance before merging into the plateau. There were goat tracks through the scrub, but few humans cared to climb so far; and even had they done so they might well have failed to notice the pavilion, for its outlines were lost against the weather-worn bulk of the *Mor Minar*.

Ash and Kairi, pursuing a truant marmoset, had clambered over the rubble that choked the ruined tower, and looking up the topless funnel had spied the fugitive half way up it. There must once have been rooms in the tower, but although no part of the floors remained, there were still traces of the stairway that had led up to them: broken stumps of stone, some barely large enough to provide foothold for the marmoset. But where a monkey can go an active child can often follow, and Ash had had plenty of practice on the rooftops of the city, and possessed an excellent head for heights. Kairi too could climb like a squirrel, and the broken staircase had proved easy enough to negotiate once they had removed the untidy bundles of twigs and egg shells deposited there by generations of owls and jackdaws. They had scrambled up it, and following the marmoset through a doorway, found themselves in a carved and canopied balcony that hung dizzily over empty space, as secure and inaccessible as a swallow's nest.

Ash had been delighted with their find. Here at last was a hidden place to which he could retreat in time of trouble, and from where he could look out across the world and dream of the future—and be alone. The claustrophobic atmosphere of the palace, with its incessant whispers of treachery and intrigue, its cabals and plots and place-seeking, was banished by the clean air that crooned through the marble tracery and kept the little pavilion swept and garnished; and best of all there was no one to dispute his possession of it, for apart from the monkeys and owls, the hill crows and the little yellow-crested bulbuls, no one could have set foot in it for fifty years and by now, in all likelihood, its very existence was forgotten.

Given the choice, Ash would have traded the balcony for permission to visit the city whenever he chose, and had he been given it would not have run away—for Sita's sake, if for nothing else. But deprived of that liberty, it was doubly satisfying to have a safe hiding place where he could escape from the quarrels and the gossip, the tantrums and the talk. The humble quarters that he shared with Sita did not fill this need because any servant sent to find him always came there first, so it was preferable to have a safer place of retreat, one from which he could not be haled forth to undertake some trivial errand or answer an idle question that had been forgotten by the time he reached the Presence. The discovery of the Queen's balcony made his life in the Hawa Mahal more bearable. And the possession of two such friends as Koda Dad Khan, the *Mir Akhor*—the Master of Horse—and Koda Dad's youngest son, Zarin, almost reconciled him to staying there for ever . . .

Koda Dad was a Pathan who as a youth had left his native Border hills to wander among the northern fringes of the Punjab in search of his fortune. He had come by

76

chance to Gulkote, where his skill at hawking had attracted the attention of the young Rajah, who had newly succeeded to the throne on the death of his father only two months previously. That had been more than thirty years ago, and except for occasional visits to his own Border-country, Koda Dad had never returned home. He had remained in Gulkote in the service of the Rajah, and as *Mir Akhor* was now a man of considerable reputation in the state. There was nothing that he did not know about horses, and it was said of him that he could speak their language and that even the wickedest and most intractable became docile when he spoke to it. He could shoot as well as he could ride, and as his knowledge of hawks and falconry equalled his knowledge of horses, the Rajah himself—no mean authority on both—asked his advice and invariably took it. After his first visit home he had returned with a wife who in due course presented him with three sons, and by now Koda Dad was the proud possessor of several grandsons and would occasionally talk to Ash of these paragons. "They are myself when I was young; or so says my mother, who sees them often; our home being in the Yusafzai country, which is not far from Hoti Mardan* where my son Awal Shah serves with his Regiment—as does my second son Afzal, also."

Koda Dad's two eldest sons had taken service under the British in that same Corps of Guides that Ash's Uncle William had belonged to, and now only Zarin Khan, the youngest, still remained with his parents, though he too had set his heart on a military career.

Zarin was nearly six years older than Ash, and by Asian standards a grown man. But apart from the difference in height, the two were very alike in build and colouring, for Zarin, like many Pathans, was grey-eyed and fair-skinned. They might easily have been taken for brothers, and indeed Koda Dad treated them as such, addressing them both as "my son" and cuffing them with equal impartiality when he considered that they deserved it: an attention that Ash regarded as an honour, for Koda Dad Khan was a re-incarnation of the friend and hero of his baby days—the shadowy but never-forgotten figure of Uncle Akbar, wise, kind and omniscient.

It was Koda Dad who taught Ash how to fly a hawk

---

*pronounced Ma-darn

and train an unbroken colt, how to spear a tent-peg out of the ground at full gallop with the point of a lance, fire at a moving target and hit it nine times out of ten, and at a stationary one and never miss at all. It was also Koda Dad who lectured him on such matters as the wisdom of keeping his temper and the dangers of impulsiveness, and took him to task for acting or speaking before he thought —a case in point being his attack on the Yuveraj and his threat to leave the palace. "Had you held your tongue you might have left when you would, instead of getting yourself penned up in this manner," said Koda Dad severely.

Zarin too had been kind to the boy and treated him as a younger brother, cuffing and encouraging in turn, and best of all, Ash was occasionally permitted to accompany them outside the Hawa Mahal, which was almost as good as going alone, for though they too were instructed to see that he did not run away, their manner, unlike that of the Yuveraj's servants, never smacked of the gaoler, and with them he was able to enjoy the illusion of freedom.

Ash had forgotten the Pushtu he had learnt in his father's camp, but now he learned to speak it again because it was the native tongue of Koda Dad and Zarin and, boy-like, he wished to imitate his heroes in all things. He would speak only in Pushtu when in their company, which amused Koda Dad, though it ruffled Sita, who became as jealous of the old Pathan as she had once been of Akbar Khan. "He does not worship the gods," reproved Sita severely. "Also it is well known that all Pathans live by violence. They are thieves, murderers and cattle killers, and it grieves me, Ashok, that you should spend so much time in the company of barbarians. They will teach you bad ways."

"Is it bad to ride and shoot and fly a hawk, mother?" countered Ash, who considered that these accomplishments more than made up for such peccadilloes as murder and theft, and had never been able to see why cattle should be regarded as holy, despite all the teachings of Sita and the admonitions of the priests. If it had been horses now—or elephants or tigers—he could have understood it. But cows—

It was difficult for a small boy to keep track of the gods, when there were so many of them: Brahm, Vishnu, Indra and Shiv, who were the same and yet not the

78

same; Mitra, ruler of the day, and Kali of the skulls and blood who was also Parvati the kind and beautiful; Krishna the Beloved, Hanuman the Ape, and pot-bellied Ganesh with his elephant head who was, strangely, the son of Shiv and Parvati. These and a hundred other gods and godlings must all be propitiated by gifts to the priests. Yet Koda Dad said that there was only one god, whose Prophet was Mohammed. Which was certainly simpler, except that it was sometimes difficult to tell who Koda Dad really worshipped—God or Mohammed—for God, according to Koda Dad, lived in the sky, but his followers must not say their prayers unless they faced in the direction of Mecca, a city where Mohammed had been born. And although Koda Dad spoke scornfully of idols and idol-worshippers, he had told Ash about a sacred stone in Mecca that was regarded as holy by all Muslims and accorded a veneration equal to anything offered by the Hindus to the stone emblems of Vishnu. Ash could see little difference between the two: if one was an idol, so was the other.

Thinking the matter over, and unwilling to go against either Sita or Koda Dad, he decided that it might be better to choose his own idol, there being authority for this—or so it seemed to him—in a prayer that he had heard the priest of the city temple intone before the gods:

> *"Oh Lord, forgive three sins that are due to my*
> *human limitations.*
> *Thou art Everywhere, but I worship thee here:*
> *Thou art without form, but I worship thee in these*
> *forms;*
> *Thou needest no praise, yet I offer thee these*
> *prayers and salutations.*
> *Lord, forgive three sins that are due to my*
> *human limitations."*

That sounded eminently sensible to Ash, and after some deliberation he selected the cluster of snow peaks that faced the Queen's balcony: a crown of pinnacles that lifted high above the distant ranges like the towers and turrets of some fabulous city, and that were known in Gulkote as the Dur Khaima—the Far Pavilions. He found the mountain a more satisfactory object of devotion than the ugly red-daubed *lingam* that Sita made offerings to, and he could also face towards it when he said his prayers,

79

as Koda Dad faced towards Mecca. Besides, reasoned Ash, *someone* must have made it. Perhaps the same someone whom both Sita and her priests and Koda Dad and his maulvies acknowledged? As a manifestation of the powers of that Being it was worthy of veneration. And it was his own. The personally selected interceder, protector and benefactor of Ashok, son of Sita and servant of his Highness the Yuveraj of Gulkote. *"Oh Lord,"* whispered Ash, addressing the Dur Khaima: *"thou art Everywhere, but I worship thee here . . ."*

Once adopted, the beautiful, many-peaked massif acquired a personality of its own, until it almost seemed to Ash that it was a living thing, a goddess with a hundred faces, who, unlike the stone emblems of Vishnu and the shrouded rock in Mecca, took on a different guise with every change and chance of weather and season, and each hour of every day. A gleaming flame in the dawn light and a blaze of silver at mid-day. Gold and rose in the sunset, lilac and lavender in the dusk. Livid against the storm clouds or dark against the stars. And in the months of the monsoon, withdrawing herself behind veil after veil of mist and the steel-grey curtain of the rain.

Nowadays, whenever he visited the Queen's balcony, Ash made a point of taking a handful of grain or a few flowers to lay on the broken ledge as offerings to the Dur Khaima. The birds and squirrels appreciated the grain and in time became surprisingly tame, hopping and scampering over the boy's recumbent form as though he were part of the stonework, and demanding food with the persistence of professional mendicants.

"Where have you been, *piara?*" scolded Sita. "They have been looking for you, and I told them that you would surely be with the rascally Pathan and his hawks, or in the stables with his good-for-nothing son. Now that you are of the household of the prince it is not seemly that you should go running after such persons."

"The servants of the Yuveraj would seem to think I am your keeper," grumbled Koda Dad Khan. "They come here asking 'Where is he? What is he doing? Why is he not here?' "

"Where have you been?" Lalji would demand petulantly: "Biju and Mohan have been searching everywhere for you. I won't have you going off like this. You are my servant. I wanted to play *chaupur*."

Ash would apologize and say that he had been wandering in one of the gardens or down at the stables or the elephant lines, and then they would play *chaupur* and the matter would be forgotten—until the next time. The Hawa Mahal was so large that it was easy enough to get lost in it, and Lalji knew that the boy could never go outside it alone and would in the end be found. But he still liked to feel that Ashok was near by, for instinct told him that here was one person who could not be bribed or suborned into playing the traitor; though as there had been no more "accidents," he was beginning to think that old Dunmaya's fears for his safety were largely imagination and that Biju Ram might be right when he said that no one, not even the *Nautch*-girl, would dare to harm him. If that were so, then there was no longer any reason to keep Ashok in attendance on him; particularly as he did not find the boy such an amusing companion as Pran or Mohan or Biju Ram, who, though probably untrustworthy and a full ten years older than himself (Biju Ram had turned twenty), were always ready to entertain him with amusingly scandalous stories of the Women's Quarters, or initiate him into various pleasurable vices. In fact if it were not for a strong feeling that Ashok was in some way a talisman against danger, he would have been tempted to dismiss him, because there was often something very like scorn in the younger boy's steady gaze, and his refusal to be amused by Biju's salacious wit or the entertaining cruelties of Punwa implied a criticism that was lowering to Lalji's self-esteem. Besides, he was becoming jealous of him.

It had started over Anjuli; though that had been a very minor irritation, for she was only a silly baby and a plain one at that. Had she been a pretty or engaging child he might have regarded her as a rival for his father's affections and hated her—as he hated the *Nautch*-girl and the *Nautch*-girl's eldest son, his half-brother, Nandu —but as it was, he remembered the *Feringhi*-Rani's kindness to him, and repaid it by being kind to her daughter and tacitly confirming Ashok in the role of unofficial mentor, bear-leader and protector to that small unripe mango, "Kairi-Bai." But he had been displeased when one of his equerries, Hira Lal, had taken a liking to the boy, and even more displeased when Koda Dad Khan, who was something of a legend to the young bloods of the palace, had done the same thing. For Koda Dad had the ear of the Rajah and he had spoken well of the boy.

The ruler of Gulkote was a large, lethargic man whose excessive fondness for wine, women and opium had drained him of strength and given him, in his early fifties, the appearance of a much older man. He was fond of his eldest son, and would have been shocked beyond words at the very idea that anyone could wish to harm his heir, and unhesitatingly condemned to death even the *Nautch*-girl herself had it been proved to him that she had attempted to take the boy's life. But increasing age and weight had made him dislike trouble, and he had discovered that, whenever he paid any attention to Lalji, trouble with the fascinating Janoo-Bai invariably followed. Wherefore in the interests of peace he saw very little of his eldest son, and Lalji, who loved his father with a burning, jealous love, resented the neglect bitterly, as he resented, too, any word spoken to anyone else during his father's all too brief visits.

The Rajah had only spoken to Ash because Koda Dad had remarked that the boy might be worth training, and also because he seemed to remember something about his having once saved Lalji's life, which entitled him to a little attention. For these reasons he had been gracious to Ash, and would sometimes order his attendance when he rode out to try a new falcon on the game-birds that abounded on the flat lands of the plateau. On these occasions Lalji would sulk and scowl and later take some petty and spiteful revenge, such as keeping Ash in attendance on him for hours on end without allowing him to eat or drink or sit until he was dizzy with fatigue, or, more viciously, driving him to rage by some senseless act of cruelty to one of the pet animals in order to have him beaten for the resulting explosion.

Lalji's courtiers, taking their cue from their master, did their best to make life difficult for the upstart horse-boy whose sudden elevation they had always resented, the sole exception to this being Hira Lal, whose duties were vaguely defined as "Equerry to the Yuveraj."

Of them all, Hira Lal was the only one who showed Ash any kindness, and he alone never applauded Biju Ram's sadistic foolery or laughed at his prurient jokes. He would yawn instead and toy with the black pearl that dangled from his right ear, fingering it with an abstracted air that somehow managed to convey a blend of boredom, resignation and distaste. The gesture itself was no more than a habit with him, but on such occasions it never failed to infuriate Biju Ram, who suspected (rightly) that the great pearl was worn in deliberate parody of the single earring that he himself affected, and that its rarity—the jewel was the exact shape of a pear and had the subtle, smoky iridescence of a pigeon's feather—only served to make his own diamond-drop look flashy and meretricious by contrast; in the same way as the equerry's sober grey silk *achkans* had a way of making his own more colourful coats appear vulgar and not too well cut.

Hira Lal never seemed to do any work and always appeared to be on the verge of falling asleep, but his lazy-lidded eyes were not nearly as unobservant as they looked, and very little escaped them. He was a good-natured and easy-going man, with a reputation for idleness that was a joke in the palace and gave him something of the standing of a court jester whose utterances need not be taken seriously. "Do not let them worry you, boy," he would encourage Ash. "They are bored, poor mud-heads, and for lack of other amusement must cast about for some creature to torment. To witness another's discomfiture makes them feel more important themselves, even if that someone is only a child or a tame gazelle. If you do not let them see that you care, they will tire of the sport soon enough. Is that not so, *Bichchhu-ji?*"

His use of the nickname was an added insult, and Biju Ram would glare at him from eyes that were narrow slits of fury, while the others would scowl and mutter. But Lalji would pretend not to have heard, for he knew that he could not punish or dismiss Hira Lal, who had been appointed to his service by the Rajah himself (at the instigation, Lalji sometimes suspected, of his hated step-mother, the *Nautch*-girl) so that it was better, on such occasions, to feign deafness. And there was no denying that, spy or no spy, the equerry could be both witty and entertaining; he could crack jokes and invent foolish games that made one laugh on even the dullest day, and life would be a good deal less amusing without him.

Ash too was grateful to Hira Lal, and profited from his advice, which he discovered to be sound. He learned to conceal his emotions and to accept punishment stoically. But although he could in time give a convincing impres-

83

sion of indifference, his emotions were still there, unchanged, and all the stronger because having no outlet they must remain hidden and go deeper. Yet it was Hira Lal who made him see that Lalji should be pitied and not disliked, and how infinitely superior his own position was to that of the angry, bewildered little prince.

"When he oppresses you, it is only to revenge himself for the lack of love that he needs and is not given," said Hira Lal. "If he had never had love it would matter less, for many grow up without it and do not know what they have missed. But having had it he has learned what it is to lose it. And it is this that makes him unhappy. When he has teased and tormented you and had you unjustly punished, you can run to your mother who will console you and weep over your wounds. But there is no one to whom he can run except that old witch of a nurse, Dunmaya, who does nothing but croak warnings and make him frightened of his own shadow. Be patient with him, Ashok, for you are more fortunate than he."

Ash strove for patience, though it was uphill work. But a clearer understanding of the heir's predicament undoubtedly helped, and for this he was grateful to Hira Lal.

Lalji was married the following year and enmities were forgotten in the bustle and preparation and festivity. The vast, somnolent palace came alive and hummed like a beehive as painters and decorators swarmed in with their buckets of lime wash and colour, and walls, ceilings and archways that were dusty from neglect received coats of bright paint and gilding. The *Nautch*-girl, predictably jealous of all the attention bestowed upon her step-son, had alternately sulked and made scenes, and the bride's relatives had created considerable uproar on the very eve of the wedding by suddenly demanding double the previously agreed bride-price, which had so incensed the groom's father that he had come within an ace of calling the whole thing off. But as this would have brought great shame on all concerned, a compromise had been reached after hours of argument, cajolery and hard bargaining, and the preparations had gone forward.

The bride was the eight-year-old daughter of a small hill Rajah, and after the wedding she would return to her parents until she was old enough for the marriage to be consummated; though this made no difference to the

lengthy and elaborate ceremonies. It was a long and tedious business and it cost the Rajah a great deal of money
that could have been put to better use alleviating the poverty of his subjects or improving the roads in Gulkote—
not that such an idea even crossed the mind of either ruler
or subjects, and if it had it would have been unanimously
rejected by both in favour of the jollity and entertainment
offered by a really lavish wedding.

All Gulkote enjoyed the spectacle and relished the
gifts of food and money distributed to the poor, and the
sight of so much magnificence. Fireworks, bands, proces-
sions by torch-light to the city temple, prancing horsemen
and plodding elephants draped in glittering brocade and
carrying silver howdahs full of bejewelled guests, enthralled
the citizens and drained the treasury. Which troubled the
Rajah not a whit, though it angered the *Nautch*-girl,
who complained that it was all a great waste of money,
and was only placated with a gift of rubies and diamonds
from the state regalia.

5

Ash enjoyed the wedding festivities as much as anyone,
and for the first time in her short life, the four-year-old
Kairi was ordered to take part, as a Princess of Gulkote,
in an official ceremony.

As the sister of the Yuveraj, it was her privilege to
present the first gifts to the bride; and she had done so
dressed in unfamiliar finery and decked with resplendent
jewels that had at first delighted her by their colour and
glitter, and then tired her by their weight and the way
their sharp edges scratched. But as her sole ornament
hitherto had been a small mother-of-pearl fish that she
wore on a string about her neck as a "luck-piece" (it had
belonged to her mother and once been part of a set of
Chinese counters) she had greatly enjoyed the dignity they
lent her. It was nice to feel important for once, and she
had revelled in that and performed her duties with becoming seriousness.

85

The ceremonies and festivity had continued for over a week, and when at last they were over and bride and guests had returned to their own homes, Kairi's borrowed finery was whisked away from her and returned to one of the numerous chests that filled the Rajah's treasury, and only tattered decorations, fading wreaths and a smell of stale incense and decaying flowers remained to show that the great occasion had come and gone. The Hawa Mahal and its Rajah relapsed into lethargy, and Janoo-Bai the Rani set about planning far more spectacular alliances for her own small sons.

As for Lalji, now that all the excitement was over he found that the dignity of his married state added nothing to his importance, and that for all the difference it had made to life he might just as well have done without those long, tiring ceremonies. He thought his wife was a stupid little thing and not particularly pretty, and could only hope that she would grow up to look more attractive. Dunmaya said she would; but then Dunmaya would say anything to please him. With the departure of the wedding guests his father had lost interest in him, and once again time hung heavy on his hands and he felt crosser and unhappier than ever. Wherefore he quarrelled with his suite and made life so miserable for Ash that it was some time during those dismal months, in the flat aftermath of the wedding, that Ash for the first time discussed with Sita the possibility of their leaving Gulkote.

Sita had been aghast at the idea. Not on her own account, for she would have sacrificed anything for his sake; but because she did not believe that he would be better off anywhere else, or that his present mood was anything more than a boy's natural reaction to the churlish behaviour of the Yuveraj, which would pass. Sita was fully aware of the Yuveraj's problems; there were few secrets in the palace, and though it angered her that he should vent his spleen on her beloved son, she, like Hira Lal, could not help feeling a certain sympathy for the motherless, neglected heir whose father was too idle to champion him and whose step-mother prayed for his early death. His fits of ill-temper and sporadic outbursts of cruelty were surely no more than could be expected of a boy caught in such an intolerable web of circumstances, and Ashok must learn to bear with them and try to forgive them. Besides, it was certain that the Yuveraj would never willingly allow him to leave, and he must not even think of running away; it would be impossible, and even if he should succeed, where could they go? Where else could they live in such comfort and security as here, in a Rajah's palace and enjoying the salary and status of royal servants?

"Do they pay you then, mother?" inquired Ash bitterly. "Me, they do not—though it was promised me. Oh, I am given food and clothing. But never money. And if I ask for it they say, 'Later. Another time. Next month.' I have not so much as a *pice* to give or spend."

"But *piara,* we are both fed and clothed," urged Sita. "And we have a roof over our heads and a fire to warm ourselves by. Besides, do not forget that the Yuveraj will one day be Rajah, and then you will be rewarded and stand high in his favour. He is only a boy, Ashok, a young, unhappy boy. That is why he is sometimes unjust. But when he is grown he will be wiser. You will see. You have only to be patient and wait a little longer."

"How much longer? A year? Two years? Three? Oh, mother—!"

"I know, my son. I know. But I—I am not as young as I was, and . . ."

She did not finish the sentence, but Ash looked at her sharply and noticed for the first time, with a curious little stab of fear, that she seemed to have become much thinner of late and that the sprinkling of grey hairs that had grown more noticeable with each year now outnumbered the dark, so that her head was nearer silver than black. She looked tired too, and he wondered if they made her work too hard in Kairi's wing of the palace. He must talk to Kairi and tell her that his mother must not be worried or overworked. Yet it was he who was worrying her now, and realizing it, he flung his arms about her and hugged her in a sudden spasm of remorse, telling her that of course they would stay—he had only been teasing her, and as long as she was happy here they would remain in the Hawa Mahal.

He did not broach the subject again, and after that he pretended that all was well in the Yuveraj's household and did his best not to let her see that he was disgruntled or unhappy. Kairi, severely lectured for lack of consideration towards his mother, assured him earnestly that Sita's duties were not heavy: "I think perhaps she only gets tired because she is old," ventured Kairi, thinking it over. "Old ladies do get tired, you know. Dunmaya is always saying how tired she is."

But his mother was not old—not like wrinkled, white-headed Dunmaya, thought Ash; and was once again afraid. Because of that fear he spoke sharply to Kairi, telling her that she was a stupid, brainless baby who did not understand anything and he did not know why he wasted time talking to her or allowed her to follow him about like a mangy kitten, never giving him a moment's peace. "Miaow! Miaow!—*Girls!*" said Ash with masculine scorn, and added unkindly that he was thankful that he hadn't any sisters. Whereupon Kairi wept and had to be comforted by being allowed to tie a strand of floss silk about his wrist, which made him her "bracelet-brother" in accordance with an ancient custom that permits a woman to give or send a bracelet to any man, who, if he accepts it, is thereafter honour-bound to aid and protect her if called upon to do so, as though she were in truth his sister.

But although Kairi's persistent adoration frequently exasperated him, Ash had, in the end, become genuinely fond of the little creature and developed a strong sense of ownership, something that he had not felt since the death of Tuku. Kairi was a more satisfactory pet than even Tuku had been, for she could talk to him. And like Tuku, she loved him and followed him about and depended upon him, so that in time she came to fill the empty place in his heart that had once belonged to the little mongoose. It was good to know that here at least was a creature he could pet and protect without any fear of harm befalling it from Lalji or anyone else. But caution made him warn Kairi not to show her partiality for him too openly: "I am only your real brother's servant, and so he and the others might not like it," he explained.

Young as she was, she had understood; and after that she seldom addressed him directly unless they were alone or with Sita. They had devised a way of communicating with each other through the medium of a conversation ostensibly directed at a third person, and such was their rapport that they soon learned to translate the real meaning from an apparently casual sentence addressed to Lalji or one of his household or, more frequently, to a macaw or a pet monkey. It was a game that delighted both of them, and at which they grew so expert that no one save Hira Lal—who seldom missed anything of significance—ever suspected that the little girl's chatter and the boy's occasional remarks had two meanings and were directed at each other. In this way they would openly arrange to meet at certain times, and at certain places for which they had invented code words: either in Sita's courtyard or, more often, in the Queen's balcony, where they would feed the birds and squirrels, discuss the doings of the palace, or sit in companionable silence gazing out at the far snows.

Ash lost one of his few friends that year, for in the autumn Zarin left to join his two elder brothers, who were sowars in the Corps of Guides.

"I have taught him all I know of marksmanship and swordplay, and he was a horseman born," said Koda Dad. "It is time he made his own way in the world. Fighting is a man's trade, and there is always war along the Border."

Koda Dad had seen to it that his son was provided with the finest horse that Gulkote could supply, for vacancies in the Corps were much sought after, and went only to the finest riders and best shots among a long list of applicants. Neither Ash nor Zarin doubted for one moment that a vacancy would be won, and Zarin rode confidently away, assuring Ash that he would return on his first leave.

"And when you are full grown, you shall come to Mardan and be a sowar too," promised Zarin, "and we will ride in cavalry charges and see the sack of cities. So look to it that you learn all that my father can teach you, so that you do not disgrace me when you come as a recruit."

Life in the Hawa Mahal had seemed more irksome than ever after Zarin had gone, and when word came from Mardan that he had won a vacancy in the *rissala* (cavalry) and was now a sowar in the Guides, Ash's restlessness had increased: and with it, a determination to emulate his friend and become a soldier. With this in mind he missed no chance to ride or shoot with Koda Dad; though Sita did her best to discourage this new plan for the future. The very mention of the Guides terrified Sita, and a large part of her hostility towards Koda Dad and his son stemmed from their connection with that Regiment. It had been a severe shock to her to discover that even here in Gulkote, where she had thought herself so safe, Ashok had made friends with men who might one day bring him to the notice of his *Angrezi* uncle, and she had done everything in her power to avert this calamity.

Soldiers, asserted Sita, were brutal, ill-paid men who lived dangerous and disorganized lives, sleeping in tents or on the hard ground with never a roof over their heads or the security of a settled home for their families. Why should Ashok suddenly desire to become a soldier?

She had appeared so upset that Ash had dropped the subject and allowed her to suppose that he had not been serious. He imagined that she had only taken a dislike to it because it had been suggested to him by Koda Dad and Zarin, neither of whom she had ever approved of, and did not suspect that there was any other reason for her opposition. But though he did not mention it again to Sita, he continued to discuss it with Koda Dad, and would often talk of it to Kairi, who despite her tender age and limited understanding, made an admirable and uncritical audience.

Kairi could be relied upon to listen by the hour to anything he had to say, and he found that he did not have to explain things to her, for she seemed to understand him by instinct; though it is doubtful if she remembered any of it for long—except when he spoke of the valley. Kairi preferred that subject to all others, for by now the valley had become as real to her as it was to Ash, and she took it for granted that she would go too and help to build their house. The two children would plan the house together room by room, adding and embellishing, turning it from a cottage to a palace, until—tiring of grandeur— they would demolish it with a wave of a hand and begin it again, this time as a miniature dwelling with low ceilings and a thatched roof. "Though even that will cost a lot of money," said Kairi anxiously. "Tens and tens of rupees" —she still could not count further than ten.

One day she brought him a silver four-anna piece as a beginning, telling him that they should start saving up for the house. The little coin was more money than Ash had held in his hand for a long time, and to him even more than to Kairi it represented something approximating to riches. There were a dozen things he would like to have spent it on, but he hid it instead under a loose stone in the floor of the Queen's balcony, telling her that they would add to it when they could. They never did so, for money was hard to come by in the Hawa Mahal; and though there was always enough to eat, and clothing could be had if one could prove the need of it, Ash looked back on his life in the city as a time of affluence as well as freedom, and recalled with longing his modest wages as a horse-boy in Duni Chand's stables.

It was humiliating to realize that in these days he could not even match Kairi's meagre contribution, and that if he should ever obtain permission to leave the service of the Yuveraj, and overcome Sita's prejudice against soldiering as a career, he would not be able to join Zarin. For Koda Dad told him that the Guides Cavalry was recruited on the *Silladar* system, by which each recruit brought his own horse and also a sum of money with which to buy his equipment, the latter being refunded to him on discharge. Zarin had had both money and a horse, but Ash could see little prospect of acquiring either.

"When I am married, I will give you all the money you need," consoled Kairi, whose betrothal was already being discussed in the Women's Quarter of the Hawa Mahal.

"What's the good of that?" retorted Ash ungratefully. "It'll be too late then. You won't be married for years and years—you're only a baby."

"I shall be six soon," urged Kairi, "and Aruna says that this is old enough to be married."

"Then they will take you away, perhaps days and days of marches from here; and however rich you are, you won't be able to send money back to Gulkote," said Ash, determined to look on the dark side of things. "And anyway, your husband might not give you any money."

"Of course he would. If I were a Maharani I should have crores and crores of rupees to spend—like Janoo-Rani has. And diamonds and pearls and elephants and—"

"And an old, fat, bad-tempered husband who will beat you, and then die years and years before you do, so that you will have to become a suttee and be burned alive with him."

"*Don't say that.*" Kairi's voice shook and her small face turned pale, for the Suttee Gate with its pathetic frieze of red hand-prints had always filled her with horror, and she could not bear to pass that tragic reminder of the scores of women who had made those marks—the wives

91

and concubines who had been burned alive with the bodies of dead Rajahs of Gulkote, and who had dipped their palms in red dye and pressed them against the stone as they passed out through the Suttee Gate on their last short journey to the funeral pyre. Such slender, delicate little hands, some of them no-bigger than her own. The British had forbidden the barbaric custom of suttee, but everyone knew that in remote and independent states, where white men were seldom seen, it was still practised; and half the population of Gulkote could remember seeing Kairi's grandmother, the old Rani, immolating herself in the flames that consumed the body of her husband, together with three lesser wives and seventeen women of the Zenana.

"If I were you, Juli," said Ash thinking it over, "I wouldn't get married at all. It's too dangerous."

Few Europeans had ever visited Gulkote, for although the state was now officially part of the territory that had come under the jurisdiction of the British Crown after the sepoy mutiny of 1857, its lack of roads and bridges continued to discourage travellers, and as it had given no trouble, the authorities were content to leave well alone until such time as they had settled the more pressing problems of the sub-continent. In the autumn of '59, the Rajah, with an eye to forestalling interference, had prudently sent his Prime Minister and a deputation of nobles to negotiate a treaty of alliance with the new rulers, but it was not until the spring of '63 that Colonel Frederick Byng of the Political Department paid a formal visit to His Highness of Gulkote, accompanied by several junior secretaries and an escort of Sikh Cavalry under the command of a British officer.

The occasion was one of considerable interest to His Highness's subjects, whose acquaintance with Europeans had so far been limited to that colourful Cossack adventurer, Sergei Vodvichenko, and his hapless, half-caste daughter, the *Feringhi*-Rani. They were curious to see what these Sahib-log looked like and how they would comport themselves. And more than ready to enjoy the festivities that would mark the occasion. It was to be a right royal *tamarsha* (show), and no one looked forward to it with keener anticipation than Ash, though Sita made it clear that she disapproved strongly of foreigners visiting the state, and did her best to dissuade him from attending any of the ceremonies, or even appearing at court during the time that the Englishmen would be present.

"Why should they wish to come here and interfere with us?" complained Sita. "We do not want *feringhis* here, telling us what we should or should not do and creating worry and trouble for everyone . . . asking questions. Promise me, Ashok, that you will have nothing to do with them."

Her vehemence puzzled Ash, who had never quite forgotten a certain tall, grey-haired man who had lectured him repeatedly on the crime of being unfair . . . he could remember nothing else about this man except a curious and uncomfortable memory of his face seen fleetingly by lamplight, drained of life and colour; and afterwards the sound of jackals snarling and quarrelling in the moonlight, a sound that had, for some reason, left so strong an impression of fear that even now he could never hear the yelling of a jackal pack without shuddering. But he had early discovered that his mother disliked any mention of the past and could not be persuaded to talk of it. Perhaps the *feringhi* had been unkind to her, and that was why she was so anxious to prevent him from having any truck with the English visitors? It was, however, unreasonable of her to expect him to absent himself from duty for the duration of their stay; this would not be possible, as Lalji would need the services of all in his household during the visit.

But on the eve of Colonel Byng's arrival, Ash was unaccountably taken ill after a meal prepared by his mother, and for the next few days he remained prone on his bed in her quarters, unable to take any interest in anything but the acute discomfort in his head and stomach. Sita nursed him devotedly, accusing herself, with tears and lamentations, of giving him bad food, and while refusing to admit the hakim (doctor) who had been sent by Hira Lal to treat the sufferer, dosed Ash with herbal brews of her own concoction that had the effect of making him drowsy and heavy-headed. By the time he was on his feet again the visitors had gone, and he had to be content with a second-hand account of the junketings, relayed to him by Kairi, Koda Dad and Hira Lal.

"You did not miss very much," said Hira Lal sardonically. "The Colonel was old and fat, and his secretaries young and foolish, and only the officer in command of their escort spoke our tongue with any fluency. His Sikhs said that he was a pukka devil—which they meant to be a compliment. Are you well now? Kairi-Bai said she was sure you had been given poison to keep you from seeing the *tamarsha,* but we told her not to be a little owl, for who would care whether you saw it or no? Not Lalji, whatever his foolish little sister may think. Our beloved Yuveraj is too full of his own importance these days to bother his head over such matters."

This last was true enough, for as his father's heir, Lalji had played a prominent part in the various official functions in honour of Colonel Byng, and enjoyed the lime-light. It had been more entertaining and far less tiring than the ceremonies that had attended his wedding, and as part of his father's design to dazzle the barbarians, the clothes and jewels he had been given to wear had been even more magnificent than his wedding finery. Lalji had a fondness for fine clothes and display, and few opportunities for indulging it, so he had thoroughly enjoyed pea-cocking it at his father's side, decked out in embroidered coats stiff with gold and silver thread, wearing brilliant gauze turbans, ropes of pearls and collars of glittering jewels, and carrying a diamond-hilted sword with velvet scabbard that was sewn with seed pearls.

The fat Englishman who spoke such execrable Hindu-stani had been most affable, and treated him as though he were already a man grown, and although his father had also presented the *Nautch*-girl's eldest son to the visitors, little Nandu had not created a good impression, for he was a spoilt child and had screamed and whined and been so naughty that the Rajah had lost all patience with him and had him removed half-way through the first reception. He had not been allowed to appear again, so it was Lalji, and Lalji alone, who had sat, stood or ridden by his fa-ther's side throughout the four days of festivity; and when it was all over the splendid robes and jewels had not been taken away from him, but left in his charge, and his father had continued to command his presence and treat him with unusual affection.

Lalji was happier than he had ever been before, and his happiness showed itself in a hundred ways. He ceased to tease his little sister or torment his pets, and was gracious and good tempered to all his household. It was a pleasant change from his former tantrums, and only Hira Lal predicted trouble in the future. But then Hira

Lal was known to be a cynic. The other members of the Yuveraj's household basked in the relaxed atmosphere created by their young master's change of temper, and saw it as a sign that the boy was becoming a man and preparing at last to put aside childish things. They were also pleasantly surprised at the Rajah's continuous predilection for his son's society: they had not expected it to outlast the departure of the visitors, and were amazed to find that the young Yuveraj now spent a large part of each day in his father's company and was actually being instructed in affairs of state. All of which was deeply gratifying to the *Nautch*-girl's enemies—and they were many—who regarded the situation as a sign of the favourite's declining power (particularly as the child she had lately borne her lord was a small and sickly girl). But as subsequent events were to show they had once again underestimated her.

Janoo-Rani had been thrown into an imperial rage by the removal of her screaming son from the Durbar Hall, and the favourable impression created by his hated half-brother, the heir. She had raged for two days and sulked for a further seven. But, for once, without the anticipated effect. The Rajah had retaliated by avoiding her apartments and keeping to his own part of the palace until such time as she should have recovered her temper, and this unexpected reaction had frightened her as much as it had delighted her enemies.

Janoo looked at herself in the glass and saw in it something that she had hitherto refused to recognize— that she had lost her figure and was becoming stout. Time, childbearing and soft living had taken their toll, and the seductive, golden-skinned girl of a few years ago had gone, leaving in her place a short, plump little woman whose complexion was already beginning to darken and who would soon be fat, but who had, as yet, lost none of her wit or her power to charm. Taking stock of the situation, Janoo had hastily stage-managed a reconciliation, and so successfully that she was soon firmly back in the saddle. But she did not forget that short-lived taste of terror, and now, to the surprise of the court, she set out to win the friendship of her step-son.

It had not been easy, for the boy's jealous hatred of the woman who had supplanted the *Feringhi*-Rani and enslaved his father was a strong growth whose roots went deep. But Lalji had always been fatally susceptible to flattery, and now the *Nautch*-girl fed his vanity with fulsome compliments and extravagant gifts. Reversing her previous policy, she encouraged the Rajah to make much of his eldest son, and in the end she achieved, if not friendship, at least a truce.

"Someone," said Koda Dad, unimpressed by the Rani's apparent change of heart, "should remind that boy of the tiger of Teetagunje, who feigned to be a vegetarian and invited the buffalo's child to dine."

The court too regarded this new situation with a sceptical eye and predicted that it would not last. But as the weeks went by and it was seen that the Rani continued to remain on good terms with her step-son, it lost its novelty and in time came to be accepted as a normal state of affairs; which delighted the Rajah and pleased the majority of the Yuveraj's household—with the exception of old Dunmaya, who could not be brought to trust the *Nautch*-girl, and Hira Lal, who for once found himself in agreement with her. "Never trust a snake or a harlot," quoted Hira Lal sardonically.

Ash too had benefited briefly from the changed atmosphere, for Lalji's happiness and high spirits made him wish to make amends for his former unkindness to the boy who had, after all, once saved his life; though Lalji no longer believed that his step-mother had been in any way involved in that incident. It must have been an accident, he felt certain of that now; and also that there had been no need for him to insist on Ashok's presence in the palace, or any valid reason why he should continue to restrict his liberty. The obvious thing to do now would be to permit him to come and go as he chose. But Lalji was nothing if not obstinate and his pride forbade him to go back on any orders he had once given. He resolved, however, to be kinder to Ashok in the future.

For a time it almost seemed that Ash had been reinstated in his original position of companion and confidant to the Yuveraj. But it did not last. He was not aware of having done anything to offend, and he could not understand the reason for his second fall from favour—any more than he had understood the previous, and equally sudden, reinstatement. But the fact remained that once again, and without warning, Lalji turned against him, and from then on treated him with unreasonable and increasing hostility. A trinket mislaid or an ornament broken, a curtain torn or a parrot ailing—there and a dozen other petty mishaps were laid at his door and he was duly punished for them.

"But why *me?*" demanded Ash, bewildered by Lalji's inexplicable change of heart and, as always, taking his troubles to Koda Dad. "What have I done? It's not fair! Why should he treat me like this? What has happened to him?"

"Allah knows," shrugged Koda Dad. "It may be that one of his household became jealous of his renewed favour towards you, and has whispered falsehoods against you to bring you down. The favour of princes breeds envy and makes enemies; and there are some who have no love for you. He they call '*Bichchhu*' for one."

"Oh, him. Biju Ram has always hated me; though I do not know why he should, for I have done him no harm and I have never stood in his way."

"Of that I am not so sure," said Koda Dad.

Ash looked a question, and Koda Dad said dryly: "Has it never occurred to you that he might be in the pay of the Rani?"

"*Biju?* But—but that cannot be so," stammered Ash, aghast. "He could not . . . not while Lalji holds him in such favour and gives him rich presents and . . . He would not—"

"Why? Was it not the Yuveraj himself who dubbed him '*Bichchhu*'?—and with good reason? I tell you, Biju Ram's blood is as cold as that of his namesake. Moreover, we have a proverb in the country beyond the Khyber, that says 'A snake, a scorpion and a Shinwari have no heart to tame' (which Allah knows is true of a Shinwari). Listen, my son; I have heard it whispered in certain quarters of the city, and here too in the Hawa Mahal, that this man is a creature of the Rani's and that she pays him well to do her work. Should this be true—and I think it is—then surely both he and the woman should have every reason to hate you?"

"*Yes.*" The boy's voice was almost inaudible and he shivered, feeling as though the very ground under his feet was no longer solid. "Poor Lalji . . . !"

"Poor Lalji, indeed," agreed Koda Dad soberly. "Have I not told you many times that life is not always easy for those in high places?"

"Yes; but he had been so much better of late. So

much happier; and kinder, too. To everyone, not only me. Yet now all of a sudden I seem to be the only one he is unkind to, and always for things I have not done. It isn't fair, Koda Dad. It isn't *fair*."

"*Bah!* that is a child's saying," grunted Koda Dad. "Men are not fair—neither the young nor the old. You should have found that out by now, my son. What does Hira Lal say?"

But Hira Lal had only pulled at his earring and said: "I told you there would be trouble." And as he refused to add anything to this comment, it could hardly be considered helpful.

A few days later Ash had been accused of damaging Lalji's favourite bow, which had snapped during target practice. He protested that he had not touched it, but was disbelieved and soundly beaten; and it was after this that he had begged permission to resign from the Yuveraj's service and quit the Hawa Mahal. It was not granted. Instead, he was informed that he would not only remain in the service of His Highness, but that in future he would not be permitted under any circumstances to leave the fortress, which meant that he was no longer allowed to accompany Lalji or the Rajah when they rode out to hunt or hawk on the plateau or among the hills; or go into the city with Koda Dad or anyone else. The Hawa Mahal had turned, at last, into the prison that he had visualized on the day that he first entered it: its gates had closed behind him and there was no way of escape.

With the advent of the cold weather Sita contracted a chill and a small dry cough. There was nothing new in this; she had suffered from such things before. But this time she did not seem to throw it off, though she refused to seek advice from the hakim, and assured Ash that it was nothing and would pass as soon as the clean winds of winter rid them of the lingering heat and dampness of the monsoon. Yet already the heat had gone from the plateau and the air that blew off the mountains carried the faint cool tang of pine-needles and snow.

News had come from Zarin in Mardan, but it was not good news. The Guides had been in action against one of the Border tribes, and in the fighting his brother Afzal, Koda Dad's second son, had been killed. "It is the will of Allah," said Koda Dad. "What is written is written. But he was his mother's favourite . . ."

It was a sad autumn for Ash, and would have been sadder but for the staunch support of that small but faithful ally, Kairi-Bai. Neither disapproval nor direct orders had the slightest effect on Kairi, who evaded her women with the ease of long practice and would slip away daily to meet Ash in the balcony on the *Mor Minar,* bringing with her, as often as not, an assortment of fruit or sweetmeats smuggled out from her own meals or stolen from Lalji's.

Lying there and looking out towards the white peaks of the Dur Khaima, the two children would devise endless schemes for Ashok's escape from the palace; or rather, Ash would propound while Kairi listened. But the schemes were not serious, for both knew that Ash would not leave his mother, who was getting daily frailer. She who had always been so hard working and energetic was now often to be found sitting tiredly in her courtyard, her back against the trunk of the pine tree and her hands lying idle in her lap, and by common consent the children were careful not to mention Ash's troubles to her; though there were many troubles, not least of them his knowledge that once again someone was actively attempting to murder the heir of Gulkote.

Three years are a long time in a child's life, and Ash had almost forgotten the poisoned cakes that had been left in Lalji's garden, until suddenly a similar incident recalled them vividly and unpleasantly to his mind.

A box of the special nut-sprinkled *halwa* that Lalji was particularly fond of was found lying on one of the marble seats in the pavilion near the lily pool, and the Yuveraj pounced upon them, supposing them to have been left there by one of his attendants. But even as he did so, Ash recalled in an ugly flash of memory a trio of fat carp floating belly upwards among the lily pads, and springing forward he snatched the box from the Yuveraj's hand.

The action had been purely instinctive, and faced with a furious demand for an explanation he found himself in a trap. Having never told anyone of those cakes, he could not speak of them now without being disbelieved, or accused of concealing an attempt on the Yuveraj's life: either way the truth would not serve him, so he took refuge in a lie and said that the sweets were his own, but were unfit to be eaten, having been handled in error by a sweeper—a man of the lowest caste—and that he had brought them

99

here intending to feed them to the pigeons. Lalji had backed away in horror, and Ash had been punished for bringing them into the garden. Yet that three-year-old memory had not betrayed him, for later that evening he threw one of the sweets to a crow. And the crow had died. But because he had not spoken before, he dared not speak now.

The following week there had been another unnerving incident, involving a cobra that had somehow found its way into Lalji's bedroom. A dozen servants were ready to swear that it could not have been there when the Yuveraj went to bed, but it was certainly there in the small hours of the morning, for something had woken Ash, and within a few minutes of his waking he heard a clock strike two. His pallet lay across the threshold of the Yuveraj's room and no one could pass in without disturbing him: not even a snake. Yet lying awake and listening in the darkness, he had heard something that he could not mistake: the dry rustle and slither of scales moving across the uncarpeted floor.

Ash possessed all the European's horror of snakes, and instinct urged him to be still and make no move that might attract the creature's attention to himself. But the sound had come from inside the Yuveraj's room, and he knew that Lalji was a restless sleeper who might at any moment throw out an arm or turn over with an abruptness that would invite attack. So he rose, shivering with panic, and groped his way over to the curtained doorway that led into an outer room. There was an oil lamp there, its wick turned low, and he set it flaring and woke the servants.

The cobra was investigating the fruit and drink set out on a low table by Lalji's bed, and it was killed to the accompaniment of shrieks from Lalji and considerable uproar from a milling mob of servants, courtiers and guards. No one had ever discovered how it had managed to enter the room, though it was generally supposed to have found its way in through the bathroom sluice, and only Dunmaya saw its appearance as a deliberate plot against her darling.

"She is a foolish old woman, that one," said Sita, listening to the tale of the night's doings. "Who would dare to catch a live cobra and carry it through the palace? And if they could do such a thing they would certainly have been seen, for it was not a small snake. Besides, who is there in Gulkote who would wish to harm the boy? Not the Rani; all know how fond she has become of him. She treats him with as much kindness as though he was her own son, and I tell you it is not necessary to have given birth to a child in order to become fond of it. Dunmaya did not bear the Yuverai, yet she too loves him—even to seeing plots everywhere. She is mad."

Ash remained silent and did not tell her of those long-ago cakes and the *halwa* that had so recently appeared in the same garden and had also been poisoned, or what Koda Dad had said about the Rani and Biju Ram. He knew that such ugly tales would only frighten her, and he did not intend that she should hear them. But all too soon there came a day when it was no longer possible to keep them from her, for Kairi stumbled upon something that was to alter their lives as drastically as the cholera had done in that terrible spring when Hilary and Akbar Khan had died.

The Princess Anjuli—"Kairi-Bai," the little unripe mango—was barely six years old at that time, and had she been born in any Western country she would still have been considered a baby. But she had not only been born in the east, but in an eastern palace, and a too early experience of the plotting and intrigues of an Indian court had sharpened her wits and made her wise beyond her years.

Mindful of Ashok's warning and knowing him to be out of favour with her brother Lalji, Kairi no longer spoke to him or even glanced his way in public. But the system of secret signs and code words by which they could communicate under the eyes of the whole household without being detected served them well, and it was three days after the incident of the cobra that she ran to the Yuveraj's quarters and managed to convey an urgent signal to Ash. It was one that they were only to use in a dire emergency, and obeying it, Ash had slipped away at the earliest opportunity and made his way to the Queen's balcony, where Kairi had been waiting for him, white-faced and dissolved in tears.

"It's your own fault," sobbed Kairi. "She said you threw away some sweets and saved him from a cobra. I truly didn't mean to listen but I was afraid she would be angry if she found me in her garden, and Mian Mittau had

101

flown in there and I had to catch him—I *had* to. So when I heard her coming I hid in the bushes behind the pavilion and I heard . . . I heard what she said. Oh Ashok, she is bad! Bad and wicked. She meant to kill Lalji, and now she is angry with you about the cobra and because of some sweets. She said it showed that you know too much, so they must kill you quickly and she doesn't care how it is done, because it won't show by the time the kites and crows have finished with you, and who will mind about the death of a bazaar brat—that's you Ashok, she meant you. And she told them to throw you over the wall afterwards so that people will think you were climbing and fell off. It's true what I'm telling. They are going to kill you, Ashok. Oh what shall we do—what shall we do?"

Kairi threw herself at him wailing with terror, and Ash put his arms round her and mechanically rocked her to and fro while his thoughts scurried round in frantic circles. Yes, it was true . . . he was sure of that, for Juli could never have invented such a conversation. Janoo-Rani had always meant to kill Lalji and set her own son in his place, and to her certain knowledge he, Ashok, had stood in her way at least three times—four, if she was aware that it was also he who had found and thrown away those cakes. Had she known? He did not think anyone had seen him do that. But it made no difference now. She meant to see that he did not interfere again, and he would be a much easier target than Lalji, for no one would inquire too closely into the death or disappearance of such an unimportant person as the son of a serving-woman in the household of the neglected Kairi-Bai. He had never told Lalji of those cakes, or the truth about the *halwa*, and it was too late to tell him now. Particularly as Lalji had long ago persuaded himself that the falling slab of sandstone had been no more than an accident, and only two days ago had told Dunmaya that she was an evil-minded old trouble-maker who deserved to have her tongue cut out, because the old woman had voiced suspicions regarding the cobra. There was no help to be expected from the Yuveraj.

"Juli was right," thought Ash despairingly. "It is my own fault for not telling Lalji about it and showing him what those cakes did to the fish years ago, and the sweets poisoning that crow." He hadn't any proof now; and even if he had it wouldn't help him because Lalji was so sure that the Rani was his friend, and he, Ashok, could not prove that she did it, or tell them what Juli had heard because they would say that she was only a baby and had made it up. But the Rani would know that she hadn't and perhaps kill her too—and his mother as well, in case Sita should ask too many questions if he were killed ...

Twilight was gathering under the dome of the Queen's balcony, and Kairi had wept herself into exhaustion and now lay still and silent, soothed by the monotonous motion as Ash rocked to and fro and stared above her head at the far-away snows. The breeze was cold with the coming of winter, for October was nearly over and the days were drawing in. The sun had almost vanished and the distant peaks of the Dur Khaima made a frieze of fading rose and amber against an opal sky in which a single star shimmered like one of Janoo-Rani's diamonds.

Ash shivered, and releasing Kairi said abruptly: "We must go. It will soon be too dark to see, and—and they may be looking for me." But he did not go until the snows had turned from pink to violet and only the top-most peak of the Far Pavilions—*Tarakalas*, the "Star Turret"—still held the last of the sunset.

He had brought no rice with him today, but Kairi wore a little bracelet of late rosebuds around one wrist, and he stripped it off and scattered the buds at the edge of the balcony, hoping that the Dur Khaima would understand the emergency and forgive him for not bringing an offering of his own: "Help me," prayed Ash to his personal deity. "Please help me! I don't want to die ..."

The light faded from the peak and now the whole range was no more than a lilac silhouette against the darkening sky, and there was not one star, but a thousand. As the night wind strengthened it blew the rosebuds away, and Ash was comforted, for it seemed to him that the Dur Khaima had accepted his offering. The two children turned together and groped their way down through the ruined tower and back to Sita's courtyard, hand clutched in hand and eyes and ears strained to catch the smallest sound or movement that would betray a lurker in the shadows.

Sita had been cooking the evening meal, and Ash left Kairi with her and fled back to the Yuveraj's rooms through the maze of corridors and courtyards that formed a third of the Hawa Mahal, his heart thumping wildly and a queer cold feeling between his shoulder-

103

blades at that spot where a knife might most easily be driven in. It was an enormous relief to find that he had not been missed because Lalji had received a set of jewelled chessmen from the Rani, and was engaged in a game with Biju Ram.

Half-a-dozen sycophantic courtiers surrounded the chess players and applauded their young master's every move, and at the far end of the room a solitary figure sat cross-legged under a hanging lamp, absorbed in a book and paying no attention to the game. Ash tiptoed over to him and begged in a whisper for a word in private, and Hira Lal's lazy eyes scanned the boy's face for a brief moment before returning to the book.

"No. Tell me here," said Hira Lal in an unhurried undertone that did not carry to the group of courtiers. "If it is important, it is better not to go apart, for then someone might follow to find out what it is that you do not wish overheard. Turn your back to them so that they cannot see your face, and do not speak in a whisper. They will never believe that you would talk secrets in so public a place, so you may say what you will."

Ash obeyed him. He had to have advice, and of all the Yuveraj's household only Hira Lal had befriended him. He would have to trust him now because there was the night to be got through, and he did not know how many of the household were in the *Nautch*-girl's pay: perhaps half of them—or all of them. But not Hira Lal. Instinct told him that he could rely on Hira Lal, and instinct was right. Hira Lal listened without comment, his slim fingers absently toying with his dangling earring while his gaze strayed about the room in a manner calculated to suggest to the group by the chess players that he was bored and paying very little attention. But when Ash had finished, he said quietly: "You did well to tell me. I will see to it that you come to no harm tonight. But the Rani is a dangerous woman and she can afford to pay highly to achieve her ends. You will have to leave Gulkote—you and your mother both. There is no other way."

"I cannot"—the boy's voice cracked. "The Yuveraj would never give me leave and the guards will not let me pass the gate alone."

"You will not ask for leave. As for the gate, we shall find some other way. Tomorrow go to the Master of Horse and tell him what you have told me. Koda Dad is a wise

104

man and he will devise something. And now I think we have spoken together long enough; that is the second time Biju Ram has looked our way."

He yawned largely and closing his book with a bang, rose to his feet and said in a carrying voice: "Horses I can endure, but hawks, no. You must not expect me to show interest in creatures that bite and smell and shed feathers and fleas all over the floor. Grow up, boy, and study the works of the poets. That may improve your mind—if you have a mind."

He tossed the book to Ash and strolled over to join the group surrounding the chess players. But he was as good as his word. That night one of the Rajah's personal bodyguard shared the ante-chamber with Ash, his presence being explained as a mark of His Highness's disapproval at the laxity that had permitted a cobra to enter his son's bedroom.

There were no alarms in the night; but Ash did not sleep well, and as soon as he could escape next morning he went off to see Koda Dad Khan. Hira Lal had been before him.

"It is all arranged," said Koda Dad, checking him with an upraised hand. "We are agreed that you must leave tonight, and as you cannot go through the gate you must go over the wall. For that we shall only need rope; much rope, for the drop is a long one. But there is enough and to spare in the stables, so that will be easy. It is the last part that will be difficult, for you will have to climb down the rocks by goat tracks, which are hard enough to find by daylight and will be more so by night. It is fortunate that there is a moon."

"But—but my mother?" stammered Ash. "She is not strong and she can't—she could not . . ."

"No, no. She must leave by the gate. There is no order forbidding it. She must say that she wishes to purchase cloth or trinkets in the bazaar, and means to pass a night or two with an old friend. They will not question it, and once she is gone you must pretend to be ill so that you need not sleep in the Yuveraj's quarters tonight. You have only to cough and make believe to have a sore throat, and he will instantly agree to let you sleep elsewhere for he is afraid of infection. Then as soon as the palace is quiet, I myself will let you down on a rope, and after that you will have to get away quickly. Can your mother ride?"

"I don't know. I don't think so. I have never—"

"No matter. The two of you together cannot weigh as much as a full-grown man, and she can mount behind you. Hira Lal will arrange for a horse to be waiting for you among the *chenar* trees by Lal Beg's tomb beyond the city. You know the place. You cannot enter the city, as the gates are closed at night, so your mother must leave it during the afternoon when many people are about and no one notices who goes in or out. Tell her to take food and warm clothing, for the winter is coming and the nights are cold. And when you have her on the horse, ride hard for the north, since they will be sure you will go southward where the climate is kinder and the crops more abundant. With luck they may not search for you for a full day or more, for at first the Yuveraj will think that you are ill, and by the time he finds that you are gone you must be far away. Yet it is not he, but the Rani that you have to fear. She will know very well why you have fled, and desire your death the more—for fear of what you may know and who you might tell. The *Nautch*-girl is a ruthless and dangerous enemy. Do not forget that."

Ash's young face whitened and he said hoarsely: "But Juli knows too—Kairi-Bai knows. If the Rani finds out who told me, she will have her killed too. I shall have to take her with me."

"*Chup!*"* snapped Koda Dad angrily. "You talk like a child, Ashok. You must be a man now, and think and act as one. You have only to tell Kairi-Bai to keep her mouth shut, and even the *Nautch*-girl will not suspect her, for the child comes and goes like a sparrow and no one troubles to notice her. But if you run off with the Rajah's daughter, do you think that he would swallow such an affront to his honour? Why, he would hunt you to the death; and there is no man in all Hind who would not think him right and help him to do so. So let us have no more of such foolishness!"

"I'm sorry," apologized Ash, flushing. "I didn't think."

"That has always been your besetting sin, my son," growled Koda Dad. "You act first and think afterwards: how many times have I not said so? Well, think now if there is a safe place from where we may lower you over the wall on the northern side, because there the ground

---

*Be silent!

106

below is more broken and there are bushes and goat tracks among the rocks. But it will not be easy, for I know of no place on that side where you could not be seen by a man looking out from the wall or a window."

"There is one," said Ash slowly. "A balcony . . ."

So for the first time he went to the Queen's balcony by night, to leave it for the last time; clinging to the end of a rope that Koda Dad Khan and Hira Lal lowered down the forty-foot drop on to the tumbled rocks, where thorn bushes made black patches of shadow in the clear October moonlight, and the wandering goat tracks wound steeply downwards towards the milky levels of the plateau.

He had said goodbye to Kairi earlier that day after Sita had left, and had not expected to see her again. But she had been waiting for him in the Queen's balcony, a small, forlorn shadow in the moon-flooded night.

"They don't know I'm here," she explained hurriedly, forestalling criticism. "They think I'm asleep. I left a bundle in my bed in case anyone looked, but they were b-both snoring when I went out and they didn't hear me. Truly they didn't. I wanted to give you a present, because you are my bracelet-brother, and because you are going away. Here—this is for you, Ashok. To—to bring you luck."

She thrust out a thin, square little palm and the moonlight glinted on a small sliver of mother-of-pearl carved in the semblance of a fish. It was, Ash knew, the only thing she had to give: the sole trinket she possessed and her dearest and greatest treasure. Seen in these terms it was perhaps the most lavish present that anyone could or would ever offer him, and he took it reluctantly, awed by the value of the gift.

"Juli, you shouldn't. I haven't anything to give you." He was suddenly ashamed that he should have nothing to offer in return. "I haven't anything at all," he said bitterly.

"You've got the fish now," consoled Kairi.

"Yes, I have the fish."

He looked down at it and found that he could not see it clearly because there were tears in his eyes. But men did not cry. On a sudden inspiration he broke the little slip of mother-of-pearl in two, lengthways, and gave her back half of it. "There. Now we have each got a luck-charm. And one day, when I come back, we'll stick them together again and—"

"Enough," interrupted Koda Dad roughly. "Go back

to bed, Kairi-baba. If they find you gone and raise an outcry we shall all be ruined; and the boy must leave at once, for he has a long way to go before moonset. Say goodbye to him now, and go."

Kairi's small face puckered woefully and the tears that streamed down it drowned the words that she was trying to say, and Ash, embarrassed, said hastily, "Don't cry, Juli, I'll come back one day, I promise."

He hugged her briefly and pushing her towards Hira Lal, who was standing silent in the shadows, said urgently: "See that she gets back safely, won't you, Hira Lal? Her women mustn't know that she has been out to-night, for the Rani might hear of it, and then when it is found that I have gone—"

"Yes, yes, boy. I know. I will see to it. Now go."

Hira Lal moved out into the moonlight, and as he did so the grey silk of his *achkan* became one with the night sky, and his face and hands took on the neutral tint of the stonework, so that for a moment it seemed to Ash that he was looking at a ghost, and that Hira Lal was already only a memory. The thought sent a chill through him, and for the first time he realized how much he owed to this man who had befriended him. And to Koda Dad and Kairi, and others who had been good to him: falconers, syces, mahouts from the elephant lines; and before that, all the playfellows and acquaintances of his happy days in the city. It was strange that only now, when he was leaving Gulkote, did he see that there had been almost as many good times as bad ones.

The great black pearl that hung from Hira Lal's ear glimmered faintly as its wearer moved, and as the moonlight fell on it, it glinted like a flake of opal—or a falling tear—and Ash stared at it fixedly, willing himself not to cry and wondering when, if ever, he would see it again . . .

Hira Lal said curtly: "Make haste, boy. It grows late, and you have no time to waste. Go now—and may the gods go with you. *Namaste.*"

"I have let down the loop. Put your foot in it, so, and hold fast to the rope," directed Koda Dad. "And when you reach the rocks, be sure of your footing before you let go. From there your way will be more difficult, but if you move slowly and do not slip on the goat tracks you should do well enough. May the All-Merciful permit that you and your mother reach safety. Do not forget us. Farewell, my son. *Khuda Hafiz!*" (God protect you!)

He embraced the boy, and Ash bent to touch his feet with quivering hands and then turned quickly away, making a pretence of adjusting the heavy bundle of clothing for fear that Koda Dad should see the tears in his eyes. Behind him he could hear Kairi sobbing in helpless, childish grief, and, peering downwards he was suddenly appalled by the drop below him and the steep fall of rocks and scrub that plummeted towards the plain.

"Do not look down," warned Koda Dad. "Look up!"

Ash jerked his gaze from the gulf at his feet and saw, across the vast moon-washed spaces of the night, the Far Pavilions, their glittering peaks high and serene against the quiet sky. Fixing his gaze upon them he groped with one foot for the dangling loop, and grasping the rope, was lowered from the edge of the balcony, down and down, turning and swaying through dizzy space, while tears stung his eyes and Kairi called from above him in a sobbing whisper that was loud in the night silence: "Goodbye, Ashok. Goodbye. You will come back, won't you? *Khuda Hafiz! . . . Khuda Hafiz . . . Jeete Raho—Jeete Raho!*"*

Her tears fell on his face as she leaned from the edge of the Queen's balcony, and at last his feet touched the rocks at the foot of the wall and he steadied himself, and releasing the rope, saw it drawn up again. For the last time he waved to the three friends who watched from above, and then turning away, scrambled down between the rocks and prickly thorn bushes in search of a faint track he had spied earlier that afternoon when plotting his route from the balcony.

6

The distance from the foot of the wall to the level ground was less than two hundred yards, but it took Ash the best part of an hour to traverse it. Once he had almost come

---

*a Hindu form of blessing, literally "Live long"

to grief through losing his balance on a steep slope of shale, and it had taken him a long time to crawl back to firmer ground. But after that he had been more cautious, and at long last, scratched, bruised and breathless, with his clothes in tatters but his bundle still intact, he had reached the level ground.

Above him he could see the sheer cliff of the fortress wall and the dark bulk of the Peacock Tower. But the balcony was no longer visible, for it was lost in shadow; and he knew that no one would be there now. Perhaps no one would ever enter it again, unless Juli sometimes went there out of sentiment. But he did not think she would go there often; she was only a baby and in time she would forget, and the way to the balcony be lost—as it had been before he and Juli found it. Everything would change. Lalji would become a man and the *Nautch*-girl would grow old and fat, and lose her beauty and with it her power, Koda Dad would retire and a younger man become Master of Horse. Hira Lal too would grow old, and one day the old Rajah would die and Lalji would be ruler of Gulkote. Only the Dur Khaima would not change. The months, the years, the centuries would pass, and when the Palace of the Winds was no more, the Far Pavilions would still be there, unchanged and unchanging.

Ash knelt on the stony ground and bowed to them for the last time, bending until his forehead touched the dust, as Koda Dad bent when he prayed to Allah. Then, rising, he shouldered his bundle again and set off across the moonlit country towards the grove of *chenars* beyond the city.

Sita had not failed him: and neither had Hira Lal. A sturdy country-bred horse was tethered among the shadows where Sita waited anxiously, clutching a heavy bundle containing the food and clothing for the journey that she had purchased that afternoon in the bazaars. There was a man in charge of the horse, a stranger who gave no name but put a small packet into Ash's hand, saying that it was from Hira Lal.

"He said you might need money and this should help you on your way. The mare is a better animal than she looks," added the stranger, tightening the girths. "She will cover many miles a day and you may keep her to a trot for two or three hours at a stretch, for she has drawn a

110

*ghari** and does not tire easily. Your best road is that way——" He pointed with a lean forefinger and then bent to draw a rough map in the moonlit patch of dust: "Thus. There is no bridge over the river, and the main ferry will be too dangerous, but there is a small one here——to the southward——that is used only by a few farming folk. But even after you have crossed, be careful, for Hira Lal says that the Rani may well pursue you beyond the borders of Gulkote. May the Gods protect you. Ride swiftly"——and as Ash gathered up the reins he sent the horse forward with a slap on its rump.

It was fortunate that Ash not only possessed a good eye for country but had, in the old days, ridden out so frequently on hunting and hawking expeditions with the Rajah, Lalji or Koda Dad. Otherwise he would certainly have lost his way a dozen times before the night was out. But even by moonlight he had been able to follow the route roughly laid out for him by the man who had waited for him among the *chenars* by Lal Beg's tomb, and when the sky lightened to the dawn he recognized a circle of rocks on a hillside from where he had once seen the Rajah shoot a leopard, and knew that he was on the right road.

The drama and excitement of the previous day had exhausted Sita, and she slept soundly, her head against Ash's shoulder, and tied to him by a length of *pagri* (turban) cloth that prevented her from falling. When at last she awoke, aroused by the early sunlight, they could glimpse the river at the far end of a little stony valley between the hills, and Sita had insisted that they eat their morning meal before approaching the ferry, for to appear too early and too eager would only arouse curiosity. "And because inquiries will soon be made as to all those who have passed this way, we will dress you as a woman, my son," said Sita. "Those who come seeking us will ask for a woman and a boy on foot, not two women on horseback."

Draped in one of Sita's saris and decked with a few cheap brass ornaments, Ash made a very good girl, and Sita warned him to keep his head modestly bent and the sari pulled well forward to hide his face, and to leave the talking to her. The horse had been the only difficulty, for

---

*cart or carriage

111

it did not fancy entering the leaky flat-bottomed boat that provided the sole means of crossing the river, and at first the ferryman had demanded an exorbitant sum for transporting it. But though Hira Lal's packet had proved to contain the sum of five rupees in copper and silver coins, Sita had no intention of wasting money and still less of owning to such wealth, and she haggled with the man until the matter had been settled to the satisfaction of both, and the horse coaxed on board.

"Now we are safe," breathed Sita, looking back from the far bank. But Ash remembered the words of Koda Khan and the man in the *chenar* grove, and he knew that they had only won the first throw. The Rani would make others, using loaded dice; and realizing this, he turned north towards the inhospitable country where the foothills would soon be powdered with snow, instead of southward to the warm air and the lush croplands where, in the circumstances, they would be expected to go.

It seemed to him a very long time—a lifetime—since the day that they had arrived in Gulkote and imagined that here they would find peace and freedom and security. But there had been little freedom or peace in the Hawa Mahal, and no security, and now once again they were homeless and hunted and must search for a safe hiding place. There must be some place, somewhere, where people were not cruel and unjust and interfering—where they could live peacefully, minding their own business and being happy. "Somewhere where they won't bother about us, but just leave us alone," thought Ash desperately.

He had had less than three hours' sleep since Kairi had told him what she had overheard in the Rani's garden. He was eleven years old, and very tired.

The nights became colder as they journeyed north, and Sita's cough seemed to be a good deal worse. Though perhaps this was only because Ash was continually with her now, and so noticed it more. Mindful of Hira Lal's warning he had sold the horse as soon as they were well clear of the borders of Gulkote, because he knew that they would be less conspicuous if they travelled on foot. But no sooner had he done so than he regretted it, because Sita could only manage a very short distance each day, and sometimes they covered less than a mile.

He had not realized before how frail she had become,

112

and it worried him. However, they did not always have to go on foot, for with the money Hira Lal had given them, together with the price of the horse, they could afford to travel by tonga or bullock cart. But such journeys, in addition to being undertaken in the company of others, provided an ideal opportunity for questions and gossip, and after enduring a friendly catechism from their fellow-travellers during a long day spent in a bullock cart, and a similar experience from the driver of an *ekka*, they decided it was safer to go slowly on foot.

As the days went by without any sign of pursuit, Sita became less anxious and Ash began to think they had outwitted the Rani and could now relax and start planning for the future. It was obvious that they could not be continually on the move; their purse was not bottomless, and besides, Sita needed rest and quiet and a roof over her head—their own roof, not a different one every night, or the open sky when they failed to reach other shelter. He would have to find work and a hut for them to live in, and the sooner the better, for even at mid-day the air was sharp and chilly, and there was snow on the hills to the north. They had put enough distance between themselves and Gulkote to make it safe enough to stop running, and the Rani would realize that he could do little to harm her now, for even if he were to tell what he knew, who would be interested in the affairs of a small and far-away state, or place any credence in the tales of a vagabond boy?

But Ash had not only underestimated the Rani's agents, but failed to understand the real reason for her determination to destroy him. It was not so much fear of the Rajah, as fear of the British Raj . . .

In the old days of happy independence it would have been enough for Janoo-Rani to know that the boy Ashok had fled the state. But the old days were over and the *Angrezis* were all-powerful in the land, making and unmaking kings. Janoo-Rani still intended to set her son on a throne, and to do that she must first remove his half-brother. The fact that she had made several attempts to do so, and failed, did not worry her unduly; there were other methods and in the end she would find one that succeeded. But it was vital that none save her most trusted confederates should be aware of this, and she had been enraged to discover that one of Lalji's servants, a beggar-brat whom he had introduced into the palace—presumably as a spy

113

—had somehow come to know of it. Well, there was nothing for it but to see that he died before he could carry tales to the Rajah, who had unfortunately taken a fancy to him and might even believe him. She had given the necessary orders, but before they could be carried out both the boy and his mother had fled; and now Janoo-Rani was not only angry but afraid.

Lalji too had been angry, and he had sent out search parties to arrest the boy and bring him back under guard. But when they failed to find any trace of the runaways he had lost interest, and said that they were well rid of Ashok—a view that the Rani might have endorsed had it not been for the British. But the Rani had not forgotten the unwelcome visit of Colonel Frederick Byng of the Political Department, whom her husband had been compelled to receive with honour, and she had also heard tales of ruling princes who had been deposed by the British Raj for murdering their relatives or rivals. If the boy Ashok were to hear one day that the heir of Gulkote had met with a fatal accident, he might carry tales to those in authority, and then perhaps there would be inquiries; and who knew what might not come to light as a result of officious questioning and inquisitiveness? The boy must not be allowed to live, because as long as he remained alive he was both a danger to her and a stumbling block in the way of her son's advancement. "At whatever cost, he must be found," ordered Janoo-Rani. "He and his mother both, for he will have told her all he knows, and until they are dead we dare not move against the Yuveraj . . ."

Ash obtained work with a blacksmith in a village near the Grand Trunk Road, and with it the use of a ramshackle *godown* (storeroom) behind the forge for himself and Sita. The work was arduous and poorly paid and the room small and windowless and devoid of any furniture. But it was a beginning, and they spent the last of Hira Lal's bounty on a second-hand string bed, a cheap quilt and a set of cooking pots. Sita hid what money remained from the sale of the horse in a hole under her bed, and when Ash was out, dug a second hole in the wall for the sealed packet and the wash-leather bags that she had brought away from her quarters in the Hawa Mahal. She made no attempt to find work for herself, which was unlike her, but seemed content to sit in the sun outside the door of

114

their room, cook their scanty meals and listen of an evening to the tale of Ashok's doings. She had never asked much of life, and she did not regret the Hawa Mahal; she had seen too little of her boy there and knew that he had been unhappy.

Ash was certainly happier now than he had ever been in the service of the Yuveraj, and his meagre wages were at least put into his hand in solid coin; which was more than they had been in the Palace of the Winds. He felt that he was at last a man, and though he had not abandoned his grandiose plans for the future, he would have been content to remain in the village for a year or two. But early in the new year two men had arrived at the village inquiring for a hill-woman and a boy—a grey-eyed boy who, they said, might be disguised as a girl. The pair were wanted for the theft of certain jewellery, the property of the State of Gulkote, and there was a reward of five hundred rupees for their capture and fifty for information that would lead to their arrest . . .

The men had arrived late one evening, and fortunately for Ash had been given lodging for the night in the house of the *tehsildar,** whose young son happened to be a friend of his. This boy had overheard their conversation with his father, and there being no other couple answering to that description in the village, he had crept out into the darkness and woken Ash, who slept on the ground outside Sita's door. Half an hour later the pair were hurrying down a field path in the uncertain starlight, making for the main road where Ash hoped to beg a lift from a passing bullock cart, as it was only too clear that Sita could not go far or fast on foot. They had been lucky, for a kindly tonga driver had taken them up and driven them five miles and more to the outskirts of a small town, where they had taken to the open country, doubling back slowly and painfully to the southward in the hope of throwing their pursuers off the trail.

For the next two months they lived from hand to mouth, continually haunted by the fear of pursuit and never daring to stop in any place where they might attract attention. The larger towns seemed safer than small villages where strangers aroused comment, but work was not easy to find and the living was expensive. Their small

---

*village headman

115

hoard of money dwindled, and the close air of the crowded cities did not agree with Sita, who longed for the hills. She had never liked the plains, and now she was afraid of them; and then one evening, gossiping with a group of coolies outside a timber yard, Ash heard again the tale of a rich reward being offered for the capture of two thieves who had stolen a Rajah's jewels, and began to lose heart. Were they never to escape?

"Let us go north again, to the hills," begged Sita. "We shall be safe among the hills; there are few roads and many hiding places there. But where can one hide in these flat lands where there are a hundred paths leading to every town?"

So once again they turned northwards, but on foot and very slowly. There was no money now for tongas or bullock carts, and little enough for food, and as they could not afford to pay for lodgings they slept in the streets of towns or under trees in the open country: until there came a day when Sita could go no further . . .

They had spent the previous night in the shelter of an outcrop of rock on the banks of the Jhelum River, within sight of the Kashmir snows; and when the dawn broke over the dew-wet plain the long rampart of the mountains lay high above the morning mists, rose-flushed with the first rays of the coming day. In the clear air of the early morning they seemed no more than a few miles away and as though they could be reached in a mere day's march; but Sita, raising herself on her elbow to gaze longingly at them, knew at last that she would never reach them.

There had been nothing to eat that morning save a handful of parched grain, carefully hoarded against an emergency. Ash ground it between two stones and mixed it to a paste with water, but Sita could not swallow it, and when he wished to move on—their present refuge being too precarious—she shook her head.

"I cannot, *piara*," whispered Sita. "I am too tired— too tired."

"I know, mother darling. I too. But we cannot stay here. It is too dangerous. There is no other cover near by, and if anyone should come this way we should be caught like rats in a trap. And—and I think they may come soon. I . . ." He hesitated, reluctant to add to her trouble, but forced to it because she must understand that they dare not delay. "I did not tell you before, but yesterday I saw

116

someone I knew in that *serai* where we stopped for a while. A man from Gulkote. That is why I would not let you stay there. We must walk down-stream and see if we can find a ford, or a boatman who will take us across, and then we can rest for a little. You can lean on me. It will only be a short way, mother dear."

"I cannot, Heart's-dearest. You must go alone. You will make better speed without me, and be safer too. They are hunting a woman and a boy travelling together, and I know that I should have parted from you long ago except —except that I could not endure to."

"That's silly. You know I wouldn't have gone," said Ash indignantly. "Who would have looked after you if I had? Mother, *please* get up. Please! We'll walk very slowly."

He knelt beside her pulling at her cold hands and coaxing her. "You want to get to the mountains, don't you? Well, there they are—look, you can see them plain. You'll be better once you reach them. Your cough will go in the hill air and you'll feel well again, and then we'll look for our valley. You haven't forgotten the valley and the goat and—and the almond tree and . . ." His voice wavered suddenly and he tugged at her hands again, trying to lift her to her feet. "Only a little way more, I promise."

But Sita knew that she had come to the end of the road. Her strength was almost spent, and what little she had left must be used for one last, bitter task that must be done quickly, before it was too late. She freed her hands from his grasp and fumbled among the folds of her sari for a sealed packet and four small, heavy, wash-leather bags that she had carried tied about her waist in a length of cloth, and looking at them the tears gathered in her eyes and rolled slowly down her wasted cheeks; the fact that Ashok believed himself to be her son had been so sweet to her that even now, when she knew that the truth might save him, she could not bear to tell him. Yet he must be told. There was no other way in which she could help him to escape; and even this might not serve . . .

"I am not your mother. You are not my son," whispered Sita, forcing the words through trembling lips. "You are the son of an *Angrezi* . . . a Sahib . . ."

The words made no sense to Ash, but her tears frightened him more than anything that had ever happened to him during the years of servitude in the Hawa Mahal or the dreadful weeks since their escape: the death of Tuku, the poison and the cobra, the terror of pursuit—nothing had been as bad as this. He put his arms about her and clung to her, begging her not to cry and telling her that he would carry her if she could not walk: he was strong, and if she would hold about his neck he was sure that he could carry her. The things she said made no sense to him, and it was only the sight of the money that at last shocked him into attention. He had never seen so much money before in all his life, and at first it only meant one thing to him: they could afford to hire a cart—to buy one if necessary. His mother need not walk now, and they could out-distance their pursuers and pay for doctors and medicines to make her well. They were rich. "Why didn't you tell me before, mother?"

"I did not want you to know that you were not my son—my own son," wept Sita. "I would have thrown it away had I dared, but—but I did not dare . . . for fear that one day you might have need of it. That day is here, for the Rani's men are close on your heels and if you are to escape them you must leave me and go on alone, and take refuge with your own people where even she will not dare to follow you. You will be safe with them. There is no other way . . ."

"What people? You have always said we had no people. And of course I am your son. You mustn't say things like that. It's only because you are feeling ill and you've had nothing to eat, but now we can buy some food, and a horse and a cart and—"

"Ashok! Listen to me." Fear and urgency sharpened Sita's voice and her thin hands clutched his wrists with unexpected strength. "You cannot go back to buy food, and if you show that money they will say you stole it, for it is too great a sum for a boy such as you to possess. You must hide it as I have done, and keep it until you reach your own people. There is much written stuff in the packet, and more on this paper here. You must find someone who can read *Angrezi* and they will tell you who to take it to. Your father wrote it before he died, and—and I would have obeyed his commands and taken you to his people but for the great rising and the slaughter of the Sahib-log in Delhi. But I kept the papers and the money for you, and I did as he asked: I took care of you. He said: "Look

118

after the boy, Sita." And that I have done . . . But for love's sake; because alas, alas, I am not your mother. She too was *Angrezi*, but she died at your birth and it was I who took you from her arms and gave you the breast . . . I who cared for you from the first—the very first! But I can do so no longer. So now must I send you back to your own people, for with them you will be safe. And because I can go no further, you must go alone. Do you understand?"

"No," said Ash. "You are still my mother and I won't leave you. You can't make me! And I don't believe any of it; any of the rest. Or if it is true, it doesn't matter, for we can burn these papers and then no one will ever know, and I shall still be your son."

"If you are my son, you will obey me—I do not ask you to do this. As your mother, I command you. Stay with me if you will until I go. It will not be long. But afterwards take the papers and the money and go quickly. Do not destroy them. If you love me, promise that you will not destroy them, but that you will use them and return to your own people. And if you will not do it for love's sake, then do it because I am . . . because I have been your mother. Promise me, Ashok?"

"I—promise," whispered Ash. She could not be dying . . . it wasn't true. If only he could fetch help—a hakim. Or some hot food: that might revive her. Yet she looked so ill, and supposing he were to leave her and run to the nearest village, and be caught?

He dared not risk it; she was too weak to move and she would die slowly of thirst and starvation. Yet even if he did not go, they would both die, because sooner or later someone would find them here, for there was no other cover for more than a mile in any direction—only the flat, treeless plain and wide reaches of the river. He would never have taken refuge in such a place except that it was dusk when they fled from the *serai*, and not daring to keep to the highroad he had turned towards the open country. They had reached the rocks by the riverside an hour after moonrise and had been forced to stay there because Sita could go no further; yet, recognizing the danger of such an isolated spot, he had meant to leave it at first light and find some safer place of refuge. But now the sun was already shredding away the morning mists and he could see the foothills, and above them the snows were no longer pink and amber but sharply white. The day was here—and his mother was dying . . .

"It isn't true. I won't let it be true!" thought Ash frantically, his arms tight about her as though to hold her safe. But suddenly and hopelessly he knew that it was, and that she was leaving him. Grief and terror and desperation tore at his heart, and he hid his face against her shoulder and wept wildly, as a child weeps, shuddering and gasping. He felt Sita's frail hands patting him and soothing him, and her beloved voice against his ear, murmuring endearments and telling him that he must not cry for he was a man now—he must be brave and strong and outwit his enemies and grow up to be a Burra-Sahib Bahadur, like his father and old Khan Bahadur Akbar Khan for whom he had been named. Did he not remember Uncle Akbar who had taken him to see a tiger shot? He had been no more than a babe then, yet he had not been afraid and they had all been so proud of him. He must be as brave now, and remember that death came in the end for everyone—Rajah and Beggar, Brahmin and Untouchable, man and woman. All passed through the same door and were born again . . .

"I do not die, *piara*. I rest only, and wait to be reborn. And in that next life, if the gods are kind, it may be that we shall meet again. Yes, surely we shall meet again . . . perhaps in that valley—"

She began to talk of it in a slow, halting whisper that struggled for breath, and presently, as his sobs quieted, she turned from that dear familiar tale to the old nursery rhyme with which she had been used to sing him to sleep —"*Nini baba, nini, muckan, roti, cheeni*," crooned Sita. "*Roti muckan hogya; hamara . . . baba . . . sogya*—"

Her voice died away so softly that it was a long time before Ash realized that he was alone.

The blue far-reaching shadows of the early morning shortened into the scanty shade of mid-day, and slowly lengthened again as the afternoon wore away and the sun moved down towards the far horizon.

There were partridges calling out on the plain now, and wild duck quacking on the river, and along the white banks of the Jhelum the mud turtles that had basked all day in the hot sunlight were slipping back into the water. It would be dusk soon, and he would have to go, thought

120

Ash numbly. He had promised to go, and there was nothing left to stay for.

He stood up slowly and with difficulty, for he had crouched all day by Sita's body, holding her stiffening, work-worn hand in his. His muscles were cramped and his mind dazed with grief and shock. He could not remember when he had last eaten, but he did not feel hungry, only very thirsty.

The river was bright with the sunset as he knelt on the wet sand and scooped up the water and drank greedily, and afterwards splashed handfuls of it over his aching head and hot, dry eyes. He had not cried again after Sita died; and he did not cry now, for the boy who had wept so bitterly in the dawn was dead too. He was not yet twelve years old, but he would never be a child again. He had grown up in the short space of a single afternoon and left his childhood behind him for ever. For it was not only his mother whom he had lost that day, but his identity. There was no such person—there never had been—as Ashok, son of Sita who had been the wife of Daya Ram, syce. There was only a boy whose parents were dead and who did not even know his own name or where to find his own kin. An English boy—a *feringhi*. He was a foreigner, and this was not even his own land . . .

The coldness of the water helped to clear his head and he began to wonder what he should do now. He could not go away and leave his mother lying there, for an ugly memory from the almost forgotten past came back to him, and he shivered uncontrollably, recalling a hot night that had been made hideous by the sound of jackals and hyenas quarrelling in the moonlight.

Out on the quiet surface of the river something moved. It was only a piece of driftwood, floating down on the current, but as he watched it slide past him, Ash remembered that his people—no, his mother Sita's people —burnt their dead and cast the ashes into the rivers so that they might be carried at last to the sea.

He could not make a pyre for Sita for there was no fuel. But there was the river. The cool, deep, slow-flowing river that had risen among her own hills, and that would take her gently and carry her to the sea. The setting sun flamed on it with a dazzling brilliance that was brighter than fire, and he turned from it and went back to the shallow cave among the rocks, and wrapping Sita's wasted

121

body in her blanket as though to keep her warm, carried her down to the river and waded through the shallows until the water took her weight. She was stiff already, and so painfully light that the task was easier than he supposed. And when he released her at last she floated away from him, borne up by the blanket.

The current drew her out and down-stream, and he stood waist-deep in the water, straining his eyes to watch her go until at last her small shape was lost in the sun dazzle and he could see it no more. And when the brightness faded and the river turned from gold to opal, she had gone.

Ash turned and waded back to the shore, his legs numbed with cold and his teeth clenched together to keep them from chattering. He was hungry now, but he could not bring himself to eat the paste that he had made for Sita and that she had been unable to swallow, and he threw it away. He would have to find something to eat soon or he would not have the strength to go very far, and he had promised her . . . He lifted the sealed packet and the little wash-leather bags that were heavy with gold and silver coins, and weighed them in his hands, wishing he could leave them and knowing that he must not. They were his and he would have to take them. Removing only a single rupee for his immediate needs, he wrapped them again in the length of cloth and tied it about his waist as Sita had done, concealing it under his ragged garments. The folded sheet of paper with the faded, spidery writing that he could not read he hid in his turban, and now there was nothing left in the shallow cave to show that anyone had ever been there . . . Nothing but the footmarks and a slight depression in the sand where Sita had lain down to sleep on the previous night and where she had died in the dawn. He touched it very gently, as though she were still there and he feared to wake her.

As he did so, the first breath of the night wind blew in from across the river, and eddying about the cave, stirred up the dry silver sand and left it smooth again.

Ashton Hilary Akbar Pelham-Martyn shouldered his bundle and his burdens, and turning his back on the past, set out in the cold twilight to search for his own people.

"It is for a Captain-Sahib. A Captain-Sahib of the Guides," said the bazaar letter-writer, peering at Hilary's last letter through a pair of scratched spectacles. "Yes, see—here it says 'Mardan.' That is by Hoti Mardan, which is up Malakand way. Beyond Attock and the Indus, and across the Kabul River."

"The Guides," breathed Ash in an awed whisper. He would have made for Mardan long ago had he dared, but he knew that the Rani's men would expect him to go there and would lie in wait for him, for his friendship with Koda Dad's son had been no secret in the Hawa Mahal. But by now the watchers must surely have decided that he was too cunning to make such an obvious move, and they would have left to search elsewhere. Even if they had not, the situation itself had been drastically altered by the fact that he was no longer a friendless bazaar brat, hoping to find shelter with a sowar of the Guides, but a Sahib who could demand protection from his fellow Sahibs. Not only for himself, but for Zarin. And if necessary, for Koda Dad too.

"The Guides," repeated Ash softly. And suddenly his eyes were bright with excitement and the grey despair that had filled his mind and heart for so many days began to shred away like mist at morning. His luck had changed at last.

"It is the name of a *pulton* (regiment) that is stationed at Mardan," explained the letter-writer importantly, "and the Sahib's name is As-esh-taan. Captain Ash-tarn. As for the rest—" he made as though to open the folded paper, but Ash snatched it back, explaining that it was only the Sahib's name and address that he needed, the rest was no importance.

"If it is a recommendation, it is better to know what has been said," advised the letter-writer sagely. "Then if harsh things have been written, one can tear it up and say that one has lost it. Or if it is a good recommendation, it

123

may be sold for much money. Such things fetch good prices in the bazaars. Do you hope to take service with this Sahib, then?"

"No, I—go on a visit to my cousin's wife's brother, who is his servant," improvised Ash glibly. "They told me the address, but I had forgotten it and I cannot read *Angrezi*."

He paid over the half-anna that had been agreed upon and having made sure that he had memorized the name correctly, tucked the paper back among the folds of his turban and spent the other half-anna on a handful of roast *chunna* and a stick of peeled sugar-cane.

Ash had come a long way since the night he left the cave by the Jhelum River. It had not taken him long to discover how much farther and faster he could travel now that he was alone; or how right Sita had been when she had told him that he would be safer by himself, for he had heard of inquiries made in the villages and was aware that the hunt was still up. But since the men who hunted him knew that he would never leave his mother, they still looked for a hill-woman and a grey-eyed boy travelling together, and were not concerned with a single ragged ur-chin whose colouring, in the north-west of India where the Khyber hills lay along the horizon, was nothing out of the common.

He had not been questioned, but because he was afraid of doing anything that might draw attention to himself, he had not dared to ask for a translation of that paper in any of the smaller towns where such an inquiry might arouse interest. Only when he reached one large enough to boast half-a-dozen letter-writers had he felt safe enough to risk it; and now the name and address on it had turned out to be that of an officer of the Guides —Zarin's regiment. It was almost too good to be true.

Ash remembered that his mother had said she did not know what was written on that paper. But he thought that she must have had some suspicion, and that this perhaps explained her antipathy towards Koda Dad and his son, and her opposition to his plan of joining Zarin one day and enlisting in the same Corps. Yet in the end it was she who had set him on the road to Mardan, where he would see Zarin and become a sowar in the Guides—or even an officer, if this Captain-Sahib should prove to be a relative and prepared to help him. But that last was something he was never to know, for William Ashton was dead.

The Guides had taken part in the Ambeyla expedition, a campaign launched against certain hostile Border tribes in the autumn of the previous year, and William, still unaware that he possessed a nephew, had been killed in action only a few weeks after his sister's son escaped over the walls of the Hawa Mahal. But now it was spring, and the almonds were in bloom and the willows in bud as Ash took the road that leads from Attock to Peshawar.

The Kabul River ran red with the red earth of the Khyber that the spring rains and the melting of the snows in far-off Afghanistan had washed down on the flood, and the fords were impassable, so that he must cross by the bridge of boats at Nowshera. Ash had already made a detour of some dozen miles to avoid crossing the Indus by the Attock ferry, it having occurred to him that it would be an easy matter for a single man to keep a check on all who passed that way: in which he was wise, for there had indeed been a man on watch, an innocent-seeming traveller who appeared to be in no hurry, and who had made friends with the boatman and spent his days idly observing all those who used the ferry. Ash had crossed instead some five miles down-stream, having begged a lift on a farmer's raft, and from there made his way back to the Peshawar road. And now once again providence was kind to him, for in Nowshera a kindly villager on his way to Risalpur with a load of vegetables gave him a lift, and on pretence of being sleepy he burrowed down behind the cabbages and knole-kole and crossed the bridge of boats unseen. So towards evening on that same day—dusty, footsore and very weary—he reached the cantonment of Mardan and asked for Sowar Zarin Khan of the Guides.

The Corps of Guides were back once more in their barracks after months of hard campaigning and harder fighting in the Yusafzai country, and eighteen months of active service had aged Zarin so that he was barely recognizable as the gay youth who had ridden away so light-heartedly from Gulkote. He had grown taller and broader, and acquired an impressive moustache in place of the budding growth that Ash remembered. But he was still the same Zarin, and he had been delighted to see Ashok.

"My father sent word that you had left Gulkote, and

125

I knew that you would come here one day," said Zarin, embracing him. "You will have to wait until you are full grown before you can enlist as a sowar, but I will speak to my eldest brother, who is now a Jemadar since the battle on the road to Ambeyla, and he will find you work. Is your mother here?"

"She is dead," said Ash flatly. He found that he could not speak of her even to such an old friend as Zarin. But Zarin appeared to understand: he asked no question and said only, "I am sorry. She was a good mother to you, and I think it must be hard to lose even a bad one, for each of us has only the one to lose."

"It seems that I have had two," said Ash bleakly. And squatting down tiredly to warm himself at Zarin's fire, he told the tale of his escape from the Hawa Mahal and of the things that he had learned from Sita in the cave by the river, producing at last, in proof of the latter, a sheet of paper that bore the address of a dead officer of the Guides.

Zarin could not read the writing, but he too had been startled into belief by the sight of the money, for the coins spoke for themselves and did not need any translation. There were over two hundred of them, of which less than fifty were silver rupees and the rest sovereigns and gold mohurs; and that Sita should have concealed this small fortune for so many years seemed to prove that there must be at least some truth in her story.

"I think we had better show this to my brother," said Zarin, looking doubtfully at the paper that Ash had thrust into his hand. "Perhaps he will be able to advise you, for I cannot. It is too dark a matter for me."

Zarin's brother, the Jemadar, had no such doubts. There was only one course to take. Ashton-Sahib being dead, the whole affair must now be laid before Colonel Browne-Sahib, the Commandant, who would know how to deal with it. He himself, Awal Shah, would accompany the boy Ashok to the Colonel-Sahib's quarters immediately, because if there was any truth in this extraordinary story, the sooner both money and papers were placed in safe hands the better.

"As for you, Zarin, you will say nothing of this to anyone. For if the Rani of Gulkote desires the boy's death, she will revenge herself on those who helped him to escape, and if she should hear that he is with us, she will suspect that our father had a hand in the matter. So it is better for all our sakes that the trail should be lost. I will go now to the Commandant-Sahib, and you, Ashok, will follow me, walking a little behind so that we are not seen to be together, and waiting outside until you are sent for. Come."

The Jemadar stuffed the evidence into his pocket and strode out into the late sunlight, and Ash followed at a discreet distance and spent the next half hour perched on the edge of a culvert, tossing pebbles into the ditch below, and keeping a watchful eye on the Commandant's windows while the shadows lengthened on the dusty cantonment road and the sharp spring evening filled with the scent of woodsmoke and dung fires.

It was, though he did not know it, his last hour of independence. The last, for many years, of peace and freedom and idleness, and perhaps if he had realized that he might have broken his promise to Sita and run away while there was still time. Though even if he had escaped the Rani's assassins it is doubtful that he would have got very far, for Colonel Sam Browne, v.c., the Officiating Commandant of the Corps of Guides, having read the unfinished letter that Professor Pelham-Martyn had started to write to his brother-in-law William Ashton, was now engaged in removing the seals from a packet that had been wrapped in oiled silk almost exactly seven years ago. It was already too late for Hilary's son to run away.

Three weeks later Ash was in Bombay, dressed in a hot and uncomfortable suit of European clothes and shod with even more uncomfortable European boots, *en route* for the land of his fathers.

His passage had been arranged and paid for by the officers of his uncle's Regiment, all of whom, after flatly refusing to believe that this beggar-brat could possibly be the nephew of poor William, had eventually been convinced by the evidence in the packet (which included a daguerreotype of Isobel, whose likeness to her son was startling, and another of Ash seated on Sita's lap and taken in Delhi on his fourth birthday—both sitters having been unhesitatingly identified by Zarin), together with a searching verbal and physical examination of the claimant. Once converted, William's friends could not do enough for the nephew of an officer who had served with the Corps since Hodson built the fort at Mardan, and whom everyone had liked. Though his nephew was not in the least grateful for their efforts on his behalf.

Ash had obeyed his foster-mother's last commands and handed over to the Sahib-log the papers and the money she had given him. Having done so, he would have preferred to live in the lines with Zarin and Awal Shah, and earn his living as a stable boy or a grass-cutter until he was old enough to join the Regiment. But this had not been permitted. Why couldn't people leave him alone? thought Ash resentfully. Why, always and everywhere, must there be dictatorial people who gave him his unpalatable orders, restricted his liberty and over-rode his wishes—and others, who at a word from an evil and ambitious woman, were even prepared to hunt him across Hind and take his life, though they had no quarrel with him and he had done them no harm? It wasn't fair!

He had been happy in the bazaars of Gulkote and he had not wanted to leave the city and move to the Hawa Mahal. But he had been given no choice. And now it seemed that he must leave his friends and his homeland and go to his father's country; and once again there was no choice—and no appeal. He had walked into a trap as surely as on the day that he had entered the Hawa Mahal, and it was too late to try and escape from it, for the doors were already closing behind him. Perhaps when he grew up he would be allowed to do as he pleased—though in a world filled with oppression, assassins and interfering busy-bodies, he began to think it unlikely. But at least the Sahibs had promised that when the years of servitude in *Belait* were over, he would be permitted to return to Hind.

Colonel Sam Browne, the Commandant, told him that telegrams had been sent to his father's people, who would send him to school and turn him into a Sahib. Also that if he worked hard and did well in examinations (whatever those were) he would obtain a commission in the army and return to Mardan as an officer of the Guides; and it was that hope, rather than his promise to Sita or his fear of the Rani's men, that prevented Ash from making a break for freedom. That, and the fact that he was to travel to England in the care of a Sahib who was taking home two Indian servants; which meant that he would not

128

be entirely alone and friendless. This last had been largely due to a chance remark of Jemadar Awal Shah's.

"It is a pity," said Awal Shah to his Commanding Officer, "that the boy will forget the speech and the ways of this land, for a Sahib who can think and talk as one of us, and pass as either a Pathan or a Punjabi without question, would have made his mark in our Regiment. But in *Belait* he will forget and become as other Sahibs; which will be a great loss."

The Commandant had been much struck by this observation, for although every Englishman in the service of the Government of India was expected to become fluent in one or more of India's languages, very few learned to speak well enough to pass as a native of the country. And those few were for the most part half-castes whose mixed blood debarred them from employment in the higher ranks of the army or the Civil Service—even so gifted a soldier as Colonel George Skinner of Skinner's Horse, the famed "Sikundar Sahib," having been refused a commission in the Bengal Army because his mother was an Indian lady. But it was plain that William Ashton's nephew was a native of India in all but blood, and one of the few who could go deeper than the skin. As such he might one day prove of inestimable value in a country where accurate information often meant the difference between survival and disaster, and Awal Shah was right: such potentially valuable material ought not to be wasted.

The Commandant brooded over the problem, and eventually hit upon an admirable solution. Colonel Ronald Anderson, the District Commissioner, whose retirement had been enforced by ill-health, would be leaving for England on the following Thursday, taking with him his Pathan bearer, Ala Yar, and his *khansamah* (cook) Mahdoo, whose home was in the hills beyond Abbottabad, both of whom had been in his service for over twenty years. Anderson had been a friend of both John Nicholson and Sir Henry Lawrence, and had in his youth spent several years in Afghanistan on the staff of the ill-fated Macnaghton. He spoke half-a-dozen dialects and had an exhaustive knowledge and a deep love for the North-West Frontier Province and the land beyond its borders, and he would be an ideal person to keep an eye on young Ashton during the long voyage home, and for as many school holidays as the Pelham-Martyns would permit—always supposing he could be persuaded to accept such a task. The Commandant of the Guides Corps had wasted no time, but calling for his horse had ridden off that same day to lay the whole matter before Colonel Anderson. And the retiring Commissioner, intrigued by the story, had instantly consented.

"But of course you will return," said Zarin, reassuring the anxious Ash. "Only first it is necessary to acquire learning, and that, they say, must be done in *Belait*. Though I do not myself . . . Well, no matter. But it is even more necessary to remain alive, and it is certain that you are not safe in this country while there is a price upon your head. You cannot be sure that the Rani's spies have lost your trail, but we can at least be sure that they will not follow it across the sea, and that long before you return, both she and they will have forgotten you. I and my brother Awal Shah have been sworn to secrecy and cannot even send news of you to our father, for as letters may be opened and read by the curious, it is better that he should be kept in ignorance rather than risk betraying your whereabouts and your changed fortunes to those who wish you ill. But later, when the *gurrh-burrh* has died down, if the Colonel-Sahib thinks that it is safe to do so, I will write to you to *Belait;* and remember that you do not go there alone. Anderson-Sahib is a good man and one whom you may trust, and he and his servants will see to it that you do not wholly forget us while you learn to be a Sahib—and you will find that the years will go quickly, Ashok."

Yet there Zarin had been wrong, for they had not gone quickly. They had crawled by so slowly that every week had seemed a month and every month a year. But he had been right about Colonel Anderson. The ex-District Commissioner had taken a liking to the boy, and during the long, tedious days of the voyage he had managed to teach Ash an astonishing amount of English, having impressed upon him that to be speechless in a foreign land would be a grave disadvantage and, moreover, humiliating to pride.

The point had been taken, and Ash, who had inherited his father's gift for languages, had applied himself with such diligence to the mastering of his new tongue that a year later you would never have known that he had spoken any other, for with the natural imitativeness of youth he had come to speak it with the exact drawl and inflection of upper-crust England—the voice of pedantic tutors and elderly Pelham-Martyns. Yet try as he would, he could not learn to think of himself as one of them, nor did they find it easy to accept him as such.

He was to remain a stranger in a strange land, and England would never be "Home" to him, because home was Hindustan. He was still—and always would be—Sita's son; and there were endless things about this new life that were not only alien to him, but horrifying. Trivial things in the opinion of Englishmen, but to one brought up in the religion of his foster-mother's people, incredibly shocking. Such as the eating of pork and beef; the one an abomination and the other sacrilege unspeakable—the pig being an unclean animal and the cow a sacred one.

No less appalling was the European habit of using a toothbrush not once but many times, instead of a twig or a small stick that could be plucked daily and discarded after use; saliva, as everyone knows, being of all things the most polluting. Apparently the English did not know, and there were bitter battles before Ash could be brought to accept this and other practices that seemed to him barbaric.

That first year had been a difficult time for all concerned, not least for Ash's relatives, who were equally horrified by the habits and appearance of this young "heathen" from the East. Rigidly conservative and possessing all the in-bred insularity of their race, they flinched from the prospect of displaying Hilary's son to the critical gaze of their friends and neighbours, and hastily revised their original plans, which had included sending their nephew to the famous public school that had been responsible for the education of seven generations of Pelham-Martyns. Instead, they engaged a resident tutor, together with the weekly attendance of an elderly cleric and a retired Oxford Don, to "lick him into shape," and thankfully agreed to an arrangement whereby he should spend his holidays with Colonel Anderson.

Pelham Abbas, the seat of Hilary's elder brother, Sir Matthew Pelham-Martyn, Bart, was an imposing property consisting of a large, square Queen Anne house, built on the site of the earlier Tudor one that had been destroyed by Cromwell's men in 1644, and surrounded by

131

terraced lawns, walled gardens, stables and greenhouses. There was also an ornamental lake, an extensive park in which Ash was permitted to ride, a trout stream, and on the far side of a belt of woodland in which Sir Matthew's gamekeeper raised pheasants, a home-farm consisting of some four hundred acres. The house itself was full of family portraits and Regency furniture, and the Pelham-Martyns, who had feared that their uncivilized young nephew might be over-awed by it, were disagreeably surprised to discover that he considered it cold and uncomfortable, and not to be compared in either size or magnificence to some Indian palace with an unpronounceable name in which, so he said, he had lived for "many years."

It was the first of several surprises, not all of them disagreeable. That the boy should prove to be equally at home with a horse or a gun was something that they had not expected, and for which they were profoundly grateful: "As long as he can shoot and ride, I suppose he'll scrape past," said his cousin Humphrey. "But it is a pity we didn't catch him younger. He doesn't seem to have any of the right ideas."

Ash's ideas remained unorthodox and frequently led him into trouble; as witness his refusal to eat beef in any form (this was the last and strongest remnant of Sita's training, and the one that took him the longest time to overcome despite the many difficulties involved—not to mention the lectures and punishments it brought down on his head from teachers and schoolmasters, and the anger, resentment and irritation it aroused among his relations). Then, too, he could not see why he should not offer to teach Willie Higgins, the boot-boy, to ride, or invite twelve-year-old Annie Mott, the thin, overworked little scullery maid who always looked half starved, to share his tea in the schoolroom. "But it's my tea, isn't it Aunt Millicent?" asked Ash. Or: "But Uncle Matthew gave me Blue Moon for my own horse, so I don't see why . . ."

"They are servants, my dear, and one does not treat servants as equals. They would not understand it," explained Aunt Millicent, annoyed at being argued with in broken English by this impossible offspring of her eccentric brother-in-law. How *like* Hilary—he had always been a problem, and now that he was dead he was still capable of causing them grave embarrassment.

132

"But when I was Lalji's servant," persisted Ash, "I used to ride his horses, and—"

"That was in India, Ashton. You are in England now, and must learn to behave properly. In England we do not play with the servants or invite them to share our meals. And you will find that Annie is adequately fed in the kitchen."

"No she's not. She's always hungry, and it isn't fair, because Mrs. Mott—"

"That's enough, Ashton. I have said 'No,' and if I hear any more of this I shall have to give orders that you are to be kept away from the kitchen and not allowed to speak to any of the underservants. Do you understand?"

Ash did not. But then neither did his relatives. Later on, when he had learned to read and write in English as well as speak it, his uncle, in a praiseworthy attempt to encourage industry and lighten the tedium of lessons, had given him a dozen books on India, saying that they would of course be of special interest to him. The books had included several of Hilary's later works, together with such stirring tales as *The Conquest of Bengal*, Sleeman's account of the suppression of Thuggery, and Sir John Kaye's *History of the Sepoy War*. And Ash had certainly been interested; though not in the way that his uncle had intended. He found his father's books too dry and erudite, and his reactions to the others had seriously annoyed Sir Matthew, who had been rash enough to request his opinion on them.

"But you asked me what I thought!" protested Ash in some indignation. "And that is what I think. After all, it was their country and they weren't doing you—I mean us—any harm. I don't think it was fair."

"Shades of Hilary!" thought Sir Matthew with exasperation, and he explained tartly that, on the contrary, they had been doing a great deal of harm—what with murdering, oppressing and making war on each other, strangling harmless travellers in honour of some heathen goddess, burning widows alive, and generally obstructing trade and progress. Such horrors could not be allowed to continue unchecked, and it was both the duty and responsibility of Britain, as a Christian nation, to put a stop to these barbarities and bring peace and tranquillity to the suffering millions of India.

"But *why* was it your responsibility?" asked Ash,

genuinely puzzled. "I don't see that it had anything to do with you—I mean with us. India isn't even anywhere *near* us. It's at the other side of the world."

"My dear boy, you have not been giving proper attention to your books," said Sir Matthew, striving for patience. "If you had read more carefully you would have learned that we had been granted trading posts there. And trade is not only vital to us, but to the prosperity of the entire world. We could not permit it to be disrupted by continual vicious and petty wars between rival princes. It was necessary to preserve order, and that we have done. We have, under God's providence, been able to bring peace and prosperity to that unhappy country, and bestow the blessings of progress on a people who have for centuries suffered atrocious persecution and oppression at the hands of greedy priests and quarrelling overlords. It is something we may be proud of, and it has not been without grave cost to ourselves in labour and lives. But one cannot hold back the march of progress. This is the nineteenth century, and the world is becoming too small to permit large portions of it to remain in a state of medieval depravity and barbarism."

Ash had a sudden vision of the white pinnacles of the Dur Khaima and the wide sweep of the plateau across which he had ridden out hawking with Lalji and Koda Dad, and his heart sank: it was terrible to think that one day there might be no wild, beautiful places left where one could escape from the things that Uncle Matthew and his friends called "Progress." He had formed an unfavourable opinion of Progress, and he did not continue the conversation, it being obvious to him that he and his uncle would never see eye to eye on such subjects.

Ash was aware (as Uncle Matthew was not) of a great many things in Pelham Abbas that were in need of reform: the waste and extravagance, and the feuds that raged in the servants' hall; the tyranny of the upper servants and the miserably inadequate wages that were considered sufficient payment for long hours of gruelling work; the unheated attics in which such despised underlings as kitchen and scullery maids, boot-boys and underfootmen slept; the long flights of uncomfortable stairs that the housemaids must toil up and down a dozen times a day carrying cans of boiling water, slop-pails or loaded trays, with the dread shadow of instant expulsion without recompense or reference hanging over them should they commit any fault.

The only difference that Ash could see between the status of the Pelham Abbas servants and those in the Hawa Mahal was that the latter led pleasanter and more idle lives. Yet he wondered what his uncle would think if Hira Lal or Koda Dad—who were both wise and incorruptible men—were suddenly to appear before the gates of Pelham Abbas accompanied by the guns, war elephants and armed soldiers of the Gulkote State Forces, and take over the management of the house and estates, setting them to rights according to ideas of their own? Would Uncle Matthew gratefully accept their domination and willingly obey their orders because they were running his house and his affairs better than he could run them himself? Ash doubted it. People everywhere preferred to make their own mistakes, and resented strangers (even efficient and well-meaning ones) interfering with their affairs.

He resented it himself. He hadn't wanted to come to *Belait* and learn to be a Sahib. He would far rather have stayed in Mardan and become a sowar like Zarin. But he had not been given the choice, and felt in consequence that he understood more about the feelings of subject races than his Uncle Matthew, who had spoken so patronizingly of "bestowing the benefits of peace and prosperity on the suffering millions of India."

"I suppose they look on me as one of the 'suffering millions,'" thought Ash bitterly, "but I'd rather be back there, and working as a coolie, than here, being told what to do all day."

The holidays had been oases in a dry wilderness of lessons, and but for them he often felt that he would not have been able to endure this new life; for although he was encouraged to walk and ride in the park, it was never alone but always under the watchful eye of his tutor or a groom. And as the park was surrounded by a high stone wall and he was not allowed beyond the lodge gates, his world was in many ways as restricted as that of a prisoner or a mental patient. Yet the loss of freedom had not been the worst thing in those years, for Ash had experienced much the same restriction in the Hawa Mahal. But then Sita had been there, and he had had friends; and at least Lalji had been young.

135

The age of his present gaolers irked him, and after the colourful muddle of an Indian court he found the decorous and inflexible ritual of Victorian country-house life dreary and meaningless—and alien beyond words. But since his pocket money, like the servants' wages, was too meagre to permit him to think of escape—and in any case, England was an island and India was six thousand miles away—there was nothing he could do about it except endure it, and wait for the day when he could go back to join the Corps of Guides. Only obedience and hard work could hasten that day; so he had been obedient and had worked hard at his lessons, and his reward had been the end of tutors and life at Pelham Abbas, and four years at the school his father and grandfather and great-grandfather had attended before him.

Nothing in Ash's formative years had prepared him for life in an English public school, and he detested every aspect of it: the regimentation, the monotony and the lack of privacy, the necessity to conform and the bullying and brutality that were meted out to weaklings and all whose opinions differed from those of the majority; the compulsory games and the reverence paid to such gods as the Head of Games and the Captain of Cricket. He was not given to talking of himself, but the fact that one of his names was Akbar had elicited questions, and his replies having revealed something of his background, he had promptly been nicknamed "Pandy," a name applied for many years by British soldiers to all Indians, whom they termed "Pandies" in reference to the Sepoy, Mangal Pandy, who had fired the first shot of the Indian Mutiny.

"Young Pandy Martyn" had been treated as a species of foreign barbarian who must be taught how to behave in a civilized country, and the process had been a painful one. Ash had not accepted it in the proper spirit, but attacked his tormentors with teeth, nails and feet in the manner of the Gulkote bazaars, which was apparently not only uncivilized but "unsporting"—though it did not appear to be unsporting for five or six of his opponents to set upon him at once when it became clear that in the matter of muscle he was a match for any two of them. But numbers invariably triumphed, and for a time he had again seriously contemplated flight; only to reject it once more as impractical. He would have to endure this as he had endured the lesser evils of Pelham Abbas. But at least he would show these *feringhis* that on their playing fields he could be as good or better than they.

Koda Dad's training in marksmanship having encouraged a naturally good eye, it had not taken long for Ash's schoolmates to discover that "young Pandy" could more than hold his own at any form of sport, and it had made a great deal of difference to their attitude towards him—particularly once he had learnt to box. When he eventually graduated from the Second Eleven to the First, played fives and football for his House and later for the school, he became the object of considerable hero-worship among the junior forms; though his contemporaries found him difficult to know. Not unfriendly, but apparently uninterested in any of the things that they had always believed in, such as the supremacy of the Anglo-Saxon races, the importance of being well-bred, and the Divine Right of the British to govern and control all coloured (and therefore unenlightened) peoples.

Even Colonel Anderson, in most matters so wise and understanding, had little sympathy with Ash's views, for his own opinions inclined more in the direction of Sir Matthew's. He too had pointed out that with the triumph of the steam-engine and the improvement of medical standards, the world was becoming smaller and more overcrowded every year. It was no longer possible for either nations or individuals to go their own way and do exactly as they pleased, for if everyone were free to do as they liked, the result would not be contentment, but anarchy and chaos. "You'll have to find a desert island, Ash, if you want to live your life without anyone else interfering with it. And I don't suppose there are many of those left."

The English climate had not improved Colonel Anderson's health as much as had been hoped, but though he had been forced to resign himself to a life of semi-invalidism he continued to take an active interest in Ash, who still spent the greater part of the school holidays under his roof. The Colonel's house was a small one on the outskirts of Torquay, and though in no way comparable to Pelham Abbas, Ash would have preferred to spend all his free time there, since those portions of the holidays that had to be spent in his uncle's house continued to be a severe trial to both of them, Sir Matthew being annoyed to find that, except in the matter of sport, his nephew

137

showed no signs of turning into a credit to him and every sign of being as intransigent as his father Hilary had been, while Ash, on his part, was equally baffled and exasperated by his uncle, his relatives and his relatives' friends. Why, for instance, would they persist in asking for his views, and then be affronted when he gave them? "What do *you* think, Ashton?" might be a well-meaning remark, but it was also a singularly stupid one if he were not expected to give an honest reply. He would never understand the English—or feel at home in their country.

Colonel Anderson never asked stupid questions and his conversation was astringent and stimulating. He loved India with the single-minded devotion that some men give to their work—or their wives—and would talk by the hour of its history, culture, problems and politics, and the knowledge and guile that must be acquired by those who aspired to serve and govern its peoples. On these occasions he invariably spoke in Hindustani or Pushtu, and as neither Ala Yar nor Mahdoo ever addressed his protégé in English, he was able to report to Mardan that the boy still spoke both languages as fluently as ever.

The Colonel had been ill in the winter of 1868, so Ash had spent the Christmas holidays at Pelham Abbas, where his education—if it could be called that—had taken a new turn. He had been seduced by a recently engaged housemaid, one Lily Briggs, a bold, brass-haired girl some five years his senior, who had already caused considerable rivalry and dissension among the men in the servants' hall.

Lily had a loose mouth and a roving eye, and she had formed a habit of coming in last thing at night in her dressing-gown to make sure that Ash's bedroom windows were open and his curtains properly drawn. Her heavy corn-coloured plaits fell almost to her knee, and one night she combed them out and sat on the edge of Ash's bed to show him, she said, that she could sit on her hair. From there things had moved very fast and Ash was never quite sure how she had come to be in his bed, or who had put out the light; but it had been wildly exciting. His own inexperience had been more than compensated for by Lily's extreme proficiency, and he had proved such an apt pupil that she had enjoyed herself immensely and contrived to spend the next six nights in his bed. She would certainly have spent the seventh there as well had they not been discovered by Mrs. Parrot, the housekeeper, *in flagrante delicto*—though that was not precisely the term Mrs. Parrot had used when reporting the incident to Ash's Aunt Millicent ...

Lily Briggs was dismissed without a character, while Ash received a sound thrashing and a lecture on the evils of concupiscence from Uncle Matthew, and a black eye and a split lip from the second footman, who had been one of the faithless Lily's most fervent admirers. The remainder of that holiday passed without incident and the next one saw him back with Colonel Anderson.

Once or twice a year there would be a letter from Zarin. But on the whole these contained little news; Zarin could not write, and the bazaar letter-writer he employed had a flowery style and a habit of beginning and ending every letter with polite and protracted inquiries as to the recipient's health, and long-winded prayers to "the Almighty God" for his continued well-being. Sandwiched in between would be a few disconnected items of news, and by this means Ash learned that Zarin was to be married to a second cousin of Awal Shah's wife; that a young squadron officer, Lieutenant Ommaney, had been murdered by a fanatic while attending band practice in Mardan; and that the Guides had been out against the Utman Khel, who had been raiding villages in British territory.

Sometime during those early years Zarin's mother died, and shortly afterwards Koda Dad Khan resigned his post and left Gulkote. The Rajah had been loth to part with his old and trusted servant, but Koda Dad had pleaded ill-health and his desire to end his days among his kinsmen in the village where he had been born. His true reason, however, had been a lively distrust of Janoo-Rani, who had made no secret of the fact that she suspected him of complicity in Ashok's escape. She had done her best to poison the Rajah's mind against him, but without success. The Rajah valued the old man and had been curt with Janoo-Rani, and Koda Dad knew that he had nothing to fear from her while he enjoyed her husband's favour and protection.

But there came a day when the Rajah decided to journey to Calcutta in order to see the Viceroy and personally press his claim to the neighbouring state of Karidarra, whose late ruler, a distant cousin, had left no heir. He announced that his eldest son, the Yuveraj, would

139

accompany him, and that during his absence the Rani would act as Regent—a piece of folly which (in Koda Dad's opinion) many people besides himself might have cause to regret. The list of officials who were to travel to Calcutta in the Rajah's suite did not include the Master of Horse; and noting that omission, Koda Dad knew that the time had come for him to leave Gulkote.

He was not sorry to go, because now that his wife was dead and his sons were soldiering in the north, there was little to stay for: a few friends, his horses and his hawks, that was all. The Rajah had been more than generous to him, and he had ridden away on the finest horse in the royal stables, with his favourite hawk on his wrist and his saddle-bags crammed with enough coins to ensure a comfortable old age. "You are wise to leave," said Hira Lal. "Were it not for the Yuveraj—who, the gods know, needs at least one servant who is not in the pay of the *Nautch*-girl—I would follow your example. But then I am to go to Calcutta with him; and I do not think she suspects me, for I have been very careful."

But it seemed that Hira Lal had not been careful enough. He had allowed himself to forget that Lalji, spoilt, vain and gullible, had never been capable of distinguishing between his friends and his enemies, and could be counted upon to prefer the latter because they pandered to him and flattered him. Lalji's chosen favourites, Biju and Puran, were both spies of the Rani, and they had always distrusted Hira Lal. One hot night on the long journey to Calcutta, Hira Lal had apparently left his tent in search of air and been attacked and carried off by a tiger. There had been no signs of a struggle, but a fragment of his blood-stained clothing had been found caught on a thorn bush a hundred yards from the camp; and there was known to be a man-eating tiger in the territory. The Rajah had offered a hundred rupees for the recovery of his body, but the surrounding country was full of thickets, elephant grass and deep ravines, and no further trace of him had been found.

Hira Lal had vanished. But as Koda Dad's friends were not addicted to writing him letters, he never heard the tale—or anything further from Gulkote. And neither did Ash, since Koda Dad's departure from the state had severed his last link with it. Inevitably, the past retreated, for life in England allowed him little time for retrospect.

There was always work to be done and games to be played, school to be endured and holidays to be enjoyed, and in time the memory of Gulkote became shadowy and a little unreal, and he seldom thought of it, though at the back of his mind—ignored but ever-present—there lurked a curious feeling of emptiness and loss, a haunting sense of being incomplete because something that was vitally necessary to him had gone out of his life. He had no idea how long that feeling had been there, and he made no attempt to analyse it for fear that it might lead him back to the day of Sita's death. But he was convinced that just as soon as he returned to his own country and saw Zarin and Koda Dad again, it would vanish; and in the meantime he accepted it much as a man with one arm or one leg accepts his disability and learns to live with it; and to ignore it.

He made no close friends and was never particularly popular among his contemporaries, who found him difficult to know and continued to regard him as something of a freak—a "loner." But in a world where the ability to hit a ball or out-run one's fellows was prized above scholarship, his prowess at sports at least earned him their respect (and in the case of his juniors a large measure of admiration), and in his last year at school he had a batting average of fifty-two point nought three, took seven wickets for sixteen in a house match, made a century at Lord's and passed into the new Royal Military College at Sandhurst by a comfortable margin.

It was a come-down, after those three final terms, to find himself once more in the position of an obscure "new boy" at the bottom of a ladder. But on the whole he preferred the R.M.C. to his public school, and did well there; well enough, at all events, for some of his fellow cadets to try and dissuade him from going into the Indian Army—especially now that the purchase of commissions was to be abolished, which meant that the sons of rich men would in future be obliged to rely on ability instead of their purses to obtain promotion. Thus handicapped, few gentlemen would now care to plump for an army career, and Ash's advisers prophesied (correctly as it happened) a disastrous drop in cadets; their own term being the last to enter before the new rule came into force. It was going to be bad enough in a decent regiment, let alone going off to soldier among a lot of pushing, provincial nobodies. "And you don't want to do that, you know. After all, it's not as if you were short of the ready, so why go off and bury yourself in some colonial backwoods among a lot of blacks and second-raters? My pater says . . ."

Ash had retorted with some heat that if the speaker and his father and his friends really thought along these lines, then the sooner the British cleared out of India and left her to run her own affairs the better, for she could probably do so more successfully with her own first-raters than with anyone else's second-raters.

"Pandy's up on his elephant again!" jeered his Company (the nickname had followed him to the Military College). But a Senior Instructor, who had overheard the exchange and repeated it to the Company Commander, had been inclined to agree with him.

"It's the old Horse Guards' attitude," said the Senior Instructor. "All those fellows were as caste-ridden as Hindus, and used to regard an India Army officer as some form of Untouchable. Why, old Cardigan wouldn't even eat in mess with one. But if we want to have an Empire, we need our best material to serve overseas, not our worst. And thanks be to God there are still enough of the former who are prepared to go."

"Would you class young Pandy Martyn among the best?" inquired the Company Commander sceptically. "Damned if I would. If you want my opinion, he's as wild as a hawk and liable to fly off at a tangent at any moment. Doesn't take any too kindly to discipline either, for all that surface appearance of docility. I don't trust the type. The army's no place for Radicals—especially the Indian Army. In fact they're a downright danger, and if I had any say in it I'd keep 'em out of it. And that goes for young Pandy!"

"Nonsense. He'll probably end up as another Nicholson. Or a Hodson, anyway."

"That's just what I'm afraid of—or would be, if I were his future C.O. Both those two were mountebanks. Useful ones, I grant you. But only because of the particular circumstances. It was probably fortunate that they died when they did. From all one hears, they must have been quite insufferable."

"Oh, well, perhaps you're right," conceded the Senior Instructor, losing interest in the subject.

As at school, Ash made no close friends at Sandhurst,

142

though he was liked, and to a great extent admired—the latter again almost solely on account of his success as an athlete. He won the Pentathlon, played football, cricket and fives for the College, took first place in the riding events and marksmanship, and passed out twenty-seventh in a list of two hundred and four cadets.

Uncle Matthew and Aunt Millicent, Cousin Humphrey and two elderly female Pelham-Martyns attended the Passing-Out Parade. But Colonel Anderson had not been present. He had died in the previous week, leaving a small legacy to each of his two Indian servants, in addition to a sum sufficient to cover their return to their own country, and a letter to Ash asking him to see that they reached their homes in safety. His house and its contents had been left to a nephew, and Ash, Ala Yar and Mahdoo had spent their last month in England at Pelham Abbas; embarking at the end of June on the S.S. *Canterbury Castle*, for Bombay. The years of exile were over, and for all three of them, home lay ahead.

"It will be good to see Lahore again," said Mahdoo. "There be many larger cities in *Belait*, but save only in the matter of size, none can rival Lahore."

"Or Peshawar—or Kabul," grunted Ala Yar. "It will be pleasant to purchase proper food in the bazaars once more and to smell the morning among the Khyber hills."

Ash said nothing. He leaned upon the rail and watched the foam-streaked water widen between the ship and the shore, and saw life opening before him like a vast sunlit plain stretching away and away towards unimaginable horizons. A plain across which he could travel at will, choosing his own path and taking his own time.

He was free at last. He was going home, and the future was his to do what he liked with. The Regiment first: the Guides and Zarin and soldiering among the wild hills of the North-West Frontier . . . perhaps one day he would command the Corps; and after that a Division. In time—who knew?—he might even become *Jung-i-Lat Sahib*—Commander-in-Chief of all the armies in Hind —but that would be a long way ahead . . . he would be old then and all this would be in the past. He did not have to think of the past just now: only of the future . . .

BOOK TWO

Belinda

8

Ash had returned to India in the late summer of 1871.

It was a year that had not been without interest to many millions of people. France had seen the capitulation of Paris, heard Prince William of Prussia proclaimed Emperor of Germany at Versailles, and once again declared herself a Republic. In England, Parliament had finally legalized trade unions, and an end had been put to the long-established and iniquitous system by which commissions in the British Army could be purchased by the highest bidder, irrespective of merit. But none of these events had been of any interest to Ashton Hilary Akbar, compared to the fact that he was returning at last to the land of his birth after seven long years in exile.

He was home again. He was in his nineteenth year—and he was engaged to be married . . .

Until recently, Ash had had very little to do with girls of his own class, for after Lily Briggs the well-bred and well-behaved sisters and cousins of his schoolmates had seemed painfully prim and colourless, and he had gone out of his way to avoid them. Lily had had her successors, but they had made no lasting impression and already their names and faces were becoming dim, for his heart had

144

never again been involved. As a cadet he had gained the quite unfounded reputation of being a misogynist by refusing invitations to tea-parties, picnics and dances, and announcing grandly that he "had no time for women." But there had been plenty of time—hours and days and weeks of it—on the long sea voyage from London to Bombay. And Miss Belinda Harlowe was not only a young lady, but far and away the prettiest girl on board.

There was nothing prim or colourless about Belinda. She was as pink and white and gold as Ash's romanticized memory of Lily, as gay as Dolly Develaine of "The Seaside Follies" and as seductively shaped as Ivy Markins, who had worked in a hat shop in Camberley and been so generous with her favours. She was also sweet and innocent and young (two years younger than Ash) and, in addition to a charming, wilful face that was set off to admiration by a wealth of pale gold ringlets, was the fortunate possessor of a small straight nose that wrinkled deliciously when she laughed, a pair of large cornflower-blue eyes that sparkled with interest and eagerness for life, and a kissable mouth made more inviting by the fact that a dimple hovered near each corner.

None of these assets would have aroused much emotion in Ash (beyond a natural feeling of admiration for a pretty girl), had he not discovered that Miss Harlowe, who like himself had been born in India, was delighted at the prospect of returning there. She had said as much one evening during dinner, when the *Canterbury Castle* had been at sea for close on ten days, and several of the older ladies, including Belinda's mother, had been lamenting the fact that they were journeying east once more. They had been cataloguing the many discomforts of life in India —the heat, the dust, the disease, the appalling state of the roads and the difficulties of travel—when Belinda had intervened with a laughing protest:

"Oh no, Mama! How can you say such things? Why, it's a delightful country. I can remember it clearly—that lovely cool bungalow with the purple creeper climbing over the porch, and all the gorgeous flowers in the garden; the ones like spotted lilies and those tall scarlet ones that were always covered with butterflies. And riding my pony on the Mall and seeing lines of camels, and being carried in a dandy when we went up to the hills for the summer— those great tall pine trees and the yellow wild roses that smelled so sweet . . . and the snows: miles and miles of snow mountains. You've no *idea* how ugly Nelbury and Aunt Lizzie's house seemed after that; and her servants were always scolding me, instead of spoiling me like Ayah and Abdul and my syce. I can't wait to get back."

This artless speech had displeased a Mrs. Chiverton, who evidently deciding that young Miss Harlowe was a forward chit who had no business to intervene in a conversation between her elders, remarked dampingly that no one who had endured the horrors of the Mutiny would ever be able to trust an Indian again, and that she envied dear Belinda's happy ignorance of the dangers that must face any sensitive Englishwoman forced by circumstances and a sense of duty to live in that barbarous land. At which Belinda, wholly unabashed, had laughed, and throwing a sparkling glance around the men seated about the long table, said sweetly: "But only think how many brave men we have to defend us. One could not be afraid. Besides I'm sure that nothing of that nature could happen again"—and leaning forward she appealed to Ash, who was seated on the opposite side of the table and had been listening with interest—"don't you agree, Mr. Pelham-Martyn?"

"I don't know," replied Ash, incurably honest. "I suppose that will depend on us."

"On *us?*" repeated Mrs. Chiverton in a tone that told Ash he had made a suggestion that she not only found totally unacceptable, but coming from such a very junior officer, positively insulting.

Ash hesitated, unwilling to offend her further, but Miss Harlowe had rushed gaily in where an ensign feared to tread: "He means that provided we deal justly with them, they will have no reason to rise against us"; here she turned to him again and added: "That was what you meant, wasn't it?"

It was not exactly what Ash had meant, but it was Belinda's use of the word "justly" that made him cease from that moment to see her only as a pretty girl; and after that, despite the fact that strict chaperoning, a plethora of admirers and the crowded conditions that prevailed on shipboard made it well-nigh impossible to have any speech with her alone, he seized every opportunity that offered to talk to her or listen to her talk to him, of the land to which both were returning with such high hopes and happy anticipation.

Belinda's mother, Mrs. Archibald Harlowe, was a stout, well-meaning and fluffy-minded woman who had once been as pretty as her daughter; but the climate and conditions that prevailed in India, together with her distrust of "the natives" and fear of a second Mutiny, had not suited her health or her temperament. The heat and constant pregnancies had thickened a once admirable figure, her husband, now in his late sixties, was still only a Major in an Indian infantry regiment, three of the seven children she had borne him had died in infancy, and a year ago she had been forced to take her five-year-old twins, Harry and Teddy, home to England to leave them in the care of her sister Lizzie—for India was still regarded as a death trap for the young; cantonment cemeteries up and down the country being crowded with the graves of children who had died of cholera, heat-stroke, typhoid or snakebite.

Nothing would have pleased Mrs. Harlowe more than to be able to stay in England with her darling boys, but after exhaustive discussions with her sister the two ladies had agreed that it was her plain duty to return to India: not her duty to her husband, but to her daughter Belinda, who at the age of seven had also been consigned to Lizzie's care. That had been ten years ago, and as Lizzie pointed out, the girl's chances of making an advantageous match in a small provincial town such as Nelbury were slight. In British India, however, eligible bachelors were two-a-penny, so it was only sensible to give Belinda the chance to meet and marry some suitable gentleman, after which her Mama would be able to return to her precious boys, and make her home with dear Lizzie until such time as Archie gained command of his regiment or was retired.

No one (with the possible exception of Major Harlowe) could have found fault with this programme, and Mrs. Harlowe's confidence in her decision had been speedily vindicated when no less than eleven gentlemen out of the twenty-nine who had taken passages on the S.S. *Canterbury Castle* began to pay marked attention to her pretty daughter. True, these were for the most part mere boys; either penniless ensigns, junior Civil Servants or

147

youthful recruits to Trade, and the five other unmarried ladies on board were not remarkable for good looks. But the gentlemen did include an infantry Captain in his mid-thirties, a rich middle-aged widower who was the senior partner in a firm of jute exporters, and young Ensign Pelham-Martyn, who (according to Mrs. Chiverton, the ship's gossip) was not only the nephew of a baronet, but sole heir to a more than comfortable fortune left him by his father, who had been a distinguished scholar with a world-wide reputation.

From the purely financial aspect, Mrs. Harlowe considered that Mr. Joseph Tilbery, the widower, was probably the most eligible prospect. But though his attentions to her daughter had been marked, he had not as yet made any declaration, and Belinda herself had been heard to refer to both him and the infantry Captain as "old fogies." The ensigns and young Civil Servants were much more to her taste, and she flirted with them light-heartedly and enjoyed herself enormously, playing off one against the other and revelling in being young and pretty and admired.

The heady atmosphere of that long voyage had been further heightened for her by a romantic event—a wedding at sea. Admittedly the bride and bridegroom had neither of them been handsome nor in the first blush of youth, and as both were travelling steerage she had not previously laid eyes upon them. But the Captain, having been prevailed upon to exercise the powers invested in him as master of an ocean-going vessel, had married Sergeant Alfred Biggs of the Supply Corps, returning from leave, to Miss Mabel Timmins, travelling to Bombay to join a brother working for the Bombay-and-Baroda Railway, the wedding taking place in the First-Class Saloon in the presence of every passenger on board who could be crammed into it, and being followed by speeches and toasts drunk in champagne donated by the Captain. Later on, the entire company had danced on deck, and no less than three of Belinda's suitors had begged her to follow the bride's admirable example and spend the remainder of the voyage on honeymoon.

In the circumstances, it is hardly surprising that if the other young ladies were unfriendly and their mothers openly disapproving, Belinda did not notice it. She had been cooped up in her aunt's house for ten long years, minding her lessons, stitching away at interminable sam-

148

plers and saying "Yes, Aunt Lizzie" and "No, Aunt Lizzie," and the only young men she met (at strictly chaperoned parties) were the sons of her aunt's friends: awkward, gawking schoolboys who had known her since she was in pinafores and treated her as a sister. The transition from that confined and stultifying atmosphere to the delightful freedom of life on an ocean liner and the attentions of a dozen admiring young gentlemen was an exhilarating experience, and Belinda revelled in it and was perhaps as completely happy as anyone can hope to be in the course of one lifetime. Her only difficulty had been to decide which of her many admirers she preferred, but by the time the ship reached Alexandria she was no longer in any doubt.

Ashton Pelham-Martyn might not be as handsome as George Garforth (who, though gauche and really tediously shy, possessed a Grecian profile and Byronic curls); nor was he as witty or amusing as Ensign Augustus Blain, or as rich as Mr. Joseph Tilbery of Tilbery, Patterson & Company. He was, in fact, rather a silent young man, except when he talked about India, which she encouraged him to do whenever her importunate admirers allowed her any private conversation with him, for he made it sound like her childhood memories of it: a magic place. He could, she found, be excessively charming when he chose, and there was something about him that she found fascinating: something different and exciting . . . and a little disquieting: the difference that lies between a wild hawk and a tame cage-bird. He was also undeniably good-looking in a dark, thin-faced way, and moreover a certain air of romantic mystery hung about him; there was some story of his having been brought up in an Indian palace, and that old gossip, Mrs. Chiverton, had unkindly hinted that the swarthiness of his complexion and the darkness of his hair and lashes was possibly the result of mixed blood. But then everyone knew that Mrs. Chiverton was a cat and would have been only too pleased if he had taken some notice of her own exceedingly plain daughter, Amy.

Belinda turned her sunniest smiles on Ensign Pelham-Martyn, who ended by falling helplessly and hopelessly in love, and by the last day of the voyage had summoned up enough courage to approach Mrs. Harlowe and ask her permission to propose for her daughter's hand.

Ash had been in dread of a rebuff on the score of his youth and his unworthiness, and he could not believe his good fortune when Belinda's mother assured him that she had no objection at all to his doing so, and was certain that dear Bella's Papa would agree with her, as he too believed in early marriages. Though the latter statement was far from being true, for Major Harlowe, like most older army officers, strongly disapproved of young officers ruining their prospects and reducing their usefulness to their regiments by getting tied up too early to some girl who would inevitably take their attention off their work, and involve them in domestic trivia to the detriment of the men under their command.

The Major himself had been more than twice his wife's age and nearer forty than thirty when he married; but although Mrs. Harlowe was not ignorant of his views, she had no hesitation in pledging his consent, for she had managed to convince herself that Archie must certainly wish to see his only daughter so suitably bestowed. After all, it was not as though the young people would have to live on an ensign's pay; Ashton's allowance was more than generous, and in a little more than two years' time he would come of age and inherit the whole of his father's fortune. So of course Archie must consent. Ashton might be still in his teens, but anyone could see that he was old for his age. Such a quiet, well-mannered young man. So devoted to Belinda—and so *very* eligible.

Mrs. Harlowe shed a few emotional tears, and half an hour later, in a quiet corner of the forward deck while the sun was setting and their fellow passengers were changing for dinner, Ash proposed to Belinda and was accepted.

The engagement was supposed to be kept secret, but somehow it leaked out, and dinner was barely over before Ash found himself receiving the envious congratulations of his rivals and an assortment of chilly stares from the ladies; most of whom had already declared Miss Harlowe to be a shocking flirt and were now convinced that her mama, far from being the foolish but good-natured creature they had supposed, was nothing more than a shameless, scheming, cradle-snatcher.

Mr. Tilbery and the infantry Captain had been particularly frosty, but only George Garforth had registered an active protest.

George had turned as white as a sheet, and after attempting to drown his disappointment in drink had offered to fight the successful suitor, though, luckily for all concerned, he had been taken ignominiously ill before his challenge could be accepted. Belinda had retired early, and George having been carried to his cabin, Ash had gone up to the deserted deck, where he had spent the night lying in a deck chair under the stars, dizzy with champagne and happiness.

It had been a wonderful night, and watching the dear, familiar constellations of his childhood wheel overhead, it seemed to Ash that whatever else he might forget, he would remember this night forever—and that he would never be so happy again. His first love-affair had ended in disaster, and it had taken him a full six months to realize that Lily Briggs, far from being a golden goddess who had miraculously fallen in love with him, was nothing more than an amoral slut who had amused herself by seducing a schoolboy. Yet because she had been the first woman he had ever slept with, he knew that he would never quite forget her. Her successors had been no more than brief, sordid adventures in sex, and soon he would not even be able to remember their names, and could only be sorry that he had ever known any of them. To have done so seemed in some way a betrayal of Belinda; but at least she need never know about them, and there were so many other things that he could tell her about: the whole fantastic story of his childhood, and all the secrets and sorrows and enchantments of those years.

He would have told her all this before had it been possible, but with half-a-dozen jealous rivals competing for her attention there had been no chance of doing so, and there had been many occasions when he had felt like murdering Gus Blaine or that pompous old fool Mr. Tilbery—or, for that matter, the entire roster of Belinda's beaux. Yet with so many to choose from, she had, incredibly, chosen him. He was the luckiest man in the world, and tomorrow—no, today, for it was well after midnight—he would be back in his own land at last. Soon now he would cross the Ravi River again and see the mountains, and Zarin . . .

Zarin—

Ash found himself wondering a little uneasily if Zarin would have changed very much during the past years, and if he would even be able to recognize him on sight. There had been nothing of the old Zarin in those stilted, flowery letters that had come so infrequently and told him so little. He knew that Zarin was now a Daffadar and the father of three children, but that was all. The rest had merely been a brief chronicle of regimental events and he no longer knew how Zarin thought or felt. Would they be able to take up the old relationship where they had left it seven years ago?

It had never occurred to him before that they might not, but now, quite suddenly, a doubt crept in, for he remembered that their positions would be reversed. He was returning as a British officer and Zarin Khan, that "elder brother" whom he had admired and envied and striven to emulate, would be under his command. How much difference was that going to make? None, if he could help it; but circumstances might make a great deal—such things as regimental custom and etiquette. And then there would be his fellow officers, and even Belinda . . . no, not Belinda: she loved him, and so she would feel as he felt. But it might be difficult at first for both Zarin and himself.

He wished now that it had been possible for them to meet on neutral ground instead of in the strictly military atmosphere of Mardan, where they would be under the critical eye of a dozen men who knew something of his story and would watch to see how he comported himself. However, it was too late to worry about that, and he would just have to behave circumspectly and try to remember not to rush his fences (always, according to both Koda Dad and Uncle Matthew, his besetting sin). In the meantime there was the long journey north, and the dismal prospect of parting with Ala Yar and Mahdoo, this last being the one black cloud on his bright horizon.

Recalling it now he was conscious of a sharp pang of guilt, because there was no blinking the fact that his preoccupation with Belinda had made him neglect them of late, and beyond an occasional stroll with one or other in the early morning before the passengers were astir, and a few words each day when Ala Yar came to his cabin to lay out clean linen or put studs in his shirt, he had seen very little of them. And it was too late to make amends now, for tomorrow—today—they would say goodbye to him. The three of them would be going their separate ways, and he knew that for his part he would miss both of them more than he could say. They were a link between the old days of his childhood and the new days and the new life that would begin when the sun rose, which would be very soon now, for already the stars were losing their brightness and to the East the sky was faintly green with the first, far-off glimmer of the dawn.

Bombay was still below the horizon, but the dawn wind carried the scent of the city far out to sea, and Ash could smell the mingled odours of dust and sewage, of crowded bazaars and rotting vegetation and a faint scent of flowers—frangipani, marigold, jasmine and orange blossom. The smell of home.

9

Daffadar Zarin Khan of the Guides had asked for three weeks' leave "on urgent private affairs," and travelled to Bombay at his own expense to meet the S.S. *Canterbury Castle,* bringing with him a bearer for Ash: one Gul Baz, a Pathan, who had been specially selected for the post by Awal Shah.

The years had left few marks on Zarin, and at a casual glance there was little difference between the man who stood watching the ship approach and the young sowar who had waved farewell to a disconsolate boy nearly seven years ago. He was taller now and broader, and his moustache was more luxuriant. There were also lines about his mouth and eyes that had not been there before, and in place of the sand-coloured uniform and puttees he had been wearing when Ash had last seen him, he wore the holiday dress of a Pathan: voluminous trousers, a flowered waistcoat and a flowing white shirt.

The sun blazed down on the grimy dock with its jostling jabbering crowd of coolies, port officials, hotel touts and friends and relatives who had gathered to meet the ship, and as the tugs manoeuvred her alongside and the gang-planks ran out, Zarin's eyes scanned the lines of faces that peered down from the deck rails, and it occurred to him for the first time that although Ashok should have small difficulty in recognizing him, he himself might find it less easy to identify a boy who would now be a man. But almost in the same moment his gaze checked and he drew a quick breath of relief. Yes, that must surely be Ashok. There could be no mistaking him.

He was not as tall as Zarin had expected him to be, being just under six foot; but a fair enough height, and with the lean good looks of a northerner or a Pathan. His dress proclaimed him a Sahib, yet his complexion, which had always been swarthy, was now as dark as an Asiatic's from the suns of the long lazy days on shipboard, and his hair as black. Put him in the proper clothing and he could still pass as a Pathan or a hillman, decided Zarin with a wry grin—always provided the years had not changed him in too many other ways.

This was something that only time would show, for though he had written with great frequency and his letters, except for the earlier ones, had been in Urdu script (Colonel Anderson having tutored him in this) they had had to be translated to Zarin by a munshi, and had lost much in the process. But at least they proved that the boy had not forgotten his friends. It remained to be seen if it were possible for them to adjust to a new relationship. He could see that Ashok was not expecting anyone to meet him, for unlike the majority of his fellow passengers he was not scanning the faces of the crowd in search of familiar features, but gazing above them towards the rooftops and the lush green gardens of the beautiful, flamboyant city. Even from that distance Zarin could see his expression; and reading it, was satisfied. It was indeed Ashok and not a stranger who had returned home.

"There is Pelham-Sahib," said Zarin, pointing him out to Gul Baz. He raised a hand to signal to his friend, and then dropped it without doing so. For a woman had come to stand beside Ashok, a very young woman who took his arm and clung to it as though by right, laughing up into his face and demanding his attention. Ashok turned immediately and his expression changed; and noting it, Zarin's brows twitched together in a frown. A memsahib . . . a young memsahib. This was one complication he had not bargained for.

From the first, it had been the memsahibs who had created distrust and raised social barriers between white men and brown in the territories of the Raj. In the old

154

days—the brave days of "John Company" that had seen the birth of the Bengal Army—there had been few memsahibs in India, because the climate had not been considered suitable for them, while the length and discomfort of voyages by sailing ship had discouraged many of them and kept them away. Deprived of their society the Sahibs had married or taken mistresses from the local population, and had in consequence come to know and understand the country and its people—and to speak its languages with great fluency. There had been friendship and brotherhood between white men and brown in those days, and a great measure of mutual respect. But when the harnessing of steam had made sea voyages quicker and more comfortable, the memsahibs had flocked to India—bringing with them a full complement of snobbery, insularity and intolerance.

Indians who had hitherto been treated as equals became "natives" and the term itself lost its dictionary definition and became an opprobrious word, signifying members of an inferior—and coloured—race. The memsahibs preferred not to have any social contact with "natives," though they were not above accepting the lavish hospitality of Indian princes, and prided themselves on being patient with their numerous household servants. But they rarely invited Indians into their homes, or exerted themselves to make friends among them; and few showed any interest in the history and culture of the land which the majority looked upon as heathen and barbaric. Their menfolk no longer married Indian brides or kept Indian mistresses, and the memsahibs reserved their greatest scorn for the numerous half-castes that their own countrymen had fathered in happier times, referring to them contemptuously as "Eurasians" or "Blacky-whites," and ostracizing anyone whom they suspected of having what came to be termed "a touch of the tarbrush." There were of course many exceptions, but they were swamped by the bigoted majority, and as social contact between the races dwindled, sympathy and understanding waned, and a large part of the camaraderie of the old days was lost, to be replaced by distrust, suspicion and resentment.

Zarin Khan, standing in the hot sunlight on the dock at Bombay and watching his one-time friend solicitously helping a yellow-haired girl down the gang-way, felt his heart sink. He did not know what the years in *Belait*

155

might have done to Ashok, but he had not expected any complications of this kind, and he could only hope that it might prove to be no more than a passing affair that would burn itself out in a matter of weeks. But he did not like the complacent and proprietary expression on the face of the short stout memsahib, undoubtedly the girl's mother, whom he now recognized as the wife of Harlowe Sahib, second-in-command of a regiment at present stationed at Peshawar. It boded no good, and Peshawar being less than four hours' ride from Mardan, the girl would be able to keep Ashok dancing attendance upon her at a time when his attention should be concentrated upon more important matters. Zarin frowned and was suddenly unsure of his welcome.

Major Harlowe had been unable to meet his family in Bombay, for the Frontier regiments were preparing for autumn manoeuvres and he had too much work on his hands to permit him to take leave at this time. But he had sent his bearer and his wife's *ayah* to see to their comfort on the long journey north, and felt sure that they would find an acquaintance or two on the train and not be too dull.

"Of course we shall not be dull," cried Belinda, looking about her with sparkling eyes. "Ash will be with us. Besides, there will be so much to see. Jungles and tigers and elephants and—oh, do look at that adorable baby; it's only wearing a bangle. Just imagine taking one's baby out in England dressed in nothing but a bangle! Why has Mr. Tilbery got all those garlands round his neck? How comical he looks, all smothered in flowers and tinsel. Mrs. Chiverton has got some on too: I wish—Ash, there's a native over there who keeps staring at us. The tall one in a white turban with gold ends. I believe he knows you."

Ash turned to look, and stood suddenly still. *Zarin* . . .

The years rolled back and for a brief moment he was a boy again, listening to Zarin telling him why he must go to England and assuring him that he would one day return: *"the years will pass quickly, Ashok."* They had not passed quickly; but they had passed. He had come home again, and here, waiting for him as he had promised, was Zarin. He tried to call to him but there was a lump in his throat and he could only smile foolishly.

"What's the matter, Ash?" inquired Belinda, tugging

156

at his coat-sleeve. "Why are you looking like that? Who is that man?"

Ash found his voice: "Zarin. It's Zarin——"

He brushed her hand from his arm and broke into a run, leaving Belinda to stare after him, startled and more than a little shocked by the sight of her betrothed publicly embracing a strange native with a fervour that she would have considered excessive even if they had been Frenchmen. Why, they were actually *hugging* each other. Belinda turned away abruptly, scarlet-cheeked with embarrassment, and met the malicious gaze of Amy Chiverton who had also been a witness to the encounter.

"Mama always said that there was something fishy about Mr. Pelham-Martyn," remarked Miss Chiverton spitefully. "Do you suppose that man is his half-brother, or a cousin or something? They are certainly *very* alike. Oh, I forgot you were engaged to him. How dreadful of me. I'm *so* sorry. But of course I was joking. I expect it's only one of his old servants came to meet him. Ours have come too. I expect yours are here as well."

But surely one did not embrace one's old servants? thought Belinda; and anyway, the man was far from old. She turned to look at them again and saw with a sharp pang of unease that in one respect Amy Chiverton had been right. The two men were not unlike, and if Ashton were to grow a moustache they could almost pass as brothers . . .

"Really, Belinda dear," scolded Mrs. Harlowe, hurrying back from saying her goodbyes to a Colonel and Mrs. Philpot who had occupied the next door cabin. "How many times have I told you that you must not stand about in the sun without a parasol? You will ruin your complexion. Where is Ashton?"

"He—he had to see someone about his luggage," lied Belinda, catching her mother's arm and pulling her away in the direction of the customs shed. "He will only be a moment. Let us get into the shade."

It was suddenly unbearable to her that Mama should see Ashton and that native hugging each other, for although Mama would never dream of saying—or even thinking—the sort of things that Amy Chiverton had just said, she would certainly be disapproving, and just at that moment Belinda felt that she could not bear to listen to anything else on the subject. Ashton would probably have some perfectly reasonable explanation, but he should never have abandoned her like that. He had no right to run off and leave her alone and unattended among a crowd of jostling coolies, just as though she was someone of no importance at all. If *this* was the way he intended to treat her—

Belinda's blue eyes filled with angry tears, and all at once the bustling, colourful scene about her lost its charm and she was aware only of the heat and noise and discomfort, and the fact that the bodice of her flowered muslin dress was already drenched with sweat and clinging unattractively to her shoulder blades. Ash had behaved abominably and India was horrid.

For the moment, at least, Ash had forgotten all about her. And forgotten too, as he laughed and exclaimed and embraced his friend, that he was now a Sahib and an officer.

"Zarin—Zarin. Why didn't anyone tell me that you would be here?"

"They did not know. I asked for leave and came away, not telling anyone where I meant to go."

"Not even Awal Shah? How is he? Did you recognize me at once, or weren't you sure? Have I changed very much? You have not, Zarin. You haven't changed at all. Well, a little perhaps. But not enough to matter. Tell me about your father—is he well? Shall I see him in Mardan?"

"I do not think so. He is well, but his village lies two *koss** beyond the Border and he seldom leaves it for he is getting old."

"Then we must take leave and visit him. Oh Zarin, it is so good to see you. It is so good to be back."

"I too am glad. There have been times when I feared that you might grow away from us and be reluctant to return, but I see now that you are still the same Ashok with whom I flew kites and stole melons in the days when we lived in the Hawa Mahal. I should have known that you would not change. Have the years in *Belait* seemed very long?"

"Yes," said Ash shortly. "But they are over, thank God. Tell me about yourself and the Regiment."

---

*1 *koss* = 2 miles

The talk turned to the Guides and the rumours of a winter campaign against certain of the Frontier tribes who had been raiding villages and stealing women and cattle, and presently Zarin presented Gul Baz and was introduced in his turn to Ala Yar and Mahdoo. One or two of the departing passengers paused curiously, surprised by the sight of young Pelham-Martyn laughing and chattering with such joyous animation to a group of "natives," for he had been anything but talkative on board and had, in fact, been voted a dull dog; though his success with the little Harlowe girl suggested that there must be more to him than met the eye. There was certainly no trace of reserve in his manners at the present moment, and those of his fellow passengers whose attention had been briefly attracted to the strangely assorted group raised their eyebrows in astonished disapproval and hurried on again, feeling vaguely affronted.

The crowds on the quayside began to thin and the mountains of luggage to dwindle, and still Belinda and her mother waited impatiently for Ash to return. Their companions of the last two months piled into carriages and were driven away in the direction of the city, and above their heads the sun beat down on the corrugated iron roof of the customs shed, and the temperature soared. But Ash had lost all count of time. There had been so much to talk of and to tell; and when at last Zarin dispatched Gul Baz to seek out his luggage and engage coolies to carry it from the dock, Ala Yar had announced unexpectedly that both he and Mahdoo would be accompanying Ash to Mardan.

"You will not require that new bearer," said Ala Yar, "for before he died I made a promise to Anderson-Sahib that I would see to your welfare. Mahdoo too wishes to take service with you. We have discussed the matter between us, and though we are both old men we do not desire to retire and sit idle. Nor do we wish to seek employment with some new Sahib whose ways will be strange to us. Therefore I will be your bearer and Mahdoo your cook; and there is no need to trouble yourself over the matter of payment, as Anderson-Sahib made ample provision for us both and our needs are small. A few rupees will suffice."

No argument could move either old gentleman from this decision, and when Zarin pointed out that a junior sub-

159

altern living in the mess would have no need of a cook, Mahdoo said placidly that in that case he would be a *khidmatgar* (butler); what did it matter? But he and Ala Yar had served together for many years and were used to each other's ways—and to Ash-Sahib's too—and they preferred to remain together.

Nothing could have suited Ash better, for the prospect of parting with them had been the only thing that marred his return to India, and he was delighted to agree to this arrangement, and to the suggestion that Gul Baz should be retained as "assistant bearer." "I will send him to the station to buy the tickets and to reserve a compartment for us as near to yours as may be," said Zarin: "No, we cannot travel with you . . . Or you with us. It would not be fitting. You are now a Sahib, and if you do not behave as one it will cause trouble for us all, for there are many who would not understand it."

"He is right," agreed Ala Yar. "And there are also the memsahibs to be thought of."

"Oh, to hell with—" began Ash and stopped on a gasp. *"Belinda!* Oh God, I forgot her. Look—I'll meet you at the station, Zarin. Tell Gul Baz to bring along my luggage. Ala Yar, you've got the keys haven't you? You know my gear. I must go—"

He ran back to where he had left Belinda, but she had gone. So too had all the other passengers, together with their baggage and those who had come to meet them. The S.S. *Canterbury Castle* lay silent and apparently deserted in the mid-day heat, and an official in the custom shed informed Ash that two ladies who had been waiting there for the best part of an hour had only just left. No, he did not know where they had gone: probably to a hotel on Malabar Hill, or to the Yacht Club, or the Byculla. One of the *ghari-wallahs** outside might be able to tell him. Both ladies, added the official unkindly, had appeared upset.

Ash hired a tonga and set off in pursuit, but as the pony proved to be a jaded animal and incapable of any speed, he failed to overtake them. Having spent an anxious and exhausting afternoon driving about Bombay making fruitless inquiries at a number of hotels and clubs,

---

*drivers of horse-drawn vehicles

he was left with no alternative but to make for the railway station and await them there.

The mail train was not due to leave until the late evening, so he spent the intervening hours loitering unhappily in the entrance hall and anathematizing himself for a selfish, unthinking clod who was in every way unworthy of such a superlatively lovely creature as Belinda. Only last night he had told her that if she would entrust her future to him, he would love and cherish her for ever and do everything in his power to make her happy. Yet at the first test he had failed her. What must she be thinking of him and where had she gone?

Belinda and her mother had, in fact, gone to the house of an acquaintance who lived within easy reach of the harbour, where they had spent the day; it being too hot, in Mrs. Harlowe's opinion, for sight-seeing, and of course there was no question of Belinda being allowed to go out alone. They left for the station after an early supper and arrived to find Ash on the platform, though unfortunately for him, not alone. His luck was plainly out that day, because had they arrived five minutes earlier he would still have been standing forlornly by the ticket office. But Ala Yar had friends in the city and he had taken Zarin and Mahdoo to visit them, leaving Gul Baz to make all the necessary arrangements at the station. The three men had driven up in a tonga not five minutes before the arrival of Mrs. Harlowe and her daughter, which could not have been more unfortunate, as seeing them in animated conversation with her betrothed, Belinda not unnaturally concluded that he had spent the day with them, preferring their company to her own and making no attempt to find her.

Anger and unshed tears formed a hot hard lump in her throat, and despite her training and the fact that the platform was crowded with travellers, baggage coolies, and vendors of food and drink, if she had possessed an engagement ring she would at that moment have torn it off and flung it in Ash's face. Deprived of such an outlet for her wounded feelings, she was preparing to sweep past him with her head in the air, when unkind fate sent her a weapon that few women, in these circumstances, could have resisted making use of.

It was to prove, in long run, one of those trivial incidents that can change the character and course of events in the lives of many more people than those immediately involved, though no one, least of all Belinda, could be expected to know that. She merely saw a chance of repaying Ash in his own coin, and took it; and young George Garforth—he of the Grecian profile and Byronic curls—hurrying down the platform in search of his carriage, found himself being greeted with every appearance of delight by the girl to whom he had already lost his heart. Overcome by this reception, he now lost his head as well.

A combination of love, shyness and an acute sense of inferiority had hitherto prevented him from expressing his devotion, and though Belinda admired his looks, she considered him deplorably dull and had agreed wholeheartedly with Amy Chiverton's malicious observation that "poor Mr. Garforth would have made an excellent tailor's dummy." Such looks ought, by rights, to have bestowed confidence, if not conceit, on their owner. But George Garforth quite obviously lacked any trace of either quality, and was not only painfully unsure of himself, but apt, at times, to be unbelievably gauche, pushing himself forward in an unseemly manner at quite the wrong moments, and then retreating in scarlet-faced confusion that created even further embarrassment. Ash, who rather liked him, had once said, "The trouble with George is that he was born with one skin too few, so everything seems to touch him on the raw."

Belinda had certainly done so. On the only occasion that George had nerved himself to make a bid for her attention, he had set about it in a manner calculated to irritate the mildest of girls, and she had been compelled to give him a sharp set-down that had sent him back into his shell, sore, blushing and humiliated. Yet here she was, advancing on him with an outstretched hand and a smile of such dazzling sweetness that poor George stopped in his tracks and cast an involuntary look over his shoulder to see who could be standing behind him.

"Why, Mr. Garforth. What a pleasant surprise. Are you travelling on this train? I do hope so. It will make the journey so much pleasanter if we have friends on board."

George stared at her as though he could not believe his ears, and then dropping the packet of letters he held, he clutched her proffered hand with the fervour of a drowning man catching at a rope. The blood drained out

162

of his face and his tongue seemed to tie itself into knots, but his inability to answer her did not appear to offend his divinity, for having freed her hand from his grasp she tucked it confidingly under his arm and begged his escort to her carriage.

"If I had known that you would be on this train, I should not have worried," declared Belinda gaily. "But I confess I was a trifle hurt that you had not even said goodbye to me this morning. I looked for you everywhere, but the dock was so hot and crowded."

"D-did you?" stammered George, finding his voice. "Did—did you really?"

They were approaching Ash and his disreputable friends, and Belinda laughed up into her escort's pallid face, and giving his arm a little squeeze, said: "Yes, *really*."

The colour rushed back into George's face, and he took a deep breath that seemed to fill not only his lungs but his whole body with a heady exhilaration that no wine had ever given him before. All at once he felt taller and broader, and for the first time in his life, full of confidence.

"I *say!*" said George. He began to laugh, and Ash looked round and saw them arm in arm, laughing together as though neither had a care in the world. He started forward and Belinda said carelessly: "Oh, hallo, Ashton," and passed by with a casual little inclination of the head that was infinitely more wounding than any cut direct.

Ash followed them to the Harlowes' carriage where he found himself compelled to make his apologies and explanations to Mrs. Harlowe, as Belinda seemed far too occupied with George to pay much attention to what he was saying—beyond telling him graciously that there was no need for him to apologize, it did not matter at all. Which not only took the wind out of his sails, but left him feeling uncommonly foolish.

He was to feel a good deal worse in the days that followed, for Belinda continued to treat him with maddening politeness when he presented himself at her carriage during the leisurely and frequent stops at wayside stations, and never once invited him to sit with them in their carriage, or take her strolling on the platform during the evening halts. This behaviour afflicted Ash and alarmed poor Mrs. Harlowe, but its effect upon George was little short of electrifying. No one who had travelled out with him on the S.S. *Canterbury Castle* would have believed that the gauche, tongue-tied and over-sensitive youth of the voyage could have blossomed so swiftly into this talkative and assured young man, who squared his shoulders and threw out his chest as he walked in the twilight with Belinda on his arm, or monopolized the conversation in the carriage.

Ash himself was far too crushed and remorseful to take offence at his love's behaviour, or even notice George's growing jealousy and truculence, for he had already convicted himself of almost every crime in a lover's calendar, and felt that no punishment could be too severe—except the unthinkable one of losing her. As for Zarin, finding that he could do nothing to lighten Ashok's mood, he abandoned the attempt, and consoled himself with the more congenial company of his fellow-countrymen until such time as his friend should come to his senses. The journey that both had looked forward to had become slow and tedious, and Ash had no attention to spare for the vast landscape that streamed past his window, though it was seven long years since he had last seen it, and for the greater part of those years had dreamed of little else than seeing it again.

The tree-clad gorges and lush greenness of the south gave place to the parched emptiness of rock and sand: to jungle and cropland, little lost villages and ruins of dead and gone cities, and wide, winding rivers where crocodiles and mud-turtles basked on the sand bars and white egrets fished in the shallows. At night-fall the thickets and the elephant grass shimmered with fire-flies, and at dawn peacocks cried from every cane-brake and the yellow sky mirrored itself in ponds and ditches that were starred with water-lilies. But Ash lay on his back and stared at the ceiling, rehearsing speeches to soften Belinda's heart, or replying to the conversational efforts of his travelling companions—an enthusiastic young man in the Political Department and a middle-aged Forest-Officer—very much at random.

Mrs. Harlowe was also not enjoying the journey, which was only to be expected. Experience had taught her that travelling in India by whatever means was bound to be hot, dusty and excessively uncomfortable; but on the present occasion it was neither the tediousness or the discomfort that was upsetting her, but Ashton and Belinda, whose behaviour had plainly demonstrated that both were still little more than children. A great many girls married at seventeen—she herself had done so; but they married grown men who could be relied upon to take care of them, not thoughtless and irresponsible boys in their teens, which Ashton had shown himself to be when he ran off and left Belinda alone and unprotected on a crowded quayside while he gossiped for over an hour with a parcel of natives.

His excuse for this behaviour had merely made matters worse. To explain that one of them (and a mere daffadar at that—not even an Indian officer) was an old friend who had travelled from the Khyber to Bombay to meet him, and that he had been so pleased to see him that he had "lost all count of time," might reflect credit on his honesty, but it certainly proved him to be lacking in wisdom and tact, and Mrs. Harlowe fully sympathized with her daughter's rejection of such a clumsily phrased apology. Ashton really should have known better. And know better, too, than to be on such exceedingly friendly terms with sepoys and servants. Such behaviour was not at all the thing, and only went to prove that he did not yet know how to conduct himself—and also that she herself knew far too little about him. She had, in fact, allowed his eligibility in the matter of birth and fortune, and her anxiety to see her daughter swiftly and safely bestowed, to override good sense and caution. And now Belinda was flirting shamelessly with another, and quite ineligible young man, and really she felt distracted with worry. It was all most upsetting, and she did not know *what* Archie was going to say when he heard . . .

Poor, foolish, conscience-stricken Mrs. Harlowe took refuge in tears and an attack of vapours, and three days of this atmosphere proved more than enough for Belinda, who began to discover that a sense of outrage was not equal to sustaining her through the boredom of endless hours penned up in a hot and dusty railway carriage, with nothing to do but listen to Mama's tearful observations on the subject of Ashton, early engagements and what Papa was likely to say about it all. Of course Ashton had behaved abominably, but he had been punished enough. Besides, she was beginning to tire of George Garforth's increasing bumptiousness and the protective and proprietary airs he had begun to adopt towards her, and thought that it was really time she put him in his place.

When the train next stopped at a station and Ash as usual knocked humbly at the door, he was admitted, and the unhappy George found himself suddenly relegated to the position of odd-man-out and left to hang about the platform, or make laborious conversation with his divinity's mother. But for Ash and Belinda the rest of the journey passed pleasantly enough—apart from a tiff in Delhi, where the railway stopped and anyone wishing to travel further northward must proceed in the manner of an older day by dâk-*ghari*,* palanquin, bullock cart or on foot. The travellers had put up at Delhi dâk-bungalow, and Ash, after two afternoons devoted to sightseeing, had absented himself for an entire day.

He had, in fact, been absent for a full twenty-four hours, but fortunately neither Mrs. nor Miss Harlowe was aware of this, for Ash was learning wisdom, and this time he had accounted for his absence by producing a very pretty pearl and diamond ring, explaining that he had had to visit at least twenty or thirty shops in the old city and along the Chandi Chowk, Delhi's famous "Silver Street," before finding something good enough to give Belinda. Both ladies had been charmed with the ring; though it could not of course be worn until Ash had spoken to Belinda's Papa. And as George Garforth had taken advantage of Ash's absence to take them for a picnic to the Kutab Minar, they had passed the day very pleasantly. Ash was forgiven, and neither Belinda nor her mother had thought to ask him any further questions, which was just as well, for he had, in point of fact, spent less than half an hour over the purchase of the ring and the rest of the time in quite another fashion.

Mahdoo had relations in Delhi, and on the previous night Ash had donned the dress of a Pathan (borrowed for the occasion from Gul Baz) and roistered in the city until dawn, eating and drinking and merry-making with Mahdoo's relatives, and later sampling the night-life of the crowded bazaars with Zarin. He was filled with an exhilarating sense of freedom, as though he had broken out

---

*mail carriage (*dâk* literally post, mail, posting-house)

166

of gaol. The Western veneer so painfully acquired during the cold years at school and Pelham Abbas fell away from him as easily as though it had been no more than a winter overcoat, discarded on the first warm day of spring, and he slipped back effortlessly into the ways and speech of his childhood. The rich, spicy food tasted ambrosial after a diet of boiled beef and carrots, watery cabbage and suet puddings, while the heat and smell and noise of the city was an intoxication and a deep delight. England, Sahib-hood, the Guides, Belinda—all were forgotten, and he was once more Sita's son Ashok, who had come home and inherited a kingdom.

Having no idea which temple Sita had taken him to (even if he had, he would not have been able to enter it in his present guise) he gave alms to several ash-smeared *sadhus* and a dozen Hindu beggars in her name, and the following morning, in company with Zarin, Ala Yar, Mahdoo and Gul Baz, he joined a vast congregation in the great courtyard of the Juma Masjid and said a prayer for her and for Uncle Akbar—the one an orthodox Hindu and the other a devout Mussulman—in the belief that the One God, to whom all creeds are one, would hear and not be offended.

There had been a group of tourists in the gallery above the great gate, European men and women who had looked down at the worshipping throng below, laughing and talking the while as though they were watching the antics of animals in a zoo. Their plangent voices cut through the murmured prayers, and Ash was wondering angrily what they would think if a group of Indians behaved in a similar manner during a service in Westminster Abbey, when he was disconcerted to see that one of them was Mrs. Harlowe and another his betrothed. "It's only ignorance . . . they don't mean any harm; they don't understand," he excused them to himself.

The red-walled city of the Moguls was as intriguing by day as it was exciting by night, but towards evening his conscience belatedly reminded him of the enormity of his behaviour and its probable consequences, and he reluctantly changed back into his own clothing and spent half an hour in a jeweller's shop in the Chandi Chowk before presenting himself at the dâk-bungalow.

Only a handful of passengers who had travelled on

the mail-train from Bombay were going further north into the Punjab, and the remainder of the journey had been undertaken in dâk-*gharis,* rickety horse-drawn vehicles that resembled closed boxes on wheels. This time Ash had only one companion to share his carriage with him, but as it turned out to be George Garforth he would have been happier on his own or with a full complement of passengers.

George had no intention of relinquishing the hopes that Belinda had encouraged by her treatment of him during the first three days out from Bombay. The fact that she considered herself engaged to Ashton Pelham-Martyn made no difference to his feelings for her (beyond adding jealousy and despair to the other emotions he was suffering on her behalf) and as he saw no reason why he should not discuss the subject of his wounded heart with her betrothed, Ash found himself listening to a good deal of talk from his love-sick rival, and was often hard put to it to keep his temper.

It was sad that Belinda, by encouraging George to talk about himself, should have released such an uninhibited torrent of speech, for once having got the bit between his teeth, George showed every sign of bolting. But as Ash could see no way of stopping him that did not involve unpleasantness, he merely took the easier way of spending a large part of each day in the company of Zarin, Ala Yar and Mahdoo; not only because he found their society infinitely preferable to Mr. Garforth's, but because it was no longer possible for him to get Belinda to himself—her Mama having invited an old acquaintance, a Mrs. Viccary, to share their dâk-*ghari.*

The presence of a third, and middle-aged lady, effectively put an end to any hope of his being invited to pass an occasional hour or so in the Harlowes' carriage, or of spending much time alone with them at the various stopping places where rooms and meals were available and the horses were changed. Yet in spite of this disappointment he did not, as might have been expected, take a strong dislike to the interloper, for Mrs. Viccary turned out to be a delightful person, wise, tolerant and understanding, with a talent for making friends and a genuine interest in other people that made her very easy to talk to. As she was also an excellent and sympathetic listener, it was not long before Ash found himself telling her more of his history than he was ever to tell Belinda; which surprised him—though it did not surprise her.

Edith Viccary was used to receiving confidences (and had never been known to betray one, which probably accounted for the fact that she received so many). Moreover in the present instance, having listened to a voluble account of young Mr. Pelham-Martyn's prospects, relatives and background from his prospective mother-in-law, she had exerted herself to draw him out, as she not only fully understood but shared his passion for his adopted country, which was, in a sense, her own, because she too had been born in it. She had also by now spent the greater part of her life there, for having been sent home to England at the age of eight, she had come back as a young lady of sixteen to rejoin her parents who were at that time stationed at Delhi; and it was there in the capital city of the Moguls that a year later she met and married a young engineer, Charles Viccary.

That had been in the winter of 1849, and since then her husband's work had taken her to most parts of the vast sub-continent in which men of both their families, Carrolls and Viccarys, had served for three successive generations—initially in the East India Company and later under the Crown. And the more she saw of it, the more she came to love the land, and to appreciate its peoples, among whom she was proud to number many close friends, for unlike Mrs. Harlowe, she had set herself to master at least four of India's main languages and learned to speak them with enviable fluency. When cholera deprived her of her only child, and the great Sepoy Rising of '57 took the lives of her parents, and of her sister Sarah and Sarah's three small children who died in the terrible *Bibi-gurh* at Cawnpore, she did not give way to despair or lose her sense of proportion and justice; and even during the bitter aftermath of the Mutiny she did not allow herself to hate.

In this, as in all else, she was by no means unique. But as she happened to be the first of her kind whom Ash had met, it was Edith Viccary who was responsible for erasing for ever an uneasy suspicion that he had lately begun to entertain—that Mrs. Harlowe and those of her fellow-sightseers who had laughed and talked so loudly during the prayers at the Juma-Masjid were typical of all the British-born "memsahibs" in India. For this alone he would have been willing to forgive her almost anything

169

—even for being the unwitting cause of preventing him from seeing as much of Belinda as he had hoped to do on the journey north.

Apart from that deprivation, the days passed pleasantly. It was good to be with Zarin again and listen to familiar talk while the remembered scenes unrolled beyond the windows; to eat the food that Gul Baz bought from the stalls of vendors in the villages—curries and dals, rice, chuppattis and sticky sweetmeats shimmering with beaten silver—served as often as not on green leaves, and washed down with draughts of buffalo milk or water from the wells that were to be found at every hamlet. The names of towns and rivers and the aspect of every little village was suddenly familiar to him, for this was the country across which he and Sita had wandered in the months that followed their escape from Gulkote.

Karnal, Ambala, Ludhiana, Jullundar, Amritsar and Lahore, the Sutlej and the Ravi Rivers. He knew them all . . . The temperature at mid-morning and for the best part of the afternoon remained uncomfortably high, and the sun still blistered the paintwork on the roofs and sides of the *gharis*. But as the teams of starveling ponies rattled them forward across the rich croplands of the Punjab, the air became noticeably cooler, and there came a day when Ash, descending in the early dawn to stretch his legs on the quiet roadside, saw above the far horizon to the north a long, jagged line of pale rose glowing bright against the cool green of the sky: and knew that he was looking at the snow peaks of the Himalayas.

His heart seemed to turn over as he looked, and his eyes filled with tears. And all at once he wanted to laugh and cry and to shout aloud—or to pray, as Zarin and Ala Yar and a dozen of their co-religionists were doing. Only it was not towards Mecca that he would face, but to the mountains. His own mountains, in whose shadow he had been born—to the Dur Khaima to which he had prayed as a child. Somewhere over there lay the Far Pavilions, with *Tarakalas,* the "Star Tower," catching the first rays of the sunrise. And somewhere, too, the valley that Sita had so longed to reach before she died, and that he himself would reach one day.

They had stopped for the previous night on the outskirts of a little village, and there was a food-stall near by. Ash bought a handful of cooked rice, and remembering

170

the offerings he used to make to the Dur Khaima in the Queen's balcony at Gulkote, he strewed it on the dew-wet ground. Perhaps it would bring him luck. A grey-headed plains crow and a famished pariah dog swooped upon the feast, and the sight of the emaciated mongrel recalled him abruptly from the past. Gulkote and the Dur Khaima were forgotten, and it was Ashton Pelham-Martyn and not Ashok who bought half-a-dozen chuppattis and fed them to a starving dog; and Isobel's son, not Sita's, who boarded the *ghari* again, hands in pockets and whistling "John Peel" as the sun rose above the horizon and flooded the plains with brilliant light.

"Ah! This smells like my own country again," said Ala Yar, snuffing the wind like an elderly horse that scents its stable. "Now it will not matter so much if these *gharis* should break down, for if need be we can walk the rest of the way." (Ala Yar distrusted hired vehicles and was convinced that the frequent halts were due to faulty driving.)

The *gharis* did not break down, but a culvert and half a mile of road that had been swept away by the flooding of a river caused a delay of two days, and the travellers were forced to put up in a near-by dâk-bungalow until the road was mended.

There is little doubt that but for George Garforth, Ash would not have been able to resist the temptation to play truant in the company of Zarin and Ala Yar. But he had not forgotten Belinda's graciousness to George during those three dismal days after leaving Bombay, or that George had been quick to step into the breach when he, Ash, had absented himself in Delhi, so to Zarin's disgust he spent every possible moment in her company during that two days' delay.

Mr. Garforth had been equally assiduous, though once again he had been compelled to spend most of the time talking to Mrs. Harlowe rather than to her daughter. He had, however, won golden opinions from that lady by holding her knitting wool and telling her at length about his childhood. She had always considered George Garforth to be a very personable and presentable young man, but Byronic features, chestnut curls and melting brown eyes did not compensate for lack of means, and it had to be owned that Mr. Garforth's prospects, for the moment anyway, were not bright.

171

As a new and very junior member of a firm which dealt in beer, wines and spirits, his salary was modest and his social position even more so; for except in the great ports such as Calcutta, Bombay and Madras, where Commerce was King, Anglo-Indian society ranked the "box-wallah" (a scornful term applied to all who engaged in trade) well below the level of those two ruling castes, the army and the Civil Service, and in such a military stronghold as Peshawar, a junior "boxwallah" would count for very little indeed; which was a pity, thought Mrs. Harlowe, because if only things had been different she would have been far happier with George Garforth as a son-in-law than with Ashton Pelham-Martyn, who was so . . . who was so . . . It was difficult to explain what she felt about Ashton. On board he had seemed such a quiet and dependable young man, and the fact that he was rich (or, at least, so comfortably off) and that as his uncle had only the one son, there was always the chance that Ashton might one day inherit a baronetcy, had made him appear an excellent matrimonial prospect; but ever since that dreadful day in Bombay she had been beset by doubts.

If only George had been as eligible as Ashton, sighed Mrs. Harlowe, how much happier she would feel about dear Bella's future. George, for all his spectacular looks, was so comfortably normal and uncomplicated, and his parents certainly seemed to be well off; his description of his home made it plain that they lived in far greater style than she herself had ever been accustomed to. Two carriages, no less—it made one wonder if he were not a better prospect than he appeared. His father, he had told her, was Irish by extraction, and his maternal grandmother a Greek lady of title (which would account for the romantic profile), and though he himself had wanted to go into the army, his mother had been so set against it that to please her he had given up the idea and agreed instead to go in for commerce. The romance of the East had appealed to his adventurous spirit and led to his accepting a post in the firm of Brown & Macdonald, in preference to some well-paid sinecure obtained for him through family influence in England; for, fond as he was of his parents, George had confessed that he preferred to stand on his own feet and start at the bottom of the ladder, a sentiment that won Mrs. Harlowe's full approval.

What a nice boy he was. Now Ashton never mentioned his parents, and what little he had told her of his childhood was so exceedingly odd that she had been forced to discourage him from saying any more, and had told him (tactfully of course) that the less he said about it the better as such a story was likely to be . . . well . . . misunderstood. A Hindu foster-mother, the wife of a common syce, whom he actually spoke of as "my mother" as though she had been the real one! Mrs. Harlowe shuddered at the thought of what people would say if they knew, and wished she had not been so precipitate over agreeing to his betrothal to Belinda. She would never have done such a thing if it had not been for little Harry and Teddy and her longing to be with them again. People did not understand how terrible it was to be separated from one's children for years at a time. Even Archie did not. She had only wanted Belinda to be safely and happily married and she did so hope Archie was not going to be cross. After all, she had done it for the best. The best for Harry and Teddy . . .

By dusk on the second day the repairs to the road were completed and the passengers rounded up and re-embarked, and shortly after moon-rise the *gharis* rattled forward upon the last leg of the journey to Jhelum, where there was a British military cantonment of some size.

The Jhelum River was running high and swiftly, swollen by heavy autumn rains in far-away Kashmir, and there was nothing in the sight of that turbulent brown flood to remind Ash of the quiet river that had carried Sita away from him so many years ago. The town itself, together with the cantonments, lay on the far side, but as there had been a military exercise that day, there were a number of British officers idling on the near bank waiting for boats to ferry them back, and Belinda viewed the younger ones with lively interest and thought how very different (and how much more exciting) these cheerful, sunburned young officers were from the stolid and soberly clad townsmen of Nelbury, who, viewed in retrospect, might have belonged to a different race from these gaily uniformed men whom the furnace summers and bitter Khyber winters, warfare, responsibility and hard exercise had welded into a type that had become as instantly recognizable as a Red Indian or the cowboys of Texas.

The very sight of them served to restore Belinda's spirits, which had sunk considerably during the last day or two. The mounting tedium and discomfort of the dusty, interminable journey had depressed her, and the group of young officers on the bank was a welcome reminder that civilization and gaiety had not been left behind. No pretty girl need ever feel bored or neglected with so many men to squire her to picnics and partner her at dances, and it was almost a pity that she had engaged herself to marry Ashton. But then she was in love with him, and so of course she wished to marry him; though perhaps not too soon. It would be pleasant to be free for a few years longer and to enjoy all the delights of being courted by half-a-dozen young men instead of only one; and it wasn't as though Ash would even be in the same station. He would be miles away in Mardan and probably unable to ride over and see her more than once a week at most, yet as an engaged girl she would be unable to accept invitations from other men; that would be considered shockingly fast.

Belinda sighed, admiring the scarlet coats and luxuriant moustaches of the young officers, and somewhat naturally did not spare a look for the older ones, as she was not expecting to see her father. Even if she had been, she would not have recognized him. The man she dimly remembered had seemed a giant to his seven-year-old daughter, while the small and elderly gentleman who now appeared at the door of their *ghari* was an unimpressive figure, and Belinda was as shocked as she was startled when her mother uttered a piercing cry of "Archie!" and warmly embraced the stranger. Could this really be the alarming autocrat of whom her resolute Aunt Lizzie and her stout and voluble Mama had so often said, "Your Papa would never permit it"?

But if Belinda was disappointed in her Papa, it was plain that he was far from disappointed in his daughter. She was, he told her, the very image of her dear Mama at the same age, and it was the greatest pity that the Brigade would be going off on manoeuvres so soon, for he was afraid she might find Peshawar a trifle slow with all the young sparks away under canvas. But by Christmas the regiments would all be back in cantonments, and after that she would have nothing to complain of, as Peshawar was a very gay station.

Major Harlowe pinched his daughter's chin, and

174

added that he could see they would soon have all the young fellows lining up to take his pretty little puss out riding and dancing—a remark that caused Belinda to blush uncomfortably and her mother to hope that Edith Viccary would not say anything indiscreet, or Ashton put in an appearance before she had been able to explain matters to Archie. It was really *very* vexing that Archie should have elected to meet them at Jhelum, for she had counted upon being able to choose her time and broach the subject of Belinda's engagement in the privacy of their own bungalow before there was any chance of his meeting Mr. Pelham-Martyn, who would be parting company with them at Nowshera.

The next quarter of an hour had proved a difficult one, but Mrs. Viccary had said nothing untoward, and when Ash put in an appearance he was so closely followed by George Garforth that it had been possible for Mrs. Harlowe to introduce both young men as shipboard acquaintances, and to get rid of them on the excuse that she and her husband and dear Bella had so much to say to each other after so long a separation . . . she was *sure* they would understand.

Ash certainly understood that this was not the time or the place for him to present himself to Major Harlowe in the character of a future son-in-law, and he had retired to the dining room of the dâk-bungalow to eat a four-course meal while Zarin arranged transport and accommodation for the rest of the journey, and George prowled up and down the verandah in the hope of catching a last glance from Belinda's blue eyes.

"I can't understand you," said George bitterly, joining Ash at the table when the Harlowes had finally departed. "If I had only had the luck to be in your shoes, I'd be with them now, tackling the old man and staking my claim before the whole world. You don't deserve that angel, and it'll serve you right if some other fellow cuts you out. I bet you there'll be dozens of them hanging about her in Peshawar."

"There were at least a dozen on the boat," observed Ash amicably. "And if you think this is a good place to line up before a complete stranger and demand his daughter's hand in marriage, *you're* the one who must be mad. Damn it, he hasn't seen her since she was in short socks.

175

I can't embark on a subject like that five minutes after he's met her; and in a crowded dâk-bungalow at that. Talk sense."

"I believe I *am* mad," groaned George, striking his forehead in a manner that would have done credit to Henry Irving. "But I can't help loving her. I know it's hopeless, but that doesn't make any difference. I love her, and if you let her down——"

"Oh, stow it, George!" interrupted Ash impatiently. "You've just announced that she'll probably throw me over for someone else, and you can't have it both ways. Tell a *khidmatgar* to get you something to eat and let me get on with my dinner."

He sympathized with the unsuccessful suitor, and as the accepted one, felt in honour bound to treat him kindly; but George's dramatics were beginning to pall, and Ash could only regret that he would be stationed in Peshawar where, if he intended to haunt the Harlowes' bungalow, they were bound to meet. As for any fears that Belinda might change her mind, Ash had none. She had assured him of her love, and to have harboured any doubts on that score would have seemed to him a lack of trust and an insult to them both. By which it can be seen that he was still young enough to be pompous in the matter of his emotions.

He was also sufficiently lacking in vanity to feel no surprise when neither Belinda nor Mrs. Harlowe made any move to single him out for attention, or bring him to the notice of his future father-in-law when they met on the road at the various dâk-bungalows between Jhelum and Nowshera where the dâk-*gharis* changed horses while their passengers ate, and where they put up at night. George might say what he liked (and he said a good deal, since they were still, unfortunately, sharing the same dâk-*ghari*) but it seemed only reasonable to Ash that a daughter who had been separated from her father for so many years should hesitate to spoil their meeting by informing him that she planned to leave him before too long. Once the Harlowes were safely settled into their own house and had recovered from the fatigue of the journey, Belinda would be sure to write and let him know when he might call, and he would ride over to Peshawar and talk the whole matter over with her father—and perhaps— who knew?—they might even be married by the spring.

It must be owned that such an idea had not previously occurred to him, for he had imagined that Belinda's Papa would insist that they wait until he came of age, and he had not been prepared to quarrel with that. But his meeting with Major Harlowe had made him begin to revise his plans. Ash too had pictured someone far more formidable than the undersized and—it must be admitted—insignificant-looking gentleman to whom he had been introduced at Jhelum, but now that he had seen the Major, he was no longer surprised that Mrs. Harlowe should have taken it upon herself to consent to the engagement instead of telling him (which he had fully expected her to do) that he must wait until he had seen Belinda's Papa, because if looks were anything to go by, Major Archibald Harlowe was the kind of man who would allow himself to be over-ruled by the opinions of his women-folk; in which case they might well be able to talk him into allowing an early wedding. It was an exciting prospect, and Ash gave himself up to day dreams.

Major Harlowe, for his part, had paid no particular attention to Ensign Pelham-Martyn beyond vaguely noting that his pretty little daughter seemed to have attracted two personable young admirers. He had acknowledged his wife's introductions to Ash and Mr. Garforth, and promptly forgotten their names, though he would nod amiably to them whenever they met at one of the staging posts on the road, and twit his daughter on having acquired two beaux already.

The road wound through the desolate Salt Ranges that lay between Jhelum and the great cantonment of Rawalpindi, and swept onward, past the ruins of Taxila and among low rocky hills that showed above a barren plain like the bones of starving cattle, to end on the banks of the Indus under the grim shadow of Attock Fort. Here the travellers descended, and having paid off their drivers, crossed the river by ferry and continued their journey in fresh relays of dâk-*gharis* along the road that ran parallel to the Kabul River. The autumn rains had turned the river to a swirling, rust-stained torrent, but the plains were still parched and dusty, and beyond the swollen river the land stretched away towards the hills, lion-coloured and rock-strewn, its trees and fields dried to a uniform gold by the furnace heat of the summer months.

The hills were nearer now, and the horizon no longer limitless but bounded by bleak folds and ridges of rock that changed colour with every hour of the day: at one moment seeming fifty miles away and as blue and transparent as glass, and at another a mere furlong distant, rust-brown and streaked with the black shadows of innumerable gullies. Behind them the Border hills and the mountains of Malakand rose up in ridge after ridge like frozen waves breaking on the rim of the plain, guardians of a harsh land inhabited by a score of turbulent tribes who recognized no law save that of force, lived in fortified villages and indulged in savage blood-feuds, and waged perpetual war either with each other or the British. For this was the North-West Frontier: the Gateway of India through which Alexander of Macedon and his conquering Legions had marched when the world was young. Beyond its inhospitable passes lay the Kingdom of Sher Ali, Amir of Afghanistan. And beyond that, the vast and menacing Empire of the Tsars.

To Belinda, the countryside seemed depressingly bleak and empty, but at least there was no lack of traffic on the Peshawar road, and looking out from the window of the dâk-*ghari* she could see an occasional Englishman on horseback or driving a trap, as well as the now familiar country carts and plodding pedestrians; and once a column of British soldiers on the march tramped past, a file of laden baggage elephants rolling in their wake, and the thick dust dimming their scarlet coats to an indeterminate and rusty grey.

There were camels too, creatures that she could remember seeing as a child: long lines of them carrying enormous loads that jolted and swayed like bumboats in a choppy sea, high above the inevitable goats and cattle that were being herded from one village to the next. As they neared the outskirts of Nowshera the traffic thickened and the drivers of phaetons and *tikka-gharis*, tongas and *ekkas*, whipped up their ponies for a final burst of speed and raced each other into the town, scattering pedestrians like startled chickens and raising a smothering cloud of dust that set their passengers choking. The town was a small one with a dâk-bungalow that differed very little from a dozen others on the road, and it was not until Ash came to say goodbye that Belinda realized that this was where he must leave them.

He stood hat in hand in the late evening sunlight, gazing at her with his heart in his eyes and finding that it was impossible to say any of the things he had meant to say, because her parents were listening and it was plain to him from Mrs. Harlowe's flustered manner and her husband's polite indifference that nothing had as yet been said on the subject of an engagement. In the circumstances he could only press Belinda's hand, and assure her that he would ride over to Peshawar at the first opportunity to give himself the pleasure of calling upon her. Mrs. Harlowe said that they would be happy to see him; though not for a week or so, for what with all the unpacking . . . perhaps next month? and her husband said vaguely: "Of course, of course," adding that around Christmas most of the young fellows managed to get a few days' leave from their regiments and he dared say that Mr.—er —er? would be able to do so too and must certainly look them up. Belinda blushed and murmured something to the effect that she hoped Mr. Pelham-Martyn would be able to visit Peshawar long before Christmas, and at this point the driver of the Harlowes' *ghari,* who had been superintending a change of horses, announced that he was now ready to take the road.

Major Harlowe embarked his family once more, the doors slammed shut, a whip cracked and they were gone in a cloud of dust, leaving Ash standing in the roadway feeling depressed and inadequate and wishing that he had summoned up enough courage to kiss Belinda before them all and thereby force the issue. Mrs. Harlowe's reference to "sometime next month" had not been encouraging, but it was her husband's remark about "a few days' leave at Christmas" that had given him a really disagreeable jolt, for he had looked forward to riding over to Peshawar within a day or two of his arrival, and until that moment it had not occurred to him that leave to do so might not be granted to a newly joined subaltern; or not unless he could give some particularly pressing reason for requesting it, and he could hardly discuss the subject of his engagement to Belinda with his Adjutant or the Commanding Officer before it had even been mentioned to her father. He could only hope that once Mrs. Harlowe had explained matters to her husband, Major Harlowe might demand his presence in Peshawar, or else ride over himself to Mardan. But that would depend largely on his reception of the news, and Ash was suddenly a lot less confident that he would approve it.

"The Regiment have sent a tonga," said Zarin, appearing abruptly at his side. "It will not take us all, so I told Gul Baz to hire a second for himself and Mahdoo, and they have gone on ahead with the baggage. The day grows late and there is more than ten *koss* to be covered before we see Mardan. Let us go."

10

Night falls swiftly in the East, for there is no lingering dusk to soften the transition from daylight to darkness. The Kabul River had been gold with the sunset as Ash and his three companions crossed the bridge of boats at Nowshera, but long before they reached Mardan the moon was high and the shadow of the little star-shaped fort that Hodson built in the years before the Great Mutiny lay black on the milk-white plain.

In the old days, when the Land-of-the-Five-Rivers (the Punjab) was still a Sikh province, and the only British troops within its borders were East India Company regiments stationed at Lahore to uphold the authority of a British Resident, the idea of an elite and highly mobile force, capable of moving to any trouble-spot at a moment's notice, had been conceived by Sir Henry Lawrence, that great and wise administrator who was to die a hero's death during the Mutiny, in the beleaguered Residency at Lucknow.

This "fire-brigade" would consist of one troop of cavalry and two companies of infantry, unhampered by tradition and run on entirely new lines, in that it would combine soldiering with early and accurate intelligence work, and its members—handpicked men commanded by handpicked officers—would wear a loose, comfortable, khaki-coloured uniform that would blend into the dusty background of the Frontier hills, instead of the regulation scarlet coat and tight stock in which a majority of regiments marched, sweltered and suffered in temperatures that made such clothing a torment—and which could be seen from miles away. As a further break with tradition, Sir Henry had named his brain-child "The Corps of Guides" and entrusted the raising of it to one Harry Lumsden, a young man possessed of exceptional ability, character and courage, who had fully justified the choice.

The original headquarters of the new Corps had been at Peshawar, and at first its duties had consisted of dealing with the marauding Frontier tribes, who preyed on the peaceful villagers, carrying off women, children and cattle into the inhospitable Border hills, in defiance of the Sikh Durbar who were nominally in control of the Punjab and in whose name a handful of British officials exercised authority. Later on the Corps had been sent south to fight in the plains round Ferzapore, Mooltan and Lahore, and had served with distinction in the bloody battles of the Second Sikh War.

It was only when the war had ended and the Punjab been annexed by the Company's Government that the Guides had returned once more to the Frontier—though not to Peshawar. The Border having become more settled, they had selected a site near the Kalpani River where the tracks from Swat and Buner meet, and exchanged their tents for a mud-walled fort at Mardan on the plain of Yusafzai. It had been a desolate and treeless spot when Hodson had begun work on the fort, and his wife, Sophia, writing home in January of 1854, had said of it: "Picture to yourself an immense plain, flat as a billiard table but not as green, with here and there a dotting of camel-thorn about eighteen inches high by way of vegetation. This, far as the eye can see on the west and south of us, but on the north the everlasting snows of the mighty Himalayas above the lower range which is close to our camp."

The view had not changed: but the Corps had grown in size and the Guides had planted trees to shade their cantonment, and on this autumn night the garden that Hodson had made for his wife and their only and dearly loved child, who was to die in infancy, was sweet with the scent of jasmine and roses. In the cemetery where the dead of the Ambeyla campaign lay buried, a dozen tombstones gleamed white in the moonlight; and near by, at the junction of three roads, a mulberry tree threw a black patch of shadow above the place where Colonel Spottiswood, Commanding Officer of the Bengal Infantry Regiment that had been sent to relieve the Guides in the black year of 1857, shot himself when his beloved regiment mutinied.

The familiar scents and sounds of the cantonment drifted out to Ash like a greeting. The smell of horses and wood-smoke, of water on parched ground and spiced food cooking over charcoal fires, the stamp and whicker of cavalry chargers tethered in the lines, and the beehive hum of men gossiping after a hard day's work. In the Officers' Mess half-a-dozen voices were singing a popular music-hall ballad to the strains of a tinny piano, and somewhere in the bazaar a tom-tom beat a monotonous counterpoint to the doleful howling of pariah dogs baying the moon. A conch brayed in a temple and from far out on the milky plain beyond the river came the mournful cry of a jackal pack.

"It is good to be back," said Zarin, sniffing the night air with approval. "This is better than the heat and noise of the south and the racket of trains."

Ash made no reply. He was looking about him and realizing that this small, man-made oasis between the foothills of the Himalayas and the wide sweep of the plain would be his home for many years. From here he would ride out with his Regiment to keep the peace of the Border and to fight battles among those hills that showed like folds of crumpled cloth in the moonlight, or to dance, hunt and race in any one of a dozen gay stations from Delhi to Peshawar; but for whatever reason he left it, either on duty or for pleasure, as long as he served with the Guides he would always come back to Mardan ...

He turned to grin at Zarin and was about to speak when a figure detached itself from the shadow of a neem tree by the roadside, and moving out into the moonlight, brought the tonga to a halt.

"Who is it?" asked Ash in the vernacular—but even as he spoke the memory of another moonlight night came back to him, and without waiting for an answer he leapt from the tonga and was in the dusty road, stooping to touch the feet of an old man who stood by the horse's head.

"*Koda Dad!*—it is you, my father." There was a break in Ash's voice and the past came back to him as though lit by bright flashes of lightning.

The old man laughed and embraced him. "So you have not forgotten me, my son. That is good, for I do not think I should have known you. The little boy has grown into a tall strong man—almost as tall as I; or is it that old age has shrivelled me somewhat? My sons sent word that you were coming, so I made the journey to Mardan, and Awal Shah and I have waited by the roadside these last three nights, not knowing when you could come."

Awal Shah stepped out of the shadows and brought his hand up to a salute; his father and Zarin might forget that Ash was an officer, but Jemadar Awal Shah would not.

"Salaam, Sahib," said Awal Shah. "The *gharis* being delayed, it was not known when you would reach here. But my father wished to see you before you made your salaams to the Colonel Sahib. Therefore we waited."

"Yes, yes," nodded Koda Dad, "for tomorrow will not do. Tomorrow you will be an officer-Sahib with many duties to perform, and your time will not be your own. But tonight, before you have reported yourself to those in authority, you are still Ashok and may, if you will, spare half an hour to speak to an old man."

"Willingly, my father. Tell the tonga-wallah to wait, Zarin. Do we go to your quarters, Jemadar Sahib?"

"No. That would not be wise or fitting. But we have brought food, and there is a place behind these trees where we can sit and talk together and be out of sight of the road."

The Jemadar turned and led the way to a small patch of ground, blackened by the ashes of old camp fires, where a handful of charcoal glowed red among the roots of the neem tree. Someone had set out several covered *dechis* (cooking pots) and a hookah, and Koda Dad Khan squatted down comfortably in the shadows, grunting approval as Ash followed his example, for few Europeans find it easy to adopt that characteristically Eastern pose—the cut of Western clothes discourages such attitudes, nor are Western men accustomed from youth to squat on their hunkers while eating, talking or idling. But Colonel Anderson, like Awal Shah and the Commandant of the Guides, had had his own ideas as to the education and training of Ashton Pelham-Martyn, and he had seen to it that the boy did not forget things that might one day be of use to the man.

"My son Zarin sent a message from Delhi to tell his brother that all was well and that you had not become a stranger to us. Therefore I came over the Border to welcome you back," said Koda Dad, taking a long pull at the hookah.

"And what if he had sent word that I had become altogether a Sahib?" inquired Ash, accepting a chuppatti heaped with *pilau* and falling to with a good appetite.

"Then I should not have come, since there would have been nothing that needed saying. But now there are things that must be said."

There was that in his voice that made Ash say sharply: "What things? Is it bad news? Are you in trouble?"

"No, no. It is only that Zarin and Ala Yar both say that you are still in many ways the Ashok of Gulkote days; which is good news. But——" The old man paused to glance at his sons, who nodded as though in agreement with a spoken question, and Ash looked from Koda Dad to Zarin and from Zarin to Awal Shah, and seeing the same expression on all three faces, said abruptly "What is it?"

"Nothing that need disturb you," said Koda Dad tranquilly. "It is only that here in Mardan, or wheresoever the Guides are sent, you and my son can no longer be the Zarin and Ashok of the old days, for it would not be fitting that a daffadar and an *Angrezi* officer should behave as blood-brothers. It would cause too much talk. And also—who knows?—the fear of favouritism among the men; there being Pathans of many different clans in the Guides, and also many men of different faiths, such as Sikhs and Hindus, all of them equal in the sight of their officers, which is just and right. Therefore only when you and Zarin are alone, or on leave, can you be yourselves as once you were; but not here or now, in the presence of the Regiment. Is it understood?"

The last three words were spoken quite softly, but they were less a question than a command, and the tone was a reminder of the old days when a Master of Horse had befriended a lonely little boy in the service of a spoilt princeling, cuffing him when he needed it, consoling him in his misfortunes, and treating him in all ways as a son. Ash recognized it and reacted to it in the same spirit,

184

though with reluctance. It seemed absurd to him that he should not be able to treat Zarin as a friend and brother without giving rise to criticism. But then he found a great many things that his elders and betters did absurd, and had seldom found any profit in arguing with them. In the circumstances Koda Dad's advice was probably sound and must be accepted, so he said slowly: "It is understood. But . . ."

"There are no buts," interrupted Awal Shah sharply. "My father and I have discussed this between us, and we are agreed. Zarin also. The past is the past, and it is best that it should be forgotten. The Hindu boy from Gulkote is dead and in his place is a Sahib—an officer-Sahib of the Guides. You cannot alter that; or try to be two people in one skin."

"I am that already," said Ash wryly. "Your brother helped to make me so when he told me that it would be best for me to go to *Belait* to the care of my father's people, and to learn to become a Sahib. Well, I have learned. Yet I am still Ashok, and I cannot alter that either, for having been a child of this land for eleven years I am tied to it by something as strong as the tie of blood, and shall always be two people in one skin—which is not a comfortable thing to be."

His voice held a sudden note of bitterness and Koda Dad laid a consoling hand on his shoulder and said gently: "That I understand. But you will find it easier if you keep the two separate and do not try to be both at one time. And some day—who knows?—you may discover in yourself a third person who is neither Ashok nor Pelham-Sahib, but someone whole and complete: yourself. Now let us talk of other things. Give me the hookah."

Awal Shah pushed the pipe towards him, and the familiar bubbling purr and the scent of country-grown tobacco took Ash back to long-ago evenings in Koda Dad's quarters in the Palace of the Winds. But as the pipe circulated it was not of the past that the old man spoke, but of the present and the future. His talk was of the Border, which had been unusually peaceful of late, and as they spoke the moon swung clear of the surrounding tree-tops and drowned the red glow of the coals in a flood of cold, clear light. From the direction of the road came a sharp jangle of bells as the tonga-pony shook its head restlessly, impatient for its stable, and presently its driver coughed discreetly to indicate that time was passing and that he had already wasted the best part of an hour.

"It grows late," said Koda Dad, "and if I am to get any sleep I must go, for tomorrow I set out for my own village before sunrise. No, no, my mind is made up. I wished only to see you, Ashok, and that being done I return to my own house—" his hand pressed heavily on Ash's shoulder as he levered himself to his feet. "Old men become like horses; they like their own stable best. Farewell, my son. It is good to have seen you again; and when next you obtain leave, Zarin shall bring you across the Border to visit me."

He embraced Ash and left, striding stiffly away into the shadows and disdaining the proffered help of his eldest son, who spoke briefly to Zarin, saluted Ash and followed in the wake of his father.

Zarin scuffed out the remnants of the fire and gathering up the cooking pots and the hookah, said: "I too must go now. Our holiday is over and my father is right— we would do better not to arrive together. The tonga will take you to the Adjutant Sahib's quarters where you should report your arrival. We shall see each other; but only in the way of work."

"But there will be other holidays."

"Beshak!" (without doubt). "When we are on leave we can be what we choose. But here we are on duty in the service of the Sirkar. Salaam, Sahib."

He vanished among the tree shadows and Ash went slowly back to the road where the tonga waited in the moonlight, and was bowled away into the fort to report himself to the Adjutant.

Those first days in Mardan had not been entirely happy ones for Ash, a circumstance that probably accounted for much that was to happen in the future, since it altered, at the outset, his approach to army life, and intensified an inborn impatience for rules and regulations, and a critical attitude to the arbitrary decisions of his elders and betters.

He should of course have foreseen it all, though the fact that he had not done so was not entirely his own fault. At least three other people must be held partly responsible: his Uncle Matthew, who had naturally never dreamt of warning his nephew against engaging himself to be married before he had so much as joined his regiment, Colonel Anderson, who had given him a great deal of good advice but (himself a confirmed bachelor) had neglected to touch on matrimony, and Mrs. Harlowe, who should have scouted the idea instead of welcoming it with such alacrity and instantly pledging her own and her husband's consent. In the circumstances Ash could hardly be blamed for thinking that lack of means, not years, was the sole reason why young officers were discouraged from marrying at the outset of their careers, and as this did not apply to him, that there could be no serious objection to his betrothal.

He was very speedily disillusioned, for Mrs. Harlowe's worst fears had been realized. Her husband had taken an exceedingly poor view of the whole affair; and so too, when he heard of it, had the Commandant of the Guides. Ash's intention of riding over to Peshawar at the first opportunity had been forestalled by Major Harlowe, who had driven to Mardan two days after his arrival and had a private talk with the Commandant.

Both men had been in complete agreement on the subject of early marriages and the fatal consequences attending young officers who acquired wives before they had, metaphorically speaking, cut their wisdom teeth. Ash had been sent for and treated to an embarrassing lecture that had left him feeling bruised and humiliated and, worse, infuriatingly callow. He had not been refused permission to see Belinda—it would perhaps have been kinder if he had been—but Major Harlowe had made it painfully clear that there could be no question of an engagement, official or otherwise, and that the matter must not be raised again for several years, by which time it was to be hoped that both young people would have learnt wisdom and acquired more sensible views on life (and, by implication, Belinda would have met and married some older and more suitable man). Provided that was clearly understood, Major Harlowe would have no objection to Mr. Pelham-Martyn calling on his family, if at any time he should happen to be in Peshawar.

"You must not think me hard-hearted, my boy," said Belinda's father. "I know just how you feel. But really, you know, it will not do. I am aware that financially you are well able to support a wife, but that don't alter the fact that you are both far too young to be think-

187

ing of marriage. Or if Bella is not, you are. Cut your milk teeth first my boy, and learn your trade; and if you have any sense you'll give yourself at least another eight or ten years before you tie yourself to petticoats and perambulators. That's my advice."

It was also the Commandant's. When Ash had attempted to argue his cause, he had been tersely instructed not to be a young fool, and that if he felt himself unable to support life without Miss Harlowe, then he was obviously unsuited to such a Corps as the Guides, and had better arrange a transfer to some more sedentary branch of the service as soon as possible. In the meantime, as it seemed that there had been some talk of an engagement, he had permission to take leave the following weekend in order to ride over to Peshawar and put matters straight with Miss Harlowe.

Ash had been prepared for a certain amount of opposition to his matrimonial plans and would undoubtedly have settled for a long engagement, but it had never crossed his mind that Belinda's father and his own Commanding Officer would refuse to recognize any engagement at all. After all, it was not as though he were a fortune-hunter or a penniless nobody; compared with the average Indian Army officer he could be considered extremely well-off, and it was therefore palpably unjust that his proposal to Belinda should be dismissed in this cavalier fashion.

Suddenly convinced that he could not possibly live without her, he decided on the instant that there was nothing for it but to elope. If he and Belinda were to run away together, her father would consent to the marriage in order to avoid a scandal, and if the Guides refused to keep him, well, there were plenty of other regiments.

Looking back on it, Ash could never remember very much about that first week in Mardan: there had been so much to learn and so much to do. But though the days had been full of interest, the nights had turned into a long battle for sleep, for it was only then that he had leisure to think of Belinda.

He would lie awake in the darkness evolving wild plans, and when at last he slept it was always to dream of riding headlong across a stony plain between low barren hills, with a girl on the crupper behind him who clung to him and urged him to ride faster—faster. A girl whose face he could not see, but who was of course Belinda; though the long hair that streamed out behind her like a flag in the wind, impeding his view of their pursuers, was not yellow but black. He would hear the thunder of following hoofbeats coming louder and nearer, and would wake sweating with terror—to find that the sound of galloping horses was his own heart-beats thumping as though he had been running a race.

It was disturbing, too, to realize that although he was back once more in the land of his birth and able to see and speak with Zarin and Koda Dad again, he had not after all lost that nagging sense of emptiness that had haunted his years in exile. It was still there, but he felt sure that if Belinda would only agree to defy her father and marry him, with or without permission, he would be free of it for ever—together with all restlessness and anxiety and doubt. It was the nights that made the week seem long. Yet almost before he knew it, it was Saturday.

He left Mardan well before sunrise, accompanied by Gul Baz, and they breakfasted a mile beyond Nowshera on chuppattis and dal curry bought from a food-vendor by the side of the Peshawar road. Parrots screamed and preened among the branches of the shade-trees lining the road and Gul Baz, though now in his thirtieth year, so far forgot himself as to break into song, and Ash recovered his spirits and was suddenly full of optimism. Somehow and in some way his problems would be solved, and tomorrow when he rode back to Mardan the future would be clear and everything settled.

Ash had sent a brief letter to Belinda, telling her that he would be riding over to Peshawar and hoped to reach there by mid-day, and a longer and more formal one to Mrs. Harlowe, asking permission to call. But though he arrived at their bungalow a little earlier than he expected he found it empty but for a portly Mohammedan bearer, who informed him that the Major-Sahib had gone into camp with his regiment on the previous day, and the memsahibs were out shopping and would not be back until three o'clock, as they were taking *tiffin* with the Deputy Commissioner's memsahib. There was, however, a note for Ash . . .

They were so sorry, wrote Belinda, to be out, but the luncheon engagement was one that could not be missed, and as Mohan Lal's shop had announced the arrival of a new consignment of dress materials and printed cottons from Calcutta, there was no help for it but to leave early. She was sure Ash would understand, and Mama hoped that he would take tea with them at four o'clock.

The note contained three spelling mistakes and had obviously been written in a hurry, but it was the first that Ash had ever received from her, and as she had signed herself his affectionate Belinda, he stowed it carefully away in the breast-pocket of his coat, and leaving a message to say that he would return at tea time, remounted his horse and rode slowly away to the dâk-bungalow. There he engaged a room for the night, left Gul Baz and the horses, and having sent for a tonga, had himself driven to the Club. At least it would be cool there and probably quiet—which was more than could be said for the dâk-bungalow. But it proved to be an unfortunate choice.

The Club was certainly cool and comfortable, and it was empty except for a sprinkling of bored *khidmatgars* and two middle-aged Englishwomen who were drinking coffee in a corner of the lounge. Ash retired to the opposite corner with a mug of beer and a six-month-old copy of *Punch*, but the quacking voices of the two women made it impossible to concentrate, and presently he rose abruptly, and marching out of the lounge, took refuge in the bar where, owing to the fact that most of the garrison were out on manoeuvres, he found himself the sole occupant and was alone with his thoughts, none of which were particularly pleasant.

It was a measure of his disquiet that barely a quarter of an hour later he greeted the appearance of George Garforth with something approaching relief, though normally he would have been at pains to avoid George's company, and within minutes was regretting that he had not done so. For George, having accepted his offer of a drink, had immediately embarked on a harrowing description of Belinda's impact on Peshawar society and the compliments paid to her by several eligible bachelors who, asserted George, should know better than to pester such a young and innocent creature with their loathsome attentions.

"It's downright disgusting, when you think that Foley and Robinson are both old enough to be her father—or her uncles, anyway," said George bitterly. "As for Claude Parberry, anyone can see that he is nothing but a *roué*

190

and not to be trusted to take one's sister out riding. I can't think why her mother permits it: or why you do."

He glowered resentfully at Ash, and having refreshed himself with a long pull at his glass, cheered up slightly and remarked that he happened to know that Belinda was merely embarrassed by the attention of these officers—he would not call them "gentlemen"—but the poor child was too inexperienced to know how to deal with them as they deserved. He could only wish she would give him the right to do so, said George, adding truculently that he felt it only fair to warn Ash that she might yet do so.

"I may as well tell you," declared George loudly, "that as she is not wearing your ring, I do not regard her as irrevocably bound to you, and I shall do my best to make her change her mind. After all, 'All's fair in love and war' you know, and I was in love with Belinda before you were. Have another drink?"

Ash refused, saying curtly that he had ordered lunch and did not intend to keep it waiting. But George was impervious to snubs and merely said that he too was feeling peckish and would join him. The meal was hardly a convivial one; Ash did not talk at all while George never stopped talking, and judging from his conversation, he appeared to be very much *persona grata* at the Harlowes' bungalow. He had already squired Belinda to a picnic in addition to accompanying her and her mother on a shopping expedition, and that very evening was to dine with them and go on afterwards to the "Saturday Hop" at the Club.

"Belinda says I am quite the best dancer in Peshawar," observed George complacently. "I daresay I—" he broke off abruptly as a new and obviously disagreeable thought struck him. "Oh, I suppose you are going to be there tonight. Well, you won't find many people there. I believe it's no end of a crush when the military are in town, but as most of 'em are marching around the Kajuri Plain just now, the hops are pretty small affairs. I can't think why Belinda didn't mention that you'd be coming. But perhaps you don't dance? I believe some of the fellows don't, but for my part—"

George continued to talk his way steadily through four courses, and Ash was profoundly relieved when at last he took himself off. A post-luncheon silence descended upon the Club, and he returned to the deserted lounge and the unread copy of *Punch*, and watched the hands of the clock crawl slowly round the dial until at last it was time to leave.

Mrs. Harlowe was waiting for him in her drawing-room, and although she greeted him kindly enough, she appeared ill at ease and plunged at once into a disjointed flood of small talk. It was plain that she did not intend to discuss personal matters and was determined to treat his visit as nothing more than a social call, and she was becoming a little breathless by the time her daughter tripped in, wearing white muslin and looking enchantingly young and pretty.

Framed in the doorway of that common-place bungalow drawing-room with its drab-coloured chintzes, numdah rugs and Benares-brass trays, Belinda glowed like a freshly blown rose in an English garden, and Ash forgot the proprieties and the fact that her mother was present, and ignoring her outstretched hand, caught her in his arms and would have kissed her if she had not turned her head away and twisted free.

"Ashton!" Belinda's hands flew to her hair, patting her curls into place as she backed away from him, blushing vividly, and uncertain whether to laugh or be scandalized: "Whatever will Mama think? If you are going to behave so abominably I shall go away. Now do sit down and be sensible. No, not over there. Here, beside Mama. We both want to hear about your Regiment and Mardan and what you have been doing with yourself."

Ash opened his mouth to protest that he had not come to talk about such things, but he was foiled by Mrs. Harlowe, who rang for tea; and in the presence of a hovering *khidmatgar* there was nothing for it but to give a brief account of his doings, while Belinda poured and the *khidmatgar* proffered plates of cakes and sandwiches.

Listening to his own voice, it seemed to Ash that the day had taken on a queer dream-like quality in which nothing was real. Their whole future, his and Belinda's, was at stake; yet here they sat, sipping tea and nibbling egg sandwiches, and talking trivialities as though nothing else mattered. The entire day had been a nightmare from the moment that he had arrived at the Harlowes' bungalow and learnt that Belinda had left to go shopping: George's unwelcome conversation, the long, slow hours of waiting, Mrs. Harlowe's nervous chatter, and now this.

The room seemed to be full of an invisible glue in which he struggled feebly like a fly trapped in a pot of jam, while Mrs. Harlowe talked of Zenana Missions and Belinda gleefully listed the various gay functions she had attended during the past week, and drew his attention to the impressive array of engraved cards that stood ranged on the chimney-piece.

Ash glanced at them and said abruptly: "I saw George Garforth at the Club. He says he has seen you fairly frequently during the past week."

Belinda laughed and made a little moue. "If he has, it is only because nearly all the presentable men are out in camp, so he is almost the only one left who can be trusted not to tread on one's dress at a dance. Do you dance, Ashton? I do hope so, for I find I enjoy it more than anything."

"Then perhaps you will give me some dances tonight," said Ash. "I understand there is to be a dance at the Club, and though I cannot undertake to dance as well as George, I will at least try not to tread on your dress."

"Oh, but—" Belinda stopped and looked appealingly at her mother, and poor Mrs. Harlowe, distracted by the whole situation and finding herself quite incapable of dealing with it, issued a flustered invitation to Ash to join their party that evening, which she had certainly not meant to do. She had only asked him to tea in order to give the young couple an opportunity to talk the matter over in the garden and decide—as of course they must decide—that there was no point in continuing the association and that it would be better to part. Belinda could then return Ashton's ring, and after that the poor boy would naturally wish to leave Peshawar immediately, as the very *last* thing he would want to do would be to return an hour or so later in order to dine with them. She could not imagine why she had invited him to do so, but perhaps he would have the sense to refuse.

Ash had disappointed her: he had accepted with alacrity, under the mistaken impression that the invitation showed Mrs. Harlowe to be still on his side and prepared to support his suit; and when she suggested that Belinda might like to show him the garden, he took it as a further proof of her goodwill. Once again, as on the Peshawar road in the early morning, his spirits soared, and he followed Belinda out into the garden and kissed her behind

193

a kindly screen of pepper trees, feeling light-headed with love and optimism. But what followed was worse than anything that he had endured or imagined in the dismal days since his interview with Major Harlowe and the Commanding Officer . . .

Belinda had certainly returned his kiss, but having done so she had also returned his ring and had left him in no doubt as to her parents' opposition to the engagement. Ash learnt that Mrs. Harlowe, far from supporting his suit, had gone over to the enemy and was now fully persuaded as to the folly of the whole affair. There was no question of either parent relenting, and as Belinda herself would not be of age for another four years, there was nothing to be gained by arguing or protesting.

Her reaction to Ash's suggestion that they elope had been blank dismay and an emphatic refusal to consider it for a moment. "I wouldn't *dream* of doing anything so— so silly and outrageous. Really, Ashton, I think you must be mad. You'd be dismissed from your Regiment and everyone would know why, and there'd be a vulgar scandal and you'd be disgraced; and so would I. I'd never be able to hold up my head again, and I think you are quite horrid to—to even *mention* such a thing to me."

Belinda burst into tears, and only the most abject of apologies on Ash's part had prevented her from running back to the house and refusing to see him again. But though she had eventually agreed to forgive him, the damage had been done, and she would not agree to any private contract between them. "It's not that I don't love you any more," explained Belinda tearfully. "I do, and I would marry you tomorrow if Papa approved. But how can I know what I shall feel like when I'm twenty-one?— or if you will still be in love with me by then?"

"I shall always be in love with you!" vowed Ash passionately.

"Well, if you are, and if I am still in love with you, then of course we shall get married because we shall have proved that we must be the right people for each other."

Ash insisted that he already knew that, and for his part he would be willing to wait for any length of time if only she would promise faithfully to marry him some day. But Belinda would not promise anything. Nor would she take back the ring. Ashton must keep it, and perhaps one day when they were both older, if her parents and his

Commanding Officer approved and if they themselves were still of the same mind—

"If—if—if," interrupted Ash savagely. "Is that all you can offer me? 'If your parents approve,' 'If my C.O. permits.' But what about *us* my darling?—you and me? It's *our* life and *our* love and *our* future that is being decided. If you loved me—"

He stopped, defeated. Belinda was looking hurt and upset and it was obvious that if he were to continue in this strain it would only lead to another quarrel and more tears, and the possibility of an immediate and permanent break. That last was something he could not bear to contemplate, so he reached for her hand, and kissing it, said contritely: "I'm sorry, darling. I shouldn't have said that. I know you love me and that none of this is your fault. I'll keep your ring for you, and one day, when I've proved myself worthy of you, I shall ask you to take it back again. You know that, don't you?"

"Oh, Ashton, of course I do. And I'm sorry too. But Papa says—Oh well, don't let's talk about that any more, because it doesn't do any good."

Belinda dabbed her eyes with a sodden scrap of lace and cambric and looked so forlorn that Ash would have kissed her again. But she would not let him do so, on the grounds that having returned his ring and thereby formally ended their betrothal, it would not be proper. She hoped, however, that they could remain friends, and that he would not feel obliged to change his mind about joining the party that evening, for she was sure that he would dance delightfully; and in any case, an extra man was always useful. On which deflating note the conversation ended and Ash escorted her back to the bungalow with a face of doom and a strong desire to cut his throat —or get drunk.

The reflection that his presence that evening as an extra man would be "useful" was not calculated to soothe the feelings of a rejected suitor. But as he could not bring himself to forgo even a moment of Belinda's company, he swallowed his pride and attended the party.

He had not expected to enjoy it, but it had proved a surprisingly pleasant evening. Belinda had danced with him three times and been kind enough to commend his waltzing, and emboldened by this success, he had begged as a keepsake the yellow rose-bud she wore at her breast.

195

She would not give it to him (George had already made the same request and been refused, and besides, Mama would be sure to notice), but she had allowed him to take her for a stroll on the lantern-lit terrace, which prevented him from feeling unduly depressed by the fact that she had also given three dances to George Garforth, and two waltzes and the supper dance to a tall, chinless young man who was, apparently, an aide-de-camp to some high-ranking General. But then Belinda in a ball-gown was such a bewitching sight that Ash felt himself quite unworthy of her and even deeper in love than before—if that were possible. The thought of having to wait for her, even if it should mean serving seven years, as Jacob had for Rachel, no longer seemed an intolerable injustice, but only reasonable and right. Such dazzling prizes should be earned, not snatched carelessly and in haste.

Mrs. Harlowe, who had feared that the presence of Belinda's discarded lover would cast a gloom over her party, was relieved to find that his behavior could not be faulted, and that he had actually contributed a great deal to the evening's success, being pronounced a delightful young man and an asset to any party. While as for Belinda herself, the impression that Ash had made on the other young women present had not been lost upon her. Being confident of his devotion it pleased her to know that she possessed something that others found desirable, and on parting with him she returned the pressure of his hand with so much warmth and such a speaking look from her blue eyes that he went back to the dâk-bungalow walking on air.

Her mother too had been unexpectedly kind and had actually said that she hoped he would call on them when next he was in Peshawar, though she was sorry that prior engagements would prevent them from seeing him on the following day. But this had not depressed him, for as their carriage drove away down the dark cantonment road, Ash looked down at the thing that Belinda had pressed into his palm under cover of the conventional farewell, and was comforted and uplifted to find that he held a much crushed and faded yellow rose-bud.

11

Mardan looked friendly and familiar in the evening light, and Ash was surprised to find himself glad to get back to it. The sounds and smells of the cavalry lines, the little star-shaped fort and the long line of the Yusafzai hills, rose-red in the sunset, already seemed like home to him; and though he had not expected to be back until late, Ala Yar was waiting on the verandah, ready to talk or be silent as the mood took him.

In the months that followed there had been little time in which to brood over Belinda and the unsatisfactory state of their love-affair, and there were even days—sometimes several in succession—when he did not think of her at all; and if he dreamed of her at night he did not remember it by morning. For Ash was discovering, as others had done before him, that the ways of the Indian Army (and in particular the ways of the Corps of Guides) differed a great deal from the pattern laid down by the Military Academy at Sandhurst. That difference was very much to his taste, and had it not been for Belinda, he would have had nothing to complain of and much to commend.

As a junior officer of the Guides he was expected to devote a part of each day to the study of Pushtu and Hindustani, the former being the language of the Border and the latter the lingua-franca of India and the Indian Army. But though he needed no instruction in either, he had still not learned to read or write them with the same facility with which he used the spoken word, and now he studied hard under an elderly munshi (teacher) and being Hilary's son made rapid progress. Which, it may here be noted, availed him little, for when he subsequently sat for the written examination in the Higher Standard, he failed to pass, to his own bewilderment and the fury of his munshi who took the matter up with the Commandant, asserting angrily that it was impossible for Pelham-Sahib to have failed; never before had he taught such a pupil and there must be some fault on the part of the examiners —a misprint perhaps? The papers were not returnable, but the Commandant had a friend in Calcutta who on the promise that no action would be taken, borrowed them from the files, only to discover, scrawled across them in red ink, the terse comment: *Flawless. This officer has obviously used a crib.*

"Tell the boy to make a few errors next time," advised the Commandant's friend. But Ash never sat for an examination again.

November saw the beginning of squadron training, and he exchanged his hot, high room in the fort for a tent on the plains beyond the river. Camp life, with its long hours in the saddle and frosty nights under canvas or the open sky, was far more to his taste than the routine of the cantonment; and after sundown when the tired squadron had finished their evening meal and his fellow officers, sated with fresh air and hard exercise, had fallen asleep, Ash would join a group around one of the fires and listen to the talk.

This to him was almost the best part of the day, and during it he learned a great deal more about his men than he would ever have learned in the normal course of his duties, not only about their families and personal problems, but the dissimilarities in their characters. For men who are relaxed and at ease show a different side of themselves from that which appears when they are on duty; and as the firelight faded and the ring of faces became shadowy and unrecognizable, they would discuss many things that would not normally have been raised in the presence of a *feringhi*. The talk would range widely, from tribal matters to theology; and once a Pathan sowar who had recently met and conversed with a missionary (to the mystification and deep misunderstanding of them both) had demanded of Ash an explanation of the Trinity: "For the Missionary-Sahib," said the sowar, "says that he too believes that there is only the One God, but that his god is three gods in one person. Now, how can that be?"

Ash hesitated for a moment, and then, picking up the lid of a biscuit-tin that someone had been using as a plate, poured a drop of water into three of the corners and said: "Look—here are three things, are there not? Each separate to itself." The assembly having looked and agreed, he tilted the tin so that the three drops ran together and formed a single and larger one: "Now tell me, which is which of the three? There is now only one, yet all three are in that one." His audience had applauded and the tin was handed round to be peered at and argued over, and Ash achieved an overnight reputation for great wisdom.

He was sorry when the camp broke up and they returned to the cantonment, but apart from the blow to his hopes of an early marriage, he thoroughly enjoyed his first cold weather in Mardan. He got on well with his fellow officers and was on excellent terms with his men—all of whom, by the mysterious grapevines of India (for neither Zarin nor Awal Shah had talked), knew something of his story and took a keen and faintly proprietary interest in his progress. Because of this his troop soon acquired the reputation of being the smartest and best disciplined in its squadron, for which Ash received more credit than he deserved, as it was his background rather than any special talent for leadership or force of character that was responsible for this state of affairs. The men knew that "Pelham-Sahib" not only spoke but thought as they did, and therefore could not be fooled by lies or tricks such as might serve occasionally with other Sahibs. They knew too that it was safe to bring him their private disputes, because he could be counted upon to make allowances for certain factors that would for ever be beyond the comprehension of those born and bred in the West. It was Ash, for example, who while out on detachment with his troop gave a judgement that was remembered and appreciated for many years on the Border . . .

His men had been told to keep a look out for a grey polo pony stolen from an officer stationed at Risalpur, and on the following night a missionary doctor, riding a grey horse, had jogged past in the moonlight and been challenged by a sentry. The horse had taken fright and bolted, and the sentry, supposing this to be the action of a thief putting spurs to his steed, fired at the doctor and fortunately missed. But the shot had gone uncomfortably close and the doctor, an elderly and choleric gentleman, had been exceedingly angry and lodged a complaint against the sentry. The man had come up for judgement the next morning and Ash, using the judiciary powers of a detachment commander, had sentenced him to fifteen days' de-tention with loss of pay: two days for firing at a Sahib, and the remainder for having missed him when he did. The sentence had been received with considerable acclamation, and the fact that the Commandant had later put it aside on the grounds that the sowar in question had acted in good faith did nothing to affect the popularity of the verdict; the men being well aware that Ash could not have enforced it and had merely taken this way of showing his disapproval of poor marksmanship. His seniors, however, had not been amused.

"We shall have to watch that young man," said his Squadron Commander. "Good stuff in him, but he lacks balance."

"Too rash, too unadvised, too sudden," quoted Lieutenant Battye. "I agree. But he'll learn."

"I suppose so; though there are times when I have my doubts about it. If only he had a cooler head and a bit more steadiness, he'd be first-class material for a Corps like this. But he's too apt to go off at half-cock. Frankly, he worries me, Wigram."

"Why? The men think the world of him. He can do anything with them."

"I know. They treat him as though he were some sort of minor deity, and I believe they'd follow him anywhere."

"Well, what's wrong with that?" demanded the Lieutenant, puzzled by his senior's tone of voice.

The Squadron Commander frowned and tugged unhappily at his moustache, looking baffled and irritated: "On the face of it, nothing. All the same, and just between the two of us, I'm not at all sure that in a crisis he wouldn't leap before he looked and lead them into something he couldn't get them out of. He's got plenty of courage, I'll grant you that. Possibly too much. But he seems to me to be guided too often by his emotions and not enough by . . . And there's another thing: in a pinch, and supposing he had to make a decision, which way would his loyalties lie? With England or India?"

"Good God," gasped the Lieutenant, genuinely shocked. "You aren't suggesting he'd turn traitor, are you?"

"No, no, of course not. Well . . . not exactly. But with a fellow like that—with that background I mean—there's no knowing how it might look to him. It's a deal simpler for you and me, Wigram, for we are always going to

200

assume that our side of any question is the right one; because it's ours. But which *is* his side? See what I mean?"

"Can't say that I do," admitted the Lieutenant uneasily. "After all, it's not as though he had any Indian blood in him, is it? Both his parents were as British as—as beer. And just because he was born out here—Well, I mean, dozens of fellows were. You were, for one."

"Yes, but I never once thought of myself as an Indian! Well he did, and that's the difference. Oh well, time will show. But I'm not at all sure that we didn't make a hell of a mistake in fetching him back to this country."

"Couldn't have stopped him," said the Lieutenant with conviction. "He'd have got back even if he'd had to walk—or swim. Seems to look upon it as his home."

"Exactly what I've been saying—but it isn't: not really. And one day he's going to find that out, and when he does, he'll realize that he doesn't belong anywhere—unless it's in Limbo, which as far as I remember is somewhere on the fringes of Hell. I tell you, Wigs, I wouldn't be in that boy's shoes for all the tea in China; and I probably wouldn't have cared a damn about it if he'd managed to get back here off his own bat, because that would have been his own affair. As it is, we—the Corps—saddled ourselves with the responsibility for it, so it's ours too, and that's what worries me. Though mark you, I like the boy."

"Oh, he's all right," said the Lieutenant easily. "A bit difficult to get to know, if you know what I mean. You get just so far and no further. But there's no denying that he's the best all-rounder on the sports side that we've had in years, and we ought to knock spots off the rest of the Brigade at next month's gymkhana."

Neither Awal Shah nor Zarin were in Ash's squadron, and he saw comparatively little of them in Mardan, though whenever possible one or other of them would accompany him out shooting. When neither of them could do so, he would either go alone or take one of his sowars—Malik Shah or Lal Mast, tribesmen from the country beyond the Panjkora, whose company he enjoyed and from whom he had learned much.

Malik Shah was an excellent *shikari* would could stalk a herd of gurral so cunningly that not one would see him until he was well within range; and in this his cousin, Lal Mast (the relationship was so remote that it was impossible to work out the degree), was almost his equal. But though Ash spent many hours in the hills with one or other of them when Zarin was otherwise occupied, he never learned to move as skilfully or as silently as they did, or mastered completely their trick of melting into the landscape and becoming so much a part of it that one would have sworn that there was no human being within miles.

"It has to be learned when young," said Malik Shah consolingly as the buck they had been stalking threw up its head and bounded away across the plain. "In my country, to move unseen, taking advantage of every stick and stone or blade of grass, may often mean the difference between living and dying; for we are all good shots and we make many enemies. But with you, Sahib, it is different; you have never had to lie as still as a stone, or slither from rock to rock as silently as a snake because an enemy waits for you on the far slope—or you yourself stalk one for his life. Had I a gun such as this one" (he had been shooting with his army-issue carbine) "I should make myself master of our valley and a score of villages among the hills. Wait here, Sahib, and I will drive the buck this way again—between that nullah and those thorn bushes yonder. That should give you a good shot."

Ash acquired a number of friends among the villages and spent many nights as the guest of headmen beyond the Border, where few if any of the inhabitants had ever seen a white man before. The men of his own troop were drawn largely from the Border tribes: Yusafzai, Orakzai and Khattak, with a sprinkling of Afridis. But the Guides also recruited a large number of Sikhs, as well as Hindus from the Punjab, Gurkhas from Nepal, Dogras, Farsiwans (Persians) and Punjabi Mussulmans; and Ash would sometimes head southward across the Indus to shoot snipe and *chinkara* in the company of Risalder Kirwan Singh of the Sikhs, or Bika Ram, one of the Hindu noncommissioned officers; cheerful men whose talk reminded him of the play-fellows of his youth—those merry companions of his careless, carefree years in the bazaars of Gulkote city. Yes, it was a good time—or would have been, if it had not been for Belinda.

For Belinda's sake Ash would willingly have spent all his free time dancing attendance upon her in Peshawar. But Major Harlowe would not permit him to visit her more than once a month, and then only to take tea; and even Mrs. Viccary, who was often a fellow-guest on these occasions, and would ask him back to dine and listen sympathetically to his woes, refused to concede that the Major's behaviour was unreasonable, advising him instead to try putting himself in the anxious father's place. Only at Christmas time (proverbially a season of Peace and Goodwill) had there been any relaxation of this rule, but by then the Peshawar Brigade were back from the Kajuri Plain and Belinda was involved in a festive whirl of parties, race-meetings and balls.

Ash rode over to deliver his Christmas presents at the Harlowes' bungalow, and to enter his name for the Boxing Day Point-to-Point, which to Belinda's delight he subsequently won by a short head. She seemed for some reason to regard the exploit as reflecting credit upon herself, and rewarded him with two waltzes and the supper-dance at the Boxing Day Ball that night. As a result, he enjoyed the evening, and in the course of it had a long talk with Mrs. Viccary, danced with several other young ladies and made himself so pleasant to their mamas that he was later to receive a flattering number of invitations to other parties and balls. But in the event, he never attended another dance in Peshawar. He saw the New Year of 1872 in with Zarin, and in very different surroundings, for they took two days' casual leave and spent them with Koda Dad.

January and February were icy months that year: snow whitened the Border Hills, the Regiment donned poshteens (sheepskin jerkins) to keep out the cold, and Ala Yar kept a log fire burning in Ash's room in the fort where the Munshi came daily to instruct the Sahib in reading and writing. By early April the poplars and willows along the Peshawar road were in bud and the orchards were once again bright with almond blossom; and as spring came and went there was still no sign of trouble on the Frontier and—outwardly at least—the tribes remained at peace with one another and the British.

In Mardan the Guides played a new game called polo, fought mock battles on the plain and instructed their new recruits as they had done for many seasons, and the routine of the Regiment became as familiar to Ash as the walls of his room or the view from the mess verandah. Day began with the scalding mug of tea, sweetened with *gur* and tasting faintly of woodsmoke, that Ala Yar brought to his bedside; and while he shaved and dressed, the old Pathan would discuss the doings of the previous day and tell him the news of Mardan and the Border and the gossip of the bazaars. After that came musketry on the ranges, breakfast in mess, stables, a session in the office, and, at intervals, durbar—the regimental parliament where complaints, requests for leave, and all matters pertaining to policy and justice came up before a *panchayat* ("five elders"). This last being the system by which Indian villages have governed themselves from time immemorial. Here the *panchayat* consisted of the Commanding Officer, the Second-in-Command, the Adjutant and the two senior Indian officers, the men attending not as spectators, but to see that justice was done, for under the *Silladar* system every man in the Regiment was to all intents and purposes a shareholder in a private company, owning his own horse and his gear, as an apprentice owns the tools of his trade. The Guides were none of them landless men, but came of yeoman stock. They enlisted for honour and the love of fighting (and for loot if loot was to be had) and when they had had their fill of military service they would retire to farm their own acres—and send their sons to join the Regiment.

When work was over, Ash spent most of his free time out shooting, and divided the remainder between polo and hawking. Once every week he would write to Belinda (who was not permitted to reply) and once every month he would ride over to Peshawar to pay the formal afternoon call allowed by Major Harlowe.

There had been a time when he had fondly imagined that it would be a simple matter to beat this restriction by attending various Peshawar functions at which Belinda was bound to be present, such as Club dances, hunts or race meetings. But this had not proved a success; she had been far too strictly chaperoned to allow him to have any speech with her, and to have to watch while she rode and talked with other men, or danced with George Garforth (still, apparently, a favoured partner), had been so depressing that it was almost a relief when his Commanding Officer, hearing of these visits, had vetoed them and placed Peshawar out of bounds to him except for the one day a month permitted by Belinda's father.

Ash became savagely jealous of George, which was an unnecessary waste of emotion. Belinda's parents might permit Mr. Garforth to call with great frequency, and have no objection to her dancing or riding with him; but they were shrewd enough to realize that she stood in no danger of falling in love with him, and in the normal course of events would probably not have invited him to their house at all, as Mr. Garforth's position in the social hierarchy of Peshawar was a humble one. But the fact that his arrival had coincided with the autumn manoeuvres and a resulting shortage of dancing partners had been greatly to his advantage, while his good looks had made an instant impression on every young lady in the station. This, coupled with his newly acquired confidence and his talk of a titled grandmother (the daughter, it was rumoured, of a liaison between a beautiful Greek countess and no less a person than George Gordon, Lord Byron), lifted him out of the ruck, and Belinda would not have been human had she failed to take pleasure in the fact that a man whom other girls admired had eyes only for herself. Besides, as she had once told Ash, George was such an excellent dancer.

She therefore continued to see a great deal of him even after the regiments returned to Peshawar, for her father not only had no objection to her being squired about by a young man whom she would never consider marrying, but hoped that it might help her to forget that ridiculous engagement. As for George's feelings, he did not give that a moment's thought; according to Major Harlowe, every young man at one time or another fell in love and had his heart broken, and the majority of them did it half-a-dozen times over. Nor was he disposed to waste any concern over Ash's feelings either: marriage, indeed—at nineteen—the boy must be half-witted. Either that or his early up-bringing had warped his thinking, for had he indeed been a native of this country he could have married at fifteen without causing any comment. But then Ashton was British and should behave as such.

Ash was trying his best to do so, but he found it hard going. The very qualities that nine years ago Awal Shah and the then Commandant of the Guides, and later Colonel Anderson, had regarded as valuable future assets were proving to have their drawbacks, and Ash often envied his fellow officers, who could make decisions with such cheerful confidence. To them so many matters were either right or wrong, necessary or unnecessary, the obvious, or the sensible, or the just course to pursue: it was as simple

205

as that. But it was not always so to Ash, who was apt to look at a question as much from the viewpoint of Lance-Naik Chaudri Ram or Sowar Malik Shah as from that of a product of the British public-school system and a cadet of the Royal Military Academy; which tended to complicate matters rather than simplify them, for to know what was going on in the mind of a sowar up for judgement, and to understand only too well the mental processes that had led the culprit to commit whatever crime he was accused of, did not always help towards giving a quick and clear-cut verdict.

Too often, Ash's sympathies lay with a man for no better reason than that he himself could and frequently did think as a native of the country. And there is a wide and fundamental difference between the reasoning of East and West—a fact that has before now confounded many a well-meaning missionary and zealous administrator, and led them to condemn whole nations as immoral and corrupt because their laws and standards, habits and customs, differ from those evolved by the Christian West.

"A Sahib, for instance," explained the Munshi, attempting to illustrate that difference to his pupils, "will always give a truthful answer in reply to a question, without considering first whether or not a lie might have served better. Now with us it is the reverse; which in the end causes less trouble. We of this country recognize that truth can often be most dangerous and therefore should on no account be scattered carelessly abroad, like husks for the chickens, but used only with great caution."

His pupils, junior officers who had been brought up by parents and tutors to consider lying a deadly sin, were shocked by this open admission on the part of an elderly teacher that in India a lie was regarded as entirely permissible (and for reasons that seemed to an Englishman both sly and cynical). They would learn better in time, as other British officers, officials and businessmen had learned before them. And as their understanding increased, their usefulness to their country and to the Empire that their country governed would increase proportionately. But the chances were that with the best will in the world they would never fully understand more than a little of the motives and processes of thought that dictated Asiatic reasoning: the tip of the iceberg only. Some few would learn to see further, and many would imagine that they could,

206

though there would be many more who were unwilling or incapable of making the effort to do so. But blood and environment, custom, culture and religion divided them, and the bridges between those gulfs were still too few; or at best, slender and insubstantial structures that were apt to break down at unexpected moments if overmuch reliance were placed upon them.

Ash would have found life easier if, like his fellow officers, he could have concentrated upon building and making use of such bridges, instead of standing with one foot on each bank, uneasily balanced between the two and unable to throw his full weight onto either. It was an invidious position and he did not relish it.

His happiest times were when he was out with Zarin, though even Zarin had changed. The old relationship that both had imagined they had recaptured, and could keep, was being altered by circumstances beyond the control of either of them. Zarin found it increasingly difficult to forget that Ash was a Sahib and an officer set in authority over him, and this inevitably raised a barrier between them: a flimsy one it is true, and Ash, for his part, was barely aware of it. But because of those years in England, his official position in the Regiment and some of the things he would say or do, Zarin was no longer quite sure what his friend's reactions would be in certain circumstances, and therefore felt it safer to walk a little warily. For Ashok was also "Pelham-Sahib," and who could be certain which one, at any given moment, would be in the saddle?—Sita's son, or the British officer?

Where Zarin was concerned, Ash would have preferred to be the former only; but he too had realized that the relationship between them could never be quite the same again. The lordly elder brother and the hero-worshipping small boy of the Gulkote days had both, inevitably, outgrown the past. And in growing up they had drawn level with each other. Their friendship remained, but it had changed its quality and now contained hidden reservations that had not been there before.

Only Koda Dad had not changed; and whenever possible Ash would cross the Border to visit him and spend long hours in his company, riding or hawking or merely squatting comfortably by his fireside while the old man discussed the present and reminisced about the past. It was only with Koda Dad that he felt completely relaxed and at ease, for though he would have hotly denied that there was any change in his relationship with Zarin, he knew that something was there: "a cloud no bigger than a man's hand."

Neither Ala Yar nor Mahdoo, or Awal Shah either, would ever treat him as anything but a Sahib, since none of them had known him in the days when he was merely Ashok. But Koda Dad had never had any contact with the "Sahib-log," and in his long life had seen very few of them: a handful at most. All that he knew of them had been learned at secondhand, so their influence on him had been minimal, and the fact that Ashok's parents had been *Angrezis,* and that he was therefore a Sahib by right of blood, in no way altered Koda Dad's feelings towards him. The boy was the same boy, and no child could be held responsible for his parentage. To Koda Dad, Ash would always be Ashok and not Pelham-Sahib.

Regimental routine changed with the coming of the hot weather; officers and men now rose before dawn in order to make use of the coolest hours of the day, and during the fierce heat of the morning and early afternoon they remained indoors, emerging again as the sun began to slide once more towards the horizon. Ash no longer rode over to Peshawar, for Mrs. Harlowe and her daughter had retreated to the cool of the hills, and he could only keep in touch with Belinda by letter (his letters, not hers). Once, as a great concession, Belinda had been allowed to reply, but the stilted little note, obviously written under Mrs. Harlowe's eye, told him nothing except that Belinda appeared to be having an exceedingly gay time in Murree, which was not the sort of news he really wished to hear. She had mentioned no names, but he learned by chance from an officer in Razmak that the firm of Brown & MacDonald, who employed George Garforth, had a branch in Murree, and that George, having suffered an attack of heat-stroke in Peshawar, had been transferred there for the summer.

The thought of his rival picnicking in the pine-woods with Belinda and partnering her to dances was intolerable. But there was nothing he could do about it, for when he applied for permission to take hot-weather leave in Murree, the Adjutant had brusquely informed him that if he wished to go on leave he could go and shoot in Kashmir

—and via Abbottabad, not Murree—which would do him a deal more good than poodle-faking at tea-parties.

Zarin had been equally unsympathetic. In his opinion, to go running like a tame puppy-dog, begging for scraps, after a woman who would neither marry or bed with one, was both undignified and a waste of time that might be put to better use. He advised Ash to abandon any thought of marriage for at least five years, and suggested instead a visit to one of the better-known houses of ill-fame in Peshawar or Rawalpindi.

Ash was strongly tempted to accept, and it would probably have done him a great deal of good, for the life of an unmarried subaltern in the Indian Army was a monastic one. The majority of his fellow-officers, similarly placed, kept their sexual appetites within bounds by taking violent exercise, while the remainder risked contracting unpleasant diseases and being robbed of their valuables by paying surreptitious visits to brothels in the bazaar, or indulging in less orthodox affairs with local youths after the fashion of the Frontier tribesmen, who have never seen anything wrong in such behaviour. Ash, however, had no leanings towards homosexuality, and being enamoured of Belinda he could not bring himself to purchase the favour of harlots—even those of such notable charmers as Masumah, the wittiest, prettiest *kasbi* in Peshawar. He went fishing in the Kangan Valley instead.

By September the nights were cooler, even though the days were still intolerably hot. But by the middle of October there was a freshness in the air, and once again duck and teal appeared on the *jheels* and the quieter reaches of the rivers, and long lines of geese flew high overhead, making for their winter feeding-grounds in central and southern India. Zarin was promoted to Jemadar, and Belinda and her mother arrived back in Peshawar.

Ash rode over to take tea with the Harlowes. He had not seen Belinda since the spring, nearly six months ago—though it seemed to him more like six years, and might almost have been so, for she had altered a great deal. She was still as pretty as ever, but she no longer looked like a gay, heedless school-girl who had only recently escaped from her lesson-books and was revelling in newly acquired freedom and her first heady taste of life. She had acquired a good deal of assurance and was suddenly very much a young lady. And although she was just as gay, it seemed to Ash that her gaiety was no longer spontaneous, and that her laugh and the pretty airs and graces, that had once been wholly charming and unself-conscious, now held a trace of artificiality.

The change in her disturbed him and he tried without success to convince himself that he had imagined it, or that after so long a parting Belinda felt shy and possibly a little awkward at seeing him again, and that once this had worn off she would be her own sweet, familiar self again.

The only gleam of consolation in that dismal afternoon was the fact that George Garforth, who had also been invited, had received even less attention from Belinda than he himself had done. On the other hand, George was obviously very much at home in Mrs. Harlowe's drawing-room, and on excellent terms with her (she had addressed him on several occasions as her "dear boy") while polite-ness had compelled Belinda to devote most of her at-tention to entertaining a stout and elderly civilian who rejoiced in the name of Podmore-Smyth and was a friend of her father's.

It would be interesting to know what course Ash's life might have taken if he had never met Belinda, or having met her, had avoided provoking her into flirting with George Garforth. Only one of the three was to avoid suf-fering from the fact that the threads of their separate lives had become entangled, and now both George and Belinda were to play a part—though admittedly a very small one—in setting in train something that was to make all the difference to Ash's future, since both were responsi-ble for the state of mind in which he had returned from Peshawar, and it was the thought of them that had later driven him out to walk in the moonlight.

He had gone to bed early, and when at last he fell asleep it was only to dream the same dream that had haunted his sleep during his first week in Mardan. Once again he found himself riding for his life—and Belinda's —across a stony plain between low, barren hills, while behind him the thud of pursuing hoof-beats grew louder and nearer until he awoke to find that the sound was no more than the hammering of his own heart . . .

The night was fresh and cool, but his body was wet with sweat, and he threw off his blanket and lay still, waiting for his racing heart-beats to slow down to their proper pace, and still subconsciously listening for sounds of pursuit. Beyond the open window the fort lay bathed in moonlight, but even the pariah dogs and jackals were silent, and except for the sentries the whole cantonment seemed asleep. Ash got up and went out onto the verandah and presently, seized by a sudden spasm of restlessness, he returned to don a dressing gown and a pair of *chupplis* —the heavy leather sandals that are the common footwear of the Border—and went out to walk off his disquiet in the night air. The sentry recognized him and let him pass with a murmured word in place of the conventional challenge, and he turned towards the parade ground and the open country that stretched away beyond it to meet the hills, his shadow dark before him on the dusty road.

There were a number of piquets encircling Mardan to give warning in case of an attack, but knowing the precise location of each one, Ash found little difficulty in avoiding them, and soon he had left the cantonment behind him and was striding out towards the hills. The plain was seamed with gullies and dotted with camelthorn, boulders and sudden outcrops of rock, and the iron studs on the soles of his *chupplis* clicked on the stony ground and made a sound that was magnified out of all proportion by the silence. The noise disturbed his train of thought and became an active irritation, but eventually he came on a goat track where the dust lay inches deep, and after that he moved without sound.

The track wandered out across the plain in the aimless manner of goat tracks, and he kept to it for the best part of a mile, before turning aside to sit above it on the crest of a small hillock where a flat-topped rock, shaded by pampas grass and a pile of boulders, offered an inviting seat. The hillock was barely more than a mound, but seated on the rock with his back against a boulder, Ash looked out across the moon-washed levels and had the illusion that he was sitting high above the plain—as high and secluded as in the Queen's balcony on the Peacock Tower.

There had been a light fall of rain on the previous day, and in the clean, cold air even the peaks of the far mountains seemed very near: a day's march at most—or an hour's. Looking at them, Ash stopped thinking of Belinda and George and thought instead of other things: of

211

another moonlight night, long ago, when he had made his way across just such a plain as this one towards a grove of *chenar* trees by the Gulkote road. He wondered what had become of Hira Lal. He would like to meet Hira Lal again, and repay a part of the debt he owed him for the horse and the money. One of these days he must take leave and . . . His thoughts came suddenly back from the past and his eyes narrowed and became intent.

Something was moving out on the plain and it could not be cattle, for there was no village near enough. Presumably, some kind of deer; *chinkara* perhaps? It was difficult to tell, for moonlight played tricks with one's eyesight. But as they were moving towards him and there was no wind to carry his scent to them, he would know soon enough. He had only to remain still and they would pass very close, for his clothing was the same colour as the rock, and sitting motionless in the shadows he would be almost invisible even to the keen eyes of a wild creature.

His interest was at first no more than idle. But all at once it ceased to be so, for the moonlight glinted on something that was not horns, but metal. He had been watching men, not wild game: armed men who carried muskets.

As they came nearer Ash could see that there were only three of them, and the sudden tension of his nerves relaxed. He had imagined for a moment that they might be a party of raiders from across the Border, swooping down to attack some sleeping village and carry off cattle and women. But three men could not do much harm and possibly they were only *Powindahs*—wandering, gipsy-like folk who live in tents and are always on the move. He did not think this very likely, for now that the days were pleasantly cool again, few men would choose to travel on foot by night. But whoever they were he preferred not to meet them, as their reasons for being abroad at such an hour were almost certainly discreditable, and cattle-thieves and outlaws were apt to shoot first and ask questions afterwards. He therefore stayed very still and was grateful for the lengthening shadows, and for the fact that the moon was behind him and shining straight into the eyes of the advancing men.

Secure in the knowledge that if he did not move they were unlikely to see him, he was able to relax and watch them approach with curiosity and a touch of impatience. He was beginning to feel chilly and he wished that the strangers would quicken their pace, for until they had passed and were well out of range, he himself would not be able to leave. Ash yawned—and a split second later was tense and listening.

The sound he had heard was a very small one, but it had not been made by the men who were moving towards him. It had come from much nearer and from somewhere behind him: at a guess, from not more than twenty or thirty yards away—though in that windless silence any sound would carry a considerable distance. This one had been no more than the rattle of a displaced pebble; but except for the mound on which he sat the plain for several hundred yards in every direction was as flat as a board, and no pebble could have dislodged itself, or struck against another with that degree of force, without assistance. He held his breath to listen and heard another sound that was as easy to recognize as the first had been: the click of an iron-studded *chuppli* striking against a stone. There was at least one other man approaching the mound, but from a different direction.

Several separate possibilities flashed through Ash's mind, all of them unpleasant. Blood-feuds bedevilled the Border country, and the man or men behind him might be laying a trap for those ahead. Or was he himself the quarry and had he perhaps been seen and followed by someone who had cause to hate the Guides? It had been a mistake to come out unarmed. But it was too late to regret that now, for once again metal clicked on stone and a pebble rattled, and Ash turned his head cautiously in the direction of the sound and waited with every nerve and muscle in his body tensed and ready.

There was a rustle close by as someone brushed against a thorn bush below the mound, and a moment later a lone man hurried past and went on without turning. He had gone too quickly for Ash to gain more than a fleeting impression of a tall figure, muffled in a coarse woollen blanket and further protected from the night air by a length of cloth wound about his head and neck. Once past he was only a hurrying shape in the moonlight, and if he were armed it was certainly not with a musket, though the blanket probably concealed a Pathan knife. It was also

213

clear that he had neither seen Ash nor suspected his presence. Yet there had been an indefinable suggestion of furtiveness about him—in the hunch of his shoulders and the way his head turned sharply from left to right, giving an impression of nervous haste and the fear of being followed.

The four men met some fifty yards from the mound and stood talking together for several minutes. Presently they squatted down on their hunkers to continue the conversation in more comfort, and Ash saw the flash of flint on tinder as a hookah was lit and passed round. They were too far away for him to be able to catch more than a faint murmur of voices and an occasional laugh, yet he knew that if he attempted to leave they would see him, and he did not think they would take at all kindly to the idea that they had been spied upon. The very fact that they had chosen to meet at such an hour and in such a place was a clear indication that their business was not one they wished to advertise, and in the circumstances it seemed safer to stay where he was.

He had stayed there for the better part of an hour, becoming colder and crosser with every passing minute, and cursing himself for being such a fool as to indulge in nocturnal rambles. But at last the long wait was over and the four rose to their feet and went their separate ways: three of them heading back towards the hills while the fourth man returned the way he had come, passing again within a few feet of the mound. This time the moon was full on his face instead of behind him, but he had wrapped the loose end of his headcloth about his mouth and chin so that only a hawk-like nose and a pair of deep-set eyes were visible. Yet despite this, something about him struck Ash as familiar. The man was someone he knew: he was quite certain of that, though he did not know why he should be; but before he had time to think it out the man had passed him and gone.

Ash waited for a moment or two before turning to peer cautiously around the boulders and watch the tall figure hurrying away in the direction of Mardan, and only when he could see it no longer did he get to his feet, cramped and cold and with all thoughts of Belinda driven out of his head, and set out on the long walk homeward to the fort.

214

Looking back on it next morning in the brilliant light of a blue and gold autumn day, the incident lost the sinister overtones that moonlight had lent it, and appeared singularly innocuous. The four men had probably only met to discuss some urgent matter of purely tribal interest, and if they preferred to do so by night that was their affair. Ash put the whole thing out of his mind, and would probably never have thought of it again but for a chance encounter in the dusk some six days later . . .

There had been no polo on that particular evening, so he had taken a gun and gone after partridge in the scrub-land along the river, and returning shortly after sunset he met a man on the cantonment road by the cavalry lines: a sowar of his own squadron. The light was fading fast and it was only when they were almost abreast that Ash recognized him. Returning the man's salute, he walked on, and then stopped and turned, checked by a sudden memory. It was partly the man's gait—he had a trick of hitching one shoulder very slightly to match his stride. But there was something else: an old scar that divided his right eyebrow into two and that Ash had seen, without realizing it, on the upper part of a face glimpsed briefly in bright moonlight.

"Dilasah Khan."

"Sahib?" The man turned and came back. He was an Afridi-Pathan, and his tribe was one of many who in theory owe allegiance to the Amir of Afghanistan, but in practice acknowledge no law save their own. Recalling this, it occurred to Ash that the men Dilasah Khan had gone out to meet were almost certainly kinsmen bringing him news from his village, and that in all probability it concerned some blood-feud with a neighbouring tribe, one or more of whose members might be serving with him in the Guides.

British territory was held to be neutral ground and no blood-feud might be carried into it. But one step beyond the Border things were different, and Dilasah's fellow tribesmen might not wish to be tracked there. In any case, he had not been breaking the law, so it was hardly fair, thought Ash, to catechize him about something that he obviously wished to keep private. As he himself had suffered from similar interference in his time, and resented it, he did not say what he had meant to; which was, per-

215

haps, a mistake, for if Dilasah had taken fright he might have changed his mind and his plans, and thereby saved, amongst other things, his own life. Though as his creed taught him that his fate was tied about his neck and could not be avoided, he would presumably have refused to believe that any action of his own, or anyone else's, could have altered it.

In the event, Ash said nothing of having seen him out on the plain by night, and spoke instead of some trivial matter concerned with the riding school, before sending the man on his way. But the incident, now that it had been recalled, refused to be dismissed from his mind, and for some unknown reason it nagged at him with the persistence of a fly that keeps settling on the face of a drowsing man. Because of this he paid more attention to Sowar Dilasah Khan than he would otherwise have done, and decided that he did not like him. The man was a good soldier and a more than adequate horseman, and there was no fault to be found with him on that level. But there was something about him that Ash could only define as "shifty." Something in his manner which was tinged with obsequiousness (a most uncharacteristic quality in a tribesman) and in the way his eyes slid away, avoiding a direct gaze.

"I don't trust that fellow Dilasah," confessed Ash, discussing the troop with his Squadron Commander. "I've seen one or two horses with that sort of look in their eyes, and I wouldn't have one if it was being given away with a pound of tea."

"Dilasah? Oh, nonsense," said the Squadron Commander. "Why, what's he been up to?"

"Nothing. It's just that . . . I don't know. He gives me an uncomfortable feeling between my shoulder blades, that's all. I saw him out on the plain one night—"

Ash described the incident and the Squadron Commander laughed and dismissed it with a shrug of the shoulders and an interpretation that was similar to Ash's original one: "Ten to one there's been a row between his lot and the next-door village, and they were merely warning him to watch out for himself next time he goes on leave, because his cousin Habib has just shot their headman's son, Ali, and Ali's relations will be gunning for all or any of Habib's. Bet you it's that."

"I thought so too at first, but it can't have been, be-

216

cause he went out to meet them. That means that it was all arranged beforehand. The meeting, I mean."

"Well, why not? They'd probably sent a message to say that they had news for him. If it was about a killing, they wouldn't have risked saying more than that."

"I expect you're right. All the same, I've a feeling we ought to watch that fellow."

"You do that," agreed the Squadron Commander cordially. His tone conveyed a distinct suggestion of "run away and play" and Ash flushed and dropped the subject. But he did not forget it and he was sufficiently interested to ask Ala Yar to make a few inquiries into the history and background of Sowar Dilasah Khan.

"There are five others of his clan in the *rissala* (cavalry)," reported Ala Yar. "All proud, fierce men—Afridis who have joined the Guides for *izzat* (honour) and because they love a fight. And also perhaps because their clan is rent by many blood-feuds, and here they cannot be ambushed and shot down without warning. There are two of them in your own troop: Malik Shah and Lal Mast."

"I know that. And they are both good men—the best. I have been out on *shikar* with Malik half a dozen times, and as for Lal Mast—"

Ala Yar held up a hand: "Hear me out. I had not finished. Their clan is a small one and so they are all in some way tied by blood—third, fourth and it may be fifteenth cousins a dozen times removed. Yet it is a fact that not one of them has any liking for their kinsman, Dilasah. They say he is a cheat and sly; and like yourself, they distrust him."

"Why? In what way?"

"Oh, for a dozen small things done in childhood. You know how it is with children: one of their number lies or cheats or runs tale-bearing to those in authority, and for this his playmates hold him in dislike. Even when they grow up and became men, the dislike remains. The others were not pleased when he joined the Guides, and they say that they do not understand why he did so, for it was unlike him. But he came with a good horse and rode it well, and he is also a fine marksman; he won his place fairly in competition with others, and as his officers speak well of him his kinsmen can have no complaint and from pride in their clan they will stand by him. Nevertheless they still dislike him, for he has at one time or another done

217

each of them an ill turn—boy's tricks only: but men, as I have said, do not forget. Ask Malik or Lal Mast, next time you go out shooting with them."

Ash had done so. But he had learned no more than Ala Yar had told him.

"Dilasah? He is a serpent," said Malik Shah. "His blood runs slow and his tongue drips poison. When we were boys—" He told a long tale of a childhood escapade that had ended in punishment and tears for all save Dilasah, who had instigated the whole affair and then betrayed his playfellows to authority and avoided the consequences by some spirited lying. It was plain that the episode still rankled, yet Malik admitted that a year in the Regiment had improved Dilasah out of all knowledge: "He has made a good soldier, and when we of the Guides are again called upon to fight battles, he may even bring credit upon us, and on his clan also. Still, it is strange that he should have wished to serve under the Sirkar and submit himself to discipline, for I would have said that he was the last man to choose this way of life. Yet—who knows? —he may have done some killing that has made life in our hills too dangerous for him, and so has sought safety here for a while. He would not be the only one to do so!"

Malik laughed, and Ash, who knew that last was true enough, did not pursue the subject. But less than a week later it became all too clear why Dilasah Khan had enlisted in the Guides. And equally clear that his kinsmen's distrust and Ash's suspicions had been well founded.

12

There had been no moon on the night that Dilasah disappeared from Mardan, taking with him his own and one other Government-issue cavalry carbine. Nor had anyone seen him go, for he, like Malik, could move like a shadow when he chose.

He had been on sentry duty in the last watch before dawn, one of two men who were patrolling the lines, and the fact that he had not knifed his fellow sentry was probably due to a dislike of being involved in further blood-feuds rather than any respect for human life. But the man had suffered a bad case of concussion and it was some time before he could tell his story. He had naturally not expected any attack from such a quarter and could not remember being hit; but it was obvious that Dilasah had felled him with the butt of his carbine before gagging and binding him with his own turban, and dragging him away into the shadows out of earshot of the sleeping camp. The aggressor had them made off into the darkness, and must have had at least an hour's start before the groans of the bound man at last aroused someone to investigate, for although patrols on horseback had galloped out to scour the countryside and track him down, they failed to find him.

By nightfall there was still no sign of him, and the following morning the Commandant demanded to know how many other members of his clan were serving with the Regiment. These were summoned to his office and ordered to remove every piece of uniform or equipment that was the property of the Corps, and they had obeyed in silence, each in turn adding to the pile of the matting-covered floor before returning to his place to stand rigidly at attention.

"Now go," said the Commandant. "And do not let me see your faces again until you have brought back both rifles."

The men had gone without a word, and no one had questioned the Commanding Officer's action except Ash, to whom it had come as the culmination of a particularly harrowing week.

"But he can't do that," stormed Ash to his Squadron Commander, white-lipped with anger. "What's it got to do with them? It wasn't *their* fault. Why—why they don't even like the man! They never have."

"They belong to the same clan," explained the Squadron Commander patiently, "and the C.O.'s a very shrewd bird who knows what he's doing. He wants those carbines back because we can't afford to have that kind of weapon being used in the passes—and because we can't afford to allow one of our fellows to get away with this kind of thing either. It might give a lot of other men ideas. No; he's done the only thing he can. It's a question of *izzat*. Dilasah has let his clan down and his fellow clans-

219

men will get those carbines back for their own sakes. You'll see. They've probably got a pretty good idea where he's heading for, and the chances are that they'll be back inside forty-eight hours with the rifles."

"What if they are?" demanded Ash. "They've had their uniforms stripped off them and they've been flung out—punished and publicly disgraced for something that had nothing whatever to do with them. If there was any justice, *I'm* the one who ought to be punished—or *you!* I knew that man was up to no good, and so did you. I warned you, and you brushed it off as though I'd brought you some footling fairy-story. But I could still have done something to prevent this, and Malik and the others couldn't. It isn't fair!"

"Oh for God's sake grow up, Pandy," snapped the Squadron Commander, losing his patience: "You're behaving like a child of two. What's got into you? You've been going round like a bear with a sore head for the last few days. Aren't you feeling well?"

"I'm perfectly well, thank you," retorted Ash angrily. "But I don't like injustice and I'm going to see the C.O. myself."

"Well, rather you than me. He's not in a particularly good mood at the moment, and after you've heard what he has to say you'll wish you'd had more sense."

But Ash was beyond the reach of reason, not only on account of Dilasah Khan's defection and the dismissal of his fellow clansmen. That had merely been the last, and by no means worst incident, in a week that he was to look back on as the blackest period of his life. Ever afterwards, nothing would ever seem so bad again, because he himself was never again to be the same kind of person that he had been until then . . .

It had begun with the arrival of a letter by the morning post, and he had not even recognized the writing on the envelope, but had opened it casually in the mess, expecting it to contain only another invitation to a dinner-party or a dance. Mrs. Harlowe's well-meant letter, informing him that her daughter was engaged to be married, had been as unexpected as the first shock of an earthquake.

Belinda was so very, *very* happy, wrote Mrs. Harlowe, and she did *so* hope that he would do nothing to

220

spoil that happiness, but be sensible about it and not en-
act them any tragedies, for it must have become plain
to him by now that he and Belinda were *quite* unsuited
to each other, and in any case he was much too young to
be thinking of marrying and settling down. Ambrose was
in every way a far more suitable husband for Belinda,
and she felt sure that Ashton would be unselfish enough
to rejoice in her daughter's great happiness and wish her
the best of good fortune in the future. Belinda had asked
her to break the news to him, as owing to all the foolish
talk there had been between them, the dear child felt that
he might prefer it that way . . .

Ash sat staring at the letter for so long that eventually one of his friends had inquired if he were feeling all
right, and had had to repeat the question three times
before receiving an answer.

"Yes—I mean, no. It's nothing," said Ash confusedly.

"Bad news?" asked Wigram Battye sympathetically.

"No. Only a headache—touch of the sun, I expect.
Think I'll go and lie down," said Ash. And added unexpectedly: "I don't believe it!"

"Believe what? I say, old fellow, hadn't you better see
the M.O.? You're looking like death," observed Wigram
candidly. "If it is sun-stroke—"

"Oh, don't be an ass," said Ash unkindly, and went
back to his room to sit on the edge of his bed and re-
read Mrs. Harlowe's letter.

He read it half-a-dozen times, and each time it
seemed to be less believable. If Belinda had really been
falling in love with someone else, surely he would have
sensed it when he last saw her—which was barely three
weeks ago? But her last words to him had given no indication of any drastic change of heart, and he did not
believe that after all that there had been between them,
she would have asked her mother to write such a letter. If
it were true, she would have written to him herself; she
had always been honest with him. *Ambrose*—Who the
hell was Ambrose? It was all a plot on the part of her
parents. A plot to separate them. Either that, or they
were forcing Belinda into a distasteful marriage against
her will.

Mrs. Harlowe's letter had arrived on a Friday, and

there were still eight days to go before Ash was officially allowed to see Belinda again. But on the following day he defied orders and rode over to Peshawar.

Once again, as on the occasion of his first visit, the Harlowes' bungalow was empty and a servant informed him that the Sahib and the memsahibs were out to lunch and not expected back until mid-afternoon. Ash retired, as he had done before, to the Club; and here too, history repeated itself, for though the Club was far from empty and the lawns and terraces were packed with a gay and chattering Saturday morning crowd, the first person to accost him was George Garforth.

"Ash!" cried George Garforth grabbing at him as he passed. "Mus' talk to you. Don't go. Have a drink—"

Ash had no desire at all to talk to George—or to anyone else, apart from Belinda. But two things prevented him from disengaging himself and walking away. The first, that George was tipsy, and the second that here was someone who would certainly know if there was any truth in this tale of an engagement. Though the very fact that George was drunk—and at this hour of the morning—made his heart shrink with foreboding.

"Jus' the fellow I wanted to shee," babbled George hoarsely. "Wan' t' talk to you, Ash. Only one I can talk to. But not here . . . too many people here . . . too many b-bloody stuck-up snobs sitting around and listening. Le's go t' my bungalow for *t-tiffin*."

In the circumstances it seemed a sensible suggestion, for Ash could think of nothing worse than having to listen to what George had to say (if, as seemed only too likely, it concerned Belinda) in the presence of half the members of the Peshawar Club. In any case, the sooner Mr. Garforth removed himself from such a public spot the better, for his behaviour was obviously attracting a considerable amount of attention. Far too many people were staring at him in patent disapproval and whispering to their neighbours, and it was plainly only a question of time before the Secretary or some irate member requested him to leave—a disgrace that to someone of George's over-sensitive temperament would cause a degree of suffering and humiliation out of all proportion to the offence. Ash sent for a tonga and took the inebriated Mr. Garforth back to his bungalow, which turned out to be a large, square building, part office, that was owned by his firm.

George's portion of it was a modest one, consisting of a small back-bedroom with an adjoining bathroom and one end of a verandah (screened off from the remainder by a *chik**) that did duty as a combined sitting-room and dining-room. The whole bore a depressing resemblance to a dâk-bungalow, but the servant who appeared at the sound of the tonga bell was able to produce a three-course lunch, accompanied by two bottles of Brown & MacDonald's light ale, so that despite his forebodings Ash contrived to make a tolerable meal. His host, on the other hand, rejected every dish with expressions of loathing, and sat slumped in his chair muttering belligerently and scowling at the *khidmatgar*. It was only when the table was eventually cleared and the servant went away that he abandoned this truculence in a startling manner.

The verandah *chik* had no sooner dropped into place behind the departing *khidmatgar* than George leant forward, and laying his folded arms on the table, dropped his head onto them and burst into tears.

Ash retired precipitately to the dusty compound where a solitary neem tree provided an oasis of shade in the mid-day glare. He would have liked to walk back to the Club, but he could not bring himself to abandon George at this particular juncture, even though he was by now fairly certain that the cause of both drunkenness and grief must be Belinda's engagement, and he was no longer sure that he wanted to hear what George had to say on the subject. He sat down on a root of the neem tree, feeling angry with himself and angrier with George, and waited. The harsh, gulping sobs were not a pleasant sound to listen to, but they stopped at last and he heard George blow his nose and stumble away to the bedroom where, judging from the noise of splashing, he appeared to be emptying the contents of the water *chatti* over his head.

Ash rose and came back to his chair on the verandah, and presently George reappeared wearing a towel around his shoulders and with his hair dripping water. He poured himself out a cup of black coffee from the pot that the *khidmatgar* had left on a tray, and subsided heavily into a sagging cane chair where he sat sipping the hot liquid and looking utterly demoralized. There seemed to be nothing left of the talkative and bumptious young man

---

*sun-blind made of split cane

who for over a year had been such a success at tea-parties and Club dances. Even his good looks had vanished, for his pallid face was puffy and unshaven and his eyes red with weeping, while his sodden hair had lost its Byronic curls and straggled limply down his neck and forehead.

Confronted by this spectacle Ash's irritation became diluted with sympathy, and resigning himself to the role of confidant and comforter, he got up and helped himself to coffee and said with an effort: "You'd better tell me about it. I suppose it's this engagement."

"What engagement?" asked George tonelessly.

Ash's heart gave a leap that set his pulses racing, and the coffee slopped all over the floor. So he had been right after all. Mrs. Harlowe had lied to him, and it wasn't true.

"Belinda's of course. I thought that was why—I mean . . ." He was incoherent with relief. "I'd heard she was engaged to be married."

"Oh that," said George, dismissing it as something of no account.

"Then it isn't true? Her mother said—"

"It wasn't really her," gulped George. "She—Mrs. Harlowe—tried to be nice about it, I think. She really did like me, you know. But Belinda . . . I—I wouldn't have believed that *anyone* . . . no, that isn't true; I suppose it was just because I did believe it that I tried to keep it quiet. I should have known that someone would find out one day."

"Find out what? What the blazes are you mumbling about, George? Is she engaged or isn't she?"

"Who? Oh, Belinda. Yes. They got engaged after the Bachelors' Ball, I believe. Look, Ash, do you mind if I talk to you about something? You see, I don't know what to do. Whether to stick it out, or give in my notice and quit, or . . . I can't stay on here. I won't. I'd—I'd rather shoot myself. She'll tell everyone—she's started already. Didn't you see the way they were all staring at me and whispering at the Club this morning? You must have noticed. And it will get worse. Much worse. I don't think I can—"

But Ash was not listening. He had put down his cup with a hand that was noticeably unsteady and now he sat down with some suddenness. He did not want to hear any-

224

thing more or to talk to anyone. Not to George, anyway. And yet . . .

He said abruptly: "But that can't be true. The Bachelors' Ball was right at the beginning of the month. That's nearly six weeks ago, and I've seen her since then. I had tea with her, and if it was true she would have told me then. Or her mother would. Or someone."

"They didn't want to announce it too soon. They kept it quiet until his new appointment came through—I suppose it sounded grander then. Marrying a Resident, you know."

"A *Resident?* But—" Ash broke off and scowled at George, who must be even drunker than he had thought, because a Residency was a senior appointment: a "plum job" of the Indian Civil Service. Only men who had served that department for many years were sent to represent their Government in some independent native state with the title of "Resident."

"Bholapore—one of those states somewhere down south," said George indifferently. "It was in the papers last week."

"Bholapore?" repeated Ash stupidly. "But—Oh, you must have made a mistake. You're drunk. That's what it is. How would Belinda ever meet anyone like that, let alone get engaged to him?"

"Well, she has," said George flatly and as though it did not matter very much. "Friend of her father's. You must have noticed him: stout party with a red face and grey whiskers. He was having tea with them the last time you were here, and Belinda was all over him."

"*Podmore-Smyth!*" gasped Ash, appalled.

"That's the fellow. Pompous old bore, but I'm told he's no end of a catch. Sure to be knighted before long and end up as a Lieutenant-Governor, and all that. His wife only died last year, and his daughters are older than Belinda, but she doesn't seem to mind that. He's got a lot of money of course—his father was one of those Calcutta Nabobs, so he's simply rolling in it. And I suppose she likes the idea of being Lady Podmore-Smyth. Or Her Excellency the Governess. Or possibly even Baroness Podmore of Poop one day." George gave a hollow crack of laughter and helped himself to more coffee.

"I don't believe it," said Ash violently. "You're making it up. She wouldn't do a thing like that. Not Belinda. You don't know her like I do. She's sweet and honest and—"

"She's honest, all right," agreed George bitterly. His lip quivered and once again his eyes filled with tears.

Ash disregarded them: "If she's engaged to him it's because she's been forced into it. Her parents are behind this—that dried-up old stick of a father and her idiotic, gossiping mother. Well, if they think I'm going to let them ruin Belinda's life and mine, they're wrong."

"You're the one who's wrong," said George. "Her parents didn't like it above half, but she coaxed them round. She's a taking little thing, as you should know by now. But then you don't really know her at all. Neither did I. I thought I did, and I would never have believed . . . Oh God, what am I going to do?"

The tears brimmed over and trickled down his cheeks, but he made no attempt to brush them away or any effort to control them. He merely sat there slumped in his chair and staring into vacancy, with his jaw slack and his fingers clenching and unclenching on the coffee cup. He was an embarrassing sight and his unashamed misery exasperated Ash. What right had George to behave like this? It was not as though Belinda had even been engaged to him, or ever would have been. Ash told him so with considerable sharpness, and found a perverse comfort in doing so. But though he had not minced his words they drew no answering spark of anger from George.

"It's not that," said George dully. "You don't understand. Of course I knew she'd never marry me; I'm not a fool. I was too young and I hadn't any prospects. I hadn't . . . *anything!* I suppose that's why I invented all that stuff. To make myself more interesting . . . But I never thought—I didn't dream that she'd take it like that if she found out."

"Found out *what?*" demanded Ash, justifiably bewildered. "For God's sake, George, pull yourself together and stop babbling! What is all this about? What did she find out?"

"About me. You see I—I've told a lot of lies about myself. And that woman Mrs. Gidney, who Belinda's mother is so thick with, has a friend in Rangoon who knows someone who—Well, it was like this . . ."

It was a simple and rather sordid little story, and no

one came out of it very well. Mrs. Gidney, writing to a dear friend in Rangoon, had happened to mention George's name and comment on his romantic ancestry, and by an unfortunate coincidence the friend was acquainted with a certain Mr. Frisby in the teak trade. And that was how it had all come out . . .

George's grandmother, far from being a Greek countess, had been an Indian woman of humble parentage whose union with his grandfather—a colour-sergeant in a British regiment stationed in Agra—had been of a strictly temporary nature, but had resulted in the birth of a daughter who had eventually been placed in a home for the orphaned or abandoned children of mixed parentage. At the age of fifteen the child had been found employment as a nursemaid in an army family, and subsequently married a young corporal in her master's regiment, one Alfred Garforth. Their son George, who had been born in Bareilly, was the only one in the family to survive the Mutiny of 1857, his parents, his baby brother and three small sisters having all been murdered in the space of fifteen frenzied minutes.

George had been spending the day with the family of a friendly storekeeper who had escaped the massacre, and during the few years that remained before the regiment returned to England, the same kindly couple had given him a home, for as his father too had been an orphan, there were no relations to take care of the boy. It was during this period that little George learned from his playmates that a "half-caste" was an object of scorn. There were several such among the barrack children, and they and he were teased and despised by those whose parents and grandparents were white, and looked down upon with almost equal scorn by Indian children with parents and grandparents who were brown.

"Yer grandma was a sweeper-woman!" or "Yah, yah, yer a bleedin' blacky-white," were familiar taunts in scuffles among the barrack children, while the vocabulary of the bazaar children could be even more wounding. Yet George, by the irony of fate, was fairer than many of his white tormentors, and had he possessed a tougher character, or been less good-looking, he might have lived down the unknown grandmother. But he was not only a very pretty little boy, but a painfully timid one, a combination that endeared him to adults but made his own generation yearn to kick him—which they did with enthusiasm and on every possible occasion.

George developed a bad stammer and burning hatred of his schoolmates and the barracks and anything and everything to do with the army, and when the regiment sailed for England, taking him with them, it was only the kindness of the storekeeper and his wife, Fred and Annie Mullens, that saved him from being sent to an army orphanage, for they had arranged for him to be educated at their expense at a small boarding school near Bristol that catered exclusively for children whose parents were overseas. A large number of these children spent both holidays and term time at the school, and nearly all of them had been born abroad, which was George's misfortune, for they too spoke of "half-castes" with scorn, and one of their number who had the misfortune to be black-eyed and dark-complexioned was cruelly teased on this score— George, to his shame, joining in with the best of them. For with the possible exception of the Headmaster, no one at the school knew anything about him, and he was therefore able to invent a family-tree for himself.

At first this was a comparatively modest affair. But as he grew older he enlarged it, adding mythical grandparents and great-grandparents and a variety of picturesque ancestors. And because he was always afraid that one day his eyes would become darker and his skin betray him by turning brown (as his baby curls, once blond, had done) he gave himself an Irish father—the Irish being prone to black hair—and added a Greek grandmother for good measure. Later he was to discover that a majority of waiters and small shopkeepers in Soho were immigrants from Greece, and as by then he could hardly change this mythical woman's nationality, he decided to make her a countess.

Towards the end of his school-days his benefactor, Mr. Mullens, who had a friend in Brown & MacDonalds', arranged for his protégé to enter that firm as a clerk, imagining that by doing so he had done young George an excellent turn and started him on what might one day prove to be a profitable career in the wine business. Unfortunately, the news had been anything but welcome to George, who left to himself would never have returned to India, but he lacked both the courage and the means to refuse such an offer. When he had served his apprenticeship and was eventually ordered to Peshawar, the only bright spot on his horizon was the fact that close on four hundred miles separated Peshawar from Bareilly, and that he would not, in any case, be expected to visit Mr. and Mrs. Mullens; for barely a month before his departure he had heard that Mr. Mullens had died of enteric and his broken-hearted widow had sold the store and sailed for Rangoon, where her son-in-law was doing well in the teak trade.

Mr. Mullens, charitable to the last, had left George fifty pounds and a gold watch, and George spent the money on clothes and told his landlady that the watch had been his grandfather's. His Irish grandfather—the O'Garforth of Castle Garforth . . .

"I didn't think they would ever find out," confessed George miserably. "But Mrs. Gidney has a friend whose husband is in the teak trade and knows old man Mullens's son-in-law, and it seems that the friend met Mrs. Mullens one day and they began talking about the Mutiny and all that, and Mrs. Mullens told her about me and how her husband paid for my schooling and got me this job, and how well I was doing, and—Well, just about *everything*. She even had a photograph of me. I'd forgotten that. I sent it to them my last term at school. I used to write to them, you know. And then this friend wrote to Mrs. Gidney . . ."

Mrs. Gidney had apparently conceived it her duty to "warn" her dear friend Mrs. Harlowe, and Mrs. Harlowe, greatly upset by George's duplicity, had somewhat naturally told her daughter. But where the two older ladies had merely been shocked, Belinda had been outraged, not so much because she had been lied to, but because she considered that she had been made to look foolish. After all it was she and her mother who had, in effect, sponsored George and helped to launch him on Peshawar society, because although his looks alone would have attracted a certain amount of attention, they would never have obtained for him the social recognition that Mrs. Harlowe's partiality and her daughter's friendship for him had bestowed on him from the start. Besides, Belinda had more than half believed that romantic tale of a liaison between his mythical great-grandmother and Lord Byron (though to give George his due, this was one rumour for which he was not responsible), but though she had found nothing

229

shocking in an illegitimate grandmama born of such exalted parents—in fact, quite the reverse—the bastard
daughter of a colour-sergeant and a low-caste Hindu
woman was a very different affair, and sordid in the
extreme. Why, George's mother was nothing more than
a half-caste—an illegitimate Eurasian who had married
a corporal in a line regiment—and George himself had
more than a "touch of the tar-brush," for he was one
quarter Indian; and low-caste Indian at that. This—*this*
was the man that she, Belinda, had helped to foist onto
Peshawar society and had danced and dined with and
bestowed her smiles on. Now all the other girls were going to laugh at her, and she would never live it down.
Never."

"She was so *angry*," whispered George. "She said
such terrible things—that all half-castes told lies and she
never wanted to see me again, and . . . and if I ever spoke
to her again she'd c-cut me d-dead. I didn't know anyone
could be so cruel. She didn't even look p-pretty any more
. . . she looked ugly. And her voice . . . Her mother k-kept
saying 'You don't mean that, dear. You can't mean that.'
But she did. And now she's started t-telling people. I know
she has, because they look at me as though I was s-some
sort of insect and . . . What am I going to do, Ash? I'd k-
kill myself if I could, but I haven't got the g-guts to do it.
Not even when I'm drunk. But I can't stay here any longer. I can't! D-do you think that if I made a c-clean breast
of it to my boss he'd send me s-somewhere else? If I
begged him to?"

Ash did not answer. He was feeling dazed and sick,
and in spite of everything, disbelieving. He would not
and could not believe it of Belinda. Of George, yes. The
story explained a great deal about George: his appalling
sensitiveness and lack of confidence; that abrupt transformation from tongue-tied timidity to brashness and truculence when Belinda set out to charm him and Mrs. Harlowe treated him with consideration and kindness, and he
began to believe in himself at last; and most of all, his
complete moral and physical collapse now that his make-
believe world had been exposed as a sham. But Belinda
could never have behaved in the manner he described.
George was inventing again and allowing his guilty conscience to put into her mouth sentiments that he had
already applied to himself. Because these were the sort of

230

things he was afraid she might say, he was punishing himself by pretending she had actually said them—and quite possibly, too, that she was engaged to Mr. Podmore-Smyth, which was something else that he, Ash, was not prepared to believe until he heard it from her own mouth. Then if her parents were really putting pressure on her to force her into marrying some dirty old man in his dotage, he would expose them for what they were.

He stood up and jerked the *chik* aside, and shouted for the servant to call him a tonga.

"You aren't going?" gasped George, in a panic. "Don't go yet. Please don't go! If you leave me I'll—I'll only get drunk again, and it's worse when I'm drunk. Besides, b-brandy only makes me feel braver. I might g-go out and d-do something stupid. Like going to the Club this morning and m-making a fool of myself."

"Then don't get drunk," snapped Ash, exasperated. "And for God's sake, George, stop feeling so damn' sorry for yourself. You don't have to go to pieces just because you've been found out telling a pack of silly taradiddles about your grandmother. Who the hell cares what your grandmother was or wasn't? You are still you, aren't you? It's sheer poppycock to pretend that people only liked you because they thought your grandmother was a Greek or an Italian or whatever it was. And if you imagine for one minute that Belinda or anyone else is going to spread around any stories about her, you must be mad. You know what it is, George?—you've exaggerated the whole thing out of all proportion, and been so busy being sorry for yourself that you haven't even stopped for a minute to think about it sensibly."

"You didn't hear what Belinda s-said to me," gulped George. "If you'd heard her——"

"I daresay she was damned angry with you for telling her a lot of fatuous lies, and only wanted to punish you for that. Try and use your head for half a second and stop behaving like a hysterical rabbit. If Belinda is what I believe her to be she'll keep quiet about it for your sake, and if she's what you like to think she is, she'll keep it even quieter for her own—and that goes for her mother and Mrs. Gidney too, for I don't suppose either of them will care to advertise the fact that they've been a pair of gullible old tabbies."

"I never thought of that," admitted George, cheering

231

up slightly. "Yes, I suppose . . ." His shoulders slumped again. "But then no one spoke to me at the Club this morning except Mrs. Viccary. The rest just looked at me and whispered and sniggered and—"

"Oh, stow it, George," interrupted Ash angrily. "You turn up at the Club on a Saturday morning as drunk as an owl and are surprised because people notice it. For the love of God, stop dramatizing yourself and try to keep a sense of proportion."

He reached for his hat as a clatter of hooves and the jangle of a bell announced the arrival of a tonga, and George said wistfully: "I'd hoped you'd stay on a b-bit and—and advise me. It's been awful just sitting here alone and thinking; and if I could just talk about it—"

"You've talked about it for over an hour," observed Ash tartly. "And if you really want my advice, you'll forget all about this and shut up about your great-aunts or grandmothers or whoever they were, and just go on behaving as though nothing had happened, instead of making a public exhibition of yourself and inviting comment. No one else is ever going to hear about it if only you'll keep your head and shut your mouth."

"You—you really think so?" stammered George. "Perhaps you're right. Perhaps it won't ever get out. I d-don't think I could bear it if it did. If it does . . . Ash, honestly now, w-what would you do, if you were me?"

"Shoot myself," said Ash unkindly. "Goodbye George."

He leapt down the verandah steps and was driven back to the Club where he collected his horse and rode over to the Harlowes' bungalow; and for once luck seemed to be with him; for Belinda's parents were still out, while she herself had returned and was resting. The bearer, roused from his afternoon nap, was loath to disturb her, but when Ash threatened to walk in on her himself he hurried away and tapped on her door, telling her that a Sahib had called to see her and would not go away until he had done so. But when Belinda entered the drawing-room some five minutes later it was instantly and painfully clear that she had expected to see someone entirely different. She ran gaily into the room and then stopped dead, the smile wiped from her pretty face and her eyes widening in apprehension and anger.

"*Ashton!* What are you doing here?"

Something in her voice and expression daunted Ash and he said uncertainly, stammering a little, as George too had stammered: "I—I had to see you, darling. Your m-mother wrote to me. She said you were . . . you were engaged to be married. It isn't true is it?"

Belinda did not answer the question. She said instead: "You shouldn't have come here. You know quite well you should not. Please go, Ashton. Papa will only be angry if he comes back and finds you here. Abdul should never have let you in. Now *do* go."

"Is it true?" repeated Ash, ignoring the appeal.

Belinda stamped her foot: "I asked you to go, Ashton. You've no right to come forcing your way in here and cross-questioning me when you know I'm alone and—" She shrank away as Ash came towards her, but he walked past her without touching her, and closing the door, locked it and put the key into his pocket and went back to stand between her and the french windows, blocking her retreat.

Belinda opened her mouth to call the bearer and then closed it again, daunted by the prospect of embroiling one of the servants in such an embarrassing situation. An interview with Ashton, however distasteful, seemed the lesser of two evils—and as she would probably have to endure one sooner or later, she might as well get it over now. So she smiled at him and said coaxingly: "Please don't let's have a scene, Ashton. I know you must feel badly about it. That's why I asked Mama to write—because I couldn't bear to be the one to hurt you. But you must have realized by now that when we first met we were both much too young to know our own minds, and that we'd grow out of it, just like Papa said."

"Are you going to marry that man Podmore?" asked Ash stonily.

"If you mean Mr. Podmore-Smyth, yes, I am. And you needn't use that tone of voice either, because—"

"But my darling, you can't let yourself be bullied into this. Do you think I don't know that this is all your father's doing? You were in love with *me*—you were going to marry me—and now he's forcing you into this. Why don't you stand up for yourself? Oh Belinda, darling, can't you *see?*"

"Yes, I can," said Belinda crossly. "I can see that you don't know anything about it, for if you must know, Papa was very much against it. And Mama too. But I'm not seventeen any longer: I shall be nineteen this year and quite old enough to know my own mind, so there was really nothing they could do about it, and in the end they had to agree, because Ambrose——"

"Are you trying to pretend that you're in love with him?" interrupted Ash harshly.

"Of course I'm in love with him. You don't suppose that I'd marry him if I wasn't?"

"You can't be. It isn't true. That fat, prosing, pompous old man who's the same age as your father . . ."

The blood rushed up into Belinda's face and quite suddenly Ash remembered what George had said about her losing her prettiness and looking ugly. She had lost it now and her voice was strident and furious:

"He's not as old as my father! He's not. How *dare* you talk to me like that? You're jealous of him because he's a man of the world——because he's mature and interesting and successful. Someone I can rely on and look up to, and not a silly, callow boy who——" She checked and bit her lip, and controlling herself with an effort said in a more reasonable voice: "I'm sorry, Ashton. But it makes me so angry when people say things like that. After all, you were just as angry when Papa thought you were too young. You said age had nothing to do with it, remember? and it's true. Ambrose understands me, and he's kind and generous and clever and everyone says that he's bound to be a Governor. He might even be Viceroy one day."

"And I gather he's rich as well."

Belinda missed the sarcasm and accepting the comment at its face value said happily: "Yes, he is. He's given me such lovely presents. Look."

She held out her left hand in unaffected pleasure and Ash saw with a pang that it was adorned with a band of enormous diamonds, any one of which was at least twice the size of the pearls in that pretty but unpretentious ring that he had bought for her in Delhi over a year and a half ago. It seemed much longer than that; five years at least. Too long for Belinda, who was going to marry a man old enough to be her father. A fat, rich, successful widower who could give her diamonds and make her Lady Podmore-Smyth——and present her with two ready-made step-children the same age as herself.

There appeared to be nothing left to say. The sight of those diamonds on Belinda's finger proved that all the arguments and pleas that he had meant to use would be a waste of time, and all he could do now was to wish her happiness and go. It was strange to think that he had planned to spend his whole life with her and that now he was probably seeing her for the last time. Outwardly she was as pink and white and pretty as ever, yet it was obvious that he had really never known what went on inside that golden head, but had fallen in love with someone who had existed largely in his imagination.

He said slowly: "I suppose I've been doing it too. Inventiong stories to suit myself and make me feel more comfortable, just like George did."

Belinda stiffened, and once again, and shockingly, her face was scarlet with anger and her voice high-pitched and shrewish: "Don't you speak to me about George. He's nothing but a low-bred, lying hypocrite. All those stories about a Greek grandmother——"

Something in Ash's face checked her and she broke off and gave a shrill laugh that was as ugly as her voice: "Oh, I forgot you wouldn't know about that. Well, I'll tell you. She was no more Greek than I am. She was a bazaar woman and if he thinks I'm going to keep my mouth shut, he's mistaken."

Ash said haltingly, through stiff lips: "You can't. You don't mean it . . . You couldn't . . ."

Belinda laughed again, her eyes bright with anger and malice. "Oh, yes I could. And I have, too. Do you think I'm going to sit and wait until someone else finds out and starts telling everyone, and people begin laughing at me and Mama behind our backs, and sympathizing with us for being taken in? I'd rather die! I shall tell them myself; I shall tell them that I always suspected it and that I trapped him into admitting it, and——"

Her voice was shaking with resentment and wounded vanity, and Ash could only stare at her, appalled, while her pretty pink mouth went on and on manufacturing malice and pouring out spite as though she could not stop herself. Had he been older and wiser, and less badly hurt himself, he might have recognized it for what it was: a tantrum thrown by a spoilt child who has been courted and flattered and over-indulged to a point where good sense and

235

youthful high-spirits have turned to conceit and vanity, and any opposition—any fancied slight—is magnified into an unforgivable injury.

Belinda was young and not very wise. She had been foolish enough to accept the compliments of her beaux at their face value, and after a heady year as a reigning belle had come to expect adulation, approval and envy as her due. She had, in fact, become insufferably set up in her own esteem, and having flaunted the handsome George as one of her conquests, she could not endure the thought of what several jealous young ladies would have to say when they discovered how she had been hoodwinked. How *dare* George lie to her and make a fool of her?—that, in effect, was her instinctive reaction to Mrs. Gidney's disclosures. The pathos of George's lies and posturing, the personal tragedy that underlay it and the humiliation that he must now be suffering were aspects of the affair that she had not even thought of, for in the shock of discovery she could only think of how it might affect Miss Belinda Harlowe.

Ash was the first person apart from her Mama and George himself to whom she had been able to unburden herself of all the pent-up forces of resentment and wounded vanity that had been accumulating within her ever since she learned of George's duplicity, and she found it a great relief. But to Ash, listening to the angry spate of words, it was the final betrayal: the collapse of all that he had believed her to be—sweet, kind, innocent and good. The owner of this shrewish voice was none of those things. She was a worldly and grasping woman who was prepared to marry an old, fat man for the sake of money and position. A heartless snob who could judge a man and condemn him for the sins of his grandparents, and an evil-tongued virago who was not above ruining a man's reputation in order to save a few scratches on her own.

He had not spoken or made any attempt to interrupt the tirade, but his disgust must have shown plainly on his face, for Belinda's voice rose suddenly and her hand darted out with the swiftness of a cat's paw to slap his cheek with a violence that jerked his head back and made her palm tingle.

The action took them both by surprise, and for a frozen moment they stared at each other in mutual horror, too startled to speak. Then Ash said grandly: "Thank

236

you," and Belinda burst into tears and whirling round, ran to the door, which was, of course, locked.

It was at this juncture that the crunch of wheels on gravel announced the inopportune return of Major and Mrs. Harlowe, and the next ten minutes had been, to say the least of it, confused. By the time Ash had been able to get the key out of his pocket and unlock the door, Belinda was in hysterics, and her startled parents were greeted by the sight of a sobbing, screaming daughter bursting out of the drawing-room to rush wildly across the hall and into her bedroom, slamming the door behind her with a bang that reverberated through the bungalow.

Major Harlowe had been the first to recover himself, and what he had had to say on the subject of Ash's manners and general disposition had made unpleasant hearing. Mrs. Harlowe had contributed nothing to the interview, having hurried away to comfort her afflicted daughter, and her husband's trenchant summing-up of Ash's character had been conducted against a background of muffled wails and agitated maternal appeals to know what that "horrid boy" had been doing.

"I intend to take this up with your Commanding Officer," announced Major Harlowe in conclusion, "and I am warning you that if I ever catch you so much as attempting to speak to my daughter again, I shall take great pleasure in giving you the thrashing you so richly deserve. Now get out."

He had given Ash no opportunity to speak, and even if he had done so there was very little to be said that would not have exacerbated the situation still further; apart from an abject apology, which might possibly have been accepted, though it would not have changed anything. But Ash had no intention of apologizing. The boot, he considered, should be on the other foot, and he had confirmed the Major's opinion of him by looking that irate gentleman up and down in a manner that could hardly have been bettered by his Uncle Matthew, and leaving without so much as a word of explanation or regret.

"Insufferable young puppy," fumed the Major, justifiably incensed; and he retired to his study to compose a forceful letter to the Commandant of the Corps of Guides, while Ash rode back to Mardan with his mind in a turmoil of anger and disgust and sheer, concentrated bitterness.

It was not Belinda's engagement that stuck in his

throat. He could have found excuses for that: the Victorian age approved the marriage of young girls to much older men, and it was no uncommon thing for a girl of sixteen or seventeen to marry a man of forty. Mr. Podmore-Smyth, whatever his physical disadvantages, was rich, respected and successful, and Belinda had probably been flattered by his attentions and ended by mistaking her admiration for his qualities as something much warmer, and persuading herself that it was love. She was, after all, young and impressionable, and she had always been impulsive. Ash might have forgiven her engagement, but he could neither excuse nor condone her behaviour in the matter of George.

George had undoubtedly told a lot of silly lies, but the revenge Belinda was taking on him was cruelly unjust, for it was not as though he had intended to marry her under false pretences. He knew very well that neither she nor her parents would ever have seriously considered him as a possible husband, and the most he had hoped to do was to make himself more interesting in her eyes and be accepted as an equal by the narrow, insular society of the cantonment. Yet now she was planning to expose him as a liar and a half-caste to that same society, knowing full well that although they might forgive the first, they would neither forgive nor forget the second. George would be ruined socially, for Anglo-India was intensely parochial and the story would follow him up and down the country. Wherever he went there would always be someone who knew it, or had heard it from someone else, and the virtuous middle-class matrons would whisper behind their fans while their daughters snubbed him and their menfolk laughed—and blackballed him at their Clubs.

"It's not fair!" thought Ash passionately. What did it matter who a man's grandmother was? Or his father or mother, if it came to that? He wished now that he had swallowed his pride and his bile and put in a plea for George to Belinda's father. He ought to have spoken up and told that old puffing-billy what his daughter was up to, and that she must be stopped. Except that it was already too late for that, as according to her she had already told several people, and for all he knew, her father might agree with her. Her mother and that tattling woman Mrs. Gidney obviously did, and so, presumably, would their friends and acquaintances, all of whom would sympathize with that conceited little bitch, Belinda, and turn on poor George like a pack of wolves. The ugliness and injustice of it stuck in Ash's throat and choked him, and he felt physically ill with disgust.

He had arrived back in Mardan in a black rage and blacker disillusionment. And a few days later Dilasah had absconded with the carbines, and five sowars of his clan, including Malik Shah and Lal Mast, had been stripped of their uniforms and expelled from the Regiment with orders to bring back the stolen carbines or never again show their faces in Mardan . . .

Ash had intended to demand an interview with the Commandant in order to protest against the action that had been taken. But he had been forestalled by the belated arrival of a letter from Major Harlowe, and had been sent for instead to explain himself. The dressing-down he had received from Belinda's father had been nothing to the one he received from his C.O., though most of it went over his head, for once again he was obsessed with an injustice. It was not *fair* that five men of Dilasah Khan's tribe, with impeccable records—men who had never even liked Dilasah, let alone helped him!—should be driven out of the Guides like criminals. He could barely wait for the Commandant to finish speaking before making his own protest; and the fact that he had obviously paid little attention to anything that had been said to him did nothing to improve his case, or the Commandant's temper.

"If anyone is responsible, it's me," declared Ash with a fine disregard for grammar. "*I'm* the one who ought to be sacked or sent after Dilasah, because I knew there was something wrong somewhere, and I ought to have seen that he didn't get a chance to do anything like this. But Malik and the others had nothing whatever to do with it, and it's not fair that their faces should be blackened in this way. It's not their fault that he belongs to their tribe, and it's downright unjust that—"

He got no further. The Commandant told him in one brief, blistering sentence what others had previously told him at greater length but with less clarity, and dismissed him from the Presence. Ash took his troubles to Zarin, but once again received no encouragement from that quarter, for Zarin considered the Commandant's action to be a wise one. So too did Risaldar Awal Shah.

"How else will he get our rifles back?" demanded

Awal Shah. "We of the whole Guide Corps have scoured the countryside and have not caught so much as a glimpse of Dilasah. But it may be that his own kin will be able to read his mind and follow his trail, and in two days, or three, they will return with the rifles. Thus their honour and ours will be saved."

Zarin grunted in agreement, and Koda Dad, who happened to be paying a rare visit to his sons, not only sided with them but took Ash to task.

"You talk like a Sahib," said Koda Dad crossly. "To prate of injustice in such a matter is foolishness. The Commandant-Sahib is wiser, for he is thinking not as an *Angrezi* but as a Pathan, while you—you who were once Ashok—are looking at this as though you had never been anything but Pelham-Sahib. *Chut!* how many times have I not told you that it is only children who cry 'it is not fair' —children and Sahib-log? Now at last," added Koda Dad acidly, "I see that you are indeed a Sahib."

Ash returned to his quarters sore and discomforted, and as angry as before. Yet even then he might have saved himself from folly if it had not been for George— for George and Belinda . . .

Walking into the mess that night, Ash met one of his fellow subalterns, newly returned from a visit to Head-quarters in Peshawar.

"Heard the news about that fellow Garforth?" in-quired Cooke-Collis.

"No. And I don't want to, thanks all the same," re-torted Ash rudely. He had not expected the story to spread quite so quickly, and the thought of having to listen to some second-hand or third-hand version of it sickened him.

"Why, didn't you like him?"

Ash ignored the question, and turned his back, hailed a *khidmatgar* and ordered himself a double brandy. But Cooke-Collis was not so easily put off: "Think I'll have one too. *Hamare waste bhi,** Iman Din. I need it, by jove. Nasty business at any time, but when it's someone you know, it's a bit of a shock, even if you didn't know them very well, and I didn't really; though I'd met him at several dinner-parties and dances and all that sort of thing, because he got asked all over the place. Very popular with the ladies, even though he was only a junior box-

---

*for me too

240

wallah. Not that I've anything against boxwallahs, you know; daresay they're a very pleasant lot. But Garforth was the only one you seemed to meet almost everywhere, and I won't deny that it was a nasty shock to hear that he——"

"Was a half-caste," finished Ash impatiently. "Yes, I know. And I don't see that it is any concern of yours or anyone else's, so you needn't go on about it."

"Was he a half-caste? I didn't know that. Are you sure? He didn't look it."

"Then what on earth are you talking about?" demanded Ash, angry with himself for betraying George's secret to someone who obviously did not know it and would now inevitably hand it on.

"Garforth, of course. He shot himself this afternoon."

"What?" Ash's voice cracked. "I don't believe it."

"Perfectly true, I'm afraid. I don't know what he'd been up to, but it seems that several people cut him at the Club last night. Then this morning he got a couple of letters cancelling invitations that he had already accepted, so at lunch time he took two bottles of brandy from the shop, drank 'em both and then shot himself, poor devil. I got it from Billy Carddock who'd just met the doctor coming away from the firm's bungalow. He said they'd no idea what was behind it."

"I was," whispered Ash, his face grey and drawn with shock: "He asked me what I'd do if I were in his place, and I told him . . . I told him——" He shuddered, and pushing the unbearable thought away, said aloud: "Belinda was behind it. Belinda and all those narrow-minded, bigoted, bourgeois snobs who purred over him while they thought his grandmother was a countess and cut him when they found out that she was only a bazaar woman from Agra. The ——, ——!" The end of the softly spoken sentence was in the vernacular and happily unintelligible to young Mr. Cooke-Collis, but its virulent obscenity startled the *khidmatgar* into dropping a box of cigars, and drew a shocked protest from a senior Major who happened to be standing within earshot.

"Here, I say," objected the Major. "You can't talk like that in mess, Ashton. If you must spout filth, go and do it somewhere else, will you."

"Don't worry," said Ash, his voice deceptively gentle. "I'm going."

241

He lifted his glass as though drinking a toast, and having drained it, tossed it over his shoulder in the manner of an earlier day when it had been the custom in some regiments to drink a young queen's health in broken glass. The crash brought conversation to a stop, and in the brief lull that followed, Ash turned on his heel and walked out of the mess.

"Silly young ass," observed the Major without heat. "I shall have to give him a talking-to in the morning."

But Ash was not there in the morning.

His room was empty and his bed had not been slept in, and the sentry who had come on duty at midnight reported that Pelham-Sahib had left the fort shortly after that hour, saying that he could not sleep and would walk for a while. He had been wearing a poshteen and a pair of Pathan trousers, and as far as the sentry could remember had not been carrying anything. His horses were still in the stables, and Ala Yar, questioned by the Adjutant, said that apart from the poshteen and a pair of *chupplis* and some money, the only thing missing from his room was a set of Pathan clothing and an Afghan knife that his Sahib always kept in a locked box on top of the *almirah* (cupboard). The box had not been in its accustomed place when he, Ala Yar, had brought in his Sahib's *chota hazri* (small breakfast) that morning; it had been on the floor, open and empty. As for the money it was a matter of a few rupees only, and it was certain that no thief had taken it, for his Sahib's gold cuff-links and silver-backed brushes lay on the dressing table where no one could have failed to see them. It was Ala Yar's opinion that his Sahib, being troubled in his mind, had taken leave and followed after the father of Risalder Awal Shah and Jemadar Zarin Khan, who had been visiting his sons and had left in the late afternoon of the previous day to return to his village.

"Koda Dad Khan is as a father to my Sahib, who has a great affection for him," said Ala Yar. "But yesterday there was some small disagreement between them, and it may be my Sahib desires to mend matters and make his peace with the old man, and when he has done so he will return swiftly. No harm will befall him beyond the Border."

"That's all very well, but he's got no damned business to be beyond the Border—now or at any other time," re-

242

torted the Adjustant, forgetting for a moment whom he was addressing. "Just you wait until I get my hands on that young—" He recollected himself and dismissed Ala Yar, who returned to the Sahib's quarters to remove the *chota hazri* tray that he had placed on the bedside table in the dawn, and in the agitation of the morning omitted to remove. It was only then that he saw the letter underneath it, for in the dim light of the early morning the envelope had not shown up against the clean cloth that he himself changed daily on the Sahib's table.

Ala Yar had learned to read a little English during his years in *Belait,* and ten minutes later, having deciphered the address, he was in the Commandant's office.

Ash had indeed gone over the Border. But not to visit Koda Dad. He had gone to join Malik Shah and Lal Mast and their fellow clansmen, who had been sent to track down Dilasah and bring back the two stolen rifles. And though search parties were sent out to bring him in, they could find no trace of him. He had vanished as completely as Dilasah had done, and nothing more was heard of him for almost two years.

That afternoon Zarin had gone to the Commandant and asked for special leave so that he might go in search of Pelham-Sahib. But this had been refused, and a few hours later, after a long talk with Mahdoo and a shorter and slightly acrimonious one with Zarin, Ala Yar had gone instead.

"I am the Sahib's servant and he has not yet dismissed me from his service," said Ala Yar. "There is also the promise that I made to Anderson-Sahib that I would see to it that the boy came to no harm, and as you cannot go after him, I must do so. That is all."

"I would go if I could," growled Zarin. "But I too am a servant. I serve the Sirkar and I cannot do as I please."

"I know. Therefore I go in your stead."

"You are an old fool," said Zarin angrily.

"Maybe," agreed Ala Yar without rancour.

He left Mardan an hour before sunset, and Mahdoo accompanied him for a mile along the track that leads towards Afghanistan and stood to watch him grow smaller and smaller against the vast, desolate background of the plain and the Border hills, until at last the sun went down and the dusty purple twilight hid him from sight.

BOOK THREE

World out of Time

13

"There are men out there. Beyond the nullah, to the left," said one of the sentries, peering out at the moonlit plain. "Look—they are moving this way."

His companion turned to stare in the direction of the pointing finger, and after a moment or two laughed and shook his head. "Gazelle. This drought has made the *chinkara* so bold that they do not fear to approach within a stone's throw. But if those clouds yonder do not fail us, there should soon be grass in plenty."

The summer of 1874 had been a particularly trying one. The monsoon had been late and scanty and the plains around Mardan were burned to a dry golden-brown in which no trace of green showed. Dust-devils danced all day among the mirages and the parched thorn bushes, and the rivers ran low and sluggishly between banks of blinding white sand.

There was no grass on the hills either, and most of the game had moved up the far valleys in search of food. Only a few wild pig and *chinkara* had remained, and these plundered the fields of the villagers by night, and would occasionally even venture into the cantonment to eat the shrubs in Hodson's garden, or nibble the leaves of the mulberry tree that marked the place where Colonel Spottiswood had killed himself over seventeen years ago. The sentries had become so accustomed to the sight of them that a dark shape skirting the parade ground or moving among the shadows no longer brought a challenge followed by the crack of a carbine; and in any case, the section of Frontier adjacent to Mardan had been quiet for so long that men were becoming used to peace.

There had been no "Border incidents" for over five years, and the Guides had had no active soldiering to occupy them. They had provided an escort under Jemadar Siffat Khan to accompany a new Envoy on a mission to Kashgar, and a year later two of the escort had carried the completed treaty from Kashgar to Calcutta in sixty days. A sepoy of the Guides Infantry had been detailed to accompany a messenger across the Oxus and from there, by way of Badakshan and Kabul, to India, and a sowar of the Cavalry, who had been sent to Persia with a British officer bound on a special mission, had been killed on the road to Teheran while defending the baggage from a gang of robbers. The Corps itself had taken part in a year-long "camp of exercise" at Hasan Abdal, from where it had returned to Mardan in February of that year, to occupy itself with the normal routine of cantonment life, and pray throughout that hot weather for rain to temper the remorseless heat.

September had been as scorching as July, but now October was almost out, and the mercury in the thermometer that hung in the mess verandah retreated daily. Men went abroad again at midday, and the wind that blew off the mountains at sunset carried a refreshing edge of coolness. But apart from a few brief and isolated showers there had been no sign of the autumn rains—until tonight, when for the first time in many months there were clouds in the sky . . .

"This time—*Shukr Allah**—they will not fail us," said the sentry devoutly. "The wind is behind them and I can smell rain."

"I too," said his companion. The two men sniffed appreciatively, and as a sudden gust whirled up the dust and obscured any further movement on the plain, they turned together and continued on their rounds.

---

*thanks be to God

The wind had been blowing only fitfully since moon-rise, but now it steadied and blew strongly, driving the banked clouds before it until presently they reached the moon and blotted it out. A quarter of an hour later the first swollen drops of rain splashed down out of the darkness: forerunners of a lashing torrent that within seconds turned the dust of the long, scorching summer into a sea of mud, and transformed every dry nullah and ditch into a fully fledged river.

Under cover of darkness and that raging bedlam of noise and water, the handful of men that one of the sentries had mistaken for *chinkara* passed the outposts unseen. But head-down against the wind-driven rain, they missed their way and were challenged by the guard on the gate of the fort.

It had been no part of their plan to be dragged before Authority that night. They had hoped to reach the cavalry lines without being detected, and to lie up there until morning; but as it was, the havildar in charge of the guard had sent for the Indian officer on duty, who in turn sent for the Duty Officer; and presently the Adjutant was fetched from the mess where he had been playing whist, and the Second-in-Command, who had retired early, aroused from his bed.

The Commandant had also retired early, but not to sleep. He had been writing his weekly letters home when he was interrupted by the entrance of two of his officers, accompanied by as sorry an object as had ever been seen in that room. A gaunt, bearded tribesman with a bandaged head, from whose tattered blanket, worn cloak-wise in the manner of the Frontier, a dozen little rivulets poured onto the Commandant's cherished Shiraz carpet. The bandage too leaked a steady red-stained trickle down one hollow and unshaven cheek, and the blanket that clung wetly to the man's scare-crow body failed to conceal that he held something long and bulky under its sodden folds. He let his arms drop, and the carbines that he had been carrying slid down and fell with a clatter into the circle of light shed by the oil lamp on the writing table.

"There they are, sir," said Ash. "I'm sorry . . . we took so long . . . about it, but . . . it wasn't as easy as . . . we'd thought."

The Commandant stared at him and did not speak.

246

He found it difficult to believe that this was the boy who had stormed into his office nearly two years ago. This was a man. A tall one, for he had come late to his full height, and lean with the leanness of hard muscle and harder living. His eyes were sunk deep in his head, and he was ragged, unkempt and wounded, and dazed with fatigue. But he held himself erect and forced his tongue to the English that it had not spoken for so long:

"I must . . . apologize, sir," said Ash haltingly, the words blurred by exhaustion, "for . . . letting you see us like—like this. We didn't mean . . . We meant to spend the night with Zarin and—make ourselves presentable, and in the morning . . . But the storm—" His voice failed and he made a vague and entirely oriental gesture with one hand.

The Commandant turned to the Adjutant and said curtly: "Are the others out there?"

"Yes, sir. All except Malik Shah."

"He's dead," said Ash tiredly.

"And Dilasah Khan?"

"He too. We got back most of the ammunition. He hadn't used much of it. Lal Mast has it . . ." Ash stared down at the carbines for a long moment, and said with sudden bitterness: "I hope they're worth it. They cost three lives. That is a high price to pay for anything."

"For honour?" suggested the Commandant in the same curt voice.

"Oh—*honour!*" said Ash; and laughed mirthlessly. "Malik and Ala Yar . . . Ala Yar." His voice broke and his eyes were suddenly full of tears. He said harshly: "May I go now, sir?" And almost as he spoke he fell forward, as a tree falls, and lay sprawled and unconscious across the cavalry carbines that had been stolen two years ago and recovered at the cost of three lives. One of them Ala Yar's . . .

"He'll have to be cashiered, of course," said the Second-in-Command.

His tone made the remark less an assertion than a query, and his Commanding Officer, who had been drawing complicated patterns on the blotting paper, looked up sharply.

"Well, I mean—it seems a pity," said the Major defensively. "After all, when you come to think of it, it was a damned fine show. I've been talking to Lal Mast and the others and they——"

"So, oddly enough, have I," interrupted the Commandant with some asperity. "And if you intend to play Devil's Advocate, you're wasting your time. I don't need one."

Two days had passed since Ash and his four companions had stumbled into Mardan, but the rain was still falling and the little fort was loud with the sound of water drumming upon the flat roofs, cascading from pipes and gutters, and splashing into the inch-deep lake that had replaced the dusty paths and parched lawns of the previous week. Malik Shah's family were to be awarded a pension, and his four fellow-tribesmen had been congratulated and reinstated, their uniforms returned and two years' back-pay handed over to them. But Lieutenant Pelham-Martyn, who faced a charge of Absent Without Leave for the space of twenty-three months and two days, was technically under close arrest—though in actual fact confined to bed in the quarters of the Medical Officer, Ambrose Kelly, with a high fever due to a head wound that had become septic. His fate and his future were still under discussion.

"You mean you agree with me?" demanded the Major, startled.

"Of course I do. Why else should I have bothered to go over to Peshawar yesterday? You don't suppose I spent over an hour jawing with the Commissioner, and two more arguing with an assortment of brass-hats, just for the fun of it, do you? Ashton's an insubordinate young bastard, but he's too valuable to throw away. Look—what's the most useful thing to any military commander who is planning a campaign or trying to keep order in a country like this? Information! Early and accurate information is worth more than all the guns and ammunition one could ask for, and that's why I'm going to fight like a steer to keep that young idiot. I don't imagine any other Corps could get away with it; but then we're not like any other Corps. We've always been pretty unorthodox, and if one of our officers can spend a couple of years on the other side of the Border without being spotted as an Englishman or shot as a spy, he's too bloody useful to lose and that's all there

248

is to it. Though mark you, what he really deserves is a Court Martial. *And* they'd cashier him."

"But what the hell are we going to do with him?" demanded the Major. "We can't just let him stay on here as though nothing had happened, can we?"

"No, of course not. The sooner he leaves Mardan the better. I propose to see if I can't get him transferred to another unit for a couple of years. Preferably a British one, where he can cool his heels and mix with his own people for a change. He needs to get right away from his friends and the Frontier for a while; and it won't do him any harm to go somewhere down south."

"He'll probably get into even more trouble there," observed the Major pessimistically. "After all, he was brought up as a Hindu, wasn't he?"

"What of it? The point is, he can't stay here just now. It would have a bad effect on discipline."

Which is why Ashton Pelham-Martyn came to be stationed in Rawalpindi that winter.

If his Commanding Officer had had his way, Ash would have been sent somewhere a good deal further off. For although Rawalpindi is hardly true Frontier country (which in the north-west is held to start at Hasan Abdal, once a posting-stage of the Mogul Emperors on their journeys to Kashmir) it lies only one hundred and thirteen miles to the south-east of Mardan. But as the main object of those in authority had been to remove the offender from his regiment as soon as possible, and as the 'Pindi Brigade had been able to provide an immediate vacancy (Ash would have been surprised to learn how many strings had been pulled to engineer that unorthodox posting), it would have to do for the present. Meanwhile the Commandant of the Guides had been promised that at the first opportunity Mr. Pelham-Martyn would be moved further down south, and that on no account whatever would he be permitted to put so much as a foot inside the North-West Frontier Province, or go back across the Indus.

In the unlikely event of there being anyone there who could recall having seen him when he stopped at the 'Pindi dâk-bungalow on his way from Bombay to Mardan, over three years ago, they would certainly not have known him now, for he had changed beyond recognition—and not only outwardly. As a child in the Gulkote days he would, by European standards, have been considered old for his age; the city and the Hawa Mahal made few concessions to youth, and he had made an early acquaintance with the facts of life and death and evil. Yet later on, as a boy among boys of his own blood, he had seemed curiously young, for he had retained a child's way of looking at a problem and seeing it in the simplest possible terms, without realizing—or perhaps merely ignoring—the fact that every question is likely to have more than two sides to it.

Arriving back in Rawalpindi that winter he was still only twenty-two. But he had grown up at last—though he was always to retain a trace of the child and the boy and the young man he had once been, and despite the strictures of Koda Dad, to continue to see things as "fair" or "unfair." But he had learned many things in the land beyond the Border, not least among them to ride his temper on a tight rein, to think more carefully before he spoke, to curb his impatience and (surprisingly enough) to laugh.

Superficially, the change in him was more noticeable. For though he had removed both beard and moustache, the boyish look had gone for ever and his face bore deep, unyouthful lines that had been etched there by hunger and grief and hard living. It also bore a long, angry-looking scar that ran up into his hair above his left temple, pulling up one eyebrow and giving him a quizzical look which oddly enough was far from unattractive, and looking at him now one would have said he was a remarkably handsome man—and also, in some indefinable way, a dangerous one: someone to be reckoned with . . .

Accompanied by Gul Baz and Mahdoo, who was very shrivelled now and beginning to feel his years, Ash arrived in Rawalpindi to find that he had been allotted a half share in part of a small, dilapidated bungalow largely given over to offices and the storing of files. The quarters were cramped and dark, but compared with the places he had slept in during the past two years they seemed palatial; and having lived cheek-by-jowl with his fellow men for months on end, he had no objection at all to sharing them. The cantonment suffered from a chronic shortage of accommodation, and he was, in fact, lucky not to be sharing a tent. And even luckier, as it turned out, in his stable-companion; though a gangling young ensign almost four years his junior, newly arrived from Home and addicted to writing bad verse, was probably the last person whom Ash himself would have selected for a roommate. Yet surprisingly, it proved to be a great success. The two had taken to each other from the outset and were soon to find that they had a great deal in common.

Ensign Walter Richard Pollock Hamilton of the 70th Foot was at that time only a year younger than Ash had been when he landed at Bombay. And like Ash, he saw India as a wonderful and mysterious country, full of endless possibilities for excitement and adventure. He was a pleasant youth, good-tempered, high-spirited and intensely romantic—and he too had fallen desperately in love with a yellow-haired chit of sixteen during the voyage from England. The girl had had no objection to flirting with the tall handsome boy, but his suit had been rejected out of hand on the score of his youth, and two days out of Bombay she had become engaged to an elderly gentleman who must have been at least twice her age: "Thirty, if he was a day," declared Walter disgustedly. "And a civilian too. Some dreary fellow in the Political Department. Would you believe it, now?"

"Only too easily," said Ash. "Belinda, let me tell you—"

But that story, as he told it now, was no longer a tragic one, and any bitterness that remained was sorely on George Garforth's account. For this was something else that had altered during the past two years; and looking back on his abortive romance, Ash could not only recognize it for the foolish and ephemeral thing it had been, but also see the comic side of it. Retold to Walter, the chronicle of his misfortune lost all trace of tragedy, and eventually became so hilarious that the ghost of Belinda was exorcized for ever, swept away on a gale of laughter into the limbo that is reserved for forgotten love-affairs. Walter's flirtatious sixteen-year-old had followed her there, and he celebrated the fact by writing a ribald poem entitled "Ode to Forsaken Subalterns," that would have surprised and pained his fond relatives—who were used to more elevated out-pourings from "dear Wally."

Wally rather fancied himself as a writer of verse. It was the only thing in which his sense of humour failed him, and his letters home were apt to contain deplorably amateur poems that were passed round the family circle and greatly admired by doting aunts and similar biased and unqualified critics, who considered them to be quite as good as "dear Mr. Tennyson's." And wrote to say so. The "Ode," however, was in a very different style from any of his previous effusions, and Ash translated it into Urdu and had it set to music by a Kashmiri singer of his acquaintance. It subsequently achieved quite a success in the 'Pindi bazaar, and versions of it (the more colourful ones) were sung for many years throughout the Punjab.

Wally himself was no mean singer, though the songs he sang were less secular. He had been a member of his school choir for several years, and nowadays, when he felt the urge to sing (which was often, for he sang whenever he was happy or exhilarated), he would launch into one of the more militant hymns of his youth: "Fight the good fight," "Onward Christian Soldiers!," "Forward be our watchword!" or "For all the Saints"—the last being a special favourite. There was no irreverence in this: Wally approved the sentiments and genuinely liked the familiar melodies (he said they were "corking tunes") and could see no reason why hymns should only be sung in church; particularly the ones that conjured up for him visions of banners and trumpets and legions of armed men charging into battle to smite the troops of Midian. His fondness for these stirring anthems meant that the days in the bungalow invariably began with the sound of a baritone voice, accompanied by much splashing of bath water, announcing melodiously that "Time like an ever-rolling stream bears all its sons away," or, alternatively, demanding "Oh, let thy soldiers, faithful true and bold, fight as the Saints who nobly fought of old, and win with them the Victor's crown of gold—Alle—luia! *Al—le—lu—ia!*" Similar hymns frequently enlivened the evening rides, and once Wally had raced down the polo ground and scored the winning goal in the last two seconds of a hard-fought match, chanting "Forward into battle see our banners go!"

These and other "Wally-isms," such as his occasional use of brogue, were an endless source of amusement to Ash. Though it is probable that in anyone else he would have found them tiresome or dismissed them, scornfully, as affectation. But then Wally was . . . Wally—*fidus Achates.*

252

Apart from Zarin, who had been more like an elder brother to him, Ash had never had a really close friend. He seemed to have no talent for friendship with those of his own blood. At school and the Military Academy, and later in the Regiment, he had always been something of a loner; an observer rather than a participant; and even at the height of his popularity as an athlete, no one had been able to claim that they knew him well or were on particularly friendly terms with him, though many would have liked to do so. But then he had never cared whether he was liked or not, and though, on the whole, he had been, it had been a luke-warm emotion, which was largely his own fault. Yet now, and entirely unexpectedly, he had found the friend that he had missed in those earlier years.

From the moment of their meeting he had felt at ease with Walter; so much so, that he had told him what he had told no one else, not even Zarin—the full tale of the grim tracking-down of Dilasah Khan and the death of Ala Yar and Malik. The savage revenge that the hunters had taken on the thief and killer, the long, terrible journey back through territory held by hostile tribes who had hunted the hunters, and the ambush that had been laid for them on the very fringe of the Border by several men of the Utman Khel who had seen and coveted the carbines, and from which they had barely escaped with their lives after Ash and Lal Mast had been wounded . . .

It was a story that the Commandant of the Guides had heard, in part, from the four men of Dilasah's tribe, though not from Ash, who had initially been too ill to be interrogated, and had later confined himself to answering questions in the fewest possible words. Ash's official account of those two years had been colourless in the extreme. But the full story was anything but colourless, and Walter—himself the stuff of which heroes are made—had listened enthralled and become a hero-worshipper in his turn. There was no one like Ash! And, naturally, no regiment like the Guides.

Walter had always meant to be a soldier. The heroes of his childhood had been Joshua and David, Alexander the Great and Rupert of the Rhine, and all his dreams were of military glory. They were very private dreams and he had never imagined himself being able to talk of

253

them to anyone. Yet he had talked of them to Ash, and without embarrassment, and taken a good deal of ribbing on the subject with unimpaired good temper.

"The trouble with you, Wally," said Ash, "is that you've been born too late. You ought to have been a cavalier. Or one of Henry's knights at Agincourt. But there are no worlds left to conquer now—and precious little glamour or chivalry about modern warfare."

"Perhaps not in Europe," agreed Wally, "but that's why I wanted to come out here. It's different in India."

"Don't you believe it."

"But it *is!* It must be, in a country where guns are still dragged by elephants and the rank and file of a Regiment like yours have competed for the honour of serving in it. Your sowars and sepoys are not pressed men, or riffraff from the slums of big cities like Lahore and Peshawar. They're yeomen—gentlemen adventurers who have enlisted for honour. It's magnificent."

"I can see that you are a hopeless idealist," said Ash drily.

"And it's a misbegotten cynic you are," retorted Wally. "Haven't you ever wanted to storm an impregnable position or defend an impossible one? I have. I'd like to lead a cavalry charge, or a forlorn hope. And I'd like my countrymen to remember me as they remember men like Philip Sidney and Sir John Moore. And him over there: '*Nikalseyne*'—"

They had been riding across the open country west of 'Pindi, and Wally flung out an arm to point at a rocky hillock on the horizon, crowned by a granite obelisk that commemorated the name of John Nicholson, killed while leading an assault during the battle for Delhi, seventeen years ago. "That's the way I'd like to die. Gloriously—with a sword in my hand and at the head of my men."

Ash observed dampingly that Nicholson's men had failed to follow him, and that he had in fact lingered on in agony for at least three days after being shot.

"What if he did? That's not the way he'll be remembered. Alexander said it all more than two thousand years ago"—there was a glow in the boy's eyes and his face had flushed like a girl's—"'*It is a lovely thing to live with courage, and to die leaving behind an everlasting renown.*' I read that when I was ten, and I've never forgotten it. That's exactly—"

He broke off as a sudden shiver made his teeth chatter, and Ash said: "Goose walking over your grave—and serve you right. Speaking for myself, I'd rather play safe and live to a ripe and undistinguished old age."

"Oh, rats!" retorted Wally scornfully, firm in the conviction that his friend was a hero. "It's getting damned chilly out here. Race you to the road."

Ash was no stranger to hero-worship. He had received a good deal of it from his juniors in the days when he had been a member of the first eleven at his school, and later when he had played for the Military Academy; and once, long ago, from a little girl; "a small sour-looking little thing like an unripe mango." He had never taken it very seriously and had in general found it either irritating or embarrassing; and on occasions, both. But Wally's admiration was different, and it warmed his heart because it was a tribute from a friend, not slavish adulation for mere physical prowess and skill at games, regardless of whether the possessor of it was, in himself, an admirable or a despicable character; or a dull one.

The two became known in Rawalpindi as "The Inseparables" and if one were seen without the other there was always someone to call out: "Hullo David—what have you done with Jonathan?" or "Blowed if it ain't Wally! I didn't recognize you without Pandy—you look improperly dressed." These and other equally foolish pleasantries had at first attracted the disapproving attention of several senior officers, none of whom would have objected very much to their juniors keeping half-caste mistresses or visiting the harlots' quarter of the bazaar (always provided they were discreet about it) but who had a horror of what they termed "unnatural vice."

To these grey-beards any close friendship between young men was suspect, and they feared the worst; but careful inquiry revealed nothing that could be termed "unnatural" about the vices of either young officer. In that respect at least, both were unquestionably "normal"—as Lalun, for one (the most alluring and expensive courtesan in the city), could have testified. Not that their visits to such establishments were very frequent; their tastes lay in other directions, and Lalun and her kind merely represented experience: one of many. Together they rode, raced and played polo, shot partridge on the plains and *chikor* among the hills, fished or went swimming in the rivers, and spent far more than they could afford on buying horses.

They read voraciously—military history, memoirs, poetry, essays, novels: De Quincey, Dickens, Thackeray and Walter Scott; Shakespeare, Euripides and Marlowe; Gibbon's *Decline and Fall*, Balzac's *La Comédie Humaine* and Darwin's *Descent of Man* ... Tacitus and the Koran, and as much of the literature of the country as they could get their hands on—their tastes were catholic and all was grist to their mill. Wally was working for his Lieutenancy and Ash coached him in Pushtu and Hindustani, and talked to him by the hour of India and its peoples; not the British India of cantonments and Clubs, or the artificial world of hill stations and horse shows, but that other India: that mixture of glamour and tawdriness, viciousness and nobility. A land full of gods and gold and famine. Ugly as a rotting corpse and beautiful beyond belief ...

"I still think of it as my own country, and that I belong here," confessed Ash, "even though I've learned that feeling one belongs doesn't mean much, unless one is accepted as belonging; which I am not—except by Koda Dad, and sometimes by strangers who don't know my history. To those who do, it seems I am and always will be a 'Sahib.' Though when I was young I was, or thought I was, a Hindu for almost seven years—a life-time, to a child. In those days it never occurred to me or to anyone else that I was not one, yet now no high-caste Hindu would care to sit at the same table with me, and many would have to throw away their food if my shadow fell on it, and wash themselves if I so much as touched them. Even the humblest would break any dish or cup that I had eaten or drunk from, so that no one else would be defiled by using it. That sort of thing isn't so with Mohammedans, of course; but when we were hunting Dilasah Khan and I lived and fought and thought as one of them, I don't think that any of the men who knew who I was ever really forgot it. And as I can't seem to learn to think of myself as a Sahib or an Englishman, I presume that I am what the Foreign Office would call 'A stateless person.' A citizen of no-man's-land."

" *'That Paradise of Fools, to few unknown,'* " quoted Wally.

"What's that?"

"Limbo—according to Milton."

"Oh. Yes, you may be right. Though I wouldn't have described it as a Paradise, myself."

"It might have its advantages," suggested Wally.

"Maybe. But I admit I can't think of any," said Ash wryly.

Once, sitting out in the warm moonlight among the ruins of Taxila (the 'Pandi Brigade was in camp), he had spoken of Sita, which was another thing that he had never been able to do before. Not even to Zarin and Koda Dad, who had known her.

". . . so you see, Wally," concluded Ash reflectively, "whatever people say, she was my real mother. I never knew the other one and somehow I can't believe in her; though I've seen a picture of her of course. She must have been a very pretty woman, and I don't suppose that *Mata-ji* —Sita—was pretty. But then she always looked beautiful to me, and I suppose it's because of her that I feel that this country, and not England, is my own. Anyway, Englishmen don't talk about their mothers. It's considered to be either 'soppy' or 'bad form'—I forget which."

"Both, I think," said Wally, and added smugly: "Though I'm allowed to, of course. It's one of the privileges of being Irish. Sentiment is expected of us. It's a great relief. Your foster-mother must have been a remarkable woman."

"She was. I didn't realize just how remarkable until much later on. One takes such a lot for granted when one is young. She had more courage than anyone I have ever known. The best kind of courage, for she was always afraid. I know that now, though I didn't then. And she was such a little woman. She was so small that I . . ."

He broke off and sat staring out across the plain, remembering how easy it had been for an eleven-year-old boy to lift her in his arms and carry her down to the river . . .

The night wind smelt of wood-smoke from the camp fires, and very faintly of pine trees from the near-by foothills that lay like wrinkled velvet in the moonlight. Perhaps it was that last that had recalled the ghost of Sita. "She used to talk to me about a valley in the mountains," said Ash slowly. "I suppose it must have been her home, where she was born. She was a hill-woman, you know. We were going to go and live there one day and build a house

257

and plant fruit trees and keep a goat and a donkey. I wish I knew where it was."

"Didn't she ever tell you?" asked Wally.

"She may have done once. If she did, I've forgotten. But I imagine it's somewhere in the Pir Panjal; though I always used to think it must be in the mountains below the Dur Khaima. You don't know about the Dur Khaima, do you? It's the highest mountain in the range you can see from Gulkote: a great crown of snow peaks. I used to say my prayers to it. Silly, isn't it?"

"Not really. Did you ever read *Aurora Leigh?*— '*Earth's crammed with heaven, and every common bush afire with God; but only he who sees takes off his shoes.*' You were merely taking off your shoes—that's all. And you aren't the only one either: millions of people must have felt the same, for there are holy mountains all over the world. And then there was David, of course: '*Levavi oculos*'—"

Ash laughed. "I know. It's funny you should say that. I used to think of the Dur Khaima every time we sang that in chapel." He turned to face the foothills and faraway line of the mountains that rose up behind them, dark against the stars, and quoted in an undertone: " 'I will lift up mine eyes unto the hills, from whence cometh my help.' D'you know, Wally, when I first came to England and didn't know any better, I tried to find out in what direction the Himalayas lay so that I could face that way when I said my prayers, like Koda Dad and Zarin, who always faced towards Mecca. I remember my aunt was simply horrified. She told the vicar that I was not only a heathen, but a devil-worshipper."

"You can see her point," said Wally tolerantly. "Now I was luckier. Fortunately for me, my family never discovered that for years I thought I was praying to my godfather. Well, you can see how it was—'God-the-Father'—it was perfectly obvious to me. Particularly as the old boy had an impressive set of white whiskers and a gold watch-chain, and every one was terrified of him. I can tell you it gave me no end of a jolt when I finally discovered that he wasn't really God and that I'd been sending my petitions to the wrong address. All those years of earnest supplication straight down the drain. It was a disaster, so it was."

Ash's shout of laughter woke the occupant of the

nearest tent, and an irate voice urged them to shut up and let a fellow sleep.

Wally grinned and lowered his voice. "No, seriously now, it was the waste that worried me most. But I've come to the conclusion that it's the intention that counts. My prayers had been perfectly genuine, as I expect yours were too, so the fact that they were wrongly addressed was an error for which I do not believe the Almighty will hold us responsible."

"I hope you're right. Do you still say your prayers, Wally?"

"Of course," said Wally, genuinely surprised. "Don't you?"

"Sometimes. Though I'm not sure who I address them to." Ash stood up and slapped the dust and dried grass from his clothes. "Come on, Galahad, it's time we turned in. This bloody exercise is due to start at 3 a.m."

In the circumstances it was hardly surprising that Wally should have set his heart on joining the Guides, though there was, as yet, very little that he could do about it because he must first pass for his Lieutenancy. Ash had been in some doubt whether a good word from him might not hinder rather than help his friend's chances of being offered a vacancy, so he had used a more oblique method and introduced him to Lieutenant Wigram Battye of the Guides, who had twice been over to Rawalpindi on duty. And, later on, to Zarin.

Zarin had taken short leave in the heat of June and ridden into 'Pindi bringing messages from his father and brother, and news of the Regiment and the Frontier. He had not been able to stay for long as the monsoon was due at any moment, and once it broke, the fords would be impassable and travelling become a slow business; but he had stayed long enough to gain an excellent impression of Ashok's new friend. Ash had made certain that Zarin should see for himself that the boy was an admirable shot and a born rider, and had encouraged the two to talk, knowing that under his own unorthodox tutorage, and the more scholarly methods of a Munshi, Wally had already made great strides in the two main tongues of the Frontier. And though Ash had said nothing in his praise, Mahdoo had said a great deal:

"That is a good Sahib," said Mahdoo, gossiping with Zarin on the back verandah. "One of the old kind, such as

259

Anderson-Sahib was in his youth. Courteous and kind, and with the bearing and courage of a king. Our boy has become a changed man since they met. Cheerful again, and full of laughter and jokes. Yes, good boys both."

Zarin had learnt to respect the old man's judgement, and Wally's own character and personality did the rest. Wigram Battye too watched and listened and approved; and both he and Zarin carried favourable reports back to Mardan, with the result that the Guides, always on the look-out for good material, took note of Ensign Walter Hamilton of the 70th Foot as a possible future addition to their Corps.

The hot weather that year had not been as abominable as the previous one, but it was Wally's first and he suffered all the torments that can beset the novice undergoing his first experience of soaring temperature. Prickly-heat, boils and sandfly-fever, dysentery, dengi and other hot-weather maladies plagued him by turn, and eventually he went down with a severe attack of heat-stroke and spent several days in a darkened room, convinced that he was dying—and with nothing done of all the many things he had hoped to do. On the advice of the M.O., his Colonel had packed him off to the hills to recuperate, and Ash had managed to get leave and gone with him.

Accompanied by Mahdoo and Gul Baz, the two had left by tonga for Murree, where rooms had been booked for them in one of the hotels that at this time of year were full of summer visitors escaping from the blazing heat of the plains.

Wally celebrated his own escape by falling in love with three young ladies at once: a pretty girl who sat with her mother at a near-by table in the dining-room, and the twin daughters of a High-Court Judge who had hired a cottage in the hotel grounds. His inability to choose between them prevented any of these affairs from becoming serious, but they inspired him to write a good deal of love-lorn verse, all of it deplorable, and led him to accept so many invitations to dine, dance or take tea that if Ash had not intervened, his chances of enjoying the rest and quiet advocated by the doctor would have been minimal. But Ash had no intention of wasting his leave dancing attendance on "a bunch of bird-witted girls and giddy grass-widows," and said so with considerable force—adding a

260

rider to the effect that in his opinion the objects of Wally's divided devotion were three of the most insipid damsels this side of Suez, and his doggerel was worthy of them.

"The trouble with you," retorted the incensed poet, touched on the raw, "is that you have no soul. And what's more, if you're going to go on posing as a misogynist for the rest of your life just because some silly chit gave your fresh young illusions a black eye and a bloody nose a few years ago, you haven't any sense either. It's about time you got over Bertha or Bella or Belinda or whatever her name was, and realized that there are other women in the world—and very charming ones too. Not," conceded Wally generously, "that you have to marry them, of course. I don't think, myself, that a soldier should get married until he's at least thirty-five."

" 'A Daniel come to judgement'!" mocked Ash. "Well, in that case, the sooner we remove ourselves from temptation the better."

They removed themselves to Kashmir, leaving most of their luggage behind in the hotel and hiring hill ponies for the long trek between Murree and Baramullah, from where they turned aside to shoot duck on the Wula Lake and red bear and *barasingh* in the mountains above it.

It was Wally's first experience of high mountains, and gazing at the white crest of Nanga Parbat, the "Naked Mountain," rising tall and stately above the long range of snows that ring Lalla Rookh's fabled valley, he could understand the awe that had moved Ash as a small boy to pray to the Dur Khaima. The whole country seemed extravagantly beautiful to him, from the lotus-strewn lakes and the winding, willow-fringed rivers, to the vast forests of deodar and chestnut that swept upwards to meet the shale and the great glaciers that lay above the snow line. He was loth to leave it, and 'Pindi seemed hotter and dustier and more unpleasant than ever as their tonga rattled along the cantonment road on the last day of leave, bringing them back once more to their bungalow. But the mountain air and the long days spent in the open had done their work. He returned fit and well, and suffered no more illness during the remainder of that hot weather.

The heat had not worried Ash, but desk work bored him to distraction and there was always too much of that in Rawalpindi. Zarin, riding over from Mardan, told him

261

that the Guides were to provide an escort for the eldest son of the *Padishah* (the Queen) when he visited Lahore during his tour of India in the coming cold weather.

"It's a great honour," said Zarin, "and I grieve that you will have no share in it. How much longer do they mean to keep you here, tied to a desk? It is nearly a year now. Soon it will be three years since you last served with the Guide Corps, and that is far too long. It is time you came back to us."

But the authorities did not agree with this view. They had made a promise to send Lieutenant Pelham-Martyn further away from the Frontier as soon as a suitable opportunity presented itself, and now, nearly eleven months later, they roused themselves from the lethargy induced by the hot weather, and redeemed it.

A letter had come from the Governor of the Punjab's First Secretary requesting them, on behalf of His Excellency, to nominate a suitable British officer to escort the two sisters of His Highness the Maharajah of Karidkote to Rajputana, to be married to the Rana of Bhithor. The officer's principal duty on the march would consist of seeing that His Highness's sisters were received with due honour and the proper salutes by any British garrisons on the route, and that their camp was adequately provisioned. On arrival in Bhithor he would be expected to see that the agreed bride-price was paid and the brides safely married, before accompanying the camp back to the borders of Karidkote. Taking all this into account, and bearing in mind that the camp was likely to be a large one, it was essential that the officer selected should not only be a fluent linguist, but have a thorough knowledge of the native character and the customs of the country.

It was that final paragraph that had brought Lieutenant Pelham-Martyn's name to mind; and the fact that the assignment would certainly take him well away from the North-West Frontier had served to clinch the matter. Ash himself had not been invited to express any opinions or allowed the option of refusing the appointment. He had merely been sent for and given his orders.

"What they appear to want," said Ash disgustedly, describing the interview to Wally, "is someone to act as a combination of sheep-dog, supply officer and nursemaid to a parcel of squealing women and palace parasites; and

262

I'm it. Oh well, bang goes polo for this season. Who'd be a peace-time soldier?"

"Faith, if you ask me, it's a lucky divil you are," said Wally enviously. "I only wish they'd chosen me. Just think of it—jaunting off across India in charge of a pair of beautiful princesses."

"Pair of bun-faced dowds, more likely," returned Ash sourly. "Bet you anything they're fat, spoilt and spotty—and still in the schoolroom."

"Blather! All princesses are ravishingly beautiful. Or they should be, anyway. I can just picture them: rings on their fingers and bells on their toes, and hair like Rapunzel's—no, she was a blonde, wasn't she? They'll be brunettes. I adore brunettes. You wouldn't be asking if I could go along with you, would you now? As a sort of right-hand-man: head cook and bottle-washer? You're sure to need one."

"Like rabies," observed Ash inelegantly.

Fifteen days later he said goodbye to Wally, and accompanied by Mahdoo and Gul Baz, his head-syce Kulu Ram, a grass-cutter and half-a-dozen lesser retainers, set out for Deenagunj, a small town in British India where the wedding party, at present under the charge of a local District Officer, awaited his arrival.

14

Deenagunj lay on the fringe of the foothills, a day's march from the border of the independent State of Karidkote and some twenty miles from the nearest British garrison.

Barely more than a village, it was indistinguishable from a hundred other little towns in the northern half of the territory that is watered by the Chenab, the Ravi and the Beas Rivers, and its population seldom rose above two thousand. At the present moment, however, this figure had been disastrously increased, the Governor's secretary having under-stated the case when he expressed the opinion that the bridal camp was "likely to be a large one," as it was, in point of fact, enormous.

The assembly sent by the Maharajah of Karidkote to escort his sisters to their wedding outnumbered the citizens of Deenagunj by almost four to one, and Ash arrived to find the town a mere annex to the camp, the bazaar sold out of all foodstuffs and fodder and rapidly running short of water, the city-fathers in a state of near hysteria and the District Officer, nominally in control of the camp, down with malaria.

It was a situation that might well have daunted a great many older and more experienced men than Ash. But the authorities had, after all, not chosen so badly when they nominated Lieutenant Pelham-Martyn (temporarily elevated to the rank of Captain by virtue of his office) for this particular mission. The uproar and confusion that would have conveyed, to an alien eye, an impression of riot, aroused no dismay in one who had been brought up in the bazaars of an Indian city and become accustomed at an early age to the extravagance, muddle and intrigue of life in the palace of an Indian prince.

The size and disorganization of the camp did not strike Ash as in any way remarkable, for he had not forgotten Lalji's wedding and the army of attendants that had accompanied the bride to Gulkote and settled like a swarm of locusts on the city and the Hawa Mahal. Yet Lalji's bride had only been the daughter of some small hill Rajah, while the brother of the Karidkote princesses was a full-blown Maharajah and ruler of no small state, so it was only to be expected that their escort would be proportionately larger. All that was needed was someone to make decisions and to give the necessary orders, and Ash had not served with the Guides and been tutored by Koda Dad's two sons for nothing. This was familiar ground.

He sent Gul Baz to find a guide who could take them to the District Officer, and presently they were riding through the mêlée, led by an elderly individual in uniform—presumably that of the Karidkote State Forces—who laid about him with the scabbard of a rusty tulwar as he cleared a passage for them between the shifting, shouting crowd of men and animals.

The District Officer's tent had been pitched under a *sal* tree and its occupant lay prone on a camp bed, shivering helplessly in the grip of fever. His temperature

264

was a hundred and three (which was much the same as that in the tent) and he was unfeignedly glad to see his replacement. Mr. Carter was both young and new to the district, and as it was also his first experience of malaria, it is hardly surprising that he should regard the whole situation as some form of nightmare. The endless stream of petitions, complaints and accusations, the chaos and the heat and the noise—particularly the noise—made his head feel as though it was an anvil on which iron hammers beat unceasingly, and the sight of Ash, who would relieve him of responsibility, was as welcome as water in a desert.

"Sorry about this," croaked the District Officer. "Devilish nuisance. Afraid you'll find things are in a . . . bit of a mess here. Undisciplined beggars . . . better get 'em on the move again, soon as you can . . . before there's a scrimmage. There's this business about the boy, too . . . Jhoti—H.H.'s brother. The Heir Apparent. Arrived last night. Ought to tell you—"

He did his best to give Ash an outline of the position and some idea of the responsibilities and problems involved, but it was plain that he found it almost impossible to marshal his thoughts or make his tongue obey him, and he eventually abandoned the effort and sent instead for a native clerk, who reeled off a tally of the dowry contained in a score of iron-bound chests and the amount of ready money available for the journey, produced lists of men, waiting-women, baggage-animals, tents, supplies and camp-followers, but admitted that the numbers were only approximate and the actual total was probably somewhat higher. Even on paper the entourage was formidable enough, for it included a battery of artillery and two regiments of the Maharajah's soldiery, together with twenty-five elephants, five hundred camels, innumerable horses and at least six thousand camp-followers.

"No need to have sent so many. Bit of swank—that's all," whispered the District Officer hoarsely. "But then he's only a boy still. Not seventeen yet . . . H.H., I mean. Father died a few years ago, and this . . . this is his chance to show off to the others—fellow princes. And to us, of course. Waste of money, but no arguing with him. Difficult young man . . . tricky . . ."

It appeared that the young Maharajah had escorted

265

his sisters as far as the border of his state, and then turned back to go hunting, leaving the cumbersome camp in charge of the District Officer, whose orders were to accompany it as far as Deenagunj, where he would hand it over to Captain Pelham-Martyn of the Guides Cavalry. But neither His Excellency the Governor of the Punjab nor the military authorities at Rawalpindi had realized how large that camp would be. Nor had they known that there would be a last-minute addition to the party in the person of His Highness's ten-year-old brother, Jhoti.

"Don't know why they sent him. Though I can guess," mumbled the District-Officer. "Nuisance, though . . . didn't even know he was here until last night . . . More responsibility. Oh well—your pigeon now, thank God! Sorry for you . . ."

There were a good many other formalities that had to be completed, and by the time these had been dealt with the day was far advanced. But the sick man insisted upon leaving, not only because he craved for quiet and for clean air to breathe, but because he recognized the pitfalls of divided authority. The camp was no longer "his pigeon" and therefore the sooner he left it the better. His servants transferred him to a waiting palanquin and jogged away into the dusty glow of the late afternoon, and Ash went out to take over control of his command.

That first evening had been a chaotic one. No sooner had the District Officer's palanquin disappeared from sight than a clamouring horde converged upon his successor with demands for payment of bills, accusations of theft, brutality and other forms of *zulum* (oppression), and loud-voiced complaints on a score of matters ranging from inadequate accommodation to a dispute between the camel-drivers and the mahouts from the elephant lines over an allocation of fodder. Their behaviour was understandable, for the age and rank of the new Sahib who had taken over from "Carter-Sahib" presupposed inexperience, and judging solely by this yardstick, it seemed to the camp (and also to the city-fathers) that the Sirkar had sent an almost insultingly inadequate representative to act as "sheep-dog, supply-officer and nursemaid." They therefore reacted to this belief in a predictable manner, and discovered their mistake in something under five minutes.

"I addressed them," wrote Ash, describing the scene

in a letter to Wally, "and after that we managed to get things straightened out all right." Which is probably as good a description as any, though it hardly conveyed the impact that his words and personality had on the noisy gathering in the Karidkote camp. No Sahib of their acquaintance had ever possessed such a fluent and picturesque command of their language as this young Sahib—or been able to compress so much authority and sound commonsense into half-a-dozen trenchantly phrased sentences. The few *Angrezi-log* whom they had previously come across were either polite officials, earnestly striving to understand a point of view that was alien to them, or, on occasions, some less polite Sahib on survey or *shikar*, who lost his temper and shouted at them when crossed. Pelham-Sahib had done none of these things. He had spoken to them in the manner of an experienced *sirdar* (headman), wise in the ways of his fellow men and the customs of the district, and used to being obeyed. Ash, it will be seen, had learned much from the regimental durbars.

The camp listened and approved: this was someone who understood them and whom they could understand. By the time the tents were struck on the following morning and they were ready to move on, the townsmen's accounts had been paid, a majority of the disputes settled, and Ash had managed to meet and exchange courtesies with most of the senior members of the bridal party; though he had not had time to sort them out, and retained only a confused impression of scores of faces momentarily concealed by hands pressed palm to palm in the traditional Hindu gesture of greeting. Later he must get to know them all, but at the moment the most important thing was to get the camp on the move. The District Officer's advice on that head had been sound, and Ash resolved to hurry them forward with as much speed as they could make, and if possible avoid stopping for more than one or two nights in any one place, so that they did not repeat the mistake of wearing out their welcome as they had done at Deenagunj. Close on eight thousand humans and more than half as many baggage animals were worse than a plague of locusts, and it was clear that without planning and forethought their effect upon the country they passed through could be quite as devastating, and equally disastrous.

He found little attention to spare for individuals on that first day's march, for he rode up and down the long column, taking note of its numbers and composition and estimating their capacity for speed, thereby unconsciously enacting one of the roles that he had mentioned to Wally—that of sheep-dog. This was easy enough to do, for progress was slow. The mile-long column moved at a foot's pace, plodding through the dust at the same leisurely pace as the elephants and stopping at frequent intervals to rest, talk or argue, to wait for stragglers or draw water from the wayside wells. At least a third of the elephants were baggage animals, while the remainder, with the exception of four state elephants, carried a large number of the Karidkote forces and a weird assortment of weapons that included the heavy iron cannons of the artillery.

The four state elephants bore magnificent howdahs of beaten gold and silver in which the Rajkumaries* and their ladies, together with their younger brother and certain senior members of the bridal party, would ride in procession on the day of the wedding, and it had also been expected that the brides would travel in them on the journey. But the slow, rolling stride of the great beasts made the howdahs sway, and the youngest bride (who was also the most important one, being the Maharajah's full sister) complained that it made her feel ill, and demanded that both she and her sister, from whom she refused to be parted, be transferred to a *ruth*— a bullock-drawn cart with a domed roof and embroidered curtains.

"Her Highness is very nervous," explained the chief eunuch, apologizing to Ash for the delay caused by this alteration in the travelling arrangements. "She has never before been outside the Zenana walls, and she pines for her home, and is greatly afraid."

They covered less than nine miles that first day— scarcely three as the crow flies, for their road wound and twisted downwards between low, scrub-covered hills that were barely more than folds in the ground. It was clear that they might often do less, and Ash, poring over the large-scale survey map that evening and calculating their weekly advance at an average of fifty to sixty miles, real-

---

*Princesses

ized that at this rate it was going to be many months before he saw Rawalpindi again. The thought did not depress him, for this nomadic open-air life with its constant change of scene was going to be very much to his taste, and he found it exhilarating to be free from supervision and senior officers, in sole charge of several thousand people and answerable to no one.

Halfway through the following day he belatedly recalled that the Maharajah's young brother had arrived, but on inquiring if he might pay his respects to the little prince, he was told that His Highness was unwell (the result, it was reported, of eating too many sweetmeats) and that it would be better to wait a day or two. The Sahib would be informed as soon as the child was feeling fully recovered. In the meantime, as a special mark of favour, he had been asked to meet the prince's sisters.

The brides' tent was the largest in the camp, and as it was always the first to be pitched, the remainder formed a series of circles about it, those in the inner ring being occupied by ladies-in-waiting, serving women and eunuchs, and the next by high officials, palace guards, and the little prince and his personal servants. By rights, Ash's tent should have been included in the latter circle, but he preferred a quieter and less central position, and had arranged for it to be pitched on the outskirts of the camp, which on this particular evening was some considerable distance from the brides' pavilion. He had been escorted to the meeting by two officers of the guard and an elderly gentleman who had been introduced to him on the previous evening as the Rao Sahib, a brother of the late Maharajah and uncle to the two princesses.

The custom of purdah—the veiling and seclusion of women—was adopted by Hindu India from Mohammedan conquerors and does not go far back into the roots of the country, so the fact that Ash was permitted to meet his two charges was not really surprising. As a Sahib and a foreigner, and more particularly as the representative of the Raj whose duty it was to see to their safety and comfort on the journey, he merited special treatment and was therefore accorded the honour of speaking with them; a privilege that would not have been accorded to any other man who was not a near relative. The interview, however, had been a brief one, and by no means private, having been conducted in the presence of their uncle and a second elderly kinsman, Maldeo Rai, as well as their duenna and distant cousin Unpora-Bai, several waiting women, a eunuch and half-a-dozen children. The decencies were preserved by the fact that the brides' faces, and that of Unpora-Bai, were partially covered by the fringed and embroidered saris that they held in such a way that only their eyes and a small segment of forehead were visible. But as the saris were of the finest silk gauze from Benares, this was more a token gesture than anything else, and Ash was able to gain a fairly accurate idea of their looks.

"You were quite right about them," he wrote to Wally in a lengthy postscript to the letter describing his arrival in camp, "they are as pretty as pictures. Or the younger one is, anyway. She's not yet fourteen, and just like that miniature of Shah Jehan's Empress, the lady of the Taj. I managed to get a good look at her because one of the children tried to catch her attention by tugging at her sari, and twitched it out of her hand. She's the prettiest thing you ever saw, and it's thankful I am that you can't see her, you susceptible Celt, for you'd fall in love with her on the spot and there would be no holding you. You'd be rhyming heart, part and cupid's dart all the way from here to Bhithor, and I'm not sure I could endure it. Thank God I'm a soured and unimpressionable misanthropist! The other sister kept a bit in the background and is quite old, at least eighteen, which in this country is practically on the shelf, and I can't think what they were about not to marry her off years ago; except that I gather she is only the daughter of some secondary wife, or possibly a concubine of the late Maharajah's, and from what I could see of her I wouldn't say she was exactly the Indian idea of a beauty. Or mine either, for that matter. Much too tall and with one of those rather square faces. I prefer oval ones, myself. But her eyes are magnificent—'like the fishpools in Heshbon by the gate of Beth-Rabbin'—not black like her sister's but the colour of peat-water, with little gold flecks in them. Don't you wish you were in my shoes?"

Ash might choose to describe himself as soured and unimpressionable, but the fact that the Karidkote princesses were far from unattractive undoubtedly added a fillip to the situation; though as he was unlikely to see very much of them their personal appearance, one way or another, was a matter of little importance. Nevertheless, the thought that he was escorting two charming young creatures to their wedding instead of the "pair of dowds" that he had visualized made the whole affair seem more romantic. It even lent a redeeming touch of glamour to the din and dirt and inconvenience of the enormous camp, and he strolled back to his tent humming the old nursery rhyme that tells of a lady who rode to Banbury Cross "with rings on her fingers and bells on her toes," and mentally recalling the names of legendary beauties whose stories are chronicled in Tod's *Rajasthan:* Humayan's wife, the fourteen-year-old Hamedu; lovely Padmini, "the fairest of all flesh on earth," whose fatal beauty had led to the first and most terrible Sack of Chitor; Mumtaz Mahal, "Splendour of the Palace," to whose memory her grieving husband had raised that wonder in white marble, the Taj Mahal. Perhaps Wally was right after all, and all princesses were beautiful.

Ash had been far too interested in the brides to spare more than a cursory glance at the remainder of the company, several of whom would have repaid a little more of his attention. And as the next day's march was to end on the outskirts of a town where there was a small garrison of British troops, he had ridden on ahead to speak to the officer in command, and seen little of anyone in the camp during that day, for the Garrison Commander had invited him to dine in mess.

Unlike Wally, his host that night appeared to think that a British officer landed with Ash's present task was greatly to be pitied, and had said as much over the port and cigars. "Can't say I envy you the job," said the Garrison Commander. "Thank God I'm never likely to be told off to do anything in that line! It must be nearly impossible to live in among that lot without putting your foot in it twenty times a day, and frankly, I can't think how you manage it."

"Manage what?" inquired Ash, puzzled.

"Coping with this caste business. It's no problem with Mussulmans, who don't seem to mind who they eat and drink with or give a damn who cooks or serves the stuff, and don't appear to have too many religious taboos. But caste Hindus can pose the most appalling problems, as I've learnt to my cost. They're so hedged about with complicated rules and customs and restrictions imposed upon

271

them by their religion, that a stranger in their midst has to walk like Agag to avoid offending them—or at the very least, embarrassing them. I don't mind telling you that I find it a devil of a problem."

The speaker had gone on to illustrate the pitfalls of the caste system with a long story about a sepoy who had been wounded in battle and left for dead, but recovering, had wandered for days in the jungle, famished, delirious and half mad with thirst, and eventually been found by a little girl who had been herding goats, and who had given him a drink of milk that had undoubtedly saved his life, for he had been at his last gasp. Not long afterwards he had come across some men of his own regiment who had carried him to the nearest hospital, where he had lain gravely ill for many months before being discharged and returning to duty. Several years later he had obtained leave to go to his home, and on arriving there had told his story. His father had immediately said that from his description of the child she could have been an "untouchable," and if so, his son was defiled and must not stay in his own home, for his presence would pollute it. No arguments had been of any use, and not only his own family but the entire village recoiled from him as an outcaste and unclean. Only after costly ceremonies (for the performance of which the priests demanded every anna of his life's savings) was he declared "purified" and allowed to enter his family home again.

"And all this," said the Garrison Commander, summing up, "because the poor devil had once, when crazed with wounds and thirst and at his last gasp, accepted a cup of milk from the hands of a child who might possibly have been an 'untouchable.' Apparently he ought to have preferred death to the remote possibility of defilement. Can you beat it? And I assure you that the story is true, because a cousin of mine had it from the sepoy himself. Just shows you what we're up against in this country. But I suppose you've found that out for yourself by now."

Ash had found it out many years ago. But he refrained from saying so and merely said that he thought that in these matters a fanatical regard for the letter-of-the-law and an obsessive terror of pollution was, in general, confined to the priests (who benefited greatly from it) and to the middle classes, both upper and lower. The nobility tended to be less hag-ridden by it, while royalty, secure

272

in the knowledge of their own superiority over men of lesser birth, usually felt free to stretch the rules to suit themselves—fortified no doubt by the knowledge that if they overstepped the mark they could well afford to pay the Brahmins to put them right again with the gods. "It isn't so much that they are more broad-minded," said Ash, "but they are firm believers in the Divine Right of Kings; which is not surprising when one thinks that a number of the princely houses claim to be descended from a god—or from the sun or the moon. If you believe that, you can't really feel that you are quite like other men, so you can afford to do things that people with less exalted ancestors wouldn't dare do. Not that the great are irreligious—far from it. They can be just as devout. But possibly less bigoted."

"You may be right," acknowledged the Garrison Commander. "But then I have to admit that I don't know any of the ruling princes. Have some more port?"

The conversation had switched to pig-sticking and horses, and Ash had not returned to his tent until well after midnight.

The following morning had dawned wet and windy, so that he was able to sleep late, for under such conditions the camp took longer than usual to get on the move. And because of the weather, he again had little opportunity to take note of his fellow-travellers, who unlike himself were shrouded and unidentifiable under cloaks or blankets worn to keep out the wet. Not that this worried him, as there would be plenty of time later on, and he was more than content to jog along in silence; even the discomfort of spending the day in a damp saddle, head down against a gusty wind that tugged at his sodden cloak and drove the rain into his eyes, being infinitely preferable to being tied to an office desk in Rawalpindi. The almost total lack of paper-work was, in his opinion, one of the main advantages of this present assignment, another being that any problems that arose were likely to be familiar ones, differing only in degree from those that cropped up frequently at regimental durbars, and just as easily dealt with.

But in this he was mistaken, for that self-same evening he was to come up against one that was not only unfamiliar, but very difficult to deal with. And, potentially, extremely dangerous.

The fact that he was entirely unprepared for it was largely his own fault, though insufficient consultation between Army Headquarters in Rawalpindi and the Commandant of the Corps of Guides, together with inadequate briefing by the Political Department and the illness of the District Officer, could also be held responsible. But it was Ash's original attitude to his appointment—that disgusted dismissal of it as a mere matter of playing sheep-dog and chaperone to "a pair of dowds and a parcel of squealing women"—that had led him into the old error of his early school-days: neglecting to do his homework.

He had no one to blame but himself, since he had, quite simply, not bothered to find out anything about the background and history of the state whose princesses he was to escort to their wedding, while the authorities in Rawalpindi, for their part, had given him no information on that head because they assumed that Mr. Carter, the District Officer, would deal fully with it; and they could hardly have been expected to know that an attack of malaria would prevent the District Officer from doing anything of the sort. But as a result, Ash had entered on his command in a blithe state of ignorance and wholly unaware of the pitfalls that lay ahead. Even the information that a young brother of the Maharajah's had elected to join the camp at the last possible moment, and would be travelling with them, had not struck him as particularly interesting. After all, why shouldn't the child accompany his sisters to their wedding? He had dismissed young Jhoti's presence as something of no importance, and beyond sending a polite inquiry as to his health, gave the matter no more thought. But that evening, as darkness fell, a servant brought him a message to say that the little prince was now fully recovered from his indisposition and would like to see him.

The rain had stopped some hours before and the sky was clear again as Ash, wearing mess dress in honour of the occasion, was once more conducted through the roaring, lamp-lit camp to a tent near that of the princesses, where a sentry armed with an ancient tulwar provided a token guard and a yawning servant waited to usher him into the Presence. A solitary hurricane lamp hung on an iron pole outside, but passing in under the tent-flap Ash was met by a blaze of light that momentar-

274

ily dazzled him, for the interior of the tent was lit by half-a-dozen European-style lamps that had been designed to carry shades of silk or velvet, but that now stood, unshaded, on low tables set in a half-circle about a pile of cushions on which sat a plump, pallid little boy.

He was a handsome child, despite his plumpness and his pasty complexion, and Ash, blinking in the glare, was suddenly reminded of Lalji as he had seen him on that first day in the Hawa Mahal. This child must be about the same age as Lalji had been then, and was sufficiently like Ash's memory of the Yuveraj for the two to be brothers, though Lalji, thought Ash, had been a far less personable child than this one, and he would certainly not have risen to his feet to greet his visitor, as Jhoti was doing. The resemblance was mainly a matter of dress and expression, for Lalji had worn similar clothes and he too had looked sour and cross—and very frightened.

It occurred to Ash, bowing in acknowledgement of the boy's greeting, that if (as Wally maintained) all princesses were beautiful, it was a pity that all young princes should be plump and cross and frightened. Or, at least, all the ones that he himself had met so far.

The absurdity of this reflection made him grin and he was still smiling when he straightened up . . . to find himself looking directly at a face that even after all these years he recognized instantly and with a paralysing sensation of shock—the face of a man who stood immediately behind the little prince and less than three paces away, and whose narrow eyes held the same slyness, the same chilling look of calculation and malice that had been so familiar in the days when their owner had been Lalji's favourite courtier and the *Nautch*-girl's spy.

It was Biju Ram.

The smile on Ash's face stiffened into a fixed grimace and he felt his heart jerk and miss a beat. It was not possible—he must be mistaken. Yet he knew that he was not. And in the same instant he knew too, and without any shadow of doubt, why the boy Jhoti reminded him of Lalji. Because Jhoti was either Lalji's brother or his first cousin.

He could not be Nandu: he was too young for that. But there had been at least two more children, and for all he knew the *Nautch*-girl might have borne many others later on. Or could this be Lalji's son . . . ? No, that was not

275

likely. A cousin, then?—a child or grandchild of one of the brothers of the old Rajah of Gulkote . . . ?

Ash became aware that several people were beginning to look at him curiously, and also that there was no trace of recognition in Biju Ram's narrow-eyed gaze. That slyness was habitual; and so was the malice. As for the look of calculation, it probably only meant that Biju Ram was assessing the calibre of the new Sahib and wondering if it would be necessary to placate him, because in no circumstances could he have recognized this Sahib as the "horse-boy" who had saved the life of the Yuveraj of Gulkote so many years ago.

Ash forced himself to look away and to reply to the polite questions of the little prince; and presently his pulse steadied and he was able to glance casually about the tent and assure himself that there was no one else there whom he knew. There were at least two. But even then he could surely not be in any danger of discovery, for apart from Koda Dad (and he would never have told), no one else in Gulkote could have learned that Sita's son was an *Angrezi*. There was nothing to connect the boy Ashok with a Captain Ashton Pelham-Martyn of the Guides, and little enough resemblance between the two. It was only Biju Ram who had not altered. True, he was much fatter and beginning to grow a little grey, and the lines that dissipation had already begun to draw on his face when he was a young man were deeper now; but that was all. He was still smooth and spruce and sly, and he still wore a large diamond drop in one ear. But why was he here, and what was the relationship between the Yuveraj of Gulkote and the ten-year-old Jhoti? And who, or what, was the child frightened of?

Ash had seen fear too often not to recognize it, and the signs were all there: the wide, over-bright eyes and the swift glances that flickered to left and right and back over the shoulder; the tensed muscles and jerking turn of the head, and the uncontrollable quiver and clench of the hands.

This was how Lalji too had looked; and with good reason. But then this child was not heir to a throne. He was merely a younger brother, so it seemed inconceivable that anyone should wish to harm him. A more likely explanation was that he had run away to join the wedding party against the wishes of his elders, and was only now beginning to assess the possible consequence of his escapade.

"He's probably only a spoilt brat who has gone too far and is now scared of being spanked," thought Ash. "And if he is playing truant, I'll bet anything that Biju Ram put him up to it . . . I must find out about his family. About all of them. I should have done it before . . ."

The little prince had begun on introductions, and Ash found himself greeting Biju Ram and exchanging the few formal sentences suitable to the occasion before passing on to the next in line. Ten minutes later the interview was over and he was outside in the semi-darkness, and shivering a little, not only because the night air struck cool after the heat in the over-lighted tent. He drew a deep, shuddering breath of relief as though he had escaped from a trap, and was ashamed to discover that his palms were sore where his nails had pressed into them—though he had not even realized until this moment that he had been holding his hands tightly clenched.

That night his tent had been pitched under a banyan tree, some fifty yards beyond the perimeter of the camp and screened from it by the cluster of smaller tents that housed his personal servants. Passing these, he changed his mind about sending for one of the Karidkote clerks, because Mahdoo was sitting out in the open smoking his hookah, and it occurred to Ash that by this time the old man had probably picked up as much information about the royal family of Karidkote as any denizen of that state. Mahdoo enjoyed gossiping, and as he came into contact with many people whom Ash did not meet, he heard things that are not usually spoken of to Sahibs.

Ash paused beside the old man and said in an undertone: "Come and talk with me in my tent, Cha-cha (uncle), I need advice. There are also many things that it may be you can tell me. Give me your hand. I will carry the hookah."

A hurricane lamp with the wick turned low had been left hanging in Ash's tent, but he preferred to sit outside under the narrow awning, from where he could look out past the dense shadows of the banyan tree to the wide plain that lay beyond it, dim in the starlight. Mahdoo squatted comfortably on his hunkers while Ash, impeded by mess dress, had to content himself with a camp chair.

"What is it that you would know, *beta* (son)?" inquired the old man, using the familiar address of long ago, which was something that he did very rarely in these days.

Ash did not reply to the question immediately, but was silent for a space, listening to the soothing bubble of the hookah and arranging his thoughts. At last he said slowly: "Firstly, I would know what connection there is between this Maharajah of Karidkote, whose sisters we take to their wedding and whose brother travels with us, and a certain Rajah of Gulkote. There must be one, I am sure of that."

"But of course," said Mahdoo, surprised. "They are one and the same. The territories of His Highness of Karidarra adjoined those of his cousin the Rajah of Gulkote, and when His Highness died, leaving no heir, the Rajah left for Calcutta to lay claim before the *Lat*-Sahib himself to the lands and titles of his cousin. There being no one nearer in blood, it was granted to him, and the two states were merged into one and re-named Karidkote. How is it that you did not know this?"

"Because I am blind—and a fool!" Ash's voice was barely more than a whisper, but it held a concentrated bitterness that startled Mahdoo. "I was angry because I knew that the Generals in Rawalpindi were only using this appointment as a pretext to send me further away from my friends and the Frontier, so I would not even take the trouble to ask questions, or to find out anything. Anything at all!"

"But why should it matter to you who these princely folk are? What difference does it make?" asked the old man, troubled by Ash's vehemence. Mahdoo had never been told the story of Gulkote. Colonel Anderson had advised against it on the grounds that the fewer people who knew that tale the better, as the boy's life might depend on his trail being lost. It was the one thing that Ash had been forbidden to mention before Ala Yar or Mahdoo, and he did not wish to go into it now. He said instead:

"One should know all that one can about those under one's charge, for fear of . . . of giving offence through ignorance. But tonight I have been made to realize that I know nothing at all. Not even . . . When did the old Rajah die, Mahdoo? And who is this old man whom they say is his brother?"

"The Rao-Sahib? He is a half-brother only: the elder
278

son by some two years, though being the son of a concubine he could not inherit the *gadi* (throne), which went to a younger son whose mother was the Rani. But all the family have always held him in great affection and respect. As for the Rajah—the Maharajah—he died some three years ago, I think. It is his son, the brother of the Rajkumaries, who now sits on the *gadi* in his place."

"Lalji," said Ash in a whisper.

"Who?"

"The eldest son. That was his milk-name. But he would have been—" Ash stopped, remembering suddenly that the District Officer had spoken of the Maharajah of Karidkote as only a boy and "not yet seventeen."

"Nay, nay. This is not the son of the first wife, but a younger one: the second son. The first one died of a fall some years before his father. It is said that he was playing with a monkey on the walls of the palace and fell and was killed. It was an accident," said Mahdoo; and added softly: "—or so they say."

"An accident," thought Ash. The same kind of accident that had so nearly happened before. Had it been Biju Ram who pushed him over to his death? or Panwa, or . . . Poor Lalji! Ash shuddered, visualizing that last hideous moment of terror and the long, long fall onto the rocks below. Poor Lalji—poor little Yuveraj. So they had done for him at last and the *Nautch*-girl had won. It was her son, Nandu, the spoilt brat who had been banished, shrieking, on the occasion of Colonel Byng's visit to Gulkote, who was now Maharajah of the new State of Karidkote. And Lalji was dead . . .

"It seems that the family has suffered many misfortunes of late years," said Mahdoo reflectively, and sucked again on his pipe: "The old Maharajah also met his death from a fall. I am told that he was out hawking when his horse bolted and fell into a nullah, breaking both their necks. They think the horse must have been stung by a bee. It was very sad for his new bride—did I tell you that he had recently taken another wife?—yes, indeed, his fourth, the first two being dead. They say she was young and very beautiful: the daughter of a rich *zemindar* . . ." The hookah bubbled again and it seemed to Ash as though the sound was a malicious chuckle, laden with sly innuendo. "It is said," continued Mahdoo softly, "that the third Rani

279

was greatly angered, and had threatened to kill herself. But there was no need, for her husband died and the new bride burned with him on his pyre."

"Suttee? But that has been forbidden," said Ash sharply. "It is against the law."

"Maybe, child. But the princes are still a law unto themselves, and in many states they do as they wish and no one hears until it is too late. The girl was in ashes long before anyone could interfere. It seems that the Senior Rani would have joined her on the pyre had her women not locked her in a room from which she could not escape, and sent a word to Political Sahib, who was on tour and could not be reached in time to prevent the Junior Rani from becoming a suttee."

"Very convenient for the Senior Rani—who I presume became the power behind the throne in Karidkote," observed Ash dryly.

"I believe so," admitted Mahdoo. "Which is strange indeed, for they say she was once a dancing-girl from Kashmir. Yet for more than two years she was the true ruler of the state, and at least she died a Maharani."

"She is dead?" exclaimed Ash, startled. Somehow it did not seem possible. He had never even seen Janoo-Rani, yet her presence had so dominated the Hawa Mahal he found it difficult to believe that the violent, ruthless woman who had ruled the old Rajah and plotted Lalji's death—and his own—was no longer alive. It was as though the fortress-palace itself had fallen, for she had seemed indestructible . . . "Did they say how it happened, Cha-cha?"

Mahdoo's wise old eyes glinted in the faint glow from the hookah as he looked sideways at Ash, and he said softly: "She quarrelled with her eldest son, and soon afterwards she died—from eating poisoned grapes."

Ash caught his breath in a harsh gasp: "You mean—? No. That I will not believe. Not his own mother!"

"Have I said that he did it? *Nahin, nahin,*" Mahdoo wagged a deprecatory hand. "There was of course a *tálash* (inquiry) and it was proved to be an accident; she herself had poisoned the grapes for the purpose of ridding the garden of a plague of crows, and she must in error have left a few of them on her own dish—"

The hookah chuckled slyly again, but Mahdoo had not finished: "Did I not tell you that the ruler of Karidkote has

280

suffered much misfortune? First his elder brother and then his father; and two years later, his mother. And before that there were also one or two small brothers and another sister who died when they were babes in a year of sickness, when cholera killed many children—and not a few grown men and women too. The Maharajah now has only the one brother left—the little prince who is here in the camp. And only one full sister, the younger of the two Rajkumaries who are being sent far away to be wed, for the elder is only a half-sister, the child of his father's second wife, who they say was a foreigner."

"*Juli!*" thought Ash: and was stunned by the thought. That tall, veiled woman whom he had seen in the brides' pavilion two nights ago was the *Feringhi*-Rani's neglected little daughter, Anjuli; the child whom the *Nautch*-girl had scornfully likened to an unripe mango, and who had been known thereafter to everyone in the Palace of the Winds as "Kairi-Bai." It was Juli—and he had not known it.

He sat silent for a long time, staring into the starlight and re-living the past, while behind him the camp settled down to sleep. The voices of men and animals sank to a murmur that lost itself in the rustle of leaves as the night wind breathed through the branches of the banyan tree, and beside him Mahdoo's hookah bubbled a rhythmic accompaniment to the monotonous tunk-a-tunk of a distant tom-tom and the howl of a jackal-pack out on the plain. But Ash heard none of these sounds, for he was a long way away both in distance and in time, talking to a little girl in a balcony on a ruined tower that looked out upon the snows of the Dur Khaima . . .

How could he possibly have come to forget her almost completely, when she had been so much a part of his years in the Hawa Mahal? No—not forget her—he had forgotten nothing. He had merely pushed her into the back of his mind and not troubled to think of her: perhaps because he had always taken her for granted—

Later that night, after Mahdoo had gone, Ash unlocked the small tin cash-box that he had bought with his first pocket-money and in which he had kept his most treasured possessions ever since: a little silver ring that Sita had worn, his father's last and unfinished letter, the watch that Colonel Anderson had given him on the day they arrived at Pelham Abbas, his first pair of cuff-links and a dozen other trifles. He turned them over, looking for something, and finally emptied the contents of the box onto his camp bed. Yes, it was still there. A small flat square of yellowing paper.

He carried it over to the lamp, and unfolding it, stood looking at the thing it contained: a sliver of mother-of-pearl that was half of a Chinese counter shaped like a fish. Someone—the *Feringhi*-Rani, perhaps?—had bored a hole through the fish's eye and threaded a strand of twisted silk through it so that it could be worn as a medallion, as Juli had worn it. It had been Juli's most precious possession, yet she had given it to him for a keepsake and begged him not to forget her; and he had hardly ever thought of her again . . . there had been so many other and more urgent things to think of: and when Koda Dad had left Gulkote there had been no one to send him news of the palace, because no one else—not even Hira Lal—knew what had befallen him or where he had gone.

Ash slept little that night, and as he lay on his back looking up into the darkness, a hundred trivial incidents that had been lost with the years came trooping back again to dance before his mind's eye. A night full of fireworks and feasting that celebrated the birth of a son to Janoo-Rani—Nandu, who was now Maharajah of Karidkote. The names and faces of the boys he had played with in the streets of Gulkote—Gopi and Chitu, Jajat and Shoki and a dozen others. The death of Tuku the little mongoose, and Hira Lal telling him that he should be patient with Lalji, for he, Ashok, was more fortunate than his master. Juli bringing him a silver four-anna piece so that they could begin saving up for the house they would build in Sita's valley, and the two of them hiding the precious coin under a loose stone on the floor of the Queen's balcony. They had meant to add other coins to it from time to time, but had never been able to do so, and it was curious to think that unless Juli had taken it out after he had gone, it must still be there, hidden away and forgotten—like his half of her luck-piece that had lain so long in the bottom of the tin cash-box, out of sight and out of mind.

The stars were beginning to pale by the time he fell asleep, and just as his eyes closed, an odd fragment of a conversation returned to him out of the past—something that he himself had once said, though he could not recall the occasion, or why he should have said such a thing:

"If I were you, Juli, I wouldn't get married at all. It's too dangerous."

Why dangerous? thought Ash drowsily as he drifted into sleep.

15

"Ahsti! Ahsti! Khabadar, Premkulli. *Shabash, mera moti —ab ek or. Bas, bas! Kya kurta, ooloo—? . . . Nikal-jao! Arré! Arré! Hai! Hai! Hai! . . ."*

The camp was fording a river to the usual accompaniment of shouts, yells and confusion, and inevitably a cart had become bogged down half-way across and was being pulled out by one of the pad elephants.

Mulraj, who commanded the contingent of Karidkote State Forces, had ridden on ahead with Ash to test the depth of the ford, and now the two sat at ease on the far bank, and from the vantage point of a bluff overlooking the river, watched the unruly multitude straggle across.

"If they do not make haste," observed Mulraj, "it will be dark before the last is across. *Hai mai,* what a business they make of it!"

Ash nodded absently, his gaze still on the men splashing through the shallows or wading knee-deep in mid-river. Three days had passed since he had come face to face with Biju Ram and learned that the Princely State of Karidkote was one and the same as the Gulkote of his youth, and since then he had looked more closely at the men about him and found himself identifying several of them. There were more than half-a-dozen among the mahouts alone, men who had served in the elephant lines of the Hawa Mahal. And there were others too: palace officials, syces, members of the State Forces and a handful of servants and courtiers who four days ago would probably not have attracted his attention, but in the light of his new knowledge were suddenly familiar.

283

Even the elephant, Premkulli, who was being exhorted by his mahout to be careful, was an old friend whom he had fed many times with sticks of sugar cane . . . The last rays of the sinking sun caught the river, glittering on the water in a blaze of gold that dazzled Ash's eyes so that he could no longer make out the faces of those who were crossing, and he turned away to discuss various matters of administration with Mulraj.

The servants and camp-followers, with the baggage animals, had been the first to cross, for there were tents to be pitched, fires lighted and food cooked. But the brides and their immediate entourage preferred to follow at a slower pace and delay their arrival until all was in readiness for them. They had picnicked today in a grove of trees half a mile from the ford, and knowing that their camp would be pitched at the first suitable spot on the far side of the river, had passed the afternoon there, waiting for the word to move on. But the trees had been full of birds coming home to roost by the time a messenger brought word that they might now proceed, and before they were ready to do so the sun had disappeared below the horizon. Accompanied by a rear guard of some thirty men of the State Forces, they had moved on at last in a leisurely manner that brought them to the ford in the twilight.

A covered cart full of waiting-women normally followed immediately behind the gaily caparisoned *ruth* in which the brides travelled, but tonight it had fallen some way behind, and when the *ruth* entered the water it was escorted only by a handful of soldiers and servants, and by the brides' uncle, who had announced his intention of walking the last mile, and having sent his palanquin on ahead, was dismayed to discover that the ford was not nearly as shallow as he had supposed.

On the far bank Ash had already called for his horse, and he was back in the saddle and moving down towards the level ground when a further outburst of shrieks and curses arose from the rapidly darkening river, and he stood up in his stirrups and saw that the near bullock of the *ruth* had fallen in midstream, snapping a shaft and throwing its driver into the water. Held fast by the traces, the animal was struggling and kicking in a frantic attempt to avoid drowning, and the *ruth* was already tilting over on one side. From behind its tightly laced curtains came the piercing shrieks of one of its occupants, while a dozen vociferous men milled about it in the dusk, pushing and pulling as the floundering bullock began to draw it towards deep water.

With night closing in it was difficult for the majority of those in the river to see what had happened, but looking down on the scene Ash had a clear picture of it, and he dug his heels into his horse's flanks and rode down the slope and into the river at a gallop, scattering the gaping crowd in the shallows. The shouting men who surrounded the *ruth* jumped back to give him room as he leaned from the saddle and wrenched at the curtain fastenings until they tore.

A soaked and screaming woman, lifted by a pair of firm, capable hands, seemed to leap at him from the darkness, and he snatched her out just as the off-side wheel broke and the *ruth* fell on its side and began to fill with water.

"Quick, Juli! Come on, get out!" Ash was unaware that he had called to the remaining occupant by name as he shouted to make himself heard above the tumult of yelling voices and the ominous sound of water rushing through the half-submerged *ruth,* but in fact his words had been lost in the din, for the small figure in his arms was clinging to him in a frenzy of terror and still shrieking at the top of her voice. He beat down the clutching hands and thrust her at the nearest person, who happened by good fortune to be her uncle, though it might just as easily have been a sowar or a bullock driver. The next second he was off his horse and in the river, with the water swirling above his waist.

"Get out, girl!"

There was a choking, spluttering sound from the darkness and a hand reached out between the torn curtains. Ash gripped it and dragged its owner up and out, and lifting her off her feet, carried her to the bank.

She was no light and fragile creature like the little sister whom he had thrust out of the *ruth* into his arms, nor did she scream or cling to him as the younger girl had done. But though she made no sound he could feel the quick rise and fall of her breast against his own, while the weight of her warm, wet body, and every slender curve and line of it, spoke eloquently of a woman and not of a child.

285

He was breathing a little unevenly himself by the time he reached dry land, though his reasons for doing so were not emotional but physical, and few men, called upon to carry approximately a hundred and twelve pounds across a river, with the current tugging at their knees and a crowd of excited spectators splashing and jostling alongside, would not have done the same. It seemed a long way to the shallows, and when he reached the bank there was no one to whom he could hand over his burden. He called for torches and the Rajkumaries' women and waited in the dusk, holding Anjuli's dripping figure in his arms while his syce set off to retrieve his horse, and far too many helpers struggled to free the bullocks and drag the broken *ruth* out of the way, so that the cart with the princesses' waiting-women could cross in safety.

Above him the stars came out one by one, and as the night wind arose and blew strongly off the river, the girl in his arms began to shiver in the cold air and Ash called for a blanket and wrapped it about her, drawing one end over her head to shield her from the gaze of the crowd as torches began to flower in the darkness and the women's cart creaked into view at last.

Judging from the noise, the younger bride was already inside it, though her shrieks had now given place to hysterical sobbing. But Ash did not pause to inquire after her. His muscles were beginning to ache, and he bundled Anjuli in without ceremony and stood back as the cart jolted on its way to the camp, aware for the first time that his clothes were soaking wet and that there was a distinct nip in the night air.

"*Mubarik ho*, that was well done, Sahib," approved Mulraj, materializing out of the darkness. "I owe you my life, I think. I and many others, for had you not been here the Rajkumaries might both have drowned, and then who knows what vengeance His Highness their brother would have taken on us his servants?"

"*Be-wakufi*,"* retorted Ash impatiently. "They were never in the least danger of drowning. Only of getting wet. The river is not nearly deep enough there."

"The driver of the *ruth* was drowned," observed Mulraj dryly. "The current took him into deep water and it seems that he could not swim. The Rajkumaries would

---

*nonsense (literally, stupidity)

286

have been trapped inside by the curtains and drowned also, but it was their good fortune that you should have been on horseback and watching—and most of all, that you are a Sahib, for no other man there, save only their uncle who is old and slow, would have dared to lay hands on the daughters of a Maharajah, and by the time I myself had seen what was toward and was in the saddle, it was all over. They should fill your hands with gold for this night's work."

"At this moment I would rather have a hot bath and dry clothes," said Ash with a laugh. "And if anyone deserves praise it is Anjuli-Bai, for keeping her head and getting her younger sister out, instead of screaming and struggling to escape herself, when she must have known that the *ruth* was filling up with water. Where the devil is my syce? *Ohé*, Kulu Ram!"

"Here Sahib," said a voice at his elbow: the horse's hooves had made no sound on the sandy ground. Ash took the reins and swung himself into the saddle, and having saluted Mulraj, touched the horse with his heel and cantered off between the clumps of pampas grass and the thorny *kikar* trees to where the lights of the camp made an orange glow in the night sky.

He turned in early, and the next day had been a busy one, for he had ridden off at dawn with Jhoti, Mulraj and Tarak Nath, a member of the camp's *panchayat*, and an armed escort of half-a-dozen sowars, to reconnoitre the next ford. The boy had been an unexpected addition to the party, having apparently teased Mulraj into bringing him. But as he proved to be an excellent rider, and was obviously eager to please and be pleased, he was no trouble to anyone. And it occurred to Ash that it would be no bad thing to get him away from his attendants and out into the fresh air, on horseback, as often as possible, for a day in the open had plainly done the little prince a world of good, and he already looked a different being from the pallid and anxious-eyed child of their first meeting.

The ford had proved impassable, and as it had been necessary to find out, by personal inspection, which of two alternative crossing places would save the most time and cause the least inconvenience, the sun was setting and the day almost over by the time they returned to the camp. Ash had intended to ask for an early start on the following morning, but this had been frustrated by Shushila-Bai, the younger princess, who sent word that she was suffering from shock and sickness and did not intend to move anywhere at all for at least two or three days—if not longer.

Her decision was not so tiresome as it would have been two days earlier, for food stocks were high and the river provided an unlimited supply of water. And as it happened, Ash himself was by no means averse to remaining in one place for a few days, for there were both black-buck and *chinkara* out on the plain, and he had seen snipe on a jheel near by and any amount of partridge in the scrubland. It would, he thought, be pleasant to go out shooting with Mulraj instead of shepherding this flock across country.

Having been informed that the Rajkumari Shushila was indisposed, he was surprised when a second messenger arrived with a politely worded request that he would pay the Maharajah's sisters the honour of visiting them. And as the messenger on this occasion had been no less a person than the brides' uncle, affectionately known throughout the camp as "Kaka-ji Rao,"* it had been impossible for him to refuse, even though the hour was late and he would have preferred bed to social conversation. However, there being no help for it, he duly changed into mess dress, and almost as an after-thought, slipped the broken half of the mother-of-pearl fish into his pocket before accompanying the Rao-Sahib through the lamp-lit camp.

The "durbar tent" in which the princesses received guests was large and comfortable, and lined throughout with a rust-red cloth embroidered in gay colours and lavishly decorated with tiny circles of looking-glass that winked and glittered as the material billowed to the night breeze or the flames of the oil lamps swayed in a draught of air. The floor was strewn with Persian rugs and squabby silk and brocade cushions which served in place of chairs, and there were a number of low tables, carved from sandalwood and inlaid with ivory, on which an assortment of fruit and sweetmeats had been set out in silver dishes. But except for Kaka-ji Rao and the elderly duenna, Unpora-Bai, and two serving women who

---

*kaka = paternal uncle

sat in the shadows beyond the circle of light, the only other persons present were the brides themselves and their younger brother, Jhoti.

The Rajkumaries were dressed much as they had been before. But with one noteworthy difference. To-night they were both unveiled. "It is because they owe their lives to you," explained the little prince, coming forward to greet Ash and do the honours for his sisters. "But for you, they would both have drowned. This very day their pyres would have been lit and the river received their ashes, and tomorrow we others should have returned home with our faces blackened. We have much to thank you for, and from now on you are as our brother."

He waved away Ash's assertion that there had in fact been no danger, and his sisters rose to make their bows while Unpora-Bai made approving noises from behind her veil, and Kaka-ji observed that modesty was a virtue to be prized above valour, and that it was plain that Pelham-Sahib possessed both in full measure. One of the serving-women then shuffled forward with a silver tray that bore two ceremonial garlands fashioned out of tinsel ribbon ornamented with gold-embroidered medallions, and first Shushila and then Anjuli solemnly hung one about Ash's neck, where they glittered incongruously against the drab khaki of his mess jacket and gave him something of the appearance of an over-decorated General. After which he was invited to seat himself and plied with refreshments, and as a singular mark of favour (for it is pollution for those of high caste to eat with casteless men) the company ate with him—though not from the same dishes.

Once Shushila-Bai had been coaxed out of her shyness, the party relaxed and spent a very pleasant hour nibbling *halwa*, sipping sherbet and talking; and even cousin Unpora-Bai, while remaining closely veiled, contributed her mite to the conversation. It had not been easy to draw out the younger princess and persuade her to talk, but Ash, when he chose, had a way with him, and now he exerted himself to put the nervous child at her ease, and was eventually rewarded by a shy smile and then a laugh, and presently she was laughing and chattering as though she had known him all her life and he was indeed an older brother. It was only then that he felt free to turn his attention to her half-sister, Anjuli-Bai—and was startled by what he saw.

Anjuli had been sitting a little behind her sister when he entered, and directly under the shadow cast by the hanging lamp; and even when she rose to greet and garland him, he had not really been able to study her, for she had kept her head bent and wore the peak of her sari drawn so far forward that its broad edging of embroidery shadowed what little he could see of her face. Later, when they were all seated, he had been too occupied with his efforts to coax the younger princess into joining in the talk between himself and her brother and uncle to spare much attention for the elder one. That could wait. And though Anjuli had so far barely spoken, her silence neither suggested the nervous timidity that appeared to afflict her young half-sister, nor conveyed the impression that she was uninterested in what was being said. She sat quietly, watching and listening and occasionally nodding in agreement or shaking her head in smiling dissent, and Ash remembered that "Kairi-Bai" had always been a good listener . . .

Looking fully at her at last, his first thought was that he had made a mistake. This was not Kairi. It was not possible that the thin, plain, shabby little creature who never seemed to have enough to eat, and who, as he had once complained, followed him around like a starving kitten, could have grown into a woman like this. Mahdoo had got it wrong, and this was not the daughter of the old Rajah's second wife, the *Feringhi*-Rani, but of someone else . . .

Yet because her head was no longer bent, her sari had slipped back a little, and the signs of her mixed blood were clearly to be seen. They were there in the colour of her skin and the structure of her bones; in the long, gracious lines of her body, the breadth of shoulder and hip, and the small, square-jawed face with its high cheek bones and broad brow; in the set of the wide-spaced eyes that were the colours of bog-water, the tilted tip of that short nose, and the lovely, generous mouth that was too large to suit the accepted standards of beauty that were so admirably personified by her half-sister.

By contrast, Shushila-Bai was as small and exquisite as a Tanagra figurine or the miniature of some legendary Indian beauty: golden-skinned and black-eyed, her face a flawless oval and her mouth a rose-petal. Her small-boned perfection made her seem as though she were fashioned from a different clay from the half-sister who sat beside and a little behind her—and who was not quite as tall as Ash's first impression of her, for standing, he had topped her by half a head. But then he was a tall man, and her co-bride, Shushila, stood barely four foot ten in her heelless silken slippers.

The elder girl lacked the delicacy of the East, but that did not prove that she was the *Feringhi*-Rani's daughter . . .

His gaze fell on a bare arm that was the colour of warm ivory, and there, just above the golden bangles, was a crescent-shaped scar: the mark left by the teeth of a monkey, many years ago . . . Yes, it is Juli all right, thought Ash. Juli grown up—and grown beautiful.

Long ago, during his first year at a public school, Ash had come across a line in one of Marlowe's plays that had caught his imagination and stuck fast in his memory ever since: Faust's words on seeing Helen of Troy: *"Oh thou art fairer than the evening air, clad in the beauty of a thousand stars!"* It had seemed to him then, and still did, the perfect description of beauty, and later he had applied it to Lily Briggs, who had giggled and told him that "he wasn't 'alf a one," and later still to Belinda— who had reacted in a similar manner, though she had phrased her comment a little differently. Yet neither of them bore the least resemblance to the Maharajah of Karidkote's half-sister, Anjuli-Bai, for whom, thought Ash, astounded, those lines might have been expressly written.

Looking at Juli, it was as though he were seeing beauty for the first time in his life, and as though he had never realized before what it was. Lily had been blowsily attractive and Belinda had certainly been pretty—a great deal prettier than any of his previous loves. But then his ideal of feminine good looks had been shaped by his childhood in India, and unconsciously influenced by fashion—Victoria's England, as may be seen from countless paintings, picture-postcards and illustrated books of the period, still admired large eyes and a small rose-bud of a mouth in a smoothly oval face, to say nothing of sloping shoulders and a nineteen-inch waist. The era of Du Maurier's stately goddesses, who were to usher in an entirely new fashion in beauty, had not yet dawned; and it had never occurred to Ash that any form and face

291

so diametrically opposed to the Victorian—and Indian—ideal could not only be immeasurably more arresting, but make the prettiness he had hitherto admired seem slightly insipid. But though his personal preference was still for dainty and delicately built women such as Shushila, Anjuli's looks, which threw back to her Russian great-grandmother, were a revelation to him, and he could not take his eyes off her.

Becoming aware of his regard and embarrassed by it, she half turned from him and drew the peak of her sari forward again so that her face was once more in shadow; and Ash suddenly realized that he had been staring—and also that Jhoti had just asked him a question and that he had no idea what it was. He turned quickly towards the boy, and for the next ten minutes became involved in a discussion on falconry; and only when Jhoti and Shushila began to tease their uncle to let them go hawking on the far side of the river was he able to turn back again to Anjuli.

The two elderly waiting-women were already beginning to yawn and nod, for it was getting late. But though he knew that it was time he took his leave, there was something he meant to do before he left. He put his hand in his pocket, and a moment or two later reached out and made believe to pick something off the carpet.

"Your Highness has dropped something," said Ash, holding it out to Anjuli. "This is yours, I think?"

He had expected her to look surprised or puzzled—probably the latter, for he thought it unlikely that after all these years she would remember either the luck-piece or the boy she had given it to. But she did neither. She turned her head when he spoke, and seeing the sliver of mother-of-pearl on his palm, took it with a smile and a brief murmur of thanks.

"*Shukr-guzari*, Sahib. Yes, it is mine. I do not know how it can have—"

She stopped on a gasp, for she had put a hand to her breast; and Ash knew in that moment that he had been wrong. Juli not only remembered, but she still wore her half of the luck-piece where she had always worn it, hanging from a strand of silk about her neck. And she had just realized that it was still there.

Ash was suddenly aware of a disturbing mixture of emotions that he did not wish to analyse, and turning

292

to Shushila-Bai, he begged her forgiveness for keeping her up so late and asked for leave to withdraw. Yes, yes, agreed Kaka-ji, rising with alacrity, it was quite time they all retired to bed; the hour was late and though young people might be able to do without sleep, he himself could not. "It has been a very pleasant evening. We must have other parties," said Kaka-ji Rao.

Anjuli said nothing. Nor did she move. She sat quite still, holding the missing half of her luck-piece clenched in her hand and staring at Ash with wide, startled eyes. But Ash was already regretting the impulse that had made him give it to her, and as he said his farewells he avoided her gaze, and leaving the tent walked back through the camp feeling angry with himself and wishing that he had thrown away the piece of pearl shell—or at least had the sense to leave well alone. He had an uneasy feeling that he had started something, the end of which he could not see, like a man who carelessly flicks a pebble at an over-hanging ledge of snow, and thereby sets in motion an avalanche that may overwhelm some hamlet in a valley far below.

What if Juli were to talk of the strange return of the missing half of her luck-piece? He had no way of knowing how many people were in her confidence these days, or how much she had changed. Nor had he any idea where her loyalties now lay, for the sad little Kairi-Bai of his Gulkote days appeared to have nothing in common with this bejewelled princess of Karidkote who was being conveyed to her wedding with such pomp and splendour, and it was clear that her circumstances had altered surprisingly and everything turned out well for her. As for himself, he had no desire to be identified in any way with the boy who had been her brother's servant. Janoo-Rani might be dead but Biju Ram was still very much alive; and, in all probability, just as dangerous. He at least would not have forgotten Ashok, and were he to hear the tale of Juli's luck-piece he might well take fright and decide to deal with this Sahib as he and Janoo-Rani had plotted to do all those years ago with Ashok. And for the same reason—for fear of what he might know or guess; and, now that Lalji was dead, of the ghosts that he might raise . . .

Thinking of all this, Ash was uneasily conscious of a cold feeling in the pit of his stomach and a compul-

293

sive urge to look over his shoulder as he walked back through the camp. He had been a fool and once again, as so often in the past, acted on impulse and without giving due thought to the possible consequences of the action; which was something he had sworn to himself that he would never do again.

That night he slept with the tent-flap laced shut and a revolver under his pillow, having made a mental note to pay more attention to the siting of his tent, which at present could be too easily approached from three sides without disturbing either Mahdoo or Gul Baz, or any of his personal servants. From now on he would have their tents pitched in a half-moon behind his own, with their guy-ropes interlocking, while the horses should be tethered to the right and left instead of bunched together in the rear. "I'll see to it in the morning," decided Ash.

But the morning was still several hours away when he was awakened from sleep by the sound of a hand trying the fastening of the tent-flap.

Ash had always been a light sleeper and the stealthy sound woke him instantly. He lay still, listening, and presently heard it repeated. Someone was trying to enter the tent, and it was not one of his own men; they would have coughed or spoken to attract his attention. Nor could it be a prowling dog or a jackal, for the sound did not come from ground level but from higher up. Ash slid a hand under his pillow and drew out his revolver, and was easing back the safety catch when someone again scratched softly but imperatively on the canvas and a whispering voice called: "Sahib, Sahib."

"Kaun hai?" (who is it?). "What do you want?"

"No harm, Sahib. Indeed no harm. A word only—" The speaker's teeth chattered from cold, or possibly from fear or nervousness.

Ash said curtly: "Speak then. I am listening."

"The Rajkumari . . . my mistress, Anjuli-Bai, says . . ."

"Wait."

Ash felt for the knot and unlacing the flap threw it back and saw that his visitor was a woman, a veiled and shrouded figure bundled in shawls, who was presumably one of the royal serving-women. He himself was more scantily clad, for his sole garment was a pair of loose

294

cotton trousers, and the woman drew back with a startled gasp, disconcerted at being faced with a half-naked Sahib who clutched a revolver in one hand.

"Well, what is it?" demanded Ash impatiently. He did not relish being woken at such an hour and was ashamed of the fear that had stabbed through him in the moment of waking. "What is it that your mistress wishes to know?"

"She wishes—she prays that you will tell her from whom you received a certain piece of pearl-shell, and asks if you can give her news of him . . . and of his mother also; and tell her where they may be found. That is all."

And quite enough, thought Ash grimly. Was it only Juli who wanted this information, or had the return of the missing half of the luck-piece already been talked of in the camp, and could Biju Ram have sent this woman to question him?

He said brusquely: "I cannot help the Rajkumari. Tell her that I am sorry, but I know nothing."

He made as though to close the tent-flap, but the woman reached out and catching his arm said breathlessly: "That is not true. You must surely know who gave it to you, and if so . . . Sahib, I beg of you! Of your charity, tell me only if they are alive and well."

Ash looked down at the hand on his arm. The newly risen moon was in its last quarter, but its light was still bright enough to show him the shape of that hand, and he caught it about the wrist and holding it in a hard grasp, reached out and jerked aside the *chuddah* that hid the woman's face. She made one frantic attempt to free herself, and finding that she could not, stood quite still, staring at him and breathing a little quickly.

Ash laughed and made her a half bow. "I am greatly honoured, Your Highness. But is this wise? As you see I am not dressed to receive visitors; and were you to be found here at such an hour it would cause great trouble for us both. Besides, you should not go unattended through the camp. It is too dangerous. You would have done better to send me one of your women. Let me advise you to return quickly before they awake and rouse the guard when they find you gone."

"If it is for yourself that you are afraid," said Anjuli

295

sweetly, "you have no cause to be, for I sleep alone and therefore no one will miss me. And if I feared for myself, I would not be here."

Her voice was still barely more than a whisper, but there was so much scorn in it that the blood came up into Ash's face and for a fraction of a second his fingers tightened cruelly about her wrist.

"Why, you little bitch," said Ash softly and in English. He laughed, and releasing her, stepped back and said: "Yes, I am afraid. And if Your Highness is not, I can only say that you should be. Myself, I cannot believe that your brothers or your uncle would treat such an escapade lightly; or your bride-groom, either. They might consider that it in some way touches your honour, and as I confess I have no wish to get a knife between my ribs one of these nights, I would urge you again, with all respect, to go quickly."

"Not until you tell me what I wish to know," said Anjuli stubbornly. "I will stay here until you do, though as you well know, if I am found here it will go hard with me. Even my worst enemy could not wish me so much ill, and you have already saved my life. Only tell me what I ask and I will trouble you no more. I swear it."

"Why do you want to know?"

"Because the thing you gave me tonight is the half of a luck-charm that once, very long go, I myself gave to a friend; and when I saw it I—" A movement behind her made her spin round: a patter and a rustle in the stillness. "There is someone there—!"

"It is only a *lakar bagha* (hyena)," said Ash.

The grotesque, shadowy creature that had been scavenging in the camp scuttled past and loped away across the plain, and the girl drew a deep, shuddering breath of relief and said haltingly: "I thought it was . . . I thought I had—been followed."

"So you *are* afraid after all," said Ash unkindly. "Well, if you wish to talk you had better come inside. It cannot be more dangerous than standing out here where anyone might see us."

He stood back to let her enter the tent, and after a moment's hesitation she went in past him, and Ash closed the tent-flap and said: "Don't move. I'll light a lamp."

She heard him groping in the darkness and then a match flared, and when the wick of the hurricane lamp was

296

burning steadily, he pulled up a canvas chair for her and, without waiting to see if she took it, turned away to put on his dressing gown and slippers. "If we are going to be caught talking together at this hour of night," observed Ash, tying the cord about his waist, "it will look better if I am wearing a few more clothes. Won't you sit down? No? Then you won't mind if I do." He seated himself on the end of the camp bed and looked up at her, waiting.

The carriage-clock on the table behind him ticked audibly in a silence that he made no attempt to break, and a moth that had found its way in from the night began to flutter around and around the lamp, throwing whirling, wavering shadows across the walls of the tent.

"I . . ." began Anjuli, and paused, biting her lip in a way that was suddenly and sharply familiar to Ash. It was a trick she had as a child and his mother used to scold her for it, saying that it would spoil the shape of her mouth.

"Go on," said Ash unhelpfully.

"But I have already told you: I gave that charm to a friend many years ago, and I wish to know how you came by it because—because I would like to know what became of my friend and his mother, and where they are now. Is that so hard to understand?"

"No. But it is not enough. There must be more than that, or you would never have risked coming here. I want to know the whole. Also, before I answer your questions, I want to know whom you would tell."

"Whom I would tell? I do not understand."

"Don't you? Think—are there no others besides yourself who might also wish to know where this friend of yours is?"

Anjuli shook her head. "Not now. Once, perhaps; for there was an evil woman who wished him ill and would have killed him if she could. But she is dead now and cannot harm him; and I think she had forgotten about him long ago. As for his friends, except for myself they left Gulkote, and I do not know where they are, or if they know where he is or what became of him. It may be that they too are dead. Or that they have forgotten him as everyone else has."

"Except yourself," said Ash slowly.

"Except myself. But then, you see . . . he was a brother to me—a true brother, as my own were not—and I do not remember my mother. She fell into disfavour before she died, and afterwards my father's new wife saw to it that I was kept out of his sight, so that he became a stranger to me. Even the servants knew that they need not treat me well, and only two were kind to me: one of my serving-women, and her son Ashok, a boy some few years older than myself who was in the service of my half-brother, the Yuveraj. Had it not been for Ashok and his mother I should have been friendless indeed, and you cannot know what their kindness meant to the child that I was . . ."

Her voice wavered uncertainly and Ash looked away from her, for there were tears in her eyes and once again he was ashamed because he had allowed himself to forget a little girl who had loved his mother and looked up to him as a friend and a hero, and whom he had left behind, friendless, in Gulkote and never thought of again . . .

"You see," explained Anjuli, "I had no one else to love, and when they went away I thought that I should die of grief and loneliness. They had no choice but to go . . . But I will not tell you that tale, for it is one I think you must know, or how else would you have known who had the other half of the luck-piece? I will only say that when we parted I gave the charm to Ashok for a keepsake, and he broke it in two and gave half back to me, promising that he would surely return one day and then—then we would join the two pieces together again. But I never learned what had become of him or even if he and his mother had escaped to safety, and there were times when I feared that they were both dead, for I could not believe that they would send me no word, or that Ashok would not come back. You see—he had promised. And then . . . and then tonight, when I saw that what you had given me was not my own half of the charm, but his, I knew that he was alive and that he must have asked you to give it to me. So I waited until all the camp was asleep, and came here to ask for news of him."

The moth had fallen down the chimney of the oil lamp and set the wick flaring, and another clumsy night-flying insect was battering itself against the glass, making a monotonous sound that now Anjuli was no longer speaking seemed as loud as the beat of a drum in the silence. Ash rose abruptly and went over to trim the wick, standing with his back to her and apparently giving his whole attention to the task. He had not made any comment, and as the silence lengthened and he still did not speak, she said with a catch in her voice:

"Are they dead, then?"

Ash spoke without turning: "His mother died many years ago. Not long after they left Gulkote."

"And Ashok?" She had to repeat the question.

"He is here," said Ash at last; and turned towards her, the light at his back falling full on her face and leaving his own in shadow.

"You mean—here in the camp?" Anjuli's voice was a startled whisper. "Then why did he not . . . Where is he? What is he doing? Tell him—"

Ash said: "Don't you know me, Juli?"

"Know you?" repeated Juli bewildered. "Ah, do not make game of me, Sahib. It is not kind."

She wrung her hands together in a gesture of despair and Ash said: "I am not making game of you. Look at me, Juli—" he reached for the lamp and lifting it, held it so that the light fell on his face. "Look carefully. Have I changed so much? Do you really not know me?"

Anjuli backed away from him, staring and whispering, "No! no, no, no—" under her breath.

"Yes, you do. I can't have changed as much as all that: I was eleven. It was different with you. You were only a baby of six, or was it seven? I would never have recognized you if I hadn't known. But you still have the scar where the monkey bit you. Do you remember how my mother washed the bite and tied it up for you, and told you the story of Rama and Sita and how Hanuman and his monkeys helped them? And afterwards I took you to Hanuman's temple near the elephant lines? Have you forgotten the day that Lalji's marmoset ran away and we followed it into the *Mor Minar*, and found the Queen's balcony?"

"No," breathed Anjuli, her eyes wide and enormous. "No, it cannot be true. I do not believe it. It is a trick."

"Why should I trick you? Ask me anything; something that only Ashok could know. And if I cannot answer—"

"He could have told you," interrupted Anjuli breathlessly. "You could be repeating things that you learned from him. Yes, that is it!"

"Is it? But why? There is nothing to be gained. Why should I trouble to tell you this if it were not true?"

"But—but you are a Sahib. An *Angrezi* Sahib. How can you be Ashok? I knew his mother. He was the son of my waiting-woman, Sita."

Ash put the lamp back on the table and sat down again on the camp bed. He said slowly: "So he always thought. But it was not so. And when she came to die, she told him that the woman who bore him was an *Angrezi* and the wife of an *Angrezi*, and that she, Sita, whose husband was his father's head syce, had been his foster-mother—his own having died at his birth. It was something that he—that I—did not wish to learn, for she had been, in every way but one, my real mother. But that did not make it any the less true, and truth is truth. I was, I am, Ashok. If you do not believe me you have only to send word to Koda Dad Khan, who lives now in his own village in the country of the Yusufzais, and whom you must surely remember. Or to his son, Zarin, who is a Jemadar of the Guides, in Mardan. They will tell you that what I say is true."

"Oh, no!" whispered Anjuli. Her voice failed, and turning from him she leaned her head against the tent pole and wept as though her heart would break.

It was, perhaps, the one reaction he was not prepared for, and it not only disconcerted him but left him feeling embarrassed and helpless, and more than a little indignant.

What on earth had she to cry about? *Girls!* thought Ash—not for the first time—and began to wish that he had kept his mouth shut. He had meant to do so; though admittedly only after it had occurred to him that others besides Anjuli-Bai might be interested in the fate of Ashok, and that it had probably been a grave mistake to resurrect the memory of that long-forgotten little boy. But the fact that Juli had remembered him and his mother with so much affection for so many years had melted his resolution, and it had suddenly seemed cruel not to tell her the truth, and allow her to believe, if it was any comfort to her, that he had kept a promise that, to be honest, he had forgotten all about until now. He had presumed that she would be pleased. Or at least excited. Not appalled and tearful.

What did she expect? thought Ash resentfully. What else could he have done? Fobbed her off with some cock-and-bull story of a stranger who had given him that piece of pearl-shell? Or refused to tell her anything and sent her away with a flea in her ear—which is what she deserved for behaving in this embarrassing manner. He scowled at the haze of insects that by now were circling the lamp and tried to shut his ears to the sound of that stifled sobbing.

The clock on the table by his bed struck three, and the small, brisk chimes made him start violently, not because they reminded him of the lateness of the hour, but because, subconsciously, his nerves were on the stretch. He had not realized until then just how apprehensive he was, but that involuntary spasm of alarm was a reminder of the dangers of the present situation and the horrifying risk that Juli had taken in coming to see him. She had brushed it away lightly enough, but that did not make it any the less real; if she were missed, and found here, the consequences for them both did not bear thinking of.

For the second time that night Ash found himself thinking how easily he could be murdered (and Juli too, for that matter!) without anyone ever knowing, and his exasperation mounted. How like a woman to compromise them both and then, having landed them in this dangerous and ridiculous position, make matters worse by collapsing into floods of tears. He would like to shake her. Didn't she realize—?

He turned his head to look at her, still scowling, and his mood changed abruptly; for she was crying very quietly and there was something in her pose that reminded him vividly of the last time he had seen her cry. Even then it had been on his account—because he was in danger and was going away—and not because she herself would be left alone and friendless. And now once again he had made her cry. Poor Juli—poor little Kairi-Bai! He stood up and came to stand beside her, and after a moment or two said awkwardly: "Don't cry, Juli. There isn't anything to cry about."

She did not reply, but she shook her head in a helpless gesture that might have been either agreement or dissent, and for some reason that small, despairing gesture cut him to the heart and he put his arms about her and held her close, whispering foolish words of comfort and saying over and over again: "Don't cry, Juli. Please don't cry. It's all right now. I'm here. I've come back. There isn't anything to cry about . . ."

For a minute or so the slender, shuddering body

301

made no resistance. Her head lay passively against his shoulder and he could feel her tears soaking through the thin silk of his dressing-gown. Then all at once she stiffened in his arms and tore herself free. Her face was no longer beautiful: the lamplight showed it blurred and distorted with grief, and her lovely eyes were red and swollen. She did not speak; she merely looked at him. It was a chill and contemptuous look, as wounding as the lash of the whip, and turning from him, she ripped back the tent-flap and ran out into the night, and was swallowed up by the moonlight and the chequered shadows.

There was no point in following her, and Ash made no attempt to do so. He listened for a while, but hearing no sound of voices or any challenge from the direction of the camp, he went back into the tent and sat down again, feeling dazed and curiously breathless.

"No," whispered Ash, arguing with himself in the silence. "No of course not. It's ridiculous. It couldn't possibly happen like that . . . not in just one minute, between one breath and the next. It *couldn't* . . ."

But he knew that it could. Because it had just happened to him.

16

In obedience to the younger bride's wishes, the tents had not been struck on the following morning and word had gone out that there would be no further move for at least three days—a respite that was welcomed by all, for apart from a rest from marching it provided an opportunity for clothes to be washed and food to be cooked in a more leisurely manner, and a thousand repairs and re-adjustments made to tents, trappings and saddlery.

The banks of the river were soon lined with *dhobis* busied with piles of washing, mahouts bathing their elephants, and hordes of children splashing and playing in the shallows. Grass-cutters scattered in search of fodder and hunting parties rode out after game; and Jhoti and Shushila wheeled their uncle into arranging a day's hawking that the girls could attend without the necessity of keeping strict purdah.

Kaka-ji had needed a lot of persuading, but he had eventually given way on condition that they kept well out of sight of the camp, and a party had been made up that included Ash and Mulraj, half-a-dozen falconers, three of the brides' women and a small escort of palace guards and servants. It also included Biju Ram (who would be in attendance upon Jhoti) and Kaka-ji Rao, who announced that he himself would be accompanying them solely in order to keep an avuncular eye upon his nieces —which had deceived no one, for the old gentleman had a passion for falconry and they were all aware that he would not have missed it for anything; and also that he would have preferred to go without either of his nieces.

"It is not that they cannot ride well enough," he explained to Ash in a burst of confidence, "but they know little of falconry, which is a man's sport. A woman's wrist is not strong enough to support a hawk. Or at least, Shushila's is not, though with her half-sister it is different. But then Anjuli-Bai has no liking for the sport and Shushila tires too easily. I cannot think why they should wish to come with us."

"Kairi did not wish to," volunteered Jhoti, who had been listening to the conversation of his elders. "She wanted to stay behind. But Shu-Shu said that if Kairi wouldn't go she would not go either, and she began to cry and say that she was so tired of the noise and the smells of the camp, and of being shut up in a *ruth* or a tent, and that if she didn't get away from it and out into the open air for a while she would die. *You* know what she is like. So of course Kairi had to agree to come. Oh, here they are at last—Good. Now perhaps we can start."

They rode away across the plain, holding their horses to a sedate trot in order not to out-distance the cart containing the waiting women, who could not ride, or the Rajkumari Shushila, who in spite of what Kaka-ji had said was an indifferent horsewoman and rode on a lead-rein held by an elderly retainer.

Both girls wore light head scarves that concealed their faces and left only their eyes uncovered, but once clear of the camp and in the open country they allowed the flimsy material to blow free. But Ash noted with interest that except for Jhoti and Kaka-ji, none of the men-

303

folk—not even Mulraj, who was related to the royal family—ever looked directly at them even when replying to a question: an exhibition of good manners that impressed him, though he did not emulate it. Having been told to consider himself one of the family, he saw no reason why he should not claim an honorary brother's privilege and look as long and as openly as he pleased, and he had done so. But at Anjuli rather than at her younger sister; though little Shushila, laughing and excited by the sport and the heady taste of freedom, was well worth looking at: a princess from a fairy-tale, all gold and rose and ebony, and sparkling with gaiety.

"She will be ill tonight. You'll see," said Jhoti cheerfully. "She is always ill after she gets excited. Just like a see-saw, up in the air or down in the mud—*bump!* I think girls are silly, don't you? Fancy having to marry one."

"Hmm?" said Ash, who was not listening.

"My mother," confided Jhoti, "had arranged a marriage for me, but when she died my brother Nandu broke it off, which was a good thing, for I did not wish to get married. He only did it to spite me—that I know well. He meant to do me an ill turn, and did me a good one by mistake, the silly owl. But I suppose I shall have to marry some day. One has to have a wife in order to get sons, does one not? Has yours given you any sons yet?"

Ash made another indeterminate noise and Mulraj, who was riding on the other side of him, answered on his behalf: "The Sahib has no wife, Prince. His people do not marry young. They wait until they are old and wise. Is that not so, Sahib?"

"Umm?" said Ash. "I'm sorry—I didn't hear what you said."

Mulraj laughed and threw up a protesting hand. "You see, my Prince?—he has heard nothing. His thoughts are far away today. What is it, Sahib? Is there something that troubles you?"

"No, of course not," said Ash hastily. "I was only thinking about something else."

"That is plain—you have already missed a chance at three birds because of it. *Ohé!*—there goes another. A fine, fat pigeon. No . . . you are too late. The prince is before you."

Jhoti had in fact been the first to see the pigeon, and

304

before Mulraj had finished speaking his hawk was in the air and he himself spurring excitedly in pursuit.

"He has been well taught," approved Mulraj, watching the child race away; "and he rides like a Rajput. But I do not like the look of his saddle. It seems to me ... Forgive me, Sahib."

He set spurs to his horse and left at a gallop, abandoning Ash, who, left alone with his thoughts, was not ungrateful for a period of silence. He was not feeling at all sociable that morning; or particularly interested in the day's sport either, though he too had been well taught and the falcon on his wrist was a gift from Kaka-ji Rao. Normally he would have enjoyed nothing better than a day's hawking in such country, but today his mind was on other things.

The younger princess appeared to have shed a large part of her previous shyness, for she had talked gaily to him and obviously accepted him as a friend, but Anjuli had not spoken, and this time her silence was one of withdrawal and Ash discovered that he could not even make her look at him. He had tried to force her into conversation, only to find his questions answered with a slight gesture of the head or at best a faint polite smile, while her eyes continued to look past him as though he were not there. And she was not looking well. Her face was swollen and colourless and he suspected that she had not had enough sleep, which was not surprising considering that it was after three when she had left his tent. He did not think it would be possible for her to look ugly, for her beauty was bone deep, and the way her small square face was set on the column of her throat, the shortness of her upper lip and the width between her eyes, would always be there. But today, riding beside her little sister, she appeared almost plain, and he wondered why that should make no difference at all to the way she looked to him.

Months ago he had told Wally that he could never fall in love again because he was cured of love for ever— immunized to the disease like a man who has recovered from smallpox. And only a few hours ago, eight at most, he would have repeated that statement and been confident that it was true. He still could not understand why it should no longer be so, or how it had come about. His feelings for the child Juli, though protective, had certainly never been either fond or sentimental (small boys being seldom interested in, let alone deeply attached to little girls much younger than themselves) and given the choice he would undoubtedly have preferred a playmate of his own age and sex. Besides, he had known who she was when he carried her through the river and stood holding her for an unconscionably long time in the dusk; yet his only emotion then had been impatience . . .

Two nights later, staring at her in the durbar tent and discovering with amazement that she was beautiful, his pulses had not quickened or his emotions been stirred; and when she came to his tent he had been suspicious, irritated and vaguely sentimental by turn, and ended up feeling angry and embarrassed. So why on earth should a few minutes in which she had sobbed in his arms, and the sight of her wet, distorted face, change the world for him? It did not make sense—yet it had happened, all the same.

One minute he had been furious with her for coming and wishing angrily that she would stop crying and go away—quickly. And thirty seconds later, holding her, he had known without a shadow of doubt that he had found the answer to that nagging feeling of emptiness that had bedevilled him for so long. It had gone for ever, and he had been made whole again, because he had found the thing that was lacking—it was here in his arms: Juli . . . his own Juli. Not part of his past, but quite suddenly, and for always, a part of his heart.

As yet he had no idea what, if anything, he intended to do about this. Prudence told him that he must put her out of his mind and do his best to avoid seeing or speaking to her ever again, because to do so could only end in disaster for them both: a point he had seen clearly enough last night and that was still as clear, if not clearer, in the harsh light of morning. The Rajkumari Anjuli was the daughter of a ruling prince, the half-sister of another, and soon to become the wife of a third. Nothing could alter that, so his wisest course—the only course—was to forget last night and be thankful that something he had said or done had succeeded in offending her so deeply that she obviously did not intend to have anything further to do with him.

But then prudence had never been Ash's long suit;

306

nor, for that matter, had caution. All he could think of at the moment was that he must and would talk to her, though that was going to be difficult enough to do even with her co-operation, and almost impossible without it. But he would manage it somehow. He must. There were still weeks of journeying ahead of them, and though up to the present he had done his best to hurry the camp forward and keep it on the move, this was something that could be altered.

From now on he would let the pace slow down, and stay longer at each stopping place—a day or two at least, which alone would add several weeks to the journey. And in order to ensure that Juli should not avoid him he would take special care to make friends with Shushila, Jhoti and Kaka-ji, who would invite him to the durbar tent, where Juli would have to join them. For judging from her little sister's dependence upon her, she would find it hard to refuse—and harder still to find a valid reason for doing so, as somehow he did not think she would be prepared to explain the true circumstances to her sister, or anyone else.

"*Hai mai!*" sighed Ash, and he did not know that he had spoken aloud until Kaka-ji, who had drawn rein beside him, said: "What is it that troubles you?"

"Nothing of any importance, Rao-Sahib," said Ash, flushing.

"No?" Kaka-ji's tone was gently teasing. "Now I would have said, from the signs, that you were in love and had left your heart behind in Rawalpindi. For thus do young men look and speak and sigh when they think of the beloved."

"You are too acute, Rao-Sahib," said Ash lightly.

"Ah, but then I too have been young; though to look at me now, you might not believe that."

Ash laughed and said: "Did you ever marry, Rao-Sahib?"

"Assuredly—and when I was far younger than you. But she died of the cholera five years later, having given me two daughters; and now I have seven grandchildren —all girls, alas; though doubtless they will in time give me many great-grandsons. I must hope so."

"You should have married again," said Ash severely.

"So my friends said; and my family also. But at the time I was in no haste to add yet another woman to a

307

household that seemed over-full of them. Then, later—much later—I fell in love . . ."

The last words had been spoken in such a lugubrious tone that Ash laughed again and said: "To hear you speak, anyone would think that was the greatest of misfortunes."

"To me, it was indeed so," sighed Kaka-ji, "for as she was not of my caste I knew that I should not think of her, and that my priests and my family would oppose it. But while I hesitated her father gave her in marriage to another man, who cared less for such matters than I; and afterwards . . . Afterwards I found that no other woman could take her place in my heart, or blot out her face from my mind. Therefore I could not bring myself to marry again, which was perhaps as well, for women can cause a great deal of trouble and noise, and when one is old, as I am, one requires peace and quiet."

"And leisure to go hawking," grinned Ash.

"True, true. Though with age one's skill at such pursuits grows less. Let me see now how you shape, Sahib . . ."

They talked no more of love, and Ash turned his attention to hawking, and during the next hour or so won golden opinions from Kaka-ji for his handling of the merlin-falcon. The mid-day meal was served in a large grove of trees near the edge of a *jheel*, and when it was over the brides and their women retired to take an afternoon siesta in a makeshift tent, while the men disposed themselves comfortably in the shade and prepared to sleep away the hottest part of the day.

By now the fresh breeze of the morning had dwindled to a mere breath of air that whispered among the branches but did not stir the dust below, and the chattering of the *saht-bai* and the little striped squirrels was stilled. Somewhere out of sight a pair of ring-doves kept up a soft, monotonous cooing that blended pleasantly with the drowsy rustle of the leaves and an occasional tinkle of bells as a hawk stirred and shook itself in the shadows. The soft combination of sounds was soothing enough to lull any average adult to sleep, and only Jhoti—who like most ten-year-olds considered sleeping in the afternoon a shocking waste of time—was alert and restless. Though not all his elders were asleep: Captain Pelham-Martyn, for one, was awake.

Comfortably settled between the roots of an ancient neem tree, his shoulders fitting snugly into a deep groove in the trunk, Ash was once again engaged in pondering the problems presented by Juli, while at the same time listening with one ear to a low-pitched conversation between two people whom he could not see, and who were presumably unaware that there was anyone else on the far side of the tree—unless they imagined him to be asleep. It was a singularly uninteresting conversation and only its content told him that one of the speakers was Jhoti, who apparently wished to go off on his own to try his hawk on the far side of the *jheel,* and was being discouraged from doing so by some un-cooperative adult. As Ash saw no reason to make his presence known and thereby be drawn into an argument in which both sides would appeal to him for support, he stayed where he was and kept silent, hoping that the two would soon go away and leave him in peace. The low-pitched voices interfered with his thoughts and made it impossible for him to concentrate, and he listened to them with increasing irritation.

"But I want to go," said Jhoti. "Why should I waste the whole afternoon snoring? If you don't want to come with me, you need not. I don't want you, anyway. I'd much rather go alone. I'm tired of being followed about as though I were a baby and never being allowed to do anything by myself. And I won't take Gian Chand, either. I can fly a hawk just as well as he can, and I don't need *him* to tell me how to do it."

"Yes, yes, my Prince. Of course." The whispering voice was soothing and placatory: "Everyone knows it. But you cannot go about unattended. It is not fitting, and His Highness your brother would never permit it. Perhaps when you are older—"

"I am old enough now," interrupted Jhoti hotly. "And as for my brother, you know quite well that he would do anything to prevent me enjoying myself. He always has. He knew how much I wished to accompany my sisters to Bhithor, so of course he said I could not go just to spite me. But I tricked him finally and came after all."

"You did, my Prince. But as I warned you then, it was a rash deed and one we may all live to regret, as he may yet send to fetch you back and revenge himself upon those of us who came with you. This escapade of yours has already put me in grave jeopardy, and were any

309

harm to befall you on the journey, my head would surely pay for it."

"Bah! That is child's talk. You said yourself that he would never have me dragged back for fear that it would create too much talk, and make him look foolish because I had out-witted him. Besides, you were in his service before you were in mine, so—"

"Nay, Prince, I was in your mother the Maharani's service. It was only by her orders that I served him; and by her order that I left his service for yours. Ah, she was a very great lady, the Maharani."

"You do not need to tell *me* that," said Jhoti jealously, "she was my mother. And she loved me best—that I know. But because you were once in Nandu's household, you can always pretend that you only came away with me in order to see that I came to no harm."

The reply was a curious giggling laugh that instantly identified the boy's companion and jerked Ash to sudden attention, for even after all these years he remembered that sound. Biju Ram had always giggled like that at Lalji's jokes and his own obscenities, or at the sight of any creature, human or animal, being tormented.

"Why do you laugh?" demanded Jhoti resentfully, his voice rising.

"Hush, Prince—you will wake the sleepers. I laughed because I was thinking of how your brother would look if I said any such thing to him. He would not believe it, though the gods know it is true. Yet you have shown him that you can think and act for yourself, and cannot be tied by the leg like one of his tame macaws, or followed about by women and old men crying 'Take care,' 'Be careful,' 'Do not tire yourself,' 'Do not touch.' *Hi-ya!* you are a true son of your mother. She ever took her own path and no one had the courage to gainsay her—not even your father."

"They will not gainsay me either," boasted Jhoti. "And I am not going to be followed about any longer. I'm going to go out by myself and fly my own hawk; now, this minute, instead of lying around snoring. And you can't stop me."

"But I can arouse your syce, and Gian Chand also. They will see that you come to no harm."

"Don't you *dare!*" whispered Jhoti fiercely. "I thought you were my friend. Why did you help me escape from my brother if you were going to behave just as he does and stop me from doing anything I want to do? You are just like everyone else. 'Don't do this—don't do that. Take care. Be careful.' "

"My Prince, I *beg* of you—"

"No! I will go. And I will go alone."

*"Hazrat,"** sighed Biju Ram, capitulating. "Well, if you will not let me go with you or take Gian Chand, at least do not ride Bulbul; he is too fresh today and may be hard to manage. Take Mela, who is quieter and will give you no trouble, and do not, I beg you, ride too far or too fast. Keep to a trot only and stay within sight of us, for if you were to fall—"

"Fall!" snorted Jhoti, outraged by the very idea. "I have never fallen off a horse in my life!"

"There is always a first time," observed Biju Ram sententiously, and giggled again as though to rob the platitude of offence.

Jhoti laughed, and a moment later Ash heard the pair move away between the trees. But though the afternoon was now silent he found himself oddly uneasy. There was something about the conversation he had overheard that did not ring true. Why, for instance, had Biju Ram, of all people, elected to side with the younger son against the elder, and carry his partisanship to the extent of helping to smuggle Jhoti out of Karidkote in defiance of the Maharajah's wishes? That his reasons were not altruistic could be taken for granted—unless his character had changed out of all knowledge during the past decade, which was something that Ash was not prepared to believe. Biju Ram had always known on which side his bread was buttered, and it was safe to assume that he still did so. On the other hand he had been Janoo-Rani's creature for many years, and if there was any truth at all in Mahdoo's slanderous hints as to the reason for her sudden demise, it was just possible that he might have turned against the parricide and transferred his allegiance to her younger son. Though not, decided Ash, unless there was a good chance of that son being able to reward him liberally one day for doing so.

Could there, then, be a move on foot to kill Nandu, the new Maharajah, and put Jhoti in his place? If so, then

---

*Highness

Biju Ram's behaviour was easily explained, as was his anxiety to keep the boy from running any risks. No wonder he too was attempting to molly-coddle the child, for if there was conspiracy against the Maharajah, it was possible that the Maharajah knew it and might kill his brother in order to deprive the plotters of a rallying point for revolt. And if Biju Ram's task was to remove the heir to a safe place until the throne was made vacant, it stood to reason that he would take very good care to see that the boy came to no harm.

Ash clasped his hands about his knees, and propping his chin on them, thought about Biju Ram and Karidkote. Ought he perhaps to send a word of warning to Mr. Carter, the District Officer? or better still to the British Resident in Karidkote (there was bound to be one by now)? But then he had no proof. It would not be enough to say, "I used to know Biju Ram, and therefore I know that if he is befriending young Jhoti it must be because he knows that Nandu is due to be murdered, and that Jhoti will soon be Maharajah." No one would believe him. And in any case it might not be true. The whole thing was probably only a figment of his imagination; though Mahdoo had said . . . But then that too was merely a rumour, the idle gossip of some camp-follower and therefore no more reliable than his own random suspicions. There was obviously nothing he could do, and anyway the internal affairs of Karidkote were none of his business.

Ash yawned and leaning back against the tree trunk prepared to follow the example of the majority and go to sleep. But the afternoon was destined to be a disturbed one. The muffled clip-clop of a horse's hooves on thick dust was barely audible in the silence, but it was still loud enough to attract his attention, and he turned his head and saw Jhoti ride past, carrying a hooded falcon on one wrist and keeping his horse to a walk for fear of waking the sleepers in the grove. He was riding the bay gelding, Bulbul, and he was alone: proof enough that he had won his point against Biju Ram.

Ash could sympathize with the child's desire to escape from supervision, but watching him turn away from the *jheel* and head for the open country, he found himself in unexpected agreement with Biju Ram. This was probably the first time that Jhoti had ever ridden out alone, for up to now there must always have been several men in attendance on him, one of whom would ride ahead to make sure that he did not venture into country where there were such traps for the unwary as nullahs and concealed wells, patches of bog or unexpected outcrops of rock.

"It isn't safe," thought Ash. "Someone should have gone with him!" Hadn't Mahdoo said something about Lalji's father and a riding accident?—that the late Maharajah had been out hawking when his horse bolted and fell into a nullah, breaking both their necks? His uneasiness increased and he scrambled to his feet and began to walk quickly back through the trees to where his own horse, The Cardinal, was tethered.

There was no sign of Biju Ram, and falconers, syces and guards were all asleep. But Mulraj, who was not, saw him pass and inquired in an undervoice where he was going in such haste. Ash paused briefly to explain and Mulraj looked startled.

"So? Then I think I will go with you," said Mulraj. "We can pretend that we wished to spy out the land for game while the others slept, and took the same path as the boy by chance. Then he will not think that he has been followed. Let us be quick."

Some of Ash's disquiet seemed to have communicated itself to Mulraj, for he began to run. They did not take long to saddle their horses, but to avoid rousing the others they rode through the grove at a walk, as Jhoti had done, and only when they were well clear of the trees did they break into a gallop. At first they could see no sign of the boy, for the plain shimmered under the mid-afternoon sun and the dancing heat-haze hid him from sight. But presently they caught sight of the little figure on horseback and reined their own mounts to a sedate canter.

Bulbul was still jerking his head and sidling impatiently, but Jhoti seemed to have no difficulty in controlling him. He was riding quite slowly through a patch of scrub, presumably in the hope of putting up a hare or a partridge, and Ash breathed a sigh of relief. The child had more sense than he had given him credit for and was evidently right when he asserted that he was quite old enough to look after himself. There had been no need at all for Mulraj and himself to go chasing off after the brat like a pair of anxious nursemaids, since he was plainly no milk-sop, and obviously at home on a horse. If he could only be persuaded to take more exercise and eat less *halwa*, and lose some of that puppy-fat, he would make a first-class rider one of these days; and as Malraj had already pointed out, he knew how to handle a hawk.

"We're wasting our time," observed Ash irritably. "That child knows what he's doing and you and I are behaving like a pair of old women. It's just the sort of thing he complains of, and I don't blame him."

"Look—" said Mulraj, who had not been listening, "he has put up a partridge—no, a pigeon I think. Two of them!"

"Teal," said Ash, whose eye-sight was keener. "There must be grass among those bushes."

They saw Jhoti rein in and heard his shrill, excited *"Hai-ai!"* as he rose in the saddle and flung up his arm to help the falcon take off. For a moment bird and boy were motionless: Jhoti standing in his stirrups to gaze upwards and the falcon hanging above him, threshing the air with its wings like a swimmer treading water, until, sighting its prey, it was away with the speed of an arrow. The boy plumped back into the saddle, and was almost unseated as his horse responded with a frenzied bound and plunged forward through the bushes to bolt wildly out onto the stony plain.

"What on earth—?" began Ash puzzled; and had no time to finish the sentence, for the next instant he and Mulraj together were racing in pursuit, using whip and spur in a desperate attempt to overtake the run-away.

There was no need for questions, as they could see clearly enough what had happened: Jhoti must have saddled his own horse to avoid waking the syces, and he had failed to pull the girth tight enough, for now the saddle was sliding over to one side, taking him with it and making it impossible for him to check Bulbul's headlong flight. But there was good blood in the boy—Rajput blood, than which there is no finer—and though his mother's birth had been lowly, she had possessed courage and a quick brain, and her youngest son had inherited both. Feeling the saddle slide to the right and finding himself unable to prevent it, he freed his right foot and stood in the left stirrup, and using that as a lever, flung himself forward onto his horse's neck where he clung like a monkey. The saddle swung over and crashed to the ground, striking against one

314

of the flying hooves as it fell and putting the final touch to Bulbul's panic.

"*Shabash*, Raja-Sahib!" called Ash, yelling encouragement. "Oh, well done."

He saw Jhoti throw a quick glance over his shoulder and force a grin. The child's face was pallid with terror, but there was determination in it, and pride too: he was not going to be thrown if he could help it. In any case, to let go now would mean the certainty of breaking an arm or a leg, if not his backbone, for the ground was as hard as iron and he knew that the few bushes that grew on it were armed with thorns that were capable of tearing his eyes out. There was nothing for it but to hold on, and he did so with the tenacity of a limpet. But because his cheek was pressed to the horse's neck and Bulbul's mane blinded him, he did not see what both Ash and Mulraj now saw: the death-trap that yawned ahead of him. A wide, steep-sided nullah that the rains of many monsoons had scoured deep into the plain, dry now and thickly strewn with stones and water-worn boulders.

The horse had not seen it either, for in the manner of bolting horses it was crazed with panic and capable of running straight into a picket fence or over a cliff. It also had a long start on its pursuers and was carrying considerably less weight. But the child's head pressing against its neck made it bear to the left, which gave Ash and Mulraj an advantage, since they rode on a straight line—and on far better horses. Ash's roan, The Cardinal, had recently won two flat races and a point-to-point in Rawalpindi, while Mulraj's mare, Dulhan, had the reputation of being the finest horse in camp.

Yard by yard they narrowed the distance, but the lip of the nullah was barely ten paces away when at last Mulraj drew level and dropped his reins. Guiding Dulhan with his knees alone he leaned out, and gripping the child around the waist, snatched him away just as Ash, coming up on the opposite side, caught Bulbul's trailing reins and attempted to turn him.

As a horseman, Mulraj had few equals and no superior, though had he been riding any other horse that day the whole affair would even then have ended in disaster, if not tragedy. But man and horse had known each other for years and established a rare accord that made

315

them seem, at times, to be part of a whole that was half equine, half human. Mulraj had made his calculations, and coming up on the left of the bolting horse was already riding on a line that would take him parallel to the nullah. Because of this, and despite the fact that he was hampered by the boy in his arms and unable to use his reins, he was still able to turn Dulhan away from the rim.

But Ash was unable to check The Cardinal, and the bay and the roan together tore on and over the lip of the nullah, to end up in kicking, threshing turmoil among the stones and boulders ten feet below.

17

Ash did not recover consciousness for some considerable time, which was just as well, because in addition to concussion and a large number of cuts and bruises, he had broken his collar-bone, cracked two ribs and dislocated a wrist; and under these circumstances, a jolting, three-mile journey in a bullock cart would have been almost as unpleasant as the subsequent setting of broken bones without the help of anaesthetics. Fortunately, however, he came through both ordeals without being aware of them.

Even more fortunately, Kaka-ji Rao's personal hakim was an expert bone-setter, for had Ash been left to the tender mercies of the Rajkumaries' doctor, whose services had been offered by Shushila-Bai, it would have gone hard with him, the royal physician being an elderly and old-fashioned practitioner who pinned his faith to herbal remedies and the curative properties of earth-currents and incantations, combined with offerings to the gods and various concoctions made from the dung and urine of the cow.

Luckily Kaka-ji, though a devout Hindu, had little faith in such medicines when it came to mending broken bones, and he had tactfully declined his niece's offer and sent his own doctor, Gobind Dass, to deal with the matter. Gobind had done so with great success; he knew what he was about and few college-trained European doctors could have done better. Aided by Mahdoo, Gul Baz, and one of the Rajkumari Anjuli's women, Geeta, who was a notable *dai* (nurse), he brought his patient safely through the two days and nights of high fever that had followed on the period of coma—in itself no small feat, for the sick man tossed and raved and had to be held down by force for fear that he should do himself further injury.

Ash was conscious of very little during those days, but once—it was at night—he thought he heard someone say, "Is he going to die?" and opening his eyes saw a woman standing between him and the lamp. She was only a dark silhouette against the light, and he looked up into a face he could not see and muttered: "I'm sorry, Juli. I didn't mean to offend you. You see, I——" But the words clotted on his tongue and he could not remember what it was he had meant to say; or to whom. And in any case the woman was no longer there, for he was looking at the unshaded lamp and he shut his eyes against the glare and sank back into blackness.

The fever left him on the third day and he slept the clock round, awaking to find that it was again night and the lamp was still burning, though its flame was shielded from him by something that threw a black bar of shadow across the bed. He wondered why he had not turned it out, and was still puzzling over this trivial point when he discovered that his mouth was as dry as a desert and that he was very thirsty, but when he attempted to move, the pain that shot through him was so unexpected that it wrenched a groan for him. The bar of shadow that lay across the upper half of his bed moved instantly.

"Lie still, child," said Mahdoo soothingly. "I am here . . . lie still, my son."

The old man spoke in the voice of an adult addressing a child who has awakened from a nightmare, and Ash stared up at him, mystified by the tone and even more by Mahdoo's presence in his tent at such an hour.

"What on earth," inquired Ash, "are you doing here, Cha-cha-ji?"

The sound of his own voice surprised him as much as Mahdoo's had done, for it was no more than a hoarse croak. But Mahdoo's expression altered surprisingly and he threw up his arms and said wildly: "Allah be praised! He knows me. Gul Baz—Gul Baz—send word to the Hakim that the Sahib is awake and in his right mind again.

317

Go quickly. Praise be to Allah, the Merciful, the Compassionate—"

Tears rolled down the old man's cheeks and flashed in the lamplight, and Ash said weakly: "Don't be an owl, Cha-cha. Of course I know you. For heaven's sake stop playing the fool and give me something to drink."

But it was Gobind Dass, hurriedly aroused from sleep, who finally gave him a drink. Presumably one with a drug in it, because Ash fell asleep again, and when he awoke for the third time it was late afternoon.

The tent-flaps had been thrown back and through the open door he could see the low sunlight and the long shadows, and far away across the dusty plain, the faint line of the distant hills, already tinged with rose. There was a man squatting by the tent door and idly throwing dice, left hand against right, and Ash, watching him, was thankful to see that Mulraj at least had managed to avoid crashing into the nullah. The fog had lifted from his brain at last and he could remember what happened; and lying there he attempted to assess the extent of his injuries and was relieved to discover that his legs were not broken, and that it was his left arm and shoulder that was bandaged and not the right—proof that he had managed to fall on his left shoulder after all. He could remember thinking as The Cardinal plunged over into the nullah that he could not afford to lose the use of his right arm and must throw himself to the left, and there was a crumb of comfort in the fact that he had evidently managed to do this.

Mulraj gave a grunt of satisfaction at the fall of the dice, and glancing over his shoulder, saw that Ash's eyes were open and lucid.

"Ah!" said Mulraj, gathering up the dice and coming to stand beside the bed. "So you are awake at last. It was time. How do you feel?"

"Hungry," said Ash with the ghost of a grin.

"That is a good sign. I will send at once for the Rao-Sahib's Hakim, and it may be that he will permit you to have a little mutton broth—or a bowl of warm milk."

He laughed at Ash's grimace of disgust and would have turned away to call a servant, but Ash reached out with his uninjured arm, and clutching a fold of his coat, said: "The boy. Jhoti. Is he safe?"

Mulraj appeared to hesitate for a moment, and

then said reassuringly that the child was well and Ash need not trouble his head about him. "All you have to think of now is yourself. You must get well quickly; we cannot move camp until you have regained your strength, and we have already been here for nearly a week."

"A *week?*"

"You were without your senses for a full night and day, and for the best part of the next three you raved like a madman. And since then you have been sleeping like a babe."

"Good lord," said Ash blankly. "No wonder I'm hungry. What happened to the horses?"

"Jhoti's horse, Bulbul, broke his neck."

"And mine?"

"I shot him," said Mulraj briefly.

Ash made no comment, but Mulraj saw the betraying flicker of his eyelids and said gently: "I'm sorry. But there was nothing else that I could do. He had broken both forelegs."

"It was my fault," said Ash slowly. "I should have known that I couldn't turn that horse of Jhoti's. It was too late. . . ."

Another man might have uttered consoling denials, but Mulraj had taken a liking to Ash and so he did not lie. He nodded instead and said: "One makes these mistakes. But what is done is done, and there is no profit in bewailing what cannot be undone. Put it behind you, Pelham-Sahib, and give thanks to the gods that you are alive; for there was a time when we thought that you would surely die."

The last words reminded Ash of something, and he frowned in an effort to remember what it was, and then said abruptly: "Was there a woman in here one night?"

"Surely. The *dai*. She is one of the Rajkumaries' women and she has come every night; and will come for many more, being skilled in massage and the healing of torn ligaments and strained muscles. You owe her much —and the Hakim, Gobind, even more."

"Oh," said Ash, disappointed. And closed his eyes against the low sunlight.

Considering all things, he made a remarkably quick recovery; for which his constitution as much as Gobind's ministrations could take the credit. Those two hard years in the mountains beyond the North-West Frontier had

319

paid dividends at last, for they had toughened him as nothing else could have done. The unorthodox nursing and insanitary conditions that prevailed in the camp—the dust and the flies, the cheerful disregard for even the most elementary rules of hygiene and the total lack of peace and quiet, all or any of which would have horrified a Western doctor—seemed almost luxurious to Ash when compared to the horrors and hardships that he had seen injured men endure in tribal territory. He considered himself lucky—and rightly so, because as Kaka-ji took care to point out, he could easily have been dead; or at the very least, crippled for life.

"Of all fool-hardy things to do!" scolded Kaka-ji severely. "Would it not have been far better to let one horse die than to kill both, and but for a miracle, yourself as well? But then you young men are all alike—you do not think. Nevertheless, it was bravely done, Sahib, and I for one would willingly exchange all the caution and wisdom that the years have brought me for a little of such rashness and valour."

Kaka-ji Rao was by no means Ash's only visitor. There were others, members of the camp's *panchayat* such as Tarak Nath and Jabar Singh, and old Maldeo Rai who was Kaka-ji's third cousin: too many others, according to Mahdoo and Gul Baz, who disapproved of this stream of callers and did their best to keep them at bay. Gobind too had advocated quiet, but changed his mind when he saw that his patient was less restless when listening to gossip about Karidkote, or to any talk that kept him abreast of the day-to-day doings of the camp.

Ash's most frequent visitor was Jhoti. The boy would sit cross-legged on the floor, chatting away by the hour, and it was from him that Ash received confirmation of something that had occurred to him only as a vague suspicion. That Biju Ram, who for so many years had enjoyed the protection of Janoo-Rani—and during that time amassed a comfortable fortune in bribes, gifts and payments for unspecified services—had fallen on evil days.

It seemed that after the *Nautch*-girl's death, those who had stood highest in her favour had suddenly found themselves relegated by her son, Nandu, to positions of comparative unimportance and deprived of all their former influence, together with most of the perquisites of

320

power, which had infuriated Biju Ram, who had grown vain and over-confident in the Rani's shadow. He had apparently been foolish enough to show his resentment, and the result had been an open quarrel, in the course of which Biju Ram had been threatened with arrest and the confiscation of all his property, and only saved himself by appealing to Colonel Pycroft, the British Resident, to intercede for him.

Colonel Pycroft had spoken to Nandu, who had said a great many rude things about his dead mother's stool-pigeon, but eventually agreed to accept a grovelling apology and a large fine, and forget the matter. But it was clear that Biju Ram had no confidence in Nandu doing any such thing, and when Nandu, barely a week after accepting that humiliating public apology, had refused permission for his Heir Apparent to accompany the bridal party to Bhithor, Biju Ram had instantly set about inciting the boy to revolt and planning Jhoti's escape—and his own.

For Ash had been right about that too. The idea had been Biju Ram's, and he and two of his friends, both of whom had been adherents of the late Rani and were now out of favour, had planned the escape and carried it through. "He *said* it was because he was sorry for me," said Jhoti, "—and because he and Mohun and Pran Krishna had always been loyal to my mother, and they knew she would have wished me to go to Shu-shu's wedding. But of course it was not that at all."

"No? What then?" asked Ash, regarding his youthful visitor with increasing respect. Jhoti might be young, but he was obviously not gullible.

"Oh, because of the quarrel. My brother Nandu doesn't like anyone to disagree with him, and though he might pretend to forgive Biju Ram, he wouldn't: not really. So of course Biju Ram thought it would be safer to leave Karidkote as soon as possible, and to stay away as long as he could. I suppose he is hoping that in the end Nandu's anger may cool, but I don't think it will. Pran and Mohun only came with me because just now Nandu does not like any of the people who my mother appointed, and so they feel safer here too; and they have brought away all the money they could, in case they can't ever go back. I wish I didn't have to. I think I shall stay behind

321

in Bhithor with Kairi and Shu-shu. Or perhaps I shall run away again and become a robber chief, like Kale Khan."

"Kale Khan was caught and hanged," observed Ash dampingly.

He did not intend to encourage Jhoti in any further forms of rebellion; and in any case, he imagined that Biju Ram and his friends would be only too eager for Jhoti to extend his stay in Bhithor for as long as the Rana could be persuaded to have him. Unless, of course, news of Nandu's untimely demise was received even before they got there, in which case they would turn back at once and hurry homeward with the new Maharajah.

But Jhoti did not often talk of Karidkote. He much preferred to hear about life on the North-West Frontier; or better still, in England. He was an exhausting companion, for his thirst for knowledge forced Ash to talk a great deal at a time when talking was still something of an effort. But though Ash would have been only too pleased to do without Jhoti's endless questions, it was one way of keeping him out of mischief; and a disturbing conversation with Mulraj had made him uneasy on the boy's behalf . . .

Mulraj had not intended to broach the subject until Ash was feeling stronger and better able to deal with such matters, but his hand had been forced, since despite all his efforts to change the conversation, Ash had persisted in discussing the accident and speculating upon its causes.

"I still can't make out," said Ash, frowning at the tent pole, "how that saddle came to fall off. I suppose it was Jhoti's fault for not fastening the girth properly. Unless Biju Ram or one of the syces did it for him. Who did? Do you know?"

Mulraj had not answered immediately, and Ash became aware that the older man had tried to avoid the whole subject. But he was tired of being treated as a feeble-minded invalid, so he scowled at Mulraj and repeated his question with a certain tartness, and Mulraj shrugged his shoulders, and bowing to the inevitable said: "The child says that he alone saddled the horse, because Biju Ram refused to help him and went away, thinking that he could not do it single-handed and would therefore be prevented from going off alone, or be compelled to wake one of the syces, who would in turn rouse some servant who could not be prevented from following him."

"Young idiot," observed Ash. "That'll teach him."

"Teach him what?" inquired Mulraj dryly. "To see that the straps on the girth are properly fastened? Or to look first—and very carefully—at the underside of a saddle?"

"What do you mean by that?" demanded Ash, startled by something in Mulraj's face and voice rather than by the words themselves.

"I mean that the straps were securely fastened, but the girth itself broke. It had worn thin . . . and in a mere matter of hours, too. For by pure chance I examined the saddle earlier in the day. Do you remember how the boy flew his hawk at a pigeon that you had not even seen, your mind being elsewhere, and how I, watching him gallop away, thought that his saddle looked a trifle loose and rode after him?"

"Yes, now you mention it. You said something about not liking the look of it. But . . . Go on."

"By the time we recovered his hawk and the pigeon," continued Mulraj, "we had outdistanced the rest of you and were alone, so I myself adjusted the girth; and I tell you, Sahib, that save for the fact that it could with advantage have been tighter, there was nothing wrong with it then. Yet only a few hours later it had become so worn that it broke when the horse began to gallop."

"But that's impossible."

"You are right," agreed Mulraj grimly, "it is not possible. Yet it happened. And there can be only two explanations: either that it was not the same girth, but an old and rotten one that had been substituted for the other, or —which I myself think more likely—that while we ate and rested, someone had worked on it with a sharp knife, scraping it almost through, and so cunningly that it could be fastened without breaking or attracting notice, yet must part if too much strain were placed upon it . . . the strain, let us say, that would be occasioned by a bolting horse."

Ash stared at him under frowning brows, and observed with some tartness that if it had broken while the boy was in the company of half-a-dozen others there wouldn't have been very much danger, and no one was to know that he would go off alone like that. Only Biju Ram, who for once was on the side of the angels and tried to stop him.

Mulraj shrugged in agreement, but added that there were certain things that the Sahib was not aware of: among them, that it was Jhoti's habit to gallop after his hawk, and that when he did so he hated to have someone riding at his heels. Therefore it would not have mattered how many people were out with him, because as soon as his hawk was away he would have spurred after it while everyone else would have waited and watched, and when his horse bolted, the extra strain on the girth would have made it part quickly; and as the speed of a run-away horse carrying little weight was likely to be greater, for a time, than one still under control and bearing a full-grown man, the chances were that the boy would have fallen before anyone could reach him. "And to be thrown from a bolting horse in such country as this can kill a man, let alone a child. But those who planned it failed to make allowance for the boy's courage and quick thinking, nor did they foresee that his very size would enable him to cling on where a grown man could not."

Ash made an impatient noise and inquired irritably how Mulraj imagined that "they," whoever "they" were, could possibly have foreseen that the horse would bolt? The whole thing hinged on that, and it was impossible.

Mulraj sighed and rising to his feet, stood looking down at Ash, his hands thrust through his belt and his face suddenly grim. He said very softly: "You are wrong; that too was arranged. I could not understand why the horse should have bolted in that fashion, for Jhoti has always risen in his stirrups and cried aloud as he throws his hawk into the air, and Bulbul was as accustomed to that action as the child himself. Yet on this occasion we both saw the horse leap forward as though it had been shot. You recall?"

Ash nodded, and the pain of that incautious movement made him reply with more asperity than he had intended: "Yes I do. And I also happen to remember that there was no one else within sight of us and no sound of a shot either. If you ask me, you've got a bee in your—"

He stopped suddenly, checked by a memory: the same that had sent him in search of his horse after seeing Jhoti ride off alone. Mahdoo's story of how the old Rajah had met his death while out hawking, and the old man's sly, sideways glance as he said: "They think that perchance it may have been stung by a bee."

Mulraj appeared to have followed this train of thought, for he said dryly: "I see that you too have heard that tale. Well, it may even be true—who knows? But this time I meant to make sure, and therefore when I had dragged you from under your horse and found that you were not dead, I did not go to fetch help myself, but sent Jhoti instead. A risk, I own; though only a small one, for he would be riding Dulhan, who as you know is a horse in ten thousand and even a babe would be safe with her. When he was gone I went in search of his fallen saddle—"

"Go on," said Ash tersely, for Mulraj had paused to look over his shoulder and appeared to be listening. "It's only Mahdoo, who is not near enough to hear and will cough if anyone else approaches."

Mulraj nodded as though satisfied. But when he took up the tale it was in a voice that would not have carried beyond the walls of the tent: "It was no bee this time, but the double thorn of a *kikar* tree which the boy drove home when he plumped back into the saddle after throwing up his hawk. It had been cunningly hidden in the padding in such a way that the movement of a rider would work it down, little by little, until in the end it must be driven into the horse's flesh. One day, when you are up and about again, I will show you how it is done. It is an old trick—and a very evil one, because no one can swear that such a thorn might not get there by chance. Have we not all, at some time or another, plucked such thorns out of our clothes and blankets and saddle cloths? Yet I will wager you my mare against a dhobi's donkey that this one did not find its way there by chance. The thorn alone —or the broken girth. But not both."

There was a long silence in the tent, broken only by the buzz of flies, and when at last Ash spoke his voice was no longer sceptical:

"What have you done about it?"

"Nothing," said Mulraj curtly. "Except to try and keep a watch on the boy, which is no easy task, for he has his own people about him, and I am not one of them. I left the saddle where I found it and made no mention of the thorn—it being a thing I might well have missed seeing. As to the girth, which both you and I had seen break, I raised a great tumult about it when we returned to camp, berating the prince's syces for carelessness and saying that they must be dismissed. Had I not done this there are those who would have wondered why I kept silent; and that is something I do not desire."

"But do you mean to say that you haven't told *anyone?*" demanded Ash incredulously.

"Whom should I tell? How do I know how many people, or how few, are involved in this matter?—or even the reason for it? Sahib, you have no knowledge of Karidkote, and you know nothing of the intrigues that infest the palace like a plague of flying-ants in the monsoon. Even here in the camp we are not free of it. I had not intended to speak of this matter to you until you were stronger, as worry is not good for a sick man; but now that I have done so I am glad, because two heads are better than one and together we may devise some way of protecting the child from his enemies."

They had been able to talk no more about it that day, for the arrival of Gobind and Kaka-ji had put an end to the conversation. Gobind, declaring that his patient was looking feverish, had banned any further visitor for the remainder of that day, and Ash spent the rest of the afternoon and evening, and a good many hours of the following night, in worrying over the problem of Jhoti. Which was at least a change from worrying about Juli—though it did nothing towards improving his health or sweetening his temper. He found it intolerable to be tied to his bed at such a time, and it was then that he decided to encourage Jhoti to visit him as often and for as long as possible. A decision that he carried out in face of considerable opposition from Gobind, Mahdoo and Kaka-ji.

18

"You have been causing us all a great deal of trouble, you know," remarked Jhoti chattily.

"*Afsos*, Highness," murmured Ash; and placing his hands together in a mock gesture of abasement, added

326

meekly that he was doing his best to get well as quickly as possible and should with luck be up and about in a few days.

"Oh, I didn't mean *that*," said Jhoti. "I meant with the priests."

"The *priests . . . ?*" Ash looked blank.

"Yes. They have been very cross with my sisters. And with me and Mulraj too, and with my uncle most of all. And do you know why? Because they have been told that when you came to visit us in the durbar tent you sometimes sat on the same carpet as we did, and that when we offered you things to eat—fruit and sweets and things —we ate with you instead of just pretending to eat. They don't like that, because they are very strict, you know, so that they have been making a great fuss about it."

"Have they, indeed?" said Ash, frowning. "Yes . . . I suppose I ought to have thought of that. Does this mean that I am not to be asked to the durbar tent in future?"

"Oh no," said Jhoti blithely, "for when they complained to my uncle he got much crosser than they were, and told them to remember that you had saved us all from great shame and disaster—for of course it would have been terrible for everyone if Shu-shu had been drowned —and that, anyway, he took all responsibility for this. So after that there wasn't anything else they could say, because they know very well how devout he is, and how he spends hours every day at his *pujah*" (devotions), "and gives alms to the poor and money and rich gifts to the temples. Besides, he *is* our father's brother. I was very cross too—with Biju Ram."

"Why with Biju Ram?"

"Because he had asked me a lot of questions about what we did when you came to the durbar tent, and I told him; and then he went straight off and told the priests. He said he had only done it to protect me, because he was afraid that if it came to Nandu's ears, Nandu would spread it about to discredit me, and everyone would be angry with me for allowing it. As if I cared what Nandu or the bazaar-log think! Biju Ram interferes too much. He behaves as if he were my nurse, and I won't have it . . . Oh, here is my uncle coming to visit you. *Salaam,* Kaka-ji."

"I might have known that I should find you here, tiring the Sahib with your chatter," said Kaka-ji reprovingly.

327

"Run away now child, for Mulraj is waiting to take you out riding."

He shooed his nephew away, and as Jhoti ran off, turned to shake an admonitory finger at the invalid. "You are far too patient with that boy," said Kaka-ji severely. "How many times have I not told you so?"

"I have lost count," admitted Ash with a grin. "Have you only come here to scold me, Rao-Sahib?"

"You deserve to be scolded."

"So it seems, for your nephew has been telling me that I have caused trouble for you with your priests."

"Chut!" said Kaka-ji, annoyed. "The child talks too much. There was no need to worry you with that matter. I have taken it on my own head, and it is now settled."

"Are you sure? I would not wish to be the cause of any trouble between you and—"

"I have said that the matter is settled," interrupted Kaka-ji firmly. "If you wish to please me you will forget it; and also cease from allowing Jhoti to pester you. It is folly to permit him to tire you. You are letting that child worry you and giving your mind no rest."

This was certainly true, though not in the sense that Kaka-ji meant. But Ash was not prepared to argue the point. His mind was very far from being at rest, and, as it happened, his worries on Jhoti's account had been greatly increased of late by certain things that Kaka-ji himself had let slip in the course of his frequent visits.

The old gentleman's intentions were admirable, and he would have been shocked to realize that his well-meant efforts to alleviate the invalid's boredom had proved far more disturbing than all Jhoti's questions put together. But there was no denying that Jhoti's uncle loved to talk, and Pelham-Sahib, immobilized by splints and bandages, proved an ideal audience. Kaka-ji had seldom found so good a listener—or Ash acquired so much valuable information by the simple expedient of keeping his mouth shut and looking interested. On the subject of Nandu, Maharajah of Karidkote, for instance, Ash had learned a great deal—far more, in all probability, than Kaka-ji had intended, for the old gentleman's tongue was apt to run away with him, and even when he was being discreet it was not difficult to read between the lines.

Janoo-Rani had undoubtedly been a clever woman, but as a mother she appeared to have been singularly unintelligent. Doting upon her sons, she had allowed no one to correct or punish them, and her first-born, Nandu, had been indulged to the point of foolishness, his easy-going father being too idle to take a hand in disciplining the boy. "I do not think," said Kaka-ji, "that my brother really liked children, even when they were his own. He would tolerate their presence while they behaved well, but the moment they cried or were in any way troublesome he would send them from his presence and often refuse to see them again for many days, which he chose to believe was a punishment; though I do not think it was regarded as such by any save Lalji, who was his first-born and died many years ago. Lalji, I think, loved him greatly and would have given much for his father's favour; but the younger ones saw too little of him to love him, and though Jhoti might in time have taken his dead brother's place in his father's affections, Nandu was no horseman . . ."

This, it seemed, was once again Janoo-Rani's fault —one could hardly blame the boy, who was barely three years old when he took his first toss off a pony's back. Unaccustomed to being hurt, Nandu had screamed from fright and the pain of a few small scratches, and Janoo-Rani would not let the child ride again, insisting that he had suffered great injury and might easily have been killed. Even now he would not ride one if it could possibly be avoided. "He uses elephants instead," explained his uncle. "Or drives out in a carriage—like a woman."

Janoo would undoubtedly have done the same to his youngest brother had he not been made of different stuff, for the first time Jhoti took a fall he too screamed aloud. But when he had finished howling he insisted on mounting again and would not let the syce put him back on a leading rein, which delighted his father who had been watching—though Nandu, said Kaka-ji, was not so pleased. "I think there has always been a certain jealousy there. It is not so unusual between brothers, when one has talents that the other lacks."

Fortune had evidently favoured Nandu in many ways. Firstly, he was his mother's darling, her first-born and the favourite child. Then the death of his half-brother, Lalji, had made him heir to the throne, and now he was Maharajah of Karidkote. But it seemed that he could still be jealous, and that he was wholly the *Nautch-*

329

girl's child both in character and physique. Like her he possessed a violent and ungovernable temper: and no one had ever made any attempt to control his rages, for his mother thought them royal and high-spirited and the servants were afraid of them, while his father, seeing little of him, was unaware of them. He had never excelled in any sport, and had not the build for it, being short and stout, like his mother; though, unlike her, he had few claims to beauty and was strangely dark-skinned for a northerner: A *"Kala-admi,"* said the citizens of Karidkote scornfully, a "black man." And they would cheer when Jhoti rode past, and keep silent when it was Nandu who drove through the city or the countryside.

"Jealousy is an ugly thing," mused Kaka-ji, "but alas, few if any of us can claim to be free of it. I myself was often afflicted by it in my youth, and though I am now old and should by rights have outgrown such unprofitable emotions, there are still times when I can feel its claws. Therefore I am afraid for Jhoti, whose brother is both jealous and powerful . . ."

The old man broke off to select another sugared plum from a box of candied fruit that he had brought as a present to the invalid, and the invalid inquired in a deceptively casual tone: "And not above doing away with him, you think?"

"No, no, *no!* You must not think—I did not mean . . ." Kaka-ji swallowed the plum in his agitation and had to be restored with a drink of water, and Ash realized that he had made a grave mistake in trying to rush the old gentleman and put words into his mouth. There was nothing to be gained by such methods, and much by letting him ramble on umprompted. But if Kaka-ji was indeed afraid for Jhoti, what exactly was he afraid of? To what lengths did he think his nephew the Maharajah would go to injure a young brother of whom he was jealous, and who had had the temerity to flout him?

Ash was well aware that Jhoti had joined the bridal camp without permission and against his elder brother's expressed wishes. But the very fact that Jhoti had found it possible to ride after the camp, accompanied by at least eight persons and a not inconsiderable amount of baggage, proved that there could not have been any serious restriction of his liberty, and there was something about the whole affair that Ash did not understand; something that did not quite agree with his mental portrait of a jealous and tyrannical young ruler, who, for the pleasure of spiting his young brother, had banned him for accompanying his sisters to their wedding, and on hearing that the ban had been defied, flew into a fury and planned his assassination. There was, for instance, the question of time . . .

The Maharajah would not have heard of Jhoti's escapade (it could hardly be termed an "escape") for several days. In fact it was probably much longer, because according to Kaka-ji, Nandu's reason for accompanying his sisters to the border of his state had been less a brotherly gesture than because it suited him to do so, it being on his route to the hunting grounds in the foothills to the north-east where he had planned a fortnight's sport, taking only a small party with him so that they could keep on the move, camping in a different spot each night and following the game by day. He did not often indulge in such expeditions, but when he did, he preferred to forget the affairs of state and shelve all such matters until he returned from the forest. Runners with messages were therefore discouraged, and as the hunting party was continually on the move, news of his little brother's behaviour was unlikely to catch up with him for some time. This fact was probably well known to Jhoti—and certainly known, thought Ash, to the men who had accompanied the boy on his flight from Karidkote, for however faithful and devoted to his interests they might be, they would hardly have agreed to take the risk of being stopped at the border or overtaken within a few miles of it, and ignominiously brought back to face the Maharajah while his anger was at white heat.

In Ash's opinion they would have been wiser not to have come at all, but Kaka-ji took a different view: they were all, said Kaka-ji, loyal members of Jhoti's household who had been appointed to his service by his mother the late Maharani, and it was not only their duty to obey him, but to their interest also; their fortunes being bound up with his.

"Besides," admitted Kaka-ji, "Jhoti too can be very obstinate, and I understand that when they attempted to dissuade him he threatened to go off alone, which of course they could not permit. The boy being in their care, it would have brought great shame on them had they allowed him to go alone and unattended; though I do not think that they would have dared accompany him had

331

they not known that his brother would hear of his flight too late to stop him before he reached this camp. But once here, they can feel safe for a time, since they are no longer in the territory of the Maharajah but in that of the Raj. They are also under your protection, Sahib, and they reason that His Highness cannot know how you might regard an attempt to drag an unwilling child away from his sisters and return him to Karidkote to be punished—for all must know that Jhoti would never go willingly. Therefore his servants hope that His Highness will realize that there is nothing to be gained by sending men to arrest the child, particularly when he has only to wait until this wedding is over, as after that Jhoti will of course return. But by then we must all hope that the Maharajah's rage will have had time to cool, and he will be less inclined to deal harshly with something that is, let us admit it, only a boy's prank."

Kaka-ji's words were optimistic, but the tone of his voice was less so, and he had changed the subject a little abruptly and begun to talk of other matters. However, he had already provided Ash with plenty of food for thought in the long night watches when the discomfort of splints and bandages kept sleep at bay.

The difficulties that he had foreseen, or been warned of in the prosaic, official atmosphere of Rawalpindi, had all had to do with such matters as provisioning or protocol and the possibility (considered to be negligible) of the camp being attacked by raiders in the remoter parts of the country through which it must pass. But neither he nor his military superiors had visualized the far more complicated and dangerous problems that now confronted him, and which, for the present at least, he had no idea how to deal with.

For this reason, if for no other, he had cause to be grateful for the injuries that tied him to his bed, as they not only gave him time for thought, but postponed the need for action. There was nothing he could do at the moment beyond encouraging Jhoti to spend as many hours as possible in his company, and trusting to Mulraj to keep an eye on the child for the rest of the day. Though there was always the night . . . But possibly Jhoti was safer then than at any other time, for he slept surrounded by his personal servants, all of whom, according to Kaka-ji, were devoted to him. Or if not to him, decided Ash cynically, at least to his interests, which must also be their own.

On the face of it, these men had taken a grave risk in order to let the little prince enjoy himself for a strictly limited time—possibly only for a day or two, supposing a search-party had set out at once to fetch him back, and at best a few months, since after that both he and they must return. How did they expect to be received on their return? Did they, like Kaka-ji, hope that the lapse of time would have cooled the Maharajah's wrath and allowed him to regard the episode as no more than a childish prank? Or was there some other plan? . . . Perhaps the murder of Nandu, who had as yet no son, and whose Heir Apparent was still his younger brother, Jhoti?

But then it was not Nandu but Jhoti who had very nearly been murdered—and here in the camp; though to the best of Ash's knowledge (it was a point on which he had taken the trouble to inquire) no one had followed after them or joined the camp since he himself had taken over from the District Officer in Deenagunj, nor had there been any messages from Karidkote. This suggested that the attempt had no connection with the boy's escape but must be the work of one of the rival party; some adherent of Nandu's, who, like Ash, concluded that there must be something more behind Jhoti's unexpected arrival than a "boyish prank," and had decided to take no chances, but to scotch any further plotting by the simple expedient of killing the heir.

"If only I could talk to Juli," thought Ash. She if anyone would know what went on inside the frowning walls and fretted wooden screens of the Hawa Mahal. The things that were whispered in its planless maze of rooms and corridors or gossiped about behind the purdahs of the Zenana Quarter . . . Juli would know, but there was no way of reaching her; and as Kaka-ji had taken fright, it would have to be Mulraj instead. At least Mulraj should know whom to watch, for the number of suspects must be limited to someone who was out with the hawking party that day. There had not been very many of them, and all those with alibis could be eliminated as a start.

Mulraj, however, had not proved helpful.

"What do you mean, 'not very many of them'?" he demanded. "It may have seemed a small party to you, but then your thoughts were not with us that day and you did not even see the game we put up—let alone who was there. Do you know how many there were? One hundred and eighteen, no less—and two thirds of them paid servants of the state, which means the Maharajah. Of what use to interrogate them? We should hear nothing but lies and would only succeed in putting the true assassins upon their guard."

"Well, why not?" inquired Ash, ruffled by the impatience in Mulraj's voice. "Once they realize that we know there has been an attempt on the boy's life, they may think twice before they make another. It will be too dangerous to try such tricks again, knowing that a watch will be kept."

"Just so," said Mulraj dryly. "And were you dealing with your own people, your plan might be a good one. I myself have met few Sahibs, but I am told that it is their custom to go straight for an objective, looking neither to the right nor to the left. This is not so with us. You would not scare off those who meant to kill the child: you would only warn them. And being warned, they would, as you say, play no more tricks, but use instead such methods as would be less easy for us to guard against."

"Such as?" asked Ash.

"Poison. Or a knife. Or perhaps a bullet. Any of those things would eliminate chance."

"They would not dare. We are in British territory and there would be a strict inquiry. The authorities . . ."

Mulraj grinned derisively and said that naturally some more discreet method would be preferred, as plain murder would necessitate the provision of a scapegoat to pin the blame on, and there would also have to be a reason for the killing; one that would have no connection with the true one, and yet be acceptable as the truth. Neither of these things, in his opinion, would be impossible, but they would be a little more difficult to arrange, and as those who desired the boy's death would not want questions asked, an accident would serve them far better.

"And I am very sure that they will set about arranging another, provided they think that the first has gone unsuspected. I am also sure that knowing what we know, we shall be able to prevent it from being successful, and may even discover whose hand prepared it, and why:

thereby putting an end to these attempts once and for all. It is our best chance. Perhaps our only one."

Ash was forced to agree. Reason told him that Mulraj was right, and as the present state of his health debarred him from taking any action, he decided that the only thing to do was to try and collect more information as to the character and habits of Jhoti's elder brother; which sounded simple enough, but proved to be more difficult than he imagined. As he grew stronger the number of his visitors increased, and most of them remained to gossip; but although their talk was largely concerned with their home state, and certainly increased his knowledge of the politics and scandals of Karidkote, it taught him little more than he already knew about its ruler, and merely prevented him from having much private conversation with Kaka-ji or Mulraj—not that those two gentlemen appeared over-anxious to talk of the Maharajah either.

Jhoti, on the other hand, would have been only too willing to discuss his brother, but in such uncomplimentary terms that it was not safe to allow him to do so. There remained the *dai*, Geeta, a gaunt, pock-marked crone who under Gobind's orders continued to treat Ash's dislocated wrist and wrenched muscles, and to remain on watch for part of each night, squatting silently in the shadows in case her patient should wake and be in pain.

As a poor relation distantly connected to the late ruler's first wife, it was safe to assume that she would know all the gossip of the Zenana and prove a mine of information. But she had proved a sad disappointment, for she was far too timid; so much so that even a direct order from Shushila-Bai had not been able to persuade her to venture out except after dark and at an hour late enough to ensure that most of the camp would be asleep, and then only when shrouded in a cotton bourka such as Mohammedan women wear, for fear that a strange man should catch a glimpse of her face. (Ash, who had had that privilege, considered these precautions unnecessary, as he could not imagine any man in his senses wishing to spare her wrinkled and respectable visage so much as a passing glance.) Nevertheless he welcomed the lateness of her visits, for he found it difficult to get to sleep by the end of the day, and the *dai*'s belated appearance and skilful ministrations

335

came at an opportune moment and always helped him to relax. But try as he would he could not coax her into talking. Her bony hands were firm and sure, but she was too shy and far too much in awe of the Sahib to do more than titter nervously when spoken to, or at most, reply in monosyllables.

Ash gave up the attempt, and deprived of more direct sources of information fell back on Mahdoo, who could be trusted to hold his tongue when necessary and at the same time collect a great deal of miscellaneous gossip from acquaintances in the camp. This he would relay of an evening when the lamps were lit and the visitors had gone, sucking at his hookah between the leisurely sentences while the smoke from the camp fires and the fragrances of cooking drifted out across the plain, and Gul Baz kept watch to see that no one crept near to listen.

Much of what he related could only have been apocryphal, and most of the rest was a hodge-podge of hearsay, speculation and scandal-mongering: the usual buzz of the bazaars, in which little credence could be placed. But here and there a nugget of useful information could be sifted from the spate of gossip and these put together, not only told Ash a good deal about the conditions that prevailed in the one-time state of Gulkote, but shed considerably more light on the temper and disposition of its present ruler. A score of anecdotes testified to his vanity and love of display, while many others hinted at a streak of cold-blooded and precocious cunning that had shown itself in childhood and grown with the years, and if even a fraction of the latter were true the picture that emerged was far from prepossessing.

Among the plethora of rumors, guess-work and gossip, two things stood out quite clearly: that Nandu could not endure to be defeated, and that he had very unpleasant ways of dealing with those who displeased him. An instance of this last was his treatment of a tame cheetah, one of a pair of hunting leopards that had been loosed after a buck on the plain below the Hawa Mahal, and which Nandu had backed with twenty gold mohurs to reach and pull down the quarry first. It had failed to do so and he had lost his money and his temper, and sending for a tin of kerosene oil, flung it over the wretched animal and set alight.

This tale, unlike many others, was not based on hear-

336

say, for a number of men in the camp had seen the cheetah burned alive. And though it had later been given out
that its trainer had fled the state, few believed it. "They
say that he too died that same night," said Mahdoo. "But
as to that, there is no proof; and though it is certain that
the man was never seen again, that is not to say he is dead.
It may be that he feared for his life and ran away. Who
knows?"

"At a guess, the Maharajah," said Ash grimly.

Mahdoo nodded in agreement. "So it is believed. The
Maharajah is young, but already he is greatly feared by his
people. Yet it would be unwise to suppose that he is
hated by all, for the people of Karidkote have never
cared for weaklings, and many are pleased that their new
ruler has shown himself both cunning and ruthless; taking
this to be an assurance that they will not lose their independence and be swallowed up by the British, as other
princely states have been. There are also many who admire him for those very qualities that make him the evil
youth he is."

"And many others, I suspect," said Ash, "who hate
him enough to plot against him, and hope to pull him
down so that they may set another in his place."

"You mean the young prince?" Mahdoo pursed his
lips and looked sceptical. "Well, maybe. Yet if so, it is
something I have not heard spoken of among the tents;
and for myself, I do not think that in these times even the
worst of the grumblers would desire to be ruled by a
child."

"Ah, but they would not be. That is the point. They
would be ruled by that child's advisers, and it is certain
that those advisers would be the ones who plotted to place
him on the throne. It would be they and not the boy
who would rule Karidkote."

"Biju Ram," murmured Mahdoo, as though considering the name.

"Why do you say that?" inquired Ash sharply. "What
have you heard about him?"

"Nothing good. He is not liked, and I have heard
him called many evil names: scorpion, snake, jackal, spy
and pander, and a dozen more. He is said to have been a
creature of the late Maharani's and there is a tale . . . But
that was many years ago and is of no consequence."

"What tale?" demanded Ash.

Mahdoo shrugged his shoulders by way of reply and sucked at his pipe, brooding like an elderly parrot while the hookah bubbled gently in the silence. He refused to say anything more on the subject. But when Gul Baz came in to settle Ash for the night and he rose to take his leave, he returned to it briefly:

"Touching the matter we were discussing, I will make inquiry," said Mahdoo, and went away to gather his nightly quota of gossip from around the camp fires that flickered in the darkness.

But the tittle-tattle of the camp produced nothing new, and Ash realized that if there was any more to be learned it must come from some other source, preferably from one of Nandu's immediate family—the Rajkumari Anjuli for choice. Juli was only a few months older than Nandu, and being the nearest to him in age must surely know more about him and be a better judge of his nature than anyone else in the camp. She had also known Biju Ram for many years, and she would not have forgotten Lalji . . .

"If only I could talk to her," thought Ash for perhaps the twentieth time. "Juli will know. I must manage it somehow . . . it can't be impossible. As soon as I can get on my feet again—"

But he did not have to wait as long as that.

19

"My sister Shushila," announced Jhoti, presenting himself at Captain Pelham-Martyn's tent some two days later, "says she wishes to see you."

"Does she?" inquired Ash without much interest. "What about?"

"Oh, just to talk, I think," said Jhoti airily. "She wanted to come with me to visit you, but my uncle said she must not: he does not think it would be proper. But he said that he would speak to Gobind, and if Gobind agreed, he did not see why you should not be carried

338

across to the durbar tent this afternoon, where we can all eat and talk together."

Ash's gaze ceased to wander and he was suddenly alert. "Has Gobind agreed?"

"Oh, yes. He said you could be carried across in a *dhooli*. I told my sister that I did not think you would wish to go, because girls only giggle and chatter like a lot of parrots and never seem to have anything sensible to talk about. But she says that it is your talk she wishes to hear. My uncle says that this is because she is bored and afraid, and the things you speak of, being strange to her, cheer her up and make her laugh, so that she forgets her fears. Shu-shu has no courage at all: not one grain. She is even frightened of mice."

"And your other sister?"

"Oh, Kairi is different. But then she is quite old, you know; and besides, her mother was a *feringhi*. She is strong too, and taller than my brother Nandu—a whole two inches taller. Nandu says she should have been a man, and I wish she had been; then she would have been Maharajah instead of him. Kairi would never have tried to stop me going to the wedding like my brother did—fat, spiteful bully that he is."

Ash would have liked nothing better than to talk of Kairi-Bai, but he had no intention of allowing Jhoti to make uncomplimentary remarks about the Maharajah in his presence, particularly when there were at least two of the boy's attendants within call, not to mention several of his own. He therefore turned the conversation into less dangerous channels and spent the rest of the morning answering endless questions on the subject of cricket and football and similar pastimes of the *Angrezi-log,* until Biju Ram came to fetch Jhoti away for the mid-day meal.

Biju Ram had not stayed long, but to Ash even those few minutes had seemed interminable. It was all very well to come under that sly, hostile scrutiny by lamplight and in a crowded tent—and when one was wearing mess dress and presumably looking very much a foreigner and a Sahib. But it was quite a different matter to endure it in broad daylight while lying propped up and helpless on a camp bed, and as he looked up into the familiar face of his old enemy and listened to the smooth tones of that well-remembered voice mouthing glib compliments and inquiring solicitously after his health, Ash found it difficult to believe that the man could fail to recognize him.

Biju Ram himself had changed so little that seeing him again at close quarters the years dwindled away until the gap that separated the past from the present seemed negligible, and it was only the other day that a boy named Ashok had been the favourite butt of his malicious wit, and the victim of a hundred cruel and humiliating practical jokes that had made Lalji laugh and the courtiers snigger. Surely he could not have forgotten? But though Biju Ram's eyes were as crafty as ever, there was still no trace of recognition in them, and if his fulsome compliments were anything to go by, he seemed to be genuinely grateful for Ash's part in the rescue of Jhoti. This was not surprising if he were indeed out of favour with the Maharajah and hoping to lead a rival party, for Jhoti alive might one day prove to be a trump card, while Jhoti dead could only mean disaster for the handful of men who had accompanied him when he fled from Karidkote.

It occurred to Ash that probably the strangest aspect of the whole situation was that he and Biju Ram should find themselves on the same side of the fence—any fence. But although he would have preferred to do without such an ally, there was no denying that Biju Ram's ambition, combined with fears for his own skin, might in the end be a better guarantee of Jhoti's safety than any protection that Mulraj or he himself could devise. All the same, the very sight of the man had been enough to tighten his nerves and send a shudder down his spine, and it was a relief to turn his thoughts to the prospects of seeing Juli again in a few hours' time.

That she would do her best to avoid the meeting he was certain. But then he was equally certain that she would not succeed: Shushila would see to that, for the younger girl plainly leaned heavily on her half-sister for support and was unlikely to make any move without her. He was therefore not surprised to see her enter with her sister a few moments after he himself had been carried there, though what did surprise him was that she made no attempt to avoid his gaze, but looked gravely back at him, and with an interest as great as his own.

She had returned his greeting without a trace of embarrassment, and as she bowed to him in the graceful, conventional gesture of *namaste*, palm pressed to palm

340

and lifted to touch her forehead, the slight sideways inclination of her head and the shape of her hands—those firm, square hands that were so different from the slender hands of most Indian women—were suddenly so familiar that he could not understand why he had not recognized her at sight.

Anticipating this meeting, he had been afraid she would be cold to him, if not openly hostile, and he had wondered how he could deal with this and made various plans for doing so. But there was neither coldness nor animosity in the eyes that he had likened to the "fishpools of Heshbon," and no fear, merely interest. Evidently Juli had accepted the fact that he was, or had been, Ashok, and was studying him closely in an effort to trace in the features of a strange Englishman the face of a little Hindu boy she had once known; and as the evening wore on he also discovered that she was listening not so much to what he said as to the sound of his voice: testing it, perhaps against her memory of that boy's voice talking to her in the Queen's balcony long ago.

Ash had very little recollection of what he said during the earlier part of that evening, and he was uneasily conscious of talking at random. But with Juli sitting barely a yard away he found it almost impossible to concentrate. She had always been a rather solemn little girl, unassuming and old beyond her years, and it was clear that she still retained much of that early gravity. It did not take much discernment to see that here was a woman whose life was narrow and busy, and who had lost the habit (if she had ever possessed it) of attaching any importance to her own feelings and desires because the needs of others pressed upon her and absorbed her to the exclusion of all else. An unassertive young person, completely unaware of her own beauty and already, in her attitude towards Shushila, over-burdened with a responsibility that seemed akin to that of a mother or a devoted nurse rather than an older sister.

It did not surprise Ash that her unusual looks should be unappreciated by her people or herself, for they diverged too widely from the Indian ideal. But he was disturbed by her acceptance of Shushila's dependence on her and all that it implied, though he did not know why it should make him so uneasy. He could not possibly be afraid of Shushila? He dismissed that thought almost before it entered his mind, and decided that it was because it offended him to think of Juli taking second place to the *Nautch*-girl's daughter, and cherishing and worrying over a spoilt, pretty, highly strung child, who could force her to do things she did not want to do by the simple expedient of bursting into tears and resorting to moral blackmail of the "If you won't come with me, then I shan't go" variety. Yet there was nothing weak about Juli's firm chin or the line of her level brows. And that she was also quick-witted and courageous had been proved by the episode in the river.

He found it difficult to keep his gaze off her, and did not try very hard to do so, for it was refreshment beyond words merely to look at her. It was only when Jhoti tugged at his sleeve and inquired in a penetrating whisper why he kept staring at Kairi that he awoke to the unwisdom of his behaviour; and after that he was more careful. The hour that Kaka-ji had permitted passed very pleasantly and was an agreeable break from lying on a camp bed with nothing to look at, day after day, but the stretch of barren plain and sun-dried *kikar* trees that was all Ash could see through the open flaps of his own tent, and of which he was by now heartily tired. "You will come again tomorrow," said Shushila, her tone making the words a command rather than a query as he prepared to leave. And somewhat to Ash's surprise, Kaka-ji had seconded the invitation; though in fact the old man's reasons for doing so had been simple enough.

Kaka-ji was tired of listening to his youngest niece's woes. And tired, too, of attempting to soothe the nervous fears that had been temporarily forgotten in the novelty of meeting a foreigner, and the subsequent excitement of Jhoti's rescue and Pelham-Sahib's narrow escape from death, but that had now returned in force as a result of the boredom and inactivity of the past days.

His niece Kairi was accustomed to work, and even here there were numerous tasks that she was expected to do, such as dealing with the servants, listening to complaints and doing what she could to set matters right, supervising the waiting-women, settling quarrels, ordering meals, cooking and sewing—there was no end to it. But with Shushila it was different, for having been waited on all her days, she found the present state of affairs intolerable. As long as the camp was on the march she could at

342

least count on there being something of interest in each day, and at least they would be moving—even though it was towards a future she dreaded. But owing to Pelham-Sahib's injuries the camp had remained static for far too long, and there was little to occupy a spoilt princess who must stay cooped up in tents that were hot and airless by day and draughty by night.

Anjuli had done her best to keep her little sister entertained, but such games as *chaupur* and *pachesi* soon began to pall, and Shushila complained that music made her head ache, and wept because she did not want to be married and because her cousin Umi, who was Kaka-ji's granddaughter, had died in childbirth, and she did not want to die in a strange country—or at all.

Kaka-ji, like his brother the late Maharajah, was a peaceable man, but he was rapidly being driven to the limit of exasperation by the tears, fears and megrims of his brother's youngest daughter, and by now was prepared to clutch at any straw that might help to alleviate them. Under normal circumstances he would not have considered it at all proper for any man outside the immediate family circle to continue to meet and converse with his nieces in such a relaxed and friendly fashion, but then the present situation was far from normal. They were, in effect, in the wilderness where every-day rules need not apply; and the man in question being a foreigner to whom they were greatly indebted, if his talk of *Belait* and the ways of foreigners amused Shushila and served to distract her attention from such things as homesickness and a morbid terror of the future, what harm? In any case, it was not as though he was ever likely to be alone with her; there would always be at least half a dozen others present, and this (and the fact that he was at the moment incapable of moving out of a chair without assistance and therefore could hardly be regarded as a threat to any woman) decided Kaka-ji to second Shushila's command that the Sahib should repeat his visit on the following day.

The Sahib had done so, and after that—though Kaka-ji was never quite sure how it had come about—it became an accepted thing that he should be carried to the durbar tent every evening, where he and Jhoti and Kaka-ji, and sometimes Maldeo Rai or Mulraj (who by virtue of his relationship and his office was permitted the entrée) would sit and talk with the brides and their women, or play foolish games and gamble for sweets or cowrie shells. It all helped to pass the time and ease Shushila's nervous tension, and she, like Jhoti, delighted in Ash's descriptions of life in *Belait*, many of which struck them as excruciatingly funny.

The two would explode into giggles over such things as hunt balls and the absurdity of men and women prancing around in couples to music; of Londoners groping through a pea-soup fog and families bathing in the sea at Brighton; or descriptions of the ludicrously uncomfortable clothes that an *Angrezi* woman wore: her tight, high-heeled, buttoned boots and tighter corsets—armoured with steel and whalebone and laced to suffocation; the horse-hair bustles worn under innumerable petticoats, the pads of wire and wool over which her hair was rolled and pinned, and the hats that were skewered to this edifice with yet more pins, and decorated with flowers, feathers and fur; or even, on occasions, an entire stuffed bird.

Of them all, only Anjuli-Bai seldom spoke. But she listened, and sometimes laughed, and though ostensibly Ash talked to the company at large, his conversation was in fact almost entirely directed at Anjuli. It was Anjuli he exerted himself to please, and for her that he tried to describe something of his life in England, so that she might know what had happened to him and how he had lived in the years since his escape from Gulkote.

He found it astonishingly easy to say things he knew would have one meaning for the others but a different one for Juli, who because of her special knowledge would be able to interpret it in a way that no one else could have done; and often her smile or a faint movement of her head would tell him that she had understood an allusion that had passed the others by. It was as though the clock had turned back, and once again, as they had done in the presence of Lalji and his courtiers, they were speaking to each other in code and using a language that only the two of them understood, for in this respect, if in no other, the rapport that had existed between the children they had once been had survived the years.

The last time they had played that game Juli had been little more than a baby, and until recently Ash himself had forgotten the way they used to speak to Lalji, or pretend to talk to a pet monkey or one of the macaws

344

when they were in reality talking to each other—exchanging news or arranging where and when they would meet, and indicating times and other details by means of hand signals, coughs or the rearranging of a vase or a cushion. He could even remember their code word for the Queen's balcony: *Zamurrad* (emerald), which was also the name given to the pampered peacock that lived with his harem in the Yuveraj's garden. The connection, a reference to the Peacock Tower, was easy to follow, and there had been a hundred ways in which one or other of them could bring that word into a conversation.

There had also been a word that stood for his mother's quarters, but he could not remember it: or their signals either, for though the outline of those remained, the details had been lost in the debris of the years and try as he would he could not recapture them. It was only when he had given up the attempt that suddenly, lying awake one night, the lost word slid unbidden into his mind: Hanuman. Of course: Hanuman the Monkey-God, whose legions had made a living bridge across the sea to Lanka, each holding his neighbour's tail so that Rama might cross in safety to rescue his wife Sita, kidnapped and held prisoner there by a Demon.

Did Juli remember that? Or had she been too young? Yet she had remembered so much—far more than he had done—and her response to his oblique conversation had made it clear that she had not forgotten their old method of communicating with each other when they were not alone. Perhaps he could make use of it again and press his advantage one step further. It was worth trying, thought Ash; and he had tried it on the following evening. But this time Juli had made no response, or given any sign that she understood him or remembered, and though she did not avoid his gaze, she could not have been said to return it.

Ash went back to his tent feeling tired and defeated, and was rude to Mahdoo and short with Gul Baz. And when later that night the *dai* scratched timidly on the canvas, he called out to her to go away, saying he was no longer in need of treatment and did not wish to see anyone. In proof of which he reached out and deliberately extinguished the lamp, knowing that she could not work in the dark and must accept the dismissal without argument —not that he imagined for a moment that she would think of arguing it. But apparently the *dai* possessed more obstinacy than he had credited her with, for the darkness thinned as the canvas was pushed aside and a bright bar of moonlight accompanied the familiar shrouded figure into the tent.

Ash raised himself on one elbow and repeated crossly that he did not need her that night and would she please go away and leave him in peace, and the woman said softly: "But you yourself told me to come."

It seemed to Ash as though his heart tried to jump into his throat so that for a moment he could not breathe or speak, and the next instant it had jerked back again and was hammering so wildly that he thought she must hear it. *"Juli—!"*

There was a ghost of a laugh; a familiar laugh but with an odd catch in it, and his uninjured hand shot out to clutch a fold of coarse cotton and grip it as though he was afraid she would vanish as silently as she had come.

Anjuli said: "Did you not mean me to come? You spoke of Hanuman, and that was always our word for your courtyard."

"My mother's," corrected Ash involuntarily.

"Yours too. And as she is gone it could now have only meant one place. Your tent. That is right is it not?"

"Yes. But you were only a child—a baby. How could you possibly have remembered?"

"It was not difficult. Once you and your mother had gone, there was nothing else for me to do but remember."

She had spoken quite matter-of-factly, but that brief sentence brought home to him as never before how lonely those years must have been for her, and once again he found that there was a lump in his throat and he could not speak.

Anjuli could not have seen his face, but she seemed to have followed his thought, for she said gently: "Do not let it trouble you. I learned not to mind."

Perhaps she had indeed done so. But he found that he minded—that he minded unbearably. It appalled him to think of the child Juli left cruelly alone and neglected, with nothing to live for but memories and the hope that he could keep his promise and return. How long had it been, he wondered, before she gave up hoping?

Anjuli said: "And you too remembered."

346

But that was not entirely true. In fact had it not been for Biju Ram, he might still not have known who she was, let alone recalled the old game of double-talk and the code-words that he himself had invented. Ash cleared his throat and spoke with an effort: "Yes. But I did not know if you would remember . . . if you would understand." And then, suddenly, panic gripped him as he realized for the first time the stupidity and selfishness of what he had done. "You shouldn't have come here. It's too dangerous."

"Then why did you ask me to?"

"Because I didn't dream that you would. That you *could.*"

"But it was very simple," explained Anjuli. "I had only to borrow one of old Geeta's bourkas and persuade her to let me come in her stead. She is fond of me because I once did her a favour. And I have come before, you know."

"Then it *was* you—on the first night after the accident. I was sure it was, but Mulraj said it was only the *dai* and I—"

"He did not know," said Anjuli. "I came with Geeta because I had been angry with you for being—for behaving like a Sahib. And because you had not thought of me for years while I—I . . ."

"I know. I'm sorry, Juli. I thought you might never want to speak to me again."

"Perhaps I would not have done if you had not been injured. But I thought you might be dying, and so I made Geeta bring me with her. I came with her more than once, and sat outside in the darkness while she worked over you."

"Why, Juli? *Why?*" Ash's grip tightened on the fold of cloth, jerking at it imperatively, and Anjuli said slowly: "I suppose—to hear your voice. So that I could be sure that you were really who you said you were."

"Ashok."

"Yes, my brother Ashok. My only brother."

"Your—?"

"My bracelet-brother. Had you forgotten that? I had not. Ashok always seemed more my true brother than Lalji ever was—or Nandu or Jhoti. It was always as though he were my only brother."

347

"Was it?" Ash sounded oddly disconcerted. "And are you now sure that I am that same Ashok?"

"Of course. Would I be here if I were not?"

Ash pulled at the cotton bourka to draw her nearer, and said impatiently: "Take this thing off and light the lamp. I want to look at you."

But Anjuli only laughed and shook her head. "No. That would indeed be dangerous; and very foolish too, for if someone were to surprise us they would only think that I was old Geeta, and as she seldom speaks, I would be safe. Loose me now, and I will sit here for a space and talk to you. It is easier to talk thus, in the dark; for while I cannot see your face, or you mine, we can make believe to be Ashok and Juli again, and not Pelham-Sahib, who is an *Angrezi,* or the Rajkumari Anjuli-Bai who is to be—"

She stopped a little abruptly, and leaving the sentence unfinished, subsided onto the carpet to sit cross-legged and comfortable beside the camp bed: a pale, shapeless form that might have been a ghost—or a bundle of washing.

Later on, trying to recall what they had talked of, it seemed to Ash that they had talked of everything. Yet no sooner had she gone than he remembered a hundred things he had meant to ask or forgotten to say, and he would have given anything to call her back. But he knew that he would see her again somehow, and there was enormous comfort in that. He had no idea how long she had stayed, for there had been so much to tell that they had lost count of time. But the bar of moonlight from the open tent-flap had crept upward until it showed him the small square of coarse mesh that concealed Juli's eyes, and he could catch a glint of them as she smiled or turned her head. A little later it lay in a pale lozenge on the roof above her head, and later still, as the moon reached its zenith, it vanished altogether, and left them in darkness with only the glimmer of stars showing in the segment of sky beyond the tent door.

They spoke in whispers for fear of arousing Ash's servants, and had it not been for the intervention of the *dai,* Geeta, who taking her courage in both hands had scuttled through the silent camp to find out why her mistress had not returned, it is possible that they might have talked on into the dawn and never noticed it. But Geeta's

348

anxious voice had jerked them abruptly back from the past and to a realization of the lateness of the hour, and of the risk that they ran; for neither of them had heard her approach and it might well have been someone other than the old *dai* who tiptoed to the tent door while they talked.

Anjuli rose swiftly and moved to the doorway, blotting out the stars. "I'm coming, Geeta. Goodnight, my brother. Sleep well."

"But you will come again, won't you?"

"If it is possible. But even if not, we shall see each other often in the durbar tent."

"What is the good of that? I can't talk to you there."

"Oh yes you can. As we used to do in the old days, and as you did tonight. It is late, brother. I must go."

"Juli, wait—" His hand went out in the darkness, but she had moved out of reach, and a moment later he could see the stars again and though he had heard no sound he knew that she had gone.

20

Ash leaned back against the pillows and stared out at the night sky, brooding with dismay on that word "brother." Was that really how she thought of him? He supposed that she must. And if that was why she felt free to visit him, he ought not to complain. But he did not think of her as a sister—though honesty compelled him to admit that he had certainly treated her as one, both in his neglect for her feelings and his forgetfulness of her existence. Yet the last thing he wanted from her now was sisterly affection, even though he realized that as long as she thought of him as a brother they were comparatively safe, while should their relationship change to anything deeper, the dangers ahead were incalculable.

He lay awake for a long time, making plans and discarding them, but when at last he fell asleep, only one thing was still clear to him: the need for caution. He would have to be very careful—for Juli's sake more than his own, though he was well aware of the peril in which he would lie should anyone suspect that his feelings towards one of the brides whom he had been charged with conveying to their wedding were far from detached.

He had not needed Mulraj to point out to him how easy it would be for young Jhoti to die on the march—ostensibly from an accident—without any inquiry being made by the British authorities; and he knew that it would be equally easy for his own death to be arranged. There were so many ways in which a man could die in India, and provided he were to do so at some stage in the journey where the camp was conveniently out of reach of an English doctor or anyone else capable of giving a professional opinion on his corpse before heat, vultures and jackals had effectively disposed of it, his murderers would run no risk of being found out. Nor would his death be a lingering one, as for their own sakes they would kill him quickly. But it would be otherwise with Juli.

Ash remembered the tale of the cheetah that Nandu had burned alive because it had lost him a wager, and he shivered at the thought of what might be done to Juli. Whatever happened, she must not risk coming to his tent again. They would have to find some other way of meeting—for if she imagined for a moment that he would be content to see her only in the presence of her relations and her women in the durbar tent, she was very much mistaken. Nevertheless, they must be careful . . .

On that decision, Ash fell asleep. And waking in the cheerful sunlight of another idle, cloudless morning, straightway abandoned it. The dangers that had been so easy to visualize in the darkness seemed far less menacing by daylight, and by the time he was carried to the evening meeting in the durbar tent and saw her smile at him as she sketched the familiar gesture of greeting, he had forgotten his good resolutions and decided that she must come just once more, if only so that he could explain to her why she must never come again, which was something that he found too difficult to convey to her by oblique and roundabout methods.

Three hours later she was seated on the end of his camp bed while old Geeta crouched in the shadows among the guy-ropes outside and kept watch, trembling with anxiety and muttering prayers to a variety of gods. But

350

Ash had not succeeded in making Juli see the rashness of her behaviour.

"Are you afraid that Geeta will talk? I promise you she will not. And she is so deaf that we would have to talk much louder than this before she could hear what we were saying."

"That is not the point, and you know it!" said Ash. "What matters is that you are here, and you should not be. What could you say if you were discovered?"

Anjuli laughed at him and said lightly that there was not the least danger of her being discovered there, but that even if she were, no great harm would result from it. "For has it not been agreed that you are now as our brother, having done us all great service in rescuing my sister and myself from the river, and injuring yourself in attempting to save our little brother from death? And should a sister not be permitted to visit a sick brother? Particularly when she comes after dark when strangers cannot gape at her, and is accompanied by an elderly and respectable widow."

"But I am not your brother," said Ash angrily. He would have liked to add that he had no wish to be, but as this did not seem to be an appropriate moment to say so, he said instead: "You are talking like a child! and if you were still now one this would not matter, but the trouble is that you are not. You are a woman grown, and it is not fitting that you should come to my tent alone. You must know that."

"Surely," agreed Anjuli; and though he could not see her face for the darkness and the bourka that she still wore, he knew that she was smiling. "I am not entirely foolish. But if I am discovered here I can pretend to be. I shall say what I have just said to you, and though I shall be severely scolded and forbidden to come again, that is the worst that would happen."

"To you, perhaps," retorted Ash. "But what about me? Would anyone believe that I—or any man for that matter—can see no harm in entertaining a woman in the privacy of my tent and by night?"

"But then you are not a man," said Anjuli sweetly.

"I'm not—What the devil do you mean?" demanded Ash, justly incensed.

"Only not in the way you meant," explained Anjuli soothingly. "Or not at present. My uncle himself has said

351

that no woman could possibly consider herself endangered by the presence of an invalid who was trussed like a fowl in splints and bandages and incapable of moving freely."

"Thank you," observed Ash caustically.

"But it is true. When you are well again it will be different. But at present you could hardly be suspected of doing any harm to my virtue, even if you wished to."

Ash could think of no adequate retort, though he knew that it was not as simple as all that, and that even the kindly Kaka-ji would not take a lenient view of his niece's behaviour, or his own either. But the temptation to let Juli stay was too great, and he made no further attempt to send her away or discourage any further visits. She had not stayed very long that night, nor had she allowed him to dispense with the *dai*'s treatment. She had sent the old lady in to knead and massage him while she herself waited outside in the moonlight, and the two had left together. But despite Geeta's ministrations, Ash had once again endured a wakeful night.

He was in no hurry to get the camp on the move again, but there were a great many disadvantages in letting it remain for too long in one place; not the least of them being the risk of depleting the surrounding country-side of food and fodder. He had no desire to risk a repetition of the situation that he had found on his arrival at Deenagunj, and he also knew that the presence of so large a number of men and animals encamped in one spot would be bound to foul the locality to an extent that would soon become painfully noticeable. Already the wind blowing in through his tent door had brought him warning of this. Yet as long as they stayed there, Juli would probably continue to visit him, while once they moved on it might not be too easy. For that reason alone he would have given anything to stay, but he could not bring himself to disregard his responsibilities to the camp, and on the following morning he discussed the matter with Mulraj and informed Gobind that he was now perfectly capable of travelling; not on horseback, possibly, but in one of the baggage carts or on an elephant.

Gobind had been dubious, but after some argument had given way on condition that Pelham-Sahib allowed himself to be carried in a *palkee*, and a sedan having been procured, orders had gone out that the camp would march next day.

352

The decision had been generally welcomed, though not by the younger bride, who only a few days ago had been complaining of the inaction, yet now that they would shortly be on the move again, was reminded by all the bustle and preparation of what awaited her at their journey's end. Thinking of it, she wept and wrung her hands and clung to her sister for comfort, wailing that she felt ill and that the very thought of having to travel in that hot, stuffy *ruth* again was more than she could bear.

There had been no meeting in the durbar tent that evening, and later the *dai* had arrived alone and overcome her timidity sufficiently to whisper that Anjuli-Bai sent her salaams and regretted that she would not be able to visit the Sahib that night, or on the next one either. But during the following week she came nightly, though her visits were brief and she did not come alone, but always with Geeta, who would treat Ash and then retire out of earshot to wait while her mistress and the Sahib talked together.

The old lady's hearing might be poor, but her eyesight was still excellent, and her fears made her an admirable watch-dog, for the smallest movement attracted her attention. Her nervous little cough signalled a warning if anyone came too near, and the two in the tent would fall silent. But no one interrupted them, and Ash's servants, who would not have allowed anyone else to approach unchallenged, were used to the sight of the *dai* and the lateness of her visits, and being aware of her timidity were not surprised that she had taken to bringing a companion with her. They saw the women arrive and leave again, and were not troubled.

The friendly sessions in the durbar tent were no longer an accepted part of each day, for after long hours spent in a closed *ruth*, Shushila was often too weary for company. The roads, where they existed, were little better than cart-tracks between villages, and where there were none the surface of the plain was almost preferable. On both, the dust lay thick and the hooves of the trotting bullocks stirred it up in choking clouds that forced their way between the closely drawn curtains of the *ruth*, covering everything within, clothing, cushions, hands, faces and hair, with a thin grey film of grit.

Shushila coughed and wept and complained ceaselessly of the dust and the jolting and the discomfort, so

353

that by the day's end Anjuli was often exhausted, and there were times when she came near to losing her patience and giving her little sister a good shaking. The fact that she did not do so was due to the habit of years as much as to her affection and sympathy for Shushila, for Juli had learned very early to control her emotions and hold her tongue. And to shoulder, without complaint, burdens that many an adult would have found hard to bear.

She had been six years old when Ashok and Sita fled from Gulkote, and during the next few months her position in the palace had been unenviable. But there came a day when by chance she succeeded in quietening little Shushila, who was cutting a tooth and had been screaming for hours on end, after everyone else had failed to do so. Her success was probably due to the fact that she happened to pick up the child at a moment when it had howled itself into exhaustion and was ready to stop anyway. But the equally exhausted Zenana thought otherwise, and Janoo-Rani, who while doting on her sons took little or no interest in a mere daughter, said carelessly that in future Kairi-Bai could make herself useful by helping to look after her half-sister.

There can be little doubt that the *Nautch*-girl derived a certain malicious satisfaction from seeing the *Feringhi*-Rani's daughter dancing attendance upon her own offspring, but Kairi-Bai had enjoyed the sudden sense of responsibility. Her days were no longer empty or aimless, for this latest of Janoo's children was a sickly and fretful little creature and its attendants had been only too willing to let someone else do their work for them—even when that someone was only a six-year-old child. Kairi-Bai was kept fully occupied, and it was not surprising that as the years went by Shushila should have come to look on her less as an older sister than a combination of nurse, playfellow and slave.

Kairi had been all those things: but her reward was love. A selfish, clinging, demanding love, it is true; but love all the same, which was something she had never had before—the poor *Feringhi*-Rani having died too soon to be remembered; and though Ashok had been kind to her and Sita had given her affection and understanding, she knew that those two loved only each other while

354

Shushila, on the other hand, not only loved her, but needed her. To be needed was an equally novel experience, and such a comforting one that she did not begrudge the long hours of servitude that the idleness of the child's servants thrust upon her.

Had Kairi been given a free hand, it is even possible that she might have succeeded in bringing up her baby sister to be a tolerably healthy and well-adjusted young woman. But she was far too young and inexperienced to be able to combat the pernicious influence of the Zenana women, whose anxiety to curry favour with Janoo-Rani led them to make much of little Shushila, and vie with each other to pet and spoil the child.

The *Nautch*-girl's own treatment of her daughter was governed entirely by her moods. As these were unpredictable, little Shushila could never be certain if she would be received with a caress or a slap, and as a result she developed a morbid sense of insecurity which was aggravated by the fact that she admired her mother even more than she feared her, and craving as she did for her affection, the careless caresses could not compensate for the misery of being rebuffed. It was this that bred in her a passionate attachment for anything that was safe and familiar: the privacy and protection of the Zenana walls, the faces and voices of all those who peopled her small world, and the unchanging routine of each day. She had no interest in anything that lay beyond the Women's Quarters or in the world outside the Palace of the Winds, and no desire to venture there.

Kairi, who had watched her grow up, was aware of this, and perceptive enough to divine the reason for it, though Shushila herself would never have been able to put it into words, even supposing she had recognized the forces that drove her, which she did not. She was not given to analysing her emotions, any more than the women who pandered to them and by doing so encouraged her to be hysterical and selfish. It was only Kairi-Bai, made wise by harsh experience, who came to realize that her little sister's headaches and the attacks of nervous hysteria that caused so much anxiety in the Zenana were largely imaginary and always self-induced; and that these, together with her fear of the unfamiliar and her high-handed treatment of servants and the humbler members of the Zenana who were incapable of retaliation, were a form of revenge

355

for the lack of interest that her fascinating and imperious mother showed towards her.

Nevertheless it seemed quite natural to Kairi, who was devoid of vanity, that Shu-shu's love for her mother should be immeasurably greater than her love for so unspectacular a person as herself—even though Janoo-Rani, apart from giving birth to her, had done nothing to earn it, while she herself had watched over her and waited on her with tireless devotion, played with her, comforted her and encouraged her, understood her and loved her. Yet with all her understanding, Kairi had never fully realized the depth of Shu-shu's idolatry until Janoo-Rani died.

Shushila's behaviour on that occasion had been so frenzied that the Zenana had confidently predicted that she would die of grief. She had wept and shrieked and tried to throw herself from one of the windows, and when Kairi had prevented this, turned on her half-sister like a wild cat, clawing at her face until the blood ran. Shut into a room with barred windows she had refused all food; and the fact that she had held out for five days proved conclusively that she possessed more stamina than her frail appearance and frequent illness had led anyone to suppose. To all Kairi's coaxing and efforts to console her she had turned a deaf ear, and in the end it had been Nandu who put a stop to the whole nerve-wracking business by storming in and berating his little sister in terms that only an angry and exasperated brother would have thought of using.

Astonishingly, it had worked, partly because as Maharajah of Karidkote as well as her elder brother he was doubly in authority over her, but mostly because he was a man, and as such, a magnificent and all-powerful being whose wishes must be regarded as law by any mere woman. Every Indian woman was taught that her first duty was obedience; and there was no woman, and no Zenana in all the land, that was not under the unquestioned control of some man. Shushila had meekly submitted to her brother's commands, his wrath having succeeded where Kairi-Bai's loving patience had failed, and peace had returned to the Zenana.

But as a result of Nandu's high-handed treatment of her, Shushila had somewhat unexpectedly transferred to him all the obsessive admiration she had felt for her mother; and the Zenana women, who had expected to see her half-sister's influence over her become greatly increased as a result of the Rani's death, were surprised (and in some cases relieved) to find that this was not so. Kairi-Bai's position in this respect remained unaltered, though in other ways it had changed a good deal; and for the better because Nandu had a keen sense of his own position and regarded any lack of respect shown to a member of his immediate family as a slight to his own dignity, and Kairi-Bai was a princess of the royal house and his own half-sister.

She did not look ahead, for she had learned long ago that it was better to live for the present and let the future rest in the lap of the gods, though she took it for granted that she would be married one day—marriage, after all, being the fate of every girl. But her father had been too indolent to bestir himself in the matter, and her step-mother too jealous to arrange a good match for her—yet too afraid of the Rajah to try marrying his eldest daughter to a nobody. The question of a husband for Kairi-Bai had therefore been shelved, and in time it began to seem unlikely that one would ever be found for her. After all, she was getting old: far too old for a bride.

When her father died, and later her step-mother, the old stumbling-block still remained; only now it was Nandu's pride that would not permit him to entertain the idea of giving his half-sister in marriage to anyone of inferior rank. Nor did he intend to let her take precedence over his full-sister even in such a matter as this: Shushila must be married first—and to a ruling prince. When that was done he would dispose of Kairi to some less important personage; though he realized that this might not be too easy, for as well as getting on in years she was no beauty: a tall, gawky woman with high cheek bones, a big mouth and the hands of a working woman —or a European. But his own father's daughter, nevertheless.

Little Shushila, on the other hand, gave promise of exceptional beauty, and already a number of offers had been made for her hand, though none so far had met with her brother's approval. Either their rank or their riches were not sufficiently impressive, or, in two cases where this was not an obstacle, the suitors' own lands lay too near to Karidkote.

Nandu had not forgotten how his father had acquired the disputed State of Karidarra, and he had no intention of providing any loophole that might one day allow some descendant of his sister Shushila's to lay claim to his own territories. He was nothing if not thorough. When, eventually, an offer had come from the Rana of Bhithor, he had accepted it, though the match could hardly be termed a splendid one, Bhithor being a small and backward state with an unspectacular revenue, and its Rana a middle-aged man who had already been married and widowed twice over, and fathered no less than seven children—all of them girls. Both his previous wives had died in child-bed, the last one only a year ago (assisted, according to rumour, by poison), and of his seven daughters, the five who had survived their infancy were all considerably older than Shushila. But his lineage was superior to Nandu's and the gifts he had sent were impressively rich. Best of all, his state lay more than five hundred miles to the southward, which was much too far away from Karid-kote to allow any future Rana to dream of annexing it. In Nandu's opinion it was a sensible and satisfactory match. But his little sister had been appalled.

Shushila had always known that she must marry one day, but now that the day was actually in sight she was overwhelmed by panic. The thought of leaving her home and all the safe, familiar people and surroundings that she had grown up amongst terrified her, while the prospect of travelling hundreds of miles across India to a strange place and a strange man—a middle-aged widower—was unendurable. She could not face it. She would not—she *would* not. She would rather die . . .

Once again hysterical shrieks and lamentations rang through the Zenana Quarters, and this time even Nandu at his angriest could not move her, though he had threatened to have her beaten within an inch of her life if she did not obey him. But then Nandu did not understand, as Anjuli did, that at the heart of her terror and resistance lay the dread of a far worse death. Death by fire. Against that, a beating seemed a trivial thing . . .

"It was the *Nautch*-girl's doing," Anjuli had explained during one of those visits to Ash's tent. "Janoo-Rani gave orders that her daughter should be strictly instructed in all those things that a well-born woman should

358

know. Not only in religious observances and the proper ritual of *pujah*, but in all matters of ceremony and etiquette, and the duty of a wife towards her husband. This Shushila was taught almost from the time she could first speak, and she was only five when she was taken to see the hand-prints on the Suttee Gate—you remember it?—and told that if she herself were ever widowed, she must burn herself on her husband's pyre. Thereafter she was made to stir boiling rice with her little finger, in order to teach her to bear fire without flinching."

Ash's comment had been savage and unprintable, and though he had spoken in English, Anjuli had not needed a translation; his tone had been enough and she had nodded agreement and said thoughtfully: "Yes, it was cruel, and it did not serve its purpose, for it only succeeded in making Shu-shu more afraid. She became terrified of pain. She cannot endure it."

Ash observed caustically that Janoo-Rani obviously could not endure it either, because she had certainly not practised what she preached when her own husband died, and he, for one, did not believe for a moment that anyone could have locked her in a room against her wishes. Or prevented her from doing anything else she wanted to do.

"That is true," agreed Anjuli. "I think she would not go to the pyre because she was very angry with my father for taking another wife, and she hated the woman so much that she would not even burn with her, for then their ashes would have mingled."

Ash made a rude noise and said it was a good story, but it was obvious that she never had any intention of burning herself. As for Shushila, there was no need for her to worry, since suttee was now forbidden by law.

"An English law," scoffed Anjuli. "Have you really become so much an *Angrezi* that you believe your people have only to say 'It is forbidden,' for such old customs as this to cease immediately? Bah!—widows have burned themselves with their husbands for centuries, and the tradition will not die in a day—or a year or a score of years—at the bidding of *feringhis*. In places where there are large numbers of *Angrezis* and police and *pultons* to enforce the law, there will be those who will obey. But many others will not, and your Raj will never even

359

know of it; for this is too vast a land for a handful of *feringhis* to keep watch over. Only when women themselves refuse to submit to this custom will it cease."

Yet Anjuli knew that Shushila, for one, would never refuse. That early teaching had made too deep an impression on her, and though the very thought of such a death terrified her beyond words, it would not occur to her to avoid it, for she knew that not one of her father's predecessors had burned alone (those tragic prints on the Suttee Gate bore witness to that) and her father himself had been accompanied through the flames by his latest wife, the scheming little interloper, Lakshmi-Bai. It was the inescapable duty of a royal widow.

Had her prospective bridegroom been a boy of her own age, or even a youth in his teens, Shushila's reaction to the news of her betrothal might have been very different. But the Rana was almost forty and might die at any moment, and then her worst nightmare would come true and she would be burned alive. The finger with which she had been forced to stir that boiling rice had shrivelled to the bone, and she had learned to hide it very cleverly, looping the edge of her sari over it so that no one would ever have noticed it. But though it had become numb and nerveless long ago, she had never forgotten the agony of those early days; and if one small finger could cause such excruciating pain, what must it be like to have one's whole body thrust into a fire? It was this thought that now drove her to a hysterical frenzy and made her declare wildly that she would not marry the Rana—or anyone else.

Perhaps if she had explained this to Nandu he might have had some sympathy for her, though he would certainly not have changed his plans. But she could not bring herself to admit to anyone that it was not marriage that she was afraid of but widowhood, because that would mean that she, a Rajkumari and the daughter of a royal line, shrank from accepting a fate that millions of humbler women had accepted without question, and she would never disgrace herself by such an admission of cowardice. If Anjuli knew, it was not because Shushila had confided in her, but because she loved her, and therefore did not need words to explain the real cause of this stubborn and hysterical refusal to marry the husband that Nandu had chosen for her.

360

It had proved a trying time for almost everyone in the palace, not least for Anjuli. Patience and sympathy for the sufferer had very soon run out, and as the hysterical scenes continued, tempers had worn thin. Intimidation, bribery and entreaty had been tried in turn, but all to no effect, and eventually Nandu had carried out his threat and had his sister soundly beaten. Physical violence had won the day, for Shushila, as Anjuli had said, could not bear pain; and though there could be no comparison between a beating and being burned alive, the latter calamity was, after all, in the future (and might conceivably be avoided), whereas this—the cruel, cutting strokes of a bamboo cane that raised great weals on her tender flesh —was happening now, and she could not endure it. She had capitulated almost immediately. But not unconditionally. She would obey her dear brother and marry the Rana—but only if Kairi could go with her and remain with her. Were this granted, she promised to make no more trouble and to be a dutiful wife and do everything in her power to please her husband and her brother. But if it were not—

The prospect of more scenes was not to be borne, and Nandu was perceptive enough to recognize that despite her fragile appearance, beauty was not the only legacy that Shushila had inherited from their mother: somewhere inside that spoilt, highly strung and over-imaginative little girl there lurked a thin core of Janoo's own steel, and if driven too hard, she might well kill herself: not by poison or a knife, or anything that would involve too much pain, but by leaping from a window or into a well, which she would imagine to be quick and easy—or even by starving herself to death. She could be surprisingly obstinate when she chose, and once she had left Karidkote and was no longer under his eye there was no knowing what she might do, if she had left unwillingly. Obviously, then, it was better that she should go willingly; and if the Rana could be persuaded to take two brides instead of one, it would provide a neat solution to yet another problem: the question of a husband for Kairi-Bai.

The Rana's emissaries had been agreeable and Nandu had experienced the satisfaction of one who brings down two birds with one shot; though admittedly the dowry demanded for Kairi-Bai was greatly in excess of the sum he had had in mind, and there had been considerable argument on the subject, some of it verging on the acrimonious. The matter had eventually been settled to the advantage of the Rana, for as Nandu's current favourite had pointed out, it was only fair that Kairi-Bai's deficiency in the matter of breeding, age and beauty should be compensated for by a substantial dowry. And besides, the cost of a double wedding was bound to be less than two separate ones.

This last was certainly true, for Nandu had been able to economize in the matter of jewels and bride-clothes for his half-sister, giving as his excuse that it was only fitting that her trousseau should be smaller and less valuable than that of the more important bride, Shushila-Bai. Also the retinue he had sent to escort his two sisters to Bhithor would have been just as large and as lavish if only one of them had gone, it being, in reality, less a bridal procession than a public display of the might, splendour and importance of His Highness the Maharajah of Karidkote. For Nandu, as Mr. Carter, the District Officer, had pointed out, was showing off.

All these arrangements had taken time, since the Rana himself had remained in Bhithor and the envoys he had sent to negotiate the marriage had not been able to accept an extra bride without consulting him. Messengers had ridden back and forth between the two widely separated states, and the journey being a slow and arduous one even for a rider with relays of fast horses, it was many months before Nandu's sisters at last set out for Bhithor.

Anjuli had had no say in all this: her future had been decided by her half-brother and his favourites, and there was nothing she could do about it. Even if her wishes had been consulted (and, even more unlikely, had carried any weight), she would never have dreamed of deserting Shushila. Shu-shu had always needed her, and now she needed her more than ever. It would have been unthinkable to let her go away alone, and Anjuli had quite simply not thought of it. She had not even given much thought to their future husband, or what her feelings might be for a man who was prepared to marry her solely in order to get the younger sister. That the bargain did not hold out much prospect of happiness for her was of minor importance, because Anjuli had never expected very much of marriage. It seemed to her a gamble in which the dice were heavily loaded in favour of the opposite sex, for no woman could choose her husband; yet, having married him, even though he proved to be cruel and unjust to her, or physically repulsive, she must worship him as a god, serving him and doing his will to her life's end, and if he died before her, immolating herself on his pyre. A bridegroom who was disappointed when he lifted his bride's veil and saw for the first time the face of the girl he had married could console himself with other women; but a disappointed bride had nothing but her sense of duty and the hope of children to sustain her.

In the circumstances, it did not do to build too heavily on the chance of a happy marriage, and Anjuli had not done so; partly, it must be admitted, because somewhere in the back of her mind there had lurked the hope that one day Ashok and his mother would come back for her, and she would be able to go away with them to live for the rest of her life in a valley among high mountains.

That hope had never quite faded; though it had grown fainter as the years passed and they had not returned. But as long as she remained unmarried it seemed to her that somewhere a door was still open: and as she grew up and left childhood behind her, and there was still no talk of a husband for her, she began to think that perhaps there never would be.

For Shushila of course, it would be different. Shushu was going to be as beautiful as her mother: that had been clear from the first. She was also a person of considerable importance, so an early and splendid marriage for her was a certainty. Anjuli had long ago resigned herself to the fact that it would separate them—perhaps for ever—and the news that this would not happen, and that they were to stay together after all, had compensated her for many things. For the closing of that door and the final abandonment of a dream. For having to leave Karidkote and live out her days in a hot and arid country far and far to the southward, where no one had ever seen a deodar or a rhododendron or a pine tree, and there were no mountains—and no snow . . .

She would never see the Dur Khaima again, or smell the scent of pine-needles when the wind blew in from the north. And if Ashok were now to keep his promise and return, it would be too late, for he would find her gone.

21

Not many people in the camp were able to sleep late. There was too much work to be done, and the majority rose early in order to feed and water animals, milk cows and goats, light fires and prepare the morning meal. Or, like Mahdoo and Kaka-ji, to pray.

Mahdoo's prayers did not take too long, but Kaka-ji's *pujah* was a protracted affair. The old man was keenly aware of the existence of God—though he confessed to being uncertain as to whether God was also aware of him. "But one must hope," said Kaka-ji. "One must live in hope." The Unseen was very real to him, and as he had no intention of allowing the fact that he was on a journey to interfere with his religious observances, he took to rising well before dawn in order that he might devote his customary two hours to his *pujah*.

His niece Shushila was one of the few who lay late abed, but her sister, Anjuli-Bai, rose almost as early as Kaka-ji; though for a different reason. Habit had something to do with it, but in the early days of the march she would be up by cockcrow in order to peer out between the tent-flaps and gaze at the mountains.

For a time the snow peaks of the Himalayas had remained clearly visible in the dawn, floating silver and serene in the cool air of morning. And though at mid-day the dust would hide them, when the day waned they would emerge again, rose-tipped now against the green of the evening sky. But as the weeks wore away, the snow-capped ranges receded, dwindling and growing fainter and further away, until finally they vanished. And Anjuli looked for them no more.

There came a day when the Punjab too, with its five great rivers, its friendly villages and fat crop-lands, was left behind. And with it, British India. They were crossing Rajputana now: Tod's fabled Rajasthan—the "Country of the Kings." A land of feudal states ruled over by the descendants of warrior princes whose deeds colour the chronicles of Hindustan with blood and violence and splendour, and whose names read like a fanfare of trumpets—Bikaner, Jodhpur, Gwalior and Alwar; Jaipur, Bhurtpore, Kotah and Tonk; Bundi, Dholpur, Udipore, Indore . . .

This was very different country from the fertile and densely populated Punjab. Here towns and villages no longer stood cheek-by-jowl, but were widely scattered, and the land itself was for the most part flat and featureless. A place of limitless horizons and little shade, where the light seemed harsher than in the north, and men, as though in compensation for the lack of colour in their surroundings, painted their houses blinding white or sugar-pink, and decorated their walls and gateways with gay murals of fighting elephants or legendary heroes. Even the horns of their cattle were often brightly tinted, and the country-women did not wear saris but favoured voluminous skirts in vivid tones of sapphire and scarlet, cerise, orange, grass-green and saffron, printed and bordered in black. With their tight, bright bodices and head-scarves of strongly contrasting colours, they were as brilliant as a flock of macaws, and they walked like queens, balancing vast brass cooking pots, water *chattis* or heavy loads of fodder on their heads with graceful ease, and moving always to the clash and jingle of silver, since every ankle and wrist bore its load of bracelets.

"Like dancing girls," sniffed Mahdoo, disapprovingly.

"Like *Houris*,"* retorted Ash. "Like peonies, or Dutch tulips." The aridity of the landscape depressed him, but he approved of the gay garb of its women, and of the fact that this sandy and rock-strewn country was by no means as barren as it appeared at first sight, but supported more wild life than he had seen during all their days in the Punjab. Herds of black-buck and *chinkara* roamed the plain, and the scanty scrub seemed alive with partridge and quail and flocks of pigeons. And once, in the early dawn, he had seen a great cloud of sandgrouse that must have numbered many thousands, rising from a lonely pool of water in a treeless waste of sand. Apart from the

---

*nymphs of the Mohammedan paradise

beauty of these sights, it was a relief to realize that there would be no need for him to follow the example of such orthodox Hindus as Kaka-ji, and turn vegetarian.

A dâk-runner arrived in camp bearing a large packet of mail addressed to Captain Pelham-Martyn. Most of it was of little interest, and having skimmed through this dispiriting collection of waste paper and consigning it to its proper place, Ash turned gratefully to the only two items that interested him: a short letter from Zarin, and a much longer one from Wally, who was frankly envious and complained of the dullness of Rawalpindi and wished that he was in Ash's shoes.

"I told you those girls were bound to be beautiful, but you wouldn't believe it," wrote Wally. "They're wasted on you!" And then went on to belie his complaints by giving Ash a lyrical description of a Miss Laura Wendover, who unfortunately (or perhaps fortunately?) had turned out to be betrothed to a civil engineer. There was also a poem written to commemorate a fellow officer who had died of enteric, that began "Lo, e'en ere his day had reached full morn," and ran to seven lengthy verses, each worse than the last.

Ash waded through the first two before crumpling it up and tossing it away, and as the wind caught the paper and carried it out of sight, wondered idly what a stranger, finding that effusion and unacquainted with Wally, would make of the poet. Any impressions gained from such turgid stuff would be nothing in the least like the writer, yet Wally's six-page letter conjured him up as though he were there in the flesh and talking aloud, and Ash laughed over it and re-read it, and for a moment almost wished himself back in Rawalpindi.

Zarin's letter, on the other hand, consisted of a single page and was a curious document. For one thing it had been written in English, which was surprising, as Zarin knew perfectly well that there was no longer any necessity for this, and Ash had received two letters from him while in Rawalpindi, both in Arabic script. This one like all the others had been dictated to a professional letter-writer, and apart from the usual flowery compliments and prayers for the recipient's health and prosperity, it contained only a few quite unimportant items of regimental news, and ended with the information that Zarin's mother was in excellent health and desired him to urge the Sa-

366

hib to have a care for his own, and to take special precautions against such things as snakes, centipedes and scorpions—the latter being very prevalent in the wilds of Rajputana . . .

As Zarin's mother had been dead for a good many years, Ash came to the conclusion that Zarin too had made the belated discovery that Karidkote and Gulkote were one and the same, and was attempting to convey a warning. He would know that the use of her name would arrest Ash's attention and put him on his guard, supposing he had not already discovered this for himself, and that remark about scorpions was plainly a reference to Biju Ram, whose nickname in the Hawa Mahal had been "*Bichchhu,*" while the fact that the letter was written in English suggested that Zarin was taking precautions against the possibility of it being opened and read by someone else.

This last had obviously been a prudent move, as a close examination showed Ash that every single envelope that the dâk-runner had delivered to him had been tampered with—an unpleasant discovery, but one that did not worry him unduly, for he knew very well that there was no one in the Karidkote camp who could read English well enough to make much sense of them; and at least it proved that the risks that Zarin was trying to warn him against were not entirely imaginary.

Ash put Wally's letter aside, and tearing up Zarin's sent it to join the others in the waste-paper basket, and went out to exchange compliments with the local *Tulakdar* who had agreed to deliver a supply of sugar-cane to the elephant lines.

The camp had been on the march again for less than a week when he abandoned the sedan and insisted that he was now perfectly capable of riding once more, and impatient to try the paces of the mettlesome Arab, Baj Raj—"the Royal steed"—that Maldeo Rai, in the name of the *panchayat,* had presented to him in replacement of his dead roan, The Cardinal.

That he was able to ride at all was a tribute to Gobind's skill and the ministrations of Geeta, the *dai;* and though his first day in the saddle had been more of a strain than he cared to admit, the next one had been better, and the next better still, and by the following week he was back to normal and feeling as fit as he had

367

ever been. But the pleasure of being free of pain and bandages and on his feet again was not entirely unalloyed, because it also meant that there was no longer any need for the *dai's* treatments; and once her visits ceased it became too dangerous for Juli to come alone.

For the time being there seemed no alternative to seeing her only in the durbar tent, which in Ash's view was a thoroughly unsatisfactory state of affairs and comparable to standing in the snow and looking through a plate-glass window at a warm room and a blazing fire. Besides, the evening meetings were still subject to the whims of Shushila, and now that the Sahib was no longer an invalid, Kaka-ji would have preferred to have discontinued them altogether, though he did not forbid them and appeared to enjoy them as much as anyone whenever Shushila happened to convene one. But Ash had become too used to being able to see Juli alone and talk with her freely to give that up, and he had no intention of doing so. There must be some other way in which they could meet.

Once again he lay awake at night making and discarding plans and weighing risks. But he could have saved himself the trouble and the hours of lost sleep, for Jhoti unwittingly solved the problem for him by complaining to Kaka-ji that his sisters were growing dull and tiresome and that even Kairi, who was never ill, had twice refused to play chess with him because she had a headache. And no wonder, declared Jhoti scornfully—what else did she expect?—cooped up for hours on end in a stuffy *ruth* when she wasn't shut up in a purdah tent, never taking the air or any exercise at all, and walking at most a dozen steps a day. At this rate, by the time they reached Bhithor she would be as bad as Shu-Shu—always ill and no use to anyone.

As for Shu-Shu, if she wasn't careful she wouldn't get there at all, for in addition to all the ailments she complained about, she was now not even eating properly, and if she went on like this she'd shrivel up and die, and then the Rana would find himself left with only Kairi, and probably refuse to have her. And *then*, added Jhoti, his imagination running away with him, they would all have to turn round and go back to Karidkote with nothing to show for all the trouble and expense, and Nandu would be so enraged that he would probably have everyone beheaded—or anyway sent to prison. Or perhaps he might even have a fit and fall down dead.

This final flight of fancy seemed to cheer Jhoti considerably. But there had been enough truth in his previous remarks to alarm Kaka-ji, and the next time he saw his nieces he looked at them with more attention and decided that Jhoti had been right. Kairi-Bai appeared tired and heavy-eyed and there was a listlessness in her manner that he had never noticed before. It alarmed him, for if she fell ill what would become of Shu-shu? None of the other women would be able to take her place, and it was easy to see that even she was finding the task of keeping her little sister's megrims within bounds a taxing one. The younger girl was also looking far from well, and Kaka-ji, studying her, decided that she was growing too thin and that it did not become her. She was beginning to look like . . . yes, like a skinny brown monkey, all eyes.

The thought shocked him profoundly, for until this moment he had always considered Shushila to be an exquisitely beautiful girl; and though he had no apprehensions that she might die before they reached Bhithor (as her little brother had so gloomily predicted) it would be almost as great a disaster if she were to lose her looks. After all, the Rana had not only been promised a beautiful bride but, as part of her bride-price, compelled to accept her much older half-sister as well; so there was no knowing how he might react were he to feel himself cheated on the deal. Something must be done at once, and Kaka-ji hurried away to see Pelham-Sahib; and spent the next half-hour discussing his predicament with an interested and sympathetic listener.

From Ash's point of view, the situation might have been tailor-made to suit his convenience, and seizing the opportunity with both hands he suggested that what both girls needed was more exercise. A daily ride, perhaps—preferably of an evening while the tents were being pitched and the air was cool and refreshing. Something of this nature could not fail to do them good, and coming at the end of a long day spent in the dusty discomfort of the *ruth*, it would provide a welcome relief for their cramped muscles and not only give them an appetite for the evening meal, but help to ensure a good night's sleep as well. He was sure that a quiet mount could be provided for the Rajkumari Shushila, and there would be no necessity for a guard to accompany them, for Kaka-ji, Mulraj and himself would be sufficient protection. Also it might be a good idea to encourage Jhoti to give his younger sister riding lessons, and there was even a chance that Shushila-Bai might become a good enough horse-woman to ride for some part of the journey instead of travelling the whole way in the *ruth*.

By using all the guile and diplomacy at his command he contrived to convey the impression that the whole scheme was in reality Kaka-ji's own idea from start to finish, and that all he, Ash, had done was to agree with it. With the result that later that evening, after consulting Gobind (who had agreed that the effect of exercise in moderation could be as beneficial as tonics and purges), the old gentleman had produced it to Mulraj as his own solution to the problem, and charged him with procuring suitable mounts for the brides and making any other arrangements that might be necesary.

Jhoti had been delighted at the prospect of showing off to Shushila, and was only too willing to instruct her. The plan had been put into effect on the very next day and been a success from the start; particularly from Ash's point of view, for the evening rides were an enormous improvement on those gatherings in the durbar tent, as they allowed far more latitude for private conversation and were free from the observant eyes of waiting-women.

The *ruth* would be stopped a mile short of the selected camping site, and Ash, with Jhoti, Mulraj and Kaka-ji, would ride back to meet it, taking two spare horses for the girls; a slow, sedate and well-mannered animal for Shushila-Bai and a more mettlesome one for Anjuli.

Sometimes they would bring hawks with them, and sometimes a shot-gun if there was a chance of game. But mostly they rode for exercise and pleasure. And as Shushila preferred to keep to a walk, or at most a gentle trot, while Jhoti, in the role of instructor, stayed close beside her with Mulraj to keep an eye on them both, and Kaka-ji was usually too tired by a day in the saddle to do more than jog along behind, Ash and Anjuli-Bai found it the easiest thing in the world to ride ahead and explore the countryside together without arousing any comment. Once again it became possible for them to talk freely, and this time without any fear that what they

370

said might be overheard; for out in the open country they were safe and Ash could watch Juli's face as she talked, instead of only listening to a voice that whispered in the darkness from behind the folds of a bourka.

Jhoti had insisted on Shushila wearing male attire, as no one, he declared, could possibly manage to ride comfortably—let alone well—while swathed in a sari. And though Kaka-ji had protested at this, he had been overruled, for Shushila was enchanted at the prospect of dressing up, and Mulraj, who also considered a sari an impossible garment to ride in, pointed out that it would arouse less curiosity in any strangers they might happen to pass, if they gave the appearance of being a party of men out for an evening canter.

Dressed in borrowed clothing, Shushila made a charming boy and Anjuli a handsome young man. And even Kaka-ji had to admit that their costume could hardly be considered immodest, and was certainly more sensible; though he failed to notice that this change of dress resulted, inevitably, in an easier and far more informal atmosphere—a phenomenon that can be observed at any costume ball, where the mere donning of a false moustache or a farthingale seems to convince the wearers that they are no longer recognizable, and enables them to lose their inhibitions and frolic in a manner that they would never dream of doing on any other occasion.

The fact that his nieces were wearing what to them was fancy-dress made it possible for Anjuli-Bai to ride off with Pelham-Sahib in pursuit of a jackal, or to see what lay beyond a ridge of higher ground, without anyone, including himself, thinking that there was anything undesirable in it. For without the flowing lines of a sari to remind him of her sex, his elder niece seemed to shed her identity and become only an anonymous young person who could safely be allowed a certain amount of freedom. Harmless freedom naturally, for was not he there himself to keep a close eye on them all?

Kaka-ji congratulated himself on the success of his plan, because there was no doubt that the health and spirits of both girls had greatly improved. Shushila had already lost the wizened look that had so alarmed him and would soon be as pretty as ever, and her women assured him that her appetite was returning and her nerves were far better of late. He could also see that she enjoyed

371

the riding lessons almost as much as Jhoti enjoyed giving them, and as he listened to his nephew's shrill little voice shouting advice and encouragement, and Shushila's answering laughter, Kaka-ji felt a glow of satisfaction at his own ingenious solving of a troublesome problem.

Much the same could be said of Ash, who had only one fault to find with the present situation: the fact that the evening rides were all too short and far too quickly over. The nights and the long, dusty days became no more than a preparation for that single hour in which he could be with Juli, even though he could not expect to spend more than a portion of the time with her, since caution and good manners forced them both to ride and talk with the others for at least some part of it. Nor was it always an hour, for like Ash, Jhoti and Mulraj and Kaka-ji had also ridden all day, and sometimes they too were tired— not that Ash, for one, would ever have admitted it. When that happened the hour would be cut by a quarter, or a half. But Ash was still grateful for every minute of it.

As the camp crawled southward across Rajputana like a vast and colourful circus procession (or, as it often seemed to Ash, an insatiable horde of locusts) the weather became warmer and he realized that the time would soon come when it would be too hot to march when the sun was high. But there was no need to start planning for that yet, as the temperature was still tolerable even at noon, and the nights remained mild.

The days slid into weeks almost without his noticing it, and he enjoyed every one of them: though it was far from being an idle time, for each day brought its own crop of difficulties, ranging from the routine ones of provisioning (which included dealing with claims for damages to crops and grazing-grounds by irate village headmen) to arbitrating in a wide variety of disputes within the camp, and, on more than one occasion, helping to beat off an attack by armed raiders. These and a hundred other matters kept him fully occupied. But he would not have changed places with anyone in the world, for he found the constant and varying demands upon him stimulating, while the fact that there had been a serious attempt to murder young Jhoti—and would probably be others— added a spice of danger to the journey that offset any element of tedium. And at the end of each day there was always Juli, and riding beside her in the quiet hour before sunset he could relax and forget his responsibilities to the camp and to Jhoti, and become Ashok again instead of "Pelham-Sahib."

It was on one of these evenings—a hot, still evening at the end of an even hotter day—that he heard for the first time the story of how Hira Lal had accompanied Lalji and the old Rajah to Calcutta, and had vanished from his tent one night and never been seen again—taken, it was said, by a tigress, a notorious man-eater who was known to roam the district and had already accounted for more than a dozen villagers. The proof of this had been a fragment of Hira Lal's blood-stained clothing, found among the bushes. But there had been no pug-marks and no trace of the drag, and a local *shikari* (game hunter) had tactlessly insisted that he did not believe that this was the work of the man-eater—an opinion that was later borne out by the news that the tigress had killed a herdsman near a village some twenty-five miles away on the very night that Hira Lal disappeared ...

"No one in the Hawa Mahal believed it either," said Anjuli, "and there were many who said he had been made away with by order of the Rani—though they did not say it out loud, but only in a whisper: very small whispers. I think, myself, that they were right; everyone knew that she had been enraged when she learned that my father had decided to take Lalji with him when he travelled to Calcutta to lay claim before the Viceroy to the throne of Karidarra, and it was no secret that it was Hira Lal who had persuaded him to do so—perhaps because he did not trust him not to bring about Lalji's death as soon as my father's back was turned. She was always jealous of Lalji."

"And I imagine she made away with him in the end," observed Ash grimly. "Lalji and Hira Lal both. It almost makes one hope that there may be a hell after all; with a special section reserved for people like Janoo-Rani who do their murdering at second-hand."

"*Don't!*" said Anjuli in a low voice, and shivered. "You do not have to wish for that. The gods are just, and I think she paid in this life for all the evil she did —and more. Much more, for she did not die an easy death, and towards the end she shrieked out that it was Nandu himself who had poisoned her, though that is something I will not believe; no son could have done such a

373

thing. Yet if she believed it, how terrible it must have been for her to die thinking that. There was no need for a hell after death for Janoo-Rani, for she found it here; and as we know that those whose conduct is evil attain an evil re-birth, she will also have to pay in her next life, and perhaps for many lives afterwards, for every ill deed that she committed in this one."

" 'Take what you want,' says God. 'And pay for it,' " quoted Ash. "Do you really believe all that, Juli?"

"That we must pay for all we do? Of course."

"No: that we are born over and over again. That you and I, for instance, have already lived many lives and will live many more."

"If one has been born once, why not again?" asked Juli. "Besides, the Upanishads* tell us that this is so, and according to that teaching it is only those who attain to the knowledge of the identity of the Soul of Brahma who reach 'the way of the gods' and do not return to earth. Therefore it follows that you and I have not yet freed ourselves from the cycle of re-birth; and as I do not think either of us are seekers after holiness—or anyway, not yet—we shall surely be born again."

"As a worm or a rat, or a pariah dog?"

"Only if we have committed some terrible sin in this life. If we are kind and just, and give to the poor—"

"And the priests," interjected Ash derisively. "Don't forget the priests."

"And the priests also," amended Anjuli gravely, "then—who knows?—we may even be born as great ones. You a king or a famous warrior; or even a Mahatma. And I a queen—or a nun."

"The gods forbid!" said Ash with a laugh.

But Anjuli did not smile and her face was suddenly sober as she said slowly, and almost as though she were speaking to herself: "But I had forgotten . . . I will soon be a queen in this one. The Junior Rani of Bhithor . . ."

Her voice died out in a whisper and they rode on without speaking, until presently Ash reined in to sit watching the sun go down. He knew that Juli had drawn rein beside him, but though he would not look at her, he was acutely aware of her presence—of the faint fragrance of dried rose-petals that clung about her and the

---

*part of the Vedic literature

fact that he had only to move his hand a little way to touch hers. The sun slid below the horizon and was gone, and from the shelter of a patch of high grass a peacock called mournfully into the silence. Ash heard the girl beside him draw a slow breath and let it out on a sigh, and he said abruptly, still without looking at her: "What are you thinking about, Juli?"

"The Dur Khaima," said Juli unexpectedly. "It is strange to think that I shall never see the Dur Khaima again. Or you either, once this journey is ended."

The peacock cried again, its harsh call a loneliness in the gathering dusk. And like an echo of that sound came Jhoti's high-pitched voice calling to them that it was time to go back, and there had been nothing for it but to turn their horses and rejoin the others.

Ash had been noticeably silent as they rode back to the camp, and that night for the first time he took stock of the situation, and made a serious attempt to sort out his emotions and decide what, if anything, he meant to do about Juli. Or could do.

To the consternation of Gul Baz, he announced that he was going to take a long walk and would not be returning for some hours; and having brusquely refused to allow anyone to accompany him, he strode off into the darkness, armed only with a stout, iron-bound *lathi* (staff) such as country folk carry.

"Let him be, Gul Baz," advised Mahdoo. "He is young, and it is too hot for sleeping. Also I think there is something that troubles him, and it may be that the night air will serve to clear his mind. Go to bed, and tell Kunwar that I will be *chowkidar* tonight. There is no need for us both to wait up for the Sahib."

The wait had proved much longer than Mahdoo expected, for the Sahib did not return until shortly before dawn; and long before that the old man fell asleep at his post, secure in the belief that Ash must arouse him in order to re-enter the tent, and untroubled by any serious fear for the safety of one who had learned caution on the Border and was well able to take care of himself. Any anxiety he felt was solely on the score of his Sahib's state of mind, which the old man had divined with far more accuracy than Ash would have given him credit for—or appreciated.

"Unless I am greatly mistaken, and I do not think

I am," mused Mahdoo, communing with himself before sleep overtook him, "my boy is in love . . . and with someone he sees daily yet cannot win—which can only be one of the two Rajkumaries. Unless it is one of their women—that could well be. But whoever it is, there can be nothing in it but danger and disappointment for him; and let us hope that he has realized this, and that his night-walking will serve to cool his blood and permit prudence to prevail before matters go too far."

Ash had not only realized it. He had seen the danger from the beginning and had not underrated it, but for one reason or another he had put off thinking about it. Stubbornly refusing to look ahead and see where all this was leading, or where it would end—perhaps because at the back of his mind he knew only too well, yet could not bring himself to face it.

He had, in effect, been indulging in a form of mental sleep-walking, and Juli's reminder that she would soon be a queen—"Junior Rani of Bhithor"—had acted as a dash of ice-cold water thrown in his face, awakening him at last to the discovery that the path he was on was no wide and level one, but a narrow ledge on the face of a precipice.

Her words had been a reminder, too, of another thing he had chosen to ignore: the swiftness with which the days were slipping by, and the fact that far more than two thirds of their journey was over. By now half Rajputana lay behind them; they had long since skirted the deserts of Bikanir, passed south of Ratangarh and Sikar, and from there marched north-eastward up through the harsh, rock-strewn ridges that guard the great Sambhar Lake and the approaches to Jaipur. Now, having crossed the Luni River and forded two tributaries of the Banas, they were facing south once more and it would not be long before they reached their journey's end; and then . . . Then he would attend the wedding ceremonies and watch Juli walk seven times round the sacred fire with the Rana of Bhithor, and when it was all over he would ride back to the Punjab alone, knowing that this time she was lost to him for ever.

It did not bear thinking of. But he would have to think of it now.

There was no moon that night, but Ash had always been cat-eyed in the dark, and grim necessity during his years in tribal territory had helped to sharpen his sight so that now he could walk confidently where many others would have had to grope forward with caution. He had brought the *lathi* with him as a walking-stick and not a weapon, for he had no fear of being attacked, and as for losing his way in unfamiliar country, there was little danger of that because he had ridden across it earlier that evening and noticed that half a mile away, in a direct line from his tent, the level ground narrowed to form a natural roadway between a wilderness of thorn-scrub and pampas grass and a wide belt of broken rock. As this provided the shortest and easiest way to reach the open country beyond, he was not likely to miss it even in the darkness, particularly with the lights of the camp providing a beacon that could be seen for miles across the plains.

The ground underfoot was hard and dry, and once his eyes had grown accustomed to the starlight he walked quickly; intent only on putting as much distance as possible between himself and the camp, because it seemed imperative to him that he should get beyond the range of the sound and smell of men and animals, and the sight of oil lamps and cooking fires, before he even began to think of Anjuli and himself.

Always, until now, the affairs of the camp had come between him and any serious consideration of personal matters, since he could not afford to be dilatory where his command was concerned but must deal promptly with every difficulty as it arose, however petty it might be, for unless solutions were found and arguments settled in the shortest possible time, chaos could easily result. But with Juli it had been different. The problem that she posed was a strictly personal one and so could be set aside to be dealt with later; there was no need to hurry, for he would be seeing her that evening—and tomorrow evening, and the evening after that ... They had plenty of time ...

But now, all at once, it could be put off no longer; time was running out, and if there was anything to decide he must decide now—one way or another.

The roar of the camp dwindled by degrees to a gentle hum and then a faint murmur that faded and was finally lost, and now at last the night was quiet: so quiet that for the first time in many weeks Ash found that he could hear the sough of the wind and a dozen small sounds that were suddenly audible in the silence. The whisper of dry grass and casuarina fronds stirring in the breeze. The

377

hoot of an owl and the scutter of some small nocturnal animal foraging around a clump of pampas. The chirr of a cricket and the flitter of a bat's wing, and from somewhere very far away, the sound that is the night-song of all India—the howl of a jackal-pack.

For a mile or so the plain remained level, and then it sloped sharply upwards, and Ash crossed a long, low ridge that was barely more than a spine of rock thrusting up from the naked earth, and once on the far side of it, found that he could no longer see the glow of the camp fires or any trace of human habitation. There was nothing now but the empty land and a sky full of stars; and there was no point in going any further. Yet he walked on mechanically, and might have done so for another hour if he had not come on a dry watercourse that was full of boulders and smooth, water-worn pebbles that slid treacherously underfoot.

To have crossed that by starlight would have been to risk a sprained ankle, so he turned aside, and selecting a patch of sand, settled down cross-legged in the classic Indian posture of meditation, to think about Juli . . . or at least, that was what he had meant to do. Yet now for no reason, he found himself thinking instead of Lily Briggs. And not only Lily, but her three successors: the soubrette of the seaside concert party, the red-haired barmaid of The Plough and Feathers and the provocative baggage from the hat-shop in Camberley, whose name he could no longer remember.

Their faces rose unbidden from the past and simpered at him. Four young women, all of whom had been older and far more experienced than he, and whose appeal to men had been unabashedly erotic. Yet not one of them had been mercenary, and it was ironic that he should have wished to marry Belinda Harlowe, who had the soul of a huckster, because by contrast she had seemed to epitomize all that was sweet and good and virginal—and was, in addition, a "lady." He had told himself that he loved her because she was "different"—different from four over-generous wantons whose bodies he had known intimately but whose minds he had known nothing about and had never been interested in—and it had taken him more than a year to discover that he knew nothing about hers either, and that all the admirable qualities that he had believed her to possess had been invented by him-

378

self and forcibly bestowed on some mental image of his own devising.

"Poor Belinda!" thought Ash, looking back a little wryly at that pasteboard paragon of his own devising, and at the tedious young prig that he himself had been. It was not her fault that she had failed to live up to that idealized portrait; he doubted if anyone could have done so. The real Belinda had been no angel, but merely a very ordinary and rather silly young woman who happened to be pretty and was vain of her prettiness, and had been spoiled by too much flattery and adulation. He could see that quite clearly now, and realize, too, that the worldliness that had made her accept Mr. Podmore-Smyth's offer, and the vindictive outburst that had destroyed poor George, could hardly be condemned as unusual failings when it was clear that a good many other people shared them. He himself would probably have shrugged off the first as a sensible if unromantic decision, and the second as a natural display of feminine pique at being lied to, had some other woman been involved. But because it was Belinda who had done these things he had chosen to regard it as a personal and appalling betrayal, and his revulsion had been so violent that for a time he had not been quite sane.

Even now the thought of what she had done to George gave him a momentary twinge of nausea. And George's face, as he had last seen it that hot Sunday afternoon in Peshawar, was still painfully clear in his memory. But Belinda's eluded him, and trying to recall her, Ash discovered that he could only remember that her eyes had been blue and her hair yellow; but not what she had actually looked like, or how she had spoken or moved or laughed. She seemed to have faded as an old daguerreotype will do if left too long in the sun, and considering all the emotional agonies he had suffered on her account, it was disconcerting to discover that he could remember Lily Briggs far more clearly. Though perhaps that was not so surprising for Lily had encouraged him to explore and caress every inch of her warm nakedness, while with Belinda, respect had kept his love-making strictly within bounds, and on those rare occasions when he had been permitted to take her befrilled and trimly corseted shape in his arms, his kisses could hardly have been more reverent had he been a Russian peasant kissing an ikon.

379

Sensuality had had no place in his affair with Belinda, while sensual pleasure had been the sole purpose of all the previous ones. With the result that, having experienced these two extremes, he had decided that he had now learned everything about women; and disliking what he knew, was cured for ever of falling in love (in the circumstances, an understandable reaction, though hardly an original one). Yet now, like many a disillusioned lover before him, he had fallen in love again. And it seemed like the first and only time: and would, he knew without any doubt, be the last.

There had been no joy in this discovery, for it was something that he would have given a great deal to avoid; and had there been any choice he would, even now, have elected to escape it, because he could see no solution that did not spell despair either for himself or Juli: or possibly for both of them. But as far as he was concerned, there was nothing he could do about it; it had been too late from the night that he had given her back his half of the little mother-of-pearl fish and had taken her into his arms, and known in the same instant that they belonged together just as surely as the two halves of the broken charm, and that it was not only Juli's luck-piece but he, Ash, who had been made whole again—and happy beyond words. He could not change that even if he would, nor could he analyse it or explain it away. It was simply there—like sight or sunlight or the air he breathed. An integral part of him . . .

Juli was as unlike any other woman he had ever known as a blue day in the Himalayas is unlike a grey one on Salisbury Plain. There was nothing that he could not tell her or that she would not understand, and to lose her now would be like losing his heart and his soul. And what man can live without the one, or hope for Heaven without the other?

"I cannot give her up," thought Ash. "I cannot . . . I *cannot!*"

A night-jar flitted down the dry watercourse and came to rest on a boulder, unaware that the motionless figure within a yard of it was a man, and a foraging mongoose paused, nose a-twitch, and deciding that the human was not dangerous, crept forward to investigate. But Ash was not aware of them: he was locked away in a private world, and so lost in thought that had there been dacoits

380

abroad that night he might never have returned to camp, because the discovery that he could not face losing Juli was merely a first step on a long and dangerous road, and it was only when he had taken it that he began to see clearly how formidable were the barriers that separated them, and how difficult to surmount.

That Juli shared his own feeling of completeness and belonging was something he knew without having to be told; just as he knew that she was fonder of him than anyone else in the world—as she had always been. But fondness was not love, and if what she felt for him was only the same single-hearted devotion that had been given him by an adoring little girl who had trotted at his heels and thought him the wisest and best of all brothers, it was not enough, and unless he could change that into something deeper he would surely lose her . . .

It was not as her brother that he could ask her to throw in her lot with him and face the consequences: the disgrace and the difficulties, and the incalculable dangers that might follow. And his own love for her was not in the least brotherly; it was as a wife that he wanted her. But even if she had grown to love him in the same way, that too was only a first step, for she was still Anjuli-Bai: a princess and a Hindu. And though the question of rank might seem trivial to her, that of caste might prove too strong for her to overcome.

Ash's foster-mother had been a devout Hindu, and as her son he had been brought up with a proper knowledge of religious matters. He had studied the Rig-Veda and was familiar with the tale of the sacrifice of Purusha, the primeval man, from whose immolation came all creation, together with the four Hindu castes. From Purusha's breath had come the Brahmans, the priestly caste; from his arms, the warriors, or Kshatriyas; from his thighs, the Vaisyas—agriculturalists and traders; and from his feet the servile caste, the Sudras. All other men were outcasts; "untouchables" whose very presence was defilement. Wherefore, to a Hindu, caste was the most important thing in life, for it decreed every person's social status and the work they were permitted to do, and affected in one way or another every aspect of living. Nothing could change it. A man born a Sudra, in the lowest caste, must live and die as one; no riches or power that he might acquire could raise him to a higher

381

one, and his children and grandchildren, and their children after them to the end of time, would always be Sudras. Only a life of great piety and good works might, after his death, make it possible for him to be reborn as a member of a higher caste. But apart from that, there was no other way in which he could escape his destiny.

Sita's people had been farmers: hill-men, claiming Rajput blood. Her husband too had been a Vaisya, and she had brought Ash up as strictly as though he had been her son. Juli's mother, on the other hand, had been a half-caste, and therefore, in the eyes of orthodox Hindus, tainted by her foreign blood. But her father had belonged to the warrior caste, and like many Kshatriyas, considered that they, and not the Brahmans, should by rights hold pride of place. He also happened to be an autocrat, a Rajput and a Rajah. On these counts he regarded himself as being above caste, and had he wished to marry the daughter of the lowliest of Untouchables, he would probably have done so and carried it off with a high hand. Nevertheless, on the grounds of caste alone he would certainly not have considered the foster-child of the waiting-woman, Sita (and even less the only son of Professor Pelham-Martyn), in any way a suitable husband for his daughter by the *Feringhi*-Rani. Nor would his heir—that was something that Ash could be certain of, despite the lowly origins of Nandu's own mother, or the fact that the dubious status of his half-sister, Anjuli-Bai, had caused so much argument and hair-splitting with the emissaries from Bhithor that only a lavish bribe and the promise of a munificent dowry had finally induced them to accept her as a suitable wife for their Rana.

At this date, however, the question of Nandu's approval or disapproval was wholly irrelevant; the fact remained that as the marriage contracts had been agreed and betrothal gifts exchanged, his sisters were to all intents and purposes already the legal property of the Rana, and the wedding ceremony would do no more than supply the final seal to a bargain that had been approved and was regarded as binding. So except for a miracle, there was no way out that would not involve a major scandal and considerable danger; and Ash was no believer in miracles.

Unless he could persuade Juli to run away with him, the wedding would take place. And once she was married to the Rana he would never be able to see her or speak to her again, for she would vanish into the sealed and secret world of the Women's Quarters, and be lost to him as surely as though she were dead. He would not even be able to write to her or to receive any news of her, unless, perhaps, through Kaka-ji—though that was highly unlikely, as Kaka-ji would not consider it proper to discuss the Rana's wife with another man, and the only information he would be likely to pass on would be the kind that would be unbearable to hear. That Anjuli-Bai had become a mother. Or was dead . . .

The thought of either was so intolerable that Ash flinched involuntarily as though ducking a blow, and the mongoose that had finally crept out across the sand to investigate this strange creature who sat so still, whisked away with a chatter of rage and vanished into the shadows.

Ash did not see it go, but the sound reminded him briefly of another mongoose: Tuku. It surprised him a little to find that after all these years he should still remember that name; and remember, too, the look of satisfied malice on Biju Ram's face, and the feel of Tuku's small body lying lifeless between his hands. But the memory of that day only served to bring his thoughts back to Juli, for it was she, "Kairi-Bai," who had filled the void left by Tuku's death.

There were very few memories of the Hawa Mahal, now that he came to think of it, that did not include her; for though his attitude towards her had been a mixture of irritation and lordly condescension, she had come to be an integral part of his days, and but for her he would never have left the palace alive. Yes, he owed a great debt to Juli; and he had done nothing to repay her—unless possibly by forgetting his promise to come back for her, for honesty forced him to the conclusion that it might have been better for her if she had never seen him again and been able to think of him as dead. He remembered now that even as a child she had never questioned her fate but accepted it as inevitable—the decree of the gods —and had he not returned she would have come to terms with it, and at the very least have enjoyed a certain amount of comfort and security as the wife of a ruling prince. But what would her life be like if she ran away with a *feringhi*—a mere junior officer in the Guides—and just how far would they be allowed to run? That, after all, was the crux of the matter . . .

"Not very far, I imagine," decided Ash grimly.

There was no blinking the fact that everyone in the camp, and in all India for that matter, would regard such an elopement as indefensible: a shameless and dishonourable betrayal that insulted Bhithor and brought black disgrace on both Karidkote and the Raj.

The British would take an equally strong view, though from a somewhat different angle. They would dismiss Juli's part in it with a careless shrug: "What else can you expect from some illiterate little bint in purdah?" But there would be no mercy for Captain Ashton Pelham-Martyn, who had betrayed his trust and "let his side down" by running off with a woman (and a "native woman," at that) whom he had been charged with escorting across India and delivering safely into the care of her future husband.

"I would be cashiered," thought Ash.

A year ago he had fully expected to face a Court Martial for his part in the affair of Dilasah Khan and the stolen carbines, and he knew that this had only been avoided by the narrowest of margins. But were he to run away with Juli there would be no question of avoiding it again. He would be court-martialled and dismissed from the army in disgrace: *Her Majesty having no further use for his services.*

He would never see Mardan again . . . or Zarin and Awal Shah—or Koda Dad. The men of his troop and his fellow officers, the Corps of Guides, and old Mahdoo, too . . . they would all be lost to him. And so would Wally; for even that inveterate hero-worshipper would not be able to condone this.

Wally might talk a great deal of nonsense about love and romance, but his views on such matters as duty were uncompromising, and he would see this in simple terms as a breach of trust: a sacred trust, because to Wally duty was sacred, and had he found himself in Ash's situation he would certainly have been able to say, like Lovelace: "I could not love thee, dear, so much, loved I not honour more." For it would never occur to him that Juli, or any woman in the world, could be worth more than honour . . .

"I should lose him, too," thought Ash. And for the second time that night, flinched at a thought as though from a physical pain. Wally's friendship, and Wally's admiration, had come to mean so much to him that the withdrawal of both would leave a gap in his life that he would never be able to fill; or to forget. And there was another thing . . . why should he suppose that Juli would like living in England, when he himself had not?

The British in India invariably referred to their island as "Home." But it had never been home to him, and staring back into the past he knew very well that even if Juli went with him, he did not want to go back there. Yet they could not remain in India, for quite apart from the fact that they would be socially ostracized by British and Indians alike, the danger of reprisals from the offended rulers of Bhithor and Karidkote would be too great.

The former consideration carried little weight: Ash had never cared very much for social approval or the opinions of his fellow men. But for Juli's sake he could not risk the latter, so they would have to leave the country and live elsewhere—if not in England, then in America. No, not America . . . Americans, like "memsahibs," held strong views on miscegenation, and even in the northern states Juli would be regarded as a "coloured woman" and treated accordingly.

South America, then? Or perhaps Italy—or Spain?

But he knew in his heart that it would make no difference which country they chose, for wherever they went it would only mean one thing for both of them. Exile. Because India was their country: his as much as Juli's. And if they left it they would be going into banishment just as surely as he had done once before, when he had sailed from Bombay as a forlorn twelve-year-old in the care of Colonel Anderson.

Only this time, he would know that he could never come home.

22

The night was almost gone when Ash at last rose stiffly to his feet, and having slapped the sand from his clothes and retrieved the *lathi,* turned to make his way back to the camp.

He had not meant to stay away for so long, and it was only when a small, cool wind arose and blew down the dry river-bed, stirring up the sand between the boulders and driving it into his eyes, that he realized how late it must be; for this was the wind that blows across Rajputana in the dark hour before the dawn, and dies before sunrise.

Standing once more on the crest of the ridge that had shielded him from sight of the camp, Ash saw that the myriad fires and lamps that had earlier made a red glow in the sky had burned out or been extinguished long ago, and now there were only a few scattered pinpoints of light to show him where the camp lay. He would need them, as it was far darker now than it had been when he had set out; the stars had already begun to pale, and though there was now a segment of moon in the sky, it lay wan and lemon-coloured in the dregs of the night and gave little or no light.

The darkness forced him to walk slowly in order to avoid stumbling over rocks or into holes, but even this failed to prevent his brain from continuing to bedevil itself with the problem that had sent him out into the night some hours ago, and which he was now carrying back with him, still unsolved. It had not seemed particularly complicated when he set out—a mere matter of clearing his mind and deciding upon a course of action. It was only when he realized that he could not give Juli up, and began to plan ways and means of running away with her, that the appalling difficulties that would have to be faced and overcome rose up before him; and now as he made his way back to the camp, the problems seemed to multiply with every step . . .

Should they attempt to escape together they would certainly be followed: and this was not British India —this was Rajputana—"King's Country"; an amalgam of sovereign states ruled over by independent princes, where the writ of the Raj meant little. The hereditary rulers paid lip-service to the Queen-Empress, but apart from that they did very much as they pleased, and their rank protected them from prosecution in any court of law. A paternal Government provided them with "advisers" in the form of Residents, Commissioners, Political Officers and an Agent-General, and decided such vexed questions as how many guns each should be entitled to have fired in salute on ceremonial occasions. But otherwise it made a point of not interfering with them unless actually forced to do so, and there would be little safety for a runaway princess and her lover in such country.

Once the word of their flight had gone out, every man's hand would be against them and no state in all Rajputana would give them refuge. So for the present there was nothing he could do but wait upon events and trust to the inspiration of the moment, hoping, like Mr. Micawber, that something would turn up—a miracle, for preference, for he was beginning to think that they would need nothing less. "Yet what have I ever done to deserve a miracle?" thought Ash.

He could find no answer to that, and when, half an hour later, something did indeed turn up, it was not the miracle he hoped for, but a confirmation of all his fears, and proof—if he had needed proof—that the dangers he had visualized were very far from imaginary.

Because the light was still poor enough to make the going treacherous, he had been keeping his eyes on the ground, and it had not occurred to him that his movements would be of any interest to anyone save Mahdoo and his own servants, or that he might be attacked.

The shot took him by surprise, and for a moment he did not realize that he had been the target. The bullet struck the *lathi* and spun it out of his hand in the same instant that he heard the report, and it was instinct alone made him throw himself flat among the stones; though even then it did not occur to him that he had done anything more than cross the line of fire of some local hunter who was shooting for the pot, and he raised his head and shouted angrily into the darkness.

The answer was a second shot that whipped above his head, missing him by less than an inch. The wind of its passing stirred his hair, but this time he made no sound, for though the first shot could have been accidental the second was not. He had seen the flash, and realized that the man who had fired was standing little more than fifteen yards away and could not possibly have failed to hear him call out, or mistaken his voice for that of a wounded animal. And in the next moment, as though to confirm this, he heard quite clearly in the silence the snick of a breech block as the man reloaded.

It was a frightening sound, and the cold deliberation of it made his heart lurch and miss a beat. But at the same time it seemed to clear his brain, and make him think a good deal more quickly and more concisely than he had done for many days. The vacillation of the past hours fell away from him and he found himself assessing the situation as coolly as though he were on a training exercise on the plains beyond Mardan.

The unknown man was certainly no wandering *bud-marsh* shooting at a stranger for sport or viciousness; rifle bullets were far too valuable to waste without the certainty of reward, and he carried nothing worth stealing. His assailant was also plainly aware that his quarry was unarmed, for in spite of having fired twice, he had not troubled to move his position, but was standing confidently upright, concealed but in no way protected by the tall clump of pampas grass where he had been waiting for his victim to pass . . .

That last was something else of which Ash was suddenly certain, for this was the one place where the lie of the land dictated his route, and anyone wishing to waylay him would know that he must come this way, and had only to wait. Someone had known, and waited; and even in the darkness the shot must have been an easy one, since at that range the chance of missing was almost negligible. Moreover Ash had been walking very slowly and without troubling to move without noise, and had it not been for the *lathi* he would have died or been seriously wounded.

But the watcher with the gun would not know about the *lathi*, and having seen Ash fall, the chances were that he imagined the bullet to have gone home and that his victim was either dead or dying—the latter, probably: it had been a mistake to call out. On the other hand, many men did so at the moment of impact, and as he had made no further sound he could only hope that his assailant, thinking him dead, would refrain from wasting a third bullet on a corpse. It was not much of a chance, but the fact that the man must be reasonably confident that he had not missed was the only card that Ash held, and unless he could make good use of it he would die.

His assailant made no move for the best part of
388

five minutes, but stood motionless in the shelter of the tall grass. Then at last he began to creep forward, treading as softly and as warily as a cat and pausing between every step to listen.

He was barely more than a dark outline against the shadowy background of pampas and thorn-scrub, but the sky was becoming lighter and objects that a few minutes ago had been unidentifiable were beginning to take shape and reveal themselves as rocks and bushes, and Ash could make out the barrel of the rifle that was still trained on him. From the angle at which it was held he knew that there was still a finger on the trigger, and that for his life's sake he must not move or breathe.

The wind had dropped with the approach of dawn, and the world was so quiet that he could hear the soft crunch of dry earth and pebbles under shoe leather, and presently, the sound of his would-be murderer's breathing, quick-drawn and uneven. The man was now less than a yard away. But that was still too far, for his rifle remained ready and unwavering and any premature movement would be the signal for a third bullet—fired this time at point-blank range. He was standing motionless, listening, and it seemed hardly possibly that he could fail to hear his quarry's heart-beats when to Ash's own ears they sounded as loud as trip-hammers falling on iron. But apparently he did not, for after a moment or two he came forward and touched the supposed corpse with his foot. When it did not move, he kicked it, this time with some violence.

His foot was still in the air when a hand closed like a vice about his other ankle and jerked it savagely, and losing his balance he fell forward across something that appeared to be made of steel and whipcord.

The gun exploded in a deafening crash of sound and the bullet slammed into a rock and filled the air with a hornets' nest of flying splinters, one of which slashed across Ash's forehead, leaving a shallow cut that filled his eyes with blood.

But for this he would almost certainly have killed his adversary, because that kick had made him lose his temper with a thoroughness that he had never previously equalled, and driven anything he had ever been taught about Queensberry Rules out of his mind. He was intent only on killing—or being killed, though there was never much chance of the latter. His opponent might be dangerous with a gun in his hands, but deprived of it he proved to be no match for Ash, being not only shorter but inclined to stoutness, and judging from his frantic gasps for breath and the flabbiness of his muscles, sorely out of condition.

Nevertheless he fought hard for his life, scratching, clawing and biting with the desperation of a cornered rat as the two rolled over and over among the stones, until with a sudden frenzied wrench he was free. Ash, blinded by his own blood, grabbed at him but missed his hold, and was left clutching a handful of clothing that had torn in his grasp as their owner, sobbing and gasping, scrambled to his feet and bolted like a terrified animal for the cover of the pampas grass.

There had been no point in following him, for by the time Ash had cleared the blood out of his eyes the man had disappeared. And though the darkness had by now thinned to an indeterminate grey, there was still too little light to make tracking a fugitive through that maze of scrub and grass a feasible proposition, while any attempt to do so by ear alone would be equally fruitless, since the noise of his own passage would drown all other sounds. There was obviously nothing for it but to get back to the camp as quickly as possible and institute a few inquiries there.

Ash tied a make-shift bandage round his head to keep the blood out of his eyes and picked up his *lathi* and the fallen gun. The *lathi* had splintered and was of little further use, but the gun was evidence, and it should not be too difficult to trace the owner, for by the feel of it it appeared to be a modern sporting rifle similar to the one he himself owned. There could not be many other men in the camp who possessed such a weapon; and as only someone who was familiar with that type of rifle would think of using it for such a vital assignment as murder, the task would not have been given to a servant or an underling.

He did not doubt that the owner had come from the camp, and the rifle should be able to prove it. But he was daunted by the discovery that he possessed an enemy who was not only prepared to kill him, but had, to that end, kept so close a watch on him that when on the spur of the moment he had walked out on the plain that night, he had given the watcher an opportunity to put into practice a scheme that had probably been decided on much earlier—the death of Captain Ashton Pelham-Martyn.

Oddly enough, it had not occurred to Ash until now to wonder who had tried to kill him. But then the whole ugly incident, from the first shot to the moment when his assailant had wrenched himself free and escaped to the shelter of the thickets, had lasted no more than ten to fifteen minutes, and during that time he had had more urgent things to think of than the identity of the killer. But now the point seemed vitally important, and looking back on his own actions during the past two months, Ash wondered why it had not occurred to him before that he might have an enemy in the camp, when the person or persons who had attempted to murder Jhoti must still be with them, and could well hate him for his part in preventing it—and for the pains he had taken afterwards to keep an eye on the boy. Then, too, there was Juli . . .

It was not beyond the bounds of possibility that there were others besides the old *dai*, Geeta, who had learned of Juli's visits to his tent, and if so it might well be regarded as a matter of honour to kill him, since it would be assumed that he had seduced her. Or then again, there was always a chance that someone—possibly Biju Ram?—had somehow managed to trace a connection, through the Guides, with Zarin and Koda Dad, and from there to the Hawa Mahal, and had recognized the one-time servant of the late Yuveraj of Gulkote: the boy Ashok.

Ash considered this last and rejected it as unlikely. That trail was cold, and with Lalji and Janoo-Rani both dead there was no one in the newly named State of Karidkote who would derive any benefit from his death on that score, or even trouble to remember him. Nevertheless, after setting that aside, it was clear that there were several reasons to account for his having an enemy in the camp; and realizing that there was likely to be more than one, Ash took particular pains during the remainder of his return journey to keep well clear of any rock, bush or fold in the ground that might provide cover for a marksman, and registered a vow that never again would he go anywhere without a revolver.

The dawn light was flooding across the plain by the time he reached his tent, and Mahdoo, snoring peacefully, did not stir as he stepped over him. The lamp that hung from the tent pole had burned out, but he did not need it now; there was enough light to see by, and he stowed the rifle and the broken *lathi* under the bed, and having removed his shoes and coat, lay down in his shirt sleeves and was instantly asleep.

There had seemed no point in arousing Mahdoo, and it had not occurred to Ash that he would give the old gentleman the fright of his life, for he had not yet seen his own face in a looking-glass and had no idea of the spectacle he presented. But Mahdoo, waking half an hour later in the clear light of early morning and entering the tent to see if the Sahib had returned, imagined for one nightmare moment that he was looking at a corpse, and very nearly suffered a heart-attack on the spot.

Reassured by the sound of breathing, he tottered out to fetch Gul Baz, who came running and after a short inspection declared that there was no need for anxiety, as the Sahib was obviously not badly hurt.

"I think he has only been in a brawl," observed Gul Baz reassuringly. "Those marks on his cheeks are such as are made by finger-nails and little stones. Also there is not much blood on the cloth about his head, and he is sleeping peacefully. It would be wiser not to wake him, and later we will get a piece of raw goat's meat to bind over his eye to reduce the discoloration and the swelling."

The raw meat had been duly applied to an eye that by then had turned every colour of the rainbow, and may conceivably have done it some good. The rest of Ash's injuries were equally superficial and faded quickly, and within a week there was nothing to show that he had been in a fight but the ghost of a black eye and a faint scar that might have been mistaken for a frown line on his forehead. But however quickly these faded, the marks had been there and the man he had fought must have had similar ones: gravel rash, at least, and with luck an impressive collection of bruises, which should make it a simple matter to identify him.

It had not, however, been at all simple, because Ash had overlooked something: the fact that in a camp as vast as this one, any number of men incurred minor injuries every day of the week, and though the majority of cuts and bruises were due to carelessness or the normal hazards of daily life, a great many were acquired as a result of arguments that had ended in fights: "and as for Gunga Dass," reported Mahdoo, "it seems that his wife and his wife's mother, finding that he had spent much money on one of the harlots, attacked him with cooking pots and broke a *chatti* on his head. Then there is Ram Lalla who . . ."

There were many such tales; too many. "Were there only a hundred men in the camp, it would be a different matter," said Mulraj. "But there are thousands, and even if we should find the man we seek, he is sure to have a tale ready and a dozen witnesses to swear to its truth and tell how he came by such injuries; and who could disprove it?"

The only thing that had been easily proved was the ownership of the rifle, because as Ash had surmised, it was no old-fashioned musket but a modern, precision-made weapon, a Westley-Richards sporting rifle, capable of great accuracy up to a range of four hundred yards. He had felt sure that there could be few weapons of this type in the camp, and in this too he had been right: there was only one. His own.

To find that he had very nearly been murdered by his own rifle annoyed him every more than the attempt itself. The colossal impertinence of it added insult to injury, and he promised himself that when he found the man he would give him the thrashing of a lifetime. But the fact that the rifle had been removed from his tent under Mahdoo's very nose, and without one of his servants hearing a sound, was perhaps the most disturbing part of the affair, for it showed that he had little or no protection against assassination, and proved what he had already suspected: that someone, or possibly several people, had been keeping a close watch on him.

His attacker had obviously seen him start out last night, unarmed except for a *lathi,* and having overheard enough to know that he had intended to be away for several hours had been sufficiently cunning to realize the opportunity this offered. He must have seen the servants retire and Mahdoo settle down at the tent door to keep watch, and once the old man fell asleep it could not have been difficult to creep in at the back without disturbing him. The hurricane lamp would have been burning, but it would have been turned down low, providing only a glimmer of light that would have been enough to enable the thief to move without noise. And once in possession of the rifle he had only to leave as he had come, and

393

following the same route that Ash had taken, lie up in the gully to wait, in the sure knowledge that his quarry would return that way.

Once again it occurred to Ash to wonder how many people had seen Juli come to his tent, and the very thought of it made him cold with fear and anger and a sudden sickening apprehension. If that attempt on his life had been on Juli's account, then he had made a serious mistake in mentioning it at all—let alone discussing it in detail with Mahdoo and Gul Baz and Mulraj, and speculating with them as to the possible reasons for it. He should have kept his mouth shut and invented some plausible story of a fall in the dark to account for that black eye and the other souvenirs of the night.

But then he had been in no state to concoct lies, or even consider whether or not to tell the truth when he had awakened late in the day, after hours of exhausted slumber, to find Mulraj staring at him in frowning concern while Mahdoo and Gul Baz hovered anxiously in the background. He had merely explained the circumstances, and it had been the sight of his own face in the glass that had prompted him to remark that all they had to do was to keep a look-out for someone who bore similar marks—a man of medium height and inclined to plumpness, who was known to be a good marksman and . . .

It was at this point that Ash, turning towards his bed with the intention of producing the rifle, was sidetracked by a suggestion from Gul Baz that inquiries among the *dhobis* might prove profitable since one of them might remember washing a garment that was badly torn and stained. Ash had agreed, but the reference to washing reminded him that he himself was sorely in need of a bath, and as it was now late afternoon and he had eaten nothing since the previous evening, that he could also do with a meal.

The two servants had hurried off to see to the matter, and as luck would have it, a *bheesti* began to pour the bath just as Ash was groping under the bed for the rifle, with the result that he did not even look at it, but handed it to Mulraj and continued the conversation from the far side of a canvas partition while splashing in the tub and shaving.

Mulraj agreed that there could be few such weapons

394

in the camp and that it should be a simple matter to trace the owner. "For it is of the same pattern as the one that you yourself use to shoot black-buck. An *Angrezi* rifle," said Mulraj, and replaced it under the bed. He was far more intrigued by the *lathi*, and after examining it, declared that the Sahib had clearly been born under a lucky star, for the bullet had struck one of the narrow iron rings that strengthened the stout bamboo, and with such force that although it had been deflected, the ring was almost flattened and the bamboo inside it reduced to a pulp. "The gods were surely on your side last night," commented Mulraj, and left, promising to lose no time in setting a few private inquiries on foot. So it was not until a full hour later, when Ash had dressed and done justice to a large and satisfying meal, that a closer inspection of the rifle disclosed its ownership; and by then it was too late for second thoughts.

He could hardly tell Mulraj, or even Mahdoo, that he had changed his mind and no longer wanted any help in tracking down the man who had tried to murder him, for they would want to know why; and the truth would not serve, because he could not explain that he was afraid that they might also uncover a motive—a motive for murder that had nothing whatever to do with Jhoti or jealousy (or even the fact that he, Pelham-Sahib, had once been a boy called Ashok) but was solely concerned with the Rajkumari Anjuli-Bai and the honour of the royal houses of Karidkote and Bhithor . . .

It was a relief when both Mahdoo and Mulraj discovered, separately, that to try and find a man with a scratched and bruised face in a camp numbering close on eight thousand was like looking for one particular windfall in an apple-orchard after a stormy night. And also when Gul Baz's investigation failed for the same reason (according to the *dhobis*, so much clothing became torn and stained on the march that it was impossible to keep count of it).

Any inquiries, however artfully pursued, would inevitably arouse curiosity, and Ash was now thankful that he had not also thought to hand Gul Baz a piece of evidence that some *dhobi* might well have recognized. But then he himself had not realized—or not until much later—that the strip of pewter-grey cloth that he had used as a bandage was not his, but part of the man's clothing—the entire left front of a thin cotton coat that had torn away in his hands, and by doing so allowed his assailant to escape.

He must have tied it about his head without thinking, and on removing it, thrown it aside and never noticed it again until after he had found out about the rifle; by which time he could only feel grateful that no one else had shown any interest in it either, for the colour and material—a handwoven mixture of cotton and silk in two shades of grey that produced a "shot" effect—was a valuable clue, and as such, the fewer people who knew about it, and the sooner it was destroyed, the better.

From now on he would keep quiet about any new clues and with luck the investigation that he had so rashly set on foot would come to nothing, and the whole affair be forgotten—except by himself, for he had every intention of trying to discover the identity of the man who had attempted to kill him. But he would do it without assistance; this was something he must handle alone or not at all, and if the incident had done nothing else, it had at least forced him to make up his mind about Juli . . . he supposed he should be grateful for that.

The absurd, unformed hopes that had lurked for so long at the back of his mind, and that only yesterday had crystallized with startling suddenness in an urgent problem that must be solved without delay—all the fears and the wild plans that he had taken out onto the plain to wrestle with for the whole of one long night and carried back with him, still unresolved—had been settled by a bullet fired from his own gun; because it had brought home to him, as nothing else could have done, that he had been right to be afraid for Juli.

Ash had not been blind to the dangers of his own position in the camp, for unlike too many of his countrymen (and most of his countrywomen), who had already forgotten the lessons of the Mutiny, he knew that India as a whole had little love for the Raj. India had always respected strength, and she accepted the realities of power and was prepared to tolerate, if not enjoy, a situation that there seemed little prospect of putting an end to at present—and that on the whole happened to suit her fairly well. But she was like a bamboo ticket that sways to every breeze and bends gracefully before a gale yet never

396

breaks, and hides among its canes a sleeping tiger that may awake at any moment, and kill.

As the sole representative of the authority of the Raj and the only European in camp, Ash's position was bound to be a little precarious, and he had taken certain precautions to safeguard himself. The siting of his tent, for instance, and its position in relation to his servants and his horses; the fact that he slept with a revolver under his pillow and an Afghan knife on the table by his bed, and that once his tent was pitched one or other of his servants would always be on guard unless he himself were in it. Yet despite all this his tent had been entered and his rifle stolen, and he himself had been spied upon, followed and ambushed as easily as though he had been a child, or a sheep. He meant to be a great deal more careful in future, but he knew that the advantage would always lie with the enemy, who could choose his time while he, the victim, even though forewarned, could not be perpetually on guard and suspicious of everyone. Sooner or later, not knowing who to suspect, there would come a time when the guard would be dropped; and then . . .

It was not his own body that Ash visualized lying sprawled and bleeding in the dust, but Juli's. And he knew that he could not bring her to her death. He must do nothing to prevent her marriage to the Rana, and perhaps after all she would find a measure of happiness —in motherhood, if in nothing else, though that thought still stabbed as cruelly as a dagger in the heart. But to picture Juli lying dead was infinitely worse; and at least in Bhithor she would be with Shushila, and as a Rani— even a Junior Rani—she would possess a certain amount of influence and considerable prestige, and live in comfort surrounded by waiting-women and servants. Her life might not be too unbearable, and though at first she would miss the mountains, the memory of them would fade; and in time she would forget the Peacock Tower and the Queen's balcony. And Ashok.

Juli would accept her fate and endure it without complaint. And at the worst, it would be better than death, for as long as one was alive there still was a chance, even though it might only be what Wally termed "a fighting chance"—a chance of being able to twist fate to suit one's purpose, of making something out of the impossible, a chance that life might take a sudden unexpected turn, and disaster become victory. But to die and be buried, or burned . . . that was for the old, not for someone young and strong and beautiful, like Juli. Yet if she were to run away with him now, death would catch up with them very quickly.

They should have gone earlier, while they were still in British India . . . but it was too late to think of that now, and even if they had done so it would only have meant postponing the inevitable a little longer. Ash had not forgotten how the *Nautch*-girl's henchmen had once hunted him throughout the length and breadth of the peaceful Punjab, where there were British troops in a dozen cantonments and a police-post in every village, and he knew that they would almost certainly have caught him in the end if the Guides and Colonel Anderson had not turned him into a Sahib and whisked him out of the country.

Juli would be far easier to find than that little bazaar boy had been, and what chance would she have of getting safely out of the country if he himself were under arrest? There would be endless delays, and while officials argued and prevaricated, Nandu would act—that at least was something he could be certain of, as there was nothing in all the tales that Ash had heard about the new ruler of Karidkote to suggest that he would permit his half-sister to disgrace him in this fashion without taking immediate steps to wipe out the stain. And if Nandu was dilatory in exacting vengeance, there would still be the Rana to reckon with.

British India or no British India, they would hunt Juli down as remorselessly as a wolf pack on the trail of a hind, and long before Ash could arrange to get her out of the country they would have closed in for the kill.

Death, or the Rana? He would never know which one Juli would have chosen. Or whether she loved him enough to prefer the first, or still only thought of him as a favourite brother. But whichever way she chose, he would still have lost her.

Ash laid his head on his arms and sat motionless for a long time, looking into a future that was bleak and empty and devoid of all meaning. And that evening he did not join the riding party, but excused himself on the score of work.

398

When he did not go again, the rides were discontinued, though he was unaware of this. Shushila sent several times, inviting him to the durbar tent, but he pleaded a headache and did not go. He knew that he could not withdraw completely from that circle, but it was preferable to feign illness and pressure of work, or even to risk giving offence by appearing boorish, rather than to see too much of Juli.

The less they saw of each other the better it would be for both of them—particularly for her, if the attempt on his life had been on her account—but now that he no longer had the evening rides to look forward to the days seemed endless and the business of the camp an intolerable burden, and it became increasingly difficult to keep his temper and listen patiently to the innumerable complaints that were brought before him daily and that he was expected to settle. Because although Mulraj and his officers and such elder statesmen as Kaka-ji Rao dispensed justice in the camp, Ash had come to be regarded as the court of final appeal, and all too many cases came up before him for judgement.

Men quarrelled and came to blows, stole, lied and cheated, contracted debts that they did not pay, or accused each other of a variety of crimes that ranged from murder to giving short weight at the food stalls; and Ash would sit for hour after hour, looking attentive while accuser and accused produced their witnesses and talked interminably. And as often as not he would realize, suddenly, that he had not heard one word of what anyone had said and had no idea what the dispute was about. Then it would all have to be said over again; or, more frequently, he would set the case aside "for further consideration" and go on to the next—and often hear very little of that too.

The effort not to think about his own affairs seemed to be affecting his ability to think about anything, though fatigue probably had a good deal to do with it. He was sleeping badly and was always tired; and the weather did not help, for each day it grew hotter, and already the *louh* had begun to blow—the hot wind that whines across Rajputana when the cold weather is over, and dries the moisture from ponds and plants and the bodies of men. Later, when the rivers ran low and the countryside was parched with heat, there would be dust-storms; dense, brown, smothering clouds that could blot out the sun and turn noon-day into night; and though the season for such storms still lay well ahead, the prospect of it provided Ash with yet another reason for urging speed. Yet in the circumstances, any exhortations to hurry were a waste of breath, since the camp no longer marched in the daytime but moved only in the early hours of the morning.

Each evening scouts rode on ahead to spy out the land and select the best available stopping place for the following day, and the tents were struck before first light so that the long procession could crawl forward in the comparative coolness that preceded the dawn, to stop again as soon as the sun was far enough above the horizon for the heat of its rays to become unbearable. Very often the distance between one camp site and the next would be no more than five miles, and sometimes it was less, because their progress was governed by the need for water and shade—though the latter could, and of necessity often was, dispensed with. But canvas and carts and straw were a poor protection against the blazing sun; and only the animals, tethered in the open and suffering torments from the heat, had reason to be grateful for the scorching wind which at least kept them free of flies. As the pace became slower and slower, men and women alike became irritable and intolerant, and tempers flared; yet however slowly they moved, each day's march brought them inexorably nearer to the border of Bhithor, and it would not be long now before they reached the end of their journey.

It could not be too soon for Ash, who had once wished that it would never end and now only wanted to get it over quickly. The physical discomforts of the march were becoming enough to try anyone's temper, but combined with acute mental stress and the mounting problems of the camp, they verged on the intolerable. On top of which he now suffered from a disagreeable sense of insecurity, for only three days after the attack on him, his tent had again been burgled, this time in broad daylight, it having been the first occasion on which the camp had moved off before dawn in order to avoid marching in the heat, and stopped when the sun was high.

The site chosen that day had been near a shallow expanse of weed-choked water that had evidently once been a man-made tank, dug many centuries ago to supply

400

some long-forgotten city, the traces of which still surrounded it in the form of low mounds, crumbling sandstone blocks and the remains of ruined walls that were
barely higher than the rustling, lion-coloured grass, and
split by the roots of neem and *kikar* and *sal* trees.

As usual, Ash's tent had been pitched under a tree
on the outskirts of the camp, with his servants' tents arranged in a half circle some way behind it. The waist-high
grass had been cut or trampled down for twenty yards
around to ensure that no one could approach unseen, yet
some time during the hottest part of the day someone had
done so.

No less than two of Ash's men had been on guard at
the time, squatting in the shade of a neem tree at the
edge of the clearing from where they could keep the
tent under observation. But the fact that neither had
seen anything suspicious was not altogether surprising—
they had been up since four o'clock that morning, and
having eaten their mid-day meal were replete and lulled
into drowsiness by heat and the hot wind. Both had dozed
off at intervals—secure in the conviction that their mere
presence would be enough to deter any wrong-doer from
approaching—and they had heard nothing to rouse them,
for their ears had been filled with the dry rustle of leaves
and grass in the wind.

Ash had been busy elsewhere, and he had returned
to find his belongings in considerable disorder: the locks
of his boxes forced and their contents strewn about the
floor. Even his bed had been stripped, and the entire tent
showed signs of being searched in great haste, yet with
a thoroughness that he found oddly disquieting. Every
piece of furniture had been moved and the matting rolled
back to see if anything had been buried in the earth underneath it. His mattress had been slit open with a knife and
both pillow-slips had been removed. But the search had
proved unrewarding, as apart from a handful of small
change—most of it copper—there had been neither money nor firearms in the tent, for Ash had taken to carrying
his revolver, and had given the two cash boxes, the rifle
and shot-gun and his spare ammunition to Mahdoo, who
had hidden them in a shabby canvas bedding-roll which he
added to his own luggage.

The only other mitigating circumstance—if it could
be called that—was the fact that the thoroughness of

the search seemed an indication that the thief had been looking for money, and was therefore not the man who had previously stolen the rifle. Ash drew what comfort he could from that, because although it was unpleasant enough to find that someone had managed to enter his tent without being seen, ransack it and leave again, all in broad daylight and with two of his servants in plain sight, it was better than wondering if once again one of his own weapons had been needed to use against him, and if so, why. To make a murder look like suicide?—or because suspicion would naturally fall on his servants if he were found shot with his own gun?

That last seemed the most likely explanation, as all the camp knew that the Sahib's tent stood apart and was not easy to approach unseen, so who but one of his own people would have been able to enter it and take the rifle? The reasoning would have appeared sound enough, and the majority would have accepted it because the alternative (that in a camp where there were literally thousands of firearms—muskets, muzzle-loaders and jezails without number, most of them easily stolen—a man bent on murder would go to immense trouble in order to steal the Sahib's gun) would seem absurdly far-fetched. The only question would be which one of the Sahib's servants was the murderer.

Ash would have liked to discuss this latest piece of unpleasantness with Mulraj, and had he been certain that the thief was only after money he would have done so and found it a great relief. But he was not certain, and so he said nothing. He told Mahdoo and Gul Baz that he did not wish it talked of, and Gul Baz had tidied up the tent without assistance, and later confided to Mahdoo that the sooner they were done with this wedding and free to return to Rawalpindi again, the better he would be pleased. "I have had enough of Rajputana," said Gul Baz. "And more than enough of this camp. There is something here that I do not understand: some evil which threatens the Sahib, and perhaps others too. Let us pray that we may separate ourselves from these Karidkoties and turn our faces to the north before it overtakes us."

Much the same thoughts were in Ash's mind, but with one difference, for he had few illusions about himself and knew that what he must pray for was patience and self-control.

He found that he could get through the days provided he filled every moment of them with some form of activity that would prevent his thinking of Juli, but the nights were a different matter; however hard he drove himself, and however tired he became, the moment he lay down to sleep her face rose before him and he could not banish it. He would turn and toss and stare into the darkness, or rise again to light the lamp and write unnecessary reports or check columns of figures—anything to shut her out of his mind, and Gul Baz, coming to wake him before first light with a mug of tea, would find him asleep at the table with his head on a pile of foolscap.

As the world turned pearl-grey before dawn and men and animals awoke reluctantly to a new day, he would climb wearily into the saddle and ride off to do what he could towards getting the camp on the move, while his servants struck his tent and loaded it with the rest of his belongings on to the bullock cart, where Mahdoo would already be ensconced among the cooking-pots, squatting comfortably on a pile of baggage that included a shabby canvas bedding-roll. The air would still be cool from the night, and at this hour there was no wind, for the *louh* did not blow before sunrise. But no one had leisure to notice, let alone enjoy it, for the uproar and activity that preceded departure, and the artificial heat of torches, oil lamps and cooking fires made an inferno of the early mornings.

As the crow flies, Bhithor was no great distance ahead. But now they were no longer crossing a featureless plain, and the country here was full of low, barren hills whose slopes were slippery with shale and dry grass and whose ridges were bare rock. A traveller on foot could cross them without much difficulty and thereby save himself many miles, but it was impossible for a cart to do so. The camp must go round them, winding to and fro along the wide, shallow valleys that meandered between the hills, and doubling on its tracks with monotonous regularity, as though caught in a maze. It was a particularly tedious form of progress, and when at last they came out into comparatively open country again no one was surprised when the younger bride put her foot down and demanded a halt of at least three days, announcing that if it were not granted she would refuse to move another step. She was, she said, aware that only a few more marches would bring them to the borders of Bhithor, but she had no intention of arriving in her new country ill from exhaustion, and unless she were allowed a few nights' uninterrupted sleep she would collapse.

Her ultimatum had been well timed, for that day's march had brought them to the banks of a river where there were trees in plenty; and no one, with the exception of Ash, was averse to a halt. It was an excellent site for a camp, and although the river had shrunk in the heat to no more than a narrow channel threading a shimmering waste of sandbanks, it was still capable of providing an inexhaustible supply of water, besides being easily fordable. Better still, on the far side there were several villages surrounded by cultivated land, and the inhabitants were eager to sell such things as grain and vegetables, milk, eggs and sugar-cane, while the country being more open here there would be plenty of fodder for the animals, as well as black-buck and *chinkara* on the plain, and fish in the river. As a camping site it could hardly have been improved upon, and Ash found no support when he wished to push on.

"What do a few days matter?" said Kaka-ji, fanning himself. "There is no great need for haste, and we shall all of us benefit from a short rest. Yes, even you, Sahib! For I fear your health is not good these days. You have become much thinner, and have lost your spirits and no longer laugh, or talk and ride with us as before. No, no . . ." a raised hand checked Ash's apologies. "It is the heat. The heat and this hot wind. We all suffer from it. You and Mulraj who are strong and I who am old, and Jhoti who is young—and pretends that it is the heat and not too many sweetmeats that have turned his stomach. Shushila too, for she has always been sickly, though I think that with her it is partly fear. Shu-shu is afraid of the future, and now that we are so nearly at Bhithor she would delay her arrival, even if only for a day or two."

"You have only yourself to blame, Sahib," shrugged Mulraj. There was an unaccustomed edge to his voice and his tone was unsympathetic. "You know how it is with Shushila-Bai, and had she been kept amused and occupied she might have given less thought to the future —and found the heat easier to bear. But when first you and then Jhoti ceased to ride with us of an evening or

404

join in the gatherings in the durbar tent, those things no longer amused her and she turned to fretting and complaining."

"I have been too busy," began Ash uncomfortably. "There have been so many—" he broke off abruptly, and frowned: "What's all this about Jhoti? Why did he stop coming?"

"To begin with, I suppose because you did. And when he was taken ill, he could not."

"*Ill?* Since when? Why was I not told?"

Mulraj's brows lifted and for a moment he stared in astonishment; then his eyes narrowed and he said slowly: "I see now: you were not even listening. I should have known as much when you did not ask after him or try to see him."

His voice changed and was no longer unfriendly: "I told you myself four days ago, and spoke of it again on the following morning. When you said nothing, but only nodded your head, I thought that you no longer wished to be troubled with such things. I should have known better. What is the matter, Sahib? You have not been yourself of late. Not since that attack upon you. It is not pleasant to know that someone waits and watches for an opportunity to put a bullet through one's head or a knife in one's back; as I myself know only too well. Is it that, Sahib? Or is it something else that troubles you? If I can be of help, you have only to ask."

Ash flushed and said hurriedly: "I know. But there is nothing, only the weather, and you cannot change that. Now tell me about Jhoti. Kaka-ji Rao said something about the heat being too much for him."

"Not the heat," said Mulraj dryly. "*Datura*—or so I think. Though one cannot be sure."

Now *datura* is a plant that grows wild in many parts of India, though more especially in the south. Its white, lily-like flowers are sweetly scented and very beautiful. But its seed, which is round and green, is known as the "apple of death," for it is exceedingly poisonous—and being easily obtained it has been used for centuries as a handy method of getting rid of unwanted husbands, wives or elderly relatives. It is one of the commonest of all poisons, and can be ground into a powder and mixed with almost any food (though bread is the usual choice) and death follows quickly or slowly, depending on the size of the dose or the amount that has been eaten. According to Mulraj, Jhoti must have eaten a good deal of it, but he had vomited most of it up and thereby saved himself. He had been moved to his sisters' tent, where he was making a rapid recovery under the care of the *dai*, Geeta ...

"But where did he *get* it from?" demanded Ash. "What was it in? Have you questioned the *khansamah* and the rest of his servants? Surely all his people eat the same food, don't they?—he can't have been the only one made ill by it."

But it seemed that he was. The poison, said Mulraj, had apparently been in some *jellabies,* a form of fried sweetmeats that Jhoti was particularly fond of, and that he had found in his tent. Fortunately, he had gobbled the lot—more than enough to make any child sick without there being any sinister ingredients. And equally fortunately, one of his servants, alarmed by the excessive vomiting, had run at once for Gobind instead of losing his head like the rest of them.

"Did Gobind say it was *datura?*" asked Ash.

Mulraj made a gesture of negation with one hand. "No. Only that it might be. The boy, as I have said, had eaten them all, even to licking the honey from the leaves on which they had lain, so that nothing remained. His own people said that it was only the excessive number and greasiness of the sweetmeats that was causing him to vomit."

Apparently Gobind had not been so sure of that; and though he said nothing then of his suspicions, he had treated the child as though for poison and made inquiries among the servants as to where the sweets had come from. But as he told Mulraj later, even if there had been nothing wrong with the *jellabies* and they had been placed there as a small surprise by someone who was fond of the child and only meant to please him, the very fact that they had made him sick would ensure that the giver would deny all knowledge of them. So he had not been surprised when no one would admit to knowing anything about them.

"But someone must have seen the boy eating them. Did Gobind ask about that?"

"Of course. But those who saw supposed—or said they did—that the Rajkumar had brought the *jellabies* himself. And I myself was only told that in his opinion the child had been poisoned, probably with *datura,* and that had he not been so greedy he would have died. But all that grease would have helped to coat his stomach and prevent the poison from being too quickly absorbed, and the grease and the sweetness together had made him feel sick, so that he had vomited everything up before it was too late; or that is what Gobind thinks, though he says that it would be difficult to prove. After I had spoken to him, I arranged for Jhoti to be nursed by his sisters. The elder is a woman of sense, and it gives Shushila-Bai something to think of other than the heat and her own troubles."

Ash said: "But there is a guard on the boy's tent. How could anyone—" and stopped, recalling that there had been a guard on his own tent, yet it had twice been entered without anyone having been seen. He pushed a hand through his hair, looking harassed and angry, and said: "I told you we should have spoken out about that first attempt to kill the boy, so that whoever was responsible for it would know that we knew and be afraid to try again. But you wouldn't have it, and now look what has happened. It's been tried again. This time you should have told everyone."

"I told *you,* Sahib," observed Mulraj dryly. "But it seems that you had other things on your mind, and did not hear."

Ash said nothing, for he knew that there had been too many occasions of late when, drunk with tiredness, he had only made a pretence of listening without taking in a single word that was being said. He had not let this disturb him overmuch, because he had been sure that if anything of real importance had been mentioned he would certainly remember it, and if he did not, it would only mean that the subject had been of no interest; yet Mulraj had spoken to him about Jhoti and he had not listened to a word. How much more had he missed? . . . how many other people had told him things that he had not listened to as he went about his duties in a daze, attempting not to think of his own troubles and thinking of nothing at all, and imagining himself to be doing useful work?

Mulraj, watching him, noticed for the first time how much thinner he seemed to have become; not only thinner, but older—which was something that Kaka-ji had noticed even earlier, and remarked on. But then Mulraj, like Ash, had had other things on his mind.

"I am sorry," said Mulraj contritely, regretting his last remark. "That was unkind."

"It was deserved!" admitted Ash ruefully. "I am the one who should apologize. I have been behaving like . . . like George!"

"George?" Mulraj looked puzzled. "Who is George?"

"Oh . . . just someone I once knew. He used to dramatize himself. It's a bad habit. Now, what are we going to do about Jhoti?"

23

There was, when they came to discuss it, very little they could do towards protecting Jhoti from assassination, beyond what they had done already; which was not much.

It was not possible to police the boy for every minute of every hour, unless he was to be followed everywhere by a guard of picked men from the State Forces, and though Mulraj would not have admitted it, he could not be wholly certain that even among his own best men there might not be one or two who were untrustworthy. Nandu was, after all, their hereditary overlord and ruler of their state and their destinies, and their duty was to obey his orders. Besides, there would also be large rewards, for he would not be niggardly when it came to paying for something he desired—such as the death of his heir-presumptive.

Mulraj was no cynic, but he had few illusions on the subject of human nature. He knew that most men can be bought if the price is high enough, and had therefore decided to say nothing about that first attempt to kill the little Rajkumar, but instead to pray to the gods and hope that vigilance and fore-knowledge would be able to foil a second one.

But it seemed that the gods had not listened to him,

and as it was no thanks to him, or to Ash either, that the second attempt had failed, this time they would have to speak out. There was obviously nothing to be gained by keeping silence, and though they had little to offer in the way of proof, the boy would at least be warned of his danger and would never again be careless as to what he ate or drank. It was the course that Ash had originally favoured; yet now that it came to the point, he opposed it. Because once again he remembered a face from the past, not George's this time, but the face of the frightened boy who had been Jhoti's half-brother and Yuveraj of Gulkote . . .

Lalji too had been threatened with assassination, and had lived in terror of it—starting at shadows and never knowing who if anyone he could trust. And though he had been warned (his old nurse, Dunmaya, had never ceased warning him) it had not saved his life. All that it had done was to make a hell of his short life, and his rages and cruelty and vindictiveness were a not unnatural reaction to a burden of fear that was too great for a child to bear.

Jhoti too was no stranger to fear. He had been afraid on the night when Ash had first seen him and been struck by his resemblance to another plump and pallid little boy. He had good reason to shake in his shoes, for he had just defied Nandu and run away, and he knew enough of his brother to be frightened—though not, Ash thought, of being murdered; only of being punished. But if he knew . . .

"It's no good. We can't do it," said Ash harshly. "It would be too cruel. He's only a child and it would scare him out of his wits to learn that there is someone here in this camp who means to kill him and who has not only nearly done so twice, but will certainly try again. He'll grow afraid of everything and everyone. Afraid of trusting anyone, or eating anything, or drinking or sleeping or riding. It's too much to expect any child to bear. But there's no reason why we shouldn't tell his sisters and Kaka-ji. They can see to it that his food is tasted by someone else before he touches it. And we'll get Gobind to tell him not to eat sweets, or anything else he finds lying around, because the ones that made him sick must have been stale, or fried in bad *ghee* or something like that. Gobind will know what to say, and he and the girls and Kaka-ji can all help to keep an eye on the boy. It's the best we can do."

Mulraj frowned and pulled at his lip, and agreed that it would be kinder not to frighten the child, but that if they wished to keep him in ignorance they would not be able to tell either Kaka-ji or Shushila-Bai—particularly Shushila, who would never be able to keep it to herself. She would only work herself into a state of hysteria over it, and the tale would be all over the camp within a matter of hours. As for Kaka-ji, he was too old and frail to be worried by such violent matters, as well as being far too talkative—and too transparent. Which left only Anjuli-Bai . . .

"Jhoti is fond of her, and she of him," said Mulraj. "Also I know her to be a sensible woman and one who does not lose her head and become distracted by danger. I have not forgotten her behaviour on the night that the *ruth* foundered in the river and the driver of the bullocks was drowned. She did not shriek or show fear, but saw to it that her sister was saved; and I am very sure that she would do no less for her brother. It is a heavy responsibility to lay on one woman's shoulders, but we need help, and Anjuli-Bai is perhaps the best person to give it. At least we know that we can trust her. Which is more," added Mulraj grimly, "than can be said of many others in this camp."

Yes, Juli could be trusted, thought Ash. She would do everything in her power to protect her little half-brother from harm, and she would neither panic nor talk unwisely—or lose her head in a crisis. She was the obvious person to turn to for help, and it had been a mistake not to tell her the truth about Jhoti long ago, after that near-fatal riding accident. He had fully intended to do so, yet somehow he had not. He could not remember why.

Another thought struck him, and he said abruptly: "But Anjuli-Bai is never alone, so how are you going to tell her?"

"*I?*" Mulraj sounded surprised. "*Nahin*, Sahib. It is you who will have to do that; if I did I would surely be overheard. But on our evening rides, which have lately ceased, it was your custom to gallop on ahead with the Rajkumari Anjuli, and if the rides are resumed you

410

could do so again without occasioning any remark. It is the only way."

Which is why Ash, despite all his good intentions, came to be riding beside Juli on the following evening . . .

He had, in point of fact, seen her on the previous day, as after speaking to Mulraj he had asked if he might see Jhoti, who was still convalescent and in his sister's care. The tent had been crowded with people, for the East has never believed in the theory that segregation and quiet are necessary to the sick, and in addition to the princesses and their women, both Kaka-ji and Maldeo Rai were present.

Jhoti was looking better than expected, and well on the way to recovery. But his greeting had contained a strong suggestion of reproach. He had obviously been hurt by Ash's failure to visit him earlier, and only forgave it when Ash cravenly put the blame on Gobind, who, he said, had forbidden him to do so until the patient was in better health. He had not stayed long, and there had been no opportunity to speak to Juli beyond the usual polite greetings. He thought she looked pale and tired, and when he met her gaze it was puzzled, and like Jhoti's, a little reproachful, and his heart contracted.

He did not look at her again, because he was afraid that if he did he would not be able to stop himself from reaching out in front of them all to smooth away that faint, bewildered frown, and tell her that he loved her and had only stayed away because he could not bear to endanger her. Turning away quickly he spoke instead to Shushila, and afterwards he could not remember who had brought up the subject of a riding party on the following evening, or what arrangements had been made. He remembered only that he had agreed to go. And as he walked back to his tent, he realized that he should not have done so.

"But it is for Jhoti's sake," thought Ash, arguing with himself. There were so many ways in which Juli could help—she *had* to be told about Jhoti, and because he, Ash, was the only one who could do it, he had no choice in the matter.

But there was a flaw in that argument, and he knew it. It was not that Juli could not help, because she could and would do more than anyone else to protect her

411

young brother from harm, and her help would be invaluable; but there was a time limit to any help she could give, and it was a very short one. In a few days they would reach Bhithor, and then there would be the wedding; and once that was over she would not be able to help Jhoti any more, so there was not much point in telling her anything for the sake of what little she could do in the few days that were left . . .

"I should have told her long ago," thought Ash. But he had not, and it was no good telling her now. It was too late . . . He ought to send word that he could not join the riding party tomorrow. He ought not to see her again . . . it would only make matters worse. He would not go.

But he knew that he would, because he could not resist seeing her and talking to her just once more. After all, it would be for the last time. The very last . . .

That night he fell asleep the moment his head touched the pillow and awoke next morning feeling enormously refreshed; and though the future, when analysed, remained as bleak as before, the fog of fatigue and despair that had enveloped him had lifted, and life did not seem so intolerable after all.

Even the weather had improved. As the sun moved up the sky and the temperature rose, the tents did not flap maddeningly or the trees and grass whine in the wind, and today there were no veils of sand hissing along the river-bed. For once, the *louh* was not blowing, and the relief of being free from its hot, fretting breath was as great as though a persistent drum had suddenly stopped beating. Men's nerves relaxed and the whole atmosphere of the camp changed and lightened, for the cessation of the wind was almost as great a boon as the prospect of a few days' rest in a spot where there was both shade and water. The camp settled down to enjoy both, and although by the afternoon the day had become airless and stifling and the hordes of flies that the wind had previously kept at bay were back in force, these were considered a small price to pay for rest and quiet.

The late afternoon continued breathlessly still, but as the shadows lengthened and the shimmering heat-haze that had danced all day above the sandbanks died away, a faint current of air stirred along the river and crept be-

412

tween the tents. "It will be cooler out on the plain," said Kaka-ji.

But it had not been cooler. If anything, it had been hotter, because apart from the belt of trees and the cultivated land that bordered the river, the plain beyond was dry and stony, and the low hills that surrounded it had been absorbing heat all day and were now giving it off again in the manner of a flat-iron that has just been removed from the stove.

To the riding party it felt as though they were moving towards an open furnace and away from what little there was of coolness and shade, and even the horses and the trotting bullocks that drew the *ruth* appeared reluctant to go forward. A sudden gust of wind, the first that had blown all that day, whipped up a small whirl-wind of dust and dead leaves and sent it spinning across the plain like some fantastic ghostly top, and presently others arose, twirled briefly among the stones and died again. But otherwise the evening was very still, and except for the dust-devils nothing moved on the plain.

The spot chosen as a starting place for the ride lay over a mile from the camp and had been selected by Mulraj, who had ridden out at dawn accompanied by some of his officers and a local *shikari* to shoot black-buck for the pot, and had decided that it would suit them very well. It was out of sight of the camp and the villages and well away from any beaten track, and the *shikari* had told him that although men had once lived among the hills, that was long ago, before the river changed its course and left them waterless. No one now came this way except to shoot; and there would be no game to shoot of an evening, for as the day waned the black-buck moved off towards the river and the croplands and did not stay out on the plain.

Anjuli and her sister had left camp in the *ruth*, together with one of Shu-shu's women; their horses following behind in the charge of an elderly syce and two grey-bearded members of the body-guard, while Ash, Kaka-ji and Mulraj rode ahead. Jhoti had not come out with them, though he had meant to, insisting that he was quite recovered. But Gobind had produced a new and fascinating game that one played with coloured pegs, so he had decided at the last moment that he would prefer to stay behind after all, and that anyway it was too hot for riding: Shu-shu and Kairi must go without him.

The *ruth* came to a stop near a tall outcrop of rock near the mouth of a mile-wide amphitheatre where the hills made a half-circle about the plain, and syces and escort discreetly turned their faces away as the brides descended and the riding party set out across the level ground. Ash had been afraid that without Jhoti to keep her entertained, Shushila might insist on their all keeping together; but luckily Kaka-ji proved an excellent substitute. The old man rode beside her and complimented her on her progress, offered useful suggestions and chatted about various incidents in the camp, while Mulraj as usual kept near by. It was as easy as it had ever been for Ash and Juli to ride on ahead—though less easy to tell her about Jhoti, because the moment they were out of earshot she forestalled him by speaking first.

"Why have you kept away from us for so long?" demanded Anjuli. "It was not because of work, and you have not been ill for I made Geeta make inquiries for me. There is something the matter. What is it, Ashok?"

Ash hesitated, taken off guard. Juli had always been direct, and he should have borne that in mind and been ready with an answer that would have satisfied her; but there was no time to think of one now—and he had already decided that he could not tell her the truth. The impulse to do so was suddenly so strong that he had to clench his teeth to keep back the words, and Anjuli must have seen it, for a small crease appeared between her brows—that same frown line that he had ached to smooth away last night, because he could not bear to see her troubled.

The sight of it was just as unbearable today, and he thought that if he had not known before that he loved her, he would know it now, if only because of the pain that that small shadow caused him. Once again he would have given anything to be able to smooth it away and to tell her that he loved her and that there was nothing he would not do to protect her from unhappiness. But because he could not do so he took refuge in anger, and told her furiously that he had had more important things to do than sit about making social conversation in the durbar tent, and though she might not be aware of it, there had already

414

been two attempts to murder her young half-brother: the second of them by poison, and only a few days ago.

This was not in the least how he had planned to break the news to her and the sight of the white shock on her face made him ashamed of himself. But he could not unsay the words, and as it was too late now to try softening the blow, he told her the tale harshly and in detail, leaving nothing out. When he had finished she said only: "You should have told me after the first time; not now, when I have so few days left."

It was what Ash himself had thought; though it had certainly not occurred to him immediately—or to Mulraj at all, unless Mulraj considered that any help, for however short a period, was worth having. But Anjuli had seen it at once, and the crease between her brows deepened, though now it was no longer on Ash's account but on Jhoti's. She looked very white and shaken, and he saw for the first time that there were dark shadows under her eyes, as though she too had not been sleeping.

He said: "I'm sorry, Juli." And thought as he said it that in the circumstances it was a singularly useless statement to make—a polite and automatic expression of regret that could serve as an apology for overturning a tea-cup or inadvertently jostling someone in a doorway. But there did not seem to be anything else he could say, and he *was* sorry: deeply and sincerely sorry . . . and for so many more things than neglecting to tell her about Jhoti. Perhaps most of all for having given her back the broken half of her little mother-of-pearl fish, for if he had not done that . . .

The sound of Shushila's laughter, borne on another brief gust of wind, was a reminder that unless he quickened their present pace they would soon be overtaken, because as they talked they had unwittingly slowed to a walk. He said urgently, "Come on," and they spurred forward again and raced across the plain towards a gap in the encircling hills, and entering it, found themselves in a quiet valley that was awash with evening shadows.

The ground here was less rough and stony than on the open plain, but the hillsides were largely rock and there were caves among the tumbled boulders, some of which had clearly been occupied at some time or another by either men or cattle, for the rock faces bore the traces of old fires, and here and there on the ground about

415

them were marks left by cow-droppings that had long since been dispersed by sun and wind and the dung-beetles. But though Ash looked closely, he could see no sign of present habitation, and having assured himself that they had not been followed and that the valley was untenanted, he drew rein, and once more both horses fell into a walk. But though there was no longer any danger of being overheard, he did not speak, and Anjuli too was silent.

The shadow of the hills to their right covered two thirds of the valley, and although those nearest them were still bright in the sunset and aglow with the heat of the burning afternoon, it was cooler here than it had been out on the plain. The wind that had whipped up the dust-devils was blowing more strongly now, and the occasional gust that swept in from the plain dried the sweat between their shoulders and put an end to the hot, brooding stillness that had prevailed all day. Ahead of them the sky was already green with the evening and the hills were no longer lion-coloured, but brilliant with rose and cerise and apricot where the sunlight still lingered, and deep blue and violet in the swift-gathering shadows below. But Ash had no eyes for such things . . .

He was looking at Juli and realizing that although he might see her again during the next few days, and once more, and finally, at her wedding, he would never again be alone with her and be able to look his fill.

She was dressed, as always for the evening rides, in men's clothing: trousers and *achkan* and a small muslin turban that covered her hair and showed only the deep widow's peak in the angle where its folds crossed. The severity of the headgear only served to heighten the beauty of her features, drawing attention to the lovely lines of cheek and chin and the size of the wide-set eyes with their heavy fringe of lashes, while its colour, a vivid ruby-red, deepened the ivory tones of her skin and was repeated in the warm curve of her lips and the caste-mark between her brows. She sat tall and straight-backed in the saddle, and her shoulders had nothing of the sloping delicacy of Shushila's, but were slim and square.

Any casual passer-by would have taken her to be a handsome youth, for she held her head erect like a man instead of submissively bent as becomes a gently nurtured woman. But to Ash, riding beside her, her present garb seemed to emphasize her femininity far more than the graceful folds of a sari. The straight lines of the *achkan* showed the swell of her breasts which a sari could hide, and her slender waist and rounded hips were not those of a boy—though her hands might well have been. So much of Juli's character, thought Ash, was written in those hands. He studied them as they rested quietly against her horse's mane, the reins looped between the strong, square-tipped fingers. Dependable hands . . .

He had forgotten Jhoti. But Anjuli had not, and when she spoke at last it was in an undertone, as though she was thinking aloud: "This is Nandu's doing," said Anjuli quietly. "It must be so, for who else could gain any profit from Jhoti's death, or have any reason for wishing to kill him? The camp is full of Nandu's men . . . though I cannot believe that there can be many who would be willing to kill a child. But then it would not need many, only one or two, and if we do not know who they are it will be difficult to guard him. We must decide who can be trusted and see to it that there is always one of them with him to keep watch."

She turned to look at Ash, and said: "Who else knows of this, besides Mulraj and yourself and my uncle's Hakim, Gobind Dass?"

"No one," said Ash, and explained why it had seemed best that first time to keep the matter secret, and to tell only herself and Gobind now. Anjuli nodded and said thoughtfully: "Yes, you were right. It would only frighten Shu-shu, and as she would never believe that Nandu could have ordered such a thing, she would see it as part of a plot to kill us all—our family. My uncle would believe, but what can he do? Besides, if he knew he would find it difficult to conceal his alarm from Shu-shu, or from Jhoti either. But there are others whom I think we can safely trust. Old Geeta, for one. And Jhoti's own body-servant, Ramji, who has been with him since he was born, and whose wife is one of my women. Ramji would surely know which, if any, of his fellow servants could be trusted. Let us think now . . ."

The horses wandered forward unchecked, pausing occasionally to crop a mouthful of parched grass and moving on again while their riders discussed ways and means of preventing the murder of a child, and behind them the sky darkened. Presently another and far stronger gust of wind swept down the valley, driving the dust before it and snatching the turban from Anjuli's head to send it bowling away, unwinding as it went. Her hair whipped about her face and streamed forward on the blast like sea-weed in a tide-rip, and both horses threw up their heads and snorted and began to trot.

"High time we turned back," said Ash. "You'd better tie something round your head or you won't be able to see where you're going. Here—"

He pulled a handkerchief from the pocket of his riding breeches and put it into her hand, and turning his horse caught his breath and said in English: "Good God!"

They had both been too occupied to pay much attention to their surroundings, and neither of them had thought to look behind them or to wonder why the light seemed to be fading unusually quickly. The sky ahead had been clear and calm, and even now the last of the sun lay gold along the crest of the near hill. But as they turned they saw that behind them lay nothing but darkness: a brown, turgid curtain of darkness that spanned the horizon from left to right and was advancing with such speed that it had already blotted out the entrance to the valley. The wind that drove it forward was no longer blowing in gusts, but had steadied to a gale, and now they could smell the dust and see that the sky above them was turning brown. "But it's too early," thought Ash dazedly. "A month too early . . . more!" He stared at the advancing dust-storm as though he could not believe what he saw.

Juli said: "Shushila," and caught her breath on a sob. "Shushila—"

She dropped her hands and let the handkerchief that she had been trying to tie about her head vanish on the wind, and snatching up the reins, urged her horse to a gallop, riding headlong for the wall of darkness that had swallowed up the plain where they had left Shushila. But Ash had recovered himself and he was too quick for her. He had never before used more than the lightest touch of a spur on Baj Raj, but he used both now, and the horse bounded forward and was level with Anjuli's mare and riding it off, turning her back up the valley.

"No!" cried Anjuli. "No—I must go to Shushila."

She wrenched at the reins in an attempt to check the frantic animal, and Ash cut her across the wrists with his whip and called savagely: "Don't be a fool. Mulraj will look after her"—and brought the whip down again,

418

this time on Baj Raj, though the horse needed no urging, for the towering, boiling darkness that was sweeping down on them was something he had never seen before, and he desired to escape from it every bit as urgently as Ash did.

The mare too was galloping at full stretch, and it is doubtful if anyone could have turned her; but Anjuli made no further effort to do so, because she had realized even as he spoke that Ashok was right and that what she had meant to do would have been an act of madness. Once caught in the heart of such a storm she could have seen nothing and helped no one; and Mulraj was with Shu-shu. He and the others could be counted upon to see that no harm came to her, and in all probability they had seen the approaching storm long ago and ridden straight back to camp, and were safe by now. But she and Ashok . . .

Anjuli had never seen a dust-storm either, but she did not need to be told that it was not a thing to be caught in out in the open, and she settled down to ride as she had never ridden before, crouching over the saddle-horn with her weight thrown forward to help the labouring animal, and without any idea where they were going, for she was half blinded by her own hair blowing about her face in wild, black confusion.

Ash was making for a cave that he had noticed earlier that evening in the brief moment before the shadow of the far hills reached it. He would not have seen it if the sun had not been on it, for at the time it had been a good half mile ahead, and though they had been moving slowly towards it they had barely covered more than half that distance. But Ash had been trained among the Frontier hills, and in the sunlight there was a sharp difference between the work of nature and that of man . . .

Even at that range it had been possible to see that below a jutting overhang of rock someone, at some time, had closed in the front of a large cave with mud bricks, leaving an entrance large enough to admit a man or a cow. It was the shape of that doorway—a black, straight-sided oblong—and the bleached colour of the mud that did not quite match the surrounding hillside, that had caught Ash's attention and made him narrow his eyes and stare at it to make sure that the cave behind it was not occupied. But nothing had moved in the valley or on the hillsides, and he knew that if there had been any men about, there would have been smoke, for it was the time of

419

the evening meal. The sunlight had retreated and the cave had been lost among the advancing shadows, and Ash had turned to look at Juli, and forgotten it: only to remember it again in the instant that he had realized the significance of that ominous pall of darkness.

There were other and nearer caves, but it was difficult to judge how deep they were, and a shallow one would offer no protection against such a storm as this. But one that had been worth blocking in with a mud wall was likely to run far back into the hillside, and that narrow doorway would keep out the worst of the dust—if only they could reach it in time, for Ash was sharply aware that if the storm overtook them before they did so they would never find their way to it, the air already being so thick with dust and flying fragments of dry grass and leaves that they seemed to be riding through a fog.

Had the ground been less level they might never have reached it; boulders would certainly have brought one or both of their horses down, and bushes would have slowed them, but mercifully there were neither, and the only difficulty had been preventing their horses from racing past it and on up the valley. But Ash, who was in the lead, reined in with a violence that forced Baj Raj back on his haunches, and was out of the saddle and leaping at the mare as it shot past, Anjuli tugging on the reins with all her strength.

The mare swerved wildly and came to a sliding, slithering stop, and Anjuli tumbled from the saddle, and picking herself up, ran to catch Baj Raj, who was trotting in an aimless circle stumbling over his reins, and led him through the empty doorway into the darkness beyond, to be followed a moment later by Ash with the mare.

There was not enough light to see how big the cave was, but judging by the hollow sound of the horses' hooves it was a large one; and they had reached it in time—but only just in time. The storm had been so close on their heels that even as they turned to face the entrance, a dark curtain appeared to be drawn across it and the daylight was blotted out as a churning, choking maelstrom of dust whirled down the valley, driven by a wind that shrieked as though the Valkyries rode it, or witches from the Brocken.

The noise of the gale filled the quiet cave with sound and made the darkness reverberate with a hollow, high-pitched drone that seemed to come from all points of the compass at once, and dust poured in through the doorway until the close air within was suddenly so thick with it that breathing became difficult, and Anjuli began to cough and choke.

She heard Ash calling something, but the words were lost in the howl of the wind and the echoes that they awoke in the recesses of the cave. Then his hand closed upon her arm and he was shouting into her ear: "Take your coat off and put it over your head. And get back into the cave—as far as you can." He brushed away the silky hair that was getting into his mouth, and added: "Carefully now, Larla; don't go falling over anything."

The old endearment had slipped out unconsciously, and he did not know that he had used it, for he had other things on his mind; notably the horses, who were backing and snorting in an effort to escape from the stifling dust, and might panic at any moment and lash out in the darkness, injuring each other if not Juli or himself. And if the horses went lame it was going to mean a long walk back to camp—if there was still a camp. He did not want to think of what might be happening there, and in any case there was no point in worrying about a situation that was completely beyond his control. But at least he should be able to do something about Baj Raj and the mare.

He had given his handkerchief to Juli, so there was nothing for it but to remove his shirt and tear it into strips; and he did so—using his teeth to start it tearing and tying the first strip over his nose and mouth as a filter. It was easier to breathe after that, and he kept his eyes shut against the dust and did the rest by touch, soothing the horses and knotting up their reins out of harm's way, and finally fastening a loop of cloth between each animal's forelegs, just above the fetlock, in the time-honoured fashion of the Indian villager who slips a similar loop of grass rope on his pony so that it can only hobble, and lets it out to graze in the sure knowledge that it cannot stray too far or come to much harm.

That done, he turned his attention to exploring the cave in order to see if it went far enough back to allow them all to get out of this stifling smother and into cleaner air.

The wind was blowing slantwise down the valley and slightly away from the cave, and the overhang of rock

421

helped in some small way to deflect it. But there was no way of blocking the entrance, and the dust fumed in through it like steam from a boiling kettle. The further away they could get from it the better for all of them, and Ash moved back cautiously into the darkness, feeling his way along one wall.

He had gone perhaps twenty yards when his hand touched something that was unmistakably metal, and further investigation showed that someone, presumably the long-ago occupant who had closed in the cave mouth with those mud bricks, had driven several short iron staples into the rock wall; though for what purpose was not clear. The staples were spaced in a long slanting line, and there were five of them, and may well have been others higher up the wall and out of reach. But at least four were at a reasonable level, and Ash blessed the unknown man who had put them there, for though they were corroded by rust and one snapped off in his hand, the others would serve his purpose, as the air in this part of the cave was more breathable than that by the open doorway.

He groped his way back to the horses and returned with Baj Raj, who was jerking his head wildly from side to side in an effort to escape the dust, and had to be coaxed to follow. But once out of the worst of the smother, and with his reins hitched to a staple in the wall, he stopped shivering and stood quietly, and Ash went back for the mare, and having tethered her in the same manner, wiped the caked dust from his eyes and opened them a fraction to see if there were any signs that the storm was abating. But the doorway still showed barely lighter than the surrounding blackness of the cave, and outside the wind still howled past with the racket of an express train whistling in a tunnel.

It looked, thought Ash, as though it was going to be a long business, and he wished that he had paid more attention when the headmen of villages in their line of march had spoken of hot winds and dust-storms and other vagaries of the Rajputana weather. But having learned that the season of such storms was still well ahead, he had not troubled to ask questions about them, imagining that that was something that could safely be left until later and need not concern the Karidkote camp until the wedding ceremonies were over and they were free to start north again. But he regretted now that he had not asked them earlier, but he had no idea how long a dust-storm could be expected to last. Hours?—or only minutes?

It seemed to him that this one had been raging for close on an hour already, but on reflection he revised that estimate. He could not have taken more than ten minutes to tear up his shirt and find those providential staples, and to tether the horses. Say fifteen at most, and surely there could not be enough dust in all Rajputana, dry as it was, to sustain such a storm as this for more than a limited period? Unless, of course it was blowing in a circle—which was something else he did not know. But at least it could not last indefinitely; as soon as the wind expended its first violence and began to die down, the clouds of dust would sink back to earth and it would be over. Though not, at this rate, until the sun had set.

There was a watch in the pocket of Ash's riding breeches, but he had not looked at it since he left the camp, and as he could not see it now he had very little idea of what time it was. But it occurred to him that the storm alone might not account for the fact that he could barely make out the entrance to the cave. Once the sun had set, the interval of twilight was very short, for here night did not come slowly, as in the West, but hastily, on the heels of day. And if the sun was already down they were going to have to find their way back in the dark, across unfamiliar country and through a maze of hills.

"Mulraj will send out men to search for us," thought Ash; though with more hope than confidence, because it seemed to him only too likely that the camp would have been thrown into such appalling chaos that Mulraj and the rest of them would have their hands full and be forced to wait until daylight before sending out search-parties, by which time, with any luck, he and Juli would have got back on their own. Meanwhile, for as long as the storm raged they would have to stay where they were and make the best of it.

He pulled down the strip of cambric that he had tied over his nose and mouth, and sniffing the air, found that it was a good deal better than he had expected. It would probably be better still further back in the cave—particularly if, as the echoes suggested, there were side caves leading out of this one, which the dust would not have entered—and at least it was pleasantly cool in here. The heat of the sun's rays had not been able to penetrate this

423

far into the hillside, and after the burning heat outside, the drop in temperature was considerable; he hoped that Juli would not catch a chill, for she was wearing only a thin cotton *achkan;* and possibly nothing under it.

He called out to her, and once again the cave filled with echoes that fought with the weird drone of the wind as a dozen voices shouted from different points in the darkness, some close and some far away, their words lost in the clamour. The echoes faded but the noise of the wind remained, and Ash did not know if Juli had answered him or not, for her voice would have been drowned in the medley of sounds. But suddenly and unreasonably, half-a-dozen hideous possibilities sprang into his mind, and his heart contracted in a spasm of sheer terror. He had warned her to be careful, but suppose there was a pit in the floor of the cave?—a well, even? Or some deep fissure that went far down into the rock, into which she could have fallen? Or were there other caves heading out of this one in a chain of caverns and passages going back and back into the hillside, branching and twisting so that anyone groping through them would soon become hopelessly lost . . . ? And supposing there were snakes . . .

Panic gripped him and he ran forward into the darkness, his hands outstretched, calling, "Juli—Juli. Where are you? Are you all right? Answer me, Juli!" And the echoes reverberated round him, mocking him; now fading, now rising above the deafening croon of the wind: *Juli . . . Juli . . . Juli . . .*

Once he thought he heard her answer; but he could not be sure where the sound had come from and he would, at that moment, have sold his soul for a light or a few seconds of silence. Straining to listen, he could hear nothing but the bagpipe drone of the wind and the maddening echoes of his own voice, and he stumbled on blindly, groping in the inky blackness and meeting only rock and rough earth, or emptiness.

He must have turned a corner into a side cave without knowing it, because all at once the volume of noise diminished as sharply as if a door had closed behind him, and the air was almost free from dust. He heard no new sound and the blackness was still as impenetrable; but suddenly he knew that it was from here that Juli had answered him, and that she was still here, for there was a

424

faint fragrance of rose-petals in the stale, cool air. He turned towards it, and caught her in his arms.

Her arms and shoulders, her breasts and her slender waist were smooth and warm and naked against his own bare flesh, for having thrown the *achkan* over her head as a protection against the choking dust, she had pulled it away in order to call to him, and lost it somewhere in the darkness. The cheek that was pressed to his was wet with tears and she was breathing in hard gasps as though she had been running, for she had heard him shouting and had turned back to go to him, afraid that it had been a cry for help, because there had been so much urgency in the sound. But confused by the echoes she had lost her bearings and blundered round in the dark, bruising herself against unexpected outcrops of rock and sobbing and calling as she searched for him in the clamorous darkness.

They clung together for a long minute, not moving or speaking, and then Ash turned his head and kissed her.

24

If the dust-storm had not blown up so quickly . . . If they had noticed its approach earlier . . . If the cave had been smaller and they had been able to see; or hear . . .

Much later, Ash was to think of that and to wonder if it would have made any difference? Perhaps. Though not if old Uncle Akbar, after whom he had been named, had been right.

Uncle Akbar and Koda Dad had both assured him that all men are born into the world with their fate tied about their necks, and cannot escape it.

"What is written, is written." How many times had he heard Koda Dad say that? And Akbar Khan had said it before him—once when Ash stood looking down at the dead body of a tiger, shot five minutes earlier from the machan where they had waited for hours; and again, on an equally memorable occasion, in the courtyard of Shah

Jehan's great mosque in Delhi, where the crowd had been so great that two men had fallen from the gateway and been killed, and Ash had demanded explanations. But in the present instance, the question of predestination versus free-will was of purely academic interest; the fact remained that he had failed to notice the storm, and because the cave in which they had taken refuge had been very large and dark and full of noises, he had been seized by panic at the thought of Juli lost in it—breaking her neck by falling into some hideous underground cavern, or treading on a cobra in the dark.

Had he kept his head he would almost certainly have succeeded in keeping his good resolutions as well. In which case the two of them would have sat out the storm without touching each other, and set off for the camp the moment they heard the wind drop. Yet if they had done so they would have missed Kaka-ji and the *ruth*, and returned, innocent, to find themselves the centre of a major scandal and facing serious charges.

In the event, they had no idea of how long the storm lasted or when the wind dropped. It could have been an hour, or two hours, or ten. They had lost all count of time, and even the silence and the fact that they could hear each other's smallest whisper did not remind them of its passing.

"I never meant this to happen," murmured Ash; which was true enough. But if there had been any hope at all of his making a last effort to avoid it, it was lost when Juli, found at last, had flung her arms about his neck and clung to him. And then he had kissed her—

There was nothing of tenderness in that kiss. It was hard and violent, but though it bruised her lips and took the breath from her body, she did not draw back from it but clung closer, and the moment was almost one of desperation, as though they strove against each other as enemies, intent on inflicting pain and careless of receiving it.

The brief frenzy ended, and Juli's taut body relaxed as the panic ebbed away from her, leaving her soft and supple in his arms. Desperation died and gave place to a slow delight that burned its way through every vein and nerve and fibre. Her tears were salt on Ash's tongue, and he could feel the ripple of her hair all about him: long, silky strands that smelt of roses and slid over his skin like a cloak of feathers, or caught and clung to him as though they had a life of their own. Her lips were no longer tense with terror, but warm and eager and sweet beyond relief, and be kissed them again and again until at last they opened under his own, and he felt her whole body shiver with desire.

He would have lifted her then and laid her down on the floor of the cave, but even as his arm tightened, he checked himself and broke off that kiss to ask what seemed, in the circumstances, a superfluous question. Yet he too had been panic-stricken in the inky darkness, and knowing that Juli had been equally frantic, he had to be sure that her passionate response to his kisses was not merely an emotional reaction from terror. Therefore he spoke harshly, forcing himself to say the words, because he was suddenly afraid of how she might reply. "Juli, do you love me?"

The cave, and caves beyond the cave, repeated it after him, again and again: *do you love me? . . . you love me . . . love me . . .* And Anjuli laughed very softly—but so lovingly that his heart seemed to turn over—and answered against his ear, too low for the echo to catch her voice: "How can you ask me that when you know I have loved you all my life? Yes, always! From the very beginning."

Ash's hands went up to grip her smooth shoulders, and he shook her roughly and said: "As a brother. But that is no use to me. I want a lover—a wife. I want all of you—for my own, for always. Do you love me like that? Do you, Juli?"

She leaned her cheek against his left hand, rubbing it caressingly as it held her shoulder, and said slowly, as though she were reciting a poem or repeating a profession of faith: "I love you. I have always loved you. I have always been yours and I always will be; and if I loved you first as a brother, it was not a brother that I waited for as I grew up and became a woman, but a lover. And—and —" She leaned forward to lay her cheek against his own and he felt the taut nipples touch his chest like light fingertips: "—this you do not know: but when you returned again I loved you before ever I knew who you were, for when you lifted me out of the *ruth* that night in the river, and held me in your arms while we waited for my women, I could not breathe for the beating of my heart. And I

427

was ashamed, because I thought you were a stranger. Yet something in my blood rejoiced to be held so, and would have had you hold me closer and closer. Like this——" She tightened her arms about his neck and kissed the hollow below his cheek bone, and said in a shaken whisper: "Oh, my love! Love me—love me now, before it is too late for me."

The whisper ended in a gasp as Ash's hands slid down from her shoulders to catch her again into a close embrace and pull her down with him onto the floor of the cave.

The dry, silver sand was cool and smooth and very soft, and Juli's black hair spread a silky coverlet over it as she lay in the darkness and felt Ash's hands strip away the only garment she still wore, and move up again slowly and caressingly: warm and firm and very sure. For a moment only she knew a pang of fear, but it passed as quickly as it had come, and when he said: "I'm going to hurt you," she tightened her arms about him, and did not cry out at the lovely cruelty that ended her girlhood.

"I never meant this to happen," Ash had murmured. But that had been hours later—they did not know how many—and after it had happened. And again . . .

"I did," whispered Juli, lying quiet and relaxed in the curve of his arm, with her head pillowed on his shoulder.

"When, Larla?"

Juli did not answer immediately, but Ash was already thinking of something else, and the question had been an idle one for his mind had turned to plans. He was trying to visualize the large-scale Ordnance Maps that he had studied almost daily as the camp moved down across India, and decide which route would be the safest to take. Because the sooner they quit Rajputana and the south, the better. They had their horses, but no money . . . They would need money, yet they could not go back to the camp. He felt Juli move her head, and the cool touch of the jewel in her ear reminded him that the stones she wore that day were pigeon's-blood rubies, set in gold, and not only in her ears, but as buttons on her *achkan*. If they were careful they should be able to get a good price for them, and they could dispose of them one by one as the need arose.

"A long time ago," said Juli softly, answering his question at last. "A month or more; though I did not

428

plan it this way. How could I know that the gods would be so good to me as to send a storm in which we two would be caught, and find refuge here, together? You will think me shameless, but I planned to come if I could to your tent, and if you would not take me willingly, to beg of you . . . because I was desperate, and I thought that if only—"

"What are you talking about?" asked Ash, recalled abruptly from his own plans.

"The Rana," whispered Juli, and shivered. "I—I could not endure to think that I must lose my maidenhead to another man, one whom I neither knew nor loved and who did not love me, yet who would use me, by right—for lust or to beget heirs from my body. An old man and a stranger . . ."

She shuddered convulsively and Ash tightened his arm about her, holding her hard against him, and said: "Don't, Larla. You don't have to think of it any more. Ever."

"But I must," insisted Juli, her voice shaking. "No—let me speak. I want you to understand. You see, I knew from the beginning that I must submit to him, and also that—that even if he did not find me desirable he would use me, because I was a woman and his wife, and he desires sons. That much I could not escape. But that he should be the first—and the last . . . That I must be taken without love and submit with loathing, and never, never know what it was to lie with a lover and rejoice in being a woman—It was this that I could not endure, and therefore, Heart's-heart, I planned that I would ask you, would beg of you if need be, to save me from it. Now you have done so, and I am content. No one can ever take these hours away from me, or spoil or defile them. And—who knows?—the gods may even add to their kindness and permit me to conceive from this night. I will pray to them that it may be so, and that my first-born will be yours. But even if that is not granted me, at least I have known love . . . and having known it I can endure the lust and the shame, and not mind it too much."

"You won't have to mind it at all!" said Ash violently. He pressed his fingers through her hair and pulled her head back so that he could kiss her: her eyes, her forehead, her temples, her cheeks and chin and mouth. He kissed them in turn and spoke between the kisses:

"My love . . . my foolish love. Do you really think I would let you go now? I might have done so before, but not now. In spite of everything, I couldn't now . . ."

He told her then how he had planned to ask her to run away with him and been forced to decide that he must not do so, because the danger was too great—for both of them, though for her most of all—but that the dust-storm had changed all that. It was the miracle that he had needed so badly and despaired of, since it gave them a way of escaping unsuspected—and without any fear of pursuit. They had horses with them, and if they set off as soon as the wind died down they should be able to cover a good many miles that night, and by sunrise be far beyond the reach of any search, for the confusion and havoc that the storm must have wrought in the camp would make it impossible to send out search parties to look for them before daylight. When they were not discovered it would be assumed that they had lost their lives in the storm, and were lying dead and buried in some sand drift among the hills; and the search for their bodies would soon be abandoned because the country for miles around would be changed by dust and blown sand, and too many gullies and hollows would be newly silted up with it.

"They'll give up after a day or two, and go on to Bhithor," said Ash. "They'll have to, because of the heat if nothing else. And we don't even have to worry about money, for we can sell my watch and your rubies—those earrings and the buttons on your coat. We can live on those for months. Probably for years. Somewhere where no one knows us: in Oudh, or among the foothills in the north, or in Kulu Valley. And I can find work, and then when they have forgotten all about us—"

Anjuli shook her head. "They would not. Me they might forget, for I am of little worth to anyone. But with you it is different. You might hide for a year, or for ten years; but when you showed your face again, either here in Hind, or in *Belait,* and tried to claim your inheritance, you would still be an officer in the army of the Raj who had run away without leave; and for that they would catch you and punish you. And then all would become known."

"Yes," said Ash slowly. "Yes; that's true." There was a note of surprise in his voice as though he had made a new and disconcerting discovery. In the intoxication of the past hours he had genuinely forgotten about the Guides.

"I could never go back. But—but we shall be together, and—"

He stopped, for Anjuli had laid a hand over his mouth.

"No, Ashok." Her voice was a pleading whisper. "Do not say any more. Please, please do not, because I cannot go with you . . . I cannot. I could not leave Shushila . . . I promised her that I would stay with her. I gave her my word, and I cannot go back on that . . ."

For a while Ash had not believed her. But when he tried to speak, her fingers pressed tighter against his mouth and her voice hurried on in the darkness, explaining, pleading. Each word a hammer blow. Shu-shu loved her and depended upon her, and had only agreed to marry the Rana on condition that she, Anjuli, stayed with her. She could not possibly abandon her little sister now and leave her to face the terrors of a new life alone. Ashok did not understand how frightened and homesick and unhappy Shu-shu was. How terrified of the prospect of marriage to a middle-aged stranger and of living among people whose ways would be different from hers, in surroundings that were so unlike those she had hitherto known and loved. Shu-shu was only a child still. A frightened and bewildered child—

"How could I ever be happy, knowing that I had deserted her?" whispered Anjuli. "She is my little sister, whom I love; and who loves and trusts me—and needs me, too . . . she has always needed me, ever since she was a baby. Shu-shu gave me love in the years when I had nothing else, and if I failed her now, when her need is greatest, I would feel guilty all my days and never be able to forgive myself; or to forget that I had run away and left her . . . broken my word and—and betrayed her—"

Ash caught her wrist and wrenched her hand away: "But *I* love you too. And *I* need you. Does that mean nothing to you? Do you care so much more for her than you do for me? Do you?"

"You know that I do not," said Anjuli on a sob. "I love you more than life. Beyond anyone and anything else. Beyond words—beyond shame! Have I not proved that to you tonight? But—but you are strong, Ashok. You will go on living and learn to put all this behind you and make yourself a good life without me; and one day—"

"Never. Never. *Never,*" broke in Ash vehemently.

"Yes, you will. And I too. Because—because we are both strong enough to do it. But Shu-shu is not; and if I am not there to give her courage when she is afraid, and to comfort her when she is ill or sad or wild with homesickness, she will die!"

"Be-wakufi!" said Ash roughly. "She's probably a lot stronger than you suppose, and though she may be a child in some ways, she's her mother's daughter in a good many others. Oh, Juli, my darling, my Heart's-love—I know she's your sister and you're fond of her, but underneath all that shyness and charm she's a spoilt, selfish and demanding brat who likes her own way; and you've allowed her to have it, and to tyrannize over you for far too long. It's high time you let her stand on her own feet and realized that she isn't your baby sister any more, but a grown girl who will be a wife within a month and a mother inside a year. She isn't going to let herself die. Don't you believe it."

Anjuli was silent for a moment or two, and then she said in a curiously flat and unemotional voice: "If Shu-shu were told that I had perished in the storm, and that she must go on alone to Bhithor, she would go mad with grief and fear, and there would be no one who could control her. Nandu is not here, and only he was able to do so before. I tell you I know her; and you do not. And though I love her, I am not blind to her faults—or to my own. I know that she is spoilt and selfish and self-willed; and Janoo-Rani's daughter. But I also know her to be gentle and loving and very trusting, and I will not bring her to her death. If I did, how could you love me?—knowing that I too was selfish and self-willed, as well as faithless? And cruel, too! For I should be all those things if I were willing to jeopardize my little sister's life and reason for the sake of my own happiness."

"And *my* happiness?" demanded Ash, his voice harsh with pain. "Does mine not matter?"

But it had been no good. Nothing that he could say had made any difference. He had used every argument and every plea he could think of, and at last he had taken her again, ravaging her with an animal violence that had bruised and hurt, yet was still sexually skilful enough to force a response from her that was half pain and half piercing rapture. But when it was over and they lay spent and breathless, she could still say: "I cannot betray her."

432

And he knew that Shushila had won, and that he was beaten. His arms fell away and he drew aside and lay on his back staring up into the darkness, and for a long time neither of them spoke.

The silence was so complete that he could hear the sound of his own breathing, and from somewhere in the outer cave the faint jingle of metal as one of the tethered horses moved restlessly. But it was not for an appreciable time that the significance of this dawned on him, and he realized that the wind had died, and that it must have done so some time ago, because he could not remember when he had last been aware of that vibrating drone. Not for at least an hour; and it was probably longer than that. In which case the sooner they made a start the better, for if they were going to return to the camp it would be wiser to do so under cover of darkness, and trust that in the general confusion their arrival would not be too public.

It was going to be bad enough, from Juli's point of view, to have been missing for several hours in the company of a single man. But the dust-storm would excuse that; and provided they returned as quickly as possible, scandal might be avoided by the mere fact that conditions had hardly been conducive to dalliance, and the camp itself likely to be in such a state of disarray that few people would have any time to waste on idle gossip and speculation. With luck, Juli would escape with no more than a scolding for riding too far ahead of her sister and uncle, and no one could ever suspect . . . A thought struck Ash with jarring suddenness, and he said sharply: "You can't go through with it, Juli. It's too dangerous. He's bound to know."

"Who will know?" Anjuli's voice was muffled, as though she had been crying. "Know what?"

"The Rana. He'll find out that you're not a virgin just as soon as he beds with you, and then there'll be the devil to pay. He isn't likely to forgive a thing like that, or take another man's leavings. He'll want to know who and when, and if you won't tell him he'll beat it out of you and send you back to your half-brother with your nose cut off, and without returning your dowry. And when your precious brother gets his hands on you, he'll either see to it that you die as painfully as possible, or he'll cut your feet off and let you live a cripple as a warning to other

433

women. And what use are you going to be then to Shushila? You can't do it, Juli. You've burnt your boats now, and you can't go back."

"I must and I can," said Anjuli huskily. "He will not know, because . . ." Her voice wavered and died, but she controlled herself with an effort: "Because there are . . . ways."

"What ways? You don't know what you are talking about. You couldn't possibly know——"

"Harlot's tricks? But I do"—he heard her swallow painfully. "You forget that I was brought up by servants in the Women's Quarters of a palace, and that a Rajah keeps many women besides his wives: concubines who know every art and trick that can please a man or fool him, and who talk freely of these things because they have little else to talk of, and because they think it only right that all women should be instructed in them . . ." The young voice paused for a moment, and then went on again, very steadily: "I do not like to tell you this, but had I not known that when the time came I could deceive the Rana, I would not have taken you for my lover."

The words fell like drops of ice water into the darkness, and as the little echoes reverberated softly round the cave they sent a thin cold trickle through Ash's heart, and he said harshly and with deliberate cruelty: "And I suppose you have thought too of what may happen to the child—my child—if you have one? Its legal father will be the Rana, and what if he chooses to bring it up to be another Nandu, or Lalji? Or appoints scorpions like Biju Ram to its service—perverts and panders who love to do evil? Have you thought of that?"

Anjuli said quietly: "It was the *Nautch*-girl and not my father who appointed Biju Ram to Lalji's household. And—and I believe that it is a child's mother who can, if she chooses, shape its early years and set its feet on a given path, for it is to her that it will look when it is small, and not to its father. If the gods grant me your child I will not fail him: that I swear to you. I will see to it that he shall grow up to be a prince that we can be proud of."

"Of what use will that be to me, when I shall never see or know him? When I may never even hear that he exists?" demanded Ash bitterly.

For a moment he thought that she was not going to answer him, and when she did it was in a whisper. "I am

434

sorry," said Anjuli. "I . . . I did not think—It was for myself, for my own comfort that . . . that I wished it. I have been selfish. . . ." Her breath caught on a sob, and then her voice steadied again: "But it is done now: and what may come of it is out of our hands."

"It is not! It is still in our hands. You can come away with me—for the child's sake, if not for mine. Promise me that if there should be a child you will come to me. Surely you can do that? I won't believe that Shu-shu means more to you than any child of mine could do, or that you would sacrifice its future for her sake. Promise me, Larla!"

Only the echoes answered him, for Anjuli did not speak. Yet her silence spoke for her, repeating, wordlessly, what she had told him before; that she had already given a promise to Shu-shu. And that a promise was sacred . . .

A tightness built up in Ash's throat but once again anger drove him to speech, and he forced words past the constriction and threw them viciously at that obdurate silence: "Can't you understand what it will be like for me to have to live—as I may do—with the knowledge that my child, *my child,* is the property of another man to do what he likes with? To sell in marriage one day to whoever he chooses—as you and your sisters were?"

"You . . . will have other children—" whispered Anjuli.

"Never!"

"—and I shall not know," continued Anjuli as though he had not spoken. "It may even be that you have some already, for I know that men are careless of their seed. They think nothing of lying with harlots and light women, and do not trouble their minds as to what may come of such matings. Can you tell me that you yourself have never, until this night, lain with any other woman . . . ?" She paused briefly, and when he did not reply said sadly: "No. I did not think I was the first. For all I know there may have been more than one; perhaps many. And if that is so, how can you be sure that there is not, somewhere, some child who could call you father? It is the custom for men to buy their pleasure, and when they have taken it and paid, to walk away and think no more of it. And though you say now that you will never marry—and you may not—I do not believe that it is in your nature to

435

become an ascetic. Sooner or later, in the years to come, you will lie with other women and—it may be—father other children without knowing it, or caring. But I, if I should conceive one, will know . . . and care. I shall carry it in my body for many months and suffer all the discomforts that come from that, and at the end risk death and endure much pain to give it life. If I pay that price, surely you could not begrudge it me? . . . You could not."

You could not, sobbed the echo. And he could not. For Juli was right. Men were careless with their seed, yet they reserved the right to pick and choose among the fruit of their matings: to ignore, repudiate or claim paternity as it suited them. It had never occurred to Ash before that he might have fathered a child, and now that it did he was horrified to realize that it was not only possible, but that he had not cared enough to take any precautions against it, presumably because he had always thought (if he had thought about it at all) that precautions were something for women to worry about and to deal with.

Yes, he supposed it was quite possible that there could be a child of his alive at this moment, living in 'Pindi Bazaar or some smoke-filled hut among the Border hills, or in the poorer quarters of London. And if that were so, and Juli were to bear one—braving the "pains and perils of child-birth" to do so—then what possible right had he to lay claim to it? Or even to insist that he would make a better father than the unknown Rana?

He tried to speak and found that he could not, because his mouth was drawn as though he had swallowed acid; and because there was nothing left to be said. The echoes had faded and the silence shut down again, and presently he became aware of movements in the darkness and knew that Juli was drawing on the tight-fitting riding trousers that he had stripped off—how long ago? It seemed, suddenly, a life-time away, and he felt cold and defeated and drained of all emotion. The air in the cave struck so cold that he shivered, and the sharp, absurd sound of his own teeth chattering reminded him that unless they found Julie's *achkan* and the remnants of his shirt, there would be no hope of avoiding an appalling scandal, because they would both be forced to ride back to camp half-naked. He retrieved his riding breeches and boots and stood up tiredly to put them on, and having buckled the belt about his waist and made sure that he had dropped nothing from his pockets, spoke curtly into the darkness:

"What did you do with your coat?"

"I don't know"—her weariness was as vivid to him as though it had been his own. "I had it over my head, and I must have dropped it when I heard you call."

"Well, you can't go back without it, that's certain," said Ash roughly. "We'll just have to walk round in circles until we find it. Give me your hand. There's no point in losing each other in the dark."

Her hand was cold and oddly impersonal. It did not clasp his, but remained entirely passive, and he held it as he would have held a stranger's: lightly and almost at arm's length, and solely as a means of keeping in touch in the inky darkness as they moved forward slowly, guiding themselves by the rock wall.

It took them nearly an hour to find the *achkan*. The shirt had been easier, as Ash had dropped it near the horses in the main cave, and now that the storm had passed, the entrance showed up as a grey, sharp-edged oblong that provided them with a landmark in the waste of blackness.

The depths of the cave had been cold, but the air outside was hot and still and heavy with the smell of dust, and the few stars that could be seen shone hazily, as though through a veil. The moon was either hidden by the hills or by dust clouds, and the valley was in shadow; but after the unrelieved darkness of the caves, both earth and sky seemed astonishingly light, and it was some time before Ash realized that this was not solely due to the fact that the storm had spread a pale-coloured shroud of dust and river sand over many miles of country, but because the dawn was near.

The discovery jolted him badly. He had never imagined for a moment that it could be as late as this, or that so many hours could have passed without his knowing it. He would have put it at two or three: four at most. Instead, it was almost a whole night, and his plan of smuggling Juli back into the camp under cover of darkness and confusion was useless, for by the time they reached it the sky would be light. No wonder there was no sign of the moon; it must have set hours ago. The stars were already fading and despite the dust there was a smell of morning in the air, that faint, indefinable smell that tells of a coming day as clearly as the growing light and the sound of a cock crowing.

"Hurry," said Ash peremptorily, and urged Baj Raj into a gallop. But less than a minute later Juli's mare stumbled and slowed to an uneven trot, and he was forced to stop and turn back.

"I think it is only a pebble," said Anjuli, dismounting to investigate. But it proved to be a piece of flint as sharp-edged as glass, and so deeply imbedded that lacking a knife and hampered by bad light, it had taken Ash the best part of ten minutes to remove it; and when he had done so the mare still limped, for the cut was a deep one.

"You'd better take Baj Raj and get back as fast as you can, and I'll come on later," decided Ash. "In fact it's probably a good idea in the circumstances for you to arrive back alone. You can pretend we got separated in the storm, and you spent the night alone in a cave and started back as soon as it began to get light. It will sound better that way. You can tell them you don't know where I am."

"When I am riding your horse? And you mine? They would never believe it!" said Anjuli scornfully: "Any more than they would believe that you would have permitted me to get lost."

Ash grunted and said: "No, I suppose not. It would take a lot of explaining and at the moment I can't think of a good enough story. Anyway, I suppose the fewer lies we tell the better."

"We do not need to tell any," said Anjuli curtly. "We will tell the truth."

"All of it?" inquired Ash dryly.

Anjuli did not answer, but remounted her horse in silence and they moved on again, this time at a walk. But although there was still very little light, and no sound but the creak of saddle-leather and the soft clop of hooves on thick dust, Ash knew that she was crying. Crying very quietly with her eyes wide open, as she used to do in the old days when she had been Kairi-Bai, and in trouble.

Poor little Kairi-Bai. Poor Juli . . . He had failed them both: forgetting the one, and now blaming the other because she had wanted to snatch a brief moment of glory out of the drabness and servitude that was her life,

438

and had laid plans to keep it secret; not for her sake, but for Shushila's—because if she were to be cast off by the Rana and sent back in disgrace to Nandu, what would happen to her frail, hysterical, selfish little sister? It was unjust to blame Juli. But the descent from the heights of love and rapture and extravagant hope had been too violent, and that ugly picture of serving-women and concubines instructing their juniors in sexual tricks had so sickened him that for a dreadful instant he had wondered if the physical ecstasy he had experienced had been artfully heightened by what she herself had termed "harlot's tricks," and if her own response had been real, or only simulated in order to add a sharper edge to his pleasure.

That suspicion had vanished as quickly as it had come. The intangible bond that linked them, and that made him aware at this moment that she was crying, could not have deceived him as they lay embraced, but something of the chill and the distaste still stayed with him. Enough, at least, to prevent him from further speech; though he had the grace to feel ashamed of himself for hurting her, and for keeping silent instead of apologizing and reaching out a hand to comfort her.

This was a sorry ending to an episode that she had risked a great deal for, and had hoped to treasure as a golden memory that would sustain her in the loveless years that lay ahead. He knew that if he let her go like this, without further words or even a touch of the hand, he would regret it until the end of his life. But at the moment he could not bring himself to do either, for his own disappointment was too bitter to be borne, and weariness and a crushing sense of failure pressed so heavily on him that he felt curiously numb and apathetic—as though he were a punch-drunk boxer, beaten to his knees on the canvas and vaguely aware of the necessity of getting to his feet before he was counted out, but unable to make any effort to do so. He would talk to Juli presently. Tell her he was sorry, and that he loved her and would always love her; even though she herself did not love him enough to desert Shushila for his sake . . . It was strange to think that although Janoo-Rani was dead she could still strike at both of them through her daughter, who was going to wreck their chance of happiness and ruin their lives . . .

The last star faded in a wash of pale light that crept

439

slowly upward from the horizon and drained the darkness from the plain, turning it from black to a pearly grey in which the scattered boulders and occasional bushes cast no shadow. They were clear of the hills now, and ahead of them, in the far distance, a tall outcrop of rock thrust up out of the wide amphitheatre of plain, cutting a dark silhouette against the prevailing greyness. It was the spot where they had left the *ruth* and its escort on the previous evening, and Ash recognized it with relief, for he had paid little attention to the countryside yesterday and was not entirely sure where they were. But that jagged pile was the one unmistakable landmark in a colourless, treeless land where the outlines of the encircling hills presented few distinctive features, and once they reached it, they should be able to find their way back to the camp easily enough. But the sky was already beginning to turn yellow in the east and it would not be long now, thought Ash grimly, before the day broke and displayed them both in the merciless sunlight, dirty and dishevelled and still a long way from the camp.

He turned to look at Anjuli, and saw that she was drooping with fatigue and paying no attention to where she was going, but sitting slack in the saddle and allowing the limping horse to choose its own path between the stones and the low scrub. Even in that dim light her coat showed sadly crumpled and her attempt to confine the tangled mass of her hair into a single heavy plait, using her fingers for a comb, had not been particularly successful. Her head was turned away from him in order to hide the fact that she was crying, but even if he had not already known it intuitively the growing light would have betrayed her, for it glinted wetly on the outline of her averted face.

Perhaps a similar perceptiveness had made her aware of his gaze, because as he watched her she straightened her shoulders, and lifting a hand as though to push back her hair, brushed away the tell-tale wetness in a gesture that appeared so unstudied that anyone else would have been deceived.

It did not deceive Ash, and he felt his heart contract with love. There had been so much gallantry in that small, seemingly casual action, and in the determined straightening of her back. She had not asked for pity, and she would hide her grief and face the future with courage, and without complaining.

There was good Rajput blood in Juli, and the fire and rashness inherent in it had been cooled and balanced by a strong Cossack strain that was a legacy from her grandfather, old Sergei Vodvichenko—that hard-headed, aristocratic Soldier-of-Fortune who had sold his sword to the highest bidder and won battles for Ranjit Singh and Holkar and Scindia of Gwalior, and bequeathed his gold-flecked eyes and his high cheek bones to his granddaughter Anjuli, Princess of Karidkote.

Rajput and Cossack . . . it was a strange amalgam, and an unlikely one. But it had produced Juli, who was loving, faithful and passionate, and who possessed, in addition to courage, that particular brand of quiet fortitude that is rarer and far better than courage—together with the strength to keep a promise, once given, even if it meant the sacrifice of her own happiness.

Ash had once made her a promise and forgotten it. Though there was some excuse for that; he had, after all, been barely eleven at the time. Yet he was uncomfortably certain that had their positions been reversed and she had made him a similar promise, she would neither have forgotten it nor broken it. Juli, like Wally, took a disconcertingly literal view of such things; and it occurred to Ash that in some ways they were remarkably alike.

His mouth twisted in a wry grimace of self-contempt, and he reached out a hand to her. But he had left it too late, for even as he did so she reined in and pointed at something that moved in the half-light, separating itself from the shadowy bulk of the rocky outcrop ahead of them. An object that lurched away across the plain looking like a prehistoric animal with a double hump. It was the *ruth*.

"Look!" cried Anjuli. "It is Shu-shu. So they did not get back either."

But it was not Shu-shu. It was only Kaka-ji and the driver of the *ruth*.

Ash stood up in his stirrups and shouted out to them, and then spurred forward, leaving Anjuli to follow slowly in his wake coughing in the white clouds of dust that had been churned up by Baj Raj's galloping hooves. By the time she came up with them, Kaka-ji had told his own

441

story and heard something of theirs, and there had been no need for Ash to make any suggestions, for one look at Anjuli had been enough for the old man.

"*Arré-bap!*" exclaimed Kaka-ji, startled. "Get inside the *ruth* at once, my child." He hurried to help her dismount, and then turning to peer at Ash, took in for the first time the enormity of that tattered shirt.

"It will be better," decided Kaka-ji, looking from one dishevelled figure to the other, "if we let it be supposed that we have all been together this past night. No"
—he raised a peremptory hand to forestall any argument, and having bundled his niece into the *ruth,* turned to address the driver: "Budoo, should anyone inquire, you will say that the Sahib returned with the Rajkumari only a moment or two after the dust overtook us, and that she took refuge in the *ruth* while we three men together lay beneath it. That is an order. And if I hear that there has been any talk to the contrary, I shall know who has spoken—and whom to punish. Is it understood?"

"*Hukum hai,* Rao-Sahib," murmured the driver placidly, lifting a curved palm to his forehead in salute. He was an elderly man who had been promoted to his present employment after the original driver had drowned in the river, and having been in the service of the family for many years, he could be trusted to obey an order and keep his mouth shut.

"And you, Sahib," said Kaka-ji authoritively, turning back to Ash, "you will take off those rags and wear my shirt in their stead. There are shawls in the *ruth* that will serve to cover me, but it is not fit that you should ride into the camp half-naked. The less talk we occasion the better, so do not argue with me."

Ash had no intention of arguing, and the transfer having been accomplished, Kaka-ji joined his niece in the *ruth* and ordered the driver to proceed. The bullocks ceased chewing the cud and trotted obediently forward, while Ash took the mare on a leading-rein and followed behind, keeping well to one side and out of the dust; and as he listened to the rise and fall of Kaka-ji's voice re-telling the events of the past night to Juli, he realized that they were doubly fortunate, in that the old man was far more interested in his own experiences than in theirs.

Kaka-ji had accepted a brief and colourless account of their adventures without question, and embarked with

442

enthusiasm on a description of his own trials, which had lost nothing in the telling. It seemed that neither he nor Mulraj, nor Shushila either, had noticed the approaching storm for some time; and when they did, it was only because Mulraj, like Ash, had happened to glance over his shoulder and seen that the sky behind them had become a dingy brown. The escort and the driver of the *ruth* were equally ignorant, for they were squatting in a shallow cleft among the rocks smoking and gossiping, facing an unclouded sky and well shielded from the wind and all view of the eastern horizon. At that time the storm was still some way off, but anyone could see that it was racing towards them with such alarming swiftness that if they hoped to get back to the camp before it struck, there was no time to be lost—and certainly no time to go chasing after the other two members of the riding party.

Kaka-ji had not actually said so in so many words, but it was perfectly clear to Ash that when the chips were down there was only one bride whose safety and well-being were vital to both Karidkote and Bhithor: young, lovely Shu-shu, whose beauty would compensate the Rana (together with that substantial bribe) for having to wed her plain, part-foreign half-sister as well. Neither Nandu nor the Rana was likely to lose much sleep over the loss of Kairi-Bai, but the loss of Shushila would spell disaster for them all, because even if Kairi-Bai survived, the Rana would never accept her in her sister's stead.

There would be no marriage, and the enormous sums that Nandu had spent on gifts and bribes and baksheesh, on clothes and jewels for his sisters' trousseaux and on the absurdly extravagant escort that he had sent to accompany them south would all have been wasted, and he would be mad with rage. Many heads would fall and both Mulraj and Kaka-ji knew it—and knew also that theirs would be among the first. With that ominous brown stain reaching up into the sky and spreading outward to span the horizon, there had been no time to waste in worrying over the whereabouts of Kairi-Bai and Pelham-Sahib, who would have to look after themselves. The important thing was to get Shushila back to the camp before the storm overtook them, for though she might just as easily come to harm in her own tent as out here among the rocks, at least if she did they would not be called upon to explain what she was doing there.

Mulraj had eyed the dust-cloud and made a swift calculation, and sacrificing convention and the proprieties, had taken Shushila up behind him and set off at full gallop, leaving Kaka-ji to follow with her riderless horse. The escort, still in ignorance of the approaching storm and seeing Mulraj racing towards them with the Rajkumari clinging to his waist like a monkey, had leapt up, expecting him to stop, and when he flashed past them, heading for the camp, they had barely waited for Kaka-ji's explanations before riding in pursuit, taking the waiting-woman with them.

Kaka-ji had not accompanied them. He had made them take Shushila's horse and his own, and had elected to stay behind with the *ruth*, whose driver, realizing that it could not possibly reach the camp ahead of the storm, was making hurried preparations to shelter his bullocks in a cleft among the rocks. "We will wait here for my niece and the Sahib, who will shortly return and be dismayed if they find us all gone," said Kaka-ji, peering anxiously in the direction of the hills. "It is not fitting that the Rajkumari should be seen to return alone on horseback, accompanied only by the Sahib, and they cannot be long."

But the minutes had passed and there was still no sign of the missing riders. Old Budoo, the driver, had backed the *ruth* as far as it would go between the rocks, and unyoking his bullocks had edged them past and tethered them in the cramped space behind it, after which he pulled out the rugs, shawls and bolsters that had cushioned the Rajkumaries and their women against jolting, and fastened them to form a rough-and-ready screen against the dust and sand that was roaring down on them. The smell of it was already in the air and now they could hear it; but still Kaka-ji waited, hoping to see horses galloping towards him. It was only when the bow-wave of dust struck the far side of the hillock of rock where they refuged that he allowed Budoo to drag him into the *ruth*; and there, deafened and half stifled, the two old men had crouched together while the storm raged outside.

Kaka-ji's account of his own sufferings was vivid in the extreme, and he had enjoyed telling it. But he too was uncertain how long the storm had lasted, and when it had passed and all was quiet again, he and Budoo had both fallen asleep and had not woken until the sky was beginning to pale. They had intended, he said, to set out in search of his niece and the Sahib, for whose safety he entertained the gravest fears, imagining that they would have been caught out in the open with no form of shelter; but they had barely started when they had heard the Sahib shouting aloud.

He had seen no reason to doubt Ash's story and he had not thought to question his niece, for having experienced all the discomforts of the storm himself, he was convinced that nothing of an improper nature could possibly have occurred between them. Not even the lustiest of men and the most ardent of young women would be likely to think of such things—let alone put them into practice—while fighting for breath with a cloth over the head, and eyes, mouth and nostrils full of grit. In Kaka-ji's opinion, a dust-storm was a more efficient guarantee of proper behaviour than a dozen duennas, though this did not prevent him from impressing on Anjuli that she must on no account let anyone suspect that she had not spent the night in the *ruth*. Not even Shu-shu.

"For you are shortly to be wedded," said Kaka-ji, "and it is most unseemly for a bride to go apart with any man, even if he be a Sahib. There are too many loose-tongued people who delight in slander, and if evil things were to be whispered about you, both the Rana and your brother would be gravely displeased. Therefore you will say only that you reached the *ruth* just as the storm struck, and stayed in it all night. And I and the Sahib and old Budoo will say the same."

Anjuli could only nod wordlessly. She was too tired to speak—too tired to feel grateful for the way in which fate had played into her hands by letting her get caught in the storm with Ashok and then sending her uncle to save them both from scandal. Too tired even to think . . .

It was much lighter now, and presently, as the sun rose and a bright golden ray pierced between the embroidered curtains and lit up the dusty interior of the *ruth*, she fell asleep, and was still sleeping when they arrived at the camp.

Roused by Kaka-ji with the reassuring news that Shu-shila was safe, she stumbled out into the arms of Geeta and was instantly hurried off to bed.

25

The arrival of the *ruth* had created a small stir, but no more than that. For Ash had guessed right: the camp had been too badly hit for anyone to waste much thought on a single unusual incident when more than a hundred startling ones clamoured for attention.

Even the sudden and melodramatic return on the previous evening of Mulraj and the youngest bride had passed virtually unnoticed, for by then the whole camp was in a ferment and taking frantic measures to withstand the storm. Tent-pegs were being hammered home and guy-ropes tightened, and everything that was liable to be blown away was being battened down or otherwise secured. Syces, bullock-drivers and herdsmen were seeing to the safety of their animals, while the elephants had been hurried across the river and shackled to the stout trunks of a grove of palm trees in case they should grub up their pickets in panic and run amok through the camp.

Few people had leisure to spare even a glance for Mulraj and Shushila, galloping between the embattled tents only minutes before the storm whirled down upon the camp. And while it raged they could only crouch down under cover, with their mouths and noses bandaged against the dust, or struggle grimly to prevent their tents and carts and make-shift shelters from blowing away or being overturned.

When at last it was over, the havoc it had caused was so great that there was no time to think of anything but how to repair the damage, and the arrival of the brides' *ruth* shortly after sunrise, bearing the Rajkumari Anjuli and her uncle (who had been caught by the storm while out on the plain), had been greeted with relief, but aroused little curiosity. There were, as Ash had surmised, too many other things to think of, and his own arrival, jogging in slowly with the limping mare on a leading rein, had been unspectacular enough to attract no interest except among his own servants.

446

His tent was still standing, but unlike Anjuli, he had no sleep that day, because the damage to the camp was even worse than he had expected and it was clear that he and Mulraj, and every able-bodied man and woman in the place, were going to have their work cut out to repair it.

Considering the enormous number of men and animals in the bridal retinue, it was a matter for congratulation that only three people had lost their lives in the storm, and of the hundred or so who had been injured, most had received only minor cuts and bruises. The animals had suffered far more severely, for the majority had panicked in the choking dust, and the toll of broken necks and broken bones, and runaways who might or might not be recovered, was high.

Inspecting the incredible profusion of assorted debris, the snapped tent poles, torn canvas and tangled guy-ropes, and the endless drifts of dust and sand that had silted up against the sides of everything that had withstood the gale, Ash could only be grateful for the river, which although it had helped to deluge them with sand, would at least ensure that there was no shortage of water. To have had to contend with that on top of everything else, and in this heat, would have been the last straw. He gave thanks for small mercies, and went off to find Mulraj and discuss ways and means of making good the damage.

A large number of tents had been bodily uprooted or else blown flat on their cowering occupants, but the palace guard had had the sense to dismantle the big durbar tent and use its canvas to reinforce the smaller ones in which Shushila and her women slept. They, and Jhoti with them, had in consequence suffered less discomfort than anyone else, and had never been in any real danger. But as they did not know this, they made the most of their experiences, with the result that Anjuli, who had expected to face a barrage of questions, found to her relief that they were all far more interested in telling her everything that had happened to them, and there had been no need for her to tell lies. Or, indeed, to say anything at all, for all that had been required of her was to listen.

"You were lucky to have been out of it and safe in the *ruth*," Shu-shu told her, voicing the opinion of everyone present except Jhoti, who commiserated with her for missing the fun.

"You've no idea how exciting it was, Kairi!" declared Jhoti. "The tent flapped and flapped and the dust came pouring up under it, and I made Shu-shu get under my *charpoy* (bedstead), and covered it with shawls because she howled and cried and said that the roof would fall on us and we should all be smothered. Such a fuss."

"I did not *howl!*" protested Shu-shu angrily.

"Yes, you did—like a jackal. Like six jackals!"

"I did not!"

"You *did!*" . . . The conversation relapsed into bickering, and neither then nor at any other time did anyone bother to ask Anjuli where she had been when the storm broke, and how or when she had managed to get back to Kaka-ji and the *ruth*.

There were to be no more evening rides, or any further meetings in the durbar tent. Both Ash and Mulraj were too busy to spare any time for social gatherings, and as Jhoti followed them about the camp all day, chattering incessantly and convinced that he was giving valuable assistance, he was tired enough by nightfall to welcome the prospect of early bed, which left only Kaka-ji, who continued to drop in for a chat with his nieces, but found it dull without the others, and did not stay long.

As though in apology for that unseasonable storm, the weather improved out of all knowledge. The day-time temperatures fell below ninety, while the nights were once again cool. But no one was prepared to risk getting caught by another dust-storm, and men toiled like galley slaves to repair the damage and get the camp ready to move again. And not only for fear of a second storm, for by now the vast majority were tired of this nomadic existence and only too anxious to stay in one place for a time, and to enjoy the fleshpots of Bhithor and all the festivities that would attend the wedding.

Most of the errant livestock had been rounded up, fresh fodder had been procured and food supplies, though still low, were adequate, Ash having ranged far afield to supplement the meagre amounts that the near-by villages, also hard hit by the storm, had been able to spare them. The camp rang with the sound of hammers and saws as tent poles and vehicles were repaired, but with the best will in the world it was obviously going to be at least a week before the order to march could be given.

It had, in fact, taken a little more than that, eight

days, to be precise, and in all that time Ash had not had a glimpse of Juli, or of Shushila either. He had been too busy. But Kaka-ji and Jhoti gave him scraps of news about them, and he told himself that as soon as the camp was on the move again he would make a point of seeing them, if only to make his peace with Juli. That was something he could do no matter how many other people were present; there were words and ways that she would understand, and he could not endure the thought of parting from her without her knowing that he was sorry for being unkind to her, and that he would love her all his life. It was unthinkable to let her go without another word and with the bitter memory of his churlishness unerased, though had it not been for that, he would have avoided seeing her again, since to do so would only be driving a knife further into his own heart. And into hers also.

Ash had imagined that an opportunity to pay a call at the durbar tent would soon present itself, but there had been no suggestion that he should go there, and when he mentioned the matter to Kaka-ji, the old man had shrugged it aside and said that there was no need to trouble himself. "You would find it very dull. My nieces are busy preparing for their arrival in Bhithor, and can talk of nothing now but what saris and which jewels they will wear."

That did not sound like Juli, and Ash had been unable to resist saying so. Kaka-ji had agreed, but said with a chuckle that although it was Shu-shu who was exercised in her mind over the question of dress, he suspected Kairi of fostering it as a means of keeping her sister's mind off other matters. "And she is quite right," approved Kaka-ji. "Anything that will distract Shu-shu's attention and keep her from tears and bewailing is a good thing for us all."

Jhoti had echoed his uncle's opinion (though in cruder words as he had little sympathy with "all this silly fussing about what to wear") while Mulraj had hinted that it might be better, now that they were so near Bhithor, for both the Sahib and himself to keep their distance from the durbar tent, as the Rana was known to be a stickler for etiquette.

Indirect methods having failed, Ash sent to ask when he might call upon the Rajkumaries, and received a

449

flowery but evasive reply, intimating that Shushila-Bai did not feel strong enough at the moment to entertain visitors, and would therefore have to postpone the honour of receiving him until a later day. The refusal had been sweetened with a great many compliments; but it remained a refusal. Did Juli too, like Mulraj, consider it advisable for her sister and herself to retire into strict purdah now that they were almost within reach of their future husband's territory? Or did she really intend not to see him again? Either way it would mean that he would now never be able to put things right between them, and that the memory of the manner in which they had parted would be an unhealed wound all his days: a punishment —and a just one.

But he had misjudged Anjuli. It was not in her nature to be unforgiving, and she had not blamed him for that sudden repulsion. She had understood the reason for it as clearly as though he had spoken his thoughts aloud, and she knew him too well to imagine that it would last, or that he would not regret it; and perhaps wonder, too, if she blamed him. Well, there was still a way of telling him that she did not. A very simple one.

One evening, at the end of a long, tiring day in the saddle, a basket of oranges had been handed to Ash by one of the royal servants who explained that it was a gift from the Rajkumari Anjuli-Bai. The Rajkumari regretted that her sister's health prevented them from receiving the Sahib, but trusted that the Sahib himself would remain in excellent health, and that he would enjoy the fruit. Ash looked down at the oranges, and suddenly his heart was thudding violently and for a dizzy moment it was all he could do not to snatch the basket from the man's hands, and search it there and then for the message he was sure it would contain. But he managed to control himself, and having rewarded the bearer, carried the basket into his tent, and spilling the oranges onto his bed, found nothing.

But something must be there, otherwise why should Juli, of all people, have bothered to send him a conventional gift of fruit? It was not in character, and the polite verbal message that accompanied it had certainly not contained a hidden meaning. Ash picked up the oranges and examined them one by one. The skin of the fifth bore a small mark, as though a sharp knife had cut into it, and

450

he broke it open and was immediately lifted out of despair. The malaise of the past days, the pain of guilt and self-loathing and the ache of loss were suddenly eased as he looked down at Juli's message, and felt hope return to him and the tiredness and strain fall away and be forgotten.

She had not written to him. There had been no need to, for she had sent him something that said more than the longest letter could have done. The half of the little mother-of-pearl fish that she had given him once before on the night that he had escaped from Gulkote.

Ash stood for a long time looking at it; not seeing it, because he was reliving that night. Remembering the silence and the fear and the whispering, urgent voices: seeing again the moonlight shimmering on the snow peaks of the Dur Khaima and flooding the Queen's balcony with a cold radiance that glinted on the pearl in Hira Lal's ear and turned to silver a little slip of carved shell that was Juli's most precious possession.

She had given it to him because he was her bracelet-brother, and to bring him luck; and because she loved him. And he had broken it in two and told her that they would each keep half, and that one day, when he came back, they would mend it and make it whole again. And now she sent him back his half, knowing that he would understand what she meant . . . that they themselves were still two halves of a whole, and that while they lived there would always be the hope that perhaps one day, far in the future and when their actions had ceased to be of any importance to anyone else, they might even be able to come together again. It was a tenuous hope at best; but to have any at all was like coming upon a spring of fresh water after wandering for days in a burning desert. And even if it were never realized, the piece of pearl-shell was in itself a tangible proof that Juli still loved him, and that she had forgiven him everything.

Ash touched it as gently as though it were a sentient thing, and saw it through a haze of tears. And it was only when his sight cleared that he realized that Juli had not sent him back the piece that he had originally possessed, but her own. The half that she had worn for so many years above her heart in the warm hollow between her breasts, and that still held the scent of her skin: a faint, faint

451

fragrance of dried rose-petals. It was an additional message from her, as loving and as intimate as a kiss, and he held it to his cheek and was immeasurably comforted.

A discreet cough announced the return of Gul Baz and a *khidmatgar* with his evening meal, and Ash put the broken luck-charm in his pocket, hurriedly replaced the oranges, and went out to eat with a better appetite than he had shown for some time past.

Unless wind or weather prohibited it, he preferred to eat out of doors rather than in his tent, and this evening the table had been laid under a *kikar* tree whose yellow, mimosa-like blossoms diffused a dusty incense on the warm air and a film of pollen over table-cloth and dishes and Ash's dark head. The sky was still tinged with the sunset, but by the time the meal had been cleared away and the coffee drunk, it was full of stars; and Ash sat out under them, smoking a cigarette and thinking of Juli, and making a promise to her—and to himself. That he would never marry anyone else, and that even if he never saw her again he would always think of her as his wife, and in the words of the marriage service, "Cleave only unto her as long as ye both shall live."

A lamp glowed in the tent behind him and he could hear Gul Baz moving about, laying out his night shirt; and struck by a sudden thought, he called out to him to ask Mahdoo for the small japanned tin box that ever since the theft of his rifle had been in the old man's charge. Mahdoo himself brought it and stayed awhile to smoke and talk, and when he had gone Ash carried it into the tent and put it on the table, and took the luck-charm out of his pocket.

The strand of silk that it had hung from had been removed in order to insert it into the orange, and he would have to find another, as even the finest chain would probably end by breaking the shell. There was nothing in the tent that would serve and he would ask Gul Baz to find him something tomorrow, and in the meantime lock away Juli's half of the charm in the same place where his own had stayed, safe and out of mind, for so many years.

He removed the cheap brass key from his watch-chain and unlocked the box, and was surprised when the lid flew up as though it had been held by a spring. But there had not really been enough room for that piece of blood-stained material that he had crammed into it days ago; and he remembered now that he had had to force the lid to shut—though until this moment he had not spared another thought for the torn strip of cloth that he had hidden away from prying eyes and had meant to destroy.

At the time, the tin box had been the nearest thing to hand that was safe from inspection by Gul Baz, who had charge of all the other keys, so he had stuffed that ill-omened bandage into it and locked it, intending to take the thing out again at the first opportunity and burn it or bury it, or merely throw it away in open country. But then he had given the box to Mahdoo, together with his money and firearms and the spare ammunition, and forgotten all about it.

He took it out now and looked at it with a grimace of distaste, wondering again whom it had belonged to and what to do with it. He still could not burn it without the risk of bringing one of his servants at a run, imagining that his tent had caught fire. Nor could he drop it on the floor to be thrown away, for the sight of it would only remind Gul Baz of an episode that had best be forgotten. Probably the best course would be to take a short walk and discard it somewhere in the darkness beyond the range of the camp fires.

He crumpled it into a ball and was about to push it into his pocket, when he became aware of something that he remembered noticing, subconsciously, before. Something small and hard was attached to it, presumably a button or possibly a lead weight such as Indian tailors sometimes use to make a seam fall straight.

Apart from a cursory inspection Ash had never really examined that bit of torn material, for once having decided that it was a piece of evidence that he did not wish anyone else to see, he had been in too great a hurry to hide it before one of his servants, or Mulraj, should realize what it was and start asking questions that he did not want answered. Now for the first time he spread it out and looked at it more carefully.

The whole thing was blotched and stiff with blood, for that cut on his forehead had bled freely. But here and there between the stains it was possible to see that the grey, shadow-patterned material was a hand-woven mixture of silk and cotton that must have been expensive. The

453

stuff was thin and unlined (the weather had been very hot) and it was the stitching and not the cloth that had parted; the entire left-hand front of the coat having come away along the seams, leaving collar and sleeve behind. There was a line of gaping button-holes and a single small breast-pocket on the inner side, rather oddly placed in that it was low down and below the armhole. The pocket had a double flap that prevented anything placed in it from falling out, and Ash, investigating, found that it had also been sewn up: presumably to ensure the safety of the small, hard object it contained.

Probably a jewel, thought Ash—a valuable one, if its owner had gone to the trouble of having his coats made with a special pocket in order to carry it about with him.

The stitches were caked with dried blood and as he picked at the thread he grinned to himself, picturing the would-be murderer's consternation on discovering his loss. All in all, an expensive evening for the gentleman in the grey coat, and it was to be hoped that it had taught him a salutary lesson. This, of course, explained that curious burglary and the meticulous manner in which his tent had been searched. He had been puzzled by that at the time, for it was obvious that the thief had been looking for something much smaller than a shot-gun or a box of cartridges, or even a bag of rupees. And but for the fact that only a few hours earlier the japanned tin box had been one of the things handed to Mahdoo for safe keeping, he would have found it.

"What I should have done," thought Ash, giving up the attempt to break the stitches and looking around for a pair of nail-scissors, "was to go back as soon as it was light and hide in the grass where I was ambushed. I bet that bastard went scuttling back as soon as he realized what he'd lost, and crawled over every inch of it—and serve him right: a nice piece of poetic justice if ever there was one." But then at the time it had not occurred to him to go back for he did not know that his assailant had lost anything of value; and even if he had known, he would have been too late, because he had not woken until well into the afternoon. So much for hindsight.

Ash found the scissors, and without bothering to unpick the stitches, cut through the centre of the pocket.

The trinket that it had contained fell out and rolled over the edge of the table onto the floor, where it lay in a pool of light thrown by the hurricane lamp that hung from a hook on the tent pole. A single pear-shaped jewel with the subtle, smoky iridescence of a pigeon's feather . . .

It was Hira Lal's earring.

Ash's body emptied itself of breath and he stood rigid, staring down at it for a full three minutes before he bent stiffly and picked it up.

It was incredible that after all these years he should actually have thought of this thing only an hour or so ago, and seen it clearly in his mind's eye. The fabulous black pearl that had so infuriated Biju Ram, who suspected—rightly—that it was worn in deliberate parody of the single earring that he himself wore, and that its rarity made his own diamond look flashy and meretricious by contrast.

The pearl glowed in the lamp-light as though it was alive, and looking at it Ash knew beyond any shadow of doubt who had killed Hira Lal. And who had ordered it.

Biju Ram would certainly have accompanied Lalji on that fateful visit to Calcutta, and Biju Ram had hated Hira Lal and envied his possession of the black pearl. The murder itself would have been the brain-child of Janoo-Rani, who had probably planned it down to the last detail before the travellers even set out, so that Biju Ram would only have had to wait until they were in tiger country—preferably in an area where there was known to be a man-eater—before putting it into operation. But Janoo should have known that he would never be able to resist keeping that priceless bauble, even though its retention would brand him a murderer and he would never dare wear it. Its beauty, as well as its rarity and value, had obviously overweighed those considerations and made it seem worth any risk, and Biju Ram must have carried it about with him ever since.

There must still be any number of people who even now would recognize that pearl on sight, as Ash had done, because no one who had seen it was likely to have seen another. It was doubtful if a pair to it could have been found in all India, and only greed—or hate?—could have made Biju Ram keep such a damning piece of evidence

455

against himself. No wonder he had torn Ash's tent apart trying to find it. The thing was as dangerous as a *krait*, the little brown snake whose bite is swift death.

Ash weighed it thoughtfully in his hand and wondered why on earth he had not instantly known the identity of the man he had grappled with in the dark. Looking back on it there were so many things that should have made it perfectly clear, like size and shape—and smell. Biju Ram had always used scent, and the man who had ambushed him had smelled of orris-root. But at that time he had been far too angry to be conscious of anything except the desire to kill, and it was only now that he recalled the reek of orris-root, and realized, too, that Biju Ram no longer wore the vivid colours that he had been addicted to in the old days, but in conscious (or unconscious?) imitation of his dead rival, had taken to wearing grey. And only grey.

The blood-stained rag on the table smelt unpleasantly —though not of orris-root—and Ash tossed it out of the tent door and did not care who saw it or how many questions it evoked, because he knew now that it had nothing whatever to do with Juli. She had never come into it at all, and if he had not had a guilty conscience on her behalf he would have seen the real reason for that murderous attack long ago, and not wasted time concealing clues from his friends and hiding his own head in the sand for fear that any investigation must involve her.

The motive had been a very simple one. He had merely been looking at things the wrong way round, and it had taken the sight of Hira Lal's earring to set his brain working clearly. Now, suddenly, it was as though he had been presented with a mirror, and facing it, could make sense at last of something that had hitherto confused him because it had been written backwards ...

Biju Ram had no interest at all in Anjuli-Bai, nor had he recognized, in Pelham-Sahib, the little boy who had once been the butt of his cruel jokes. He had meant to kill Ash for precisely the same reason that Janoo-Rani had meant to kill Ashok—because he had interfered, and was interfering, with a plot to assassinate the heir. It was as simple as that—and he had not seen it because he had been blinded by a preconceived idea.

Knowing that Biju Ram had been in the late Rani's pay for many years, and that it was she herself who had appointed him a member of Jhoti's personal suite, Ash had persisted in thinking of him as the *Nautch*-girl's creature—and Jhoti was the *Nautch*-girl's son. So, if it came to that, was Nandu. But then, if rumour was true, Nandu had murdered his mother and later (this at least was true, for there were a number of witnesses to prove it) he had quarrelled violently with Biju Ram. The enmity between them had reached such proportions that when Nandu had refused to allow his young brother to accompany the bridal party to Bhithor, Biju Ram had taken it upon himself to incite Jhoti to defy the order and escape, and had then metaphorically burned his boats by personally accompanying the runaway.

Taking all these events into consideration (and bearing in mind that Biju Ram was, in truth, about as trustworthy as a scorpion) Ash had decided that his old enemy was involved in a plot to have Nandu either murdered or deposed and replaced by Jhoti—who on account of his age would for some years be only a puppet ruler, and therefore could be used by the plotters to further their own ends and feather their own nests. It had seemed a reasonable assumption, since it fitted in with all the known facts—except one that Ash, from his knowledge of Biju Ram, should not have missed: that Biju Ram had always known on which side his bread was buttered, and that the moment it became clear that Nandu, and not the *Nautch*-girl, was going to be the real power in the state, he would have lost no time in changing his allegiance.

Looked at in this light, the pattern altered like the design in a kaleidoscope when the tube is twisted. The same pieces were there, but in a different order, and Ash saw now why there had had to be a loud and public quarrel, and why Jhoti had been refused permission to leave Karidkote and then allowed to escape. And why no one had been sent after him to fetch him back.

"I should have seen it before," thought Ash bitterly, which was true enough, for the reasons were perfectly clear and would have been all along if only he had taken the trouble to question the evidence instead of accepting it at its face value. It was no consolation to realize that others had been equally gulled, for he, of all people, should have known better—and if this was what falling in love did to one, then perhaps there was something to be said after all for the official view, so in-

457

furiatingly expressed by his Commanding Officer and Major Harlowe when he had wanted to marry Belinda, that any junior officer who allowed himself to "lose his head over a petticoat" was no use to the army and had better retire from active service and grow turnips.

Ash sat down on the end of his camp bed and looked at the evidence from another angle—something he should have done long ago . . .

Nandu regarded his brother as a rival and a possible focus for discontent, and therefore intended to get rid of him. But there had already been too much unpleasant speculation concerning the death of Janoo-Rani, and if Jhoti were also to die suddenly, the British resident, who had shown a tendency to ask disagreeable questions after Janoo's death, would almost certainly ask a good many more; and then who knew what trouble might be stirred up? Better by far that Jhoti should leave Karidkote and meet with a fatal accident somewhere well beyond its borders; and just to underline Nandu's innocence and provide an additional artistic touch that should serve to disarm even the most suspicious, the boy must be shown to have left against his brother's wishes, and in circumstances that would prevent Nandu from hearing of his "escape" in time to prevent it, or let it seem worth while sending after him to bring him back. Hence that convenient hunting party.

It had been a good plan, based on a sound knowledge of Jhoti's character and the assumption that no one was going to believe that a man who helped him to escape to his sister's camp, and accompanied him on the venture, could be anything but a sympathizer and a partisan. That last provided an alibi for Biju Ram, who would appear as an ally of the Heir Apparent (and by inference no friend of the Maharajah's), which would serve to clear him of all suspicion when the heir met with a fatal accident.

The details of the plan had obviously been thought out carefully, and Biju Ram would have had helpers—two at least, and possibly three. Ash thought it unlikely that there would have been more than that, for to involve too many would mean increasing the risk of discovery. Mohan and Pran Krishna, and perhaps Sen Gupta, he decided, making a mental selection from among the members of Jhoti's suite. The first two certainly, the latter probably.

And the personal servants of all three would be open to bribery and therefore equally suspect.

Pran Krishna was a particular crony of Biju Ram's, and had always made a great show of admiring and sympathizing with their young master. He was also a superlative horseman, and had been a member of the hawking party on the day that Jhoti's saddle had been tampered with. He if anyone would have known how to play that trick; and had it succeeded he would have stood a good chance of being able to recover the evidence before anyone else thought to examine the saddle, for with Jhoti dead there would have been a good deal of confusion, and attention would have been centred on the boy and not the horse.

Ash remembered the conversation he had overheard on that afternoon, and realized now that far from dissuading Jhoti from going off to ride alone, Biju Ram had actually been using his knowledge of the child's character to goad him into doing so. And if Jhoti had not come back it would have been Biju Ram who would have raised the alarm and made a great to-do over it. He and Pran Krishna, with everyone else, would have galloped off to search for the boy, and had Jhoti been found dead, Biju Ram would have displayed extravagant grief and blamed the syce, while Pran Krishna disposed of the evidence under pretence of examining the saddle.

Few plans, however, are wholly water-tight, and this one was no exception; for though Jhoti could hardly avoid being thrown, he might only be injured and not killed. But that, too, had almost certainly been taken into account, and if his injuries alone had not been fatal, he could easily have been assisted to succumb to them by a surreptitious overdose of opium, or some similar draught that would have produced coma and death—something that, in the circumstances, was only to be expected and would therefore have aroused no suspicion. One way or another it stood a good chance of success—and then Ash had ruined everything by seeing the boy ride off alone, and not only deciding to follow him, but telling Mulraj, who had gone too. No wonder Biju Ram had been angry enough to turn his attentions to removing this meddler.

Both Nandu and Biju Ram must have known from the beginning that a British officer would be accompanying the camp to Bhithor, and they had probably considered it an excellent arrangement, because the presence of a Sahib would be a guarantee that any unfortunate accident that befell the Heir Apparent would be accepted by the authorities as just that and no more. And as their experience of Sahibs was small, they had probably expected some young and gullible junior officer with a limited knowledge of the languages and customs of the country, who would be easy to hoodwink.

But Pelham-Sahib had not resembled this comfortable picture, and to make matters worse he had interfered with a very well-laid plan, and followed it up by making friends with the intended victim and showing far too much interest in the boy's welfare. At this rate he might well develop into a serious stumbling block, and Biju Ram must have decided early on that it would be advisable to get rid of him, but only safe to do so when the camp had left British India and was in a part of the country where there were no towns large enough to warrant the presence of a British official, or anyone who might inquire too closely—or too soon—into an accident that involved the death of a Sahib. For it would, of course, be an accident.

Biju Ram had probably thought of several that might serve, and whenever the camp was in suitable territory had kept watch on this meddling *Angrezi,* in the hope of being presented with the right opportunity for putting one of them into practice. When it had come, he had seen it and seized it with frightening swiftness, and had Ash been found shot with his own rifle, then clearly he must have stumbled or been handling it carelessly and shot himself by mistake . . . And since Biju Ram's servants would not have been familiar with such a weapon, *Bichchhu* the scorpion would have had to play murderer himself.

Ash got up and went to stand in the open door of the tent and stare out into the night. But there were too many patches of shadow out there and it was impossible to tell if one of them concealed a watcher, though he himself must present an admirable target, outlined against the yellow lamp-light. Not that he was disturbed by that, for he was convinced that the last thing Biju Ram and his fellow-conspirators desired was to attract the attention of the British authorities: and the one thing that

460

would attract an embarrassing amount of it would be the murder of a British officer. It must be an accident or nothing. And as another one had almost certainly been planned, he, Ash, would have to move very quickly indeed if he wished to reach Bhithor alive. But this time he must make certain that he was right and not merely guessing again. It was not enough to be sure in his own mind. He had been sure before; and wrongly so.

His gaze fell on the crumpled rag that he had thrown out of the tent door as something that need no longer be hidden, and presently he went out and picked it up, for he had suddenly thought of a use for it.

26

The start of the next day's march had been unduly delayed owing to an argument between a carter and the mahout of a baggage elephant over a redistribution of loads. A trivial matter, but tempers were short and both had attracted vociferous supporters, until eventually half the bullock-drivers and all the mahouts were involved in an exchange of insults that led, inevitably, to blows.

By the time the combatants had been separated and the dispute settled, a full two hours had been lost and it was plain that the next camping ground would not be reached until well after mid-day—an unpleasant prospect in that weather.

Their route that day followed a dry water-course that wound between high tussocks of grass, an occasional thorn tree and numerous tall ant-castles; and although the sun was still below the horizon when they at last set out, the freshness had already left the morning air and the day promised to be even hotter than the previous one. Sand rose in choking clouds from under the hooves of horses and bullocks, the wheels of carts and the plodding feet of men and elephants, and Shushila wept and complained until Jhoti, who was sharing his sister's *ruth*, lost his temper and slapped her.

"Anyone would think you are the only one who is

461

hot and uncomfortable," stormed Jhoti. "Well, you're not! And if you think I am going to travel one more yard in this silly box with a whimpering ninny who makes more fuss than a sick goat, you're wrong." With which he scrambled out into the dust, and ignoring all entreaties to return, sent for his horse and insisted on riding the rest of the way.

The slap and his sudden departure had a salutary effect upon Shushila, who was apt to react favourably to any display of male violence; and the incident also proved unexpectedly helpful to Ash, who, having gone to considerable trouble to avoid Biju Ram's society during the past weeks, was now wondering how to reverse the process without making it appear contrived.

Jhoti's sudden appearance on horseback solved this problem, because his entourage, who had of late been travelling in covered carts, were forced to abandon them in order to ride in attendance on their young master; and when he would have dismissed them, saying that he did not need them as he would be riding with the Sahib and Mulraj, Ash had intervened with the suggestion that it might be useful if they stayed with him, as later on they could ride ahead to fetch food and drink. There being no chance of making camp in time for the mid-day meal, they would all have to eat by the wayside or not at all.

For once Jhoti had not argued, and they rode on together in a group, so that for the first time since the start of their journey Ash spent several hours in the company of Biju Ram, and even managed to speak to the man as if they were on easy terms with one another. Conversation had been desultory as the temperature did not encourage talk, but from Ash's point of view the situation could not have been bettered, as it had come about naturally and with no appearance of being contrived; and later on he had found it a simple matter to fall back well behind the tail of the procession, on the excuse that it was better to arrive last when all the tents had been pitched and the dust allowed to settle. But although this had meant keeping to a walk, no one—not even the horses—was feeling energetic, and they had all been content to amble along, staying well out of range of the dust-cloud raised by the shuffling marchers ahead.

The sun had been almost directly overhead before

they found a suitable spot in which to stop for a meal, and Mohan and Biju Ram had ridden off to arrange for food to be brought to them. On their return they had reported that the camp site lay less than a mile ahead, and as the vanguard had reached it some time ago, most of the tents were already pitched and the remainder should be up within an hour.

Ash had hoped for a wind, but as luck would have it, that day the *louh* did not blow and the air was still; which in the long term might be no bad thing, though it meant that he would have to take extra care not to make the action he had planned appear contrived. Its success depended on an appearance of casualness, and it was just as important that the thing should look spontaneous as that Biju Ram should be watching; and almost equally important that the spot chosen should be easily recognizable and not too far from the camp—or too near, either.

He waited until the meal was over and they moved on again, for he could see, not too far ahead, a lone palm tree that rose above the waste of dusty ground and scattered grass clumps, and provided the landmark he needed. Beyond it, less than a mile away as the crow flies, a cloud of dust showed where the tents were rising, and soon they would be rejoining the camp. It was now or never—

Ash took a deep breath, and turned to Kaka-ji with a question about Karidkote that he knew would lead to general conversation and ensure that Biju Ram was paying attention. Then as they came abreast of the palm tree he removed his pith helmet, and remarking on the excessive heat, pulled a handkerchief from his pocket and began to mop the sweat off his neck and forehead. Only it was not a handkerchief. It was a torn and crumpled piece of material that had been part of an elegant grey *achkan* and was now stained with dark brown blotches. Ash drew attention to the fact by stopping in mid-sentence to look at it in blank surprise.

His expression suggested that he had never seen the thing before and could not understand how it had got there, and he stared at it, frowning, sniffed it and made a face of disgust, and without troubling to inspect it further, rolled it into a ball and tossed it away among the scattered clumps of pampas grass.

He did not even glance at Biju Ram until he had

finished the sentence and hunted through his pockets for the conventional square of white linen that he had (supposedly) expected to find. Discovering this in an inner pocket of his riding coat, he dabbed his forehead with it, draped it over the back of his helmet to keep the sun off his neck, and continued the conversation, taking particular care to include Biju Ram in it so that there would be no chance of his turning back to retrieve that tattered piece of cloth before they reached the camp. Once there, it would be easy enough to see that he did not go in search of it too soon, for Ash had instructed Gul Baz to site his tent on this side of the perimeter, and facing this way, so that if Biju Ram went back to look for his late property to daylight he would have to do so in full view of Ash, who intended to sit out under an awning, ostensibly scanning the plain for black-buck with a pair of field glasses. Under these circumstances, it was unlikely that Biju Ram would risk it. Yet one thing at least was certain. Provided he had recognized that piece of material (and he had certainly been given every opportunity to do so) he would go back to look for it.

They reached the outskirts of the camp some fifteen minutes later, and the rest of the day passed uneventfully. The heat discouraged any unnecessary form of activity, and men and animals sought what shade they could find and drowsed away the slow hours until the sun was low in the sky and the temperature became more tolerable. Ash had kept a desultory watch on the plain where the solitary palm tree showed small as a toothpick against the bleached sky, but except that the landscape quivered continually to the waves of heat, nothing alive moved there. And when at length the camp aroused itself and set about its evening chores, the grass-cutters did not go that way, but avoiding the well-trodden route along which they had marched that morning, fanned out to left and right where the grass would be less thickly smothered in dust and sand.

As usual Ash ate in the open, though this evening he did not sit out late, but moved back into his tent as soon as the first stars showed, and having dismissed Gul Baz, waited until darkness fell and then turned out his lamp so that anyone who might happen to be interested in his movements would imagine that he had retired to bed. He had plenty of time at his disposal, for the moon was on the wane and would not be rising for another hour and more, but he was taking no chances. He preferred to be on the ground too early rather than risk being late, and the glass of the hurricane lamp had barely had time to cool before he slid out under the side of his tent, and lying flat on his stomach, wriggled across the open to the shelter of the grass clumps with a silence and celerity that even Malik Shah—who had taught him that trick—could not have bettered. Behind him the glow and glitter of lamps, torches and camp fires lit up the sky and turned night into day, but the plain ahead was a chartless sea of shadow dotted with rustling islands of grass, and even the nearest *kikar* trees were barely visible against the stars.

He paused for a while to make sure that he had not been seen or followed, and then set off into the darkness, guided by the line of the dry water-course whose sandy bed showed white in the starlight. The track he had ridden along earlier that day ran parallel to it, and though its windings added half as much again to the scant crow-flight mile that separated him from the spot where he had discarded the torn half of Biju Ram's *achkan*, it was easy to follow. So easy that almost before he knew it the dark column of the palm tree was looming up against the star-strewn sky.

Leaving the track he walked towards it, and once there, squatted down native-fashion to wait. The moon would not be up for well over half an hour, and as Biju Ram was unlikely to leave the camp until there was enough light to see by (and once started would take at least forty-five minutes to cover the distance) the wait promised to be a long one.

Ash had learned patience—painfully—but he would never find it easy to practise, and tonight proved to be no exception. For although he had been careful to memorize the place where he had thrown that piece of material, and would have said that he knew to within a yard or two where it lay, the islands of grass seemed to have taken on different shapes in the starlight, so that now he was less sure. And there was no way of telling whether it was still there or if a hawk or a prowling jackal had carried it away, and no point in searching for it in the darkness. If it was there Biju Ram would find it soon enough, while if it had gone it would not matter, because the mere fact that he had come in search of it would be proof enough. But when at last the moon came up over the plain he saw the thing itself, lying near a clump of pampas grass some ten paces to his left.

The moonlight also betrayed his own position, for now the palm tree no longer provided any shelter, and he rose and went over to the pampas grass, and having trodden out a rough-and-ready hide from where he could watch unseen, settled down once more to wait.

It proved to be an uncomfortable hiding place, as any unguarded movement made the grass rustle and the night was so still that the smallest sound was sharply audible. Yet the silence was to his advantage, for it meant that he would be warned of Biju Ram's approach long before he came in sight. But as the slow hours crawled by and nothing stirred, Ash began to wonder if he had made a mistake, not as to the ownership of the grey coat— he knew it to be one of Biju Ram's—but in the manner in which he had discarded it. Had he thrown it away too quickly and without allowing enough time for it to be recognized? Or so casually that the gesture had not even attracted a disinterested glance? Or had he overplayed the scene, so it rang false . . . ?

Biju Ram was no fool, and if he suspected a trap he would take no chances, no matter how alluring the bait. On the other hand, if he had been deceived by that performance this morning and accepted it at its face value, then nothing would keep him away; nor would he send a deputy or bring anyone with him. He would come alone or not at all. Yet by now the moon had been up for well over two hours and still there was no sign of him and no sound of anyone approaching. If he failed to appear it might well mean that he suspected a trap, in which case the likelihood of walking into an ambush on the way back to camp could not be disregarded.

Ash stirred restlessly and was tempted to abandon the vigil and return to his tent by a circuitous route, and go to bed. It must have been close on one o'clock by then and in little more than three hours' time the camp would be astir in preparation for another early start. Besides it was not as if he needed any further proof that it was Biju Ram who had fired at him and whose coat had torn in his hands as they struggled together in the dark. Or, for that matter, that it was Biju Ram, on behalf of the *Nautch*-girl, who had engineered the disappearance of Hira Lal and the death of Lalji, and was now, at the bidding of a new master, striving to dispose of Jhoti as well. There was surely no need for anything more, and this quixotic conviction that he must, in all fairness, obtain at least one concrete piece of evidence to support his suspicions before taking any action, was absurd: what could it do but confirm what he knew already? And what had fairness ever had to do with Biju Ram?

"Nothing," decided Ash angrily. *"Nothing"* . . .

Yet he knew that he could not leave until Biju Ram came. Or did not come. The conviction might be quixotic, but it was there and he could not free himself from it. The past was too strong for him. Hilary and Akbar Khan had, between them, sown better than they knew when they had impressed upon a small boy that the one unforgivable sin was injustice, and that he must at all costs be fair. And the very laws of England held that any accused person is presumed to be innocent until he is proven guilty.

"Ad vitam aut culpam," thought Ash wryly, recalling one of Colonel Anderson's favourite tags, which the Colonel had chosen to translate as "until some misconduct is proved"; while the Commandant of the Guides, discoursing on the same subject (the proper administration of justice), had been fond of quoting the opinion of Dickens's judge that "what the soldier said was not evidence." Yet the case against Biju Ram was founded on gossip and guesswork, strongly biased by a personal antipathy that dated back to the days of Ash's childhood, and he could not bring himself to condemn a man to death on suspicion alone.

To death . . . The words gave him an odd shock of surprise, for strangely enough it was the first time that he had consciously realized that he meant to kill Biju Ram. Yet here the influences of the Hawa Mahal and the Border tribes took over and Ash ceased to think as an Englishman . . .

Faced with a similar situation, ninety-nine out of a hundred British officers would have arrested Biju Ram and handed him over to be tried by the proper authorities, while the hundredth would probably have allowed Mulraj and the senior members of the Karidkote camp to deal with

467

the matter. None would have dreamt of taking the law into their own hands, yet Ash saw nothing untoward in doing so.

If Biju Ram was guilty of murder and attempted murder, then there was nothing for it but to deal with him here and now—if he came. And if he did not? "But he will," thought Ash. "He must. He won't be able to resist coming on the off-chance of finding that pearl."

The shadows had shortened as the moon travelled up the sky, and by now the light was so bright that small print could have been read by it. A hot-weather moon over the plains of India has little in common with the cool silver globe that floats above colder lands, and even the smallest beetle scurrying across the dusty spaces between the grass clumps was as clearly visible as though it had been daylight. The torn piece of cloth with which Ash had baited his trap now lay starkly exposed as a dark blotch on the white dust, and the silence of the night was no longer unbroken.

A faint clattering sound announced the arrival of a young porcupine that had been attracted by the smell of stale blood, but having nosed the cloth and found it inedible, it scuttled off with an indignant rattle of quills. Far away a jackal pack broke into a wailing, yelping chorus that echoed across the plain and died on a long mournful howl, and shortly afterwards there was a patter and a rustle as a hyena loped past, making for the camp where there would be rich pickings for scavengers. But there was still no sound that suggested the approach of a man, and Ash flexed his stiffening muscles and longed for a cigarette. The moonlight was bright enough to neutralize the momentary flare of a match and he could easily conceal the glowing tip in his hand. But he could not risk lighting one; the scent of tobacco smoke would carry too far on the windless night, and Biju Ram would smell it and be warned.

Ash yawned tiredly and closed his eyes; and he must have dozed for a few minutes, for when he opened them again a little vagrant breeze was stirring the grasses with a sound like far-away surf on a pebble beach. And Biju Ram was standing in a patch of moonlight less than a dozen yards away . . .

For a moment it seemed to Ash that his hiding place had been discovered, for the man appeared to be staring straight at him. But Biju Ram's gaze passed on. He was looking about him, glancing from the palm tree to the mile-distant camp and evidently calculating the line that he and the others had ridden along on the previous day. It was clear that he had no suspicion that he had walked into a trap or that anyone might be watching him, for he stood out in the open without any attempt at concealment and with his coat half unbuttoned to allow the breeze to cool his plump, bare chest.

Presently he began to move forward between the scattered clumps of knee-high grass and the tall islands of pampas, searching as he went. Once or twice he leant forward to peer more closely into the shadows and poke among them with the heavy silver-mounted walking-stick that he carried, and once he swooped to pick up something that he dropped again with a gesture of disgust, pausing to wipe his fingers on his coat sleeve before moving on again.

He was within a few feet of Ash's hiding place when he saw the thing that he came in search of, and his sudden in-drawn breath of satisfaction was audible even above the susurration of the grasses. For an appreciable length of time he stood wide-eyed and rigid, staring at it, and then he dropped his stick and ran forward to pick it up and crumple it between frantic hands.

An uncontrollable spurt of laughter proclaimed his discovery that there was still some small hard object hidden among its folds, and he tore at the concealed pocket in such a frenzy of haste that the earring leapt out and fell at his feet . . .

The diamonds in the tiny leaf glittered with a frosty brilliance and the black pearl lay like a drop of glowing darkness on the white dust, a thing of beauty and wonder that seemed to gather and reflect the moonlight. Looking down at it, Biju Ram laughed again—that familiar giggling laugh that had almost always been an expression of satisfied malice rather than honest amusement, and that now held an unmistakable note of triumph.

He had been too obsessed with his search for the lost jewel to sense the near presence of another human, and now, as he stooped to pick it up, he was not aware that though the breeze had died as suddenly as it had arisen, the grass was still rustling. And when he saw the shadow it was too late.

A hand like a steel trap closed about his wrist and twisted it so savagely that he cried out with pain and let go of the pearl, which fell back onto the dust.

Ash picked it up and put it in his pocket, and releasing his grip, stood back.

Biju Ram was quick and cunning, and he had shown himself capable of thinking very fast and of translating thought into action with equal speed. But this time he was taken off guard, for he had thought himself safe and the shock of Ash's sudden appearance drove him to incautious speech: "Sahib! What—what do you do here? . . . I did not know . . . I came out to—to search for that trinket that I—that I lost this morning. Give it back to me, Sahib. It is mine."

"Is it?" inquired Ash grimly. "Then the coat that it was concealed in must also be yours. Which means that you have twice, to my knowledge, tried to kill me."

"To kill you?" Biju Ram was recovering himself and his face and voice expressed complete bewilderment. "I do not understand, Sahib. What coat?"

"This," said Ash, touching it with his foot. "You left this much of it in my hands when you escaped from me—having failed to kill me. And later you ransacked my tent looking for it, because you knew, as I did not, what it contained. But last night I too found out, and so I threw it down here for you to find, knowing that you would come back for it. I have watched you search for it and seen you take the pearl from it, so there is no need for you to waste breath pretending that you do not know what I am talking about, or that the coat was none of yours."

A mixture of emotions compounded of rage, fear, indecision and wariness showed fleetingly on Biju Ram's face, to be succeeded by one of half-humorous deprecation as he smiled and spread out his hands in a gesture of resignation, and said wryly: "Now I see that I shall have to tell all."

"Good," said Ash, surprised at this swift capitulation.

"I would have spoken long ago, Sahib, had I dreamt that you might suspect me. But such a thought did not enter my mind, so when my servant, Karam, confessed all and threw himself upon my mercy, and I learned that no grave harm had been done and no complaints raised, I foolishly agreed not to betray him—though you must not think that I did not punish him. I assure you I did, most severely. But he told me—and I believe him—that he never intended to steal the gun; only to borrow it so that he might shoot *kala hirren*" (black-buck) "who come out to graze at night; there being those in our camp who eat meat and will pay good money for it. He had meant to replace the gun before it was missed, but in the darkness he mistook the Sahib for a buck, and fired, and on discovering his mistake was overcome with terror, for he said that until you leapt upon him he thought that he had killed you; and when at length he escaped from you, having dropped the gun and left a piece of clothing in your hands, he said nothing of all this but gave out that he had been injured in a fall. I myself would never have learned of it had it not been that only the day before I had given him an old coat of mine, forgetting that I had left an earring in one of the pockets, and when I realized what I had done I asked him for it, and it was then that he confessed all. Sahib—you may imagine my horror!"

He paused as though in expectation of some comment, and when Ash offered none, sighed deeply and shook his head over the recollection of that moment. "I should have hauled him before you on the instant—I know it," confessed Biju Ram magnanimously. "But he begged me with tears to be merciful; and as you, Sahib, had made no report of the matter and by good fortune had been unharmed, I acceded to his request, and did not find it in my heart to denounce him. He promised, too, that he would find and return my earring, but had I known that he would search your tent for it, or that you had recognized the coat as mine and suspected me of being the culprit, I would have come to you at once and told you the truth, and you would have given me my earring and all would have been well. The fault was mine—I admit it— I was too lenient with my rascal of a servant, and for that I ask your pardon. But had you been in my place, and the offender one of your own men, would you not have done the same? I am sure of it! And now, Sahib, having told you all, I would beg leave to return to the camp. Tomorrow my *budmarsh* of a servant shall present himself before you to make full confession of his fault and receive whatever punishment you think fit. This I can promise you."

"Yes, I am sure you can," said Ash dryly. "And I can

471

also be sure that he will repeat what you have told me, word for word; because he will not dare to do otherwise. Also I imagine that you will see that he is well rewarded for acting as scapegoat."

"The Sahib wrongs me," protested Biju Ram, injured. "I have spoken only the truth. Moreover, there are many who can bear witness that I did not leave my tent that night, and—"

"And that on the following morning your face showed no signs of cuts or scratches," finished Ash. "Of course. Though I think I have heard otherwise. But no matter— even if that could be proved I am sure that you and your friends would have some plausible story to account for it. Very well then. Since it seems that you can produce so many witnesses to swear that you speak truth, let us pretend that it was not you but one of your servants who stole my gun and tried to shoot me with it while wearing, by chance, a cast-off garment that you had generously given him only a day before. But what of the earring? Have you witnesses to prove that it is indeed yours?"

The moonlight betrayed the sudden, startled widening of Biju Ram's eyes, and Ash saw it and knew that he had been right in thinking that no one else would know about that pearl and that it could never be worn. To have admitted possessing it would have been to invite blackmail, if not murder. For even after all these years there would still be men who would recognize it, and recall how its owner's disappearance had never been satisfactorily explained. Biju Ram could bribe or threaten any number of people into giving false evidence, but he would not risk producing the black pearl in public or attempting to bribe anyone—even the most venal of his fellow conspirators—into testifying to his ownership of that jewel.

There was a noticeable interval before he replied to the question, and becoming aware of this he essayed a smile and said: "The Sahib is pleased to jest. What need of witnesses? The trinket is mine, and surely the fact that I came here to search for it is proof enough, because had I myself not placed it for safe-keeping in an inner pocket of that coat, how could I have known it was there?—or what to look for? Besides, I doubt if even my servants would recognize it, as I have never worn it. It belonged to my father, who gave it to me as he lay dying, so it saddens me to see it, but I have carried it with me ever since in memory of him. I look upon it as a charm to remind me of a great and good man, and to keep me from harm."

"Very filial of you," commented Ash. "And very interesting too. I would have said that he was not nearly old enough to be your father, as there cannot have been more than five years between you, if that. But then perhaps he was a particularly precocious child."

Biju Ram's smile became a little fixed, but his voice remained smooth and once again he spread out his hands in a deprecatory gesture: "You speak in riddles, Sahib, and I do not understand you. What can you know of my father?"

"Nothing," said Ash. "But I used to know the man who owned that earring and always wore it. His name was Hira Lal."

The sharp hiss of indrawn breath was harshly audible in the silence as Biju Ram stiffened and stood rigid, and once again his eyes were wide and revealing. But this time they reflected shock and disbelief, and the dawn of something that was half-way between rage and terror. He ran his tongue over his lips as though they had suddenly become dry, and when he spoke at last it was in a grating whisper that seemed forced from him against his will:

"*No*," whispered Biju Ram. "No . . . it is not true. You could not . . . it is not possible . . ." A shudder went through him, and he appeared to wrench himself awake from the grip of a nightmare. His voice shot up:

"Some enemy has told you lies about me, Sahib. Do not believe them. There is no truth in this—none. This man you speak of, this Mera—no, Hira Lal, was it not? There must be many of that name in Karidkote. It is not an uncommon one, and it is possible that one of them has an earring somewhat similar to this one of mine. But is that any reason to accuse me of theft and falsehood? Sahib, you have been misled by someone who wishes to ruin me, and if you are a just man—and we know all Sahibs to be just—you will tell me the name of this perjurer so that I may confront him and make him admit that he lies. Who is it who accuses me?" demanded Biju Ram in throbbing tones, "and of what am I accused? If you know his name, speak, Sahib. I demand justice!"

"You will get it," promised Ash grimly. "His name is Ashok. He was once in the service of the late Yuveraj

473

of Gulkote, and you of all people should remember him well."

"But—he is dead," breathed Biju Ram. "He could not . . . This is a trick. A clumsy plot. You have been deceived by an impostor. That boy died many years ago."

"Did the men you sent to hunt him down tell you so? If so, they lied. No doubt because they feared to return and admit that they had failed. No, *Bichchhu-ji*"—Biju Ram jerked like a startled horse at the old nickname—"your men lost him, and though his mother died, he lived; and now he has come back to accuse you of the murder of his friend Hira Lal, whose pearl you stole, and of the attempted murder of the boy, Jhoti; and of myself, whom you would have shot. There is also the matter of the death of Lalji, for though I cannot know if it was your hand that thrust him from the battlements, I am very sure that you contrived it—you and his step-mother, who between you hastened the death of my mother, Sita, by hounding us back and forth across the Punjab until she died from exhaustion."

"Us? . . . *your* mother—?"

"Mine, *Bichchhu*. Do you not recognize me? Look closer. Have I changed so much? You have not. I knew you again the moment I saw you—that first night in Jhoti's tent; as I knew the pearl too the instant it fell from the hidden pocket you had made for it in a coat that had torn in my hands."

"But . . . but you are a Sahib," whispered Biju Ram through dry lips, "a Sahib—"

"Who was once Ashok," said Ash softly.

Biju Ram stared and stared. His eyes seemed to stand out from his head, and great beads of sweat that had nothing to do with the warmth of the hot night formed on his forehead and glittered in the moonlight. "No, it is not true"—the words were barely more than a breath of sound—"it cannot be . . . it is not possible . . . I do not believe . . ." But the muttered denials were contradicted by a dawning recognition on his face, and suddenly he said loudly: "If it is true, there should be a scar, the mark of a branding—"

"It is still there," said Ash, and pulled open his shirt to show the silvery-white ghost of a half-circle, still faintly visible against his brown, suntanned skin. A mark made long ago by the mouth of an old-fashioned blunderbuss.

He heard Biju Ram's involuntary *"Wah!"* and glanced down at the scar; which was unwise. He should have known better than to look aside from a man who had not been nicknamed "the scorpion" for nothing and would not have ventured out unarmed. The heavy silver-mounted stick lay just out of Biju Ram's reach, but he carried a particularly deadly knife in a slit pocket in his *achkan,* and as Ash looked down he whipped it out and struck with the speed of his namesake.

The blow only missed its mark because Ash too could move swiftly; and though he had momentarily lowered his gaze he was aware of the quick movement and dodged instinctively, flinging himself to one side so that the thrust went harmlessly past his left shoulder. The force of it sent Biju Ram plunging forward, and Ash had only to put out a foot to trip him up and send him sprawling full length in the dust.

As he lay there, winded and gasping, Ash turned to snatch up the fallen knife and was tempted to plunge it between those heaving shoulders and be done with it. And had he indeed been of Zarin's blood he would have done so, for the sons of old Koda Dad had no pettifogging scruples in the matter of dealing with an enemy. But now, quite suddenly, Ash's ancestry and those tedious years at a public school betrayed him, for he could not bring himself to strike: not because to do so would have been murder, but for a more trivial reason—because he and his forebears had been taught that it is "not cricket" to stab a man in the back or strike a fallen one; or to attack an unarmed man. It was the unseen presence of Uncle Matthew and a score of pastors and masters that stayed his hand and made him stand back and urge Biju Ram to get up and fight.

But it seemed that Biju Ram had no stomach for fighting, for when his breath returned to him and he began to scramble to his knees, the sight of Ash standing there, knife in hand, made him shrink back with a scream, and he fell on his face again to grovel in the dust and babble incoherent pleas for mercy.

The spectacle was not an edifying one, and though Ash had always known Biju Ram to be a vile creature, it had not occurred to him that the sadistic ogre of his childhood might be a coward at heart. It was a shock to discover that *Bichchhu*'s pleasure in inflicting pain was only equalled by his aversion to enduring it himself, and that he could go to pieces so completely when faced with a taste of his own medicine. Deprived of supporters and a weapon, the ogre had suddenly become a thing of straw.

Ash jeered and taunted, stirred the grovelling figure with a scornful foot and used every insult that he could lay his tongue to. But to no effect. Biju Ram refused to stand up, for instinct told him that once he rose to his feet the Sahib would attack him; and the Sahib not only held the knife, but was, by some terrifying wizardry, Ashok —Ashok returned from the dead. What were a few insults compared to that? A combination of superstitious awe and the fear of death kept Biju Ram flat on his face and deaf to abuse, until at last Ash turned away in disgust and told him roughly to get up and go back to camp.

"And tomorrow," said Ash, "you and your friends will make an excuse to part company with us. I do not care what excuse you use provided you leave, or where you go as long as it is not to Bhithor or back to Karidkote. But if I ever hear that you have been seen in either of these states I shall go straight to the authorities and tell everything that I know, and they will have you hanged or transported. And if they should not, then I shall deal with you myself and kill you with my own hands. That is an oath! Now go—and quickly, before I change my mind and break your fat neck here and now, you lying, thieving, crawling murderer. Up and run, son of a swine. Go—*go!*"

His voice shot up and cracked with a rage which was directed at himself as much as the grovelling creature whom he had intended to kill, because he knew that this was no occasion for mercy; yet it seemed that he was not yet emancipated from the tradition of those hated schooldays and was still adrift in Limbo, neither wholly of the East nor of the West, and therefore still unable to react to any situation with an undivided heart.

Biju Ram stumbled to his feet, and with his gaze riveted to the knife in Ash's hand, began to back away cautiously, a step at a time. Evidently he found it difficult

476

to believe that he was to be allowed to go free, and did not dare turn his back for fear that the knife would be driven home between his shoulder blades.

He had taken no more than three steps when he trod on the discarded walking-stick and tripped and almost fell, and Ash said scornfully: "Take it up, *Bichchhu*. You will feel braver with a stick in your hand."

Biju Ram obeyed, groping for it with his left hand while his eyes still watched the knife; and apparently Ash was right, for when he straightened up a measure of confidence seemed to have returned to him. He began to speak in a voice that was once again smooth and obsequious, addressing Ash as *"Huzoor"** and thanking him for his clemency, and assuring him that his orders would be obeyed to the letter. Tomorrow, with the dawn, he would take his departure from the camp—though the *Huzoor* misjudged him, for at no time had he ever intended harm to anyone. It was all a terrible mistake— a misunderstanding—and had he only known . . .

Still talking he continued to back away, and having edged crab-wise past a clump of grass and put at least ten paces between himself and Ash, he paused and said with a shrug of the shoulders: "But of what use are words? I am the *Huzoor's* servant, and I will obey his orders and go. Farewell, Sahib—" He bowed deeply, bringing his hands together in the traditional manner.

The gesture was so familiar that the fact that he still held the stick appeared unimportant, and for the second time that night Ash was caught off guard. For the stick was not all it seemed: it happened to be the work of a gunsmith who specialized in lethal toys for the rich, and it had been acquired by the late ruler of Karidkote, whose widow, shortly before her death, had given it to Biju Ram as a reward for unspecified services. But as Ash did not know this he was unprepared for what followed.

Biju Ram had been holding the stick in his left hand, and as he brought his two hands together the right twisted the silver-mounted top; and when he straightened up from his bow he held a slim-barrelled pistol.

The explosion shattered the moonlit silence with a brilliant flash of orange and a crack of sound, but though the range was a mere matter of six or seven yards, the events

---

*Your honour

477

of the past quarter of an hour had so shaken Biju Ram that not only were his hands unsteady, but in the agitation of the moment he had forgotten that this particular weapon tended to throw to the left, and omitted to make allowances for it. As a result, the bullet that had been intended for Ash's heart did no more than scorch his shirtsleeve and flick a fragment of skin from his arm as it passed harmlessly by to be lost on the plain.

"*You bastard!*" said Ash viciously and in English; and flung the knife.

Rage does not make for good marksmanship and Ash's aim was no better than Biju Ram's had been—the knife point missed the throat and a collar bone that was so well protected by fat that the blade came nowhere near reaching it. But as the knife fell to the ground and a small trickle of blood ran down from the wound, Biju Ram dropped the pistol and began to scream on a thin high-pitched note of pure terror.

There was something inhuman in the sound of that screaming, while the spectacle of a grown man reduced to a frenzy of fear by the sight of his own blood trickling from a cut that would hardly have discommoded a child was so nauseating that Ash's rage turned to scorn, and instead of leaping at Biju Ram to knock him down and beat him to a pulp with his own stick, he stayed where he was and began to laugh—not at the absurdity of the sight, but because it seemed incredible to him that this miserable craven should ever have been able to terrorize anyone. Seeing him now, it was difficult to believe that so lily-livered a thing could have murdered Hira Lal, and Ash's laughter was, in its way, as ugly a sound as those womanish screams.

The blood drew a thin dark line down Biju Ram's pale chest, and he stopped screaming and bent his head in a ludicrous attempt to suck the wound. But the cut was too high to allow his mouth to reach it, and when he realized this he shrieked again and began to run to and fro like a chicken that has had its head cut off, stumbling among the grass clumps and the scattered stones in an aimless frenzy of terror, until at last he tripped and fell, and once again lay writhing on the ground.

"I die!" wept Biju Ram. "I die . . ."

"You deserve to," said Ash unfeelingly. "But I am afraid that scratch is unlikely to do more than give you

478

a stiff shoulder for a day or two, and as I still dislike
the idea of killing anyone as spineless as you in cold
blood, you can stop play-acting and get up and start
back to the camp. It's getting late. Stand up, *Bichchhu-
baba*. No one is going to hurt you."

He laughed again, but either Biju Ram did not trust
him or the shock of that second failure had finally broken
his nerve, for he continued to writhe and weep.

"Help me!" moaned Biju Ram. *"Marfkaro"* (have
mercy), *"Marfkaro . . .!"*

His voice died on a curious gasping wail, and Ash
walked over to him, still laughing but moving warily in
case this was merely a trap designed to lure him within
range of another unsuspected weapon. But a glance at
Biju Ram's grey, contorted, sweat-drenched face checked
his laughter. There was something here that he did not
understand. He had heard that there are people who cannot endure the sight of their own blood and are literally
overcome by it, but the man on the ground, while patently in the grip of fear, was also suffering from genuine
physical agony. His body arched and twisted convulsively,
and Ash bent down and said roughly: "What is it,
Bichchhu?"

"Zahr . . ." (poison), whispered Biju Ram. "The
knife . . ."

Ash straightened up with a jerk and took a quick step
backwards, suddenly enlightened. So that was why the
man had shrieked and cowered. He had misjudged Biju
Ram: it was not fear of pain that had made him grovel
on the ground, but the fear of death—swift and horrible
death. Nor had he been afraid of Ash. His fear had been
for the knife in Ash's hand—his own knife with a blade
that was steeped in poison to ensure that any wound it
inflicted would prove fatal. No wonder he had watched
it with such hypnotized terror, and shrieked in panic when
he saw that small bright trickle of blood. The wound
was indeed a small one and "no more than a scratch."
But, like Mercutio's it was enough: it would serve.

Biju Ram had been hoist with his own petard and
there was nothing that Ash could do. It was already too
late to try and suck the poison from the wound, and he
had no antidote or any knowledge of what poison had
been used. The camp was over a mile away, and even
if it had been half that distance he could not have reached

479

it and got back again in time to offer any help—if help were possible, which he doubted, for it was plain that the poison was a deadly one.

Biju Ram deserved to pay with his own life for the lives he had taken, or helped to take, and the irreparable harm that he had done. But even those who had most cause to hate him might have pitied him now. Yet Ash, watching him die, remembered Lalji's young, frightened face and haunted eyes—and a slab of sandstone that moved and slid as a boy in a blue satin coat rode under the Charbagh Gate in Gulkote bazaar. There were other memories too. Several carp floating belly upwards among the lily pads in a palace pool; a king cobra that had somehow found its way into the bedroom of the Yuveraj; Sita, dying of exhaustion under the rocks by the Jhelum River; Hira Lal, who had vanished in the jungle, and Jhoti—Jhoti who but for the grace of God would have died weeks ago, the innocent victim of another "accident" arranged by Biju Ram.

Remembering all the evil that this man had done it was difficult to feel anything except that his fate was richly earned. And it was one that he had brought on himself, for Ash had not spoken idly when he had told him that he could go free provided he left the camp and kept away from Bhithor and Karidkote. Had he gone then he might have lived to wreak more harm and plan other murders for many years to come; but he had chosen instead to fire that shot, and it was this last act of treachery that had killed him. He had lived like a mad dog and it was only right that he should die like one, thought Ash. But he wished that it could have been over sooner, for it was not pleasant to watch, and had there been a second bullet in that ingenious pistol he would have used it unhesitatingly to put Biju Ram out of his misery. As he could not do so, he stayed, resisting the urge to turn and walk away, because it appalled him to think that anyone should have to die in this manner alone. At least he was another human being; and perhaps the fact that he was—or had been—an enemy did not matter any more.

He stayed until it was over. It did not in fact take long. Afterwards he stooped and closed the staring, sightless eyes, and retrieving the knife, cleaned it very thoroughly in the earth to remove any trace of poison. The pistol had fallen into a clump of grass and he had some difficulty in finding it, but having done so he fitted it back into place and laid the walking-stick down within reach of one of the dead man's hands.

Biju Ram would not be missed for some hours yet; and long before there was any chance of his body being found, the dawn wind would have swept the dust clear of footprints. There was therefore no point in leaving evidence that might suggest a quarrel and lead to questions being asked, and as it would be obvious that the cause of death was poison, it would be better, from every point of view, if it were put down to snake-bite.

Ash picked up the knife and having stained it with the fast-congealing blood, dropped it again and went off to search for one of the long double-pronged thorns that grow on *kikar* trees. Returning with this, he jabbed it into the dead man's flesh just below the wound. The two small punctures were almost exactly the marks that a striking snake would have made, and the cut above it would be taken for a fruitless attempt by the victim to stop the venom from spreading upwards. The only mystery would be why Biju Ram should have left the camp alone and at night, and strayed so far. But the heat would probably be blamed for that. They would decide that he could not sleep and so had gone out to walk in the moonlight, and that feeling tired he must have sat down to rest, and been bitten by a snake, which, remembering that Hira Lal's death had been arranged to look like the work of a tiger, was singularly apt. "The gods, after all, are just," thought Ash, "for if it had been left to me, I would have been fool enough to let him go."

There remained only Hira Lal's earring.

Ash took it out of his pocket and looked at it, and saw the black pearl gather and reflect the moonlight as it had done on that last, long-ago night in the Queen's balcony. And as he looked, the words that Hira Lal had spoken then came back to him, and it was almost as though the man himself was speaking to him again, very softly, and from very far away: *"Make haste, boy. It grows late and you have no time to waste. Go now—and may the gods go with you. Namaste!"*

Well, he—or perhaps the black pearl—had avenged Hira Lal. But the pearl held too many memories, and remembering how Biju Ram had come by it, it seemed

481

to Ash a thing of ill-omen. Its possession could have brought little satisfaction to the thief, since to own it was proof of murder, so it had to be kept hidden away, with an ever-present risk of discovery, for as long as anyone remembered Hira Lal; and in the end it had brought only death. The pearl had done its work, and now Ash could not wait to be rid of it.

There was a rat hole near the clump of pampas grass in which he had lain in wait for Biju Ram, and judging from the lack of tracks about it, one that was no longer tenanted. Ash went back to it, and having dropped in the earring, filled it in with earth and small stones that he stamped hard down; and when he had scattered a handful of dust over the spot there was no longer any trace of the hole, or any indication that there had ever been one.

He stood for a moment or two looking down at the spot and thinking that perhaps, one day, someone as yet unborn would unearth the earring and wonder how it came there. But they would never know, and anyway, by then the thing would be almost valueless, for pearls too can die.

The dawn wind had begun to stir the grasses when Ash turned on his heel and started back to the camp. But the sun had been well above the horizon by the time that one of Biju Ram's servants (that same Karam who had been allotted the role of scapegoat) reported that his master was missing.

He would, explained Karam, have disclosed this much sooner had he not imagined that his master must have gone out unexpectedly early and would soon return. It was not his business to question his master's comings and goings, but he had become increasingly anxious when tent after tent came down and still his master had not returned to eat his morning meal or give any orders for the day. Tentative inquiries among the servants and the other members of the young prince's entourage having proved fruitless, Karam had finally reported the matter to an officer of the guard, who had raised the alarm.

The search for the missing man was complicated by the enormous size of the camp and the fact that it was by then on the move, and it is more than likely that Biju Ram's body would never have been found had it not been for the kites and the vultures. But the sun had not yet risen when the first winged scavenger dropped out of the skies, to be followed by another and another; and presently one of the searchers had seen them and ridden out to investigate.

The discovery had been made only just in time, for half an hour later there would have been nothing to show how Biju Ram had died, and there would have been talk of foul play and, inevitably, exhaustive inquiries. As it was, in spite of a good deal of damage from beak and claw it was still possible to see that his death was due to poison and that his body bore the mark of a snake's fangs—two small punctures near the collar bone. How or why he had come to be in that spot was less easy to explain, but as Ash had surmised, this was eventually put down to a combination of heat and insomnia, and this solution seemed to satisfy everyone.

Mulraj had sent word that the camp would halt until further orders, and later that day Biju Ram's remains were cremated with due ceremony on a pyre of *kikar* wood and dry grass, hastily collected from the surrounding country and drenched with *ghee*. Next morning, when the night wind had dispersed the ashes and the charred earth had cooled, the fragments of bone that remained were carefully collected in order that they could be taken to the Ganges and thrown into that sacred river. "And as there are none of his relatives here, it is only right that his friends should take it upon themselves to perform this pious duty," said Mulraj, straight-faced. "Therefore I have arranged that Pran and Mohan, and Sen Gupta, with their servants and those of Biju Ram's, shall leave at once for Benares. For saving only Allahabad, there is no more sacred spot at which a man's ashes may be consigned to the waters of Mother Gunga."

Ash received this Machiavellian announcement with a respect that verged on awe, for with Biju Ram dead, there was still the problem of how to rid the camp of those who had been his closest associates, and Ash could see no way out of it that would not involve argument and uproar and a good deal of dangerous speculation. Mulraj's solution was an admirably simple one, though there could be a flaw in it—

"What will Jhoti say to this?" inquired Ash. "These men are of his party—or so he thinks—and he may not agree to let them go."

"He has agreed already," said Mulraj blandly. "The prince sees clearly that it would not be fitting for the ashes of one of his entourage, a man of standing who served his late mother faithfully and for many years, should be thrown into any river and at any spot. Therefore he gives them leave to go."

"But will they do so?"

"Assuredly. For how could they refuse?"

"Oh, *shabash*, Bahadur-Sahib," murmured Ash in an under-voice. "It is indeed well done. I salute you."

He suited the action to the word, and Mulraj permitted himself a faint smile, and returning the salute said equally softly: "And I you, Sahib."

Ash looked a question and Mulraj held out his hand. In the palm lay a small shirt button made from pearl-shell—a common enough object, except that it was of European manufacture and had a metal shank.

"I found this by chance, within ten paces of the body," said Mulraj quietly, "my foot having struck against it where it lay hidden in the dust. Later I showed it to your bearer, saying that I had found it in my tent, and he claimed it as one of yours and said that he had noticed yesterday that one was missing from a shirt that you had worn the evening before. I told him I would return it to you myself—making a jest of it."

Ash was silent for a moment or two, realizing that he must have jerked the button off when he pulled open his shirt to show the scar on his chest, and thinking that it was lucky that Mulraj and not one of Biju Ram's associates had found it—except that no one else would have seen anything in the least interesting in it. He reached out, and taking it said lightly: "I must have lost it when we rode into camp."

"Mayhap," said Mulraj with a shrug. "Though had I been asked I would have said that you wore a khaki shirt with horn buttons that morning. But no matter—it is better that I should know nothing. We will not speak of this again."

They had not done so. Neither then nor later had Mulraj asked any questions, or Ash volunteered any information. Pran, Mohan and Sen Gupta, with their servants, had left before dawn on the following day, presumably for Benares, and the camp moved on again. But though it was too much to hope that it was now free of spies and plotters, those who remained were unlikely to do any serious harm, largely because they were now leaderless, but also, in part, because they would not be certain that the death of their leader and the sudden departure of his closest colleagues was merely a coincidence, and if it were not, how much had become known of their doings. Being unsure, they would lie very low and take no action, which meant that, for the time being at least, Jhoti was safe. Or as safe as he ever could be, decided Ash.

Anjuli remained invisible, and he knew that there was little chance of seeing her again save as a sari-shrouded figure on the occasion of her marriage; for with the Rana's territory only a few marches away the casual easy-going conditions that had prevailed for so long were abandoned, and rules that had been allowed to lapse were once again strictly enforced. He could not even send her a message, because the brides were now kept closely secluded. Additional guards surrounded their *ruth* on the march and kept watch on their tents at the stopping places, and there was nothing that he could do except wear the luck-charm openly at her wedding in the hope that she might see it, and knowing that he had found it, know too that he understood why she had sent it back to him.

The half of that little mother-of-pearl fish was not only a token of her forgiveness, but a reminder that the other half was still in her possession; and that perhaps some day—one day—they might come together again.

Ash took what comfort he could from that thought. It was not a great deal, yet it would have to do, for he had nothing else. But for the most part he tried not to think of Juli; or of the future. Because a future without her presented nothing more than a vista of empty, fruitless years, stretching away in front of him like an endless road that led nowhere, and the thought of it frightened him.

BOOK FOUR

―⋙⋘―⋙⋘―⋙⋘―⋙⋘―⋙⋘―⋙⋘―⋙⋘―

Bhithor

27

―⋙⋘―⋙⋘―⋙⋘―⋙⋘―⋙⋘―⋙⋘―⋙⋘―

With the low range of hills that formed the northern border of Bhithor clearly in sight, an embassy from the Rana rode into camp.

The emissaries brought gifts, garlands and messages of welcome, and were accompanied, somewhat disconcertingly, by what appeard at first sight to be a horde of masked bandits; though these turned out to be nothing more alarming than royal servants, who in accordance with a local custom wore the ends of their turbans wound about nose, mouth and chin in the manner of the veiled Tuaregs of the Sahara—an effect that was distinctly unnerving, in that it suggested footpads and violence, but was in fact (or so they were informed) a mark of respect in Bhithor—"a symbolic veiling of humble features from the effulgent glory of the countenances of the highly born." All the same, the sight of that faceless horde was far from reassuring, and Ash was not the only one to wonder what sort of country they were entering. However, it was too late to worry about that now.

There was nothing for it but to go forward, and three days later the vast cavalcade that had set out from Karidkote so many weeks ago crossed into the Rana's territory, where they were greeted by an escort of State Cavalry and a number of dignitaries, headed by the Diwan—the Prime Minister—who presented more garlands and made more long and flowery speeches. But if Ash had imagined for one moment that his troubles were almost over, he was to be disappointed. They were, on the contrary, about to begin.

The Diwan having taken his leave, Ash and Mulraj and several of the senior members of the camp rode off with the Rana's men to be shown the place where they would pitch their tents for the duration of their stay, and where all but a handful of them would live until the time came for them to return to Karidkote. The site, which had been personally selected by the Rana himself, proved to be in a long, level valley, some three miles from the ancient walled city of Bhithor from which the state took its name. At first glance it seemed to be an admirable choice: it was large enough to accommodate the camp without any over-crowding, and was, moreover, bisected by a stream that would provide all the water they would need. Mulraj and the others had expressed approval, but Ash had been markedly silent.

As a Guides officer trained in Frontier warfare, the site appeared to him to possess certain drawbacks that more than outweighed its advantages. There were, for instance, no less than three forts in the valley. Two were clearly visible at the far end of it, crowning the hilltops that flanked the city, and not only guarding the approaches to the capital, but commanding the full stretch of the level ground. The third dominated the narrow, steep-sided gorge through which they had ridden in order to reach the valley, and even a casual observer (which Ash was not) could see that its ancient walls were still in an excellent state of repair and its bastions armed with a formidable number of heavy cannon.

These last, like Bhithor itself, were relics of an earlier and more barbarous age—great, green-bronze things that had been cast in the reign of Akbar, greatest of the Moguls and grandson of Barbur the Tiger, but still capable of hurling an iron cannon ball with deadly effect against anyone attempting to force a passage through the gorge.

Taking all this into consideration, the valley had the appearance of a trap, and Ash surveyed the terrain with

487

a jaundiced eye and did not fancy the prospect of walking into it; for though he had no reason to distrust the Rana, he was well aware that last-minute disputes over such matters as the payment or non-payment of the bride-price, and similar monetary transactions connected with a marriage, were not uncommon. As witness the drama that had preceded Lalji's wedding, when the bride's relatives had suddenly demanded double the sum originally agreed upon.

His orders having expressly stated that he was to protect the interests of the Maharajah's sisters and see that the proper payments were made, it seemed unwise, to say the least of it, to allow them and their followers to make camp in such a vulnerable spot; because once under the Rana's guns, negotiations would be difficult if not impossible, and unless he wished to risk bloodshed he might well find himself forced to accept any settlement that the prospective bridegroom chose to make. It was a possibility that did not appeal to him, and to the unconcealed annoyance of the Bhithor dignitaries he had not only refused to move the bridal camp into the valley, but had actually withdrawn it to a position some two miles on the far side of the gorge that gave access to it, and dispatched a special messenger with a letter to the Political Officer responsible for that part of Rajputana, advising him of what he had done, and why.

The decision had been an unpopular one with all save Mulraj and some of the more cautious and level-headed elders, for the entire camp had been looking forward to roaming through the bazaars of Bhithor and seeing the sights of the city. They could still do so, but only at the cost of covering some sixteen miles there and back, and the days were very hot. Therefore they grumbled and protested, and the Rana sent two elderly relatives with another deputation of high-ranking officials to inquire why the Sahib would not permit the brides and their entourage to set up their tents within easy reach of the city, and on the excellent site that had been specially selected for them.

The deputation was plainly aggrieved, and Ash's reply that the camp did very well where it was did nothing to mollify them. They withdrew in so much dudgeon that Kaka-ji took fright and suggested that it might be wiser to fall in with the Rana's wishes, for if they offended

488

him he might withdraw from the marriage contract altogether. Ash did not think this in the least likely—considering that half the bride-price had already been paid and that the preparations for the wedding must by now have cost the state a pretty penny. But Unpora-Bai and several of the elders had become infected by Kaka-ji's fears, and they urged him to reconsider.

Even Mulraj began to look a little doubtful, and when, eventually, a reply came from the Political Officer, it proved to be a frostily worded note that rebuked Captain Pelham-Martyn for being over-zealous and advised him to accept the proffered site without any further delay.

According to the Political Officer, such an uncalled-for display of caution could only offend the Rana, who was not in the least likely to back out of his obligations or attempt to dictate unacceptable terms, and therefore the sooner the camp was moved the better. The note, and its tone, was not something that Ash could afford to ignore, so bowing to the inevitable, he gave the order to march.

Two days later the last of the long column passed through the gorge under the guns of the fort crowning the ridge above it, to pitch their tents in the valley: and within a matter of hours Ash's fears were fully realized and the Political Officer's confidence proved groundless.

The Rana sent a junior minister to announce that the terms of the marriage contracts drawn up in the previous year with His Highness the Maharajah of Karidkote were, on reflection, adjudged to be unsatisfactory, and the council had therefore decided that they must be re-negotiated on a more realistic scale. If the Sahib and such of the elders who chose to accompany him cared to present themselves at the city palace, the Rana would be pleased to receive them and discuss the matter in more detail, after which they would undoubtedly see the justice of his claims, and the affair would be speedily settled to the satisfaction of all.

The minister sweetened his message with a few fulsome compliments, and having tactfully ignored the Sahib's statement that there was nothing whatever to discuss, set the time of the meeting for the following morning and removed himself with some haste.

"What did I tell you?" demanded Ash. The question was not untinged by a certain gloomy satisfaction, for he

489

had not relished the barely concealed accusation of timidity that the Political Officer's strictures on "undue and unnecessary caution" had implied. Or the angry grumbling in the camp and the reiterated fears of those who had agreed with Kaka-ji that the Rana must not be annoyed.

"But he cannot do this to us," exploded a senior official, finding his voice at long last. "The terms were agreed. Everything was settled. He cannot in honour go back on them now."

"Can't he?" returned Ash sceptically. "Well, all we can do is wait and see what he has to say before we decide what we can do about it. With luck it may not turn out to be as bad as we think."

On the following morning Ash, Kaka-ji and Mulraj, attended by a small escort of cavalry, had ridden to the city to meet the Rana.

The ride was not a pleasant one. The unshaded road was little more than a cart-track, inches deep in dust and full of ruts and potholes, and the sun was very hot. The valley must have been a good two miles wide at the point where their camp had been pitched, but nearer the city it narrowed until its sides were less than half that distance apart, the gap between them forming a natural gateway that gave on to a wide plain encircled by hills and containing the life-blood of Bhithor—the great Rani Talab, the "Queen's Lake." It was in the centre of this gap, midway between the two fort-crowned heights that flanked it, that the first Rana had built his capital in the reign of Krishna Deva Raya.

The city had changed very little since then. So little, that had its builders been able to return they would have found themselves on familiar ground, and still felt themselves at home, for here old customs and old ways still prevailed, and the lives of the inhabitants had altered almost as little as the solid sandstone of which their city was built or the jagged outline of the low hills that enclosed the valley. There were still only four gateways in the massive outer wall: the *Hathi Pol*—the "Elephant Gate" —facing down the length of the valley, the Water Gate that looked eastward across the lake and the open country towards the far hills, and on the north and south, the *Mori* and the *Thakur* Gates, both of which faced an almost identical view—a belt of cultivated land three quarters of a mile wide, with beyond it the steep rise of a hillside topped by an ancient fort.

The cultivation gave the city the appearance of a rock standing in a river gorge and splitting the current into two streams: a green river made up of fields where the farmers grew grain and vegetables and sugar-cane, interspersed with groves of mango, papaya, lichi and palm trees. But the cultivated area did not stretch far, and beyond it the valley, grazing-grounds, plain and hills lay bleached and colourless under the glare of the sun, so that Ash was thankful to reach the shade of the great gateway, and more than grateful for the prospect of being able to dismount and sit in coolness and comfort in the Rana's palace, even though the accompanying interview might prove to be a trying one.

Just how trying it was likely to be was at once made clear by the behaviour of the guards at the gateway, who did not trouble to salute them, and the fact that the one person waiting there to conduct them to the palace was a very minor official who ranked little higher than a flunkey. This in itself was a discourtesy that verged on insult, and Mulraj spoke between his teeth in a muttered aside:

"Let us go back to the camp, Sahib. We will wait there until such time as these people" (yeh-log—the term is one of contempt) "have learned manners."

"Not so," said Ash softly. "We will wait here." He lifted his hand, and as the escort clattered to a halt behind him, raised his voice and addressed the solitary courier:

"I fear that in our haste to greet the Rana we have arrived too early and caught him unprepared. Perhaps he has overslept, or his servants have been dilatory in attending to him. These things happen, and no court can be perfect. But we are in no hurry. You may tell your master that we will wait here in the shade until we hear that he is ready to receive us."

"But—" began the man uncertainly.

Ash cut him short: "No, no. Do not apologize, we shall find the rest pleasant. Ijazat hai."*

He turned away and began to talk to Kaka-ji, and the man shifted uneasily and cleared his throat as though about to speak again, but Mulraj said curtly: "You heard what the Sahib said—you have his leave to go."

---

*You have permission to go

491

The man went, and for the next twenty minutes or so the delegation from Karidkote sat at ease in their saddles under the shadow of the great gateway, while their mounted escort held off an ever-growing crowd of interested citizens, and Mulraj favoured Kaka-ji with a long monologue (delivered sotto-voce but still clearly audible to most of the by-standers) deploring the muddle and disorganization, the shocking lack of discipline and total ignorance of polite procedure that was to be met within many small and backward states.

The men of the escort grinned and murmured agreement, and Kaka-ji added injury to insult by rebuking Mulraj for being so hard on men who had not had his advantages and therefore knew no better. It was not their fault, said Kaka-ji, that being ignorant of the ways of the great world they lacked polish, and it was unkind to censure them for behaving in a manner that appeared uncouth to men of superior culture.

Mulraj acknowledged the justice of the reproof and complimented Kaka-ji on his charitable outlook and kindness of heart, and raising his voice began to admire the size of the gateway, the smartness of the guard and the arrangements that had been made for the comfort of the camp. He appeared to be enjoying himself, and the obvious discomfort of the guard, and those by-standers who had been near enough to overhear the preceding conversation, suggested that the Rana's slighting treatment of his guests—presumably designed to put them at a disadvantage and make them realize the weakness of their position—was proving a boomerang by making it appear instead that he and his courtiers and subjects were nothing but ignorant yokels, unversed in etiquette and lacking in courtesy.

Ash alone held his tongue, for he had no illusions as to their position. They might win a point by forcing the Rana to accord them an outward show of civility, but the victory would be a trivial one. The real struggle lay ahead, when the marriage settlements came to be discussed; and here the Rana held all the cards. It only remained to be seen if he would dare to play them—and how far he could be bluffed.

A clatter of hooves announced the arrival of the Rana's personal bodyguard with two senior ministers and an elderly royal relative, who was profuse in his apologies for having mistaken the hour of the guests' arrival and thereby failed to be on time to receive them. It was all due to a sad mishap (it seemed he had been misinformed by an officious secretary) and he assured them that the man responsible for it would be severely punished, as not for the world would anyone in Bhithor have inconvenienced such honoured guests.

The honoured guests accepted the apologies and permitted themselves to be escorted in state through a maze of narrow streets towards the city palace, where the Rana awaited them.

Ash had not forgotten the Gulkote of his childhood, and he had, at one time or another, seen many Indian cities. But none of them had been in the least like this one. The streets and bazaars of Gulkote had been clamorous and colourful, and as crowded with people and full of life as the teeming rabbit-warren that was Peshawar, or the old walled cities of Delhi and Lahore with their shops and street-merchants and jostling, chattering citizens. But Bhithor was like something out of another age. An older and more dangerous age, full of menace and mystery. Its pale sandstone walls had an oddly bleached look, as though the burning suns of centuries had drained them of colour, while the sharp-edged shadows were grey rather than blue or black. The planless labyrinth of streets, and the blank and virtually windowless faces of the houses that hemmed them in gave Ash an uncomfortable feeling of claustrophobia. It seemed impossible that sunlight could ever penetrate into those narrow, man-made canyons, or the winds blow through them, or that ordinary people could live behind those barred doors and closely shuttered windows. Yet he was aware of eyes peering down through those shutters—women's eyes, presumably, for all over India the upper storeys of houses are woman's territory.

There were surprisingly few women in the shadowed streets however, and those few kept their faces hidden, holding their cotton head-cloths close so that once again nothing could be seen but eyes; wary and suspicious eyes. And though they wore the traditional dress of Rajputana, full-skirted and boldly patterned in black, their preferences seemed to be for such colours as rust-red, ochre and burnt orange, and Ash saw none of the vivid blues and greens that flaunted so gaily through the bazaars and by-

493

ways of neighbouring states. As for the men, a number of these too gave the impression of being veiled, since even here in the city streets there were many who kept one end of their turbans wrapped about the lower part of their faces; and judging by their narrow gaze, a European was a novelty in Bhithor—and not a popular one, either.

The citizens stared at Ash as though he were some form of freak, and the expressions of those whose faces were uncovered betrayed more hostility than interest. It was, he thought, as though he were a dog walking down an alley full of cats, and he felt the hair on the back of his neck prickle in animal response to that silent antipathy —the enmity of closed minds towards all that is strange or new.

"One would think, to look at them, that we have come here for some evil purpose instead of for a wedding," muttered Mulraj under his breath. "This is an ill place, and one does not need to be told that they worship the Drinker-of-Blood. *Phew!* Look there—"

He jerked his head in the direction of a shrine to Kali, who is also Sitala the goddess of smallpox, that stood at the junction of two streets; and as they rode past it Ash caught a glimpse of the frightful goddess in whose honour the Thugs had strangled thousands of victims, and whose temples had benefited by a tithe of their loot. The nightmare deity, with her multiplicity of arms, her glaring eyeballs, protruding tongue and long necklace of human skulls, is worshipped throughout India as the wife of Shiva the Destroyer. A singularly appropriate patroness, thought Ash, for this sinister city.

A strong stench of corruption and a buzzing cloud of flies showed that her devotees were not backward in satisfying her thirst for blood, and it was a measure of his unease that he actually caught himself wondering if it were only goats that were being sacrificed to appease that thirst. He shook the thought from him with impatience, but was nevertheless inordinately relieved when at last they left the streets behind them, and dismounting in the entrance courtyard of the city palace, the "Rung Mahal," were conducted through a maze of dusty rooms and dark stone passageways to meet the Rana. Though here too there was the same claustrophobic atmosphere that had been so noticeable in the streets: the same stillness and stifling heat, the same haunting sense of an unforgotten past . . . of old times and old evil, and the unquiet ghosts of dead kings and murdered queens.

Compared to the Palace of the Winds, the Rung Mahal—the "Painted Palace"—was a modest building comprising half-a-dozen courtyards, a garden or two, and not more than sixty or seventy rooms (no one had ever counted those in the Palace of the Winds, though the number was believed to be in the region of six hundred). Possibly it was for this reason—among others—that its owner had begun by treating his guests in a manner calculated to damp any pretensions they might have, and now followed it up by simultaneously dazzling them with magnificence and chilling their blood with as barbaric a display of military strength as Ash, for one, had ever seen—or imagined.

It had been no surprise to find that the outer courtyards bristled with armed men, but the sight of the Rana's personal bodyguards, who policed the inner ones and lined the long dark corridors, had startled Ash considerably, not on account of their numbers, though there must have been several hundred of them, but because of their weird attire, and because here, once again, were masked faces.

The officers wore helmets of a pattern that the Saracens must have worn in the days of the Crusades. Antique iron casques with long flat nose pieces, damascened in gold and silver and deeply fringed with chain mail that protected the wearer's jaw and neck and partially concealed his cheeks, leaving only the eyes visible. The helmets of the rank and file, though similar in style, were fashioned of leather, and the effect in that half light was oddly inhuman, as though the macabre figures who lined the corridors were masked headsmen or the mummified bodies of dead warriors. Their surcoats too were of chain mail, and instead of swords they carried short spears. "Like lictors," thought Ash with a shiver.

He regretted that he had not brought his revolver with him, for the sight of these mailed figures brought home to him, as nothing else had done, that this was a place in which no rules—and no law as the West understood law—held sway. Bhithor was of another age and another world: she stood outside of present Time, and was a law unto herself.

In a final ante-chamber at least fifty servants, dressed in the Rana's colours of scarlet, sulphur-yellow and orange, divided to let the visitors through, and preceded by the royal relative with the senior officials bringing up the rear, they were ushered into the *Diwan-i-Am*, the "Hall of Public Audience," where the Rana and his Prime Minister the Diwan, together with the councillors and courtiers, waited to receive them.

The *Diwan-i-Am* was a beautiful building, though at that season of the year unsuited for a morning audience, as it consisted of an open-sided pavilion formed by a triple row of columns, and was closed only at each end. With the sun blazing down upon it and no breath of breeze, the heat under the pillared arches was considerable, but its beauty made amends for any deficiencies in the way of comfort; and certainly the temperature did not appear to trouble the serried ranks of courtiers and noblemen who sat cross-legged on the uncarpeted floor, packed as closely as sardines in a tin, and dressed in their festive best.

At the far end of the hall a shallow flight of steps led up to a raised platform on which a central dais served as a throne for the ruler when he gave audience, received distinguished visitors or dispensed justice, and behind this stretched a solid wall of black marble with a polished surface that reflected the assembly as though in a mirror. The sides of the platform were enclosed by screens of pierced marble through which the ladies of the Zenana could watch the proceedings, but elsewhere the stonework had been plastered over with polished *chunam* and decorated in low relief with formal designs of beasts, birds and flowers that had once been brightly coloured, but had faded in the course of the slow centuries to pale ghosts of their former glory. Yet the *Diwan-i-Am* did not lack colour, since the Rana's courtiers, unlike his humbler subjects, were so gaily attired that a foreigner entering the hall might well have thought for a dazzled moment that he had walked into a flower-garden—or a fairground.

Turbans of scarlet and cerise, sulphur-yellow, sugar-pink and purple vied with *achkans* of every shade of blue and violet, turquoise, vermilion, grass-green and orange; while to add to the mass of colour, the centre aisle was kept clear by a double rank of crimson-turbaned retainers, gaudily uniformed in yellow muslin sashed with orange, and carrying huge, plumed fly-whisks made of horsehair that had been dyed a vivid shade of magenta.

496

There were more retainers on the raised platform, two of them standing behind the dais and playing fans of peacock feathers, and the remainder armed with naked tulwars—the long curved swords of Rajputana. And on the dais itself, cross-legged on a carpet sewn with pearls, ablaze with jewels and clad from top to toe in gold, sat the focal point of all this splendour: the Rana of Bhithor.

The warrior races of Rajputana are famous for their good-looks, and it is doubtful if any similar assembly of Western men could have matched the present one in the matter of physical beauty, distinction and panache. Even the grey-beards among them retained traces of the hawk-faced handsomeness they had possessed in youth, and held themselves as erect as though they sat in a saddle instead of cross-legged upon the ground. The white, tightly fitting jodhpurs and the sleek lines of flared, brocaded coats showed off each lean, broad-shouldered, slim-hipped figure to perfection, while the crisp folds of their brilliant turbans added inches to their height and made every man seem a giant. There were, of course, exceptions to the rule. Scattered here and there under the arched roof of the *Diwan-i-Am* were men who were fat or withered or ill-favoured, the most noticeable of these being their ruler himself.

The Rana's dress, jewels and diamond-hilted sword were magnificent. But his person did not do them credit, and Ash, gazing up at him from the bottom step of the stairs, was conscious of a violent sense of shock.

This—this misshapen baboon—was the bridegroom that Nandu had chosen for Juli. For Juli and Shushila . . . No, it could not be—there must be some mistake: the man on the dais could not possibly be in his late thirties. Why, he was *old*. Sixty, at least, if not seventy. Or if he was not, he certainly looked it, and Ash could only suppose that his way of life must have been singularly unsavoury to give him the appearance of old age before he was forty.

Discounting prejudice, the Rana was certainly an un-prepossessing spectacle, and Ash could not have been the first person to be struck by his resemblance to a baboon. Anyone who had visited a zoo or been to Africa could hardly fail to notice it, and it was probably just as well that no citizens of Bhithor had ever done so and therefore did not realize how strikingly their ruler's facial structure, with its close-set eyes, abnormally long nose and wide, flaring nostrils, resembled a mandrill's—an old, sly, vicious mandrill, with an evil temper. As if that were not enough, the thin, hatchet-shaped and almost chinless face was deeply scored with the tell-tale lines of debauchery and self-indulgence, and the close-set eyes were as watchful and unblinking as a cobra's—their stillness in marked contrast to the ceaseless movement of the long, loose-lipped mouth; for the Rana was chewing *pan*. The betel-nut stained his lips and teeth and made small wet, red patches at the corners of his mouth, so that he might almost, like Kali, have been drinking blood.

In complexion he was fairer than most southern Europeans, for his lineage was impeccable (the royal house of Bhithor claimed descent from a god) but the pale golden tone of his skin was overlaid by an odd greyish tinge, and there were dark purple pouches, like bruises, under the cold, unblinking eyes. All in all, he presented a singularly unattractive picture, and the magnificence of his attire seemed to emphasize his physical shortcomings rather than detract from them.

Ash had been prepared for a good many things, but not this. The shock momentarily deprived him of words, and as the Rana remained silent it was left to Kaka-ji to step into the breach and fill the awkward pause with a graceful speech, to which the Rana replied a good deal less gracefully.

It was an inauspicious beginning, and the remainder of the morning did nothing to rectify it. The compliments proper to the occasion were duly exchanged—and at unconscionable length—and when at last they were over the Rana rose, and dismissing the assembled courtiers, retired to the "Hall of Private Audience," the *Diwan-i-Khas*, accompanied by his Diwan, his senior councillors and the representatives of Karidkote.

The *Diwan-i-Khas*, unlike the *Diwan-i-Am*, was pleasantly cool. It consisted of a small marble pavilion set in the middle of a formal garden, and was surrounded by water channels in which fountains played—a setting that not only charmed the eye and reduced the temperature to comfortable limits, but ensured privacy, as no shrub was large enough to conceal an eavesdropper, and even if by some miracle an intruder had been able to enter the garden unseen, the splash of the fountains would have prevented him from hearing anything that was said inside the pavilion.

A chair had been provided for Ash, but the Rana occupied a cushioned and carpeted dais similar to the one in the *Diwan-i-Am*, while the remainder of the company disposed themselves comfortably on the cool marble floor. Uniformed servants dispensed glasses of cold sherbet, and for a short time the atmosphere seemed pleasantly friendly and informal; but it did not last. No sooner had the servants withdrawn than the Diwan, acting as the mouthpiece of the Rana, proceeded to justify Ash's worst fears.

He had approached his subject obliquely and wrapped it up in a wordy cloud of compliments and polite phrases. But shorn of irrelevant verbiage, the matter was plain: the Rana had no intention of paying the full bride-price for the Rajkumari Shushila, or of marrying her half-sister Anjuli-Bai, unless the bribe for doing so was increased to over three times the sum that had originally been offered (and pocketed), for after all, the girl's birth hardly qualified her to be the wife of such an exalted personage as the ruler of Bhithor, whose line was one of the oldest and most honourable in all Rajputana, and the Rana had already made a great concession in even considering the possibility of marrying her at all.

To be fair to the Rana, the sum that Nandu had demanded as a brideprice for Shushila had been very large. But then in view of her rank, her outstanding beauty and her impressive dowry, she was a valuable commodity in the marriage market and there were others who would have paid as much, if not more, for such a wife: several of them princes of far more consequence than the ruler of Bhithor. Nandu, for his own devious reasons, had decided in favour of the latter, and the Rana's ambassadors had not quibbled over the price or demurred at paying half of it in advance—or at giving a written promise on his behalf to pay the remainder as soon as the bride arrived in Bhithor, because large as the sum was, it had been drastically reduced by the bribe demanded as the price of the Rana's consent to take Anjuli-Bai as well as the lovely Shushila; and as any question of a second bride-price had been waived, the Rana had, in fact, got a bargain.

But it appeared that he was not content with it, and

499

wanted more. Much more. The additional sum he now demanded for marrying the *Feringhi*-Rani's daughter came to a good deal more than half Shushila's bride-price, and if it were paid (and the half he himself still owed was not) it would mean that he would not only have acquired two brides, together with their dowries, for nothing, but would actually have made a handsome profit out of the transaction.

The demand was so outrageous that even Ash, who had been prepared for something of the kind, could not at first believe that he had heard aright—or if he had, that the Diwan had not exceeded his instructions. The man *could* not seriously mean what he said. But at the end of half an hour of argument and expostulation it was clear that the Diwan had done no more than speak his master's mind, and that the councillors were all in agreement with him. Plainly, now that the brides and their dowries were virtually in a trap, with their forces at the mercy of the guns and garrisons of two forts, and their camp confined to a valley from which the only exit was barred by a third, Bhithor saw no reason for keeping to the terms of the contract. The council not only approved the demand for a further extortionate bribe, but clearly considered that their ruler had shown himself to be a *chabuk sawi,* a smart fellow, who had successfully tricked a formidable opponent.

Ash could see no point in prolonging a discussion that could only lead to a loss of temper and a consequent loss of face by one or other of his own party—probably himself, for he had seldom felt angrier. It had been bad enough in all conscience to know that Juli was lost to him, without having to discover that her future husband was not only physically repulsive and prematurely aged by debauchery, but capable of going back on his word and resorting to blackmail; and not above insulting her in open council.

The fact that such a creature should dare to demand that he be paid for the privilege of making Juli his wife was beyond bearing, and Ash was aware that it was only a question of time before he lost his precarious hold on his temper, and spoke his mind in terms that would be both undiplomatic and quite unforgivable.

He therefore brought the proceedings to an abrupt close by announcing that—regrettably—the terms put

500

forward by the Diwan were wholly unacceptable and would not be met: and forestalling further argument, rose to his feet, bowed curtly to the Rana, and withdrew in good order, followed by the fuming representatives of Karidkote.

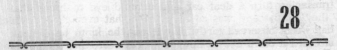

28

The escort was waiting for them in the outer courtyard, and they mounted in grim silence, and did not speak as they rode back through the narrow streets and under the great archway of the Elephant Gate where the lounging sentries grinned openly as they passed.

The valley shimmered in the heat and there was no sign of life in the forts that looked down from the low hills to the left and right of the city, for the garrisons were taking their ease in the shade. But the mouths of the guns showed black against the sun-baked stone, and Ash stared up at them, and noting their number, spoke abruptly, his voice raw-edged with rage:

"It's my own fault. I should have backed my own judgement, instead of letting a pompous Political Officer give me orders and rap me over the knuckles for insulting a ruling prince with my unworthy suspicions. Much he knows! That treacherous old spider had it all planned, and we've done exactly what he meant us to do—walked meekly into his parlour."

"It is terrible . . . terrible," moaned Kaka-ji. "I cannot believe . . . How is it possible that the Rana should refuse to pay? That *we* should pay . . . ?"

"Don't worry, Rao-Sahib. We won't," said Ash shortly. "He is merely bluffing."

"You think so?" inquired Mulraj. "*Hmm.* I wish I could feel sure of that. He has enough guns in those forts to smash the valley into dust—and all of them trained on our camp. If it should come to a fight we would have no chance, since of what use are swords and muskets against stone walls and heavy cannon?"

501

"It will not come to a fight," snapped Ash. "He would not dare."

"Let us hope that you are right. But I would not care to wager on it. The princes of Rajputana may think it prudent to pay lip-service to the Raj, but they still wield great power within their own states, and even the Sahibs of the Political Department—as you have seen—prefer to turn a deaf ear and a blind eye to much that they do."

Ash observed tartly that it was going to be difficult to turn a blind eye to this, or a deaf ear either, as he intended to raise a considerable noise about it. He proposed to write a full account to the Political Officer and have the letter sent off by special messenger that very afternoon.

"That would be as well," agreed Mulraj. And added thoughtfully—"though I do not think your messenger will get through, for they have the roads well guarded. Moreover, my spies brought me a tale last night that I do not like: they say that the city and the forts can speak to each other without words."

"You mean by semaphore?" inquired Ash, startled. "Can they, by jove. I wonder where the devil they learned that?"

"You know of it, then? It is possible?"

"Of course. It's quite simple. It's done with flags: you make signs with them and—Oh, it would take too long to explain. I'll show you one day."

"Ah, but this is not done with flags. This thing is done with the aid of small shields of polished silver that catch the light of the sun and flash warnings that can be seen from many miles away."

"That for a tale," scoffed Ash, losing interest. His scepticism was understandable, for though he had read that the Indians of North America had long since learned the trick of sending visual messages by means of smoke, the somewhat similar method of communication described by Mulraj, and that would become known as the heliograph, was as yet unknown to the Indian Army, nor would it be used by them for some years to come. He therefore dismissed it as a fabrication, and remarked that it did not do to believe everything one was told.

"Nor do I," retorted Mulraj. "But my spies tell me

that it is no new thing in Bhithor and that it has been practised here for longer than anyone can remember. They say the secret of it was brought here by a merchant of this city who was a great traveller, and who learned the art from the *Chinni-log*" (he meant the Chinese) "many years before the Company's Raj came to power. Be that as it may, it is certain that all our movements will be watched and reported on, and that no messenger that we send will leave unobserved. They will be ready and waiting for him. And even if one should succeed in slipping through their net, I will wager fifty gold mohurs to five rupees that the only answer he will bring back from the Political Sahib will be a request that you use great restraint and do nothing that might upset the Rana."

"Done," returned Ash promptly. "You'll lose, because he'll have to take action on this."

"I shall win, because, my friend, your Government does not wish to quarrel with the princes. To do so might lead to bloodshed and armed rising, and that would mean the dispatching of regiments and the expenditure of much money."

Unfortunately, Mulraj had been right—on both counts.

Ash had sent off a detailed report of the latest developments, and it was only after the best part of a week had passed without any sign of his messenger with the reply that stringent inquiries and a strongly worded protest to the Diwan revealed that the man had got no further than the far end of the gorge, where he had been stopped and subsequently held prisoner in the fort on a trumped-up charge. (He had, it seemed, "been mistaken for a notorious bandit" and the error was deeply regretted.) The second messenger did not go alone, but was accompanied by two armed troopers. They returned three days later, on foot, having been ambushed some twenty miles beyond the border by a party of dacoits who had stripped them of all they possessed, and taking their horses, left them naked, wounded and without food, to find their own way back.

Ash let it be known that he himself would be the next messenger, and that he would be taking an armed escort of over a dozen picked men of the Karidkote State Forces, all of them crack shots. And though he had not

503

actually done this—being unwilling to leave the camp to its own devices with the Rana and his councillors in their present mood and tempers running high among their angry guests—he had made a pretence of doing so by riding with the original messenger and the escort until they were well outside Bhithor.

He did not see the warning sun signals that blinked frantically behind him from a high rooftop in the city and the outer walls of the two guardian forts. But Mulraj did, and he grinned as he watched them, for his spies had not been idle and the code was a very simple one—far more so than that complicated business of dots and dashes that the Sahib had called "Morse" and tried to expound to him. The Bhithories had more sense than to waste time over such things, and like the Red Indians confined themselves to essentials. Their code was a model of simplicity, consisting of a single sustained flash for "Enemy" or, alternatively, three long ones for "Friend, do not molest," followed by short ones to indicate the numbers involved, up to a score; and if in excess of that, by a flurry of flashes. The addition of a side-to-side movement meant that the man or men in question were mounted, and not on foot, while several wide circular sweeps ordered "stop them!" To which the reply was seldom more than a single answering flash that could be translated as "Message received and understood." There were no other signals, Bhithor having found these more than adequate.

Mulraj watched the agitated flashes that commanded "friends, do not molest," and his grin turned to a laugh, for he knew that Ash intended to turn back as soon as the border had been safely crossed—being reasonably certain that this time no plans would have been made to waylay the party, as the Rana would never risk attacking a well-armed band of men commanded by the Sahib himself, and by the time it was discovered that the Sahib was no longer with them, it would be too late to arrange yet another unfortunate accident.

All this had wasted a good many days. But they had not been spent in idleness. Those who did not possess tents had busied themselves constructing grass huts that would protect them from the burning sun and the night dews, and though wood was far from plentiful in Bhithor, Mulraj—visualizing a lengthy stay and anxious for the horses now that the hot weather had begun—had set men to work felling the broom-stick palms and the scarlet *dak* trees, and presently a score of stoutly built sheds arose, well thatched with palm-fronds and bundles of reeds from the lake.

Ash and his *panchayat,* for their part, had paid repeated visits to the city palace, where they conferred endlessly with the Diwan and one or other of the senior ministers, and occasionally with the Rana himself, in an effort to break the deadlock by persuading him to honour his bond or at least moderate his demands. They had also given a number of banquets for him and his courtiers, councillors and officials, and once, when the Rana had sent word that he was unable to attend because of a painful attack of boils (an affliction he was prone to), they had proffered the services of Gobind, in the hope that Kaka-ji's invaluable Hakim might be able to relieve the pain and thereby earn his good will.

Gobind had in fact not only succeeded in doing this, but had actually effected a cure, which was something that the Rana's own hakims had signally failed to do. But though the grateful patient had rewarded him with a handful of gold mohurs and presented Kaka-ji with a large ruby set in a gold thumb-ring, his attitude towards the marriage settlements had remained unchanged. For all the results that Ash and his colleagues achieved they might just as well have addressed their arguments to the pillars of the *Diwan-i-Am* and given banquets for the local pigeons; and when at last the messenger and his escort returned with the Political Officer's long-awaited reply, it proved to be almost exactly what Mulraj had predicted.

The Political Officer confessed to being greatly disturbed by Captain Pelham-Martyn's communication. He, Major Spiller, could only suppose that Captain Pelham-Martyn had either misunderstood the Rana's proposals or been less than patient in his handling of the ruler and his ministers. He was reluctant to believe that the Rana intended any breach of faith, but on the other hand he admitted the possibility of there being faults on both sides— each had probably misunderstood the other. He advised Captain Pelham-Martyn not to rush his fences but to proceed with the greatest caution, and having stressed the necessity for exercising Tact, Courtesy, and Forbearance, ended by saying that he looked to the Captain to do everything in his power to avoid antagonizing a ruling

505

prince who had always been a loyal supporter of the Raj, and therefore . . .

Ash handed Mulraj five rupees without comment.

The ball was back in his own court, and he realized that he would have to negotiate a settlement without any help from the Political Department—or not for the time being, at all events. If he did so successfully, well and good. If not, then he and he alone would be blamed for bungling it. In short, Captain Pelham-Martyn would be convicted of "failing to exercise tact, courtesy and forbearance," while the authorities, provided with this useful whipping-boy, would still be able to remain on excellent terms with both Karidkote and Bhithor. It was not a cheerful prospect.

"Heads, they win; tails, I lose," concluded Ash bitterly.

He spent another sleepless night (there had been too many of them of late) wondering how he could get a message to Juli, and why she had not sent one to him when she could not fail to know how anxious he must be on her behalf. Was it a good sign that she had not done so, or a bad one? If only he knew, it would make it easier for him to hold to his present course. But while he did not, there would always be the fear that if he continued to conduct negotiations with the patience and caution recommended by the Political Officer, the delay might end by destroying Juli.

It was the time-factor that frightened him. By rights the wedding should have taken place within a few days of the brides' arrival in Bhithor, and it had obviously never occurred to Juli—any more than it had to him—that it might not. But already over three weeks had been wasted in fruitless talks, and by now it was almost two months since the night of the sandstorm. If her hopes had been fulfilled and she was pregnant, there would soon be very little chance of the child being accepted as a prematurely born offspring of the Rana's. And should there be any doubt at all on that score, both Juli and the child would die: that much was certain. It would be so easy. No one in authority would ask any questions, for death in childbed was all too common and the news that a junior Rani of Bhithor had died giving birth to a prematurely born infant would occasion no surprise. If only Juli would send him word. She *must* know by now—one way or another . . .

Ash did not close his eyes that night. He had watched the stars move slowly in their spheres and seen them pale in the yellow flush of another dawn, and when the sun was up he set out once more with Mulraj and the others for the city (it was the fourth time that week) to attend a meeting with the Diwan that proved no more fruitful than the preceding ones.

For the fourth successive time they were kept waiting in an ante-room for over an hour, and when they were eventually admitted, it was to no purpose. The situation remained at stalemate, because the Rana was confident that he held the upper hand and had no intention of re-treating from what he plainly regarded as an impregnable position. On the contrary, there were signs that he might demand an even larger sum for marrying the "foreigner's daughter," on the grounds that he would have to pay very highly to be "purified" by the priests for taking such a woman to wife. The amount thus expended would, hinted the Diwan, be considerable, and in the circumstances the prospective bridegroom's demands could not be regarded as unreasonable.

Ash, replying on behalf of Karidkote, pointed out that all this had been discussed in full over a year ago. Nothing had been concealed, and the settlement that had been reached had been declared satisfactory by both sides. Were they then to conclude that the Rana's emissaries had not, after all, been empowered to speak for him? If so, why had they been sent? And if it was being claimed that they had exceeded their instructions, surely it would have been a simple matter for the Rana, on their return, to arrange for a *tar* (telegram) to be dispatched to Karidkote, breaking off the negotiations until someone more competent to carry out his wishes could be sent to reopen the discussions?—or at the very least, to halt the bridal train before they had travelled too far from the borders of their own state, instead of allowing them to complete the journey. Such conduct, implied Ash, was not compatible with either the dignity or the honour of a prince, and as the expense of the journey had been heavy, there could be no question of waiving the other half of the Princess Shushila's dowry, or of adding anything to the sum already paid on behalf of her half-sister, Anjuli-Bai.

The Diwan replied that he would relay these views to his master, and was sure that the matter would eventually be settled to everyone's satisfaction. And on that all-too-familiar note, the meeting ended.

"I wonder how long they will keep it up?" remarked Ash as they rode back to the camp.

Mulraj shrugged and said morosely: "Until we give in."

"Then it looks as though we are going to be here for a long time, because I do not intend to be blackmailed, and the sooner they realize that the better."

"But what else can we do?" wailed Kaka-ji. "Perhaps if we were to offer him—"

"Not one anna," cut in Ash, brusquely interrupting the old man. "Not one pi. The Rana is going to pay all that he owes. And more—much more."

Mulraj grinned and said: "*Shabash*, Sahib. Bravely spoken! But may one ask how you mean to bring this about? It is not he, but we who are in a trap. And we cannot rush those forts, even by night."

"I don't intend to rush anything—least of all the forts. *Or* my fences," added Ash bitterly. "No one is going to be able to say that I have acted precipitately or been too impatient. I mean to give the Rana all the time he wants, and see whose patience wears out first: his or mine. Or Bhithor's."

"Bhithor's?"

"Certainly. Are we not all guests of the state? And as such, why should we pay for our keep? That is surely the privilege of a host. Presently the shopkeepers and the farmers and the cowherds, and all those who supply us with food and fuel and fodder, will demand payment. And they will not get it from us, that I promise you. The Rana and his councillors will soon find that it is costing them far more to keep us here than they bargained for, and after a time they may decide that it would be cheaper to make concessions."

Mulraj laughed for the first time in several weeks, and the faces of the others cleared.

"*Arré*, that is true," said Mulraj. "I had not thought of it. Why, if we stay here long enough, those swindling sons of faithless mothers may even pay us to go away."

508

"Or take what they want by force?" suggested Kakaji with a pessimistic nod in the direction of the nearest fort. "Ah yes, Sahib"——here he shook his head at Ash—— "I know that you think otherwise, and I wish that I was of your mind. But I cannot feel sure that the Rana will abstain from using violence once he finds that he cannot get what he desires by more peaceful means."

"By blackmail and bluff, you mean," retorted Ash. "But bluff, my father, is a game that two can play at, which is something that these faithless apes have failed to take into account. Well, we will play it with them."

He refused to be drawn further, for if the truth were known he had nothing in mind except a firm determination to resist the Rana's demands and see that he paid up to the last farthing. For the moment it behoved him to move cautiously, if only to show Major Spiller, the Political Officer, that he had done everything possible in the way of peaceful persuasion, and shown enough patience to arouse envy in Job. Once that point had been made, if the Rana continued to be intransigent then he, Ash, could hardly be blamed if he took more forceful measures to bring the bridegroom's party to their senses. But whatever happened, he must not lose his temper.

This last resolve came close to being broken two days later, when at yet another meeting in the Rung Mahal——convened to discuss "new proposals"——the Diwan (who had again kept them waiting) announced in a confidential manner and with a great show of regret that as a result of further discussions with the priests on the religious aspect of the Rana's proposed marriage to his bride's half-sister, it had, unhappily, become necessary to ask for still more money in return for this favour. He mentioned a sum that made the previous extortionate demand seem almost paltry by contrast...

"These priests they are rapacious," confessed the Diwan in a resigned, man-of-the-world voice. "We have reasoned with them, but alas, to no avail. They have now demanded that my master build a new temple as the price of their consent to this marriage. It is iniquitous——but how can he refuse? He is a most religious man, and he cannot go against his priests. Yet to build a temple will cost a great deal of money; so you will see that he has no choice but to ask that His Highness of Karidkote should defray an expense that will have been incurred on behalf

509

of His Highness's half-sister. It is all most unfortunate"
—the Diwan wagged a regretful head and spread out his
hands in a gesture of rueful deprecation—"but what can
I do?"

Ash could think of several things. But the question
was plainly rhetorical, and in any case he could not have
answered it for the simple reason that he could not trust
himself to speak, because it was Juli who was being subjected to insult by these contemptible, smirking black-
mailers. He was aware, through a red haze of rage, that
Kaka-ji was replying to the Diwan in a gentle, dignified
voice; and presently that they were all out in the sunlight
once more, mounting their horses and riding away again.
But he still had no idea what answer the Diwan had received.

"Well, and what now, Sahib?" inquired Mulraj.

Ash did not reply, and Kaka-ji took up the question,
repeating it and demanding to know what they could do
in the face of this latest outrage.

Ash came out of his dream and said abruptly: "I must
speak to her."

The old man stared at him in bewilderment. "To
Shu-shu? But I do not think——"

"To Anjuli-Bai. You must arrange it for me, Rao-
Sahib. I must see her. And alone."

"But that is impossible!" protested Kaka-ji, shocked.
"On the march, yes. There it did not matter too much.
But not here in Bhithor. It would be most imprudent
and I could not permit it."

"You will have to," insisted Ash tersely. "For unless
I do, I will take no further part in these negotiations, but
send word to Spiller-Sahib that I can do no more and that
he and the Rana must decide the matter between them."

"But you cannot do that!" gasped Kaka-ji. "What if he
should give way to the Rana for the sake of peace?—
which he might well do, as Mulraj has said. We should be
undone, for how could we pay such a sum? Even if we
had it—which we have not—it would beggar us, and
without money we could not make the return journey.
Nandu, I know, would never send us any more, for he
would be mad with anger and——"

Agitation was making Kaka-ji speak with more frank-
ness than he would normally have dreamt of using in
public, and realizing it, he broke off to throw an anguished

510

glance over his shoulder at the four other members of the party, who had fallen behind them, and was relieved to see that they were not only well out of earshot but engaged in an animated conversation of their own.

"Besides," said Kaka-ji, lowering his voice and returning to his original argument, "what good can you do by speaking to Anjuli-Bai? There is no way in which she can help us, and to tell her what the Rana has said would only be an unkindness, there being no way out for her or for Shu-shu."

"All the same, I must see her," said Ash implacably. "She has a right to know how things stand. A right to be warned beforehand, in case . . ."

He hesitated, and Mulraj finished the sentence for him: "In case the Rana refuses to wed her. Yes, I think you are right, Sahib."

"No," said Kaka-ji unhappily. "It is not wise or proper that you should do so; and I cannot think that it is necessary. But as I see that you are both against me in this, I will tell her myself. Will that content you?"

Ash shook his head. "No, Rao-Sahib, it will not. I must speak to her myself. It is not that I do not trust you, but there are things that I wish to say that you could not. But only you can arrange it."

"Nay, Sahib. It is impossible. I cannot . . . It would become known. It would be too difficult . . ."

"Nevertheless you will do it for my sake. Because I ask it of you as a great favour. And because, or so I have heard, you and her grandfather, Sergei, were friends, and you knew her mother, who——"

Kaka-ji checked him with an uplifted hand: "Enough, Sahib. You heard aright. I admired her grandfather the Russian very greatly when I was young. A strange man —a magnificent man—we feared him for his rages as much as we loved him for his laughter; and he laughed often. I have heard that even when he lay dying, he laughed and was not afraid . . ."

Kaka-ji sighed and was silent for a moment or two. And presently he said: "Very well, Sahib, I will do what I can. But only on one condition. I myself must be present."

Nothing that Ash could say would make him give way on that point. The old man was convinced that if it should come to the ears of the Rana and his council that Anjuli-Bai had talked alone with a young man who was unrelated to her, they might use it as an excuse to send her back from Bhithor in disgrace—and in all probability portionless as well. They were quite capable of impounding her dowry as "compensation" for the loss of a bride, and the fact that the young man in question happened to be a Sahib whom the Government had placed in overall charge of the camp and empowered to negotiate the marriage settlements would be neither here nor there. The only factor of importance would be his sex, and a scandal would merely strengthen the Rana's hand and stiffen his attitude on the question of Shushila's bride-price.

"You have nothing to fear," promised Kaka-ji. "No word of what passes between you will ever be spoken afterwards by me: I will promise you that. But if by some evil chance news of it were to leak out, my niece must be safeguarded. I must be able to say that I, her uncle—brother to her father who was lately Maharajah of Karidkote—was present throughout. If you cannot agree to that, then I for my part cannot help you."

Ash looked at him long and thoughtfully, recalling certain rumours he had heard about him, "old, forgotten, far-off things" that might or might not be true. If they were . . . But there was obviously nothing to be gained by arguing with him now. Kaka-ji had meant what he said and would not go back on it; and as it was going to be impossible to have any speech with Juli without his help, there was nothing for it but to accept his terms. At least he could be trusted to keep his word and hold his tongue.

"I agree," said Ash.

"Good. Then I will see what can be arranged. But I can make no promises on behalf of my niece. It may be that she may not wish to see you, and if that is so, I can do nothing."

"You can try to persuade her," said Ash. "You can tell he . . . No. Just say that it is necessary, and that I would not have asked it of her—or of you—had it not been."

Kaka-ji had arranged it. The meeting was to take place in his tent at one o'clock in the morning, at which time all the camp should be asleep. And as Ash would have to find his way there unseen, it would be as well, suggested Kaka-ji, if he disguised himself as a night-watchman, for it could be arranged that the *chowkidar* whose duty it was to patrol that part of the camp would be given a drug that night—something that would send him to sleep for an hour or so.

"Gobind will see to it," said Kaka-ji; "and also that no servant of mine is within sight or hearing. He is to be trusted, and it is necessary that I trust someone; but as we cannot be too careful, even he will not know who it is who comes to my tent by night. Now listen carefully, Sahib—"

Ash would have preferred a less complicated arrangement, and could see no reason for such elaborate precautions. But Kaka-ji was adamant, and on the score of secrecy, the meeting could not have gone better. No whisper of it had ever leaked out, and both his niece and the Sahib had come to his tent and left again without attracting any attention or arousing the least suspicion. But in all other respects it had been a sorry failure, and afterwards the old man was often to regret that he had gone back on his original refusal to have anything to do with it; and even more that having done so he had insisted on being present, as but for that he could have remained in happy ignorance of things that he would so much rather not have known.

His niece Anjuli had arrived first, shrouded in a dark cotton bourka and slipping into the tent as silently as a shadow, to be followed a few moments later by a tall, turbaned figure wearing a dingy shawl wrapped high about his mouth and nose in the time-honoured manner of *chowkidars*, who distrust the night air. Kaka-ji noted with approval that following his instructions the Sahib was carrying a night-watchman's *lathi* and the length of chain that is rattled at intervals to warn away evil-doers, and congratulated himself on his attention to detail. Now it only remained for the Sahib to say what he wanted without wasting words, and for Anjuli to refrain from unnecessary comments, and in less than a quarter of an hour the whole thing would be over and the two of them safely back in their own tents without anyone being the wiser.

Buoyed up by a warm feeling of complacency, Kaka-ji made himself comfortable on a pile of cushions and prepared to listen without interruption while the Sahib informed Anjuli of the Rana's demands and their possible consequence to herself.

The old man had been far too preoccupied with the

513

impropriety and hazards of such a meeting to give much thought as to what exactly might be said at it, or why the Sahib should have been so insistent that only he could say it; which was unfortunate for Kaka-ji, as had he done so he might have been better prepared for what followed—or taken strong measures to prevent it altogether. As it was, that pleasant glow of complacency lasted only as long as the time it took Ash to adjust his eyes to the light and make out Anjuli's shrouded figure, standing motionless among the shadows beyond the lamp.

She had not removed her bourka and as its brown folds matched the canvas walls behind her, for a moment or two he did not realize that she was there, though he was aware of Kaka-ji sitting cross-legged and unobtrusive at the far side of the tent. The slight draught of his own entrance had set the pierced bronze lamp swaying, so that it sent a dazzle of golden stars across the walls and floor. The dancing points of light confused his eyes and made the shadows shift and sway and take on a dozen different shapes, and it was not until they steadied again that he saw that one of those shadows was Anjuli.

The sound of a *lathi* and a chain falling to the floor was disproportionately loud in that waiting silence, and though Kaka-ji was not an imaginative man, it seemed to him in that moment as though something vital and elemental quivered between those two silent figures: an emotion so intense as to be almost visible, and that drew them towards each other as irresistibly as a magnet and steel. He watched, rigid, as they moved on the same instant, and as they met, saw Ash put out a hand to lift the bourka and throw it back from Anjuli's face . . .

They neither spoke nor touched each other. They only looked, long and hungrily, and as though looking were enough and there was no one else in the tent, or in the world. And there was that in their faces that made speech unnecessary, for no words and no actions—not even the most passionate of embraces—could have conveyed love so clearly.

Kaka-ji caught his breath and attempted to rise, moved by some hazy notion of throwing himself between them and breaking the spell. But his legs refused to obey him and he was forced to stay where he was, cold with dismay and unable to do anything but stare in stunned disbe-

514

lief; and when at last the Sahib spoke, to listen with horror.

Ash said softly: "It's no good, my dear love. You cannot marry him. Even if it were safe for you to do so after so much delay; and this is something you have not told me yet. Would it have been safe?"

Anjuli did not pretend to misunderstand him. She nodded wordlessly: but the small gesture of negation was so desolate that he was ashamed of his own involuntary spasm of relief. He said: "I'm sorry"—the words caught on a tightness in his throat and sounded dry and inadequate.

"I too," whispered Anjuli. "More than I can ever say." Her lips quivered and she controlled them with a visible effort and bent her head so that her mouth and chin were in shadow: "Is—is that why you wished to see me?"

"Partly. But there is something else. He does not want you, my Heart. He only agreed to take you because he could not get Shushila on any other terms, and because your brother bribed him to do so with a large sum of money, and asked no bride-price for you."

"I know"—Anjuli's voice was as quiet as his own. "I have known it from the first. There are few things that can be kept secret from the Women's Quarter."

"And you did not mind?"

She raised her head and looked at him dry-eyed, but her lovely mouth was pinched and drawn. "A little. But what difference does that make? You must know that I was given no choice—and that even if I had been, I should still have come."

"For Shu-shu's sake. Yes, I know. But now the Rana says that the bribe he accepted from your brother was insufficient, and that unless nearly three times more is paid he will not wed you."

Her eyes dilated and she put a hand up to her throat, but she did not speak, and Ash said harshly: "Well, we have not that sum to spare, and even if we had, I could not authorize such payment without instructions from your brother, who from all I hear would never agree to pay it —and rightly. Yet I do not think that he will demand the return of both his sisters. The cost of this journey has been so great that I am very much afraid that when he has thought it over he will decide that it will be wiser in the long run to swallow the affront, and let the Rana's marriage with Shushila take place."

"And . . . what of me?" asked Juli in a whisper.

"You would be sent back to Karidkote. But without your dowry, which the Rana is certain to claim as compensation for the loss of a bride that he does not want. That is, unless we are prepared to risk bloodshed to prevent him getting his hands on it."

"But—but he cannot do that," breathed Anjuli. "It is against our law."

"What law? The only law here in Bhithor is the Rana's."

"I speak of Manu's law, which even he, as a Hindu, must obey. In that law it is laid down that a bride's jewels serve as her *istri-dhan* (inheritance) and may not be taken away from her. It was written by Manu that *'The ornaments which may be worn by women during their husband's life time, his heir shall not divide. Those who divide them shall be outcasts.'* "

"But you are not his wife, so he need not regard that law. Nor will he do so," said Ash grimly.

"But . . . I cannot go back. You *know* I cannot . . . I could not leave Shu-shu."

"You will have no choice."

"That is not true." Her voice rose and she stepped back from him, and said breathlessly: "The Rana may refuse to wed me, but he will not refuse to let me stay and take care of Shu-shu, as—as a waiting-woman, or an *ayah* if need be. If he keeps my dowry it will surely pay for what little food I eat, even if I should live to be old, and when he sees that unless I stay with her his wife will pine and die, he will be glad to keep me, while as for Nandu, I know very well that he will not want me back, for after this who is there who would wish to marry one whom the Rana of Bhithor has rejected?"

"There is one," said Ash quietly.

Anjuli's face crumpled like a hurt child's, and she turned sharply away from him and said in a suffocated whisper: "I know . . . But that cannot be, and therefore . . . you will tell any who ask that I will not go back to Karidkote and that no one can make me do so. And that if I cannot stay in Bhithor as my sister's co-wife, I will stay

516

as her servant. That is all I have to say. Except . . . except to thank you for warning me, and for all . . ."

Her voice failed, and she moved her head in a small, helpless gesture that was more pitiful than words, and with shaking hands began to draw the bourka back into place.

For a moment—for just as long as a tear might take to gather and fall—Ash hesitated. Then he reached out and grasped her shoulders, and snatching away the bourka, pulled her round to face him. The sight of her wet cheeks sent a physical pain through his heart and made him speak with more violence than he had intended:

"Don't be a fool, Juli! Do you imagine for a moment that he will not bed you if you stay here as Shu-shu's servant instead of his wife? Of course he will. Once you are under his roof you will be just as much his property as if he had married you, but without the status of a Rani—or any status at all. He will be able to do exactly as he likes with you, and from what I have seen of him it will probably appeal to his vanity to use the daughter of a Maharajah as a concubine, having rejected her as a wife. Can't you see that your position would be intolerable?"

"It has often been that," returned Anjuli with more composure. "Yet I have borne with it. And I can do so again. But Shu-shu—"

"Oh, damn Shu-shu!" interrupted Ash explosively. His grip tightened and he shook her so savagely that her teeth chattered. "It's no use, Juli. I won't let you. I thought I could, but I hadn't seen him then. You don't know what he's like. He's old—old. Oh, not in years, perhaps, but in every other way: in body and face, and in evil. He's rotted with vice. You cannot mate with a creature like that—a hideous, heartless, hairless ape who has shown himself to be without honour or scruples. Do you want to breed monsters? because that is what you'll do: misshapen monsters—and bastards at that. You cannot risk it."

A spasm of pain contorted Anjuli's wet, tear-streaked face, but her voice was soft and steady and inflexible. "I must. You know why. Even if you should be right about his vanity, it will surely satisfy him to be able to treat me as a servant without troubling himself to use me as he would a concubine, and my life will not be too unhappy. I shall at least be of help to my sister, whereas back in Karidkote there would be nothing for me: only disgrace

517

and sorrow, for Nandu would vent his anger on me even more than he will on all those who will be returning there."

"You speak as though you had no other choice," said Ash. "But that is not so, and you know it. Oh, my love—my Heart's-delight"—his voice broke—"come away with me. We could be so happy, and there is nothing for you here. Nothing but servitude and humiliation and—no, don't say it, I know that Shushila will be here—but I've told you before that you are wrong about her, that she's a spoilt child who has learned that tears and hysteria will get her almost everything she wants, and so she uses them as weapons, selfishly and ruthlessly to gain her own ends. And she won't even need you after a time, or even miss you—not when she is Rani of Bhithor with a host of women at her beck and call, or when she has children of her own to love and spoil, and play with. And what about me? What if *I* cannot live without you? . . . Shu-shu isn't the only one who needs you, Heart's-dearest —I need you too . . . far more than she does. Oh, Juli—"

The tears were running down Anjuli's cheeks, blinding her eyes and choking her voice so that for a time she could not speak; but she shook her head and presently she said in a broken whisper: "You told me so before, and I said . . . I said then that you were strong but that Shu-shu is weak, and so . . . so I cannot betray her. And if the Rana is as you say, it will be worse for her. You know that I love you . . . more than anyone . . . more than life . . . But—I love her too; and you are wrong when you say she does not need me. She has always needed me. Now, more than ever. And so I cannot . . . I cannot . . ."

Once again her voice failed her, and Ash realized with a terrible, sick despair that he would have stood more chance if he had lied to her—made her believe that the Rana was handsome and fascinating, and that Shu-shu could not fail to fall madly in love with him and be far better off without any intrusive half-sister making a third in their blissful life together. Had Juli believed that, she might have weakened. But the truth had been fatal because it had shown her only too clearly what lay in store for Shushila—for whom there was no prospect of escape. And being Juli, that was enough to stiffen her resolution and make it appear even more necessary, now, to stay and

518

do everything possible to sustain and comfort and encourage the frightened little sister who must marry a monster. He should have known better, and he had not . . .

The realization of failure invaded his brain and body in a cold wave, taking his strength from him, so that his hands relaxed their grip and fell from Anjuli's shoulders and he could only stand and stare at her. She stood before him; tall and slender and lovely in the lamplight. And royal—a princess who would become a waiting-maid . . .

The silence began to fill with little sounds: the flutter of moths about the hanging lamp, the creak of a guy-rope and Anjuli's soft, sobbing breath; and through them Ash could hear the thumping of his own heart and was surprised to find that it could still beat. Unless it was Juli's heart that he could hear. For an endless interval he studied her drawn face and wide, tear-blurred eyes in a passion of love and pain, until suddenly he could bear it no longer, and reaching out he snatched her into his arms and covered her face with desperate kisses, crushing her to him in the wild hope that physical contact might accomplish what words had failed to do, and break her resistance.

For a time it almost seemed as though he had won. Her arms flew up to circle his neck and he felt her hands pressing the back of his neck while she clung to him with a desperation that equalled his own, and turned up her mouth to meet and return those frantic kisses. Time stopped and stood still for them. They had forgotten Kakaji, and everything and everyone else. The world had narrowed down into a charmed and timeless circle in which they were alone together, clinging so closely that it seemed to the old man who watched them that their two figures had merged into one and become a single entity—a flame or a shadow, swayed by an invisible wind . . .

It was Anjuli who broke the spell. Her arms slid down and she leaned back, and forcing her hands between their two bodies, pressed her palms against Ash's breast to push him away from her. And though he could so easily have held her, he did not try to do so. He knew that he was beaten. Shushila's weakness had proved stronger than his love and his own need, and there was nothing left to say. And nothing else he could do, for he had long ago abandoned any idea of abducting Juli—recognizing that even with her consent the chances of success would

519

be minimal and the risk appalling, while without it there could be no chance at all: only the certainty of death for both of them.

He released her and stood back, and watched her stoop to grope blindly for her bourka. Her hands were shaking so badly that she had difficulty in putting it on, and when she had done so she paused for a moment, holding back the voluminous folds from her face, to gaze at him with the terrible concentration of one who looks for the last time at a beloved face before the coffin-lid is closed upon it, as though she were imprinting him on her memory; learning him by heart so that she would never forget a single detail of feature or expression—the colour of his eyes and the slant of his brows, the set of a mouth that could be grave or grim or astonishingly tender, and the deep un-youthful lines that Belinda and George and life and death in the Border country beyond the North-West Frontier had scored on either side of it. The texture of his skin and the single dark lock of hair that habitually fell across his forehead and half hid a jagged, silvery scar that had been made by an Afghan knife—

Ash spoke in a flat, controlled voice: "If you should ever need me, you have only to send me the luck-charm and I will come. Unless I am dead, I will come."

"I know," whispered Anjuli.

"Goodbye—" his voice broke suddenly—"Heart's-beloved—my dear—my darling. I shall think of you every hour of every day, and be glad that I have known you."

"And I you. Farewell . . . my lord and my life."

The brown folds dropped into place and there was only a dark shrouded figure standing in the pool of light under the hanging lamp.

She went past him as noiselessly as a shadow, and he steeled himself to let her go and did not turn his head when he heard the rasp of canvas as she lifted the tent-flap, or when the lamp swayed once more to a faint draught of air and sprayed a shimmer of stars across the walls and ceiling. The flap fell with a soft thud that was, somehow, an unbelievably final sound. The lamp steadied and the stars were still: and Juli had gone.

Ash did not know how long he stood there, staring at nothing and thinking of nothing, because his mind was as empty as his arms—and his heart.

A movement in the shadows and the touch of a hand on his arm aroused him at last, and he turned slowly and saw Kaka-ji standing beside him. There was neither anger nor shock in the old man's face, only sympathy and understanding. And a great sadness.

"I have been blind," said Kaka-ji quietly. "Blind and foolish. I should have known that this might happen, and kept you apart. I am truly sorry, my son. But Anjuli has chosen wisely—for both of you, since had she consented to go with you I am very sure that you would both have died. Her brother Nandu is not one to forgive an injury and he would have hunted you to the death, the Rana aiding him, so it is better this way. And in time you will both forget. Being young, you will forget."

"Did you forget her mother, then?" asked Ash harshly.

Kaka-ji caught his breath and for a fractional moment his fingers bit into Ash's arm: *"How did you—?"* he stopped abruptly.

His hand fell away and he released his breath in a long sigh. His gaze moved past Ash's shoulder to stare into the shadows as though he could see another face there, and his own face softened. "No," said Kaka-ji slowly. "I did not forget. But then I . . . I was no longer a young man. I was already in my middle years when . . . *Chut!* no matter!—I put it away from me. There was no other course. Maybe if I had spoken earlier it would have been different, for her father and I had been friends. But she was younger than my own daughters, and having known her since she was a babe in arms she still seemed a child to me—too young for marriage, like the bud of the moonflower that will wither unopened if it is plucked. Therefore I did not speak but waited instead for her to become a woman—not realizing that she had already become one. Then one day my brother, hearing rumours of her great beauty, contrived to see her: and seeing her, he loved her—and she him . . ."

Kaka-ji was silent for a space, and then he sighed again, very deeply, and said: "After their marriage I left the state—my own children being wed—and went on a pilgrimage to the holy places, seeking enlightenment—and forgetfulness, which I did not find. And when at last I returned it was to find that she had died long since,

521

and of a broken heart, leaving a little daughter for whom I could do nothing, because there was now a new Rani in the palace: an evil woman who had usurped that other's place, and by enslaving my brother's heart and bearing him sons had attained great power and influence over him—while, I who had once been close to him, had through my own folly become a stranger and of no account. Wherefore, finding that I could in no way help her child Anjuli, I withdrew to my own estates and seldom visited the court. And though it was urged upon me, I did not take a second wife because . . . because I could not forget *her*. I am now old; but still I cannot forget."

"Yet you tell me that I shall do so," said Ash bitterly.

"Ah, but then you, my son, are young, and many years of youth lie before you. It will be easier for you."

"And what of her?—what of Anjuli? Will it be easier for her?"

Kaka-ji fended off the question with a helpless gesture of his small hands, and Ash said violently: "You know it will not! Rao-Sahib, *listen* to me—you have just told me that you could do nothing to help her when she was a child, because of Janoo-Rani. But there is no one now who can stop you from helping her if you choose and you have seen enough of that vile creature who calls himself Rana of Bhithor to know what he is like and how little regard he has for honour or promises. No one could blame you, after all that has occurred, if you decided to withdraw from the contract and take both your nieces back to Karidkote."

"But—but that is not possible," gasped Kaka-ji, horrified. "It would be madness. No, no, that I could not do."

"*Why not?*" urged Ash. "Who is there to prevent you? Rao-Sahib, I beg of you—for Shushila's sake as well as Anjuli's. No one would blame you. You need only—"

"*No!*" said Kaka-ji loudly. "It is too late. You do not understand. You do not know Nandu."

"He cannot be worse than the Rana."

"You think not? But then as I have said you do not know him. Were we now to return, bringing back his sisters unwed and dowerless, having forfeited all that has already been paid and made ourselves a laughing stock throughout all India, Nandu's vengeance would fall terribly upon all of us. My own life is of little account, but there are others to be thought of: Mulraj and Maldeo Rai, and Suraj Ram and Bagwan Singh also, and many others besides. Even Unpora-Bai—"

"He would not dare kill them," interrupted Ash impatiently. "The British Resident—"

"*Bah!*" Kaka-ji's scornful expletive cut him short. "You Sahib-log think your Raj can do many things that it cannot. Have I said that there would be a public slaying? There would be no need. There are other ways—many others. And even if we did not die, we and our families would forfeit all we had, even to the very roofs over our heads, while as for my nieces . . . who would there be after this who would wish to wed them when their names had become a byword and a jest because of this affair? I tell you, both would find their brother Nandu a crueller gaoler than even the Rana of Bhithor, and end by wishing that we had let them be. If you do not believe that, ask Mulraj—ask Maldeo Rai. Either will bear me out. Sahib, what you suggest is not possible. We must make what terms we can with the Rana. That is all we can do."

"Even though it means letting Anjuli sacrifice herself for the sake of the daughter of an evil woman—your own term, Rao-Sahib—who supplanted her mother and made her childhood a misery?" asked Ash bitterly.

"It is her own choice, my son," Kaka-ji reminded him, forbearing to take offence. "And if you think that I who am only her uncle could turn her from it, when you who love her, and whom it would seem that she loves, have failed to do so, then you cannot know her as I do."

Ash's mouth twisted, and presently he said under his breath: "I know her: I know her better than . . . anyone. Better even than myself . . ."

"Then you will know that I am right."

Ash did not answer, but his face spoke for him. And reading that look, Kaka-ji said gently: "I am sorry, my son: for both of you. But I have no choice—and she has made hers, and will abide by it despite anything you or I could say. The most we can do for her now is to see that she remains here as a wife and not as one of her sister's waiting-women; which the gods know is little enough when both of us have brought her so much sorrow —you by stealing her heart and thereby making the future sadder and more desolate for her, and I by my negligence and folly in permitting you to ride and talk with her, and

523

being blind in that I did not perceive what might—what had—become of it. I am very greatly to blame."

There was so much pain in the old man's voice that at any other time it must have awoken some response in Ash. But he was spent. His anger had drained out of him, and he was suddenly so tired that he could have dropped where he stood. He could not even think clearly, and though he knew that what Kaka-ji had said was true, and that between them they had done Anjuli a great disservice, his mind could only register the fact that he had made his last throw and lost. He could endure no more that night. Perhaps tomorrow . . . Tomorrow was another day. But a day without Juli—No more Juli for ever and ever. For ever and ever . . . *Amen.*

He turned away without another word, and stumbling out of the tent, made his way back through the silent camp, moving like a sleepwalker.

29

Maintaining a policy of patience, Ash allowed a full week to go by without making any move to re-open negotiations with the Rana, or to reply to his latest demand.

Messages and gifts of fruit and sweetmeats still arrived daily, and were received with polite expressions of thanks. But neither side suggested a further meeting, and it began to look as though the Rana, too, had decided on a waiting game.

"Having had his say, he is giving us time to realize that he means it. And to make up our minds to pay what he asks," said Mulraj gloomily. To which Ash retorted that if this was what the Rana thought they were doing, he would soon find out that he was mistaken.

"Maybe," shrugged Mulraj. "But how if in the meantime we starve? The country folk and the merchants in the city are, as you foretold, demanding payment, and we have referred them to the Diwan and the council—who have sent them back to us. Now they are refusing to supply us with foodstuffs unless we pay beforehand, and if we do not pay we shall all go hungry, because they will withhold supplies; though the gods be thanked they cannot prevent us from cutting fodder for our animals, and we still have enough cattle and goats to provide a measure of milk and butter for all if we are careful."

"And enough grain to keep us in bread for some little time," added Ash with a fleeting grin. "I have been hoarding it against just such a situation as this. Nevertheless, we will not touch it until we must, as a day may come when we need it more than we do now. Try these Bhithoris with fair words and promises, Mulraj, and see if they cannot be persuaded to give us credit for a little longer. And when they will do so no more, tell them that their bills and their demands must be given to us in writing. We must have written evidence to lay before this Political-Sahib who fears we may not be patient enough."

"I will do that," grinned Mulraj. "When do you mean to ask for another meeting with the Rana or his Diwan?"

"I don't. This time we will wait until they ask us for one. In the meantime let us go out hawking, and while making pretence of searching for game, see if we cannot find some goat-tracks across these hills by which a few men could, if it became necessary, leave the valley unseen. It might come in useful."

They had not succeeded in finding one, but a few days later the Rana had invited them to another meeting in the city palace, at which the same demands had been made and the same excuses put forward to justify them. These had once again been declared unacceptable, and the delegation from Karidkote had thereupon withdrawn in good order, leaving the position as before.

"Our turn next," said Ash philosophically. And having allowed several days to elapse he requested a further audience with the Rana, and early in the following week presented himself at the Rung Mahal to argue the case all over again, though with no better results. After that there followed a short lull in the negotiations, and then as Bhithor appeared content to leave the initiative to Karidkote and the visitors were finding it increasingly difficult to obtain supplies on credit, Ash changed his tactics and took to calling daily at the palace to confer with the Rana, or if the Rana would not see him, with the Diwan, to press for more reasonable terms. He had even (with one eye on the Political Officer) offered a few small concessions, in order to avoid any future accusations by that gentleman and his department of inflexibility or of having made no attempt at bargaining or compromise. But the result of these efforts had, predictably, merely served to convince the Rana that the opposition was weakening, and that he had only to stand firm to have all his demands met.

This conviction was shared by his Diwan, who had actually had the temerity to hint that if his royal master's terms were not accepted soon, he might well reconsider them. The inference being that the price would go up, though Ash had affected to misunderstand him and observed gravely that he sincerely hoped so, as it was high time that he returned to Rawalpindi and his military duties. Which was true enough.

The double wedding had originally been planned for early spring, and even though the journey from Karidkote had taken longer than expected, it could still have taken place before the worst of the hot weather was upon them and the temperature was still tolerable. But six weeks having passed since the great bridal camp had pitched its tents in the valley, the hot weather was by now in full blast and the camping ground had become an inferno of heat and dust and flies, in which men and animals sweltered and suffered together. A scorching wind blew all day from dawn to dusk, stirring up the dust and setting every piece of canvas and every shred of rope flapping, thrumming and clattering so that there was never a moment of silence, and when it died at night-fall the dark hours were filled with the maddening drone of mosquitoes, the ululations of jackals and the yelping of pariah dogs who prowled between the tents in search of scraps.

Had it not been for the lake and the fact that the prevailing wind, blowing in from that direction, was several degrees cooler than in many parts of Rajputana, the situation of those in the camp would have been intolerable. As it was, it could be endured—though that was the most that anyone could say of it—and at least the wind helped to keep the flies at bay and enabled the more important personages in the camp to obtain a degree of comfort by the use of *kus-kus* tatties: thick mats of woven roots that were hung in the entrances of the tents, and kept drenched with water so that the wind passing through them blew cool and refreshing. But for those without tents or tatties it was an abominable time. More especially as all in the

526

camp were hill-men and unused to temperatures that dwellers in Rajputana accepted as a matter of course.

"How much longer can we hold out?" groaned Kaka-ji, who was suffering an attack of acute depression.

The old man was looking as shrivelled and unhappy as a new-born monkey, for the wind blowing through the *kus-kus* tatties had given him a chill on the liver, and besides, he had much on his mind—and on his conscience.

"Do not fret yourself, Rao-Sahib," said Ash. "If all goes well, it should not be long before you and all in your charge will be installed in one of the guesthouses on the lake, where you will be able to live in more coolness and comfort."

"*If*," repeated Kaka-ji pessimistically. "Yet I see no sign of the Rana relenting, and very soon now we may find ourselves short of water. Should the stream dry up—and my servants tell me that it is shrinking daily—what then? Are we to suffer thirst as well as hunger?"

"The stream will not dry up. It is fed by springs in the hills as well as by the lake, and though the lake is low, it is still deep and wide. Nevertheless it is time that we took action, for by now I do not believe that even the Political Agent-Sahib could accuse me of showing a lack of patience. We will speak with the Rana again tomorrow and see if his heart—if he has one—has changed."

"You will find that it has not," grunted Mulraj. "Why waste our breath and our time?"

"In *Belait*," said Ash, with a shrug, "they have a saying, 'If at first you don't succeed, try, try again.' "

"*Bah!* We have tried a score of times—two score," returned Mulraj disgustedly. "*Hai mai,* but I grow weary of this business."

Nevertheless, on the morrow they had ridden yet again to the city—they were becoming all too familiar with that road—and after being kept waiting for an even longer time than usual, embarked on the same wearisome round of argument, with the same lack of success. But this time Ash had asked for the Rana's demands to be put in writing, in order, so he said, to cover himself (should he accede to them) in case His Highness the Maharajah of Karidkote, or the British authorities, refused to believe that they had actually been made, and suspected him of inventing the story to cover the fact that he and the other members of his party had misappropriated the additional sum and divided it among themselves.

"Unless we can show proof that such a sum was demanded of us, we dare not even consider paying it," explained Ash. "That is our difficulty, and you will, I am sure, understand that speaking for my companions, it would be as much as their lives were worth to return to Karidkote with nothing to support their word that they had expended this money on His Highness's behalf. I myself might be in great trouble with my superiors, so I would ask . . ."

To the Rana and his Diwan (and his entire council for that matter) such a request seemed perfectly sensible. Had the position been reversed, they themselves would certainly have reasoned along the same lines and taken similar steps to cover themselves, so what more natural than that the Maharajah and the Foreign and Political Department should, in their wrath, suspect the Sahib and his associates of theft and falsehood when they confessed to having parted with a sum greatly in excess of the agreed price? The Rana, scenting victory, had instantly agreed to furnish the Sahib with a written statement of his demands, and had even, at Ash's request, graciously appended his own thumbprint as proof that the document was not a forgery.

Ash read it over carefully, and having stowed it away in the inner breast pocket of his coat, thanked the Rana for his kindness with a cordiality that was, for once, quite genuine, though the Rana was wrong in supposing that it was a hopeful sign and an indication that the delegation from the camp had at last decided that they had no alternative but to capitulate to his demands.

"Well, and what have we gained by that?" inquired Mulraj as they rode out side by side through the Elephant Gate—Kaka-ji had not accompanied them that day, being confined to his bed with a chill.

"Proof," replied Ash, slapping his breast pocket. "This goes tonight with a covering letter to Spiller-Sahib, the Political Officer. And as soon as I am sure that he has received it, we will pull the Rana's nose. Even Spiller-Sahib cannot regard such an outrageous example of blackmail as something to be excused and given in to."

The covering letter was written within the hour, and because Ash was angry and in haste, it was not as tactful-

528

ly phrased as it might have been. Its curt sentences, while not actually rude, gave an impression of barely concealed irritation with official bumbling that was to cause deep offence and lead to unforeseen repercussions. But Ash did not know that.

Having finished it, he enclosed it in a sealed envelope, together with the paper setting out the Rana's demands, and once again accompanied the messenger to the frontier and set him on his way. Though this was probably an unnecessary precaution, since it would seem only natural to the Rana that the Sahib should send word to the Political Officer as a preliminary to capitulation, and it was therefore unlikely that on this occasion at least there would have been any attempt to prevent the messenger getting through. All the same, Ash preferred to take no chances, and he had watched the man ride away, and waited until he could see him no longer before turning back.

He knew very well that the action he had in mind was no more than a bluff, and that if it failed in its effect the result might be a disaster. But it was a gamble he had to take, the only alternative being to abandon Juli to the fate that must befall her if she were to be left behind in Bhithor unwed, and with no rights or privileges beyond those of any other waiting-woman in the Women's Quarters of the Rung Mahal. That was not to be thought of, for appalling as it was to leave her there at all, to leave her in such circumstances would be beyond all bearing, and he would do all in his power to ensure that she stayed as a Rani of Bhithor. That was the most he could do for her now.

He waited two days to give his messenger time to reach the Political Officer, and on the third day requested yet another audience, in order to warn the Rana not to cherish false hopes and give him one last chance to change his mind. The request having been granted, Ash rode to the Rung Mahal accompanied only by Mulraj and a small escort, and was received in a private room in the palace by the Rana and half-a-dozen of his councillors, and a few favourite courtiers.

The interview had been a short one: apart from the usual exchange of courtesies Ash had only spoken twice and the Rana once, and both had confined themselves to a few words. Ash had inquired if the Rana had reconsidered

529

his demands, and was prepared to accept the terms that had originallly been agreed upon in Karidkote by his representatives and His Highness the Maharajah, and the Rana had replied, in effect, that he had no intention of doing so, and in fact considered his demands to be not only just but exceedingly reasonable. His tone was insolent, and when his evil-genius prompted him to smile, the watching councillors, taking their cue, grinned appreciatively while one or two of the more sycophantic courtiers sniggered audibly. But it was to be the last time that any of them smiled that morning. "In that case," announced Ash curtly, "we have no alternative but to remove our camp and refer the whole matter to the Government of India. Good-day, Rana-Sahib."

He bowed briefly, and turning on his heel, left the room.

Mulraj followed, looking resigned; but they had not gone far when they were overtaken by a breathless councillor who brought a message from the Diwan. The Diwan, said the councillor, urgently desired to speak with them in private, and begged that they would grant him a few moments of their time. There being nothing to be gained by a refusal, they had turned back to find the Rana's Prime Minister waiting for them in a small ante-room near the one that they had left so unceremoniously a few moments before.

The Diwan was full of apologies for what he professed to regard as "an unfortunate misunderstanding," and he had pressed refreshments on them, talking volubly the while. But it soon became clear that he had nothing new to offer in the way of concessions; or, for that matter, to add to the endless—and unconvincing—excuses that he had made before on the Rana's behalf. He had merely retraced his steps over the same ground that had already been covered to exhaustion during the past weeks, repeating the same arguments in support of his master's claims, until at last Ash's small remaining stock of patience had given out, and he had cut through the spate of words with the brusque announcement that if the Diwan had something fresh to offer they were prepared to listen. If not, they were merely wasting their time as well as his, and would bid him goodbye.

The Diwan seemed loth to let them go, but they were not prepared to wait any longer, and after further and protracted expressions of regret he had personally accompanied them as far as the gate into the outer court-yard, where he stayed talking to them while a servant was sent to fetch their horses and their escort, who were being entertained by men of the palace guard. It was there-fore almost an hour after quitting the Rana's presence that they finally left the Rung Mahal, and as they rode out past the sentries, Mulraj said meditatively: "Now what was the purpose of all that? The old villain had nothing to say, and this is the first time that my men have ever been offered hospitality by the guard at the palace. What do you suppose they hoped to gain?"

"Time," said Ash succinctly.

"That much is clear. The old fox held us in talk for the best part of an hour, and then that servant took so long to fetch our men and our horses that it would not have surprised me to learn he had fallen asleep by the way. They wished to delay our departure—and they succeeded. But why? For what purpose?"

They had learned it within ten minutes of leaving the city.

The Rana had acted with considerable speed, for the twin forts that earlier that day had been garrisoned by no more than a handful of sentries were now manned by scores of artillerymen who swarmed on the battlements and stood ready by their guns, a sight that the delegation from Karidkote, riding back to their camp, could not fail to take note of, and that must bring home to them the vulnerability and helplessness of their own position when faced with this threat of force.

The camp had already taken note, and anxious groups of men, who would normally have been taking an afternoon siesta in the shade, were standing about in the blinding sunlight to stare at the forts and speculate un-easily as to the reason for this ominous show of force. A dozen explanations, each one more alarming than the next, were in circulation among the tents, and present-ly a rumour arose that the Rana was about to open fire on the camp with the intention of killing everyone in it, so that he might seize the money and valuables that had been brought from Karidkote.

By the time Ash and Mulraj returned, panic had spread with the speed of a whirlwind, and only drastic ac-tion on the part of Mulraj, who set the pick of his troops to keep order with lances, musket butts and *lathis*, had averted a riot. But there was no denying that the situation looked exceedingly ugly, and within an hour of his return Ash had dispatched yet another message to the palace, requesting an audience on the following day—this time in public durbar.

"Why send so swiftly?" raged Mulraj, who, had he been consulted, would have preferred to save face by ignoring the threat for as long as possible. "Could we not have waited at least until the morrow before begging that—that *dagabazik* (cheat, trickster) for an audience? Now everyone will think that his guns have thrown us into such terror that we dared not waste a moment for fear that he should loose them upon us."

"Then they are due for a disappointment," snapped Ash, whose hold on his temper was hourly becoming more precarious. "They can think what they choose. But we have already wasted too many moments, and I do not intend to waste any more."

"That would be good hearing," sighed Kaka-ji, "if only there was anything we could say to the Rana. But what is there left to say?"

"A good deal that should have been said long ago, had I had my way," returned Ash shortly. "And I trust that you will feel strong enough to accompany us to-morrow, Rao-Sahib, so that you too may hear it."

They had all accompanied him: not only Kaka-ji, but all those who had attended the first durbar. And this time they had been required to present themselves at the city palace in the late afternoon. They had gone there dressed in their glittering best and escorted by thirty splendidly uniformed lancers. And despite the fact that thermometer in his tent still registered 109 degrees, Ash himself had donned the fullest of full dress to ride with them through the sultry heat to the Rung Mahal, where they had been met by a minor official and conducted to the Hall of Public Audience. Here, as once before, they found the entire court awaiting them, seated in serried ranks between the painted arches.

Today the outer arches on the windward side were closed by *kus-kus* tatties and those on the opposite side by split-cane *chiks*, which while helping to reduce the temperature to something approaching coolness, filled the *Diwan-i-Am* with a shadowy gloom that seemed even deeper by contrast with the brightness outside. But even the combination of shadows and the low sunlight of the waning afternoon did not prevent Ash from seeing that every face in that crowded assembly room wore an expression of smug anticipation that was, in some cases, tinged with derision, and it was immediately clear to him that they were confidently expecting to witness the public humiliation of the emissaries from Karidkote and the foolish young Sahib who was their spokesman, and to enjoy the skill with which their crafty ruler had played his cards and out-witted his hapless guests. It was a pity, thought Ash sardonically, that they were to be disappointed on both counts. And dispensing with the accepted preliminaries of debate—the polite greetings, the compliments and the hollow expressions of mutual esteem and good-will that wasted so much time—he came straight to the point.

"I have noticed," said Ash, addressing the Rana in a voice that none present had ever heard him use before, "that Your Highness has seen fit to man all three forts that command the valley. For which reason I desired this meeting, so that I might inform you, in public durbar, that if so much as one of the guns that are trained upon our camp should be fired, your state will be taken over by the Government of India and you yourself will be deposed and sent away to spend the remainder of your life in exile. I will also inform you that I intend to strike camp and remove to our first site, outside the valley, where we shall remain until you are prepared to come to terms with us. *Our* terms. This is all I have to say."

The grim certainty of his own voice surprised him, for his mouth was dry and he had, in fact, no confidence whatsoever in the Government's willingness to take such action—or indeed, give him any support. They were, he thought, more likely to reprimand him for making unauthorized threats in their name and "exceeding his instructions." But then the present company was not to know that. The Diwan's jaw had dropped and the Rana's face was a study in shock. And of a sudden it seemed as if every man in those close-packed ranks of men had caught his breath and was holding it; for though the wind still whined through the *kus-kus* tatties and rattled the swaying *chiks* with a maddening, monotonous tattoo, there was no other sound under the painted arches. Noting this,

Ash realized that any further discussion could, at this point, rob the threat of half its effect, so without giving the Rana time to reply, he collected his own party with a jerk of the head and stalked out of the *Diwan-i-Am*, the jingle of his spurs and the clank of his sword sharply audible in the stunned silence.

This time no one had been sent hurrying after them, and there had been no attempt to delay their departure. The escort and their horses had been ready and waiting for them, and they had mounted without any words of farewell and clattered out of the courtyard and back through streets that were full of strolling citizens come out to "eat the evening air."

Kaka-ji had been the first to speak, but only after they were safely through the city gate and riding down the valley into the eye of the setting sun, and even then he had lowered his voice as though he were afraid of being overheard:

"Is it true, Sahib, what you told the Rana? Will the Sirkar (Government) indeed dispossess him if he uses his guns upon us?"

"I do not know," confessed Ash with a wry grin. "They should. But then one cannot tell how the affair would be reported to them, for how many of us would be left alive to tell the true tale? However, all that matters now is whether the Rana himself believes that they would do so; and that is something we shall find out as soon as we start moving off."

"So you do mean us to move?" said Mulraj. "When?"

"Now. At once. While they in the palace are still afraid that I may have spoken no more than the truth. We must be out of this valley and beyond the reach of those forts before the sun rises again."

"But will that not be too great a risk?" demurred Kaka-ji, alarmed. "What if they should fire upon us when they see us preparing to leave?"

"They will not do so while there is the least doubt in their minds as to how the Government may react; which is why we must not lose a moment, but move immediately, while they are still debating it. If there is a risk, it is one that we must take because there is nothing else we can do except give in and let the Rana have everything he asks. And that I will not consider. We march within the hour."

"It will not be easy to move by night," observed Mulraj, squinting at the setting sun. "There is no moon."

"All the better. To fire in the darkness at a moving target will not be easy either; also it might mean the destruction of much treasure—and perhaps of the brides also. Besides, in this heat a night march will at least be cooler than moving by day."

By the time they reached the camp half the valley was in shadow and the wind had fallen with the approach of sunset. Cooking fires were already being lighted and smoke hung in the still air like a long scarf of grey gauze, spanning the valley floor and touching the flanks of the hills that hemmed it in on either side. Sunlight still lay along the heights, and its rays seemed to be concentrated on the sandstone walls of the nearest fort, turning them to burnished gold and striking blinding glints from bronze cannon and the barrels of muskets.

The opposite fort was only a dark violet shape against the evening sky, but its crouching bulk was no less menacing, and Ash felt a shiver run down his spine as he looked up at it. Supposing . . . just supposing he was wrong, and that his bluff had not deceived the Rana? Well, it was too late to worry about that now; and as he had told Kaka-ji, they would soon find out. He gave orders for the camp to be struck, and went off to change his uniform for clothing more suited to the work that lay ahead.

With less than an hour-and-a-half of daylight left, few men had found time for an evening meal, and those who had, had eaten it standing, the threat presented by the manning of the forts having been clear to all of them. They were as eager to quit the valley as Ash himself, and not only had no one queried the order to march or raised any objection on the score of short notice and the difficulties involved, but every man, woman and child had set to with feverish speed and worked with such a will that dusk had barely fallen when the first laden cart moved off towards the gorge, preceded by a picked band of cavalry.

By midnight the tail-end of the long column marched out, leaving the cooking fires still burning, as Ash had given orders that the fires were to be left to die out untouched so that watchers in the forts would be uncertain as to how many men had moved, and how many remained behind. The marchers themselves had been forbidden to

535

carry lights, and seen from above and by starlight, they would be almost invisible, for as they plodded forward, the dust that rose up under their feet and made the going a torment served to screen them from view more effectively than anything else could have done, and made it difficult to guess at the numbers involved.

To Ash, riding in the thick of the press, the noise of their progress seemed appallingly loud; for though no one spoke except to give an order or urge on a reluctant animal—and then only in an undertone—there were many other sounds that could not be avoided: the creak of wheels and the crack of whips, the tread of innumerable feet, the click of hooves and the jingle of harness, the wails of children and the grunts, squeals and grumbles of cattle, sheep, camels, horses and elephants. Not to mention a continual yapping from the horde of pi-dogs that had attached themselves to the camp and could not be persuaded to leave it.

Ash consoled himself with the reflection that deafening as it might sound at close quarters, from half a mile away even this amount of noise would be inaudible, and in any case there had never been any question of keeping the Rana's men in ignorance of the move. He had told them himself what he meant to do. All the same, he preferred to keep them guessing as to how long such an operation would take, for, if they under-estimated the speed with which it could be done, and were expecting to find at least two thirds of the camp still in the valley by morning, it might discourage them from taking any precipitate action that night. The critical part of the affair was going to be the passage through the gorge, for there progress was bound to be slow, and the fort that stood guard over it was over-close. He wondered how soon he would reach it and whether the small force that Mulraj had sent to lead the way had already done so, and were safely through it. And where Juli was . . .

He had seen the *ruth* move off, surrounded three-deep by an escort of armed guards and preceded and followed by a detachment of cavalry, together with the covered carts bearing the brides' women, servants and personal effects. Mulraj and Kaka-ji had ridden alongside it, and Jhoti had travelled with his sisters. Ash had seen the boy's excited face by the smoky light of a hurricane lamp as he climbed into the *ruth*, but the brides had been no more than a fleeting glimpse of two shrouded figures, indistinguishable from their women; and but for the fact that one of them was taller than the other he would not even have known which was Juli. A moment later the escort had closed about them and the *ruth* had jolted off into the darkness, and he could not even ride within sight of it. The most he had been able to do was to arrange that if the forts opened fire, or if it should come to a fight (as it would do if the Rana's soldiers attempted to close the gorge road), Juli, Shushila and Jhoti were to be snatched out of the mêlée by Mulraj and a small band of horsemen, who would circle back and attempt to find their way out across the hills, while he himself remained behind to cover their retreat and deal with the Rana in the morning.

It was a sketchy plan and far from foolproof. But if the worst came to the worst it would have to be tried, and Ash could only hope that it would not come to that; for though he and Mulraj had searched diligently during the past weeks, the only paths they had found among the hills were goat tracks that wandered aimlessly between outcrops of rock on the steep, grassy slopes, and appeared to lead nowhere. But there was no profit in worrying about that either. The die had been cast and by now the matter was out of his hands. There was nothing else he could do—except pray that he had convinced the Rana that any attempt at force would be fatal.

"If it does come to a fight," thought Ash, "there will be no wedding. They couldn't go ahead with it after that . . . Even Nandu would not consider doing so. Nor could the Government overlook such a thing—they'd have to take *some* action, even if they didn't actually take over the state . . . perhaps appoint another ruler, and see that Nandu was repaid some if not all of what he has spent on this sorry business . . . I ought not to have interfered. I should have left well alone, and then Juli would have . . ."

But he knew that he could not have done anything else. He could not have disregarded his orders and stood aside, leaving the bargaining and the decisions to Kaka-ji and his compatriots who would have been forced in the end to pay the blackmailer in full—as well as forfeiting Anjuli's dowry and leaving her behind, unwed. All the same he found himself listening for the sounds of battle and half hoping that the Rana's soldiers would deny them passage through the gorge, for a fight was the only thing that would put an end to any further talk of a wedding. Yet if it came to fighting, men would die. Probably a great many of them . . .

Ash was suddenly filled with a sick disgust of himself. Had he really fallen so low as to contemplate, even for a moment, the death of men he knew and liked, men in whose company he had travelled southward all the long way to Bhithor, merely because their deaths might help him achieve a purely personal desire? Juli, he knew, would never dream of buying happiness at such a price. And neither could he. With that thought it was as though she moved quietly away from him, as she had done when she left Kaka-ji's tent. The night noises ceased to whisper her name or the dust to hold a scent of roses, and as his mind emptied of her, he could listen once more to the many sounds about him with his ears alert to catch the crack of a distant musket.

It was no longer necessary to fear the cannon in the two forts behind him. If their crews had been going to open fire they would have done so before now, instead of waiting until the camp had moved out of range. The real danger lay ahead in the short half-mile of track that wound through the gorge below the third fort, where it would be only too easy to entrap a large part of the column, leaving all those who had not yet entered it with no alternative but to turn and retreat back into the larger trap of the valley.

"If they attack us there," thought Ash, "we are finished."

But the threat of annexation and exile had destroyed the Rana's confidence. It did not occur to him that the Sahib could have spoken in that fashion on his own authority and without a shadow of official support. He presumed that the Sahib must be speaking as the mouthpiece of the Political Officer, who was himself the mouthpiece of the Raj; and he also knew that there had been many precedents for such action. Too many to allow him to count on the fact that as these had occurred in the days before the great uprising, when the East India Company ruled the land, they would not occur again under a Raj headed by a Viceroy representing the Padishah Victoria herself. If in the past such princely states as the great Kingdom of Oudh could be annexed, how could he be sure that a similar fate could not befall his own, which was small and by no means powerful? The Rana and his councillors had quailed at the thought, and urgent messages had been dispatched to the commanders of the forts, ordering them to abstain from any action that could possibly be construed as hostile.

The bridal camp passed unmolested through the gorge, and by the time the sun rose it was busily setting up tents and lighting new cooking fires on the old site, well out of range of the fort and in a position to defend itself against attack or, if necessary, to retreat over the border.

"Now let those sons of jackals try to threaten us," said Mulraj viciously. "*Arré!* but I am weary. I am not a fearful man, and the gods know I would fight with the best against any odds in open battle. But I tell you, Sahib, I died a thousand deaths last night as we crept through that gorge in the darkness, knowing the slaughter that a mere handful of men on the cliffs above could have wrought on us, and expecting every moment to see the cannons speak and hear armed men pouring down to attack us. Ah well, it is over: we have broken out of the trap. But what happens now?"

"That is up to the Rana," said Ash. "We shall wait and see what he will do. But I am inclined to think that we shall have no further trouble from him and that he will pretend that it has all been . . . what was it the Diwan said? . . . 'an unfortunate misunderstanding.' Tomorrow, or perhaps today, he will send us a deputation bringing gifts and soothing messages, so we had better take what rest we can before they arrive. How is young Jhoti?"

"Asleep. And sadly disappointed in the Rana. He had been hoping that there would be a great battle."

"Blood-thirsty brat," commented Ash sourly. And added that he hoped the boy's uncle was also asleep, as the old man had had a great deal to put up with of late, and the events of the previous night must have tried him sorely.

"That is so," agreed Mulraj, "but it would take more than the discomforts of a night march to keep the Rao-Sahib from his prayers. He performs his *pujah*, and only when that is finished will he rest. As for myself, being less devout, I shall follow the young prince's example and take what sleep I can before these Bhithoris descend upon us with lies and excuses and false expressions of goodwill."

"And apologies also, one hopes—though I doubt that. But there is no need for us to break our rest for them. They have kept us waiting often enough and it will do them and their misbegotten ape of a Rana no harm to get a taste of their own medicine."

"Oho! *Sahib ka mizaj aj bahut garum hai*," quoted Mulraj with a grin, repeating a comment he had heard Gul Baz make in a muttered aside to Ash's syce.

"So would you be in a bad temper," retorted Ash hotly, "if you'd had to—" He broke off and laughed a trifle ashamedly: "You are right. I'm in a foul mood, and at the moment I'd enjoy murdering the lot of them—starting with the Rana. The thought of having to pretend that all the insults and chicanery that we have been subjected to are forgiven and forgotten, and that the wedding can take place as though nothing had happened, sticks in my gullet, and when I think that . . . I'm sorry. I'd better get some sleep myself or I shall be in no fit state to conduct any further talks with anyone. Go on, get to your bed. *So-jana, bai*, and may your dreams be auspicious."

He watched Mulraj walk tiredly away and was aware that he himself was tired beyond reason, not only physically but mentally—so tired that suddenly he could not feel angry any more. His anger, together with all the fears and hopes that had tormented him for so long, seemed to have drained out of him, leaving behind a vast emptiness. He had done all that he could for Juli. And also, which was ironical, for Nandu: he had saved Nandu's pride and his purse, together with Juli's honour, and (for what it was worth) the reputations of the Rana, the Political Officer and Captain Pelham-Martyn of the Guides. And none of it meant anything any more . . .

Ash turned and went into his tent, and a few minutes later the anxious Mahdoo, hastening in with a scalding cup of tea, found him stretched out on the camp bed, fully clothed and so deeply asleep that he did no more than grunt when Mahdoo and Gul Baz eased him out of his coat and riding boots before closing the tent-flap against the dazzle of the rising sun.

30

He was riding headlong across a stony plain that was bounded by low, barren hills, and Anjuli was on the crupper behind him, clinging to him and urging him to ride faster—faster. He could not see the horsemen racing in pursuit, for when he looked back her unbound hair, streaming out on the wind like a silken scarf, impeded his view. But he could hear the thunder of galloping hoofbeats drawing nearer and nearer, and he laughed because Juli's arms were about him and nothing and no one could harm them as long as they were together. And then suddenly he realized that the silken scarf was not black but yellow, and he looked over his shoulder and saw with horror that it was not Juli at all, but a silly simpering girl with blue eyes and blond ringlets who pouted at him and said: "Do hurry, Ashton. I don't want Papa to catch us." Belinda!—he had eloped with Belinda, and now he would have to marry her and be saddled with her for the rest of his life. For ever and always ...

"No. Oh no," cried Ash. And woke, sweating and shuddering, to find Mahdoo bending over him and his tent once more lit by an oil lamp. He had slept the clock round, and the messengers from the Rana, who had arrived in the course of the morning, were still waiting to speak to him.

"The Sirdar Mulraj gave orders that neither you nor he were to be disturbed," said Mahdoo, "but the Sirdar is still sleeping, and now the Rao-Sahib sends to know what is to be done with them and whether arrangements should be made for them to spend the night here."

"Why here?" asked Ash, puzzled. His mind was still clouded with the aftermath of nightmare and he was feeling absurdly shaken and not yet fully awake.

"Because the hour is late, and the road to the city is a rough one in the darkness," explained Mahdoo.

Ash shook himself like a dog coming out of water, and his eyes became focused and aware. He said shortly:

"That last we have good reason to know. But if we could travel it, so can they. If the Rao-Sahib's servant is without, I will speak to him. Call him."

Mahdoo did so, and Kaka-ji's elderly major-domo entered and salaamed.

"Tell the Rao-Sahib," said Ash, "that there is no reason why he should put himself out to offer hospitality to these people, and that I myself will send word to them that we much regret our inability to offer them any accommodation for the night, but owing to our own lack of sleep we have not yet had time to set our camp in order. So I suggest they now return to the city and visit us again tomorrow; or preferably the next day, when we shall be in a better state to receive them."

He had done precisely that, and the Rana's envoys rode back to Bhithor by starlight in an extremely anxious frame of mind, having all wasted the greater part of a day without having been able to see or speak to a single person of consequence, or make any of the fulsome and placatory speeches they had been charged to deliver. At an early hour next morning they reported on the failure of their mission to the Diwan, who not unnaturally regarded this as proof positive that the Sahib was acting with the full approval of the Government of India—for otherwise how would he have dared to behave in this manner? The Rana fully agreed with this view, and after another urgent meeting with his councillors ordered the dispatch of large supplies of grain, fruit and fresh vegetables to the camp, as a personal gift from himself and a gesture of good-will from the citizens of Bhithor.

The arrival of these provisions relieved Ash of a major source of anxiety, for the stocks he had managed to hoard would not have lasted long, and had there been no way of augmenting them, the camp would have been forced to leave Bhithor and risk the possibility of not being invited to return, which would have spelt disaster for Karidkote. The long line of heavily laden carts that rumbled into the camp not only banished that fear, but showed that the Rana had lost his nerve and was metaphorically waving a white flag.

There had been no deputation from the palace that day, but on the following one the Diwan himself, accompanied by a number of senior councillors and nobles, had ridden into the camp and been received with all ceremony. It was immediately plain that there were to be no explanations or apologies, but that all the unpleasantness of the preceding weeks was to be treated as though it had never occurred. The Diwan had even managed to imply that any delay over the negotiations was only due to the fact that the Rana's family priest had not been in agreement with the priests of the city temple on the matter of an auspicious date for the wedding. But as this difficulty had at last been resolved, it remained only for the brides' relatives to choose which of two selected dates (both equally propitious) they preferred and the arrangements for the ceremony would at once be put in train.

No one on either side had made any reference to previous disagreements, and the talks had been conducted in an atmosphere of cordiality and sweet reason that could hardly have been exceeded among a band of bosom-friends. The Diwan had concluded by saying that the state guest-houses, together with the Moti Mahal, the Pearl Palace, were at the disposal of the brides and their entourage, and it was hoped that they would take up residence there at the earliest opportunity.

By now the entire camp had learned to place no trust in the Rana, and the thought of what he might do if he were allowed to gain possession of so many valuable hostages could not be avoided. Nevertheless, the offer had been accepted; largely because Ash considered that the danger was past and there would be no further attempts at blackmail or intimidation, but also because the Pearl Palace, and all three guest-houses, stood in the Ram Bagh, a large park on the banks of the lake and over a mile beyond the city.

"The Ram Bagh," said Ash, "has a wall about it. A high and well-built wall that we could defend if these faithless Bhithoris tried any further tricks. It is also shielded from the forts by the city, so that there will be no threat from their cannon, and we'll leave a third of our forces here, allowing it to be known that should any further 'misunderstandings' occur, they have orders to fight their way out across the border and carry a full report of the matter to the Government. Yes, I think we may safely accept the offer."

Kaka-ji and the elders had agreed, and after consulting his priest, Kaka-ji had declared in favour of the second of the two dates. That having been settled, two thirds of the camp had moved back through the gorge again, and marching down the length of the valley, had skirted the city and taken up residence in the royal park; the brides with their brother and uncle and their women in a little white marble palace on the lake's edge, Ash and Mulraj and other senior personages in the guest-houses, and the remainder in tents pitched under the shade of mango, neem and gold *mohur* trees.

The change was a welcome one, for now that the *louh* was failing the park was an infinitely cooler and more comfortable spot than the valley or the country beyond the gorge. Both palace and guest-houses were plentifully supplied with punkahs and *kus-kus* tatties, and what little breeze there was blew in off the lake and made the nights pleasant and the days far from intolerable. Nor could any fault be found with the behaviour of the Rana and his subjects, who now combined to see that the visitors lacked nothing. The Rana, with unexpected generosity, had actually decreed that the park was to be regarded as Karidkote territory for a period of six weeks, so that the brides' relatives and friends could look upon it as their home and, in effect, invite the *barat*—the bridegroom's party—to attend the wedding there.

"A truly thoughtful and courteous gesture," approved Kaka-ji, adding hopefully that it showed the Rana had good qualities as well as bad ones, and possibly he had been influenced of late by evil advisers whom he had now found out and dismissed. "It may be that in future he will be more just in his dealings," said Kaka-ji. "We must believe that this is so."

Ash did not believe anything of the sort, but he could see no point in saying so. The old man was tired and anxious, and if it consoled him to hope that the Rana had suffered a change of heart, why not leave him to his daydreams? God knew that he, Ash, would have given much to share them, but he knew very well that the Rana's advisers merely echoed their master's wishes, and that there was only one ruler in Bhithor. If, at present, their ruler was on his best behaviour, it was merely because he had been badly frightened; but leopards did not change their spots, and once the wedding was over—and the interfering Pelham-Sahib had departed—the Rana would revert to normal. Of that Ash was confident.

544

But as there was nothing he could do about it he kept silent on that subject, though he pointed out somewhat acidly that the "thoughtful and courteous gesture" of bestowing temporary territorial rights over the park to Karidkote was likely to prove an expensive one as far as Nandu was concerned, for by custom, the bride's family play host to the groom's party, the *barat,* during the three days of the marriage ceremonies. And though it is laid down that the *barat* must not exceed two hundred, in the present instance, as the wedding was to take place in the groom's own state, that number was, understandably, likely to be very much higher—a fact which had not troubled the bride's family at all, since they could hardly be expected to play host to their hosts. Now, however, as a result of the Rana's decree they must do that very thing—and pay heavily for the privilege.

Kaka-ji, who had hitherto failed to see this point, looked startled, and as its implications dawned on him, observed with grudging respect that the Rana was undoubtedly a cunning fellow and one to be reckoned with. "Too cunning for an old man such as myself," admitted Kaka-ji ruefully. "Ah well, it would not have been possible for us to refuse his offer, so we must put a good face upon it. Nor do I feel that we need grudge him this little victory, seeing that we have defeated him so soundly in all other respects. Yet I hope you do not think that he has any further tricks in mind?"

Ash thought it only too likely: probably a round dozen. But he side-stepped the question by asking if the Rao-Sahib had yet learned how many people were likely to be in the bridegroom's party?—the durbar hall of the Pearl Palace, where the marriage ceremony would take place, was not over-large, and . . .

The Rao-Sahib, instantly diverted, replied that only relatives and close friends would be in the durbar hall, but that several large *shamianahs* were already being erected in the gardens of the Moti Mahal to accommodate the remainder of the guests. He took Ash off to inspect them, and in the bustle and excitement of the preparations the Rana's "minor victory" was tactfully forgotten.

There had been no more trouble over the payment of the bride-price, and now it seemed that nothing was too good for the visitors. The bride's brother and uncle, and anyone else who chose to do so, were pressed to stay on

545

after the wedding for as long as it suited them—until the onset of the monsoon if they wished. The Pearl Palace would be placed at their disposal and no limit set to the number of attendants and other members of their entourage whom they might choose to keep with them, all of whom could be accommodated in the park.

The offer was a generous one, and Ash realized with dismay that it would probably be accepted, and that however much he personally disliked the idea of having to stay in Bhithor for even a day longer than he must, it would be no bad thing if it were, as there was no blinking the fact that the longer Jhoti stayed out of Nandu's reach the better. Biju Ram was dead and his servants and confederates banished from the camp, but there would still be men in Karidkote willing to do murder at a nod from their ruler, and it was Ash's hope (or had been, in the days before he met the Rana) that the boy's new brother-in-law might be persuaded to keep him in Bhithor until such time as he was old enough to guard himself from assassination—or until Nandu over-reached himself and was deposed, which was not so unlikely in view of the fact that the verbal report Ash would be required to make on his return to Rawalpindi would include an account of the attempts on Jhoti's life, which would certainly result in a good deal of official attention being focused on Nandu's activities, both past and present.

There was also the welfare of the camp as a whole to be considered, and Ash knew very well that the great majority of its members, including the horses, elephants, pack animals and other livestock, would gain greatly from remaining in Bhithor until the arrival of the monsoon. If all had gone as planned, they would have been half-way home by now, but delays on the outward march and the protracted negotiations that had followed upon their arrival had totalled many weeks. The worst of the hot weather was already upon them, and to start the return journey in this heat would mean great hardship for all—the old in particular; and Kaka-ji, for one, was far from robust, and unused to these high temperatures.

"They will have to stay," thought Ash resignedly. They would all have to stay, himself included. He was tied to the camp until such time as they reached Deenagunj again. When the proposal was put to him he agreed to it, even though the thought of lingering in Bhithor within

546

sight of the Rung Mahal where Anjuli would be living, wedded and bedded to that shrivelled and unscrupulous satyr, was as near intolerable as makes no matter. He would have given ten years of his life to be able to turn his back on the place now, at once, and get as far away from it as possible; and a further ten to be able to forget that he had ever seen it.

But the news that they were to stay in Bhithor for a further month was received with delight by Jhoti, who now that the wedding day was imminent had begun to think of the future and to wonder what Nandu would do to him when he got back to Karidkote. The thought made him shiver, and he therefore greeted the Rana's invitation as a reprieve and, boy-like, forgot that it would at best be only a temporary one, and that the extra time granted him would pass all too soon. Instead, his spirits soared and he began to look upon the Rana as a benefactor instead of an ogre.

Kaka-ji was equally grateful. He had been dreading the rigours of a return journey at this season, and had not looked forward to exchanging the cool marble rooms of the Pearl Palace for an airless tent in the dust and the scorching heat of the empty plains. But Mulraj was less enthusiastic, though he agreed that as far as Jhoti and Kaka-ji were concerned, it was an excellent idea: "But we cannot all stay. Our numbers are too great, and it would be a grave mistake to put so heavy a strain upon the Rana's hospitality; or his patience. Besides, there is no necessity for it. I would suggest that we divide our camp into two and that as soon as the festivities are over, one half should move off under the command of Hira Singh, who can be trusted to see to their safety and welfare, taking the heavy baggage and moving only by night —there being no need for haste. It is even possible that if the monsoon favours us, we who remain here may catch up with them before they reach the borders of Karidkote."

Ash gave his consent to this plan, but made no move towards putting it into operation. The affairs of the camp had suddenly become so meaningless to him that he found it an effort to show even a cursory interest in them, and it was left to Mulraj and his officers to work out the details and deal with the hundred and one arrangements that must be made, while Ash spent his days shooting sand-grouse or riding through the narrow valleys between the hills. Anything to escape from the past and the Pearl Palace—and the sight and sound of men preparing for the celebration of a marriage; which was only possible far out on the plain or among the hills, since not only the city itself, but every village and hamlet in the state was a-flutter with banners and garlands, while the approaches to the park were spanned by arches decorated with tinsel and coloured paper and flowers.

By the day of the wedding the very alleyways of Bhithor smelled of marigolds and jasmine instead of the more familiar mixture of dust and refuse and boiling *ghee*, while the hum of the city was drowned by the din of *fu-fu* bands and the crackle of *patarkars*. In the Pearl Palace the centre portion of the durbar hall, normally open to the sky, had been roofed in by an awning, and below this four silver posts supported a canopy fashioned from thousands of marigold heads strung on gold wire, beneath which the sacred fire would be lighted and the officiating priests perform the *shadi*, the marriage ceremony.

The ground between the silver posts had been spread with fresh cow-dung that was patted and dried to form a smooth floor, eight foot square. On this a large circle and various good-luck signs were now drawn in a white paste made from rice flour . . . for at last the long awaited day was here.

In an inner room of the Pearl Palace the brides were being bathed and anointed with scented oil, the soles of their feet and the palms of their slender hands tinted with henna, their hair combed and braided by Unpora-Bai.

Their day had begun with a dawn-hour *pujah*, to pray for a hundred sons and a hundred daughters, and they had eaten nothing because they must fast until the marriage ceremony was over. Their women crowded about them, laughing and teasing and chattering like a flock of gaily coloured parakeets as they dressed the brides in the shimmering silks and gauzes of the wedding garments, painted their eyes with *kohl*, and hung them with jewels that were part of their dowries: diamonds, emeralds, pigeon's-blood rubies and ropes of pearls from the treasury of the Hawa Mahal.

The small room was dim and airless and heavy with the scent of sandalwood, jasmine and attar-of-roses, and Shushila's convulsive sobs were lost in the prevailing din

548

of women's voices and went as unregarded as the dripping of a tap. Jhoti had been in to see his sisters and give them the benefit of his advice on what jewels they should wear, but as the mob of excited, shrill-voiced women who pressed about them had for once paid little attention to him, he had stayed only long enough to tell Shushila that if she didn't stop crying she would be the ugliest bride in all India—a brotherly piece of candour that only served to increase the flow of Shu-shu's tears and earned him an unexpectedly sharp slap from Unpora-Bai. Jhoti had withdrawn in some dudgeon, and run off to find Ash in order to show off his own wedding finery and complain of the silliness of women.

"It's true what I said, Sahib. She's done nothing but snivel until her eyes are all swollen and puffy and her nose is as red as her sari. She looks a fright and I expect the Rana will think we have cheated him on purpose and be angry with all of us. Do you suppose he'll beat her? I would, if she were my wife and all she could do was cry! And I shall tell her so. Except that Kairi said . . ."

But the Sahib was no longer listening.

Ash had been living of late in a curious half world, refusing to think and deliberately driving himself to exhaustion by means of hard exercise; or when that failed, working at reports or playing interminable games of chess with Kaka-ji or Mulraj, or of patience with himself. He had eventually managed to persuade himself that he was over the worst and could face this day, when it came, without any emotion. And now Jhoti had spoken of her, and the mention of the old nick-name had broken through his defences as though they were so much tissue paper, and clawed at his heart with a pain that was as sudden and as savage as the impact of a bullet smashing into flesh and bone. For a moment the room about him had turned dark and the walls and floor seemed to sway, and when they steadied again he became aware that Jhoti was still talking, though at first the words were no more than a jumble of meaningless sounds.

"Do you like my *achkan*?" demanded Jhoti, revolving slowly to show it off. "I was going to wear a silver brocade one, but my uncle said he liked the gold one best. Do you think he was right, Sahib?"

Ash did not speak, and when Jhoti repeated the question, replied so much at random that it was clear

549

that he had not been paying the least attention. "Are you not feeling well?" inquired Jhoti solicitously. "Is it the heat?"

"What . . . ?" Ash seemed to come back from a long way off. "I'm sorry, Prince. I was thinking of something else . . . What did you say?"

"It is nothing," said Jhoti, politely dismissing it with a wave of his small paw. He had seen men look and speak in a similar fashion after taking drugs, and presumed that the Sahib must have been dosing himself with opium against some sickness of the stomach. He had a fondness for Pelham-Sahib and was sorry that he should feel unwell, but there were so many exciting things to be seen and done that day that he did not waste time worrying over it, and ran off to show the gold brocade coat to Mulraj instead.

Ash was barely aware that he had gone; or that Gul Baz had entered the room and was saying something about it being time to go. Go where?

"The Rao-Sahib sends word that the bridegroom's procession is said to have left the Rung Mahal," reported Gul Baz.

Ash nodded, and putting up an uncertain hand to wipe the sweat off his forehead, was startled to find his fingers shaking uncontrollably. He snatched them away and stared down at his hand, forcing it to steadiness with an effort of will, and when it was still again, reached for the elaborately braided and befrogged coat that Gul Baz was holding out to him, and that would today provide the only sober note among a rainbow of colours and the sheen of gold and silver thread.

Gul Baz had earlier helped him to pull on his boots and overalls and buckle on the webbed sword belt with its dangling straps about his waist; and now he shrugged himself reluctantly into the coat and adjusted the cross belt, feeling as stale and exhausted as though he had just returned from a route march instead of doing no more than rise from his bed and eat his breakfast. The high, tight collar of his uniform felt as though it would choke him, but though the day promised to be one of the longest and worst of his life, and was already abominably hot, as a Sahib and an officer he must sit through it sweltering in full-dress uniform, gloved, booted and spurred, and with a ceremonial sword clanking at his hip—which seemed, somehow, the last straw in the whole sorry business.

His hands were steady enough as he buckled on his sword, but when Gul Baz handed him the big white pith helmet that is worn with full dress, he took it and stood looking at it as he had looked at Jhoti, as though he did not see it.

Bands of blue and gold striped the pugaree-cloth about the crown, and the light glinted on the tall gilt spike that topped it and on the links of the chinstrap that custom decreed must be worn above and not below the chin. Gul Baz cleared his throat in a deprecatory cough that was a polite reminder that time was passing, and when that had no effect, said firmly: "Put it on, Sahib. The sun is hot."

Ash obeyed mechanically, and having adjusted the chinstrap, drew on his gloves and hitched forward the hilt of his sword, and straightening his shoulders as though he were about to face a firing squad, went out to join Kaka-ji and others who were already waiting to welcome the bridegroom and his party in a covered courtyard by the main gate of the Pearl Palace.

The courtyard was a large one, but it was stiflingly hot, and also exceedingly noisy, for in addition to the many people waiting there, a three-man band sat playing in a small balcony above the arch that led into the main block of the palace.

Garlands of roses and jasmine buds hung down from the balcony's edge and were looped across the marble screens, and the close air reeked with the cloying sweetness of *itr* and incense and fading flowers, the sharp smell of *pan* and cardamom seeds, and the less pleasing odour of perspiration. Ash could feel the sweat running down between his shoulder blades, and he surreptitiously unhooked the high collar of his coat and wished that the dignity of a Sahib did not entail his having to accept a chair instead of squatting Indian fashion on the floor as his companions were doing: the marble would at least be cool, whereas the plush upholstery of the chair that had been provided for him felt as though it had just come out of an oven. He shifted restlessly and wondered how long he would be called upon to endure it, and whether it was the heat or the lack of air or the intermittent bursts of ear-piercing music that was making his head ache so abominably.

In the event the wait turned out to be even longer than expected, for the report that the bridegroom and his *barat* had left the city palace and were on their way to the park had been over-optimistic. They had intended to leave a full two hours before noon, but Asia has little regard for Time and none at all for punctuality, and the afternoon was far advanced before the procession finally set out for the Ram Bagh; and when at last it reached the park the sun was well down in the sky and the worst of the heat was over.

They could hear it coming from a long way off. At first the tunk-a-tunk of drums and the joyous squeal of flutes, the braying of horns and the shouts of watching crowds were only a distant murmur barely louder than the cawing of crows and the crooning of doves and green pigeons among the trees of the Ram Bagh. But as the minutes slid past the sounds grew in volume, and at last Jhoti, who had scampered up to the roof from where he could catch a glimpse of the road across the intervening tree-tops, came pelting down to announce that the procession was entering the park gates, and where were the garlands? The assembled company rose to smooth down their *achkans* and straighten their turbans, and Ash refastened his collar, drew a deep breath, and setting his teeth, tried to think of nothing at all, and found himself thinking of Wally and Zarin, and the snow peaks of the Dur Khaima . . .

The bridegroom had not come on horseback from the city. He had been carried instead, seated on a platform that was draped and canopied with pearl-fringed cloth-of-gold and borne by twelve gorgeously liveried retainers. His dress too was gold, as on the occasion of that first durbar so many weeks ago, but today it was even more splendid, for the brocaded *achkan* was sewn with jewels. There were more jewels on his turban: a great crescent of diamonds and emeralds pinned an aigrette to the gold tissue, and ropes of pear-shaped diamonds looped about it in the manner of tinsel on a Christmas tree. Jewels flashed on his fingers and blazed on the solid gold of his sword belt, while the sword itself—the sword that a bridegroom wears to symbolize his readiness to defend his bride against all

552

enemies—had a hilt encrusted with diamonds and topped by a single emerald the size of a rupee.

A stranger seeing that glittering figure seated on a golden platform and surrounded by liveried attendants and the gorgeously dressed members of the *barat* might well have taken it to be some Eastern idol being carried in procession by its worshippers, an impression heightened by the fact that its face was concealed by strings of marigold and jasmine buds that hung down from the turban, so that only the glint of eyes from behind the veil showed that the bedizened object was alive.

The music stopped on a long wailing note, and Kaka-ji's family priest went out to recite Vedic hymns and invoke the blessing of the gods, before calling the bride's uncle forward for the *milni*, officially the ceremony of the introduction between the fathers of the bride and groom, but today (both fathers being dead) between Kaka-ji and one of the Rana's maternal uncles. The two old gentlemen embraced, and Jhoti, as the brides' brother, assisted the bridegroom to alight and conducted him and his friends into the covered courtyard where the brides' party waited to garland the guests and present gifts to their opposite numbers in the *barat*.

Despite his dazzling dress the Rana appeared far less imposing on foot. Not even the over-large turban with its tall aigrette could disguise his lack of inches, and Kaka-ji Rao—no giant—topped him by half a head. Nevertheless the faceless figure still managed to convey a disquieting sense of power. "And danger," thought Ash.

It was as though a tiger, full-fed and therefore temporarily harmless, had come padding unconcernedly through a field full of sheep and cows, and the impression was so strong that Ash could almost have sworn that the man gave off a special smell: an animal smell, rank and menacing. He felt the hair at the base of his scalp prickle as though it were lifting, and recalled in a sudden flash of memory a long-forgotten scene: moonlight and the black shadows of trees and jungle grass, and a warning shiver that seemed to run through the silence like a cat's-paw of wind flitting across an expanse of still water, felt but not heard, and someone—was it Uncle Akbar?—saying in a whisper that was barely more than a breath of sound: "*Shere ahraha hai!*" (the tiger is coming).

The sweat that had soaked through his uniform was

suddenly cold, and Ash shivered and heard his teeth chatter. Then the bridegroom had moved past him and was being escorted towards the arch below the balcony for the *jai-mala*, the garlanding of the groom by the bride.

The arch gave onto a narrow tunnel-like entrance hall where Shushila and her sister waited with the garlands that a bride must place round the groom's neck in token of her acceptance of him. Even now, at this eleventh hour, a wedding will be cancelled should the bride refuse to do this; and when there followed an unexplained pause in which the Rana waited and those behind him jostled and peered, Ash had a desperate moment of hope, the frantic, foolish and utterly ludicrous hope that Shushila had changed her mind and meant to reject the marriage. But though the pause seemed a long one to those who could not see into the hallway and did not know the cause of the delay, it could not have lasted more than a minute or so, and then the groom bowed low, and when he straightened up the bride's garland was about his neck.

A moment later he bent again—though this time so slightly that it was more a brief inclination of the head than a bow—and those behind him saw a woman's hands lift a second garland high in order to clear the osprey plume on his gold turban. The hands were decked with jewels and the palms and finger nails had been tinted with henna and touched with gold leaf. But they were still square and capable—still unmistakably the hands of a little unloved girl who had been known as Kairi-Bai—and glimpsing them, Ash knew that he would, after all, be able to watch her go through the marriage rites and see her leave for her husband's house without flinching, because nothing that was to come could possibly hurt worse than that brief sight of Juli's hands ...

With the garlanding over, the band struck up once more and the groom and guests entered the Pearl Palace to be feasted, the *barat* being fed before the brides' party, while all those for whom there was no room indoors filed out to take their places in the gaily decorated *shamianahs* where more bands played and servants hurried to and fro laden with dishes.

By now the sun was low and presently the evening breeze arose and blew gently across the lake, its breath bringing a welcome coolness to the park, though inside the Pearl Palace the air remained stifling, and now that the rich odour of food mingled with the scent of flowers and perfume the atmosphere was rapidly becoming unbreathable. Ash, however, was not called upon to endure it, this being one part of the ceremonies that he asked to be excused from attending, in order to save Kaka-ji the embarrassment of having to tell him what he already knew: that the Rana's caste forbade him from sitting down to eat with a foreigner.

Leaving the palace by a side door he walked back to his own quarters in one of the guest-houses, to eat his evening meal alone and to watch the sun go down behind the hills beyond the city and the stars come out one by one in a sky that darkened swiftly from dusty green to midnight blue: and not only stars, for tonight as the dusk deepened a myriad pin-points of light flowered on the walls and rooftops and window-sills of Bhithor as the Rana's subjects lit thousands upon thousands of *chirags*—the little earthenware saucers filled with oil, in which a wisp of twisted cotton serves as a wick, that all over India are used for illuminations during times of festivity.

The park too was alive with lights that swayed and flickered or burned bright according to the whims of the breeze, and the Pearl Palace itself was outlined in twinkling gold, so that it shimmered against the night sky like some enchanted castle in a fairy tale. Even the forts had been decked with *chirags,* and presently the sky above the city began to blossom with showers of red and green and purple stars, as fireworks streaked upward to burst and blaze and fade slowly away on the darkness.

Ash watched them from the verandah outside his room, and wished that the Rana's caste had also prevented him from permitting a foreigner to be present during the actual marriage ceremony. But it seemed this was not so: and in any case, it would have been impossible to avoid attending, as apart from the fact that Kaka-ji and Mulraj had been particularly insistent that the Sahib should be present at the ceremony, the instructions issued to him in Rawalpindi had expressly stated that Captain Pelham-Martyn was to see the two sisters of His Highness the Maharajah of Karidkote safely married.

The actual wording was, of course, open to different interpretations. But in the circumstances it would be as well to take it literally, in case at some future date there should be any arguments as to the validity of at least one of the marriages, which was a point that Kaka-ji and Mulraj might also have had in mind.

Over an hour had passed since Gul Baz had removed the coffee tray and gone off to join in the merry-making, but the feasting was still in progress; and remembering Lalji's wedding, Ash realized that he might well have to wait for another hour or two before being summoned to witness the *shadi* ceremony. In the park and the palace, bands played on with unabated vigour, vying with the bang and crackle of fireworks and the throb of tom-toms in the city to turn the night into pandemonium, and Ash retreated to his room, and closing the doors against the noise, sat down to pass the time by writing to Wally and Zarin to let them know that he would be delayed in Bhithor for at least another month—more, if the monsoon were late—and there was small hope of his seeing either of them before the end of the summer at best.

He had finished both letters and begun a third, this time to the Political Officer, when Mulraj arrived to fetch him to the Pearl Palace where the *shadi* was about to take place; and as they walked back through the park, he saw that the moon was down, and knew that it must be close on midnight.

The durbar hall was crowded to capacity, and coming in from the night air the heat and the overpowering odour of sandalwood and incense and dying flowers met him like a tangible wave. But at least the bands were no longer playing, and except for the murmur of voices the hall was reasonably quiet. It was also surprisingly dark, for the lamps were all of coloured glass, and by now the oil in them had burned low so that it took him a moment or two to accustom himself to the dim light and be able to pick out his friends from among the sea of faces.

A chair had been placed for him near the door and in the shadow of a pillar, far back enough to make his presence unobtrusive, while allowing him to see over the heads of the men who sat cross-legged on the ground in close-packed rows in front of him. From it he could see not only the four silver posts with their golden canopy of marigolds, but the ground below it, where the circle drawn in rice-flour showed startling white against the smooth square of dry cow-dung. A brass cauldron in which the sacrificial fire would be lit stood ready, and beside it the priests had set up an altar on which they were busy ar-

556

ranging *pujah* vessels and bowls of Ganges water, lamps, godlings and incense-burners. And on low stools to one side of the square, their faces veiled by flowers, sat the bridegroom and the brides, together with Kaka-ji and Maldeo Rai (who were jointly deputizing for the brides' late father) and the shrouded figure of cousin Unpora-Bai, representing their deceased mothers—which was surely enough, thought Captain Pelham-Martyn sardonically, to cause the ashes of both ladies to rise in fury from the dust.

The rustle of talk sank to a whisper, and presently that too was silenced as one of the priests under the canopied enclosure began the *havan*, the lighting of the sacred fire. The flames illuminated his calm, smooth-shaven face so that it seemed to glow like burnished metal as he leaned forward to feed the fire with chips of scented wood and grains of incense. When it was well alight, silver platters heaped with perfumed salts were passed round to those who sat within reach of the circle, each of whom took a pinch and threw it at the fire. The salts sizzled and sputtered, giving off a strong, aromatic odour that set off a muffled chorus of coughing from the unseen women in the purdah gallery overlooking the hall. And in obedience to a signal, the Rana and Shushila rose and were led into the rice-flour circle.

A priest began to intone the *mantras*, but Ash sat too far away to catch more than an occasional word, and later, when the priest paused now and again for the bride and her groom to repeat the vows after him, only the Rana's voice could be heard. Shushila's was inaudible, but the vows were familiar to everyone present. The pair were promising to live according to their creed, to be true to each other and share each other's burdens, to beget sons and to remain firm and faithful as a rock ...

Even standing beside her wizened groom, Shushila looked incredibly small and slight, like a child who has dressed up in its mother's finery. She was wearing scarlet as a bride should—red being the colour of rejoicing—and out of compliment to the groom, the traditional full-skirted dress of Bhithor, and all Rajasthan. The pigeon's blood rubies that circled her neck and wrists and decked her fingers caught the light of the flames and shone as though they were on fire, and though she kept her head bent and spoke her vows in a whisper, she performed

557

her part in the ceremony without faltering: to the surprise (and no small relief) of her relatives and women, all of whom had fully expected a flood of tears if not a hysterical scene.

Ash could not help wondering if she would have behaved as well if she had been able to catch a glimpse of her bridegroom's face, or had any inkling of what that curtain of flower-buds concealed. But as custom decreed that a bridal pair must not look at each other until the wedding ceremony was over, and Shushila too wore a similar veil of flowers, it was not possible for her to see anything very much. The "marriage ring"—a bracelet of iron—was placed on her arm, and the thread of happiness hung round her neck; and presently a corner of her sari was knotted to the end of her bridegroom's sash, and thus tied together they took the "seven steps" round the fire: the *satapadi* that is the essential part of the whole ceremony, as without this the marriage is still revocable in law, while once the last step is taken it is established, and there can be no going back.

Shushila was now a wife and Rani of Bhithor, and her husband was addressing her in the words of the ancient Vedic hymn: *"Become thou my partner as thou hast paced all the seven steps with me. Apart from thee I cannot live. Apart from me do thou not live. We shall share alike all goods and power combined. Over my house thou shalt bear full sway . . ."*

His voice ceased and the newly wedded pair returned to the sacred circle to receive the blessing of their older relatives, and that done, seated themselves once more. The fire was fed again with wood and incense, the *mantras* chanted and the silver trays passed round, and the whole ceremony repeated. But this time with more haste and with a different bride.

Anjuli had been seated on the far side of her half-sister and concealed from Ash's view by the stout shape of Unpora-Bai. But now she in her turn was led forward into the circle. The moment that he had dreaded for so long was upon him, and he must watch Juli being married.

Almost unconsciously he braced his body as though to face a physical assault. But there had, after all, been no need to do so. Perhaps it was the absence of hope that made it possible for him to relax his tense muscles and sit motionless and detached, feeling nothing—or almost noth-

558

ing. For although he would have said that the ceremony of the garlanding had extinguished the last infinitesimal flicker of hope, a spark had survived: the chance that spoilt, highly strung Shu-shu, over-driven by the delays of the last weeks and her terror of marriage to a stranger in a strange land, might baulk at the last moment and refuse to go through with the ceremony.

It was unthinkable that a devout Hindu bride should refuse to take those final binding steps around the sacred fire, and such a thing could have happened only rarely—if at all. But then Shu-shu, by Western standards, was only a child: an over-emotional child whose reactions were often unpredictable, and who might well be capable of creating a scandalous precedent by refusing to perform the *satapadi*. But she had not done so; and as she took the seven steps, that last obstinate spark died, thereby releasing Ash from hope and enabling him to sit through that second ceremony with something approaching detachment.

He had been helped in this by the fact that there was nothing in the least familiar about the faceless and anonymous figure in the shimmering sari and the veil of flower buds. From where he sat it could have been any Indian woman; except that she was taller than most, and made her bridegroom appear wizened and stunted by comparison.

She was less splendidly dressed than her half-sister, which was understandable. But the choice of colour, jewels and material (for which Unpora-Bai had been responsible) was unfortunate, as the topaz and pearl ornaments did not show to advantage in the dim lighting, while the yellow and gold shot-silk that had seemed such an admirable foil for Shushila's scarlet paled into insignificance beside the brilliant gold of the bridegroom's coat. The material, too, was so stiff that it disguised the wearer's slenderness and grace and gave her an oddly clumsy appearance. There was nothing there of Juli: only a shapeless bundle of silk topped by a fringe of wilting marigold heads, repeating a series of actions that no longer seemed significant or charged with any emotion.

The priests hurried through the rites and the groom gabbled the final hymn, and it was all over. There followed a final ceremony in which the Rana led his wives out to introduce them to those members of the *barat* who had not been present at the wedding, in token that a bride is no longer a member of her own family but belongs from henceforth to her husband's. That being done, the two hungry and exhausted young women were free at last to return to their own rooms and take off their finery, and to eat the first food they had tasted in more than twenty-four hours.

Kaka-ji and the other men carried off the groom to a feast in the largest of the *shamianahs* in the park, and Ash went to bed and—surprisingly—slept through the din of bands and fireworks and rejoicing crowds as soundly as though he had been drugged.

The first day of the three-day ceremony had ended, and the second was several hours old and close to dawn before the bands and fireworks and voices ceased and the park was silent at last.

31

By tradition the two days that followed were given over to feasting the *barat*. But on the morning after the wedding Ash had excused himself from the celebrations and gone off shooting, accompanied by his syce, Kalu Ram, and a local *shikari*.

Returning in the dusk as the *chirags* were beginning to twinkle once more on rooftops and walls and the cattle strayed homeward from the grazing grounds around the city, he was met by a messenger who had arrived earlier in the day and who had been squatting by the door of his room, waiting for his return.

The man had ridden many miles and slept little during the past few days; but though he had accepted food he had refused to rest until he had given the letter he carried into the Sahib's own hand, and it had been impressed upon him that the matter was one of the greatest urgency—he would, he explained, have delivered it sooner if anyone had been able to tell him in which direction the Sahib had gone.

The envelope he proffered was heavily sealed, and recognizing the writing, Ash's heart sank. He had a guilty conscience over the tone of his last letter to the Political Officer, and half expected a sharp reprimand. Even without that, any communication from Major Spiller was bound to be depressing, and he wondered what he was going to be advised to do, or told not to do, this time. Well, whatever it was it was too late, for the wedding was over and done with and the bride-price had been paid.

He dismissed the messenger, and having handed over his shot-gun to Gul Baz and a brace of black partridge to Mahdoo, carried the letter into the lamp-lit sitting room and broke the seals with his thumb-nail. The envelope contained a single sheet of paper and he took it out and glanced at it, feeling bored and irritable. The message had clearly been written in haste, for it differed from any previous one he had received from the Political Officer, in that it was short and to the point. Yet he had to read it twice before he took it in, and then his first thought was that it had come too late. A week ago—even two days ago —it might have changed everything, but now there could be no going back; the thing was done. A cold tide of bitterness swelled up in him and he smashed his clenched fist against the wall and was grateful for the savage pain and the smart of bruised knuckles, because it served in some small way to counteract the less bearable pain in his heart.

He stood staring blindly before him for a long time, and it was only when Gul Baz came into the room and exclaimed at the sight of his injured hand that he roused himself and went off to wash it clean. The cold water seemed to clear his brain as well as the broken skin, and he realized that he was probably wrong in thinking that it would have made any difference if the news had arrived earlier, since after the expediture of so much time and money and effort there would have been no question of turning back.

He allowed Gul Baz to bandage his knuckles, postponed his bath for half an hour, and having swallowed three fingers of brandy, retrieved the letter and went off to read it to Mulraj.

Mulraj had been dressing for that night's banquet when Ash walked in and demanded a few words with him in private, and he had taken one look at Ash's face and dismissed his servants. At first he too had been unable to credit the news that had first been sent, over a fortnight

561

ago, to the Governor of the Punjab, passed on to the military authorities in Rawalpindi, from where it had been telegraphed to the Political Officer responsible for the affairs of Bhithor, who in turn forwarded it by the hand of a special messenger to Captain Pelham-Martyn, marked *Urgent. For Immediate Attention.*

Nandu, Maharajah of Karidkote, whose family had of late suffered more than their fair share of fatal accidents, had met with one himself: a genuine one, this time. He had been trying out some of the ancient muzzle-loading weapons in the old armoury of the Hawa Mahal, one of which had exploded in his face and killed him outright. As he had died childless, his younger brother, the Heir Apparent, was now Maharajah, and it was thought advisable that he should return immediately to take up his inheritance. Captain Pelham-Martyn was therefore instructed to escort His Highness back to Karidkote without delay. Speed being essential, they should travel light, taking with them only as many men as Captain Pelham-Martyn judged sufficient for the protection and comfort of his young charge, and it was left to his discretion to make what arrangements he considered necessary for the welfare of the remainder of the bridal camp, who would have to return in their own time and at their own pace . . .

"So it has all been useless," said Ash bitterly.

"How so?" asked Mulraj, puzzled.

"The marriages. They were arranged by Nandu because he was afraid that if he married his sisters nearer home, a day might come when he found himself with a brother-in-law who might conceivably have designs on his throne, so he took care to choose one who lived too far away to make that possible. And now he is dead, and those poor girls have been tied to that—that offal for nothing!"

"That is not so," said Mulraj. "At least the boy is safe, and but for this journey to Bhithor he would not have been. If he had stayed in Karidkote his brother Nandu would have found a way to destroy him; and certainly the gods are on the boy's side, for while his brother lived he would not have been safe even here. There are always men who can be bribed to kill, provided the bribe is large enough."

"And you do not think Nandu would have quibbled in
562

the matter of blood money," said Ash. "Neither do I. Well, we have no need to worry ourselves over such questions any longer, because this news has solved all Jhoti's problems."

It had also solved one of his own, for it meant that he could leave Bhithor at once instead of being forced to remain there for an indefinite period, within sight of the Rana's palace and with nothing to do but wait on the weather and eat his heart out for a girl who would be living less than a mile away—one who was for ever out of reach, but whose husband he might have to meet frequently and be polite to. It meant also that he would be spared the long, slow torment of a return journey without Juli, camping in familiar places that would be full of memories, and passing once more through country that they had ridden across side by side on those evening rides . . . He had dreaded that; but a small party, unencumbered by women and children and minus baggage carts, camp-followers, livestock or elephants, would be able to cut corners and move with far greater speed, and need not be tied to a route that had been dictated by the needs of a camp of thousands.

His eagerness to leave was so great that had it been at all possible, he would have gone that same night. This being out of the question, he had suggested they start on the following afternoon, but Mulraj had set his face against it: "We cannot leave tomorrow," said Mulraj.

"Why not? I know there will be much work to do, but if we set our minds to it we could be ready."

"Perhaps. But you forget that tomorrow is the last day of the wedding festivities, and that at nightfall the brides will leave for their husband's house."

Ash had not forgotten it, but he could hardly explain that it was precisely because he hoped to avoid that particular sight that he was so anxious to set out on the following afternoon. However, Mulraj insisted that to leave before the celebrations had ended would cause great offence to the Rana and his people. It would be neither seemly nor necessary to disrupt the festivity of the final day with preparations for departure, and as Nandu had already been dead for over two weeks it could make little difference if Jhoti started back in two days' time, or three or four.

"Also our preparations will be better if we do not

563

make them too hastily," said Mulraj. "For as you say, there is much to be done."

Ash had not been able to deny that, and they had eventually agreed to say nothing about the letter for another day so that the merry-making should not be marred by news that coming at such a time was bound to be regarded as ill-omened, and that however welcome it might be to some, would certainly cause grief and distress to Shushila, if to no one else. Time enough, said Mulraj, to disclose it on the morning after the brides' departure, when they themselves would be free to make their own arrangements to leave.

The banquet that night was given by Kaka-ji, who had politely invited the Sahib to attend and received an equally polite acceptance. Honour being satisfied, Ash had later sent a message regretting that a sudden and severe headache prevented him from being present, and when Mulraj had gone he went back to his own quarters and having sent for the camp records, spent the greater part of the night poring over lists of men, animals and transport, and deciding how many or how few to take with him, which to leave, and what was to be done about a score of other matters. All of this would of course have to be discussed with Mulraj and the *panchayat*, but it was going to save a good deal of time if a detailed plan could be put forward for their approval as soon as the marriage festivities were over. His lamp was still burning when Kaka-ji's guests returned from the banquet, and the cocks were crowing before he turned it out and went to bed.

The third and last day of the ceremonies was again given over to feasting, but this time Ash did not leave the park to go off riding or shooting. He walked instead; and when at nightfall a message from Kaka-ji summoned him to the Pearl Palace, he put on his full-dress uniform again and went over to watch the final act of the tragicomedy that Nandu had planned in order to guard against something that could only have been visualized by a mind as riddled with suspicion and jealousy as his own.

Certainly Jhoti would never have thought of it, and it occurred to Ash that if, as Mulraj seemed to think, the gods were on the boy's side, it was a pity that they had remained uninterested in the fate of his sisters, for had they removed Nandu a year earlier none of this would have happened. True, he himself would not have met An-

564

juli again—though in the circumstances, that would surely have been far better for both of them. But at least Shushila would have been happier and Biju Ram would still be alive; and as Jhoti took after his father's side of the family, he would not have worried his head over imaginary rivals or wasted the revenues of his state in showing off to his fellow princes—as Nandu had done when he sent that preposterously large bridal camp traipsing across half India.

Yet even now, waiting to see Anjuli leave for her husband's house, he could not feel sorry that he had met her again, and known her and loved her. The pain of loss and the prospect of the long, empty years ahead could not outweigh that, or make it less wonderful to him; and he knew that if he had been able to foresee the future when he first discovered the Rajkumari Anjuli of Karidkote, whom he was escorting to her wedding in Bhithor, was none other than little Kairi-Bai of the Queen's balcony, it would have made no difference at all. He would still have handed her his half of the luck-charm—and accepted the consequences with gladness and gratitude.

Wally, who was always falling in and out of love, had been fond of quoting lines that some poet or other had written, to the effect that it was "better to have loved and lost than never to have loved at all." Well, Wally—and Tennyson, or whoever it was—had been right. It was better, infinitely better, to have loved Juli and lost her than not to have loved her at all. And if he did nothing worthwhile in the years ahead, life would still have been worth living because he had once loved and been loved by her . . .

It had taken him long enough to realize that, and it struck him as curious that he should not have done so until now, of all times, when he was waiting to catch a last glimpse of her. But it was enough that he had done so; and the knowledge brought him the same kind of relief that an exhausted swimmer feels when he reaches shallow water, and knows that he is not going to drown after all.

The departure of the brides and the groom had been a magnificent affair, and one that would surely have gratified the vanity of the late Maharajah of Karidkote if he could have seen it. His state elephants, gorgeously caparisoned, stood in the blaze of torchlight before the main entrance of the Pearl Palace, rocking gently from one foot to another as they waited for the procession to start. Their trunks and foreheads, their fringed ears and massive legs had been decorated with painted designs in brilliant colours, and their tusks ringed with bands of gold. The shimmering fringes of their velvet housings reached almost to the ground, and the embossed gold and silver-gilt of the howdahs gathered light from the bright flame of torches and the twinkling of innumerable *chirags*.

The start had already been held up by over an hour by the time Kaka-ji's message was delivered to Ash, and another hour went by without any sign of a move. Servants handed round *pan* and *itr,* and later, trays of little cakes to the patiently waiting crowd, and the guests munched and yawned and passed the time in desultory small-talk, until at last the groom's closest friends appeared on the steps of the palace. After that, things moved swiftly: a band struck up to signal the start, and as the elephants sank ponderously to their knees, an advance guard of gaily dressed horsemen set off with a clatter of hooves into the night. The Rana, ablaze with jewels and attended by a file of courtiers and uniformed servants, came through the gateway, closely followed by a small group of women—the Ranis of Bhithor and their ladies.

Tonight Shushila's sari was of flame-coloured gauze spangled and embroidered with gold, and though she wore it pulled far forward and held close to shield her face, and gems beneath it seemed to burn through it like fire. She walked without grace, supported by two attendants and almost tottering under the sheer weight of the jewels that decked every available inch of her slight body, and at each step the *rakhri* on her forehead trembled and its central stone, an enormous spinel ruby, glinted blood-red through the gauze.

Two paces behind her came Anjuli, tall and slender in green. Her sari was bordered with silver and seed pearls, but once again she was overshadowed by Shushila's splendour. There was an emerald on her forehead, faintly visible through the woven silk that was fine enough to betray the hint of copper in her dark hair and the thin red line that coloured her parting—the streak of *kunkum* that only a wife may wear. Her hair had been threaded with pearls and braided into a thick plait that swung down almost to her knee, and as she passed him Ash caught the scent of dried rose-petals that he would always associate with her.

She must have known that he would be there among the other spectators, but she kept her head bent and did not glance to left or right. The Rana mounted a silver ladder held against the leading elephant by two scarlet-turbaned servants, and settled himself in the howdah. Shu-shu went next, half-pushed, half-carried by her women, and took her place at his side. And then Anjuli was mounting the steps, slim, straight and royal, a flash of green and silver and the end of a swinging plait of dark hair; narrow feet the colour of carved ivory and a glimpse of slender ankles circled with jewels.

The mahout shouted a word of command and the elephant lurched to its feet: and as it moved off, Anjuli looked down from her seat in the gilded howdah. Her eyes, dark-rimmed with *kohl,* appeared enormous above the close-held edge of her sari, and they did not search among the sea of faces below her, but went directly to Ash, as though the compulsion of his own intent gaze had been strong enough to tell her exactly where he stood.

For a long, long moment they looked at each other, straight and steadily. Looked with love and longing, and without grief, trying to say with their eyes all those things that did not need saying because they knew them already: "I love you . . . I will always love you . . . Do not forget me." And in Juli's wide eyes the words she had spoken long ago on a moonlit night, looking down on him as she was looking now—*Khuda hafiz*—God be with you. Then the attendants and the torch-bearers closed up on either side, another band struck up and the howdah swayed as the elephant swung slowly away, taking Juli and Shu-shu and the Rana down the avenue of shade trees towards the gates of the park and the mile-long road that led to the city and the Rung Mahal.

Ash remembered very little of what happened after that. He retained a confused impression of other elephants plodding majestically past him carrying the senior members of the *barat,* and had a vague recollection of helping Kaka-ji, Jhoti and Maldeo Rai into a gilded howdah, and seeing Mulraj and others of the Karidkote party climb into another and be borne away in their turn. After that it was a discordant blur of drums and flutes and horsemen, and of endless numbers of gaudily dressed men

567

marching off into the night accompanied by files of link-men bearing torches. The head of that long procession must have reached the Rung Mahal before the last of those who marched in it passed under the flower-decked arch leading out of the park, and Ash supposed that he must have stayed among the spectators outside the Pearl Palace and made polite conversation to the end, for it was long past midnight by the time he walked back through the hot night to his rooms in the airless guest-house.

The punkah-coolie who squatted in the verandah out-side his bedroom, and whose task it was to pull the rope that set the heavy punkah swinging to and fro to create an artificial draught, was asleep at his post. So too was the *chowkidar* who lay, sheeted like a corpse, on a string bed that he had placed in the shelter of the porch. Ash did not wake them. He turned and trod softly away to where a flight of stone steps led upwards, and climbing them came out on the flat roof and went to lean on the parapet and look out at the lake and the city.

He had fought hard against thinking of Juli during the past weeks, and though he had not always been suc-cessful he had done his best, closing his mind against her with a deliberate effort of will whenever the thought of her slipped past his defences. But it had been a con-stant battle, and one that he knew he would have to con-tinue fighting until time and old age came to his rescue, for he could not spend his days listening to echoes and liv-ing on memories. Life had to be lived, and he could not share his with Juli: he would have to come to terms with that—they both would. But tonight he could afford to de-vote a few hours to her, and who knew but that his thoughts might not be able to reach her across the scant mile that separated them, so that she would know that he was thinking of her, and be comforted.

The park below him was gradually sinking into si-lence. Dawn came early in these latitudes, and those who had not followed the procession were settling down to get what sleep they could before the birds awoke and an-other burning day was upon them. But torches still laid a jiggling ribbon of light along the road leading to the city, and Bhithor itself was ablaze with illuminations and noisy with bands and *patarkars*. High above the crowded houses, the sandstone roofs and cupolas of the Rung Mahal stood

568

out against the night sky, glowing like burnished copper in the light of thousands of *chirags,* and Ash could picture the scene in the outer courtyard as one by one the elephants came in under the arch of the great gateway, and knelt to let their riders dismount. By now Juli would be in the Zenana Quarters and seeing for the first time the rooms in which she would spend the rest of her days: her women would be removing her jewels and laying away her gala dress, and very soon—

His imagination checked abruptly, but even as his mind winced from the thought, he realized that it would not be Juli but Shushila who would have to share the Rana's bed tonight. The Rana had never wanted Juli and perhaps he never would, and if so she might be left in peace and allowed to live out her life, busy and unregarded, taking care of Shu-shu and of Shu-shu's children; though it was a poor enough outlook for a girl like Juli, who was young and beautiful and formed for love . . .

To deprive her of motherhood and shut her away from life and happiness in the narrow world of the Zenana was as great a crime against heaven as the caging of a lark; but perhaps Shu-shu would come to realize the extent of that sacrifice, and repay it in the only possible way—with love. Ash could only hope so, though without much confidence, for Shu-shu had depended on her half-sister for so long that by now she took her devotion for granted—and it is only the thirsty or starving who are grateful for bread and water.

Juli was bread and water. But when there was rich food and wine and juicy fruits for the taking, Shu-shu might well lose her taste for plain fare and end by thinking it dull and unnecessary, and turn from it. One could not trust Shu-shu, that was the rub. She might mean well, but she had always been ruled by her emotions, and no one could tell in which direction they would drive her. And after all, she was still only a child and like most children, susceptible to flattery. Among these strangers there would be many who would spare no pains to ingratiate themselves with the new First Lady of the Palace—and several who would do their best to wean her away from her dependence on her half-sister and supplant Juli in her affections.

"Oh, my darling," thought Ash, "my dear, sweet, foolhardy love—what will become of you? What is to become of me?"

Once again the future yawned before him as lonely and dark and cold as outer space, and as endless as eternity, and there seemed no point in living if he must live without Juli. Bitterness and self-pity welled up in him, bringing its own weakness and making him less a man, so that glancing down at the drop below the parapet it occurred to him for the first time how easy it would be to put an end to it all.

The morbidness of the last thought suddenly struck him, and he grimaced at the picture of himself that it presented: a spineless coward, wallowing in self-pity. How Juli would despise him if she knew. And she would be right to do so, for one thing was certain: living was going to be a lot easier for him than it would be for her. He was not condemned to stay in Bhithor, and there were many ways in which he could fill his life. The North-West Frontier was seldom quiet for long, and the Guides were more familiar with war than peace. There would be campaigns among the Border hills, and battles to be planned and fought and won; horses to ride and strange, wild places to explore; mountains to climb . . . and friends to talk and drink and laugh with—Zarin and Wally and Koda Dad, Mahdoo and Mulraj and Kaka-ji and many others. But for Juli there was only Shushila, and if Shushu were to fail her or turn against her, or fall ill and die, she would have nothing left . . .

The sky that had been dark when Ash came up onto the roof was beginning to pale, and there were no longer lights in the city, for the *chirags* had burned out or been extinguished by the dawn wind. The night was over and morning only a step away, and soon the cocks would begin to crow and a new day begin. It was time to go down to his room and try to snatch an hour's rest while the air was still faintly cool, because once the sun rose the heat would be too gruelling for sleep, and there was so much to be done and decided on in the coming day that it would be as well to avoid trying to deal with it while sodden with fatigue.

Ash straightened up tiredly and thrust his hands into his pockets, and as he did so his fingers encountered something round and rough. It was one of the small cakes that had been passed round among the guests on the steps of the Pearl Palace, and that he had accepted out of politeness and put in his pocket, meaning to throw it away later. He took it out, and looking at it was reminded of other days. A smile softened the grim weariness of his mouth and he crumbled it up and strewed it on the rim of the parapet; and when he had done that, he looked for the last time at the distant silhouette of the Rung Mahal and spoke very softly into the stillness.

It was not the prayer that he had been used to say when he made offerings to the Dur Khaima but it was, in its way, a prayer. A prayer and a vow. "Don't worry, my dear darling," said Ash. "I promise I won't forget you. I shall love you always and for ever. Goodbye, Juli. Goodbye, my dear and only love. *Khuda hafiz! . . .*"

He turned and walked back across the roof, and was asleep by the time the dawn broke in a wash of lemon yellow behind the dark line of the hills.

Two days later—which was one more than Ash had hoped for and several less than Mulraj had expected— the new Maharajah of Karidkote set out for home with a party of seventy men; twenty-four of them soldiers, a dozen officials, and the remainder syces and servants. They had received a royal send-off, being accompanied as far as the frontier of Bhithor by what appeared to be fully half the population of the state, headed by the Rana himself. And as they rode down the valley the guns of the three forts had thundered in salute.

Their departure had been preceded by three farewell interviews: an official one in the *Diwan-i-Khas*, another between Jhoti and his sisters, and a third, and private one, between Ash and Kaka-ji.

The official farewell had consisted largely of speeches and garlands, and Jhoti's had been a taxing experience. Shushila had genuinely admired her elder brother and already wept herself into a state of exhaustion on hearing of his death. Faced now with parting from the younger one, she had given way to hysteria and behaved in such a frenzied manner that Jhoti had finally been driven to slapping her. The blow having shocked her into silence he had seized the opportunity to deliver a brotherly lecture on the advantages of self-control, and made his escape before she could recover her powers of speech.

Ash's interview with Kaka-ji had been a much quieter affair. The old man had originally declared that of course he would accompany his nephew back to Karidkote, but Mulraj had managed to persuade him that his nieces must now be in sore need of his comfort and support, owing to the news of their elder brother's death, and when Ash, more bluntly, pointed out that his presence could only serve to slow down the speed of the return journey, Kaka-ji had given way and agreed (not without relief) to remain in Bhithor with the rest of the bridal camp until the monsoon broke. Later the two had spoken together alone when Ash came to say farewell before the advance party left.

"I have to thank you for many things, Rao-Sahib," said Ash. "For your friendship and understanding, but most of all for your great generosity. I know very well that you could have destroyed me with a word; and . . . and her also. Yet you did not, and for that I shall always be in your debt. If there should ever be anything that I can do to repay you, I will do it."

Kaka-ji made a small deprecating gesture, and Ash laughed and said: "That must sound like an empty boast, since at the moment I am not in a position to help anyone; as no one knows better than yourself, Rao-Sahib. Even my rank is only lent me because while I am here I represent the Raj, and as soon as my mission is completed I shall become a junior officer again, and of no importance to anyone. But I hope one day to be in a position to help my friends and repay my debts, and when that day comes—"

"Mother Gunga will long since have had my ashes," finished Kaka-ji, smiling. "You owe me nothing, my son. You have been courteous to an old man and I have taken pleasure in your company. Also it is we who are doubly in your debt: for saving my nieces from the river and also for saving their marriages; together with our honour which would have been lost had we been forced to return with them, empty-handed, to Karidkote. As for that other matter, I have put it out of my mind: and you, my son, would be well advised to do likewise."

Ash's mouth quivered and the look on his face said all that he did not put into words. Kaka-ji replied to it as though he had spoken:

"I know. I know," sighed Kaka-ji. "Who should

know better than I? But it is because I speak with a knowledge that was gained by my own mistakes that I can say to you now, 'Do not look back.' The past is the last refuge of the defeated—or the aged—and there is as yet no need for you to number yourself among either. Tell yourself that what is done is done, and put it away and forget it. Do not let yourself remember and try to live on memories. That is well enough for old men who have had their day, but it is bitter fare for the young. So be advised by me, my son, and look forward and not back, remembering always that life is a gift from the gods and therefore not a thing to be despised or wasted. Live it to the full: that is the best advice that I, who did not do so, can give you."

"I will try, Rao-Sahib," promised Ash. "And now I must go. Will you give me your blessing?"

"Assuredly; though I fear it is of little worth. Yet for what it is, you have it. I will also make prayers to the gods that they grant you a safe and swift journey to Karidkote, and a quiet heart and happiness in the years to come. I will not say goodbye for it is my hope that we will meet again: many times, I trust."

"I too," said Ash. "Will you come and visit me in Mardan, Rao-Sahib?"

"No, no. I have had my fill of journeying, and once I win home I shall not leave it again. But Jhoti I know has taken a great liking to you, and now that he is Maharajah he will certainly wish you to visit him. We shall surely see you in Karidkote."

Ash did not contradict this statement, though he knew in his heart that he had no desire to set foot there again, and that once he had escorted Jhoti safely back to Karidkote, he would never return. But that was not something that he could explain to Kaka-ji.

He was wearing full uniform in deference to the official leave-taking at the Rung Mahal, but he forgot this and stooped instead in the manner of the East to touch the old man's feet.

"The gods go with you," said Kaka-ji; and added softly: "And rest assured that if at any time there should arise a . . . a need . . . I will send word to you."

He did not have to add that the need would not be his own. That was understood He embraced Ash, and there being no more to be said, dismissed him. They would see each other again that day, because Kaka-ji would be riding as far as the border with his nephew and the advance party, but there would be no further opportunity for private talk: or any necessity for it.

Two thirds of the returning party had left at dawn with the pack-horses, to set up camp some five miles on the far side of the border in readiness for the arrival of the more important members, whose departure was likely to be delayed by protocol and ceremony. In fact it had been delayed even longer than Ash had expected, for the sun had set by the time the motley cavalcade reached the frontier of Bhithor. As Ash turned in his saddle for a last look at Kaka-ji he saw by the flare of torchlight that there were tears on the old man's cheeks, and lifting a hand in salute, was astonished to find that his own eyes were wet.

"Goodbye, uncle!" shrilled Jhoti. "Goodbye!"

The horses broke into a canter and the chorus of farewells became lost in the thunder of hoof-beats. And presently the yellow glow of the torches faded and they were riding through grey moonlight and the black shadows of the hills. The heartbreak and treachery and the claustrophobia of Bhithor lay behind them, and once again they were riding for the north.

BOOK FIVE

Paradise of Fools

32

"Two more days, if the gods are kind, and we shall be sleeping in our own beds again," said Mulraj.

"Two more days. Two more days. Only two more days," chanted Jhoti. "In two days from now I shall be riding into the city—my own city—and entering my own palace, with all the people shouting and cheering as I pass. And after that I shall really be Maharajah."

"Your Highness has been that ever since your brother died," said Mulraj.

"I know. Only I don't *feel* as if I was. But when I am back in my own state I will. I mean to be a great king. A much better one than Nandu."

"That last should not be too hard," observed Mulraj dryly.

"Two more days . . ." thought Ash, and wished that he could share Mulraj's relief and Jhoti's enthusiasm.

The long ride up from the south had been remarkably free from incident. Considering the relentless heat that had forced them to move only between sunset and sunrise and snatch what rest they could during the burning day, they had made better time than anyone had expected; though it had been a gruelling ordeal for all of them, not least for the horses but most of all for Mahdoo, who had flatly refused to be left behind despite the fact that besides being elderly, he was an indifferent horseman.

The one person who had enjoyed every moment of the journey had been Jhoti. They had all been anxious on his account and worried that the pace might be too much for him, but he seemed to thrive on heat and hard exercise—so much so that there were times when his high spirits made Ash feel at least a hundred years old, though on the whole he had enjoyed Jhoti's lively company and uninhibited conversation and endured the never-ending stream of questions with commendable patience. The boy had shed his fears along with his plumpness and his pasty complexion, and became a different person from the apprehensive run-away whom Biju Ram had so skilfully goaded into "escaping" from Karidkote, and it occurred to Ash as he watched and listened to him that the denizens of Karidkote were likely to be very fortunate in their new ruler.

Jhoti talked continuously of their arrival and the state entry he meant to make into his capital (still apparently known as Gulkote) and was full of plans for the ceremonies that would attend his installation as Maharajah. But as they neared their journey's end Ash became increasingly aware that he himself had no desire to see Gulkote again, let alone enter the Hawa Mahal.

He had never felt any great urge to return there, for he had always known that it would be unwise to do so while the *Nautch*-girl lived; and in any case his memories of the place were far from pleasant. His first years in the city had, indeed, been happy ones; but they had been overshadowed by the misery, fear and humiliation of the later ones in the Hawa Mahal, and though there had been compensations even there, in the main he remembered the Palace of the Winds as a prison from which he had escaped only just in time to save his life, and Gulkote as a place that he and Sita had fled from by night in terror of capture and death.

There was no longer anything left to draw him back there—apart from a cluster of snow peaks that he used to say his prayers to and the memory of a little girl whose devotion had consoled him in some small degree for the loss of his pet mongoose—and the prospect of returning, now of all times, had begun to fill him with something like panic. But as there was no way by which he could avoid doing so, he would have had to set his teeth and go through with it; and if Kaka-ji was right about the past being the last refuge of the defeated, then the sooner he faced it and stared it down the better.

By now the fertile plains were behind them and they were among the bad-lands: a rough and desolate region of boulders, ridges and ravines where little grew except camel-thorn and rank grasses. But ahead of them lay the foothills and behind the foothills were the mountains, no longer a dimly seen barrier along the horizon but near and blue and solid, towering above them; and sometimes the scorching, dust-laden air carried a clean smell of pine-needles, and in the early dawn, or towards evening, Ash could see the snow peaks of the Dur Khaima.

This was the country through which Sita had brought him after their escape from Delhi in the Black Year of the Mutiny. But in those days there had been no road, and Deenagunj (it had been Deena then) had consisted of half-a-dozen mud huts, huddled together on the only level spot between the plains and the river that formed the southern boundary of Gulkote. Yet despite its inhospitable surroundings, Deenagunj was now a thriving town, for when the territories of Gulkote and Karidarra had been amalgamated under the rule of Lalji's father, the Government had sent a British Resident to advise His Highness on matters of finance and policy, and followed this up by building a road through the bad-lands and a bridge of boats across the river. The Government's road-building had brought prosperity to the twenty-odd villagers of Deena, who had seen their tiny hamlet grow into a town of no mean size, and Ash, looking about him, was no longer surprised that he had failed, in the previous autumn, to recognize the frontiers of Gulkote when he rode along that wide and well-trodden road on his way to take over command of a bridal camp from a state whose name was unfamiliar to him for the mountains had been hidden by heaped haze and clouds.

Today, for the first time since leaving Bhithor, they had broken camp at dawn instead of sundown, and were riding by daylight. The thermometer still registered a temperature of 102° at noon, but the past night had been pleasantly cool, and now Deenagunj was almost within sight. They could have reached it before midnight, but

577

by common consent they did not press on, but made camp as darkness fell, and slept for the first time in many days by starlight.

Rising with the dawn, rested and refreshed, they bathed and prayed and ate a frugal morning meal. After which they sent a messenger ahead to announce their arrival, and having dressed themselves in their best, as befitted the escort of a Maharajah, rode into Deenagunj at an easy pace, where they were met by the District Officer and a deputation of senior citizens, and what appeared to be the entire population of the town, eager to witness any form of *tamarsha*.

There were several familiar faces among the waiting deputation; men who had presented bills or brought complaints when Ash had last been in Deenagunj. But the District Officer's was not one of them: Mr. Carter had apparently suffered yet another attack of malaria with the onset of the hot weather, and was on sick-leave in Murree. His replacement, a Mr. Morecombe, informed Ash that the British Resident, together with the members of his staff and at least fifty nobles of Karidkote, were waiting to receive the new Maharajah in a camp that had been set up on the far side of the bridge of boats, where it had been arranged that His Highness would spend the night. The state entry into the capital would take place on the following day; but unfortunately Captain Pelham-Martyn would not be able to see it, for he was ordered to return immediately to Rawalpindi.

A letter confirming this was handed to him by the District Officer, who commiserated with him under the mistaken impression that it would be a disappointment. "Rotten bad luck," said the District Officer over a glass of country-brewed beer. "Seems a bit hard, bringing that boy all this way and then being done out of the show, and what's the betting that when you do get to 'Pindi, you'll find there was no need at all to go chasing back there in such a tearing hurry? But that's G.H.Q. all over."

Ash thought it only too likely—and was deeply grateful to whoever was responsible for sending off the order for his return. Nevertheless, for politeness sake he did his best to appear disappointed, though not sufficiently so to encourage Jhoti to insist on his staying:

"No. Your Highness cannot send a *tar* to the *Jung-i-lat Sahib*, demanding that I remain," said Ash firmly. "Or to the Viceroy or the Governor of the Punjab either. It would do me no good. I know that you are now a Maharajah, but I am still a soldier; and as Mulraj will tell you, a soldier must obey the orders of his senior officers. The General-Sahibs in Rawalpindi have commanded my return, and even for Your Highness I cannot disobey them. But I hope that you will write and tell me about the ceremonies and rejoicings, and I promise that I will write to you as often as I can."

"And visit me, too," insisted Jhoti.

"And visit you too," agreed Ash, hoping that he might be forgiven the lie—if it was a lie. Perhaps it was not. Perhaps one day he would feel differently about returning to Gulkote and the Hawa Mahal, and if so . . .

He said his farewells, and realized as he did so how much he was going to miss them all: Mulraj and Jhoti, Kaka-ji and Gobind—and so many others . . . It was not only Juli whom he was going to miss and to think of in the years to come.

"It is my hope that we shall meet again many times," said Mulraj. "You will come here on *chutti* (leave) and we will take you out hawking on the flat lands and show you good sport among our mountains. And when I am an old man and you are a General-Sahib, we shall still meet and talk over old times together. Therefore I do not say 'Good-bye,' but 'Come again soon.' "

They had accompanied Ash for a mile and more down the road, and looking back to wave a last farewell, he knew a momentary regret that he was riding away instead of going on with them to Gulkote. If he could have changed his mind then, he might well have turned back. But it was too late for that now.

A turn of the road hid them from sight and he knew in his heart that in spite of Mulraj's confident prediction, he was unlikely to see them again, because his only hope lay in taking Kaka-ji's advice and turning his back on the past. The old man had been right: he must strive to put it all behind him and to forget; he must learn not to think of Juli at all, and as visiting Gulkote would only serve to bring back the past, he must not go there—not now, or for many years—if ever. Because were he to do so the sense of ease and comradeship that had existed between himself and those in whose company he had spent these last months could be destroyed.

In the camp he had been the only European, and because no one there spoke his language it had been possible for him to forget at times that he was a *feringhi*. But he would not be allowed to forget it in Karidkote; not now that there was a British Resident there, supported by a large staff of Europeans and possibly a guard of British troops. There would also be many old and orthodox Hindus who would strongly disapprove of his being treated with the casual familiarity that had been accorded to him on the march, and inevitably, his relations with Jhoti and Mulraj would suffer. The ease and camaraderie of the camp would be replaced by politeness, and there would, in all probability, be relief when he left—which was something he did not even like to think of.

No; much better to stay away and let them think of him with affection as someone they had known and liked, and hoped to see again some day. And then perhaps when he was old—when they were all old, and nothing mattered very much any longer because life was nearly over and the bad parts of it forgotten—he might go back for a short visit to talk over old days with any who might still remember him. And to make a last offering to the Dur Khaima.

Later, as the light began to fade and the dusk turn green about him, he reined in and turned to look back at the mountains that were already in shadow and sharply violet against the hyacinth of the darkening sky. One cluster of peaks still held a last gleam of the sunset: the crown of the Dur Khaima, rose-pink in the twilight . . . the far pavilions . . . The warm colour faded from them as he looked, and peak after peak turned from rose to lavender until at last only *Tara Kilas,* the "Star Tower," held the light. Then suddenly that too had gone, and the whole long range lost its sharpness of outline and merged into a night that was brilliant with stars.

Memories crowded upon him, choking him; and almost without knowing it, he dismounted, and placing his palms together as he used to do long ago, he bowed his head and repeated the old prayer of the Queen's balcony that asks forgiveness for "three sins that are due to human limitations."

". . . Thou art everywhere," murmured Ash, "but I worship thee here: Thou art without form, but I worship thee in these forms: Thou needest no praise, yet I offer thee these prayers and salutations . . ."

The first breath of the night wind sighed through the parched thorn bushes and brought him the scent of pine trees and wood-smoke, and mounting again, he turned his horse's head and rode slowly on to join Mahdoo and Gul Baz and Kulu Ram the syce, who had ridden on ahead and would by now have selected a camp site and set about preparing the evening meal.

Had they travelled as swiftly as they had done on the way up from Bhithor, they would have reached Rawalpindi in well under a week. But there was no longer, in Ash's opinion, any pressing need for haste; and as the temperature in the plains never fell below 110° in the daytime and 102° in the coolest part of the night, and Mahdoo was very tired and saddle-sore, they moved at a leisurely pace, rising at two o'clock in the morning to ride until just before the sun rose, when they would make camp and rest until the same hour on the following day.

In this way, averaging no more than twenty-five miles a day, they covered the last lap of their journey. And in the early dawn of the last day of May they came within sight of Rawalpindi, and found Wally waiting, as he had waited every morning for the past eight days, by the third mile-stone on the 'Pindi–Jhelum Road.

Ash had been away for eight months, during which time he had spoken English perhaps half-a-dozen times at most, and for the rest had talked, thought and dreamed in the language of his adoptive mother, Sita.

'Pindi in June is a place to be avoided. Heat and glare and dust combine to turn it into an inferno, and those whose duty keeps them tied to an office or to barracks and parade ground are liable to fall victim to a tedious variety of hot-weather ills ranging from heat-stroke to sandfly fever.

In the compound of Wally's bungalow the giant neem tree was grey with the dust of the scorching plain, and when the hot wind blew, its leaves did not rustle but clicked instead like dice in a leather shaker, or rattled like dry bones: nor could Ash any longer see the hills, for they were hidden by the dust-clouds and the heat haze.

"How does it feel like to be a lowly Lieutenant again after eight months of peacocking about as a lordly Captain in command of countless thousands?" asked Wally curiously.

"Dull," said Ash. "Dull but peaceful. How many pairs of socks do you think I'd better take?"

The best part of a week had passed since Ash's return from his travels, and he was preparing to move again, but this time on leave. He had duly presented himself at Army Headquarters, where he had given a brief report of his mission and a detailed account of the Rana's misbehaviour to a Colonel Dorton, whose habit of falling asleep during office hours had earned him the nick-name of Dormouse. The Colonel had run true to form and sat through the interview with closed eyes, only opening them (after Ash had been silent for a full two minutes) to stare vaguely into the middle-distance and remark that Mr. Pelham-er-Martyn had better report to the Adjutant General's Department, where Major Boyle would assign him to some new duty.

But the prediction made by the District Officer at Deenagunj proved correct. There had been no special reason for Ash's recall. Major Boyle had gone down with a severe attack of dysentery and no one else in the Adjutant General's department appeared to have heard of Lieutenant (lately Captain) Pelham-Martyn, let alone have any orders for him. On the face of it he might just as well have stayed away, for apart from demoting him from the honorary rank he had held for the past eight months (and sending an immediate memo to this effect to the Pay Department) no one seemed to know what to do with him. Ash had asked to be allowed to return to his Regiment, but had been told somewhat tartly that this was a matter for the Commandant of the Guides, who would send for him when he thought fit.

All in all, it had been a depressing home-coming, and but for Wally, he might well have resigned his commission on the spot and set off to explore Tibet or enlist as a deck-hand on a cargo boat—anything that would take him away from the monotony of cantonment life and let him work off the gnawing restlessness that had possessed him ever since his last sight of Juli outside the Pearl Palace in Bhithor. The speed of the journey back across Rajputana and the Punjab to Deenagunj had temporarily assuaged it, but here in Rawalpindi where there was little or nothing to do it returned to torment him, and only Wally's cheerful presence and lively interest in every detail of the Karidkote–Bhithor venture kept it within bounds.

To Wally, Ash retold the story that had aroused so little interest in the somnolent Colonel Dorton, but this time in more detail and leaving less out, though he held back the truth about Juli, and, oddly enough, did not mention the fact that Karidkote had turned out to be the Gulkote of his childhood. Even to this close friend he would not—could not—talk about Juli, and if he could have left her out of the story altogether, he would have done so. That being impossible, he referred to her only when he must, and as though she were less an individual than an abstract problem that had to be solved between the ruler of Bhithor and himself. Though why he should have remained silent on the other matter was something that he could not explain even to himself. It was, after all, the most surprising thing about the whole affair, and Wally, who already knew the saga of those early years in Gulkote, would have been enthralled to hear that the State of Karidkote was the self-same place that Ash had described to him over a year ago on a moonlit night among the ruins of Taxila.

Yet Ash had kept back that vital piece of information, and without it the tale of Biju Ram's death lost much of its point. The rest posed no special problems, and Wally had listened and asked questions as avidly as Jhoti had done; and with much the same enthusiasm.

Compared with these stirring adventures, Wally declared that his own doings during the same period had been deplorably tame. He had, predictably, fallen in and out of love with several charming young women, written a vast amount of bad poetry, broken his collar-bone playing polo and lost a month's pay in a single evening at poker. But his most important piece of news had been kept until the last.

Having finally passed for his Lieutenancy, he had been offered, and accepted, a commission in the Guides, and would be joining the Corps in August.

Wally added, after congratulations, that he had delayed putting in for joining leave in the hope that Ash would return in time for the two of them to spend it together. "Because of course you must be due for some too. You haven't had any since last summer, so it stands to reason they'll give it you without a murmur if you ask for a couple of months off now."

This was something that had not occurred to Ash, largely because he had felt himself to be enjoying a glorified form of leave during a good two thirds of his time with the Karidkote camp, and to demand more now smacked of extortion. But taking into account the fact that the Adjutant General's Department appeared to have no orders for him and Major Boyle was still on the sicklist, he could see no harm in asking. They could only refuse, and might even welcome the chance of getting rid of him for a further spell.

He therefore immediately put in for six weeks' leave, and far from being refused, was told that he could take eight—the extra two being in the nature of a bonus, in consideration of the fact that he had been constantly on duty for a period that included the New Year, the Christian holidays of Christmas, Whitsun and Easter, the Hindu festival of Diwali, and the Moslem celebration of Id-ul-Fitre.

He was not particularly grateful for the extra two weeks once he discovered that the ban on his entry into the North-West Frontier Province was still in force, because it meant that he would not be able to visit Mardan and that unless Zarin could manage to get a few days' leave and ride over to Rawalpindi, he might not see him for another year—possibly even longer, should the Commandant of the Guides decide that it would be wiser to extend the ban for a further period.

Ash returned to the bungalow to tell Wally the news and to write three letters: one to the Commandant, Colonel Jenkins, asking to be allowed to return to his unit, another to Wigram Battye, begging him to put in a good word on his behalf, and the third to Zarin. Colonel Jenkins had been away on leave and unable to reply, but his Second-in-Command wrote to say that Ash's request had been noted and would, he felt sure, receive the Commandant's sympathetic consideration as soon as he returned to Mardan, while Wigram, in a friendly letter full of regimental news, promised to do all he could to speed Ash's recall. Zarin did not write, but he sent a verbal message by an itinerant horse-dealer, well known to them both, making an assignation to meet Ash at a certain house on the outskirts of Attock.

"The Risaldar" (Zarin had been promoted) "cannot take his *chutti* at this time," explained the horse-dealer. "But as it is permitted that he absent himself for a day, he will set out at nightfall on the coming Friday, and if all goes well should reach Attock by midnight. If this should not be convenient, the Sahib has only to send a *tar*."

The messenger salaamed and was about to leave when he remembered something and turned back: *"Chut!* I had almost forgotten: Zarin Khan called after me to say that if the Sahib wishes to bring Ashok with him, all can be arranged. Would that be one of the Sahib's syces? I have heard that many down-country men make good horse-boys. My own . . ." Here he embarked on a discussion of the merits and demerits of horse-boys in general, thereby saving Ash from the necessity of answering such an awkward question, because the purport of Zarin's apparently casual afterthought was clear. The little town of Attock lies on the east bank of the Indus, and one has only to cross the river to enter the North-West Frontier Province. It would therefore be wiser if Ash were not seen there, as it might look as though he intended to defy the ban, which at the present moment could easily prejudice his chances of being allowed to return to the Guides in the near future. Yet as Zarin could only spare a day, if they could meet at Attock rather than in Rawalpindi or some half-way house, they would have more time together.

Wally put in for his leave as soon as he heard that Ash's had been granted, but whereas Ash had been told that he could take his immediately, Wally was informed that he might go on leave in ten days' time, and not a day before: "I tried everything, but the old scutt was adamant," explained Wally sadly. "It seems that they cannot spare their blue-eyed boy at present, because Johnnie Reeves has chosen this moment to join the ranks of the great majority."

"Dead?" asked Ash, startled.

"No. Dysentery. That makes six of 'em so far. Ah well, it can't be helped, so I'm thinking you'd better go on ahead. We can arrange to meet somewhere as soon as I can get away."

As it happened, this programme could not have suited Ash better, since it gave him a free hand for the next few days, and absolved him from explaining about his own plans to visit Attock, which was something he pre-

585

ferred not to discuss with Wally. The two agreed to meet at Murree and go on from there, on foot, to Kashmir; taking only Wally's bearer Pir Baksh, and hiring any other servants they might need, so that all those who had accompanied Ash to Bhithor could take leave.

Both Mahdoo and Gul Baz had protested that they had no wish to take *chutti*, but in the end they had allowed themselves to be persuaded, and Ash had engaged a seat in the mail-tonga bound for Abbottabad, and seen Mahdoo aboard: "And when you return, we will engage an assistant for you, Cha-cha-ji. One you can instruct, and who will learn to cook so well that all you will need to do will be to oversee him. It is time you had more leisure and someone to take the bulk of the work off your shoulders."

"It is not necessary," growled Mahdoo. "I am not yet so old that I cannot earn my wage. Or are you no longer satisfied with me?"

Ash laughed and told him not to talk nonsense for he knew very well that he was indispensable.

Gul Baz and Kulu Ram and the others left for their respective homes that same day, and when darkness fell Ash went out into the Mall, and hailing a passing *ekka*, told the driver to take him to a house in the Rawalpindi bazaar where he had some business to transact. He did not get back to the bungalow until long past midnight, and some five hours after breakfasting with Wally, he left again by tonga, taking a modest amount of luggage and bound, ostensibly, for Murree.

There were several rest-houses on the Murree road, and Ash stopped at the least frequented of these, where having paid off the tonga and selected the least stifling room, he stretched himself out on the bare *narwar* bed and made up for lost sleep. Awakened in the late afternoon by the sound of two horsemen riding into the compound, he went out to greet a friend of his, one Kasim Ali, whose father owned half the cloth shops in Rawalpindi bazaar, and whom it seemed that he had been expecting.

The two exchanged a few words, and the second rider having dismounted, Ash took over his horse and told the *khansamah* of the rest-house that he would be away for a couple of nights, but that his friend's servant

586

would remain to keep an eye on his luggage, and must be provided with bed and food. The horse carried a small bundle strapped to the back of the saddle, and once safely out of sight of the rest-house Ash stopped in the first clump of trees to change into the clothes it contained, before riding on across country in the guise of a Kashmiri pundit.

Reaching Hasan Abdal in the twilight, he bought food at a wayside stall and let his horse rest and graze while he ate his evening meal on a grassy hillside overlooking the tomb of Lalla Rookh. There was still another thirty-odd miles to be covered, but as Zarin would not be leaving Mardan before sunset there was no need for haste. He lingered by the quiet tomb, listening to the horse cropping the parched grasses and watching the light fade from the far hills while the sky bedecked itself with stars, until at last the moon rose in the hot dust-scented dark. With that bone-white glare lighting the road, it was possible to press on at a fair pace, and the rest and the cooler air had put so much heart into the horse that it brought Ash to the tall old house on the outskirts of Attock in far less time than he had anticipated.

The house stood in a large walled garden, and its owner, Koda Dad's sister Fatima-Begum, was an elderly widow who had often entertained her nephews and their friends there, and this would not be the first time that Ash had stayed under that hospitable roof. Tonight the old lady had already retired, for the hour was late, and as the gatekeeper said that the Risaldar-Sahib Zarin Khan had not yet arrived, Ash left his horse to be stabled and walked on down through the sleeping town, past the walls of the Emperor Akbar's great stone fort that had guarded the ferry for close on two centuries. The descendants of the first ferry-men still plied the trade of their forefathers, but they would soon be gone, for the English had constructed a bridge of boats over the Indus and nowadays nine tenths of the traffic crossed by that.

Ash stopped on a turn of the road from where he could see the bridge, and squatted down in a patch of shadow to wait for Zarin. Few people were abroad at that hour, and except for a sentry on duty at the bridge-head, only Ash seemed to be awake; and listening. The resonant voice of the "Father of Rivers" as it foamed through the Attock gorge filled the night with thunder, but the sound of horses' hooves carried far, and Ash's ears caught that beat above the water noises.

As it came nearer it changed to a hollow drumming on the wooden planks of the bridge, and he saw that there was not one horseman, but two. Zarin (there was no mistaking the set of that head and shoulders) had brought someone with him. But despite the brightness of the moonlight it was not until they breasted the rise that Ash realized who the other rider was, and leaping up he ran down the road to grasp Koda Dad's stirrup with both hands and touch his forehead to the old man's foot.

"I came to assure myself that all was well with you, my son," said Koda Dad, leaning down to embrace him.

"And also to hear news of that which was once Gulkote," grinned Zarin, dismounting.

"That too," said Koda Dad in a tone of reproof. "But I have been anxious for you ever since we learned too late what manner of folk it was whom you were escorting across Hind. If anyone had recognized you there might still have been great danger, and it is good to see that you are safe and well."

It was like a homecoming, thought Ash, as he walked up the moon-blanched road with Zarin on one side of him and Koda Dad riding at a foot's pace on the other. After the thirsty wastes of Rajputana the very sound of the river was both refreshment and reassurance; and best of all was the knowledge that he was in the company of two people with whom he could talk freely of Gulkote, for both had been so intimately linked with his childhood that there was little they did not know about it.

Except for certain facts connected with Juli, there was nothing that he could not tell them about the happenings of the last eight months; and that alone, apart from his pleasure at seeing them again, brought him an enormous feeling of relief. The need to unburden himself to someone who would fully understand the complexities of his situation had been building up in him for many weeks, though until a few days ago he had not realized how strong it had become, or how necessary it was to his peace of mind to be able to pour it all out and rid himself of doubts and guilt and anxieties—and ghosts.

33

There had been little conversation that night, as all three travellers were tired, and once in bed Ash had slept better than he had for many weeks.

His bed had been put out on a partially screened roof for greater coolness, and awakening in the pearly hot-weather dawn he looked down from the parapet and saw Zarin at his prayers in the garden below. Waiting until these were over, he went down to join him and walk and talk under fruit trees that were full of birds greeting the new day with a clamour of cawing and song. The talk had been mainly of the Regiment, for the subject of Gulkote could keep until Koda Dad was ready to listen, and Zarin had closed the long gap of the past year by bringing Ash up to date on a number of matters that for one reason or another he had not wished to entrust to a bazaar letter-writer. Details concerning his personal life and items of news about various men of Ash's old troop: the possibility of trouble with the Jowaki Afridis over the construction of a cart-road through the Khyber Pass, and the doings of those who had provided an escort for the *Padishah*'s eldest son, the Prince of Wales, when he visited Lahore during the past cold weather.

The Prince, said Zarin, had been so pleased by the bearing and behaviour of the Guides that he had written to his august mother, who had replied by appointing him Honorary Colonel to the Corps, and commanding that in future the Guides should be styled "The Queen's Own Corps of Guides" and wear on their colours and appointments the Royal Cypher within the Garter (Zarin's translation of this last would have startled the College of Heralds considerably). By the time they had eaten the morning meal the sun was up, and after they had paid their respects to the lady of the house—who received them seated behind an ancient and much broken *chik* through which she could be plainly seen, but which preserved, if only technically, the rules of *purdah*—they were free to seek out Zarin's father.

It was already too hot to be abroad, so the three of them had spent the day in the old, high-ceilinged room that had been allotted to Koda Dad because it was the coolest in the house. Here, protected from the heat by *kus-kus* tatties, and sitting cross-legged on the uncarpeted floor of polished *chunam* that was pleasantly cool to the touch, Ash told for the third time the tale of his journey to Bhithor, this time with few evasions, telling it all from the beginning and leaving nothing out—save only that he had lost his heart to the girl who had once been known to all of them as "Kairi-Bai."

Zarin had interrupted the tale with questions and exclamations, but Koda Dad, never a talkative man, had listened in silence, though it was to him rather than to Zarin that Ash spoke. The discovery of Hira Lal's earring had drawn a grunt of surprise from him and the account of Biju Ram's death a grim nod of approval, while a smile had commended Ash's handling of the Rana's attempt at blackmail. But apart from that he had offered no comments, and when at last the tale was ended, he said only: "It was an ill day for Gulkote when its Rajah's heart was caught by the beauty of an evil and covetous woman, and many paid for his folly with their lives. Yet for all his faults he was a good man, as I know well. I am sad to hear that he is dead, for he was a good friend to me during the many years that I lived in his shadow: thirty-and-three of them . . . for we were both young men when we met. Young and strong. And heedless . . . heedless . . ."

He sighed deeply and fell silent again, and after a moment or two Ash realized, with an odd sensation of panic, that Koda Dad had fallen into the light sleep of old age. It was only then that he noticed for the first time how many physical changes had come about since their last meeting: the thinness of body that the voluminous Pathan dress had partially disguised, and the many new wrinkles that seamed that familiar face; the curiously fragile appearance of the parchment-coloured skin that had once been so brown and leathery, and the fact that under the brave scarlet dye, hair and beard were now snow-white . . . and very scanty.

Ash would have noticed this at once had he not been

so taken up with his own affairs, yet now that he had done so the change both shocked and frightened him, bringing home to him as nothing else could have done the shortness of the human span and the terrifying swiftness of Time. It was as though he had come without warning upon one of those mile-stones that long after they are passed, stand out in one's memory as marking the end of a phase—or perhaps a turning point?—and something of this must have shown in his face, for when he looked away and caught Zarin's gaze there was both understanding and compassion in it.

"It comes to all of us, Ashok," said Zarin quietly: "He is now well past his seventieth year. There are not many who live as long; and few who have been as contented with their lot. My father has been fortunate in that he has had a full life and a good one; which is surely as much as anyone can ask of God. May we two be granted the like."

"*Ameen*," said Ash under his breath. "But I—I did not realize . . . Has he been ill?"

"Ill? This is not a sickness—unless old age be one. This is no more than the weight of years. And who is to say that he will not see many more of them? But among our people, seventy is accounted a great age."

Ash knew that to be true. The men of the Border hills lived hard lives, and a tribesman was considered old at forty while his wife was often a grandmother before she was thirty, and Koda Dad had already exceeded the three-score-years-and-ten that had been promised to the descendants of Adam. Of late Ash had begun to think of life as far too long, and to see it in imagination as an endless road stretching away ahead of him and leading nowhere, along which he must walk alone; yet now, abruptly, he saw that it was also cruelly short, and was unreasonably shaken by this commonplace discovery. Zarin, who was still watching him and knew him well enough to follow his train of thought, said consolingly: "There is still myself, Ashok. And the Regiment also."

Ash nodded without replying. Yes, there was still Zarin, and the Regiment: and when he was allowed to return to Mardan there would be Wally also, and Koda Dad's village lay only a mile or so beyond the Border and a short march away. Koda Dad, who had suddenly become so old . . . Studying the old Pathan's sleeping face, Ash

591

saw the lines of character that were engraved there as clearly as the lines of time: the kindness and wisdom, the firmness, integrity and humour, written plain. A strong face; and a peaceful one. The face of a man who has experienced much and come to terms with life, accepting the bad with the good and regarding both as no more than a part of living—and of the inscrutable purpose of God.

Reviewing his own achievements by the light of Koda Dad's long and eventful life, it struck Ash with stunning force that they could be summed up as a brief list of sorry failures. He had begun by making an utter fool of himself over Belinda and ended by losing Juli. And in between he had failed George, proved himself to be an intractable and disappointing officer, and—indirectly—caused the death of Ala Yar. For had it not been for his quixotic behaviour in the matter of the carbines, Ala Yar would still be alive and probably, at that moment, gossiping comfortably with Mahdoo on the back verandah of a bungalow in Mardan.

To set against that it could be said that he had saved Jhoti's life, avenged the deaths of Hira Lal and Lalji, and succeeded in rescuing Karidkote's reputation and treasury from disaster. But that was poor compensation for the dismal tale of his previous failures; or for the fact that his brief and passionate love-affair with Juli could only add to her unhappiness in the life to which her own loyalty had doomed her—a life that he did not dare allow himself to think about.

There were few things, in these days, that he cared to look back on; and even less that he could look forward to. But among the former there had always been Koda Dad, a source of wisdom and comfort and a rock to lean upon. Koda Dad and Zarin, Mahdoo and Wally. Only four human beings out of all the teeming millions in the world; yet of immeasurable importance to him. And he was about to lose them. When Koda Dad and Zarin recrossed the Indus and Wally left for Mardan in a month's time, he would be unable to follow them, for they would have entered territory from which he himself was excluded until the Guides agreed to take him back again—which, for all he knew, might not be for years. If so, this could well be the last time he would ever see Koda Dad.

As for Mahdoo, he too was growing old and frail;

and if Koda Dad, the immutable, could crumble in this fashion, how much more so could Mahdoo, who did not possess half the old Pathan's stamina and must be at least his equal in age? It did not bear thinking of. Yet he thought of it now, grimly and despairingly, seeing his life as a fragile house—an empty one, since there was no Juli—which once he had planned to cram with treasure. A house supported by four pillars, two of them now almost worn out and in the nature of things unlikely to last very much longer . . . When those two fell, as one day they must, the walls might still stand. But if a third were to fail, his case would be desperate, and if all went, the house would crash to the ground and break apart, exposing its emptiness.

Koda Dad's head nodded and fell forward, and the movement awoke him: "So now there is a new ruler in Gulkote," said the old man, continuing the conversation where it had ended when he dozed off. "That is good. Provided he does not take after his mother. But if God wills, his father's blood will prove stronger; and if so Gulkote—*Chut!* that is no longer the name. I forget the new one, but no matter. It will always be Gulkote to me and whenever I think of it, it is with affection; for until the mother of my sons died, my days there were pleasant ones. A good life . . . Yes, a good life. Ah! here is Habibah. I did not realize that it was so late."

When the sun dipped behind the hills and the air began to cool, Ash and Zarin went out to exercise the horses in the dusty evening light, and when they returned it was to find that the Begum had invited a number of her brother's old friends and acquaintances to dine with them, so there had been no further opportunity for private talk that night. The next day was Sunday, and as Zarin must be back in Mardan in time to prepare for parade on Monday morning (which in the hot weather was at 5:30 a.m.), father and son would be leaving some time after nightfall. The three spent that day as they had spent the previous one, talking together in Koda Dad's room and resting during the heat of the afternoon, and towards evening the Begum sent a servant to tell Zarin that his aunt wished to see him on some matter connected with the possible purchase of land near Hoti Mardan, and Ash and Koda Dad went up to the roof to catch the cooler air as the sun went down behind the hills around Attock.

It was the first time they had been alone together, and in an hour or so Koda Dad would be gone and there was no knowing when they would meet again. But though Ash would have given a great deal to be able to ask for advice and comfort as he had done so often in the past, both as a child in Gulkote and a junior subaltern in Mardan, he could not bring himself to do so. The problem was too personal and the wound still too raw, and he shrank from probing either, and made conversation instead: talking of his coming leave in Kashmir and the prospects of shooting, in a light, cheerful voice that would have deceived ninety-nine people out of a hundred but failed entirely to deceive Koda Dad.

The old Pathan listened and nodded, but did not speak. Then, as the sky took fire from the setting sun, the first stirring of the evening breeze carried a faint, high-pitched cry from the distant city. *"La Ill-ah ha! il ill-ah ho!"*—"There is no God but God!" It was the voice of the muezzin from the minaret of a mosque in Attock, calling the Faithful to prayer, and Koda Dad rose to his feet, and unrolling a small mat that he had carried up to the roof, turned to face Mecca and began his evening prayers.

Ash looked down from the parapet and saw that several of the household were doing the same in the garden below, and that the aged porter was also at his devotions in the road outside the gate. He watched them for a moment or two as they knelt, bowed their heads to the dust, rose and knelt again, muttering the traditional prayers that were said at this hour; and presently he turned away to face the north-east where, hidden by the heat-haze and the dust and distance, lay the Dur Khaima. But he did not say his own prayer—that ancient Hindu invocation that he had adopted so long ago. He had meant to, but before the words could shape themselves, his mental picture of the goddess of his childhood faded, and he found himself thinking instead of Juli.

He had told her that he would think of her every hour of every day, yet he had tried not to do so; partly because he had not been able to bear it, and also because he had decided that his only hope lay in taking her uncle's advice and putting the past behind him. It had been like barring a door and throwing all his weight against it to keep out a flood that was building up outside, and though it had been impossible to prevent trickles from

594

that flood seeping under the lintel and through cracks in the wood, he had managed somehow to shut out the worst of it. But now, suddenly, the bars snapped and the door gave way, and he was drowning in the same savage tide of love and anguish and loss that had swept over him in Kaka-ji's tent when he realized that he had made his last appeal and lost; and that he would never see Juli again . . .

Koda Dad finished his prayers and turned to see Ash standing by the parapet with his back towards him, facing the 'Pindi road and the eastern horizon where a full moon was drifting slowly up into the sky as the sun sank down in the glowing, dusty, golden West. The rigidity of that back and the spasmodic clenching and unclenching of the lean, nervous hands told Koda Dad almost as much as the determined lightness of Ash's conversation had done, and the old man said quietly:

"What is amiss, Ashok?"

Ash turned quickly—too quickly, for he had not given himself time to control his features, and Koda Dad caught his breath in the involuntary hiss that greets the sight of a fellow-creature in physical agony.

"*Ai, Ai,* child—it cannot be as bad as that," exclaimed Koda Dad, distressed. "No, do not lie to me"—his uplifted hand checked Ash's automatic denial—"I have not known you since your seventh year for nothing. Nor have I become so blind that I cannot see what is written on your face, or so deaf that I cannot hear what is in your voice; and I am not yet so old that I cannot remember my own youth. Who is she, my son?"

"*She—?*" Ash stared at him, startled.

Koda Dad said dryly: "You forget that I have seen you troubled in some such manner before—only then it was calf-love and no more than a boy's foolishness. But now . . . now I think it cuts deeper; for you are no longer a boy. It is Kairi-Bai, is it not?"

Ash caught his breath and his face whitened. "How did you . . . But you can't . . . I did not—"

He stopped, and Koda Dad shook his head and said: "No, you did not betray yourself in words. It was those you did not speak that warned me of something amiss. You told of two brides and spoke of the younger one by name, describing her and telling of things that she had said and done. But save when you could not avoid

595

it you did not mention the elder, and when you did, your voice changed and became without feeling and you spoke as though there was a restraint upon you. Yet this was that same Kairi-Bai whom we all knew, and to whom you owed your escape from the Hawa Mahal. Yet you told us almost nothing of her and spoke of her as you would have spoken of a stranger. That told its own tale. That, and the change in you. It could be nothing else. Am I not right?"

Ash smiled crookedly and said: "You are always right, my father. But it shames me to learn that I can be so transparent and that my face and voice are so easily read."

"There is no need," said Koda Dad placidly. "No one but myself could have done so—and then only because of my long knowledge and affection for you, and because I remember the old days very clearly. I will not press you to tell me anything that you do not wish, but I am troubled for you, my son. It grieves me deeply to see you so unhappy, and if I can be of any help—"

"You have always been that," said Ash quickly. "I leaned upon you as a child and I have done so again and again when—when I was a raw recruit. Also I know well that had I taken your advice more often I would have saved myself much sorrow."

"Tell me," said Koda Dad. He seated himself cross-legged on the warm stone, prepared to listen, while Ash leaned on the parapet, and looking out across the Begum's garden to where the Indus glowed red-gold in the sunset, told all those things he had left out of his tale on the previous day, omitting only the happenings of one night . . .

When he had finished, Koda Dad sighed and said inconsequentially: "Her father had great courage and many good qualities, and he ruled his people wisely—but not his own household. There he was both weak and idle, being one who greatly disliked tears and arguments and quarrelling. *Hai mai!*"

He fell silent, brooding on the past, and presently he said: "Yet he too never broke a promise. If he gave his word, he kept it, as befits a Rajput. Therefore it is only right that Kairi-Bai should do likewise, as from what you have told me I see that she has inherited only the good. This you may see only as your misfortune, yet in time

I think you will come to see that it was best for both of you that she had the courage to keep faith, since had she done as you desired (and lived to tell of it, which I think unlikely) you would not have found happiness together."

Ash turned from his contemplation of the darkening river and said harshly: "Why do you say that? I would have done anything—everything."

Once again Koda Dad's sinewy, authoritative hand checked him: "Do not talk like a child, Ashok. I do not doubt that you would have done all that was in your power to make her happy. But it is not in your power to build a new world; or to turn back time. Only the One God could do that—were it necessary. And it would be very necessary for you! I myself have had little or no experience of your people, but I have sons and kinsmen who know the ways of the Sahib-log; and having ears to hear, I have listened and learned much during the years since I left Gulkote. Now as I do not believe that all I have heard can be lies, you, Ashok, will now listen to me."

Ash smiled faintly and sketched a mock-humble salute, but Koda Dad frowned him down and said sharply: "This is not a matter for jest, boy. Once, long ago, in the days when the rule of the Company Bahadur" (he meant the East India Company) "was young and there were no memsahibs in Hind, the Sahibs took wives from among the women of this land and none spoke against it. But when the Company waxed strong their ships brought out many memsahibs, and the memsahibs frowned upon this practice, openly despising all those who associated with India women—above all, those who married them—and showing scorn and contempt towards the children of mixed blood. Seeing this, the people of Hind were angry and they too set their faces against it, so that now both regard it with equal disfavour. Therefore neither Kairi's people nor yours would have permitted a marriage between you."

"They could not have stopped us," declared Ash angrily.

"Maybe not. But they would have tried. And if you had persisted, and made her your wife, you would have found that few if any mem-log would have consented to meet her or invite her into their houses, or allowed their daughters to enter hers; and none would treat her as an equal—not even her own people, who would do likewise, and speak ill of her behind her back because she, a king's daughter, must accept such treatment from many *Angrezi* women whose own parents were far less well-born than hers. They would despise her as the Rana and his nobles did, because her grandfather was a *feringhi* and her mother a half-caste; for in this respect, as you will have learned in Bhithor, her people can be as cruel as yours. It is a failing common to all races, being a matter of instinct that goes deeper than reason: the distrust of the pure-bred for the half-breed. One cannot overcome it, and had you brought Kairi-Bai away with you, you would have discovered these things soon enough—and discovered too that there would be no refuge for you here; your Regiment would not have wished to have you back, and other Regiments would not have been anxious to accept one whom the Guides had rejected."

"I know," said Ash tiredly. "I too had thought of that. But I am not a poor man, and we should have had each other."

"*Beshak*. But unless you lived in the wilderness, or made yourselves a new world, you would also have had neighbours—native-born villagers or townsmen to whom you would have been foreigners. You might well have learned to like their ways and earned their friendship and acceptance, and in the end been content. But *bardast* (tolerance) is a rare flower that grows in few places and withers too easily. I know that the path you now tread is a hard one, but I believe it to be the best for you both; and if Kairi-Bai has had the courage to choose it, have you so much less, that you cannot accept it?"

"I have already done so," said Ash: and added wryly, "There was no choice."

"None," agreed Koda Dad. "Therefore what profit is there in repining? What is written is written. You should rather give thanks for that which was good, instead of wasting your time in fruitless regret for what you cannot have. There are many desirable things in life besides the possession of one woman, or one man: this even you must know. Were it not so, how lonely and desolate a world it would be for the many, the very many, who through ill-luck or by reason of being ill-favoured, or from some other cause, never meet that one? You are more fortunate than you know. And now," said Koda Dad firmly, "we will talk of other things. The hour grows late and I have much to tell you before I go."

Ash had expected him to talk of mutual acquaintances in villages beyond the Border, but he had spoken instead of far-away Kabul, where, so he said, agents and spies of the "Russ-log" had recently become so numerous that there was a jest in that city that out of every five men to be met with in the streets, one was a servant of the Tsar, two were taking bribes from him and the remaining two lived in hopes of doing so. The Amir, Shere Ali, had scant love for the British, and when Lord Northbrook, the recently retired Governor General, had refused to give him any firm assurance of protection, he had turned instead to Russia, with the result that during the past three years relations between Britain and Afghanistan had deteriorated alarmingly.

"It is to be hoped that the new Lat-Sahib will come to a better understanding with the Amir," said Koda Dad. "Otherwise there will surely be another war between the Afghans and the Raj—and the last one should have taught both that neither can look to gain advantage from such a conflict."

Ash observed with a smile that according to Kairi's uncle, the Rao-Sahib, no one learnt over-much from the mistakes of their parents and even less from those of their grandparents; for the reason that all men, using hindsight, were convinced that they could have done better, and in trying to prove it either ended up making the same mistakes, or new ones that their children and their children's children would criticize in their turn. "He told me," said Ash, "that old men forget, while young ones tend to dismiss events that occurred before they were born as ancient history. Something that happened very long ago and was naturally mismanaged, considering that everyone involved —as can be seen by looking at the survivors—was either a creaking grey-beard or a bald-headed old fool. In other words, their own parents, grandparents, uncles and aunts."

Koda Dad frowned at the lightness of his tone, and said with a trace of sharpness: "You may laugh, but it would be as well if all those who like myself can remember that first war against the Afghans, and all who like you and my son Zarin Khan had yet to be born, would consider that conflict, and what became of it."

"I have read of it," returned Ash lightly. "It does not make a pretty tale."

"Pretty!" snorted Koda Dad. "No, it was not pretty, and all who engaged in it suffered sorely. Not only Afghans and *Angrezis,* but Sikhs, Jats and Punjabis and the many others who served in the great army that the Raj sent against Shere Ali's father, the Amir Dost Mohammed. That army won a great victory, slaying large numbers of Afghans and occupying Kabul, where they remained for two years and doubtless expected to stay for many more. Yet in the end they were forced to abandon it and to retreat through the mountains—close on seventeen thousand of them, men, women and children, of whom how many think you reached Jalalabad? One!—one only out of all that great company who marched out of Kabul in the year that my son Awal Shah was born. The rest, save for some few whom the Amir's son took into custody, died among the passes, butchered by the tribes who fell upon them like wolves upon a flock of sheep, for they were weakened by cold, it being winter and the snow lying deep. Some four months later my father had occasion to pass that way, and saw their bones lying scattered thick for mile upon mile along the hillsides, as though . . ."

"I too," said Ash, "for even after all these years, many are still left. But all that happened very long ago, so why should it disturb you now? What is wrong, Bapu-ji?"

"Many things," said Koda Dad soberly. "That tale that I have just told you, for one. It is not so old a tale, since many men still living must have seen what my father saw, and there must also be others, far younger than myself, who took part in that great killing and later told their sons and grandsons of these things."

"What of it? There is nothing strange in that."

"No. But why is it that now of a sudden, and after so many years, the tale of the destruction of that army is being told again in every town and village and household throughout Afghanistan and the lands that border upon it? I myself have heard it told a score of times in the past few weeks; and it bodes no good, for the telling of it breeds conceit and over-confidence, encouraging our young men to think scornfully of the Raj and to belittle its power and the strength of its armies. And there is another curious thing: the teller is nearly always a stranger, passing through. A merchant perhaps, or a Powindah, or some wandering mendicant; a holy man on pilgrimage or someone on a visit to relatives in another part of the country, who has asked for a night's lodging. These strangers tell the story well, making it live again in the minds of folk who first heard it ten, twenty, thirty years ago, and had almost forgotten it, but who now retell it to each other and become boastful and full of wild talk. I have begun to wonder of late if there is not something behind it. Some plan . . . or some person."

"Such as Shere Ali, or the Tsar of Russia?" suggested Ash. "But why? It would not pay Shere Ali to embark on a war with the British."

"True. But it might please the Russ-log if he should do so, for then he would hasten to ally himself to them so that he might call upon them to aid him. All the Border knows that the Russ-log have already swallowed up much of the territory of the Khans; and were they to gain a firm foothold in Afghanistan, who knows but that they might one day use it as a base for the conquest of Hind? I for one have no desire to see the Russ-log replace the Raj— though to speak truth, child, I would be happy to see the Raj depart from this land and the Government return once again to the hands of those to whom it rightfully belongs: the native-born."

"Like myself," observed Ash with a grin.

"*Chut!* You know very well what I mean—to the men of Hind whose land this is and whose forefathers owned the soil, not to foreign conquerors."

"Such as Barbur the Mogul, and other followers of the Prophet?" asked Ash wickedly. "Those were also foreigners who conquered the land of the Hindus, so if the Raj goes, it may well be that those whose forefathers owned the soil will next expel all Mussulmans."

Koda Dad bristled wrathfully, and then, as the truth of the observation struck him, relaxed again and said with a rueful laugh: "I confess I had overlooked that. Yes indeed. We be foreigners both: twice over, I being a Pathan and you . . . you neither of this country or of *Belait*. But the Mussulmans came here many centuries ago, and Hind has become their homeland—the only one they know. They are grafted onto it too strongly to be separated: wherefore—" He checked, frowning, and said: "How did we come to be talking of these things? I was

601

speaking of Afghanistan. I am troubled by what is brewing beyond the Border, Ashok, and if it is possible for you to speak a word into the ear of those in authority——"

"Who—*me?*" interrupted Ash, and gave a shout of laughter. "Bapu-ji, you cannot be serious. Who do you suppose would listen to me?"

"But are there not many Burra-Sahibs in Rawalpindi, Colonel-Sahibs and General-Sahibs to whom you are known, who would listen to you?"

"To a junior officer? And one who could produce no proof?"

"But I *myself* have told you——"

"That certain men are going from village to village in the Border country, telling the tale of something that happened long before I was born. Yes, I know. But what someone else has told me is not proof. I should need more than that if I expected to be believed—much more. Without it they would laugh at me; or more likely give me a sharp reprimand for wasting their valuable time with a pack of bazaar rumours, and suspect me of trying to make myself seem important."

"But surely," urged Koda Dad, puzzled, "your elders in Rawalpindi must hold you in high favour now that you have just completed a difficult mission with honour? Had they not thought well of you, they would never have chosen you for such work in the first place."

"You are wrong there, my father," said Ash bitterly. "They chose me only because it offered a chance to remove me as far as possible from my friends, and from the frontier. And because Hindustani is my mother-tongue and the work required someone who could both speak and understand it with ease. That was all."

"But now that you are back, having done well—?"

"Now that I am back they must find some other way to get rid of me until such time as my Regiment is willing to receive me again. Until then I am merely a nuisance. No, Bapu-ji, you would do better to ask Awal or Zarin to speak to Battye-Sahib or the Commandant. They would at least be given a hearing, which I should not."

"What is that I am to say to Battye-Sahib?" asked Zarin's voice from behind them. His feet had made no sound on the stone stairway, for as Fatima Begum did not permit the wearing of shoes in her house, they had not heard him approach.

"Billah! I am getting deaf in my old age," said Koda Dad, annoyed. "It is as well that I have no enemies, for a babe could stalk me in the open. I did not hear you; and Ashok, who should have done so, was talking so loudly that his ears were full of the sound of his own foolish words."

Zarin and Ash grinned at each other, and Ash said: "Alas, Bapu-ji, they were not foolish. I still lie under the disfavour of those in authority, both in Rawalpindi and Mardan, and until I have served my sentence you cannot expect any words of mine to carry weight with them. Besides, they must know these things already. They have spies everywhere; or if they have not, they should have."

"What is the talk?" asked Zarin, seating himself beside his father. "What things should already be known?"

"Your father," said Ash, "tells me that there is trouble brewing in Afghanistan, and he fears that unless it is nipped in the bud it may lead to an alliance between the Amir and the Russ-log: which in turn would lead to another war."

"Good! We could do with one," approved Zarin. "We have eaten idleness for too long, and it is time we were given a chance to fight again. But if the Sirkar fears that Shere Ali will permit the Russ-log to gain control of Kabul, or the tribes allow them to occupy the country, then they know nothing of the Amir or his people."

"True . . . that is true," conceded his father. "And if this new Lat-Sahib" (he meant Lord Lytton, who had succeeded Lord Northbrook as Viceroy and Governor-General) "can be prevailed upon to tread carefully, using patience and friendship and much wisdom in his dealings with the problems of the Amir and the people of Afghanistan, then all may yet be well. But should his councillors continue on the present course, I am very sure that the end will be war, and though when I was young I too relished fighting and danger, I find that now I am old I have no wish to see villages burned and crops laid waste, and the bodies of all those who once lived there lying unburied; food for the foxes and the carrion crows."

"Yet the mullahs tell us that no man dies before his time," said Zarin gently. "Our fates are written."

"It may be," admitted Koda Dad doubtfully. "But that is something else that of late I have become less sure of; for how can the mullahs—or even the Prophet him-

603

self——read all the mind of God? There is also another thing——I have still three sons (for I count Ashok here as one), all of them *jawans** who serve in a regiment that will be among the very first to be called upon to fight if there should be another war with Afghanistan; and though you will say I am growing womanish, yet I would prefer that they were not cut down in their prime but lived, as I have done, to see their sons grow to manhood and beget many grandsons; and when they die at the last that they should die full of years and contentment . . . as I, their father, will do. Therefore it distresses me to hear the whispers that go up and down the Frontier, and to see the storm clouds gather."

"Do not fear, Bapu-ji," consoled Ash, stooping to touch the old man's feet. "A wind will arise and blow these clouds away, and you can be at ease again——while your three sons bite their nails for idleness, and quarrel with their friends for lack of an enemy to fight."

"*Thak!*" (let be) snorted Koda Dad, preparing to rise. "You are as bad as Zarin. You think of war only as a game or as a chance to obtain promotion and honour."

"And loot," added Ash with a laugh. "Do not forget the loot, my father. I spent eight days in Kabul searching for Dilasah Khan, and it is a rich city."

He reached down a hand to help the old man to his feet, but Koda Dad brushed it aside and rose without assistance, settling his turban and remarking austerely that the young displayed too much levity and not enough re- spect for their elders. "Let us go down. It is time that we ate, for I must see my sister and also rest awhile before we start our journey back."

They ate together in the open courtyard, and after- wards went up to pay their respects to Fatima Begum and to thank her for her hospitality. The old lady kept them gossiping for well over an hour before dismissing them to get what sleep they could before midnight; at which hour a servant awakened them and they rose and dressed, and leaving that hospitable house, rode away together down through Attock to the bridge of boats.

The Indus was a wide expanse of molten silver under the blaze of the full moon, and as ever, the voice of the

---

*Literally young men: but also used colloquially to mean soldiers.

"Father of Rivers" filled the night with sound, hissing and chuckling between the tethered boats that jerked and strained against the current, and rising to a sustained thunder downstream where the gorge narrowed. It was not too easy to make oneself heard above the river noises, and none of the three attempted it. There was, in any case, nothing more to be said, and when they dismounted at the bridge head to embrace as sons and brothers in the Border country are accustomed to do on meeting or parting, they did so without words.

Ash helped Koda Dad to remount, and taking one of the old man's hands in both his own, pressed it to his forehead, holding it there for a long moment before he released it and stood back to let the two men ride forward onto the bridge. The horses' hooves rang loud on the tarred planks, like drum beats tapping out a counterpoint to the roar and chuckle of the river. But the sound diminished swiftly, and all too soon it merged with the noise of water and was lost.

The sentry on duty at the bridge yawned largely and lit a cheap bazaar-made cigarette, and Ash's horse, taking exception to the sudden fizz and splutter of the sulphur match and the brief flare of light, threw up its head and began to snort and sidle. But Ash did not move. He waited until the two horsemen reached the far side, and as they breasted the rise of the road, saw the taller of the two lift a hand in farewell and the other check his mount to look back. At that range it was impossible to make out his features, but the moonlight was brilliant enough to show that familiar nod of admonition, and Ash smiled and held up both his hands in a gesture of acceptance. He saw Koda Dad nod again as though satisfied, and the next moment father and son rode on, and Ash watched them grow smaller and smaller until they reached a turn in the Peshawar road and were swallowed up by the shadow of the hillsides.

"You do not go with your friends, then?" asked the sentry idly.

For a moment it seemed as though Ash had not heard the question, and then he turned and said slowly: "No . . . no, I cannot go with them . . ."

"*Afsos*," commiserated the sentry with easy sympathy, and yawned again. Ash bade him good-night, and

605

mounting the restive horse, rode back alone to the Begum's house where he was to spend the remainder of the night and the best part of the following day.

The old lady had sent for him next morning and they had talked together for over an hour—or rather the Begum had talked while Ash, separated from her by the split-cane *chik*, had listened, and occasionally answered a question. The rest of the time he had been left very much to himself. For which he was grateful, as it gave him a much needed period of quiet in which to think over what Koda Dad had said on the subject of Anjuli; and when he left the Begum's house shortly after moonrise, he was in better spirits and a more equable frame of mind than he had enjoyed for some considerable time; and with a quieter heart. He did not press his horse, but took the sixty-odd miles at a leisurely pace, and having changed into his own clothes in a convenient cane-brake, arrived back at the rest-house by the Murree road well before the moon was down. The temperature in his room was well over a hundred and the *punkah* did not work, but he had spent the day there, and left on the following morning for the pines and the hill breezes of Murree.

Wally had joined him a day later, and the two had trekked into Kashmir by way of Domel and the Jhelum gorge, and spent a month camping and shooting among the mountains beyond Sopore. During which time Wally had grown a short-lived beard, and Ash an impressive cavalry moustache.

It had been a halcyon interlude, for the weather had been perfect, and there had been endless things to talk about and to discuss. But though Ash, while again omitting any reference to Juli, had told Wally in some detail about his visit to Fatima Begum's house, oddly enough (or perhaps understandably, considering how pre-occupied he had been with his personal problems) he had not thought to mention Koda Dad's tale of trouble brewing beyond the Border. It had slipped his mind, for he had, in fact, not paid over-much attention to it: there was always trouble on the Frontier, and the affairs of Afghanistan did not interest him as much as his own.

Half-way through July the weather broke, and after enduring three days of pouring rain and impenetrable mist on a mountain side, the campers beat a hasty retreat to Srinagar, where they pitched their tents in a grove of *chenar* trees near the city, and made arrangements to return by tonga along the cart-road—the prospect of long marches on foot through a continuous downpour being too dismal to contemplate.

After the keen, pine-scented air of the mountains, they found Srinagar unpleasantly warm and humid, the city itself a squalid jumble of ramshackle wooden houses, crammed together and intersected by insanitary alleyways, or narrow canals that smelt like open sewers—and frequently were. But the Dal Lake was ablaze with lotus blossoms and alive with the flashing blue and green and gold of innumerable kingfishers and bee-eaters, and they bathed and lazed, gorged themselves on the cherries, peaches, mulberries and melons for which the valley was famous, and visited Shalimar and Nishat—the enchanting pleasure gardens that the Mogul Emperor, Jehangir, son of the great Akbar, had built on the shores of the Dal.

Yet all too soon, like all pleasant times, the careless, sun-gilt days were over and they were being rattled and jolted along the flat cart-road to Baramullah at the mouth of the valley, and from there into the mountains and the pouring rain; clattering through vast rock gorges and forests of pine and deodar, jogging through the streets of little hill villages, and along tracks that were no more than narrow shelves scraped out of mountainsides that dropped sheer away to where the foam-torn Jhelum River roared in spate three hundred feet below.

They were not sorry to see Murree again, and to be able to sleep in beds that were both dry and comfortable, though Murree too had been swathed in the mist and rain of the monsoon. But as they jogged down the endless turns of the hill road, the clouds thinned and the temperature rose, and long before they reached the level of the plains they were back again in the gruelling heat of the hot weather.

Mahdoo was back from his holiday in his home village of Mansera beyond Abbottabad, and feeling, he said, rested and greatly refreshed. But though he looked much the same, it was clear that the long journey to Bhithor and that headlong return in the worst of the hot weather had left its mark on him, and that he like Koda Dad Khan was beginning to feel his age. He had brought a young relative with him: a good-tempered, gangling youth of sixteen with a deeply pock-marked face, who answered to the name of Kadera and would in time, said Mahdoo, become a good cook: "For if I am to have a 'makey-learn,' I prefer to choose my own and not be worried by some *chokra* who cannot be trusted to boil water, let alone prepare a *burra khana!*"

The bungalow smelt stalely of mildew and lamp-oil and overpoweringly of flowers, the *mali* (gardener) having filled every available jar with tight bunches of marigolds and zinnias, and there was a pile of letters on the hall table, mostly mail from Home and addressed to Wally. Two, not in English, were for Ash, and both had been written over six weeks ago and described the ceremonies and festivity that had accompanied the installation of the new Maharajah of Karidkote. One was from Kaka-ji and the other from Mulraj, and both had thanked Ash yet again for his "services to their Maharajah and the State," and passed on messages from Jhoti, who appeared to be in high feather and wanted to know how soon the Sahib would be able to visit Karidkote. But apart from that reference to his "services," there had been no mention at all of Bhithor.

"Well, what else did I expect?" thought Ash, folding away the sheets of soft, hand-made paper. As far as Karidkote was concerned that chapter was closed, and there was no point in turning back the pages when there was so much to look forward to. Besides, in India the posts were still slow and uncertain, and the distance between the two states of Karidkote and Bhithor was roughly the same as that which separated London from Vienna or Madrid. It was also unlikely that the Rana, having failed to cheat the late Maharajah, would wish to correspond with his successor or encourage Jhoti's sisters to do so.

That same evening, their first back from leave, Wally had suggested that they drop in at the Club to look up various friends and hear the latest news of the station, but as Ash preferred to stay and talk to Mahdoo, he had gone there alone—to return two hours later with an unexpected guest: Wigram Battye, who was also on his way back from leave.

Lieutenant Battye had been shooting on the borders of Poonch, and Wally, meeting him on the Mall and hearing that he intended to spend a day or two in 'Pindi,

608

had insisted that he would be far more comfortable in their bungalow than at the Club (which was not strictly true) and brought him back in triumph. For though Ash still held first place in Wally's regard, Wigram came a close second, not only because he happened to be a likeable and very popular officer, but because his eldest brother, Quentin—killed in action during the Mutiny— occupied a special niche in Wally's private hall of fame.

Quentin Battye had taken part in that famous march to the Ridge of Delhi when the Guides, at the height of the hot weather, had covered close on six hundred miles in twenty-two days, storming a rebel-held village on the way, and going into action within half an hour of their arrival at the Ridge, despite having marched thirty miles since dawn. The battle had been Quentin's first and last. He had been mortally wounded (*"noble Battye, ever to the fore"* wrote Captain Daly in his diary that evening), and dying a few hours later had muttered with his last breath the words of a famous Roman: *"Dulce et decorum est, pro patria mori."*

Wally, himself a patriot and a romantic, had been moved by that story and fully approved the sentiment. He too considered that to die for one's country would be a good and splendid thing, and in his eyes Quentin's brothers, Wigram and Fred, both now serving with the Guides, were tinged with the gold of reflected glory, as well as being what he termed "cracking good fellows."

Wigram, for his part, had taken to young Walter Hamilton at their first meeting over a year and a half ago, which was in itself no small tribute to Wally's character and personality, considering that the meeting had been arranged by Ash, whom Wigram regarded as being wild to a fault—not to mention the fact that young Hamilton obviously regarded him as some sort of hero instead of a thoroughly difficult and insubordinate junior officer who, in the opinion of his seniors (and they included Lieutenant Battye), had been more than lucky to escape being cashiered.

In the circumstances, Wigram might have been forgiven if he had decided to steer well clear of Pandy Martyn's protégé. But it had not taken him long to realize that there was nothing slavish in the younger man's attitude towards Ashton, and that his admiration for him did not mean that he would try and emulate his exploits.

Walter's head might be in the clouds, but both his feet were firmly on the ground, and he had a mind of his own. "A good boy," thought Wigram. "The kind who will make a first class Frontier officer, and who men will follow anywhere because he will always be out in front . . . like Quentin." Wigram had made a point of seeing what he could of Ensign Hamilton whenever duty or pleasure brought him to Rawalpindi, and had spoken so warmly of him to the Commandant and the Second-in-Command that it was largely due to his efforts that Walter had been offered a commission in the Corps of Guides.

Ash was not unaware that Wigram, as a dedicated soldier, regarded him with a certain amount of disapproval, and though they were on tolerably good terms, and on the whole got on well together, that it was Walter's company that Wigram enjoyed, and Walter who brought out the best in Quentin's quieter, steadier brother, making him laugh and relax and behave as though he too was a young ensign again.

Watching them now as they joked and talked together, Ash could only be grateful for Wigram's presence, though at any other time he might well have felt a twinge of jealousy at Wally's obvious admiration for the older man, and the fact that they had plainly seen a good deal of each other during the eight months that he had been away, and become fast friends. But he had not been looking forward to these last few days in the bungalow, with the rooms strewn with reminders of Wally's departure and the loneliness that would follow, and Wigram's presence would not only help to make the time pass quicker, but ease the strain of parting from the only real friend he had ever made among men of his own blood.

It would also help Wally, since as Wigram was leaving on the same day they would be riding together, which not only meant that Wally would have a companion on the journey, but that he would arrive in Mardan in the company of one of the most popular officers in the Corps. That alone should guarantee him a flying start, and his own engaging personality, together with the excellent reports that Zarin would have carried back, would do the rest.

Ash had no fears for Wally's future in the Guides: he had been born under a bright star and would one day make a great name for himself. The sort of name that he, Ash, had once imagined himself making.

The bungalow had seemed very quiet after Wally had gone, and there were no more martial hymns from his bathroom of a morning. It also seemed intolerably empty —empty and over-large, and depressingly squalid.

Ash had not noticed until now how dilapidated it had become, or how shoddy were the few bits of furniture they had hired at an exorbitant monthly rate from a contractor in the bazaar. He had thought it comfortable enough before, and despite certain obvious drawbacks, even friendly. But now it appeared sordid and inhospitable, and the smell of mildew and dust and mice that pervaded it was an active offence. The room that had been Wally's study and bedroom already looked as though it had been unoccupied for years, and the only proof that he had ever slept and worked there was a torn scrap of paper that appeared to be part of a laundry list.

Looking about that empty room, Ash was conscious of an uncomfortable conviction that he had lost Wally. They would meet again, and certainly see a good deal of each other in the future once he himself was allowed to return to the Regiment. But time and events would be bound to loosen the close ties of friendship that at present existed between them. Wally would find other and worthier men to admire—Wigram, for one—and because he was bound to be liked and to make friends wherever he went, he would be an immensely popular officer and an asset to the Guides. Ash did not do him the injustice of imagining that he would allow any new friendship to diminish the old one, yet its quality was bound to alter at the will of circumstances and pressures, and what officialdom termed "the exigencies of the service."

The morning had been dark and overcast, and now a gust of wind, forerunner of one of the violent monsoon rainstorms that periodically drenched the plains, swept through the deserted room, setting the *chiks* flapping and bringing with it a small cloud of dust and dead neem leaves from the verandah beyond. It sent the crumpled fragment of paper, sole relic of Wally's occupation, bowling across the matting to Ash's feet, and he stooped and picked it up, and smoothing it out saw that it was not a laundry list. The poet had been jotting down rhymes—

Divine. shine. pine. mine. wine? Valentine. en . . .

En—? "Entwine?" pondered Ash, amused. Or perhaps something more exotic, like "encarnadine"—? (Wally's verse was apt to be peppered with such words). Ash wondered whom he had been addressing, and if one day he would meet a girl who would not only attract his passing fancy, but capture it and keep it for good. Somehow he could not picture Wally as a sober and settled pater familias. As a love-lorn suitor, yes. But a suitor who took good care not to press his suit too hard or allow himself to be taken too seriously, and who preferred to pursue some unobtainable She.

"The fact is," mused Ash, "that he enjoys paying court to pretty girls and scribbling poems bewailing their cruelty or praising their eyebrows or ankles or the way they laugh, but that's about as far as it goes, because the thing he is really in love with is glory. Military glory, God help him. Until he gets that out of his system, no girl has a ghost of a chance. Oh well, he's bound to grow out of it one of these days: and out of me too, I suppose."

He turned the scrap of paper over and discovered on the reverse side part of an exercise in Persian. Wally had evidently been translating a passage from Genesis into that language, and it occurred to Ash that this crumpled fragment of paper provided an accurate sketch of the boy's character, in that it bore evidence of his piety, his attempts to write verse, his light-hearted philandering, and his dogged determination to pass the Higher Standard in Languages with Honours. The translation proved to be a surprisingly good one, and reading the graceful Persian script, Ash realized that Wally must have been studying even harder than he had thought—

...*set a mark upon Cain, lest any finding him should kill him. And Cain went out from the presence of the Lord, and dwelt in the land of Nod, on the East of Eden* ...

Ash shivered, and crumpling up the scrap of paper into a ball, flicked it away as though it had stung him. Despite his upbringing, he was not overgiven to superstition and a belief in omens. But Koda Dad had talked of trouble in Afghanistan and been disturbed by the possibility of another Afghan war, because the Frontier Force Regiments would be the first to become involved; and Ash knew that among men of the Border country, and throughout Central Asia, it is believed that the plain of Kabul is the Land of Cain—that same Nod that lies to the

612

east of Eden—and that Cain's bones lie buried beneath a
hill to the south of the city of Kabul, which he is said to
have founded.

The link was far fetched, and the fact that Wally
had selected that particular passage for translation could
hardly be termed a coincidence, for he had recently been
reading the memoirs of the first Mogul Emperor, Barbur
the Tiger, and on learning of that legend, had obviously
been sufficiently interested to look up the story in Genesis, and later use it as an exercise in translation. There
was nothing in the least remarkable about it, decided Ash,
ashamed of that superstitious shiver. But all the same, he
wished that he had not read the thing; because that part
of him that was and always would be Ashok saw it as
an ill-omen, and not all the Western scepticism of the
Pelham-Martyns or those years at an English public school
could wholly succeed in convincing him that this was
absurd.

A second gust of wind whisked the little ball of
paper under the flapping *chik* and across the verandah into the dusty waste of the compound beyond, and the
last trace of Wally's occupancy had gone. And as Ash
closed the door against the whirling dust the first drops
of rain splashed down, and in the next moment the day
was dark and full of the roar of falling water.

34

The downpour lasted over the weekend. It laid the dust
and lowered the temperature, and flooded out the snakes
who lived in holes below the bungalow and among the tree
roots, and who now took up residence in the bathrooms
and between the flower pots on the verandah—from
where they were evicted by the servants to the accompaniment of much shouting and noise.

Unfortunately it had not been possible to evict Captain Lionel Crimpley, who moved into the bungalow on
the Monday in place of Wally, for there happened to be a
severe shortage of accommodation in Rawalpindi at the

time, and if it had not been Crimpley it would have been someone else. Though Ash was of the opinion that almost anyone else would have been preferable.

Lionel Crimpley was a good ten years older than Ash, and he considered that his seniority should have entitled him to better quarters. He deeply resented having to share half a bungalow with a junior officer, and made no secret of the fact—or that he disliked everything about the country in which he had elected to serve, and regarded its inhabitants as inferiors, irrespective of rank or position. He had been genuinely horrified when a few days after his arrival he had heard voices and laughter coming from Ash's room, and on walking in without knocking, discovered the owner enjoying a joke with his cook who, to make matters worse, was actually smoking a hookah.

To give Crimpley his due, he had supposed that Ash must be out and that his servants had taken advantage of his absence to sit around in his chairs and gossip. He had apologized for his intrusion and left, looking inexpressibly shocked, and that evening at the Club had described the disgraceful incident to a like-minded crony, one Major Raikes, whose acquaintance he had made when their respective regiments were stationed at Meerut.

Major Raikes said that he was not at all surprised; there had been some very queer rumours going around concerning young Pandy Martyn. "If you ask me, there's something deuced fishy about the feller," pronounced Major Raikes. "Speaks the lingo a sight too well, for one thing. Mind you, I'm all for bein' able to speak it well enough to carry on out here, but that don't mean one need speak it so well that one could pass for a native provided one was blacked up."

"Quite so," agreed Lionel Crimpley, who, though like all Indian Army officers had had to pass the set language examinations, had never added to a meagre vocabulary or outgrown an unmistakably British intonation.

"Any case," continued Major Raikes, warming to the subject, "hob-nobbin' with these people on equal terms don't do us any good as a race. What happened in '57 could happen again if we don't see to it that the natives have a proper respect for us. You ought to speak to young Pandy Martyn, y'know. High time someone did, if he's started getting pally with his *nauker-log* (servants)."

614

Captain Crimpley had thought the advice good and acted upon it at the first opportunity. And Ash, who had been fortunate enough not to have encountered this particular viewpoint before (the Crimpley–Raikes species being a rarity), had begun by being amused, but on discovering, with incredulity, that his mentor was perfectly serious, ended by losing his temper. There had been an unfortunate scene, and Lionel Crimpley, enraged at being addressed in such opprobrious terms—and by an officer junior to him in rank—had complained to the Brigade Major, demanding an immediate apology and the offender's head on a platter, and insisting that he, Crimpley, be given other and more suitable quarters, or if that was not possible, that Lieutenant Pelham-Martyn should be expelled from the bungalow instantly, as he himself refused to remain under the same roof as any insolent, abusive, unlicked cub who smoked and gossiped with the servants, and moreover . . .

There had been a good deal more on this head, and the Brigade Major had not been pleased. He held no brief for Captain Crimpley, or for Captain Crimpley's views, but then neither did he approve of Lieutenant Pelham-Martyn's, for his own were strictly middle-of-the-road and he disliked extremes. In his opinion, the attitudes of both Crimpley and Pelham-Martyn were equally displeasing, and neither could be held blameless. But as no junior officer must be allowed to hurl abusive epithets at one senior to him, whatever the provocation, Ash had received a sharp dressing-down, while Crimpley for his part had been brusquely informed that for the time being both he and Lieutenant Pelham-Martyn would remain where they were, as no alternative accommodation could be provided for either of them.

"And serve them right," thought the Brigade Major, pleased with himself for this judgement of Solomon and unaware how severe a punishment he had inflicted on both offenders.

The best that either could do was to see as little of each other as their cramped quarters permitted, but the next few months had not been pleasant ones, even though the Captain did little more than sleep in the bungalow, and took all his meals in the mess or at the Club. "Couldn't possibly bring myself to eat or drink with a fellow of that stamp," confided the Captain, airing his

615

grievances to his friend Major Raikes. "And if you ask me, our Government is making a great mistake in allowing that sort of outsider to come to this country at all. They ought to recognize the kind and weed 'em out at once."

"Crimpley," wrote Ash angrily, describing him in a letter to Wally, "is precisely the type of supercilious, bone-headed bastard who ought never to be allowed to set foot in this country, for he and his kind can ruin the life-work of a thousand good men by a single fatuous display of rudeness and insularity. Thank God there are only a very few of them. But even one would be too many, and it is depressing to think that our descendants will prob-ably accept the view that dear Lionel was 'typical,' and that the whole damned lot of us, from Clive onwards, were a bunch of pompous, insular, over-bearing and man-nerless poops!"

Ash had many acquaintances in the cantonment, but no close friends. He had not needed any while Wally had been there, and now that Wally had gone he did not trouble to make any others among his fellow Club mem-bers, largely because he preferred to see as little as pos-sible of Crimpley, who could always be found at the 'Pindi Club out of office hours. Instead, he took to spending much of his free time in the company of men like Kasim Ali or Ranjee Narayan, sons of well-to-do middle-class men who lived with their families in large, rambling houses set in leafy gardens on the outskirts of the city, or in tall flat-roofed ones in the city itself. Merchants, bankers, cultivators and landowners, contractors or dealers in gems. The solid, sober backbone of any city.

Ash found their company much more relaxing and their conversation more to his taste than anything that he could find in social gatherings within the cantonments, for their talk ranged over a much wider field of subjects—theology, philosophy, crops and trade, the problems of local government and administration—and was not con-fined to horses, station-scandal and military "shop"; or to the politics and squabbles of democratic nations on the far side of the world. Yet even here he was not wholly at ease, for though his hosts were unfailingly kind and extended themselves to make him feel at home, he was always conscious of a barrier, carefully disguised, but still there. They liked him. They were genuinely in-terested in his views. They enjoyed his company and were pleased that he should speak their tongue as well as they themselves did . . . But he was not one of them. He might be a welcome guest, but he was also a *feringhi*: a foreigner and a member of the foreign Raj. Nor was that the only barrier—

Because he was not of their faith or their blood, there were certain things that they did not discuss with him or mention in his presence; and though their young children came and went freely and accepted him without question, he never caught so much as a glimpse of their women-folk. When visiting Ranjee Narayan's house or in the homes of Ranjee's relatives and friends, there was also the barrier of caste, for many of the older generation could not (to quote Captain Crimpley) "bring themselves to eat or drink with a fellow of that stamp," because their religious beliefs forbade it.

Ash saw nothing odd in this, for he realized that one cannot change immemorial attitudes in a decade or two. But there was no denying that it tended to make social intercourse between the Orthodox and the Outsider a difficult and somewhat delicate business.

There had been talk that cold weather of an important conference to be held in Peshawar between the representatives of Great Britain and the Amir of Afghanistan, on the question of a treaty between the two countries. The political implications of this had been the subject of much discussion in Rawalpindi—and indeed throughout the Northern Punjab—but despite what Koda Dad had told him, Ash had not paid over-much attention to it, mainly because he seldom went to the Club or the mess and so missed a good deal that he might otherwise have heard.

Zarin had managed to visit Rawalpindi once or twice during the autumn, and Wally had actually been able to get a week's leave at Christmas, which he and Ash had spent shooting duck and snipe on the Chenab near Morala. The week had passed very pleasantly, but by contrast the long days that succeeded it seemed even more tedious, though Wally wrote regularly and Zarin at intervals, and once in a while there would be a letter from Kaka-ji that brought news of Karidkote and messages from Jhoti and Mulraj; but no mention of Anjuli—or of Bhithor. Koda Dad too wrote, though only to say that he was well, and that things were much the same as they had been at the time of their last meeting—which Ash took to be a reminder that the situation he had spoken of last summer still prevailed and showed no signs of improving.

Captain Crimpley, who occasionally caught sight of one of these letters (the post was laid out daily on the hall table), spoke scathingly at the Club about Pandy Martyn's correspondents, and hinted that they should be investigated by Intelligence. But apart from Major Raikes, no one paid any attention to these allegations. The Captain and his crony were not popular with their fellow members, and it is unlikely that they could have done Ash much harm if it had not been for the affair of Mr. Adrian Porson, that well-known lecturer and globe-trotter . . .

January and February had come and gone. The days were warm and sunny, and Mr. Porson was among the last of these birds-of-passage to appear in Rawalpindi, the genus preferring to be out of the country well before the first of April. He had already spent several months seeing India under the aegis of such exalted personages as Governors, Residents and Members of Council, and was at present staying with the Commissioner of Rawalpindi, *en route* to his final port of call, Peshawar, before returning to Bombay and Home. The object of this tour had been to acquire material for a series of critical lectures on "Our Eastern Empire," and by now he considered himself to be an authority on the subject, and had chosen to air his views to a group of members at the 'Pindi Club one early March evening.

"The trouble is," said Mr. Porson in a voice trained to carry to the back rows of a hall, "that as I see it, the only Indians you people out here care to know are either Maharajahs or peasants. You would seem to have no objection to hob-nobbing with a ruling prince and pronouncing him to be quite a 'decent sort of chap,' but, one asks oneself, how is it that you fail to make friends with Indian men and women of your own class? That, if you will forgive plain speaking, one finds inexcusable, as it indicates a degree of short-sightedness and prejudice, not to say racial snobbery, that must strike any thinking person as offensive in the extreme. Particularly when one compares it with the patronizing indulgence extended to your 'faithful old servants' that you

618

speak so highly of—the subservient 'Uncle Toms' who wait on you hand and foot and care for all your creature comforts, the—"

It was at this point that Ash, who had dropped in to pay a Club bill and paused to listen to Mr. Porson's discourse, was moved to intervene:

"It would be interesting, sir," observed Ash, in a tone that cut across those rolling periods like acid, "to know why you should sneer at faithfulness. I had always supposed it to be one of the Christian virtues, but obviously, I was wrong."

The unexpectedness of the attack took Mr. Porson aback, but only momentarily. Recovering himself, he turned to look the interrupter up and down, and then said blandly: "Not at all. One was merely endeavouring to illustrate a point: that in this country, all you Anglo-Indians obviously get on admirably with your inferiors and enjoy the company of your betters, but make no effort at all to make friends with your equals."

"May one ask, sir," inquired Ash with deceptive mildness, "how many years you have spent in this country?"

"Oh, shut up, Pandy!" muttered an anxious acquaintance, jerking warningly at Ash's coat-sleeve. *"Stash it!"*

Mr. Porson, however, remained unruffled, not because he was used to being heckled (the type of audience he was accustomed to lecture to were far too well-bred to interrupt the speaker), but he could recognize a heckler when he saw one, and now he sat back in his chair, smoothed his waistcoat, and placing the tips of his plump fingers together, prepared to deal with this boorish young Anglo-Indian:

"The answer to your question, my dear sir, is 'none.' One is only a visitor to these shores, and—"

"One's first visit, I presume?" cut in Ash.

Mr. Porson frowned, and then, deciding to be tolerant, laughed. "Quite right. I arrived in Bombay in November, and alas, I leave again by the end of this month; one's time is not one's own, you understand. But then someone like myself, a mere visitor with a fresh eye and an open mind, is, I fancy, better qualified to see flaws in a system, it being a true saying that 'The onlooker sees most of the game!' "

"Not in this case," said Ash shortly. "The particular flaw you have singled out is one that a great many

619

globe-trotters and temporary visitors have noticed and commented on, but as far as I know, none of these critics has stayed here long enough to practise what they preach. Had they done so, they would very soon have discovered that in nine cases out of ten the boot is on the other foot, for the middle classes in this country—like their counter-parts in any other one—are a pretty conservative lot, and it is they more often than the Anglo-Indians who call the tune. I am afraid, sir, that you fall into an error common to superficial observers when you accuse your countrymen of cold-shouldering them. It is not nearly as simple as that, because it's by no means a one-sided affair, you know."

"If by that you mean what I think you mean," intervened Major Raikes angrily, "then, by George, I'd like to say—"

"A moment, please!" said Mr. Porson authoritatively, quelling the interruption with a firm gesture of one podgy hand. He turned back to Ash: "But my dear young man, one is, of course, prepared to believe that many Indians of this class might hesitate to invite into their homes *some* to the British whom one has, oneself, had occasion to meet out here. (One need not particularize, need one? No names, no pack-drill!) But surely it should be the duty of every one of you to do all in your power to break down the barriers and get on close terms with these people? Only by doing so can you come to understand one another's view-point, and help to forge those bonds of loyalty and mutual respect without which our Raj cannot hope to retain its hold on this country."

This time it was Ash who laughed, and with a genuine amusement that made Mr. Porson stiffen angrily. "You make it sound very easy, sir; and I won't pretend that it isn't possible, because of course it is. But what makes you think that they really wish to make friends with us? Can you give me one good reason, one single one, why they should?"

"Well, after all, we are—" Mr. Porson stopped himself just in time, and actually blushed.

"Their conquerors?" said Ash, finishing the sentence for him. "I see. You feel that as members of a subject race they should be gratified to receive invitations from us, and be only too eager to welcome us into their own homes?"

620

"Nothing of the sort!" snapped Mr. Porson, his empurpled countenance betraying only too clearly that this was precisely what he had thought—though he would certainly have put it in different words. "I merely intended —What I meant to say was . . . Well, one has to admit that we are in a—in a position to offer a great deal in the way of—of . . . Western culture, for instance. Our literature. Our discoveries in the fields of medicine and science and . . . and so on. You had no right to put words into my mouth, Mr.—er . . . ?"

"Pelham-Martyn," supplied Ash helpfully.

"Oh." Mr. Porson was somewhat taken aback, for he happened to be acquainted with several Pelham-Martyns and had once lunched at Pelham Abbas, where, having monopolized the conversation through two courses, he had received one of Sir Matthew's stinging set-downs. The episode was still green in his memory, and if this outspoken young man should be related to that family—

"If I did you an injustice, sir, I apologize," said Ash. "It was a natural assumption, as a great many visitors do seem to hold that view——"

Had he stopped there, the chances are that he would have been back in Mardan that summer, and much that came later would not have happened—or happened differently. But the subject under discussion was one that interested him a great deal, and so he did not leave well alone, "—but it might help you to modify it," continued Ash, "if you were to try putting yourself in the other fellow's shoes just for a minute or two."

"Putting myself . . . ?" Mr. Porson was offended. "In what way, may one ask?"

"Well, look at it this way, sir," said Ash earnestly. "Imagine the British Isles as conquered territory, as it was in Roman times, but part of an Indian Empire instead. An Imperial colony, in which Indians hold every post of real authority, with an Indian Governor-General and Council proclaiming and enforcing laws that are completely alien to your way of life and thought, but which make it necessary for you to learn their language if you hope to hold any reasonably well-paid post under them. Indians controlling all the public services, garrisoning your country with their troops and recruiting your countrymen to serve in the ranks of regiments that they themselves would officer, declaring anyone who protested against their

621

authority a dangerous agitator, and putting down any rising with all the force at their command. And don't forget, sir, that the last of those risings would have been less than twenty years ago, when you yourself were already a grown man. You would remember that rising very well, for even if you had not fought in it yourself, you would have known people who had, and who had died in it—or been hanged for complicity, or suspicion of complicity, or merely because they had a white skin, in the reprisals that followed it. Taking all that into account, would you yourself be eager to get on close and friendly terms with your Indian rulers? If so, I can only say that you must be a truly Christian person, and that it has been an honour to meet you. Your servant, sir."

He bowed, and turning on his heel, walked out without waiting to hear if Mr. Porson had anything further to say.

Mr. Porson had not. Having never considered the problem from that angle, he was temporarily silenced. But Major Raikes and his friend Captain Crimpley, who had been among those present, had both said a great deal. Neither had any liking for Mr. Porson, whose opinions and criticisms on the subject of Anglo-Indians they considered offensive, but Ash's views (and his temerity in expressing them to a stranger old enough to be his father and brought to the Club as a guest) had touched both on the raw.

"Brazen impertinence and sheer bloody bad manners," fumed Lionel Crimpley. "Butting into a private conversation and spouting a lot of seditious twaddle to a man he hadn't even been introduced to. And a houseguest of the Commissioner's, too! It was a calculated affront to the entire Club, and the Committee should force that young sweep to apologize or get out."

"Oh, rats to that," retorted Major Raikes, dismissing the Committee with an impatient sweep of the hand. "The Committee can look after itself, and as for that numbskull Porson, he's nothing but a swollen-headed snob. But no officer has a right to say the sort of things that Pelham-Martyn said, or even think them. All that tripe about supposin' the British Isles were garrisoned by Indian troops—putting ideas into their heads, that's what it is, and damned treasonable ideas, too. It's about time someone kicked that young man's backside hard, and the sooner the better."

Now there can always be found in any military station—as in any town or city anywhere in the world—a smattering of bored and muscular louts who delight in violence and are only too eager to take a hand in "teaching a lesson" to any individual whose views they do not happen to share. Major Raikes therefore had no difficulty in recruiting half-a-dozen of these simple-minded souls, and two nights later they burst into Ash's bedroom in the small hours to drag him from his bed and beat him insensible. Or at least, that had been the idea.

In the event it had not turned out quite the way they had planned it, for they had neglected to take into account the fact that Ash was a remarkably light sleeper, and had long ago, from stark necessity, learned how to defend himself; and that when it came to fighting he had no respect for Queensberry Rules or any false ideas as to "sportsmanship."

They had also, unfortunately, failed to realize that the uproar would arouse the occupants of the servants' quarters as well as the sleeping *chowkidar,* all of whom, imagining that the bungalow was being attacked by a gang of robbers, had seized any weapon they could lay hands on and charged bravely to the assistance of Pelham-Sahib, the *chowkidar* wielding chain and *lathi* with deadly effect, Gul Baz laying about him with an iron bar, while Kulu Ram, Mahdoo and the sweeper had pinned their faiths respectively to a polo-stick, the kitchen poker and a long-handled broom...

By the time lights were brought and the mêlée sorted out, both sides had sustained casualties, and Ash was certainly insensible; though not, as intended, from the attentions of Major Raikes and his bravos, but as a result of tripping over a fallen chair in the darkness and knocking himself out on the corner of the dressing-table. The Major himself had received a broken nose and a sprained ankle, and no combatant, with the sole exception of the agile Kulu Ram, had come out of the engagement unmarked.

The affray, though brief, had been far too noisy (and its impressive tally of minor fractures, black eyes, cuts, sprains and bruises, too glaringly visible) to be ignored or glossed over. Questions had been asked in official quarters, and as the answers had been considered unsatisfactory, a searching inquiry had been instituted. This had

623

revealed the shocking fact that native servants had actually taken part in the fracas, attacking and being attacked by British officers. The Authorities had been horrified: "Can't have this sort of thing going on," declared the Brigade Commander, who had served with Havelock's forces in Cawnpore and Lucknow during the Mutiny and had never forgotten it. "Could lead to anything. Anything! We shall have to get rid of that young trouble-maker, and in double-quick time."

"Which one?" inquired a senior Major, pardonably confused. "If you mean Pelham-Martyn, I can't see that he can be held responsible for——"

"I know, I know," snapped the Brigade Commander impatiently. "I'm not saying that it was his fault. Though it can be argued that he provoked the attack by speaking out of turn at the Club, and being rude to that fellow who is staying with the Commissioner. But there is no denying that, intentionally or otherwise, he is a trouble-maker: always has been——his own regiment got him transferred to us, and still don't seem to want him back. Besides, it was his *nauker-log* who attacked Raikes and Co., don't forget. They may have had every reason for doing so, and if it *had* turned out to be a raid by a band of dacoits, we'd have said they were loyal fellows for coming to his rescue. But in the circumstances, this isn't at all the sort of tale we want circulating round cantonments or told as a joke in the city, so the sooner we get rid of him the better."

Major Raikes, his nose and ankle in plaster, had been severely reprimanded for his part in the affair and ordered to take himself off on leave until his injuries were healed. His confederates had been confined to their quarters for a similar period, after receiving a tongue-lashing that they would remember for the rest of their lives. But Ash, who as the victim and not the aggressor might have been expected to escape any share of blame, had been given twenty-four hours in which to pack up his belongings, settle his debts and arrange to leave with his servants and his baggage by road to Jhelum, where they would take the mail-train bound for Delhi and Bombay.

He was to serve on attachment with Roper's Horse, a cavalry regiment stationed at Ahmadabad in Gujerat, nearly four hundred miles north of Bombay—and more

624

than two thousand miles distant by road and rail from Rawalpindi . . .

On the whole, Ash had not been sorry to leave 'Pindi. There were things he would miss: the company of several friends in the city, the foothills that could be reached so easily on horseback, the sight of high mountains clear-cut against the sky, and the hint of woodsmoke and pine-needles that sometimes tinged the air when the wind blew down from the north. On the other hand, it could not be much more than seventy miles to the border of Raj-putana, and little more than a hundred as the crow flies from Bhithor; he would be nearer Juli, and even though he could not enter the Rana's territory, that was some small consolation—as was the fact that however unfair he considered his arbitrary expulsion from Rawalpindi, he was not disposed to quarrel with a verdict that rescued him from sharing a bungalow with Lionel Crimpley.

There was also some comfort in the thought that in any case he would not have been able to see either Wally or Zarin for some time to come, as all leave for the Guides had recently been cancelled following rumours that further trouble was to be expected from the Jowaki Afri-dis, who apparently objected to some change in plan over the allowance paid to them by the Government in return for keeping the peace.

A letter from Mardan had brought Ash this piece of news only a day after the raid on his bungalow, and the reflection that neither of his friends would be able to visit 'Pindi until the Jowaki matter was resolved had gone a long way towards softening his resentment at be-ing so unjustly bundled off to Ahmadabad. But re-reading that letter from Wally, he had been reminded again of what Koda Dad had said on the roof of Fatima Begum's house at Attock, and was fretted by the thought that if there should be a war, the Guides would certainly be in-volved in it. The whole Corps would be sent, and some, inevitably, would never come back. But he, Ash, would be out of it all—kicking his heels in a dull and dusty cantonment in far-away Gujerat.

It was a lowering thought, yet on consideration he was unwilling to believe that this business of the Jowaki Afridis would develop into anything serious, or that it was connected in any way with the incidents that Koda Dad had related. The truth was that Koda Dad was getting old, and the old were apt to make much of trifles and take a pessimistic view of the future. There was no reason to take those stories too seriously.

Ash's last day in Rawalpindi had been a busy one. He had arranged the sale of two of his horses and despatched Baj Raj to the care of Wally in Mardan, paid a number of farewell visits to friends in the city, and scribbled several hurried letters to say that he was on his way to Gujerat and would probably be stationed there for at least eighteen months if not longer.

". . . and if during that time you should chance to be visiting your nieces," wrote Ash to Kaka-ji, "may I hope that you will honour me by travelling a little further, so that I may enjoy the felicity of meeting you again? The extra distance would not be too great. No more I think than fifty *koss* as the crow flies, and though it may well be half as much again by road, that is still only four or five days' journey, and I myself would come two thirds of that way to meet you. More if you would permit it, though that, I fear, you would not do . . ."

Kaka-ji would certainly not permit it. Nor did Ash have any real hope that the old man would even consider undertaking another journey to Bhithor. Yet there was always a chance that he would, and if he did he would certainly see and speak to Juli, and though he would not make any mention of her in writing, he could not, surely, refuse to speak of her if he and Ash should meet, when he must know that there were times when Ash would willingly have given an eye or a hand to hear that she was well and not too unhappy—or to have any news of her at all. Even bad news would have been easier to bear than this complete silence.

"I am getting too old for such journeys," grumbled Mahdoo, stowing his baggage aboard the mail-train on the following night. "It is time I took my *wazifa* (pension) and settled down to spend my last days in peace and idleness, instead of all this running to and fro across the length and breadth of Hind."

"Do you mean that, Cha-cha-ji?" asked Ash, startled.

"Why should I say it if I did not?" snapped the old man.

"To punish me, perhaps? But if you do mean it,
626

there is a dâk-*ghari* that leaves here in the morning and you could be in Abbottabad within three days."

"And what will become of you if I leave?" demanded Mahdoo, rounding on him angrily. "Will you ask Gul Baz for his advice as you ask for mine? Or take it when it is given, as you have on many occasions taken mine? Besides, I am tied to you by a promise that I gave many years ago to Anderson-Sahib; and also by one that I gave to Ala Yar. By affection, too, which is an even stronger bond . . . but it is true that I grow old and tired and useless, and I have no wish to end my days in the south among idol-worshippers whose hearts are as black as their skins. When my time comes I would choose to die in the north where a man may smell the clean wind that blows off the high snows."

"That will be as God wills," said Ash lightly, "nor am I being sent to Gujerat for a lifetime. It is only for a short while, Cha-cha, and when it is over I will surely be permitted to return to Mardan; and then you shall take as much leave as you wish—or retire, if you must."

Mahdoo sniffed, and went away to see to the bestowal of his own baggage, muttering to himself and looking unconvinced.

The train was only half-full that night, and Ash had been relieved to find himself the only occupant of a four-berth compartment, and thereby freed from the obligation of making conversation. But as the wheels began to turn and the lights and tumult of the railway station slid slowly past the carriage windows, giving place to darkness, he would have been grateful for a companion, for now that he was alone and idle, the optimism that had sustained him during the past two days suddenly left him, and he was no longer so certain that he would only be required to spend a year or eighteen months in Gujerat. Supposing it was two years—or three . . . or four? Supposing the Guides were to decide that on consideration they were not prepared to take him back at all?—ever!

The train rattled and jolted, and the oil lamp that swayed to every jolt stank abominably and filled the closed carriage with the stench of hot kerosene. Ash rose and turned it out, and lying back in the clamorous darkness, wondered how long it would be before he saw the Khyber again—and had the uncomfortable fancy that he could hear a reply in the voice of the clattering

627

wheels—a harsh, mocking voice that repeated with maddening insistence, "Never again! Never again! Never again . . ."

The train journey to Bombay seemed far longer than he remembered it to have been on the last occasion that he had come that way, over five years ago. He had been travelling in the opposite direction then, and in the company of Belinda and her mother and the unfortunate George. Five years . . . Was it really only five years? It felt more like twelve—or twenty.

The railways were supposed to have made great strides since then, but Ash could see very little difference. Admittedly, an average speed of fifteen miles an hour was an improvement, but the carriages were just as dusty and uncomfortable, the stops as frequent, and there being still no through-train to Bombay, passengers were compelled to change trains as often as before. As for his carriage companions (for he had not been left in sole possession for long) they could hardly have been less enlivening. But at Bombay, where the mail-train stopped and Ash and his servants and baggage transferred into another one bound for Baroda and Ahmadabad, his luck changed. He found himself sharing a two-berth carriage with a small and inoffensive-looking gentleman whose placid manner and mild blue eyes were belied by red whiskers and a cauliflower-ear, and who introduced himself, in a voice as mild as his eyes, as Bert Stiggins, late of Her Majesty's Navy and now Captain and owner of a small coastal trading ship, the *Morala*, docked at Porbandar on the west coast of Gujerat.

The mildness, however, proved to be deceptive; for just as the train was due to leave, two late arrivals pushed their way into the carriage, asserting loudly that they had reserved it for their own use and that Ash and Mr. Stiggins were occupying it illegally. The interlopers were both members of a well-known trading concern, and they had obviously dined far too well before setting out for the station, since they seemed incapable of understanding that the number of the carriage they had reserved did not tally with the one they were attempting to occupy. Either that or they were spoiling for a fight, and if a brawl was what they desired, Ash was more than willing to accommodate them. But he was forestalled.

Mr. Stiggins, who had been sitting peacefully on his

berth while Ash and the guard attempted to use reason, rose to his feet as one of the intruders kicked the guard's legs from under him, toppling him backwards on to the platform outside, while the other aimed a wild punch at Ash, who had leapt to the guard's assistance.

"You leave this to me, sonny," advised Mr. Stiggins soothingly, and put Ash aside without apparent effort.

Ten seconds later both intruders were lying flat on their backs on the platform, wondering dazedly what had hit them, while Mr. Stiggins tossed their belongings after them, apologized on their behalf to the ruffled guard, shut and fastened the carriage door and returned placidly to his seat.

"Well I'll be damned!" gasped Ash, unable to believe his eyes. "How on earth did you do that?"

Mr. Stiggins, who was not even out of breath, looked faintly embarrassed and confessed to having learnt his fighting in the Navy and "brushed up on it" in bars and other places—notably in Japan. "Them Japs is up to all sorts o' tricks; and very useful I've found 'em," said Mr. Stiggins. "They lets the other bloke do all the work and knock 'imself out, so's ter speak. Simple, if you knows the way of it."

He blew gently on the cracked skin of a knuckle, and glancing out of the window at the still recumbent gladiators, remarked in a tone of concern that "if them pore young fellers didn't look slippy" they were going to miss the train, as no one among the gaping crowd of bystanders seemed to be interested in carrying them to their carriage. "Let's 'ope it'll be a lesson to them both to go easy on the likker in future. As the Good Book says, 'wine is a mocker, strong drink is ragin'.'"

"You are a teetotaller, Mr. Stiggins?" inquired Ash, regarding his small companion with considerable awe.

"Cap'n Stiggins," corrected that gentleman mildly. "No, I likes a nip now an' then, but I don't 'old with wallowin' in it. Moderation in all things is me motto. One swaller too many, an' there y'are takin' on all comers an' like as not endin' up in the clink. Or, as it may be, missin' yore train like them pore young drunks are adoin' this very minute . . . there, wot did I tell yer?"

The guard, taking his revenge, had blown the whistle, and the train pulled out of Bombay Central Station a mere ten minutes late, leaving behind two would-be passengers who sat holding their heads and groaning amid scattered hand luggage and grinning coolies.

Ash learned a good deal about the little Captain during the remaining days of the journey, and his admiration for the Captain's fighting powers was soon equalled by his respect for the man himself. Herbert Stiggins, nicknamed "Red" for reasons not wholly confined to the colour of his hair (he was known up and down the coast as the *"Lal-lerai-wallah,"* the "Red fighting-fellow"), had parted company with the Navy almost half a century ago while still in his teens, and was at present engaged in the coastal trade, plying mainly between Sind and Gujerat. The *Morala* had recently been damaged in a collision with a dhow running without lights, and her owner explained to Ash that he had been in Bombay to see a lawyer about a claim for damages, and was on his way back.

His conversation was as salty and invigorating as the sea and interlarded with frequent quotations from the Bible and the Book of Common Prayer—the only printed works apart from manuals on sailing and navigation that he had ever read—and altogether he proved such an entertaining companion that by the time the train at last pulled into Ahmadabad, the two had become the best of friends.

35

Ahmadabad, the noble city that Sultan Ahmad Shah built in the first half of the fifteenth century, retained few traces of its legendary beauty and splendour. It was set in flat, featureless surroundings near the banks of the Sabarmati River, and the fertile land was as different from the harsh, lion-coloured Border country as the sowars of Roper's Horse were different, both in appearance and temperament, from the men of the Frontier Force regiments; the Gujeratis being by nature a peace-loving folk whose best-known proverb is "Make friends with your enemy."

Their senior officers struck Ash as being surprisingly old and staid, and far more set in their ways than those in his own Regiment; while as for their Commanding Officer, Colonel Pomfret, he might have been Rip Van Winkle in person, complete with ragged white beard and a set of ideas that were at least fifty years out of date.

The cantonment, however, differed little from the scores of similar cantonments scattered across the length and breadth of India: an ancient fort, a dusty sun-baked parade ground, barracks and cavalry lines, a small bazaar and a few European shops and a number of officers' bungalows standing in tree-shaded compounds where parakeets, doves and crows roosted among the branches and little striped squirrels scuffled among the tree roots.

Life there followed a familiar pattern of reveille, stables, musketry and office work, but on the social side Ash made a pleasant discovery: the presence of an old acquaintance from the Peshawar days—no other than Mrs. Viccary, whose husband had recently been transferred to Gujerat. The pleasure had been mutual, and Edith Viccary's bungalow soon became a second home to him since she was, as ever, an interested and sympathetic listener, and as the last time he had seen her was prior to Belinda's defection and his own disappearance over the Border into Afghanistan, there was much that he had to tell her.

As far as his work was concerned, he found himself at a grave disadvantage in the matter of language. Once, long ago, he had learned Gujerati from a member of his father's camp; but that was too far back for him to remember it, so now he must start again from the beginning, and like any newcomer, study hard to master it. The fact that he had spoken it as a child may possibly have helped him to make better progress than he would otherwise have done—certainly his fellow officers, unaware of his background (though the nickname of "Pandy" had followed him), were astonished at the speed with which he picked it up, though their Colonel, who thirty years ago had met Professor Hilary Pelham-Martyn and subsequently read at least one volume of the Professor's monumental work *The Languages and Dialects of the Indian Sub-Continent*, did not think it strange that the son should have inherited his

631

father's linguistic talents. He could only hope that the young man had not also inherited his parent's unorthodox views.

But Ash's behaviour during the first few months of his attachment gave no cause for alarm. He performed his duties in a perfectly satisfactory manner, though without over-much enthusiasm, and was voted a "dull dog" by the junior officers because he showed even less for cards and convivial evenings in the mess. Though they agreed that this could well be due to the heat, for the hot-weather temperatures were apt to cast a damper on the liveliest of spirits, and once the cold season came round he might prove more gregarious.

In this respect, however, the arrival of the cold weather had made no difference, except that his prowess on the polo field was sufficiently outstanding to permit allowances to be made for his lack of sociability and the fact that he continued to make no effort to take part in the amusements of the station, but whenever possible refused invitations to attend card-parties, picnics and paper-chases, or to act in amateur theatricals.

The ladies of the station, who had begun by taking considerable interest in the newcomer, ended by agreeing with the junior officers that he was either deplorably dull or insufferably conceited—the verdict depending on age and temperament—and in either case, no asset to station society; an opinion that had been reinforced by his shameless conduct in inviting a vulgar individual, apparently the skipper of a cargo-boat, to dine with him at the English Club (Red Stiggins had been on a brief business trip to Ahmadabad and had encountered Ash by chance in the city).

This episode had put an end to any further attempts to entice or dragoon Ash into attending purely social functions, and thereafter he had been left to go his own way and do what he pleased with his spare time, which suited him very well. He spent a large part of the latter in studying, and much of the rest exploring the countryside beyond the city, where the ground was littered with the relics of a great past, now overgrown by creepers and almost forgotten: old tombs and the ruins of temples and water tanks, built of stone that had been quarried in hills many miles to the north.

The great peninsula of Gujerat was for the most part

flat and without scenic interest, and because of its abundant rainfall, a lush and fertile land, green with crops, banana groves, mango, orange and lemon trees, palms and cotton. It was a country very dissimilar to the Rajputana that Ash remembered so vividly, yet the low hills that bordered it to the north-east marked the frontiers of the Country of the Kings, and on the far side of them—barely more than a hundred miles as the crow flies—lay Bhithor. Bhithor and Juli . . .

He tried not to think of that, but it was difficult not to do so during the slow, furnace-like months of the hot weather, when the day's work must begin at first-light if it was to be done before the temperatures reached a point that made any form of physical or mental activity almost impossible, and the hours between mid-morning and late afternoon were spent indoors with the shutters closed against the heat and the glare, with nothing to do but keep still—and if possible, sleep.

The majority of citizens, and all the Europeans, seemed to find no difficulty in doing one or the other, but to Ash these hot, idle hours were the worst part of the day . . . too much time—aeons of it—in which to think and remember and regret. Therefore he studied Gujerati in an effort to kill two birds with one stone, and mastered the language at a rate that astonished his munshi and won the admiration of the sowars . . . and was still unable to keep from thinking unprofitable thoughts.

He should have grown used to that by now, for he had been plagued in this fashion for over a year. But somehow it had been easier to accept the situation as irrevocable when hundreds of miles separated him from Juli and there was nothing in his surroundings to remind him of her. Besides, Rawalpindi, even after Wally's departure, had provided some palliatives—half-a-dozen good friends, his horses, and an occasional weekend in Murree from where he could see the Kashmir snows . . . Even the feud with Crimpley and his friend Raikes had had its uses. It had at least served as a distraction, and almost without his knowing it, the pain of loss had begun to ease a little and the gnawing sense of restlessness to decrease, until there had actually been times when he had come through an entire day without thinking of Juli at all.

But here in Ahmadabad that was no longer so and sometimes he wondered if space, as measured in miles, could have an effect on thought. Was it because he was now so much nearer to her in terms of distance that the memory of her was again so vivid and so continuously in his mind? From here Bhithor was only three days' journey away . . . four at most . . . If he were to set out now—

"You are not attending, Sahib!" the munshi would reprove him. "Read me that sentence again—remembering what I told you about the tense."

Ash would drag his mind back from the past and fix it on the present; and when the lesson ended, cast about for something else, anything else, to keep him occupied until the worst of the day's heat was over and he could go out and ride. But in October, with the end of the hot weather in sight, the outlook became considerably brighter. The cold season was a time of intense military activity, and now, as though to make up for the unavoidable idleness and lethargy of the past months, camps, manoeuvres and training exercises followed one another at speed, while any spare time was taken up by such energetic pastimes as polo, racing and gymkhanas.

Best of all, Ash acquired two things that did more than all the rest to take his mind off his personal problems and compensate him for being banished from the Frontier, and the Guides. A friend, Sarjevan Desai, the son of a local landowner. And a horse named Dagobaz.

Sarjevan, known to his intimates as Sarji, was a great-nephew of the Risaldar-Major—a fierce, wise, grey-whiskered warrior who was by now something of a legend in Roper's Horse, for he had served with it since its inception some forty years ago, joining it as a lad of fifteen in the days when the land was ruled by the East India Company.

The Risaldar-Major was a martinet and a notable horseman, and he appeared to be related to most of the local aristocracy, among them Sarjevan's late father, who had been the son of one of his many sisters. Sarji himself was no military man. He had inherited a large estate, and with it his father's passion for horses, which he bred more for his own pleasure than for profit, refusing to sell to anyone he did not personally know and like.

His great-uncle, having taken a favourable view of the newly joined British officer, had introduced Sarji to Lieutenant Pelham-Martyn with instructions to see that the Sahib was fitted out with mounts that would not disgrace the good name of the Regiment—or of Gujerat. And fortunately for Ash, the two had taken to each other. They were the same age and their mutual love of horses had cemented an immediate liking that had soon become friendship, with the result that Ash had acquired, for a not unreasonable figure, a stable that was the envy of his fellow officers and that included a pedigree black stallion of Arab descent: Dagobaz, "The Trickster."

Since the days when he had been a horse-boy in the stables of Duni Chand of Gulkote, Ash had seen and ridden and later on owned many horses. But never yet had he seen anything to equal this one for beauty, mettle and speed. Even Baj Raj, now in Wally's care in Mardan, paled into insignificance by contrast. Dagobaz was almost three years old when he came into Ash's possession, and at first Sarji had been reluctant to sell him, not because of his spectacular looks and promise, but because the stallion had not been named Dagobaz for nothing. He might have the appearance of perfection, but his character did not match his looks; he possessed a fiery and uncertain temper, together with a dislike of being ridden that no amount of patient training had so far been able to overcome.

"I do not say that he is vicious," said Sarji, "or that he cannot be mounted. He can. But unlike the others he has still not outgrown his hatred for the feel of a man upon his back. This you can sense in your bones when you ride him, and it does not make for comfort. He has a will of his own, that horse—a will of iron—and by now even the best of my syces are ready to admit defeat. They say he has a thousand tricks whereby he may rid himself of a rider, and that when one thinks one has learned them all, lo! he has a new one—and there one is again, sprawling in the dust or among the thorn-scrub and faced with another walk home. You are taken in by his beauty; but if you buy him—and I would sell him to no one else—you may well live to regret it. Do not say I have not warned you!"

But Ash had only laughed and bought the black horse for a price that in view of its looks and its pedigree was ridiculous: and never had cause to regret it. Sarji had always been good with horses and was an excellent rider, but being a rich man's son he had not gained his experience the hard way, as Ash had done, by working with them as a child in the lowly capacity of horse-boy.

Ash had made no attempt to ride Dagobaz for at least ten days, but during that time he spent every moment he could spare in the stable or in the enclosed field adjoining it, handling the horse, grooming him, feeding him raw carrots and lumps of *gur* (the crude brown stuff that is extracted from sugar-cane) and talking to him by the hour together. Dagobaz, at first suspicious, soon grew used to him and presently began to make a few tentative overtures of his own until eventually, on hearing Ash's low whistle, he would prick up his ears and answer to it with a soft whinnying, and trot over to greet him.

Rapport having been established, the rest had been comparatively easy: though Ash had suffered a few reverses and had on one occasion found himself faced with a five-mile walk back to the cantonments. Yet in the end even Sarji had to admit that "The Trickster" had been wrongly named and should now be re-titled "The Saint." But Ash had retained the old name, for in some ways it was still applicable. Dagobaz had accepted him as a friend and his master, but showed plainly that he was a "one-man" horse and that his affection and obedience were reserved for Ash alone. No one else could ride him with impunity, not even his syce, Kulu Ram; though he would grudgingly permit that individual to exercise him on the rare occasions when Ash was unable to do so—giving as much trouble as possible in the process, so that Kulu Ram was driven to declare that he was no horse but a devil in disguise. But with Ash on his back, he behaved like an angel.

He was a big horse by Arab standards, and the length of his stride was phenomenal. Ash discovered that he could, when pressed, out-distance anything else on four legs, including Sarji's pet hunting cheetahs—though the cheetah is reputed to be the swiftest of all animals and can easily run down a buck. He had, in addition, a mouth of velvet, the manners of a prince, and a truly royal temper that discouraged strangers—and syces—from taking liberties with him. But as Sarji had truly said, there was no vice in him, and once Ash had succeeded in winning his heart, he proved to be as docile and affectionate as a kit-

636

ten and as intelligent as a well-trained gun-dog. So much so, that within two months of his purchase, and notwithstanding his known foibles, Ash had received at least half-a-dozen offers for him, all of them greatly in excess of the sum that he himself had paid—and all of them refused.

There was not, Ash asserted, enough gold in all India to buy Dagobaz. In proof of which he trained the stallion to jump, entered him in a local cross-country race and won it by over fifteen lengths (to the dismay of the bookmakers, who knowing that the horse had never raced before had rashly offered long odds), and for the best part of a month rode him on parade in place of the more experienced charger that he had acquired on his arrival in the station. Dagobaz, though unfamiliar with the drill, had taken it in his stride, and apart from one attempt to keep ahead of the line, had behaved as if he had been trained to it from the beginning.

"There's nothing he can't do!" declared Ash, boasting of his performance to Sarji. "That horse is human. And a damn' sight cleverer than most humans, at that. I swear he understands every word I say. He uses his head, too. He'd make a wonderful polo-pony, except that I don't need another, so I'd rather keep him just to ride and . . . Did you see the way he took that irrigation channel with the well on the near side of it? Flew it like a bird. By God, he should have been called Pegasus. The Colonel says I can race him in Bombay next cold weather—that is if I'm still here."

"You expect to go before then?" asked Sarji.

"Not expect," corrected Ash wryly. "Only hope. Didn't they tell you I was serving a sentence? I'm on attachment; and as I shall have been here a year in March, there's just a chance that the powers in Rawalpindi may relent and send word that I may go back to my own *rissala*."

"What powers are those?" inquired Sarji, interested.

"Gods," said Ash flippantly. "Tin gods that say unto one 'go' and he goeth, and to another 'come' and he cometh. I received the first order and perforce obeyed: now I hope for the second."

"So?" Sarji was puzzled but polite. "And what of Dagobaz? Will you take him with you when you go?"

"Of course. You don't think I'd part with him, do you? If I couldn't take him any other way, I'd ride him

637

back. But if I'm to be left here to rot for another year, I mean to take him down to Bombay for the races, and the entire Regiment are planning to put their shirts on him."

"Shirts?"

"Money. They are going to bet every rupee they can lay hands on."

"Ah! I too. I shall go to Bombay with you and I shall back you with a *lakh* of rupees for your first race, and make a fortune!"

"We all will. You and I and your great-uncle the Risaldar-Sahib, and every man in the Regiment. And afterwards Dagobaz will have a silver cup as big as a bucket to drink out of."

Ash's opinion of the black horse was shared by many; though not by Mahdoo, who refused to see anything admirable in the animal and openly regretted its purchase.

"I believe that you care more for that Child of the Pit than for anyone else," complained Mahdoo crossly as Ash, returning at dusk after an evening ride, fed Dagobaz with sugar before sending him back to the stables. "It is not fitting to give one's heart to an animal, who has no soul."

"Yet Allah made horses for our use," retorted Ash, laughing. "Is it not written in the Koran, in the Sura of the War-Steeds . . . *'By the snorting of war-steeds which strike fire with their hooves as they gallop to the raid at dawn, and with a trail of dust split the foe in two: man is ungrateful to his Lord! To this he himself shall bear witness.'* Would you have me ungrateful for such gifts as these, Cha-cha?"

"I would have you spend less time talking to a brute-beast, and more on those who have your welfare at heart. Such as Hamilton-Sahib, to whom, as I know well, you have sent only one short letter since the day that you acquired that son of perdition."

Ash started and had the grace to look guilty: "Have I not? I did not realize . . . I will write to him now, tonight."

"First read what he has to say. This came by the morning's dâk, but it seems that you were in too great a hurry to glance at your letters before you went off to that creature's stable. This thick one is, I think, from Hamilton-Sahib; and we also, Gul Baz and I, would like news of him and of our friends in Mardan."

He proffered a brass salver bearing half-a-dozen letters, and Ash snatched up the bulkiest, and tearing open the envelope, carried it into the lamp-lit bungalow to read it:

"The cavalry have been having a damned dull time of it lately," wrote Wally, "but the infantry, lucky devils, have been having no end of larks. I can't remember if I told you about that trouble with the Jowaki Afridis over the Government suddenly deciding to stop bribing them (sorry, I believe I should have said 'paying them an allowance.' *Wah illah!*) in return for keeping open the road through the Kohat Pass, and offering them an equivalent sum for safeguarding the Khushalgarh road and telegraph line.

"They didn't take to the idea at all, and after a bit they began to make their displeasure felt by plundering and burning villages and attacking escorts and police stations. Then they burned down a bridge on the Khushalgarh road and that seems to have got the Powers-that-Be on the raw—a sort of last straw on their august shoulders. They decided that the Jowaki jokers must be given a sharp rap over the knuckles, and, I regret to say, that was just about all it was. A quick dash into Jowaki territory by three columns, one of them ours—201 bayonets with Campbell in command and Stuart, Hammond, Wigram and Fred in support—burn a village or two and nip back again. *Bus!* (enough). The columns were under arms in vile heat for twenty hours, marched nearly thirty miles and had eleven casualties—our fellows had two men wounded. Short and sweet, and apparently a complete waste of everyone's time, for the Jowakis remain noticeably unimpressed and are still cutting-up with unabated vigour.

"I suppose this means that we shall be having another go at them before long. If so, I hope the Big-Wigs let the cavalry get into the act. I'd like to see a bit of action for a change. Zarin sends his salaams and asks me to tell you that he is afraid his father was right. He says that you will know what he means, and I hope you do because I don't. Let us have some news of you. You haven't answered my last letter yet and it's months since I heard from you. But as no news is good news, I presume you are alive and enjoying yourself. My salaams to Mahdoo and Gul Baz . . ."

639

"When you write, send ours to him," said Mahdoo, and added sourly: "And ask him if he has need of another servant: an old man who was once a good cook."

The other servants had settled down contentedly enough, for as there was no shortage of accommodation in the Ahmadabad cantonment, Ash had a whole bungalow to himself with a large compound and plenty of servants' quarters: a luxury seldom enjoyed by a junior officer in any military station. Kulu Ram had been pleased to approve of the stables, and Gul Baz, who had left his wife and family in Hoti Mardan, had made himself comfortable by installing a local woman in the hut behind his quarters —a silent and retiring creature who kept herself to herself, cooked and washed and generally attended to the wants of her temporary protector.

Mahdoo, however, was too old for such arrangements; and he hated everything about Gujerat with the possible exception of Ahmadabad's great mosque, where the founder of the city, Sultan Ahmad Shah, lies buried. For the rest, he detested the heat and the humidity, the lush, dripping greenery in the compound, and the rain clouds that during the monsoon had driven in on a wind that smelled of the sea, to empty their contents on the roofs and roads and parade ground of the cantonment until the whole area was awash and it seemed, at times, as though the bungalows were islands floating in a waste of water. The food did not agree with him, and he distrusted the local people, whose language he did not understand and whose ways were not his.

"He is too old to change," said Gul Baz, excusing Mahdoo's crotchetiness. "He misses the scents and sounds of the north, and the food and talk and customs of his own people."

"As you do," said Ash, and added under his breath: "and I also."

"True, Sahib. But then if God is merciful you and I will have many more years to live, and therefore if we spend one or two in this place, what matter? But with Mahdoo-ji it is different, for he knows that for him the years are few."

"I should not have brought him here," said Ash remorsefully. "Yet how could I help it, when he refused to be left behind? I would send him on leave at once if I thought he would stay in his own home until we go north again, but I know he would not, so if we are to spend another hot season in this place it would be better for him to stay here now while it is cool, and leave for the north in the first half of February. That way he will miss the months of greatest heat and the worst of the monsoon; and if we are still here when it is over, I may even be able to send to tell him that he need wait only a little longer and meet us in Mardan. Because by that time I must surely know my fate."

In this last respect, Ash was to be proved right: though in a way that he had not foreseen.

Throughout that cold-weather season, whenever the Regiment was not in camp or engaged in manoeuvres, Ash would rise with the dawn in order to take Dagobaz out for an early-morning gallop. And on most evenings he would ride out alone or with Sarji to explore the countryside, returning to his bungalow only after dusk had fallen.

There was much to be seen, for Gujerat is not only drenched in history, but is the legendary scene of the chief exploits and death of the god Khrishna, the Indian Apollo. Every hill and stream has its link with some mythological happening, and the land is strewn with the ruins of tombs and temples so ancient that the names of those who built them have long been forgotten. Among the memorials to the dead—the magnificent, pillared domes of the great and the sculptured slabs of humbler men—one curious motif attracted Ash's attention, for it appeared over and over again. A woman's arm, ornamented with intricately carved bracelets and armbands.

"That?" said Sarji in answer to a question. "Oh, it commemorates a suttee. A widow who burned herself on her husband's funeral pyre. It is a very old custom, one that your Government has forbidden—and rightly. I think. Though there are still those who would not agree with me. Yet I remember my grandfather, who was a learned and enlightened man, telling me that many thinkers, himself among them, believe that this practice arose through the error of a scribe when the laws were first put down in writing, many centuries ago. The original law, they say, laid down that when a man dies his body must be given to the fire and his widow must afterwards 'go within the house'—in other words, live in seclusion for the remainder of her life—but that a scribe, writing this down long after,

641

left out the last two words by mistake, so that it came to be believed that 'go within' meant to go within the fire. Perhaps that is true; and if so it is as well that the Raj has given orders that the practice must cease, for to be burned alive is a cruel death, though many thousands upon thousands of our women have not flinched from it, but considered it an honour."

"And many more have been forced to endure it against their will, if even half the tales one hears are true," said Ash grimly.

Sarji shrugged. "Maybe. But then their lives would have been a burden to them had they lived, so perhaps they were better off dead; and you must not forget that she who becomes suttee becomes holy. Her name is honoured and her very ashes are venerated—look there." He pointed with his riding whip to where a vivid splash of colour glowed bright against the dark stone and the tangle of greenery.

Someone had draped a garland of fresh marigolds over one of the carved weather-worn arms that bore silent witness to the hideous death of a wife who had dutifully "completed a life of uninterrupted conjugal devotedness by the act of *saha-gamana,*" and accompanied her husband's corpse into the flames. The stone was half hidden by grass and creepers, but someone—another woman, surely?—had decked it with flowers, and though the afternoon was windless and very warm, Ash shivered, and said violently: "Well if we have done nothing else, at least we can mark up one thing to our credit—that we put a stop to *that* particular horror."

Sarji shrugged again; which might have meant anything—or nothing—and he began to talk of other matters as they turned their horses and made for the open country.

The two went riding together at least once or twice a week, and often at weekends or holidays they would go on longer trips together, staying away for a night or two, and choosing a route at random. Sometimes to Patri and the shallow waters of the Rann of Kutch, where the air smells of salt and seaweed and the rotting fish-heads that the boatmen fling out on the shore for the gulls to dispose of. Sometimes east towards Baroda, the capital city of His Highness Siraji Rao, the Gaekwar, or south, to the Gulf of Cambay where the great rollers drive in from the Arabian Sea between those two outposts of the Portuguese

Empire, Diu Island and Damman—and where, on several occasions, they found the cargo-boat *Morala* at anchor, and went on board to collogue with her owner, Captain Red Stiggins. But only when he was alone did Ash ride northward in the direction of the distant blue ranges that lay between Gujerat and Rajputana.

Sarji was a cheerful and entertaining companion, but when Ash chose to ride towards the hills he did not want companionship, for on these occasions he would make for a lonely, ruin-crowned knoll overlooking the river below Bijapur from where he would gaze at the jagged outline of those ancient hills, and know that Juli had only to look out of a window of the Rung Mahal to see them too . . .

They looked so easy to cross: a low and insubstantial barrier, dusty-gold in the evening light or aquamarine in the shimmering heat-haze of the early afternoon. Yet he had learned that there were few paths through them; and even fewer passes where it was possible for a man to cross on foot, let alone on horseback. The hazards of those mountain passes, and the trackless miles of tiger-jungle that clothed the lower slopes, discouraged would-be travellers to Rajputana from attempting short cuts, and led the majority to turn westward and make a detour by way of Palanpur, or else go south to Bombay, and travel by rail or road through the *ghats*. But as Ash could see no prospect of his ever being able to enter Rajputana again, the difficulty or otherwise of finding a way through those hills was unimportant. Even if there had been a paved highway between Ahmadabad and Bhithor, it would have made no difference, because the Country of the Kings was forbidden territory, and like Moses, he could gaze at the promised land but he must not enter it.

Ash would sit on the knoll for hours, absorbed and motionless—so still that the birds and squirrels and even the shy lizards would often stray within reach of his hand, or a butterfly come to rest on his head. Only when Dagobaz—turned loose to crop among the ruins—became impatient and thrust an anxious nose into his breast, would he awake as though from a deep sleep, and coming stiffly to his feet, mount and ride back across the flat lands to Ahmadabad and the bungalow in cantonments.

On these days he would invariably find Mahdoo waiting for him, squatting unobtrusively in a corner of the verandah from where he could see the front gate while at the same time keeping a watchful eye upon the kitchen and the servants' quarters in case his assistant, young Kadera, should neglect his duties.

Mahdoo was not happy. He was feeling the weight of his years and he was also deeply uneasy on Ash's account. It was not that he had any idea where Ash went, or what he had been doing on these particular occasions. But though his knowledge of geography was slight, his knowledge of Ash was extensive, and once having learned that the borders of Rajputana lay less than a day's ride to the north, his intuition had supplied an answer that alarmed him. Bhithor was not so far beyond that border.

Their proximity to the Rana's kingdom worried Mahdoo a great deal, for though he had never heard so much as a whisper involving Anjuli-Bai, he had realized long ago that something far more serious than the Rana's attempts at blackmail and treachery had occurred there. Something deeply personal to Ash-Sahib that had struck at his happiness and peace of mind, and destroyed both.

Mahdoo was no fool. He was, on the contrary, a shrewd old man who had known and loved Ash for many years, and that combination of shrewdness, knowledge and affection had enabled him to make a fairly accurate guess at the cause of his child's trouble; though he hoped very much that he was mistaken, for if he were not, then the situation was not merely tragic, but profoundly shocking. Despite his many years of service with the Sahib-log and his long sojourn in their country, Mahdoo still held firmly to the opinion that all decent women (particularly young and beautiful ones) should be kept in strict purdah —European ones excepted of course, as their customs were different and they could hardly be blamed for going about unveiled when their men-folk were foolish enough to permit such immodest behaviour.

The ones he had blamed were those who had permitted the Rajkumaries and their women to meet and talk so freely and frequently with Ash-Sahib, who had naturally (or so Mahdoo surmised) ended by falling in love with one of them, which was a terrible thing to have happened. But at least it was over and done with, and before long he would forget this woman as he had forgotten the other one—that yellow-haired miss-sahib from Peshawar. He could hardly fail to do so, thought Mahdoo, when one considered the vast distance that separated Rawalpindi from Bhithor and the unlikelihood of his ever having occasion to enter Rajputana again.

Yet little more than a year later, by some evil chance he was sent south once more—and to Ahmadabad, of all places, so that here they were, once again within range of that sinister, medieval little state from which Mahdoo, for his part, had been so profoundly thankful to escape. Worse still, his child was plainly unhappy and given to strange moods, while he himself was filled with foreboding. Surely Ash-Sahib would not be so foolish as to cross into Rajputana and attempt to enter Bhithor again? Or would he? . . . young men in love were capable of any folly, yet if he were to venture once more into the Rana's territory, this time alone, without the backing of armed men and the authority (or even the permission) of the Government, he might not leave it again alive.

In Mahdoo's opinion, the Rana was not a man to forgive anyone who had got the better of him, let alone someone who had threatened him in the presence of his councillors and courtiers, and nothing would be likely to please him more than to learn that his adversary had returned secretly (and presumably in disguise) without the knowledge or consent of anyone in authority; for then if the Sahib were simply to disappear and never be heard of again, how could anyone bring accusations against the state? It would merely be said that he must have lost his way among the hills and died of thirst or met with an accident, and who would be able to prove that he had so much as set foot in Bhithor, or even intended to do so?

Mahdoo had spent sleepless nights worrying over the possibilities, and though he had never served in any but a bachelor's establishment and had always taken a poor view of memsahibs and their ways, he now began to hope against hope that his child would meet some beautiful young miss-sahib among the British community in Ahmadabad, who would make him forget the unknown girl from Karidkote who had caused him so much sorrow.

But Ash continued to ride out alone and in the direction of the hills at least one day out of every seven, and appeared to prefer Sarji's society, or the Viccarys', to that of any of the available miss-sahibs in the station. Wherefore Mahdoo continued to worry over the possible consequences of those solitary rides and to fear the worst, and when, towards the end of January, Ash told him that he was to take long leave and go to his own village for the duration of the hot weather, the old man had been indignant.

"What?—and leave you to the care of young Kadera, who without my supervision could easily give you food that would upset your stomach? Never! Besides, if I were not here there would be no one to see that you did not commit any number of follies. No, no, child. I will stay."

"To hear you talk, Cha-cha-ji," retorted Ash, torn between amusement and irritation, "anyone would think that I was a feeble-minded child."

"And they would not be altogether wrong, *mera beta*,"* returned Mahdoo tartly, "for there are times when you behave as one."

"Do I so? Yet this is not the first time you have taken leave and left me to manage without you, and you never raised a *gurrh-burrh* about it before."

"Maybe not. But you were in the Punjab then, and among your own kind, not here in Gujerat, which is neither your country nor mine. Besides, I know what I know, and I do not trust you to keep out of trouble when my back is turned."

But Ash only laughed and said: "Uncle, if I give you my solemn oath that I will behave as soberly and circumspectly as a virtuous grandmother until you return, will you go? It need only be for a few months; and if before then my luck has changed and I am recalled to Mardan, you can meet me there instead. You know very well that you are in need of a rest and will be all the better for a month or two in the good air of the hills, with your family to cook and care for you and wait on you hand and foot. You need feeding up on good Punjabi food, and bracing with the clean winds of the mountains, after all these warm, heavy airs. *Hai mai*, I wish I could go with you."

"I too," said Mahdoo fervently. But he had raised no further objections, for he too hoped that Ash's period of exile would soon be over, and that any time now he would be recalled to his own Regiment. With Hamilton-Sahib and Battye-Sahib to plead his cause and press for his return, that day could surely not be too far off, and if

*my son

646

so, he, Mahdoo, might never have to return to this pestilential place.

He had left on the tenth of February, accompanied by one of the syces whose home was near Rawalpindi, and Ash had seen him off at the railway station and had stayed on the crowded platform watching the train chug slowly away, a prey to conflicting emotions. He was sorry to see the old man go, and he would miss the pawky advice and the nightly talks that were spiced with gossip and punctuated by the familiar bubble of the hookah. On the other hand there was no denying that it was in some ways a relief to be rid of that anxious surveillance for a while. Mahdoo obviously knew or suspected too much, and was beginning to show it too clearly for comfort. A temporary separation would do them both good, and there was no doubt that the old man's health and spirits had suffered from the move to Gujerat and his dislike for the country and its people. All the same . . .

Ash watched the train disappearing in the distance, and long after the last smudge of smoke had thinned and vanished he stood staring after it, remembering the first time he had seen Mahdoo. Mahdoo and Ala Yar and Colonel Anderson, who had taken him under their collective wing and had been good to him when he was a bewildered boy speaking, feeling and thinking of himself as Ashok, and unable to credit that he was in reality an *Angrezi* with a name that he could not even pronounce; or that he was being shipped off to an unknown land to be turned into a "Sahib" by strangers who, so he was told, were his father's people.

Remembering that day, the faces and forms of those three men were all at once as clear in his mind's eye as though they were there in the flesh and standing with him on the crowded platform: Colonel Anderson and Ala Yar, who were both dead, and Mahdoo, who was still very much alive and whom he had just seen on to the train and waved goodbye to as the Bombay-and-Baroda Mail drew out of the station. Yet there was something wrong with their faces—and suddenly he realized what it was. He was not seeing Mahdoo as he was now—grey and wrinkled and shrunk to half his former size—but as he had been then, when Colonel Anderson and Ala Yar were alive and all three men had seemed tall and strong and a little larger than life. It was as if Mahdoo had in some way joined

647

them and become part of the past . . . which was, of course, absurd.

Gul Baz, who had accompanied them to the railway station, coughed discreetly to indicate that time was passing, and Ash awoke from his reverie, and turning away, walked quickly back along the platform and out into the yard to where a tonga waited to take them back to the bungalow.

BOOK SIX

Juli

36

Perhaps it was just as well for Mahdoo that he left when he did, for his anxiety on Ash's account would have been considerably increased had he been present two days later, when an unexpected visitor arrived at Ash's bungalow in cantonments.

The Regiment had been out on a training exercise, and Ash had returned an hour after sunset to find a hired tonga standing among the shadows near the gate, and Gul Baz waiting on the verandah steps to inform him that he had a caller. "It is the Hakim from Karidkote," said Gul Baz. "The Rao-Sahib's Hakim, Gobind Dass. He waits within."

It was indeed Gobind. But the sudden spasm of terror that had made Ash's heart miss a beat on hearing his name vanished at the sight of his face. This was no bearer of bad tidings sent by Kaka-ji to break the news that Juli was sick or dying, or dead—or even that her husband was ill-treating her. Gobind looked as spruce and calm and as reassuring as ever, and he explained that he was on his way to Bhithor at the earnest request of Shushila-Rani, who had become worried about her husband's health and had no faith in the Rana's personal physician, an elderly gentleman of seventy-eight whose methods, she asserted, were several hundred years out of date.

"And as the Rani herself is at last with child, and must at such a time be saved any unnecessary anxiety," said Gobind, "my master the Rao-Sahib felt that it was not possible to refuse her request. Wherefore you see me now on my way to Bhithor. Though I do not know what good I can do—or will be permitted to do, since I cannot believe that the Rana's own hakims will be pleased at a stranger being called in to treat him."

"Is he seriously ill, then?" asked Ash, with a flicker of hope.

Gobind shrugged and spread out his hands in an expressive gesture. "Who can say? You know how it is with Shushila-Rani. She is one who will always make the most of every small ache or twinge of discomfort, and it is more than likely that she is doing so now. Nevertheless, I have been sent to see what I can do, and to remain in Bhithor for as long as I am needed."

Accompanied only by a single servant, a plump, foolish-faced yokel named Manilal, Gobind had travelled to Bombay, from where he had come by way of Baroda and Ahmadabad: "For the Rao-Sahib, knowing that you have been sent here, insisted that I should come by this way, saying that his nieces the Ranis would be pleased to have news of you, and that you in turn would wish to hear news of your friends in Karidkote. See, here are letters: the Rao-Sahib does not trust the public dâk, and so he entrusted them to me, giving strict orders that I was to put them into your own hand and no other . . . as I have now done."

There were three letters, for in addition to Kaka-ji, Jhoti and Mulraj had also written; though only briefly, as Gobind, they said, would give him all the news. Neither of their letters contained anything that could not have been read aloud to anyone—Jhoti's being largely concerned with sport and horses, and ending with a frivolous description of the British Resident (whom he seemed to have taken in dislike on the trivial grounds that the man wore pince-nez and looked at him over them) while Mulraj's merely conveyed good wishes and the hope that Ash would see his way to visiting them on his next leave.

Kaka-ji's letter on the other hand was of considerable interest. Reading it, Ash understood why it had been

650

necessary to send it by the hand of someone as trustworthy as Gobind instead of through the public post, and also why it had been essential to send Gobind to Bhithor by way of Ahmadabad.

The first part of the letter merely covered in more detail the ground that Gobind had already sketched in outline: Shushila's urgent plea for a doctor that she could trust, and the necessity of complying with it because of her condition. This was followed by a request that Ash would assist Gobind in the matter of horses and a guide and anything else that might be necessary to ensure his safe arrival in Bhithor, the money to cover all expenses being in Gobind's possession.

Having dealt with these matters, Kaka-ji had gone on to confess that he was anxious about his nieces and that it was for this reason, rather than the one he had initially given, that he had agreed at once to send Gobind to Bhithor.

"They have no one there whom they can trust," wrote Kaka-ji, "or that we here can rely upon to send us truthful reports on their well-being, since Shushila cannot write and we have as yet had no word from her half-sister, which is strange. We have reason to believe that the eunuch who writes on their behalf is untrustworthy, for the few letters we receive say nothing except that they are well and happy, yet we have learned that the *dai* Geeta, and no less than two of the waiting-women who accompanied them from Karidkote, all of whom were faithful servants and greatly attached to my nieces, are dead, though no mention of this was made in any letter.

"I doubt very much if we should have learned of it at all had not a trader visiting Bhithor heard the tale and repeated it to another in Ajmer, who in turn told it to a man who by chance has a cousin living here in Karidkote. Thus it came to our ears as no more than a traveller's tale, but the families of the three women heard it, and being greatly disturbed they petitioned Jhoti to inquire of his brother-in-law the Rana if it were true. This he did, and after much delay an answer came back to say that the two waiting-women had died of a fever, while the *dai* had broken her neck falling down a flight of stairs.

"The Rana professed himself astonished to learn that neither the Senior nor the Junior Rani had thought to mention the matter in their letters to their dear brother, and

651

could only suppose that they had not deemed the death of servants to be worthy of being brought to his notice. In which, he the Rana, agreed with them—

"But you and I know," wrote Kaka-ji, "that had they been free to write as they pleased, they would not have failed to mention it. Therefore I am sure in my own mind that what the eunuch writes are the words of the Rana or the Rana's minions, though it may well be that I am over-anxious and that all is indeed well with them. Nevertheless I would feel easier if I had some way of knowing beyond doubt that this was so, and now it seems as though the gods have provided one. The Rana was pleased with Go-bind, who, as you will remember, cured him of boils when his own hakims had failed to do so; and it is certain that he must have been feeling unwell when he permitted Shushila-Bai to ask that Gobind should come with all speed to Bhithor to heal him.

"It is an answer to prayer, as Gobind will be able to learn how it is with Jhoti's sisters, and I have instructed him to devise some method of passing on any news to you, for as you live beyond the borders of Rajasthan, you can send it on in safety to Karidkote. I would not have troubled you with this had I not known that you too would have reason to be concerned over this matter and would wish to satisfy yourself, even as I do, that all is well. If it is not, you will be able to send word to us; and then Jhoti and his advisers will decide on what action they will take."

"—if any," thought Ash grimly. For though the princes still maintained their private armies, "the State Forces," the enormous distance that separated Karidkote from Bhithor was enough to ensure that no military action could be taken by the one against the other, even supposing that the Government of India would have permitted such a thing, which they most certainly would not. Jhoti's only hope would be to lodge a complaint through the proper channels—in this case, the British Resident—from where it would be passed on to the Political Department, who would send to Ajmer, requesting the Agent-to-the-Governor-General to tell the officer in charge of the particular section of Rajputana that included Bhithor to investigate the complaint, and report on it.

Remembering the dilatoriness and disbelief of the Political Officer, and how impossible it had been to make him think ill of the Rana or take any action that might

652

conceivably be questioned by his superiors in Ajmer, Simla and Calcutta, Ash had little hope that anything useful would come of that. Particularly as there would be no question of the Political Officer (or indeed anyone else) being allowed to see or speak to either of the Rana's wives, who of course kept strict purdah. Any attempt to force such an interview would lead to uproar not only in Bhithor, but throughout India, and the most that would be granted—though even that was unlikely—would be an interview with an unseen woman seated on the far side of a curtain and undoubtedly surrounded by a number of people, all of whom would be in the Rana's pay and would keep a check on every word she said.

Under such conditions the truth was unlikely to be spoken; nor would there be any proof that the speaker was in fact one of the Ranis and not some carefully coached Zenana woman. All things considered, thought Ash, it was a thousand pities that Jhoti should have chosen to take some silly boy's *zid* against the Resident in Karidkote . . .

He looked up from the letter in his hand, and meeting Gobind's quiet gaze, said, "Do you know what is written here?"

Gobind nodded. "The Rao-Sahib did me the honour of reading it to me before he sealed it, so that I should realize how necessary it was to guard it with great care and see that it did not fall into the wrong hands."

"Ah," said Ash, and reached for the lamp.

Held above the glass chimney, the two sheets of thick Indian-made paper blackened and curled and then burst into flame, and Ash turned them this way and that, watching them burn until at length the flames neared his fingers and he dropped the smouldering fragments to the floor, and putting his foot on them, ground them to powder with a vicious twist of his heel.

"There. That has removed at least one of the Rao-Sahib's causes for anxiety. As for the rest, his fears may be well founded, but they come too late. Had he torn up the marriage contracts no one would have blamed him. But he did not do so, and now the harm is done, for the laws and customs of the land are on the Rana's side— and so too is the Political-Sahib, as we have cause to know."

"That may be true," agreed Gobind quietly. "But you

653

are less than just to the Rao-Sahib. Had you known the late Maharajah, you would have realized that the Rao-Sahib had no choice but to do as he did, and see that the marriages were performed."

"I know," admitted Ash with a sharp sigh. "I am sorry. I should not have spoken like that. I know very well that in the circumstances he could do nothing else. Besides, it is over, and we cannot alter the past."

"That even the gods cannot do," agreed Gobind soberly. "But it is the Rao-Sahib's hope, and mine also, that you and I, Sahib, may perhaps be able to do a little towards shaping the future."

There had been no more talk that night, for Gobind was very tired. Neither he nor his servant Manilal had ever been on a train before, and the journey having left them dizzy and exhausted, both were still asleep when Ash left to go on parade the following morning. It was not until the day's work was over and afternoon well advanced that he was able to speak to Gobind again, but as he had slept very little during the previous night, he had been able to give a good deal of thought to Kaka-ji's disclosures and—when this became intolerable because of the fears that it aroused in him for Juli's safety—to more mundane matters such as the arrangements that must be made for getting Gobind safely to Bhithor. These he put in hand first thing in the morning, despatching his head syce, Kulu Ram, to choose and bargain for a pair of horses from a local dealer, and sending a message to Sarji, asking if he knew anyone who would act as a guide for two travellers wishing to go to Bhithor and anxious to leave on the following day.

The horses and Sarji's reply had been waiting for him on his return to the bungalow, and both had proved equally satisfactory: Sarji wrote that he was sending his own particular *shikari*, Bukta (a hunter who knew every path, game-track and short-cut through the hills), to guide Ash's friends to Bhithor, while the horses that Kulu Ram had purchased were sturdy and reliable animals, sound in wind and limb and capable, said Kulu Ram, of covering as many *koss* a day as the Hakim-Sahib required of them.

There remained only one other matter to be settled, the most important of all: how to establish some method of communication between Gobind in Bhithor and Ash in Ahmadabad without arousing the suspicions of the Rana.

The two had discussed this for hours, riding side by side along the river bank, ostensibly to try out the newly purchased horses but in reality to ensure against being overheard; and later they had talked together in Ash's bedroom until well after midnight, their voices so low that Gul Baz, who had been stationed on the verandah outside to warn off intruders, was barely able to catch more than a faint murmur of sound.

Time was short and there was much that had to be done. A code of some sort was essential if they were to communicate at all—something simple enough to be memorized and that would arouse no suspicions in the event of a message being intercepted—and when they had worked that out to their satisfaction they had to consider ways and means of getting news out of Bhithor, because if the Rana had anything to hide he would certainly see to it that Gobind was closely watched. That problem, however, would have to be solved by Gobind alone, and then only after he had arrived in Bhithor and was able to assess the situation there and discover how much freedom, if any, he would be allowed. Yet plans must still be made, for even if the majority of them proved on his arrival to be impracticable, one at least might work.

"There is also my servant, Manilal," said Gobind, "who on account of his speech and appearance is taken to be a simpleton: a foolish yokel, incapable of guile—which is far from the truth. I think we may well find a use for him."

By the time the clock struck twelve they had discussed at least a dozen plans, one of which resulted in Gobind setting off at nine o'clock on the following morning in search of a certain European-owned shop in the city, because as he had said, "If the worst comes to the worst I can always say that I must go to Ahmadabad for more drugs with which to treat His Highness. Is there a good *dewai dukan* (medicine shop) in this city? A foreign one, for choice?"

"There is one in the cantonments: Jobbling & Sons, the Chemists, where all the Sahibs and memsahibs buy their tooth powder and hair-lotions and many patent medicines from *Belait*. You should be able to get any *dewai* you want there. But the Rana will never let you return here to fetch anything yourself."

"Maybe not. But whoever is sent here will have to

bring with them a piece of paper on which I will have written down the drugs I require. Therefore tomorrow I will visit this chemist and make inquiries as to what medicines they sell, and also try if I cannot get on good terms with the shopkeeper."

He had left for Bhithor shortly after mid-day, taking with him an assortment of pills and potions that he had bought earlier on the advice of Mr. Pereiras, the Eurasian manager of Jobbling & Sons' Ahmadabad branch, with whom he had soon come to a friendly understanding. Ash had returned from the lines in time to see him off, and the two had conferred briefly on the verandah before Gobind and Manilal, accompanied by Sarji's *shikari*, Bukta, who was to guide them to Bhithor by way of Palanpore and the foothills below Mount Abu, rode away from the bungalow and were lost to view among the flame-trees that lined the long cantonment road.

Ten days later Sarji sent word that the *shikari* was back, having led the Hakim and his servant to within a mile of the frontier of Bhithor. The Hakim had rewarded Bukta liberally for his services and sent a verbal message to Pelham-Sahib to the effect that he would pray daily that the Sahib would be blessed by health and good fortune and that all things would go smoothly in the months ahead. A pious hope that needed no decoding.

As the days became hotter, Ash rose earlier and earlier of a morning so that he could take Dagobaz out for an hour or two before the routine of Stables; and now that the seasonal training was over, there was more office work. His evenings were usually taken up with polo practice, for the game that had been a new one on the Frontier when he first joined the Guides had spread like wildfire, until now even cavalry regiments in the south had taken it up, and Ash, having played it before, was much in demand.

His days were therefore fully occupied, which was a godsend to him; though he did not see it like that, and probably would not have admitted it if he had. But at least it prevented him from thinking too much about what might be happening to Juli, and made him tired enough to sleep at night instead of driving himself to the verge of mental exhaustion by lying awake brooding and worrying about the information in Kaka-ji's letter, and its possible implications. Hard work and violent exercise were an anodyne, and one that he should have been grateful for.

Mahdoo wrote by the hand of a bazaar letter-writer to say that he had arrived safely and was pleased to be back in Mansera once more. He was in good health and hoped that Ash was too, and that Gul Baz was looking after him properly. His entire family (there were now three more great-grand-children, two of them boys) sent their earnest wishes for his continued health, happiness and prosperity—etc., etc. . . .

Ash replied to this, but did not mention Gobind's visit. And curiously enough, neither did Gul Baz when he wrote as promised to give the old man the latest news of Pelham-Sahib and his household, and to assure Mahdoo that they were all keeping well. Though as far as Gul Baz was concerned his silence on that particular point was purely a matter of instinct, since neither Ash nor Gobind had suggested that it might be wiser not to talk of it. But then he too was worried.

Gul Baz, like Mahdoo, had a healthy distrust of Bhithor, and no wish to see the Sahib involved once again in anything whatever to do with that lawless and sinister state or its unprincipled ruler. Yet this, he feared, was what the Hakim from Karidkote was striving to do—though why, and in what way, was more than he could guess (Gul Baz knew a great deal less about Ash than Mahdoo did, and that wise old man had taken care to keep certain of his suspicions to himself).

The anxiety that Gobind's unheralded arrival had aroused in him should, by rights, have subsided with that gentleman's departure. But it had not done so, for Gul Baz noticed that after that the Sahib took to making many small purchases at an *Angrezi*-owned pharmacy, the same shop, by a coincidence—or was it a coincidence?—that the Hakim had patronized on his last morning, and where, according to the driver of the hired tonga that had taken him there (a chatty individual whom Gul Baz had later questioned), he had spent over half an hour in consultation with the shopkeeper, and eventually bought an assortment of foreign nostrums.

By itself, there was nothing strange in that, it being no secret that the Hakim had been sent for to treat the Rana of Bhithor, whom he had once cured of a painful affliction and who therefore had great faith in his powers. Yet why should the Sahib, whose health was excellent, now take to shopping there as often as three or four times a week, when previously he had always left it to Gul Baz to keep him supplied with soap and tooth powder and such things?

Gul Baz did not like it. But there was nothing he could do about it and no one with whom he cared to discuss it. He could only keep his own counsel and hope against hope that an order would soon come from Mardan, summoning the Sahib back to the Guides and the North-West Frontier, for now he too was eager to be away, and hungry for the sight of his own Border-country and the speech of his own people.

Ash, on the other hand—who only a short while ago had been equally impatient to see the last of Gujerat—was suddenly afraid of having to leave it, because if he were to be recalled to Mardan before Gobind managed to smuggle out some news from Bhithor, he might never know what had happened there, or be able to send on a message to Kaka-ji, or do anything to help.

The very thought was so intolerable that at this juncture he would actually have been relieved to hear that he must serve another five years in Gujerat; or even ten or twenty, for to leave now could mean deserting Juli just when she might need help more than she had ever needed it before, and at a time when her very life might depend on his presence here in Ahmadabad, and his willingness to do anything he could to help her.

He had deserted her twice before: once in Gulkote when she was a child, and again in Bhithor—though that had been sorely against his will. He would not do so a third time. Yet if he was ordered back to Mardan, what then? Would it do any good if he were to write to Wally and Wigram Battye, asking them to use their influence to get his recall postponed if they should hear that it was being considered? But then, having told both of them how much he wanted to get back to the Guides, how did he propose to explain this abrupt *volte face* . . . ? "I'm sorry I can't tell you why I've changed my mind and would rather not come back to the Corps just now, but you'll just have to take my word for it that it's vitally important that I should be able to remain here for the time being—"

They would think he must be ill or mad, and Wally,

at least, would expect to be trusted with the truth. But as the truth could not be told there was no point in writing at all.

Ash fell back on hope. With luck the "Tin Gods" who had banished him to Gujerat had forgotten about him and would leave him alone. Or better still, Gobind would manage to get in touch with him and tell him that their fears were groundless and that all was well with the Ranis of Bhithor, in which case it would not matter how soon he was recalled to the Guides. The sooner the better in fact, for Wally's last letter had increased his longing to get back almost as much as Kaka-ji's letter had made him wish to stay.

Wally wrote to say that the Guides had been in action again, and that Zarin had been wounded, though not seriously. The letter gave a detailed description of the affray (which involved a gang of Utman Khel tribesmen who two years previously had murdered a number of coolies working on the Swat River canal-works), and sang the praises of its instigator, one Captain Cavagnari, Deputy Commissioner of Peshawar, who having heard that the leader and several members of the gang were living in a village called Sapri some five miles upstream from Fort Abazai and just inside the Utman Khel border, sent a message to the village headman demanding their surrender, together with a large sum of money to furnish pensions for the families of the murdered coolies.

The inhabitants of Sapri, fondly imagining their village to be impregnable, replied offensively, and Captain Cavagnari decided to take them by surprise and laid his plans accordingly. Under the command of Wigram Battye, three officers of the Guides, two hundred and sixty-four sowars of the cavalry and a dozen sepoys of the infantry—the latter mounted on mules—set off one night after dark for Sapri, accompanied by Cavagnari, who had managed to keep the whole operation so secret that two of the officers had actually been playing racquets up to the last moment, and left almost straight from the courts.

The first part of the march had been simple, but eight miles short of their goal the country became so rough that the horses and mules had to be sent to Fort Abazai, while the Guides groped their way forward in the darkness on foot. Sapri, still confident that the intervening wilderness of rocks, precipices and nullahs afforded ample protection against any attack, awoke in the dawn to find itself surrounded and rushed for its arms, but after a brisk spell of fighting during which the murdered coolies were fully avenged, the ringleaders and nine others who had been implicated in that massacre were taken prisoner.

"Our losses were only seven men wounded," wrote Wally, "and Wigram has put up Jaggat Singh and Daffadar Tura Baz for the Order of Merit for 'Conspicuous bravery in action.' So as you can see, we haven't exactly been living an idle life up here. What about you down there? You know, I hate to say it, but your letters seem to contain a great deal about this pearl among horses that you have acquired, but next to nothing about yourself, and it's you and your doings I want to hear about, and not his. Or does nothing ever happen in Ahmadabad and Roper's Horse-Show? Wigram says to send you his salaams. Zarin ditto. Did you hear about that young ass Rikki Smith of the 75th N.I.? Well you'd hardly credit it, but . . ." The rest of the letter consisted of gossip.

Ash put it away with a sigh. He must write to Zarin, and tell him to take better care of himself in future. It was great to hear from Wally and get all the news and gossip of the Regiment; but it would be better still to be able to talk to him again—and to serve once more with a regiment that was always in action, instead of one that had seen little or none since the days of the Mutiny, and to which he was only temporarily attached as an uninvited guest who had been wished on them by a higher authority, and who might at any moment be recalled to his own Corps; ". . . only not too soon," prayed Ash: not until he had heard from Gobind . . .

But the days dragged by and no word came out of Bhithor; though it was spring now, and over a year since he had arrived in Ahmadabad "on temporary attachment" to Roper's Horse. How long was temporary? "This year, next year, sometime . . . ?" What *was* Gobind doing?

Ash paid yet another visit to Jobbling's the Chemist, where he bought a bottle of liniment for the treatment of a fictitious sprain, and passed the time of day with Mr. Pereiras, an inveterate gossip who could be counted upon to mention any item of interest (such as a special order for medicines for a ruling prince) without any prompting.

Mr. Pereiras had been as voluble as ever and Ash had learned several things about the ailments of a number of prominent people, though nothing about the Rana of Bhithor. But that same evening, returning late to his bungalow, there on the verandah waited a fat, travel-stained figure: Gobind's personal servant, Manilal, bringing news at last.

"This oaf has been here for two hours," said Gul Baz indignantly, speaking in Pushtu (Bhithor again!), "but he refuses to eat or drink until he has spoken with you, though I have told him a score of times that when the Sahib returns it will be to bathe and change and eat hs dinner before speaking to anyone. But this man is a fool and will not listen."

"He is the Hakim's servant, and I will see him now," said Ash, beckoning Manilal to follow. "And in private."

The news from Bhithor was neither good nor bad, a circumstance well illustrated by the fact that Manilal had been allowed to travel to Ahmadabad, but that Gobind had not dared send a letter with him for fear that he would be searched. "Which was done," said Manilal with a ghost of a smile, "—very thoroughly." The message was therefore a verbal one.

The Rana, reported Gobind, was suffering from a combination of boils, indigestion and headaches, due largely to chronic constipation. His physical condition, as was only to be expected considering his mode of life, was poor, but improving—the foreign medicines having proved most efficacious. As for the Ranis, from what he had heard, all was well with them.

The younger and Senior Rani, whose confinement was imminent, was reported to be in good health and eagerly awaiting the birth of her child, whom the soothsayers, astrologers and midwives all confidently predicted would be a son. Already preparations were being made to celebrate this auspicious event in a most lavish manner, and a messenger stood ready to ride with the news to the nearest telegraph office (a distance of many miles) from where it would be sent to Karidkote. But Gobind was somewhat disturbed to learn that this was not, as he had supposed, the Senior Rani's first pregnancy but the third . . .

He was at a loss to know why no hint of the two previous pregnancies had ever reached Karidkote, since one would have expected such a pleasant piece of news to be announced immediately, but the fact remained that she had twice miscarried in the early months. This, he imagined, might well have been due to grief and shock, as the first miscarriage had coincided with the deaths of her two waiting-women, and the second with that of the faithful old *dai*, Geeta: which hardly seemed like a coincidence. But though he still suspected that there was some mystery connected with those deaths, one thing was quite clear: the Senior Rani was neither ill-treated nor unhappy.

Extraordinary as it might seem, the marriage that had begun so ominously for her had, if gossip was to be believed (and he personally was inclined to credit it), turned out to be an unqualified success, the little Rani having taken it into her head to fall wildly in love with her unprepossessing husband, while the Rana, for his part, had found the combination of exquisite beauty and extravagant adoration so refreshing to his jaded palate that he had actually lost interest in his catamites, and to please her had dismissed the two handsome and degenerate young men who had previously been his favourite companions. All of which made good hearing.

The Junior Rani, on the other hand, had been less fortunate. Unlike her sister she had not found favour with the Rana and he had refused to consummate the marriage, declaring openly that he would not deign to father a child by a half-caste. She had been banished to a wing of one of the smaller and seldom-used palaces outside the city, from where, after only a month, she had been recalled at the insistence of the Senior Rani. Later she had again left the Zenana Quarters—this time for the Pearl Palace—only to be recalled once more after some months of separation. Since when she had been permitted to remain in the Rung Mahal, and now lived quietly retired in her own suite of rooms.

Gobind was of the opinion that the Rana probably intended to divorce her, and to send her back to Karidkote as soon as her sister the Senior Rani became less dependent upon her, which could be expected to happen once there were little sons and daughters to occupy Shushila-Bai's attention. But this of course was only conjecture, for the Sahib must realize that it was almost impossible (and indeed extremely dangerous) for anyone in Gobind's position to ask leading questions about the Ranis of Bhithor, or to show too much interest in their welfare and their relations with the Rana. Therefore he could well be

662

mistaken in this, as well as in other matters. But though a wife only in name, at least the Junior Rani appeared to be safe and in good health, and it was to be hoped that the same could soon be said for the Senior Rani.

Gobind trusted that the Sahib would write as soon as possible to Karidkote to set the Rao-Sahib's mind at rest. For the present there would appear to be no cause for anxiety, and but for the fact that the deaths of the *dai* and the waiting-women had been concealed from their relations he, Gobind, would have said that there was nothing wrong in Bhithor, or at least, not so far as the two Ranis were concerned. Nevertheless, he confessed that those deaths continued to trouble him: there was something not quite right about them—something unexplained.

"What does he mean by that?" asked Ash. "What sort of thing?"

Manilal shrugged and said slowly: "There are too many stories . . . moreover, no two of them agree, which is a strange thing. Like my master, I too am from Karidkote and therefore a stranger and suspect. I cannot ask too many questions or betray too much interest: I can only listen. But it is not difficult to guide the talk into certain channels without seeming to do so, and sitting among the palace servants or strolling in the bazaars of an evening, I have now and then dropped a little word that like a pebble in a pool has set ripples circling outwards . . . If these women did indeed die of a fever, why should there be any talk? Why should anyone trouble themselves over something that happens so often, and to so many? Yet these three deaths have not been forgotten, and those who speak of it do so in whispers; some saying that the serving-women died from this cause and others from that, but none agreeing except on one point— that no one knows the real cause.

"What do they say of the third woman, the *dai* Geeta?" asked Ash, who remembered the old lady with gratitude.

"They say it was given out that she fell by accident down a steep flight of stairs, or from a certain window, or from the rooftops of the Queen's Palace—for again the stories are all different. There are those who whisper that she was pushed and others who hold that she was dead before she fell—strangled or poisoned, or killed by a blow on the head, and afterwards flung down from a high

663

place so that it would appear to be an accident. Yet no one has put forward a reason why these things should have been done, or by whom—or upon whose orders. Therefore it may be that they are nothing more than the invention of babblers and scandalmongers who like to pretend to more knowledge than their neighbours. But it is curious . . . Curious that there should still be so much talk when two of the women have been dead for well over a year, and the *dai* for close on one."

That was all the news from Bhithor, and apart from the death of old Geeta, it was better news than Ash had expected. But Manilal was not too sure that he would be allowed to come to Ahmadabad a second time—

The men who had stopped and searched him had found nothing on him except two empty medicine bottles and some money. But they had questioned him exhaustively as to what messages his master had charged him to deliver, to which he had replied, gabbling parrotwise: "I require six more bottles of the medicine that was formerly in the larger bottle and two more of that in the smaller, here is the money in payment." Adding that he meant also to buy on his own account some chickens, the Rao-Sahib being fond of eggs, and perhaps some melons and a certain kind of sweetmeat, and . . .

When they put a stop to this by twisting his arm and demanding to know what further messages the Hakim had sent, he wept copiously (it was one of his accomplishments) and asked *what* other messages? His master had strictly instructed him to take these bottles to the *dewai dukan* in Ahmadabad, and to say to the shopkeeper: "I require five bottles of . . ." or was it *three* bottles? . . . there now—they had muddled him with their questions and put it out of his head, and the Hakim would be angry.

In the end they had given up and released him, deciding that he was much too foolish to remember more than one thing at a time. "Also," said Manilal thoughtfully, "I do not think that the Rana any longer distrusts the Hakim-Sahib, whose skill and medicines have afforded him much relief, for when the Hakim-Sahib said that he required a further supply of a certain *Angrezi dewai* and desired that I, knowing the *dewai* shop, should be sent to fetch it, there was no objection; though at first they would have had me buy fifty or a hundred bottles, but the

664

Hakim-Sahib said that long before a fraction of that number had been used, the rest would be bad. Even so, the eight will last a long time, so as my master has done as the Sahib suggested in the matter of pigeons, he has charged me to acquire a pair of birds from the Sahib's friend to take back with me."

This last referred to one of the many plans that had been discussed during Gobind's short visit. Sarji kept carrier-pigeons, and Ash had suggested that he ask for one or two of the birds for Gobind to take with him to Bhithor.

Gobind had refused to do anything so foolish, pointing out that to do this would merely give rise to the suspicion that he intended to send messages to someone outside the state. But he had agreed that something might be made of the idea, and it had been decided that as soon as he was settled in Bhithor he would show a great interest in birds and collect as many as possible—including pigeons, of which there were always great numbers in any Indian city.

Once the people had become accustomed to the sight of the Hakim from Karidkote feeding parrots and putting up nesting boxes and dovecotes, he would see if it was possible to find some way of smuggling in a pair of Sarji's carrier-pigeons.

Manilal's arrival had now solved that particular problem. And as Gobind, on his part, had established a reputation as a bird-lover, it only remained for Ash to acquire the pigeons; though in view of what he had just heard, it seemed to him unnecessary, as there was no great urgency about sending good news out of Bhithor—that could safely be left to the Rana and the Telegraph Office. But if Gobind thought it wise, Ash was not disposed to argue, and he had acquired the birds that same night, riding over to Sarji's estate by moonlight and returning with two pigeons in a small wire cage.

He had pledged Sarji to secrecy after telling him as little as possible (and even that little was not strictly accurate), and Manilal had left next morning, taking with him half-a-dozen bottles of Potter's Sovereign Specific for the Relief of Indigestion and two of Jobbling & Sons' best castor oil, together with an assortment of fruit and sweetmeats and a large wicker-work basket that appeared, on inspection, to contain live poultry: three hens and a cockerel—the fact that it also contained two pigeons being unnoticeable, owing to a cunningly contrived false bottom and the presence of the clucking fowls.

37

"Anyone would think there were no eggs to be had in Bhithor," sniffed Gul Baz, watching the Hakim's servant ride away. "And being a fool, he will certainly have been cheated over the price of those chickens."

Gul Baz was glad to see the back of Manilal, and afraid that his visit might have the same depressing effect upon the Sahib's spirits that the Hakim's had done. But he need not have worried. Manilal's news had lifted a crushing load off Ash's mind, and his spirits soared. Juli was safe and well—and she had "not found favour with the Rana."

The relief that those few words had brought him had been so great that hearing them he had, for a moment, felt light-headed. All the intolerable things he had imagined happening to her—the thought of what she might be called upon to endure, and the ugly pictures that would rise before his mind's eye whenever he could not sleep—none of them were true. She was safe from the Rana; and perhaps Gobind was right and once the child was born, Shu-shu would cease to cling to her sister and the Rana would divorce Juli and send her back to Karidkote. She would be free. Free to marry again . . .

Lying awake in the dark after returning with the pigeons, he had known that he could wait now; and without impatience, because the future that had looked so bleak and meaningless was suddenly filled with hope, and there was something to live for again.

"Pandy seems to be in pretty high feather these days," remarked the Senior Subaltern a week later, glancing out of a mess window as Ash ran down the steps, vaulted onto his horse and rode off singing "Johnnie was a Lancer." "What do you suppose has come over him?"

"Whatever it is, it's an improvement," observed the Adjutant, looking up from a tattered copy of *The Bengal*

666

Gazette. "He hasn't exactly been a ray of sunshine up to now. Perhaps someone has left him a fortune."

"He doesn't need one," put in a married Captain a shade sourly.

"Well, he hasn't been, because as a matter of fact I asked him that," confessed the first speaker ingenuously.

"And what did he say?" inquired the Adjutant, interested.

"Snubbed me. Said he'd been given something a damn' sight better: a future. Which I imagine was his way of saying 'If you ask a silly question you'll get a silly answer'—in other words, 'mind your own business.'"

"Did he, by Jove?" said the Adjutant looking startled. "I'm not so sure about that. Sounds to me as though he may have heard something, though I'm blowed if I know how he could have done. We only got it an hour ago, and I know the C.O. hasn't passed it on yet."

"Passed on what?"

"Well, I suppose there's really no reason why you shouldn't know, now that Pandy obviously does. He's to return to his own regiment. An order to that effect came by this morning's dâk. But I imagine that someone at Military Headquarters in 'Pindi blabbed in advance and one of his friends passed on the good news a week or so ago, which would account for his sudden rise in spirits."

The Adjutant was mistaken. On the contrary, by the time Ash learned of his impending departure the entire mess and most of the rank and file of Roper's Horse had already heard the news, so that in fact he himself was among the last to hear of it. But as far as he was concerned it could not have come at a better time. A fortnight ago he would have received it with dismay, but now there was no longer any urgent reason for wishing to stay here; and coming at this moment, the news seemed to him an omen that his luck had changed at last.

As if to bear this out, the order for his recall ended with the welcome information that Lieutenant Pelham-Martyn was to take any leave due to him before, and not after, rejoining. This meant that he could take at least three months if he wished, as apart from an occasional weekend and a brief visit to Kutch, he had taken no leave since the summer of '76 when he had trekked to Kashmir with Wally—the two of them having decided to save up their leave against the day when Ash returned to the

Frontier, when they could go on another trek together, this time to Spiti and across the high passes into Tibet.

"How soon are you proposing to leave us, Pandy?" inquired the Adjutant as Ash came through the outer office after seeing the Colonel.

"As soon as it's convenient," said Ash promptly.

"Oh, I fancy it's convenient now. We haven't got much on at the moment, so it will be up to you to decide. And there's no need for you to look so damned pleased about it, either!"

Ash laughed and said: "Was I looking pleased? I'm sorry. It's not that I'm glad to leave. I've had some good times here, but—Well, you might say I've been serving a sentence for the last four years: 'doing a stretch.' Now it's over and I can go back to my own regiment and my old friends and to my own part of the world again, and I can't help feeling pleased about it. No reflection on Roper's Horse. They're a fine lot."

"Don't mention it," said the Adjutant graciously. "Though I take it we are not to be compared with the Guides. Ah well, I expect I should feel the same, in your shoes. Strange how absurdly attached one becomes to one's own particular crowd. I suppose you won't be selling that horse of yours?"

"Dagobaz? Not likely!"

"I was afraid not. Well, even if we don't exactly break our hearts over losing you, Pandy, we're going to miss that black devil. He'd have won every race you entered him for, next season; and we'd have cleaned out every bookmaker in the Province. How do you propose to get him to Mardan?"

"Take him up by train. He won't like it, but I can always doss down with him if necessary. He'll have his own syce, anyway."

"If you'll take my advice," said the Adjutant, "you'll nip down and see the station-master this evening. It's not all that easy to reserve a truck, and if you plan to leave fairly soon, you'd better make sure that you can get one. Otherwise you may find yourself being held up for a good deal longer than you expect."

"Thanks for the tip," said Ash gratefully, and took himself off then and there to the railway station, where he discovered that the Adjutant had been right. If he meant to travel on the same train as Dagobaz, it did not look as

668

though he would be able to leave Ahmadabad within the next ten or fifteen days. And even that would entail a judicious amount of bribery and corruption.

"Arranging accommodation for quadruped is veree difficult affair and will occupy much time, for it will mean much booking ahead," explained the Eurasian station-master. "You see, Mr. Martyn, there are too many trains, all of different gauges. Now if I obtain a horse-van for you on thee Bombay-and-Baroda line, this is veree fine. But then that is only small part of your journey, and what, I am asking, will occur when you arrive at Bombay Central and find that none is available on thee G.I.P. railway, to which you will there transfer yourself? Or when you must change again at Aligarh onto thee East Indian Railway Line, which is again different gauge, and there is likewise no van? I am fearing veree greatly, sir, that you will endure many vexatious delays if you leave hastily and before all these bookings are pukka."

Ash had hoped to leave within a day or two, but he accepted the station-master's verdict with good grace. There was, he decided, no tearing hurry. The delay would give him more time in which to dispose of the rest of his stable, and allow Wally more time to arrange matters at his end. There was no point in trying to rush things, and anyway, another week or so in Ahmadabad would be no great hardship.

He returned to the bungalow in high spirits, and that night he wrote several letters before he went to bed. A long one to Wally, full of plans for their leave, a brief one to Zarin, sending messages to Koda Dad whom he said he hoped to see again before long, and another to Mahdoo, telling him the good news and urging him to stay where he was until further notice and to be prepared to come to Mardan in two to three months' time—Gul Baz, who would also be going on leave, would come and fetch him when the time was ripe.

"The old one will be pleased," beamed Gul Baz, collecting the finished letters. "I will see that Gokal takes these at once to the dâk-*khana* (post-office) so that they go out with the morning dâk and there is no delay."

Wally's telegraphed reply arrived a few days later. It read: *Unable get leave before end May owing unforeseen circumstances can meet you Lahore thirtieth three rousing cheers writing.*

669

Coming on top of the station-master's gloomy assessment of the time needed to complete travelling arrangements for Dagobaz, this was not as disappointing as it might have been, for at most it meant delaying his departure for a few more weeks—unless he left as soon as possible and made straight for Mardan, from where he could reach Koda Dad's village in a day and put in the extra time there until Wally's leave was due.

The prospect was an alluring one, but on consideration he discarded it—largely because it occurred to him that in view of the reason for his four-year exile from the North-West Frontier Province, it would hardly be diplomatic to celebrate the lifting of the ban by spending the first few days of his leave on the wrong side of the Border. Besides, it would also entail a lot of extra travelling, as Lahore was the obvious starting-point for the trek he had in mind.

On both these counts his reasoning was sound; but the decision proved to be a vital one, though at the time he did not realize this. It was only long afterwards, on looking back, that he recognized how much had hung upon it. Had he chosen to leave for the Punjab at the first possible date, he would not have received Gobind's message, and if he had not had that . . . But in the event he elected to stay and having been given permission to take a month's local leave "pending departure" in addition to the three he had already put in for, he went off to shoot a lioness in the Gir Forest with Sarji and Sarji's wise, wizened, little *shikari*, Bukta, leaving Gul Baz to deal with packing up the bungalow.

The lioness they were after was a notorious man-eater who for two years had terrorized an area larger than the Isle of Wight, and was reported to have killed more than fifty people. A price had been put on her head and a score of sportsmen and *shikaris* had gone after her, but the man-eater had grown too cunning, and so far the only hunter to lay eyes on her had not lived to tell the tale.

That Ash succeeded where so many had failed was due in part to beginners' luck, but even more to the genius of Bukta, who—so Sarji averred—had more knowledge of *shikar* in his little finger than any other ten *shikaris* between the Gulfs of Kutch and Cambay. In recognition of this, and remembering his services to Gobind and Manilal, Ash had presented the little man with a Lee Enfield rifle, the first that Butka had ever seen, and on which he had cast covetous eyes.

Butka's delight in the rifle and its performance more than equalled Ash's satisfaction in bringing down the man-eater, though his pleasure in this success would have been keener if it had not been that on the very day before they were to leave for the forest, one of the pigeons that Manilal had taken with him to Bhithor returned.

Sarji had seen it come homing into the pigeon-loft above the stables, and had sent a servant to Ash's bungalow with a sealed packet containing the scrap of paper that had been fastened to its leg.

The message was a short one: Shushila had given birth to a daughter and mother and child were both well. That was all. But reading it, Ash was conscious of a sudden sinking of his heart. A daughter . . . a daughter instead of the longed-for son . . . Would a girl succeed in filling Shu-shu's heart and mind to the extent that a boy would have done?—enough to make her lose her dependence on Juli and allow her to go?

He tried to console himself with the reflection that, son or daughter, the baby was Shushila's first-born; and if it took after her it would be beautiful, so that once she got over the disappointment at its sex she was bound to love it dearly. Nevertheless a doubt remained: a small, lurking shadow in the back of his mind that spoilt some of his enjoyment in the tense, exciting, frightening days and nights in the Gir Forest that followed.

Returning in triumph to Ahmadabad with the scraped and salted hide of the man-eater, he encountered an *ekka* being driven at a rattling pace in the opposite direction, and was almost past it when he recognized one of the occupants and pulled up to hail him.

"Red!" yelled Ash. "Hi, Captain Red—belay there."

The *ekka* came to a stop and Ash ranged alongside, demanding to know what Captain Stiggins was about, where he was off to, and why hadn't he sent word that he would be visiting Ahmadabad?

"Bin seeing an agent. I'm on me way back to Malia. Didn't know I'd be a comin' 'ere until the last minute," said Captain Stiggins, answering the questions in strict rotation. He added that he had called at Ash's bungalow on the previous day and been told by Gul Baz that the

Sahib was away on leave in the Gir Forest, pending his return to the North-West Frontier.

"Then why didn't you wait? He must have told you that I was expected back today, and you know very well that there's always a bed for you any time you want it," said Ash indignantly.

"Couldn't, son. I gotter get back to the old *Morala*. We're shippin' a cargo o' cotton over to Kutch termorrer. But I was right sorry to 'ear that you were orf up ter the Frontier and that I'd missed seein' you ter say goodbye and good luck."

"Come on back with me, Red," urged Ash. "Surely the cotton can wait? After all, if there was gale or a fog or something like that it would have to, wouldn't it? Dammit, this may be the last time I'll see you!"

"Wouldn't be serprised," nodded the Captain. "But that's life, that is. 'Ere today and gorn tomorrer; 'Man fleeth as a shadder an' never continueth in one stay.' No son; carn't be done, not no 'ow. But I gotter better idea. Seein' as you're on leaf, why don't yer come along o' me for the trip? Land yer back nex' Toosday, cross me 'eart."

Ash had accepted with alacrity and spent the next few days on board the *Morala* as the guest of the owner, lazing on deck in the shadow of the sails, fishing over the side for shark and barracuda, or listening to tales of the old East India Squadron in the days of John Company's greatness.

It was a peaceful and relaxing interlude, and when the Captain disclosed that the *Morala* would be sailing in a few weeks for the coast of Baluchistan, and suggested that Ash and Gul Baz should come half-way and be put off at Kati on the Indus, from where they could go by river boat up to Attock, he was tempted to agree. But there was Wally to be thought of—and Dagobaz too, The *Morala* had no proper accommodation for a horse, and on the open deck Dagobaz would have had a bad time of it in anything more than a gentle swell. He was obliged to refuse the offer, though he did so with regret, the more so because he realized that he was unlikely to meet Red Stiggins again, and he had enjoyed knowing him.

That was the worst of making friends like Red and Sarji: people who were not "members of the Club"—that closed society of Anglo-Indians who were moved across the vast map of India from this station to that and back again, on order from Simla or Calcutta or some other Seat of the Mighty, so that in time most of them came to know each other by repute even if they never actually met.

There was always a chance that in the course of his military career he would meet Mrs. Viccary or one or other of the officers of Roper's Horse once more. But the odds were against his ever seeing either Sarji or Red again, and the thought depressed him, for in their different ways both had helped to make his stay in Gujerat far more enjoyable than it might otherwise have been: Sarji more than Red, for while Captain Stiggins had been something of a shooting star, flashing briefly into view and disappearing again with equal abruptness, Sarji had been a frequent and valued companion. Gay and talkative or restfully silent to suit the occasion, seldom if ever out of temper, he had been an invaluable ally in times of restlessness and despair, and had provided a means of escape from the restricted life of the cantonment.

"I shall miss Sarji," thought Ash. "And Red too." But there would be Wally waiting for him at Lahore and Zarin in Mardan, with Koda Dad a mere afternoon's ride away across the plain. And old Mahdoo would be in his quarters at Mardan ahead of him, pleased to be on familiar territory once more and waiting to welcome him back. It was a pleasant prospect, and suddenly he could not wait to leave.

But he was never to see Mahdoo again. The letter that he had written telling the old man of his recall to Mardan had arrived too late, for Mahdoo had died in his sleep less than twenty-four hours before it should have reached him, and by the time it was delivered he was already in his grave. His relations, who did not understand the workings of the telegraph, sent the news by dâk to young Kadera, his assistant, and Gul Baz was waiting with it when Ash returned to Ahmadabad.

"It is a great loss to us all," said Gul Baz. "He was a good man. But he has fulfilled his years and his reward is sure since it is written in the Sura of the Merciful 'shall the reward of goodness be anything but good?' Therefore do not grieve for him, Sahib."

But Ash had grieved deeply for Mahdoo, mourning the loss of someone who had been part of his life ever since that far-off day when he had been handed over to the care of Colonel Anderson and sent off on the first stage of the long journey to Bombay and England, a journey that would have been a nightmare had it not been for the presence of Mahdoo and Ala Yar, who had talked to him in his own tongue; and on many occasions during the years that followed given him advice and comfort and support. When he returned to India they had come with him, and when Ala Yar died, Mahdoo had remained at his post. Now he too had gone, and Ash could not bear to think that he would never see that kindly wrinkled face again, or hear the bubble of his hookah in the twilight.

The blow had been all the worse for coming at a time when the future had taken a rosier hue, and on the heels of those exhilarating days in the Gir Forest and that peaceful voyage on the *Morala*. Ash took it hard, and attempted to work off his grief by going for long, solitary rides across country, giving Dagobaz his head and taking banks, irrigation ditches, thorn hedges and sunken roads as they came, and at a reckless speed as though he were striving to out-distance his thoughts and memories. But both kept pace with him, and the restlessness and disquiet that had temporarily left him was back once more.

However fast and far he rode, and however tired he was on his return, he could not sleep; and Gul Baz, coming to wake him with the morning mug of tea, would find him standing on the verandah, staring out across the acre of trees and dusty grass that passed for a garden. And would know from his haggard face and the lines about his eyes that the night had again been a white one.

"It is not right that you should grieve in this manner," chided Gul Baz disapprovingly, "for it is written in the Book that 'all who live on earth are doomed to die.' Therefore to mourn thus is to question the wisdom of God, who of His goodness permitted Mahdoo-ji to live to a peaceful and honourable old age, and decreed both the hour and the manner of his death. Put aside your sorrow and be thankful that so many good years upon this earth were granted to one who is now in Paradise. Moreover, very soon now you will be back in Mardan and among friends again, and all this will be behind you. I will go again to the railway station and inquire if the carriages have been arranged for yet. All is packed and ready here, and we can leave within a day."

"I'll go myself," said Ash. And he had ridden down to the station and received the welcome news that the reservations he had asked for had been made at last—but for the following Thursday, which meant that he would have to spend the best part of another week in Ahmadabad.

The thought of sitting around among the packed and corded luggage that stood ready in the bungalow was dispiriting, and he decided that he would ride over to Sarji's house and ask if he could stay there for part of the time. But he was saved the trouble, for on returning to his bungalow he found Sarji himself waiting for him on the verandah, comfortably ensconced in one of the long wicker chairs.

"I have something for you," said Sarji, lifting a languid hand. "The second pigeon came back this morning, and as I had business in the city I thought I would play *chupprassi* (peon) and bring you the message myself."

Ash snatched the small scrap of paper from him, and unrolling it, read the first lines with a sudden lift of the heart. *"The Rana is ill of a fatal sickness and will not live for more than a handful of days,"* wrote Gobind. *"This has become clear to all . . ."*

"Dying!" thought Ash, and smiled without knowing it—a wide, grim, glittering smile that showed his clenched teeth—"he may be dead already. She will be a widow—she'll be free." He felt no sympathy for the Rana. Or for Shu-shu, who if gossip could be believed had fallen in love with the man, because he could only think of what this would mean for Juli and himself: Juli widowed, and free . . .

He steadied himself and read on; and all at once the day was no longer hot or the sunlight bright, and there was a constriction about his heart.

". . . and I have now learned that when he dies his wives will become suttee, being burned with him according to the custom. This is already spoken of, for his people follow the old laws and pay no heed to those of the Raj, and unless you can prevent it, it will surely be done. I will strive to keep him alive for as long as possible. But it will not be long. Therefore warn those in

675

authority that they must act swiftly. Manilal will leave for
Ahmadabad within the hour. Send more pigeons and . . ."

The lines of minute writing blurred and wavered
before Ash's eyes and he could no longer focus them. He
turned blindly away and groping for the back of the nearest chair, gripped it as though to steady himself and spoke
in a breathless whisper: "No—it's not possible! They
couldn't do it!"

The words were barely audible, but the horror in
them was unmistakable and it shocked Sarji out of his
lounging attitude. He said sharply: "It is bad news, then?
What is it? What is not possible?"

"Saha-gamana," whispered Ash without turning. "Suttee . . . The Rana is dying, and when he dies they mean
to see that his wives are burnt with him. I must see the
Commissioner—the Colonel—I must . . ."

"Ah, *chut!*" said Sarji impatiently. "Do not distress
yourself, my friend. They will not do it. It is against the
law."

Ash jerked round to glare at him. "You do not know
Bhithor!"—his voice had shot up, and Gul Baz, appearing
in a doorway with a tray of refreshments, froze at the
sound of that hated word—"or the Rana. Or—" He broke
off and, turning, leapt down the verandah steps shouting
for Kulu Ram to bring Dagobaz back.

A moment later he was again in the saddle and galloping down the drive like a maniac, raising a cloud of
dust and grit and leaving Sarji, Gul Baz and Kulu Ram
to stare after him in open-mouthed dismay.

38

"I can only suppose that you have taken leave of your
senses," said Colonel Pomfret austerely. "No, of course I
cannot send any of my men into Bhithor. Such an action
would be quite out of order; nor, I may say, would I
do so if it were not. Matters of this nature are best left
to the civil authorities or the police, and not to the army;
though I would advise you against bursting in on anyone

676

else in this unceremonious manner with some wild rumour that no one in their right minds would take seriously. I cannot understand what you are doing here, anyway. I thought you were on leave and off shooting somewhere."

Two white patches showed on Ash's lean cheeks, but he managed to keep his voice under control and said briefly: "I was, sir."

"Then you had better go back there. No point in hanging about cantonments doing nothing. Haven't they been able to arrange your reservations on the trains yet?"

"Yes, sir. They're for next Thursday. But—"

"*Hmm.* Wouldn't have given you leave if I'd known that you'd be staying here at a loose end for all this time. Well, if you've said all you want to say, you will oblige me by leaving. I have work to do. Good-day."

Ash withdrew, and disregarding the Colonel's advice, called on the Commissioner; only to find that the Commissioner shared Colonel Pomfret's views—particularly on the subject of junior officers who demanded to see him towards mid-day and on being told that the hour was inconvenient, and they should either come later in the day or earlier on the following one, burst into his presence with some cock-and-bull story and a demand that he, the Commissioner, should take immediate action on it.

"Poppycock!" snorted the Commissioner. "I don't believe a word of it: and if you knew these people as well as I do, you wouldn't either. It don't do to believe more than a fraction of what they tell you, as most of 'em will always tell a lie rather than speak the truth, and trying to find out what really happened is like drawing eye-teeth or hunting for that proverbial needle in a haystack. This friend of yours—Guptar or Gobind or whatever his name is—is either pulling your leg or else he's too gullible by half. I can assure you that no one nowadays would dare to be party to such a thing as you suggest, and it's easy to see that your credulous friend has been the victim of a hoax. And you too, I fancy! Well, let me remind you that this is 1878 and that the law against suttee has been in force for over forty years. It is not likely to be flouted now."

"But you don't know Bhithor!" cried Ash, as he had to both Sarji and Colonel Pomfret. "Bhithor doesn't belong to this century, let alone this half of it. I don't believe

677

they have taken in that there is such a thing as the British Raj, or if they have, that it has anything whatever to do with them."

"Gammon," snapped the Commissioner, annoyed (he lunched at noon and it was already past that), "you exaggerate. It is obvious that—"

"But you haven't *been* there," interrupted Ash.

"What has that to say to anything? Bhithor is neither in my Province nor under my jurisdiction, so even were I inclined to place any credence in this ridiculous tale, which I fear I am not, I could still do nothing to help you. Your informant would have been better advised to approach the Political Officer responsible for that section of Rajputana—that is, if he really believes his own story, which I doubt."

"But sir, I have told you that he cannot get any message out of Bhithor," persisted Ash desperately. "There is no telegraph or post office, and though they may allow his servant to come here to buy medicines and drugs, they would never permit him to go anywhere else. If you would only send a telegram to the Political Agent—"

"I shall do no such thing," said the Commissioner testily, and rose to his feet to show that the interview was at an end. "It has never been the policy of my Department to interfere with the administration of other provinces or to instruct those in charge of them, who are, believe me, more than able to deal competently with their own affairs."

Ash said slowly: "Then . . . you will not do anything?"

"It is not a question of 'will not,' but 'cannot.' And now, if you will excuse me—"

Ash ignored the request and stayed where he was, arguing, pleading and explaining for a further five minutes. But to no avail, for the Commissioner had merely lost his temper, and having informed him tersely that he was meddling in matters that he did not understand (and that were, in any case, no concern of his) had ended by ordering him to leave immediately or be forcibly removed by the guard.

Ash left, realizing that he had wasted the best part of two hours and that if he had had his wits about

678

him he would have sent off a telegram before attempting to talk to anyone.

The Telegraph Office was closed to the public during the time of the mid-day meal and afternoon siesta, but he routed out an indignant clerk and induced him to send off four urgent telegrams: one to Kaka-ji, another to Jhoti, the third to that same Political Officer who had been so unhelpful in the matter of the Rana's chicanery over the marriage contracts, and finally (in case that obstinate official proved to be as useless now as he had been on that occasion) a fourth to the Honourable the Agent to the Governor-General, Rajputana—familiarly known as the A.G.G.—in Ajmer: an afterthought that was to prove disastrous, though it had seemed an excellent idea at the time. But then Ash had no idea who the present incumbent was, and had not taken the trouble to find out.

It had not been at all easy to cajole the Eurasian telegraph clerk into transmitting these telegrams. The contents of all four had alarmed him, and he had protested strongly against "such high matters" being sent in clear. Messages of this kind ought, in his opinion, to be sent in code or not at all. "I am telling you, sir, that telegrams, they are not secret things. By no means. They are getting sent on from one *tar-khana* to another, and veree many cheeky fellows are seeing them by the way—peons and such-like too—and they will be chitter-chattering about them to one and all."

"Good," said Ash shortly, "I'm delighted to hear it. The more talk the better."

"But sir—!" wailed the clerk, "there will be much unfortunate gossip and scandal. And what if this Rana-Sahib should not after all die, and you are finding yourself in loads of trouble for misrepresentation and libels and such things? And me too, because I am sending out these accusations? I may be blamed for this and get into hot waters, and if I am losing my job—"

It had taken fifteen minutes and fifty rupees to overcome the clerk's scruples, and the telegrams had been sent. After which Ash had gone to the bungalow of Mr. Pettigrew, District Superintendent of Police, in the hope (a faint one by now) that the police might prove more helpful than the military or the civil arm.

Mr. Pettigrew had certainly been less sceptical than

either Colonel Pomfret or the Commissioner, but he too had pointed out that this was a matter for the authorities in Rajputana, adding that they probably knew a good deal more about what went on there than Lieutenant Pelham-Martyn would seem to think. However he had at least promised to send a personal telegram to a colleague in Ajmer—one Carnaby, who was a personal friend of his.

"Nothing official, you understand," said Pettigrew. "One doesn't want to stick one's neck out and sound like a meddling nosey-parker. And to be honest, I can't say that I take this pigeon-post message of yours all that seriously. You'll probably find it's all a hum. On the other hand, it's just possible that there might be something in it, so there's no harm in dropping a hint to Tim Carnaby —just to be on the safe side. He's not the type of fellow who prefers to let sleeping dogs lie, and he'll certainly see that it's looked into. I'll get a wire sent off to him at once, and you can be sure that if anything needs to be done he'll do it."

Ash thanked him with a good deal of fervour and rode away feeling much easier in his mind. After the agonizing frustration of the morning, it was reassuring to find someone who did not dismiss Gobind's warning as pure nonsense, and was actually prepared to do something about it—even though that something was no more than an unofficial hint to a personal friend.

But as matters turned out he might have saved himself the visit, for the D.S.P.'s efforts on his behalf came to nothing. The friend had gone on leave three days before the telegram was dispatched, and owing to Pettigrew's anxiety to avoid any suggestion of interfering with another man's work, the information it contained had been presented in such casual and chatty terms that it failed to convey any suggestion of urgency. The officer deputizing for the absent Tim Carnaby had, in consequence, not thought it worthwhile to send it on and had thrust it into a drawer with other letters that Carnaby could read on his return.

The effects of Ash's own telegrams had been equally abortive. Jhoti, with Kaka-ji's approval, had sent one of his own to the A.G.G. Rajputana, on receipt of which the A.G.G. had in turn wired the British Resident in Karidkote, whose reply had been non-committal. It was, he said, well known that the Rana's health was not of the best, but this was the first anyone in Karidkote had heard that he might be dying, and he had reason to believe that the source of this information was not entirely trustworthy. Anything emanating from that particular quarter should be treated with reserve, as the officer in question not only appeared to have too much influence over the young Maharajah, but was by reputation both eccentric and undisciplined.

Unfortunately, these observations had arrived in Ajmer only hours before a letter from the Political Officer; and taken together the two communications had effectively destroyed Ash's credibility—and with it any chance that his warnings would be taken seriously. For by an unkind quirk of fate the newly appointed Agent to the Governor-General, who had taken office only a few weeks previously, happened to be that same Ambrose Podmore-Smyth—now Sir Ambrose—who six years earlier had married Belinda Harlowe. And what with Belinda and her father and the gossips of the Peshawar Club, everything he had heard of young Pelham-Martyn had inspired him with a dislike for his wife's former suitor that time had done nothing to eradicate.

Sir Ambrose strongly disapproved of Englishmen who "went native," and his wife's garbled account of her ex-admirer's early history (it was perhaps fortunate that Belinda could not recall the name of the state in which Ash had lived—and very little else either) had scandalized her husband. No wonder the fellow lacked steadiness and a proper sense of moral values, and had brought disgrace upon his race and his regiment by absconding into tribal territory with a handful of dismissed sepoys. One could only hope that he would meet a speedy and merciful death there and no more would be heard of him.

Sir Ambrose had been unpleasantly surprised to find that a telegram from Ahmadabad, sent in clear and containing startling allegations, was from someone signing himself Pelham-Martyn. He could not believe it was the same Pelham-Martyn, but as the name was an uncommon one it might be worthwhile to check, and he had directed his Personal Assistant to do so immediately; and also to see that a copy of the telegram was sent to the Political Officer whose area included Bhithor, inviting his comments. After which, conscious of having done all that could be expected of him, he had retired to his wife's drawing-room for a pre-tiffin drink, where he happened to mention the odd coincidence of that name from the past.

"You mean *Ashton?*" cried Belinda (a Belinda, alas, whom Ash would barely have recognized). "Then he did get back safely after all! Well I must say, I never thought he would. Nor did anyone else. Papa said it was good riddance of bad rubbish. But I don't think Ashton was bad, only rather wild. Just fancy his turning up again."

"He has not 'turned up,'" said Sir Ambrose tartly. "There is no reason to believe it's the same fellow. Might be a relative: though I doubt it. Probably no connection at all, and we shall find—"

"Oh fiddlesticks!" interrupted his wife. "Of course it's Ashton—it's so like him. He was always getting mixed up with things that were none of his business; and with natives, too. Now here he is doing it again. It must be him. It couldn't be anyone else. I wonder what on earth he's doing in this part of the world? Do you suppose he's still . . ." She broke off, and leaning back in her chair, surveyed her lord and master with a dissatisfied eye.

Time and the climate of India had not been kind to Sir Ambrose. They had changed him from a portly, self-satisfied man into an obese, bald and insufferably pompous one, and Belinda, studying that purple countenance with its fringe of grey whiskers and plethora of chins, caught herself wondering if it had been worth it. She was Lady Podmore-Smyth, the wife of a tolerably rich and important man, and mother of two healthy children (both girls, which was not her fault though Ambrose seemed to think otherwise) and yet she was not happy.

Life as a Resident's lady had not been nearly as amusing as she had imagined: she missed the gaiety of a military station in British India, disliked the whole tedious and painful business of child-bearing, found her husband dull and existence in a native state boring beyond words. "I wonder," mused Belinda aloud, "what he looks like now? He used to be very handsome . . . and so madly in love with me."

She preened herself complacently, sublimely unaware that the years had been even more unkind to her than they had to her elderly husband, and that she was no longer the slim slip of a girl who had once been the belle of Peshawar, but a stout matron with faded blond hair, an acid tongue and a discontented expression. "Of course, that was why he did it—ran away from his regiment I mean. I've always known that he did it because of me and that he went in search of death; or to forget. Poor Ashton . . . I have often thought that if only I had been a little kinder—"

"Rubbish," snorted Sir Ambrose. "If you have given so much as one moment's thought to him from that day to this, I confess I should be exceedingly surprised. As for his being madly in love with you . . . Now, now, Belinda, there's no need to make a scene about it; I'm sorry I mentioned the fellow. I should have known better . . . I am *not* shouting—!"

He stamped out of the room in a fury, banging the door behind him, and was not best pleased when his Personal Assistant's inquiries disclosed that the author of that impertinent telegram was indeed none other than the Ashton Pelham-Martyn who had once aspired to his wife's hand and subsequently caused a great deal of talk by behaving in a manner that could only be described as unbalanced. Nor was his temper improved when later on the Political Officer's reply to his request for comments on the contents of the telegram arrived.

Ash's chickens were coming home to roost with a vengeance, for Major Spiller, the Political Officer (who had never forgiven what he had taken to be a rude and insufferably high-handed letter, sent from Bhithor over two years ago), began by saying that he himself had received a similar telegram from the same source, and went on to comment at length—and forcefully.

He had already, wrote Spiller, had some experience of Captain, now Lieutenant, Pelham-Martyn in the past, and considered him to be an officious trouble-maker bent on creating a scandal and causing dissension. A few years ago the fellow had done his utmost to disrupt relations between the Government of India and the State of Bhithor (which until then had always been cordial in the extreme) and had it not been for his, Spiller's, firmness, he might well have succeeded in doing so. Now, once again, for reasons best known to himself, he was endeavouring to stir up trouble. However, as no reliance could be placed on anything he said, Major Spiller for one intended to treat these wild allegations with the contempt they deserved: particularly in view of the fact that those whose business it was to know what went on in Bhithor had assured him that the Rana's illness was no more than a slight recurrence of the malarial fever with which he had been plagued at intervals during the past few years, and there was not the least danger of his succumbing to it. The whole thing was a mare's nest, and it might be as well if Lieutenant Pelham-Martyn was given a sufficiently strong reprimand to discourage him from any further meddling in matters that were no concern of his; and it was inexcusable that . . .

Sir Ambrose had not bothered to read further, since the writer's opinion merely confirmed his own: Belinda had been right and that insufferable young blackguard was at his old tricks again. Sir Ambrose threw the entire correspondence into the waste-paper basket, and having dictated a soothing reply to His Highness the Maharajah of Karidkote, assuring him that there was no need for anxiety, sent a frosty letter to Army Headquarters, complaining of Lieutenant Pelham-Martyn's "subversive activities" and suggesting that it might be as well if his present interests and past history were investigated with a view to his being deported as an Undesirable British Subject.

At about the same time as his telegram (together with Jhoti's, and the Resident's and the Political Officer's comments) was being consigned to the Honourable the Agent to the Governor-General's waste-paper basket, Ash was greeting a tired and dusty traveller who had arrived that morning from Bhithor.

Manilal had set out for Ahmadabad less than twenty minutes after Gobind had released the second pigeon. But while the pigeon had covered the distance in a few hours, Manilal had taken the best part of a week, for his horse had strained a tendon and thereafter he had been forced to go slowly, the roads being rutted by cartwheels and deep in dust, which did not make for easy going at the best of times.

"What news?" demanded Ash, running down the steps as the tired man dismounted under the shadow of the porch. Ash had ridden out three days running in the hope of intercepting Manilal, and had become increasingly anxious when there had been no sign of him, or any reply from the District Superintendent of Police's friend in Ajmer (he had not been so sanguine as to imagine that his own telegrams would be answered). To tempt Fate, he had stayed indoors that morning, and towards noon Fate had rewarded him by sending Gobind's servant to the bungalow.

"Very little," croaked Manilal, whose throat was dry with dust: "except that he was still alive when I left. But who knows what may have happened since? Has the Sahib warned the Government and Karidkote of what is toward?"

"Assuredly, within a few hours of that pigeon reaching home. I have done all I could."

"That is good news," said Manilal hoarsely. "Have I your leave, Sahib, to eat and drink and perhaps rest a little before I talk further? I have not slept since the horse injured himself shying in terror at a tiger that crossed our path."

He slept for the rest of the day and reappeared after sundown, still heavy-eyed, to squat on the verandah and tell Ash all that Gobind had not been able to send by pigeon-post. Apparently the palace physicians still said that the Rana would recover, insisting that he was only suffering an unusually severe attack of malarial fever to which he had been subject for many years. But in Gobind's view this was no mere fever, but a sickness of the body for which there was no cure, and the most that could be done was to administer drugs to relieve the pain—and hope to delay the end until the Government sent someone in authority to see to it that when he died it would mean one death only, and not three.

Gobind had apparently managed, by devious means, to establish contact with the Junior Rani through a serving-woman whose relatives were susceptible to bribery, and who was herself said to be much attached to Kairi-Bai. In this way several messages had been smuggled into the Zenana Quarters, and one or two had even been answered, though the replies had been short and uncommunicative, and told Gobind nothing beyond the fact that the Junior Rani and her sister were well—which should have satisfied him, but failed to do so because there was something about those letters that made him uneasy—perhaps the very fact that they were too cautious. Was Nimi, the serving-woman, not to be trusted, and did Kairi-Bai know or suspect this? But if that were so it could only mean that there was something that must be concealed . . . unless he was being needlessly suspicious.

Then the baby had been born, and on the following morning Gobind had received a letter from Kairi-Bai that was not in answer to one of his own. It had been a frantic plea for help, not for herself, but for Shushila-Rani, who was in a serious condition and must have attention at once—if possible, a European nurse from the nearest *Angrezi* hospital. It was a matter of the utmost urgency and Gobind must send for one immediately and in secret, before it was too late.

There had been a withered *dakh* flower enclosed in the letter, which is the sign for danger; and seeing it Gobind had been seized with the terrifying suspicion that the Senior Rani, having failed to produce an heir, was perhaps being poisoned—as rumour said the previous one had been—

"Yet what could the Hakim-Sahib do?" asked Manilal with a shrug. "It was not possible for him to do as Kairi-Bai desired. And even if he had been able to send such a message out of Bhithor, the Rana would never have permitted any foreign woman, doctor or not, to force her way into the Zenana and examine his wife. Not unless such a one came with a strong escort of soldiers, guns and police-Sahibs, or unless he himself could be persuaded to send for one."

Gobind had courageously tried the latter course, but the Rana would not hear of it and was angered that such a suggestion should even have been put to him. He despised all foreigners as barbarians and would, if he had his way, have refused to allow any of them to set foot in his state, let alone have any personal contact with him. Had not he, alone among all his neighbouring princes, refused to appear at any of the durbars arranged by the Raj to announce that the Queen of England had been declared *Kaiser-i-Hind* (Empress of India), excusing himself on the grounds that he had fallen ill and was unfortunately unable to travel?

The suggestion that he of all people should now invite an *Angrezi* woman to come and poke her nose in his wife's affairs was offensive. Besides, what could a foreign woman possibly know of Hindu medicine and the arts of healing? There was nothing wrong with the Rani that rest and proper care would not put right, and if

686

the Hakim doubted it he was at liberty to question the *dai* who had presided at the birth.

Gobind had taken advantage of this unexpected offer, and been favourably impressed by the midwife; though she had been strangely uncommunicative on the subject of her predecessor, old Geeta from Karidkote, and when questioned about the dead woman had muttered that she knew nothing—nothing at all—and hastily changed the subject. Apart from that, she struck him as a sensible woman with a sound knowledge of midwifery.

The *dai* had assured him that contrary to all expectations, the birth had proved an easy one. There had been no complications and the Rani was in good health. Her disappointment at the infant's sex had affected her spirits, but that was understandable as she had set her heart on having a son, and the astrologers and soothsayers, not to mention her own women, had foolishly bolstered her hopes by assuring her that the coming child would be a boy. However, she would get over that before long, and if the gods were kind the next one, or the one after that, would be a son. There was plenty of time for she was young—and also far stronger than her frail appearance suggested.

The *dai* had given Gobind a good deal of technical information on the subject of the Rani's physical condition following her delivery, and left him feeling reassured as to her health and no longer so uneasy as to her safety, since he did not believe that the woman was lying. He came to the conclusion that Kairi-Bai must have heard those ugly whispers about the death of the Rana's previous wife, and was in consequence afraid that now her sister too had borne a daughter she might be removed in the same way. This was highly unlikely, if only for the reason that Shushila-Bai was an exceptionally beautiful woman whom the Rana loved, while her predecessor, from all reports, had been plain, fat and stupid, and wholly lacking in charm.

Gobind had sent a reassuring note to the Junior Rani, but had received no answer; and a week later the baby had died.

There had been a rumour in the palace that the *dai* too was dead, though some said that she had only been dismissed following a dispute with the Rani's half-sister, who had accused her of failing to take proper care of

687

the child. It was also said that the Rana, angered by the Junior Rani's interference, had given orders that she was to keep to her own rooms and neither see nor speak to her sister until further notice: an edict that Gobind feared would cause even more distress to the Senior Rani than the Junior one . . . if it were true.

But then a great many of the palace rumours were not. The Rung Mahal, said Manilal, stank of evil and bred rumours as a midden breeds flies, being crammed with idle courtiers, place-seekers and hangers-on, in addition to hordes of servants, none of whom had enough to do and therefore relieved their boredom by engaging in feuds and generally making mischief. "They sit about and chew *pan* and talk scandal—when they are not asleep," said Manilal scornfully. "And most of their talk is lies, for each one wishes to make out that he is privy to more than the others, and invents a tale to draw attention to himself and gain importance; and if the tale is a scandalous one, so much the better, virtue being too often very dull."

Nevertheless the rumours had disturbed Gobind and he had done his best to discover if there was any truth in them, but however much the Rana's people might gossip among themselves about the affairs of the Zenana, they were at pains to avoid that subject when talking to the men from Karidkote, and the most that Gobind learned was that no one could be blamed for the baby's death. It had been an undersized and sickly little creature whose hold on life had been precarious from the start, and the Senior Rani was prostrated with grief at its loss, having become very fond of it once she recovered from her disappointment that it was a daughter instead of a son.

About the Junior Rani and the *dai* there had been no further information, and Gobind could only hope that if it were true that Kairi-Bai had again been parted from her sister, the Rana would soon rescind the order for the sake of the bereaved mother—unless of course, he had lost interest in her and was using this method of punishing both women: the one for interfering and the other for having failed to give him a son. That was more than possible.

"But surely this serving-woman or her family could have given you or your master news of the Junior Rani? And of the *dai* too?" said Ash.

Manilal shook his head and explained that although

the woman Nimi had acted as a go-between in the matter of the letters, it had at no time been possible to have any speech with her, the Hakim-Sahib's only contact with her being through her parents who accepted payment on her behalf, and to whom he gave his letters and received the occasional reply. But either they knew nothing of what went on in the Zenana, or considered it safer to pretend that they did not.

"They profess to being ignorant," said Manilal, "and we have learned nothing from them beyond that they have this daughter Nimi, who they say is devoted to her mistress the Junior Rani, but who is certainly rapacious, for she demands more and more money for each letter that she takes in or out of the Women's Quarters."

Ash said: "If you have only their word for that, it may be that she does what she does for love, and knows nothing of the sums they extort in her name."

"Let us hope so," said Manilal earnestly, "for many risks are cheerfully undertaken for love. But those who take them only for payment may turn traitor if another is willing to pay more, and if it becomes known that the Hakim-Sahib is corresponding in secret with the Junior Rani, then I think all our lives will be endangered: not only his, but hers too—and mine also, together with the woman's relatives. As for the woman herself, her life would not be worth so much as a grain of corn."

Manilal shivered involuntarily and his teeth made a little chattering sound. They had, he told Ash, learned nothing more when the Rana fell seriously ill, and before very long it became plain to all that the illness could be mortal.

"Only then did we learn by a chance whisper overheard in the palace—and later through the open talk in the city and certain unseemly jests in the bazaars—that if he died his wives would burn with him; for save for his father, the old Rana, who died of the cholera, no ruler of Bhithor has ever gone to the pyre alone—and for him it was only because there had been no wives to become suttee as they too, and his favourite concubine also, had already taken the disease and died of it. But it seems that when his predecessor died, in the year that Mahadaji Sindia retook Delhi, fourteen women—wives and concubines—followed him into the flames; and before that never less than three or four and often more than a score.

Now the wits say that this time there will be only two, there being no concubines but only catamites."

Ash's mouth twisted in a tight-lipped grimace of disgust, and Manilal said: "Yes, it is an ugly jest. Though well deserved. But what matters is that even the jesters take for granted that the Ranis will become suttee, as do all in Bhithor. It is, they say, the custom; though the common folk no longer observe it, and only a very few of the noble families have done so during the life-time of the present Rana. Yet the people still consider it incumbent upon the royal house to respect the old laws, for the honour of Bhithor and all who dwell there—particularly those who do *not* keep them. For when the Rana's wives become suttees they will stand, as it were, as a symbol and a substitute for all those widows who have shrunk from doing so, or been prevented from it by their relatives.

"In fact," said Ash savagely, and in English, "it is still expedient that one man should die for the people. In this case, two women." He saw that Manilal was looking startled, and reverted to the vernacular: "Well, they are not going to die, so Bhithor will just have to do without its scapegoats and burnt offerings. When do you return?"

"As soon as I can procure more pigeons and another six bottles of useless medicines from the *dewai dukan*. Also a fresh horse, for my own will not be fit to ride for some days yet and I dare not delay my return. I have lost too much time already. Can the Sahib perhaps help in the matter of a horse?"

"Surely. You may leave that to me. The pigeons and medicines also. What you need is rest, and you had best get as much of that as you can while you have the chance. Give me the empty bottles. Gul Baz shall fetch what you require as soon as the shop opens tomorrow morning."

Manilal handed them over, retired to his charpoy and was asleep again within minutes: a deep, refreshing sleep from which he did not awake until the sun was up and the crows, doves and parrots were quarrelling over the spilt grain by the stables, while the well-wheel squeaked in descant to the clatter of cooking pots and all the familiar sounds of an Indian morning. But by that time Ash had already been gone two hours, leaving a message telling Manilal to procure such things as he needed and meet him at Sarji's house.

690

The message had been delivered by Gul Baz, in a voice laden with disapproval, together with half-a-dozen bottles of patent medicines from Jobbling & Sons, the Chemists. Manilal made his way to the bazaar, where he bought a large wicker basket, a quantity of food and fresh fruit, and three chickens. The basket, like the one he had previously taken into Bhithor, had a false bottom. But this time it had not been used, for Ash had made other plans: ones that did not include carrier-pigeons.

Unlike Manilal, Ash had stayed awake for most of the night. There had been a great many things to think about, but his mind had discarded the larger issues and fastened instead on a comparatively trivial one: Manilal's curious use of an old and unkind nickname, *Kairi*. Who could have been unkind enough to see that even someone like Manilal, mixing with the other servants in the Rung Mahal and listening to their gossip, and to the talk in the bazaars, could use it automatically when speaking of her? It was a small thing. But as a straw in the wind shows the direction in which the wind is blowing, it was a clear indication of the contempt in which Juli was held by her husband's people, and—more disturbingly—that only someone from Karidkote could have been responsible for repeating that cruel nickname and encouraging its use in the Zenana, from where it would have spread to the rest of the palace.

Half-a-dozen of their own women had remained with Juli and Shu-shu, and Ash could only hope that the one responsible was among the three who were now dead (though he could not believe it was Geeta), because if not, there was a traitor among those closest to the Ranis: a female counterpart to Nandu's spy, Biju Ram, unsuspected by her young mistresses because she came from Karidkote, and currying favour with the Rana by denigrating the wife he so despised. It was an unpleasant thought, and also a frightening one because it meant that even if the Rana lived or the Raj sent troops to enforce the law against widow-burning, Juli and her sister might still be exposed to more dangers than Gobind suspected.

Ash did not doubt that the Government of India would see to it that if the Rana died there would be no suttee. But if the Rana lived they might not be able to protect Juli from punishment (or Gobind and Manilal either, should he find out about those smuggled letters) for that would be a purely domestic matter. Even if all three

691

were to die or simply disappear, it was doubtful if the authorities would ever hear about it. And if they did, and asked questions, they would not ask soon enough; for in a country of vast distances and poor communications these things took time, and once the trail was cold, any explanation, such as a sudden fever, or the bland statement that the Hakim and his servant had left the state and were presumably on their way back to Karidkote, would have to be accepted, for there would be no evidence. And no way of proving anything . . .

Ash shivered involuntarily, as Manilal had done, and thought in panic: "I must go myself. I can't sit here and do nothing while Juli . . . Manilal was right: the Rung Mahal stinks of evil and anything could happen there. Besides if Gobind can get letters to her, so can I . . . not from here, but I could from there . . . I could warn her to be on her guard because one of the Karidkote women may be disloyal, and ask about the *dai* and what really is happening. She wouldn't run away with me before, but she may feel differently now, and if so I'll find a way of getting her out—and if she still won't, at least I can satisfy myself that the police and the Political Department are taking steps to see that if that animal dies, no one is going to try to force his widows onto the pyre."

It would have to be force with Shu-shu. They'd have to drag her to the burning ground, or tie her up and carry her, and Ash imagined that she would probably die of fright long before they got her there. Juli had told him once that Shu-shu had always been terrified at the very idea of suttee, and that it was for this reason she had not wanted to get married, because her mother . . . "I hope," thought Ash viciously, "that there is a special hell for people like Janoo-Rani."

When Gul Baz brought in the tea at dawn, he found the Sahib already up and dressed, and engaged in packing the small *bistra*—a leather-bound strip of canvas that he took with him on night exercises rolled up and strapped to the back of the saddle. Yet a glance was enough to show that he was not planning on being away for a mere night and a day. On the contrary he was, he said, going on a journey that might keep him away for anything up to a month, though on the other hand he could be back again in a matter of eight or ten days—his plans were uncertain.

There was nothing unusual about this, except that always before any packing that had to be done was left to Gul Baz, and there was generally far more of it than could be contained in that small roll of canvas: several changes of clothing, for a start. But this time Gul Baz saw that the Sahib meant to travel light, and was taking only a cake of soap, a razor and a single country-made blanket in addition to his service revolver and fifty rounds. There were also four small and disproportionately heavy cardboard boxes, each containing fifty rounds of rifle ammunition.

Recognizing these, Gul Baz had allowed himself to hope that the Sahib was only going on another trip to the Gir Forest—though why he should take the revolver and need such a vast amount of ammunition ...

The hope died as Ash went over to the dressing-table, and unlocking a drawer, took out and pocketed a small pistol and a handful of rounds (items that he could certainly have no use for on any shooting expedition) and a tin cash-box that he emptied onto the table, remarking that it was a stroke of luck that Haddon-Sahib should have decided to pay cash for the two polo-ponies, as it would save him a trip to the bank. He began to sort it into separate piles of gold, silver and notes, counting under his breath, and did not look up when Gul Baz said heavily, and not as a question: "The Sahib goes to Bhithor, then."

"Yes," said Ash "—though that is for your ear alone ... three fifty, four hundred, four fifty-nine, five ... six—"

"I knew it," exclaimed Gul Baz bitterly. "This was what Mahdoo-ji was always afraid of; and on the day that I saw that hakim from Karidkote drive up to this bungalow I knew that the old one had been right to be afraid. Do not go, Sahib, I beg of you. No good can come of meddling in the affairs of that ill-omened place."

Ash shrugged and went on counting, and presently Gul Baz said: "Then if you must, at least let me go with you. And Kulu Ram also."

Ash looked up to smile and shake his head. "I would if I could. But it would not be safe—you might be recognized."

"And what of yourself?" retorted Gul Baz angrily. "Do you suppose they will have forgotten you so soon, when you gave them such good cause to remember you?"

"Ah, but this time I shall not be going to Bhithor as

693

a Sahib. I shall go in the guise of a boxwallah; or a traveller on pilgrimage to the temples at Mount Abu. Or perhaps a hakim from Bombay . . . yes, I think a hakim might be best, as that will give me an excuse to meet a fellow doctor, Gobind Dass. And you can be sure that no one will know me—though some might know you, and more would know Kulu Ram, who often rode with me to the city. Besides, I shall not be going alone. I shall have Manilal with me."

"That fat fool!" said Gul Baz with a scornful sniff.

Ash laughed and said: "Fat he may be, but fool he is not: of that I can assure you. If he chooses to let people think him one, it is for a good reason, and believe me, I shall be safe in his hands. Now let me see, where was I?—Seven hundred . . . seven eighty . . . eight . . . nine hundred . . . one sixty-two—" He finished counting the money, and having stowed away a large part of it in the pockets of his riding coat, returned the rest to the cashbox and handed it to Gul Baz, who received it in grim silence.

"Well, there you are, Gul Baz. That should be more than enough to cover the wages and expenses of the household until I return."

"And what if you do not?" demanded Gul Baz stonily.

"I have left two letters which you will find in the small top drawer of my desk. If after six weeks I have not returned and you have received no word from me, give them to Pettigrew-Sahib of the police. He will act upon them and see that you and the others do not suffer any hardship. But you need not worry: I shall come back. Now as to the Hakim's servant, when he wakes tell him that when he is ready to leave, to come to the Sirdar Sarjevan Desai's house near the village of Janapat, where I will meet him. Also to take the bay mare in place of his own horse that is lame. Tell Kulu Ram to see to it, and —no, I had better tell him myself."

"He will not be pleased," said Gul Baz.

"Maybe not. But it is necessary. Do not let us quarrel, Gul Baz. This is something that I must do. It is laid upon me."

Gul Baz sighed and said half to himself: "What is written, is written," and did not argue any more. He went off to tell Kulu Ram that the Sahib required saddle-bags, and to bring Dagobaz round to the porch in a quarter of an hour's time; and having done that, fetched fresh tea —the original mug by now being cold. But when he would have brought the sporting rifle, Ash shook his head and said that he did not need it—"For I do not think a hakim would own such a weapon."

"Then why take the bullets?"

"Because these I shall need. They are of the same calibre as those that the *pultons* use; and over the years many Government rifles have found their way into other hands, so I can safely take the other." He had taken the cavalry carbine, and, as an after-thought, his shot-gun and fifty cartridges.

Gul Baz dismantled the shot-gun and stowed it in the *bistra,* and when all was ready, carried the heavy canvas roll out to the porch. And as he watched Ash mount Dagobaz and ride away in the crystal-clear light of dawn, he wondered what Mahdoo would have done if he had been there.

Would Mahdoo perhaps have been able to turn the Sahib from his course? Gul Baz thought it highly unlikely. Yet for the first time he was glad that the old man was no longer alive so that he, Gul Baz, was spared from having to explain how it had come about that he had stood by and seen Pelham-Sahib riding away to certain death: and been unable to do anything to prevent it.

39

Ash's first call had been at the house of the District Superintendent of Police, whom he had found lightly clad in a dressing-gown and slippers, eating *chota-hazri* on his verandah. The sun was still below the horizon, but Mr. Pettigrew, a hospitable soul, did not seem to mind receiving a caller at such an early hour. He waved aside Ash's apologies and sent for another cup and plate and more coffee.

"Nonsense, my dear chap. Of course you can stay for a few minutes. What's the hurry? Have a slice of papaya—or what about a mango? No, I'm afraid I still haven't had a word from old Tim. Can't think what he's playing at. I thought I was bound to get an answer to that telegram. But I expect he's too busy. However, you needn't worry, he's not the sort of chap who'd stick it in a drawer and forget it. In fact, he probably went off to Bhithor to see that there's no hanky-panky. Have some more coffee?"

"No thanks," said Ash, rising. "I must go. There are one or two things I have to do." He hesitated for a moment, and then added: "I'm going off into the country for a few days' shooting."

"Lucky beggar," said Mr. Pettigrew enviously. "Wish I was. But then I don't get my leave until August. Well, good hunting."

Ash had no better luck at the Telegraph Office. The clerk on duty said that there were no telegrams for him, and assured him yet again that if any had been received they would have been sent immediately to his bungalow. "This I am telling you before, Mister Pelham. We are never losing or mislaying such things. That I can promise. If your correspondents have unfortunately not sent reply, can I help it? Should they do so you shall receive same within a flash."

The clerk was obviously ruffled, and Ash apologized and left. He was not particularly worried by the absence of any replies. He realized that as there was not much that could be safely said, the most he could expect would be a bare acknowledgement. But he had hoped for that, if only because experience had taught him that even urgent messages can, on occasion, be pigeon-holed through error or idleness—it being a matter of history that the frantic telegram from Delhi, warning of the outbreak of the Great Mutiny, had been handed during a dinner-party to a high official who had put it in his pocket unread, and forgotten all about it until next day; by which time it was far too late for him to do anything about it.

In the present circumstances, Ash would have welcomed any form of acknowledgement, however curt, for the sake of his own peace of mind. But as Mr. Pettigrew had pointed out, it did not follow that because he had received none, no action was being taken, but on the contrary probably showed that it was being taken, and that

696

there was no time to spare for sending unnecessary messages.

Sarji's land lay some twenty-odd miles to the north of Ahmadabad, on the west bank of the Sabarmutti, and the morning was far advanced before Ash reached his friend's house. The servants, who knew him well, informed him that their master had been up since dawn overseeing the accouchement of a valuable brood mare, and had only recently returned. The Sirdar was at the moment breaking his fast, but if the Sahib would have the goodness to wait? Dagobaz, whose black satin coat was now sandy-grey and rough with dust, allowed himself to be led away by one of Sarji's grooms while Ash, after being given water to wash with, was politely ushered through a swaying bead curtain into a side room, and served with food and drink.

He was not invited to share Sarji's meal, and did not expect to be. For though Sarji was broad-minded, and capable when in camp or away from his home of relaxing a great many rules, here on his own ground and under the eye of his family priest it was a different matter. Among his own people a greater strictness was expected, and as his caste forbade him from sitting down to eat with one who ranked as an outcaste, his *Angrezi* friend must eat alone—and from cups and dishes that were kept solely for his own use.

Sarji was a close friend, but the rules of caste were strict and not to be lightly broken, but Ash could never avoid a pang that was part hurt and part surprise whenever he encountered those rules in action. The fact that he understood them far better than the vast majority of his fellow *feringhis* never diminished that automatic sense of shock at being made to feel a pariah—someone with whom even a close friend could not sit down to eat and drink without risking ostracism, because that simple, human act defiled the doer, and until the defilement was cleansed no one would willingly associate with him.

Drinking iced sherbet and eating vegetable curry, *kachoris* and *kela halwa* in that cool, ground-floor room in Sarji's house, Ash wondered if the family priest was aware that Sarji had often broken this particular taboo when they were out together. Somehow, he doubted it. When the dishes had been removed and he was alone

697

again, he lit a cigarette and sat blowing smoke-rings at the ceiling and thinking.

He was remembering something that Sarji's *shikari* Bukta, who had guided Gobind and Manilal to Bhithor, had told him one day when they were out shooting, when he, Ash, had been speaking of that journey. Bukta had mentioned the existence of another and shorter way into the valley of Bhithor: a secret way that avoided the forts and the frontier posts and came out a mere *koss* from the city itself, and that he had been shown many years ago by a friend, a Bhithori, who claimed to have discovered it and had used it for the purpose of smuggling stolen goods in and out of the Rana's territory.

"Horses, mostly," Bukta had said with a reminiscent grin. "One could safely ask a good price in Gujerat or Baroda for a horse that had been stolen in Bhithor, as its owner would never think to look for it here because no one else (or so my friend said) knew of this path. In those days, being young, I had little respect for the law and would often help him—with much profit to myself. But he died, and I became respectable. Yet though it is now many years since I followed his secret path, it is still clear in my mind, and I know that I could find my way along it as easily as though I had only used it yesterday. I did not speak of it to the Hakim-Sahib, as it would have been neither wise nor fitting for him to arrive by such a road."

Ten minutes later, when his host appeared in the doorway, Ash was so deep in thought that he did not even hear the clash of the bead curtain.

Sarji came in with apologies for keeping his guest waiting, but something in Ash's face checked the polite phrases that were on his tongue, and he said sharply: "*Kia hogia, bhai?*"

Ash looked up, startled, and coming to his feet said: "Nothing has happened—as yet. But it is necessary that I go to Bhithor, and I have come to ask for your help because I cannot go as I am. I must go in disguise—and as quickly as possible. I need a guide who knows the secret ways through the jungles and across the hills. Will you lend me your *shikari*, Bukta?"

"Of course," Sarji said promptly. "When do we start?"

"We? Oh no, Sarji! This is not a shooting trip. This is serious."

"I know that. The look on your face told me so as

698

soon as I came in. Besides, if you cannot enter Bhithor except in disguise, then it can only mean that it is dangerous for you to go there at all. Very dangerous."

Ash shrugged impatiently and did not answer, and Sarji said thoughtfully: "I never asked you any questions about Bhithor, because it seemed to me that you did not wish to speak of it. But ever since you asked me to send Bukta to guide some hakim who wished to go there—and later, over the matter of the pigeons—I admit I have often wondered. You do not have to tell me anything you do not wish, but if you go into danger, then I will go with you; two swords being better than one. Or do you perhaps not trust me to keep a still tongue?"

Ash said irritably: "Don't talk nonsense, Sarji. You know it is not that. It is only . . . well, this is something that concerns no one but myself and . . . and it is not a thing that I would wish to speak of to anyone. But you have already been of great help to me; and now again you are willing to help, and without question. I am more than grateful for that, and it is only fair that you should have some explanation of . . . of what is toward."

"Do not tell me anything you would rather not," said Sarji quickly. "It will make no difference."

"I wonder? Perhaps not. But then again it is just possible that it might, so I think it may be better for you to know what errand I go on before you decide whether to help me or not, since it touches upon a custom that your people have honoured for many centuries. Can anyone overhear us?"

Sarji's eyebrows lifted, but he said briefly: "Not if we walk outside among the trees." He led the way into a garden where roses, jasmine and canna lilies wilted in the heat, and here, safely out of earshot of any loitering servant, listened to the tale of the two princesses of Karidkote whom a young British officer had been detailed to escort to their wedding in Bhithor; of the tribulation and treachery they had encountered on arrival, and the terrible fate that threatened them now.

The story was incomplete and to some extent inaccurate. Ash saw no reason to mention his previous connection with the State of Karidkote, and as he had no intention of disclosing his own involvement with the elder princess, he could not give his main reason for returning to Bhithor, only the secondary one—his need to assure himself that steps were being taken to guard against the Rana's wives becoming suttees, if and when the Rana died; which was something that Sarji, as a Hindu, might feel disinclined to interfere with, for it was a custom hallowed by centuries of use, and one that even now would probably be regarded as a meritorious act by his priests and the great majority of his people.

Apart from these omissions the tale he told was accurate, and included an account of his abortive interviews with Colonel Pomfret, the Commissioner and the Superintendent of Police, and of the telegrams that had been sent and not answered:

"So you see why I have to go myself," said Ash in conclusion. "I cannot just sit here and hope for the best when I know only too well how slowly and cautiously the Raj can act at times; and how reluctant it has become to interfere in the affairs of the princes. The officials of the Raj require proof and they will not move without it. But in a case like this the proof will be a handful of ashes and charred bones, and nothing they can do then will undo what has been done, for even they cannot bring the dead back to life . . . Once the pyre has been lit it will be too late to do anything, except gaol a handful of people and levy a fine upon the state—and make excuses for themselves for not acting sooner, which will not help those poor girls . . .

"Sarji, *I* brought those two to Bhithor. You may say that I had no choice, but that doesn't make me feel any better about it, and if they are burned alive I shall have it on my conscience to the end of my life. That's no reason, though, why you should get involved in this, and if you feel you would rather have nothing to do with it—I mean . . . as a Hindu—"

"*Chut!*" said Sarji. "I am no bigot to desire the return of a cruel custom that was outlawed before I was born. Times change, my friend; and men change with them— even Hindus. Do your Christians in *Belait* still burn witches, or fellow-Christians who do not agree as to the manner in which they shall worship the same God? I have heard that this was once your custom, but not that it is still so."

"Of course not. But—"

"But you think we of this country are incapable of any similar progress? That is not so—though there are

700

many things that we do not see in the same light as your people do. I myself would not have any widow burn herself unless she desired it above all things, loving her husband so greatly that she could not endure to live without him and so chose of her own free will to follow him. That, I confess, I would not prevent, since unlike your people, I do not consider that I have a right to decide that a man or a woman may not take their own life if they choose to do so. Perhaps this is because life is less important to us than it is to you, who being Christians have only the one life on this earth, whereas we have many. We die and are re-born again a hundred thousand or a thousand thousand times; or it may be many more. Who knows? Therefore what matter if we choose to shorten one of these lives by our own desire?"

Ash said: "But suicide is a crime."

"To your people. Not to mine. And this is still my country, and not yours. As my life is also mine. But to contrive the death of another is murder, which I do not condone; and because I have seen and spoken with the Hakim from Karidkote, I am ready to believe him if he says that the Ranis of Bhithor stand in danger of being forced to the pyre against their will, for I judged him to be a good man, and no liar. Therefore I will do all that I can to help you and him, and the Ranis also. You have only to tell me what you need."

Manilal, arriving at mid-day, was met by the *shikari* Bukta, and taken into the presence of the master of the house and a man whom he did not immediately recognize: which was understandable. Sarji and Bukta had taken great pains with Ash's disguise, and walnut juice when properly applied is an admirable dye, though it does not last over-long. Ash had also shaved off his moustache, and it would never have occurred to anyone that this was not a compatriot of Sarjevar's. A sober, middle-class Indian, with a parent or ancestor who hailed from the hills where men are fairer of skin than in hotter parts of the country, and whose dress proclaimed him a professional man in good standing. A vakil (lawyer), perhaps, or a hakim, from somewhere like Baroda or Bombay.

Manilal, that stolid and imperturbable person, was for once betrayed into a startled gasp, and stood open-mouthed, staring at Ash as though he could not believe

701

his eyes. *"Ai-yah!"* breathed Manilal, awed, "it is wonderful. And yet . . . yet it is only a matter of clothes and a razor. But what is the meaning of this, Sahib?"

"Ashok," corrected Ash with a grin. "In this garb I have another name, and am no longer a Sahib."

"What does the—what does Ashok mean to do?" inquired Manilal.

Ash told him, and Manilal listened, looking doubtful, and when he had finished, said cautiously that it might serve, but that the Sahib—Ashok—must take into account that the Bhithoris were a surly and suspicious folk, apt to suspect any stranger of being a spy. More especially in the present circumstances. "They have no liking for strangers at the best of times," said Manilal, "and should their Rana die, they would think nothing of slitting all our throats if they thought that we stood in the way of anything that they desired."

"Such as a *tamarsha*," said Ash, spitting out the word as though it were a bad taste in his mouth. "What you mean is that they are looking forward to the enjoyable spectacle of two high-born and beautiful young women walking unveiled to the burning ground, and being burned alive there before their eyes."

"That is true," agreed Manilal quietly. "To look on the face of a queen, and to watch her die, is something that few will see more than once in a lifetime; so to many it will indeed seem a great *tamarsha*. But to others—maybe to all—it will be a holy occasion: one that bestows merit on everyone who is present. Therefore on both counts the people of Bhithor will be enraged if any should attempt to prevent it, and only a strong force of well-armed soldiers or police of the Raj will be able to restrain them. But one man, or two or three, can do nothing. Except lose their lives needlessly."

"I know," said Ash soberly. "And I have already thought deeply. I go because I must. It is laid on me. But there is no reason for anyone to go with me, and my friend the Sirdar here knows that."

"He also knows," put in Sarji, "that anyone riding such a horse as Dagobaz would not be travelling alone without a servant or a syce. I can act the part of one or other; or if need be, both."

Ash laughed and said: "You see how it is? The Sirdar comes of his own free will and I cannot prevent him. Any more than you can prevent me. As for Bukta, he goes only to show us the secret paths into Bhithor, so that we may go swiftly and not lose ourselves among the hills, or be stopped and questioned and perhaps turned back by those who guard the known ways. Once our road ahead is clear, there will be no need to take him further and he can return here in safety. You of course must go back to Bhithor by the same road that you came by, and be seen to return openly. It would not do for you to return secretly."

"And you?" asked Manilal, still doubtful. "When you have reached the city, what will you do then?"

"That is in the lap of the gods. How can I know until I see what the situation is and have talked to the Hakim-Sahib, and learned what measures the Sirkar has taken."

"If they have taken any," muttered Manilal sceptically.

"Indeed so. Which is why I go. I must discover if they have done so; and if they have not, take what steps I can to see that they do."

Manilal shrugged and capitulated. But he warned Ash to be very careful about approaching Gobind; his master had never been *persona grata* with the palace circle in Bhithor, and the Rana's councillors and courtiers had been hostile to him from the first.

"The Hakim-Sahib has many enemies," said Manilal. "Some hate him because he is from Karidkote, and some because he is more skilled in the arts of healing than they —while others hate him because he, a stranger, has the ear of the Rana. Me they dislike because I am his servant. But fortunately they also look upon me as a simpleton, which means that we can meet any day as strangers, and by chance, in the main bazaar or the Street of the Coppersmiths, where there are always crowds."

For the next quarter-of-an-hour they had discussed their plans in some detail, before Manilal left, riding one of Sarji's country-bred hacks in place of Ash's bay, which was thought too showy an animal for a hakim's servant to have acquired. He would take longer to reach Bhithor than the two who meant to go there by way of a smugglers' route across the hills, but he did not think that the difference would be more than a few days: two or three at most.

In fact, it was nearer five. For no one in all Gujerat

had a better knowledge of the trails through the jungles and hills than Bukta, whose father, having fled to Gujerat as a youth (according to Bukta he had killed a powerful man of his own country, somewhere in Central India), had taught his son to hunt and track almost as soon as he could walk.

Bukta had made them wait a full half hour so that Manilal should get well ahead, yet still managed to bring them to the fringes of the jungle by the time the sun had set. Despite the difficulties of the terrain, they had actually covered close on fifty miles in less than six hours, in the course of which they had crossed the Hathmati by ferry-boat, and Sarji declared that at this rate they would be in Bhithor tomorrow. But Bukta shook his head, saying that although up to now the going had been easy (which was not how Ash would have described it) once among the jungle-clad foothills they would find it increasingly difficult, and much of the trail could only be taken at a foot's pace.

They made camp near a stream, and being tired, slept soundly, taking it in turn to keep watch, as there were both tiger and leopard in these jungles and Bukta feared for the horses. Sarji, who had taken the last watch of the night, woke them at first light, and by mid-morning they were free of the jungle and among the bare slopes of the hills, where, as Bukta had predicted, they could only cover a few miles an hour, moving in single file.

Ash had brought a compass with him, but even with this to aid him he realized that left to himself among these hills he would have become hopelessly lost within a matter of minutes. The spurs and ridges ran this way and that in an aimless, featureless maze. But Bukta appeared to see and recognize landmarks that were invisible to his companions and he pressed ahead unhesitatingly, riding where the ground permitted, and where it did not, plodding forward on foot, leading his pony along narrow rock ledges or across precipitous slopes of shale or slippery, sun-bleached grass.

Once they halted for an hour by a spring among a wilderness of rocks, and later, as the afternoon drew towards evening and the folds and gullies filled with shadow, they descended a hair-raising cliff and came upon a little wooded valley, less than half-a-mile long, that lay like

704

some lost oasis among the harsh, treeless hills. Here another spring debouched from the rocks above to send a thin silver waterfall tumbling down into a deep pool that was fringed with grass and rushes and shaded by trees —a surprising sight in that barren land, and a most welcome one, for the day had been very hot and the horses were parched with thirst.

There were many animal tracks leading down to the pool and marking the damp verges, but no sign that it had been recently visited by men; which seemed to relieve Bukta, though he must have realized hours ago that for many seasons neither men nor horses could have used the trail he had been following all day, since had they done so they would have left unmistakable traces—horse droppings and the ashes of old fires.

There was nothing of that description to be seen now, and only after digging down among the roots of a certain old and twisted wild fig tree did Bukta unearth a few blackened stones, and announce with a grunt of satisfaction that this was where he and his smuggling friend used to light their cooking fire. "I was a young man then and neither of you can have been born, as that was many years ago. But it is clear to me that none save wild creatures have come to this place for a long time; which is as well, for I can light a fire here in safety."

They spent the night there, keeping the fire alight as a protection against the wild creatures that Bukta had spoken of, and were away again before the sun gilded the crests of the hills. That day was a repetition of the previous one; except that as there had been places where it was possible for the horses to trot, they had made better time, so that when evening came Ash had been all for pressing on. But Bukta had been adamant, pointing out that they were all tired, and tired men were prone to make mistakes—and weary horses apt to stumble. Also that the miles that lay ahead of them were among the most difficult, and to attempt them by night would be courting disaster, for he could easily miss the path.

The prospect of being lost in that trackless sea of hills was one he, Bukta, did not fancy; and besides, had not the Hakim's servant told them that it was the custom in Bhithor to close the city gates an hour after sunset? If that were so, there was nothing to be gained by pressing forward, and in his opinion they would be well advised to time their arrival for dusk on the following day, when men and cattle and flocks of goats would be streaming homeward from the fields and the grazing grounds that surrounded the city, and they would be unremarked among the crowds.

"He is right, you know," said Sarji. "In the evening, when the cooking fires are lit and the air is full of smoke and dust, the light is poorer—and men less inclined to curiosity, their thoughts being fixed on rest and food."

Ash had reluctantly agreed, and they found a cave among the rocks on a high ridge, and having turned the horses loose to graze, ate a cold meal for fear that a fire might attract attention, and spent the night there, going forward again only when the sun was up.

There was still no sign of a path to follow, and as far as Ash could see, not so much as a goat-track marked the bare hillsides where the scanty grass of winter was already turning brown and brittle with the approach of the hot weather. But Bukta led the way as confidently as ever, and the others followed: today for the most part on foot across steep slopes where they and their horses slithered on the brittle grass or picked their way among broken rocks, riding only occasionally in single file along some narrow ravine between sheer hillsides.

There were no springs here, and they were parched with thirst by the time they crossed a high ridge at mid-afternoon and looking down, saw below them, in a rocky hollow, a small pool of water that glittered in the slanting sunlight like a jewel in a setting of brass. It was shaded by a solitary and incongruous palm that had somehow managed to find a foothold among the rocks, and must have been fed by a spring, for the water was unexpectedly cool. To the dry-throated men and thirsty horses it tasted like nectar, and when they had drunk their fill, Bukta allowed them half an hour's rest before they scrambled up the far slope, and reaching the top of another ridge, once again moved downwards.

An hour later they reached the floor of a narrow canyon that wound and twisted between the folds of the hills like the track of some giant snake, and for the first time that day they rode forward at a brisk pace on level ground. It was a welcome change but it did not last long, for after less than a mile the canyon ended abruptly in what appeared to be an impassable barrier: the debris of

706

some ancient landslide that blocked it with a forty-foot wall of boulders and scree.

Ash and Sarji pulled up and stared at the obstruction in dismay, imagining that Bukta had taken a wrong turning and that they would have to go back. But the *shikari* dismounted, and beckoning them to do the same, walked forward leading his horse; and following doubtfully behind him they rounded a boulder the size of a small house, passed between two more, and entered a narrow crevice some twenty feet in length, where the saddle flaps brushed the rock on either side.

Like the canyon, this too appeared to come to a dead end. But Bukta turned sharply to the left, and after a further ten or twelve paces, right again—and suddenly Ash found himself out in the open, and facing the self-same stretch of valley where the Karidkote camp had been pitched two long years ago.

There was little to show where that great sea of tents and carts had once stood. All that remained of it were the dilapidated ruins of the stout, thatched-roofed sheds that Mulraj had had built to shelter the horses and elephants from the fierce glare of the sun; and of these only a handful were still standing, for sun, rain and wind, and the depredations of white ants, had combined to bring them down.

Bukta heard Ash gasp, and turned to him grinning. "Did I not say that the road here was well hidden? No one who did not know it would dream that there was a way through those rocks, or think of searching for one."

Ash glanced behind him and saw nothing but tumbled boulders and the steep flank of a hill, and realized that he himself must have looked out at this spot at least a hundred times, and ridden past it on numerous occasions, without ever suspecting that there was a way through those rocks and back into the folds of the hills behind them. He turned to study the place carefully so that he would recognize it again in case of need, noting such landmarks as a triple-fanged ridge on the hillcrest above, with a patch of shale in the shape of an arrow-head lying immediately below it.

The shale should be easy to see from a long way off, as it was several shades lighter than the hillside, while the tip of the arrow pointed directly downwards to the spot where he now stood. And nearer at hand, a mere dozen yards away, stood a twelve-foot-high boulder, liberally streaked with bird droppings and flaunting a tall tuft of grass that had sprouted from some crevice on the summit. He would recognize that boulder again, thought Ash, for combined with those parallel white streaks, the grass gave it the appearance of a plumed helmet, and he took careful note of its position in relation to the rocks that concealed the entrance to the canyon.

The old *shikari*, watching him, nodded in approval. "The Sahib does well to mark this place carefully," said Bukta, "for it is not easy to find again from this side. Well, there lies your way to the city. You had better leave me fifty rounds—and the shot-gun and cartridges also. It will cause talk if you carry more than one weapon apiece. I will remain here until such time as you return."

"That may be much longer than you think," observed Ash grimly.

Bukta waved a negligent hand. "No matter. There is both water and grazing here, and having food and the Sahib's shot-gun—not forgetting the beautiful new *Angrezi* rifle that the Sahib gave me, and my own old one also —I shall neither go hungry nor fear attack, so can wait a long time. Besides, it is in my mind that you may wish to leave in haste and by this same road, it being the only one that is not guarded, and I do not think you would find your way back to Gujerat without me."

"That much is certain," agreed Sarji with a curt laugh. "Stay then, and wait for us. For I too think that we may need to leave in haste."

The city being no more than a few miles distant and the sun still well above the horizon, they returned to the canyon and rested in the shade until the light mellowed and the shadow of the hills at their back crept forward and engulfed the valley, leaving only the opposite range warm gold against an evening sky. Only then did they rise, and whistling up the horses, led them back through the narrow passage between the rocks, mounted, and having bade goodbye to Bukta, rode out across the valley towards the dusty, beaten track along which Ash had ridden so often in the days when he and Kaka-ji and Mulraj had gone again and again to argue with the Diwan and the Rana's councillors over the disputed marriage contracts of the brides from Karidkote.

The valley had not changed, nor had the forts that overlooked it, or the frowning walls and flat, jostling roof-tops of Bhithor that blocked its far end and masked the great lake and the wide, enclosed amphitheatre of plain beyond. Nothing had changed: except himself, thought Ash wryly. In appearance, at least, he bore no resemblance to the young British officer who had ridden along this same track on a blazing spring morning, bound for the Rung Mahal and his first sight of the unpleasant despot who was to become Anjuli's husband.

He had been wearing the elaborately frogged cere-monial full-dress of his Corps, a sword had clanked at his hip and spurs jingled on his boot heels and an escort of twenty armed men had ridden behind him. While today he rode with only one companion, a man like himself, an unremarkable, middle-class Indian, clean-shaven and soberly clad, well mounted as befitted a traveller on a long journey, and armed, as a precaution against dacoits and other chance-met malefactors, with a rusty second-hand carbine of a type that was officially restricted to the army, but could be acquired—at a price—in almost any thieves-market from Cape Comorin to the Khyber.

Ash had taken pains to give that serviceable weapon the outward appearance of neglect, an effect that was purely illusory and in no degree altered its performance, and Dagobaz too had suffered a similar transformation; Bukta having insisted on altering his coat with touches of bleach and an application of reddish-brown dye before they started out, on the grounds that someone might rec-ognize the horse, if not its rider, and it was better that both be disguised so that if any accident befell them they could not be easily traced.

In addition to this the black stallion's once gleaming coat was rough with dust, while the expensive English saddle had been changed for a shabby though stoutly-made one, normally used by one of Sarji's peons, so that his whole appearance, like that of his rider, was now undis-tinguished enough to escape notice. For though anyone with an eye for horseflesh could not fail to recognize his quality, the average passer-by would not have spared him a second glance; and as Sarji had predicted, such citizens as were to be met with at that hour had other things on their minds, for by now the sun was almost down, and those who had worked in the fields all day were coming

709

home. The air was full of dust and the low, blue haze of smoke, and there was a rich smell of cattle and goats and of cooking pots simmering over innumerable fires.

The ancient bronze lamp that hung under the arch of the Elephant Gate was already being lit, and two of the three guards, their muskets laid aside, were squatting on the stone plinth by the guard-room door, intent on a game of chance and completely oblivious of the noise and the jostling throng of men and animals. The third was engaged in a wordy warfare with a carter whose off-wheel had become jammed against the gate-post, and no one challenged the two tired and dusty riders who had joined the hurrying stream of the homeward-bound.

Few if any even noticed them, and those who did were not sufficiently interested to take a second look, for it is only in small villages that men are familiar with the names and faces of every member of their community, and Bhithor was a city of close on thirty thousand inhabitants—of which at least a tenth were attached in one capacity or another to the court, and since these lived within the precincts of the royal palace, many were not personally known to a large number of the citizens, particularly to those who lived in the poorer quarters of the town.

Ash had good reason to know every turn and twist of the streets that lay between the *Hathi Pol* and the Rung Mahal, having ridden that way far too often to have forgotten it, but he knew very little of the rest of the city and must rely on the information that Manilal had given him. There was no inn or any public *serai* where a traveller could put up for a night, as Bhithor lay well off the beaten track and few travellers, it seemed, cared to visit the place: nor were they welcome.

The ease with which Ash and Sarji had entered the city was counter-balanced by the difficulty they experienced in finding a place to lodge, and night had fallen before they managed to rent a room over a charcoal-seller's shop, with permission to stable their horses in a rickety shed that occupied a corner of the yard below.

The charcoal-seller was old and infirm, and like most Bhithoris, distrusted all strangers on principle. But he was also avaricious, and though his sight and hearing were bad, both were still good enough to enable him to catch the gleam of silver and the chink of coins. He asked no questions, but after some haggling agreed to take them in

710

for a sum that was, in the circumstances, not too excessive, and raised no objection to their staying as long as they chose, providing that they paid for each day in advance.

This being settled and the first day's rent paid over to him, he took no further interest in them, and fortunately for his lodgers, the members of his household were to prove equally incurious. These consisted of three women (a humble, silent wife, an equally silent mother-in-law and an ancient servant) and his only son, a simple-minded youth who helped in the shop, and was apparently dumb, for neither Ash nor Sarji ever heard him speak.

All in all, they had good reason to be grateful to the anonymous Samaritan who had chanced to hear them being refused lodging in another house and advised them to try this one, for they could not have been better suited. Their landlord did not trouble to ask where they came from or what business had brought them to Bhithor, and plainly did not care. Also—which was equally plain and far more important—neither he nor his family were addicted to gossiping with their neighbours.

"Surely the gods were with us when they brought us to this place," said Sarji, who had anticipated having to answer a great many searching questions. "These folk are not friendly, but they do not seem to me as bad as the Hakim's servant made out that all Bhithoris were. They are at least harmless."

"As long as we pay them," observed Ash dryly. "But do not make the mistake of thinking that because they are old and blind and wholly uninterested in us, they are typical of the inhabitants of this city. They are not; and you would do well to remember that and be always upon your guard when you go abroad. We cannot afford to attract attention."

During the next few days, except for an hour each morning and evening when they exercised the horses, they spent their time strolling about the city, looking and listening and gleaning what information they could from the talk in the bazaars and wine shops. To those who asked, they gave the tale that had been agreed upon: that they were members of a party travelling to Mount Abu, who had become separated from their companions, and in endeavouring to overtake them had lost their way among the hills. Faced with the prospect of dying with thirst, they had been overjoyed at finding themselves in such a salubrious and hospitable spot as this, and intended to remain here for a few days in order to recover from their ordeal and rest their horses.

The story apparently sounded feasible, for it had been accepted without question. But if this was a weight off Ash's mind, it was the only one, because those who heard the tale had all made the same comment: that he would have to resign himself to staying longer than a few days, as only a week ago an edict had gone out forbidding anyone to leave the state until further notice—this by order of the Diwan and the council, acting on behalf of the Rana, who was "temporarily indisposed." "So it may be many days before you will be free to continue your journey to Mount Abu; perhaps a month; or even more . . ."

"But why?" Ash had asked, disquieted by this news. "For what reason?"

The answer had invariably been either a shrug, or the classic reply of those who accept every dictate of Government or fate as something beyond comprehension: "Who knows?" But one man, who had been listening while a vendor of fruit served Ash with a seer of loquats and gave him this familiar answer, had been more outspoken.

According to this citizen, the reason was perfectly obvious to anyone but a donkey. The Diwan (and everyone else in Bhithor) knew that the Rana was dying, and had no wish for the news to reach the ears of some officious *feringhi,* who might think it necessary to stir up trouble with the authorities and start interfering with matters of purely domestic interest. Therefore the Diwan had very properly "barred the gates of the state," to ensure that no spy in the service of the Government of India, or any idle chatterer either, should carry lying tales and evil talk to the Sahib-log in Ajmer—or to anyone else for that matter. "For what we choose to do, or what we choose not to do, is our affair; and we in Bhithor do not brook interference from foreigners."

So that was it: the Diwan was making certain that the only news leaving Bhithor would be such as he and his fellow-councillors approved, and that it could be carried by his own men and no one else. Ash wondered if Manilal would be denied entry, and if so, how he, Ash, was going to contact Gobind. But this was a minor worry compared with the fact that there was as yet no sign of any detachment of police or soldiery from British India, or the least indication that the Government intended to interest itself in the affairs of Bhithor.

Past experience had led Ash to talk slightingly of the Political Agencies' "see-no-evil, hear-no-evil" attitude towards the independent states of Rajputana, and their kid-glove handling of the princes. But knowing that the great majority of Political Officers did invaluable work and were not as he had chosen to describe them, he had never really believed that in the present instance those concerned would not act with speed and firmness once they were aware of what was in the wind. And as both he and Mr. Pettigrew of the police had taken steps to see that they should be made aware of it, he had arrived in Bhithor expecting to find a strong detachment of troops or police quartered in the city; or at the very least, that Spiller, the Political Officer, was occupying one of the royal guesthouses in the Ram Bagh.

The last thing he had expected to find was that no officer representing the authority of the Raj had arrived in Bhithor—or, as far as he could discover, intended to arrive. And now that the "gates of the state" had been closed and he and Sarji, like Gobind, were shut off from the outside world, it was going to be very difficult, if not impossible, to get any word out to the British authorities —except by means of Bukta's road, which would be a slow and circuitous route to Ajmer, and might well take too long to be of any use. Because the hot season was already here, and should the Rana die he would be cremated within a matter of hours—and Juli and Shushila with him.

"I don't understand it," said Ash, pacing to and fro in the room above the shop like a caged wolf. "One telegram might have gone astray, but surely not all *four*—! It's not possible. Kaka-ji or Jhoti are bound to have done something. They at least know what these people here are capable of—and so does Mulraj. They must have warned Simla. In fact they probably wired the Viceroy direct, and the A.G.G. Rajputana, too. Yet no one seems to have moved a finger. I can't understand it. I cannot!"

"Be calm, my friend," urged Sarji. "Who knows but that the Sirkar has already posted agents here in disguise?"

"What good would that do?" demanded Ash angrily.

"What do you suppose two or three spies—or six or a dozen—could do against all Bhithor? What is needed here is some senior Sahib from the Political Department or the police, with at least two companies of troops, or a strong detachment of police—Sikhs for choice. But there is no sign that the Government of India means to move in the matter, and now that the frontier has been closed, its spies—if any were sent here, which I doubt—cannot get out. And you and I can do nothing. *Nothing!*"

"Except pray that the gods, and your friend the Hakim, will prolong the life of the Rana until such time as the Burra-Sahibs in Simla and Ajmer choose to bestir themselves and make inquiries as to what goes on in Bhithor," observed Sarji unhelpfully.

He removed himself, leaving Ash to his pacing, and went down to see to the horses; and that done, sauntered through the bazaars again in search of news and in the hope of seeing a fat, foolish-seeming face among the drifting crowds. But there was still no sign of Manilal, and Sarji returned to the little room above the charcoal-vendor's shop in low spirits, convinced that the Hakim's servant must have met with some accident or else been stopped by the frontier guards and refused permission to re-enter the state; in which case the Sahib—Ashok—would undoubtedly go to the Hakim's house and demand to see him, thereby attracting to himself the attention of the Hakim's enemies—all those jealous physicians whose noses he had put out of joint and the many courtiers, councillors and priests who strongly resented the favour shown by their Rana to this interloper from the north.

Sarji had been in Bhithor for five days, but two had been more than enough to convince him that Ash's account of its ruler and his people had not been exaggerated; and that night, for the first time, it occurred to him that this masquerade on which he had embarked so light-heartedly was likely to prove a far more dangerous affair than he had imagined, and that if that fat and cunning man Manilal failed to return to Bhithor, the odds on his own chances of leaving it alive were too small to be worth betting on.

Lying awake in the hot darkness and listening to Ash's quiet breathing and the reverberating snores of the dumb youth in the shop below, Sarji shivered and wished fervently that he was back in his own safe and pleasant house

714

among the lush green fields and banana groves near Jana-pat. Life was good, and he had no wish to die, particularly at the hands of these medieval-minded Bhithoris. He heard a horse snort and stamp and a hoof thud against the wooden side of the shed as Dagobaz or his own Moti Raj lashed out angrily at some foraging rat or mongoose, and the sounds reminded him that there was still a way of escape open to them: Bukta's road. That at least was neither closed nor guarded, and tomorrow, if the fat servant again failed to put in an appearance, he, Sarji, would put his foot down.

He would have a straight talk with Ashok, and make him see that in the circumstances it was futile to invite suspicion and discovery by remaining any longer in Bhithor, and that their wisest course would be to leave by the way they had come and make for Ajmer by way of Deesa and Sirohi. True, this would take time, as it involved a considerable detour. But once there Ashok, in his own guise, would be able to see and speak to senior representatives of the Political Department and the police, explain the situation and inform them (if they did not already know it) that Bhithor had sealed itself off from the outside world and was now virtually a fortress.

Sarji distrusted the telegraph and all new-fangled means of communication, and was not in the least surprised that his friend's wires had evoked no response. A letter delivered by a trustworthy peon was, in his opinion, far more reliable. And better still was a face-to-face talk, for that way there could be no mistakes.

But as it happened there was no need for them to go to Ajmer, for Manilal was already in Bhithor. He had arrived late that evening, just as the gates were closing. And on the following morning he went to the bazaar to make some small purchases, where he fell into conversation with two visitors to the city: a tall, lean-faced man from Baroda and a small-boned Gujerati, who were debating the rival merits of mangoes and papayas with the owner of a fruit shop.

40

Gobind had not been pleased to see the Sahib.

The doctor from Karidkote had hoped against hope that when Manilal returned it would be with news that help was on the way, and during the past week he had looked to see the Political Officer or some senior Police-Sahib ride up to the Elephant Gate with a strong contingent of armed men at their back. Instead, he learned that Pelham-Sahib, having sent off several urgent telegrams that had not been answered, had insisted against all advice on coming to Bhithor himself, and was presumably at that moment somewhere in the city, disguised, and accompanied by a Gujerati friend posing as his servant.

Gobind's dismay at official lethargy was only equalled by his alarm at this disclosure, and though he seldom lost his temper, he did so now—for which he could be forgiven, as he had been living under considerable strain and Ash's presence only increased it. Gobind could not see that any good purpose could be served by the Sahib coming to Bhithor at this juncture unless he had been able to do so openly, and with the full backing of the Government. It was a piece of suicidal folly, for apart from the fact that he could do no good, if he were to be recognized he would certainly be killed; and not one of his own people would ever know what had happened to him, since according to Manilal he had left without telling anyone of his intentions.

The whole venture, in Gobind's opinion, was foolhardy to the point of madness, and could only add a further hazard to a situation that was already fraught with more dangers than he cared to contemplate. He could not understand it. Until now he had regarded Pelham-Sahib as a man of sense, and would have expected him to make straight for Ajmer to discover for himself why his telegraphed warnings had not been answered, and what action had been taken or decided upon—not dress up as a Hindu and come play-acting to Bhithor, as though it were possible for one man to turn several thousand from their purpose.

"He must leave at once," declared Gobind, turning on Manilal. "His presence here endangers us all: you and I and those few remaining waiting-women from Karidkote as well as the Ranis, whose peril is great enough already without this folly. If either he or his friend should be unmasked there is no one here who would not believe that we sent for him, and they will see to it that not one of us leaves Bhithor alive. He can do nothing here but much harm. You should have told him so, and done everything in your power to turn him from this madness."

"I did what I could," protested Manilal, "but his heart was set on it and he would not listen to me."

"He will listen to me," said Gobind grimly. "You shall bring him here tomorrow. But think carefully how you go about it, for as you know, we walk on egg-shells and cannot afford to draw attention to him or suspicion on ourselves."

Manilal had been careful. The following morning, within an hour of his meeting Ash and Sarji at a fruit-stall, half the bazaar had learned from him that the man from Baroda had studied Ayurvedic medicine in the sacred city of Kashi (Benares) and had hopes of becoming a practitioner in that ancient science. So no one thought it strange that such a person should desire to meet and talk with a hakim of a different school, it being known that professional men of opposing views delighted in argument and discussion. He had taken special pains to see that anyone he suspected of spying on his master heard the tale, and in order to avoid any suggestion of secrecy, arranged that the visitor should call openly on the Hakim-Sahib—and in daylight.

This last had not been too easy, as shortly before the hour set for the visit, Gobind had been summoned to the palace, from where he had not returned until the late afternoon, tired and dispirited, and in no mood to receive guests, particularly one on whom he had pinned so many hopes, only to be disappointed.

He greeted Ash unsmilingly, accepted without comment his explanation as to why he had thought it necessary to come to Bhithor, and when he had finished, said in a colourless voice: "I had hoped that you would be able to summon help, and when none came I feared that a

717

hawk must have slain the last pigeon before it won home, and that my servant here had either been stopped at the frontier and held on some trumped-up charge, or had met with an accident and failed to reach you. But it did not enter my mind that you could have dispatched warnings to the Sahib-log in Ajmer and to His Highness of Karidkote and my master the Rao-Sahib, and received no help from any quarter. It is beyond my understanding."

"And mine," confessed Ash bitterly.

"If you ask me," said Sarji, who had accompanied Ash to the interview, "the clerk who accepted those telegrams was a rogue, and must have kept the money himself instead of sending on your messages. It would not be the first time that such a thing has happened, and—"

"Oh, what does it matter what happened to them?" interrupted Ash impatiently. "Something did, and that's the important thing. The point is, what do we do now?"

"Leave at once for Ajmer," said Sarji promptly, repeating the solution he had arrived at during the watches of the night and already urged upon Ash. "And when we get there, demand to see the Agent-General-Sahib himself, and the police Sahibs too, and tell them—"

This time it was Gobind who cut him short. "It is too late for that," said Gobind curtly.

"Because the frontiers are closed? But there is another way out of Bhithor. The way that we came in by. That is still open, for none here know of it."

"So my servant Manilal told me. But even if you could leave by any road you chose, it would still be too late. Because the Rana will die tonight."

He heard Ash catch his breath in a gasp that was harshly audible in the stillness that followed, and turning to look at him, saw the blood drain from his face and realized with a sharp sense of incredulity that the Sahib was afraid, desperately afraid. And in the next moment, and with as much certainty as though it had been shouted aloud, he knew why—

So this was the reason for the Sahib's presence in Bhithor. Not mere foolishness and bravado, or an egotistical belief that no "black man" would dare lay hands on a member of the conquering race, and that one *Angrezi* should be able to over-awe the Diwan and the council and put the fear of the Raj into the local inhabitants.

No—the Sahib had come because he could not help it. Because he had to come. Manilal had spoken no more than the truth when he had said "his heart was set on it."

It was a complication that Gobind would never have dreamed of, and the discovery appalled him as much as it had appalled Kaka-ji and Mahdoo, and for the same reasons. "A casteless man . . . a foreigner . . . a Christian," thought Gobind, shocked to the depths of his orthodox soul. This was what came of relaxing the rules of purdah and permitting young maidens to meet and talk freely with a strange man, Sahib or no. And when the man was young and well-looking and the maidens beautiful, what else could one expect? It should never have been allowed; and he blamed the Rao-Sahib and Mulraj and young Jhoti, and everyone else whose duty it had been to see to the safety and welfare of the future Ranis. Unpora-Bai most of all.

But he knew that such thoughts were futile. What was done was done; and in any case, there was no reason to suppose that the Sahib's feelings had been reciprocated, as in all probability the one to whom he had lost his heart had remained wholly unaware of it. Gobind could only hope so. But this sudden insight into the Sahib's motives did nothing to improve his own disquiet. It merely added to his anxiety, since who could tell what folly a man in love might be capable of committing?

For a space there was silence in the room, and even Sarji seemed unwilling to break it. Gobind watched the blood come slowly back to the Sahib's face and knew what he would say before he said it . . .

"I must see the Diwan myself," said Ash at last. "That is our only chance."

"It will not serve," said Gobind curtly. "That much I can tell you now. If you think differently, then you do not know him, nor have you any understanding of the temper and disposition of his fellow councillors or the people of this city."

"Maybe. But I can at least warn him that if he permits the Ranis to burn, he and his fellow councillors will be held responsible, and that the Raj will send a Political-Sahib and a regiment from Ajmer to arrest him and to take over the state and make it a part of British India."

"He will not believe you," said Gobind quietly. "And he will be right: for even to so small and remote a place as this there has come talk of unrest in the north and of the *pultons* gathering for war. This you too must have heard as your own *pulton* will surely be among them, and having heard you must also know that the Raj will not move in this matter once it is done and cannot be undone. They will have no desire to stir up a hornets' nest in Rajasthan at a time when they have such grave matters as Afghanistan on their minds. And consider, Sahib: news of the suttee may not reach the ears of those in authority for many days—even weeks—and when it does, it will be too late to do more than send Spiller-Sahib to speak to the Diwan and council and perhaps impose a fine. But necks are not broken by hard words, and a fine can be paid from the Treasury or by means of a tax upon the people. Neither the Diwan nor his purse will suffer."

"There is also another thing," put in Sarji, addressing Ash. "Unless he is a fool he will know very well that you did not come here as an accredited spokesman of your Raj, for had you done so you would not have entered Bhithor secretly. Like a thief, and in disguise."

"That is so," confirmed Gobind. "And as the Diwan is not a fool, you will neither turn him from his purpose nor save the Ranis from the fire. You will only throw away your life to no purpose—and ours with it, for you and your friend have come openly to this house, which is watched, and once your identity is known, all our heads will fall to ensure that there is no one left to carry tales of your fate. Even those who gave you lodging will not be spared in case they might have noticed more than they should during the past few days, and be tempted to speak of it."

Ash might have argued some of Gobind's previous statements, but he was forced to recognize the truth of this one; and to be silenced by it. Had it only been a question of risking his own life in an attempt to save Juli's, he would have done so gladly and without a second's thought. But he had no right to sacrifice the lives of eight other people (for the charcoal-seller and his wife would not be the only ones in that house to have their throats cut; all five would die for the crime of having rented him a room to lodge in).

He sat staring blindly out at the view beyond the window where the low sunlight glowed rose-red on the outer walls of the Rung Mahal, his mind desperately engaged with wild plans for rescuing Juli, each one more hazardous and impractical than the last . . .

If only he could find some way of getting into the palace he could shoot down the Zenana guard, and having barred the door behind him, snatch Juli from among her women and lower her over the walls on a rope and follow himself while the enemy battered on the door; and then . . . No, that was patently impossible—it would entail tying up a score of screaming women who if left at liberty would unbar the door the instant his back was turned. He would have to have help—

Between them, he and Sarji could muster five weapons, while Gobind and Manilal could surely contrive to get possession of a musket or two. Then if Gobind was right about the Rana, it should be possible, under cover of the confusion that would reign in the palace that night, for five determined men to force their way into the Zenana Quarters and liberate two women, as everyone who could would be in or near the dying man's room, and few would have any attention to spare for the women. Vigilance was bound to be relaxed, and it might even be possible to enter the palace in the wake of Gobind, who would be admitted without question and—

Why, of course—that was how they could do it! Gobind must introduce him as a fellow-physician, a well-known practitioner of Ayurvedic medicine whose opinion could be valuable in this crisis. Sarji could pass as his assistant while Manilal, being the Hakim's servant carrying drugs, was unlikely to be questioned, and having gained admission to the palace the worst would be over, as from there they could probably bluff their way to the door of the Zenana without recourse to violence, and once inside, the rest should be comparatively simple. With the Rana dead or dying, screams and lamentation from the Women's Quarters would cause no remark, and there would be an ample supply of sheets and saris that could be used to gag and tie up the more troublesome women and knot into ropes by which the Ranis and their rescuers could descend to the dry ditch below the outer wall, from where they could escape while the city slept. It was a hare-brained scheme, but it might work: and anything, however desperate, was better than leaving Juli to her fate. But if it failed . . .

"I should have made straight for Ajmer," thought Ash.

"I could have made them listen to me. I ought to have realized that this could happen . . . that telegrams might go astray or be read and pigeon-holed by some underling who didn't realize . . . I should never have . . . Juli, oh God, *Juli!* My dear love . . . It can't happen . . . there must be some way, something I can do. I cannot stand aside and let her die . . ."

He did not realize that he had spoken those last few words aloud until Sarji said: "Her? Do you think then that it is planned that only one will follow her husband's body to the burning ground, and the other be permitted to live?"

The blind look left Ash's eyes and two spots of colour showed darkly on his cheeks. He said confusedly: "No, I didn't mean . . . I suppose they will both go. But we must not let it come to that. I have been thinking——"

He propounded his plan and the two men listened to it: Gobind impassively and the more volatile Sarji occasionally nodding approval and sometimes shaking his head. When he finished it was Sarji who spoke first: "It could succeed. But to win free of the palace would not be enough, as the city gates are closed and barred at nightfall. We should still be trapped, for even if we tied up every woman in the Zenana so that the alarm would not be given until after dawn, we could not ride out unseen and unremarked."

Ash said: "We would have to leave the horses outside the walls, and as for getting out of the city, we can do that in the same way as we shall get out of the palace ——over the wall with ropes; and if all goes well we should join Bukta and be out of the valley before the sky begins to lighten. I know it will be difficult and dangerous. I know there will be a great many risks and that things may go wrong. But it is a chance."

"It is not one that we can afford to take," said Gobind flatly.

"But——"

"No, Sahib. Let me speak. Perhaps I should have told you earlier that I can no longer return to the Rung Mahal. When I left today, it was for the last time."

According to Gobind, the Rana's councillors had been urging him to adopt an heir ever since it was learned that the Senior Rani's child was another daughter, and when he had fallen ill they had redoubled their pleas, but to no avail. He would not believe that his sickness was mortal: he would recover and sire other children, sons who would grow up to be strong men—they would see. Meanwhile, as he had no near relations apart from a pair of sickly daughters (who had failed to give him grandsons and whose husbands he despised) he refused to jeopardize the future of his line by adopting some other man's brat. His mind was made up.

Nothing that anyone could say had changed that . . . until this morning. Today, some time during the small hours, he had recognized at last that he was dying; and appalled by the prospect of descending to that hell called *Pât*, to which men who have no son to light their pyre are doomed, he had agreed to adopt an heir—though not, as had been feared, a child from the family of the Diwan, or one or other of his current favourites.

His choice had fallen instead upon the youngest grandchild of a distant relative on his mother's side—that same semi-royal relative who had been sent to greet the brides from Karidkote on their arrival in Bhithor. The boy had been sent for in haste and such ceremonies as were necessary had been rushed through, because though the choice might be a disappointment to many, even those who had cherished hopes on behalf of their own sons preferred that it should be an unimportant six-year-old rather than the child of some rival. The Rana, in fact, had remained shrewd to the end; but the effort involved had drained the last of his strength, and the affair being concluded he had collapsed and passed into a coma.

"He no longer knows me," said Gobind. "Or anyone else. Wherefore his priests and his own physicians, who have always deeply resented me, have seized their opportunity and had me expelled from his sick-room. They have also prevailed upon the Diwan, who has no love for Karidkote, to forbid me to set foot again in the palace. Believe me, they will see to it that I do not return, so you cannot use me as a cover for any attempt to enter the Rung Mahal yourself. And if you think to shoot your way in you are mad; kings are not permitted to die alone and in peace, and tonight there will be more guards and many more wakeful people in the palace than ever before, since all now know that the Rana is dying. Every passage-way and courtyard will be thronged with men who wait to hear that he has drawn his last breath, and because there is much of value in the palace, the Diwan has ordered extra guards on every door of every room—fearing, so it is said, that various trifles such as jade vases and ornaments made of gold and ivory might vanish before he himself has had time to abstract them. That last may be only slander, but I can tell you that any attempt to enter the palace by force of arms will fail."

Ash said nothing but his face spoke for him, and Gobind said gently: "Sahib, I am not so wedded to my life that I would hesitate to risk losing it if I thought that there was even the smallest chance that your plan would succeed. It is because I know there is not that I would restrain you from it. And also because if it fails, as it must, the very ones whom you hoped to save may be suspected of complicity in the plot and condemned to an even worse death than the fire. Whereas if you wait and do nothing rash, it is possible that even at the eleventh hour the Sirkar may move to prevent the burning—Yes, yes, Sahib! I know that it does not appear likely. But how do we know that they too have not laid their plans? We cannot be sure, and if we throw away our lives needlessly—killing many in that fight, as we should do, and further endangering the Ranis—it may well prove we have, as they say, 'lost Delhi for the sake of a fish.'"

"He is right," affirmed Sarji abruptly. "If he can no longer enter the palace there is no hope of our being admitted, and to attempt to force our way in would be madness. I may be foolish, but I am not mad—nor, I hope, are you."

Ash's mouth twitched in a parody of a smile, and he said: "Not yet, but—but I still cannot bring myself to believe that there is nothing I can do, and that I must resign myself to seeing . . ."

He stopped with a shudder and fell silent again, and Gobind, observing him with a professional eye, decided that madness might not be so very far off. The Sahib, it was plain, had endured much during the past week or two, and the accumulated effects of strain, fear and anxiety—and a stubborn refusal to despair contending with the gradual death of hope—had stretched his nerves almost to breaking point. In his present mood he was a danger to them all, and the next thing he would suggest was sure to be some wild scheme for snatching the Ranis as they walked through the crowds on their way to the burning

724

ground, relying on surprise, and hoping to escape under cover of the uproar and confusion that such an act would create among a milling and unmanageable mass of sightseers.

Gobind himself had, in fact, already given some thought to this particular line of action; but on consideration he had been forced to reject it, realizing that the crowd itself would wreck any such enterprise, for the people of Bhithor would be worked up to a high pitch of excitement and anticipation, and the threat of being robbed of the spectacle they had gathered to see would turn them in an instant into a raving mob. They would tear the impious intruders to pieces, and there would be no hope of escaping from them. Gobind knew this even if the Sahib did not, and he could only hope that he would be able to convince him that any such attempt would be worse than useless. But he was not called upon to do so, though he had been right in supposing that Ash was bound to think of it.

Ash had done so; but only to come to the same conclusion as Gobind. He too was aware that a crowd keyed to a high pitch of excitement can be more dangerous than a wounded leopard or a charging elephant—and that a mob is hydra-headed. If there was a way of saving Juli, it was not that one.

He rose to his feet stiffly, as though it was an effort to move, and said in a flat, formal voice: "There does not seem to be anything else to say. If either you or Manilal can think of any plan that might succeed, I would be grateful if you would let me know. I will do the same for you. We still have a few more hours of daylight and the whole of the coming night in which to think of one, and if the Rana's hold on life is stronger than you suppose, we may even have another day and another night as well; who knows?"

"Only the gods," said Gobind soberly. "Let us pray to them that tomorrow the Sirkar will send us a regiment, or at least a Political-Sahib from Ajmer. If you will take my advice, Sahib, you will try to sleep tonight. A tired man is apt to make errors of judgement and you may have need of all your wits and your strength. Be assured that I will send Manilal to you if there is any news, or if I should see any way out of this tangle."

He bowed gravely above his lifted hands, palms

725

pressed together, and Manilal saw them out and barred the door behind them.

"Where are you going?" demanded Sarji suspiciously, as Ash turned left into an alleyway that led in the opposite direction to the quarter of the town where they lodged.

"To the Suttee Gate. I must see the way that they will come, and the road they will take. I would have done so before if I had not been so sure that the Sirkar would step in before it was too late."

The alleyway skirted that side of the Rung Mahal where the Zenana Quarter lay, and presently they came to a narrow gateway cut through the thickness of the palace wall. It was an unobtrusive gate, barely wide enough to take two people walking abreast, and decorated with a curious formal pattern that on closer inspection proved to be made up of the prints of innumerable slender hands, the hands of queens and concubines who down the long centuries had walked through that gate on their way to the fire and to sanctification.

Ash had seen and noted it on his previous visit to Bhithor, and now he did no more than glance at it as they passed. His interest was not in the gate but the route that the procession would take from there to the pyre. The burning-ground lay some distance from the city, and as the city gates would be closed within an hour of sundown there was no time to waste, and he hurried Sarji forward, taking note as they went of every turn and twist and alleyway between the Suttee Gate of the Rung Mahal and the *Mori* Gate, which was the nearest of the city gates.

Ten minutes saw them out in the open country and walking along a dusty road that led straight as a narrow towards the hills. There were no houses here, and no cover, but there was a good deal of traffic on the road, mostly pedestrian and all of it moving towards the city. Presently Ash said: "There should be a path leading off to the right somewhere here. I used to ride across this bit of country, but I never actually visited the memorial *chattris* and the burning-ground. I did not think then that . . ." He left the sentence unfinished to stop a herd-boy who was driving his cattle back to the city, and inquire the way to the burning-ground.

"You mean Govidan? Are you strangers that you do

not know where the burning-ground of the Ranas lies?" asked the boy, staring. "It is over there—where the *chattris* are. You can see them above the trees. The path is no more than a stone's throw ahead of you. Are you holy men, or do you go to make arrangements for the Rana's burning? Ah, that will be a great *tamarsha*. But he is not dead yet, for when he dies the gongs will beat, and my father says they can be heard as far as the Ram Bagh, so that all . . ."

Ash thrust an anna into the boy's hand and left him, and a few minutes later they came to the spot where a side path led right-handed out of the main road towards the lake. The path, like the road, was deep in dust, but here there were no cartwheel tracks and few traces of cattle or goats. But a party of horsemen had obviously ridden down it and returned again fairly recently, for the least breath of wind would have smoothed away those hoof-prints.

"They came to select a site for the funeral pyre," said Sarji.

Ash nodded without speaking, his gaze on the dark patch of greenery ahead. Behind him the evening was full of sounds: the bleating of goats and the lowing of cattle, the shrill cries of herd-boys and the soft cooing of doves, the clamorous call of a partridge and from somewhere on the road the squeak and squeal of cart-wheels rumbling homeward to the city. Comfortable, everyday sounds; pleasantly familiar and very different from the deafening babble of the peering, jostling, wailing crowd that would gather here only too soon, jammed together shoulder to shoulder and pressing in on either side of this same dusty path that he was walking along now . . .

If he rode here he would have to leave Dagobaz tethered somewhere well beyond the crowds, for apart from the multitudes who would flock here to watch the cremation, thousands more would accompany the bier and its escort, milling about it and moving slowly forward in a rolling tide of humanity, resistless and terrifying. Visualizing the scene, Ash realized that the only advantage to be gained from it would be anonymity. No one was going to pay the least attention to him if he joined that crowd. He would merely be one of them, another onlooker, unremarkable and unremarked—provided he came on foot.

A mounted man would be far too conspicuous; and in any case, Dagobaz was unused to such crowds and there was no knowing how he would react to one.

"It would not be possible," muttered Sarji, whose mind had evidently been moving on similar lines. "Had this place only been on the other side of the city, there might have been a chance. But we could never get away from here even if we could cut our way through the crowd at our backs, since those hills there hem us in on one side and the lake on the other, while over there——" he jerked his chin to the eastward "——there is no way out, so we should have to ride back towards the city and everyone here would know it."

"Yes, I realized that."

"Then why are we here?" There was more than a trace of uneasiness in Sarji's voice.

"Because I wanted to see the place for myself before I made up my mind. I thought perhaps that there might turn out to be some . . . some feature of it that could be turned to advantage, or that might suggest something to me. There may yet be. If there is not, we shall be no worse off."

The hoof-prints stopped within the fringe of a dense grove of trees, and it was easy to see where the riders had dismounted and left their horses before entering the grove on foot. Ash and Sarji, following the same path between avenues of tree-trunks and out into the open again, found themselves in a large clearing in the centre of what appeared to be a deserted city: a city of palaces or temples, set among the trees.

There were buildings everywhere. Memorial *chattris*. Vast, empty, symbolic tombs, built of the local sandstone and intricately and beautifully carved, some of them three and four storeys high so that their airy, domed pavilions, screened in pierced stone and piled one upon the other in the manner of a fantastic house of cards, stood well above the tree-tops.

Each *chattri* commemorated a Rana of Bhithor, and had been raised on the spot where his body had been burned. And each, in the manner of a temple, had been built to surround or face on to a large tank, so that any who came to pray could perform the proper ablutions. It did not appear that many did so, for the water in the tanks was mostly green and stagnant and full of weeds and mud fish, and many of the *chattris* were half ruined. Pigeons, parrots and owls had built nests in crevices between the stones and among the weathered carvings that decorated pediments, archways and domes, a troop of monkeys pranced along the walls and the trees were full of birds quarrelling with each other as they came home to roost. But apart from the birds and monkeys and a solitary priest who was saying his prayers while standing waist-deep in one of the tanks, the place appeared to be deserted, and Ash surveyed it with the eye of a General planning a battle.

That open space over there was the obvious site for a new pyre, and to judge from the many footprints that patterned the dust at that particular spot, it had been inspected during the past day by a large number of people who had walked all over and around it, stood talking together for a considerable time, and gone away without visiting any other part of the grove. These marks were proof that this was where the next Rana would be cremated and where in time his *chattri* would be built, and there was also enough space here for several thousand onlookers as well as the protagonists—and an excellent field of fire for anyone standing above the crowd, say on the terrace of a near-by *chattri* . . .

Sarji touched his friend's arm and spoke in a whisper that had been forced on him by the brooding atmosphere of the place: "Look—they have hung *chiks* up there. What do you suppose that is for?"

Ash's gaze followed the direction of Sarji's pointing hand, and saw that one storey of the nearest *chattri* had indeed been enclosed with split-cane *chiks* that hung between each pair of pillars, thus turning the top-but-one pavilion on the near side into a small room.

"Probably for some of the purdah women who want to watch. The Diwan's wife and daughters—people like that. They'll get an excellent view from there," said Ash, and turned away quickly, nauseated by the thought that not only the ignorant and humbly-born women, but pampered, aristocratic ones would be equally eager to watch two members of their own sex burned alive—and think themselves blessed by being present.

He made a circuit of the grove, walking between the crowded *chattris* and the silent tanks that mirrored walls and terraces and domes that had been built before the days of Clive and Warren Hastings; and by the time he returned to the central clearing it was deep in shadow.

"Let us get away," urged Sarji with a shiver. "This is an ill-omened spot, and the sun is almost down. I would not be caught near this place when night falls for all the gold in the Rana's treasury. Have you seen all that you wish to see?"

"Yes," said Ash. "All and more. We can go now."

He did not speak again during the walk back to the *Mori* Gate, and for once Sarji too showed no desire to talk. The sight of that silent, tree-enclosed city of tombs had shaken him more than he cared to own, and once again he found himself wishing that he had never become involved in this affair. Admittedly, Ashok had acknowledged that any last-minute attempt at a rescue from the grove was out of the question, but Sarji had an uneasy conviction that he had something else in mind—some scheme that he intended to carry out alone and without asking advice or assistance from anyone. Well, if he must, he must. There was little one could do to prevent him. But it was bound to end in disaster, and as the Hakim had pointed out, failure would inevitably end in death for all of them. How long, wondered Sarji, would Bukta wait before realizing that his master and the Sahib would never return . . . ?

There were many more people than usual in the city that night, for by now the news that the Rana was dying had reached every village and hamlet in the state, and his subjects were flocking into the capital in order to witness his obsequies, and to look upon the suttees and acquire merit by being present at their sanctification. The talk in the streets was all of the approaching ceremonies, every temple was crowded, and by nightfall the square in front of the palace was overflowing with townsfolk and peasants who gaped at the main gate of the Rung Mahal while they waited for news.

Even the charcoal-seller and his silent wife seemed to have caught some of the excitement, for they greeted the return of their lodgers with unexpected loquacity and a hail of questions. Where had they been and what had they seen and heard? Was it true that they had visited the Rana's foreign physician, a hakim from Karidkote, and if so had he told them anything new?

Did they know that when a Rana of Bhithor died,

the great bronze gongs that hung in a gate-tower on the walls of the Rung Mahal were beaten so that all might know of his passing? Should the gongs sound by night, the twin forts that guarded the city would light beacon fires on hearing them; thus signalling the news to every hamlet and village in Bhithor, while in the city itself the outer gates would instantly be thrown open so that the ruler's spirit might pass out—choosing by which it would leave, east or west, north or south.

"And also in order that any who wish to take up positions on the road along which the bier will be carried can do so," said the charcoal-seller. Adding that it was a wise precaution, as otherwise people who wished to be in the forefront of the crowd would gather near the gates in great numbers before dawn, causing considerable confusion and probably trampling women and children and elderly persons to death in the rush to be first through the gates when the bars were lifted.

"For myself," said the charcoal-seller, "I mean to go to the Suttee Gate and stand in the ditch below the wall. From there one should see well, and I would advise you to do the same, because you will be looking upwards instead of trying to peer over the heads of taller men who may block your view. Ah, it will be a sight worth seeing. It is not often that one has the chance to see a Rani unveiled, and this one is said to be a very queen of beauty. Though the other, her sister whom they call Kairi-Bai, is clumsy and ill-favoured; or so I have heard."

"Yes indeed," said Ash, mechanically filling the pause but with his mind so clearly elsewhere that Sarji looked at him sharply and the charcoal-seller, taking offence, turned his back on him and began to shout angrily at the idiot boy. The noise served to rouse Ash from his abstraction, and he inquired abruptly if anyone had left a message for him. But no message had come from Gobind: nor was there any sign that the Government of India intended to exert its authority and enforce its laws.

"There is still time," consoled Sarji as they left the yard after seeing to their horses and he preceded Ash up the narrow staircase, carrying a lighted lamp and the key. "The Rana is not dead yet, and for all we know, a *pulton* may arrive here this very night. And if that old fool speaks truth and the gongs have sounded, they will find the gates open."

731

"Yes," said Ash thoughtfully. "That is going to make it a lot easier."

Sarji looked back at him with a grin, taking the remark for sarcasm, but Ash's face was serious and intent as though he were concentrating deeply, and there was a look in his eyes that Sarji did not like—an odd, fixed look that boded no good. What had he decided to do? wondered Sarji in sudden panic. Surely he did not *still* believe that the Sirkar would send a regiment to Bhithor? What had the gates got to do with it? *What* was going to be easier?—and for whom? Sarji stumbled on the top step and took an unconscionable time fitting the key into the clumsy iron padlock because his hands were shaking.

The small room was stiflingly hot and reeking of charcoal fumes and the odours of cooking that had drifted up from below in the course of the day, and Ash unbarred the single window and flung it wide to let in the night air, and leaning out over the sill, sniffed the familiar smell of horses. The yard below was in darkness and he could not make out Dagobaz's black shape among the shadows, but Moti Raj's grey coat showed up as a pale blur, and he could hear Dagobaz stamp and snort, disturbed by a rat or the mosquitoes, and angry at being denied his evening exercise.

"Those two will be as glad to get out of this place as I shall," observed Sarji, groping in a saddle-bag for matches. "*Phew!* it is as hot as a potter's kiln and it stinks of bad *ghee* and stale cabbage—and worse things."

Ash turned away from the window and said: "Cheer up. If the Hakim-Sahib is right, this will be the last night you will have to spend here, and by this time tomorrow you will be twenty *koss* away and asleep under the stars, with old Bukta to keep watch."

"And you?" said Sarji. He had found the matches and lit a second oil lamp, and now he held it up so that the light shone on Ash's face. "Where will you be?"

"I? Oh, I shall be asleep too. What else?" said Ash, and laughed. He had not laughed like that—or at all—for many days, and it took Sarji aback, for it appeared completely unforced. A gay, relaxed sound; and a reassuring one.

"I'm glad you can still laugh," observed Sarji. "Though I do not know why you should do so. The gods know there is little enough to laugh at."

732

"If you really want to know," said Ash, "I laugh because I have given up. I have 'thrown in the towel,' as my countrymen say. I admit myself defeated, and it's a relief to know where I stand and to see the future with a clear eye. They say drowning is quite pleasant once you stop struggling, and that is what I have done. To change the subject, have we anything to eat here? I'm starving."

"I too," laughed Sarji, his attention instantly diverted by the thought of food—they had not eaten since morning, and then only sparsely; anxiety is not conducive to good appetite and both men had passed a restless night. "There should be a chuppatti or two and some *pekoras*. That is, if the rats have not got them."

The rats had not, but the ants had shown more enterprise. What little was left went out of the window, and as Ash refused to patronize one of the eating-houses in the city on the grounds that all would be grossly overcrowded that night and he did not feel equal to waiting for hours on the chance of getting a vacant place, Sarji went off to buy what they needed from a food stall, leaving with a lighter heart and in better spirits than he would have thought possible half an hour ago.

He was relieved beyond measure that his friend should at last come to his senses and see the futility of trying to battle against impossible odds. For to Sarji, Ash's sudden return to normality, and the fact that he could laugh again—and feel hungry—proved that he had indeed made up his mind and was no longer tortured by indecision or torn this way and that between fear and hope and doubts. Now they need not even stay until the Rana died, for as they could not prevent what would follow, there was no point in their remaining in Bhithor one moment longer than necessary.

They would leave at dawn as soon as the gates were open, and Ashok would have no reason to blame himself. He had done all he could and it was not his fault that he could not achieve the impossible. If there was blame let it rest on the shoulders of the Government, who had been warned and refused to take action; and on the Diwan and his fellow-councillors, together with the priests and people of Bhithor, who intended to turn the clock back and practise the old customs of an age that was already over. This time tomorrow he and Ashok and Bukta—and perhaps the Hakim and his servant too—would be safe among the

733

hills. And if they made good time and moved by night (for now there would be a moon to help them) another two days should see them across the border and back once more in Gujerat.

"I will make a thank-offering to my temple in gratitude for my safe return: the price, in silver, of the best horse in my stud," vowed Sarji. "And once I am free of this ill-omened place I will never again set foot in it—or in Rajasthan either if I can help it."

He brought hot food from a cook-shop. Steaming rice and fire-hot vegetable curry, *dal, pekoras,* and half-a-dozen freshly made chuppattis. And from a sweet-stall in another part of the bazaar, *hawla-sharin* made in the Persian manner with honey and nuts, and an anna's worth of crisp, sticky *jellabies.*

It had been a slow business, for as Ash had predicted, the bazaars were crowded; and though many of the farmers and village-folk who had flocked to the city had thriftily brought their own provisions with them, others had not, and the food shops and stalls were besieged by hungry customers. But it was done at last, and Sarji extracted himself from the press and walked back heavily laden, nibbling *jellabies* and humming the refrain of a song composed by one of Ahmadabad's best-known courtesans.

He was still singing as he mounted the rickety stairs and flung open the door of the rented room. But at the sight of Ash the song stopped short and the singer's eyebrows rose in surprise.

Ash was sitting cross-legged in front of a make-shift desk formed by Dagobaz's saddle, and he was writing a letter—the last of several it seemed, for at least five neatly folded squares of paper lay on the floor beside him. He was using ink and a reed pen that he must have borrowed from the shop below, and writing on pages torn from a cheap loose-leaf notebook; and there would have been nothing surprising about it, except that he was writing in English.

"Who is that for?" demanded Sarji, coming to peer over Ash's shoulder. "If it is for some Sahib in Ajmer, you will not find a messenger to take it. Not at this hour, or for the next few days either. Have you forgotten that no one may leave the state?"

"No," said Ash, continuing to write. He finished the letter, and having run his eye over it and made one or two minor corrections, signed his name at the bottom of the paper and handed the pen to Sarji. "Will you write your name there, below mine? Your full name. It is only to show that you are a witness that I myself wrote this letter, and that this is my signature."

Sarji stared at him for a moment under frowning brows, and then squatted down and added his name to the paper, the neat, stylized script in strange contrast to the careless Western scrawl above it. He blew on the wet ink to dry it, and returning the letter said: "Now tell me what all this is about?"

"Later. Let us eat first and talk afterwards. What kept you? You must have been away for hours, and my stomach is as empty as a dry gourd."

They ate in companionable silence, and when they had finished, Ash strewed the remains of his meal on the window-sill for the crows and sparrows to dispose of in the morning; but when Sarji would have followed suit, he said quickly: "No, don't do that. No need to waste good food. Wrap it up and put it away in one of the saddle-bags. You may have need of it, for if the crowds are as thick tomorrow as they were tonight, you may find it difficult to buy more before you leave, and it is certain that Bukta will have none to spare by now."

Sarji stood rigid, his hand still outstretched and his startled gaze asking the question that he could not force his tongue to utter. But Ash answered it as though it had been spoken aloud: "No, I shall not be coming with you. There is something I have to do here."

"But—but you said . . ."

"That I had given up. So I have. I have had to give up all hope of rescuing her. It cannot be done. I can see that now. But I can at least save her from being burned alive."

"*Her?*" repeated Sarji, as he had done earlier that day in Gobind's house when Ash had unconsciously used the singular instead of the plural. But he had not used it so now: he had used it deliberately, because there was no longer any point in concealment. The time for that had gone—together with the need to keep silent.

"Her," said Ash softly. "Anjuli-Bai, the Junior Rani."

"*No*," breathed Sarji, the barely audible syllable as eloquent of horror as though he had screamed it.

Ash did not misunderstand him, and his smile was

rueful and a little bitter. "That shocks you, doesn't it? But they have a saying in *Belait* that 'a cat may look at a king'; and even a casteless *Angrezi* can lose his head and his heart to a princess of Hind, and be unable to regain them. I'm sorry, Sarji. If I had known that it would end like this I would have told you before. But then I never dreamed that it would or could end like this, and so I only told you part of the truth. What I did not tell you, or any-one, was that I had come to love one of the brides whom I had been charged to bring to Bhithor . . . to love her be-yond reason. There is no blame on her, for she could not have prevented it. I saw her married to the Rana . . . and came away, leaving my heart in her keeping. That was more than two years ago; but it is hers still—and always will be. Now you know why I had to come here: and also why I cannot leave."

Sarji released his breath in a long sigh and put a hand on Ash's arm, gripping it. "Forgive me, my friend. I did not mean to insult you. Or her. I know well that hearts are not like hired servants who can be bidden to do what we desire of them. They stay or go as they will, and we can neither hold nor prevent them. The gods know that I have lost and regained mine a dozen times. For which I have cause to be grateful, for my father lost his once only: to my mother. After she died he was never more than the shell of a man. He would have felt for you. But he could no more prevent my mother's death than you can prevent the Rani's."

"I know that. But I can and will save her from death by fire," said Ash with shut teeth.

"How?" Sarji's fingers tightened on his arm and shook it angrily. "It is not possible, and you know it. If you mean to break into the palace—"

"I don't. I mean to reach the burning-ground ahead of the crowd and take up a position on the terrace of that *chattri*: the one overlooking the spot where they will build the pyre. From there I shall be able to see over the heads of the crowd below, and if by the time the women reach the clearing there has been no intervention by the Sirkar, and I know that the end is near, I shall do the only thing I can for her . . . put a bullet through her heart. I am too good a shot to miss at that range, and it will be a quick death and far more merciful than the fire. She will not even know that she has been hit."

736

"You are mad!" whispered Sarji, his face grey with shock. "Mad." He snatched his hand away and his voice rose: "Do you think that those nearest you will not know who has fired the shot? They will tear you in pieces."

"My body, perhaps. But what will that matter? There are six bullets in a revolver, of which I shall only need two: the second will be for myself. Once I have fired it I shall neither know nor care what the mob does to me, and if, as you say, they tear me to pieces, it will be the best thing that could possibly happen, because then no one will ever be able to say who I was or where I came from —or even if I was a man. So we must hope that they will do so. All the same, you would be advised to leave as early as you can: you and the Hakim-Sahib and Manilal . . .

"I have written to the Hakim, telling him that you will meet them at the spot where the road crosses the stream and there are two palm trees and a wayside shrine. Manilal will know it well. They must leave the city by the *Mori* Gate, to make it appear that they mean to attend the cremation; and once in the open country they should be able to separate themselves from the crowd without being observed, and make their way to the valley. I'll deliver that letter myself before I leave. There will be too many people in the square for the watchers to keep tally of everyone who passes the Hakim-Sahib's door."

"And the other letters?" asked Sarji slowly, glancing at the pile on the floor.

"Those I hope you will take back with you and post at the dâk-*khana* in Ahmadabad." Ash picked them up and handed them over one by one: "This is the one that you put your name to: it is my Will and I have addressed it to a lawyer in *Belait*. And this, which is also in *Angrezi*, is for a Captain-Sahib in my Regiment in Mardan. These two are for an old man, a Pathan, who has been as a father to me, and for his son who has been my friend for many years. And this—No, this one too I will deliver myself to the Hakim-Sahib to take to Karidkote, as it is for the Ranis' uncle. This last is for my bearer, Gul Baz. Will you see that he gets it? And that he and the other servants get back safely to their homes?"

Sarji nodded wordlessly, and having scanned the letters carefully, stowed them away under his shirt without making any further effort to argue or plead.

Ash said: "There is one other thing you can do for

me—as a great favour. I would give much not to ask it of you, for it will mean delaying your departure, and delay could be dangerous. But I can't see any other way, because unless I am to risk getting caught up in the crowds and finding myself in the thick of the press from where I may not even be able to see her, I must reach the burning-ground ahead of the rest, which means that I cannot go on foot. But if it's true that the city gates will be thrown open if the gongs sound tonight to signal the Rana's death, when we hear them I have only to saddle Dagobaz and ride for the nearest gate, and from there in my own time to the *chattris*. The sooner I go the less likely I am to be stopped by the crowds, but it would be wiser for you to come later and with less haste, and . . . if you will give me an hour's start I will leave Dagobaz at the edge of the grove, on the side furthest from the city and behind the ruined *chattri* with the triple dome—the crowds will not reach as far back as that, and you should find him easily enough. Will you take him with you Sarji, for my sake? I would not ask it of you except that I could not bear to abandon him in such a place as this. Will you do that for me?"

"You do not need to ask," said Sarji brusquely.

"Thank you. You are a true friend. And now, as there may be much to do tomorrow, let us take the Hakim-Sahib's advice, and sleep."

"Can you do so?" asked Sarji curiously.

"Why not? I have not slept well for many nights because my mind would not let me rest. But now that all the problems are settled and the way ahead is clear, there is nothing to keep me awake. Besides, if Gobind is right about the Rana, I shall need a clear eye and a steady hand tomorrow."

He rose to his feet, yawned and stretched, and crossing to the window looked out at the night sky and wondered what Juli was doing, and if she was thinking of him. Probably not, since by now Shushila must be half mad with terror, and Juli would have no thought to spare for anyone or anything else. Not for her lover or her old uncle, or for the mountains and deodar forests of Gulkote. Least of all for herself, even though she faced the same fate as Shu-shu. It had always been this way, and would be to the last. Dear Juli . . . dear, loving, faithful Kairi-Bai. He found it difficult to realize that tomorrow or the

738

next day he would actually see her again. Only very briefly, and then—

Would the crash of his revolver herald darkness and nothingness? Or afterwards would they meet again, and be together for ever and ever? Was there a life after death? He had never been sure, though all his close friends seemed to be certain enough. Their faith was firm, and he envied them that. Wally, Zarin, Mahdoo and Koda Dad, Kaka-ji and Sarjevan might differ as to what form it would take, but they did not doubt that there was one. Well, he would soon know if they were right . . .

Wally was a believer. He believed in God and in the immortality of the soul, "the resurrection of the body, and life in the world to come." And also in such old-fashioned deities as duty and courage, loyalty, patriotism and "the Regiment"; for which reason—quite apart from the fact that there was no time now to write a lengthy letter—it had been impossible to tell him the truth.

To have written to him at all was probably a mistake, thought Ash. It might have been kinder, in the long run, if he had merely dropped out of Wally's life without a word or a sign, and let him think what he liked. But the thought of Wally waiting and wondering, hoping against hope that one day his friend and hero would return, was not to be borne; and besides, there was another consideration—the fact that Wally (and only Wally) could be counted upon to do everything in his power to have his friend's disappearance investigated, which would ensure that the burning of the Rana's widows would not be kept secret, as Bhithor would wish . . .

True, Gobind would know what had happened; and so would Kaka-ji and Jhoti and some others. But Ash did not believe that Karidkote would take the matter up officially once the thing was done. The Ranis' family were, after all, devout Hindus, and it was difficult to expect them to regard a suttee in the same light as it appeared to foreigners. They would certainly have done what they could to prevent it, but having failed, they would see no profit in raising a scandal, particularly when in their heart of hearts they—and the majority of their co-religionists—must still regard the act in question as a meritorious one.

As for Koda Dad and Zarin, they too would keep silent, on the grounds that what Ashok chose to do was his own affair. And though the Guides and the military authorities in Peshawar and Rawalpindi would of course make inquiries, his past history would tell against him, since it would be argued that he had done this sort of thing before—disappeared for the best part of two years and been presumed dead—so that when he failed to report back to his Regiment he would once again be listed as "Absent Without Leave," and after a time his name would be struck from the records and he would be written off as *"Missing, believed dead."*

But Wally could be trusted to go on hoping and to badger senior army officers, importune officials of the Government, and write letters to *The Times of India* and *The Pioneer,* until someone would eventually have to take notice of the affair. And though it was unlikely that the true facts of Lieutenant Pelham-Martyn's disappearance would ever emerge, at least there would be no more suttees in Bhithor.

Ash watched the moonlight creep up the side of a house that backed on to the yard, and remembered a night among the ruins of Taxila, when he had talked for hours, telling Wally the incredible tale of his childhood, as he had never been able to tell it to anyone else except Mrs. Viccary. It was strange to think that of all his friends, Wally should be the only one who could not be told the truth now. With the others, it was different: for one thing, they had no built-in prejudice against a man taking his own life. They did not regard that as a sin, as Christians were taught to do. Nor did they hold that a man was master of his fate.

But to Wally—a practising Christian, and a dedicated soldier in love with his regiment—suicide would seem unforgivable: a sin not only against God, but the Guides, because at this particular time, when "wars and rumours of wars" were the talk of the North-West Frontier, it would be regarded as a form of cowardice comparable with "Desertion in the face of the enemy." For if hostilities on a scale of the first conflict with Afghanistan broke out the Guides were going to need the services of every officer and every man, and since cowardice and "letting the side down" were the two cardinal sins in Wally's lexicon, he would undoubtedly think that the needs of Queen and Country should take precedence over any purely personal attachment, however deep, and that if Ash was set on dying, then the proper and honourable course would have been for him to hurry back to Mardan and take up his duties, and hope to be killed in battle, leading his men.

But then Wally had never known Anjuli-Bai, Princess of Karidkote and Rani of Bhithor, so the letter addressed to him was, in consequence, a very brief one and would allow him to suppose (if or when he should hear that Ash was dead) that he had died at the hands of a mob, following an unsuccessful attempt to prevent the burning of a widow. That way he would still be able to think of his friend as a hero—and keep his illusions.

"He'll grow out of them one day," thought Ash. "And no one else will talk: certainly not the Bhithoris. The Bhithoris will lie and evade and pervert the truth until even those who were there and saw it all won't be quite sure what happened—if anything. In the end it will probably be given out that the Ranis died of typhoid fever, and the authorities may even pretend to believe it in order to save their faces and avoid having to take any action."

As for him, no one but a handful of his friends would ever know or care what had become of him . . . "This time tomorrow, it may all be over," thought Ash; and was surprised to find that he could face the prospect with so little emotion. He had always imagined that the phrase about the "condemned man eating a hearty breakfast" had been meant as a grim joke, but now he realized that it was probably true, for once one gave up all hope, a curious peace took its place. One accepted the inevitable, and ceased struggling. He had been hag-ridden for days by fear and hope and the need to make plans that had invariably proved impossible to carry out, and now that all that was ended he could only feel a sense of exhausted relief, as though he had been freed from a burden that had become too heavy to carry.

The stars were growing pale as the moonlight brightened, and now the line of hills beyond the city was no longer a vague shadow against the indigo of the night sky, but sharp-edged with silver as though they were covered in snow; and for a magical moment it seemed to Ash as though he saw the Dur Khaima itself, transported to this hot and arid corner of Rajputana to bestow a last blessing on a some-time worshipper. He picked up a handful of the

741

crumbs that he had strewn on the window-sill, and let them fall again, murmuring the old prayer . . . *O, Lord, forgive . . . Thou art everywhere, but I worship thee here . . .*

The years had gone so fast . . . so fast. But it had been a good life, and he had much to be thankful for; and so many memories to take with him—wherever it was that one went. If it were true, as some said, that when men died their spirits returned to the place that they had loved best during their lifetime, then he, Ash, would awake to find himself among the mountains, perhaps at long last in that very valley that Sita had described so often that he could almost believe that he had seen it. The valley in which they would build themselves a hut out of deodar logs, and where they would plant cherry trees and grow corn and chillies and lemons, and keep a goat. And allow Kairi-Bai to come with them . . .

The thought brought him the first comfort he had found that day, and when he turned from the window and lay down, fully dressed on the string bed, he was smiling.

41

Gobind had been right: the Rana did not live through the night. He died in the dark hour before dawn, and not long afterwards the stillness was shattered by the boom of the great bronze gongs that have announced the death of every ruler of Bhithor since Bika Rae, the first Rana, founded the city.

The sound shuddered through the hot darkness and reverberated among the surrounding hills like a roll of thunder, the echoes passing it on and on down the valley and out across the quiet lake. It woke the sleeping city and sent flocks of roosting crows wheeling and cawing above the rooftops, and brought Ash from his bed, instantly awake and alert.

The little room was still breathlessly hot, for the night wind had died. The moon too had gone, hidden by the hills and leaving the room in such darkness that it took Ash a minute or two to find and light the lamp. But once that was done the rest was easy, and five minutes later he was down in the yard with Sarji and saddling Dagobaz.

There had been no need for silence or caution. The night was filled with the deep-throated booming of the gongs, and by now lamps were being relit in every house and the crowds who had slept in the open were awake and vocal.

Dagobaz did not care for the gongs. His ears were laid flat back and his nostrils flared as though, like the horses in the Old Testament who cried "Ha Ha!" among the trumpets, he could smell *the battle afar off, the thunder of the Captains, and the shouting.* He had flung up his head and whinnied when he heard Ash's step, and for once stood quietly without backing or sidling, or playing any of his usual tricks.

"This is the first time I have known him behave so well," said Sarji. "He is one who likes to show that he has a will of his own and does not wear a saddle from meekness—or choice. You would almost think that he knows there is serious work afoot."

"Of course he does. He knows everything, don't you, my son?"

Dagobaz bowed his head to nuzzle Ash's shoulder as though in affectionate agreement, and Ash rubbed his cheek against the velvet nose and said with a catch in his voice: "Be good to him, Sarji. Don't let him . . ." He broke off abruptly, aware of a constriction in his throat, and for the next few minutes busied himself with the remaining straps. When he spoke again his voice was curt and unemotional:

"There, that's done. I've left you the carbine, Sarji. I shan't need it, but you and the others may, so you must take it with you. You know what to do, don't you? There's no need to go over it again. We have been good friends, you and I, and I'm sorry that I let you get involved in this affair and brought you into danger—and that it had to end like this. I should never have let you come, but then I'd hoped that . . . Oh well, it doesn't matter now. But be careful, Sarji—be very careful. For if anything were to happen to you—"

"It won't," said Sarji quickly. "Do not worry, I will be

careful, I promise you. Here, you had better take my whip. It may come in useful to clear a way through the crowds. You have the revolver?"

"Yes, open the yard door for me, will you? Goodbye, Sarji. Good luck . . . and thank you."

They embraced as brothers do, and then Sarji went ahead with the lamp, and unbarring the door, held it open while Ash led Dagobaz out onto the street. "It will be light soon," said Sarji, holding the stirrup while Ash mounted. "The stars are already pale and the dawn is not far off. I wish . . ."

He broke off with a sharp sigh, and Ash leant from the saddle to grip his shoulder for a brief moment, then touching Dagobaz with his heel, he rode away without looking back.

It had not proved as easy as he had thought to reach Gobind's house, for the eerie clamour seemed to have drawn half the population of Bhithor to the Rung Mahal, and not only the square in front of the palace but every street and alleyway leading to it was packed to suffocation. But somehow he had managed to force a way through, using Sarji's whip mercilessly on the surrounding heads and shoulders, and urging Dagobaz onward a foot at a time while the crowd shouted and cursed and gave way before him.

The door of Gobind's house was barred, and anyone deputed to keep watch on it must have been swept up and carried along with the crowd minutes ago, as Ash himself would have been had he not come on horseback. But being mounted gave him another advantage, for by standing up in his stirrups he could just reach a first-floor window that had been left open because of the heat of the night. There was no light in the room behind it—or, as far as he could see, in any part of the house. But when he hammered on the lattice with the butt of the whip, Manilal's round, pale face appeared in the opening.

"What is it? Who is it?"

Ash thrust the two letters at him by way of reply, and without speaking wrenched Dagobaz round and began to force his way back down the street against the moving torrent of people. Ten minutes later he was clear of them and riding hard through dark and almost deserted alleyways towards the *Mori* Gate. Here there were lights again: oil lamps, lanterns and cressets. And more people,

744

though not too many; one or two guards and nightwatchmen, and a few small groups of country folk from outlying villages, who had evidently been camping out under the great archway and were now busy preparing an early meal before setting off to join the crowds about the palace.

The glare from the cressets and the wavering gleam of half-a-dozen little cow-dung fires made the sandstone walls glow like burnished copper, and by contrast the landscape that lay beyond the gateway appeared as a square of blackness—for the charcoal-seller had not lied about the opening of the gates: they stood wide and unguarded, so that the spirit of the dead ruler might pass through if it so wished . . .

Legend had it that the gate most favoured on these occasions was the *Thakur* Gate, because of its proximity to the city temple. But until now no one, not even the priests, had ever claimed to see a spirit pass. Tonight, however, all those who had the good fortune to be near the *Mori* Gate were to declare that they had actually seen this happen: that the Rana himself, clad all in gold and mounted on a coal-black horse whose hooves made no sound, had swept past them as silently and swiftly as a sudden gust of wind, and vanished into thin air.

The gold, of course, was pure invention. But then it must be remembered that the spectators were simple folk and saw only what they expected to see. To them, a Rana would naturally be splendidly dressed. It is also possible that a combination of torch-light and the glow from those small cooking fires, falling on Ash's light-brown clothing (and aided by the haze of smoke), could have lent it a fleeting illusion of splendour. But for the rest, the clatter of Dagobaz's hooves had been drowned by the mourning of the gongs, and in order to avoid any risk of being stopped, Ash had taken him through the gateway at full gallop, where once beyond the range of the firelight and the flares, horse and rider had instantly been lost to view.

All unaware that he had destroyed one legend and created another that would be told and re-told for as long as superstition survived or men believed in ghosts, Ash rode away from the city along the dust-laden north road.

For a moment or two the transition from light to darkness made the countryside seem an inky waste and the grey ribbon of the road barely visible for more than a few yards ahead. Then his eyes adjusted to the change and he realized that the dawn was already at hand and the near hills sharply distinct against a brightening sky in which the stars no longer blazed and glittered, but showed as pale as the petals of faded jasmine blossoms.

The little wind that is the forerunner of morning had begun to breathe across the fields, rustling the standing crops and lending an illusion of coolness to the air, and already it was possible to make out objects twenty and thirty yards distant: a boulder, a shrub, a *kikar* tree or a feathery tuft of pampas grass; and further off still, a herd of black-buck trotting sedately away across the plain after a night spent foraging in the cultivated land, and the lean grey shape of a wolf loping steadily towards the hills.

Dagobaz had always revelled in early morning gallops over open country, and of late he had spent too many hours shut up in a shed in the charcoal-seller's yard. In addition to which that frightening and inexplicable booming had set every nerve in his body on edge, and even out here he could still hear it, fainter now, for the breeze was carrying it away down the valley, but still all too audible. He redoubled his efforts to escape it, and as they were now beyond the crop-lands, swerved from the road and took to the rougher ground, his rider making no effort to restrain him.

The wolf glanced over its shoulder and broke into a canter, imagining itself pursued, while further to the left the black-buck herd took fright and went bounding away across the shadowy plain. And for a brief space Ash forgot what lay ahead and was suddenly caught by the familiar intoxication of speed and of being at one with his horse. A tremendous, all-possessing excitement that seemed to hold him rigid, his hands motionless on the reins, his thighs clamped to the saddle. What did it matter if he died today or tomorrow? He had lived. He was alive now—joyously and intensely alive—and if this was the last morning he would ever see, what better way to spend it?

The black stallion's body and his own were one, and his blood sang in rhythm with the pounding hooves as the air fled past them and the ground flowed away beneath them as smoothly as a river. The sound of the gongs dwindled away until it was no louder than the sough of wind under a door, and ahead a water channel cut a wide

dark furrow across the plain. Dagobaz took it in his stride
and raced on towards a wicked barrier of thorn bushes.
Gathering himself together he rose to it smoothly, cleared
it with ease, and landing on the far side as lightly as a
bird was off again without a check.

Quails, partridges and an occasional sandgrouse
whirred up and scattered before him, and a young cobra,
rudely disturbed, reared up hissing from the grass and
struck out furiously at the flying hooves. But Dagobaz ignored them all and swept on, nostrils wide and mane and
tail streaming out on the wind, racing to meet the morning . . .

"You beauty," crooned Ash, "you wonder!" He began to sing at the top of his voice, swaying in the saddle
in time to the tune and the swift, effortless stride of the
horse:

"Thou wast their rock, their fortress and their might!
Thou, Lord, their Captain in the well fought fight.
Thou, in the darkness drear, their one true light—
Alleluia . . . ! Alleluia . . . !"

He laughed aloud, realizing that he had without
thinking been singing one of the rousing hymns that he
had so often heard Wally sing in his bath of an early
morning—and on many other occasions when they had
ridden together galloping neck and neck across the plains
around Rawalpindi—it being one of Wally's favourite descriptions of a particularly fine day that it was "A day for
singing hymns on." But the laugh froze in his throat, for
suddenly he heard a far-away voice, faint but clearly
audible above the pounding hoofbeats, chanting in answer
to him: *"Al-le-lu-ia!"*

For a moment his heart stopped and he tried to
check Dagobaz, because he thought it was Wally. Yet
even as he pulled on the rein he realized that what he had
heard was only the echo of his own voice thrown back
at him from the far hillsides. The discovery sobered him
a little; there were villages among those hills, and realizing that if he could hear that sound so clearly there might
be others who had done so too, he sang no more. Yet
some of the exhilaration that had caused him to do so
remained, and instead of feeling sad or apprehensive he
was conscious of a curious sense of excitement: the taut,

747

ice-cold excitement of a soldier on the eve of a battle.

By the time Dagobaz slowed down they were far beyond the dark grove of Govidan, and all about them the great amphitheatre in its circle of hills lay bathed in a pearl-pale light that cast no shadows. The quiet stretch of the lake mirrored a sky that was already yellow with the dawn; and as the light brightened and partridges and peacocks awoke and began to call, the gongs in the city stopped beating, and Ash turned back towards the burning-ground.

He rode slowly now, drinking in the beauty of the early morning, the sight and the sound and the scent of it, like a man parched with thirst and slaking it with spring-water. Few people would have found much to admire in such scenery, and to the majority of Europeans the flat, featureless plain and the circle of barren hills would have appeared ugly and daunting. But though Ash had every reason to dislike Bhithor, the dawn sky and the cool pale light slowly flooding the land, the clamour of partridges and peacocks and the scent of dust and smoke and *kikar* blossoms were an integral part of the world that he had loved and was leaving, and he savoured them with a new sense of awareness and a deep feeling of gratitude for benefits received.

He rode with a slack rein, and Dagobaz, having worked off his suppressed energy, was content to keep to a walk for a time. There was no need to hurry, as it was unlikely that the Rana's body would arrive at the burning-ground much before mid-day. For though the funeral would take place as soon as possible because of the heat, the procession would take time to organize, and there were bound to be endless delays. On the other hand the crowds would get there early in order to secure good places, and already there were signs of activity in the grove. Pin-points of brightness, barely visible in the fast-growing light, betokened cow-dung fires, and gossamer veils of smoke crept out from among the tree-trunks, creating an illusion that the place was an island surrounded by shallow water.

As he came nearer Ash could glimpse the saffron-clad figures of priests moving to and fro, and looking towards the city he saw that there were horsemen on the road, riding at a gallop to judge by the dust cloud that rose up behind them and partly obscured the groups of pedestrians that followed in their wake. Presently the twin forts that crowned the hills to the left and right of the city caught the first rays of the sun and flamed red-gold against the cool aquamarine of the sky, and now from every corner of the plain pale smudges of dust told of parties of people converging on the burning-ground in carts and dhoolies, on horseback or on foot. It was clearly time to get to the grove, and obedient to the pressure of Ash's knee, Dagobaz quickened his pace.

Once among the trees on the eastern fringe of the grove, Ash dismounted and led his horse towards the ruins of an ancient *chattri* surmounted by a triple dome. There were several tunnel-like passages in the massive plinth, some of them leading directly to a central tank that was open to the sky, while others sloped sharply upward and had once contained stairways that led up to the broad terrace overlooking it. The stairs had fallen long ago, and nowadays no one visited the ruined *chattri*, but one of the passages was still in good repair, and as a temporary stable would be far cooler and more comfortable than the charcoal-seller's shed.

Ash tethered Dagobaz to a fallen block of masonry and fetched water from the tank in a canvas bucket that he had brought with him. He had also brought grain and a small bundle of *bhoosa* in a saddle-bag, for he knew that Sarji might not be able to collect the horse for another hour or two, and that after that there would be no stopping until they were clear of the valley and far along the trail through the hills. So it was necessary to supply Dagobaz with food and water now.

The water was green and stagnant, but that wild gallop across the dusty plain had made Dagobaz thirsty and he drank it gratefully. When he had finished, Ash fetched a second bucket-full and wedged it carefully between two blocks of sandstone so that it would not collapse. Dagobaz smelt it but did not drink, and ignoring the *bhoosa*, dropped a wet affectionate nose onto his master's shoulder, nuzzling him as though he sensed that there was something wrong.

"You'll be all right with Sarji," consoled Ash huskily. "He'll take care of you . . . you'll be all right." He put an arm about the black head and gave it a brief, hard hug,

749

and then pushing it aside, turned on his heel and walked out of the shadowed archway into the brightness of the sunrise.

The fringes of the grove were still deserted, but near the centre the sound of bird-song gave place to the voices of men. Where the trees stopped behind the *chattris* that faced the open sweep of the burning-ground, groups of people could be seen hurrying to and fro: enterprising vendors of food and drink busily setting up their stalls under the shade of the branches, and already serving a handful of early customers. But as yet there did not appear to be many spectators, and although there were a score of priests and officials and a number of men in the uniform of the palace guard in the clearing, none showed any interest in Ash, since all were far too busy supervising the construction of the pyre and talking among themselves.

The *chattri* nearest to them was a larger and more elaborately decorated version of the far older one where he had left Dagobaz, being built in the form of a hollow square surrounding a vast tank. But here the stairways in the thickness of the outer wall were in excellent repair, and Ash climbed one, and reaching the broad stone terrace without being molested, took up a position in the angle between the outer parapet and the wall of a small pavilion that flanked a much larger central one consisting of three tiers of diminishing width, each tier composed of graceful pillared arches with the final one topped by a number of hump-backed domes.

Similar though smaller structures adorned the other three sides of the square, and below them, from the level of the terrace and facing inward, wide, shallow stone steps led down to the water's edge. The *chattri* had been built to face eastward into the sunrise and the clustered trees, but directly behind it lay the open ground, and today the western pavilions looked down onto a hastily constructed brick platform not thirty yards from the foot of the terrace wall, where half-a-dozen priests were constructing a pyre from logs of cedar and sandalwood strewn with aromatic spices.

The newly risen sun striped the ground with brilliant bars of light and long blue shadows, but as it moved up the sky the shadows shrank and changed their shapes and the dawn wind died; and suddenly the freshness was gone from the morning and the day was breathlessly hot. "There will be a breeze soon," thought Ash. But today there was no breeze. The leaves hung limp and still and the dust lay unstirred, and behind him the green, glassy surface of the tank mirrored every detail of the *chattri* so clearly that had he moved to the back of the terrace he would not have needed to look up to where the purdah-screens formed a make-shift room out of the second storey, because it lay there in the water.

For the present it appeared to be untenanted; there was no flicker of movement from behind the split-cane *chiks* that faced towards the burning-ground, but by now there were many more people in the grove: a number of early arrivals from near-by villages, several ash-smeared Sadhus and a further influx of minor officials, puffed up with their own importance and issuing orders to the men who had brought the logs and to those whose task it would be to hold back the crowds and keep a way clear for the funeral procession.

It was as well for Ash that he had taken up his stand when he did, for before long what had begun as a trickle increased to a flood as the thousands from the city poured into the grove, turning the wide, dusty space and the long, narrow aisles between the trees into a sea of humanity that stretched back on either side of the road by which they had come.

Above this, men clustered as thick as swarming bees on the walls and terraces, the stairways, pavilions and rooftops of the surrounding *chattris*, and soon every branch of the nearer trees bore its load of determined spectators. The voice of that multitude was a corporate sound—a deep and deafening one that rose and fell like the purr of some giant cat. And still the wind did not blow . . .

The dust that fumed up under the restless feet of the crowd hung in the air like the smoke trails of the early morning fires, and with every passing minute the heat increased as the sun blazed down on the stone-built *chattris* and glittered blindingly on the quiet surface of the tanks. But the crowd were impervious to these discomforts. They were used to dust and heat and cramped conditions, and it was not often that they had the opportunity to witness such a notable ceremony as the one that would be enacted here today. If it involved a certain amount of discomfort, well, that was a small price to pay for something that all who were privileged to be present would talk of for years to come, and describe to generations yet unborn. For even here, in this remote corner of Rajasthan, there were few who were not becoming uneasily aware that in the India beyond their borders the old ways were changing and old customs dying out, and that if the Raj had its way, this might be the last suttee that anyone in Bhithor would ever see.

Ash, from his vantage point on the terrace, was equally unaffected by the dust and din and the soaring temperature. He would probably not have noticed if it had suddenly begun to rain or snow, for all his faculties were concentrated upon keeping calm and relaxed. It was essential that his eye should be clear and his hand steady because there would be no second chance; and remembering what Kaka-ji had told him about the benefits of meditation, he fixed his gaze on a crack in the top of the parapet and counted his heartbeats, breathing slowly and evenly and forcing himself to think of nothing.

The crowd pressed upon him from the left, but his back was against the wall of the pavilion, and the space between his knees and the edge of the parapet was too narrow to allow room for even the smallest child to squeeze in front of him. So far, this side of the terrace was still in shadow, and the stone at his back still retained some of the coolness of the previous night. Ash relaxed against it and felt curiously peaceful; and very sleepy, which was hardly surprising considering how poorly he had slept ever since Manilal's arrival in Ahmadabad, though in the present circumstances, with the prospect of eternal sleep a mere hour or so away, it seemed a little ridiculous.

Ridiculous or not, he must actually have dozed off; for aroused by the sudden impact of a solid body and a sharp pain in his left foot, he opened his eyes to find that the sun was directly overhead and the crowd were no longer facing away from him, but had turned and were staring up at the *chattri*.

On the terrace itself half-a-dozen helmeted members of the Rana's palace guard were laying about them with their staves in an attempt to clear the way to the stairway leading to the second storey, and as the crowd surged back before them, the stout gentleman on Ash's left had been forced to give ground and had jerked him into wakefulness by stepping on his toes.

"Your pardon," gasped the stout one, recovering himself and struggling to remain upright. He appeared to be in imminent danger of falling backwards over the parapet to land on the heads of the citizens twenty feet below, and Ash put out a hand to steady him, and inquired what was happening.

"It is some high-born women who have arrived to see the burning," explained the stranger breathlessly, replacing his turban which had fallen off in the struggle. "Doubtless the family of the Diwan. Or perhaps that of the heir? They will watch from above—from behind the *chiks* up there. Though the boy himself will walk in the procession and set light to the pyre. They say that his mother . . ."

The man talked on and on, gossiping, speculating and commenting, and Ash nodded now and then, but after a time he ceased to listen. His mouth was dry and he wished he had thought to bring his water-bottle with him instead of leaving it strapped to Dagobaz's saddle. But one of the many things that he had learned during those years in Afghanistan, when he had been masquerading as a Pathan and had to keep the Moslem fast of Ramadan, was how to endure thirst. And as Ramadan lasts a month (during which time no food or water may be taken between dawn and sunset) when it falls in the hot weather it can be no mean test of endurance.

Juli too must be thirsty, thought Ash. It would be another torment to add to those she must suffer on that long, last walk in the dust and the sun between the peering, jostling crowds. And she must be so tired . . . so very tired . . . It was difficult to believe that soon he would actually see her again in the flesh: the real Juli, instead of the one he had only seen in his imagination for the past two years. Her sweet grave eyes and tender mouth; the wide tranquil brow and the faint hollows at her temples and below her cheek bones that he always longed to kiss. His heart turned over at the thought, and it seemed to him that to see her again, if only for a moment, was worth dying for . . .

He wondered what the time was. To judge by the sun it must be well past mid-day, so it could not be long now before the Rana's body was carried out of the Rung Mahal to begin its last, slow-paced journey from the city. And behind it would come Juli . . . Juli and Shushila, Ranis of Bhithor . . .

They would be dressed in all their wedding finery: Juli in yellow and gold and Shu-shu in scarlet. But this time their spangled saris would not be pulled forward over their faces, but thrown back, so that everyone could see them. The suttees. The holy ones . . .

Ash knew that in the past many widows had been given drugs in order that they should not shrink from their duty or make any attempt to avoid their fate, but he did not believe that Juli would go drugged to her death; though she could be trusted to see that Shu-shu did, and he could only hope that the drugs would be strong ones— potent enough to numb Shushila's senses and shut out reality, while still enabling her to walk. For they would be expected to walk. That was the custom.

He shut his eyes against the glaring sunlight, but found this time that he could no longer shut out thought. Pictures formed behind his closed eye-lids as though he were seeing lantern-slides flashed on a screen: Juli in her yellow and gold wedding-dress with her black hair rippling unbraided to her knees, supporting the dazed, ruby-decked figure of her little sister . . . The two of them moving out from the shadows of the Queen's Palace into the blazing afternoon, walking towards the Suttee Gate and pausing there to dip their hands into a bowl of red dye before pressing them against the stone sides of the archway, where the imprint of their palms and fingers would join those of many former queens of Bhithor who had in their turn passed through that cruel gate on their way to death.

Well, at least it would bear no more prints, thought Ash. And perhaps some time in the next century, fifty, sixty or a hundred years hence, when even such dark corners as this would probably have been tamed and become respectable and law-abiding—and dull—parties of earnest globe-trotters would come to stare at the archway and be told the tale of the Last Suttee. The very last in Bhithor. And of how an unknown madman . . .

Ash had not noticed when the gossiping voice at his elbow ceased, or when the deafening babble of the crowd began to die away until even the hucksters and the children stopped shouting and stood quiet to listen. It was

754

the unexpected silence that broke his waking dream. The watchers had seen puffs of white smoke and bright flashes from the forts that overlooked the city, and now that silence had fallen, they could hear the boom of cannon. The forts were firing a salute as the dead Rana left his capital city for the last time.

A man in the crowd cried shrilly, "Hark! They come," and Ash heard a far-off sound, harsh, ululating and indescribably mournful—the screech of conch-shells blown by the Brahmins who walked at the head of the funeral cortège. As he listened there came another sound, equally far away, but as unmistakable: a great roar as thousands of voices greeted the appearance of the suttees with shouts of *"Khaman Kher! Khaman Kher!"*— "Well done!"

The crowded terraces and the close-packed masses below stirred and swayed like a field of corn when a gust of wind blows over it, and the babble broke out again, less noisily than before, but so fraught with anticipation that the very air of the hot afternoon seemed to vibrate to the tension that gripped the waiting crowds.

The hum of voices drowned those distant sounds, making it impossible to hear them or to judge how long it would be before the cortège reached the grove. Half an hour, perhaps? The distance by road between the *Mori* Gate and the grove was less than a mile and a half, though the sound of the conches had not to travel so far, it being considerably less as the crow flies. But then Ash had no way of knowing how far the procession had come already. The trees and the *chattris,* the dust and the heat-haze made it impossible to see the road, and it might be nearer than he supposed.

The only thing that he could be sure of was that it would come very slowly, because of the crowds who would press forward to throw garlands upon the bier and make obeisance to the dead man's widows, struggling to touch the hems of their saris as they passed, begging for their prayers and stooping to kiss the ground they had trodden on . . . Yes, it would be a slow business. And even when the cortège reached the burning-ground there would still be plenty of time, for he had taken the trouble to learn all that he could of the rites that would be performed.

Tradition dictated that a suttee should wear her wedding-dress and also deck herself with her finest jewels; but not that it was necessary for her to take such valuable things into the flames. One must, after all, be practical. This meant that Juli would first strip off all her glittering ornaments. The rings, bracelets, earrings, pins and anklets, the necklaces and brooches that had been part of her dowry—all must be removed. After which she must wash her hands in Ganges water and walk three times round the pyre before she mounted it. There would be no need for haste and he would be able to choose his moment.

Only half an hour more . . . perhaps less. Yet all at once it seemed an eternity and he could not wait to have it over and be done with it. To be done with everything—!

And then, without warning, the incredible thing happened:

Someone clutched his arm, and supposing it to be his talkative neighbour he turned impatiently on him, and saw that the garrulous gentleman had been elbowed out of his place by one of the palace servants, and that it was this man who had hold of his arm. In the same moment it flashed across his mind that his purpose must have been discovered, and instinctively he tried to jerk free, but could not because of the wall at his back, and because the grip on his arm had tightened. Before he could move again, a familiar voice spoke urgently from behind the concealing folds of muslin that covered the lower part of the man's face: "It is I, Ashok. Come with me. Hurry."

"*Sarji!* What are you doing here? I told you—"

"Be quiet," muttered Sarji, glancing apprehensively over his shoulder. "Do not talk. Only follow me."

"No." Ash tore at the clutching fingers and said in a furious undertone: "If you think you can stop me, you are wasting your time . . . Nothing and no one is going to stop me now. I meant every word I said, and I'm going to go through with it, so—"

"But you cannot; she is here. *Here*—with the Hakim."

"Who is? If this is a trick to get me away . . ." he stopped short because Sarji had thrust something into his hand. Something thin and small and hard. A broken sliver of mother-of-pearl carved in the semblance of a fish . . .

Ash stared down at it, dazed and disbelieving. And Sarji seized the opportunity to draw him away and drag him, unresisting, through the close-packed crowd that

756

gave them right of way only because of the dress that Sarji wore: the famous saffron, scarlet and orange of a palace servant.

Behind the mass of spectators, a number of soldiers of the State Forces were keeping a path clear between the side exit from the terrace and the stairway leading up to the screened second storey of the central pavilion. But they too recognized the palace colours and let the two men through.

Sarji turned right, and without relaxing his grip on Ash's arm, made for a flight of stairs that plunged downward into shadow and ended at ground level in a short tunnel similar to that in which Dagobaz had been tethered. Only privileged spectators had been permitted to use this route, and there was no one on the stairs, the guards being outside the entrance—those below watching for the cortège and those on the terrace holding back the public. Halfway down there was a break in one wall where a low doorway led into a narrow, dog-leg passage that presumably came out by the central tank, and there was no one here either, for the same reason. Sarji plunged into it, and releasing Ash, loosened the wide end of the muslin turban that had been swathed across his face, and leant against the wall, breathing fast and unsteadily as though he had been running.

"Wah!" gasped Sarji, mopping the sweat from his face. "That was easier than I expected. Let us hope the rest will be." He stooped and picked up a bundle that lay on the floor. "Here, put these on quickly. You too must be one of the *nauker-log* from the Rung Mahal, and there is no time to waste."

The bundle consisted of clothing similar to Sarji's, and while Ash put them on, Sarji gave him a brief account of what had occurred, speaking in a disjointed and barely audible whisper.

He had, he said, been preparing to leave when Manilal arrived at the charcoal-seller's shop with news that upset all their plans. It seemed that the Senior Rani, realizing that she must die, had determined to use the considerable power and influence that she still possessed to save her half-sister Anjuli-Bai from sharing the same fate. This she had done.

On the previous night she had arranged to have her sister taken secretly from the Rung Mahal to a house outside the city, asking only that Anjuli-Bai should witness the final ceremonies; to which end a screened enclosure would be prepared for her use and she would be taken there on the day of the funeral by a picked band of guards and servants, all of whom had been selected because of their known loyalty to the Senior Rani. Word of all this had been brought that very morning by the serving-woman who had often acted as a go-between, and the Hakim had instantly sent Manilal to fetch the Sahib—only to find that the Sahib had already gone.

"So we went back on foot to the Hakim's house," said Sarji, "and it was he who devised all this. He even had the clothing in readiness, because, he said, it occurred to him many moons ago that one day he might have to escape from Bhithor—and how better to do this than in the guise of one of the palace servants, who go everywhere without question? So he caused Manilal to buy cloth in the bazaar and to make two sets of their use, in case of need. And later, thinking that he might be able to take one or both of the Ranis with him, two more; and then a fifth and sixth, in case there should be more from Karidkote who would go. We put on those clothes and came here, no one preventing us and—are you ready? Good. See that the end of the turban does not slip down and betray you. Now follow me—and pray to your God that we are not questioned."

They had not been. The affair had been absurdly easy, for the beauty of Gobind's scheme lay in the fact that the Rung Mahal and the various other royal palaces of Bhithor swarmed with servants; many more than could possibly have been necessary, and certainly too many for any one of them to know more than a third of the others by sight even when they were not on duty and able to leave their faces uncovered. Also on this occasion there was too much of interest going on for the guards on the terrace to notice that two men wearing the dress of royal servants had come up the stairs where only one had gone down.

After the semi-darkness of the passage below, the glare was so intense that Ash had to screw up his eyes against the sunlight as he followed Sarji into the lower storey of the main pavilion, where half-a-dozen members of the Rana's personal bodyguard had been posted to see that the public did not enter. But these too took no interest in a pair of palace servants, and Sarji walked boldly past them and up a curving stairway that led to the second storey, where purdah screens hung between the open archways.

Ash, a pace behind him, could hear him muttering beneath his breath, and realized that he was praying—presumably in thankfulness. Then they had reached the top and Sarji was holding aside a heavy curtain and motioning him to enter.

42

The make-shift room was cooler than might have been expected.

It was also very dark, for all but one of the split-cane *chiks* that enclosed it were lined with a coarse, brick-red cloth embroidered in black and yellow and sewn with little circles of looking-glass after the fashion of Rajputana. The single exception hung between the two centre pillars facing the burning-ground, its fragile slats letting in the only light and providing an excellent view to anyone looking out, while preventing anyone outside from seeing in.

The shadowy enclosure was roughly fifteen feet square and it appeared to be full of people, some of whom were seated. But Ash saw only one. A slim figure standing a little apart from the rest in an attitude that was curiously rigid, and that suggested, starkly, a captive wild animal immobilized by terror.

Juli . . .

He had not really believed it until then. Even after those hasty explanations, and though he held the proof in his hand, he had not been sure that it was not some trick on the part of Sarji and Gobind to lure him away and keep him prisoner until it was all over and too late for him to intervene.

She was standing in front of the unlined *chik*, so that at first he only saw her as a dark figure outlined against the oblong of light: a faceless figure dressed like the others in the garments of a palace servant. Because of those clothes, a stranger entering the room would have taken her for a man. Yet Ash had known her instantly. He would, he thought, have known her even if he had been blind, because the tie between them was stronger than sight and went deeper than externals.

He pulled away the folds of orange and red muslin that had been wrapped about his face, and they looked at each other across the width of that shadowed room. But though Ash had put aside the loose end of his turban, Anjuli did not follow his example, and her face remained hidden except for her eyes.

The beautiful, gold-flecked eyes that he remembered so well were still beautiful—they could never be anything else. But as his own became accustomed to the subdued light he realized that there was neither gladness nor welcome in them, but such a look as might have belonged to the child Kay in Hans Andersen's fairy-story *The Snow Queen,* whose heart had been pierced by a sliver of glass: a blank, frozen look that appalled him.

He started forward to go to her, but was prevented by someone who moved quickly between them and laid a restraining hand on his arm: Gobind, unfamiliar in the same disguise as Juli wore, but with his face uncovered.

"Ashok," said Gobind. He had not raised his voice, but both tone and touch conveyed a warning so vividly that Ash checked, remembering just in time that except for Sarji, and Juli herself, no one present knew that there was anything between the widowed Rani and himself— and must not know it; especially at this juncture, since there was not one of them who would not be as shocked by it as Sarji or Kaka-ji had been, and the situation was dangerous enough already without his making it worse by alienating his allies.

He forced his gaze from Anjuli though it was an effort to do so, and looked instead at Gobind, who permitted himself to draw a deep breath of relief—he had feared that the Sahib was about to shame the Rani and embarrass them all by some open demonstration of feeling. That danger at least had been averted, and he withdrew his hand and said: "I thank the gods that you have come; there is much to do, and these here will need watching. The woman most of all, for she would scream if she could, and there

760

are a score of guards within hearing—in the pavilion above us, as well as below."

"What woman?" said Ash, who had seen only one.

Gobind gestured with a slim hand and for the first time Ash became aware of the others in the curtained room. There were seven of them, not counting Manilal, and only one of these was a woman—presumably a waiting-woman of Juli's. The obese, slug-like man whose pallid cheeks and numerous chins were as smooth as a baby's could only be one of the Zenana eunuchs, and for the rest, two from their dress were palace servants, another two troopers of the State Forces, and one a member of the Rana's bodyguard. All of them were seated on the floor, and all had been gagged and trussed up like fowls—except the last, who was dead. He had been stabbed through the left eye, and the handle of the stiletto-like knife that had been driven into his brain still protruded from the wound.

Gobind's work, thought Ash. No one else would have known how to strike with such deadly accuracy, and it was the only vulnerable spot. The surcoat of chain-mail and the heavy leather helmet with its deep fringe of linked metal would have deflected any attack on the wearer's head, throat or body. There had been only one chance . . .

"Yes," said Gobind, answering the unspoken question. "We could not stun him with a blow on the head as we had done with the others, so it was necessary to kill him. Besides, he spoke through the curtain to the eunuch, not knowing that we had the creature safely tied, and from what he said, it became plain that there are those who mean to see that Anjuli-Bai is punished for escaping the fire and thereby failing to do her duty as a Rani of Bhithor. She is not to be allowed to return to Karidkote or retire to one of the smaller palaces, but will go back to the Women's Quarters of the Rung Mahal, where she will spend the rest of her life. And lest she should find that life too pleasant, it has been arranged that as soon as her sister, the Senior Rani, is dead and can no longer intervene to save her, her eyes are to be put out."

Ash caught his breath in a choking gasp as though the air had been driven from his lungs, and Gobind said grimly: "Yes, you may well stare. But that is what was planned. The brazier is out there in readiness, and the

761

irons too; and once the pyre was well alight the thing would have been done—here, in this place and by those two, the eunuch and that carrion who lies there with my knife in his brain, the woman and these others helping. When I think of it I am sorry that I did not kill them all."

"That can be remedied," said Ash between his teeth. He was shaken by a cold, killing rage that made him long to get his hands on the fat eunuch's throat, and the woman's too, and choke the life out of them—they and the four others, bound and helpless as they were—because of the inhuman thing they had planned to do to Juli. But Gobind's quiet, commanding voice cut through the murderous fog that filled his brain, and brought him back to sanity.

"Let them be," said Gobind. "They are only tools. Those who ordered or bribed them to do this thing will be walking in the funeral procession and beyond the reach of our vengeance. It is not justice to kill the slave who does as he is bid, while the master he obeys goes free. Besides, we have no time for vengeance. If we are to leave here alive we shall need that man's gear, and one of the servants' also. Manilal and I will see to that if you and your friend will watch the prisoners."

He did not wait for an answer, but turned away and began to remove the dead man's accoutrements, starting with the padded leather helmet that was as yet comparatively free from blood, for he had been careful not to withdraw the knife and the wound had bled very little.

Ash allowed himself a brief glance at Juli, but she was still gazing out at the burning-ground and the waiting multitudes; and with her back towards him she was once again only a dark figure silhouetted against the light. He looked away again, and taking out his revolver, stood guard over the prisoners while Sarji watched the entrance and Gobind and Manilal worked swiftly and methodically, unfastening buckles and stripping off the surcoat, which for all their care was not a silent process.

The chain-mail clashed and clinked against the marble floor and jingled as they handled it, and the noise it made seemed very loud in that constricted space. But the surrounding curtains shut it in, and the sound of the enormous crowd outside was more than enough to cover anything less than a scream—or a shot; it would take a considerable commotion to cover that last, and Ash was well aware that the revolver was useless, for if he fired it the guards and servants on the floors above and below them would come running.

Fortunately the captives did not appear to realize this. The mere sight of it had proved enough to make them stop straining at their bonds and sit very still, their eyes above the clumsy gags white-rimmed with terror and staring fixedly at the unfamiliar weapon in his hand.

Gobind and Manilal finished disrobing the corpse and began to help Sarji remove his palace livery and replace it with the dead man's. "It is fortunate that you are of a size in the matter of height," observed Gobind, slipping the chain surcoat over his head, "though I could wish you were stouter, for that thing there was more heavily built than you. Well, it cannot be helped, and luckily those outside will be too interested in the funeral ceremonies to notice small details."

"—we hope," amended Sarji with a curt laugh. "But what if they do?"

"If they do, we die," said Gobind unemotionally. "But I think that we shall live. Now let us see to these—" he turned his attention to the bound captives and looked them over critically.

The woman's dark-skinned face was green with fear and the eunuch's pallid one twitched and trembled uncontrollably. Neither expected any mercy (and with good reason, since they themselves would have shown none to the widowed Rani), and having seen their fellow-torturer killed, they probably imagined that the manner of it— the swift upward stab through the eye—had been in retaliation for the injury he himself had intended to inflict on the Junior Rani, and that they, as his partners in guilt, would be dealt with in the same way.

They could well have been had it not been for Gobind—and for something that Manilal found hidden among the woman's clothing—for neither Sarji nor Ash would have had the least compunction in putting an end to them by that or any other method, if their continued existence in any way threatened Anjuli's safety, or their own. Both were in agreement with Manilal, who said flatly: "We had best kill them all: it is no more than they deserve, and no more than they would do to us if they stood in our place. Let us kill them now and thus make certain that they cannot raise an alarm."

But Gobind had been trained to save life and not to take it, and he would not agree. He had killed the helmeted guard because there had been no other way of silencing him; it had been necessary and he did not regret it. But to kill the others in cold blood would serve no useful purpose (provided that they were secured so that they could not summon help) and would only rank as murder. At this point Manilal, stooping to tighten the woman's bonds, had discovered that she had something hard and bulky hidden in a fold of cloth wrapped about her waist, and removing it, found it to be a necklace of raw gold set with pearls and carved emeralds: a thing of such magnificence that no waiting-woman could possibly have come by it honestly.

Manilal handed it to Gobind with the comment that the she-devil was clearly also a thief, but the woman shook her head in frantic denial, and Gobind said shortly that it was more likely to be a bribe. "Look at her"— she had cringed in her bonds and was staring at him as though hypnotized—"this was blood-money, paid in advance for the foul work she had agreed to do. *Pah!*"

He dropped the necklace as though it had been a poisonous snake, and Ash stooped quickly and picked it up. Neither Gobind nor Manilal could possibly have recognized that fabulous jewel, but Ash had seen it twice before: once when the more valuable items listed in the dowries of the brides from Karidkote had been checked in his presence, and again when Anjuli had worn it at the formal departure from the Pearl Palace. He said harshly: "There should be two bracelets also. See if the eunuch has them. Quickly."

The eunuch had not (they were found on the two palace servants) but he had something else that Ash had no difficulty in recognizing: a collar of table-cut diamonds fringed with pearls.

He stood looking at it with unseeing eyes. So the vultures were already dividing the spoils!—the Rana had only died last night, but Juli's enemies had wasted no time in seizing her personal possessions, and had actually used some of her own jewels to bribe her would-be torturers. The irony of that would appeal to someone like the Diwan, who had once hoped to retain her dowry while at the same time repudiating her bridal contract and having her returned in disgrace to Karidkote. And from his knowledge of the man and his devious mind, Ash did not believe for a moment that the Diwan would pay such lavish bribes in return for something that he could order to be done for nothing.

It was far more likely that the choice of those jewels had been deliberate, for once the appalling deed had been done, the Diwan would be able to deny all knowledge of it and have the woman and her accomplices arrested. Then, when the jewels were found on them, they could be accused of having blinded the Rani so that she would not discover that they had been stealing her belongings, and they would be condemned to death and garotted. After which he would have nothing to fear, and with his cat's-paws dead, could safely take back the jewels. "A neat, Machiavellian piece of treachery in fact," thought Ash cynically.

He looked down at the gagged and bound creatures that only a minute ago he had wanted to murder, and thought: "No. It's not fair." And with that old, familiar protest of his childhood, a large part of his rage against them died. They were vile and venial, but Gobind was right; it was not fair to take revenge upon a mere instrument while the hand and brain that guided it escaped scot-free.

He bent above the eunuch and the man's eyes bulged with terror, expecting that the end had come; but Ash had only wanted a piece of muslin. He ripped it from the man's clothes, and knotting the jewels in it, stowed them away in the bosom of his robe, and said curtly: "It is time we went. But we had better see to it first that these vermin do not raise an alarm too soon. There is nothing to stop them rolling over to the curtains and wriggling out from underneath them the moment we have gone. They should be tied together and then lashed to one of those pillars. Have you any more rope?"

"No, we have used all that we brought with us," said Gobind. "But there is plenty of cloth."

He stooped for Sarji's discarded turban, and using that and the turbans of the prisoners, who were already gagged with their waist-cloths, they lashed the six side by side in a circle with their backs to one of the central pillars, and bound them to it in a cocoon of vividly coloured muslin.

"There. That should keep them safe enough," said

Ash, tying a final reef knot and jerking it tight. "And now for God's sake, let us go. We've wasted too much time already, and the sooner we get out of here the better."

No one stirred. The bound woman was breathing noisily with an odd bubbling sound, and a wandering breath of wind shook the curtains and set the scraps of looking-glass that decorated them glinting and winking like watching eyes. Down below on the terrace and the burning ground, the waiting crowds were comparatively silent as they listened to the distant tumult that accompanied the approaching cortège. But in the curtained enclosure no one moved.

"Well, come on," said Ash, the curtness of his voice betraying the extent of his inner tensions. "We cannot afford to wait. The head of the procession will be here any moment now and raising enough noise to cover any moaning these creatures in here will make. Besides, we must be well clear of the valley before dark, and the later we leave the sooner someone is going to come in here and find the Rani gone. We must go at once."

But still no one moved, and he glanced quickly from one face to the next, and was baffled by the mixture of exasperation, embarrassment and unease that he saw there: and the fact that they were not looking at him, but at Anjuli. He turned swiftly to follow the direction of their gaze, and saw that her back was still towards them and that she too had not moved. She could not have avoided hearing those last words he had spoken, for he had not lowered his voice. Yet she had not even turned her head.

He said sharply: "What is it? What is the matter?"

His question had been addressed to Anjuli rather than to the three men, but it was Sarji who answered it:

"The Rani-Sahiba will not leave," said Sarji, exasperated. "We had decided that if our plan succeeded, the Hakim-Sahib and Manilal would take her away as soon as she had donned the disguise, leaving me to find you and follow after them. That would have been best for us all, and at first she agreed to it. But then suddenly she said she must wait and see her sister become suttee, and that she would not leave before then. See if you can make her change her mind. We cannot—though the gods know we have tried hard enough."

Anger blazed up in Ash, and heedless of the watching

766

eyes, he strode across the room, and grasping Anjuli's shoulders, jerked her round to face him:

"Is this true?"

The harshness in his voice was only a small measure of the fury that possessed him, and when she did not answer he shook her savagely: *"Answer me!"*

"She . . . Shushila . . . does not understand," whispered Anjuli, her eyes still frozen with horror. "She does not realize what . . . what it will be like. And when she does—"

"Shushila!" Ash spat out the name as though it were an obscenity. "Always Shushila—and selfish to the end. I suppose she made you promise to do this? She would! Oh, I know she saved you from burning with her, but if she'd really wanted to repay you for all you have done for her, she could have saved you from reprisals at the hands of the Diwan by having you smuggled out of the state, instead of begging you to come here and watch her die."

"You don't understand," whispered Anjuli numbly.

"Oh, yes I do. That's where you are wrong. I understand only too well. You are still hypnotized by that selfish, hysterical little egotist, and you are perfectly prepared to jeopardize your chances of escaping from Bhithor and a horrible form of mutilation—and risk all our lives into the bargain, Gobind's, Sarji's, Manilal's and my own, just so that you can carry out your darling little sister's last wishes and watch her commit suicide. Well, I don't care what she made you promise. You are not keeping it. You are going to leave now if I have to carry you."

His rage was real; yet even as he spoke, a part of his brain was saying, "This is Juli, whom I love more than anything else in the world, and who I was afraid I should never see again. She is here at last—and all I can do is to be angry with her . . ." It didn't make sense. But then nor did his threat to carry her, for if anything were to draw attention to them, that would. He could not do it, and she would have to walk; and to go with them willingly. There was no other way. But if she would not . . . ?

The funeral cortège must be very near by now. The discordant braying of the conches and the shouts of *"Khaman Kher!"* and *"Hari-bol!"* were growing louder every minute, and already isolated voices in the crowd below had begun to take up the cries.

Anjuli turned her head to listen, and the movement was so slow and vague that Ash recognized suddenly that in her present state of shock, his anger had not reached her. He drew a long breath and steadied himself, and his hands on her shoulders relaxed to tenderness. He said gently, coaxing her as though she were a child: "Don't you see, dear, as long as Shu-shu thinks you are here, watching her and praying for her, she will be satisfied. Listen to me, Juli. She will never know that you are not, for though you and I can see out through this *chik*, no one out there can see us, so you cannot even signal to her. And if you called out to her, she could not possibly hear you."

"Yes, I know. But . . ."

"Juli, all you can do is to hurt yourself cruelly by watching a sight that may haunt you for the rest of your life; and that is not going to help her."

"Yes, I know . . . but you could. *You* could help her."

"I? No, dear. There is nothing that I or any of us can do for her now. I'm sorry Juli, but that is the truth and you must face it."

"It isn't. It isn't true." Anjuli's hands came up to his wrists, and her eyes were no longer frozen but wide and imploring, and at last he saw her face, for the turban-end had become loose when he shook her, and now it fell down about her throat.

The change in that face was like a knife in Ash's heart, because it was terribly altered—more so than he could have dreamed possible. The flesh had wasted from it leaving it thin and drawn and desperate, and as drained of colour as though she had spent the last two years penned up in a dungeon where no gleam of light ever penetrated. There were lines and deep hollows in it that had not been there before, and the dark shadows that circled her eyes owed nothing to the artful use of *kohl* or antimony, but told of fear and intolerable strain; and tears—an ocean of tears . . .

There were tears in her eyes now, and in her breathless, pleading voice, and Ash would have given anything in the world to take her in his arms and kiss them away. But he knew that he must not.

"I *would* have left," sobbed Anjuli. "I would have gone at once with your friends, for I could not bear to see what I had been brought here to see, and had they not

768

come I would have shut my eyes and ears to it. But then they—the Hakim-Sahib and your friend—told me why you were not with them, and what you had meant to do for me so that I should not burn to death but die quickly and without pain. You can do that for her."

Ash took a quick step back and would have snatched his hands away, but now it was Anjuli who held him by the wrists and would not let him go.

"Please—*please*, Ashok! It is not much to ask—only that you will do for her what you would have done for me. She could never endure pain, and when . . . when the flames . . . I cannot bear to think of it. You can save her from that, and then I will go with you gladly—gladly."

Her voice broke on the word and Ash said huskily: "You don't know what you are asking. It isn't as easy as that. It would have been different with you, because—because I had meant to go with you; and Sarji and Gobind and Manilal would all have got safely away, for they would have been a long way from here when our time came. But now it would mean that we would all be here; and if the shot were heard and anyone saw where it had come from, we should all die a far worse death than Shushila's."

"But it will not be heard. Not above all that noise outside. And who will be looking this way? No one—no one, I tell you. Do this for me. On my knees, I beg of you—"

She let go his wrists, and before he could prevent it she was at his feet with the orange and scarlet turban that she wore touching the ground. Ash bent quickly and pulled her upright, and Sarji, from behind them, said tersely: "Let her have her way. We cannot carry her, so if she will not come with us unless you do as she asks, you have no choice."

"None," agreed Ash. "Very well, since I must, I will do it. But only if you four will go now. I will follow later, when it is done, and meet you in the valley."

"*No!*" There was pure panic in Anjuli's voice, and she brushed past him and addressed Gobind, who averted his eyes from her unveiled face: "Hakim-Sahib, tell him that he must not stay here alone—it is madness. There would be no one to watch for other men who may come up here, or help to overpower them as you three did to these others. Tell him we must stay together."

Gobind was silent for a moment. Then he nodded,

though with obvious reluctance, and said to Ash: "I fear that the Rani-Sahiba is right. We must stay together, for one man alone, looking out through the *chik* into the sunlight and choosing his moment, could not guard his back or listen for steps on the stair at the same time."

Sarji and Manilal murmured agreement, and Ash shrugged and capitulated. It was, after all, the least he could do for poor little Shu-shu, whom he had brought from her home in the north to this remote and medieval backwater among the arid hills and scorching sands of Rajputana, and handed over to an evil and dissolute husband whose unlamented end had proved to be her death-warrant. And perhaps the least that Juli too could do for her, because although it was only Shu-shu's hysterical refusal to be parted from her half-sister that had brought her to this pass, at the end the little Rani had done what she could to make amends. But for her intervention, Juli would even now be out there in the dust and the glare, walking behind her husband's bier towards the moment when a bullet from her lover's revolver would give her a swift and merciful death: and if he had been prepared to do that for Juli, it was not fair to refuse the same mercy to her little sister . . . Yet the very idea of doing so appalled him.

Because he loved Juli—because he loved her more than life and because she was so much a part of him that without her life would have no meaning—he could have shot her without a tremor, and never felt that her blood was upon his head; but to put a bullet through Shushila's head was a very different matter, because pity, however strong, did not provide the terrible incentive that love had done. And then, too, his own life would not be involved. The next bullet would not be for himself, and that alone would make him feel like a murderer—or at best, an executioner, which was absurd when he knew that Juli would have faced the flames with far less terror and endured the pain with more fortitude than poor Shu-shu would ever do, and yet he had resolved to save her from that agony . . . and was now sickened by the thought of doing the same for Shu-shu.

Sarji broke in on the confusion of his thoughts by remarking in a matter-of-fact voice that the range would be greater from up here than it had been from the edge of the terrace below, and that as Ash would be aiming downwards, and from at least twelve to fifteen feet higher, it was not going to be easy. He might have been discussing a difficult shot from a *machan* on one of their hunting trips in the Gir Forest, and strangely enough it seemed to take some of the horror out of this supremely horrible situation. For he was talking sense.

If the thing must be done, it must be done well; and at the last possible moment, so that it might be thought that Shushila, having taken her place on the pyre, had fainted. To bungle it would be a disaster, not only for Shushila, but for them all; because though there was every chance that the crack of a single shot would be lost in the noise of the crowd, a second or third could not fail to attract attention, or to pin-point the spot from where it had been fired.

"Do you think you can do it?" asked Sarji, coming to stand beside him.

"I must. I can't afford not to. Have you a knife?"

"You mean for the *chik*. No, but I can cut you a gap in it with this thing——" Sarji set to work with the short spear that all members of the Rana's bodyguard carried, and sliced a small oblong out of the split cane. "There. That should serve. I do not think the cane would deflect a shot, but it might; and there is no need to take chances."

He watched Ash take out the service revolver and sight along the barrel, and said in an undertone: "It is all of forty paces. I have never handled one of those things. Will it reach as far?"

"Yes. But I don't know how accurately. It was never intended for such distances, and I——" He swung round abruptly: "It's no good, Sarji. I daren't risk it from here. I shall have to get closer. Listen, if I go down there again, will you and the others——Yes, that's it. Why didn't we think of it before? We will all leave now, at once, and when we reach the terrace you three can go on ahead with the Rani-Sahiba, and I will get back to my place near the parapet and——"

Sarji cut brusquely across the sentence: "You could not get there. The crowds are too thick. It was all I could do to get to you before; and even wearing this livery they would never make room for you now. Besides, it is too late. Listen——they come."

The conches sounded again. But now the mournful and discordant bray was deafeningly loud, while the roar

771

that followed it came from the crowd lining the last short stretch of pathway that lay within the grove itself. In another minute or so the funeral cortège would be here, and there was no longer time to make for the terrace and try to force a way to the front of the close-packed and half-hysterical multitude that thronged it. It was too late for that.

The crowds on the ground below were swaying backwards and forwards as a flood-tide surges between the supports of a pier, pushing, jostling, craning to see over the heads of those in front, or striving to dodge the indiscriminate blows of men who laid about them with *lathis* in order to keep a way clear for the slow-moving procession. And now the advance guard were emerging from the tree shadows into the golden blaze of the afternoon sun, a phalanx of shaven-headed Brahmins from the city's temples, clad in white loin-cloths, with ropes of *tulsi* beads adorning their naked chests and the trident mark that is the fork of Vishnu splashed upon their foreheads.

The leaders blew on conches while the rear rank whirled strips of brass bells above the heads of those who walked between, and behind these came a motley company of other holy men, a score or more of them: saints, sadhus and ascetics, jangling bells and chanting; naked and ash-smeared or soberly dressed in flowing robes of saffron or orange, dull red or white; some with their heads shaved and others whose matted hair and beards, having never been cut, reached half-way to their knees. As wild a crew as Ash had ever seen, they had gathered here like kites who can see death from a great distance away, converging together from every corner of the State to attend the suttee. Behind them came the bier, borne high above the crowd and rocking and dipping to the pace of its bearers like a boat on a choppy sea.

The body that it bore was swathed in white and heaped about with garlands, and Ash was astonished to see how small it looked. The Rana had not been a big man, but then he had always been magnificently dressed and glittering with jewels, and always the centre of a subservient court; all of which had tended to make him seem a good deal larger than he was. But the spare, white-shrouded corpse on the bier looked no larger than an under-nourished child of ten. An insignificant object; and a very lonely one, for it was not the focus of the crowd's attention. They had not come here to see a dead man, but a still living woman. And now at last she was here, walking behind the bier; and at the sight of her, pandemonium broke loose, until even the solid fabric of the *chattri* seemed to tremble at the impact of that roar of sound.

Ash had not seen her at first. His gaze had been fixed on the shrunken thing that had once been his enemy. But a movement near him made him turn his head and he saw that Anjuli had come to stand beside him, and that she was staring through the *chik* with an expression of shrinking horror, as though she could not bear to look and yet could not keep herself from looking. And following the direction of that agonized gaze, he saw Shushila. Not the Shushila he had expected to see—bowed, weeping and half-crazed by terror, but a queen . . . a Rani of Bhithor.

Had he been asked, Ash would have insisted that Shushu would never be able to walk to the burning-ground unassisted, and that if she walked at all and did not have to be brought in a litter, it would only be because she had been stupefied by drugs and then half dragged and half carried there. But the small, brilliant figure walking behind the Rana's bier was not only alone, but walking upright and unfaltering; and there was pride and dignity in every line of her slender body.

Her small head was erect and the little unshod feet that had never before stepped on anything harsher than Persian carpets and cool polished marble trod slowly and steadily, marking the burning dust with small neat footprints that the adoring crowds behind her pressed forward to obliterate with kisses.

She was dressed as Ash had seen her at the marriage ceremony, in the scarlet and gold wedding dress, and decked with the same jewels as she had worn that day. Pigeon's-blood rubies circled her throat and wrists, glowed on her forehead and her fingers, and swung from her ears. There were rubies too on the chinking golden anklets, and the hard sunlight glittered on the gold embroidery of the full-skirted Rajputani dress and flashed on the little jewelled bodice. But this time she wore no sari, and her long hair was unbound as though for her bridal night. It rippled about her in a silky black curtain that was more beautiful

773

than any sari made by man, and Ash could not drag his gaze from her, though his body cringed from that tragic sight.

She seemed wholly unconscious of the jostling crowds who applauded her, calling on her to bless them and struggling to touch the hem of her skirt as she passed, or of the sea of eyes that stared avidly at her unveiled face. Ash saw that her lips were moving in the age-old invocation that accompanies the last journey of the dead: *Ram, Ram . . . Ram, Ram . . . Ram, Ram . . .*

He said aloud and incredulously: "You were wrong. She is not afraid."

The clamour from below almost drowned his words, but Anjuli heard them, and imagining that they had been addressed to her instead of to himself, she said: "Not yet. It is still only a game to her. No, not a game—I don't mean that. But something that is only happening in her mind. A part she is playing."

"You mean she is drugged? I don't believe it."

"Not in the way you mean, but with emotion—and desperation and shock. And—and perhaps . . . triumph . . ."

"Triumph!" thought Ash. Yes. The whole parade smacked more of a triumphal progress than a funeral. A procession in honour of a goddess who has deigned to show herself, for this time only, to accept the homage of her shouting, exultant and adoring worshippers. He remembered then that Shushila's mother, in the days before her beauty captured the heart of a Rajah, had been one of a troupe of entertainers: men and women whose livelihood depended upon their ability to capture the attention and applause of an audience—as her daughter was doing now. Shushila, Goddess of Bhithor, beautiful as the dawn and glittering with gold and jewels. Yes, it was a triumph. And even if she was only playing a part, at least she was playing it superbly.

"Well done!" whispered Ash, in a heart-felt endorsement of all those outside who were hailing her with the same words. "Oh, well done—!"

Beside him, Anjuli too was murmuring to herself, repeating the same invocation as Shushila: *"Ram, Ram— Ram, Ram . . ."* It was only a breath of sound and barely audible in that tumult, but it distracted Ash's attention, and though he knew that the prayer was not for the dead man but for her sister, he told her sharply to be quiet.

His mind was once again in a turmoil and torn with doubts. For watching the unfaltering advance of that graceful scarlet and gold figure, it seemed to him that he had no right to play providence. It would have been excusable if she had been dragged here weeping and terrified, or dazed with drugs. But not when she showed no sign of fear.

She must know by now what lay ahead; and if so, either the stories that Gobind had heard were true and she had come to love the dead man—and loving him, preferred to die cradling his body in her arms rather than live without him—or else, having steeled herself to it, she was glorying in the manner of her death and the prospect of sainthood and veneration. In either case, what right had he to interfere? Besides, her agony would be very quickly over; he had watched the pyre being built and seen the priests heap cotton between the logs and pour oils and clarified butter on it, and had thought even then that once it was lit the smoke alone would probably suffocate poor little Shu-shu before a flame touched her.

"I can't do it," decided Ash. "And even if I do, it won't be all that much quicker: Juli ought to know that . . . Oh, God, why don't they hurry up. Why can't they get it over, instead of dragging it out like this."

His whole being was suddenly flooded with hatred for everyone out there: the presiding priests, the excited onlookers, the mourners in the funeral procession and even the dead man and Shushila herself. Shushila most of all, because—

No, that was not fair, thought Ash; she couldn't help being herself. This was the way she was made, and she could not help battening upon Juli any more than Juli could keep from allowing herself to be battened upon. People were what they were, and they did not change. Yet despite all her selfishness and egotism, at the last Shu-shu had spared a thought for her sister, and instead of insisting on her support to the end, had let her go—at what cost to herself, no one would ever know. He must not let himself forget that again . . .

The red haze of rage that had momentarily blinded him cleared away, and he saw that Shushila had moved on, and that where she had been there was another small, lonely figure. But this time it was a child: a boy of about five or six years old, walking alone a little way behind her. "The heir, I suppose," thought Ash, grateful for something else to think about. "No, not the heir—the new Rana, of course. Poor little beggar. He looks done up."

The child was stumbling with weariness and plainly bewildered by the strangeness of his surroundings and his sudden elevation in rank, a rank that was clearly shown by the fact that he walked directly behind the widowed Rani and several paces ahead of the hundred or so men who followed—the nobles, councillors and chiefs of Bhithor who brought up the end of the procession. Prominent among these was the Diwan, who carried a lighted torch that had been lit at the sacred flame in the city temple.

By now the noise had risen to a crescendo as those nearest to her fought to touch the Rani and beg her blessing, and others took up the cry of *Hari-bol* or *Khaman Kher*, or shrieked with pain as the guards rained blows upon them, forcing them back. "At least the shot will not be heard," observed Sarji. "There is that to be thankful for. How much longer do you mean to wait?"

Ash made no reply, and presently Sarji muttered in an undertone that now would have been the time to leave—if they had any sense left in their thick heads. He had not intended his words to carry, but the end of the sentence was startlingly audible; for the crowds outside had suddenly fallen silent, and all at once it was possible to hear the hard breathing of the gagged prisoners and the cooing of doves from somewhere overhead under the eaves of the dome.

The cortège had reached the pyre and the bier was placed on it. And now Shushila began to divest herself of her jewels, taking them off one by one and handing them to the child, who gave them in turn to the Diwan. She stripped them off quickly, almost gaily, as though they were no more than withered flowers or valueless trinkets of which she had tired and was impatient to be rid of, and the silence was so complete that all could hear the clink of them as the new Rana received them and the late Rana's Prime Minister stowed them away in an embroidered bag.

Even Ash in the curtained enclosure heard it, and

wondered incuriously if the Diwan would ever relinquish them. Probably not; though they had come from Karidkote, and being part of Shushila's dowry should have been returned there. But he thought it unlikely that either Shu-shu's relatives or the new Rana would ever see them again once the Diwan had got his hands on them.

When all her ornaments had been removed except for a necklace of sacred *tulsi* seeds, Shushila held out her slender ringless hands to a priest, who poured Ganges water over them. The water sparkled in the low sunlight as she shook the bright drops from her fingers, and the assembled priests began to intone in chorus . . .

To the sound of that chanting, she began to walk round the pyre, circling it three times as once, on her wedding day and wearing this same dress, she had circled the sacred fire, tied by her veil to the shrunken thing that now lay waiting for her on a bridal bed of cedar-logs and spices.

The hymn ended and once again the only sound in the grove was the cooing of doves: that soft monotonous sound that together with the throb of a tom-tom and the creak of a well-wheel is the voice of India. The silent crowds stood motionless, and none stirred as the suttee mounted the pyre and seated herself in the lotus posture. She arranged the wide folds of her scarlet dress so as to show it to its best advantage, and then gently lifted the dead man's head onto her lap, settling it with infinite care, as though he were asleep and she did not wish to wake him.

"Now," breathed Anjuli in a whisper that broke in a sob—"Do it now . . . *quickly,* before—before she starts to be afraid."

"Don't be a fool!" The retort cracked like a whip in the quiet room. "It would make as much noise as a cannon and bring them all down on us like hornets. Besides—"

He had meant to say "I'm not going to fire," but he did not do so. There was no point in making things worse for Juli than they were already. But the way in which Shu-shu had cradled that awful head in her lap had made up his mind for him at last, and he had no intention of firing. Juli took too much upon herself: she forgot that her half-sister was no longer a sickly infant or a frail and highly strung little girl who must be protected and cosseted—or that she herself was no longer responsible for her. Shu-shu was a grown woman who knew what she was doing. She was also a wife and a queen—and proving that she could behave as one. This time, for good or ill, she should be allowed to make her own decision.

The crowd outside was still silent, but now a priest began to swing a heavy temple bell that had been carried out from the city, and its harsh notes reverberated through the grove and awoke echoes from the walls and domes of the many *chattris*. One of the Brahmins was sprinkling the dead man and his widow with water brought from the sacred river Ganges—"Mother Gunga"—while others poured more *ghee* and scented oil upon the logs of cedar and sandalwood and over the feet of the Rana.

But Shushila did not move. She sat composed and still, looking down at the grey, skull-like face on her lap. A graven image in scarlet and gold: remote, passionless and strangely unreal. The Diwan took the torch again and gave it into the trembling hands of the boy-Rana, who seemed about to burst into tears. It wavered dangerously in the child's grasp, being over heavy for such small hands to hold, and one of the Brahmins came to his assistance and helped to support it.

The brightness of that flame was a sharp reminder that evening was already drawing near. Only a short time ago it had been almost invisible in the glaring sunlight, but now the sun was no longer fierce enough to dim that plume of light. The shadows had begun to lengthen and the day that had once seemed as though it would never end would soon be over—and with it, Shushila's short life.

She had lost father and mother, and the brother who, for his own ends, had given her in marriage to a man who lived so far away that it had taken months and not weeks to reach her new home. She had been a wife and a queen, had miscarried two children and borne a third who had lived only a few days; and now she had been widowed, and must die . . . "She is only sixteen—" thought Ash. "It isn't fair. It isn't *fair*!"

He could hear Sarji's quickened breathing and the thump of his own heart-beats, and though Anjuli was not touching him he knew, without knowing how he knew, that she was shivering violently as though she was very cold or stricken with fever. He thought suddenly that provided he fired a shot she would not know if the bullet had done its work or not, and that he had only to aim over the heads of the crowd. If it comforted Juli to think that her sister had been spared the flames, then all he needed to do was pull the trigger—

But the trees on the far side of the clearing were full of men and boys who clung like monkeys to the boughs, while every *chattri* within range swarmed with spectators, and even a spent bullet or a ricochet could cause death. It would have to be the pyre itself; that was the only safe target. He lifted the revolver and steadied the barrel on the crook of his left arm, and said curtly and without turning his head: "We leave as soon as I have fired. Are you ready to go?"

"We men are," said Gobind very softly. "And if the Rani-Sahiba—"

He hesitated, and Ash finished the sentence for him: "—will cover her face, it will save time. Besides, she has already seen more than enough of this and there is no need for her to stand staring any longer."

He spoke with deliberate harshness in the hope that Juli would be forced to busy herself rewinding the free end of her turban across her face and so miss the last act of the tragedy. But she made no move to cover her face or turn away. She stayed as though rooted to the spot: wide-eyed, shivering and unable to stir hand or foot, and seemingly unaware that he had spoken.

All of forty paces, Sarji had said. It did not look as far as that, for now that there was no movement in the vast crowd the dust had settled; and with the sun-glare no longer dazzling his sight, the faces of the chief actors in the tragedy could be seen as clearly as though they were only twenty feet away instead of thirty-five to forty paces.

The little Rana was crying. Tears poured down the pallid, childish features that were crumpled with fear and bewilderment and sheer physical exhaustion, and if the Brahmin beside him had not held his small hands firmly about the torch, he would have dropped it. The Brahmin was evidently exhorting him in an undertone, while the Diwan looked scornful and the nobles exchanged glances that varied according to their temperaments—and the degree of their disappointment over the selection of the next ruler. And then Shushila looked up . . . and suddenly her face changed.

779

Perhaps it was the brightness of the torch, or the sound of it as the flames streamed up on the still air, that woke her from the dream-world in which she had been moving. Her head came up sharply and Ash could see her eyes widen until they looked enormous in her small, pale face. She stared about her, no longer calmly, but with the terrified gaze of a hunted animal, and he could tell the exact moment when reality broke through illusion and she realized, fully, what that flaming brand signalled . . .

The boy's hands, guided by the Brahmin's, lowered the torch until it touched the pyre near the feet of the dead man. Bright flowers of fire sprang up from the wood and blossomed in orange and green and violet, and the new Rana having performed his duty to the old one—his father by adoption—the priest took the brand from him and went quickly to the other end of the pyre and touched it to the logs at the suttee's back. A brilliant tongue of flame shot skyward, and simultaneously the crowd found its voice and once again roared its homage and approval. But the goddess of their worship thrust aside the head on her lap, and now, suddenly, she was on her feet, staring at those flames and screaming—screaming . . .

The sound of those screams cut through the clamour as the shriek of violin strings cuts through the full tempest of drums and wind-instruments and brass. It drew a gasping echo from Anjuli, and Ash lifted his aim and fired.

The screams stopped short and the slender scarlet and gold figure stretched out one hand gropingly as though searching for support, and then crumpled at the knees and pitched forward across the corpse at her feet. And as she fell the Brahmin flung the torch on the pyre, and flames gushed up from the oil-drenched wood and threw a shimmering veil of heat and smoke between the watchers and the recumbent figure of the girl who now wore a glittering wedding-dress of fire.

The crash of the shot had sounded appallingly loud in that small confined space, and Ash thrust the revolver into the breast of his robe and turning, said savagely: "Well, what are you waiting for? Get on—go on Sarji—you first." Anjuli still seemed dazed, and he pulled the cloth roughly across her nose and mouth and made sure that it was secure, and having adjusted his own, caught her by the shoulders and said: "Listen to me, Juli—and stop looking like that. You've done all you can for Shushila. She's gone. She has escaped; and if we hope to, we must stop thinking of her and think of ourselves. We come first now. All of us. Do you understand?"

Anjuli nodded dumbly.

"Good. Then turn around and go with Gobind, and don't look back. I shall be behind you. *Walk*—!"

He turned her about and pushed her ahead of him towards the heavy purdah that Manilal was holding open for them, and she followed Sarji through it and down the marble stairway that led to the terrace and the crowds below.

43

He was riding headlong across a stony plain between low, barren hills, and there was a girl on the crupper behind him who clung to him and urged him to ride faster—faster. A girl whose long, unbound hair streamed out on the wind like a black silk flag, so that when he glanced back he could not see the riders who pursued them, but only hear the thunder of following hoofbeats that became louder and nearer . . .

Ash awoke, sweating with terror, to find that the sound of galloping horses was only the desperate beating of his own heart.

The nightmare was a familiar one. But the awakening was not, because this time he was not in his own bed, but lying on hard ground in a dark patch of shadow thrown by a boulder. Below him a belt of scree fell steeply away down a gully that was bright with moonlight, and on either hand the bare hillsides swept upwards to shoulder a sky like a sheet of tarnished steel.

For a moment or two he could not remember how he came to be there, or why. Then memory returned in a scalding flood and he sat up and stared into the shadows. Yes, she was still there; a pale huddled shape lying in a hollow that Bukta had scraped out for her between two boulders and lined with his horse-blanket. At least they had brought her this far in safety, and when Bukta returned—if he returned—

Ash's thoughts checked sickeningly, balking like a horse that suddenly recognizes the dangers of a fence and refuses to face it; for the position of the moon told him that it was long past midnight, and by rights Bukta should have arrived back at least two hours ago.

He stood up cautiously, moving with extreme care to avoid making any noise that might disturb Anjuli, and peered over the boulder; but nothing moved on the bare hillside, and the only sound that he could hear was made by the night wind whispering through the dry grass and between the tumbled rocks. He could not believe that he had slept so soundly that he would not have heard the noise of returning footsteps, yet even if he had, there would still be the horses . . .

But there were no horses on that empty expanse of hillside, and no sign of Bukta, or of anyone else; though far away, in the sky above the valley, a red pulsating glow told of camp fires, and by inference, the presence of a large force bivouacked there for the night and only waiting for dawn before taking up the trail.

Ash rested his arms on the boulder, and staring out across the grey folds of the moon-washed hills towards that distant brightness, coldly calculated his own and Juli's chances of survival in an almost waterless region where there were no recognizable paths or landmarks; or none that he himself could recognize, even though he had come that way barely a week ago. Yet if Bukta did not return he would have to find the path back through this trackless maze of ridges himself, and by way of the few places where there had been springs in the parched wilderness —and later on through the many miles of jungle-clad foothills that lay across the northern borders of Gujerat.

It had been no easy road before, but now . . . Once again the train of Ash's thought jarred to a halt and he dropped his head on his folded arms, shutting out the moonlight. But he could not shut out the memory of all that had happened, and now he saw it again, printed searingly behind his closed eyelids . . .

They had walked out of the screened enclosure, Sarji leading, and down the narrow stairway to the terrace where the crowd—spectators and sentries alike—craned to watch the suttee's last moments, and swept by emotion, prayed, shouted or wept as the flames shot upwards and the pyre became a blazing, blinding pyramid of fire. No one present had spared a glance for the small party of four palace attendants led by a helmeted member of the Rana's bodyguard. They had left the *chattri* unhindered and unremarked, and within minutes had reached the shelter of the older and more ruined buildings.

Dagobaz had been standing with his ears pricked, listening; and despite the roar and crackle of the fire and the cries of the crowd he must have heard Ash's step and recognized it, for he whinnied in greeting before he saw him. There were four other horses tethered to a tree near by, one of which was Sarji's own Moti Raj and another the hack he had lent Manilal for the return journey to Bhithor. The third belonged to Gobind, as did the fourth, which he had acquired with one other some weeks earlier, in the hope that it might be possible to rescue both the Ranis.

"I bought one for each of them," explained Gobind in an aside to Ash as he adjusted the girths, "but this is the better of the two, so I have left the other behind, which is no loss—we cannot cumber ourselves with spare horses. If the Rani-Sahiba will be pleased to mount—?"

They rode out of the grove and circled back across the dusty plain towards the entrance of the valley, where the walled city stood like a vast block of sandstone in the centre of the valley mouth. The sun had not yet sunk behind the hills, and because here their route lay west they rode directly towards it. Its glare dazzled the eyes of both riders and horses and the heat rose in waves from the stony ground and beat against them—and Ash had forgotten about that nameless merchant of Bhithor who had been a great traveller, and had brought back from foreign parts the secret of how men could speak to each other over great distances with the aid of small shields of polished silver.

Even if he had remembered it would not have helped much—except that he might have been warned. As it was, riding into the eye of the setting sun and half blinded by its glare, he did not see the brief flicker from a high rooftop in the city, or the one from the walls of the right-hand fort, that could be translated as "Message understood." And Sarji, who did see them, supposed them to be only sunlight flashing on a window-pane or the burnished barrel of a cannon.

Neither of them was ever to know how their escape came to be discovered so soon, though the explanation was very simple, and proved that Manilal's advice on the score of killing their prisoners had been sound. A gag, however efficient, does not prevent a man—or a woman —from making a certain amount of noise, and when six people combine to moan in chorus, the noise they produce is not inconsiderable. The captives were unable to move but they could moan, and they did so to such good purpose that before long one of the guards below, on his way up to the top storey of the *chattri* from where he hoped to obtain a better view, stopped to listen as he passed the curtained entrance, and supposing the sound to come from the Junior Rani, could not resist twitching it very slightly aside and putting his eye to the crack.

Within minutes all six were free and pouring out a wild tale of murder, assault and abduction. And shortly afterwards a score of soldiers set off in pursuit, guided by the long, betraying cloud of dust that Ash and his companions had raised as they rode away, and that showed like a white streak across the face of the plain. The chances of overtaking the runaways were slight, for they had too good a start and should have got clean away. But as luck would have it, one of the bodyguard had been provided with a signalling shield and charged with keeping in touch with the city and the forts in order to report the safe arrival of the funeral cortège. He now made use of it to flash a warning to both that said, in effect—*Enemy. Five. On horseback. Intercept.*

The signal was seen and acknowledged, and though the hilltop forts could do little, the city took immediate action. There were no more than a handful of troops within its confines that day, the majority having been called on to keep a clear pathway for the funeral procession or sent to control the crowds at the burning-ground. But the few who had remained on guard at the palace were hastily rounded up and dispatched at full gallop to the *Hathi Pol*, the Elephant Gate, with instructions to cut off a party of five horsemen who were presumed to be making for the border.

But for a zealous gunner in the right-hand fort, they would have done so, as by now the fugitives were riding through the gap between the hillside and the northern wall of the city, and were as yet barely level with the *Mori* Gate. Having not seen the signals, or realized that their escape had been discovered, they were not pressing their horses overmuch, for fields of grain and stubble, criss-crossed by irrigation channels, are hardly the safest places to take at a gallop. Besides, the valley with its hard, sun-baked ground lay ahead, and once there, with the city behind them, they would be able to go more quickly.

The sudden appearance of a party of yelling horse-men, who having left by the Elephant Gate were not only well ahead of them but riding at a tangent with the obvious intention of cutting them off before they could reach the valley, was a shattering blow; as was the si-multaneous spatter of shots from somewhere away to the right. Yet even then, for a brief moment it seemed to all of them that they must be mistaken and that it was not possible that the shouting men could have any interest in them or the shots be aimed at them, for there had not been time . . . But the moment passed and suddenly they knew without a shadow of doubt—as the fox knows when he hears the hounds give tongue—that the hunt was up and that they were the quarry.

It was too late to turn back; and there was no point in doing so, since by now there would be other men on their heels striving to overtake them. There was nothing for it but to go forward, and reacting as one, they set spurs to their horses and made for the narrowing gap that the men from the city were racing to close.

Whether they would have reached it in time is doubtful. But it was at this point that Fate, in the form of a gunner in the fort, intervened on their behalf.

The garrison of the fort had seen the sun-signals, and had been manning the walls and excitedly watching the approach of the five fugitives and the progress of the pur-suit. Their eyrie on the hilltop gave them an advantage that the five did not possess, because from here they could not only see the quarry, but the pursuers who galloped far behind them following their trail, as well as the handful of armed men who had suddenly debouched from the *Hathi Pol* and were now riding to head them off.

The latter had been visible to the garrison from the moment they left the city. But though the fort provided an excellent grandstand from which to view the drama, the antiquated matchlocks and jezails with which the garrisons opened fire on the fugitives were almost useless at that range, while the dust and the dancing, shimmering heat-haze did not make for good marksmanship. Their shots did not take effect, and looking down from the heights it seemed to them that the runaways were in danger of winning the race and breaking through into the valley.

The great bronze cannons had already been fired once that day, but as by tradition they would be fired again to welcome the new Rana back to his city, they were primed and ready. An eager gunner leapt to load one and busied himself lighting a taper while his crew, following his lead, helped to train the monster ahead of the galloping target. The port-fire was applied to the touchhole and the flash and roar of the explosion was as impressive as ever. But in the excitement of the moment the speed of the riders below had been miscalculated, and the cannon ball missed the fugitives and landed full in the path of the on-coming soldiers from the city.

No one was seriously hurt, but the sudden and totally unexpected fountain of dust, dirt and debris that exploded a bare yard or two ahead, showering them with stones and clods of earth, panicked the already over-excited horses, who instantly reared and bolted. Several of the riders were thrown, and by the time the others had got their mounts under control the quarry had escaped through the gap and were riding like the wind down the long, straight stretch of the valley.

It had been an incredible ride. Terrifying, nerve-racking and at the same time so wildly exhilarating that, if it had not been for Juli, Ash would actually have enjoyed it. Sarji had certainly done so: he had laughed and sung and urged Moti Raj to greater efforts with cries of encouragement and extravagant endearments. Dagobaz too had been in his element, and had he been given his head he would have outdistanced his companions and left them far behind in the first half-mile. But there was Juli to be thought of, and Ash's hands were firm on the reins and he held back, glancing over his shoulder every few seconds to see that she was safe.

The wind had whipped the folds of muslin away from her face and Ash saw that it was set and intent: a pale mask in which only the eyes were alive. She was handling her horse in a manner that would have done credit to her Cossack grandfather, and Ash felt a sudden rush of gratitude towards that old free-booter—and to her father, the old Rajah, who in the face of Janoo-Rani's opposition had insisted that his daughter Kairi-Bai should be taught to ride: "God bless him, wherever he has gone," thought Ash fervently.

Gobind too was a good horseman. But Manilal was no more than an adequate one, and the pace was clearly beginning to tell on him; yet he hung on grimly and had the sense to leave everything else to his horse. As for the pursuit, from what little they could see of it through the dust that fumed up in their own wake, it was still in a state of disarray and too far behind to pose a serious threat.

They had avoided the beaten track with its potholes and cart ruts, and kept well to one side of it—the left side, since it was on this side that the entrance to Bukta's road lay—and they had covered more than two thirds of the distance when Anjuli's horse put its foot in a rat hole and came down heavily, pitching her over its head to land spread-eagled in the dust.

The fall had knocked the breath out of her body and she lay still, fighting for air, while her horse struggled to its feet and stood with drooping head and labouring sides. Manilal, who had been following behind, tugged wildly on his near rein to avoid riding over her, and missing her by inches, was carried helplessly onwards, completely out of control and reduced to clinging to the arch of his saddle. But the other three pulled up and circled back.

Ash flung himself off Dagobaz and snatched Juli into his arms; and for a dreadful, heart-stopping moment he thought that she was dead, because she did not move. But one look was enough to reassure him, and he whirled round, holding her, and saw that the hunters were still on their trail, and getting dangerously near.

Gobind too was looking back. He had not dismounted, but was holding Dagobaz's reins as well as Moti Raj's, while Sarji examined the injured horse, and he did not speak—there was no need to for they were all aware of the danger. Sarji said breathlessly: "The off-fore is badly strained. Dagobaz will have to carry two. Give me the Rani and get back in the saddle. Be quick."

Ash obeyed, and though Juli was still dazed by her fall she was getting her breath back and she had not lost her wits. When Sarji tossed her up onto the crupper she put her arms about Ash's waist and held on, and they were away again, racing after Manilal who was by now far ahead of them; Gobind and Sarji a length behind to left and right, riding wide of them to avoid being choked by their dust.

The additional weight made no difference at all to Dagobaz, who swept on with the effortless speed of a hawk. But the delay had been fatal, for it had not only reduced their lead to a mere matter of a few hundred yards, but had served to break the headlong impetus of the other two horses, so that now Gobind must use both whip and spur while Sarji rode crouched like a jockey, far forward on Moti Raj's straining neck, and singing no more.

Ash heard the crack of a shot and saw the dust spurt as a musket-ball ploughed into the ground ahead and well to one side, and realized that one of the pursuers had fired at them, and that he should have foreseen this when he took Juli up behind him. He ought to have put her in front, so that his body would have protected her from any aspiring marksmen, but it was too late to do anything about it now; they could not stop, and in any case, the risk of a shot taking effect was minimal, for a muzzle-loading jezail is an unhandy weapon when fired from the back of a galloping horse—and impossible to reload under those conditions.

There was unlikely to be another shot, but that one, though well off target, showed that the pursuit must be gaining on them; and also reminded him that he carried a revolver. Knowing that Dagobaz would answer to the least pressure of his leg, he fumbled in the breast of his robes and guiding Dagobaz by knee, swerved to avoid the dust-cloud behind him, and telling Anjuli to hold close, turned in the saddle and fired at a man on a rangy, country-bred grey who was leading the field by several lengths.

There was no luck about the shot: Koda Dad Khan had been too good a teacher for that, and Ash did not watch to see if it took effect. He looked to his front again, hearing the fall and the hoarse yells of rage from behind, and Sarji's exultant shout as the riderless grey careered past them.

Ahead of them loomed the triple-fanged ridge with the wide, arrow-shaped fall of shale immediately below it: a pale landmark that pin-pointed the position of a tall

grass-plumed, white-streaked rock near which—please God!
—Bukta the *shikari* would still be waiting for them.
Bukta with a spare shot-gun and two boxes of cartridges,
and another fifty rounds of rifle ammunition.

If only they could increase their lead and reach the
passage through the rockfall with even a minute to spare,
they would be able to hold off any number of pursuers,
and inflict such damage in the process that by the time
darkness fell the survivors would be unlikely to follow them
into the hills. But the shouts and the thunder of pursuing
hooves were becoming nearer and louder . . . and of a
sudden, uncannily familiar, until with a violent sensation
of shock and incredulity Ash realized that this was the
dream . . .

It had all happened before. Many times. Only this
time he was not dreaming. This time he was awake and
it was real—the flat, stony plain, the low hills, the sound
of pursuing hoofbeats on hard ground and the girl on the
crupper who had once been Belinda—except that even
then her hair had been black.

The nightmare had come true at last, and as if to
prove it, Juli began urging him to go faster—faster. But
when he turned, revolver in hand, he found that he could
not fire, because she had lost her turban when she fell,
and now her loosened hair streamed out behind her like a
black silk flag on the wind and made it impossible for him
to see the men who galloped behind him.

This was far worse than any of the dreams had been,
because he knew that he would not awake from it to find
himself sweating with fear, but safe. And he had no idea
how it would end. He could only urge Dagobaz to greater speed and pray that they would reach the haven among
the rocks in time.

The sun vanished with the abruptness of a snuffed
candle as they rode into the shadow of the high ridges;
and now they were nearing their goal. Half a mile to go
. . . a quarter . . . four hundred yards . . . The white streaks
of bird-droppings showed clearly against the purple
hillside, and there was someone standing near the
grass-crowned rock: a man with a rifle. Bukta, his dun-
coloured *shikari*'s clothing almost invisible among the shadows. So he had not gone. He had waited for them; and
now he was here and sighting along the barrel of his
beloved Lee-Enfield.

Ash had seen Bukta hit a tree-rat at fifty paces and bring down a galloping leopard at twice that range in thick grass; and with the light in his favour and the pursuing soldiery ignorant of his presence, he should be able to pick off at least one of them before they realized their danger, and thereby sow enough confusion among the rest to enable their quarry to reach cover.

There was barely two hundred yards to go now, and Ash found himself laughing exultantly as he waited for the flash: but it did not come—and suddenly he realized that it would not, because he and Sarji and Gobind were in the line of fire, and together they masked the enemy so effectively that the old *shikari* did not dare risk a shot.

They had all forgotten Manilal. The fat man had been carried past the rocks where Bukta waited, but his horse was tiring and he managed to turn it in a wide arc that brought him round facing the way they had come, though from much further out in the valley. Galloping back from this direction, Manilal was able to see what was happening and to size up the situation a good deal more clearly than any of the other actors in the drama.

The passage through the rock-fall had been described to him and, always a quick thinker, he realized that his companions would never reach it with enough time in hand, and that the *shikari* could not help them, for he must hold his fire until they were past him—by which time it would be too late. Manilal did not wear spurs, but he still had a whip that he had prudently carried on a loop round his wrist, and now he used it mercilessly, keeping his horse at full gallop and making not for the rocks, but for the bunched and yelling pack from the city.

Ash saw him sweep past and heard the crash and the confusion as he drove full tilt into the pursuers. But there was no time to turn round and see what had happened. There was only time to pull up and leap to the ground, to catch Anjuli as she tumbled off, and grasping her wrist, to pull Dagobaz after them while Sarji and Gobind flung themselves from their horses and followed, and Bukta fired and re-loaded and fired again . . .

The shadowed canyon behind the wall of rock and scree seemed a very peaceful spot after the heat and dust and frenzy of that wild ride. Bukta had been camping there for the past week, and his few belongings, together with the shot-gun and cartridges and the two boxes of ammunition, were neatly laid out on a ledge, and conveniently within reach. His pony, its forefeet hobbled, country-fashion, with a loop of cloth to prevent it straying, was placidly grazing on the dying grass, and the place looked curiously home-like. A haven of peace and safety enclosed by the cliffs of the steeply sloping hillsides, and only to be reached by a passage that was so narrow that a single man armed with a stout sword, let alone a revolver, could have held it against an army . . .

Or so Ash had once thought. But faced now with the reality, he was less sanguine, for there was a limit to the time they could hold out. A limit set by their supply of ammunition and water. There might be enough of the first, but the latter would not last over-long in this dry, torrid heat—especially when there were horses to be considered. Bukta had presumably watered his pony and drunk his fill at the stream in the valley, but that source was now closed to them, and the nearest supply—the little pool among the rocks with its solitary palm-tree—was over an hour's journey away. Other than that they had only the contents of their water-bottles, which might tide them over for a time, but do little for their horses. And it was now several hours since Dagobaz had last drunk; and longer still since he himself had done so.

Ash was suddenly conscious again of his own thirst, which until now had been no more than a minor discomfort when compared with the mental emotions of that eventful day. But he knew that he did not dare slake it for fear that he would not be able to stop himself from draining every drop from the bottle; and they might all be in worse need of its contents soon, and he must endure a little longer. By nightfall there would be dew and then it would not be so bad, but two things were clear: they could not afford to stay here, for without water the quiet canyon could soon cease to be a place of refuge and become a trap; and the sooner they left the better, because once darkness fell even Bukta would find it next to impossible to follow that barely visible track that led back through the hills, dipping and climbing and crossing seemingly impossible slopes and precipitous rock-strewn ridges.

Yet as soon as they left there would be nothing to prevent their pursuers from pouring through the gap and taking up the trail again. Unless someone stayed behind and held them off until the others . . .

Ash looked quickly at the narrow cleft through which they had just come, and then back at Anjuli, who had dropped to the ground when he released her, and was sitting with closed eyes, her head thrown back against the wall of the canyon. Her dishevelled hair was grey with dust and he saw that there was a snow-white streak in it, like a wide bar of silver laid across the darkness. Her face was so drawn with exhaustion that a stranger would have been forgiven for thinking her an old woman, and it did not seem possible that she was not yet twenty-one.

Ash wished that he could have let her rest there a little longer. She looked as though she needed it—as they all did, horses as well as riders—and though the air in the canyon was stiflingly hot with the accumulated heat of the blazing day, at least the shadows lent it an illusion of coolness, and the tired horses had already begun to nibble at the sun-dried grass. But there was no help for it: they would have to press on, for despite the steep hillsides on either hand and the great wall of rock and scree that lay between them and the valley, they could still hear the muffled crack of Bukta's rifle and the answering spatter of shots that told them that their pursuers had halted and were returning his fire.

Ash's own carbine was still strapped to Sarji's saddle, and he took it down and re-loaded it, and reaching for the boxes of ammunition, stowed them in one of the saddle-bags and said curtly: "Sarji, you and Gobind must go on ahead with the Rani while I take over from Bukta and hold this rabble off. He will have to go with you because he's the only one who knows the way; and——" He stopped and looked round: "Where is Manilal? What happened to him?"

But neither Sarji or Gobind could tell him. There had been no time to look back, or to do anything but urge on the flagging horses; and once they were among the rocks they could no longer see what was happening in the valley. "But Bukta will have seen that he came to no harm," said Sarji confidently. "He never misses, and there will soon be many dead men out there. Hark to him!—he is firing as fast as he can load. If we three go back and help him we should be able to kill them all."

Ash said sharply: "No, Sarji. You must leave this to me. We came here to save the Rani, and her safety comes first. We cannot afford to take risks with her life, and

792

though there may be only a handful of men out there now, there will soon be more coming up behind them from the burning-ground. Besides, once it is dark none of us will be able to move, so just do as I say and don't argue—we haven't time. Gobind, see that the Rani-Sahiba is ready to leave as soon as Bukta and Manilal get here. She'll have to ride behind one of you, so if there is any doubt about the other horses being able to take a double load, Sarji must ride Dagobaz and leave one of the others for me. Throw me over that shot-gun; I may as well take that too: and the cartridges—Thanks, Sarji. I'll be back as soon as it's safe to go on. Don't stop unless you have to. You won't be safe until you're well beyond the border."

He shouldered the two guns, picked up the laden saddle-bag, and without looking at Anjuli went quickly away.

The narrow cut that wound between the rocks was very quiet and deeply shadowed, for the light was already draining from the thin sliver of sky that showed high overhead, and it occurred to Ash that long before the sun was down it would be dark in there: too dark to see, which might be to his advantage, as anyone unfamiliar with the passage would probably be held up by the first sharp turn, imagining that it was a dead-end, whereas he would be able to grope his way back without much difficulty . . . that was, if he came back.

"No. Not if, when," thought Ash soberly, for he had remembered something: a voice from the past saying *"The Sahib-log do not understand that Truth should be used sparingly, and they call us liars because when we of this country are asked questions by strangers, we prefer to lie first and then consider whether the truth would have served us better."* And another more recent one that said, "It don't do to believe more than a fraction of what these people tell you, for most of 'em will always tell a lie rather than speak the truth, and trying to find out what really happened is like drawing eye-teeth or hunting for that proverbial needle in a haystack."

He would have to come back. There was no "if" about it, for were the others to return to Gujerat without him there was no knowing what trouble they might find themselves involved in, because their story could so easily be disbelieved (or at best dismissed as the exaggerated out-pourings of a hysterical widow, her uncle's hakim and his servant, and a local breeder of horses, none of whom

793

could speak a word of English). Officialdom, as he had good reason to know, was never very easy to convince; and if there was one thing he could be certain of it was that everyone in Bhithor, from the Diwan to the lowliest palace servant, could be counted upon to lie like a trooper in order to conceal the truth. It was even possible that his friends might end up being suspected of murdering him for the sake of his shot-gun and rifle, should he fail to return.

For a moment Ash was almost tempted to go back. But he did not do so. Sarji had many friends in Gujerat and his family was not without influence in the province, while Juli was a princess in her own right, and both she and Gobind would have the support of her brother Jhoti, who was Maharajah of Karidkote. It was the height of absurdity to imagine that they would not be able to manage without him.

He found Bukta strategically ensconced between two large boulders, with his front protected by a flat-topped rock on which he had rested the barrel of his rifle. There were gaps in his cartridge belt and spent cases on the ground about him; and out in the valley a number of frightened horses galloped to and fro with empty saddles and trailing reins, their late riders lying still among the stones and dust, in proof of Sarji's statement that Bukta did not miss. But though the opposition had been drastically reduced it had not been eliminated, and those who survived had taken cover and were returning Bukta's fire.

Their antique weapons could not compare in the matter of range and accuracy with the Lee-Enfield, but they had the advantage of numbers. They could fire four or five shots to every one of Bukta's, and the fusillade that spattered around him filled the air with flying chips of rock, spurts of dust and showers of small stones, and made it too dangerous for him to venture into the open. He could retreat in safety, but that was all; and though the enemy were in no better case, they had time on their side, and reinforcements on the way.

Bukta glanced briefly at Ash and said: "Go back, Sahib. You can do no good here. You and the others must go quickly into the hills. It is your only chance. We cannot hope to stand against an army, and there are many coming—look there."

But Ash had already seen. It was indeed an army that was spurring towards them down the valley. The low sunlight glinted on lances, tulwars and jezails, and judging by the size of the dust-cloud that whirled up behind the advancing horde, half the forces of the state had been sent to recapture the widowed Rani and her rescuers. They were still a long way off, but they would be here all too soon.

A bullet smacked into the rock within inches of Ash's head and he ducked to avoid the shower of splinters and said curtly: "We cannot go without a guide. You know that, Bukta. I will stay here in your place while you get the others away. Now go quickly."

Bukta did not waste time arguing. He wriggled out backwards, and standing up in the lee of a boulder, slapped the dust from his clothes, and said briefly: "Do not let anyone get too close, Sahib. Keep them at a distance and fire as often as you can so that they will be unable to tell how many of us are here among the rocks. When it is dark, come away, and if I can I will come back and meet you."

"You will have to bring one of the horses, for if Manilal is hurt—"

"He is dead," said Bukta shortly,"—and but for him, all of you would be too, for those dogs were so close on your heels that you could not have dismounted without being overtaken; and I could not fire. But the Hakim's servant rode into them and brought down the leading riders, and fell himself, and as he lay on the ground one coming up behind him smote his head from his body. May he be reborn a prince and a warrior. I will come back for you after moonrise. If not . . ." He shrugged and went away, and Ash lay down behind the flat-topped rock and surveyed the battle-ground, rifle and shot-gun at the ready.

The reinforcements, though much closer now, were still out of range. But one of the original posse, finding that a full two minutes had gone by without a shot being fired by the marksman among the rocks, took this to mean that he must either be dead or had run out of ammunition, and sustained by this belief was incautious enough to show himself. Ash's carbine cracked and the man jerked upright as though pulled by an unseen wire and fell back dead. After that his remaining comrades were careful to keep their heads well down while continuing to fire wildly in the general direction of the rockfall, which allowed Ash to give his full attention to the oncoming horsemen.

The cavalry carbine was accurate up to three hundred yards, though beyond that its effects were more a matter of luck than skill. But remembering Bukta's advice, Ash began to fire into the brown at extreme range, and with deadly effect, for a target provided by upwards of fifty men riding ten to fifteen abreast, and bunched together in a solid phalanx, is one that is almost impossible to miss.

Even at that distance the first shot told, and though it was difficult to see if it was man or a horse that had been hit, the formation disintegrated as if by magic, and a dust-cloud spread out to cover the mêlée as some riders reined in hard and those behind crashed into them, while others swerved out of harm's way and milled around in the smother.

Ash added to the confusion by continuing to fire, and he was reloading for the sixth time when a hand touched his shoulder and he spun round, his heart in his mouth. *"Sarji!* Oh God, you frightened me. What the hell do you think you're doing? Didn't I tell you—" He stopped in mid-sentence for behind Sarji stood Gobind.

Another fusillade of shots whined overhead but he did not heed them: "What is it? What has happened?"

"Nothing," said Sarji, reaching out to take the carbine from him. "It is only that we have decided that you must be the one to go on ahead with the Rani-Sahiba, for if there should . . . if things go wrong, you, being a Sahib, can speak better for her and for us all to your countrymen, and obtain justice from the Government. It is three to one, Ashok, for Bukta too agrees that it is wiser so. He will go with you and see that you travel in safety. Now leave us and go; they are waiting for you and will not start until you come."

"But Gobind cannot use a rifle," began Ash. "He—"

"I can load them," said Gobind, "and with two rifles your friend will be able to fire quicker than you could do, so that perhaps those out there will come to believe that there are more of us than they thought, and be less bold in consequence. Do not waste time, Sahib, but go swiftly and get the Rani-Sahiba to safety. You need not fear for us, as it will be dark soon, and until then we can hold this

796

place against all Bhithor. Take this with you"—he thrust a small packet into Ash's hand—"and now go."

Ash looked from one face to the other, and what he saw there made him realize the futility of argument. Besides, they were right, because it was what he had thought himself. He could probably do more for Juli than they could. He said: "Be careful."

"We will," said Sarji. Their hands met in a hard grip and they smiled at each other, the same fleeting tight-lipped smile. Gobind nodded in dismissal and Ash turned obediently and left them.

There was another burst of musketry from the invisible enemy and he heard the rifle crash in reply, and broke into a run . . .

The narrow slit between the rocks had been easier to negotiate now that he was no longer burdened by firearms and ammunition, and at the far side of it Bukta and Anjuli stood waiting for him. He had only to mount Dagobaz and pull Juli up behind him and canter away down the shadowed canyon in the wake of Bukta's little cat-footed pony.

The sound of firing faded and presently all they could hear was the beat of their horses' hooves, the creak and jingle of saddles and bridles, and the croon of the evening breeze blowing through the dry grasses on the hillside. And it was only as they began to climb that he remembered the packet that Gobind had given him, and taking it out, saw that it was the letters he had written last night. All of them. And realized the significance of that. But by then it was too late to turn back, even if he could have done so.

They climbed steadily until the valley lay well below them and hidden from sight by a sea of grassy spurs and high ridges, where the air was no longer tainted by dust and the wind blew cooler. But Bukta showed no sign of halting and pressed on swiftly, leading them forward and upward along paths that to Ash's eyes appeared almost invisible, and across long slopes of shale where they must dismount and lead the horses, whose hooves slipped and slithered among the loose stones.

The sun set in a blaze of gold and amber, and suddenly the sky was green and the corn-coloured hills were

797

blue and indigo and violet—and there below them, cupped in its rocky hollow and half hidden by its solitary palm tree, the lonely pool glinted in the last of the light.

Bukta had led them unerringly to the sole small spot in all those barren hills where they could slake their thirst and gain the energy to press on. But for one of them it was to prove the end of the road . . .

Dagobaz could not have seen the water, for Ash had been leading him. But he must have smelt it, and he too was parched with thirst—and very tired. Bukta's pony, who was familiar with rough country and had not lacked rest or water that day, went down the steep and stony slope as lightly as a cat. But Dagobaz, made incautious by thirst, had been less sure-footed. He had plunged forward eagerly, taking his tired owner unawares, and before Ash could do anything to check him he was sliding helplessly downwards, struggling to keep his footing in a welter of dry earth and loose stones, dragging Ash with him and falling at last among the rocks at the water's edge.

Anjuli had managed to jump to safety and Ash had suffered no more than a few minor cuts and bruises. But Dagobaz could not get on his feet; his right fore-leg had snapped and there was nothing that anyone could do for him.

Had this happened in the plains it might have been possible to have him conveyed to Sarji's farm, where he could have been treated by an experienced veterinary surgeon; and though he would always have been lame and could never have been ridden again, he could at least have spent the rest of his life in honourable retirement among the shade trees in the pastures. But here there was no hope for him.

At first Ash had refused to believe it. And when he did, it was as though everything that had happened that day—the long hours of waiting on the terrace of the *chattri,* the killing of Shushila, the headlong flight down the valley and the death of Manilal—had been building up to this moment, bit by bit, until the accumulated weight had become intolerable. Now it crashed down upon him, beating him to his knees beside the fallen horse, and he took the dusty, sweat-streaked head into his arms and hiding his face against it, wept as he had only done once before in all his life—on the morning that Sita had died.

There is no knowing how long he would have remained there, for he had lost all consciousness of time. But at last a hand gripped his shoulder and Bukta's voice said sternly: "Enough, Sahib! It grows dark, and we must leave this place while we can still see to do so, for it is overlooked on every side, and should we be caught here we should be trapped without hope of escape. We cannot stop until we reach higher ground, where we shall be safer."

Ash rose unsteadily, and stood for a moment or two with closed eyes, striving for control. Then he stooped to remove bit and headband and loosen the girth so that Dagobaz might be more comfortable. Untying the water-bottle from its fastening, he emptied the luke-warm contents on the ground and taking it to the pool, refilled it with cool water.

He had forgotten his own needs, but he knew that Dagobaz had been lured to disaster by thirst, and that at least should be assuaged. The black horse was dazed and in pain, and very weary, but he took the water gratefully, and when the flask was empty, Ash handed it over his shoulder to be refilled without looking round or realizing that it was not Bukta but Anjuli who stood beside him and filled it again and again.

Bukta was keeping an anxious eye on the fast-fading light, and when he saw that Dagobaz would take no more, he came forward and said: "Leave this to me, Sahib. He will feel nothing, I promise you. Put the Rani-Sahiba on my pony and go on a little way."

Ash turned his head and said harshly: "There is no need. If I can shoot a young woman I knew well, I can surely do the same for my horse."

He took out the revolver, but Bukta stretched out a hand for it and said gravely: "No, Sahib. It is better that I should do this."

Ash stared back at him for a long moment, and then he sighed deeply and said: "Yes, you are right. But you will have to do it while I am here, for if I go away he will try to get up and follow me."

Bukta nodded, and Ash relinquished the revolver and knelt to gentle Dogobaz's weary head and whisper loving words in his ear. Dagobaz nuzzled him and whickered softly in reply, and when the shot came he jerked once. And that was all.

"Come," said Bukta shortly. "It is time we left. Do we take the saddle and bridle?"

"No. Leave them." Ash got to his feet as slowly and stiffly as though he had been an old, old man, and reeling to the pool, sank down by the edge to plunge his face into the water and gulp it down in great mouthfuls like a parched animal, drenching his head and neck and washing away the dust and the tears and the dear, familiar smell of Dagobaz. His thirst quenched he arose, dripping, and shook the water out of his hair and eyes. Anjuli was already seated on the pony, and Bukta turned without a word and set off up the steep hillside in the gathering dusk.

Ash's foot touched something and he looked down and saw the empty water-bottle—and would have left it, because after this he would never be able to drink from it again without remembering all the fleetness and beauty and strength that had once been Dagobaz. But there would be no more water until they reached the spring among the trees, and that was many miles distant. Juli would be thirsty before then. He picked up the bottle and refilled it, and slinging it over his shoulder, followed after the others without looking back to where Dagobaz slept his last sleep among the shadows.

By the time they reached the ridge the stars were out, but Bukta hurried them on and only stopped at last when Anjuli fell asleep in the saddle and would have toppled out of it if they had not happened to be on a level stretch of ground. Even then he had insisted that they camp for the night among a number of large boulders that formed a rough circle in the centre of a wide fall of shale, though it had not been a particularly comfortable spot or one that was easy to reach.

"But you will be able to sleep in safety here," said Bukta, "and with no need to keep watch, for not even a snake could approach without setting these stones aslide and rousing you with the clatter."

He had coaxed the pony across the treacherous, shifting surface, and having tethered it on a grassy slope on the far side of the shale, returned to clear away the larger stones and loose debris from between the boulders to make a sleeping place for Anjuli. That being done, he had produced food for them all: chuppattis that he had cooked himself that morning, and *pekoras* and cold rice and *huldoo* that Sarji had purchased in the city and hurriedly transferred to Bukta's saddle-bags when it was decided that he and Gobind would stay behind to act as rearguard.

Neither Ash nor Anjuli had eaten anything that day, but both were bone-weary and too exhausted by mental and physical stress to have any desire for food. But Bukta had forced them to eat, saying angrily that they would need all their strength if they hoped to make good progress on the morrow, and that to starve themselves would be the height of folly as it would only weaken them and thereby assist their enemies: "Also you will sleep all the better for a little food, and awake refreshed."

So they had eaten what they could, and afterwards Anjuli had curled up on the saddle-blanket that Bukta had spread for her, and fallen asleep almost immediately. The old *shikari* had grunted approval, and having urged the Sahib to follow her example, had turned to go away. "Do you go back for them now?" asked Ash in an undertone.

"What else? It was arranged between us that they would await me near the top of the nullah, and that I would set out as soon as I had placed the Rani-Sahiba and yourself in this spot, which is as safe a one as any in these hills."

"You are going on foot?" asked Ash, remembering that the pony was tethered on the far side of the shale.

Bukta nodded. "I shall go quicker on foot. If I rode I would have to wait until the moon was up, as it is still too dark for riding. But the moon will not rise for another hour, by which time I hope to be within eye-shot of the nullah. Moreover a man cannot lead two horses in these hills, and it may be that either the Sirdar-Sahib or the Hakim was suffered a wound or is over-wearied, and if so I can lead while they remain in the saddle. All being well, we should be back before midnight, and on our way again by first light. So sleep while you can, Sahib."

He shouldered his rifle and went away, walking gingerly across the shale that clattered and slid under his hard, bare feet. The stone-noises stopped when he reached the grass, and a moment later the grey starlight had swallowed him up and the night was quiet again, and nothing moved in it but the wind and the pony cropping the sun-dried grass of the hillside.

Ash had never felt less like sleeping, but he knew that Bukta was right and that it was only sensible to get what rest he could, so he lay down among the great boulders and closing his eyes tried to relax his tense muscles, and to make his mind a blank because there was so much that he could not bear to think of: Shushila and Manilal. And now Dagobaz—But he must have been wearier than he knew, for sleep overtook him before he was aware of it; and when the familiar nightmare came on him and he awoke sweating with terror, the moon was high up in the sky and the hills were awash with silver.

Juli was still asleep, and after a time Ash abandoned his fruitless survey of the empty hillside, and turning to look at her, experienced none of the emotions that he would have expected the sight and the nearness to her to arouse in him.

She was here beside him, freed at last from her bondage to a hateful husband and an adored sister, and he should by rights have been light-headed with joy and triumph. Instead it was as though all feeling and emotion had drained out of him, and he could only look at her dispassionately and think "poor Juli"—and feel sorry for her because she must have suffered so much. But then he was sorry for himself too. For having had to kill little Shu-shu, and for his part in bringing about the deaths of Manilal and Dagobaz, whose mortal remains would soon be mangled and made hideous by jackals and vultures and other eaters of carrion.

If only he could have buried them—! Or burned them, as Shushila had burned, so that their bodies like hers could have become clean ash instead of tattered flesh and reddened bones . . .

Absurdly, it was this thought that hurt most. It seemed in some way a final betrayal that the headless body of fat, faithful, heroic Manilal should be left lying out in the valley, a prey to the corruption and the kites; and that all the strength and grace that had been Dagobaz should be torn in pieces by jackals and carrion crows. Not that Dagobaz would care. But Manilal . . .

If Fate had permitted Manilal to return to his home in Karidkote and to live out his life there in peace, he too, when he died, would have been taken to the burning-grounds. And afterwards his ashes would have been cast into a mountain stream that would carry them down to the Chenab River, and from there to the Indus—and so at last to the sea. It was not right that his corpse should be left to rot in the open like that of an ownerless dog.

As for Dagobaz——But he would not think of Dagobaz. There was no point in looking back. What was written, was written. The thing to do was to look forward and make plans for the future. Tomorrow . . . tomorrow they would reach that small green oasis among the barren hills and camp there for the night. And the next day they would be among the jungle-clad foothills, and after that it would not be too long before they reached a made road; though the return journey would be slower, for they could not all ride now that Dagobaz . . .

What *was* Bukta doing? The moon had not yet risen when he left, but now it was sinking again, and the breeze that blows steadily between sunset and the small hours was already dwindling down towards the lull that lies between night and morning and ends only with the rising of the dawn wind. He should have been back hours ago. Unless . . . A cold, unpleasant thought slid into Ash's mind and made his skin crawl.

Supposing Bukta had met with an accident on his way to the canyon . . . ? Supposing he had missed his footing in the dark and slipped and fallen—as Dagobaz had done? He might even now be lying stunned and helpless at the foot of some precipitous slope, or creeping painfully on hands and knees up a stony ridge with his ankle broken. Almost anything could have happened to him in these treacherous hills, and as the others would not dare to start without him, they would still be somewhere in the canyon, waiting for him. But how long would they wait?

That faint pulsating glow in the sky above the valley showed that their enemies were still camped there in force, so they would have to leave before the dawn broke, because as soon as it was light enough someone was going to discover that the entrance into the canyon was no longer guarded, and within minutes a hundred men would be on their trail again. If Bukta had met with an accident . . .

"I ought to go and look for him," thought Ash. "If he is hurt, I can always come back for the pony and put him up on it. And after all, I've been over that ground twice now, so there is no reason why I should lose my way."

But he turned to look at Anjuli again, and knew that he must not go. He could not leave her here alone, for if anything happened to him—if he missed his footing on a steep path or lost his way among the hills, and if Bukta were never to come back—what would become of her? How long would she be able to keep alive if she was left to fend for herself among this maze of parched and desolate hills?

She did not even know in which direction Gujerat lay, and could easily wander back into the valley, where she would be captured and almost certainly killed. He could not take the risk of leaving her. He would have to stay and possess his soul in patience, and pray that Bukta and the others would appear before morning.

The hours that followed had seemed interminable. The shadows lengthened as the moon moved down the sky, and when the breeze died the night became so still that he could hear the sound of Juli's soft breathing and from somewhere very far away the faint, faint howl of a jackal pack; but though he strained his ears to catch the click of hooves on hard ground or the murmur of men's voices, he heard no other sounds. The silence had remained unbroken until at last the dawn wind began to blow, softly at first, and then gathering strength as it swept across the hills, flattening the grass and displacing small stones that went clattering down the gully.

It drove the night before it as a housewife drives dust with her broom, and as the moon paled and the stars vanished, the dawn broke in a flood of yellow light along the eastern horizon—and Ash saw a small dark figure appear on the crest of the ridge, to be briefly silhouetted against that saffron sky before it moved downwards, slowly and tiredly towards the gully.

He ran out to meet it, stumbling across the shale and calling out, light-headed with relief and careless of how much noise he made; and it was only when he was half-way up the grassy slope that he stopped, and a cold hand seemed to close about his heart. For he realized that there was still only one figure. Bukta was alone; and as he came nearer Ash saw that his clothes were no longer dust-coloured but hideously dappled with great dark stains.

"They were both dead"—Bukta's voice was flat with exhaustion and he dropped down wearily and without apology, hunkering on the grass like a tired old crow. But the dried blood on his coat was not his own, for he had, he said, arrived only after it was all over.

"It was clear that some of those sons of dogs had climbed up into the hills, and coming down from behind had taken them by surprise. There had been a fight in the nullah and their horses too were dead—and I think very many of their enemies must also have died, for the ground between the rocks and in the nullah was red with blood, and there were many spent cartridges—so many that I doubt if they left so much as one unfired. But by the time I came, the Bhithori dogs had taken away their own dead and wounded. It must have taken many men to carry them back to the city, as only four men had been left behind to keep watch by the entrance to the nullah . . ."

A flicker of a smile showed briefly on Bukta's brown, nut-cracker face, and he said grimly: "Those four I slew with my knife. One after the other, and without noise; for the fools slept, thinking themselves secure—and why not? They had slain three of us five and must have thought that the other two, one of whom was a woman, would be flying for their lives and far away among the hills. I knew that I should have come away then. But how could I leave the bodies of my master the Sirdar-Sahib, and the Hakim and his servant, lying there unburned at the mercy of wild beasts? That I could not do, and therefore I carried them out one by one to a disused shed that stands near the bank of the stream, making four journeys, for I could not carry Manilal's head and body at one time . . .

"When at last I had brought them all, I pulled down the old, dry thatch and made a great pile of it, and placing the bodies upon it, each a little apart, strewed them with powder from my cartridges, and then cut down the roof-poles and supports so that these fell inwards. When all was done I fetched water from the stream and said the proper prayers, and taking flint and tinder, set fire to it and came away, leaving it burning . . ."

His voice died on a sigh, and Ash thought numbly, "Yes. I saw it. I thought it was camp fires. I didn't know—" It appalled him to think that he had actually seen that pulsating glow and had not known that it was Sarji burning . . . Sarji and Gobind and Manilal . . .

Bukta said tiredly: "It burned very fiercely, the wood being old and dry. And it is my hope that when it has burned out the wind will carry the ashes of the Sirdar-

Sahib and the others into the stream which is hard by, and thus by favour of the gods will they be taken onward to the sea."

He glanced up at Ash's stricken face and added gently: "Do not look like that, Sahib. To us who worship the gods, death is a very little thing: a brief halt only on a long journey during which birth and death are succeeded by re-birth, and again death; and thus on and on, until at last we achieve Nirvana. Therefore why grieve that these three have completed another stage on that journey, and may even now be embarking on the next?"

Ash did not speak and the old man sighed again; he had been greatly attached to Sarjevar. He was also very tired. The night's work had involved enough gruelling labour to have exhausted many a younger man, and he would have liked to stay where he was and rest awhile, but that was not possible.

Had all gone well he and his companions would by now have been many miles away and no longer in fear of pursuit. But things had gone ill, and to make matters worse he had killed the sleeping sentries and removed and burned the bodies of Sarjevar and the two others, and by doing so, ensured that before long the chase would be taken up again—though probably not before sunrise.

The flames of the pyre he had kindled would have been clearly visible in the city, but he did not think that anyone would have been sent to investigate, since it would be thought that the men who had been left on guard had set fire to the abandoned shed for sport, or to scare away jackals and other night-prowlers who would have been attracted by the scent of blood.

But with the dawn it was certain that many men would come, this time bringing experienced trackers, so that they might be able to follow the trail of the Rani and her surviving rescuers into the hills; which would have done them little good had all gone well, as he had fully expected to be far on the way by this time—too far to fear pursuit. As it was, when the enemy returned in strength they would find the four who had been left on guard lying dead, and the bodies of the three strangers gone; and would know by this that their quarry could not be far off.

Bukta struggled to his feet and said hoarsely: "Come,

806

Sahib, we are wasting time. There is far to go and great need of haste; and from now on you and I must both go on foot, for there is only the one pony."

Ash had still not spoken, and now he turned without a word and together they went back down the hillside in the growing light.

44

In the end it had been Bukta and not Anjuli who had ridden the pony.

Anjuli had been aroused by the noise of Ash's tumultuous departure, and when the two men returned they found her awake and waiting. Her eyes widened at the sight of the *shikari*'s blood-stained clothing and she looked at Ash's haggard face and drew her own conclusions. The little colour that a night's sleep had brought to her cheeks drained away and left her looking paler and even more drawn, but she asked no questions, and would have fetched food for them if Bukta had not refused to let them wait. They could, he said, eat later in the day, but now they must leave at once and press on with all the speed they could muster, for there would be men on their trail.

He shouldered the saddle-bags, and Anjuli followed him across the shale to where the pony was grazing placidly on the far slope. But when it had been saddled and Ash told her to mount, she refused to do so, saying that anyone could see that the *shikari* was exhausted, and if speed was essential they would make better time, if he rode; she herself was well rested and could easily walk.

Bukta had not bothered to argue. He was too tired and too anxious to waste time over something that was, after all, only sensible. He had merely nodded and said that they must watch to see that he did not fall asleep, for if he should do so, the pony, being surefooted, would choose its own path and might lead them badly astray. The Rani-Sahiba must walk beside him so that she could hold onto a stirrup-leather on the upward slopes.

Ash, who was still numbed by grief, had agreed, though he was less anxious than Bukta. He thought their lead was sufficiently great and did not see how their pursuers could overtake them when they did not even know the road and so must move slowly, searching the ground for signs that would show them which way the quarry had gone.

But Bukta knew that a woman who had spent the last few years penned up in strict purdah, and an elderly *shikari* who for the moment at least was physically exhausted, would never be able to match the speed of angry men who were rested and well fed and burning for revenge. He was also well aware that as soon as the sun rose and the kites came for Dagobaz the men on their trail would see the birds dropping down out of the sky, and so be led to the spot that was no great distance from the gully in which his companions had spent the night.

Therefore he hurried them on, and only when the full heat of the morning was beating down on them, and Anjuli showed signs of flagging, did he pause to change places with her, declaring himself sufficiently rested to go forward on foot. But he would not let them stop, except for a short time at mid-day when they ate a frugal meal in the shade of an overhanging rock and he slept for a space.

That brief cat-nap ended, he urged them on again, plodding steadily forward, and turning whenever they crossed a ridge to look back and search for signs of pursuit. But nothing moved except the landscape, which appeared to quiver in the dancing heat, and in the brassy sky behind them a handful of dark specks that wheeled round and round and told their own tale. The kites and vultures had been driven from their meal by the arrival of men—probably a good many men—and were circling overhead waiting for the intruders to leave.

"They have found the pool," muttered Bukta, "and now they will know that we have only one horse between the three of us and must keep to a foot's pace. Let us hope they will take their time drinking the water and quarrelling over who shall have your saddle and bridle."

Perhaps they had done so. At all events, they did not succeed in coming within eye-shot of the fugitives, and by the time the sun was low in the sky and the parched hillsides were once again streaked with violet shadows, it had become clear that they would not do so now. So clear that when at last, and by starlight, they came to Bukta's old camping ground in the little tree-filled valley, he felt secure enough to light a fire in order to cook chuppattis and discourage any prowling leopard from approaching. And also to wash his blood-stained clothing and spread it out to dry.

They had all three been too exhausted to sleep well that night, and Bukta and Ash had taken it in turns to keep watch, for there were pug-marks in the damp earth at the water's edge and they could not risk losing the pony. By first light they were on the move again and, except that there was less sense of urgency and they did not pause so often to look behind them, the day was a repetition of the one before; though even hotter and more tiring. They rested only when Bukta permitted it, with the result that nightfall found them footsore, weary and parched with thirst, but among the foothills.

The old *shikari* had slept soundly that night, and so also had Anjuli, worn out by the strain of a long, hot day in the saddle. But though Ash too was very tired, he had slept only fitfully and once again his sleep had been troubled by dreams, not of pursuit or of Dagobaz, but of Shushila. The same dream, endlessly repeated, from which he awoke shuddering: only to dream it again as soon as consciousness slipped from him . . .

Each time he slept, Shushila appeared before him dressed in her bridal array of scarlet and gold, and implored him with tears not to kill her, but he would not listen and raising the revolver he pressed the trigger and saw the lovely, pleading face dissolve in blood. And woke again . . .

"But what else could I have done?" thought Ash angrily. Wasn't it enough that he should have to bear the responsibility for Sarji's death, without being haunted by the reproachful ghost of Shushila, whose end he had merely hastened as Bukta had hastened Dagobaz's? But then Shushila was not an animal: she was a human being, who had decided of her own free will to face death by fire and thereby achieve holiness; and he, Ash, had taken it upon himself to cheat her of that.

He had done more—he had interfered in something that was a matter of faith and a very personal thing; and he could not even be sure that Shushila's convictions were wrong, for did not the Christian calendar contain the names of many men and women who had been burned at the stake for their beliefs, and acclaimed as saints and martyrs?

"If I couldn't save her, I should not have interfered," thought Ash. But as he had done so and could not undo it, he decided that he must put it out of his mind for ever; and turning over, he fell asleep again—only to meet once more a girl who wrung her hands and wept, and begged him to spare her. It had been a wretched night.

By sunrise next morning they were across the border, and three days later Ash and Bukta were back in Sarji's house, from where they had set out in such haste less than three weeks ago. But Anjuli had not been with them, for on their last night of the jungle Bukta had proffered some advice, waiting until she was asleep before doing so, and speaking very softly to avoid waking her.

He had, he said, been thinking of the future, and he had come to the conclusion that it would be better if they did not disclose the identity of Rani-Sahiba. She would get no sympathy, for not only did many people secretly approve of the old customs and would have every wife become suttee when her man died, but even those who did not tended to look upon a young widow as an ill-omened creature and little better than a slave.

Nor did he believe it advisable to tell anyone the true story of the Sirdar Sarjevar's death. It would be better for all if the Sirdar's family and friends were kept in ignorance of what had happened in Bhithor, as his identity (together with their own) could not have been known there; and in Bukta's opinion it had much better remain unknown, since there was no denying that they had all three entered Bhithor secretly with the intention of spiriting away the late Rana's wives; or that once there they had killed a member of the royal bodyguard, assaulted, gagged and bound a number of palace servants, and having abducted the Junior Rani, had opened fire on the local soldiery (who were very properly attempting to prevent their escape) and succeeded in killing a great many of them . . .

"I do not know your mind," said Bukta, "but for my part, I have no wish to be haled before a Magistrate-Sahib and required to make answer to such charges, and maybe spend the rest of my days in gaol—if I am not hanged for the killings. We know that the Bhithoris would lie and lie, and that even if they were not believed, the Sahibs would still say that we had no right to take the law into our own hands and slay those sons of swine. For that we should receive punishment, and though yours might be no more than hard words from your elders, I am very sure that mine would be gaol; and also that if ever I were released, the Bhithoris would see to it that I did not live to enjoy my freedom for more than a day—which is yet another thing to be thought of, Sahib: we have blackened their faces by putting such an insult upon them, and they will neither forget it nor forgive, and if they were to learn the names of those concerned—"

"They know the Hakim-Sahib's," said Ash curtly. "And Manilal's."

"True. But those two were both from Karidkote, and therefore it will be supposed that their accomplices were also from that state. The Bhithoris can have no reason to think otherwise, for they will never connect you, an officer-Sahib of a *rissala* in Ahmadabad, with the escape of one of the widows of the late Rana. Nor will they try and revenge themselves upon the Rani's people, who are too powerful—and too far away. But you and I are neither nor is the Rani-Sahiba until such time as she is safely back in her own state, which may not be for many weeks if there are to be police inquiries. The law moves slowly, and once let it become known that she is in Gujerat and will be required to give evidence on our behalf and her own, her life will not be worth an anna's purchase. Or yours or mine either. If you think awhile, Sahib, you will know that what I say is true."

"Yes . . . Yes, I know," said Ash slowly. The British authorities were going to take a very poor view of the whole affair—even though they bore a large part of the responsibility for it, having failed to take any action of their own—because the fact remained that a large number of men had died, and it was not as if the band of amateur knight-errants could claim to have saved the Ranis from death; Ash himself had actually hastened Shushila's, while Anjuli, by her sister's contrivance, would in any case have escaped being burned on the Rana's pyre. (She would have been blinded instead—but would anyone believe that story when all Bhithor would deny it flatly?)

The Diwan and his fellow-ministers would also claim,

with some justification, that the Senior Rani had insisted on her right to immolate herself on her husband's pyre, and that no one had been able to dissuade her; or to put a stop to it either, as she had the support of the common people who would have brooked no interference from officials or guards. All of which would sound very plausible —far more so than Ash's own story. In the end the court would inflict a fine on Bhithor, which would inevitably be paid by increasing the taxes on the peasantry; and as the new Rana was too young to be held responsible, the Political Department would lecture the Diwan and his accomplices on the evils of breaking the law and the dire consequences that would follow any further misdemeanours and probably recommend that a detachment of British-Indian troops be quartered on the state for a short period to make a show of strength. And that, as far as Bhithor was concerned, would be that.

But what of Lieutenant Pelham-Martyn and Bukta, *shikari?* How would they come out of the affair? And Juli . . . what would become of her if everything became known? When it was learned that she had escaped from Bhithor in the guise of a male servant, with a band of men who were not even related to her and in whose company she had subsequently spent several days and nights, would it be said that she was a brave young woman and much to be pitied? or a shameless one who, careless of rank and reputation, had eloped with a Sahib?—the very Sahib who three years ago had escorted her and her sister to their wedding! Because it would not be long before that too was discovered; and when it was, heads would be shaken and tongues would wag, and before long it would be believed by all that the Sahib and the Rani had been lovers for many years.

Juli's name would become a "hissing and an abomination" throughout half India, as even if there had been no grain of truth in it, the tale would have sounded plausible. How else to explain Lieutenant Pelham-Martyn's excessive display of anxiety on behalf of the Ranis? . . . his interviews with his Commanding Officer, the Commissioner and the District Inspector of Police? the telegrams he had dispatched on his own responsibility to several important officials, and his subsequent action in journeying to Bhithor in disguise, abducting the Junior Rani and firing on those who had attempted to prevent him?

The fact that there was actually a great deal of truth in it meant that he would have to watch his words and lie about his motives, and make certain that his lies carried conviction. Even then . . .

"I must have been mad," thought Ash, remembering how he had meant to come back to Ahmadabad and so shock the authorities with the tale of Shu-shu's death and Juli's wrongs that they would be galvanized into taking punitive action against Bhithor and assuming the reins of government until such time as the new Rana came of age.

"Well?" asked Bukta.

"You are right," said Ash heavily, "we cannot tell the truth. We shall have to tell lies instead. And they will have to be good ones. Tomorrow I will speak with the Rani-Sahiba and persuade her to agree. While as for our story, we have only to say that you and I and your master the Sirdar went into the jungles to shoot, as we have often done before, and that adventuring beyond the foothills, he and his horse fell from a steep path and were killed; as was my horse also—I myself receiving only bruises. We can also say with truth that it being impossible to bring his body back, we burned it near a stream that will carry his ashes to the sea."

"And the Rani-Sahiba? How do we explain her?"

Ash thought for a minute or two and then said that she would have to pretend to be the wife of his bearer, Gul Baz; or better still a widowed daughter. "Tomorrow when we are free of the jungle and can buy food, you must find us a place where the Rani-Sahiba and myself can lie hid while you take the pony and ride to cantonments to fetch Gul Baz—and also a bourka such as Moslem women wear, which will be an excellent disguise for her as it hides all. He and I will decide together on a tale to tell, and when you come for us the Rani-Sahiba can return with him to my bungalow while you and I go to the Sirdar-Sahib's house with our news."

"And afterwards?"

"That lies with the Rani. But she loved her sister, the suttee, very dearly; and if she should agree to keep silent her sister's death will go unavenged and the Diwan and those others will escape punishment. Therefore for her sister's sake she may prefer to speak out and take the consequences."

Bukta shrugged and observed philosophically that no

one could predict what a woman would do or fail to do, and they must hope that this one would be reasonable, as however dearly she loved her sister she could not undo what had been done, and her sister was dead. "Let us sleep on it, Sahib. It may be that in the morning you will think differently. Though I trust not, for we both know that the truth is too dangerous to be told."

Ash had not thought differently in the morning. The cost of this venture had already been appallingly high: it had taken the lives of Sarji, Gobind and Manilal (not to mention Dagobaz and Sarji's beloved Moti Raj), and any number of Bhithoris. And that was too high a price to pay for saving Juli's life if she must lose her reputation and become a byword among Indians and British alike, while Bukta ended his days in gaol and he himself was cashiered and deported. However strongly she might feel about Shushila's fate, she must be brought to see reason.

Ash foresaw difficulties and prepared his arguments accordingly; but they were not needed. Surprisingly, Anjuli had offered no opposition and had consented without demur to everything that had been suggested, even to wearing a bourka and masquerading as a Mohammedan woman, though Ash had pointed out that this could entail spending more than one night in the servants' quarters behind his bungalow, and pretending to be a relative of his bearer's. "What does that matter?" returned Anjuli indifferently. "One place is as good as another—and I myself have already been a servant in all but name . . ."

Her agreement brought considerable relief to Bukta, who had expected a good deal of opposition to the suggestion that she should pose as a relative of Gul Baz's—both on the score of caste and her royal blood—and he confided to Ash that the Rani-Sahiba was not only a brave woman, but a clear-headed one; which was much rarer.

Stopping on the outskirts of the first small town they came to, he bade the two to keep hidden while he went ahead on the pony to purchase food and more suitable clothing for them (the garments in which they had left Bhithor being far too conspicuous in Gujerat) and they had continued their journey in the sober dress of the hardworking local villagers—Anjuli still in male attire, as Ash had considered this safer. He had also taken the precaution of burning every shred of those gaudy palace uniforms, for he did not believe in taking chances.

In the late afternoon Bukta brought them by circuitous ways to a ruined tomb that stood among thickets of thorn trees and pampas grass in a desolate stretch of uncultivated land. No paths ran near it and not many people could have known of its existence, since it lay far from the beaten track and there were no villages within several miles. Part of the dome had fallen in many years ago, but the shell of the building remained standing and the tomb-chamber below still contained a pool of brackish water, the remnants of flooding from the rains of the last monsoon. Dust, twigs and fallen feathers littered the ground, but it was cool and dark under the arches, and Bukta swept a space clear, and cutting armfuls of dry grass, strewed it on the paving stones and covered it with the saddle-blanket to make a bed for Anjuli.

He would, he said, be as quick as he could, but it was unlikely that he would return much before sundown on the following day, and if he were later than that they were not to worry—and taking the tired pony he led it away through the tangled thickets and the tall grass. Ash accompanied him as far as the open ground and watched him mount and ride off into the dusty evening sunlight towards Ahmadabad, and only when he could see him no more did he turn and walk slowly back to the ruined tomb.

The thickets that hid it were alive with birds that had spent the heat of the day resting in the shade, while overhead, flights of parrots streamed out from the ruin, making for the distant river. The pigeons, following their example, wheeled up and up before setting off in the same direction, and a peacock woke from its afternoon siesta and paraded up and down between the tall clumps of grass.

But there was no movement from inside the tomb, and finding it empty, Ash suffered a crippling moment of panic, until a movement above him made him look up and he saw that Anjuli had not run away: there was a stairway in the thickness of the wall, and she had climbed it and was standing high above him, outlined against the sky and gazing out across the tree-tops to where the hills rose up along the northern horizon; and something in her face told him that she was not thinking of the country on the far side of them or of the beloved little sister who had died there, but of other hills—the true Hills, the high Himalayas

815

with their vast forests and glittering snow peaks thrusting up into the diamond air of the north.

He had made no noise, but she turned quickly and looked down at him, and once again he was made sharply aware of the toll that Bhithor had taken from her . . .

The girl that he had known and loved and whose picture he had carried in his heart for three long years had gone, and in her place was a stranger. A thin, haggard woman with great haunted eyes and a startling streak of whiteness in her black hair, who looked as though she had endured torture and famine and suffered a long term of imprisonment, shut away from the sunlight and fresh air. There was something else too: something less definable. A curious sense of loss. A deadness. Adversity and sorrow had not broken Anjuli, but they had numbed her.

Ash too was aware of a deadening of his senses. He loved her still: she was Juli, and he could no more stop loving her than he could stop breathing. But now, as they looked at each other, he was not seeing her face only, but the faces of three men: Sarji and Gobind and Manilal, who had lost their lives so that he and she could escape together. The tragedy of those deaths was an open wound in his mind, and for the moment love seemed a trivial thing in comparison with the cruel sacrifice that had been exacted from his friends.

He found the stairway in the wall, and climbing it, joined her on the flat strip of roof that circled the ruined dome. Below them the thorn trees and thickets and the tall grass that had grown up around the tomb were full of shadows and the tomb itself was very dark, but up here the evening sun was bright among the tree-tops and the countryside basked in the dusty golden light of an Indian evening. Out on the plain every stick and stone and blade of grass threw a long blue shadow on the ground, and soon the parrots and the pigeons would be returning to their nests and dusk would sweep down, bringing the stars and another night. And tomorrow—tomorrow or the next day—Bukta would return; and after that the lying would begin . . .

Anjuli had returned to her silent contemplation of the hills along the far horizon, and when at length Ash reached out and touched her, she flinched and took a swift step backward, putting up her hands as though to fend him off. His hand dropped and his brows drew together as he stared at her, frowning, and said harshly: "What did you think I meant to do? You can't think that I would harm you. Or . . . or is it that you no longer love me? No, don't turn away." He reached out again and caught her wrists in a grasp that she could not break. "Look at me, Juli! Now tell me the truth. Is it that you've stopped loving me?"

"I have tried to," whispered Anjuli bleakly. "But . . . but it seems—that I cannot help myself . . ." There was such despair in her voice that she might have been admitting to some physical disability like blindness, an affliction that could neither be cured nor ignored and that she must learn to accept and to live with. But Ash was not chilled by it for her mood matched his own.

He knew that though their love for each other had endured and would always endure, it had been temporarily submerged by a smothering weight of guilt and horror, and that until they had struggled free and could breathe again they had no desire for any active demonstration of it. That would return. But for the moment they were both in some way strangers to each other, because it was not only Anjuli who had changed. So much water had flowed under the bridges since they parted that even if they had met again under far happier circumstances it would have been surprising if they had found themselves able to pick up the threads again at the point where they had been cut off. But time was on their side—all the time in the world. They had come through the worst and were together again . . . the rest could wait.

He raised Anjuli's wrists and dropped a light kiss on each, and releasing her said: "That's all I wanted to know; and now that I know it I know too that as long as we are together nothing can really harm us again. You must believe that. Once you are my wife—"

"Your *wife*—?"

"What else? You can't think that I would lose you a second time."

"They will never permit you to marry me," said Anjuli with tired conviction.

"The Bhithoris? They won't dare open their mouths!"

"No, your people; and mine also, who will be of the same mind."

"You mean they will try and prevent it. But it's no business of theirs. This is our affair: yours and mine. Be-

817

sides, didn't your own grandfather marry a princess of Hind, though he was a foreigner and not of her faith?"

Anjuli sighed and shook her head again. "True. But that was in the days before your Raj had come to its full power. There was still a Mogul on the throne in Delhi and Ranjit-Singh held sway over the Punjab; and my grandfather was a great war-lord who took my grandmother as the spoils of war without asking any man's leave, having defeated the army of my grandmother's father in battle. I have been told that she went willingly, for they loved each other greatly. But the times have changed and that could not happen now."

"It's going to happen now, Heart's-dearest. There is no one who can forbid you to marry me. You're no longer a maid and therefore a chattel to be disposed of to the best advantage. Nor can anyone forbid me to marry you."

But Anjuli remained unconvinced. She could see no possibility of any marriage, based on religion, between two persons of widely differing faiths; and in their own case, no reason for it either. Or for any legal tie, as for her part she was more than content to spend the rest of her life with Ashok for love's sake, and no ceremony involving words spoken by a priest or magistrate, complete with documents in proof that it had taken place, would ever make any difference to that. She had already taken part in one such ceremony, yet it had not made her a wife in any sense except a purely legal one: a chattel of the Rana's— a despised chattel on whom, after those ceremonies, he had never again deigned to lay eyes. Had it not been for Ashok she would still be a maiden, and he was already the husband of her body as well as of her heart and spirit . . . his to do as he liked with. So what need had they for empty phrases that to one or other of them would mean nothing? or scraps of paper that she herself could not read? Besides—

She turned from him to watch the setting sun that was painting the tree-tops below her bright gold, and said in an undertone as though she were speaking to herself rather than to him: "They had a name for me in Bhithor. They called me . . . 'the half-caste.' "

Ash made a small involuntary movement, and she glanced back at him over her shoulder and said without surprise: "Yes, I should have known that you would hear that too," and turning her head away again said softly:

"Even the *Nautch*-girl never called me that. She did not dare while my father lived, and when he died, and she taunted me with it, Nandu turned on her. I suppose because it touched his pride, he being my half-brother, and therefore he would not have it spoken of. But in Bhithor it was thrown in my teeth daily, and the priests would not permit me to enter the temple of Lakshmi that is in the gardens of the Queen's House, where the wives and women-folk of the Rana worship . . ."

Her voice died out on a whisper, and Ash said gently: "You don't have to trouble yourself about such things any longer, Larla. Put them away and forget them. All that is over and done with."

"Yes, it is over and done with; and being a half-caste there is no need for me to trouble myself as to what my people or my priests will do or say, since it seems that I have neither the one nor the other. Therefore from now on I will be a half-caste, and a woman of no family, from nowhere . . . one whose only god is her husband."

"Her *wedded* husband," persisted Ash obstinately.

Anjuli turned to look at him, her face dark against the sunset. "It may be . . . if you truly desire it, and if . . . But until you have seen those who are in authority over you and spoken with your priests, you cannot know if it is possible, so let us talk no more of it now. The sun is almost gone and I must go down and prepare food for us while it is still light enough to see."

She slipped past him and went down the dark stairway, and Ash let her go without making any attempt to stop her. Instead he went to stand by the parapet, and leaning his arms on it, looked out towards the hills, as she had done, and reviewed all the difficulties that lay ahead.

45

"I shall have to be careful," thought Ash. "Very careful."

Last night after Bukta had left him he had contemplated flight. Juli and he must leave Gujerat at once, and on no account must he return to Ahmadabad. They could board the Bombay train at some small wayside station, and long before the Diwan's men could pick up their trail they would have left Central India and the Punjab behind them, crossed the Indus and be safely back in Mardan.

It had seemed the obvious thing to do. But then that was the trouble: it was too obvious. It was what he would be expected to do, and therefore he could not do it. He would have to be a lot cleverer than that—and pray that whatever decision he came to was the right one, for if it were not, neither Juli nor he would live long enough to regret it.

He had still not made up his mind when Anjuli called him down to eat. She had made a small fire in the corner of the tomb, and before it went out, Ash burned the packet of letters that he had written in the room above the charcoal-seller's shop in Bhithor, and that Sarji and Gobind had known they dared not keep, because had the Bhithoris found them they would have been evidence that would have betrayed him. He watched them shrivel and turn black, and later, when Anjuli was asleep, he went noiselessly out into the starlight to sit on a fallen block of stone near the entrance of the tomb, to think and plan . . .

He did not doubt that Bhithor and its Diwan would require vengeance for the lives of those who had died—and a lingering death for the widowed Rani, who would be blamed for everything. The hunt would be called against her, and it would not be abandoned until the hunters became convinced that she and her two remaining rescuers had lost their way among the trackless hills and died of thirst and starvation. Only then would Juli be safe. Juli and Bukta. And incidentally, he himself.

He had allowed Bukta to suppose that the Bhithoris would have no reason to connect an officer-Sahib from a cavalry regiment in Ahmadabad with the disappearance of one of the late Rana's widows. But that was not so, since was it not a Captain-Sahib, one Pelham-Martyn of the Guides, who had escorted the Ranis to their wedding and outwitted the Rana and his councillors in the matter of the bride-price and dowries? And had not an officer of the same name recently warned certain British officials in Ahmadabad that if and when the Rana died his widows would burn?—and sent off several strongly worded telegrams to that effect?

820

Besides, as it was already known in Bhithor that the Hakim-Sahib had arrived there by way of Ahmadabad, and that his servant Manilal had subsequently visited that city on two separate occasions in order to purchase medicines, the Bhithoris would certainly not neglect to send spies there in search of the missing Rani. In fact it was only too likely to be among the first places they would think of; and once there, decided Ash grimly, they would find abundant evidence that he had interested himself in the widows, and almost certainly discover that both Gobind and Manilal had stayed at his bungalow. That last would be the vital link, and unless he was much mistaken, from there it would be only a short step to murder: his own as well as Juli's. And probably Bukta's too.

The odds were frightening, because the one thing he could be certain of was that Bhithor would move quickly. The Diwan could not afford to be dilatory, and search parties would already be hurrying to cover every possible escape route to Karidkote, while others would soon be on their way to Gujerat. Yet after careful consideration Ash came to the conclusion that the best thing he could do—in fact the only thing—was to return to his bungalow and brazen it out.

Juli would have to go on ahead with Gul Baz, while he followed a few days later with Bukta, arriving as though from the direction of Kathiawar in the southern half of the peninsula, instead of from the northern districts that bordered on Rajputana—and with a different lie to account for Sarji's death and the loss of the horses.

They must say that they had changed their plans and gone south together, and that Sarji and the horses had been drowned while crossing a tidal river, the bodies being swept out to sea and lost in the waters of the Gulf of Kutch. His own grief at the loss of his friend (genuine enough, God knew), not to mention the loss of a much-valued horse, would more than account for his showing no further interest in the fate of the Ranis of Bhithor.

He still had a good deal of leave at his disposal: those weeks that he had planned to spend with Wally on trek through the high country beyond the Rotang Pass. The trek would have to be cancelled, for he must spend the next week or so idling about cantonments, disposing of unwanted property and making leisurely arrangements

821

for the homeward journey to Mardan, in order to demonstrate to any who might be interested that he had nothing to hide and was in no particular hurry to leave the station.

The presence of an additional woman in the servants' quarters was unlikely to arouse much interest (even if it were noticed) for who would expect to find a high-born lady, daughter of a Maharajah and widow of a Rana of Bhithor, agreeing to live in seclusion among the Sahib's Mohammedan servants, in the guise of his bearer's wife? Such a thing would be unthinkable, and even those Bhithoris who had termed her "the half-caste" would not credit it. They would probably watch him for several days, taking careful notes of his behaviour and his every move, and in the end they would come to the conclusion that he could have taken no part in the escape, but had lost interest in the Ranis after sending off those telegrams, and did not intend to do anything more on their behalf. They would return to Bhithor and report as much to the Diwan, who would turn his attention elsewhere. And Juli would be safe.

It was a pity about that trek; Wally was going to be disappointed. But he would understand that it could not be helped, and they could always go another year. There was plenty of time . . .

His mind made up, Ash lay down across the entrance to the tomb so that no human or animal could pass in without waking him, and was asleep before the moon rose. But though tonight his sleep was untroubled by dreams, it was not so with Anjuli, for three times that night she cried out in the grip of a nightmare.

On the first occasion Ash, jerked into consciousness by that choking scream, scrambled up to find that the tomb was filled with a cold radiance. The moon had risen while he slept and was shining in through the broken dome, and by its light he could see Anjuli crouching against the far wall with her arms across her face, as though to blot out some intolerable sight. She was moaning, "No! No, Shu-shu, no . . . !" and he caught her in his arms and held her close, rocking her shuddering body and murmuring endearments and comfort, until at last the terror left her and for the first time in all those desperate, terrible days, she broke down and wept.

The storm of tears ceased at last, and it seemed to

have washed away some of her tension, for presently she relaxed and lay still, and after a time he realized that she had fallen asleep again. Moving very gently so as not to wake her he lay down, still holding her, listening to her shallow breathing and appalled by her thinness.

Had they starved her? . . . from what he knew of the Rana and the Diwan, he would not put it past them, and his mind blackened with rage at the thought as he tightened his arms about the skeletal form that had once been so smooth and firm and sweetly slender, and whose every lovely line and curve his hands and lips had explored with such heart-stopping delight.

Less than an hour later she began to toss and turn, and once more started up, screaming Shu-shu's name. And again, shortly before dawn when the tomb was dark because the moon no longer shone into it, the nightmare trapped her for the third time that night, and she woke in the black darkness and struggled frantically against his restraining arms as though she imagined herself to be in the grip of an enemy come to drag her to a pyre—or towards a brazier where a fire-iron glowed white-hot among the coals.

It had taken longer to quieten her after that last awakening, and as she clung to him, shuddering with the aftermath of terror and begging him to hold her—hold her—the physical desire that had once been a living flame between them, and that Ash had thought lost, blazed up in him so fiercely that he would at that moment have sacrificed their hope of safety to be able to take possession of her body and obtain comfort and release for his own—and with it a temporary forgetfulness of all the problems that pressed upon him.

But there was no answering urge in the wasted body in his arms, and he knew that if he were to take her now it would be by force, for she would recoil from him; and also that if he were to give way to his own desires and to succeed in awakening a like response in her, their situation would be a great deal worse than it was already, because once the barriers were down it would be next to impossible for them to keep apart during the following days. Neither of them would be capable of it, yet if suspicion was to be disarmed it was essential that Juli should spend the next week or ten days in one of the servants' quarters behind his bungalow, and that he himself should go nowhere near her. If he were seen to do so it could be fatal for them both, and this way was better. There would be plenty of time for love-making once they were married and the nightmares were over.

Anjuli fell asleep at last, and presently Ash too slept, and did not wake until she stirred in his arms and drew away from him, aroused by the joyous chorus of parrots, pigeons, doves and weaver-birds greeting the dawn. When the sun was up, and after they had eaten, he told her of the plans he had made during the previous night, and she listened to him, raising no objection and seeming willing enough to fall in with any decisions that he might choose to make: but apart from this they talked very little. Anjuli was still suffering from shock and exhaustion, and for both of them that long day in the ruined tomb had been haunted by the thought of Shushila. Neither of them had been able to put her out of their minds; and though Ash had done his best to do so, the thought of her had returned to him so persistently that he was almost tempted to believe that her uneasy little ghost had followed them there, and was watching them from the shadows of the *kikar* trees.

In the late afternoon Bukta returned accompanied by Gul Baz and two spare horses, and though Anjuli had been awake and heard their voices, she had remained on the roof and let the three men talk together. Bukta had approved of the new plan, for he and Gul Baz had discussed the matter at length, and come to a similar conclusion: "But I have said that this tale of a wife or a widowed daughter will not serve," said Gul Baz. "I have a better plan—"

He had: and what was more, he had already taken steps to put it into operation. After discussing the matter with Bukta they had, he said, decided that the only thing to do was to substitute the Rani-Sahiba for the shy, silent woman whom he had installed more than a year ago in the hut behind his own quarter—and who had in any case been expecting to leave in the near future, since she was aware that the Sahib and his servants were about to return to the North-West Frontier Province, and had always known that the irregular but useful arrangement she had made with the Sahib's bearer would automatically cease when he went back to his own country. As that day was almost here it was only a question of terminating it a little earlier than expected; and this Gul Baz had done.

When he left the bungalow early that morning he had gone in a hired tonga, and taken the woman with him, having let it be known that she wished to visit her mother in her home village, and that they would be returning late. In fact, she would not be returning at all. It would be the Rani-Sahiba who would come back with him, though his fellow-servants would not know that there had been any substitution—one woman in a bourka being very like another. As for the other one, the Sahib need not fear: she had been well paid and there would be no danger from that quarter, for apart from being a close-mouthed woman, there was no chance of her returning to the cantonment area, or even the city, until well after they themselves were back in Mardan.

"But tonight when we return it will be seen that she has come back with me as I said, so if any stranger should come asking questions he will learn nothing, there being nothing to tell. I have here a bourka for the Rani-Sahiba, old but clean. It belonged to that other one and I took it from her, saying it was too worn and mended, and that I would buy her a new one in the bazaar; which I did. Also by good fortune she is a tall woman, for the *shikari* tells me that the Rani-Sahiba is also tall. We shall return after dark, and no one will notice any difference; and once installed in the hut the Rani-Sahiba will be safe, for I shall say she is suffering from some slight sickness and must keep to her bed. There will be no need for her to speak to anyone, or even be seen."

Ash said: "And what happens when the time comes for us to leave Gujerat?"

"We have thought of that too," said Bukta. "There will be no difficulty. Your servant has only to say that his woman wishes to visit a relative in the Punjab and that he has agreed to take her with him as far as Delhi—or Lahore, if you prefer, it makes no matter. He will arrange all that. He has a head upon his shoulders, has that Pathan. Moreover the woman is known to have lived under his protection for close on a year, while the Rani-Sahiba has only been missing for a handful of days. Now, as to our own return—"

Some twenty minutes later a party of four horsemen could have been seen riding swiftly across the croplands towards the dusty main highway that runs between Khed Brahma and Ahmadabad, and on reaching it they broke into a gallop, heading south.

Twilight overtook them when they were still many miles from the city of Ahmad Shah. But they pressed on through the dusk, and later in the starlight; and when at last they came within sight of the twinkling lights of the cantonment, the moon was rising. They drew rein near a clump of trees and Ash lifted Juli down from the saddle. They did not speak, for they had already said everything that was necessary; and besides all four were anxious and more than a little weary. Gul Baz handed over his horse to Bukta and salaamed to Ash, and followed by Anjuli, who walked a pace behind him as befitted a woman, he went away in the moonlight towards a village on the outskirts of the cantonments where he could hire a tonga to take them back to the bungalow.

Five days later Ash returned to Ahmadabad, riding one of Sarji's horses and attended by one of the syces from Sarji's stables.

The syce had been entertained by Kulu Ram and others before taking the horse back with him later that day, and before he left he told his hosts, with a wealth of detail, the story of the death of his master, who had been tragically drowned while attempting to swim his horse across one of the many tidal rivers that ran into the Gulf of Kutch, and of how the Sahib's horse had also been drowned, and the Sahib himself only saved by a miracle. The tale had lost nothing in the telling, and Gul Baz had been able to report later that it had obviously not occurred to the teller—or to anyone else—to doubt it.

"So that is another ditch safely crossed," said Gul Baz. "As for the other matter, that too was passed over in safety. No one has thought to question the identity of the one who returned here with me. Nor will they, for she keeps to her room, feigning poor health; which I think is in part true, for during her second night here she cried out in her sleep so loudly that I awoke and ran out to her hut, fearing that she had been discovered and was being abducted. But she said that it was only a dream and that—" He broke off, seeing Ash's expression, and said: "Has this happened before, then?"

"Yes. I should have thought of it, and warned you,"

said Ash, angry with himself for the omission. He himself had not been troubled by any further dreams of Shushila, but she continued to weigh on his conscience: her small, reproachful face was still apt to rise up before him at unexpected moments, and if this was so with him, how much worse must it be for Juli, who had loved her?

He asked if any of the other servants had been awakened, but Gul Baz did not think so. "For as you know, my quarter and the one that was Mahdoo-ji's stand apart from the others, and the hut in which the Rani-Sahiba lies is close behind it and thus well shielded from those that are occupied by the other servants. But on the next day I purchased opium and made a draught for her to take after sundown, since when she has slept soundly and made no further outcries in the night—which is as well, for the *shikari* spoke truth when he said that the Sahib might be spied upon."

According to Gul Baz, on the previous day several strangers had come to the bungalow, one asking for work, another purporting to be a vendor of drugs and simples, and a third inquiring after an errant wife, who, so he said, was believed to have run off with the servant of some Sahib. This last one, on hearing that Pelham-Sahib had left for a shooting trip in Kathiawar earlier in the month and had not yet returned, had asked many questions . . .

"All of which," said Gul Baz, "we answered. Sympathizing with him in his distress and telling him many things: though none, I fear, that were of help to him. As for the seller of drugs and such-like, by good fortune he was here again today when the Sahib returned, and he stayed to listen to all that the syce had to tell. Afterwards he packed up his wares and went away, saying that he had many other customers to attend to and could waste no more time here. I do not think he will return, for he has seen for himself that the Sahib came back alone, and learned from that syce, whose tongue wagged as freely as an old woman's, that no third person accompanied the Sahib and the *shikari* when they brought the sad news of the drowning in Kathiawar to the family of the Sirdar Sarjevar Desai."

"There will be others," observed Ash pessimistically. "I do not believe that the Diwan's spies will be satisfied so easily."

Gul Baz shrugged and said that in his opinion they

827

would very soon tire of hanging about the compound to exchange gossip with people who had nothing of the least interest to disclose, and of shadowing the Sahib round cantonments only to find him engaged in such unsuspicious and mundane matters as social calls and farewell parties, and the tedious but necessary arrangements that must be made with railway officials and booking clerks regarding his return journey to Mardan.

"You have only to go to-and-fro daily," said Gul Baz, "letting it be seen that you have nothing to conceal and are in no haste to be gone, and the watchers will soon weary of the game. Another week or ten days should suffice, and after that it will be safe enough for us to shake the dust of this ill-omened place from our shoes and board the rail-*ghari* for Bombay. And may the All Merciful ordain," he added fervently, "that we never have reason to return here."

Ash nodded absently, for his thoughts were on Juli, who must spend a further eight or ten days cooped up in the hot and stifling little hut, not daring to show herself for even a short breath of air, or to sleep at night without the aid of opium. But he had taken Gul Baz's advice, and had seen to it that every minute of the succeeding days should find him openly employed in some leisurely and innocuous activity, because the fact that someone, or more probably several people, were interested was soon clear to him. For though he was careful not to look over his shoulder to see if he was being followed, he realized that even if he had not been warned he would still have been aware that he was under constant surveillance. It was purely a matter of instinct, the same instinct that tells the jungle creatures that they are being stalked by a tiger, or that can warn a man waking in darkness and silence that there is an intruder in his room.

Ash had experienced that feeling before, and recognizing it (with him it took the form of a coldness between his shoulder-blades and a prickling of the hairs at the back of his neck, coupled with an intense and uncomfortable alertness) he had his bed moved up to the flat roof of the bungalow, where anyone who so desired could keep an eye on him and see for themselves that he did not leave it to engage in any surreptitious meetings by night.

The tale of Sarjevar's untimely death and the loss of the peerless Dagobaz had spread through the cantonment, and Ash received a good deal of sympathy from the officers and sowars of Roper's Horse and various members of the British community. And also from the dead man's great-uncle, the Risaldar-Major, who was touched by the Sahib's grief for his lost friend and urged him not to blame himself—which was not in Ash's power, as he knew very well that he was to blame, because he could so easily have refused to let Sarji go with him to Bhithor.

The fact that Sarji's family and friends believed that cock-and-bull story that he and Bukta had invented, and repeated it as the truth to all who called to commiserate, was of great service to Ash, as it conveyed the impression that they had known all along that the two had been shooting in an area that was a great deal further to the south of Ahmadabad than the border of Rajasthan was to the north. And this, taken in conjunction with Ash's behaviour and the absence of any evidence that the late Rana's widow was in Gujerat (or even that she was still alive), evidently succeeded in convincing the Diwan's spies that they were on the wrong track, for by the end of the week Gul Baz was able to report that the bungalow was no longer being watched.

That night there had been no skulking figure among the shadows, and next morning when Ash went riding he did not have to be told that he was not being followed or spied upon, for he could feel it in his bones. All the same he took no chances, but was careful to behave as though the danger still existed; and only when a further three days and nights passed without sign of a watcher did he feel able to relax and breathe freely again—and began to think of the future.

Now that he was no longer under surveillance, there was no reason to linger in Ahmadabad a moment longer than necessary. But it was not possible to leave immediately, because two of the three dates proffered by the station master on which he could guarantee accommodation on the train to Bombay with a through booking to Delhi and Lahore had already been lost. The remaining one entailed a further delay of several days, but now Ash closed with it and told Gul Baz to see to all the necessary arrangements for the move, he himself having other things to occupy him.

Despite the anxieties that bedevilled the tense days that followed upon his return to cantonments, the need to engage in trivial pursuits had proved a blessing, for together with the long hours of enforced idleness and the longer nights it had provided him with ample time in which to sort out the problems of the future. Yet the major one still remained unsolved: what to do about Juli?

It had all seemed so simple once; if only she were free he could marry her. Well she was free now, free from both the Rana and Shushila, and there should have been nothing to prevent him doing so. But the trouble lay in the fact that the gap between day-dreaming about remote possibilities and dealing with the reality was so wide as to be almost unbridgeable . . .

The same could be said of his feeling for the Corps of Guides, for at one stage of the unforgettable journey with the bridal camp he had actually considered deserting —leaving India, with Juli, to take refuge in another country and never see Mardan or Wally or Zarin again. It astonished him now that even in the first fever of his passion for Juli he could ever have contemplated such a thing: except that he had been in disgrace at the time, banished from the Regiment and the Frontier, and with no idea how long his exile would last—or any certainty that some future Commandant would not decide that it would be better not to have him back at all. But things were different now . . . he had been recalled to Mardan to take up the duties he had abandoned when he joined the hunt for Dilasah Khan and the stolen carbines, and there was no question of his refusing to return. The ties that bound him to the Guides stretched too far back into the past and were too strong to be easily broken; and even for Juli's sake he would not—could not—bring himself to sever them and lose both Wally and Zarin. Nor was there any point in doing so, when even if he could persuade someone to marry him to Juli, he would never be able to claim her openly as his wife.

"The problem is this—" explained Ash, discussing the matter with Mrs. Viccary, who, besides being the only person in Gujerat whom he felt able to tell the story to, could be trusted not to let it go any further and to listen to it without being swayed by any prejudice on the score of Juli's ancestry or his own.

It was not advice that he needed (being well aware that if it ran contrary to his own wishes he would not

830

take it) but someone to talk to. Someone sensible and sympathetic who loved India as he did and with whom he could discuss this whole situation, and by doing so get it straightened out in his own mind. And Mrs. Viccary had not failed him: she had neither blamed nor praised, or been shocked by his desire to marry a Hindu widow, or by Anjuli's view that no legal marriage was necessary.

"You see," said Ash, "once it was known that we were married she wouldn't be safe."

"Or you either," observed Edith Viccary. "People would talk, and news travels fast in this country."

That of course was the point; and Ash was inexpressibly grateful to her for seeing it at once instead of bringing up all the more obvious arguments against such a marriage—beginning with the fact that, until he reached the age of thirty or the rank of Major, he could not marry without the consent of his Commanding Officer (which in the circumstances he would certainly not get) and going on to point out that in a regiment such as the Guides, which recruited Mussulmans, Sikhs, Hindus and Gurkhas, a British officer who married a Hindu widow would be anathema. By doing so he would sow dissension among the men under his command, offending not only the caste Hindus, but probably the Sikhs as well, causing the Mussulmans to despise him for thinking so little of his own religion, and Sikhs, Mussulmans and Gurkhas together to suspect him of favouring his wife's co-religionists whenever he was called upon to judge between a Hindu and a man of another faith, or to recommend one or other for promotion. The Guides would ask him to leave, and no other Indian Army regiment would accept him for the same reasons.

Ash knew all about that; and so did Mrs. Viccary. But none of it was worth worrying about for the simple reason that even if he could arrange to marry Juli, to do so openly would be tantamount to signing her death warrant—together with his own—since such a marriage, once made public, was bound to cause a great deal of talk and speculation and scandal. And in a country such as India where not only regiments but members of the Civil Service, medical officers, policemen, clergymen, men in trade and numerous other Britishers, all accompanied by large numbers of Indian servants, were moved about from one end of the country to another at short notice, a story of this kind would be gossiped over in the Clubs of every military station from Peshawar to Trivandrum, and in every bazaar where the servants of the "Sahib-log" gathered to talk over the doings of the *Angrezis* and retail the gossip of the station they had just left. And the Indian grape-vine was the swiftest and most efficient in the world . . .

It would not be long before Bhithor came to hear that the same Guides officer who had escorted the late Rana's wives to their wedding (and been stationed in Gujerat at the time of the Rana's death and the disappearance of one of his widows) had subsequently married a Hindu widow. The Diwan would add two and two together, and coming up with the correct total, would send someone to investigate; after which it would only be a matter of time —probably only a very short time—before Juli died. For Bhithor would require vengeance for their own dead—all those who had died (and there must have been many of them) in the fight to defend the entrance to Bukta's secret road—as well as for the insult that had been put upon them by the abduction of their late Rana's widow.

"It would have to be kept secret," said Ash.

"Then you still mean to marry her? Even though you tell me that she herself can see no reason for it?"

But Ash was nothing if not obstinate. "What else? Do you think I want her as a mistress . . . a concubine? I want to know that she's my wife, even though I can't acknowledge her as such. It's—it's something I *have* to do. I can't explain . . ."

"You don't have to," said Edith Viccary. "If I were in your place I'd feel the same. Of course you must marry her. But it isn't going to be easy."

The difficulty, she explained, was that marriage being a Sacrament of the Church, no clergyman would consent to employ it to unite a Christian to a Hindu, unless it could be proved that the latter had undergone a genuine conversion. "God is not mocked, you know," added Mrs. Viccary softly.

"I didn't mean to mock. But then I never think of Him as being an Englishman—or a Jew or an Indian or any other nationality that we've invented for ourselves. Nor do I believe that He thinks of us like that. But I did realize, as soon as I began to think about it, that the

Church wouldn't marry us, any more than Juli's priests would, even if I dared risk asking them, which I don't. But I thought perhaps a magistrate——?"

Edith Viccary shook her head decidedly. She knew the local British magistrate a good deal better than Ash did, and Mr. Chadwick, she assured him, was the last person to consent to such a thing. He could also be trusted to report Ash's request for a marriage licence to the Commissioner, who apart from being equally horrified would ask a great many awkward questions. And once inquiries were set on foot, the fat would be well and truly in the fire.

"Yes," said Ash bitterly. "We can't risk that."

There seemed to be no way out. It was inconceivable—fatuous and unjust and totally unfair—that two grown people who only wanted to marry each other should not be permitted to do so, when their marriage would harm no one. It was a purely personal matter, and if people could get married at sea without the aid of magistrates and licences, like that couple on the *Canterbury Castle*, there should be some equally simple method by which those on land could do the same, and he——

"By God, that's it!" cried Ash explosively, leaping to his feet. "Red Stiggins—the *Morala*. Why on earth didn't I think of that before?"

Red had said something about sailing for Karachi "in a few weeks' time" and had invited him to come along for the voyage. And if the *Morala* had not left yet . . .

Pausing only to bestow a fervent hug on the bewildered Mrs. Viccary, he ran from her drawing-room, shouting for Kulu Ram to fetch his horse, and ten minutes later anyone happening to be abroad at that hottest hour of the day would have seen a Sahib riding hell-for-leather down the glaring cantonment road towards the city.

The shrewd Gujerati who looked after Captain Stiggins's business interests in the peninsula had a small office in a street near the Daripur Gate, and he had been enjoying his customary afternoon's siesta when the Sahib burst in on him, demanding to know if the *Morala* had already set sail for Karachi, and if not, when she would be leaving and from where. And this time Ash's luck was in, for the *Morala* had not yet sailed, though she would be doing so very shortly—in the next day or two if all went well, and certainly not later than the end of the week. The ship was at Cambay at the head of the Gulf, and if the Sahib wished to send a message—?

The Sahib did, and was grateful for the offer as he had no time to spare for writing letters. "Tell him that I accept his invitation and to expect me tomorrow; and that whatever he does, he is not to sail without me."

There was a great deal to be done and not much time in which to do it, for the port of Cambay was all of sixty miles from Ahmadabad, and Ash rode back to his bungalow at the same break-neck speed at which he had left Mrs. Viccary's.

46

Captain Stiggins scratched the copper-coloured stubble on his chin with a horny thumb and stared thoughtfully at Ash for a full two minutes, pondering the matter. Then he said slowly: "Well now ... I can't say as I'm pre-cisely the same kind of animal as one of them gilded skippers of a steam packet—no more'n the old *Morala* is a fancy passenger ship. Still, I'm the master of this 'ere craft, and so I don't see as 'ow that shouldn't give me the right to do anything a cove in a frock-coat and brass buttons can do aboard one of them swanky great P & O boats."

"Then you'll do it, Red?"

"Well, son, I ain't never done such a thing before, so I can't say as I'll go bail for its bein' legal. But I reckon that's yore 'eadache, not mine. And seein' as we're pals, I'm willin' to chance me arm and splice yer ... now, now—'old yore 'orses, son. I've said as I'll do it as a favour—but I ain't a goin' to do it 'ere and now. Not for you nor no one will I go pretendin' that this 'ere duck-pond is an ocean, so you'll just 'ave to wait until we're standin' well clear o' the land and a good 'arf way between 'ere and Chahbar, see? That's goin' to make it look a sight better in the log-book; and it seems to me, young feller, that yore goin' to need to do everything you can t' make this caper o' yores look ship-shape and

834

above board. Them's my terms, son. Take 'em or leave 'em."

"Where the hell is Chahbar? I thought you were bound for Karachi."

"So I am—on the way back. But there's bin a change of plan. I reckon you bin too busy with yore own affairs to notice that there's bin a famine around for nigh on three years now—particular in the south. That's why I'm shippin' a cargo o' cotton to Chahbar, which is way up on the coast of Mekran, and bringin' back a load o' grain. It's a longish haul, but on the way back I could put you ashore any place you fancy. Are you on?"

Ash had hoped to get married with the least possible delay, but he could see the sense of Captain Stiggins's argument, and in any case he had no option but to agree to his terms. It was decided that the ceremony had best be postponed until such time as Sind and the mouth of the Indus lay well astern and the *Morala* was headed north towards Ras Jewan. In the meantime, Red gallantly placed his own cabin at Anjuli's disposal and moved in with his mate, one McNulty, for the duration of the voyage, though in the event all three men (and everyone else on board for that matter) elected to sleep on deck, and only Anjuli kept to her cabin.

The *Morala* only boasted four cabins, and though Red's was certainly the best of these it was far from large and at that season of the year was stiflingly hot. But Anjuli spent the first part of the voyage in it, because she proved to be a poor sailor, and succumbed to a bad attack of sea-sickness that lasted for several days, by which time they had crossed the Tropic of Cancer, and were sailing through a sea that was stained with the silt brought down by the Indus and its four great fellow-rivers of the Punjab.

Gul Baz, who had insisted on accompanying Ash, had also been most vilely ill, but it was not long before he acquired his sea-legs and was up and about again. Anjuli, on the other hand, made a slow recovery. She spent the greater part of the day sleeping, for she was still plagued by bad dreams, and as she found these less frightening by day she stayed awake at night and kept two oil lamps burning from dusk to dawn, despite the fact that they greatly increased the heat in the cramped little cabin.

Ash had nursed her and waited upon her, and he too

took to sleeping by day so that he could sit up with her for at least part of the night. But even when she had recovered from her sea-sickness he found that she was still disinclined to talk, and that any reference to Bhithor or the immediate past, however oblique, would make her stiffen into rigidity and bring back that disturbing frozen look to her eyes. He therefore confined himself to speaking only of his own doings and his plans for their joint future, though he suspected that half the time she did not hear what he was saying because she was listening to other voices.

He had confirmed this on several occasions by breaking off in mid-sentence, only to find that she was unaware that he had stopped speaking. Asked what she was thinking of, she would look troubled and say, "Nothing" . . . until one evening, when that question had broken into her silent brooding so abruptly that she had been startled into an unguarded reply, and answered "Shushila."

It was hardly reasonable of Ash to hope that she would by now have stopped tormenting herself with thoughts of Shushila when he himself was unable to do so. But he had got up without a word and left the cabin, and half an hour later it had been Gul Baz and not Ash who had knocked on her door bringing the evening meal, for Ash had been otherwise occupied.

He had taken his problems to Captain Stiggins, and fortified by the Captain's ferocious brandy, was engaged in pouring the whole story into that gentleman's sympathetic ear. "The trouble is that her sister has always come first with her—right from the beginning," explained Ash bitterly. "I used to believe that I was the only one she really loved, and that it was only affection and a strong sense of duty that made her stay with Shu-shu. But it seems I was wrong. I tried to make her run away with me before, you know, but she wouldn't do it because of Shu-shu . . . God! how I came to hate the very sound of that name."

"Jealous, were you," nodded Red.

"Of course I was. Wouldn't you have been, in my place? Dammit Red, I was in love with her. I still am. I always will be. And but for that sister of hers—!"

"Well, now that the pore girl's dead, you've no call to be jealous of her any more 'av you?" put in Red soothingly.

"Oh, yes I have, because even now—in fact now more than ever—she's coming between us. I tell you, Red, she might just as well be here on this ship, battening upon what little strength Juli has left, and weeping and whining for sympathy and attention like she used to do. There are times when I'm even ready to believe that there are such things as ghosts, and that hers has followed us here and is doing its damnedest to take Juli away from me."

"Don't be daft!" snapped the Captain crossly. "I never 'eard such poppy-cock. Ghosts indeed!—whatever next?" He pushed the bottle over to Ash and said: "Better 'av another good swig o' that, son. Won't do you no 'arm to get good n' bosky for a change an' drown yore sorrows, for it sounds to me as though you bin battenin' down yore 'atches too 'ard of late. It'll do you good to open 'em up and let some of the bad air out. It ain't sense to go a bottlin' things up until you gets jealous of a pore lass wots dead and gorn. T'ain't 'ealthy."

"It's not that," said Ash, re-filling his glass with an unsteady hand. "You don't understand, Red. It's because now that she's dead I'm afraid . . . I'm afraid—" His teeth chattered against the rim of the glass as he gulped the raw spirit.

"Afraid o' wot?" demanded Red, frowning. "That yore Juli won't forget 'er sister? Wot's so bad about that? If she did you'd likely begin to think she was an 'ard 'earted piece, and that's the truth. You just give the pore girl a bit o' time, and you'll find you ain't got nothin' to be afraid of, for she's bound to stop grievin' one day."

Ash drained his glass and reached for the bottle again, observing impatiently that of course she would; and of course he didn't expect her to forget her sister. It was not that he was afraid of.

"Wot then?"

"That she won't be able to forget that it was I who killed Shushila."

"You *wot*!" exclaimed Red, startled.

"Didn't I tell you that? I shot her," said Ash.

He explained how this had come about, and when he had finished Red breathed heavily for a few moments, and downed a further generous helping of brandy before replying. But his verdict when it came brought little comfort: "It's 'ard to know wot else you could 'ave done," declared Captain Stiggins thoughtfully. "But I see wot

837

you mean. At the time like, all she'd be thinkin' of would be 'ow she could save 'er little sister from the pain of bein' roasted alive. But now that it's all over she's maybe blamin' 'erself for not letting the lass 'ave her own way— and you for playin' 'angman, so to speak."

"Yes. That's what I'm afraid of. She seemed so set on it at the time. She *begged* me to do it. But now . . . now I don't believe she could have been in her right mind. She was half mad with grief, and thinking back I'm not sure I was quite sane myself. Perhaps none of us were . . . but it was far worse for her, because Shu-shu meant more to her than anyone else in the world and she couldn't bear the thought of what she must suffer. She wanted me to shoot her before the flames reached her, and I did. I shouldn't have done it and I've wished ever since that I hadn't, because I cheated her out of sainthood. And now I'm afraid that Juli has begun to find that she can't look at me without remembering that it was I who killed her darling Shu-shu."

"Bollocks!" retorted Red inelegantly.

"Oh, I don't mean that she blames me for doing it. She knows damned well I only did it for her, and that if it had been up to me I wouldn't have dreamed of risking all our lives by hanging around waiting to shoot the wretched girl. But however clearly she may see that with her head, she knows in her heart that I didn't give a damn about Shu-shu—and that makes a difference."

"Yes, I can see that," said Red reflectively. "If you'd 'ad a fondness for the lass and done it for that reason— for love as you might say—it wouldn't 'ave mattered s'much . . . you shootin' 'er."

"That's it. But then I wasn't fond of her. You'll say because I was jealous of her, but it was more than that: I resented the hold she had over Juli, and now I think Juli is probably remembering that, and adding it to the rest and finding that in spite of herself it has changed her feelings for me. One can't really blame her, for though I still don't see what else I could have done, I've never stopped regretting that I shot that damned girl—and if I can feel like that, why shouldn't Juli feel equally mixed up about it? Oh, God, what a mess it all is! Let's open another bottle, Red—I'm going to take your advice and get drunk."

They had both got drunk: Red rather less so than Ash, by reason of having a harder head. And either the advice had been good, or else the dictum that confession is good for the soul had proved to be sound, because afterwards Ash certainly felt more relaxed and less apprehensive about the future, though he did not again make the mistake of asking Anjuli what she was thinking of. She was still painfully thin; and very pallid, which Ash put down to the airless heat of Red's cabin. He was sure that once they were married and he could coax her out onto the open deck and into the fresh air, her health was bound to improve, and with it her state of mind.

They had been married two hours after the shores of Sind faded from sight and the *Morala*'s bows were ploughing towards Ras Jewan and Chahbar. The ceremony had taken place at 2.30 in the afternoon, in the cramped little saloon, the witnesses being the Mate, Angus McNulty (who hailed from Dundee and admitted cautiously that he 'might be a Presbyterian'), and an old friend of Red's, one Hyem Ephraim, an elderly Jew from Kutch who had business interests in Persia and had arranged to sail with Captain Stiggins to Chahbar. Red himself claimed to be a "free thinker"—whatever that meant —but he had dignified the occasion by wearing his best suit and speaking in a voice of such portentous gravity that Gul Baz, who had watched the brief ceremony from the doorway, had been convinced that the *Morala*'s Captain must, in private life, be a particularly wise and holy *guru*.

Gul Baz, a pious Mohammedan, had been full of misgivings. But he had not voiced them, for it was too late for that. It had been too late from the day that the Hakim from Karidkote and his fat servant, Manilal, had driven up to the Sahib's bungalow in a hired tonga and he, Gul Baz, had failed to send them away. This Hindu widow was not at all the sort of wife that he had expected his Sahib to choose, and he did not approve of mixed marriages any more than Koda Dad Khan—or Mr. Chadwick. Nor did he look forward to explaining to Koda Dad and his sons how this had come about, or the part that he himself had played in it; though how he could have refused his assistance, or prevented his Sahib from leaving for Bhithor in the first place, he did not know. Nevertheless, today he put up his own private prayers for the safety, well-being and future happiness of the bridegroom and his chosen bride, and petitioned the All-Wise to grant them long life and many strong sons.

Anjuli, once a devout Hindu, had not prayed for several years, having come to believe either that the gods did not exist, or that for reasons of their own—possibly because of the foreign blood in her veins—they had turned their faces from her. She did not pray now, and she wore the bourka in place of a wedding dress, which struck no one there as strange, since Western brides traditionally wore white and went veiled to the altar, while in the East a widow's weeds are not black but white.

Ash had cut a slit at one side of the tent-like garment so that he could take her hand, and as all else was hidden by the bourka, that small, square hand was all that the wedding guests saw of the bride. Yet strangely enough each one of them, on that evidence alone, was immediately convinced that Leiutenant Pelham-Martyn's bride was a woman of rare beauty and charm. They were also convinced that she spoke and understood English, for Ash had taught her the few words she must say, and when the time came she spoke them in a low clear voice that copied his intonation so exactly that anyone who did not know her story might well have supposed that the cheap cotton bourka disguised some well-bred Victorian miss.

Ash had not thought to buy a ring in Ahmadabad, and as he did not wear a signet ring, he had removed part of his watch-chain and joined it into a slender circle of gold links. It was this that he now put on Anjuli's finger: *"With this ring, I thee wed . . ."* The brief ceremony that made her his wife had taken less than ten minutes, and when it was over she had returned to her cabin, leaving him to drink the wine that Red had provided, and accept congratulations and good wishes.

The day had been uncomfortably hot, and even with the sea wind blowing, the temperature in the saloon was over ninety degrees; but it would drop towards evening, and when darkness fell the poop deck would be a cool and pleasant place to spend the first night of the honeymoon—always provided that Juli would consent to leave her cabin.

Ash hoped that it would not be too difficult to persuade her, for he had no intention of sweltering in it himself. It was high time that Juli stopped brooding over the death of Shushila and began to look forward instead of back, and to realize that there was nothing to be gained by continuing to mourn. Mourning could not bring the dead back to life, and it was not as though she had anything to reproach herself for. She had done everything she could for Shu-shu, and she should take comfort from that and have the courage to put the black years and the beloved ghost of her little sister behind her.

As a first step, he had asked Red to give them the use of the poop deck above his cabin, and that good-natured man had not only agreed to do this, but had also arranged for the deck to be screened off with canvas for greater privacy, and provided with a small awning that would afford shade by day and protection from the dew by night.

Ash had expected the bride to put up a certain amount of opposition to his plans for her emancipation, and been prepared to coax and persuade her into acceptance. But that had not been necessary. Anjuli had agreed to spend the greater part of her days on deck rather than in the cabin. But with a listlessness that conveyed such a total lack of interest that he had had the sudden and startled impression that her thoughts were elsewhere, and that the coming night—their first as man and wife —held no special significance for her, but was merely another night; so what did it matter whether she spent it on deck with him or by herself in the cabin? For a terrible moment he had actually been afraid that she would, if given the choice, prefer the latter, and he had not dared ask her for fear of what she might say.

His confidence in his ability to make her forget the past and be happy again evaporated, and he found himself wondering if she still had any love for him at all, or if the events of the past few years had worn it away as the wind and water will wear away an apparently solid rock. All at once he did not know, and terrified by the doubt he turned from her and stumbled out of the cabin, to spend the remainder of the afternoon alone on the poop deck, watching the slow-moving shadows of the sails and dreading the coming night because of the possibility that Juli might reject him—or submit to him without love, which would be far worse.

Towards sundown the breeze had freshened a little,

tempering the salty heat of the day. And as the sea darkened and the sky turned from green to amethyst and then to indigo, the foam under the cut-water began to glimmer with phosphorus, and the stretched canvas showed iron-grey against a brilliant expanse of stars. Gul Baz, wooden-faced, brought a tray of food to the poop deck and later spread a wide, padded *resai* on the planks below the awning, added a few pillows, and observed in a voice devoid of all expression that the Rani-Sahiba —the Memsahib, he should have said—had already eaten, and had the Sahib any further orders?

The Sahib had none; and Gul Baz, having served coffee in a brass cup, went away taking the almost untouched tray with him. The ship's bell sounded the watch, and from somewhere below and amidships Red, who had been celebrating with the Mate and old Ephraim, bellowed up a convivial good-night to which McNulty added something that Ash did not catch, but that appeared to amuse his companions. The sound of their laughter faded and not long afterwards the murmur of voices from the after-deck were the lascars gathered of an evening also ceased, and the night was silent except for the swish of the sea and the monotonous creak and croon of timber and hemp and taut canvas.

Ash sat listening to those sounds for a long time, reluctant to move because he still did not know how his wife would greet him, and he dreaded a rebuff. Today had seen the fulfilment of a dream, and this night should have been the crowning moment of his life. Yet here he sat, racked with doubts and tormented by indecision— and afraid as he had never been afraid before, because if Juli were to turn from him it meant the end of everything. The final and permanent triumph of Shushila.

As he hesitated, putting off the moment of decision, he suddenly remembered Wally declaiming lines written two centuries earlier by one of his many heroes, James Graham, Marquis of Montrose—*"He either fears his fate too much, Or his deserts are small, That puts it not unto the touch, To win or lose it all . . ."*

Ash smiled wryly, and lifting a hand in a gesture of acknowledgement said aloud, as though his friend were actually present: "All right. I'll go down. But I'm afraid my deserts are minimal."

The little cabin was brightly lit, and after the cool

freshness of the night air unbearably hot and strongly tainted with the smell of lamp oil. Anjuli was standing by the open port-hole looking out across the shimmering beauty of the phosphorescent sea, and she had not heard the latch lift. Something in her pose—in the tilt of her head and the line of the long black plait of hair—reminded him so strongly of the child Kairi-Bai that almost without knowing it, he spoke to her by that name, whispering it very softly: "Kairi—"

Anjuli whipped round to face the door, and for the flash of a second there was a look in her eyes that could not be mistaken. It was gone immediately: but not before Ash had seen it and recognized it for what it was—stark terror. The same look that he had once seen in the eyes of Dilasah Khan, thief, traitor and sometime trooper of the Guides, when they had cornered him at last in a cleft of the hills above Spin Khab. And in Biju Ram's on a moonlight night three years ago, and more recently in the terrified gaze of five bound and gagged wretches in the *chattri* at Bhithor.

To see it now in Anjuli's was like receiving a sudden and savage attack from a totally unexpected quarter, and the impact of it made his heart miss a beat and drained the blood from his face.

Anjuli's own face was grey with shock and she said with stiff lips: "Why did you call me that! You have never . . ." Her voice failed her and she put her hands to her throat as though there was a constriction there that prevented her breathing.

"I suppose—because you reminded me of her," said Ash slowly. "I'm sorry. I should have remembered that you did not like me calling you by that name. I didn't think."

Anjuli shook her head, and said disjointedly: "No. No, it was not that . . . I don't mind . . . It was only . . . You spoke so softly, and I thought . . . I thought it was . . ."

She faltered to a stop, and Ash said: "Who did you think it was?"

"Shushila," whispered Anjuli.

The rustling, swishing water beyond the port-hole seemed to take up the lilting syllables of that name and repeat it over and over again, *Shushila, Shushila, Shushila—* And without warning, rage exploded in Ash, and he

843

slammed the door shut behind him and crossing the cabin in two strides, gripped his wife's shoulders and shook her with a violence that forced the breath from her lungs.

"You will not," said Ash, speaking between clenched teeth, "say that name to me again. Now or ever! Do you understand? I'm sick and tired of it. While she was alive I had to stand aside and see you sacrifice yourself and our whole future for her sake, and now that she's dead it seems that you are just as determined to wreck the rest of our lives by brooding and moping and moaning over her memory. She's dead, but you still refuse to face that. You won't let her go, will you?"

He pushed Anjuli away with a savage thrust that sent her reeling against the wall for support, and said gratingly: "Well, from now on you're going to let the poor girl rest in peace, instead of encouraging her to haunt you. You're my wife now, and I'm damned if I'm going to share you with Shu-shu. I'm not having two women in my bed, even if one of them is a ghost, so you can make up your mind here and now; myself or Shushila. You can't have us both. And if Shu-shu is still so much more important to you than I am, or you blame me for killing her, then you had better go back to your brother Jhoti and forget that you ever knew me, let alone married me."

Anjuli was staring at him as though she could not believe what she had heard, and when she could command her voice she said with a gasp: "So that is what you thought!"—and began to laugh: high-pitched and hysterical laughter that shook her emaciated body as violently as Ash's hands had done, and that went on and on . . . until Ash became frightened by it and slapped her across the face with an open palm, and she stopped, shuddering and gasping for breath.

"I'm sorry," said Ash curtly. "I shouldn't have done that. But I won't have you behaving in the way she did, as well as making her into a sainted idol."

"You fool," breathed Anjuli. "You *fool!*"

She leaned towards him and her eyes were no longer blank and frozen, but bright with scorn. "Did you speak to no one in Bhithor? You should have done so, and learned the truth; for I cannot believe that it was not common talk in the bazaars. Even if it were not, then the Hakim-Sahib should have known—or at least suspected. And yet *you*—you thought I was grieving for her!"

"For whom, then?" asked Ash harshly.

"For myself, if anyone. For my blindness and folly in not seeing what I should have seen many years ago; and my conceit in thinking that I was indispensable to her. You do not know what it has been like . . . no one can know. When Geeta died there was no one left whom I could trust . . . no one. There were times when I thought that I should go mad from fear, and others when I tried to kill myself and was prevented—because she did not want me to die—that would have been too easy. You warned me once that she was the *Nautch*-girl's daughter and that I must never forget it. But I would not listen to you. I would not believe . . ."

Her voice failed her and Ash took her hands and drew her towards the nearest chair and pushing her down in it, fetched a cup of water. He stood over her while she drank it, and then sat down opposite her on the edge of the bunk and said quietly: "I never thought of that. It looks as though we have been at cross-purposes. You had better tell me about it, Larla."

47

It was a long and ugly story, and listening to it Ash was no longer surprised that the widow whom he had snatched from Bhithor bore so little resemblance to the bride he had escorted there barely two years previously.

For he had been right about Shushila. She had indeed proved herself to be a true daughter of Janoo-Rani —the one-time *Nautch*-girl who had never let anything stand in the way of her own desires, or had the least compunction in eliminating anyone she considered to be a stumbling block in her path.

Anjuli told it as though she had known Shushila's mind from the beginning, though that was not so. "You must understand," she said, "that I did not discover this until almost the end. And even then there were many things that only became clear to me after we had escaped from Bhithor and I was lying hidden in the hut behind your bungalow, where I had nothing to do but sit alone and think—and remember. I believe that I know it all now, so if I tell the tale as though I knew Shushila's thoughts and words as well as those of other people with whom I had little or no contact, I am not pretending to a knowledge that I cannot have had. And I did in some sort know them, for few things can be kept secret in the Women's Quarters where there are always a score of watching eyes and listening ears, and too many wagging tongues.

"Geeta and my two serving-women, and a Bhithori servant-girl who also wished me well, told me all that they heard. And so also did that evil creature whom you left bound and gagged in the *chattri*, for she delighted in tale-bearing and would repeat to me anything that she hoped would hurt me. But I could not bring myself to think ill of Shushila . . . I could not. I believed that she was ignorant of the things that were done in her name, and was sure that they were done by order of the Rana, without her knowledge or consent. I believed that those who wished me well and tried to warn me were mistaken, and that those who wished me ill only told me these things in the hope of wounding me; so I closed my eyes and ears against both. But in the end . . . in the end I had to believe. Because it was Shushila herself—my own sister—who told me.

"Concerning the Rana, there too I should have known what might happen, for I had seen it happen before: only then it had been our brother, Nandu. I told you about that, I think. Nandu treated her harshly, and everyone thought she would hate him for it. Instead she became devoted to him, so much so that sometimes I felt a little hurt by her devotion, and was ashamed of myself for feeling so. Yet it taught me nothing. When she fell in love with that evil, perverted and disease-ridden man who was her husband, I could not understand it, though for her sake I was more than happy that it should be so, and being blind to what might follow, I was truly grateful to the gods for permitting her to find happiness in a marriage that she had fought to avoid and dreaded so greatly."

Ash said: "I can believe anything of your half-sister,
846

but not that she loved the Rana. She was probably only play-acting."

"No. You do not understand. Shushila knew nothing of men and therefore was no judge of one. How could she be, when except for her father and her brothers Nandu and Jhoti, and her uncle, whom she saw only rarely, the only ones to frequent the Women's Quarters were the eunuchs, both of them old and fat? She knew only that it is the sacred duty of a woman to submit herself in all things to her husband, to worship him as a god and to obey his commands, to bear him many children and, lest he should turn to light women, to please him in his bed. In this last, as I know, Janoo-Rani arranged for her to receive instruction by a famous courtesan, so that she should not disappoint her husband when the time came for her to marry. It may be that this aroused in her a hunger that I did not suspect, or else she had been born with that hunger, and kept it hidden from me. Whichever way, it was there . . .

"I would not have believed that such a man as the Rana, who preferred young men and boys to women, could have satisfied it. Yet he must have done so, for from the night that he first lay with her she was his—heart and mind and body. And though I did not know it, from that same night she hated me, because I too was his wife, and the eunuchs who wished to make trouble between us had whispered to her that the Rana admired tall women because they were more like men, and had spoken favourably of me. There was no truth in this, but it aroused her jealousy; and even though he treated me like an outcaste whose touch is defilement, and would neither speak to me nor see me, she became afraid (as I too was afraid) that one day he might come to think differently and have me brought to his bed—if only to wound her, or because he had drunk too much, or was crazed with *bhang* (hashish)."

That first year had been the worst, for though Anjuli had expected little happiness for herself in her new life, it had never occurred to her that Shushila would turn against her. She tried to convince herself that this was only a passing phase that would end when Shu-shu's first passionate adoration of her husband waned and she discovered, as she must, that the god of her idolatry was a middle-aged libertine, rotted by vice and capable of behaviour that in a less exalted personage would be regarded as unacceptable even by criminals.

But then Anjuli had never really understood Shushila. She was not analytical, and she had quite simply loved Shu-shu from the day that she first took the wailing little girl into her arms and was given charge of the child because its mother was disgusted with it for being a daughter and did not wish to be troubled with it. And to Anjuli love was not something to be loaned and taken back again, or proffered in the hope of reward. It was a gift— a part of one's heart, freely bestowed, and with it as a matter of course went loyalty; the two were indivisible.

She had never been blind to Shushila's faults. But she put the larger part of these down to the spoiling and silliness of the Zenana women, and the remainder to the little girl's nervous temperament and unstable health, and therefore did not hold Shu-shu to blame for them; or realize that in them lay the seeds of darker things that could one day come to flower.

The unbalanced passion that the Rana had so unexpectedly aroused in his youthful bride had set those seeds sprouting, and now they grew at a frightening pace, turning almost overnight into monstrous growths, as certain weeds and toadstools will do in the first downpour of the monsoon rains. In the face of this new and absorbing passion, all the love and care and sympathy that Anjuli had lavished upon her little half-sister for years went for nothing, swept away on an ugly tide of jealousy.

The Rana, and all those who had supported him in his endeavours to avoid taking "the half-caste" to wife, and who now—together with the Zenana women, the eunuchs and the palace servants—resented her elevation to the rank of Rani and were jealous of her influence over the senior wife, combined to humiliate her, until between them Anjuli's life became a misery.

An order was given that in future "Kairi-Bai" must keep to her rooms and not be permitted to enter those of the Senior Rani unless expressly summoned; the rooms in question being two small, dark and windowless cells, with doors opening out onto an inner courtyard less than ten foot square and surrounded by high walls. Her jewels had been taken from her, together with the greater part of her trousseau, the shimmering saris of silk and gauze being replaced by cheap stuff such as only poor women wear.

It seemed that no weapon was too petty to use against the girl whom Shushila had insisted on bringing with her to Bhithor—and whose only crime was that she too was a wife of the Rana. Anjuli must also be hidden from his gaze, and such looks as she possessed (little enough in the general opinion, but then there was no accounting for men's tastes) must be spoiled by near starvation to a point where she would appear to be a gaunt and elderly woman. Her title was never to be used, and for fear that faithful old Geeta and her own two serving-women from Karidkote might show her too much consideration and loyalty, they were taken from her and she was given instead one Promila Devi, that same hard-faced creature whom Ash had seen bound and gagged in the *chattri*.

Promila's role had resembled that of gaoler and spy rather than servant, and it was she who had reported that the two serving-women and the *dai* Geeta were still paying surreptitious visits to "the half-caste" and smuggling extra food to her. All three had been soundly whipped, and after that even loyal old Geeta had not dared approach Anjuli's apartments again. Then Shushila had become pregnant, and for a time her joy and triumph were so great that she became again the Shu-shu of the old days, demanding her half-sister's attendance whenever she felt tired or out of sorts, and behaving as if there had never been any break in their relationship. But it did not last . . .

A few weeks later her pregnancy ended, following a violent attack of colic brought on by eating too many mangoes. "She was always greedy over mangoes," explained Anjuli. "My father had them sent up from the plains each year, picked while still green and packed in great *kiltas* among straw, and Shu-shu could never wait until they ripened properly; afterwards she would have terrible pains in her stomach and cry and scream and blame something else—bad *ghee*, or under-cooked rice. Never the mangoes."

Now once again Shushila had gorged on her favourite fruit, and by doing so lost her longed-for child. She must have known that the fault was her own, but she could not bear to face it, and because this time the results of greed had been far worse than any passing stomach-ache, she did not put the blame on bad or poorly cooked food, but persuaded herself that some jealous person had tried to poison her. And who else, whispered her Bhithori women—fearful that suspicion might alight on one of them—then the co-wife, Kairi-Bai?

"But by good fortune, I had had no chance to touch her food or drink at that time," said Anjuli, "as Shu-shu and her ladies had gone to spend three days at the Pearl Palace on the lake-side, and I had not been asked to go with her. Nor had Geeta, so it was not possible to accuse us. But the two who had been my serving-maids were not so fortunate, for they had been of the party and had helped to pick and wash the mangoes, which came from a grove in the palace grounds. Also both of them were from Karidkote, having come to Bhithor in my service, wherefore the Bhithori women, perhaps fearing that the Rana would blame them for allowing his wife to eat unripe mangoes at such a time, and hoping to deflect his anger, banded together to accuse the foreigners."

Shushila had been frantic with pain and grief and disappointment, and in her frenzy she had listened to the traducers and had the two women poisoned. "This, Promila told me," said Anjuli. "Though it was given out that they had died of a fever, and I strove to believe it was true; I *made* myself believe it. It was so much easier for me to believe that Promila was lying than that Shu-shu could do such a terrible thing."

Anjuli herself had been banished to one of the smaller houses in the royal park where she had lived in virtual imprisonment, deprived of all comforts and compelled to cook her own scanty food, while the story had been spread about that she had insisted on remaining there for fear of contracting the fever from which her women had died.

By the late autumn, Shushila was again pregnant. But this time her triumph was marred by her fear of losing a second child, for the early stages of this second pregnancy were accompanied by headaches and morning-sickness, and she felt queasy and frightened—and much in need of comfort, which her husband was incapable of supplying. The Rana's strange penchant for his beautiful wife had still not burned out, but he had never had any patience with ill-health in others, and preferred to keep away when Shushila was not feeling well, and this had added another terror to her fear of losing the child: the terror that she might also lose his favour. Tormented by sickness and anxiety, she turned as she had always done to her half-sister, and Anjuli was brought back to the city palace and once again expected to take up her role of comforter and protector as though nothing had happened.

She had done her best, for she still believed that it was the Rana who was responsible for everything that had happened to her, and that even if Shushila was not entirely ignorant of it, she would not dare to take her older sister's part too openly for fear that it might enrage him and merely drive him into acting even more harshly in future. Geeta too was back in favour once more, her recent disgrace apparently forgotten. But the old lady had not appreciated the favour shown her; she had not forgotten the accusations of attempted poisoning that had followed the disastrous outcome of the mango-colic, and as her long experience as a *dai* warned her that Shushila-Bai's new pregnancy was likely to be a short one, she was in deadly terror of being commanded to prescribe a remedy to cure the Rani's headaches or relieve the racking bouts of sickness. When, inevitably, the command came, she took what precautions she could to protect both herself and Anjuli.

"She told me that I must pretend to be gravely displeased with her," said Anjuli, "and to let it be known that I would not speak to her or have any dealings with her, so that afterwards no one could say that we had plotted together. She warned me also that I must never touch anything that my sister was given to eat or drink, and I obeyed her, for by this time I too had learned to be afraid."

For her own protection, Geeta refused to make use of any herbs or drugs from her own store of medicaments, but demanded fresh ones and saw to it that these were pounded and prepared by other women; and always in full view of the Zenana. But it did her no good.

As she had foreseen, there was a second miscarriage. And as before, Shushila raved and wept and cast about for someone to blame, while the Bhithori women, looking for a scapegoat, talked of poison and the Evil-eye. But though they would probably have liked to accuse "the half-caste" and thereby curry favour with the Rana by

851

giving him an excuse to be rid of her, Geeta and Anjuli had played their part too well for that. Their enmity had been accepted as truth and sniggered over too often for any *volte face* to be possible now. Therefore only Geeta was blamed.

Despite all her precautions, the old *dai* had been accused of causing this second miscarriage by the use of the potions she had prescribed, and that night she had been killed by Promila Devi and one of the eunuchs, and her frail body taken up to a rooftop overlooking one of the flagged courtyards and thrown down so it would appear that she had fallen to her death by accident. "Though this I did not learn until much later," said Anjuli. "At the time, I heard only that she had fallen, and that it was an accident. And I believed it, for even Promila said so . . ."

On the following morning "the half-caste" had been sent away again: ostensibly at her own request. She was told that "permission had been granted for her to retire for a time to the Pearl Palace," and she had in fact been taken there—but to what amounted to solitary confinement in a single underground room.

"I was there for almost a year," whispered Anjuli, "and in all that time I only saw two persons: the woman Promila, who was my gaoler, and a *mehtarani* (female sweeper and disposer of filth) who was forbidden to speak to me. Nor did I see the sunlight or the sky, or have enough to eat. I was always hungry—so hungry that I would eat every crumb of the food that was given me, even when it was so rancid and foul that it made me ill. And for all those months I was forced to wear the same clothes that I had been wearing when I was taken from the Zenana, because I was given no others; and no water in which I might wash the ones I wore, which became ragged, and stank . . . as did my hair also, and my whole body. Only when the rains broke was I able to clean myself a little, for then the gutters overflowed and flooded the courtyards, and the water came into my cell and lay inches deep on the floor, so that I was able to bathe in it. But when the rains ended it dried up; and— and the winter was very cold . . ."

She shivered violently, as though she were still cold, and Ash heard her teeth chatter.

By the beginning of February, Anjuli had lost all

count of time; and now at last she began to give up hope, and for the first time to have doubts about Shushila and to wonder if her half-sister had forgotten her or preferred not to know what had become of her. Surely she could have done something to help? But then there was bad blood in Shu-shu: her mother had contrived the deaths of her own husband and a co-wife, his fourth bride, while her brother Nandu had been guilty of matricide. Was it possible that Shushila too was capable of evil? Anjuli could not bring herself to believe it, for after all Jhoti too was the *Nautch*-girl's child; though it was true that he favoured his father. Yet the doubts persisted, creeping back to torment her however hard she strove to drive them away . . .

No news from the outside world ever penetrated to her cell, for Promila Devi seldom spoke to her, and the *mehtarani* never. She was therefore unaware that her half-sister had again conceived, or that this time there was every hope of a happy conclusion: there had been no recurrence of the headaches and sickness, and when the child quickened the Zenana confidently predicted a safe delivery, while priests and soothsayers hastened to assure the Rana that all the omens pointed to a son. Nor did Promila make any mention of the Rana's illness and the failure of his doctors to effect a cure, or that the Senior Rani had sent for her uncle's Hakim, Gobind Dass, to treat him.

It was only when Anjuli was suddenly brought back to her rooms in the city palace that she learned these things, and wondered if she did not owe her release to Gobind's imminent arrival rather than to any change of heart on the part of the Rana. Her uncle's personal physician would certainly be charged to inquire as to the health and welfare of both Ranis, and to send news of them to Karidkote; so it would obviously look better if the Junior Rani was known to be in the Women's Quarters of the Rung Mahal with her sister, rather than alone in the Pearl Palace.

Whatever the reason she had come back again to the city palace, where she had been given clean clothes to wear and proper food to eat. But she was still not permitted to leave her own room except to walk in the small enclosed courtyard that faced it—a paved space no bigger than a fair-sized carpet and walled in by the backs of other buildings. But after the long months of semi-darkness in the Pearl Palace, it had seemed almost like Paradise to her, particularly as she saw far less of Promila, for she had been given a second serving-maid, a young and unskilled village-girl, afflicted with a hare-lip and so painfully shy that she conveyed the impression of being half-witted. Anjuli would try and coax her to talk, but Nimi never had much to say for herself, and when Promila was present she would tiptoe around like a terrified mouse, dumb with fear and unable to do more than nod or shake her head when spoken to.

Apart from Promila, Nimi and the inevitable *mehtarani,* no other woman ever entered the little courtyard, but Anjuli could hear their shrill voices and laughter on the far side of the surrounding walls, or, of an evening, from the rooftops where they gathered to gossip and enjoy the evening air. It was through listening to them that she learned of the Rana's illness and the arrival of her uncle's Hakim, Gobind Dass, and was seized by a wild hope that he might somehow be able to arrange for her escape.

If she could only manage to speak to him, or to smuggle out a letter to him explaining her predicament, surely he would not refuse to help her? Even if he could do nothing himself he could appeal on her behalf to Jhoti and Kaka-ji, who had always been fond of her and would demand that she be sent back to Karidkote. Or perhaps he could get in touch with Ashok, who could be counted upon to rescue her even if Promila Devi were to be replaced by ten dragons and the entire palace guard.

But try as she would, she could think of no way of getting in touch with Gobind; and she knew that he for his part would never be permitted to cross the threshold of the Zenana however high he might rise in the Rana's esteem; not even if Shushila were dying. Nevertheless she refused to despair; as long as he was in Bhithor there was hope—someday, somehow, by some means, she would be able to make contact with him. Then one warm evening, when the lamps had just been lit and the courtyard was a well of darkness, it seemed that her faith was to be justified for Nimi, bringing in the evening meal, had brought also a letter from the Hakim . . .

It was, as she learned later, the second that he had

written to her. But the first had not reached her, for on his arrival in Bhithor Gobind had sent two letters: one to each Rani, with enclosures from Kaka-ji and their brother the Maharajah. He had sent them openly by the hand of the head eunuch, and both had been taken to Shushila, who had read them and torn them up, and returned a verbal reply that purported to come from both Ranis.

This third letter, addressed to Anjuli, had also been handed to Shushila, and as its contents were innocuous (it asked only for an assurance that both sisters were well) it occurred to her that it might be a good move to let Kairi read it and answer it herself. If the answer contained nothing unsuitable, then it would satisfy the Hakim and keep him from making further inquiries: and if it did, it could be used as proof that Kairi-Bai was a traitress who was plotting to stir up trouble between Bhithor and Karidkote, and attempting to blacken the names of her husband and her half-sister.

The letter had been carefully re-sealed and given to the foolish servant girl Nimi, with instructions to hand it to her mistress after dark and to say only that she had received it from a stranger who had stopped her as she was returning from a visit to the bazaar, and promised her much money if she would hand it to the Junior Rani when no one else was present and bring back an answer when she next went out into the city. The girl had been made to repeat the story until she had it by heart, and warned not to add anything to it—or to answer any questions that her mistress might put to her, on pain of having her tongue torn out. On the other hand, if she did as she was told she would be suitably rewarded . . .

The horrifying threat, coupled by the promise of a reward, should have been more than enough to ensure obedience. But though Nimi might be ignorant and timid, she was not devoid of commonsense and she happened to possess more character than the plotters gave her credit for. Anjuli-Bai had been kind to her (which was something that no one else, not even her parents, had ever been before) so not for worlds would Nimi harm her— and that harm was intended she was sure. Why else would she have been commanded to relate this foolish tale of a stranger, and threatened with torture if she failed to do so? She would deliver the letter, but she would also tell

855

her mistress exactly how she had come by it, and what she had been told to say—leaving it to Anjuli-Bai in her wisdom to decide what to do about it.

That last had not been easy. Anjuli feared a trap and could not be sure who was setting it: was Nimi playing her false, or was the girl's story true? If it was, it confirmed those doubts she had about Shushila, and meant that Shushila had indeed turned against her . . . It was still hard to believe that, yet harder to believe that Nimi was lying, and if she was not . . . ? Perhaps it would be better to play safe and do nothing at all. Yet on consideration, Anjuli realized that if Nimi had not warned her, she would have been only too ready to believe that the letter had reached her in the way described, and would have answered it. Therefore she could be reasonably certain that if she did nothing, Nimi would be suspected of putting her on her guard, and probably tortured into confessing as much.

Paper and pen having been procured, Anjuli had composed a courteous and colourless reply, thanking the Hakim for his inquiry and assuring him that to the best of her knowledge her sister the Senior Rani was in good health, and she herself was well. Nimi had duly delivered the note to Shushila, who had read it and sent it on to Gobind; and the next time Nimi visited her parents she had dropped the suggestion that if one of them could devise a method of approaching the doctor from Karidkote in secret, there might be much money to be made by using her as a go-between—an idea that had not been her own, but Anjuli's. The bait had been snapped up, and thereafter Nimi had carried other letters from Gobind to the Junior Rani, and Anjuli had replied to them—though still with extreme caution, for she could not be sure that Nimi was not watched, or that this might not be another and more devious trap.

But Shushila was unaware of the correspondence. Having seen her half-sister's reply to the first letter, she had apparently come to the conclusion that imprisonment and harsh treatment had reduced Kairi to such a state of cowed subjection that there was nothing to be feared from her, and now Anjuli was informed that provided she did not enter the Senior Rani's apartments or the gardens, there was no reason why she should not go freely about the Women's Quarters again if she chose to do so.

As the time of the confinement approached, the Zenana women became infected by a heady mixture of anxiety and excitement, and the tension mounted daily until even Anjuli, a disregarded spectator, was disturbed by it and began to fear what its effect must be on her highly strung sister. But to everyone's astonishment, Shushila alone remained immune from the mass emotion. Her spirits had never been higher, and far from giving way to nerves—as anyone acquainted with her would have expected—she continued to glow with health and beauty, and apparently had no qualms. Only Anjuli, learning of this from the chatter of the women, suspected that the reason for it could be traced to those two miscarriages, both of which had occurred so early that they could not in fact be termed "miscarriages" at all.

She thought it probable (and in this she was right) that Shu-shu had been encouraged to believe—or had persuaded herself to believe?—that the comparatively mild discomforts she had suffered then were all that she need expect now, and that neither the new *dai* nor any of her women had summoned up the courage to undeceive her. It was when the labour pains began that the real trouble would start—and this time there would be no Geeta to help her, and no loving half-sister to cling to for comfort and support.

Shushila's pains had begun shortly before ten o'clock on a warm spring night. And all through the following day, and for part of the next night, her agonized screams rang through the Zenana Quarter and echoed eerily along the colonnades surrounding the gardens. At some time during that interminable day one of her women, grey-faced from fear and lack of sleep, had come running to Anjuli and gasped out that she must come at once—the Rani-Sahiba was calling for her.

There had been nothing for it but to obey. Though Anjuli was under no illusion as to why Shushila should suddenly wish to see her: Shu-shu was in pain and very frightened, and it was the pain and fear that had impelled her to send for the one person who had never failed her and whom she knew, instinctively, would not fail her now. Nor was Anjuli ignorant of the risks she ran in entering her sister's apartments at such a time. If anything went wrong someone would be blamed for it, and it would not be the gods or natural causes, or any of the Bhithoris:

it would be pinned on her. This time it would be Kairi-Bai, "the half-caste," who from spite or jealousy or a desire to be revenged for the way in which she had been treated, had put the Evil-eye on the child or on its mother, and would be made to pay for it.

Yet even knowing that—and had it been possible to refuse to go to Shushila which it was not—she would still have gone. Only someone deaf or stony-hearted could have remained unmoved by those harrowing screams, and Anjuli was neither. She had hurried to Shushila's side, and for the remainder of that agonizing labour it was to her hands that Shushila had clung; dragging at them until they were sore and bleeding and imploring her to call Geeta to stop the pains . . . poor Geeta who had supposedly broken her neck in a fall, over a year ago.

The new *dai* who had replaced Geeta was a capable and experienced woman, but she lacked her predecessor's skill with drugs. Moreover she had never before been required to deal with a patient who not only made no attempt to help herself, but did everything in her power to prevent anyone else from doing so.

The Senior Rani flung herself from side to side, shrieking and screaming with ear-splitting abandon and clawing wildly at the faces of those who strove to restrain her, and had it not been for the timely arrival of her half-sister she would, in the *dai*'s opinion, have ended by doing herself a serious injury or going out of her mind. But the despised co-wife had succeeded where everyone else had failed, for though the screams continued they were less frequent, and presently the frantic girl was striving to bear down as the pains waxed and to relax when they waned, and the *dai* breathed again and began to hope that all might yet be well.

The day ebbed into evening and once again it was night; but few in the Women's Quarters were able to sleep, while those in the birth-chamber were unable even to snatch a mouthful of food. By now Shushila was exhausted, and her throat so sore and swollen that she could no longer scream but only lie still and moan. But she continued to cling to Anjuli's hands as though to a life-line, and Anjuli, aching with weariness, still bent above her, encouraging her, coaxing her to swallow spoonfuls of milk in which strengthening herbs had been brewed, or to sip a

858

little spiced wine; soothing, petting and cajoling her as she had done so often in the past.

". . . and for a while—for a short while," said Anjuli, telling the story of that frenetic night, "it was as though she was a child again and we were friends once more, as in the old days; though even then I knew in my heart that this was not so, and that it would never be so again . . ."

Apart from Shushila's uninhibited and hysterical behaviour, there had been no major complications, and when at long last, just after midnight, the child was born, it came into the world very easily: a strong, healthy infant who bawled lustily and beat the air with tiny waving fists. But the *dai*'s face paled as she lifted it, and the women who had pressed forward eagerly to witness the great moment drew back and were silent. For the child was not the longed-for son that the soothsayers had so confidently promised, but a daughter.

"I saw Shushila's face when they told her," said Anjuli, "and I was afraid. Afraid as I have never been before: for myself . . . and for the babe also. For it was as though the dead had come back to life and it was Janoo-Rani who lay there: Janoo-Rani in one of her white rages, as cold and as deadly as a king cobra. I had never seen the resemblance before. But I saw it then. And I knew in that moment that no one in the room was safe. Myself least of all . . . Shushila would strike out like a tigress who has been robbed of its cubs—as she had struck twice before (yes, that too I knew now) when she had been disappointed of a child. But this time it would be worse: this time her rage and disappointment would be ten times greater, because she had carried this child for its full time and been assured that it must be a son, and having endured agony beyond anything she had ever dreamed of to give it birth, it was a daughter."

Anjuli shuddered again and her voice sank to a whisper. "When they would have given the babe to her, she stared at it with hatred, and though she was hoarse from screaming and so weak that she could barely whisper, she summoned up breath to say: 'An enemy has done this. It is not mine. Take it away—and kill it!' Then she turned her face from it and would not look at it again, though it was her own child, her first-born: bone of her bone and flesh of her flesh. I could not have believed that anyone

859

. . . that any woman . . . But the *dai* said that it was often so with those who had endured a hard labour and were disappointed of a son. They would speak wildly, but it meant nothing; and when they were rested and had held their infants in their arms they came to love them tenderly. But—but I knew my sister better than the *dai* did, and was even more afraid. It was then I think that I came near to hating her . . . yet how can one hate a child, even a cruel one?—and children can be far crueller than their elders because they do not truly understand—they only feel, and strike out, and do not see the end; and Shu-shu herself was little more than one. But I feared her . . . I feared her . . ."

The exhausted *dai* had given Shushila a strong sleeping draught, and as soon as it had taken effect the other women had crept away to spread the dire news to the waiting Zenana, while a trembling and reluctant eunuch had left to inform the sick Rana that he had become the father of yet another daughter. Anjuli had stayed for a while to allow the *dai* to get some rest, and had returned to her own rooms before Shushila awakened; and it was then that she had written that letter to Gobind, imploring his help for Shushila, and begging him to use his influence with the Rana to see if a nurse, an *Angrezi* one, could be sent for immediately to take charge of the mother and child. "I thought that if perhaps one of them could be brought to Bhithor, she might be able to cure Shushila of her hate and her rages, which were in some way a sickness, and to persuade her that no one was to blame for the sex of the child; least of all the child itself."

Gobind had received that letter, but no European woman had been summoned to Bhithor; and in any case, admitted Anjuli, there would not have been time. The Zenana was full of rumours and those that came to her ears confirmed her worst fears: Shushila had not repeated her wild outburst against the child, but she still refused to see it, explaining her refusal by saying that the infant was so frail and sickly that it could not possibly live for more than a few days at most, and she dared not face further pain and grief by becoming deeply attached to a child that must shortly be reft from her.

But at least a dozen women had been present when the child was born, and all had seen it and heard its first cries. Nevertheless, the rumour that it was a frail and sickly infant who was not expected to live was repeated so often that even those who had good reason to know otherwise began to believe it; and soon there were few in Bhithor who had not heard that the poor Rani, having been disappointed of a son, must now suffer the added grief of losing her daughter.

"I do not know how it died," said Anjuli. "Perhaps they let it starve to death. Though being a strong child that might have taken too long, so they may have chosen a quicker way . . . I can only hope so. But no matter whose hand did the work, it was done by Shushila's orders. And then—then the day after the child's body was carried to the burning-ground, three more of her women and the *dai* also fell ill and were taken away from the Zenana in *dhoolis*—for fear, it was said, that the sickness might spread. Later it was rumoured that all four died, though that may not have been true. At least they did not return again to the Women's Quarters; and when it became known that the ailing Rana had suffered a relapse, they were forgotten in all the turmoil and anxiety that followed, because at such a time who could trouble themselves to inquire what had happened to a few unimportant Zenana women?"

Shushila, who had recovered very quickly from her ordeal, flatly refused to believe that her husband's illness could not be cured. Her faith in her uncle's Hakim remained unshaken and she insisted that the relapse was no more than a temporary set-back, and that another month would see the Rana on his feet again and completely recovered: it was unthinkable that this should not be so. In the meantime she turned her attention to repairing the ravages of pregnancy and parturition, and regaining the slenderness that had previously delighted him, so that when he was well again he would think her as beautiful as ever—and have no eyes and no thoughts for anyone else.

Not until the very end could she be brought to believe that he was dying, and when finally she was forced to believe it, she tried to go to him so that she might hold him in her arms and shield him with her own body from this enemy that threatened him. She would fight Death itself for his sake—and she had fought with teeth and nails against those who had prevented her from running to his bedside. Her fury and despair had been so terrible

861

to see that her women had fled from her and hidden themselves in the furthest and darkest rooms of the Zenana, while the eunuchs listening outside her door shook their heads and muttered that she was deranged and should be put under restraint. But when the first frenzy of grief had spent itself she shut herself away in her apartment to pray, refusing to eat or drink or to allow anyone to approach her.

It must have been during this time that she made up her mind to die a suttee, and also what she intended to do about her half-sister. For when the news was brought to her that her husband was dead, her plans had been made. She had apparently sent at once for the Diwan, and speaking to him in the presence of the chief eunuch and the woman Promila Devi (who had been at pains to describe that interview to Anjuli) had informed him that she intended to die on her husband's pyre.

She would follow the bier on foot, but she would go alone. "The half-caste" could not be permitted to defile the Rana's ashes by burning with him, for being no true wife it was not fitting that she should share the honour of becoming suttee. Other arrangements would be made for her . . .

Even the Diwan must have shuddered as he listened to those arrangements, but he had not opposed them, possibly because his failure to have "the half-caste's" marriage contract repudiated and the woman herself sent back dowerless to her home still rankled, and that if he thought of her at all it was with enmity and resentment, and anger at his own defeat. At all events he had agreed to everything that the Senior Rani had decreed, before hurrying away to consult with the priests and his fellow councillors as to the funeral arrangements. When he had gone, Shushila sent for her half-sister.

Anjuli had not seen her sister since the night of the child's birth, or had any message from her. And when the summons came she imagined that she had been called because Shu-shu was frantic with grief and terror, and desperately in need of support. She did not believe that there would be any talk of suttee, for Ashok had told her that the Raj did not permit the burning of widows and that there was now a law forbidding it. So there was no need for Shushila to fear that she would be forced to die on her husband's pyre. "But this time I did not go to her willingly," said Anjuli.

Until recently she had been able to believe, or had made herself believe, that Shushila was innocent of much that had been imputed to her; but now she knew better—not only with her head but in her heart. Yet she could not refuse the summons. She had expected to find the new-made widow weeping and distraught, her hair and clothing torn and her women wailing about her. But there had been no sound from the Senior Rani's apartments, and when she entered there was only one person there: a small erect figure that for a moment she did not even recognize . . .

"I would not have believed that she could look like that. Ugly, and evil—and *cruel*. Cruel beyond words. Even Janoo-Rani had never looked like that, for Janoo had been beautiful and this woman was not. Nor did it seem possible that she could ever have been beautiful—or young. She looked at me with a face of stone and asked me how I dared come into her presence showing no signs of grief. For in this too I had sinned: it was intolerable to her that I should escape the agony of grief that was tearing at her own heart . . .

"She said . . . she told me . . . she told me everything: how she had hated me from the moment she fell in love with her husband, because I too was his wife and she could not endure the thought of it; that she had had me starved and imprisoned to make me pay for that crime, and also in order that I might look old and ugly so that if by chance the Rana should remember my existence, he would turn from me in disgust: that she had ordered the killing of my two serving-maids, and of old Geeta . . . She threw it all in my face as though each word was a blow, and as though it eased her own pain to see me suffer—and how could I *not* suffer? When—when she had finished she told me that she had resolved to become suttee, and that the last thing I would ever see would be the flames uniting her body with her husband's, because she had given orders that when I had seen it my eyes were to be put out with hot irons, and afterwards—afterwards I would be taken back to the Zenana to spend the rest of my life in darkness—as a drudge.

"I—I tried to reason with her. To plead with her. I

863

went on my knees to her and begged her in the name of all that lay between us—the years . . . the tie of blood and the affection we had had for each other in the past, the love—but at that she laughed, and summoning the eunuchs, had me dragged away . . ."

Her voice failed on the last word, and in the silence that followed Ash became aware once more of the sound of the sea and all the many small ship noises; and that the cabin smelled strongly of hot lamp oil and the fried *puris* that had been served with the evening meal and that there was still a lingering odour of stale cigar-smoke to remind him that this had been Red's cabin for many years. But up on the deck it would be cool and the stars were once again familiar ones, for the skies of the south had been left behind—and with them Bhithor and its harsh stony hills, and all that had happened there.

It was over—finished. *Khutam hogia*! Shushila was dead, and all that remained to show that she had ever lived was the print of her small hand on the Suttee Gate of the Rung Mahal. Sarji, Gobind and Manilal had gone; and Dagobaz too . . . They were all part of the past, and though he would not forget them, it would be best not to think of them too often until enough time had passed to allow him to do so calmly, and without pain.

He drew a long slow breath, and reaching out, took Anjuli's hands in his and said gently: "Why didn't you tell me all this before, Larla?"

"I could not. It was . . . it was as though my heart and mind had been so bruised that I could not endure any more emotion. I only wanted to be quiet; and not to have to answer questions and to put it all into words. I had loved her for so long, and I had thought that she—that she was fond of me. Even when I thought that I hated her, I found that I could not forget what she had once meant to me . . . how sweet she had been as a child. And then—then when I saw her walk to the pyre, and knew what would happen when she realized what she had done and that there was no escape, I—I could not bear to have her suffer so terrible a death. *I could not*! Yet if I had only gone when you wished, perhaps all those others would not have died. Their blood was on my head and I could not bear it—or bear to hear my own voice relating things that—that even now I can hardly believe can really have happened. I wanted to hide it all away

864

. . . to bury it and pretend that it could not be true. But it would not stay buried."

"It will now, my Heart," said Ash, and pulled her up into his arms. "Oh, my love, I have been so afraid. So terribly afraid. You do not know! All this time I have thought that you were grieving for her, and that you had found out that I could not replace her because she had taken all your love and there was none left for me. I thought I had lost you—"

His voice broke, and suddenly Anjuli's arms were tight about his neck and she was crying, "No, no, no—it was not so: I have always loved you—always, always. More than anyone in the world—" And then the tears came.

But this time Ash knew that they were healing tears, washing away some of the horror and bitterness and guilt from her bruised heart, and easing the terrible tension that had held her in a vice-like grip for so long. When at last they were spent, he lifted her head and kissed her, and presently they went out together into the cool, star-spangled darkness, and for that night at least, forgot the past and the future and everything and everyone but each other.

48

Ten days later, on a still and pearly morning before sunrise, the *Morala* dropped anchor off Keti on the delta of the Indus, and landed three passengers: a burly Pathan, a slim, clean-shaven man whose dress and bearing proclaimed him to be a citizen of Afghanistan, and a woman in a bourka who was presumably the wife of one or other of them.

The Afghan dress had been acquired on the previous day by Gul Baz, in the course of a brief stop at Karachi where the *Morala* had unloaded a small consignment of dressed hides and dried fruit, taken on, with the grain, a week earlier at Chahbar. It was Red who had suggested its purchase, for Sind was a harsh land, much of it sparsely inhabited, and its people were not noted for hospitality towards strangers: "But they're leary of Afghans, an' as from wot you've tole me, you can pass yoreself orf as one any day of the week, I'd advise you to do it now. It'll be a sight safer."

So Ash had gone over the side wearing Afghan dress, and whether it was due to this, or merely a matter of luck, the long journey from the coast of Sind to Attock had been accomplished in safety, if not in comfort.

A *dundhi,* a flat-bottomed river boat normally used for carrying cargo, hired on their behalf through the agency of one of Red's many friends in the coastal-trading business, had taken them up the Indus, initially under sail (during those hours when the tide was in their favour) and later, if the wind failed, by means of a tow rope. Teams of coolies had pulled the clumsy craft forward from village to village, a fresh team taking over each evening while the previous one turned homeward, each man clutching the few small coins that were doled out for his day's labour by the owner of the boat, the *manji,* who with his two sons formed the permanent crew.

In this wise they travelled slowly up the enormous mile-wide river. Past Jerak and Naidarabad and Rohri, to Mithankote where the waters of four of the five great rivers of the Punjab, the Sutlej, Ravi, Chenab and Jhelum, channelled by the Chenab, join the Indus on their way to the sea—and on northward past Dera Ghazi Khan, with the mountains of Baluchistan and Zohb rising up along the western horizon and the flat, burning plains of the Sind Sagar Doab stretching away eastward, to the junction of the Luni River below Dera Ismail Khan. From where, on a night of brilliant moonlight, they saw the crest of the Takht-i-Suliman, a far point of silver, high above the foothills of Baluchistan, and Anjuli had wept tears of joy at seeing snow again.

At first, irked by inactivity, Ash and his bride would leave the boat and walk for part of the way. But by now the hot weather was upon them, and even in the cool of the morning, or towards sunset, the heat turned the bourka into a stifling tent. Then Ash had managed to buy two horses, and after that they rode each day, ranging far afield so that the bourka could be thrown back, and returning to the boat at mid-day to rest in the shade of the small shelter constructed out of planks and matting that did duty for a cabin.

Ash had wished to buy a third horse for Gul Baz. But Gul Baz had no desire to go riding around the countryside. He thoroughly approved of this leisurely method of travelling and enjoyed spending his days sitting in lordly ease under an awning in the bows, though he would ride one of the horses and take the other on a leading rein whenever the Sahib and the Rani-Sahiba decided to travel on the boat.

Time moved slowly on the river, but for Ash and Anjuli it could not move slowly enough, and if they could have had their way the journey would never have ended. The discomforts (and there were many) counted for nothing compared to the delight of being together and free to talk and laugh and make love without fear.

The food might be plain and ill-cooked, but Anjuli, who had known starvation, found no fault with it. And after sleeping for more than a year on the dank stone floor of an underground cellar, what did it matter that the single string bed provided by the *manji* should prove to be so densely populated by bugs that Ashok had thrown it overboard, and thereafter they had slept on the floor with only a thin *resai* (quilt) between them and the rough planks?

As for their tiny, ramshackle cabin with its Noah's Ark roof and matting walls, it might be exceedingly hot and far from comfortable; but then her room in the Women's Quarters of the Rung Mahal had been far hotter, for no breeze ever reached it, while here the matting could be rolled up at will—and there outside lay the river and the white sandbanks, with beyond them the wide, sun-scorched, empty spaces that stretched away and away until they were lost in the heat-haze or made magical by moonlight. To one who had lived penned up in a small windowless room in the Rung Mahal and endured months of solitary confinement in a dark cellar, this alone was a never-failing source of wonder.

For Ash it was enough to see his wife lose her skeletal thinness and regain much of the beauty and health and serenity that the years in Bhithor had taken from her. Though this had not happened overnight: that would have been too much to expect. The road back to normality had been a slow one; almost as slow as their present progress up the "Father of Rivers." But the telling of the true story of those years had been the first step, and those long, peaceful days on the *Morala*—the hours of talk and the hours of companionable silence, the shared laughter and the wonderful star-splashed nights when they made love and fell asleep to the music of the waves and sea winds —had all helped to heal the cruel wounds that Shushila and Bhithor had inflicted. Ash watched his wife come alive again and was happier and more deeply content than he would have believed possible.

The Father of Rivers ran deep and wide: so wide that it often seemed more like an inland sea than a river, and there were days when the heat-haze or blowing sand made it impossible to see the far bank—or either bank, if the boat was under sail. Much of the countryside was barren and desolate, but palm trees, oleanders, tamarind and tamarisk grew by the river, and even where there were no towns or villages, there was always life to be seen.

Myriads of birds preyed on the swarms of *chilwa* and other small fish who teemed in the shallows. Mud-turtles and *ghariyal*—the long-snouted, fish-eating alligators of the Indian river—basked on the sandbanks, and sometimes a porpoise could be seen leaping and turning in deep water, or a great salmon-like *mahseer,* its silver-pink sides flashing in the sun. In the late evening, when the river ran gold and the hills of Baluchistan seemed to move nearer across the shadowed plains, flight after flight of wild duck, geese, pelicans and paddy-birds would pass overhead, while parties of nomads with their goats and camels would straggle past on their way to new camping grounds. And at dusk the deer and antelope, and creatures such as pig and jackal and porcupine, would come down to drink.

Sometimes they saw bands of horsemen far out across the plain, galloping furiously towards a horizon that was hidden by dust. And on the river itself there were always other boats: country-boats laden with fodder or grain, wood, sugar-cane or vegetables, and others crammed with wooly, bleating cargoes of sheep or goats; ferry-boats plying their trade and fishermen paying out their nets or setting fish-traps; and during the earlier days, an occasional river steamer huffing and puffing its way upstream under a cloud of black smoke, or sweeping past with the current on its way to the coast.

Lessons in English and Pushtu, begun on the *Morala,* became part of the daily routine, and Anjuli proved to be an apt pupil. She made rapid progress, astonishing Ash by the quickness and accuracy with which she assimilated words and phrases and mastered the complicated rules of grammar, and he realized that she must always have had a good brain but until now had lacked the opportunity to use it—women in purdah not being expected to interest themselves in anything but domestic matters. But now that she had escaped from the almost exclusively feminine world of the Zenana, her intelligence leapt to meet the challenge, and by the time the Kurram hills and the Salt Ranges of Kundian came into sight, she could express herself in her husband's language with a fluency that did credit to her instructor: and even more to her own powers of concentration.

Realizing that they would reach Kala Bagh almost a month before his leave was up, Ash had planned to tie up the boat at some pleasant spot and spend the time exploring the countryside on horseback rather than returning to Mardan before he need do so. But with the Salt Range closing in to hem the river between high banks and shut out the breeze, even the nights were no longer cool, while the days had become so hot that the cliffs of rock salt and the blinding white sand by the water's edge, the ground underfoot and even the planks of the boat felt as though they had come fresh-baked from a furnace.

In these conditions, the sooner he got Juli under a proper roof and into a house where there were solid walls and wide verandahs to shut out the cruel heat, and *punkahs* and *kus-kus* tatties to cool the air, the better. And it was then that he remembered Zarin's aunt, Fatima Begum, and the quiet house that stood back from the Attock road, protected by high walls and a garden full of fruit trees. He could leave Juli there in safety, and though it meant that he would have to take the Begum into his confidence, he felt sure that the old lady could be relied upon to keep the matter secret, and also to think of some story that would satisfy the curiosity of her household and prevent her servants from talking.

He would get Zarin to arrange it; and that same evening Gul Baz set off on Ash's horse to ride with all speed to Mardan, charged with delivering a verbal message to Zarin and a letter to Hamilton-Sahib, after which he would rejoin the party at Attock. The distance across country was probably no more than seventy *koss,* so two days should be enough to bring him to Mardan, and a night's ride would cover the rest. But it had taken the best part of a week for Ash and Juli to complete the last part of the journey to Attock, for above Kala Bagh the Indus, that for hundreds of miles divides its waters into two, three and sometimes four separate streams—each one larger than an English river—narrows into a single one where a boat must fight its way up against the full force of the current. So that even though the wind had favoured them it was not until six days later, and well after midnight, that they came within reach of Attock. And once again, as on his last visit there, Ash came to Fatima Begum's house by moonlight: only this time he did not come alone.

The path that led up to it was inches deep in dust, but either the horse's bridle chinked or else a nail in Ash's *chuppli* clicked against a pebble, for before he reached the gate it creaked open, and a man moved forward to greet him: *"Stare-mah-sheh!"* said Zarin. "I told Gul Baz that you would not face that last mile through the gorges."

"Khwah-mah-sheh?" replied Ash, returning the conventional greeting. "You were right. My courage failed at the sound of the water and the sight of those whirlpools, and I preferred to come dry-shod across the hills."

He dropped the reins and turned to help Anjuli down from the saddle, and though he knew that she was exhausted by the heat and the hours of riding at a walk along precipitous ways after a long day in the stifling shelter on the boat, he did not attempt to support her, since in the East a respectable woman, when visiting abroad, is an anonymous figure to whom no attention should be paid, and Ash knew that in a country where most people sleep out of doors in the hot weather, the night is apt to be full of eyes. For the same reason he made no introductions, but turned away to take the horse's bridle and follow Zarin through the gate, leaving Anjuli to bring up the rear in the time-honoured fashion that prevails throughout Islam.

The household had evidently retired to bed, but **a**

faint light gleamed in the inner courtyard where Fatima Begum's most trusted attendant, an elderly close-mouthed woman, had been waiting, lantern in hand, to whisk Anjuli away to an upper room. When they had gone, the two men turned to take stock of each other by the light of an oil lamp that had been left burning in a niche by the door; and both thought sharply, and with a curious feeling of loss, how greatly the other had changed since their last meeting in that same house . . .

It was barely two years, yet there were grey hairs in Zarin's beard that had not been there before. And new lines too—one a long, puckered scar that ran from his temple to the corner of his mouth, barely missing his right eye: the mark of a slashing stroke from a tulwar, received, among other wounds, during the attack on Sipri. He had been promoted to Risaldar after that action, and bore in addition to the scar the indefinable stamp that authority and responsibility give to those upon whom they fall.

In Ash the change was less obvious, and possibly someone less well acquainted with him would have missed it, but to Zarin it was striking. His face no longer wore the strained, restless, reckless look that Zarin had found so disturbing at their last meeting, and though it was thinner than ever, the eyes under the black brows were quiet and contented. "He has found happiness," thought Zarin with foreboding. "This alters everything."

They looked long and searchingly at each other, and a stranger seeing them would have said that they were saying farewell rather than greeting each other after a long absence—and in a sense would have been right, for both were realizing a little sadly, that someone they had once known had gone for ever. Then Ash smiled, and the brief moment of regret vanished. They embraced in the old manner, and Zarin took down the lamp and led the way to a room where cold food had been set ready, and they ate and talked. And talked . . .

Ash learned that Koda Dad had not been too well of late, but that Zarin had sent him word of Ash's arrival and was sure that if he felt well enough to travel he would set out for Attock immediately. Hamilton-Sahib had been away on leave, and Gul Baz was not (as Ash had supposed) waiting on the river bank for the boat, but somewhere in the vicinity of Abbottabad where he had gone in search of the Sahib, who was reported to be on his way back from the Kangan Valley.

"He said you had given him a letter for Hamilton-Sahib and told him to give it into the Sahib's own hand," said Zarin. "So, finding him gone, he took it upon himself to go to Abbottabad. He must have met with some delay on the road. Or perhaps Hamilton-Sahib has not yet reached there and Gul Baz has gone on a little way, knowing that I would be here to meet you. I have sent the gate-keeper to watch for the boat and see that your gear is brought up."

There had been a good deal of regimental and Frontier gossip to catch up on, for Ash had received no news since Wally's last letter, which had been written nearly three months ago, and Zarin had also talked at length of the prospects of war with Afghanistan. But Ash did not touch upon his own doings, or make any mention of Anjuli; and Zarin was careful to ask no questions. That subject could wait until such time as Ashok felt able to discuss it, which would probably be after a good night's rest—something he was unlikely to have had in the raging heat of the Indus gorges.

Ash had indeed slept well that night, and during the following day he had told the whole story of the past months, from the time of Gobind and Manilal's sudden appearance in Ahmadabad to the day when Anjuli had become his wife in a brief ceremony on board the *Morala*, together with a short sketch of the events of three years ago that had led up to it: first to Zarin and later, of necessity, to Fatima Begum, both of whom had been deeply interested.

Zarin had, to some extent, been forewarned; Gul Baz having told him that the woman for whom the Sahib requested Fatima Begum's hospitality was a high-born Hindu widow who he had brought with him from the south, and with whom he had been through some sort of ceremony that purported to make them man and wife (though as this had resembled no form of *Shadi* that Gul Baz had ever heard of, there being no priest and the whole affair lasting less than five minutes, it need not be taken seriously). But it had naturally not occurred to Zarin that the widow in question was a woman he himself knew, or rather one whom he had known, long ago, as the *Feringhi*-Rani's daughter, little Kairi-Bai.

872

The news that Ashok regarded himself as married to her saddened him, for Zarin had hoped to see his friend contract a suitable marriage to some girl of his own race who would solve his problem of identity, and breed strong sons to follow their father into the Guides and be ideal officers, as they could not fail to inherit his love and understanding of India and its peoples. Yet if he remained faithful to Kairi-Bai this would never come about, since his children would be both illegitimate and half-caste (Zarin too did not consider that the shipboard ceremony described by Gul Baz could be binding), and as such, unsuited to enter the Corps.

On the other hand it was a relief to know that despite his insistence that the ceremony was legal and Kairi-Bai his lawfully wedded wife, Ashok intended to keep the marriage a close secret and install the bride in some discreet little house in Hoti Mardan, where provided he was careful he would be able to visit her without anyone in the cantonment being aware of it. His reasons for acting in this sensible manner obviously did not include any doubts as to the validity of his marriage, but were entirely due to his fears for his so-called wife's safety—fears that Zarin, remembering Janoo-Rani and all that he had been told about Bhithor, considered to be justified. Yet whatever the reasons, he could only be grateful that they had been strong enough to prevent Ashok from wrecking his career by producing the ex-Rani in Mardan and demanding that the Corps accept her as his wife, for if there was one thing that he, Zarin, was sure of, it was that not one of them, from the Commandant-Sahib down to the newest-joined recruit, would have done so. And knowing Ashok as he did, he was inclined to feel grateful to the Diwan of Bhithor and his fellow assassins.

Fatima Begum, being a relic of an earlier age, saw nothing out of the way in the Sahib's desire to keep an Indian girl in some quiet little *Bibi-gurh* (women's house) near his place of work, and said as much to her nephew. Such arrangements, said the Begum, were far from uncommon and would bring no discredit upon the Sahib: when had anyone thought the less of any man for keeping a mistress? She dismissed the tale of a marriage with an impatient wave of the hand, for she had been talking to Anjuli, to whom she had taken a strong fancy, and Anjuli herself, despite all Ashok's assurances, had never been

873

able to believe that anything as devoid of ritual and as quickly over as that strange ceremony on board the *Morala* could possibly be binding in law.

Zarin's aunt had insisted that Anjuli and her husband should spend the remainder of the Sahib's leave as her guests, and told her nephew that she herself would see to it that a suitable house was found for the ex-Rani within easy reach of Mardan; one in which she could live quietly and find no difficulty in keeping her true identity a secret, for no virtuous housewife, declared the Begum, would think of prying into the antecedents of a courtesan; and as she would not be setting up in competition with others in that trade, she would be able to live in safety and seclusion.

This last observation had not been repeated to Ash, who had gratefully accepted the offer. He had not been looking forward to spending the next few weeks scouring the countryside in search of a secluded hideaway for Juli, in a temperature that frequently reached a hundred and fifteen degrees at mid-day, and the Begum's house was large, cool and comfortable—and safe.

On the following day, as there was still no sign of either Koda Dad or Gul Baz, Ash set off for Hasan Abdal, hoping to meet Wally on the Abbottabad road. The house was still in darkness when he arose and left his drowsy wife and went very quietly downstairs, but early as it was, Zarin was up and waiting for him in the courtyard, since he too had to be away before first light. Their roads lay in different directions, for Zarin was returning to Mardan, but he had had Juli's mare saddled for Ash, and the two men mounted in silence, and rode out of the gate as the stars began to pale and from somewhere behind them in the Begum's garden a cock crowed—to be answered by another in the town, and that one by a third in the fort by the river, until presently a dozen cocks were crowing.

The air was still cool, but there was no freshness in it, and already it held more than a hint of the coming day's heat, for the stillness was undisturbed by even a breath of wind, and below the town the veil of mist on the river lay motionless above the swirling water that flowed past the walls of Akbar's fort. The riders drew rein at the junction between the lane and the high road, and for a moment or two sat listening, hoping to hear the distant clop of hoofbeats that might herald the arrival of Koda

Dad Khan or Gul Baz. But the long white road lay empty, and except for the cocks and the river there was no sound.

"We shall meet them on the road," said Zarin, answering the unspoken thoughts of both. "How soon do you expect to be in Mardan?"

"In three weeks' time. So if your father has not already set out, send word to him to stay in his house, and say that I will come to see him as soon as I can."

"I will do that. But it may be that I will meet him on the way, and if so he will be waiting here for you in my aunt's house when you return. Well, we must be on our way. *Pa makhe da kha*, Ashok."

"*Ameen sera*, Zarin Khan."

They touched hands briefly and parted. And two hours later, as the sun rose, Ash passed through Hasan Abdal, and leaving the 'Pindi road, turned left on to the one that leads to the hills and Abbottabad.

Wally had been eating breakfast under a clump of trees by the roadside near the bank of a small stream that crossed it a mile or so above the town, and he had not at first recognized the lean, travel-stained Afridi who pulled up at sight of him and dismounted among the freckled shadows of the acacias.

BOOK SEVEN

My Brother Jonathan

49

"I suppose it was because I wasn't expecting you," explained Wally, plying his friend with stewed tea, hard-boiled eggs and chuppattis. "Your letter said to meet you at Attock so I expected to find you there all togged up in one of Rankin's best sun-proof suitings, not jogging along in the dust wearing fancy-dress. I always knew you were able to do it, but I hadn't realized that you could even take me in, and I still don't know how it's done, because your face hasn't altered—or not much—and it can't be just the clothes. Yet until you spoke I took you for just another tribesman. How the divil an all do you do the trick?"

"There's no trick about it," said Ash, gulping hot tea. "Or if there is it probably lies in being able to think yourselves into the mind and skin of whoever you are pretending to be, until you become that person; which isn't difficult for someone like me, who for most of his formative years imagined himself to be a native of this country. Anyway, most people only see what they expect to see, and if they spot a fellow in a tweed-suit and a deer-stalker they automatically think 'Englishman,' while one in a *shulwa* and turban, with a flower behind his ear and a *kaisora*

876

hanging from his wrist, must of course be an Afridi. It's as simple as that."

By now the sun was high and the heat already so fierce that it would have been cruelty to take the tired horses any further; for Wally too had been in the saddle since first light, having camped the previous night near Haripur. He had hired a tonga to bring his bearer and his gear down from Abbottabad, and Gul Baz—who had ridden far and fast in the last few days—had been only too pleased to finish the journey in this vehicle while the Sahib took over the horse.

Unlike Wally, Gul Baz had recognized Ash while he was still a good way off, and had instantly made an excuse to remove Wally's bearer Pir Baksh and the tonga driver to a spot further up the road, from where they would be unable to witness the meeting between the Sahib and his friend, which could not fail to arouse the tonga-wallah's curiosity.

In Gul Baz's opinion too many people already knew that Pelham-Sahib could pass as a frontier tribesman. The story of the pursuit of Dilasah Khan had leaked out and been told and re-told with countless additions and embroideries in every bazaar from Peshawar to Rawalpindi, and Gul Baz did not want to hear it revived again. He therefore kept his two companions engaged in talk until Wally called to him by name, when he hurried over to receive his orders and returned saying that the Sahib had met with an acquaintance—an Afridi horse-dealer—and that as the day was too hot for riding he would stay and talk with the man and take the road later. Meanwhile he desired that the servants would go on ahead in the tonga to Attock dâk-bungalow, where they would engage a room and order a meal for him and wait until he arrived: they need not hurry, as he himself did not intend to set out until late in the afternoon.

"Which means that they'll probably spend the next few hours resting at Hasan Abdal, and arrive in Attock only just ahead of us," said Wally, watching the tonga rattle past and disappear round a bend in the road, before turning back to resume his interrupted conversation with the pseudo-horse-dealer.

They had not seen each other for almost two years, but in spite of all that had happened during that time it was as though they had parted only yesterday and were

877

continuing a conversation that had been temporarily interrupted. The rapport between them remained unchanged and they might almost have been back in their shared quarter in 'Pindi, talking over the day's work; for Ash had refused to launch into any explanations until he had first heard all Wally's news, partly because he wanted to establish the old footing before he told his own, but largely because he knew that once it was told, neither of them were likely to talk of anything else.

So Wally had talked, and Ash had listened and laughed as he was brought up to date on a dozen matters, regimental, social and general. He learned that the Guides were in "tremendous shape," the Commandant and the other officers the "best of fellows," and Wigram Battye (recently promoted to Captain) in particular an "absolute corker." In fact the words "Wigram says" appeared with such frequency that Ash was conscious of a fleeting twinge of jealousy, and a regret for the old days when he himself possessed the major share of Wally's admiration—together with the tallest pedestal in his private pantheon. But those days were gone, and Wally had acquired other gods and made other friends; which was not surprising in someone so eminently likeable.

He was talking now with enormous enthusiasm of the Deputy Commissioner of Peshawar—that same Major Cavagnari who had instigated and planned the operation against the Utman Khel tribesmen in which Zarin had been wounded, and a later one against Sharkot where Wally had experienced his first taste of active service. It was immediately clear that the personality and talents of this oddly named man had made a deep impression on the impressionable Wally.

"Faith, it's the jewel of a fellow he is, Ash. A real out-and-outer. His father was a French count who was an aide-de-camp or a military attaché or something of the sort to one of Bonaparte's brothers, and he speaks Pushtu like a native and knows more about the tribes than anyone else on the Frontier. And would you believe it, he's actually a kinsman of mine? We're both related to the Lawrences, because Lord John's wife is my mother's sister-in-law, and mother was a Blacker, and one of the Blackers had a daughter who married a Frenchman—an officer in the Cuirassiers—and their daughter married Major Cavagnari's father. Which makes us vaguely related."

" 'Vaguely' sounds right," murmured Ash satirically. "Holy Saint Patrick, what a mixture!"

"Be damned to you for a benighted Sassenach," retorted Wally, unruffled; and went on to describe the many excellences of his latest hero while Ash lay back and listened, watching the speaker's face and thanking heaven that Wally at least had not changed—except in one respect: the tale of his doings during the past two years did not include the mention of a single girl's name.

The Guides and matters military obviously filled his thoughts to the exclusion of all else, and the gay, careless and largely one-sided love affairs of the 'Pindi days that had inspired so much bad verse were apparently a thing of the past. If Wally wrote poems now, thought Ash, they would not be addressed to some damsel's blue eyes, but would probably be concerned with such abstract subjects as Patriotism or Immortality. And the next time he fell in love it would be for ever: he would marry the girl and settle down and raise a family.

But that would not be for a long while yet. Because it was plain that at present he was in love with the Guides and with the romance of Empire—the warring tribesmen and the wild Khyber hills, the swift night marches and the sudden dawn attack on some fortified stronghold across the Border, and the discipline and comradeship of life in a Corps that had never known what it was like to live on a peace-time footing, but had always been ready to march at a moment's notice should trouble flare up on that perennially inflammable Frontier.

Wally did not ask what Ash had been doing with himself during his term of attachment to Roper's Horse; the routine activities of a regiment stationed in some peaceful spot such as Ahmadabad being of little interest to either of them; and as Ash had written reasonably often (and most of his letters had contained some reference to the dullness of army life in the peaceful peninsula) Wally concentrated on the more enlivening topic of the Frontier in general and the Guides in particular. Only when that subject had been covered fairly exhaustively did he demand to know why Ash was masquerading in this outfit, and what had possessed him to waste a valuable leave sweating up the Indus on a *dundhi* instead of going on trek as they had planned, or even coming fishing in the Kangan Valley?

"I asked Gul Baz what you'd been up to," said Wally, "but all he would say was that 'doubtless the Sahib had good reasons for his actions and would explain them to me himself.' Well, it's waiting for an explanation I am, ye spalpeen, and if you're wishful to be forgiven, it had better be a good one."

"It's a long story," Ash warned him.

"We've got all day," returned Wally comfortably, and, rolling his coat into a ball to make a pillow, he lay down in the shade and prepared to listen. "Carry on, Sergeant-Major. You have our ear."

The story as told to Wally had taken rather longer to tell than the one Zarin had heard on the previous day, for Zarin had known Kairi-Bai and so did not need to be told anything of her background or people, or her childish attachment to the boy, Ashok. But when Ash had first told Wally of his youth in Gulkote he had not thought to mention Kairi-Bai, and later he had purposely concealed the fact that the State of Karidkote, whose princesses he had been charged with escorting to Bhithor, was the same place under a different name. So there was more that had to be told now; and after the first two minutes Wally was no longer lying lazily on his back, but sitting bolt upright, wide-eyed and open-mouthed.

Zarin had listened to that tale without any noticeable change of expression, but it was not so with Wally; he had never been adept at concealing his emotions, and now his handsome, mobile face betrayed his thoughts as clearly as though they had been written there in capital letters; and reading them Ash realized that he had been wrong in thinking that Wally had not changed.

The old Wally would have been enthralled by it and his sympathies would all have been with Ash and the sad little Princess of Gulkote who, like the heroine of a fairy-tale, had suffered much at the hands of a wicked stepmother and a jealous half-sister. But the present Wally had acquired new loyalties and put away many childish things. He had also, as Ash had surmised, fallen in love with the Guides.

The Guides were now his own Corps and an integral part of him, and he genuinely believed that the members of his own squadron were the pick of the Indian Army, and men such as Wigram Battye and Risaldar-Major Prem Singh the salt of the earth. He had been in action with them: learned in their company the terror and the fierce delight of battle, and seen men die—not just any men, the anonymous ones mentioned in brief official reports ("Our casualties were two dead and five wounded"), but men he had known and cracked jokes with, and whose names and faces and problems were familiar to him.

He would no more dream of riding rough-shod over their customs and convictions, or doing anything that might bring the Regiment in which he and they had the honour to serve into disrepute, than he would consider pilfering from the mess funds or cheating at cards. Nor, in the first flush of his love-affair with the Guides and the Frontier, could he conceive of any worse fate than to be expelled from both. Yet if Ash had really married a Hindu widow, this was exactly what he was heading for—with whip and spur.

"Well?" asked Ash when he had finished and Wally had still not spoken. "Aren't you even going to wish me happy?"

Wally flushed like a girl and said quickly: "Of course I do. It's only . . ." He did not seem to know how to end the sentence, and abandoned it.

"That I have taken your breath away?" said Ash with an edge on his voice.

"Well, what did you expect?" asked Wally defensively. "You must admit it's a bit of a facer. After all, I had no idea that those girls you were taking to Bhithor had anything to do with Gulkote, because you never said a word about that, and so I never imagined . . . Well, how could I? Of course I hope you'll be happy; you know that. But . . . but you're still well short of thirty and you know very well that you're not supposed to marry before then without the consent of the Commandant, and—"

"But I have married," said Ash gently. "I *am* married, Wally. No one can alter that now. But you needn't worry; I'm not giving up the Guides. Did you really think I would?"

"But once they know—" began Wally.

"They won't know," said Ash, and explained why.

"Thank God for that!" sighed Wally devoutly when he had finished. "How dare you frighten the daylights out of me?"

"You're as bad as Zarin. He doesn't give himself away like you, but I could see that even though he knew

881

Juli when she was a little girl, the fact that I had married her shocked him, because she is a Hindu. But I must admit I thought you'd be less prejudiced."

"What, *me*? An Irishman?" Wally gave a short and mirthless laugh. "Why, a cousin of mine once wanted to marry a fellow who happened to be a Catholic, and you've no idea the row that blew up over that. The Protestants all went into hysterics about Anti-Christ and the Scarlet Woman of Rome, while the other lot called Mary a heretic and told Michael that if he married her he'd be excommunicated and everlastingly damned, because she wasn't prepared to turn papist herself and wouldn't sign an undertaking that any children she bore should be brought up as Catholics. Yet these were all adult and presumably intelligent people, and every one of them regarded themselves as Christians. Don't talk to me of prejudice! We're all riddled with it, whatever the colour of our skins; and if you haven't found that out yet, faith, I'm thinking you must have been born with blinkers."

"No, just without that particular form of prejudice," said Ash thoughtfully. "And it's too late for me to acquire it now."

Wally laughed and observed that Ash did not know how lucky he was; and after an appreciable pause, said a little uncertainly and with an unaccustomed hint of diffidence in his voice: "Could you . . . can you tell me about her? What is she like?—I don't mean what does she look like, I mean what is it you see in her?"

"Integrity. And tolerance—*bardat*, which Koda Dad once told me was a 'rare flower.' Juli doesn't make harsh judgements, she tries to understand, and make allowances."

"What else? There must be something else."

"Of course—though I should have thought that by itself would have been enough for most people. She is . . ." Ash hesitated, searching for words that would describe what Anjuli meant to him, and then said slowly: "She is the other half of me. Without her, I am not complete. I don't know why this should be, I only know it is so; and that there is nothing I can't tell her, or talk to her about. She can ride like a Valkyrie and she has all the courage in the world, yet at the same time she is like—like a quiet and beautiful room where one can take refuge from noise and storms and ugliness, and sit back and feel peaceful

882

and happy and completely content: a room that will always be there and always the same . . . Does that sound very dull to you? It doesn't to me. But then I don't want constant change and variety and stimulation in a wife; I can get plenty of that in everyday life and see it happening all around me. I want love and companionship, and I've found that in Juli. She is loving and loyal and courageous. And she is my peace and rest. Does that tell you what you want to know?"

"Yes," said Wally, and smiled at him. "I'd like to meet her."

"So you shall. This evening, I hope."

Wally had been sitting with his legs drawn up and his hands clasped about them, and now he dropped his chin on his knees, and staring ahead of him at the sun-glare on the white dust of the road and the back-drop of the foothills that lay shimmering in the heat, said contentedly: "You don't know how much I've been looking forward to you coming back to us. And so have a lot of others; the men still talk about you, and they are always asking for news of you and when you'll be coming back. They have a name for you—they call you 'Pelham-Dulkhan'—did you know that? and when we are out on an exercise or on manoeuvres, they tell tales about your doings in Afghanistan round the camp fires at night. I've heard them at it . . . and now you really are coming back at last—I can't believe it . . . !" He drew a long, slow breath and let it out as slowly.

"Is it kissing the Blarney Stone you've been?" jeered Ash, grinning at him. "Stop spreading on the butter and talk sense for a change. Tell me about this Afghan business."

Wally returned the grin, and putting personal matters aside, talked instead, and with considerable knowledge and acumen, of the problem posed by Afghanistan—a subject which at that time was much on the minds of men who served in the Peshawar Field Force.

Ash had been out of touch with Frontier matters for many months, and very little of this had so far penetrated to Gujerat, where men had less reason to trouble themselves over the doings of the Amir of a wild and inaccessible country far and far to the north, beyond the Khyber hills and the mountains of the Safed Koh. But now he was reminded again of what Koda Dad had said to him at their last meeting—and Zarin only yesterday—and as he listened to Wally, he felt as though he had been living in a different world . . .

During the past few years the Amir of Afghanistan, Shere Ali, had found himself in the unenviable position of the "corn between the upper and the lower millstones" —the simile was his own; the northern and uppermost one being Russia and the lower Great Britain, both of whom had designs on his country.

The latter had already annexed the Punjab and the Border-land beyond the Indus, while the former had swallowed the ancient principalities of Tashkent, Bokara, Kohkund and Kiva. Now Russian armies were massing on the northern frontiers of Afghanistan, and a new Viceroy, Lord Lytton, who combined obstinacy and a lofty ignorance of Afghanistan with a determination to extend the bounds of Empire to the greater glory of his country (and possibly of himself?) had been instructed by Her Majesty's Government to lose no time in sending an Envoy to Afghanistan charged with the task of overcoming the Amir's "apparent reluctance" to the establishment of British Agencies within his dominions.

That the Amir might not wish to establish anything of the sort, or receive any foreign envoy, apparently did not occur to anyone; or if it did, was dismissed as unimportant. Lord Lytton was to impress upon the Amir that "Her Majesty's Government must have for their own agents undisputed access to its (Afghanistan's) frontier positions," together with "adequate means of confidentially conferring with the Amir upon all matters as to which the proposed declaration would recognize a community of interests." They must also be entitled to "expect becoming attention to their friendly councils," while the Amir himself "must be made to understand that subject to all allowances for the condition of the country and the character of its population, territories ultimately dependent upon British Power for their defence must not be closed to those of the Queen's officers, or subjects, who may be duly authorized to enter them by the British Government."

In return for accepting these humiliating terms, Shere Ali would be given advice from British officers as to how he could improve his military resources, together with the promise of British aid against any unprovoked attack by a foreign power, and (if the Viceroy* thought fit) a subsidy.

Lord Lytton was wholly convinced that only by bringing Afghanistan under British influence, and thereby turning that turbulent country into a buffer-state, could the advance of Russia be checked and the safety of India assured. And when the Amir proved reluctant to accept a British Mission in his capital of Kabul, the Viceroy warned him that if he refused he would be alienating a friendly power who could pour an army into his country "before a single Russian soldier could reach Kabul"—a threat that merely reinforced Shere Ali's suspicions that the British intended to take over his country and extend their borders to the far side of the Hindu Kush.

The Russians too were pressing the Amir to accept a mission of their own, and both powers offered to sign a treaty with him which included a promise to come to his assistance if the other should attack him. But Shere Ali complained, with some truth, that if he were to ally himself with either power, his people would certainly object to foreign soldiers marching into their country, whatever the pretext, as they had never at any time been kindly disposed towards interlopers.

He could have added, with even more truth, that they were a fanatically independent people, much addicted to intrigue, treachery and murder, and that among their other national traits was an intolerance of rulers (or, if it came to that, of any form of authority whatsoever, other than their own desires). The Viceroy's insistence therefore put the Amir in a very awkward position, and he took the only course he could think of. He temporized, hoping that if he could only spin out the negotiations for long enough, something might turn up to save him from the indignity of being forced to accept and protect a permanent British Mission in Kabul, which could not fail to earn him the contempt of his proud and turbulent subjects.

But the more Shere Ali prevaricated, the more determined the Viceroy became to force a British Mission upon him. Lord Lytton saw Afghanistan as an uncivilized backwater inhabited by savages, and that their ruler

---

*Before India was taken over from the East India Company by the Crown, the title was Governor-General. The last of these and the second Viceroy was Sir John Lawrence.

should have the impertinence to object to a powerful nation such as Great Britain establishing a Mission in his barbarous country was not only insulting, but laughable.

Shere Ali's Prime Minister, Nur Mohammed, travelled to Peshawar to put his master's case, and though sick and ageing and bitterly resentful of the cruel pressures that were being put upon his Amir, no man could have done more. But all to no avail. The new Viceroy had not hesitated to wriggle out of any promises and obligations entered into during negotiations with his predecessor, while at the same time accusing the Amir of failing to keep to the letter of his own undertakings. And when Nur Mohammed would not give way, the Viceroy's spokesman, Sir Neville Chamberlain, turned on him in a rage, and the Amir's insulted Prime Minister and long-time friend left the Conference Chamber in despair, knowing that his arguments and pleadings had failed and there was nothing left to keep alive for.

The British negotiators had chosen to believe that his illness was merely another excuse to gain time. But Nur had been a dying man when he arrived in Peshawar; and when he died there the rumour spread throughout Afghanistan that the *feringhis* had poisoned him. The Amir sent word to say that he was sending a new Envoy to replace him, but the Viceroy ordered that the negotiations be discontinued for lack of any common ground of agreement, and the new Envoy was sent back, while Lord Lytton turned his attention to subverting the Border tribes with a view to bringing about the collapse of Shere Ali by less open means.

Some of this Ash already knew, for the Peshawar Conference had been in session before he had left for Gujerat, and the issues that had been discussed there had been known and hotly debated in every British mess, Club and bungalow throughout the northern Punjab and the Frontier provinces, in addition to the streets and shops of cities, towns and villages—the British taking the view that the Amir was a typically treacherous Afghan, who was intriguing with the Russians and planning to sign a treaty of alliance with the Tsar that would permit free passage through the Khyber Pass to his armies, while Indian opinion held that the British Raj, in typically treacherous fashion, was plotting to overthrow the Amir and add Afghanistan to the Empire.

But once Ash had left the Punjab behind him, he had found that men talked less of the "Russian menace" than of their own affairs; while from the time he reached Bombay and boarded the slow train that chugged and puffed along the palm-fringed coast towards Surat and Baroda, he had hardly ever heard it mentioned, let alone seriously discussed—despite the fact that the two leading English-language newspapers wrote an occasional leader on the subject, criticizing the Government for its failure to take action, or attacking "alarmists" who talked of war.

Insulated by distance and the slower pace of life in Gujerat, Ash had soon lost interest in the political wrangling between the High Gods in Simla and the unhappy ruler of the Land of Cain, and it had come as something of a shock to him to discover from Zarin that here in the north men took the matter seriously, and spoke openly of a second Afghan war:

"But I don't suppose it will come to that," said Wally, not without a tinge of regret. "Once the Amir and his advisers realize that the Raj is not prepared to take 'No' for an answer, they'll give in gracefully and let us send a Mission to Kabul, and that'll be the end of it. Pity, really—No, I don't mean that of course. But it would have been a terrific experience, fighting one's way through those passes. I'd like to be in a real battle."

"You will be," said Ash dryly. "Even if there isn't an all-out war, the tribes are bound to start some sort of trouble before long, because if there's one thing they really enjoy, it's taking a slap at the Raj. It's their favourite sport—like bull-fighting is to the Spaniards. We being the bull. A peaceful existence bores them, and if there happens to be a shortage of blood-feuds, or some fiery mullah starts calling for a *Jehad* (holy war), they sharpen up their tulwars and shoulder their muskets, and *Olé!*—they're off again."

Wally laughed, and then his face sobered again and he said thoughtfully: "Wigram says that if the Amir does agree to let a British Mission go to Kabul they'll take an escort with them, and he thinks that as Cavagnari is almost certain to be a member of it, the chances are that he'll see to it that the escort is drawn from the Guides. I wonder who they'll send? Faith, what wouldn't I be giving to be one of them. Just think of it—Kabul! Wouldn't you give anything to go there?"

"No," Ash's tone was still dry. "Once was enough."

"Once . . . ? Oh, of course, you've been there before. What didn't you like about it?"

"A lot of things. It's attractive enough in its way; especially in the spring when the almond trees are in bloom and the mountains all around still white with snow. But the streets and bazaars are dirty and the houses tumble-down and shoddy, and it wasn't called the 'Land of Cain' for nothing! You get the feeling that savagery is near the surface, and could break through at any moment like lava from a dormant volcano and that the line drawn between good-will and bloody violence is thinner there than anywhere else in the world. Not that Kabul belongs to the modern world any more than Bhithor does—in fact they have a lot in common: they both live in the past and are hostile to change and to strangers, while the majority of their citizens not only look like cut-throats, but can behave as such if they happen to take a dislike to you."

Ash added that in his opinion, it was perhaps not so strange that a city reputedly founded by the world's first murderer should have a reputation for treachery and violence; or that its rulers should have been faithful to the tradition of Cain, and indulged in murder and fratricide. The past history of the Amirs being one long tale of bloodshed: fathers killing their sons, sons plotting against their fathers and each other, and uncles disposing of their nephews. "It's a grisly tale, and if it's true that ghosts are the unquiet spirits of people who died terrible deaths—and that there are such things as ghosts—then Kabul must be full of them. It's a haunted place, and I hope I never see it again."

"Well, you will if there's war," observed Wally, "because the Guides will be in it so they will."

"True—*if* there is a war. But speaking for myself . . ." the sentence ended in a yawn, and Ash settled himself back in a crotch among the tree roots and closed his eyes against the glaring day, and presently, feeling relaxed and peaceful because he and Wally were together again, he fell asleep.

Wally sat watching him for a long time, seeing the changes that he had missed to begin with, and other things that he had never bothered to notice before: the vulnerability of that thin, reckless face, the sensitive mouth that accorded so ill with the firm obstinate chin, and the purposeful line of the black eyebrows that were at odds with a brow and temples that would have better befitted a poet or a dreamer than a soldier. It was a face at war with itself, beautifully modelled and yet somehow lacking cohesion. And it seemed to Wally that, in spite of the deep unyouthful lines that scored it and the faint scar of that old wound, the sleeper, in some ways, had not really grown up. He still saw things as wrong or right, good or bad, and fair or unfair—as children did, before they learn better. He still thought that he could do something to alter them . . .

All at once Wally felt deeply sorry for his friend, who thought that because a thing was "unfair" it was wrong and ought to be changed, and who, being unable to look at any problem either from a strictly European or a wholly Asiatic standpoint, was deprived of the comforting armour of national prejudice and left with no defence against the regional bigotries of East and West.

Ash, like his father Hilary, was a civilized and liberal-minded man with an interested and inquiring mind. But unlike Hilary, he had never grasped that the average mind is neither liberal or inquiring, but is in the main intolerant of any attitudes except its own firmly entrenched ones. He had his own gods, but they were neither Christian nor pagan. And he was not and never had been the dashing, romantic and wholly admirable hero of Wally's early imaginings, but was as fallible as the next man—and because of his unorthodox beginnings, possibly more prone to error than most. But he was still Ash, and no one, not even Wigram, could ever take his place in Wally's affections. A hoopoe flew down and began to probe for insects in the hard-packed earth, and Wally watched it idly for a moment or two before following Ash's example and drifting off into sleep.

By the time they awoke the sun was well down and the countryside around them full of shadows. Ash fetched water from the stream, and with this and the food that Gul Baz had left them they made a frugal meal, deciding as they ate that Wally should spend the night at Attock dâk-bungalow after visiting Fatima Begum's house to meet Anjuli, and return to Mardan in the morning.

They had arrived at the house in the dusty amethyst twilight, where the gatekeeper received them incuriously and in answer to Ash's question said no, Koda Dad Khan

889

had not come—doubtless his son, the Risaldar-Sahib, had been able to prevent his father from setting out. He took charge of the horses while Ash sent a message to the Begum, asking her permission to allow his friend, Hamilton-Sahib, to enter her house and meet his wife.

Had Anjuli been a Muslim the suggestion might well have drawn a shocked refusal from the Begum, who by now regarded herself as standing *in loco parentis* to the girl. But as Anjuli was neither a Muslim nor a maiden, and her so-called husband not only a Christian but a foreigner, the proper rules could not be expected to apply, and if Pelham-Sahib was prepared to let his men friends hob-nob with his bride, it was no concern of the Begum's. She therefore sent a servant to conduct the two men to Anjuli's room and to tell Ash that if they desired to eat together, the evening meal would be served in a few minutes' time.

The lamps had not yet been lit, but the *kus-kus* tatties had been rolled up and the high, white-washed room was palely luminous with the last of the daylight and the first glimmer of a full moon that was rising above the low, dun-coloured hills beyond Attock.

Anjuli had been standing by an open window, looking down onto the garden where birds were flocking home to roost among the fruit trees while bats flitted out from a score of dark hidden crannies to greet the night. She had not heard the footsteps on the stairs, for the sound had been lost in the chatter of quarrelling birds, and only when the door opened did she turn.

Seeing Ash, but not the man who stood in the shadows behind him, she ran to him and threw her arms around his neck. And that was how Wally had first seen her. A tall, slender girl running towards him with outstretched arms, and with such a blaze of love in her face that for a moment it seemed to him that a light shone on it. She had taken his breath away—and his heart with it.

Afterwards, sitting alone in the moonlight on the verandah of the dâk-bungalow, he found that he had no clear recollection of what she looked like. Only that she was the most beautiful creature he had ever seen—a princess out of a fairy-tale, fashioned from ivory and gold and jet. But then he had never before seen a well-born Indian woman, and knew nothing of the wealth of grace and loveliness that is hidden away behind the purdah screens and jealously guarded from the gaze of all strangers.

Few foreigners were privileged to see or know these women; and those few tended to be the wives of senior British officials, whose views on the charms of "native women" were apt to be lukewarm, or at best, tinged with condescension. So that when Ash had tried to describe his wife, Wally had made due allowance for a man in love and supposed, indulgently, that the bride might be tolerably good looking—as were one or two of the more expensive courtesans of Ash's acquaintance, whom Wally had met in those early, carefree days in Rawalpindi: brown-skinned women who painted their eyes with *kohl*, chewed *pan* and stained the palms of their slender hands with henna; and whose supple, small-boned bodies smelled of musk and sandalwood and exuded an almost visible aura of sexuality.

Nothing that he had so far seen of India had prepared him for the sight of Anjuli. He had expected a little, dark-complexioned woman, not a long-limbed goddess —Venus Aphrodite—whose skin was paler than ripe wheat, and whose beautiful black-lashed eyes were the colour of peat-water on the moors of Kerry.

Strangely, she did not suggest the East to him, but rather the North, and gazing at her, he had been reminded of snow and pine trees and the cool fresh wind that blows in the high mountains . . . and of a line in a new book of poems recently sent to him by a doting Aunt— *"And dark and true and tender is the North . . ."* Dark and true and tender;—yes, that was Anjuli. All the heroines of fiction had come true in her—she was Eve, she was Juliet, she was Helen . . . ! *"She walks in beauty like the night, of cloudless climes and starry skies. And all that's best of dark and light meet in her aspect and her eyes,"* declaimed Wally, drunk with unreasoning happiness.

He no longer blamed Ash for marrying in haste, for he could imagine himself doing exactly the same thing if he had had the luck to be in Ash's place. There could not be many women in the world like Anjuli, and having found one it would have been madness to lose her for the sake of a career. And yet . . . Wally sighed, and some of the euphoria of the last few hours left him. No, he would probably not have done it—not if he had been given enough time to realize what it might mean in terms of the future, because the Guides had come to count so much to him. Besides, he had cherished dreams of military glory for as long as he could remember; it was something he had grown up with and by now it was too much a part of him to be rooted out and replaced by love for a woman —even such a one as he had seen that night and lost his heart to.

All at once he was filled with gratitude towards Ash and Anjuli: and to God, Who had been good enough to allow him to meet the one woman in the world, and yet put her beyond his reach; so that by losing his heart to her he was saved for ever (or at least, for a long time to come) from falling in love with some lesser star and getting married and domesticated and losing his taste for adventure and with it, inevitably, some part of his enthusiasm for his profession and devotion to the men of his own Regiment.

Now that Ash was about to rejoin the Guides, life would be perfect, and the only cloud in Wally's sky was the fact that there were still three weeks to run before Ash returned to duty. The thought of having to wait another twenty-one days after waiting so long was suddenly unendurable—yet it would have to be endured; and at least there was work and Wigram (who was now Adjutant and a Captain) to help him through it and make the time pass quickly. He had asked Ash if he could tell Wigram about Anjuli, and been pleased though not surprised when Ash had agreed. Everyone liked Wigram, and there was no denying that it would be a relief to be able to tell him about Ash's adventures and his romantic, secret marriage, particularly now that he himself had met the bride and so felt qualified to speak in the couple's defence and persuade Wigram to take a lenient view of the whole affair . . .

Wally rose from the verandah chair, and having searched for something to throw at a pi-dog that sat yelping monotonously by the compound gate, discharged a well-aimed flower-pot and went in to bed humming "Fight the good fight with all thy might." Which, in the circumstances, was a healthy sign, for it showed that he was returning to normal after the stresses and strains of that emotional day.

The sun was still well below the horizon when Wally crossed the Indus and took the Peshawar road on the following morning, leaving his bearer Pir Baksh to follow in a tonga with the luggage, and an hour later he breakfasted at the Nowshera dâk-bungalow while his horse rested, before crossing the Kabul River and pressing on towards Risalpur. Mardan was an oasis of shade in a parched land. The fort and the parade-ground, the lines and the familiar back-drop of the Yusafzai hills quivered and swayed in the dancing heat, and far out on the plain towards Jamalgarhi an occasional dust-devil arose to whirl like a spinning-top and die again. But in the cantonment not a leaf stirred, and the dust of the hot weather lay like hoar frost on every stick and stone and blade of grass, reducing greens and browns to a single tint—the colour that Sir Henry Lawrence had chosen for the uniforms of his newly raised Corps of Guides in the days before the Great Mutiny, and that had come to be known as *khaki*.

Wally had gone straight to Wigram's quarters, but Wigram was not there; he had been attending some minor conference in Peshawar, and was not expected back until after sundown. He had, however, returned in time to dine in mess, and later walked back with Wally to the latter's rooms, where he had remained until long after midnight, listening to the saga of Ash and Anjuli-Bai.

The tale had obviously interested him deeply, though the marriage ceremony on board the *Morala* had drawn an angry exclamation and a black frown, and after that he had listened to the rest tight-lipped and with a furrowed brow. But he had made no comments, and at the end of it remarked thoughtfully that he remembered the Commandant saying, at the time when the question of a Court Martial was being discussed following the return of the carbines, that Ashton Pelham-Martyn was not only an insubordinate young hot-head, but an adult enfant-terrible whose penchant for acting on the spur of the moment made him capable of doing any damned silly thing without pausing to think what it could lead to in the long run; yet it had to be remembered that these were the very defects that often proved invaluable in time of war, particularly when accompanied, as in Ashton's case, with considerable courage.

"I think he was right," said Wigram slowly. "And if there should be a war, which I pray God there will not be, we may need those defects—and the courage that goes with them."

He lay back in his chair and was silent for a long time, chewing on the butt of a cheroot that had gone out long ago, and staring abstractedly at the ceiling; and when he spoke again it was to ask a question: "Do I understand that Ashton intends to spend the remainder of his leave at Attock?"

"Yes," confirmed Wally. "He and his wife have been invited to stay with Risaldar Zarin Khan's aunt—she owns that big house in a walled garden that stands back from the 'Pindi road on the far side of the town."

"*Hmm.* I should like to go over one day and meet the bride. It would—" his gaze fell on the clock and he came hurriedly to his feet: "Good gracious, is that the right time? I'd no idea it was so late. High time I got my beauty sleep. Good-night, Wally."

He left to walk back to his own quarters, but not, as it happened, to sleep. Instead, having exchanged his mess dress for the loose cotton trousers that were the customary night-wear at that time of year, he came out onto the verandah, and subsiding into a long-sleeve chair, gave himself up to thought.

50

Captain Battye gazed out unseeingly at the hot moonlight and the black shadows, and thought of his youngest brother, Fred . . . of Fred and Wally and Ashton Pelham-Martyn, Hammond and Hughes and Campbell, Colonel Jenkins the Commandant, Risaldars Prem Singh and Mahmud Khan, Wordi-Major Duni Chand and Sowar Dowlat Ram and a hundred others . . . officers, non-commissioned officers and men of the Guides; their faces passing before him as though on review. If there should be another Afghan war, how many of them would be alive by the time it was over?

He knew that even now, after all these years, the bleached bones of General Elphinstone's demoralized army still littered the defiles where they had been trapped during the retreat from Kabul, and slaughtered like sheep by the vengeful tribesmen. This time it might be Fred's bones that were left there; or Wally's skull that would go trundling before the blast when the wind howled through those haunted passes. Fred and Wally, the forgotten debris of another useless, pointless Afghan war . . .

The first had been fought well before either of those two were born, and though the Afghans had not forgotten it, the British seldom mentioned it—those who remembered it preferring to pretend they did not; which was hardly surprising, as it was an unedifying tale.

In the early years of the century, when "John Company" ruled half India, a mediocre youth named Shah Shuja had fallen heir to the throne of Afghanistan. Having lost it after a reign that was brief even by the violent standards of that country, he fled to India where he was granted asylum by the Government and settled down to a peaceful existence as a private citizen, while following his departure, his erstwhile subjects indulged in a period of riot and anarchy that came to an abrupt end when a strong and able man, one Dost Mohammed of the Barakzi clan, brought order out of chaos and eventually made himself Amir.

Unfortunately, the Government of India distrusted men of ability. They suspected that the Dost would be difficult to manipulate and might even, if they were not careful, decide to ally himself with Russia; and discussing this possibility in the rarefied atmosphere of Simla, the Governor-General, Lord Auckland, and his favoured advisers came to the conclusion that it might be a good idea to get rid of the Dost (who had done them no harm and his country much good) and replace him with the now elderly ex-Amir Shah Shuja; their argument being that this aged nonentity, if bound to his British champions by ties of gratitude and self-interest, could not fail to become a biddable tool who would willingly sign any treaty they cared to dictate.

But though the war that Lord Auckland forced upon Afghanistan had ended in total disaster for the British, the majority of those who had helped to launch it did very well for themselves, since to mark the initial victory, medals, titles and honours had been showered upon them —none of which could be taken away. But the dead who rotted in the passes received no decorations: and within two years Dost Mohammed Khan was once again Amir of Afghanistan.

The *waste,* thought Wigram, the injustice and stupidity and the cruel, senseless waste. And all to no purpose, because now once again, after a lapse of almost forty years, it seemed that a handful of men in Simla were planning to force another Amir—the youngest son of that same Dost Mohammed—to accept a permanent British Mission in Kabul. Worse still, there had actually been a time when the Amir would have been only too willing to accommodate them. Five years ago, dismayed by threats of rebellion and the growing power of Russia, Shere Ali had made overtures to the then Viceroy, Lord Northbrook, and asked for an assurance of protection against any aggressor; but his request had been refused. Embittered by this rejection, he had decided to turn instead to Russia (who had shown a flattering eagerness to discuss treaties of friendship and alliance with him); yet now these same *Angrezis,* who had rebuffed him when he asked for help, were actually demanding, as a right, that he should welcome a British Envoy to his capital and cease "intriguing" with the Tsar.

"If I were in his shoes, I'd see 'em damned first," thought Wigram, and realized that there was no profit in thinking like that. This was how wars came about.

All those years ago Lord Auckland and his friends had sent thousands of people to their deaths on the mere supposition that Shere Ali's father might consider an alliance with Russia. Was Lord Lytton now about to do the same, and with no more proof than before, basing his decisions on suspicion, gossip and rumour, and the garbled accounts of paid spies?

In the course of the past few years Wigram had seen a good deal of Wally's kinsman the Deputy Commissioner of Peshawar, Major Louis Cavagnari; and until recently his opinion of the D.C. had been almost as high as Wally's. Pierre Louis Napoleon Cavagnari was a curious person to be found occupying such a position, for as Wally had related, his father had been a French count who had served under the great Napoleon, become Military Secretary to Jérôme Bonaparte, King of Westphalia, and married an Irish lady, Elizabeth, daughter of Dean Stewart Blacker of Carrickblacker (though despite his Gallic names the Deputy Commissioner, having been brought up in Ireland, had always regarded himself as British, and preferred his friends to call him "Louis" because it seemed to him the least foreign of his three given names).

For twenty years he had served with distinction in India's Border lands, seeing service in no less than seven Frontier campaigns, and acquiring an enviable reputation for being able to manage the turbulent tribesmen, whose various dialects he spoke with idiomatic fluency. And though as far as appearance went, the tall, bearded figure might easily have been taken for a professor rather than a man of action, those who knew him declared him to be courageous to a fault. No one had ever accused him of lack of spirit, and he combined a dynamic personality with many excellent qualities; though in common with the majority of his fellow men, these last were offset by some that were less admirable: in his case egotism and personal ambition, a quick temper and a fatal tendency to see things as he wished them to be rather than as they actually were.

Wigram Battye had only recently become aware of these failings. But then he had also had the advantage of seeing Cavagnari in action. The success of the affair at Sipri with its swift night march and surprise attack had been entirely due to the D.C.'s imaginative planning and attention to detail, and that, with several other similar incidents, had given Wigram the greatest possible respect for the man's qualities. Nevertheless, of late he had come to feel less admiring and more critical; and, it must be owned, more than a little apprehensive, for the Deputy Commissioner was a professed supporter of the "Forward Policy," whose advocates considered that the only way to protect the Indian Empire from the "Russian menace" was to turn Afghanistan into a British protectorate and plant the Union Jack on the far side of the Hindu Kush.

As this was also the Viceroy's view (and Lord Lytton was known to have a great regard for Major Cavagnari and to take his advice on Frontier matters in preference to that of older and more cautious men), it was not surprising that Wigram Battye should feel uneasy at hearing the D.C. declare—as he had recently heard him do at a dinner party in Peshawar—"If Russia gets a foothold in Afghanistan she will take over that country as she has taken over almost all the old, proud kingdoms of Central

Asia; and once she has done that the road through the Khyber will be open and there will be nothing to prevent her marching her armies down to attack and take Peshawar and the Punjab, as Barbur the Tiger did three hundred years ago. I have no quarrel with the Afghan people: my quarrel is solely with their Amir, who, by intriguing with the Tsar, is playing with a fire that unless we can prevent it will destroy his own country, and from there burn its way southward until it has consumed all India . . ."

Cavagnari's use of the first person singular was characteristic of the man and in a different context Wigram would probably have thought nothing of it: but used in this one it dismayed him. His own interest in the dispute between the Government of India and the Amir was entirely non-political, his concern being mainly with the military consequences of a possible war with Afghanistan and the part that his own Corps would be called upon to play in it. He was, after all, a professional soldier. But he also possessed a conscience, and his fear was that the Forward Policy clique intended to embroil the Raj in a second Afghan war without any real justification for doing so—and without fully realizing the enormous difficulties that would face an invading army.

Of the two, it was the former that worried him most, for having always held the view that the Afghan war of '39 had been morally indefensible as well as totally unnecessary, it horrified him to discover that once again History seemed about to repeat itself, and in his opinion it was the plain duty of all honourable men to try to prevent it doing so; the crying need, as Wigram saw it, being for accurate and unedited information as to the true intentions of the Amir Shere Ali and his people.

If it could be proved that Shere Ali was intriguing with the Tsar and about to sign a treaty that would grant Russia military posts and a firm footing in his country, then the Forward Policy men were right and the sooner Britain stepped in to prevent it the better—the prospect of a Russian-controlled Afghanistan with Russian armies stationed along the north-west frontiers of India being unthinkable. But then *was* it true? Wigram had an uneasy feeling that men like Cavagnari and Lord Lytton and other Forward Policy fire-eaters were being deluded by information supplied by Afghan spies who, knowing full well what these particular Sahibs hoped to hear, repeated only what would please, and suppressed anything else—a quirk probably due to a respect for good manners and a desire to please, rather than any deliberate intent to mislead.

Cavagnari of all people would know this, and—or so Wigram hoped—make allowances for it. But would the Viceroy and his councillors realize that the reports of such spies, faithfully forwarded to Simla by the Deputy Commissioner of Peshawar, might be one-sided and fail to give the full picture? that spies, after all, were paid, and might consider themselves to be earning their pay by telling only such news as they had reason to believe would be welcome? It was this thought that had been preying on Wigram's mind of late, and Wally's talk of Ashton had given him an idea . . .

Ashton had spent almost two years in Afghanistan and probably made a number of friends there, certainly in the village of his adoptive father Koda Dad Khan, while it was well known in Mardan that Risaldar Zarin Khan was by no means the only Pathan in the Guides who regarded him almost as a blood-brother. Now supposing Ashton could persuade his friends to organize some form of intelligence service aimed at collecting reliable information which they would pass on to him, and which he in turn could pass on to the Commandant or to Wigram himself, to give to Cavagnari—who whatever his personal views could be counted upon to report it to Simla. Ashton's friends could surely be counted on to tell "Pelham-Dulkhan" the truth (because they knew that he did not think as the "Sahib-log" thought) and Ashton himself trusted to repeat what they told him verbatim, without editing it to fit any theories of his own or anyone else's. It was at least an idea, and it might work: and at this juncture, thought Wigram, *anything* was worth trying.

Impelled by a driving sense of urgency and of time running out, he had tried it at the first opportunity, riding over to Attock with Wally at the weekend, and for reasons of secrecy arriving after dark and putting up at the dâk-bungalow with a story that they intended to do some shooting on the following day. Though as things turned out, his idea had produced a result that Wigram had certainly not expected.

Wally's syce had been sent off to the Begum's house with a note for Ash, and the reply had been handed to them as they sat at supper. An hour later the two had left the dâk-bungalow to walk in the hot starlight along the 'Pindi road, and presently, turning off it down a dusty side path, they came to a gate in a high wall where they found an Afridi waiting for them with a lantern; and Wigram —who had not previously seen Ash dressed in this fashion—did not immediately realize who it was.

Captain Battye had given a good deal of thought to the arguments he intended to use and the points he meant to make, and was confident that he had thought of everything. But he had given no thought at all to Juli Pelham-Martyn, born Anjuli-Bai, Princess of Gulkote, for he considered the marriage both ill-judged and distasteful, and had no desire to meet the ex-widow. Ash however had led his guests through the shadowy garden to a small two-storied pavilion, a *barra durri* that stood in a clearing among the fruit trees, and taking them up a short flight of stairs to the screened upper room, said: "Juli, this is another friend of mine from the Regiment. My wife, Wigram—" and Wigram had found himself shaking hands in the English fashion with a girl in white, and thinking as Wally had done—though without any of Wally's emotion—that she was the loveliest thing he had ever seen.

He saw her exchange a brief glance with Ash, and though he had never been a particularly imaginative man, it seemed to him, as it had once seemed to Kaka-ji, that an invisible current leapt between them, linking them together so that they did not need to touch each other or speak or even smile in order to prove that two people can at times be truly one. He could see too what Walter had meant when he said that she was "restful." But somehow he had not expected her to be so young—or to look so vulnerable. This slender young thing in the white *shulwa* appeared to him to be little more than a child, and he thought confusedly that it was the term "widow" that had misled him: no widow should be as young as this, and he felt as though the ground had been abruptly cut from beneath his feet; though he would have been at a loss to explain why this should be so. But the fact remained that the sight of her had been enough to upset a number of preconceived notions, and all at once he was unsure of himself, and, as a result, of the suggestion he had come here to make.

Was he perhaps being foolishly naïve in expecting

Cavagnari, or anyone else for that matter, to abandon their policies and opinions merely on the basis of information from unofficial sources, supposing that information did not agree with their own? Was he, Wigram, taking too much on himself, being conceited enough to imagine that men like Cavagnari and the Viceroy, not to mention a host of big-wigs in Simla, did not know what they were about and needed help and advice from interfering know-nothing amateurs? Yet . . . He became aware that Ash had asked him a question, and replying at random saw by the quizzical lift of a black eyebrow that his answer had betrayed his inattention.

Wigram flushed and apologized in some confusion, and turning to his hostess said: "I'm sorry, Mrs. Pelham; I'm afraid I have not been attending. It was rude of me, and I hope you will forgive my bad manners. You see . . . I came here to put a—a proposition to your husband, and I have been thinking of that instead of listening."

Anjuli studied him gravely, then she gave a little nod and said politely: "I understand. You mean you would like to speak to my husband alone."

"Only if you permit."

She gave him a brief enchanting smile, and rising, placed her palms together, and then remembering that Ashok had told her that this was not the *Angrezi* way, laughed and held out her hand and said in her careful English: "Good-night . . . Captain Battye."

Wigram took her hand in his and unexpectedly bowed over it in a gesture that was as foreign to him as a handshake was to her, and that surprised him almost more than it surprised Ash and Wally. But it had been an instinctive tribute—and also in some way an unspoken apology for the things he had thought about her. Straightening up and looking into the eyes that were almost on a level with his own, he saw that Wally had been right when he said that there were gold flecks in them—unless it was only the reflections from the pierced bronze lamp that hung from the ceiling and sprinkled the little pavilion with stars. But he did not have time to find out, for Anjuli drew her hand away and offered it to Wally before she turned and left them, and watching her retreat into the shadows he had the odd fancy that she was taking the light with her.

All the same, he was relieved to see her go, because

901

her presence would have precluded straight talking, and he had neither the time nor the inclination to defer to feminine sensibilities. As the sound of her footsteps receded on the stair he heard Wally give a little sigh, and presently Ash said: "Well?"

"She is very beautiful," said Wigram slowly. "And very . . . young."

"Twenty-one," supplied Ash laconically. "But I didn't mean 'What do you think of her?' I meant what is this proposition you mentioned?"

"Yes, come on now, out with it," urged Wally. "It's dying of curiosity I've been. What have you got up your sleeve?"

Wigram grinned but said a shade defensively that now it came to the point he was not so sure that he wanted to say anything: "The fact is, I'm afraid you may laugh."

But Ash had not laughed. He knew a good deal about the late Afghan war, and while in Gujerat had re-read Sir John Kaye's book on the subject and been as infuriated by the futility, injustice and tragedy of that bungled attempt at extending the power of the East India Company as his father, Hilary, had been over thirty years earlier.

That such a thing could happen again had seemed so impossible that even after Koda Dad had warned him of it he could not believe that anyone with any sense could consider it, largely because, like most Frontier Force soldiers, he was under no illusions as to the fighting capabilities of the Border tribesmen or the ruggedness of the country in which they lived; and knew only too well the appalling problems posed by supply and transport (quite apart from the actual fighting) that must confront any modern army attempting to advance through a hostile land where every hill-top and ravine, each rock and stone and fold in the ground, could hide an enemy marksman. A land moreover where the soil was so unproductive that at the best of times there was barely enough food for the local inhabitants, and therefore no hope of being able to feed large numbers of invading troops and an even larger number of camp-followers off the country; or of grazing the host of horses, mules and other transport animals that must accompany them. Besides, surely the Generals, if not the civilians in Simla, must have learned the lesson of the previous Afghan war?

Yet listening to Wigram he realized that the lesson, if learned, had been forgotten, and that those who were planning a repeat performance of that sorry tragedy would be at pains to see that it remained so—directing the limelight instead onto the fur-hatted figure of the Russian villain lurking in the wings. "Yet if it's true that Shere Ali is planning to let in the Russians," thought Ash, as Wigram had done, "England will have to step in, because once the Russians get their hands on anything they never let go, and it would be India next."

The thought of India added to the ever-increasing territories of the Tsar—its towns and villages under the control of Ispravniks and Starostas, Russian Governors in every Province and Russian regiments quartered in every cantonment from Peshawar to Cape Comorin, their guns commanding the great sea ports of Karachi, Bombay, Madras and Calcutta—was enough to make him shudder. But then he knew Afghanistan even better than men like Cavagnari did, and that knowledge inclined him to be sceptical of the fears expressed by the Deputy Commissioner and his fellow war-mongers.

"I remember reading somewhere," observed Ash meditatively, "that Henry I of France said of Spain that if you invaded it with a large force you would be destroyed by starvation, while if you invaded it with a small one you would be overwhelmed by a hostile people. Well, you could say the same of Afghanistan. It's an appalling country to invade, and unless the Russians think that they can walk in unchallenged, with the consent of the population as well as the Amir, I can't believe they'd try it —any more than I am prepared to believe that Cavagnari knows much about the Afghans if he thinks for one moment that the Amir's so-called 'subjects' will ever tamely submit to having Russian garrisons quartered all over their country. They may be a murderous lot of ruffians with an unenviable reputation for treachery and ruthlessness, but no one has ever denied their courage; or been able to make them do anything they don't like doing. And they don't like being dictated to or ruled by foreigners— any foreigners! Which is why, in my opinion, this whole Russian scare is probably nothing but a turnip lantern."

"Exactly," agreed Wigram. "That's precisely what I'm afraid of. But though I hope I'm wrong, I can't help wondering if—if the Forward Policy fanatics know quite well

903

that it's more than likely that Russia is merely putting out a feeler—testing the temperature of the water so to speak —but are so dead set on this scheme of turning Afghanistan into a buffer-state in order to protect India that they are using this Russian business as a stalking horse to cover their real objective. Though of course if it's true that the Amir is really thinking of signing a treaty with the Tsar—" the sentence remained unfinished, because at this point he had been interrupted by Wally, who refused to believe that his latest hero could possibly be mistaken on a matter of such vital importance, or wrong about anything that concerned the tribal territories of Afghanistan as a whole. Cavagnari, insisted Wally, knew more about that country and its peoples than anyone else in India—any European at all events. Everyone knew that!

Wigram remarked dryly that he expected a great many people had said as much of Macnaghten in '38, though that hadn't prevented him from being murdered by the Afghans three years later, after being largely responsible for attempting to foist Shah Shuja on the throne, and almost wholly responsible for allowing large numbers of British women and children and their down-country servants to join the Occupation Forces in Kabul and be massacred in the Kurd Kabul passes together with the retreating army. As Wally had also studied that disastrous campaign, he was temporarily silenced, and confined himself to listening to Ash and Wigram discussing the possibility of being able to discover what was actually going on in Kabul and whether the Russian threat was real or only a turnip lantern being used by the Forward Policy bloc to frighten the electorate into supporting another war of aggression.

"But supposing we could get the information?" said Ash some ten minutes later. "We'd have no guarantee that it would be accepted if it turned out to contradict what they want to believe."

"None," confirmed Wigram; "except that if by 'they' you mean Cavagnari, he would never suppress it. That's one thing I *am* sure about. He has his own spies of course, as we have always had ours—after all, it was in our original charter that we should employ 'men capable of collecting trustworthy intelligence beyond as well as within our borders,' and as Deputy Commissioner of Peshawar, Cavagnari probably employs a good many of the same. But I'll go bail that anything of a political nature that they send him—anything to do with Shere Ali's relations with Russia for instance—is sent on at once to Simla, as anything we ourselves could tell him in that line would be too, regardless of whether it contradicted his own theories or not. In any case, one has to try. One can't sit back with folded hands and watch a shipload of passengers heading towards a hidden reef without making any attempt to light a flare or send up a rocket or do anything at all to try and warn them, even if it's only to yell or blow a whistle!"

"No," agreed Ash slowly. "One has to do something —even when the chances are that it will prove useless."

"Yes, that's it. That's how I feel," sighed Wigram, enormously relieved. He leaned back in his chair, and grinning at Ash said: "I remember when you first joined us we used to rib you over a habit you had of saying that this or that was 'unfair'—it was a favourite word of yours in those days. Well, speaking for myself, I've no objection to fighting a war: it's my trade. But I'd prefer to think that I was fighting in a just one; or at the very least, one that could not have been avoided. And I believe that this one can be. It's not too late."

Ash remained silent, and Wigram saw that although his gaze appeared to be fixed on the dark oblong of the doorway through which his wife had left, his eyes had the blind unfocused look of one whose thoughts have travelled many miles, or perhaps years away. And indeed Ash was remembering the past and hearing once again as he had in Lalji's audience chamber in Gulkote and in the *chattri* at Bhithor, a long-dead voice exhorting a four-year-old boy not to forget that injustice was the worst sin in the world and must be fought wherever it was found . . . "even when you know that you cannot win."

Wigram, who did not know Ash nearly as well as Wally did, noticed only the abstraction. But Wally saw something in the still face that frightened him: an underlying suggestion of desolation and the bleak look of a man who is being forced to make an unpalatable decision. And as he watched, the prescience that is so often a part of the Irish heritage stirred in him, bringing a premonition of disaster that was so strong that instinctively he flung up a hand as though to ward it off . . . and in the same moment heard Ash say quietly: "I shall have to go myself."

Wigram had argued with him: they had both argued with him. But in the end they had agreed that he was right. An officer of the Guides would be more likely to be believed than any Afghan who, apart from being paid for services rendered, might well have a personal or tribal antipathy towards the central government in Kabul and so be tempted to twist or be selective with information collected on the far side of the Border. Besides, what was needed now was no longer a matter of which disaffected tribe or local mullah was planning a raid into British India or inciting the Faithful to murder a few infidels, but whether an Amir of Afghanistan was engaged in plotting with the Russians, and if so, how far had he committed himself? Was he indeed preparing to welcome a Russian Mission to Kabul and sign a treaty of alliance with the Tsar, and were his people prepared to support him in this?

Reliable information on these points would be of the greatest possible value to the negotiators in Simla and Peshawar and to Her Majesty's Ministers in London, because such knowledge could mean all the difference between peace and war—which is to say life and death for thousands of human beings. And as Ash pointed out, there was nothing in the Guides' charter to bar an officer from "collecting trustworthy intelligence beyond as well as within our borders." "Anyway, I've lived in the country and I know my way around there, so it isn't as if I shall be in any real danger," said Ash.

"Gammon!" retorted Wally angrily. "Don't talk as though we were a pair of sap-heads. You weren't alone last time, but this time you will be; which means that if ever you're tired or ill or wounded and make a slip, there'll be no one to cover it up for you. You'll be a lone stranger, and as such, an object of suspicion. Faith, it's sick you make me—both of you. But I wish to God I could be going with you and that's the truth. When do you mean to leave?"

"As soon as Wigram can fix it with the Commandant. I can't go without his permission, and for all we know he may not give it."

"He will," said Wigram. "He's been just as worried about this business as I have—and half the Frontier Force too, for that matter. We're the ones who'll have to do the fighting if that gilded crew in Simla gets hold of the wrong end of the stick and proceeds to stir up a hornets' nest with it. He may take a bit of persuading, but I think you'll find that he'll see it as a good idea and a possible life-line. And Cavagnari will jump at it. It's just the sort of thing that will appeal to him no end."

Wigram had been right on both counts.

The Commandant had been talked round, and the Deputy Commissioner had shown considerable enthusiasm for the idea. He had a love of the dramatic, and Ash's story as related to him by Captain Battye enthralled him: "But if he is to work for me I must see him before he goes, since it will be better if he reports direct to me through the only one of my agents whom I allow to come into Peshawar rather than to one of your men, who will be expected to take any message to you or your Commandant first, leaving one of you to bring it to me. That won't do: the less people involved in this the better—especially for his own safety, as I hope you will explain to him, and to your Commandant. A divided authority always leads to muddle, and as the type of information required will be of no use at regimental level, I prefer that the young man should work exclusively for me. And by the way if, as I understand, he is at present still on leave, I would suggest that he is not permitted to return to Mardan. It would look odd for him to come back to duty for a few days only to leave again."

"Yes, sir. That has already been thought of. He will be leaving from Attock: it was his own idea."

"And a very sensible one," approved Cavagnari. "Please arrange for him to meet me before he goes."

Wigram saw no point in telling him that when Ash had volunteered to go into Afghanistan as a spy he had made two conditions, one of which might well have prevented him from going at all. He had insisted that he must be allowed to discuss the whole project with Koda Dad, and that if the old man did not approve, then it would have to be abandoned. The other condition had been that the Guides must promise to look after Anjuli and see to it that she received her rights as his lawful wife in the event of his failing to return.

The latter had been agreed, but when Wigram had expressed doubts about the wisdom of allowing any outside person to learn of Ash's activities, Ash had retorted that he would in any case be telling Zarin, and that he would trust Zarin's father with his life. "I've known him since I was about six, and I value his opinion more than anyone else's. If he thinks I can do any good then I'll go; but you have to remember that he's a Pathan, and as such a citizen of Afghanistan, so he may take a poor view of spies—even those whose intentions are to prevent a war: I don't know. But I must talk to him first before I decide."

Wigram had shrugged and said: "Be it on your own head. It's your life. What do you think his verdict will be?"

"Oh, I should say the chances are that he'll agree with you, as Zarin will too. I admit I haven't much hope that he won't. In fact I'm probably wasting my time as well as his, but I have to make certain."

". . . and to receive his blessing," murmured Wigram in an undervoice. He had spoken a thought aloud without knowing it and the words had been barely audible, but Ash had caught them and said quickly and in a tone of surprise: "Yes. How did you know?"

Wigram had looked embarrassed and said awkwardly: "It may sound absurd in this day and age, but my father gave me his before I sailed for India, and I've often found it a comfort to remember that. I suppose it harks back to the Old Testament, when a patriarch's blessing really meant something."

"'And Esau said . . . bless me, even me also, O my father,'" quoted Wally, speaking for the first time in a long while. "I hope you'll get it, Ash: for all our sakes."

Wigram had risen briskly to his feet and said that it was high time they left, adding that he hoped Ash would not be too long over seeing Zarin's father, as he personally had a strong feeling that there might be very little time to spare, and that what they had was running out far too quickly. "If the Commandant agrees, how soon do you think you could start?"

"That depends on Koda Dad; and on Cavagnari. I shall try and see Koda Dad tomorrow or the next day. Are you two going back to Mardan tonight?"

"We weren't, but we can."

"When you do, will you take a message from me to Zarin. Tell him that I have to see his father as soon as possible and ask him to let me know if he thinks the old man would be well enough to receive me—I gather he's been ill of late. If so, when and where; but that I'd rather not be seen in his village if it can be avoided. He needn't send word here. Tell him I'll be at the banyan tree near the first mile-stone outside Nowshera by sunset tomorrow, and that I'll wait there until he comes. He may be on duty, but I expect you can arrange for him to get away."

But no one was ever to know what Koda Dad would have advised, for he was dead. He had died at about the same hour as Wally and Wigram Battye, on their way to Attock, rode away from Mardan; and because the weather at that season is always cruelly hot he had been buried before nightfall, so that by the time Ash reached the banyan tree on the Nowshera road where Zarin waited for him with the news, Koda Dad Khan, one-time Master of Horse in the little principality of Gulkote, had lain a full twenty-four hours in his grave.

Two days later the Deputy Commissioner of Peshawar and Captain Battye of the Guides Cavalry rode out together, ostensibly to look for possible camp sites in the open country to the south-east of Peshawar.

They went unescorted, and at a time of day when all sensible folk are taking a siesta and the land appears to be deserted. Nevertheless in the course of their ride they met and conversed with another horseman, a lone Afridi whom they found resting in the shade of a tall outcrop of rock, and who might almost have been waiting for them.

To begin with, Cavagnari had done most of the talking, while Ash had confined himself to insisting that he would only agree to collect and send back information provided it was clearly understood that he would report the truth as he found it, even if it should turn out to be a view of the question that the officials in Simla did not wish to hear. "If I cannot do that, then there is no point in my going," said Ash. To which Cavagnari had replied with a shade of acidity that naturally he would be expected to keep an open mind, that went without saying; adding that the Commandant, with permission from the appropriate authority, had assigned Lieutenant Pelham-Martyn to act as his, Cavagnari's, personal intelligence officer for a period of six months, irrespective of whether war was declared during that time or not, while giving Cavagnari the right to terminate the arrangement at any moment if he thought fit. "In which case you would of course return immediately to regimental duty. With a brevet if you wish; you will certainly have earned it and 'the labourer is worthy of his hire.' "

Ash made a face of disgust and remarked tartly that he had not volunteered for this job in the expectation of reward, and that he had thought that the whole point was having a spy who wasn't getting paid for it. His services were not for hire, and what he was doing could be regarded as repayment—repayment for benefits received, as the Guides had been very good to him and he had done little to repay them.

"You will have a chance to do so now," observed Cavagnari with an approving nod, and moved on to a discussion of other matters. There were many of these—including the question of arranging for funds to be made available not only to Ash in Afghanistan but to Juli in Attock, together with the various details that would have to be worked out if the story that Lieutenant Pelham-Martyn had been sent off on a "Course" somewhere down south on the eve of his returning to Mardan was to be believed. The meeting had lasted for some considerable time, and only when the shadows began to lengthen did the two Englishmen turn back to Peshawar, while the Afridi trotted eastward on his gaunt scissor-hocked pony, heading for Attock.

Ash had crossed the Rubicon and now it only remained to tell Anjuli; which was something he had put off doing as long as he could, just in case it should not be necessary—there being always the possibility that Cavagnari, or perhaps the Commandant, would change his mind at the last moment and cancel the venture as too dangerous or impractical; as there had once been the chance that Koda Dad would disapprove.

Telling her had been the hardest thing of all. Even harder than he had thought, for she had implored him to take her with him, insisting that her place was by his side now—doubly so if he were going into danger, because in addition to being able to cook and care for him, her presence would serve to deflect suspicion from him, since who could possibly expect to find a spy accompanied by his wife? The very idea was absurd and would therefore serve to protect him. "And I would learn to shoot," pleaded Anjuli. "You have only to teach me."

"But you cannot speak enough Pushtu, my Heart."

910

"I will learn—I will learn! I promise you I will learn."

"There is no time, Heart's-dearest, for I must go at once; and if I took you with me and you were unable to speak freely with the women-folk of the country, they would begin to ask questions, and that could be very dangerous—both for our safety and for the work that I have to do. You know that I would take you with me if I could, but I cannot, Larla; and it is only for six months. I will leave Gul Baz here, and you will be safe in the care of the Begum; and—and I will be far safer alone."

It was in the end this last statement that persuaded her, because she knew in her heart that it was true, and knowing it she pleaded no longer but said only: "Then I will send my heart with you—it is already in your keeping. Bring it back to me soon, and in safety."

Ash had assured her that she need have no fears for him. But though he could make light of the danger in words, his body betrayed him: his love-making that night had been different from other nights in that it conveyed a disturbing sense of desperation . . . almost as though he were trying to make the very most of every moment for fear that there would be no tomorrow. So might a man lie with his love on the eve of some hazardous venture: a great battle, or a long and dangerous journey from which he might never return . . .

On the following night when all the household were safely asleep and the moon had not yet risen, Ash slipped quietly out by the back gate of Fatima Begum's garden and set his face towards the hills. And less than twelve hours later he was across the Border and had vanished into Afghanistan: dropping out of sight as completely as a pebble that falls into a deep pool.

51

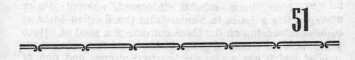

That summer of 1878, the famine that had taken such a terrible toll in the south crept northward into the Punjab. For once again, for the third year in succession, the monsoon had failed; and when at last the rain fell it was not in the steady downpour that the thirsty land needed, but in fitful and capricious gusts that did little more than turn the surface dust to mud, leaving the earth beneath still iron-hard.

There were other things, apart from the failure of the crops and the fear of war, that made this an evil year, for dissension and disease were rife.

In Hardwar, where the sacred River Ganges enters the plains and vast numbers of pilgrims from all parts of India gather to bathe in its hallowed waters, cholera had struck during the annual festival and thousands died within a matter of hours. The news that Russia had attacked Turkey, and of her victories in the field, had encouraged a number of Indian journalists (always impressed by success and military might) to fill columns in the vernacular press with a spate of inflammatory words in praise of the victors, and when the Government took no notice they became bolder and began to advocate that India join forces with Russia for the overthrow of the Raj, and to urge their countrymen to assassinate British officers. At which point the Government decided that such stuff endangered the "safety of the state" and passed the Vernacular Press Act, designed to curb the mischief-making proclivities of news-sheets that were not printed in English. But the Act caused as much disaffection as the rabble-rousing articles and incitements to murder had done; and rumour took the place of the printed word.

There were a great many rumours in circulation that year and few were encouraging, except possibly to those who favoured a war with Afghanistan. Some told of Russian armies advancing on the Oxus River in numbers that grew as the tale was passed from mouth to mouth. An army of fifty thousand . . . of sixty thousand. No, eighty thousand . . .

"I have been reliably informed," wrote Major Cavagnari in a letter to Simla, "that the Russian force at present advancing on the Oxus consists of a total of fifteen thousand four hundred men, divided into three columns: two of which are seventeen hundred strong, and one of twelve thousand. Also that a Russian Mission, consisting of General Stolietoff and six other officers with an escort of twenty-two Cossacks, left Tashkent late in May

912

in advance of the troops. It is believed that the Amir's family and friends, who fear that the Russo-Turkish affair may lead to hostilities between Russian and Great Britain, have been putting pressure on the Amir to choose between these two rival powers, but that His Highness cannot make up his mind and remains undecided. I must add that in the opinion of my informant (whose views, I would stress, are strictly personal), the Amir would much prefer to avoid declaring for either side, being convinced that his country should strive to remain independent of both. I have given the Government Agent in Peshawar a confidential letter which will be forwarded to you. It was sent to me by the same hand, and purports to be an exact copy of the terms laid down by a Russian Native Envoy who visited Kabul late last year. I cannot, of course, vouch for its accuracy, nor would it be advisable for me to disclose the source of my information. But I can assure you that I have every reason to believe that it is reliable."

The document referred to was duly forwarded to Simla, and proved to be of considerable interest, the terms stating, among other things, that the Amir should permit the location of Russian Agents at Kabul and other places within his territories; that Russian troops should be quartered at "four suitable places" on the borders of Afghanistan; and that the Russian Government should be permitted to construct roads and set up telegraph wires linking Samarkand with Kabul and Kabul with Herat and Kandahar. Also that the Afghan Government should establish agents in the capitals of Russia and Tashkent, and permit the passage of Russian troops through their territory, "if it became desirable that the Russian Government should send an expedition to wage war on India."

In return the Amir was assured that Russia would regard his enemies as theirs, in no way interfere in the administration and internal affairs of his country, and "allow the continuance of Afghanistan to the representatives, successors and heirs of the Amir in perpetuity."

Major Cavagnari had admitted somewhat grudgingly that the unnamed person who had obtained that copy and smuggled it out of Afghanistan had been at pains to point out that though, to the best of his belief, the original document was genuine and that these terms had in fact been drawn up, there was no evidence to suggest that the Amir had either seen them or would have considered accepting them if he had; while on the other hand there was ample evidence that His Highness was much alarmed by the advance of Russian troops towards his borders, and greatly angered by the news that a Russian Mission was on its way, uninvited, to Kabul.

"There are times," observed Major Cavagnari tartly to Captain Battye, who was in Peshawar for talks on Divisional Training and had asked for news of Ash, "when I begin to wonder whose side your friend is on. Ours or the Amir's."

Wigram smiled a little lop-sidedly and said with a hint of remonstrance: "I wouldn't say it was a question of sides, sir. If you ask me, I should say rather that he can't help seeing both sides of a question, while the majority of us tend to see only one—our own. Besides, he's always had an obsession about being fair: you could almost call it a bee in his bonnet. If he thought there was something to be said for the Amir, it simply wouldn't occur to him not to say it. We did warn you about that, sir."

"I know, I know. But I could wish he would not say it so often," snapped the Deputy Commissioner. "Fairness is all very well, but one must not forget that what he has to say in defence of the Amir can only be based on hearsay, and what I require is information, not personal theories. In any case his opinions do not square with the facts, since we know that General Stolietoff's Mission is on its way to Kabul, and I myself do not believe for one moment that it is going there uninvited. The Russian Government would never have allowed it to set out unless they had every reason to believe that it would be welcomed in Kabul, for they would not risk a rebuff: and that, to my mind, makes it crystal clear that Shere Ali has been intriguing with them."

"Then you don't believe," ventured Wigram, "that Ashton—"

"Akbar," corrected Major Cavagnari sharply. "I consider it essential to avoid mentioning him by any other name even in the course of a private conversation. It is safer."

"Of course, sir—that Akbar is right in thinking the

914

Amir is anything but pleased by the news that the Mission is on its way?"

"That is something that your—that Akbar cannot possibly know for certain. And to be plain with you, I am beginning to find the tone of his reports disturbing. They display an increasing tendency to put the Amir's viewpoint rather than our own, and there are times when I am not entirely sure that he is . . . let us say, *sound*."

Wigram said stiffly: "I assure you there is not the least danger of his turning traitor, if that is what you mean sir."

"No, *no!*" disclaimed Major Cavagnari testily: "I meant no such thing. You take me up too quickly. But I must confess that in spite of your warning, I had supposed that as an Englishman he would be able to recognize the Amir's double-dealing for what it is, instead of making excuses for the man—which is what he is doing. He sends me information, some of it of considerable interest, and then confuses the issue with a piece of special pleading on behalf of the Amir, with whose problems he would appear to be too much in sympathy. But there is a simple solution to those problems: let Shere Ali ally himself with Great Britain and cease trafficking with Russia. It is his refusal to do the first and his persistence in the second that is causing the present tension, and I cannot agree with the view put forward by—by Akbar, that he would lose face with his subjects if he acceded to our request, and might even be deposed. Once he has openly declared in favour of an alliance with us, there would be no further danger of Russian aggression, as they would know that any move against Afghanistan would mean war with Great Britain. And with that danger removed, their troops would go home and the situation would return to normal."

"Except," remarked Wigram reflectively, "that there would be a British Mission and British officers in Kabul, instead of Russian ones."

The Deputy Commissioner's eyebrows twitched together in a frown and he favoured Captain Battye with a long, suspicious stare, and then inquired abruptly if he had been receiving communications from his friend.

"From Ash—Akbar? No," said Wigram. "I wasn't quoting. I've heard nothing about him until now, and I did not know if you had. In fact I wasn't even sure he was alive. That's why I called in to ask if you had any

915

news of him, and it's a relief to me to learn that you have. But I'm sorry that he is not proving to be as useful as you had hoped."

"He is useful. In some ways, exceedingly useful. But he would be even more so if he would confine himself to what is actually happening in Kabul, instead of indulging in what one can only regard as thought-reading. The matter of greatest concern is the whereabouts of this Russian Mission. Has it reached the borders of Afghanistan yet, and will it be refused entry into the country? Or will the Amir throw aside deception, and show himself in his true colours by receiving it at Kabul and thereby declaring himself to be our enemy? Time will show. But we know from several sources that Stolietoff and his Mission must be nearing the end of their journey, and if your friend should send word that they have been welcomed, we shall know where we stand. And so will he, I trust. It should at least open his eyes and show him the folly of attempting to find excuses for Shere Ali's behaviour."

Time had shown even more quickly than Major Cavagnari had expected, for that very night he had received a brief message to say that the Russian Mission had entered Afghanistan and been accorded a public reception in Kabul. That was all. But the die had been cast, and from that moment a second Afghan war became inevitable.

Details had followed later. The Mission, it appeared, had been welcomed with all honour by the Amir. Elephants had been sent out to meet them, and mounted on these and attended by Afghan ministers and nobles, Stolietoff and his officers had ridden in state through the town of Kabul to the Bala Hissar, the ancient citadel that includes the royal palace of the rulers of Afghanistan, where the Amir Shere Ali and his court had waited to greet them. They had been housed in the Residency, which lies within the Bala Hissar, and accorded a strong guard: and ten days later a splendid military review had been held in their honour. But Louis Cavagnari's confident assertion that his "unsound" spy would be unable to find any further excuses for Shere Ali proved incorrect.

"Akbar" had found several. He had even suggested that in the circumstances it was to Shere Ali's credit that he had stood out against Russian pressure as long as he had, while as for that review, it had, in his opinion, almost certainly been held less from a desire to do the self-invited visitors honour than as a covert warning—a visual demonstration of the military strength that Afghanistan could bring against any would-be aggressor . . .

"It is believed in Kabul," wrote Akbar, "that the Amir has not only come to no arrangement with the Russian Envoy, but is at the moment only playing for time until he sees what action the British Government will take to counter this move. You will undoubtedly hear reports that he has spoken with great bitterness of the way in which he has been treated by Her Majesty's Government; but I have not heard it suggested that he has any intention of yielding to a new friend what he has refused to an old ally, and I would emphasize yet again, and most strongly, that everything I have seen and heard, both in Kabul and elsewhere in Afghanistan, confirms my belief that Shere Ali is neither pro-Russian nor pro-British, but merely an Afghan who is striving to preserve the independence of his country against heavy odds—to name only two, a revolt by the Herati Ghilzais and the fact that his exiled nephew Abdur Rahman, now living under Russian protection, is widely believed to be willing to accede to any terms that his hosts may choose to demand, in return for his uncle's throne."

But no amount of "special pleading" could offset the shock and anger of the Viceroy and his advisers on hearing the news that a Russian Envoy had been received by the Amir, and welcomed with all honour, after Great Britain herself had been refused permission to send a similar mission to Kabul. This was an affront that no patriotic Englishman could be expected to stomach, and urgent letters were dispatched to London, pressing for permission to demand that the perfidious Shere Ali should consent to receive a British Mission in Kabul without any further shilly-shallying.

Faced with the irrefutable fact that a Russian Envoy had indeed been received by the Amir, the Foreign Secretary had given his consent, and the Viceroy had immediately set about selecting members for the Mission. The Commander-in-Chief of the Madras Army, General Sir Neville Chamberlain, was chosen to lead it, with two officers—one of them Major Louis Cavagnari—appointed to accompany him for "political duties." The party would include a Military Secretary and two aides-de-camp, and

917

Lieutenant Colonel Jenkins was given command of the escort, drawn from his own Regiment and consisting of Major Stewart, Captain Battye, a hundred sabres of the Cavalry and fifty bayonets of the Infantry of the Queen's Own Corps of Guides.

The Mission was to set out for Kabul in September, but meanwhile a native emissary would leave immediately armed with a letter from the Viceroy to the Amir, advising him of the British Envoy's arrival and demanding that arrangements should be made for the safe passage of the Mission through His Highness's territory.

To emphasize the Government's displeasure, the emissary selected for this delicate task was a gentleman who some fourteen years earlier, before the days of Viceroys, had been appointed by the then Governor-General, Lord Lawrence, as Native Envoy to Kabul, and later been summarily recalled for abusing his position by intriguing against Shere Ali himself.

Not surprisingly, this choice of messenger did nothing to make the Amir feel more kindly disposed towards the British; while to make matters worse, Shere Ali was in ill-health and prostrated with grief at the sudden death of his favourite son, the beloved Mir Jan, whom he had chosen to succeed him. The emissary failed to make any headway, and by mid-September was writing to warn the Government that the Amir was in a bad humour, but that his ministers were still hopeful that a satisfactory solution might be achieved, and that he himself was convinced that further discussions were possible—provided the British Mission would delay its departure.

He need not have stressed that last, for travel was slow and Sir Neville Chamberlain, the Envoy Elect, had not yet arrived in Peshawar. When he eventually did so, it was to find that although the Amir had still not come to any decision, Major Cavagnari, anticipating a possible refusal, had already begun negotiating with the Maliks (headmen) of the Khyber tribes for a free passage for the Mission through their several territories. His discussions, unlike those in Kabul, were going well, and agreement had almost been reached when the Governor of the Khyber fortress of Ali Masjid, one Faiz Mohammed, came to hear of them and sent peremptory orders to the Maliks that they were to return immediately to their villages.

918

The Khyber tribes being titular subjects of the Amir, and their territories—the lands between Peshawar and Ali Masjid—part of Afghanistan, there was only one way to keep them from obeying this command: undertake to pay them the yearly subsidy that they had hitherto received from the Amir, and which would be cut off if they defied Faiz Mohammed's order.

But no one knew better than Major Cavagnari that any such action on the part of the Government would be regarded as an indefensible attempt to detach the tribes from their allegiance to the Amir, and that such hostile behaviour would only serve to convince Shere Ali that the British Mission, far from being "friendly and peaceful," was in fact the spearhead of an invading army. He therefore abandoned his talks and referred the matter to the Viceroy; who agreed that until the Amir decided for or against the Mission, any private bargaining with the tribes might provide him with legitimate grounds for complaint, but suggested forcing matters to a crisis by sending a letter to Governor Faiz Mohammed, informing him that the Mission intended to set out for Kabul at once, and asking whether he was prepared to grant it safe passage through the Khyber Pass. Should the answer be unfavourable, then Sir Neville Chamberlain was to make a settlement with the Khyber tribes and advance on Ali Masjid . . .

The letter had been dispatched, and Faiz Mohammed had sent a polite reply, pointing out that there was no need to ask his permission, as provided the Amir had given his consent to the Mission proceeding to Kabul, they could do so in safety. On the other hand, if His Highness withheld his consent and they came without it, the garrison of Ali Masjid would be forced to oppose their advance; therefore he would suggest that the Mission delayed its departure and remained in Peshawar until the Amir's decision was known.

But the Envoy, like the Viceroy, had grown impatient of continued procrastination, and come to believe that the British had a right to send a Mission to Afghanistan and that the Amir had no right to refuse them. He sent a telegram to Simla announcing that the Mission was leaving Peshawar for Jamrud, at the limits of British-held territory, and that from there Major Cavagnari, with Colonel Jenkins of the Guides and one or two others, would go forward to Ali Masjid to test the Afghan reaction. If Faiz Mohammed refused to allow them to pass, this could be regarded as a hostile act and equivalent to being fired upon, and the Mission could then return to Peshawar without the disgrace of being turned back.

Cavagnari and his party, which in addition to Colonel Jenkins included Wigram Battye, half-a-dozen men of the Guides and some of the Khyber Maliks, duly left for Ali Masjid where the Governor, true to his promise, duly turned them back; informing Major Cavagnari that considering he had come without permission, after trying to suborn certain subjects of the Amir into giving him passage through His Highness's territories—thereby setting Afridi against Afridi—he could take it as a kindness on account of remembered friendship that he, Faiz Mohammed, had not opened fire on him for the deeds that his Government had done. "After which," said Wigram, describing the incident to Wally, "he shook hands with us and we remounted and rode back to Jamrud with our tails between our legs: or that was what it felt like."

Wally whistled expressively and Wigram nodded and said: "No, not an experience I would like to repeat. For let's face it, the fellow was right. That was what was so galling. Our Government has not come out of this affair very well, and I cannot help thinking that if I had been an Afridi I'd have felt exactly as Faiz Mohammed did—and I only hope I'd have behaved as well. Yet I'm willing to lay you odds that because he stuck to his guns and refused to allow the Mission free passage through the pass except with his Amir's permission, it will now be claimed that Afghanistan has put an intolerable affront upon Her Majesty's Government and insulted the entire British Nation, so that we now have no recourse but to declare war."

"Do you really think so?" demanded Wally a little breathlessly. He came to his feet like a released spring and began to walk about the room as though he could not keep still. "Somehow it doesn't seem possible. I mean . . . well, one has got used to minor skirmishes, but war—a real war—and an unjust one. It's unthinkable: it can't be allowed to happen. Surely Ash . . ." he swung round on his heel and looked at Wigram. "Have you heard any news of him?"

"Only that he is still in touch with Cavagnari, which means that he's all right so far."

Wally sighed and said restlessly: "He did warn me that he wouldn't be able to let us know how things were going with him, because it would be too risky; and that his wife and Zarin had both agreed to this. He said we three were the only ones who knew—apart from you and Cavagnari and the Commandant of course—and that even the fellow who acts as a link between him and Cavagnari, and who is one of Cavagnari's own men, wasn't to be told who he was . . . that he wasn't an Afghan, I mean. But that Cavagnari would probably let you know that he was keeping in touch, because it had been your idea in the first place."

"Well, he has let me know, and he is in touch. So you can stop worrying about Ashton."

"Can I tell his wife?"

"Will you be seeing her?" Wigram sounded surprised and not altogether pleased.

"No. I promised Ash I'd keep an eye on her, but we decided that it would be better if I didn't call at the house. The old Begum doesn't approve; thinks it might cause too much talk, and she's probably right. But I can always send a message by Zarin, as no one would think twice about him visiting his aunt's house when he's been doing it for years. I'd like her to know that Ash is all right. It must be very hard on her . . . not knowing."

"Very," agreed Wigram. "Yes, of course you can let her know. I didn't realize she was still in Attock."

"He couldn't take her with him, so he left her with the Begum. She used to know Zarin Khan and his father when she was a little girl, so I suppose she feels safe with Zarin's aunt. I gather she's learning how to handle firearms and speak Pushtu in case Ash should be able to send for her. I wish . . ."

His voice ran out abruptly, leaving the sentence unfinished, and after a moment or two Wigram said curiously: "What is it you wish, Walter?"

Wally's unfocused gaze became alert again and he shook his head quickly in a movement that was very close to a shudder, and said lightly: "That you would give up traipsing about with the Great and return to the bosom of your own Regiment. Mardan doesn't seem the same, what

921

with you and Stewart and the Commandant off up the Khyber playing nurse-maid to this Mission we hear so much about. However, after this fiasco at Ali Masjid, I presume you'll all find yourselves out of a job."

Wally presumed right. A report on the set-back at Ali Masjid had been telegraphed to the Viceroy, who replied by disbanding the Mission.

Lord Lytton had got what he wanted: proof. Proof that "the Russian Menace" was no turnip lantern, but a grim reality with an Envoy already established in Kabul and an army advancing towards the Hindu Kush. Proof that Shere Ali was a treacherous intriguer, who having spurned the hand of friendship extended by Britain had clasped that of the Muscovite, and might even now be signing a treaty that would permit the establishment of Russian-garrisoned outposts along the very borders of India, and allow Russian troops free passage through the Passes. With General Stolietoff and his suite installed in the Bala Hissar itself, anything was possible. And if more were needed to drive home the necessity for immediate action, it had been provided by the public insult offered to Her Majesty's Envoy Sir Neville Chamberlain and a peaceful British Mission, who had not only been refused permission to enter the Amir's territory, but threatened with force should they attempt to do so. Such treatment was not to be borne, and Lord Lytton for one did not intend to bear it.

As an immediate answer to the rebuff at Ali Masjid, the Guides Corps from Mardan were sent to Jamrud, an ancient Sikh fortress that marked the limits of British-held territory; and two days after the short-lived Mission had been disbanded, orders went out for a strong force to be assembled at Multan for the purpose of crossing the Afghan border and threatening Kandahar, and for other regiments to concentrate on the outpost of Thal, where the Kurram River divided the district of Kohat from Afghan territory. A Sikh regiment and a Mountain Battery were brought from Kohat to strengthen the Peshawar garrison, and Major Cavagnari (who could see little future in attempting to re-open negotiations with the Maliks of the Khyber tribes) came up with a new and revolutionary scheme for bringing them over to the British side without wasting time in laborious talks and endless bargaining . . .

922

Asiatics were known to be inordinately impressed by success—and, conversely, to take a scornful view of losers—and as there could be no denying that the British Power had not shown to advantage in the recent confrontation at Ali Masjid, something ought to be done to wipe out that disgrace and earn the admiration of the tribesmen. And what could be better, suggested Louis Cavagnari, than to assault and capture, in a surprise attack, the very fortress whose Governor and garrison had dared to deny a British Mission passage through the Khyber? That should not only serve to teach the Afghans a lesson, but show them what the Raj could do if it chose to exert itself.

The Viceroy was delighted with this scheme, and ignoring the advice of his Commander-in-Chief and Sir Neville Chamberlain—who protested that the risks far outnumbered any advantages that might be gained—he gave the project his blessing. General Ross, in command at Peshawar, who had also protested, was curtly informed that Ali Masjid must and would be taken. The plan of action involved a swift night march, similar to the one Cavagnari had used so successfully against the Utman Khel tribesmen, followed by a surprise attack at dawn by a force consisting of the Guides and the 1st Sikhs under Colonel Jenkins, supported by 1,000 native and British troops drawn from the Peshawar garrison and supplied with three heavy guns.

As the success of the operation would depend on speed and secrecy, the greatest care must be taken that no hint of the impending attack should be allowed to leak out; and once the fortress was taken, the troops were to be withdrawn, for the Government of India had no intention of holding Ali Masjid, or leaving a garrison there. Their object was not conquest, but merely to demonstrate, by a swift and brilliant feat of arms, that the Raj could not be insulted with impunity, and what its troops were capable of.

"I don't believe it!" gasped the Commanding Officer of the 1st Sikhs when informed of this by Colonel Jenkins in the privacy of the latter's bungalow. "Are you trying to tell me that we're expected to march our fellows into Afghanistan to attack and capture a fort like Ali Masjid, and if we get it—which I'm not too sure we shall—to about-turn and march meekly back to Peshawar again, leaving the Afghans to cut up our dead and re-occupy the fort the moment our backs are turned? Why, it's crazy! They can't *all* have gone mad in Simla."

"I know, I know," sighed Colonel Jenkins tiredly. "But crazy or not, we're going to have to do what we're told. 'Ours not to reason why, ours but to do and die.'"

"But . . . but my bearer always knows where the Regiment is being posted long before I do, and in a place like Peshawar, with the city crawling with Pathans, I wouldn't be surprised if they're on to this already and busy sending word to Faiz Mohammed and his levies to prepare a warm welcome for us. 'Surprise' my foot! They'll be ready and waiting for us, and it'll be a miracle if we come out of this without being so badly scorched that the game won't have been worth the candle. Do you suppose the General's gone off his rocker?"

"It's not his idea," said Colonel Jenkins. "This is one of Cavagnari's brainwaves. He sees it as a quicker and better method of influencing the Khyber Tribes in our favour than trying to buy them over one by one—stun 'em with awe and admiration for our dash and bravery, and dazzle them with a hurricane one-innings victory. He's convinced the Viceroy that it'll work, so perhaps it sounds better on paper."

"Then all I can say is that it's a pity it can't be fought on paper!" observed the Commanding Officer of the 1st Sikhs savagely. To which Colonel Jenkins offered no comment, for he too was appalled by the scheme and could only hope that someone—anyone—would be able to bring the Viceroy and the Deputy Commissioner of Peshawar to their senses before it was too late.

Fortunately, his hope was justified. The Military Member of the Viceroy's Council, learning of it only after the order to act upon it had already been given, declared in forthright language that in his opinion the absurdity of abandoning Ali Masjid after capturing it was only equalled by the folly of taking it: a protest that might have been ignored had it not been for the timely arrival in Simla of a telegram bringing news that Ali Masjid had been strongly reinforced by Afghan troops and artillery.

In the light of this piece of information the Viceroy had no option but to cancel the project, and Louis Cavagnari, baulked of his cherished plan to dazzle the Khyber

Tribes with a brilliant *coup-de-main* that would make them decide to throw in their lot with the British, turned once more, with tireless patience, to the slow and often exasperating task of striving to attain the same end by words instead of deeds; negotiating with their Maliks, one by one.

Few men could have done it better, but the cajolery, argument and bribery involved took time. Too much time. And he was vividly aware of how little there might be left.

52

The conviction that time was running out was shared by many men that autumn. Not least by that one-time Commandant of the Corps of Guides, Sam Browne—the same who had discussed the boy Ashton's future with Zarin's elder brother. Awal Shah, so many years ago, and decided to send William Ashton's nephew to England in the care of Colonel Anderson.

Sam Browne, now Lieutenant-General Sir "Sam" and newly appointed to the command of the First Division of the Peshawar Valley Field Force, had not been among those who approved Louis Cavagnari's sensational scheme for the capture of Ali Masjid. But he realized that if war were declared the fortress would have to be taken: not as a flamboyant gesture designed to impress the tribes, but as a matter of stark military necessity. Furthermore, it would have to be attacked within hours rather than days of the declaration, because Ali Masjid was the key to the Khyber Pass, and until it was taken the road to Kabul would remain barred.

In these circumstances it shocked the General to discover how little was known of the country through which his troops might soon have to advance—and this despite the fact that a British Army had marched that way before, and on retreating, suffered one of the most appalling disasters to befall an invading army since Napoleon's *Grande Armée* melted away on the agonizing retreat from Moscow.

925

"This is ridiculous. I must have maps," said General Sam. "We can't go barging bald-headed into those hills without knowing a damn' thing about them. Do you mean to tell me there *are* no maps? None at *all*?"

"Apparently not, sir; only a few rough sketches, and I understand none of those are very accurate," said the Adjutant-General, adding in extenuation: "The tribes don't take kindly to strangers wandering around their territories with compasses and theodolites, so you see—"

"No I don't," snapped the one-armed General. "But Major Cavagnari tells me that he has already come to an agreement with two of the tribes, and is in hopes of persuading a third—the Mohmands—to allow us free passage through their territory. That being so, it should be possible to send a few men to spy out the land for us. You'd better see to it, will you."

The Adjutant-General had seen to it, and that same evening two men, Captain Stewart of the Guides and a Mr. Scott of the Survey Department, had set out from Peshawar to reconnoitre the Border country and collect what information they could as to the strength and disposition of Faiz Mohammed Khan's forces. They had been absent for the best part of two weeks, and a few days after their return Louis Cavagnari had suggested that it would be a good idea if he were to accompany them on a second reconnaissance to confirm their results: "And I think it might be as well, sir, if one or two of the officers who were with me during my interview with the Governor of Ali Masjid went with us. They already know something of the country, and a second visit should help to fix a good many important details in their minds; it seems to me that an accurate knowledge of the terrain may shortly be of incalculable value to us all."

"You are right, there," agreed the General grimly. "The more we know about the place the better. Take whom you like."

Which explains why a few days later dawn found Colonel Jenkins and Wigram Battye scrambling up a steep and almost invisible goat-track on the wrong side of the Border, in the wake of Captain Stewart, Mr. Scott and the Deputy Commissioner of Peshawar . . .

The five men had left Jamrud in the chill pre-dawn darkness, and as unobtrusively as possible. Their horses and two sowars of the Guides Cavalry had been waiting for them outside the main gate of the fort, and the small party had mounted and ridden quietly away in the darkness. The moon was down and the stars were already fading, but in the east the sky was beginning to pale, and there was just enough light for the riders to be able to take their horses at a cautious trot across the stretch of plain that lay between Jamrud and the hills; though not enough —or so Major Cavagnari hoped—to make them visible to any watcher on those hillsides. Once safely across the open ground and among the foothills they had dismounted, and leaving their horses in charge of the sowars, gone forward on foot.

It had been a long and arduous climb, and the darkness had not helped. But as the sky overhead was beginning to lighten, they reached the summit of a five-hundred-foot ridge where Scott, who had been leading, stopped at last, panting and breathless. When he was able to command his voice he spoke in a whisper, as though he were afraid that even on this remote and silent hilltop there might be other listeners: "I think, sir," he said addressing Major Cavagnari, "that this is the place you meant."

Cavagnari nodded and said equally softly: "Yes. We will wait here," and his four companions, who were hot and tired and dripping with sweat, subsided thankfully on the ground and stared about them.

They were looking out across tribal territory: the secret and jealously guarded lands of men who recognized no law other than their own desires, and whose forebears have for centuries swept down from these hills like wolf packs to rob and lay waste the villages on the plains whenever the fancy took them: tribesmen who, though titular subjects of the Amir, have always had to be paid to keep the peace and to hold the passes against the enemies of Afghanistan—or, alternatively, bribed to let those enemies through.

Even with the aid of binoculars the light was still not strong enough to allow the five men on the hilltop to detect much detail in the shadowy, treeless maze of ridges and ravines that lay below them, or to pick out Ali Masjid from the hills that surrounded it. But the higher ranges were beginning to catch the first glimmer of dawn and to stand out clearly against the paling sky.

There was frost on the higher hills, and behind them, very far away, Wigram could see the gleam of snow and the white soaring peak of Sikaram, queen of the Safed Koh. It would be winter soon, he thought; the nights would be bitterly cold, and once the snow began to fall the northern passes would be blocked. He wouldn't have said, himself, it was a good time to start a war in a country like Afghanistan ...

Glancing round at his companions he noticed for the first time that though Stewart, Scott and Colonel Jenkins were all lying at full length among the rocks, elbows propped on the ground as they raked the hills and ridges with their binoculars, Cavagnari alone had remained standing, and unlike the others, showed no interest in the scene ahead. His tall figure, outlined against the sky, conveyed a curious impression of tension, and his head was cocked a little on one side as though he was listening for something; and instinctively, Wigram too began to listen, straining his ears to pick out some unexpected sound in the dawn silence.

At first he could hear nothing but the hiss and whisper of the autumn wind through the rocks and the yellowing grasses, but presently he heard another sound: a faint click of metal on stone, followed by the unmistakable rattle of a displaced pebble rolling away down the hillside. Apparently Cavagnari had heard it too, and Wigram realized suddenly that this was something that the older man had been expecting; for though he made no movement the tension seemed to leave him.

Someone was climbing up towards them from the opposite side of the ridge, and now the others were aware of it too. Colonel Jenkins had dropped his binoculars and there was a revolver in his hand, while Scott and Stewart were on their knees and reaching for their own weapons; but Cavagnari checked them with an imperative gesture, and they waited, all five of them, making no sound and holding their breath to listen, while dawn broke over the plains below and the far snows flushed pink in the first glow of the new day.

The unseen climber was obviously an experienced hillman, for considering the difficulties of the terrain he was making excellent progress up the precipitous slope, and as though to prove what little effect the altitude and strenuous exercise had upon him, he began to hum the *Zakmi dil*, which is an old song that all Pathans know.

928

Not loudly, but hissing it through his teeth—for Asiatics do not whistle.

The tune was no more than a thread of sound, but in that dawn stillness it was clearly audible, and hearing it Cavagnari gave a sharp sigh of relief and motioning to his companions to stay where they were, walked quickly forward and down the hillside. The melody broke off and a moment later they heard him give the Pathan greeting, *"Stare-mah-sheh,"* and receive the conventional reply, and rising to their feet, looked downward and saw him in conversation with a lean, bearded tribesman who was armed with an antiquated matchlock and girt about with a bandolier stuffed full of brass-topped bullets.

It was not possible to hear what the two were saying, for after that first greeting their voices dropped to a murmur, but it was clear that Cavagnari was asking questions and the Pathan replying to them at some length; and presently, as the light strengthened, the man pointed in the direction of Ali Masjid, accompanying the gesture with an upward jerk of the head, and Cavagnari nodded, and turning, came back to the ridge, the stranger following behind him.

"One of my men," explained Cavagnari briefly. "He says that we ought to keep down and stay out of sight, as Ali Masjid is held in force. Also that there is a picket not more than two miles away, and that as soon as the sun is up we shall be able to see it for ourselves."

The Pathan ducked his head in salute to the Sahiblog, and at a word from Cavagnari, withdrew down the back of the ridge to the shelter of a tumble of rocks some twenty to thirty feet below, where he squatted down to wait, while above him the five men flattened themselves among the stones and took up their binoculars again as the featureless, pasteboard outlines of the hills took on shape and dimension and the morning mists shredded away.

The sky above them was no longer pearl-grey but cerulean, and from somewhere out of sight a partridge began to call. Then of a sudden the grass was streaked with long blue shadows, and four miles away as the crow flies, something glinted brightly in the blaze of the rising sun; pinpointing an insignificant hilltop that until then had been indistinguishable among a hundred others.

"Guns," breathed Colonel Jenkins. "Yes, that's Ali Masjid all right, and as your Pathan friend says, it's been well and truly re-inforced. Just look at those breastworks."

The fort, now suddenly visible, crowned a conical hill that barely showed above a stony ridge that was scored with lines of newly built breastworks which the binoculars showed to be well defended. There was also a cavalry encampment at the foot of the ridge, and presently a small body of horsemen emerged from among the tents, and riding up to the Shagai plateau, made their way across it to a little tower near the Mackeson road: presumably the picket that the Pathan had spoken of.

"Time we went, I think," decided Major Cavagnari, putting away his binoculars. "Those fellows have got eyes like hawks, and we don't want to be spotted. Come on."

They found the Pathan still squatting, frontier-fashion, among the rocks, his jezail across his knees, and Cavagnari motioned the others to go on ahead and went over to exchange a last word with him: but catching up with them a few minutes later as they hurried forward down the grassy hillside towards the safety of the plains and their own side of the border, he checked suddenly and called to Wigram who stopped and turned:

"Yes, sir?"

"I'm sorry, but I forgot something—" Cavagnari produced a handful of silver and a packet of cheap country-made cigarettes and thrust it at Wigram. "Be a good fellow and take this up to that man up there, will you? I usually give him a few rupees and some of these things, and I don't want him turning up in Jamrud to demand his baksheesh, and being recognized. We won't wait for you—" He turned and hurried on downward as Wigram started back up the steep slope.

The chill had gone out of the morning and now the sun was hot on Wigram's shoulders and there were butterflies on the hillside: familiar, English-looking butterflies. Fritillaries, brimstones, meadow-browns and tiny common blues that reminded him of summer holidays long ago, when he and Quentin had been boys and gone butterfly-hunting in the fields and lanes of Home. There were birds too, twittering among the grasses, and when a shred of shadow flicked over him he looked up and saw a lammergeyer very high in the blue, soaring majestically above the tumbled ridges of the Khyber.

Now that the sun was up, walking back up the hillside was warmer work than it had been in the chill starlight before dawn, and as he plodded forward, sweat soaked his shirt and ran down into his eyes. He brushed the drops away irritably and wondered if Cavagnari's Pathan would still be there, and if not, what he was supposed to do about it. But a faint sound drifted down to him: the ghost of a melody—*Zakmi dil*, that traditional love-song of a land where homosexuality has always been an accepted part of life . . . *"There's a boy across the river with a bottom like a peach, but alas, I cannot swim . . ."*

The familiar tune was half hummed, half sung, but as the climber drew nearer it changed to something even more familiar, and in that setting, startlingly unexpected: *"D'ye ken John Peel with his coat so gay—"*

Wigram stopped dead, staring upward at the bearded figure squatting in the shade of the rocks. "Well I'm damned—!" He broke into a run and arrived panting. "Ashton—you young devil. I didn't recognize you . . . I had no idea . . . Why the deuce didn't you say something? Why—"

Ash had risen to his feet to grasp the outstretched hand. "Because your friend Cavagnari didn't want the others to know. He wasn't going to let you know either if I hadn't insisted. But I said I had to speak to you, so he agreed to send you back. Sit down, and don't talk too loudly—it's astonishing how far a sound can carry in these hills."

Wigram subsided cross-legged on the ground, and Ash said: "Now tell me the news. Have you heard anything of my wife? Is she all right? I haven't dared try to get in touch with her in case . . . And how are Wally and Zarin?—and the Corps and . . . Oh, everything: I've been starving for news!"

Wigram was able to reassure him about Anjuli, one of the Begum's servants having ridden over to Jamrud only three days earlier, bringing a message to Zarin from his Aunt Fatima to say that all under her roof were well and in good heart, and that she hoped the same could be said of him—and also of his friends. At this last was clearly an oblique inquiry as to whether there was any news of Ash, Zarin had sent back a reply saying that no one need have anxiety on that score; he and his friends were in excellent health.

931

"That was because I'd told him you were getting messages through to Cavagnari, so you were obviously still alive and presumably safe and well," said Wigram, and went on to talk of Wally and what the Guides were doing, and to describe the war-like preparations that were creating chaos throughout the North-Western territories. Men and guns hurriedly transferred from one command to reinforce another; additional regiments rushed up from down-country to fill the gaps; supply trains pouring into the terminus of the North-Western Railway at Jhelum, blocking the platforms and jamming every siding with truck-loads of dead and dying transport mules and other pack animals abandoned by their native drivers. Not to mention the piles of foodstuffs, clothing and ammunition that the under-staffed Commissariat were totally incapable of coping with . . .

"It's like something out of Dante's Inferno," said Wigram, "and the only people who are really enjoying it are the *budmarshes* from every village for miles around, who are having the time of their lives looting the stuff. And to make bad worse, most of the troops from down-country have been sent up wearing tropical kit, so unless something can be done about that pretty quickly, half of them are going to die of pneumonia."

Ash observed sardonically that it sounded like a typical Staff rumpus, and that if it was like this now, God only knew what it would be like if there really was a war.

"Oh, I expect we shall muddle through all right," said Wigram tolerantly.

"Why," demanded Ash, exasperated, "is it necessary to 'muddle through'? Anyone would think that it was 'bad form' to plan ahead and—What are you laughing about?"

"You," grinned Wigram, "squatting there on your hunkers, the dead-spit of a home-grown Khyber bandit, and spouting about 'bad form.' You must admit it has its humorous side."

Ash laughed and apologized, and Wigram said: "I suppose it's that beard that changes you so completely. I'd absolutely no idea it was you. Anyway, I thought you were in Kabul."

"I was. But I wanted to see Cavagnari myself instead of writing or sending a verbal message through the usual channels. I thought that if I could talk to him I might be able to persuade him to see things differently; but I was wrong. In fact all I've done is to make him think that I'm growing far too biased in favour of the Amir, and in grave danger of becoming 'unreliable.' By which I presume he means turning traitor."

"Been losing your temper again, Ashton?" inquired Wigram with a faint smile. "Because you're talking poppycock, you know. Of course he doesn't think anything of the sort. Or if he does, it means you've gone out of your way to give him that impression. What have you been saying to upset him?"

"The truth," said Ash bleakly. "And I might just as well have saved my breath and stayed in Kabul, for he does not want to believe it. I'm beginning to think that none of them do—the fellows in Simla, I mean."

"What won't they believe?"

"That there is no danger whatever of the Amir allowing the Russians to build roads and establish military bases in his country, and that even if he were mad enough to agree to it, his people would not and it is they who count. I've told Cavagnari again and again that the Afghans do not want to take sides with either of us: Russia or the Raj—Yes, yes, I know what you're going to say: he said it too . . . 'But the Amir welcomed the Russian Mission to Kabul.' Well, what if he did? What the hell else could he do—bearing in mind that there was a Russian army across the Oxus and advancing on his borders, half his territories were in revolt, and news of Russian victories in Turkey was spreading across Asia like wildfire? He did his damnedest to put Stolietoff and his lot off, and then tried to delay their arrival; but when it became clear that they were coming anyway, he did the only thing he could do short of shooting them all and taking the consequences: he put a good face on it and gave them a public welcome. That's all there was to it. He didn't want them any more than he wants us, and the Viceroy knows it—or if he doesn't, his intelligence service must be the worst in the world!"

"You must admit that it didn't look too good from this end," observed Wigram judicially, "after all, the Amir had refused to receive a British Mission."

"And why not? We prate about our 'rights' in Afghanistan and our 'right' to have a Mission in Kabul, but

933

who the hell gave us these 'rights'? It isn't our country and it has never been a threat to us—except as a possible ally of Russia's and a base for a Russian attack on India, and everyone knows by now that any danger of that, if it ever existed, ended with the recent signing of the Berlin Treaty. So it's sheer flaming nonsense to pretend that we have anything to fear from Afghanistan herself. The whole thing can almost certainly be settled peaceably; it's not too late for that. There is still time. But it seems that we prefer to consider ourselves seriously threatened and to pretend that we have leaned over backwards to conciliate the Amir, but that our patience is now exhausted. Good God, Wigram, do our blasted Big-wigs *want* a second Afghan war?"

Wigram shrugged his shoulders and said: "Why ask me? I'm only a poor bloody cavalry officer who does what he's told and goes where he's sent. I'm not in the confidence of the great, so my opinion isn't worth much; but from what I hear, the answer is 'Yes'—they do want a war."

"That's what I thought. Imperialism has gone to their heads and they want to see more and more of the map painted pink, and to go down in the history books as great men; Pro-Consuls and modern Alexanders. *Pah!*—it makes me sick."

Wigram said: "You mustn't blame Cavagnari. I heard him tell Faiz Mohammed at Ali Masjid that he was only a servant of the Government, who did what he was told. And that's as true of him as it is of me."

"Perhaps. But men like him, men who really do know something about the Khyber tribes and can talk to them in their own dialects, should be advising the Viceroy and his fellow fire-eaters to hold their horses, instead of urging them to charge. Which is what he would seem to be doing. Oh well, I've done my best; but it was a mistake to think that anyone could ever make him believe anything that he does not want to believe."

"It was worth trying," said Wigram defensively.

"I suppose so," conceded Ash with a sigh. "You know I didn't mean to unload my bile on you. I only meant to ask you about my wife, and about Wally and Zarin and the rest, and to ask you to see that Zarin lets my wife know that you have seen me and talked to me and that I'm all right . . . and so on. I didn't mean to get side-

934

tracked into this other nonsense, but I suppose it's been weighing on my mind too much."

"I'm not surprised," said Wigram with feeling. "It's been weighing on mine too. And if it comes to that, so have you! I've found myself lying awake at night wondering if I did right in interfering and getting you involved in all this, and if I wouldn't have done a lot better to keep my mouth shut and avoid having your death on my conscience."

"I didn't know you had one," mocked Ash, grinning. "You don't have to worry, Wigram: I can look after myself. But I admit I shall be infernally glad when this is over."

"Me too!" agreed Wigram with ungrammatical fervour. "In fact I'll have a word with the Commandant, and see if he can't ask for you to be recalled."

Ash's grin faded and he said ruefully: "No, Wigram, don't tempt me. I walked into this with my eyes open, and you know as well as I do that I must go on with it as long as there is a ghost of a chance that even at this eleventh hour reason may prevail: because Afghanistan is no country to fight a war in—and an impossible one to hold if you win. And anyway, I object, on principle, to injustice."

" 'It isn't fair' in fact," murmured Wigram provocatively.

Ash laughed and acknowledged the hit with a raised palm, but remained unrepentant: "You're right. It isn't fair. And if war is declared, it will be an unjust and unjustifiable war, and I do not believe that God will be on our side. Well, it's been good to see you Wigram. Will you see that my wife gets this"—he handed over a folded and sealed piece of paper—"and give my love to Wally and Zarin and tell them that their Uncle Akbar has their interests at heart. And if you have any influence with Cavagnari, try to persuade him that I am neither a liar nor a renegade, and that to the best of my knowledge everything I have told him is strictly true."

"I'll try," said Wigram. "Goodbye—and good luck."

He rose to his feet and went away down the hillside, and reaching the plain in safety, mounted his waiting horse and rode swiftly back to Jamrud in the bright mid-morning sunlight.

Later that day he had talked with Major Cavagnari

935

about Ash. But the conversation had been brief and inconclusive, and Wigram was left with the impression that he would have done better to leave well alone.

Neither man was, at the time, aware that much of Ash's views were shared by no less a person than Her Majesty's Prime Minister, Lord Beaconsfield—Victoria's beloved "Dizzy"—who in the course of a speech delivered at the Lord Mayor's Banquet at London's Guildhall had expressed them to a nicety: though he had been careful to avoid naming names . . .

"One would suppose, from all we hear," Dizzy had said, "that our Indian Empire is on the eve of being invaded, and that we are about to enter into a struggle with some powerful and unknown foe. In the first place, my Lord Mayor, Her Majesty's Government are by no means apprehensive of any invasion of India by our North-West Frontier. The base of operations of any possible foe is so remote, the communications are so difficult, the aspect of the country is so forbidding, that we do not believe under these circumstances that any invasion of our North-West Frontier is practicable."

But though the invention of the telegraph had made it possible to send news from one end of India to the other with miraculous speed, communication with England was still painfully slow, so no one in India was aware of these sentiments. Nor would the planners in Simla or the busy Generals in Peshawar and Quetta and Kohat have paid much attention to them if they had known, for though Cavagnari's scheme of capturing Ali Masjid had been abandoned, its ultimate effects had proved catastrophic. The formidable number of the reinforcements that Faiz Mohammed had, as a result, hastily gathered for its defence had seriously alarmed the Viceroy's military advisers, who decided that the presence of so large a force within sight of the Frontier was a danger to India and must be countered by a similar mobilization of troops on the British side of the Border.

Once again couriers from India carried letters to Kabul. Letters that accused the Amir of being *"activated by motives inimical to the British Government"* in receiving the Russian Mission, and demanding a *"full and suitable apology"* for the hostile action of the Governor of Ali Masjid in refusing passage to a British one. And once again it was stressed that friendly relations between the two countries depended on the Amir's acceptance of a permanent British Mission in his capital:

"Unless these conditions are accepted, fully and plainly by you," wrote Lord Lytton, *"and your acceptance received by me not later than the 20th November, I shall be compelled to consider your intentions as hostile, and to treat you as a declared enemy of the British Government."*

But the luckless Shere Ali, who had once described himself as being like "an earthen pipkin between two iron pots" (and who by this time had come to detest the British and distrust their motives), could not decide on how to treat this ultimatum. Instead he hesitated and wavered, wringing his hands and railing against fate, and hoping that if he took no action the crisis might somehow dissolve, as previous ones had done. For after all, the Russians had left Kabul and Stolietoff was now actually writing to him to recommend that he make peace with the British—Stolietoff, whose insistence on thrusting his way into Afghanistan, uninvited, had caused all this trouble in the first place. It was too much!

In Simla the Viceroy's Private Secretary, Colonel Colley, who was as eager for war as his lord and master, was writing: *"Our principal anxiety now is lest the Amir should send an apology, or the Home Government interfere."*

Colonel Colley need not have been axious. The twentieth day of November came and went, and there was still no word from the Amir. And on the twenty-first, declaring that he had no quarrel with the Afghan people but only with their ruler, Lord Lytton ordered his Generals to advance. A British Army marched into Afghanistan, and the Second Afghan War had begun.

53

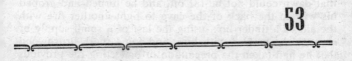

The December weather had been unusually mild, but with the arrival of the New Year the temperature had begun to fall, and there came a day when Ash was aroused in the small hours of the morning by the furtive touch of soft, cold fingers on his cheeks and his closed eyelids.

He had been dreaming again, and in his dream he had been lying half-asleep by the side of a rushing stream in a valley among the mountains. Sita's valley. It was spring and there were pear trees in blossom, and a breeze blowing through the branches loosened the petals and sent them floating down to rest upon his face.

The cool touch of those falling petals and the rushing sound of the stream combined to wake him, and he opened his eyes and realized that he must have slept for a long time, and that while he did so the wind had arisen: and it was snowing.

He had been afraid of this the previous evening. But there had been no wind then, and having lit a small fire in the back of a narrow cave among the rocks, he had cooked himself a meal, and when darkness fell, rolled himself in his blanket and gone to sleep, warmed and comforted by the glow of the firelight. The wind must have arisen some hours later, and now it moaned among the hills and drove a flurry of enormous snowflakes into the cave.

The flakes had settled on Ash's face and beard and he brushed them away, and rising stiffly shook the snow from the folds of his blanket before rewrapping it about his head and shoulders above the sheepskin poshteen that he had worn day and night for the past week or so. The poshteen smelt rankly of smoke and rancid oil, unwashed wool and unwashed humanity, but Ash was grateful for its warmth as the cave was bitterly cold, and would become colder still. Besides, he had become inured to evil smells and did not let such things trouble him.

Peering out into the whirling greyness, he realized that dawn could not be far off, and he turned and groped his way to the back of the cave to light another fire with the aid of a tinder box, using the last of a small supply of charcoal he carried with him, and some spare brushwood that he had taken the precaution of collecting the previous evening. It was not much, but it would serve to heat enough water for a bowl of tea that would warm his stomach and help to bring the circulation back to his numbed feet and cold fingers; and he still had the best part of two chuppattis.

He watched the grass flare up and catch the sticks of wood, and when the charcoal began to glow, placed his brass water-bowl on top of it and sat back to wait while it boiled; and while he waited, thought of all that had happened during the last weeks of the old year and the first few weeks of the new, and wondered how soon he would be permitted to throw his hand in and go back to Mardan; and to Juli.

Lord Lytton's war against Shere Ali (the Viceroy had made a great point of insisting that he had no quarrel with the Amir's subjects) had got off to a good start, despite a series of distressing blunders due to faulty planning. These mishaps, however, had not prevented the fall of Ali Masjid within two days of the outbreak of hostilities, with a loss to the victors of a mere fifteen killed and thirty-four wounded; or, a few days later, the occupation of Dakka and the subsequent occupation of Jalalabad. New Year's Day had seen the British firmly in possession of these three strongpoints, and there had been similar successes on other fronts, notably the occupation by the Kurram Field Force, under the command of Major-General Sir Frederick Roberts, of the Afghan forts in the Kurram Valley.

But something else had occurred in the New Year. Something that had seemed to Ash of such enormous importance that once again he had decided that he must talk directly to Major Cavagnari, who having accompanied the victorious army in the capacity of Political Officer, was at that time in Jalalabad, where he had addressed the durbar held by Sir Sam Browne on the first day of the New Year and endeavoured to explain, to the few Afghan chiefs who had attended it, the reasons for the British Government's declaration of war and its peaceful intentions towards the tribes.

Ash did not think that he would have much difficulty in arranging a meeting with Cavagnari once he reached Jalalabad, for by now the local inhabitants would have realized that they stood in no danger of being massacred by the invading infidels, and would have flocked back to their homes, intent upon selling goods to the troops at greatly inflated prices. The town would therefore once again be swarming with Afridis, and one more would not be remarked.

But he had not allowed for snow, and now he wondered if he would be able to get to Jalalabad at all, because if the present storm continued for long it could obliterate all the tracks and landmarks that he needed to guide him—if it had not done so already. The thought was a grim one and he held out his hands to the fire with a shiver that was not wholly due to the cold. But his luck was in, for the snow had stopped falling by the time it was light enough for him to start, and towards noon he fell in with a small party of Powindahs making for Jalalabad, and in their company reached the outskirts of that walled city a full hour before sunset.

The business of getting in touch with Major Cavagnari had proved reasonably easy and late that night he had been met by arrangement, at a spot outside the walls, by a shadowy figure wearing a poshteen and further protected from the freezing night by a dun-coloured shawl; the latter worn wrapped about head and shoulders without entirely concealing a cavalry turban beneath. After Ash had identified himself and answered a few whispered questions, he was taken past the sentries on the gate and along a series of narrow unlit alleyways between the blank walls of houses, to a small and unobtrusive door where a second muffled figure awaited him. A minute later he was being ushered into a lamp-lit room where the ex-Deputy Commissioner of Peshawar, now Political Officer to the Peshawar Valley Field Force, was working late on the piles of reports that littered his desk.

The news that Ash brought was both startling and tragic, though its tragic side escaped Major Cavagnari, who had never had any sympathy with Shere Ali.

The Amir, on learning that his reply to Lord Lytton's ultimatum had arrived too late and that his country was being invaded and his fortresses falling like ripe nuts in a gale, had lost his head and decided to throw himself on the mercy of the Tsar.

The mounting pressure of events had already forced him to acknowledge his eldest son, Yakoub Khan (whom he had kept under house-arrest for many years, and still hated), as his heir and co-ruler in open council, but it had been a bitter and humiliating experience for him, and the only way in which he could avoid the painful embarrassment of having to share his councils with an unfilial son, while his heart still bled for the death of a dearly loved one, was to remove from Kabul. This he had done, explaining that he intended to journey to St. Petersburg to lay his case before the Emperor Alexander, and demand justice and the protection of all right-thinking European Powers against the encroachments of Great Britain . . .

"Yes, I know all this," said Major Cavagnari patiently, adding with a tinge of rebuke that Ash must not think he was the sole source of information as regards affairs in Kabul. "We heard of the Amir's intentions. In fact he himself wrote to inform the British Government of the step he was taking, and challenged them to establish their case and explain their intentions to a Congress to be held in St. Petersburg. I presume he got the idea of this from the Congress of Berlin, where our differences with Russia were discussed and resolved. I was later informed that he left Kabul on the twenty-second of December for an unknown destination."

"Mazar-i-Sharif, in his province of Turkestan," supplied Ash. "He arrived there on New Year's Day."

"Indeed? Well, I expect we shall soon receive official confirmation of this."

"I'm sure you will. But in the circumstances I thought you should know about it as soon as possible, because of course this will make all the difference."

"In what way?" inquired Cavagnari, still patiently. "We already knew him to be hand-in-glove with the Russians, and this merely proves that we were right."

Ash stared. "But sir—Don't you see, he's no longer of any importance? He's finished himself as far as his people are concerned, because after this he can never return to Kabul or sit on the throne of Afghanistan again. If he'd stayed and stood firm, he would have become the rallying point of every infidel-hating Afghan in his Kingdom —which means ninety-nine and a half per cent of the population—but instead he chose to turn tail and run away, leaving Yakoub Khan to hold the candle. I do assure you, sir, he's finished; bust, smashed, *klas-shu*! But that's not why I came here, for it is no longer of any importance. I came to tell you that he will never reach St. Petersburg, because he is dying."

"*Dying*? Are you sure?" demanded Cavagnari sharply.

"Yes, sir. Those who are closest to him are already saying that he knows this himself and is hastening his death by refusing food and medicines. They say that he is a broken man. Heart-broken by grief at the death of the son he doted upon and the humiliation of having to acknowledge as his heir the one he detested: and also by the intolerable pressures brought to bear on him by Russia and ourselves. He has nothing left to live for, and no one believes that he will ever leave Turkestan—or would get very far if he tried to, as the Russians would certainly turn him back. Now that they have officially shaken hands with us, Afghanistan has obviously become a bit of an embarrassment to them, and I imagine they'd prefer to forget about the place . . . until the next time, of course. I have also heard on good authority that Shere Ali has written to General Kaufman asking him to intercede on his behalf with the Tsar, and that Kaufman has written back urging him not to leave his kingdom and advising him to make terms with the British. So he must know by now that there is no help to be expected from Russia, and that in leaving Kabul he has made a fatal and irreparable mistake. One cannot help feeling sorry for him; but at least it means that the war can now be ended and our troops sent back to India."

"Back to India?" Cavagnari's brows snapped together. "I don't understand you."

"But surely, sir . . . Didn't the Viceroy's proclamation say that we had no quarrel with the Afghan people, but only with Shere Ali? Well, Shere Ali has gone. He's left Kabul, and you of all men, because you understand these people, must know that he will never be allowed to go back again—Yakoub Khan will see to that! Besides, as I've told you, he's a dying man and any day now you are going to hear that he is dead. But whether he lives or dies, he doesn't count any more. So who are we fighting?"

Cavagnari did not answer, and after a moment Ash spoke heatedly into the silence:

"Look, sir, if it's true that we have no quarrel with his people, then I'd like to know what the hell we are still doing here, weeks after he threw up the sponge and did a bunk? I'd like to know what our excuse is now for invading their homes and annexing their territories, and

942

when they resist (which shouldn't surprise us), shooting them down and burning their villages and fields so that their women and children and the old and feeble are left without food and shelter—and in midwinter, too. Because that is what we are doing, and if Lord Lytton meant what he said about having no quarrel with the Afghan people, he should stop this war now, at once; for there is no longer any reason for going on with it."

"You forget," said Major Cavagnari coldly, "that as Shere Ali appointed his son Yakoub Khan co-ruler, Ya-koub will now be acting as Regent. Therefore the country still has a ruler."

"But not an *Amir*!"—it was almost a cry of pain. "How can we pretend that we have any quarrel with Yakoub, when he has been held prisoner for years and his release has been urged again and again by a number of our own officials? Surely, now that he is virtually ruler of Afghanistan, it should at least be possible to call a truce until we see how he means to behave? It couldn't do us any harm, and it would save a great many lives. But if we are going to press on with this war without even waiting to see what he will do, we shall throw away any chance of turning him into a friend, and merely ensure that he too, like the father he hated, becomes our enemy. Or is that what we want? Is it?"

Once again, Cavagnari did not answer, and Ash repeated the question again, his voice rising dangerously. "Is that what you *really* want?—you and the Viceroy and the rest of His Excellency's advisers? Is this whole blood-stained business just an excuse to take over Afghanistan and add it to the Empire—and to hell with its people, with whom we say we have no quarrel? Is it? *Is it*? Because if so—"

"You forget yourself, Lieutenant Pelham-Martyn," interrupted Cavagnari icily.

"Syed Akbar," corrected Ash with acidity.

Cavagnari ignored the correction and swept on: "And I must ask you not to shout. If you cannot control yourself you had better leave before you are overheard. We are not in British India now, but in Jalalabad, which is full of spies. I would also point out that it is neither your place nor mine to criticize the orders we are given, or to question matters of policy that lie outside the scope of our

943

knowledge. Our duty is to do what we are told, and if you are incapable of this, then you are of no further use to me or to the Government I have the honour to serve, and I feel that you would do better to sever your relations with us now."

Ash sighed deeply and relaxed. He felt as though a weight had been lifted off his shoulders: a dragging weight of responsibility that like Sinbad's Old Man of the Sea had been growing steadily heavier and more irksome to carry. Though he had the sense to realize that this was largely his own fault for being conceited enough to imagine that the information he had been at such pains to collect would be considered sufficiently important to affect the decisions of the Viceroy's council, and to weigh the scales of power in favour of peace instead of war. He should have known better.

His usefulness—if any—had lain only in the fact that his messages served to confirm or contradict the accuracy of tales sent in by native spies who were prone to exaggerate, or suspected of being over-credulous. As a check on such stories his own efforts had probably been of use, but apart from that they had counted for very little; and made no difference at all to the Viceroy's decisions—or to anyone else's. The vital issue of Peace or War must already have been decided upon before ever he himself volunteered to serve as a spy, and it would not have been altered except on direct orders from London, or the complete and absolute submission of Shere Ali to the demands of the Viceroy and the Government of India.

"I needn't have bothered," thought Ash. "Here have I been thinking of myself as the White Hope of Asia, and imagining that thousands of lives could depend on what I could find out and what use I made of it, and all the time I've been no more than just one more informer spying for the Raj—and not even drawing extra pay and allowances for it!"

The humour of it suddenly struck him and he laughed for the first time in many weeks, and then seeing the startled distaste on Cavagnari's face, apologized:

"I'm sorry, sir. I didn't mean to offend you. It's only that . . . I've been taking myself so seriously of late. Seeing myself as a sort of *deus ex machina* with the fate of my friends and the nation—two nations—depending

944

upon me. You are right to get rid of me. I'm not cut out for this sort of work, and I should have had more sense than to let myself be talked into it in the first place."

He had not expected the older man to understand how he felt, but Louis Cavagnari was only English by adoption. The blood in his veins was French and Irish, and he too was a romantic—seeing History not only as the story of times past, but as something in the making. Something that he himself could play a part in . . . Perhaps a great part . . .

His expression softened and he said: "There is no need to talk like that. You have been a great help. Much of the information that you have sent us has proved valuable, so you must not think that your efforts have been wasted. Or that I am not deeply grateful to you for all that you have done, and all that you have attempted to do. No one is more aware than I am of the grave risks you have run and the dangers you have cheerfully faced; and of the sacrifices you have made. In fact once this campaign is over, I shall have no hesitation in recommending that you be awarded a decoration for bravery."

"Rats!" observed Ash inelegantly. "I do beg you will do no such thing, sir. I hate to disillusion you, but for someone like myself there has been precious little danger, for I have never felt very different from the people I have met and talked to while I have been here. I haven't had to —to shed a skin, if you know what I mean, or grow another one. That has made it easy for me. That, and the fact that the country has been so disturbed with levies being rushed from point to point, that a stranger in one of the tribal districts no longer stands out like a sore thumb. So you see I have never really felt afraid for myself. I don't think anyone quite understands that; but it has made a great difference. The only thing I have been afraid of, and that weighed on my mind, has been my responsibility, as I saw it, for preventing a disastrous mistake: another—Oh, well, you know all about that, so there's no point in going into it again."

"None," agreed Cavagnari briefly. "On that subject we must agree to differ. But I repeat, I am sincerely grateful to you. I mean that. I am also sorry that our ways have to part. I shall of course pass on to the proper authorities the news you have just brought me regarding Shere Ali's arrival at Mazar-i-Sharif and the state of his health, and also your personal view of the situation. It may make some difference; I don't know. But the conduct of this war is not in my hands. If it were . . . But that is neither here nor there. This is goodbye then. I presume you will be returning to Mardan? If it would be of any help, I could arrange for you to travel back to Peshawar with one of our convoys."

"Thank you, sir, but I think it would be better if I found my own way back. Besides, I'm not sure yet when I shall be leaving. That will be up to my Commanding Officer."

Cavagnari gave him a sharp, suspicious look but refrained from comment and the two men shook hands and parted. The Political Officer turning back immediately to his desk and the work that demanded his attention, while his erstwhile agent was shown out into the street by the confidential servant who had admitted him, and who now locked and barred the door behind him.

After the heated office the night air felt piercingly cold, and the man who on Cavagnari's orders had brought Ash into the fortified town, and been instructed to wait and see him safely out again, had taken shelter from the wind in the doorway of the opposite house, so that for a moment Ash was afraid he had gone, and spoke anxiously into the windy darkness:

"Zarin?"

"I am here," said Zarin, coming forward. "You have been a long time talking to the Sahib and I am perished with cold. Did your news please him?"

"Not particularly. He already knew half of it, and will hear the rest within a day or two. But we cannot talk here."

"No," agreed Zarin. He led the way through the unlighted streets, moving as swiftly and silently as a cat, and presently stopped beside a low, mud-brick building below the outer wall. Ash heard an iron key grate in a lock, and then he was being shown into a small room lit by a single *chirag* and the red glow from a charcoal brazier that filled the cramped space with a welcome warmth.

"Your quarters?" asked Ash, squatting on his heels and spreading out his hands to the glowing coals.

"No. I have borrowed it from one of the nightwatchmen who is on duty at this time. He will not be back before dawn, so we shall be safe for some hours; and there is much that I wish to hear. Do you know that it is close on seven months since I last saw you? That is more than half a year—and in all that time I have heard nothing. Not one word: save only that Wigram-Sahib had seen and spoken to you on the crest of Sarkai Hill early in November, and that you had asked him to see that a letter went by a safe hand to Attock."

Zarin had carried that letter himself, and was able to report that Anjuli was in good health and much beloved by all the household, and that she had been studying Pushtu with such diligence that she could already speak it fluently. Also that both she and his aunt prayed daily for Ash's safety and his early return—as did Gul Baz and all in the Begum's house. "There. Now that I have told you what you most wish to know, you can eat with a quieter mind. Here are chuppattis and *jal frazi* that I have kept hot for you. You do not look to me as though you have fed well of late; if at all—you are as lean as an alley-cat."

"So would you be if you had come on horseback and by camel, and on foot over the Lataband, from Charikar beyond Kabul in little more than five days," retorted Ash, falling upon the food. "It is not a journey to be undertaken in winter, and as it was necessary to come quickly, I have eaten and slept in the saddle so that I need not waste the nights."

He reached for a tin mug filled with strong tea and liberally sweetened with *gur*, and drank thirstily, and Zarin, watching him, said: "Is it permitted to ask what news you carried?"

"Why not? I came to tell Cavagnari-Sahib something that he already knew. That the Amir Shere Ali has left Kabul, intending to travel to Russia in order to lay his case before the Tsar. And also, which he did not know, that the Amir is now in Mazar-i-Sharif and will never live to cross the Oxus, let alone reach St. Petersburg, for he is a dying man, and therefore his son, Yakoub Khan, is already Amir of Afghanistan in all but name."

Zarin nodded assent. "Yes. The first part was already known; the news of Shere Ali's flight was brought to Jalalabad by one of our pensioners, Nakshband Khan, who was once a Risaldar of the Guides Cavalry and now lives in Kabul."

"I know. I too have been living in Kabul. I obtained

947

work there as a scribe—in the Bala Hissar itself—and it was I who asked him to carry that news to Cavagnari-Sahib."

"*Wah-illah*! I might have known. But if that is so, why come here yourself in such haste?"

"I came because I hoped to make it clear that this flight of the Amir's means that he can no longer claim to rule Afghanistan, and that this is the end of the road for him, and therefore, if there is any justice, an end to the war also, which the Viceroy-Sahib insisted was against the Amir only. I hoped that this would mean that the fighting could now cease, but it seems not. The war will continue because the Lat-Sahib and the Jung-i-lat-Sahib and other like-minded men wish it to continue. As for me, I am a free man again. Cavagnari-Sahib having told me that he no longer needs my services."

"So? That is indeed good news!"

"Perhaps. I do not know, for there are two words about that. Zarin—is it possible for me to speak to Hamilton-Sahib without anyone knowing?"

"Not unless you can arrange to stay in Jalalabad until he returns, and I do not know when that will be; he and some others of our *rissala* have accompanied an expedition against the Bazai clan of the Mohmands. They left only yesterday and may not be back for several days."

"And Battye-Sahib? Has he gone with them? Him I must see."

"No, he is here. But it will not be easy for you to see him without anyone coming to hear of it, because he has recently been made a Major-Sahib and given command of the *rissala;* and that being so he has much work to do and is seldom alone—unlike Cavagnari-Sahib, who has many visitors who come to see him by stealth and at strange hours of the night. But I will see what can be arranged."

The news of Wigram's promotion was a surprise to Ash, who did not know that Colonel Jenkins had been given command of a newly formed Brigade consisting of the 4th Mountain Battery, the Guides Infantry and the 1st Sikhs, and he said: "Tell me what has been happening here. I know almost nothing of what our armies have done, because where I have been the talk has always been on the other side, and I have heard only that the Amir's forces inflected great casualties on the British

948

before withdrawing from their positions, with small loss to themselves, in order to lure the invaders further from their base-camps and make it easier for small parties of raiders to cut their supply lines. They also speak of the Peiwar Kotal as though it was a great victory for the Afghans, and it was not until yesterday that I learned by chance that this was not so, and that it was stormed and held by our troops. Tell me what you yourself know or have heard at first hand."

Zarin knew a good deal, and during the hour that followed Ash learned much that he had not known before; though some of it he had suspected. The Guides, being part of the Peshawar Valley Field Force, had not been involved in the battle for the Peiwar Kotal; but a kinsman of Zarin's had taken part in both attacks, and having been wounded and spent a week or two in hospital, was sent home on sick-leave. Zarin had bumped into him in Dakka and been given an account of the action, and according to the wounded man, General Roberts, commander of the Kurram Valley Field Force, had been deceived by the false reports of Turi spies, employed by the Afghans, into thinking that the enemy were retreating in disorder and the heights of the Peiwar Kotal could be taken without a fight. His troops set out in force from the Kurram Forts, only to find at the end of the long march, when all were tired and cold and hungry, that the Afghans were ready and waiting for them, strongly entrenched and in great numbers.

"It was learned afterwards, so my cousin told me," said Zarin, "that the enemy's strength had been greatly increased by the arrival of four regiments and six guns from Kabul, so that they numbered close on five thousand men with seventeen guns. Moreover they fought, he said, with great valour and fury, repulsing us again and again and inflecting such heavy losses that it took our army close on two days to capture the Peiwar Kotal. Wherefore the victory when it came proved a most costly one, both in blood and the materials of war."

Even making allowances for the boastful talk he had heard in Kabul and Charikar, Ash had suspected that all was not going too well for the forces of the Raj; and most of what Zarin told him confirmed this. The victorious advance upon Kabul appeared to have ground to a halt for lack of transport, while the troops encamped in

Jalalabad and the Kurram were suffering from sicknesses brought on by the severe cold—the hardest hit being the British regiments and those from down-country, who were unaccustomed to such freezing temperatures. There was also a chronic shortage of pack-animals, and so little fodder in the Khyber that for weeks past the chief Commissariat Officer had been complaining that unless he could send his camels back to the plains for a fortnight's grazing, he would need new ones in the spring to replace the thousands that would be dead, and whose rotting carcasses were bound to breed a pestilence.

Similar complaints, said Zarin, had come from the Kurram front; and also from Kandahar, where that part of General Stewart's army that had occupied Khelat-i-Ghilzai had been forced to fall back and were now encamped. The other part, which had been advancing on Herat, had been brought to a stop on the Helmand—as had General Sam Browne in Jalalabad. Zarin had been told by the men of a new draft that had arrived a few days ago that at Dadar, Jacobabad and Quetta there was the same crippling lack of transport, and that the desert and the passes were strewn with dead camels and abandoned stores . . .

"Were I a superstitious man," said Zarin, "which, by the mercy of the All-Merciful, I am not, I would say that this year is an ill-omened one, and that we have entered it under an evil star, not only here in Afghanistan, but eastward also. For there is news that throughout Oudh and the Punjab and the North-West Provinces the winter rains have again failed, and thousands are dying of famine. Had you heard this?"

Ash shook his head and said that he had not; but that what he did know was that here in Afghanistan the entire population were confident of victory, and that Shere Ali had issued a Royal *Firman* in which he spoke of the defeats and casualties suffered by the invaders and the victories gained by his own "lion-devouring warriors," who in fighting the armies of the Raj displayed such bravery that of those who died, not one of them went to Paradise until he had slain at least three of the enemy. Both sides always spoke like that in time of war: it was only to be expected. Yet because of the nature of the country and the lack of communication between tribes—and because they had not yet suffered a major defeat—there was no Afghan who was not convinced that their forces could easily prevent an advance on Kabul . . .

"They must know well that we have captured Ali Masjid and the Peiwar Kotal," put in Zarin grimly.

"True. But the men who fought against us there have given such a one-sided account of the fighting, boasting of the losses they inflicted upon us and minimizing their own, that it is not surprising that those who hear their talk still look for another Afghan victory such as their fathers won close on fifty years ago, when they destroyed an entire British Army in the space of a few days. They have never forgotten that tale—as your father himself warned me —and today it is repeated everywhere: even the youngest children know it. Yet I have found no one who remembers or has even heard of General Sale-Sahib's successful defence of this town of Jalalabad; or of Pollack-Sahib's victorious march through the Khyber Pass and his destruction of the Great Bazaar in Kabul. Those are matters that they choose to forget or have never been told of; and in this I think lies our greatest danger, for as long as they remain confident that they can defeat us with ease they will make no terms with us—because they think they have us trapped and can destroy us whenever they choose."

Zarin gave a short laugh and said: "Let them try it! They will soon find out that they are mistaken."

Ash did not reply, for after some of the things that Zarin had told him that night he was not so sure that he was right about this, since how could an invading army move without transport? or hold a captured fortress unless it could keep a garrison armed and fed? Carts had to be drawn and such things as food, ammunition, tents and medical supplies had to be carried by pack animals— who must also be fed. Nor did men who were cold and sick and hungry win battles, and in Ash's opinion Lord Lytton would be well advised to seize the chance that Shere Ali's flight had provided, and call a halt now. To do so would not only prove that he had spoken the truth when he said that this war was against Shere Ali alone, and not against the people of Afghanistan, but if he did it at once, while the British still held Ali Masjid and the Peiwar Kotal and such cities as this one (and could be seen to control the Khyber and the Kurram), it should be possible to come to some equitable agreement with Yakoub Khan when his father died—which would be any day now. This could well lead to a just and lasting peace between the Raj and Afghanistan. But if the war continued, Ash could see only one end to it: another massacre.

Zarin, who had been watching him, may have read his thoughts, for he said philosophically: "What will be, will be. The matter is not in our hands. Now tell me of your own doings—"

Ash told him, and Zarin brewed more tea and sat sipping it as he listened; and when the tale was ended he said: "You have more than earned your freedom from Cavagnari-Sahib's service. What do you mean to do now? Shall you join the *Rissala* here, or set out for Attock in the morning? After this, they will surely give you leave."

"That will be for the Commandant-Sahib to decide. See if you can arrange for me to see him tomorrow: not in the camp, for that would be unwise. The river bank will be best; I could walk there in the evening. Can I spend the night here?"

"Assuredly. I will tell the nightwatchman, who is a friend of mine. And as regarding the Commandant-Sahib, I will do what I can."

Zarin gathered up the dishes and withdrew, and Ash settled down contentedly to sleep, warmed not only by the fire but by the comfortable conviction that all his troubles were over, and that tomorrow or the next day he would be given permission to return to Attock to see Juli and enjoy a few days of well-earned leave, before arriving in Mardan as though he was returning from this mythical course in Poona.

There is little doubt that had he been able to see Wigram that night, or even very early next morning, Ash would have carried out this programme. But here Fate in the form of Major General Sir Sam Browne, v.c., stepped in. The General had invited Cavagnari to take *chota hazri* with him that morning in order that they might discuss a few matters in private, prior to an official conference that would be taking place in the afternoon. And it was in the final moments of this informal talk that Cavagnari, recalling that the General had once been Commandant of the Guides and might therefore be interested, spoke of Ashton Pelham-Martyn and his recent role as an intelligence agent operating from inside Afghanistan.

The General had been more than interested, and having asked a great many questions, remarked that he remembered the boy's arrival in Mardan very well, and that, by Jove, that had been a rum affair . . . curious to think that a lot of fellows who had been there, like Jenkins and Campbell and Battye for instance, had only been junior lieutenants at the time . . .

He relapsed into silence, and Major Cavagnari, taking this to be a hint, made his escape—he had a busy morning ahead of him and must find time to write to Major Campbell (who was officiating as Commandant of the Corps of Guides in the temporary absence of Colonel Jenkins), informing him that he had dispensed with Lieutenant Pelham-Martyn's services, and that as far as he was concerned, the Lieutenant was now free to return to his regimental duties. But even as he was writing this, Colonel Jenkins's replacement was reading another note: one that had been scribbled by Sam Browne and sent off by a galloper within a few minutes of Cavagnari's departure, requesting Major Campbell's presence at the General's quarters at the earliest possible moment.

Campbell had ridden over immediately, wondering what fateful plans were in the wind, and been startled to discover that the General wanted to talk to him about Ash. "I gather he's here in Jalalabad, and that Cavagnari has given him the sack and seems to think that he will now report at once for duty with the Regiment. Well, I'm sorry to disappoint him, but I have other ideas—"

The General's ideas would probably not have pleased Major Cavagnari had he heard them, for they ran counter to his own views on the reliability of Lieutenant Pelham-Martyn's information. But then, as Sam Browne pointed out, he himself was not interested in the purely political angle but only in the military one—in which sphere he considered that someone like young Pelham-Martyn would be invaluable.

"Cavagnari considers him to have become so pro-Afghan that his bias in their favour made his information suspect, if not actually unreliable. Well, I have my doubts about that. But the point is that the kind of information that we of the Peshawar Valley Field Force require has nothing whatever to do with politics, and provided you

953

can assure me that Pelham-Martyn has not turned traitor, then he is precisely what I have been looking for—someone who can send us early and accurate information as to the existence and whereabouts of hostile bands of tribesmen; their numbers and movements and how well or poorly they are armed, and so on. In a country like this that kind of knowledge is worth more than an extra army corps, and the long and short of it is that I'm asking you to see to it that this fellow carries on in his present role: only on our behalf instead of for the political Johnnies."

Chips Campbell, who until now had known nothing whatever about Ashton's work or whereabouts and supposed him to be in Poona, had agreed to the General's request, though expressing the opinion that it "seemed rather hard luck on the poor chap."

"You can put the blame on me," said General Sam. "Tell him that you are acting on my orders: which is perfectly true. Anyway, until Jenkins returns you are his Commanding Officer, and I'm yours; and there's a war on. Now listen . . ."

Ash had taken the news stoically. It had been a bitter blow, but there was nothing he could do about it. He was a serving officer and he had volunteered for this work, so he listened impassively while Wigram, who had been deputed by Campbell to meet him as though by chance on the river bank in the course of an evening ride, gave him a number of detailed instructions as to the type of information that the General required, the best methods of relaying it, and various other relevant matters . . .

"I can't tell you how sorry I am about this," said Wigram in conclusion. "I tried to talk Chips into standing up to General Sam, but he says it would be a waste of time, and I suppose he's right. Oh, by the way, the General thinks you should leave Jalalabad as soon as possible, and he suggests you continue to use Kabul as your base because sooner or later we shall have to take the place—unless the Afghans call 'Pax!' before then of course."

Ash nodded, and that night Zarin, who had arranged the meeting, met him at the same spot outside the walls where they had met on the previous night, and after a brief talk, watched him walk away into the darkness with the slouching, loose-limbed stride of the hillman. And on the following day Wally and his handful of sowars had returned to Jalalabad. But by then Ash was almost twenty miles away among the hills beyond Gandamak.

That had been in January, before the blizzards began and the passes were blocked with snow. Towards the end of the month, a letter that Ash had given to Zarin before he left Jalalabad arrived by devious means at Fatima Begum's house in Attock, and three days later Anjuli set out for Kabul.

Those few days had been fraught ones. Both the Begum and Gul Baz had been horrified at the idea of her even considering such a journey; particularly at that season of the year—and in time of war, too!—it was not to be thought of. And certainly not permitted, as a lone woman travelling through such wild country would be bound to be set upon by *budmashes,* murderers and robbers. "But I shall not be alone," said Anjuli. "I shall have Gul Baz to protect me."

Gul Baz had declared that he would have nothing to do with such a mad scheme, and that Pelham-Sahib would have his head if he agreed to it—and rightly so. Whereupon Anjuli announced that in that case she would go alone.

Had she raved and wept they might have felt more capable of dealing with the situation, but she had been perfectly calm. She had neither raised her voice nor indulged in hysterics, but merely said that her place was at her husband's side, and that though she had agreed to a separation that might last for half a year, the prospect of yet another six months—perhaps even more than that— was more than she could face. Besides, now that she could speak Pushtu and pass as an Afghan woman, she would no longer be either a danger or a hindrance to him, while as for any danger to herself, what had she to be afraid of in Afghanistan compared with what she must always be afraid of in India? Here she could never be sure that some spy from Bhithor would not track her down and kill her; but she could at least be sure that no Bhithori would ever dream of venturing over the Border into tribal territory. She already knew that her husband had found a home in Kabul under the roof of a friend of Awal Shah's, Sirdar Bahadur Nakshband Khan, so she knew where to go, and they could not stop her.

They had tried to do so, but without success. The Begum, shedding tears, had locked her in her room and set Gul Baz on guard in the garden below in case she should attempt to escape via the window (though even if she had been able to lower herself to the ground, the surrounding walls were far too high to climb). Anjuli had retaliated by refusing all food and drink, and after two days of this, realizing that she was faced with a determination even greater than her own, the Begum capitulated.

"Forgive me, Begum-Sahiba—dearest aunt—you have been so good to me, so kind, and I have repaid you by causing all this anxiety. But if I do not go I shall die of fear, for I know that he carries his life in his hands, and that if he is betrayed he will die a slow and terrible death . . . and I not there. Not even knowing for months, perhaps for years, if he is alive or dead—or held prisoner in some dreadful place, cold and starving and in torment . . . as I myself once was. I cannot endure it. Help me to go to him, and do not blame me too much. Would you not have done as much for your husband?"

"Yes," admitted the Begum. "Yes, I would have done the same. It is not an easy thing to be a woman and love with the whole heart: which men do not understand —they having many loves, and delighting in danger and war . . . I will help you."

Deprived of the Begum's support, Gul Baz had been forced to capitulate to what amounted to blackmail, since he could not possibly allow Anjuli-Begum to travel alone. She would not even wait until Ash's views could be obtained; which admittedly might have taken many weeks, for though it had been possible for Zarin to risk smuggling that letter out of Afghanistan, it was not nearly as easy for anyone in Attock to send one the other way, and even Zarin in Jalalabad would have found it difficult to get in touch with "Syed Akbar." In consequence, they set out for Kabul on the following day, taking little with them beyond food and a small sum of money—and the jewels that had been part of Juli's dowry and which Ash had brought away from the *chattri* by the burning-ground in Bhithor.

The Begum had provided Afghan dress, a sheepskin poshteen and Gilgit boots for Anjuli, and charged Gul Baz with procuring two broken-down nags in the bazaar, capable of bearing them, but unlikely to attract the attention or envy of even the most acquisitive tribesman. She had herself stayed up to see them depart unobtrusively and by night, as Ash had done; and as she bolted the little side gate behind them, she sighed, remembering her own youth and the handsome young man who had brought her to this house as a bride so many years ago, and whom she had loved so greatly. "Yes, I too would have done the same," mused the Begum. "I will pray that she will be permitted to reach Kabul in safety and find her man there. But it is ill weather for travelling, and I fear the journey will be a hard one."

It had been even harder than the Begum feared, and in the course of it they had lost one of the horses, the animal having slipped while being led along a narrow track that was barely more than a ledge of rock, and fallen to its death in a gully some three hundred feet below. Gul Baz had risked his neck climbing down the treacherous, icy slope in the teeth of a gale in order to rescue the saddle-bags, because they could not afford to lose the provisions they contained, and he had had a hard time crawling back with them to safety. Later they had twice been snowbound for several days, but the Begum's prayer had been answered: after more than a fortnight on the road they had reached Kabul safely, and knocking at the door of a house in a quiet street in the shadow of the Bala Hissar, found Ash there.

54

On the twenty-first day of February 1879, Shere Ali died in Mazar-i-Sharif in Afghan Turkestan, and his son Yakoub Khan became Amir in his stead. But the new Amir, far from making overtures to the British, was already hard at work building up and re-organizing the Afghan army.

Cavagnari's spies reported that the fighting-men in Kabul and Ghazi were determined to avenge the capture of Ali Masjid and the Peiwar Kotal, and that they already numbered seven thousand cavalry and twelve thousand infantry, together with sixty guns; though this and similar items of information had been treated with a certain amount of scepticism, as it came from native informers who had a tendency to embroider a good story. But Wigram Battye had received private confirmation of this from someone signing himself "Akbar," the writer also asserting that even those tribes who were regarded as friendly were becoming restless and hostile, and Afridis everywhere were demanding to know why, now that Shere Ali was dead, the Indian Government should continue to keep an army in Afghanistan and to build forts and barracks in their country? Did this mean that the English did not intend to keep the promises made to the people of Afghanistan at the beginning of the war?

". . . and I would strongly advise," wrote "Akbar," "that you do what you can to persuade those fatheads in authority that this is no time to allow the Survey Department to send out endless small parties to draw maps of the country; it only serves to stir up ill-feeling and confirm a widespread suspicion that the English are plotting to take over the whole of Afghanistan, for as you know, the Pathans have an inveterate hatred of the Surveyor and believe that where the Government sends one, an army will follow. So for God's sake try and get them to stop it."

Wigram had done his best; but without success.

Mr. Scott and his assistants had been savagely attacked while out sketching in the hills, four of their escort being killed and another two wounded; and three weeks later Wally had been involved in a similar incident when he and a troop of the Guides Cavalry, together with a company of the 45th Sikhs, had been ordered to escort yet another survey party. Once again infuriated villagers had attacked the map-makers, and the Sikhs' Company Commander had been mortally wounded.

"Pity about Barclay," said Wigram. "He was a good chap."

"One of the best," agreed Wally. "It seems such a waste, somehow. If it had happened in a pukka battle, I suppose one wouldn't have felt so bad about it. But this—!" He kicked an inoffensive boot-tree across the tent, and after a moment or two added bitterly: "You'd have thought that things were tricky enough in these parts without our deliberately antagonizing the locals by turning up in out-of-the-way places armed with drawing-boards, compasses and theodolites, and letting 'em see that we were making detailed maps of their home villages. Ash was right: it's a lunatic thing to do just now. I suppose you haven't heard from him again?"

"Not since then. I imagine it can't be all that easy for him to send letters. Besides, he must know that each time he does, he runs the risk of being betrayed to the Afghans or blackmailed into paying everything he has in exchange for silence. And anyway, he can have no guarantee that a letter has been delivered."

"No, I suppose not. I wish I could see him. It's been such a long time, and I miss him like the devil . . . I worry about him, too. I keep thinking what it must be like to be alone and on the run in this damnable country, week after week for months on end, knowing that if you put a foot wrong you won't live to repeat the mistake. I don't understand how he can do it. Faith, I know I couldn't!"

"Nor I," said Wigram soberly. "God knows I'm no glutton for fighting, but given the choice, I'd rather take part in half-a-dozen full-scale battles than take on the job of spying behind the enemy lines. One can be scared rigid before a battle—I always am—but the other business calls for a different kind of courage: the lonely, cold-blooded kind that most of us don't have. On the other hand, one has to remember that most of us don't happen to be human chameleons, and that Ashton is a freak in that he can think in Pushtu. Or in Hindi, when the occasion arises—it merely seems to depend on where he happens to be at the time. I've sometimes wondered if he ever thinks or dreams in English. Not very often, I imagine."

Wally turned away to jerk back the tent-flap and stand gazing up at the hills that surrounded Jalalabad, dark now against the darkening sky, while the boisterous March wind tossed his hair into disorder and swirled about the tent, setting the canvas flapping and sending files and papers fluttering to the ground: "I wonder if he's somewhere around here, watching us from those hills up there?"

"I shouldn't think so," said Wigram. "He's probably

in Kabul. Ah!—this sounds like my bath arriving—first I've had in days. The horrors of active service. Well, see you at dinner."

But Wally's surmise had been nearer the mark than Wigram's, for in fact Ash was at that moment in a little village called Fatehabad, less than twenty miles away.

Ever since the outbreak of war, a certain Ghilzai chief, one Azmatulla Khan, had been actively at work fomenting a rising against the British invaders by the inhabitants of the Lagman Valley; and late in February Colonel Jenkins and a small column had dispersed Azmatulla's forces in the valley, but failed to capture him. Now he was known to be back again, and with an even larger following, and on the last day of March Ash had dispatched a further piece of ill news to Jalalabad. The Khugiani tribesmen, whose territory lay barely seventeen miles distant to the south of Fatehabad, were also gathering in great numbers at one of their border fortresses.

On receipt of his information, the Divisional Commander had given orders that certain units were to set out with all speed to stamp out this new unrest before it gathered strength. They would march that very night, taking no tents or heavy baggage with them, and the force would be divided into three columns: one of infantry, another to consist of two squadrons of cavalry (drawn respectively from the Bengal Lancers and the 10th Hussars), and the third of infantry and cavalry combined. This last, which was under the command of General Gough and included two squadrons of Guides, would march on Fatehabad and disperse the Khugianis. Of the other two columns, one could move against Azmatulla Khan and his bravos, while the other crossed the heights of the Siah Koh to cut off the enemy's retreat.

The speed with which the operation was planned and put into execution, and the fact that the columns would move off after dark, would, the General hoped, result in Azmatulla Khan and the Khugianis being taken by surprise; though he should have known better, for Jalalabad was full of Afghan spies—there were probably scores of them in the town and as many others keeping watch by the Kabul River, and not a sabre could have stirred without it being known within the hour. Then, too, following the occupation of the town, Colonel Jenkins—now Brigadier-General Jenkins—had inspected the ford by which the

10th Hussars and the Bengal Lancers would have to cross the river *en route* to the Lagman Valley, and not only condemned it as unsafe, but advised that it should never be attempted by night even at a time when the river was low. But his report had either been pigeon-holed or lost, for though the river was at present in spate, the plan was not altered . . .

The moon was still up when the two squadrons of Hussars and Lancers left camp, but it was sinking fast, and by the time the ford was reached it had been lost to sight behind the near hills, and the valley lay deep in shadow. The river here ran a full three quarters of a mile wide, divided into two channels by a stony island in midstream, and as the trestle bridge had suffered its annual removal some weeks earlier, in order to prevent its being washed away and lost (a major disaster in an area where timber was not easily come by), the only way to cross was by the ford: a wide bar of boulder-strewn gravel that spanned the river between dangerous rapids.

The valley reverberated with the voice of the swollen river, and as the squadrons formed up in half sections, four abreast on the stony bank, even the clash and jingle of accoutrements and the clatter of the chargers' hooves could barely be heard above the roar of the rapids. But the local guide stepped confidently into the water and waded across, followed by the Bengal Lancers whose men, accustomed from childhood to the treacherous Indian rivers had reached the far side in safety. But inevitably, the pull of the current had forced the long column to give ground before it, so that by the time the ammunition mules and their drivers entered the river on the Lancers' heels they found themselves stepping off into deep water, and missing the ford, were snatched away into the rapids.

Their cries were lost in the roar of the river, and the darkness prevented the 10th Hussars—pressing too closely behind them—from seeing what had happened. Captain Spottiswood of the Hussars, at their head, urged his horse forward, felt it lose its footing, recover, and then lose it again. And within minutes the river was full of desperate men and frenzied horses, fighting for dear life as they rolled over and over in the icy grip of the foaming, furious rapids.

Some, including the Captain, survived. But many did

not. Numbed by the bitter cold and hampered by sodden uniforms and cumbersome boots, those who escaped being kicked to death by their struggling chargers were dragged under by the weight of sabres, belts and ammunition pouches, and carried downward, battered and helpless among the unseen boulders, to drown in the deep water.

Forty-two troopers, an officer and three non-commissioned officers died that night—out of a squadron that barely half-an-hour earlier had ridden out from camp seventy-five strong. The news of the disaster had been brought by dripping, riderless horses careering through the lines of the Horse Artillery, making for their own lines beyond; and all that night, by the light of bonfires and torches, men searched and called along the banks of the river.

When dawn broke, the bodies of the officer and eighteen of the rank and file were found wedged among the rocks or drifting face-downward in the eddies under the banks. The rest had been swept down on the flood and were never seen again. As for Azmatulla Khan, his spies having warned him of what was in the wind, he had promptly removed from the Lagman Valley, and the two columns that had been sent to take him had returned empty-handed.

The Khugianis, also forewarned, had shown less caution.

The mixed column whose task was to deal with that tribe had, as planned, been the last to move off. But their departure having been further delayed by the disaster at the ford, midnight had come and gone before they left, and it was close on one o'clock by the time they marched —seeing as they went the distant gleam of bonfires and flares along the river, where the frantic search for survivors continued.

"I said this was an ill-omened year," muttered Zarin to Risaldar Mahmud Khan of the Guides as the squadrons moved off in the darkness, and Mahmud Khan had replied grimly: "And it is not yet old. Let us hope that for many of these Khugianis it will grow no older after tomorrow —and that we ourselves will live to see Mardan again and draw our pensions and watch our children's children become Jemadars and Risaldars in their turn."

"Ameen!" murmured Zarin devoutly.

Despite the darkness and the difficulty of keeping to a

track that even by daylight was barely distinguishable from the rough and stony ground that stretched away on either hand, the long column of infantry, cavalry and artillery had made good progress, and it was still dark when the cavalry, riding ahead, were halted within a mile of the village of Fatehabad and ordered to wait there until the rest of the column caught up with them. By then there was not much of the night left, but Wigram and his two squadrons, old hands at this sort of campaigning, selected a spot under some trees and made themselves tolerably comfortable for what little remained of it.

The village was reported to be friendly, but when the dawn broke it was seen that no smoke rose from it, and a scouting party sent to investigate found that it was deserted. The villagers had taken all their foodstuffs and livestock with them, and except for a few pariah dogs and a gaunt cat who spat at the sowars from the doorway of an empty house, nothing moved. "So much for our intelligence," observed Wigram, eating breakfast in the shade of a tree. "'Friendly,' they said. About as friendly as a nest of hornets! It's obvious that the whole blasted jingbang have run off to join the enemy."

He had sent out patrols under Risaldar Mahmud Khan to report on the movements of the Khugianis, but though the patrols had not returned by the time the guns and the infantry appeared at ten o'clock in the morning, he had by then received news from another source:

"Ashton seems to think that they will stand and fight," said Wigram, tossing over a crumpled scrap of paper that Zarin had just brought him. The brief, scrawled message had come by way of a grass-cutter who said he had been given it by an elderly and unknown village woman, with instructions to take it at once to Risaldar Zarin Khan of the Guides *rissala*, who would reward him. He had supposed it to be a love-letter. But Zarin had known better, for it was written in *Angrezi*. And as only one person could have sent it, he had wasted no time in taking it to his Commanding Officer.

"Enemy entrenched in great strength on plateau overlooking Gandamak road," read Wally. "Estimate 5,000. No guns, but position, defences and morale tip-top. Any attempt to dislodge by frontal attack will mean heavy losses. Shelling might do it. If not, they will have to be lured out into the open, which should not be difficult as discipline nil, but warn you they mean business and will fight like demons. A."

"Good for Ash! I wonder if he is up there with them? —I wouldn't put it past him. Jove, I wish he was here with us. If only—Are you going to pass this on to the General?"

"Yes, for what it's worth," said Wigram, writing hastily in a small loose-leaf notebook. He ripped out the page, folded it, and calling up his orderly, sent him galloping off with it to General Gough. "Not that it'll be needed, because his pickets will have told him as much already. But it won't do any harm to have it confirmed."

"Did you tell him that Ash thinks we should—"

"No, I did not. I don't believe in teaching my grandmother to suck eggs. Believe me, Gough is no fool, and he doesn't need Ashton or anyone else to teach him his business. He'll have worked that out for himself."

General Gough had indeed done so. He had sent out a number of patrols, and later that day he had talked with as many of the local chiefs and Maliks as could be persuaded to meet him, in an endeavour to sound out the temper of the people, and discover, if he could, which tribes were likely to fight and which could be relied on to remain neutral—or to vanish into the hills like Azmatulla and his men.

But as the day wore on it became increasingly clear to him that the whole countryside was hostile, and when patrol after patrol reported further reinforcements hurrying to the help of the Khugianis, he began to work on his plans for the coming battle. There was nothing much that could be done that day as his baggage-animals had still not arrived, and did not do so until well after sunset— plodding wearily into camp as darkness fell and the cooking-fires filled the air with the scent of wood-smoke and a heartening smell of food.

The whole column now knew that there would be a battle on the morrow, and made their preparations accordingly. Wigram had slept soundly that night, and so too had Zarin. They had, to the best of their ability, done all those things that had to be done, and could rest with quiet minds. But Wally had lain awake for a long time, staring up at the stars and thinking.

He had been seven years old when he had seen in the window of a Dublin shop a hand-tinted engraving that depicted a cavalry regiment charging at Waterloo, sabres in hand and plumes flying, and had then and there decided that when he grew up he would be a cavalry officer and ride like that at the head of his men, fighting his country's foes. Now at last—tomorrow if Wigram was right—that old schoolboy dream would come true. For though he had been in action before, he had never yet been in a major engagement, and until now his only experience of a cavalry charge had been practice ones during squadron training. Would the reality turn out to be very different from anything he had imagined? not wildly exciting, but ugly and terrifying—and not glorious at all?

He had heard countless stories of the Afghans' methods of dealing with cavalry. They would lie on the ground, their long razor-sharp knives at the ready, and slash upwards at the legs and bellies of the horses to bring the riders down. A trick, he was given to understand, that could be remarkably successful, particularly in a scrimmage: and he could well believe it. Wigram said that sabres and lances were little use against it, and that a carbine or revolver were one's best hope, since faced with the prospect of being shot on the ground, most Afghans preferred to fight and die on their feet. It was this sort of thing that no amount of practice charges could teach one. But after tomorrow he would know . . .

He wondered where Ash was, and what he was doing. Would he be watching the battle from somewhere up on the hills? If only the two of them could have ridden together tomorrow! Wally gazed into the darkness, and remembering the past, dropped suddenly into sleep—to be awakened in the first faint light of dawn to find the camp stirring to life and his Commanding Officer shaking his shoulder.

"Awake, O Sleeping Beauty," exhorted Wigram. " 'Night's candles are burned out and jocund day stands tip-toe on the misty mountain tops'—jostling for standing-room with a few thousand belligerent tribesmen, I gather. The General suggests you reconnoitre the Khugiani country, so up with you, my young dreamer. 'Go to the ant, thou sluggard.' Breakfast will be along in about ten minutes."

Wally could not remember having seen Wigram in such tearing spirits before. He was by nature a quiet man, and except on rare occasions, such as the annual Guest Night in celebration of Delhi Day, was anything but boisterous. Yesterday, preoccupied by the cares of command and sobered by the tragedy at the ford, he had been even quieter than usual. But now he seemed to have shed ten years and put care behind him, and Wally, struggling to his feet in horror at finding that he had slept through all the stir and noise of the waking camp, caught the infection of those high spirits and found himself laughing instead of apologizing.

"I believe the old fellow is every bit as excited as I am," decided Wally, remembering, as he shaved and dressed in haste, that Wigram had once confessed to him that the sum of his ambition was to get command of the Guides Cavalry, and that anything that came after that, however exalted, would be an anti-climax. "You may think it's not much of an ambition," Wigram had said, "but it's all I've ever wanted. And if I get it I shall say *'nunc dimittis,'* and not care too much if I end up retiring as a crusty old has-been who never even rose to be a Colonel—because I shall have had my moment of glory."

"Well, he's got what he wanted," thought Wally, "and I suppose today will be just as much of a red-letter day for him as it is for me, because if there really is a battle, it will be a 'first time' for both of us. My first cavalry charge and the first time Wigram has led his beloved Command into action in a full-scale engagement."

55

The sky above the deserted village of Fatehabad was brightening with the dawn as the two officers sat down to eat a hasty breakfast. And as they ate, Wigram explained between mouthfuls that the General wished to send two members of his staff south towards Khujah, the principal village of the Khugianis, to test the reactions of the tribe, and that Lieutenant Hamilton and thirty sabres of the Guides Cavalry had been detailed to accompany them and see that they got there—and back again.

A second party, with a similar escort of 10th Hussars, would be reconnoitring the road leading to Gandamak to report on its condition, and it was hoped that both parties would avoid getting involved in a premature exchange of hostilities, and report back to General Gough as soon as possible: "In other words," said Wigram, kindly translating, "don't try jumping the gun and starting any private battles of your own. And if the local citizenry start shooting at you, 'wait not upon the order of your going,' but run like hell. What His Nibs needs at the moment is information, and not a clutch of dead heroes. So keep your eyes peeled. I should imagine you'll be all right—always provided you don't walk into an ambush."

"Don't worry, we shan't do that," said Wally cheerfully. "Zarin says that Ash will see that we don't."

Wigram helped himself to chuppatti and said with a smile: "Of course. I'd forgotten he'd be there. Well, that's something off my mind. Hullo—here comes the gilded Staff. Time you were off, Walter."

It was half past seven and the sun was drying the dew from the near hillside by the time Wally mounted his waler Mushki—"the brown one"—and rode away with the two Staff Officers, the thirty men of the escort cantering sedately behind them. An hour later, from high ground, they came suddenly within sight of a great *lashkar* of tribesmen, barely a mile or so distant across the hills. It was no peaceful gathering, for Wally could see the flutter of standards and the glint and flash of metal as the morning sunlight shone on curved swords and brassbound matchlocks, and studying the vast concourse through his field-glasses, he came to the conclusion that there must be at least three thousand Khugianis there; and possibly many more who were hidden by the folds in the ground.

A single shot, fired from no great distance, struck a shower of splinters from a rock a few yards ahead, and as he hastily put away his field-glasses and gathered up the reins, the stillness of the morning was further broken by a vicious spatter of musket balls. The enemy had not only seen them, but had obviously taken the precaution of posting pickets; and one of these, cunningly concealed behind a tumble of stones and rock barely five hundred yards away, had opened fire on the intruders. Mindful of his instructions Wally had not lingered. His small force turned tail and galloped out of range, and by ten o'clock they were safely back in camp.

The General, after listening to the report of his Staff

Officers, had ordered that a certain hilltop, from where the enemy's movements could be seen and signalled back to the camp, should be seized immediately, and Wally had gone forward with this party and remained with them for a short time, ostensibly to study the movements of the Khugianis, though in reality in the hope of locating Ash, whom he suspected of firing that first warning shot this morning, as it had certainly not come from the barrel of a Border musket. But even with the aid of field-glasses it was not possible to make out individual faces in the vast, shifting mass of tribesmen who had gathered on a stretch of high ground over a mile ahead; while a careful inspection of the nearer slopes and ridges showed no signs of life—though Wally did not doubt that at least half-a-dozen outposts were concealed among the rocks in the country between this hilltop and the insurgents.

He put away his field-glasses with a sigh and returned to camp to tell Wigram that Ash was right about the Khugianis—anyone could see that they meant business. "There must be thousands of them out there, four or five thousand at least, and they've got a whacking great red standard and a few white ones, and judging from some of their shooting this morning I'd say they've got quite a few carbines as well. What on earth do you suppose we're waiting for? Why don't we get started, instead of sitting around as though we'd only come out to look at the view and have a picnic lunch?"

"My dear Walter, Patience, we are told, is a virtue. You should cultivate it," retorted Wigram. "We—or rather the General—are waiting to hear what those fellows who went out this morning to reconnoitre the Gandamak road have to say, and as soon as they have made their report I expect we'll get our orders to move. But they haven't come back yet."

"Not come *back*?" exclaimed Wally, startled. "But it's half past twelve. I thought they were only going about five miles up the valley? Do you suppose—you don't think they've walked into an ambush, do you?"

"No I don't. If they had, there would have been a lot of firing, and at least some of them would have been able to get back and fetch help. Besides, Ashton would have known and done something about it. No, they're merely doing what they were told to: spying out the land.

They'll probably turn up in time for their *tiffin,* so we can enjoy ours with a clear conscience."

The mid-day meal was already being served, but Wally was impatient for action and far too keyed-up to feel hungry. Having swallowed a mouthful or two standing up, he strode off to see that his men had been fed and that everything was in readiness for the order to march, and Wigram, by now as familiar as Ash with Wally's habit of singing hymns when in high spirits, noticed with amusement that he was crooning "Onward Christian Soldiers" —and thought that in the circumstances it was a bizarre choice of battle song, considering that the sowars were mostly Mussulmans or Sikhs with a sprinkling of Hindus, and that all of them, in the eyes of the singer's Church, were "idol-worshipping heathens."

The Guides had not been kept waiting long. When by one o'clock the missing men had still not returned, General Gough had ordered the camp under arms and despatched Major Battye with three troops of the Guides Cavalry to search for them. He himself, following with seven hundred Sikh, Punjab and British infantry, four guns of the Royal Horse Artillery and three troops of the 10th Hussars.

"This is it!" cried Wally joyously, swinging himself into the saddle, and Zarin, to whom the words had been addressed, caught the import though he did not understand the language, and grinned in acknowledgement as the squadrons formed up four abreast and spurred forward into the shimmering heat of the stone-strewn valley.

They came up with the missing Staff Officers and their escort at a point where the road crossed the sloping ground below a plateau on which the Khugianis were gathering, and the two parties turned back together to join the General, who, hearing what they had to say, halted his infantry where they could not be seen by the enemy, and went forward to assess the position for himself. A brief survey had been enough; for as Wigram had said, Gough needed no one to teach him his business or advise him on how to deal with the situation.

The Khugianis had chosen a perfect defensive position. Their line spanned the rim of the plateau, and the hillside immediately below fell away steeply for a short distance before merging into the long, gentle slope that met the Gandamak road and the comparatively level ground on the far side. Both flanks of their line were protected by steep cliffs, while their front had been further reinforced by massive stone breastworks. Had they been able to mount guns, their position would have been virtually impregnable, and as it was, to attack it head-on would be suicidal, while to detach troops in an attempt to turn it would mean seriously weakening the small British force that was already out-numbered by five to one. The only hope, as Ash had said and the General now saw, was to lure the Khugianis out into the open.

"We shall have to take a leaf out of William's book," observed the General thoughtfully. "Nothing else for it . . ."

"William, sir?" inquired a puzzled aide-de-camp blankly.

"The Conqueror—see Battle of Hastings, 1066. By rights Harold and his Saxons should have come off the victors, and would have done, if William hadn't tempted them to leave their position on the higher ground in order to pursue his supposedly fleeing soldiery. We must do the same and try luring those fellows down. They won't have heard of that battle, and though they don't know the meaning of fear, they don't know the meaning of discipline either, and I think we can safely trade on that."

Trading on it, he had sent the Guides, the 10th Hussars and the artillery forward with orders to advance to within three quarters of a mile of the enemy, where the cavalry would halt while the gunners would gallop ahead for a further five hundred yards or so, fire a few rounds, and at the first sign of an advance, fall back a short distance before stopping to open fire again.

In the General's opinion, no tribesman would be able to resist the sight of British troops in apparent retreat— any more than Harold's militia had been able to resist the sight of Norman infantry running away in feigned disorder—and it was his hope that the Khugianis would leave the protection of their breastworks and rush out to try to capture the guns of the retiring artillery. Then, if the same manoeuvre was repeated, it should be possible to entice the enemy far enough down the slope to enable the cavalry to charge them: catching them out in the open and with little chance of being able to scramble back into their

970

entrenchments. In the meantime, while their attention was concentrated upon the pusillanimous antics of the artillery below their front, the infantry would be advancing swiftly up a nullah from where, with any luck, they would emerge, unseen and unsuspected, on the enemy's right flank.

"Told you he wouldn't need any advice," grinned Wigram as the Guides moved off. "There are no flies on the General." He brushed the sweat out of his eyes with the back of his hand and said: *"Phew*! but it's hot. Aren't you grateful you're not in the infantry?"

"By jove yes!" agreed Wally in heartfelt tones. "Faith, will you just think of having to sweat up that divil of a nullah with the sun scorching your back and every blessed rock and stone red hot. It's lucky we are."

His spirits rose as he spurred away to take up his station at the head of his troop, singing as he went, and wholly oblivious to the fact that the sun was blazing down just as fiercely on the open slope below the plateau as it was on the steep, rocky nullah and the toiling infantry; or that the tunic of his own uniform was already wet through with sweat. He was conscious only of an exhilarating chill compounded of excitement and tense anticipation, as the line of mounted men formed up and galloped forward to face the enemy position.

A trumpet blared, and obeying the signal the cavalry halted in a cloud of dust. As it settled there was a moment or two of complete silence in which Wally found himself sharply aware of innumerable small details. The way the sun gleamed along the barrels of the limbered guns; the small sharp-edged shadows under every stone, and the way the wide sweep of barren ground that sloped up ahead seemed to reflect the light like snow; the smell of horses and leather and harness oil, of dust, sweat and sunbaked earth; the tiny far-off figures of thousands of tribesmen, clustered thick as swarming bees along the rim of the plateau above, and very high overhead a single watchful lammergeyer gliding in lazy spirals—a lone dark speck in an enormous cloudless arch of blue.

The uniforms of the artillery on the right were a strong note of colour in the sun-bleached desolation of that harsh landscape, and beyond them, almost hidden by the tensely poised gun teams, he could see the khaki helmets of the 10th Hussars who, if the Khugianis could be lured down from those fortified heights, would attack their left flank while the Guides charged their centre.

"Two hundred jawans—" thought Wally "—and we shall be riding uphill to meet more than ten times that number of fanatical tribesmen who hate our guts and can't wait to get at us."

The odds were so tremendous that they should have been frightening, but instead he was aware of a curious dreamlike feeling of unreality and no real fear, or any trace of animosity towards those tiny puppet-figures up there, who in a little while would be fighting with him face to face and doing their best to kill him—as he would do his best to kill them. It seemed a little foolish and he knew a fleeting moment of regret, but it was drowned almost instantly in a heady surge of elation in which he could hear the blood begin to sing softly in his ears. He felt light-headed and joyous, and no longer impatient. Time, for the moment, seemed to have stopped still—as once the sun had stopped for Joshua. There was no hurry . . .

A breath of wind blew down the valley and dispersed the dust, and the brief spell of silence was broken by a curt command from Major Stewart of the Horse Artillery. On the word his waiting gunners sprang to life, and plying whip and spur, swept forward at a gallop, the gun wheels bounding over the stony ground and the dust whirling up behind them.

They raced on for five hundred yards, and then, pulling up, unlimbered the guns and opened fire at extreme range on the serried masses of the enemy on the heights.

The brilliance of the afternoon sunlight dimmed the flash of the explosions to no more than a fractional glitter, but in that hot stillness the smoke formed a wall that looked as white and as solid as cotton wool, and the bare hillsides threw back the sudden crash of sound and sent it reverberating round the valley until the very air seemed to shudder to it. Wally's charger, Mushki, threw up her head and backed a little, snorting. But the tribesmen on the heights jeered as the shells fell short, and fired their muskets in reply, while some, on the right, advanced boldly under cover of a ridge, bearing the red standard with them.

Seeing them move, the gunners, instantly limbered up

and galloped back to their original position, and the whole line, cavalry and artillery together, retreated a few hundred yards down the slope. It was enough. As the General had surmised, the sight of the small British force in apparent retreat proved too tempting for the undisciplined tribesmen.

Convinced that the sight of their own immensely superior numbers had struck terror into the hearts of this foolhardy handful of *Kafirs,* and seeing both gun-teams and cavalry running away, they threw all caution to the winds, and shouting exultantly, poured out from behind their entrenchments to race down the slope in an enormous, savage tidal wave of yelling humanity, brandishing banners, muskets and tulwars as they came.

Below them a second trumpet-call cut shrilly through the thunder of retreating hoofbeats and the triumphant shouts of the racing thousands, and hearing it, the cavalry pulled up and wheeled to face the enemy, while the guns unlimbered again and sprayed the converging hordes with grape-shot.

A moment later a distant rattle of musketry on the far left told that the toiling infantry had reached their objective unseen, and were attacking the enemy's flank. But the yelling Khugianis did not hear it; nor did they slow their pace, though by now they were within range of the guns. Crazed with the lust for battle—or the prospect of Paradise, which is assured to all those who slay an infidel—they paid no heed to grape-shot or carbine bullets, but came on as though each man ran a race with his neighbour for the honour of getting first at the foe.

"*Whoa,* girl!" exhorted Wally softly, steadying the mare and breathing short as he peered ahead through the dust and smoke, eyes narrowed against the glare, at that awe-inspiring torrent of fierce, eager fighting-men rushing towards the guns. He found himself mentally counting the distance: six hundred yards . . . five hundred . . . four . . .

The sun was fire-hot on his shoulders and he could feel the sweat crawling down his face from under his pith helmet, but an ice-cold shiver tingled down his spine, and the joy of a born fighter burned in his eyes as he began to sing under his breath. "Forward into battle, see our banners go!" crooned Wally joyously.

He glanced away from the on-coming multitude and

saw the officer in command of the artillery turn and cup his hands about his mouth to shout to the waiting cavalry: "This is my last round at them," yelled Major Stewart, "and then it's your turn."

Wigram Battye, who had been sitting relaxed and motionless in the saddle, out in front of his command, transferred the reins to his left hand and laid his right upon the hilt of his sabre. He did so without haste, and his Guides smiled grimly as they followed their Commanding Officer's example, and braced themselves, waiting.

The guns fired again. This time with deadly effect as the shrapnel tore great swathes through the close-packed masses of the enemy. And as the sound died, Wigram's right arm jerked upward, and from the waiting lines behind him came the answering rasp and glitter of steel as his two hundred men drew their sabres. He barked a command, and with a deafening cheer the cavalry charged . . .

They came at the enemy with the impetus of a four-hundred-yard gallop. Knee to knee, the sunlight flashing on their sabres. And now at last the triumphant Khugianis checked and looked back over their shoulders at the entrenchments behind and above them, realizing too late that it had been a fatal mistake to leave their defences on the plateau and allow themselves to be caught out in the open, since being on foot they had no hope of regaining the safety of their entrenchments before the cavalry overtook them. There was nothing for it but to stay and fight. And they did so: standing fast and firing again and again into the charging phalanx of horsemen.

In every battle the chances are that those most closely involved see only a small part of the whole; and as far as Wally was concerned, this one was no exception.

He knew that somewhere ahead and out of sight the infantry must be in action, for he had heard them firing; and also that the 10th Hussars would have charged at the same moment as the Guides. But the Hussars were on the right of the line, beyond the Horse Artillery; and as he had neither the time nor the attention to spare for anything beyond his own squadron and the enemy ahead, for him the battle, from first to last, was confined to what he himself saw—which in turn was restricted by the dust and the confusion of fighting, struggling, yelling men.

The charge had carried the Guides to within a hun-

974

dred and fifty yards of the enemy when he heard the vicious crackle of muskets and felt the wind of bullets that sang past him like a swarm of angry bees: and saw his Commanding Officer's charger, stretched at full gallop, come crashing down, shot through the heart.

Wigram pitched over its head, rolled clear and was on his feet in an instant. Only to stumble and fall again as a second musket ball smashed into his thigh.

Instinctively, seeing their leader fall, the Sikhs gave the wailing cry of their race and pulled up, and Wally too reined in savagely, his face suddenly white.

"What the hell are you stopping for?" blazed Wigram furiously, struggling to rise. "I'm all right. I'll come on directly. Take 'em on, Walter!—don't mind me. *Take 'em on, boy!*"

Wally did not pause to argue. He turned in the saddle, and shouting to the squadrons to follow him, flourished his sabre about his head, and with a wild Irish yell spurred forward up the slope towards the waiting enemy, the Guides thundering at his heels and shouting as they rode. The next minute, with the shock of wave meeting wave in a tide-race, the two forces crashed together in a pandemonium of dust and din, and Wally found himself in the thick of the smother, hacking left and right with his sabre as wild-eyed men rushed at him howling war-cries and curses and swinging great curved swords.

He sent one down with half his face cut away, and as the mare stumbled over the fallen body, heard the man's skull crack like an egg-shell; and wrenching Mushki to her feet, urged her forward, singing at the top of his voice and laying about him the while in the manner of a huntsman whipping off hounds. All around him men were shouting and cursing in a fog of dust and smoke that stank of sulphur and sweat and black powder and the cloying scent of fresh blood. Knives and sabres flashed and fell and men fell with them, while wounded horses reared up with flailing hooves, neighing with rage and terror, or bolted riderless through the mêlée, trampling down all who stood in their way.

The solid mass of the enemy had been shattered into fragments by the impact of the cavalry charging headlong into it, and now the Khugianis were fighting in small groups, clinging tenaciously to the grassy, stone-strewn slope and standing their ground with fanatical courage.

Wally caught a brief glimpse of Zarin, teeth clenched in a ferocious grin as he drove the point of his sabre into the throat of a shrieking *ghazi*, and of Risaldar Mahmud Khan—his right arm hanging useless and his sabre gone, holding his carbine left-handed and wielding it like a club.

Here and there in the press small whirlpools formed about an unhorsed sowar, defending himself with all the ferocity of a wounded boar against the tribesmen who circled about him, waiting for an opportunity to slash at him with knife or tulwar. One such, Sowar Dowlat Ram, had become entangled with his fallen charger, and the three Khugianis who had brought the horse down rushed in to kill its rider as he struggled to free himself from the dying animal. But Wally had seen him fall and now he charged to the rescue, whirling his blood-stained sabre and shouting *"Daro mut, Dowlat Ram! Tagra ho jao, jawan! Shabash!"**

The three Khugianis turned as one to meet the yelling thunderbolt that fell upon them. But Wally had the advantage of being mounted, and he was the better swordsman. His sabre took one man across the eyes and swept on and down to shear through the sword arm of the second; and as the first fell backwards blind and screaming, Dowlat Ram, still trapped by one foot, reached out and caught him by the throat, while Wally parried a wild blow from the third, and with a swift backhand cut, sliced through the man's neck, all but severing it from the crouching body.

"*Shabash*, Sahib!" applauded Dowlat Ram, freeing himself with a last frantic kick and scrambling to his feet. "That was well done indeed. But for you I would now be a dead man." He lifted his hand in salute and Wally said breathlessly: "You will be yet, if you aren't careful. Get back to the rear."

He jerked his revolver from its holster and put a bullet through the head of the thrashing horse, and wheeling Mushki, plunged back into the fray, using the maddened waler as a battering ram and shouting encouragement to his jawans, calling on them to avenge the wounding of Battye-Sahib and dispatch these sons of noseless mothers to Jehanum (hell).

The Khugianis were still holding their ground and

----

*Fear not. Be Strong. Bravo!

976

fighting fiercely, but there was little shooting now: after the first volley few found time to reload, and in the frenzy and turmoil of battle, firearms had become a liability as it was not possible to ensure that a bullet intended for an enemy would not bring down a friend. Many were using their muskets as clubs, but one man at least, a Khugiani Chief, had taken time to reload.

Wally saw the musket aimed at him and flung himself to one side; and as the bullet whipped past him, he put spurs to Mushki and rode at the man with his dripping sabre. But this time he had met his match. The Khugiani Chief was a skilled fighter and far quicker on his feet than the three tribesmen who had brought down Dowlat Ram. Unable to reload, he stood his ground, ducked the sabre stroke by dropping to his knees, and as the mare plunged past, struck upwards with a long Afghan knife.

The razor-sharp blade sliced through Wally's riding boot, but barely scratched his skin, and he dragged the mare back on her haunches and wheeled to attack again; the same fierce joy of battle in his young face as on the eager bearded one of the hardened fighter who crouched, white teeth showing in a tigerish grin, waiting for him. Once again the Chief dropped to avoid the blow, and as it missed him he sprang to his feet like a coiled spring released and ran in, the knife in one hand and a wicked curved tulwar in the other.

Wally only just managed to swing the mare round in time to parry the attack, and the Chief leapt back and stood ready, poised on his toes, his knees a little bent and his sinewy body swaying as a king cobra sways before it strikes, alert to duck again, and holding his weapons low so that when his adversary spurred forward he could strike at the easier target of the waler's legs or belly and bring down horse and rider both.

By now the duel had drawn a circle of watching tribesmen who, momentarily forgetting the larger issues, stood back, knives in hand, waiting to see their champion slay the *feringhi*. But the Chief made the mistake of repeating a successful manoeuvre once too often, and this time when Wally attacked he made allowance for it: he too aimed lower, striking at the body instead of the head. And when once again the Chief dropped to his knees to avoid the blow, the edge of the heavy cavalry sabre sheared through his left temple and he fell sideways, his bearded face a mask of blood. His tulwar scratched the mare's flank as he fell, and when Mushki reared up, screaming, the tribesmen who had rushed in as they saw him fall—and who would not have given way before that dripping sabre—scattered in the face of those murderous hooves and let horse and rider through.

Minutes later, and without warning, the tide turned.

The massed ranks of the enemy broke and scores of Khugianis turned and ran, racing desperately for the safety of their entrenchments on the plateau. And as the cavalry plunged forward, cutting and slashing as they went, the scores became hundreds, and then thousands: and the battle turned into a rout . . .

"Gone away—!" yelled Wally, hatless and triumphant: "*Shabash, jawans! Maro! Maro! Khalsa-ji ki jai!*" And gathering the scattered squadrons together, he stood up in his stirrups and gave the order: "Gallop!—*Hamla Karo!*"

The Guides obeyed, spurring recklessly forward up the long sweep of broken ground, until suddenly Wally saw for the first time something that had been hidden from him by the rise of the ground. And seeing it his heart seemed to stop.

Between the base of the steeper ground that fell sharply away below the rim of the plateau and the spot where the slope began to level out lay a natural obstacle that presented a far worse hazard than the man-made breastworks of loose rock and stone above: a deep gash in the hillside, running parallel to the rim, cut long ago by some mountain torrent that had dried up and left behind the welter of stones at the bottom of a sheer drop of eight or nine feet. On its far side the hill rose steeply, and along the crest stood the entrenchments—now filling again with wild-eyed tribesmen who turned to howl defiance and fire down into the pursuing cavalry.

It was a sight calculated to daunt many a better and more experienced soldier than young Lieutenant Hamilton. But Wally was drunk with the intoxicating frenzy of battle and he did not hesitate. He used his spur on Mushki, who leapt down into the gulf and bounded across the stones. And behind him, in a wild, slithering, shouting confusion, poured the Guides.

Once down they scattered to left and right searching

978

for a possible way up and out, and when they found one, scrambled up in twos and threes and charged straight into the attack: Wally, with his trumpeteer a close second, the first to reach the summit where the long line of breastworks barred the way to the level ground of the plateau. Here the many tribesmen who had managed to scramble back behind these defences turned at bay, firing their muskets as fast as they could load. But the breast-high wall had not checked Mushki. She rose to it with all the ease and grace of a thoroughbred hunter taking a stone wall in Kerry, and by a miracle, and her rider's skill with a sabre, came through the desperate hand-to-hand fighting that followed as she had come through the battle on the slopes below, with no more than a scratch.

There had been no co-ordination in that fight, or any time to wait for the infantry to come up on the flank, or the guns to follow and get into position. The Guides had attacked singly or in small groups, and with a ferocity that drove the undisciplined tribesmen from their entrenchments and back onto the open stretch of the plateau. For though the Khugianis fought stubbornly, most of their Chiefs and all their standard-bearers were dead. And without leaders to rally them, they failed to regroup.

Their entrenchments had been carried in a matter of minutes, and once again they broke and ran, dispersing across the level plateau like fallen leaves in an autumn gale as they fled with bursting lungs and straining muscles for the uncertain refuge of the forts and villages that nestled in the cultivated valleys beyond.

But they were not permitted to go freely. The guns of the artillery were ordered to open fire on any concentration of the tribesmen and the cavalry ordered to pursue; and Guides and Hussars together swept off in the wake of the retreating enemy, cutting down scores of fugitives as they went, and only drawing rein when they were almost under the walls of the Khugiani stronghold of Koja Khel.

The Battle of Fatehabad was over and won, and the weary victors turned and rode back across the bloodsoaked plateau, past the tragic debris of war: the mutilated bodies of dead and dying men, the discarded weapons, broken standards, *chupplis*, turbans and empty cartridge-belts . . .

General Gough's column had left Jalalabad with

979

orders to "disperse the Khugianis"; and they had done so. But it had been a terrible slaughter, for the Khugianis were brave men, and as Ash had warned, they had fought like tigers. Even when they broke and ran, groups of them had turned to fire on their pursuers, or attack them, sword in hand. Over three hundred of them had been killed, and more than three times that number wounded; but they had taken a grim toll. Gough's small force had lost nine men killed and forty wounded, and of the latter—one of whom died later of his wounds—twenty-seven were Guides: as also were seven of the dead—among them Wigram Battye and Risaldar Mahmud Khan . . .

Wally, having seen Wigram fall, had supposed that he had been carried back to the rear and out of danger. But his Destiny had been waiting for Wigram that day and he had not been permitted to escape it. He had ordered Wally, the only other British officer, to take the squadrons forward; and the boy had obeyed him—charging into the thick of the fight and coming through unscathed, with no mark on him except for a faint scratch and a slashed riding boot. But Wigram, following slowly and painfully on foot with the aid of one of his sowars, had been hit again in the hip.

As he fell for the third time a group of tribesmen, rushing in for the kill, had been beaten off, for the sowar carried a carbine as well as a cavalry sabre, and Wigram had his revolver. Five of the attackers fell and the rest drew back, but Wigram was losing blood fast. He reloaded the revolver and with an enormous effort of will managed to raise himself on one knee. But as he did so, a stray bullet fired by someone in the mêlée further up the slope struck him full in the chest and he fell forward and died without a word.

An exultant shout went up from his surviving assailants, and they rushed forward again to hack at his body, for to an Afghan the corpse of a dead enemy merits mutilation—and never more so than when the enemy is a *feringhi* and an Infidel. But they had reckoned without Jiwan Singh, Sowar.

Jiwan Singh had snatched up the revolver, and standing astride his dead Commander, fought them off with bullet and sabre. He had stood there for more than an hour, protecting Wigram's body against all comers, and when the battle was over and the surviving Guides came back from the plateau to count their dead and wounded, they found him still on guard: and around him in a circle the bodies of no less than eleven dead Khugianis.

Later, when all the official reports had been sent in, the praise and blame apportioned and decorations awarded —and when the critics who had not been present had pointed out errors of judgement and explained how much better they themselves would have handled the affair— Sowar Jiwan Singh was awarded the Order of Merit. But to Wigram Battye there fell a greater honour . . .

When the wounded had been taken away and the stretcher-bearers came for his body to carry it back to Jalalabad (as any grave near the battle-field would certainly be dug up and desecrated as soon as the column had gone) his sowars had refused to let the ambulance men touch it. "It is not fitting that such a one as Battye-Sahib should be borne by strangers," said their Sikh spokesman. "We ourselves will carry him." And they had done so.

Most of them had been in the saddle since dawn, and all, in the heat of the day, had ridden in two charges and fought a desperate hour-long battle against tremendous odds. They were weary to the verge of exhaustion and Jalalabad was more than twenty long miles away over a road that was little more than a track over stony ground. But all through that warm April night, relays of his men plodded forward, carrying Wigram's body shoulder high. Not upon a hospital litter, but laid upon cavalry lances.

Zarin had taken his turn at that sad task, and so for a mile or two had Wally. And once a man who was not a sowar, but from his dress appeared to be a Shinwari, came out of the darkness and took the place of one of the pallbearers. Strangely enough, no one had made any move to prevent him or questioned his right to be there, and it almost seemed as though he was known to them and had been expected; though he spoke only once, very briefly and in an undertone to Zarin, whose reply was equally brief and inaudible. Only Wally, stumbling tiredly in the rear, his mind blurred by fatigue and grief and the sour aftermath of battle, did not notice the presence of a stranger in the cortège. And at the next stop the man vanished as swiftly and unobtrusively as he had come.

56

They reached Jalalabad in the dawn, and a few hours later they buried Wigram Battye in the same stretch of ground where, forty-six years ago, the British had buried their dead at the time of the First Afghan War. And where nineteen new-made graves marked the last resting-place of the eighteen troopers and an officer of the 10th Hussars whose bodies, alone of the forty-six drowned below the ford, had been recovered from the Kabul River only two short days before.

Near him were laid a Lieutenant and a Private of the 70th Foot who had died in the flank attack by the infantry. But Risaldar Mahmud Khan and the five sowars who had also died in the battle of Fatehabad were men of different faiths; and according to their several religions, their bodies were carried to the Mohammedan burial ground to be laid in the earth with the proper ritual and prayers of the Faithful, or else cremated, and their ashes gathered up and cast into the Kabul River so that they might be carried down to the plains of India and from there, by the kindness of the gods, to the sea.

Not only the regiments concerned had watched these ceremonies. The army had turned out in force, and so too had the citizens of Jalalabad and its adjacent villages, and any travellers who happened to be passing through. Among the latter, unnoticed in the peering crowds, was a gaunt, baggy-trousered Shinwari who besides watching the Christian burials from a discreet distance, had also been among the spectators at the Moslem cemetery and at the burning-ground.

When all was over and the crowds and the mourners had dispersed, the Shinwari had made his way to a small house in a backwater of the city where he was presently joined by a Risaldar of the Guides Cavalry, wearing civilian dress. The two had talked together for an hour, speaking in Pushtu and sharing a hookah, and when the

Risaldar returned to the camp and his duties there he took with him a letter written on coarse paper of local manufacture with a quill pen, but addressed in English to Lieut. W. R. P. Hamilton, Queen's Own Corps of Guides.

"There was no need to write down the name; I will give it into Hamilton-Sahib's own hand," said Zarin, storing it carefully away among the folds of his clothing. "But it would be unwise for you to come into the camp to see him, or for him to be seen speaking to you. If you will wait among the walnut trees behind the tomb of Mohammed Ishaq, I will bring his reply there sometime after the moon is down. Or it may be a little earlier. I cannot tell."

"No matter. I shall be there," said Ash.

He had been there, and Zarin had handed him a letter that he read later that night by the light of an oil lamp in a room he had hired that same morning. Unlike Wally's usual letters it was very short, and mostly concerned with his grief at Wigram's death and the loss of Mahmud Khan and the others who had died in the battle. He was, he wrote, delighted to hear that Anjuli was now in Kabul, asked to be remembered to her, and ended by urging Ash to take care of himself and expressing the hope that they would be meeting again soon in Mardan . . .

It was a measure of his grief for Wigram that he had not even thought to mention something that only a short time ago would have taken precedence over almost anything else: the fact that he had just achieved his greatest ambition and the realization of a long-held and most secret dream.

General Gough, who had watched the whole battle from a vantage point on a hilltop, had sent for him to express the greatest admiration for the dash and gallantry of the Guides, and to commiserate over the heavy casualties they had suffered, in particular the death of their Commanding Officer, Major Battye, whose loss would be felt not only by his own Corps, but by everyone who had known him. But that had not been all; the General had gone on to speak warmly of Wally's own exploits, ending by informing him that in view of his taking over Wigram's command and leading it in a charge against vastly superior numbers of the enemy, together with his conduct throughout the battle and his gallant rescue of

Sowar Dowlat Ram, he, General Gough, was personally recommending in dispatches that Lieutenant Walter Richard Pollock Hamilton be awarded the Victoria Cross.

It would be untrue to say that Wally had been unmoved by this news, or that he had heard it without a lift of the heart and a sudden quickening of the pulses. That would have been a physical impossibility. But even as he listened to the unbelievable words that told him his name was to be put forward for the highest honour that can be bestowed for gallantry, the blood that rushed to his face drained away again, and he realized that he would gladly exchange that coveted cross for Wigram's life—or for Mahmud Khan's, or any of those other men of his squadron who would never ride back to Mardan again—

Seven dead, twenty-seven wounded (one of whom the doctor said would not pull through), and any number of horses killed or maimed—he could not remember how many. Yet he, who had come through without a scratch, was to be rewarded with a little bronze cross made out of cannon captured at Sebastopol, and bearing the proud inscription *For Valour*. It did not seem fair . . .

That last thought had brought Ash to mind, and Wally had smiled a little ruefully as he thanked the General, and afterwards gone back to his own tent to scribble that brief note to Ash before writing a letter to his parents giving an account of the battle and telling them that he was safe and well.

So it was from Zarin that Ash learned that Wally had been put in for the Victoria Cross. "It will be a great honour for all in the Guides if the Kaiser-i-Hind should bestow this most coveted of awards on one of our Officer-Sahibs," said Zarin. But that had not been until late on the following night when the two met once more among the walnut trees; and Ash's delight at the news had been tinged with regret because he had not been able to hear about it at first hand.

"You may do so before long," consoled Zarin, "for it is said in the camp that the new Amir, Yakoub Khan, will shortly sue for peace, and that all our *pultons* will be back in their own cantonments before mid-summer. I do not know if this is true, but any fool can see that we cannot stay here much longer when there is not enough food to feed our army, unless we let the Afghans starve. So I can only pray it is true, and if it is, we shall meet in a few months time in Mardan."

"Let us hope so. But I have had a message from the General-Sahib telling me to return to Kabul, and from what he says it may be that I shall have to stay there for some little time; which will not displease my wife, who being hill-bred has no love for the plains."

Zarin shrugged and spreading out his hands in acceptance of the inevitable, said: "Then this is goodbye. Have a care for yourself Ashok, and give my respects to Anjuli-Begum, your wife, and remember me to Gul Baz. *Salaam aleikoum, bhai.*"

"*Wa' aleikoum salaam.*"

The two embraced, and when Zarin had gone Ash wrapped himself in his blanket and lay down on the dusty ground between the walnut trees to snatch an hour or two of sleep before setting out on the road that led past Fatehabad and the Lataband Pass to Kabul.

Little more than six weeks later a Treaty of Peace had been signed in Gandamak by His Highness Mohammed Yakoub Khan, Amir of Afghanistan and its dependencies, and Major Pierre Louis Napoleon Cavagnari, C.S.I., Political Officer on Special Duty, the latter signing "in virtue of full powers vested in him by the Right Honourable Edward Robert Lytton, Baron Lytton of Knebworth, Viceroy and Governor-General of India."

By its terms, the new Amir renounced all authority over the Khyber and Michni Passes and the various tribes in that area, agreed to a continued British presence in the Kurram, declared himself willing to accept the advice of the British Government in all his relations with other countries, and, among other things, surrendered at last to the demand that his father had so strenuously resisted —the establishment of a British Mission in Kabul.

In return he had been promised a subsidy and given an unconditional guarantee against foreign aggression, while Major Cavagnari, who had been solely responsible for obtaining his signature to this document, was rewarded by being appointed to head the Mission as British Envoy to his Court at Kabul.

With a view to allaying Afghan suspicions and hostility, it had been decided that the new Envoy's suite should be a comparatively modest one. But though (apart from Major Cavagnari's) no names had yet been mentioned, camp rumour had no doubts as to one other. And as news flies fast in the East, within a day of the Amir's return to Kabul a member of his household guard had informed a personal friend—once a Risaldar-Major in the Guides and now a pensioner of that Corps—that his old Regiment had been selected for the honour of providing an escort for the *Angrezi* Mission, and that a certain officer-Sahib who had distinguished himself in the battle against the Khugianis would command it.

Sirdar Bahadur Nakshband Khan had in turn carrièd this information to a guest in his house: one Syed Akbar, to whom, with his wife and a Pathan servant, the kindly Sirdar had offered the hospitality of his home . . .

Following his dismissal by Cavagnari, Ash had given up his post in the Bala Hissar, though in obedience to the General's wishes he had continued to make Kabul his base. Yet because the type of information required by the Peshawar Valley Field Force was not so readily available in Kabul as in the countryside surrounding the headquarters of the invading army, he was often away, and Anjuli saw little of him. But from her point of view even that little compensated a thousand times for the hardships of the journey through the snowbound passages, since it was immeasurably better than not seeing him at all and getting no news of him other than an occasional oblique verbal message sent by Zarin to his aunt in Attock.

These days, when Ash left her he could never tell her with any certainty how long he would be away, or send her word of his return; but at least it meant that each day when she awoke she could think—"Perhaps he will come today." So that she lived always in hope, and when that hope was realized, was happy beyond expression—far more so than those who take happiness for granted because they feel their hold on it to be secure, and do not visualize it ending. In addition to which, as she had told the Begum, she felt safe in Kabul, safe from the Rana's people, whose spies would never track her here, so that she could forget the fears that had haunted her in India. And after the glaring sun-burned landscape of Bhithor, and the rocks and the barren salt-ranges around Attock, the air of Kabul and the sight of snow and high mountains was a perpetual source of refreshment.

Her host, who was a wise and cautious man, had taken pains to ensure that no one in his house, neither his family nor his servants, should suspect that Syed Akbar was anything other than he seemed. And when Anjuli had arrived in mid-winter and Ash had declared that they must move elsewhere, the Sirdar had insisted that they both stay, but suggested that in case Anjuli's command of Pushtu should prove inadequate when subjected to the strain of daily conversation with the women-folk of the household, it might be as well to say that she was a Turkish lady, which would account for any mistakes she might make.

The household had seen no reason to query this, and accepted her as such. They had also taken a great liking to her, as the Begum had done, and Anjuli soon became one of them, learning their ways and helping with the numerous household tasks—cooking, weaving, embroidering, grinding spices and preserving, pickling or drying fruit and vegetables. And in her spare time, studying the Koran and committing as much as possible to memory, for she could not afford to show ignorance in religious matters. The children adored her because she was never too busy to fashion toys for them, fly kites or invent enthralling stories as she had been used to do for Shushila; and here, in a land of tall, fair-skinned women, she was no longer considered raw-boned and over-large, but accounted beautiful.

Had she been able to see more of Ash she would have been completely happy, and the times when they were together were as idyllic as the honeymoon days of that long, enchanted voyage up the Indus. Nakshband Khan had rented them a small suite of rooms on the topmost floor of his house, and here they could retreat into a private world of their own, high above the hubbub of the busy, bustling life below.

Yet even when Ash was in Kabul, there was still work for him to do, and he must tear himself away from those peaceful upper rooms and go into the city to listen to the talk in the great bazaar, and discover what was being said in the coffee shops and serais, and in the outer courtyards of the Bala Hissar where an army of petty officials, place-seekers and idle servants whiled away the days in intrigue and gossip, and where he would talk with acquaintances and listen to the opinions of the citizens and men who were passing through Kabul. Merchants with caravans from Balkh, Herat and Bokhara, peasants from outlying villages bringing goods to market, Russian agents and other foreign spies, soldiers drifting back from the fighting in the Kurram or the Khyber, slant-eyed Turkomans from the north, strolling-players, horse-dealers, fakirs and men on pilgrimage to one of the city's mosques.

In this way he learned of the signing of the Peace Treaty, and after that he looked hourly for a message recalling him to Mardan: but none came. Instead, he heard one day from the Sirdar that a British Mission headed by Cavagnari would be coming to Kabul, and that its Escort would almost certainly be drawn from his own Corps and commanded by his best friend. And within an hour of hearing this, he set off hot-foot for Jalalabad to see the Commandant of the Guides.

Ash had confidently expected to be back within a week. But when he reached Jalalabad it was to find that Colonel Jenkins, who now had command of the Corps, had already left; as had Cavagnari and General Sam Browne, and Wally too —for when the Peace Treaty had been ratified in early June, the invading army began to pull out of Afghanistan. Jalalabad was to be evacuated, and those regiments still encamped there were preparing to leave.

"You are too late," said Zarin. "Hamilton-Sahib left with the advance party, and the Commandant-Sahib some days before them. If all went well, they should be back in Mardan by now."

"Then I too must go to Mardan," said Ash. "Because if it is true that Cavagnari-Sahib is to take a British Mission with an Escort of Guides to Kabul, then I must see the Commandant-Sahib at once."

"It is true," confirmed Zarin. "But if you will be advised by me you will turn back, since to go forward is to take your life in your hands, and there is your wife to be thought of. It was all very well when she was in Attock where my aunt would have cared for her, but what will become of her now if you die on the road and she is left alone in Kabul?"

"But the war is over," said Ash impatiently.

"So they say. Though as to that I have my doubts. But there are worse things than war, and cholera is one of them. Living in Kabul, you will not have heard that the black cholera is raging in Peshawar so fiercely that when it reached the garrison, the *Angrezi* troops were moved in haste to a camp six miles outside the cantonments; but to no purpose, for this time it is the *Angrezi-log* whom it is striking the hardest, and few who take it recover. They are dying like flies in a frost, and now it is sweeping up the passes to meet our army as it returns to Hind, so that it seems we shall lose more lives in quitting this country than ever we lost in taking it. I am told that so many have already died of the cholera that the roadside is lined with graves."

"This I had not heard," said Ash slowly.

"You are hearing it now! June has always been an ill month for marching; but here, where there is little shade or water and the heat and dust are worse than in the deserts of Sind, it is a foretaste of Jehanum. So take my advice, Ashok, and return to your wife. For I tell you that the road through the Khyber is so choked with troops and guns and transport, and so full of the sick and the dying, that even if you escaped the cholera you would not get through to Jamrud for several days. It would be quicker to go on foot across the mountains than to try and force a way for yourself through the press and tumult that prevails between here and the mouth of the Khyber. If your business with the Commandant-Sahib is so urgent, write it down and I will undertake to deliver it."

"No. A letter would not serve. I must speak to him myself face to face if I hope to convince him that what I say is true. Besides, you yourself will be travelling on that same road and are just as likely to be struck down by the cholera as I am."

"If I were, my chances of recovery would be greater than yours, for I am not an *Angrezi*," said Zarin dryly. "And if I died, my wife would not be left alone and friendless in a strange land. But there is little fear of my taking the cholera because I shall not be travelling by that road."

"You mean you are staying here? But I understood that Jalalabad was to be evacuated—horse, foot and guns. That everyone would be leaving."

"That is so. And I too will be going, but by way of the river."

"Then I will go with you," said Ash.

"As yourself? Or as Syed Akbar?"

"As Syed Akbar; for as I shall be returning to Kabul, it would be too dangerous to do anything else."

"That is true," said Zarin. "I will see what can be done about it."

It was a tradition with the Guides that an officer who died while serving with the Corps should, if humanly possible, be buried at Mardan. So that when his men urged that Battye-Sahib's body should not be left behind, it was agreed that the coffin should be exhumed. But because of the difficulties of taking it with them in the heat of June, it was decided to try sending it by raft down the Kabul River through the gorges north of the Khyber, and that *terra incognita* the Mallagori country, to Nowshera.

Risaldar Zarin Khan and three sowars had been assigned to escort the coffin. And at the last moment Zarin had asked permission to take a fifth man: an Afridi who had arrived in Jalalabad the previous evening, and who, said Zarin mendaciously, was a distant connection of his and would be an invaluable addition to the escort, as he had made this journey before and was familiar with every turn and twist and hazard of the river.

Permission had been granted, and in the dark hour before dawn, the raft that was to carry Wigram's remains back to their last resting place in Mardan set out on the long and hazardous voyage to the plains.

57

Daylight was beginning to fade when the look-out, who had lain all day on a ledge of cliff above the river, lifted his head and whistled in imitation of a kite. Sixty yards away a second man, concealed by a crevice in the rock face, passed on the signal, and heard it repeated by a third.

There were more than a dozen watchers lying in wait along the left bank of the gorge, but even a man with binoculars would not have suspected it; and the men on the raft had no such aids. Moreover, they needed to concentrate the greater part of their attention on keeping their unwieldy craft clear of rocks and whirlpools, for the snows were melting in the mountains to the north, and the Kabul River ran high and swiftly.

There were six men on the raft, four of whom—a tall Pathan, two black-bearded Sikhs and a burly Punjabi Mussulman—wore the dust-coloured uniform of the Corps of Guides. The fifth, a lean Afridi with a ragged red-tinged beard, was less formally clad, it being his task to wield the heavy ten-foot pole that served as a rudder; and in deference to the heat and the exertions of his office he wore only a thin shirt above the wide cotton trousers of his race. The sixth was a British officer, but he was dead. He had, in fact, been dead for close on two months—a circumstance that was all too apparent to the five who were escorting his body back to India by raft through the gorges where the Kabul River carves its way through the wild mountain country north of the Khyber, past Dakka and Lalpura and the whirlpools of the unknown Mallagori country—for the coffin had been made from unseasoned wood, and though it had been wrapped in a tarpaulin for extra protection, even the evening breeze that blew through the gorge was not sufficient to disperse the sickly odour of corruption.

The voice of the river was a rustling, hissing murmur that filled the gorge with sound but failed to drown the shrill cry of a kite, and the tall Pathan turned sharply—for the sun had already set and that call is not normally heard at dusk: "Down! there are men among those rocks," said Zarin Khan, reaching for his carbine. "Mohmands—may they fry in hell. Keep down: we are too good a target. But the light is poor and by Allah's grace we may win through."

"They may mean us no harm," said a Sikh, checking the loading of his rifle. "They cannot know who we are, and may take us for men from one of their own villages."

The Punjabi laughed shortly. "Do not deceive yourself, Dayal Singh. If there are men on the cliffs they know very well who we are and will have been waiting for us. Perhaps it was fortunate after all that Sher Afzal should have fallen from the raft and been drowned in those rapids, for had that not delayed us we should have reached this spot two hours earlier and been an easier mark. As it is—" He did not finish the sentence, for the first shot took him in the throat and he leapt up as though jerked by a string, his arms flailing, and fell backwards into the river.

The splash and the sound of the shot echoed together through the gorge, and for a brief moment a dark smear stained the colourless water and was whirled away on the current; but the Punjabi's body did not surface again. The raft swept forward into the gut of the gorge, the steersman flinging his weight on the great pole and grunting with the effort as he struggled to keep the unwieldy platform on a straight course, since he knew only too well what their fate would be if they were to run aground.

A vicious spatter of shots whipped the water about them, and the three remaining men of the escort lay flat on the logs and returned the fire with the unhurried precision of long practice, aiming for the puff and flash of the old fashioned muzzle-loaders that thrust out from a dozen crevices on the cliff. But it was an unequal contest, for the enemy lay concealed on ledges and crevices high overhead and could take their time sighting for a shot, while the men of the Guides were handicapped by lack of cover and the uneasy motion of the raft, and had only the speed of their passage and the swiftly gathering dusk in their favour. The coffin provided a narrow margin of protection; but it had been lashed dead centre, and if all three took shelter on the far side of it the raft would overturn.

"Move the stores," gasped the steersman, thrusting off from dimpled water that betrayed an unseen shoal. "Over to the left—quick! That will balance one of you."

Zarin laid aside his carbine, and crawling to the pile of tin boxes that contained the stores and ammunition for their journey, began to stack them on one side of the raft, while Sowar Dayal Singh continued to load and fire. His fellow Sikh shifted his position, and lying down beside him, rested the muzzle of his carbine on the coffin and taking careful aim, pressed the trigger.

Something that looked like a bundle of clothing fell screaming from a ledge of rock to crash down into the boulder-strewn shallows, and Zarin laughed and said: "*Shabash*, Suba Singh. That was good shooting. Almost good enough for a Pathan."

Suba Singh grinned and retorted with a crude country joke that was uncomplimentary to the prowess of Pathans, and Dayal Singh smiled. They had run into a trap in which one of their number had already lost his life, and their chance of escaping from it alive were not high; but all three were men whose trade was war. They loved a fight for its own sake, and their eyes glittered in the dusk as they laughed and re-loaded and fired at the flashes, and made grim jokes as the bullets pattered onto the raft.

A shot smashed into the coffin and the ugly stench of death was suddenly strong on the evening air, blotting out the reek of black powder and the scents of the river.

"*Apka mehrbani,** Battye-Sahib," said Suba Singh quietly, sketching a salute to the thing in the coffin. "You always had a care for your men, and but for you that would have been my head. Let me see if I cannot avenge their discourtesy towards you."

He lifted his head and sighted carefully, allowing for the jerk and sway of the raft. The rifle cracked, and a man near the cliff top flung up his arms and toppled forward to lie still, while the jezail he had held slid from his grasp and clattered down the cliff face in a shower of stones. Suba Singh might not be a Frontiersman, but he was known to be the finest marksman in his squadron.

"Two to us. Now let us see you do better, Pathan," said the Sikh.

Zarin grinned appreciatively, and ignoring the bullets that hummed about him like a swarm of angry bees, took aim at a mark that would have been invisible to any-one not bred in a country where every stone may conceal an enemy: a narrow crevice between two rocks, where the muzzle of a long-barrelled jezail protruded a few inches. The shot went cleanly home above the small circle of metal, and the muzzle dropped with an abruptness that told its own tale.

"There," said Zarin. "Are you satisfied?"

There was no reply, and turning his head he met a blind fixed stare above the coffin. The Sikh had not moved: his chin was still propped on the stiff folds of tarpaulin and his mouth was agape as though he were about to speak, but there was a bullet hole through his temple, and Dayal Singh, lying beside him, had not even known that his compatriot had been hit . . .

---

*Thank you

"Mara gaya?" (Is he dead?) asked Zarin harshly, knowing the foolishness of the question even as he asked it.

"Who? The misbegotten dog you fired at? Let us hope so," said Dayal Singh. He reached for more ammunition, and as he did so the body of Suba Singh fell sideways and lay sprawled across the raft with one arm trailing in the water.

Dayal Singh stared down at it, his outstretched hand rigid and his breath coming short. Then suddenly he began to shiver as though he had a fever. His fingers came to life again and he loaded his carbine with furious haste, cursing the while in a harsh unsteady whisper, and leaping to his feet, began to fire at the cliff, re-loading from a handful of bullets he had stuffed into his pocket.

The raft lurched dangerously, riding the full flood of the treacherous current, and the steersman flung his weight over to balance it and yelled to the Sikh to get down. But Dayal Singh was temporarily beyond the reach of reason. A red blaze of rage had swept away caution and he stood squarely astride the body of his dead comrade, facing the cliff and cursing as he fired. A bullet clipped his jaw and blood streamed into his dark beard, and presently his puttees turned red where a second shot had struck his leg. He must have been hit half a dozen times, but he neither flinched nor ceased his steady, furious swearing, until at last a bullet smashed into his chest and he staggered and dropped his carbine and fell back across the body of his fellow Sikh.

His fall tilted the raft violently to one side, and a flood of water raced across it, foaming about the coffin and sweeping away a clutter of tins and equipment; and before Zarin or the steersman could right it, the bodies of the two dead men slid down the wet logs and vanished into the river.

Relieved of their weight, the clumsy craft righted itself and Zarin rose to his knees, and wringing the water from his uniform said bitterly: "There go two good men; and in these times we cannot afford to lose even one such. This has indeed been a costly campaign for the Guides. Too many have died or been sorely wounded already, and now four more of us are gone—and if it does not get dark soon, you and I may well die too. A plague on these sons of warlocks. Would that I . . ." He broke off and his eyes narrowed: "You are hit!" he said sharply.

"A scratch only. And you?"

"I have taken no hurt—as yet."

But there had been no more shots from the cliff, perhaps because the light was now too poor and the raft no longer presented a possible mark to the watchers among the rocks. The river was a grey ribbon in the dusk and the raft no more than a bobbing shadow, as elusive as a moth or a bat flitting down the gorges. An hour later the two men and their burden were clear of the cliffs with the worst of the rapids behind them, and being swept forward in the starlight through a country less well adapted to ambush.

The day had been very hot, for the monsoon had not yet reached these northern latitudes, and among the parched and treeless hills the ground gave off the stored heat of the sun in almost visible waves, as though the doors of a furnace had been thrown open. But the Kabul River was fed by the snowfields and glaciers of the Hindu Kush, and as the night wind blew coolly off the water the steersman shivered and huddled above his pole.

The coffin had been lashed to the raft with a length of stout country-made rope, but the hemp had become sodden with the night dews and the spray from the rapids, and as the weight that it held shifted to the motion of the current, the rope stretched and sagged so that the coffin moved uneasily, as though it imprisoned someone who was alive and restless.

"Lie still, Sahib, or we lose you at the next bend," grunted Zarin, addressing the dead. "Is there a knot on your side, Ashok?"

"Two," said the steersman. "But I dare not tighten them in the dark. If we were to strike a rock or rough water while retying them, the whole thing would pull free and throw us into the river. You must wait until dawn. Besides, after steering all day my hands are too stiff for tying knots."

"And you a hillman," jeered Zarin. "Why, the night is as hot as Jehanum."

"And the river as cold as charity," retorted Ash. "It is snow water, and I have been in it twice, so I know. Had I realized that the current ran so swiftly and that the

995

Mohmands would lie in wait for us, I would have thought twice before I asked to come with you on such a journey. It is a mad one, anyway, for what difference does it make where a man's body lies? Will Battye-Sahib care if he rests in the earth by Jalalabad or in the cemetery at Mardan? Not he! Nor would he have cared if after we had gone the Afridis dug him up to spit on him or scatter his bones."

"It is we of the Guides who would care," said Zarin shortly. "We do not permit our enemies to insult the bodies of our dead."

"Of our *Angrezi* dead," corrected Ash with an edge to his voice. "This war cost us the lives of others. Yet we left their bodies among the Afghan hills and brought away only this one."

Zarin shrugged his shoulders and made no answer. He had discovered long ago the uselessness of arguing with Ashok who, it seemed, did not see things as most other men did. But presently he said: "Yet you *would* come—and not for my sake, either!"

Ash grinned in the darkness: "No, brother. You have always proved fairly capable of looking after yourself. I came, as you know, because I wish to speak with the Commandant-Sahib before it is too late. If I can only see him in time, I may be able to persuade him that this mission that they talk of is doomed to disaster and must be abandoned; or at the very least, postponed. Besides, they say that the Government will send an escort of the Guides with the new Envoy to Kabul, and offer the command of it to Hamilton-Sahib."

"So I have heard," said Zarin. "And why not? It will be a further honour for him: and a great honour for us of the Guides."

"To die like rats in a trap? Not if I can help it! I shall do my best to see that he does not accept."

"You will not succeed. There is no officer in all the armies of the Raj who would refuse such an honour. And no regiment, either."

"Perhaps. But I must try. I have made very few friends in my life—which I suppose is a fault in me. Out of those few, two have meant a great deal to me: you and Hamilton-Sahib; and I can't face losing you both . . . I *cannot*."

"You will not," said Zarin reassuringly. "For one thing, they may not send me to Kabul. And if—when—we

996

win back to Mardan, you will see things in a better light. It is only because you are over-tired, and because life has been hard for you of late, that you talk like this."

"Oh no I don't. I talk like this because I have spoken to too many men who do not know or talk to the Sahib-log or to soldiers of the Sirkar—and also to very many others who have never even seen either—and from them I have heard things that have made me afraid."

Zarin was silent for a space, then he said slowly: "I think, myself, that this has been your great misfortune: that you can talk to such people. Years ago when you were a child, my brother Awal Shah said to Browne-Sahib, who was then our Commandant, that it was a pity that you should forget to speak and think as one of us; there being few Sahibs who could do so, and such a one might be of great service to our Regiment. Therefore, because of his words, it was arranged that you should *not* forget. That was perhaps a mistake; for it has been your fate to belong to neither East nor West, yet to have one foot in both—like a trick rider at a *Pagal*-Gymkhana who stands astride between two galloping horses."

"That is so," agreed Ash with a short laugh. "And I fell between them long ago, and was torn in two. It is time I tried belonging to myself only—if it is not already too late for that. Yet if I had it all to do again—"

"You would do the same as you have done; that you know," said Zarin, "—seeing that each man's fate is tied about his neck and he cannot escape it. Give me the pole: by the sound, there are rapids ahead; and if you do not have some rest that wound in your arm will give you trouble before morning. We shall not be attacked in the dark, and I will wake you before moonrise. See if you can get some sleep, for we may need all our wits tomorrow. You had better tie one of those rope-ends about your waist before you lie down, or else you will slide off into the water if the raft should tilt."

Ash complied with the suggestion and Zarin grunted approval. "Good. Now take these. It may help you to sleep, and serve to lessen the pain in your arm." He handed over several small pellets of opium which Ash swallowed obediently. "*Faugh*! how the Sahib stinks. Have we anything with which to plug that bullet hole?"

Ash tore a piece of cloth from his turban and Zarin stuffed it into the hole. They had nothing to eat, the stores they had brought with them having been lost when the raft tilted and threw the bodies of the Sikhs into the river, but both men were too tired to feel hungry; and at least they were assured of a plentiful supply of water. Ash surrendered the pole to Zarin, and having washed his arm and bound up the wound, lay down alongside the coffin. But as the raft drifted onward down the Kabul River he found that he could not sleep. His arm throbbed painfully and he lay awake and tried to think out what he should say to Colonel Jenkins when—if—they reached Mardan.

He would have to present the information he had acquired in such a way that the Commandant would not only believe him, but be able to convince all those senior officers and officials whom he himself could not hope to make any impression on that this was the truth. But the arguments he needed eluded him, and as the opium took effect, he fell asleep.

The current swept the raft forward out of the shadow of the Mallagori hills and began to lose force as the river widened.

The slower pace aroused Ash, and he saw that the dawn had come and that the land ahead was level plain. They had won through. Though for an appreciable time that meant nothing to him, because he could not remember where he was . . . Then, as the dawn light broadened over the wide river and the wider land, his brain cleared; and realizing that it was morning, he found it hard to believe that so much time could have elapsed since Zarin had taken the pole from him and told him to rest. It seemed only a moment ago: yet the night was over—

In a little while, fifteen or twenty minutes at most if their luck held, they would be across the invisible border that divided Afghanistan from the North-West Frontier Province; and after that it would only be a matter of floating with the current that would carry them past Michni and Mian Khel to Abazai, and southward, below Charsadda, to Nowshera. They would be back in British India and Zarin could afford to tie up to the bank and sleep for an hour or two; there could have been no sleep for him during the past night, that was certain.

A breath of wind ruffled the glassy smoothness of the river and Ash shivered as it blew on him, and discovered with a vague sense of surprise that his clothes were soak-

998

ing wet and that the whole raft ran with water. It looked as though they must have had a rough passage through rapids, and fairly recently, for no dew could have been heavy enough to account for it; which presumably meant that he must have slept for at least part of the night, though he could have sworn that he had not closed his eyes. He heard a rush and a fluster of wings and water as a group of paddy-birds took off in startled haste and flew down river, and realized that the raft was no longer in midstream but drifting in towards the left-hand bank.

A minute or two later sand and pebbles crunched beneath it as it drove in on a shallow ledge below a bank fringed with tussocks of grass and a few thorn bushes and jolted to a stop, and he knew that they must be back in British India again. Zarin would not have risked tying up while they were still in tribal territory—or even within gun-shot of it.

Ash stirred at last and made the discovery that he was tied to the coffin beside him by a length of rope. He had forgotten that. He sat up, feeling dazed and stupid, and began to untie it, fumbling with numbed fingers at the sodden knot. As he did so, a voice that he barely recognized said hoarsely: "Allah be praised! You are not dead then," and turning to look across the dripping canvas he saw that Zarin's face was grey and drawn with exhaustion, that he had lost turban and *kulla*, and his uniform was dripping wet as though he had been swimming in the river.

He made an effort to reply, but the words clogged on his tongue and he could not speak, and Zarin said huskily: "When you did not stir as we were flung like a leaf in a millstream through a mile-long canyon little wider than a city gate, or when the whirlpools caught us and spun us round and round like a top, I was sure that you were dead, because you rolled to and fro at the end of that rope like a corpse and did not lift head or hand even when the waves washed over you."

"I . . . I was not asleep," said Ash haltingly. "I can't have been. I didn't close my eyes . . . at least, I don't think so—"

"Ah; that was the opium," said Zarin. "I ought not to have given you so much. But at least it must have rested you a little. I myself am an old man before my time, and I hope never to endure such a night again. I am stiff in every limb."

He drove the pole into the wet sand so as to hold the raft against the bank, and straightened himself wearily. He had fought the river all night, single-handed and without being able to relax for a moment—not even long enough to discover whether Ash had been more severely wounded than he had thought, and was either dead or bleeding to death. His hands were raw and blistered from working the heavy pole that was their only means of steering, and every muscle in his body was so cramped from strain that he could barely move. He was also hungry, thirsty and drenched to the skin. But where a European would have slaked his thirst from the river and then set about finding something to eat, Zarin first washed himself ritually and then turned to face towards Mecca and began the prayers that the Faithful say at dawn.

Ash had learned those prayers long ago. It had been necessary that he should know them (and be seen to say them), during the years when he had helped to track down Dilasah Khan through Afghanistan—and more recently, when he had gone back there at Wigram Battye's instigation in the guise of an Afridi. He had said them daily at the proper times, since they were as much a part of his disguise as the clothes he wore or the language he spoke, and to neglect them would have invited remark; so that now, instinctively, seeing Zarin begin the ritual, he too rose to face Mecca and automatically began to murmur the familiar prayers. But he did not finish them. Zarin broke off, and turning his head said angrily: *"Chup!* You are safe here. There is no need for play-acting!"

Ash stopped, open-mouthed, startled into attention by the look on Zarin's face rather than the anger in the harshly spoken words. It was a look he had never seen there before, and had never thought to see, a mixture of revulsion and animosity that was as shocking as it was unexpected, and that made him feel curiously breathless, as though he had walked into a solid object in the dark and winded himself. He was aware that his heart had begun to beat heavily, thudding like a drum in his chest.

Zarin turned abruptly back to his prayers, and Ash stared at him, frowning and intent, as if he were seeing something he recognized but had never conceived of finding here . . .

Because he had always known that to Hindus, whose gods were legion, caste was all-important, and that the

1000

only way to become a Hindu was to be born one, he had accepted the fact that as far as they were concerned he would always remain on the far side of an invisible line drawn by religion and impossible to cross. But with Koda Dad and Zarin and others of their faith (who worshipped one god only, were prepared to accept converts and had no inhibitions about eating and drinking with anyone, irrespective of creed, nationality or class) there had seemed to be no similar barrier; and even though their Koran taught them that the slaying of Unbelievers was a meritorious act rewarded by entry into Paradise, he had never felt less than at home with them. Until now . . .

That look on Zarin's face explained many things: the Mogul conquest of India and the Arab conquest of Spain, and all the many Holy Wars—the Jehads waged in the name of Allah—that have drenched the long centuries with blood. It had thrown a white light on something else too: something he had always been dimly aware of but had not troubled to think about. The fact that religion has not brought love and brotherhood and peace to mankind, but, as was promised, a sword.

The bond between Zarin and himself had been strong enough to withstand almost any strain that could be put upon it—except the stroke of that sword. For though on one level they were friends and brothers, on another, deeper one, they were traditional enemies: the "Faithful"—the followers of the Prophet—and the "Infidels," the Unbelievers to whose destruction the Faithful are dedicated. For it is written *kill those who join other gods to God wherever ye shall find them, besiege them, lay in wait for them with every kind of ambush.*

Zarin must have known that he, Ash, would for his life's sake have had to observe every ritual of the Mohammedan religion as part of his disguise, even though he had never actually seen him doing so. Yet now, seeing it for the first time—and when the necessity for it had passed—he saw it only as sacrilege; and Ash as an Infidel making a mockery of the True God.

It was strange, thought Ash, that he should never have realized before that between himself and Zarin there yawned a gulf as wide as the one that separated him from all caste Hindus, and that this too was one that he would never be able to cross.

He turned away, feeling strangely bereft, and more

shaken by that sudden revelation than he would have believed possible. It was as though the very ground under his feet had disintegrated without warning, and all at once the pearly morning was full of an aching sense of loss and sadness, because something of great value had gone out of his life and would never be regained.

In that moment of crisis his mind turned to Juli as gratefully as a man turns to a glowing fire in a cold room, holding out his hands to its comforting warmth. And as the first flush of the morning lit the snows on the Safed Koh, he said his own prayers, the same that he had said facing towards the Dur Khaima when Zarin Khan was a magnificent youth in Gulkote and he himself an insignificant little Hindu boy in the service of the Yuveraj: "Thou art everywhere, yet I worship thee here . . . Thou needest no praise, yet I offer thee these prayers . . ."

He prayed too for Juli, that she might be shielded from all harm and that he might be permitted to return to her in safety. And for Wally and Zarin, and the repose of the soul of Wigram Battye and all those who had died in the hills near Fatehabad and in the ambush last night. There was no food on the raft, so he could make no offerings: which was, he reflected wryly, just as well, for Zarin would certainly have recognized it as a Hindu rite and been even more displeased.

Zarin finished his prayers, and after they had rested a while, Ash took over the pole and thrust off from the bank. As the sun rose and the morning mists smoked off the river, they saw ahead of them the mud walls of Michini glow gold as the bright rays caught them, and presently they landed and bought food, and arranged for a man to ride to Mardan with a message warning of their arrival and asking that arrangements should be made to meet the raft at Nowshera and escort the body of Major Battye by road to the cantonment.

They saw the messenger leave, and having eaten, went on themselves by river: Ash poling their cumbersome craft and its grim burden forward through the pitiless, shadeless heat of June, while Zarin slept the sleep of utter exhaustion.

It had been an appalling day, even though the river now ran smooth and swiftly between low sandbanks and through quiet country. The sun beat down on his head and shoulders like a red-hot hammer, and with each

1002

hour the stench from the coffin became more pervasive
and intolerable. But all things come to an end, and as
twilight fell they reached the bridge of boats at Nowshera,
and saw Wally with an escort of Guides Cavalry drawn
up on the road, waiting to take Wigram home to Mardan.

58

Not having known that Ash was on the raft, Wally failed
to recognize him in the dusk, and there had been no opportunity for speech until much later, for as the condition
of the body made it necessary to re-bury it immediately,
the coffin had been hurried to the outskirts of Mardan in a
brake, where it had been transferred to a gun-carriage,
and the funeral had taken place that night by torchlight.

Only when the prayers for the dead had been recited,
the Last Post sounded and the volleys fired above the
mound of raw earth that marked Wigram's final resting
place, and when the mourners had gone back to their
quarters leaving the little cemetery to the moonlit silence
and the black shadows, had Ash been able to see Wally
alone.

He had hoped to see the Commandant first, but as
Colonel Jenkins was playing host to two senior Frontier
Force officers, friends of Wigram's who had ridden over
from Risalpur for the funeral and were staying the night,
that interview would have to be postponed until sometime next day; so Zarin had smuggled him into Wally's
rooms in the fort instead.

Wally had been delighted to see Ash, but the emotional strain of Wigram's second funeral had subdued his
normally good spirits and he was in no mood to listen to
any criticism of the proposed British Mission to Afghanistan, let alone consider refusing command of the Escort
—supposing he were offered it, which he had not been; or
at least, not officially. At the moment it was only a rumour, though everyone, according to Wally, was agreed
that Cavagnari would be the best possible choice for Envoy, if and when a Mission were sent to Kabul. "I fancy

he must have received a pretty broad hint to that effect from the Viceroy, because he was good enough to tell me that if he got the job he would ask for me as Military Attaché, in command of an Escort of Guides. And I don't believe he'd have said that unless he was fairly certain of getting the appointment. All the same, I don't mean to count my chickens before they're hatched."

"If you've any sense," said Ash, "you'll put up a prayer that this particular clutch turns out to be addled."

"*Addled*? What on earth do you mean by that?" demanded Wally blankly.

"I mean that when the late Amir, Shere Ali, was trying to get it into the heads of our Lords and Masters that his people would never take kindly to the establishment of a British presence—or, for that matter, any foreign presence—in his country, he pointed out that no Amir of Afghanistan could possibly guarantee the safety of such foreigners '*even in his own capital*.' Wally, don't you ever read anything but poetry?"

"Don't be an ass. You know I do."

"Then you must have read Kaye's history of the First Afghan War, and ought to remember his conclusions—which should have been written up in letters a foot high over the entrance to the War Office, *and* over Viceregal Lodge and Army Headquarters in Simla as well! Kaye wrote that after an enormous waste of blood and treasure we left every part of Afghanistan bristling with our enemies, though before the British Army crossed the Indus the name of England had been honoured in Afghanistan, because the people associated it with vague traditions of the splendour of Mr. Elphinstone's mission; but that all they remembered now were 'galling memories of the invasion of a desolating army.' That is still true today, Wally. And that is why this Mission has simply got to be called off. It *must* be stopped."

"It won't be. It's too late for that. Besides—"

"Well, postponed then—delayed for as long as possible, to allow time for every effort to be made to build up confidence and establish really friendly relations with the Amir and his people. Above all to allay their fears that the British mean to take over their country as we took over this one. Even at this late date that might still be done if only men like Lytton and Colley and Cavagnari could be persuaded to try a different approach—to lay

1004

aside the big stick and see what moderation and good-will can do instead. But I promise you, Wally, that if Cavagnari really means to take this disastrous Mission to Kabul, he'll never come back alive. Nor will you or anyone else who goes with him—you've got to believe that."

Wally, who had been listening with ill-concealed impatience, said: "Ah, blather!" and pointed out that the Amir himself had agreed to accept the Mission.

"Only under duress," corrected Ash sharply. "And if you think his subjects have accepted it, you're a long way out. They are as much against it as they ever were: more, if anything, after this war. And it's *their* wishes that count and not the Amir's—a fact that he is so well aware of that he came to the Gandamak Conference prepared to fight against it every inch of the way, and nothing that the Generals or the Politicals could say could make him budge. He stuck out against them all, and it was only when Cavagnari demanded that he be allowed to talk to him alone, without anyone else being present, that he—"

"I know. You don't have to be telling me. Dammit, I was there!" interrupted Wally irritably. "And what's more, Cavagnari talked him round."

"Did he? I take leave to doubt it. I imagine he threatened him, and pretty strongly. All that anyone knows for certain is that he forced the Amir to give in —and boasted afterwards that he had 'rated him as though he had been a mere Kohat Malik.' It's no use shaking your head at me, for it's true. If you don't believe me, ask him yourself—he won't deny it. But he would have done better to have kept quiet about it, because it got about, and I cannot believe that it will have helped him to make a friend of the Amir. Or of his people either, who are not ready to accept a British presence in Afghanistan because in their eyes it means only one thing: a prelude to the annexation of their homeland in the same way that the first small trading posts of the East India Company led to the annexation of India."

Wally observed coldly that they would have to lump it, and that, though he realized that the Mission would not be popular at first, once it was there it would be up to its members to see that they got on good terms with the Afghans and showed them that they had nothing to fear. "We shall all do our damnedest, I promise you. And if

1005

anyone can bring them round his thumb it's Cavagnari. That's something I *do* know!"

"Then you're wrong. I agree that he might have done it once, but riding rough-shod over the Amir has lost him a vital ally. Yakoub Khan is not one to forgive an insult, and now he will give him as little help as possible, and probably intrigue against him behind his back. Wally, I know what I'm talking about. I've lived in that damned country for months on end, and I know what is being said there—and in places like Herat and Kandahar and Mazar-i-Sharif too. The Afghans do not want this Mission, and they are in no mood to have it forced down their throats."

"Then that is their misfortune," said Wally, brusquely. "Because they are going to have it whether they want it or not. Besides, we gave them such a hell of a thrashing in the Khyber and the Kurram that they had to sue for peace, and I think you'll be finding that troops who have just been as soundly defeated in battle as these fellows have will have learnt their lesson by now and not be over-eager to get another dose of the same medicine."

Ash came to a stop, and gripping the back of a chair with both hands until his knuckles showed white, explained in a strictly controlled voice that the whole point was that they hadn't learned anything—because they didn't even know that they were defeated. "That's one of the things I came here to tell the Commandant: there have been insurrections in Turkestan and Badakshan, and as the defeated regiments have all been hurried off to deal with the situation there, the Amir is having to raise fresh ones to take their place, and the new troops are nothing but an undisciplined rabble who have never been in action against the British Army, and know nothing about the defeats. They have, on the contrary, swallowed whole a score of fairy-tales about 'Glorious Afghan Victories,' and worse still they have received no pay for months, because the Amir insists that there is no money in the exchequer to pay them. So they are preying on the wretched villagers instead, and by and large I'd say they were a far greater menace to him than having no troops at all. It's obvious that they are already pretty well out of control, and in my opinion they're likely to prove a serious threat to any British Mission foolish enough to set up shop in Kabul and trust to them to keep order; because they can't do so, and what's more they won't!"

1006

Wally retorted crossly that Cavagnari was bound to have heard all about this already as he had scores of spies collecting information for him. To which Ash agreed: "But the trouble is that they come and go, and only some-one who has actually lived in Kabul during these past months can have any inkling of the situation there. It's unstable as water and potentially dangerous as a wagon-load of gunpowder, for you can't expect reason from an undisciplined, unpaid rabble that having played no part in the recent hostilities thinks the present withdrawal of our army is a retreat, and is therefore firmly convinced that the invading British were soundly defeated and are scut-tling out of Afghanistan with their tails between their legs. Because that is how it looks to them, and so they can see no reason why their new Amir should permit a handful of the defeated, despised and hated 'Angrezi-log' to es-tablish a permanent Mission in Kabul. If he does, they will merely regard that as weakness, and think the less of him: and that isn't going to help matters, either."

Wally turned away to sit on the edge of the table, swinging a booted foot and gazing out of the window at the moonlight that filled the interior of the little fort; and presently he said slowly: "Wigram used to say that he wouldn't be in your shoes for anything in the world—be-cause you didn't know where you belonged. But I don't think he was quite right about that. I think myself that you've made up your mind and taken sides: and that it isn't our side you've chosen."

Ash did not reply, and after a brief pause Wally said: "Somehow I always thought that when it came down to brass tacks, you'd choose us. I didn't dream . . . Ah well, there it is; no use talking about it. We shall never agree as long as you apparently have adopted the Afghan view of this business, while I can't avoid seeing it from ours."

"By which you mean Cavagnari's and Lytton's, and all that lot," said Ash with something of a snap.

Wally gave a small shrug. "If you like."

"I don't. But how do you yourself see it, Wally?"

"Me? Faith, I should have thought that was obvi-ous. I may not know these people like you do—the tribes-men I mean—but I do know that they despise weakness, as you yourself have just pointed out! Well then, whatever your views are as to the rights and wrongs of it, we went to war with them and we won. We defeated them. We

1007

made their Amir come to Gandamak to discuss peace terms and sign a treaty with us, and the most important of those terms was that we should be allowed to establish a British Mission in Kabul. Now I'm not going to argue the pros and cons with you, because, praise be, I'm not a politician, but if we back down now, they'll think us a backboneless lot who haven't even the guts to insist on our rights as victors, and despise us accordingly—which you of all people must know is true. We should earn neither friendship nor respect, but only scorn, and even the men of our own Corps would despise us for it and begin to wonder if we'd lost our nerve. Ask Zarin and Awal Shah, or Kamar Din or any of them, what they think, and see what they say. It'll surprise you."

"No it wouldn't," said Ash tiredly. "They'll think the same as you. It's all this fatuous business of 'saving face.' We all suffer from that: and pay for it—in blood. We daren't risk 'losing face' even if it means throwing justice and reason and common-sense to the winds, and doing something that we know is not only foolhardy, but appallingly dangerous: and in this case, completely unnecessary."

Wally heaved a resigned sigh and said with a grin: "'It isn't fair,' in fact. God be helping us if he isn't at it again! It's no good, Ash: it's wasting your time you are."

"I suppose so," admitted Ash ruefully. "But as Wigram once said, 'One has to try.' Let's hope the Commandant can be brought to see how serious the situation is, and try his hand at persuading Cavagnari and his Forward Policy cronies to have second thoughts on the subject of this Mission. Though I admit I haven't a spark of confidence in our Simla-based decision-makers. Or in Homo-sapiens in general, if it comes to that!"

Wally laughed, and for the first time that night looked as he had done in the old days in Rawalpindi: young and gay and carefree. "Wisha, but it's a gloomy devil you are an' all, an' all. 'Tis ashamed of you I am. Ah, come now, Ash, don't be such a Jeremiah. We really aren't such a hopeless lot as you make out. I know you didn't see eye to eye with Cavagnari, but for all that I'll lay you any odds you like that he brings the Afghans round his thumb and has them eating out of his hand inside a month of our arrival in Kabul. He'll win them over just as Sir Henry Lawrence won over the defeated Sikhs in the days before the Mutiny—you'll see."

"Yes ... Yes, I shall see," said Ash slowly.

"Of course—I forgot you'd be in Kabul yourself. When do you go back?"

"As soon as I've seen the Old Man, which I hope will be sometime tomorrow. There's no point in my staying here any longer, is there?"

"If you mean you won't be able to persuade me into turning down command of the Escort if I have the luck to be offered it, no there isn't."

"When do you think you'll know?"

"I suppose when Cavagnari gets back from Simla."

"Simla! I might have known he'd be there."

"Faith, I think you might. He came out through the Khyber with General Sam and went straight up there to report to the Viceroy."

"And to be rewarded for having bullied Yakoub Khan into accepting the terms of that wretched Peace Treaty, no doubt," said Ash with an edge to his voice. "A knighthood at the least—Sir Louis Cavagnari, K.C.S.I., etc., etc."

"Why not?" demanded Wally, beginning to bristle. "He's earned it."

"No doubt. But unless he can persuade his fellow fire-eater, Lytton, to hold up this Mission until Yakoub Khan has had a chance to re-establish some sort of law and order in Kabul, it's likely to prove his death-warrant. And yours too, Wally! Not to mention the jawans, and everyone else he'll be taking with him. Have the members of the escort been selected yet?"

"Not officially, though it's more or less settled. Why?"

"I wanted to know if Zarin would be going."

"Not as far as I know. Nor is Awal Shah. In fact none of your particular cronies."

"Except yourself."

"Oh, I shall be all right," said Wally buoyantly. "You don't have to worry about me—I was born under a lucky star. It's yourself's the one you should be worrying about, ye scutt. You can't go hanging around indefinitely in a trouble-spot like Afghanistan merely in order to keep a weather-eye out for your friends, so it's I who'll be giving you a piece of advice for a change. When you see the Old Man, get him to let you come back to us. Go on your knees if necessary. Tell him we need you—which is God's truth so it is."

Ash looked at him a little oddly and started to say something, but changed his mind and inquired instead when this Mission was supposed to leave—if it did leave.

"It'll leave all right, make no mistake about that. We expect to set off as soon as Cavagnari returns from Simla. But as I told you, nothing has been decided yet, and for all I know the Viceroy may have other ideas."

"Let's hope so. They couldn't be worse than this one," observed Ash dryly. "Well, goodbye, Wally. I don't know when I shall be seeing you again, but I hope for your sake it won't be in Kabul."

He held out his hand and Wally gripped it and said warmly: "Wherever it is, it can't be too soon: you know that. And if it's Kabul, at least you'll know that I wouldn't have missed being there for anything in the world. Why, it'll be the chance of a lifetime, and if all goes well it's bound to mean promotion for Hamilton, and another long step towards getting my hands on that Field Marshal's baton. Sure now, you wouldn't want to do me out of that, would you? Sorra-a-bit! So don't say 'goodbye,' say 'I'll see you in Kabul.'"

Zarin had taken much the same view as Wally, when Ash related their conversation the following morning. And once again, as on the previous one, there had been that in his voice that sounded an ominous note of change and warning. A hint of impatience that verged on irritation, and an indefinable suggestion of withdrawal, as though he had retreated to the far side of some invisible barrier. He might almost, thought Ash, appalled by the reflection, have been speaking to a stranger.

Zarin had stopped short of telling him in so many words that his warnings were unwelcome, but that was made clear by his tone. "We your friends are no longer boys," said Zarin. "We are all grown men and can look to our affairs. Awal Shah tells me that he has spoken with the Commandant-Sahib who will see you during the afternoon, when everyone if not asleep is at least within doors."

He would not meet Ash's eyes, but rose and went out about his duties, saying that he would be back before two o'clock to take Ash to the Commandant's bungalow, and advising him to get some sleep, because he would need to be rested if he meant to set out for Kabul that night—it being too hot to travel by day.

But Ash had not slept, for apart from the fact that

Zarin's small, brick-built quarter behind the Cavalry Lines was intolerably hot, he had too many things to think of; and a vital decision to make.

The years that had once seemed to drift by so slowly were now passing with ever-increasing swiftness, like a sluggish train that pants and jerks and puffs as it draws away from a station platform, and then, gathering speed, rattles forward faster and ever faster on the iron rails, eating up the miles as time eats up the years. And Ash, sitting cross-legged on the mud floor and gazing unseeingly at a white-washed wall, looked back down the long corridor of those years and saw many Zarins. The Zarin he had first seen in Koda Dad's quarters in the Hawa Mahal: a tall, handsome youth who could ride and shoot as well as a man, and who had seemed—then and always—to be everything that was brave, splendid and admirable. A dashing, confident Zarin, riding away from Gulkote to join the Guides Cavalry. Zarin at Mardan, wearing the uniform of a sowar; consoling him for the death of Sita and mapping out his future with the aid of Awal Shah. An older Zarin, waiting to greet him on the dock at Bombay, still unchanged, still the same staunch friend and elder brother . . .

He had been afraid once that their relationship might not survive his return to Mardan as an officer in the Corps, and their sudden reversal in status. But it had done so, thanks in a large part, reflected Ash, to the astringent common-sense and level-headedness of Koda Dad's youngest son rather than to any qualities that he himself possessed. After that it had seemed to him that it would survive anything, short of death, and he had never visualized it ending like this.

Yet it was the end. He realized that quite clearly. They could not continue to see each other and talk together as they used to do, because their paths had already diverged, and the time had come when he must step to the music that he had heard.

That was something that Wigram had once quoted to him, and the words had stayed in his mind: "If a man does not keep pace with his companions, perhaps it is because he hears a different drummer: let him step to the music that he hears." It was good advice, and high time he acted upon it, for he knew now that he had never yet succeeded in keeping in step with his companions, whether European or Asiatic, because he himself was neither one nor the other.

The time had come to close the Book of Ashok and Akbar and Ashton Pelham-Martyn of the Guides; to put it away on a shelf and begin a new volume—"The Book of Juli": of Ash and Juli, their future and their children. Perhaps one day, when he was old, he would take down that first volume, and blowing the dust from it, leaf through its pages and re-live the past in memory—fondly, and with no regrets. But for the moment it was better to put all that away and forget it. *Ab kutum hogia.**

By the time Zarin returned, the decision had been made: and though Ash did not say so, Zarin was instantly aware of it. Not because of any tension between them, for they spoke together as easily as they had always done, and as though nothing had changed. Yet in some indefinable way, Zarin was aware that Ashok had withdrawn from him; and he knew without being told that in all probability they would not meet again . . .

"Perhaps when we are old," thought Zarin, as Ash had done. He put the thought away from him and talked cheerfully of the present, speaking of such things as a projected visit to Attock to see his Aunt Fatima and the necessity of purchasing new chargers to replace those lost in the recent campaign, until it was time to take Ash to see the Commandant.

This interview had lasted much longer than the one with Wally on the previous night, for in the hope of persuading Colonel Jenkins to pull any available strings that could possibly help to postpone the sending of a British Mission to Afghanistan (or better still, cause the whole project to be abandoned), Ash had gone into considerable detail as to the situation prevailing in Kabul, and the Commandant, who was well aware that his own Corps were more than likely to be involved, had listened with absorbed attention, and after asking a number of pertinent questions, had promised to do what he could to help; though he admitted that he held out no great hopes of success.

Ash thanked him, and went on to talk of more personal matters. He had a request to make, one that he had given a great deal of thought to during the past few

---

*Now it is finished

months but had only finally decided upon that same morning, during the hours that he had spent in Zarin's quarters. He asked to be relieved of his present duties, and also to be allowed to resign his Commission and leave not only the Guides, but the army.

He had not, he explained, come to this decision in haste, as the conviction that he could never settle down to becoming an army officer had been growing on him for some time. He presumed that Wigram, when Adjutant, must have told the Commandant something about Anjuli? The Commandant nodded without speaking, and Ash looked relieved and said that in that case he would understand the difficulties that had to be faced. If he had been able to return to Mardan and live openly with his wife it might have been possible for him to come to terms with army life in British India; but as there were several reasons why that could not be considered, he felt that the time had come to try and make a new life for his wife and himself . . .

Those long months on the journey to Bhithor, the weeks he had spent there and the years in Afghanistan had spoiled him for the narrow existence of an army officer—even an officer in such a Corps as the Guides—and made him realize that he would never be able to fit into any groove formed by nationality or creed. Therefore the only thing for him to do was to cut his ties with the past and start again, begin afresh as an individual who was neither British nor Indian, but merely a member of the human race.

The Commandant had been kind and sympathetic; and secretly relieved. For bearing in mind that peculiar story of the Hindu widow whom Ashton (according to poor Wigram) claimed to have married, and the scandal such a tale could cause if it were to become generally known, it seemed to him that the best thing for the Corps, as well as for Ashton, was for the young man to resign his commission and retire into civil life, where he could do what he liked.

They had discussed the matter rationally and without animosity; and as the war was now over and the British Army in the process of withdrawing from Afghanistan, and General Browne had already left that country, the Commandant had no hesitation in saying that Ash could consider that his term of duty as intelligence officer to the

Peshawar Valley Field Force had ended. He had also accepted Ash's resignation from the Guides and promised to arrange that there would be no difficulties over his resigning his commission. All that could be left to him, but in return he would like to ask a favour.

Would Ashton consent to remain in Kabul for a little longer (it might even be as much as a year) and act as an intelligence agent for the Escort of Guides?—always supposing the proposed British Mission became a reality.

"I will certainly see that all the information you have just given me is sent to Simla, and do anything else I can do to discourage the Mission being sent—though as I have said before, I am afraid that will be very little. But if it goes, young Hamilton will almost certainly go with it as Military Attaché in command of an Escort of Guides; and after what you have just told me, I would like to know that you were at hand to give him any information he may need about the state of affairs in Kabul, and the attitude of the local population, and so forth. If the Mission is abandoned or the Guides are not, after all, called on to supply an Escort, I would let you know immediately, and you can take it that you would be a civilian from that moment, and need not even return here unless you wish."

"And if it is not abandoned, sir?"

"Then I would ask you to remain in Kabul as long as the Guides are there. As soon as their term of duty expires and they are relieved by some other regiment, you are free to go. Will you do that?"

"Yes, sir," said Ash. "Yes, of course."

It would have been difficult, in the circumstances, to refuse such a request—even if it had occurred to him to do so, which it did not. In fact, it suited him very well. Juli was happy in Kabul—and besides, it would give him more time to decide what he meant to do and where they would go, for if the Corps sent an Escort to Kabul, their tour of duty would not be less than a year. Which would also mean that he would be seeing a good deal of Wally, who need not be told until the year was almost up that he, Ash, had sent in his papers and would never be returning to the Guides ...

Ash left Mardan for the last time as the moon rose, and Zarin accompanied him past the sentries and watched

1014

him stride away across the milky plain towards the Border hills.

They had embraced at parting and exchanged the formal sentences of farewell as they had done so often before: *"Pa makhe da kha"*—may your future be bright . . . *"Amin sara"*—and yours also. But both knew in their hearts that they were saying them to each other for the last time, and that this was a final farewell. They had reached the parting of the ways, and from now on their paths would lead in different directions and would not cross again, no matter how bright their separate futures might be.

Ash turned once to look back, and saw that Zarin had not moved but was still standing there, a small dark shape against the moon-washed spaces. Lifting an arm in a brief salute he turned and went on; and did not stop again until he was beyond Khan Mai. By which time Mardan had long been hidden from him by distance and the folds of the plain.

"That leaves only Wally," thought Ash. ". . . *my brother Jonathan: very pleasant hast thou been unto me . . .*"

The four pillars of his imaginary house were falling one by one. First Mahdoo and then Koda Dad; and now Zarin. Only Wally left; and even he was no longer the staunch support that he had once been, for he had grown away and acquired other interests and different values, and Ash wondered how long it would be before he too must be left behind—as Zarin had been. Not yet, at least; for they would probably be meeting in Kabul in the near future. Besides, there was no reason to fear that he would lose Wally as he had lost Zarin. And even if he did, would it matter so much, now that he had Juli?

Thinking of his wife, he saw her face as clearly as though it had actually materialized out of the moonlight before him: her grave eyes and sweet, tender mouth, her serene brow and the lovely, shadowy hollows below her cheek bones. Juli, who was his quietness and peace and refreshment: his dear delight. It seemed to him that her gaze held a faint trace of reproach, and he said aloud: "Is it selfish of me to want you both?"

The sound of his own voice startled him. The hot night was so still that although he had spoken very softly, the moonlit silence magnified the sound out of all proportion and served to remind him that he might not be the only traveller abroad that night. The reflection successfully changed the direction of his thoughts, for he knew that the people of this region had no love for strangers and a habit of shooting first and asking questions afterwards; and quickening his pace he strode on with his mind alert to danger rather than preoccupied with unprofitable hopes and regrets.

Shortly before dawn he found a safe cleft among the rocks, where he was able to sleep for the best part of the day. And when he dreamed it was not of Zarin or Wally, or anyone in the life he had left behind him, but of Anjuli.

He returned to Kabul by way of the Malakand Pass, and found the city and the plain simmering in an unaccustomed cauldron of heat and dust that made him think more kindly of the temperatures that he had left behind in Mardan, because although Kabul stood six thousand feet above sea-level, the rainfall was scanty and the earth was parched for lack of moisture. But the breeze that blew off the snowfields of the Hindu Kush at evening cooled the upper rooms of the Sirdar's house and made the nights pleasant. And Anjuli had been waiting for him.

They had not talked much that first night, and Ash had touched only briefly on his abortive trip to Mardan and his parting with Zarin. But next day, and on many of the long June days that followed, they talked of the future, though in a desultory manner and with no sense of urgency, for Nakshband Khan pressed them to stay, saying that even if a British Mission did not after all come to Kabul, there was no point in their leaving until the hot weather was over and autumn brought in cooler days. There was no hurry. The whole summer lay before them, and there was plenty of time in which to decide where they would go when they left Afghanistan—if they left at all this year, and did not decide to spend the winter there and leave in the spring, after the almond trees had bloomed, which might be the best plan.

As June gave place to July, summer lightning flickered among the hills and clouds drove across the mountain ranges, but though little rain fell, that little was enough to turn the withered grass green again, and Anjuli rejoiced in the grey days because sun-glare and dust and blazing skies reminded her of Bhithor, while Ash, watching her, would forget to make plans for the future because he found the present so deeply satisfying.

But July was barely half over when the future broke in upon them in the form of disturbing stories concerning the ruthless pillaging of lonely hamlets by bands of unpaid and undisciplined soldiers, who ever since the signing of the Peace Treaty had been converging on Kabul from all parts of Afghanistan.

Each day brought more of these masterless men to the valley, until even the Sirdar became alarmed and reinforced the bars on the doors and windows: "For if even half the tales we hear are true," said the Sirdar, "we are none of us safe. These men may call themselves soldiers, but having received no payment for many weeks they have become a disorderly rabble and no better than bandits. They are preying on the people of this valley, snatching anything they desire from the villagers and shooting down all who resist."

"I know," said Ash. "I have been among the villagers."

He had indeed; and in doing so had both seen and heard more than enough to show him that the Sirdar's fears were far from groundless, for the situation in the valley had deteriorated sharply during the past weeks. There were far too many armed and aimless men in the villages and on the road leading to the city, and on several occasions he had passed through sizeable crowds who were being exhorted by some fakir to wage a Jehad against all Infidels. As for the capital itself, it was overfull of truculent, hungry-looking soldiers who swaggered through the streets, shouldering aside the more peaceful citizens and openly helping themselves, without paying, to fruit and cooked food from shops and stalls in the bazaars.

The very air felt heavy with the threat of violence and unrest, and there were times when Ash was tempted to desert his post and take Juli away, because it seemed to him that Afghanistan was becoming too dangerous a country for her to linger in. But he had given his word to the Commandant, and he could not break it: for by now there was no one who had not heard that a British Mission, headed by Cavagnari-Sahib and accompanied by an Escort of the "Guide Corps," had already set out for Kabul.

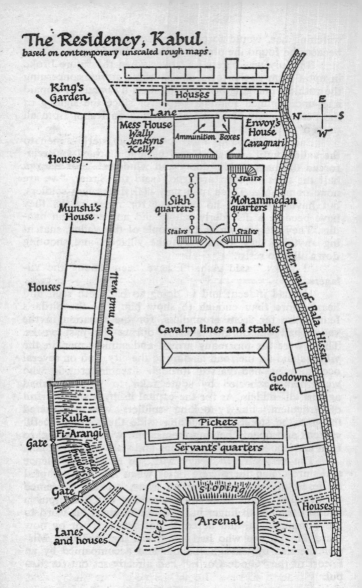

The Residency, Kabul
based on contemporary unscaled rough maps.

King's Garden

Houses

Houses

Houses

Munshi's House

Mess House
Wally
Jenkyns
Kelly

Ammunition Boxes

Envoy's House
Cavagnari

Sikh quarters

Mohammedan quarters

stairs

stairs

stairs

Low mud wall

Kulla-Fi-Arangi

Gate

Gate

Lanes and houses

Cavalry lines and stables

Godowns etc.

Pickets

Servants' quarters

Steep

Sloping land

Arsenal

Houses

Outer wall of Bala Hissar

N E S W

BOOK EIGHT

The Land of Cain

59

The solitary bird, its beak agape in the simmering heat, had been dozing on the branch of a stunted pine tree near the crest of the pass when it heard the first sounds from below, and opened a wary eye.

As yet the voices and the clop and clatter of horses' hooves were too far off to be alarming, but they were coming nearer, and as the sounds grew in volume and the creak of saddles and the jingle of harness were added to the noise of hoofbeats and voices, the bird flattened its ruffled feathers and cocked its head, listening to the racket caused by a large body of horsemen riding up the hill path. There must have been close on three hundred of them, of which less than a third were Englishmen—the others being Indian troops and Afghan soldiery—and as the two leading riders came into view the bird took fright, and abandoning its siesta, flew away with an angry chattering cry.

The General was aware that the distinguished civilian who rode beside him had put up his hand as though in salute and muttered something under his breath, and supposing himself to be addressed he said: "I'm sorry; what did you say?"

"That bird: look—"

The General glanced in the direction of the pointing finger and said: "Oh yes. A magpie. One doesn't often see them at this height. Is that what you were saying?"

"No. I was counting ten backwards."

"Counting—?" Major General Sir Frederick Roberts, known to his command as "Bobs," appeared bewildered.

Cavagnari laughed and looked a little shamefaced. "Oh, it's just a foolish superstition. It's supposed to ward off bad luck if you count ten backwards when you see a magpie. Don't you do that in England, or is it only an Irish superstition?"

"I don't know. I certainly haven't heard of it in my part of England. Though I believe we salute them. Magpies, I mean."

"You didn't salute that one."

"Nor I did. Well, it's too late now. It's gone. Anyway, I'm not a particularly superstitious chap."

"I wonder if I am?" mused Cavagnari. "I wouldn't have said so. But I suppose I must be, for I admit I would rather not have seen that bird. You won't tell my wife we saw a magpie, will you? She wouldn't like it. She's always been superstitious about such things, and she'd think it was a bad omen and worry about it."

"No, of course I won't," returned the General lightly. But the request surprised him, and it occurred to him that poor Louis must be feeling less confident about this Mission to Kabul than one had supposed, if a trivial incident like seeing a magpie could upset him—which it obviously had, because he was looking gloomy and thoughtful; and all at once, much older . . .

Major Cavagnari had arrived in Simla in early June to discuss the implementation of the Treaty of Gandamak with his friend the Viceroy, and to receive his reward for having induced the new Amir, Yakoub Khan, to sign it. When he left again in July it was as Major Sir Louis Cavagnari, K.C.S.I., Her Majesty's Envoy Designate and Minister Plenipotentiary to the Court of Kabul.

Never one to allow grass to grow beneath his feet, the one-time Deputy Commissioner of Peshawar had completed his arrangements within a few days of his return, and as soon as all was ready the British Mission had set out for Kabul.

Considering that a war had been fought in order to

establish it, the Mission was a surprisingly modest one. But Pierre Louis Napoleon was no fool, and though the Viceroy, Lord Lytton (who regarded it as the first step toward establishing a permanent British presence in Afghanistan, and, as such, a triumph for the Forward Policy), might be blithely confident of its success, the newly appointed Envoy was not so sanguine.

Unlike Lord Lytton, Louis Cavagnari's work had given him considerable experience of the Amir's subjects, and whatever Ash might think to the contrary, he was well aware of the risks involved in forcing such a presence upon a reluctant population, and equally aware that nothing short of an army could guarantee the safety of any British Mission. Consequently he saw no reason to hazard more lives than necessary, and had therefore kept the numbers down to a minimum, restricting his suite to only three men: William Jenkyns, secretary and political assistant; a medical officer, Surgeon-Major Ambrose Kelly; and a military attaché, Lieutenant Walter Hamilton, v.c., both of the Guides, the latter in command of a picked Escort of twenty-five cavalry and fifty-two infantry of the same Corps.

Apart from a single hospital assistant and the indispensable camp-followers—servants, syces and others who accompanied the Mission—that had been all. For though the Envoy designate had been careful not to damp the Viceroy's enthusiasm, he had admitted to certain close friends in Simla that he reckoned the chances were four to one that he would never return from his mission, adding that if his death were to lead to "the red line being placed on the Hindu Kush," he would not complain.

The size of the Mission had been a disappointment to Wally, who had visualized a far larger and more imposing cavalcade: one that would impress the Afghans and do credit to the British Empire. The meagreness of the Envoy's party struck him as a depressing example of Government cheese-paring, but he had consoled himself with the thought that it was an indication of the power and prestige of the Raj that where lesser nations would have found it necessary to bolster their Envoy's consequence with a horde of minor officials and an outsize Escort, a mere handful of men was sufficient for the British. Besides, the smaller the numbers the greater the glory.

It did not strike him as odd that Cavagnari proposed to travel to Kabul by way of the Kurram Valley and the Shutergardan Pass rather than by the far shorter and easier route through the Khyber, as he himself had already marched through the charnel-house that heat and drought and cholera had made of that road when the army had withdrawn from Afghanistan after the signing of the Peace Treaty, and men and baggage animals had dropped and died in their thousands on the line of march. The bodies of the former had been buried in shallow graves hurriedly scraped out of the scanty earth by the roadside, but it had not been possible to do the same for the corpses of mules and camels; and knowing that the Khyber would still be foul with the sight and stench of corruption, Wally had no desire to pass that way again until time, weather and the eaters of carrion had cleansed the road and hidden the evidence under a merciful pall of dust and grass.

By comparison the Kurram Valley, even at that season of the year, must be a paradise. And as it was no longer a part of Afghanistan (having been ceded to the British under the terms of the treaty) the victorious troops that garrisoned it had not been withdrawn; which Wally confidently supposed would ensure a peaceful passage as far as the Afghan frontier. But in this he was mistaken.

The tribes were indifferent to such things as treaties or agreements between rival governments and they continued to harass the garrisons, murdering soldiers and camp-followers and stealing rifles, ammunition and baggage animals. Deserters carried off camels under the very noses of the sentries, caravans carrying fruit from Afghanistan to India were stopped on the Shutergardan Pass and plundered by marauding bands of Gilzais, and in July alone, a British surgeon had been stabbed to death and an Indian officer of the 21st Punjabis, together with his orderly, had been attacked and killed within sight of their escort who had been riding a short distance behind. Even General Roberts himself had narrowly escaped being captured by men of the Ahmed Khel . . .

"They will all be killed. Every one of them!" exclaimed that one-time Viceroy of India, John Lawrence —brother of Sir Henry of Punjab fame—when the news reached London that the British Mission had set out for Kabul. And if conditions in the Kurram were anything to go by, the outlook was murky enough to justify that pessimistic remark.

There was certainly little sign of peace in the valley, and in order to ensure the Mission's safety a mountain battery, a squadron of Bengal Lancers and three companies of Highlanders and Gurkhas had been detailed to protect them. In addition to which General Roberts, and no less than fifty of his officers who wished to honour the new Envoy, had joined his party to set it on its way.

Thus royally escorted, Sir Louis Cavagnari and the members of his Mission had arrived at Kasim Khel, five miles from the crest of the Shutergardan Pass and barely three from the Afghan border—the cliffs known as Karatiga, the White Rock. Here, having camped for the night, they entertained the General and his staff to a farewell dinner: a function that proved to be remarkably noisy and convivial in spite of the fact that tomorrow they would be parting company, and no one could be certain as to what lay ahead.

The party broke up late, and on the following morning the Amir's representative, Sirdar Khushdil Khan, escorted by a squadron of the 9th Afghan Cavalry, rode into the camp to conduct the Mission on the last leg of its journey towards the frontier.

The Amir's representative was accompanied by the head of the Ghilzai tribe, a gaunt, hatchet-faced greybeard by the name of Padshah Khan, whom Wally, for one, distrusted on sight. Not that he thought much better of Khushdil Khan, whose sinister countenance and sly, evasive eyes struck him as even more unpleasant than the wolf-like face of the robber chief. "Wouldn't trust either of 'em as far as I could throw the mess piano," confided Wally in a whispered aside to Surgeon-Major Kelly, who smiled a tight-lipped smile and replied in an undertone that from now on they would have no alternative but to trust them, as until they reached Kabul that unprepossessing pair and the motley crew of ruffians they had brought with them were officially responsible for their safety. "Which I have to admit, I do not find particularly comforting," added the doctor thoughtfully.

The motley crew referred to were mounted on small, wiry-looking horses and decked out in what appeared to be the cast-off uniforms of British Dragoons, topped by long-discarded helmets acquired from the Bengal Horse

1023

Artillery. They were armed with smooth-bore carbines and tulwars, and Wally, eyeing them with professional interest, decided that his Guides ought to be able to handle them with ease. Apart from village hall amateur dramatics, he could not remember having seen such an outlandish assortment of warriors, and had it not been for their fierce, bearded faces and the hard gleam in their eyes, the effect would have been laughable.

But Wally's gaze held no amusement, for he was well aware that despite their ridiculous appearance and straggling, undisciplined lines, they did not know the meaning of fear—or of mercy, either. And like Major Kelly, he did not find it a reassuring thought that to such men as these the Amir of Afghanistan must look to preserve peace in Kabul and protect the lives of the British Envoy and his entourage.

"We can deal with this lot if they try anything on the road," thought Wally, "but there will always be others to replace them. Hundreds of others—thousands. And there are less than eighty of us to protect the Mission . . ."

Riding towards Karatiga, it occurred to him that Ash might not, after all, have been taking such an alarmist view of the situation in Kabul and the new Amir's uncertain grip on authority as he had liked to think. For if a sullen, shifty-eyed Sirdar, a wolf-like Ghilzai chief and this ramshackle squadron of cavalry was the best that the Amir could send to greet the British Mission and take over responsibility for its safe arrival in Kabul, then it looked as though conditions might be almost as chaotic as Ash had made out. If so, he had misjudged him. Not that he himself could have behaved any differently if he had believed every word of it—as Ash should have known.

However great the danger might be, he would still not have changed places with anyone, and as he watched the detachments that had accompanied them to the frontier turn back and ride away, he felt sincerely sorry for them, because they were having to return tamely to the Kurrum and garrison duty, while he, Walter Hamilton, would be riding forward towards Adventure and the fabulous city of Kabul . . .

The Afghan delegation had pitched a tent on a stretch of level ground near the foot of the Shutergardan Pass, and here the Amir's representative and the head of the Ghilzais gave a banquet for Sir Louis and his suite and General Roberts and his fifty British officers, before hosts and guests remounted and rode together to the summit, where carpets had been spread on the ground and glasses of tea were served. The air on the crest of the pass had been cool and bracing, and the view of the surrounding peaks and the peaceful Loger Valley far below enough to raise the spirits of any but the most dedicated of pessimists. But the sun was already moving down the sky, and Khushdil Khan hurried his guests on and downward to the Afghan camp, where after compliments had been exchanged and the last farewells said, Roberts and his officers took their leave of the Mission.

An uninstructed bystander listening to that light-hearted leave-taking would never have suspected either of the principals of harbouring any fears, for Cavagnari had long since regained the equanimity that had briefly deserted him when he saw the magpie, and both men were in the best of spirits as they renewed a promise to meet again in the cold weather, shook hands, and wishing each other God-speed, turned to go their separate ways.

But they had ridden no more than fifty yards when some impulse made them stop and turn simultaneously to look back at each other.

Wally, instinctively checking his own horse, saw them exchange a long look and then move quickly forward and, without speaking, grip hands once more before parting again. It was a curious incident, and to Wally, an oddly disturbing one. It seemed to take much of the brightness from that exhilarating day, and when the party camped for the night at the western foot of the Pass, he lay down with his carbine at his side and his service revolver under his pillow, and did not sleep any too soundly.

Five days later the British Mission was received in Kabul with the same honours that had been accorded to General Stolietoff and his Russians, the two state entries into the capital differing only in size (Stolietoff's retinue having been far more numerous and imposing) and the fact that a different National Anthem was played.

Neither entry had been regarded with favour by the population. But a show is always a show, and as before, the citizens of Kabul turned out *en masse* to enjoy a free *tamarsha* and watch the state elephants sway past, carrying another foreign Envoy and his political assistant in

1025

their gilded howdahs, and closely followed by another military escort—a mere handful this time: only two Sahibs and a detachment of twenty-five cavalrymen.

But whatever the crowds might think, Sir Louis had no criticism to make. The men of the Afghan regiments who lined the route and held back the jostling staring crowds saluted, albeit raggedly, as he passed, and as he entered the Bala Hissar the din of military bands blaring out "God Save the Queen" was almost drowned by the thunder of guns firing a Royal Salute. It was an eminently satisfactory welcome: the triumphal vindication of his policy, and the crowning moment of his life . . .

The guns and the bands, the good-tempered crowds, the capering, shouting children and the affability of the officials who had been sent out with the bedizened elephants to welcome him and escort him into the Afghan capital had all served to convince him how right he had been to insist that the Amir kept to the letter of the Gandamak treaty and accepted a British presence in Kabul without further delay. Well, that presence was now here, and establishing it was clearly going to be easier than he had thought. The moment he and his party had settled into their quarters he would set about making a personal friend of Yakoub Khan and getting on good terms with his ministers, as a first step towards forging strong and lasting ties between Great Britain and Afghanistan. Everything was going to be all right.

The Envoy was not the only one to be pleased at the reception accorded to the Mission, and heartened by the good humour of the vast crowds that had turned out to see its arrival.

The members of his suite had been equally impressed, and Wally, searching the sea of faces as he rode by in the hope of seeing Ash, had noted the expressions on those faces and thought: "What an old scare-monger the dear fellow is. Won't I just pull his leg about this when I see him! All that blather about the whole place boiling with unrest and the Afghans hating our guts and loathing the very idea of any foreigners setting up house in their capital city. Why, you only have to look at these chaps to see it isn't true. They're more like a bunch of children at a school treat, crowding up for a slice of cake." The simile was apter than he knew.

The population of Kabul was indeed, metaphorically

speaking, expecting cake, and had it occurred to Wally to turn round and look back along the route, he might have noticed that the eager expressions of the onlookers had changed to disbelief and bewilderment as they took in the fact that the British Mission consisted of no more than this handful of men. They had expected a far more lavish and formidable display of power from the British Raj, and felt cheated. But Wally did not think to look back; nor did he find the face he had hoped to see.

Ash had not been among the crowds that flocked to watch the arrival of Her Britannic Majesty's Envoy and Minister Plenipotentiary at the Court of Kabul. Having no desire to catch the eye of anyone among the visitors who might recognize him (and, by showing it too obviously, draw unwelcome attenion to him) he had purposely stayed away, contenting himself instead with listening from the rooftop of Sirdar Nakshband Khan's house to the crash of bands and the boom of guns that heralded the Envoy's arrival at the Shah Shahie Gate of Kabul's great citadel, the Bala Hissar.

The sounds had been borne clearly on the still air, for the Sirdar's house was no great distance from the citadel, and like Wally, Ash was agreeably surprised by the mood of the crowds that streamed past on their way to watch the procession. But the Sirdar, who with other members of his household had gone out to see the Mission arrive, reported that its size and lack of grandeur had disappointed the Kabulis, who had expected something far more flamboyant. True, there had been elephants, but only two of them, and as they had come from the Amir's elephant lines they could be seen on all state occasions.

"Also only three Sahibs besides Cavagnari-Sahib, and not even four-score men from my old regiment. What manner of Embassy is this? The Russ-log numbered many more. Moreover they wore rich furs and great boots of leather, and tall hats fashioned from the pelts of young lambs, and the fronts of their coats were bright with silver cartridges, row on row of them. Ah, that was indeed a great *tamarsha*. But this,"—the Sirdar spread out a lean hand and wagged it to and fro, palm downwards, to indicate something small and near the ground, "this was a poor show. The Sirkar should have arranged a better one, for many of those who watched were asking how it was possible that a Government who could not afford to send a

1027

larger embassy would be able to pay the Amir's soldiers all they are owed; and if not—"

"What is that?" interrupted Ash sharply. "Where did you hear this?"

"I have told you: from those I stood among in the press near the Shah Shahie Gate, where I went to watch Cavagnari-Sahib and those with him enter the Bala Hissar."

"No, I mean this tale that the Mission is expected to give the army its arrears of pay. There was no mention of that in the Treaty."

"Was there not? Then I can only tell you that many here believe it to be so. They say also that Cavagnari-Sahib will not only pay the army in full, but that he will put an end to compulsory military service and abate the excessive taxation that has long been a cause of great hardship to our people. Are these things also untrue?"

"They must be. Unless there was some secret agreement, which I think is unlikely. The terms of the Peace Treaty were made public, and the only mention of financial aid was a promise on the part of the Government of India to pay the Amir a year's subsidy of six *lakhs* of rupees."

The Sirdar said dryly: "Then perchance the Amir will spend those rupees, when he gets them, on paying his soldiers. But you must not forget that few here have even heard of that Treaty, and fewer still will have read it. Also, as you and I both know, half Afghanistan believes that their countrymen won great victories in the war and forced the armies of the Raj to retreat back to India, leaving many thousands dead behind them, and if they believe that, why should they not believe these other things? It may even be that the Amir himself has caused such tales to be spread abroad in the hope of persuading the people to allow Cavagnari-Sahib and his following to come here without hindrance, and to refrain from harming them, since only a fool kills the man who pays. Myself, I can only tell you that half Kabul believes that Cavagnari-Sahib is here to purchase all they need from the Amir, whether it be exemption of taxes and military service or peace from the depredations of their unpaid army; and for this reason they were dismayed when they saw how small a train he had brought with him, and at once began to doubt if it were true that he came laden with riches."

The Sirdar's disclosures came as an unpleasant surprise to Ash, who, not having come across this particular story before, went out at once into the city to see for himself how much truth there was in these statements. Half an hour had been enough to confirm them all: and if he needed further discouragement he received it on his return, when his host met him with the news that Munshi Bakhtiar Khan, the acting representative of the British Government in Kabul, had died on the previous day.

"It was given out that he died of the cholera," said the Sirdar, "but I have heard otherwise. I have been told in secret by—by someone well known to me that he was poisoned in order that he should not speak to Cavagnari-Sahib of certain things that he knew. This I think very likely, because there is no doubt that he could have told the Sahib much. But now his knowledge is buried with him in the grave. He was no friend of the late Amir's, and his appointment caused great offence in the Bala Hissar. But he was both clever and cunning and he made other friends here, several of whom are whispering behind their hands that his death was contrived by enemies—though I doubt if any word of that will reach the ears of the Sahibs."

It was enough that it had reached Ash's, and on the following day he deliberately broke a promise he had made to Anjuli, and applied for the post he had held once before in that city: as scribe in the service of Munshi Naim Shah, one of the many officials attached to the court, who lived in the Bala Hissar itself.

"It will only be for a few hours each day, Larla," he explained to Anjuli when she protested, white-faced, that he was putting his head into the tiger's mouth to no purpose; "and I shall be in no more danger there than I am here—perhaps even less, since half Kabul knows that the Sirdar-Sahib is a pensioner of the Guides, so it is always possible that his guests may be suspect. But having worked for Munshi Naim Shah before, I am known to a number of people in the Bala Hissar, and none will question my right to be there. Besides, the citadel is like a great ants' nest, and I doubt if anyone can say how many people live within its walls and how many come there daily to work or ask for favours, or to visit relatives or sell goods. I shall be no more than one ant among many."

But Anjuli, who throughout the spring and early summer had been so happy in Kabul, had recently fallen a prey to terror, and the city and its surroundings that she had once thought so friendly and beautiful had suddenly become sinister and threatening. She knew that the entire valley was subject to earth tremors, and though the first of these that she had experienced had been barely noticeable, of late there had been one or two that were far more daunting. The tall house had swayed alarmingly, and though the Kabulis accepted the frequent earthquakes as a matter of course, to Anjuli the tremors had always been eerie and frightening. Nor, in these days, did she find anything reassuring when she looked out of any window that faced the street, and saw the men who passed below.

These lean hawk-faced Afghans with their long ragged locks and unkempt beards, their cartridge-belts, muskets and tulwars, were a very different breed of men from the gentle, friendly, unarmed hill-folk she remembered from her childhood days in Gulkote, and even bearing in mind the viciousness and cruelty that had existed in Bhithor and been practised by Janoo-Rani and Nandu in Karidkote, it seemed to her now that compared with Kabul both had been places where the majority of people lived safe and very ordinary lives, undisturbed by blood-feuds, armed revolt against their rulers or the sudden outbreak of fratricidal strife between one tribe and the next, such as bedevilled this violent land. The very name of the great range of mountains that bounded the Land of Cain to the north had become a threat to her, for "Hindu Kush" meant "Killer of Hindus," and she was—she had once been—a Hindu.

She knew that the Sirdar's house had stout walls and strong doors, and that the few windows that looked out on to the narrow street were protected by carved shutters and iron bars, but the feeling of tension and danger from the streets outside seemed to seep into the house through every chink and crack, as insidiously as the pervasive dust and the evil smells of the city. And she had only to look up from the flat mud roof, or the windows of the rooms that had been allotted to Ashok and herself, to see the menacing bulk of the Bala Hissar.

1030

The great citadel appeared to loom over the Sirdar's house, its ancient towers and endless battlements blocking out the morning sun and preventing any wind from the south or east cooling the close-packed buildings below, and lately, living in its shadow, Anjuli had become aware of a recurrence of those terrors that had afflicted her during the flight from Bhithor and for so many days afterwards. But this time the source and the focus of that terror was the Bala Hissar, though she could not have explained even to herself why this should be. It was as though some evil emanated from it, and the thought of her husband entering such an ill-omened place was not to be borne.

"But why go there at all?" implored Anjuli, her eyes dark with dread. "Where is the need, when you can learn all you wish in the city? You say you will come back each evening, but what if these people should rise in revolt? If that happens, those who live in the Bala Hissar will close the gates, and it will become a trap from which you may not be able to escape. Oh my love, I am afraid ... afraid!"

"There is no need, Heart's-dearest. I promise you I shall be in no danger," said Ash, holding her tightly and rocking her in his arms. "But if I am to help my friends, it is not enough to hear only the wild tales that rumour-mongers spread in the city, because half of them are untrue. I must also hear what is said in the palace itself by those who see the Amir or his ministers daily, and so know what they say and think and how they mean to act. The four Sahibs in the Mission will not learn this, no one will tell it to them—unless I do. That is what I am here for. But I promise you that I will be careful and take no risks."

"How can you say that when you must know that every time you enter its gates, you walk into danger?" protested Anjuli. "My love, I beg of you—"

But Ash only shook his head and stifled her words with kisses, and when he tore himself away it was to go to the Bala Hissar, where, as he well knew, the room in which he would work overlooked the Residency and the compound in which the British Mission had been housed.

60

The ancient citadel of the Amirs of Afghanistan was built upon the steep slopes of a fortified hill, the Shere Dawaza, that dominated the city and a large part of the valley of Kabul.

It was surrounded by a long, rambling outer wall, some thirty feet high and pierced by four main gateways that were flanked by towers and topped with crumbling battlements. Within this were other walls, one of which enclosed the Amir's palace in the upper Bala Hissar. Higher still stood the fort, while above it the whole Shere Dawaza hill was ringed by a wall that climbed the steep flanks and followed the line of the rocky heights, so that sentries manning the blockhouses here could look out at the enormous circle of mountain ranges, and down on palace and city, the entire sweep of the valley and the wide, winding ribbon of silver that was the Kabul River.

The lower Bala Hissar was a town in itself, crammed with the houses of courtiers and officials and all those who worked for them, and possessing its own shops and bazaars. It was in this part of the citadel that the Residency stood, and from his window Ash could see the whole stretch of the compound—the clutter of servants' quarters and store rooms, the cavalry pickets and the stables at the far end, lying almost in the towering shadow of the Amir's great Arsenal, and directly below him the barracks, an oblong, fort-like structure that enclosed a line of covered quarters on either side, and was bisected by a long open courtyard entered through a deep archway at one end and a stout door at the other.

Behind that far door a narrow lane divided the barrack block from the Residency proper, which consisted of two separate houses facing each other across a walled courtyard some ninety feet square, in the nearer and taller of which Wally, Secretary Jenkyns and Surgeon Kelly had their rooms, while the Envoy himself occupied the other: a two-storey building that on the southern side was part of the outer wall of the citadel, so that the windows there had a sheer drop below them to the moat, and a magnificent view of the valley and the far snows.

Ash too shared that view, since not only the Envoy's house but the far side of the entire compound stopped at the thirty-foot drop of the wall, beyond which stretched the open country, the river and the hills and the vast panorama of the Hindu Kush. But the beauty of the view held no interest for him—his attention being reserved for the compound below, where he could catch an occasional glimpse of the Envoy and his suite, watch their servants and the men of the Escort busy about their duties, and keep a check on callers at the Residency—and an eye on Wally's comings and goings.

Wally, like Anjuli, had formed an unfavourable impression of the Bala Hissar, though for different reasons. He did not find it sinister: he thought it deplorably shoddy. Having expected the famous citadel to be a magnificent and impressive place (something along the lines of Shah Jehan's Red Fort at Delhi, only better, as it was built on a hill), he had been disgusted to find it a rabbit-warren of dilapidated buildings and fetid alleyways, huddled behind a series of irregular and often half-ruined walls and interspersed by what appeared to be waste ground on which little or nothing grew.

The grandly styled "Residency" had proved equally disappointing, being no more than a number of mud-brick buildings in a large compound that was hemmed about, on three sides, by houses built on rising ground, and on the fourth by the south wall of the citadel.

There was not even a proper entrance gate, and the sole barrier between the compound and the surrounding houses was a crumbling mud wall that a child of three could scramble over without difficulty; which augured a complete lack of privacy, as any member of the public who wished to do so could stroll in without let or hindrance to gaze at the Escort, hang around the stables watching the horses being groomed and fed, or even (if the doors of the barrack block were open) stare through the long central courtyard at the Residency itself.

"Faith, it's a combination of a gold-fish bowl and a rat-trap, so it is," pronounced Wally that first afternoon in the Bala Hissar, as he and the surgeon surveyed the place that was to be the home of the British Mission. His critical gaze travelled to the towering bulk of the Arsenal, and from there to the tiers of tall, flat-roofed Afghan houses that overlooked the compound. Behind and above these rose the walls and windows of the palace; and above again, the fortified heights of the Shere Dawaza . . .

"Glory be, will you look at that now!" exclaimed Wally, appalled. "We might just as well be living on the floor of a bull-ring or the Circus Maximus, with every seat filled with spectators staring down on us, watching every move we make and hoping to see us bite the dust. What's more, they can get in here as easy as winking, while we can't get out if they choose to stop us—bad cess to them. *Brrr*! it's enough to give one the creeps. We shall have to do something about this."

"What? If that is not a leading question?" inquired Dr. Kelly absently, surveying the surroundings from a professional viewpoint that took account of drains, smells, sanitation (or lack of it), the direction of the prevailing wind and the source of water, while Wally was interested only in the military angle.

"Well, put the place into a state of defence, to begin with," said Wally promptly. "Build a good stout wall across the entrance of the compound, with a door we can bar from this side: an iron one for choice. And get another one put up on this side of that archway bit that leads into the barracks, and close both ends of the lane that runs behind it, so that if there should be a shindy we could stop anyone getting at the Residency itself except through the barracks; or into the compound, once we'd closed the gate. As things are now, we'd be sitting ducks if anyone wanted to attack us."

"Ah, come now, no one's going to attack us," returned the doctor comfortably. "The Amir won't be wanting another war on his hands, and as he'll know that's the quickest way to get one, he'll take good care to see there's no trouble. Besides, the Bala Hissar is his own particular stamping-ground, which means that while we are here he is our host; and I'll have you know that Afghans are very punctilious on the subject of hospitality and the treatment of guests, so you can stop worrying and relax. In any case, there isn't much you can do about it, for if all those spectators you mentioned—the boyos up there in the dress-circle and the gallery—decided to

1034

turn their thumbs down, they could pick us off one by one as easy as wink your eye."

"That's just what I said," returned Wally forcefully. "I said we'd be sitting ducks, and it's not a role that appeals to me. Nor do I think it's a good idea to put temptation into the heads of the ungodly. Remember the C.O. of that Yeomanry regiment that was stationed in Peshawar a couple of years ago?"

"If you mean old 'Bloater' Brumby, yes—vaguely. I thought he was dead."

"He is. He died during a period of piping peace while the Brigade were on autumn manoeuvres near the Frontier. Took a stroll on his own one evening all dressed up in his scarlet-coated best because some big-wig had come out from Peshawar that day, and was standing around admiring the view when a tribesman picked him off. The tribal elders were most apologetic, but they insisted that it was the Colonel-Sahib's own fault for providing such a beautiful target that the temptation had been too great for poor Somebody-or-other Khan, who had not been able to resist taking a shot at him. They were sure the Sahibs would understand that there was no malice about it. *Verb. sap.!*"

"*Hmm.*" The doctor glanced up at the rooftops and the small barred or latticed windows that looked down on the British Mission's compound, and said: "Yes, I see what you mean. But we're in a cleft stick, Wally. You'll just have to grin and bear it, and trust to the luck of the Irish that no marksman finds us an equally tempting target. Because there's nothing to be done about it at all, at all."

"We'll see about that," retorted Wally vigorously. And that same evening, when the Envoy and his suite returned from paying their first official visit at the palace, he had spoken about it to William Jenkyns, and later to Sir Louis himself; only to receive a dusty answer from both. Nothing, as Ambrose Kelly had predicted, could or would be done. For the simple reason that refusal to occupy the accommodation that had been placed at their disposal would be grossly discourteous, while to demand that it be made secure against attack would be regarded as an insult not only to the Amir, but to the Commander-in-Chief of the Afghan Army, General Daud Shah, together with practically every high-ranking official in Kabul.

Nor was it possible for the members of the Mission to take matters into their own hands and set about closing off the compound or improvising defences, for to be seen doing anything of the kind could only suggest that they distrusted their host and were afraid of being attacked—which could not fail to offend the Amir and Daud Shah, and might well put ideas into the heads of many citizens who would otherwise have remained peaceably inclined.

"In any case," said Sir Louis, "it is no bad thing that the Residency should be easily accessible to anyone who wishes to walk in. The more visitors we have the better. Our first duty is to establish friendly relations with the Afghans, and I want no one turned away, or anything done that might suggest that the public are unwelcome and that we wish to keep them at arm's length. In fact, as I have just been saying to the Amir . . ."

The Amir had received the British Envoy and his suite with flattering cordiality and every sign of friendship, and appeared only too willing to accede to any demand. Sir Louis' request that members of his Mission should be free to receive visits from Afghan officials and Sirdars had been instantly granted, and Sir Louis had returned to the Residency in high feather and dictated a telegram to the Viceroy that read: "All well. Had interview with Amir and delivered presents." After which he had sat down to write his first dispatches from Kabul, and been able to retire to bed that night feeling elated and confident: everything was going smoothly and his mission to Afghanistan was going to be a triumphant success.

Wally, lying awake in the house on the opposite side of the Residency courtyard, was feeling less pleased with life, having discovered that his bed contained lodgers. It had been bad enough to be reminded of the fact that another and rival Mission had also been official guests in the Residency (and not so long ago either) by finding Russian names scribbled on the walls of his room. But bedbugs as well were beyond the line. He hoped fervently that his Russian predecessor had suffered equally badly from their attentions, and decided that if these were the best quarters that the Amir of Afghanistan could offer to high-ranking foreign guests, then the rest of the Bala Hissar must be a slum.

The house in which he lay, and the one opposite to it, were both gimcrack structures of lath and plaster supported by wooden pillars, the Envoy's house being a mere two storeys high, while the newly christened "Mess House," in which the three members of the suite were quartered, was a storey higher. Both houses, after the Afghan pattern, had flat roofs that were reached by a flight of stairs, but unlike the single-storey barrack block, neither roof possessed anything that could be called a parapet, and Wally decided that he had seen considerably better buildings in many an Indian bazaar.

He was soon to discover that large, stone-built buildings, tall towers and marble minarets are unsuitable for an area that is subject to earth tremors, and though mud-bricks, wood and plaster may not make for magnificence, they can be safer. Almost the only stone-work in the compound was to be found in the large, single-storeyed barrack block, where a line of stone pillars supported a sloping verandah roof and formed an arcade on either side of the long, open courtyard that divided the quarters allotted to the Mohammedans from those of the Sikhs. Here, despite Cavagnari's orders, Wally had eventually managed to get a second door made to close the front of the open archway that led into it, on the pretext that it would "help to keep the place warmer in the winter."

This archway ran back a full ten feet, like a miniature tunnel, to form a portico from which two flights of steps, one on either side of the entrance, led up in the thickness of the wall to the roof above. The inner end of this tunnel already boasted a massive iron-barred door, and now Wally had had another put in the outer one: admittedly a regrettably flimsy affair, as it was made from unseasoned planks. But in an emergency it would allow his men to use those stairways unseen.

There was a third stairway at the opposite end of the long courtyard near the door that opened on to the Residency lane. But as any attack would come from the front, the stairs in the thickness of the archway would be as vital to the defence of the barracks as the barracks were to the defence of the Residency. Not that Wally believed that there was the least likelihood of an attack, yet as this was his first solo command it behoved him to take what precautions he could—though they were few enough, in all conscience. But at least he had made a gesture in that line.

He was to make others. "Once we are there, it'll

be up to us to see that we get on good terms with the people," he had told Ash on that night in Mardan. And now he set about doing so with enthusiasm, organizing Mounted Sports, that because they called for skilled horsemanship would appeal to the Afghans, whom he invited to compete with the Guides at tent-pegging, lemon-cutting, spearing a ring with a lance and similar contests. Nor were the others behindhand in the task of fostering good relations; Ambrose Kelly laid plans to start a dispensary, while the Envoy and his Secretary filled their days with informal talks with the Amir, discussions with Ministers, and endless visits of ceremony from nobles and officials.

Sir Louis also made a point of being seen daily riding through the streets, though at the same time he issued an edict forbidding all members of the Mission access to the roofs of any of the Residency buildings, and ordered canvas awnings to be stretched across the barrack courtyard; the aim of both these measures being to protect the susceptibilities of neighbours in the Bala Hissar from the possibility of being affronted by the sight of the "foreigners" taking their ease.

"This is an amazing country," wrote Wally, replying to a cousin serving in India who had written to congratulate him on winning the Victoria Cross and inquire what Afghanistan was like. "But you wouldn't think much of Kabul. It's a seedy-looking place . . ."

The letter had included a light-hearted account of a well-attended *"Pagal*-Gymkhana" he had organized on the previous day, and contained no suggestion that the Herati regiments in the city were a continuing source of trouble. But the dâk-rider who carried that particular letter to the British-held outpost of Ali Khel, where all the Mission's telegrams and letters were either forwarded or received, had already carried a telegram from Sir Louis Cavagnari to the Viceroy that read: "Alarming reports personally reached me today from several sources of the mutinous behaviour of the Herat Regiments lately arrived here, some of the men having been seen going about the city with drawn swords and using inflammatory language against the Amir and his English visitors, and I was strongly advised not to go out for a day or two. I sent for the Foreign Minister and, as he was confident that the reports were exaggerated, we went out as usual. I do not

1038

doubt that there is disaffection among troops on account of arrears of pay, and especially about compulsory service, but the Amir and his ministers are confident that they can manage them."

A further telegram, sent on the following day, was considerably shorter: "State of affairs reported yesterday continues in a milder degree. Amir professing complete confidence to maintain discipline." Yet in the diary that Sir Louis wrote up every evening and sent off at the end of each week to the Viceroy, he described the arrival of the mutinous Heratis in Kabul, clamorous for pay and completely out of hand.

It was all very well, thought Sir Louis, for the Amir's Foreign Minister to assert that these men would be given their arrears of pay in full within a day or two, after which they would return to their homes; or to insist (as he did) that the reports of their lawlessness and looting were greatly exaggerated and due solely to the behaviour of a "few wild spirits." But Sir Louis had his own sources of information and he had been given several well-authenticated accounts of the conduct of the malcontents that implicated far more than a "few wild spirits." He had also heard that the troops had flatly refused to disperse to their homes until each man had had every anna of his back pay counted out into his hand, but that there was not enough money in the Treasury to pay them. None of which squared with the optimistic statements of the Foreign Minister and his master the Amir.

Yet in one way Ash had been right in thinking that Sir Louis did not fully appreciate the danger in which he and his Mission stood.

The Envoy was by no means ignorant of what was going on in Kabul, but he refused to take it too seriously. He preferred to accept the Minister's assurance that the situation was under control, and to immerse himself instead in schemes for reforming the administration of Afghanistan, together with plans for an autumn tour with the Amir, rather than concentrate on a far more urgent and immediate problem—the devising of ways and means of bolstering up the Amir's shaky authority in the face of the rising tide of lawlessness and violence that had flooded into the valley of Kabul, and was now threatening to engulf the city, and even the citadel itself.

"He cannot know what is going on," said Ash. "They

are keeping it from him. He must be told, and you are the one who must tell him, Sirdar-Sahib. He will listen to you because you were a Risaldar-Major of the Guides. For their sakes, I beg you to go to the Residency and warn him."

The Sirdar had gone and Sir Louis had listened attentively to everything he had to say, and when he had finished, smiled and said lightly: "They can only kill the three or four of us here, and our deaths will be avenged," an observation that enraged Ash when he heard it, as he felt certain that in the event of trouble not only "us," but the entire Escort, together with the numerous servants and camp-followers who had accompanied the Mission to Kabul, would also be killed.

Ash had not heard of the remark that Cavagnari was reported to have made before leaving Simla, to the effect that he would not mind dying if his death led to the annexation of Afghanistan, but nevertheless he began to wonder if the Envoy had not become a little unhinged of late and perhaps saw himself as a willing sacrifice on the altar of Imperial expansion. It was a crazy suspicion, and instantly dismissed. Yet it returned again and again in the days that followed, for there were times when it seemed to Ash that there could be no other explanation for the Envoy's lofty attitude towards all warnings.

The Sirdar, disturbed by the swaggering insolence of the Herati troops and worried about the safety of the Guides, had paid a second visit to the Residency in order to tell Sir Louis of certain things that he himself had seen and heard:

"I do not speak from hearsay, Your Honour," said the Sirdar, "but only of what I have seen with my own eyes and heard with my own ears. These regiments march through the streets with their bands playing and their officers at their head, and as they march they shout threats and vile abuse at the Amir, and revile the Kazilbashi regiments—who being loyal to him they accuse of cowardice and subservience to the infidels, jeering at them that they, the Heratis, will show the Kazilbashi slaves how to deal with foreigners. You too, Excellency-Sahib, they abuse— naming you by name. I have heard them. This you should know, for it bodes ill and should be stopped while there is yet time."

"But I do know," said Cavagnari. "And so does His

Highness the Amir, who has been before you in this, having already warned me to keep away from the city until the trouble dies down, which it will surely do. As for the Heratis, you need have no fear, Risaldar-Sahib. Dogs who bark do not bite."

"Sahib," said the ex-Risaldar-Major gravely, "these dogs *do* bite. And I, who know my people, tell you that there is great danger."

Sir Louis frowned at the implied criticism, then his face cleared and he laughed and said: "And I tell you again, Sirdar-Sahib, that they can only kill us; and if they do, we shall be terribly avenged."

The Sirdar shrugged and gave up.

"It was profitless to say more," he told Ash. "Nevertheless, after I had left his presence I saw Jenkyns-Sahib leaving the courtyard, and I followed him and asked permission to speak to him apart. We walked together by the stables in the cavalry lines while I disclosed the same matters to him, and when I had done, he spoke sharply, saying 'Have you told Cavagnari-Sahib this?' When I told him that I had just done so, and of the reply I had received, he was silent for a space, and then he said: 'What the Envoy-Sahib says is true. The British Government will not be harmed by losing three or four of us here.' Now I ask you, what can one do with men like that? I have wasted my time and theirs, for it is clear that they will not be warned."

Ash had fared little better with Wally, whom he had managed to meet on several occasions and with comparative ease, as Sir Louis' policy of encouraging visitors and keeping open house meant that the Residency was always full of Afghans, who left their attendants in the compound where they fell into conversation with the Residency servants and the men of the Escort. This had made it a simple matter for Ash to mingle with them and get a message passed to Wally making an assignation to meet at some spot where they could talk together without attracting attention, and after that first meeting they had also devised a simple code.

But though Wally was always unfeignedly glad to see him and took a deep interest in all he had to say, there was never any question of his attempting to pass on anything Ash told him to Sir Louis. The Commandant, with whom Ash had discussed this point in Mardan, had recognized the trouble this could lead to, and in briefing Wally before he left, had impressed it upon him that the Envoy would have his own sources of information and that it was no part of Lieutenant Hamilton's duties to supplement them. If at any time he had reason to believe that Sir Louis was ignorant of some vital matter that he himself had learned from Ashton, then he should mention it to the Envoy's Secretary and Political Assistant, William Jenkyns, who would decide whether to pass it on or not.

"I did that the other day," confessed Wally ruefully, "and never again. Will bit my head off. Told me that Sir Louis knew a damn sight more than I did about what went on in Kabul, and suggested that I run away and play with my soldiers—or words to that effect. And he's right of course."

Ash shrugged and remarked ungraciously that he sincerely hoped so. He was feeling worried and apprehensive, not only on account of the many disturbing things that were being said and done in the city, or his fears for the safety of Wally and the Guides, but because he was afraid for Juli. For there was cholera in the city. There had as yet been no cases of it in the Bala Hissar or near the quiet street in which Nakshband Khan's house stood, but the disease was rampant in the poorer and more congested quarters of Kabul; and there came a day when Ash heard from a friend of the Sirdar's, a well-known Hindu whose son was in the service of the Amir's brother Ibrahim Khan, that it had broken out among the disaffected troops.

Had it not been for the fact that half India, to his certain knowledge, was also suffering from a raging cholera epidemic that year, he would almost certainly have taken Anjuli away that same day and abandoned Wally and the Guides without a second thought. But there being nowhere he could take her with any certainty of escaping it, he had decided that it was probably safer for her to stay where she was, as with luck the cholera would not reach their quarter of the city; and in any case it was bound to diminish drastically with the onset of autumn. But it was an anxious time, and he grew thin from strain and found it increasingly difficult to talk to Wally of the dangers that threatened the Mission. Or, with his mind filled with fears for Juli, to sit around discussing that indefatigable poet's latest composition.

1042

A visit to the village of Bemaru, scene of the outbreak of the Kabul disaster of 1841, had inspired a particularly tedious epic, and Ash had wasted a precious afternoon listening in growing frustration while Wally strode to and fro reciting lines that only the author himself or his doting family could possibly have regarded as serious poetry—

> *"Though all is changed," declaimed Wally, "yet*
> > *remnants of the past*
> *Point to the scenes of bloodshed, and, alas!*
> *Of murder foul; and ruined houses cast*
> *Their mournful shadow o'er the graves of grass*
> *Of England's soldiery, who faced a lot*
> *That few, thank Heaven! before or since have*
> > *shared;—*
> *Slain by the hand of Treachery, and not*
> *In open Combat . . ."*

There had been more to the same effect, and the poet (who had put in a lot of hard work on it and was not displeased with the result) was disconcerted when Ash had merely remarked thoughtfully that it was curious that the four Europeans in the Residency should think and speak of themselves as "Englishmen" when one was a Scot, two were Irish, and the fourth was half Irish and half French. A comment that showed he had been thinking of something else and missed the finer points of the poem.

All the same, Wally drew more comfort than he would have cared to admit from the knowledge that his friend spent a large part of each day in a house that backed on the Residency compound. It was consoling to know that he need only glance up at a certain window to confirm whether he was there or not, for each morning, when Ash came to work, he would place a cheap blue and white pottery jar with a spray of flowers or greenery in it between the two centre bars of his window, as a sign that he was still there and had not left Kabul.

Yet even without the information he received from Ash, Wally could hardly have avoided being aware that the situation in Kabul was deteriorating daily. He knew—he could hardly fail to know—that neither the servants nor the men of the Escort any longer went singly, or even in

1043

pairs, to bathe or wash their clothes in the river, but preferred to go in groups—and armed; that even the Mussulmans did not care to venture alone into the city now,
while as for the Sikhs and Hindus, it was as much as
their lives were worth to be seen in the streets at all, so
that except when on duty they stayed within the compound. What he did not know was that Ash had already
taken action in one small sphere to defuse some of the
ill-feeling that was being generated against the foreigners.

It was a minor matter, and one that invited more
risk than Ash had a right to take. But it had had its effect.
He had taken part in the mounted sports, riding a borrowed horse and disguised as a Gilzai tribesman, and had
won several events—to the delight of the Kabulis, who
had been resentful of the prowess shown by the Guides,
and had become convinced that the contests were designed to demonstrate the superiority of the "Sahibs'
Army" over their own.

Ash's skill at this particular type of sport had helped
redress the balance a little. But he had not dared to repeat
the experiment, even though the muttered comments of
the spectators continued to worry him—as did the talk in
the bazaars. The latter to such an extent that eventually
he approached the Sirdar's Hindu friend (who, as the
Sirdar said, "knows the ins and outs of what goes on in
the houses of great men") to beg him to call at the Residency and speak to Sir Louis Cavagnari of the increasingly virulent attitude of the citizens towards the presence of
the foreign Mission in their midst.

"For His Excellency," explained Ash, "has so far
spoken only with Afghans. And who can say how much
truth they have told him, or whether it is to their advantage to make him believe that all will be well? But you,
being a Hindu, and one whose son is in the service of
His Highness the Amir's own brother, he may listen to
with attention; and believing what you say, take measures
to protect himself and his followers."

"What measures?" inquired the Hindu sceptically.
"There is only one which might serve: to dissolve this
Mission and return with it to India without delay. Though
I would not care to vouch for it reaching there in safety,
as the tribes might well fall upon it on the way."

"That he would never do," said Ash.

"No. Yet there is little else that he can do, for he

must know that the quarters in which he and his Mission live cannot be defended against attack. Therefore if he treats all warnings lightly and replies to them with brave words, this may well be because he is wise, and not, as you suppose, because he is either blind or foolish. He will know that his words will be repeated, and the very fact that they are bold and fearless may well give the hot-heads pause; and placed as he is that is wisdom, not foolishness. I have called on him before, but if you and the Sirdar-Sahib wish, I will certainly do so again and see if I cannot enlighten him as to the ill-will against the Mission that prevails in the city. Though I think you will find that he already knows this."

The promised visit had been made that very day. But this time the caller had not succeeded in seeing the British Envoy, for the Afghan sentries who by the Amir's orders stood guard by the entrance to the compound (ostensibly for the greater safety and protection of the British Mission) had not only turned him away, but had abused and stoned him as he left. "I was struck several times," reported the Hindu, "and when they saw me stagger they laughed. This is no longer a safe place for men such as myself, or for foreigners of any persuasion. I think it is time I left Kabul for a while and went south to visit my relations."

He had refused categorically to make any further attempt to see Sir Louis, and true to his word had left Kabul a few days later. But the tale of his friend's treatment at the hands of the Afghan sentries had disturbed Sirdar Nakshband Khan almost as much as it had shaken Ash, and though after his previous visit to the Residency the Sirdar too had sworn that he would not go there again, he had done so.

Sir Louis had greeted him graciously enough, but made it clear from the outset that he was already fully informed as to the situation in Kabul and needed no further information on that head, and though pleased to see the ex-Risaldar-Major, was unfortunately too busy to spare as much time as he would wish to on purely social calls.

"Indeed so. That is understood," agreed the Sirdar politely. "As is also the fact that your Honour has many sources of information and therefore knows much of what goes on in the city. Though not all, I think," and he had told Sir Louis how a well-known and much-respected Hindu who had called at the Residency desiring to speak with him, had been refused admittance and driven away with stones and abuse by the Afghan sentries.

Sir Louis' eyes blazed as he listened and even his luxuriant black beard seemed to bristle with anger. "That is untrue," rasped Sir Louis. "The man lies!"

But the Sirdar was not to be intimidated by the Envoy's wrath. "If the Huzoor does not believe me," he replied calmly, "let him ask his own servants, several of whom witnessed the stoning of the Hindu, as did many of the Guides also. The Huzoor has only to ask; and when he does so he will learn that he is little better than a prisoner. For what profit is there in remaining here if he is not permitted to see men who only desire to talk truth to him?"

The suggestion that he was not a free agent touched the Envoy on the raw, for Pierre Louis Cavagnari was an intensely proud man, so much so that he had frequently been accused by those who did not share his views, or had been treated to the rough side of his tongue, of being insufferably arrogant. It is certain that he had a high opinion of his own capabilities and did not take kindly to criticism.

Sirdar Nakshband Khan's story struck at his personal pride as well as his official dignity as the representative of Her Britannic Majesty the Empress of India, and he would have liked to disbelieve it. Instead he replied coldly that he would inquire into the matter, and having dismissed his visitor, sent for William Jenkyns and ordered the secretary to find out at once if anyone in the Residency compound had in fact witnessed such an incident as Nakshband Khan described.

William was back within fifteen minutes. The story, he reported, was unfortunately true. It had not only been vouched for by several of the Residency servants, but by two grass-cutters and a dozen men of the escort, including Jemadar Jiwand Singh of the Guides Cavalry and Havildar Hassan of the infantry.

"Why was I not informed of this before?" demanded Cavagnari, white with rage. "By God, I'll have those men disciplined! They should have reported it at once, if not to me, then to Hamilton or Kelly, or to you. And if young Hamilton knew, and did not tell me—Tell him I wish to speak to him immediately."

1046

"I don't think he's here at the moment, sir. I believe he went out about an hour ago."

"Then send him to me the minute he comes back. He has no right to slip off without letting me know. Where the devil has he gone?"

"I'm afraid I've no idea, sir," said William woodenly.

"Then you should have. I will not have my officers leaving the Residency whenever they think fit. They ought to have more sense than to go jaunting about the city at a time like this. Not that I believe . . ."

He left the sentence unfinished and dismissing William with a curt gesture, sat scowling into the middle-distance and jerking at his beard with lean, angry fingers.

But Wally was not jaunting about the city. He had ridden out to see Ash, whom he had arranged to meet on the hillside to the south of Kabul where the Emperor Barbur lies buried. For it was the eighteenth of August and his birthday: he was twenty-three.

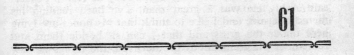

61

The last resting place of Barbur—"Barbur the Tiger," who had seized the Land of Cain only a few years after Columbus discovered America, and gone on to conquer India and establish an imperial dynasty that had lasted into Ash's own life-time—was in a walled garden on the slope of a hill to the south-west of the Shere Dawaza.

The spot had been known in Barbur's day as "The Place of Footsteps," and it had been a favourite haunt of his, so much so that though he had died far away in India, at Agra, he had left instructions that his body was to be brought back there for burial. This his widow, Bibi Mubarika, had done, travelling to Agra to claim her husband's body and take it back through the passes to Kabul.

Nowadays the garden was known as "The Place of Barbur's Grave," and few people visited it at this season, for Ramadan, the month of fasting, had begun. But as it was regarded as a pleasure park, no one would think it odd that the young Sahib who commanded the foreign Envoy's Indian escort should choose to visit such a historic spot, or that once there he should fall into conversation with one of the local sight-seers. In fact, Ash and Wally had the garden to themselves, for though the day had been sultry and overcast, no rain had fallen as yet, and the hot wind that herded the sluggish clouds across the valley was stirring up enough dust to keep all sensible Kabulis indoors.

A little stream in a formal channel flowed past the worn slab of marble and the ruined fragments of a pavilion that marked the great man's grave, and the wind strewed the water with fallen leaves and sent eddies of dust whirling between the trees and flowering shrubs, and through the carved wooden arches of a small memorial mosque—an open-sided, unpretentious building that like Barbur's tomb was sadly in need of repair. There had been only one devotee there that day, and it was not until he rose and came out that Wally realized it was Ash.

"What were you doing in there?" he inquired when they had greeted each other.

"Saying a prayer for the Tiger. May he rest in peace," said Ash. "He was a great man. I've been reading his memoirs again, and I like to think that his bones are lying here under the grass and that I can sit beside them and remember the tremendous life he lived, the things he saw and did, the chances he took . . . Let's get out of the wind."

There were other humbler graves in the garden. A number of conventional Moslem stelae in weathered marble or stone rose out of the parched grass, some still standing upright, but the majority canted to left or right by the hand of time, or lying half hidden on the ground. Ash by-passed these and having paused a moment by Barbur's grave, led the way to a level piece of ground that was sheltered from the wind by a clump of shrubs, and sat down cross-legged on the dusty grass.

"Many happy returns of the day, Wally."

"So you remembered," said Wally, flushing with pleasure.

"Of course I did. I've even got a present for you." Ash groped among his robes and produced a little bronze horse: a piece of ancient Chinese craftsmanship that he had bought in the bazaar at Kabul, knowing that it would delight Wally. It had done so; but the donor had not been pleased to discover that Lieutenant Hamilton had ridden out to meet him without an escort.

"For God's sake, Wally! Are you mad? Didn't you even bring your syce?"

"If you mean Hosein, no. But you can keep your hair on, because I gave him the day off so that I could bring one of our troopers instead: Sowar Taimus. You wouldn't know him—well after your time. He's a first-rate fellow with guts enough for six. The Kote-Daffadar says that he's a Shahzada in his own right and a Prince of the Sadozai dynasty, which is probably true. What he doesn't know about Kabul and the Kabulis isn't worth knowing, and it's due to him that we managed to sneak out without trouble, and without having a couple of Afghan troopers trotting along behind us. He's waiting outside with the horses, and if he doesn't like the look of anyone approaching this place you can be sure he'll let me know. So will you be calm now, and stop fussing like an old hen."

"I still say you should have brought at least three of your sowars with you. *And* your syce," said Ash angrily. "I would never have agreed to meet you here if I'd dreamt that you'd be such a chucklehead as to ride out without a proper escort. For God's sake, don't *any* of you realize what is going on around here?"

"Faith, and that's a foine way to talk to a feller on his birthday, so it is," grinned Wally, unabashed. "Yes, you old ass, of course we do. I'll have you know we're not nearly as stupid as you think. In fact that's precisely why I came here on the sly with only Taimus, instead of attracting a lot of attention to myself and stirring up the angry passions of the locals by clattering out with an armed escort at my heels."

"That's as maybe," retorted Ash, still shaken. "But I understand the Amir himself has advised your Chief to avoid riding through the streets for a time."

"Through the streets, yes. His Nibs seems to think it would be better if we weren't seen going about his city just now. But there are no streets here and it's a long way from the city—and where did you hear that, anyway? I thought that particular bit of advice had been given to Sir Louis on the quiet. It's not at all the sort of thing he'd like every Tom, Dick and Harry to know."

"I don't suppose they do know," said Ash. "I heard it from that pensioner of ours, Risaldar-Major Nakshband Khan. Who incidentally got it from the horse's mouth—Sir Louis himself."

"Did he now," murmured Wally, lying back on the grass and firmly shutting his eyes. "And I suppose it was yourself put that old spalpeen up to calling at the Residency to warn us that the city was full of rude, rough boys from Herat, and that if we didn't hide indoors until they went away, some of them might call us naughty names or even thumb their noses at us? Sure I might have known it. No, don't be telling me that it's all in the line of duty, because I know it is. But dammit, today's my birthday, so can't we just for once forget the political situation and all this Intelligence business and talk about other things for a change? Pleasant things . . ."

There was nothing that Ash would have liked better, but he hardened his heart and said: "No, Wally: I'm afraid we can't, because there are several things I have to say to you. To begin with, you're going to have to stop these mounted sports you've been arranging between your fellows and the Afghans."

Wally abandoned his restful pose and sat bolt upright, staring and indignant. "Stop them? What the blazes for? Why, the Afghans love 'em!—they're damned good horsemen and they thoroughly enjoy competing against my chaps. We always have a huge turn-out, and there couldn't be a better way of getting on friendly terms with them."

"I can see why you think so. But then you don't understand how these people think. They see it quite differently, and far from encouraging friendly feelings it has caused great offence. The truth is, Wally, that your sowars are too damn good at this type of sport, and the Kabulis have been saying that you hold them solely in order to show how easily you can defeat them, and that when your men ride at a dangling lemon and slash it in half with a sabre, or spear a tent-peg out of the ground on the point of a lance, they are merely demonstrating how they would cut down or spear their enemies—in other words, the Afghans. If you'd been able to stand among the spectators and listen, as I've done, and hear what they say among themselves as they watch, you wouldn't talk so glibly about 'establishing friendly relations with the Afghans,' when in point of fact all you are doing is helping to make them a deal sourer than they are already; which God knows is sour enough."

"Well if that isn't the outside of enough!" exploded Wally. "So *that's* why you were dressed up like a scare-crow and carrying off the prizes for the opposition that day. I couldn't think what you were playing at, and for two pins I'd have—" Words appeared to fail him and Ash had the grace to look ashamed of himself and say defensively: "I didn't do it for fun, whatever you may think. I hoped it might even up the balance a bit and take some of the heat out of the situation. But I didn't think you'd recognize me."

"Not recognize you? When I know every trick of riding you possess and the way you always—Holy smoke! It's yourself who's mad, so it is. Have you any idea of the risks you were running? It's all very well for me to spot you, but I'm willing to lay you a year's pay to a rotten orange that there isn't a single jawan in the Escort who doesn't know by now who you are."

"I wouldn't take you," said Ash with a crooked smile. "I imagine they know a lot more than you think. But they also know how to keep their mouths shut. Have any of them, for instance, reported to you that whenever they show their faces outside the citadel, the Kabulis don't just insult them, but make the worst kind of abusive remarks about you and Kelly and Jenkyns, and particularly about Cavagnari? No, I can see they haven't! And you can't blame them. They'd be ashamed to let any of you know the sort of things that are being said about you in the bazaars; which is your bad luck, because if they spoke out you might learn a thing or two."

"God, what a people," said Wally disgustedly. "That Sikh obviously knew what he was talking about after all."

"What Sikh?"

"Oh, just a Havildar of the 3rd Sikhs I was talking to one day when we were in Gandamak. He was scandalized by the Peace Treaty and the fact that we were pulling the army out of Afghanistan, and seemed to think we were all mad. He wanted to know what kind of warfare this was, and said, 'Sahib, these people hate you and you have beaten them. There is only one treatment for such *shaitans* (devils)—grind them to powder.' Perhaps that is what we should have done."

"Perhaps. But it's no good talking about that now, because the main thing I came here to tell you about is a deal more important than your mounted sports. I know I've brought this up before, but this time, whether you like it or not, you're going to have to talk to Jenkyns about it. As I've already told you, the Amir has allowed a rumour to get around that the Mission is only here to act as paymaster and general benefactor: in other words, to be milked of rupees like an obliging cow. Almost everyone believes this to be true, so the sooner Sir Louis persuades the Viceroy to let him act the part, and sends him enough money to pay off the arrears owed to the troops, the better. It's the only thing that may stop the pot from boiling over and scalding everyone within sight, because the minute that starving rabble from Herat have been given their just dues, they'll leave Kabul; and once they are out of the way the disaffected elements in the city can simmer down a bit and give the Amir a chance to get a firmer grip on his country and restore some respect for authority. I'm not saying that a large injection of cash will solve all that wretched chap's problems, but at least it'll help to shore him up and delay the roof falling in on him—and on your precious Mission as well."

Wally was silent for a moment or two, and then he said irritably: "It would take a deuce of a lot of money, and I don't see why we should be expected to stump up the arrears of pay that are owed to the armed forces of a country that we have been at war with—an enemy country! Do you realize that a large part of what these fellows claim they are owed seems to be back pay, so that if we were fools enough to foot the bill we'd actually be paying those men for fighting us? Paying them for killing Wigram?—and a whole lot more of our fellows too? No, it's obscene! It's a monstrous suggestion and you can't possibly mean it."

"But I do mean it, Wally." Ash's voice was as grim as his face, and there was a note in it that Wally recognized with a curious sense of shock as fear: real fear. "It may sound like a monstrous suggestion to you, and I'm not even sure that it would work, except as a temporary measure. But it would at least remove the immediate threat and give your Mission a breathing space. It would be worth it for that alone. What Cavagnari needs most is time, and it doesn't look to me as though he's going to get it unless he buys it."

"Then you're really suggesting that he sends for these mutinous divils and hands them out—"

"No I am not. I am not suggesting that he, personally, pays anything directly to the Herati regiments

1052

(who, by the way, were never in action against us and don't believe we won a single battle). But I'm willing to bet that he could galvanize the Viceroy into sending the Amir, *immediately,* a sum sufficient to cover what his troops are owed. It wouldn't even need to be a gift, because it could be counted as part of the yearly subsidy that was promised him by the terms of the Peace Treaty, which amounts to six crores a year. Damn it, Wally, that's six million rupees. Even a small part of that would wipe out the Amir's debt to his troops. But if the money isn't forthcoming soon, it won't be long before the whole Afghan Army is faced with the choice of starving or stealing; and believe me, they'll choose the latter, as the Heratis have done. And as you yourself would do, if you were in their shoes!"

"That's all very well, but——"

"There's no 'but' about it. Hunger can do a lot of strange things to people as I've learned at first hand, and I only wish I could talk to Cavagnari myself. But I promised the Commandant I wouldn't, because . . . Well, anyway, it seems young Jenkyns is our only hope; and after all he is supposed to be the Political Assistant. You'll have to pass it on to him—tell him you had it from old Nakshband Khan—tell him anything. But for God's sake get it into his head that it's deadly serious, and that if Cavagnari hasn't realized this already, which he may well have done, he has got to realize it now. As for you, Wally, if you've any sense at all, you'll stop these sports of yours and warn the Rosebud" (this was a reference to Ambrose Kelly, who for obvious reasons was known in the Guides and to his friends as "Rosie") "to write off his equally well-meaning scheme for starting a free dispensary, because it is already being said in the city that the Sahibs are planning to use this as a means of poisoning anyone who is foolish enough to attend."

"The Black Curse of Shielygh on them," sighed Wally with feeling. "May the divil fly away with the spalpeens: he's welcome to them. When I think of all we meant to do—and dammit, will do—to help these ungrateful bastards to have a better life and fairer laws, I could spit, so I could."

Ash frowned and observed with an edge to his voice that possibly they did not want to be helped by foreigners —except financially. Money was the one and only thing

1053

that could help the Amir and his people, and save the foreigners in the Residency from disaster. "If the troops get paid you may all still have a chance of scraping through with nothing worse than a bloody nose and a few bruises. But if it doesn't, I wouldn't bet a brass farthing on the safety of the Mission, or the future prospects of the Amir either."

"Faith, what a cheerful little ray of sunshine you are," observed Wally with a wry smile. "I suppose you'll tell me next that every mullah in the place is calling for a Holy War?"

"Oddly enough, they aren't. Or only a very few. There is a fiery gentleman down Herat way who is being very vocal, and an equally vocal fakir here in the city. But by and large the majority of mullahs have been remarkably pacific and seem to be doing their best to keep things on an even keel. It's a pity they haven't got a better Amir; one can't help feeling sorry for the poor fellow, but he's not half the man his father was—and he, Heaven knows, wasn't anything to write home about. What the Afghans need now is a strong man: another Dost Mohammed."

"Or a fellow like that one over there," suggested Wally, nodding his head in the direction of Barbur's tomb.

"The Tiger? God forbid!" said Ash fervently. "If *he'd* been in command here, we would never have got further than Ali Masjid. Now there's someone you should write an epic poem about: Ode to a Dead Emperor. *Hic jacet ecce Barbur, magnus Imperator. Fama semper vivat** . . . 'Lie lightly on him, gentle earth.' "

Wally laughed and said that he would try his hand at Barbur when he had finished with "The Village of Bemaru," which was still giving him trouble. The political situation was not mentioned again and the talk turned to pleasanter subjects: to books and horses, mutual friends and the prospects of *shikar* in the cold weather. "Do you remember that Christmas we spent at Morala," said Wally, "and the evening we brought down eight teal between us at one go, and seven of them fell into the river and we had to go in after them because the *shikari* couldn't swim? Do you remember—"

A sudden and stronger gust of wind whined through

---

*Here lies Barbur the great Emperor. May his fame live for ever.

the bushes and raised a cloud of dust that set him coughing. Mingled with the dust were a few rain drops, and he scrambled to his feet, exclaiming: "Glory be! I believe it's going to rain. That's something to be thankful for. We could do with a good downpour provided it doesn't wash the whole place away in a river of mud. Well, I must be off. Time I got back to my neglected duties if I don't want to get a rap over the knuckles from my respected Chief. See you sometime next week. And in the meantime I'll have a talk with William, and think about discontinuing the sports—though I suspect you're exaggerating, you old Job's Comforter. No, don't see me to the gate: Taimus is out there. *Salaam aleikoum!*"

"And the same to you, you poor purblind blinkered off-scouring of an Irish bog. And for God's sake don't go trailing your coat riding around the countryside without an escort again. It's too damned unhealthy."

" 'Too rash, too unadvised, too sudden,' " declaimed Wally soulfully. "Ah, away with you! It's a pessimist ye'are and I don't know how I put up with you at all, at all." He laughed again, and gripped Ash's hand: "Be easy now; I'll watch out for myself, I promise. Next time I'll bring a posse with me, all armed to the teeth. Will that satisfy you?"

"I shan't be satisfied until you and Kelly and the rest of our fellows are safe back in Mardan again," replied Ash with a worn smile, "But for the present I suppose I shall have to settle for an armed posse. Mind now that you don't move without it, you benighted bogtrotter."

"Cross-me-heart," said Wally cheerfully, suiting the action to the word. "Not that I shall get the chance if your depressing view of the future turns out to be correct. Ah well, as Gul Baz would say 'All things are with God.' *Ave*, Ashton, *morituri te salutant!*" He flung up an arm in the Roman salute and strode off singing "Kathleen Mavourneen" in a loud, tuneful voice and as though he had not a care in the world.

━━━━━━━━━━━━━━━━━━━━━━━━━━━━━━━━━━━━━━━

62

Apart from an occasional spatter of drops, the threatened storm did not break until close on sunset, and Wally arrived back at the Residency only lightly bespeckled by raindrops and in excellent spirits. But once there he had been brought sharply back to earth, for he was met with a message that ordered him to report to Sir Louis Cavagnari the instant he returned.

As the order had been given more than two hours earlier, the reception he received from his Chief was not cordial. Sir Louis had suffered a severe blow to his self-esteem and he was still fuming with anger and inclined to blame all those who had witnessed the mistreatment of the Hindu by the Afghan sentries, but failed to inform him of it. In particular the officer in command of the escort, whose business it was to have known of the incident and reported it at once, either to him or to his secretary, Jenkyns.

If young Walter knew about it and had said nothing, by God he'd give the boy a piece of his mind. And if he did not know, then he should have known. His Indian officers ought to have told him about the disgraceful treatment that had been meted out to a Hindu gentleman who had merely called to pay his respects to the British Envoy. How many others had also been refused admittance by the Afghans? Was this the only would-be caller who had been turned away, or merely the latest?

Sir Louis required an answer to these questions at once, and the fact that Lieutenant Hamilton, when sent for, could not be found, had done nothing to soothe his ill-humour, and Wally, who had never seen his hero really angry before and thought of him as a man whom nothing and no one could ruffle, discovered his error within minutes of his return.

The Envoy had found relief for his pent-up rage in giving his military attaché not the "rap over the knuckles" so recently and lightly referred to, but a coldly furious dressing-down of major proportions. A hail of questions had rattled about Wally's ears, and when at last he was given the opportunity to speak, he had disclaimed any knowledge of the incident involving the Hindu, promised to speak severely to all those under his command who had seen it and not reported it, and suggested that they had only kept silent out of consideration for Sir Louis, as it reflected great *shurram* (dishonour) on the Envoy and every member of the Mission that such things should be done by the Afghans, and even greater *shurram* to speak of it and thereby put the Sahibs to shame. But he would certainly talk to them and make them understand that any further incidents of this kind should be reported at once.

"That will be unnecessary," said Sir Louis icily. "I intend to ensure that there shall be no more. You will go at once to the Afghan guard and tell them that I do not desire their services any longer, and that they are dismissed and will leave immediately. See to it please. And mount a double guard of your own men. Now send Jenkyns to me."

A curt nod dismissed Wally, who saluted smartly and withdrew, conscious of an odd feeling that his knees were made of india-rubber and that he had recently been run over by a railway train. The sweat that was running down his face and neck was not solely due to the heat, and he mopped it dry with his handkerchief and having drawn a deep breath and let it out again slowly, shook himself like a dog coming out of water and went off to fetch William and dismiss the Afghan guard.

The guard commander had questioned his authority to do so, insisting that his men were there by order of the Amir and for the protection of the "foreigners." But Wally's command of Pushtu was excellent (Ash had seen to that) and smarting from the effects of that tongue-lashing from his Chief, he was in no mood to put up with what he regarded as Afghan shennanigans. Just as Cavagnari had vented his pent-up wrath on Wally's head, so Wally in turn found relief for his own feelings in telling the Afghans what they could do with themselves and why. They had not lingered.

That done, he had turned his attention to speaking strongly to his jawans on the unwisdom of keeping silence when they saw dishonour being put upon them themselves and the entire British Mission. But the replies he had received had shaken him, for they confirmed everything Ash had said about the insults that were hurled at any soldier or servant from the Residency who had the temerity to appear in the city, and the reason why this had been kept from the Sahibs.

"We were ashamed to repeat such things to you," explained Jemadar Jiwand Singh, speaking for the Guides; and later Wally's own bearer, fat Pir Baksh, had used the self-same words on behalf of the many servants who had accompanied the British Mission to Kabul.

"I suppose the Chief *does* know what's going on?" said Wally uneasily, talking the matter over later that evening with Dr. Kelly while the storm that had been threatening since late afternoon raged above Kabul. "I mean about . . . Well, things like the ill-feeling there is against us—the Mission—among the Afghans; and all that row and rumpus they are kicking up in and around Kabul."

The doctor's eyebrows rose and he said placidly: "Of course he does. He's got spies all over the shop. Don't be a young ass."

"He didn't know about the Afghan guard turning people away," said Wally, troubled. "None of us knew until today. None of us four, that is, though apparently all the rest knew what was going on inside our gates and under our very noses. Did *you* know that any of our fellows who go into the city get insulted by the Kabulis? I didn't, and it makes me wonder just how much our lot have been keeping from us, and how many of the rumours we hear are true. Or if the Chief even hears half of them. Do you suppose he knows?"

"You can be sure he does," insisted Rosie loyally. "He's always been up to every rig and row, and there have never been any flies on him. So don't be worrying your head about him. He's a great man, so he is."

"Damn you, Rosie, I'm not worrying," said Wally indignantly, flushing up to the roots of his hair. "Nor have I got the wind up. But—but I only learned today that the local population have decided that those mounted sports I've been putting on are solely designed to show 'em that the regiments of the Raj can beat the stuffing out of them with one hand tied behind our backs; and that they resent them accordingly."

1058

"Poor silly bastards," observed Rosie dispassionately. "Who told you that?"

"Oh . . . just a fellow I know."

"Well it don't do to believe every blatherumshkite you hear, for it's more than likely that your fine friend merely overheard some disgruntled competitor who'd made a fool of himself by missing the target altogether, excusing his failure by taking a swipe at the Guides and enjoying a good old green-eyed grumble."

"To tell you the truth," confessed Wally, "I was inclined to think along those lines myself at first. But then this business—all the things I learned this evening from our fellows—has made me think differently, because . . . Well he, this same chap, told me about these other things too, and he was right. And there was something else he said that is quite likely to be true. He said that you ought to give up your idea of opening a free clinic to treat the Kabulis, because it's already being said that it's only a plot to get rid of as many people as possible by giving them poison instead of medicines."

"Well of all the—!" began the doctor explosively; and then broke into laughter. "Bunkum, my dear boy—bunkum! Faith, I never heard such twaddle in me life, and you can tell your friend I said so and advise him from me to be putting his head in a horse bucket. It's as plain as the nose on your face that the feller was just pulling your leg, or as likely as not trying to put the wind up you. Even the most bigoted infidel-hating barbarian couldn't be so woollen-witted as to imagine that we'd try anything as childishly silly as that. They must have *some* sense, so they must."

But Wally's brow remained furrowed, and when he spoke again it was in an undertone that was barely audible above the noise of the wind and the rain, and as though he was speaking a thought aloud: "But he was right about . . . other things. And—and they *are* bigoted and barbaric. And they do hate us: they really hate us . . ."

"Whisht now! it's making a mountain out of a molehill you are." Ambrose Kelly wagged an admonitory finger at the youthful Commander of the Escort and by way of showing that the subject was now closed, reached for a battered tin of tobacco and turned his attention to knocking out and refilling his pipe. Wally laughed a little shamefacedly and leaning back in the creaking cane chair, felt the accumulated tensions of the last few hours seep away as his mind and his muscles relaxed under the peaceful influence of Rosie's optimism and the soothing sight of tobacco smoke weaving back and forth in the draught.

Outside the closed and shuttered windows the lightning flared and thunder rolled among the hills, while the rain and wind shook the fabric of the flimsy lath-and-plaster house, and from the next room came the *plink, plink* of water dripping into a tin basin that one of the doctor's servants had positioned below a leak in the ceiling. The flames of the two oil lamps bent and flickered in the draught that blew in under the ill-fitting doors and window frames, and Wally sat watching them with half-shut eyes as he listened gratefully to the noise of the rain and thought of what William Jenkyns had had to say earlier that evening on the subject of the unpaid troops and the advisability of paying them immediately, or at least promising that the Government of India would see to it that they were paid in full in the near future.

William had agreed that this would probably have to be done, and had told him in strict confidence that the Viceroy had already intimated his willingness to do so. "Everything will be all right, laddie. You'll see. There's precious little that goes on in Kabul that the Chief don't know about, and he'll have laid his plans and decided just how he means to deal with this particular problem long ago, I can tell you that."

But though Williams' conviction that His Excellency the Envoy was aware of all that went on in Kabul was in the main justified, his confidence in his Chief was less well-founded.

Sir Louis was certainly very well informed, and the diary that he dispatched to Simla at the end of each week would have been an eye-opener for those who thought that his confident bearing indicated ignorance of the unrest in the Amir's capital city. Both he, and via him Lord Lytton, knew what was going on, but both treated the knowledge lightly, Lord Lytton for his part being so little troubled by it that he had allowed a full ten days to drift by before forwarding, without comment, Sir Louis' account of the behaviour of the mutinous Heratis to the Secretary of State, as though it was no more than another trivial piece of information to be filed and forgotten.

As for Sir Louis, despite the fact that he had learned

early—and immediately informed the Viceroy—that the Kabulis appeared to expect him, among other things, to pay the arrears owed to the Afghan army, he made no move to deal with this particular problem; not even when he received a telegram from the Viceroy offering to provide financial assistance to the Amir if the money would help His Highness out of his present difficulties.

The offer had not been entirely altruistic (Lord Lytton having pointed out that if it was accepted, it would eventually provide the Government with a useful lever for obtaining certain administrative reforms that the Amir might be reluctant to concede), but at least it had been made. The money that Ash had seen as the only solution to the problem of the mutinous Heratis and the hatred and unrest that they were creating in Kabul was there for the asking. Yet Sir Louis did not take advantage of it —perhaps because he too, like Wally, recoiled in distaste from paying the wages of an army that had so recently been involved in a war against the British Empire.

But not even to William, who decoded all the Envoy's confidential messages, did he give his reasons. An omission that troubled his loyal secretary not a little, since to William the Viceroy's offer had seemed a godsend: a quick and easy way out of an exceedingly tricky situation, and an admirable solution to the most pressing of the problems that were bedevilling the harassed Amir, not to mention his equally harassed capital.

It had never occurred to William that his Chief would not see the offer in this light. But August wore on and Sir Louis made no move to accept it, or even to discuss the possibility of doing so, though every day brought fresh evidence that passions in the city were rapidly building up to flash-point, and that disaffection was now rife among the regiments on duty in the Bala Hissar itself.

This last was no more than a rumour that had only recently reached William at secondhand, via Walter Hamilton; yet he could not help wondering if it were true. Was it possible that the regiments at present quartered inside the Bala Hissar were in fact any more reliable than the Heratis, and if so, was the Amir playing a double game? There was no doubt that he had been exceedingly angry over the affair of the sentries who had stoned the Hindu: but not with the sentries. His wrath had been directed against Sir Louis for daring to dismiss them and

1061

refusing to allow them to be replaced—and with Lieutenant Hamilton, who had carried out Sir Louis' order.

Did the Amir, mused William, really intend to go on an autumn tour of his northern borders with Sir Louis, leaving his capital to the mercy of a mutinous gaggle of unpaid regiments and scheming ministers? Sir Louis certainly seemed to think so, and spoke of it as though it was an accepted fact.

No one could possibly have wished for a more loyal or admiring supporter than William Jenkyns. But as the summer drew to a close there were times, particularly if he happened to lie awake too long in the small hours of the night, when small pin-pricks of doubt nagged at William's mind and he caught himself wondering uneasily if Louis Cavagnari's sudden elevation in rank had not impaired his judgement and made him blind to much that would never have escaped his attention in the old days.

Wild horses could not have dragged the verbal expression of such a suspicion from the Envoy's loyal Secretary, but he was increasingly baffled by his Chief's determination to ignore what was becoming clear to others in the Mission (and glaringly obvious to many outside it, if the warning words of such visitors as the Sirdar Nakshband Khan were anything to go by). Yet as day succeeded day without any sign that the tension in the city was decreasing, Sir Louis still continued to occupy himself with ideas for reforming the administration, plans for the forthcoming tour and the prospects of partridge shooting on the *charman*—the uncultivated grazing grounds in the valley—and, despite the Amir's warnings, to ride out daily with a guard of Afghans to see and be seen by the citizens of Kabul.

William could not understand it. He was well aware that his Chief was a man who did not suffer fools gladly and was inclined to be a little too scornful of lesser men. It was part of his character, and William had once heard someone at a dinner-party in Simla saying of Cavagnari that one could easily visualize him behaving as the Comte d'Auteroches had done at the Battle of Fontenoy, when he called out to the opposing British line that the "French Guards never fired first."

At the time, William had laughed and agreed—and thought the more of Pierre Louis Napoleon in consequence. But now he recalled how that famous incident had ended, and no longer felt like laughing; for in response to those flamboyant words the British had fired first, and their murderous volley had mown down the immobile French guards, decimating their ranks and killing or wounding every one of their officers, so that the survivors, left without leaders, had broken and run.

That fellow in Simla had been right, thought William . . . Louis Cavagnari was perfectly capable of making a similar gesture . . . he was that sort of man. Brave, proud and fanatical; supremely self-confident, and contemptuous of lesser men . . .

Only last week there had been an ugly incident in the city that had arisen out of a quarrel involving a woman and four sowars of the Guides. The sowars had been attacked and only rescued with difficulty, and afterwards Sir Louis had told young Hamilton to see that his men kept clear of the city until tempers had cooled. But a few days later his own orderly, an Afridi, Amal Din, who had been with him for many years, had also been involved in a brawl, this time with a group of Afghan soldiers. Amal Din feared no one, and having taken exception to some derogatory remarks about his Sahib, he had attacked the speakers and done a good deal of damage before the fight was broken up. A formal complaint on behalf of the injured soldiers had been made to Sir Louis, who, having expressed regret in the coldest possible terms, had followed this up by rewarding Amal Din—and letting it be known that he had done so.

"That can't have done anything towards making him popular with the Afghans," brooded William in the intervals of dealing with official correspondence in the Envoy's office on the evening following this affair, "but does he care? Not him!" William gazed at the opposite wall with unseeing eyes and thought about the local women whom the men kept smuggling into the compound, though they had been warned often enough against doing so. That too was bound to lead to trouble one day, but it was difficult to know how to stop it. He began to write again, found that the ink had dried on his nib and, dipping it in the standish again, went on with his work . . .

In the Mess House on the opposite side of the courtyard, Wally too was busy writing, for the dâk-rider was due to leave at dawn for Ali Khel with the Residency post-bag, and anyone anxious to catch the next Home mail

1063

knew that their letters must be handed to the head chupprassi tonight.

Wally finished the last of his letters and reached for the fair copy of his poem on "The Village of Bemaru," which he intended to enclose in the letter to his parents. It was, he considered, one of his best, and though he had spent half the afternoon polishing it, he could not resist reading the final copy again before sending it off. Yes, not a bad effort at all, he decided with some complacency: . . . *"Yet to die Game to the last as they did, well upheld Their English name . . . E'en now their former foe Frankly avers . . ."*

Ash was going to be rude about that "E'en" . . . But then Ash was no poet and did not realize how impossible it was to make one's lines scan without resorting to such perfectly legitimate short-cuts as "e'en" and "t'were" and "were't" . . . *"Regret were uppermost, were't not for pride."* Wally frowned over the line, chewing the end of his pen, but could think of no other way of putting it. Anyway, even Ash must agree that the ending was not half bad. He read it aloud, pleased with the sound of his own lines—

> *"How England's fame shone brighter as she fought*
> *And wrenched lost laurels from their funeral pile*
> *And rose at last from out misfortunes tide*
> *Supreme—for God and Right were on her side."*

That was the stuff to give them! He repeated the last few lines again, beating time with his pen in the manner of a conductor, and had got as far as "supreme" when his baton wavered and he stopped in mid-flight, it having suddenly occurred to him that Ash would certainly not approve of that final sentiment.

Ash had never made any secret of his views on the subject of England's dealings with Afghanistan, and had expressed them pretty freely to Wally, denouncing them as unjust and indefensible. He was therefore the last person to agree that "God and Right were on her side." In Ash's opinion, England had never had any right to interfere with Afghanistan, let alone attack her, and he would undoubtedly say that God—or Allah—ought by rights to be on the side of the Afghans. Ash would say . . .

"Ah, to hell with Ash," thought Wally irritably. He

stuffed the poem in with the letter, and having sealed and addressed the envelope, added it to the pile in the "out" tray and went off to dress for dinner.

Sir Louis Cavagnari was another who had spent the latter part of the afternoon and most of the evening at his desk, bringing his diary up-to-date and writing letters and telegrams for dispatch to Ali Khel. He had been feeling considerably easier of late, for the sudden death from cholera in the course of a single night of a hundred and fifty of the Herati soldiers in the city, though a shocking piece of news, had proved to be a blessing in disguise.

The regiments concerned, panic-stricken by the sudden loss of so great a number of their comrades, had settled for part of the pay they were owed plus forty days furlough to return to their homes, and rushing to the Bala Hissar to hand in their arms, had not even waited to obtain their certificates of leave before marching away from the city, hurling threats and abuse as they went at the Commander-in-Chief, General Daud Shah, who had come to see them leave.

From Sir Louis' point of view, this could not have been better. They had caused a great deal of trouble, and the effort of preserving a bold front, and keeping up the pretence that the undisciplined behaviour of a rabble of mutinous troops was a matter of complete indifference to him instead of a constant source of anxiety, was becoming increasingly tedious. Not that he had at any time been in the least afraid of the disgruntled troops from Herat, whom he regarded as no more than hooligans.

All the same, it was a relief to know that a considerable number of them had at last been paid off (he had always known that the money would be forthcoming as soon as the Amir and his ministers realized that there was no other way of ridding themselves of a dangerous nuisance), and had handed in their arms and left the city. He fully realized that fear of the cholera had probably played a greater part than money in bringing about that welcome exodus; and also that not all the Herati regiments had left—some were still encamped in cantonments outside the city, and a number of men drawn from these were actually helping to guard the Arsenal, which on the face of it seemed a little unwise. But then the Amir had assured him that they had been carefully selected and were well disposed towards him, which Sir Louis took to mean that they had probably been paid something on account.

There remained the Ardal Regiment from Turkestan and three Orderly Regiments, whose pay was also many months in arrears. They too were pressing for their money, but had shown no signs of emulating the deplorable behaviour of the Heratis. And as General Daud Shah had apparently promised them that if they would only have a little patience they would all be paid at the beginning of September, Sir Louis felt justified in taking a more rosy view of the future.

It was unfortunate that this year the start of Ramadan, the Mohammedan Month of Fasting, should have fallen in mid-August, since during Ramadan the Faithful may not eat or drink except between sunset and the first streak of dawn, and men who have fasted all day and gone without water in the heat and dust of August are apt to be short-tempered. But then August would soon be over, and with it that long, eventful summer that had seen the metamorphosis of plain Major Cavagnari into His Excellency Sir Louis Cavagnari, K.C.S.I., Envoy and Minister Plenipotentiary. Only another week, and then it would be September.

Sir Louis looked forward to the autumn. He had heard that it was almost the best time of year in Kabul: not as beautiful as spring, when the almond trees were in bloom and the valley was white with fruit blossom, but with a spectacular beauty of its own as the leaves of poplars and fruit trees, vines, walnuts and willows flamed gold and orange and scarlet, the snow-line crept down the mountain-sides, and thousands of wild fowl on their way south flew in from the tundras beyond the great ranges of the Hindu Kush. The stalls in the bazaars of Kabul would be piled high with apples, grapes, corncobs, walnuts and chillies, and there would be snipe and quail and chikor in the uncultivated grasslands and on the lower slopes of the hills. And tempers would cool with the coming of the cooler days.

The Envoy smiled as he contemplated the day's entry in his diary, and putting down his pen he rose and went to stand by one of the windows that faced south across the darkening plain, gazing out at the far snow peaks that a short while ago had glowed bright pink in the last of the sunset, and now showed silver in the light of a sky that blazed with stars.

The storm of the previous week had been followed by several days of hot sunshine and a blustery wind that had dried up the puddles and filled the valley with a haze of dust. But yesterday rain had fallen again, not in a deluge as before but gently—the last dying tears of the monsoon —and now the new-washed air was fresh and cool.

The night was full of sounds, for after the abstinence of the day all Kabul, released from fasting by the setting of the sun, was relaxing over the *Iftari*, the evening meal of Ramadan, and the darkness hummed like a hive. A contented hive, thought Cavagnari, listening to the cheerful medley of noises that came from the Residency compound, and sniffing the scent of wood-smoke and cooked food and the pungent smell of horses. He could hear someone in the King's Garden that lay near by, behind the Residency, playing a flute; and from further up the hill came the faint sound of drums and sitars and a woman's voice singing a song of Barbur's day—*"Drink wine in this hold of Kabul—send the cup around . . ."*

Beneath his window-sill the wall of the citadel fell away into darkness, its shadow blotting out the road below. Yet here too there were sounds—the clip-clop of unseen hoofbeats on the hard earth and the sound of footsteps and voices as a party of travellers hurried towards the Shah Shahie Gate. Only the shadowy plain and the vast wall of mountains lay still and silent.

Cavagnari sniffed the night breeze, and presently, hearing feet on the stair, said without turning: "Come in, William. I've finished the letters for the dâk, so you can put the code book away; we shall not need it tonight. No point in sending another telegram to Simla when there is nothing new to report. They'll find anything they need to know when they get the next diary. What day does that go off?"

"Morning of the 29th, sir."

"Well, if anything of interest comes up before then we can always send a *tar*. But with a bit of luck, the worst is over and things should settle down a bit now that most of those pestilential nuisances from Herat have dispersed to their homes. You can take the letters. I must change for dinner."

Half-a-mile away, on the rooftop of Nakshband Khan's house, Ash too had been looking at the mountains and thinking, as Cavagnari had been, that the worst was over. After last week's downpour and the rain of yesterday there was more snow on the high hills, and tonight there was a distinct hint of autumn in the cool air, so it was more than likely that the worst of the cholera was over—or soon would be. And like Sir Louis, Ash had been encouraged by the departure of the mutinous regiments.

Now if only the Amir would pay the rest of his troops what they were owed, or the cholera scare them away—or the British Envoy buy time for himself and the Amir by insisting that the Government of India lend the Afghan treasury enough money to pay the soldiers—there was a reasonable chance that the Mission might yet succeed in turning the present hostility and distrust of a resentful people into something approaching tolerance, or even, with luck, a certain degree of respect if not liking. Time was what both Cavagnari and the Amir needed, and Ash was still of the opinion that money could buy it; and only money.

"Yet if the Amir was able to find the money to pay the Heratis," reasoned Ash, "he can probably find enough to pay off the others. He must have realized by now that he can't afford not to, and that the money must be raised somehow, even if he has to squeeze it out of his rich nobles and merchants, or from the money-lenders."

He must have spoken the last words aloud without realizing it, because Anjuli, sitting beside him in the curve of his arm with her head resting on his shoulder, stirred and said softly: "But such people do not give willingly. And if it is taken from them by force they will extort it in their turn, by one means or another, from the poor. This we know. So how shall it profit the Amir if in order to appease his soldiers he angers his nobles and rich men, and incurs the hatred of the poor? That way the unrest will not only remain, but grow greater."

"True, my wise little heart. It's a hard knot, but until it is untied or cut there will be no peace in Kabul—least of all for those in the Residency compound or in the Palace of the Bala Hissar."

Anjuli shivered at the name, and instinctively his arm tightened about her; but he did not speak, because he was thinking of Wally . . .

1068

He had not spoken to Wally since the afternoon they had spent in the garden of Barbur's tomb, though he had seen him often enough from the window of the Munshi's house—fleeting glimpses of him going about his duties in the Residency compound. He must arrange another meeting soon, which might not be so easy now; it had been tolerably simple until the day that Cavagnari had angered the Amir by insisting on the removal of the Afghan sentries, but since then none of the four European members of the Mission had been able to move a yard beyond the compound without a double guard of Afghan cavalry clattering at their heels, in addition to their own escort.

In these circumstances it had been impossible for Wally to go anywhere on his own, let alone stop and fall into conversation with some apparently chance-met Afridi. But working in the Bala Hissar had its uses, for Ash had recently learned something that was not yet known to the Residency: that from the first of September the British Mission would be required to collect the fodder needed for their horses themselves.

Hitherto, the grass and *bhoosa* for this purpose had been supplied by the Amir, but now this practice was to be discontinued. In future the Guides' own grass-cutters would have to go out to forage for what they required, and as it was certain that for their own safety the foragers would be accompanied by an escort of sowars, it would not be thought in the least odd if Wally were to ride out with them.

The inevitable Afghan guard would of course be there to keep an eye on him, but the chances were that after the first day or two they would relax their vigilance and make it possible for Ash to have speech with him without arousing anyone's suspicions. In that way the two of them ought to be able to meet at least once or twice before the end of Ramadan, by which time, if fate were kind, it was possible that the ominous tide of hate and unrest that had been washing through the streets of Kabul for the past few weeks would have turned at last and begun to ebb.

One person at least appeared to harbour no doubts as to the ebbing of that tide. Sir Louis Cavagnari was convinced that it had already turned, and on the twenty-eighth of the month he instructed William to dispatch another telegram to Simla to say that all was well with the Kabul Embassy, and two days later wrote in a private letter to his friend, the Viceroy, that he had nothing whatever to complain of as regards the Amir and his ministers: "His authority is weak throughout Afghanistan," wrote Sir Louis, "but, notwithstanding all that people say against him, *I* personally believe he will prove a very good ally, and that we shall be able to keep him to his agreements."

The only other contribution to the out-going dâk that day had been a light-hearted post-card from Wally to his cousin in India, signed only with an initial. It had clearly been written in high spirits, but William, whose duties included sealing the mail bag, had caught sight of the concluding words and been startled by them. For Wally had ended: *"Scribe a votre Cousin in exilis vale,* and now farewell till . . ."

63

"Faith, that's a fine way to begin the autumn, I must say!" exclaimed Wally indignantly. "You'd think those scutts could have given us a bit more notice, wouldn't you now? It's a shabby lot they are and no mistake."

"Oh, come now, babe," protested William. "They know very well that we have our own grass-cutters and that they are under no obligation to provide us with fodder for our horses, yet they've been giving us the stuff free, gratis and for nothing ever since we arrived. It's only fair that now we've settled down and found our feet, we should start to fend for ourselves."

"I suppose you're right," conceded Wally. "But it wouldn't have hurt His Imperial Afghan Highness to let us know beforehand that he meant to cut off supplies at the end of August, instead of waiting until the first of September to break the news that from now on we can get out and forage for ourselves. Because it's not something we can do straight off the bat, you know. At least, not in this particular country. Unless we want to find ourselves up to our eyebrows in trouble, we're going to have to make dashed certain where we are allowed to go, and even more important, where we are not—which isn't something we can sort out in five minutes."

"You mean that *I* can sort out. It'll be on my tray, not yours," retorted William wryly. "But we must have a good two days' supply in hand, surely? That last consignment ought to tide us over at least until the day after tomorrow, so I don't know what you're complaining about. I'll have a talk with the Chief about fixing up where our grass-cutters can go, and they can trot off and start earning an honest living again on the morning of the third. I suppose you will have to send a guard with them?"

"There's no 'suppose' about it," said Wally bitterly. "They wouldn't budge a yard without one."

"Bad as that, is it?"

"You know it is. It's been weeks since any of the camp-followers would risk putting a nose outside the compound unless they went in a group, and preferably accompanied by one or two jawans—Mussulmans for choice. Even my Sikhs and Hindus haven't been going about much either. Do you mean to say you didn't know that?"

"Of course I did, my wee laddie. What on earth do you take me for? I may be a few years older than you, but I'm not actually doddering yet; or deaf or short-sighted either. But I'd rather hoped that the situation would have eased a trifle after half those noisy bastards from Herat grabbed their pay and bolted."

"I daresay it has. But it's too soon for the effects to be felt, and I wouldn't dream of sending out a flock of grass-cutters without someone to play sheep-dog and keep an eye on them. In fact I shall probably go along myself at first, just to make sure that everything is all right. We don't want 'em rushing back to barracks empty-handed and in a panic because some sturdy local patriot has called them naughty names and heaved a brick at them."

"We don't indeed," agreed William, and went away to discuss a number of questions that had been raised by the abrupt announcement that in future the Residency would be responsible for feeding its own horses.

The decision had come as a surprise, but apart from

the lack of notice it was not one that could be cavilled at, because as William had pointed out, there was no earthly reason why the Afghan Government should supply fodder for the British Mission's horses—particularly when the Guides had their own grass-cutters, who were perfectly capable of getting it for them. Wally had not been blind to that, and his annoyance had been solely on account of the suddenness of the announcement, which struck him as unnecessarily discourteous.

He could see no reason why the Residency should not have been informed at the outset that this particular amenity was strictly temporary and would be withdrawn at the end of August; but apart from that, the change was not unwelcome. In fact the more he thought about it the better it pleased him, for it would give him an excuse to ride out to parts of the valley and the lower slopes of the hills that he had not yet visited, besides providing him with many more opportunities of meeting Ash.

He had been on his way back to the Mess House following his morning inspection of Stables and Lines when William met him with the news about the new arrangement for fodder, and now, turning back to pass it on to his cavalry officers, he recrossed the Residency courtyard and went out again past the sentry on the gate into the narrow lane that separated the Residency from the barrack block.

The door leading into the barracks stood open, but he did not walk through the jawans' courtyard, but turned right down the lane, and then left again to skirt the northern wall of the barracks and stroll across the dusty sun-flooded compound towards the stables that stood at the far end under the shadow of the Arsenal. As he went he glanced up casually, eyes narrowed against the sunglare, at the barred windows of the tall houses that stood on the higher ground beyond the compound wall: small, secretive windows like watchful eyes peering down from the high mud walls at the doings of the strangers in their midst.

No one seeing him glance up would have said that his gaze had rested on any particular window, or that he was in the least interested in the houses. But that brief survey had shown him that a blue and white pottery jar containing a spray of leaves stood on the sill of a certain window, and walking on he wondered if Ash already knew that in

1072

future the Guides would be sending out their own grass-cutters, or (which was more to the point) where they would be permitted to go; and if he too had seen this as an excellent opportunity for further meetings?

The final consignment of fodder sent by the Amir had been a generous one, and Jemadar Jiwand Singh, the senior Indian officer of the cavalry, was of the opinion that it would last for another two to three days and that the grass-cutters need not go out until the third. "But there is the winter to be thought of," said Jiwand Singh, "and if, as they say, the snow lies four feet deep in the valley, we shall need to lay in a great store of fodder. And for that we shall need more space."

" 'Sufficient unto the day is the evil thereof,' Jemadar-Sahib," quoted Wally lightly. "This is still only the first day of autumn and snow will not fall until late in November. But I will speak to the Burra-Sahib tonight and tell him that we shall need another store house, and space on which to build one."

"Over there," said Jiwand Singh grimly, jerking his head towards an enclosed slope of waste ground, known as the Kulla-Fi-Arangi, that lay just beyond the perimeter of the compound and separated from it only by a low mud wall. "It would be no bad thing to gain permission to build on that ground, since by doing so we could close it against the many idlers and thieves and *budmarshes* who now use it as an approach to this compound, which they enter at will. Moreover if ever the need should arise to defend ourselves, we would find that of great service."

Wally swung round to stare at the waste ground with an arrested look in his eyes. He had always been worried by the ease with which the compound could be entered, and now he muttered half under his breath, and in English: "By Jove, that's not a bad idea . . . Now why didn't I think of that before? Not walls: store houses. Good, strongly built sheds; and perhaps a few more servants' quarters. I wonder . . ."

He pondered the matter and at tea-time that day discussed it with Rosie, who agreed that it would certainly make the compound more secure if access to it could be reduced to a single entrance—preferably a narrow one that could be closed by a stout gate, instead of half-a-dozen alleyways and a slope of waste ground wide enough to drive a herd of cattle down.

"And no one," said Wally slowly, "could accuse us of insulting our hosts by building defensive walls and barricades if we asked to put up a shed to store our fodder in for the winter, and perhaps a couple of extra servants' quarters to—to ease the overcrowding."

"Not servants' quarters," said Rosie thoughtfully. "A large dispensary. I could do with one. Yes, it's not a bad scheme, and provided the Chief approves—"

"Of course he'll approve. Why shouldn't he? He can't feel any happier than we do about living in such a hopelessly vulnerable spot as this. He merely didn't want to upset the Amir by demanding defensive walls all round the shop, and I see his point. But this idea is quite different, and if anyone can bring the Amir round to it, he can. They get on together like a house on fire and hardly a day goes by without their having a long friendly blarney together—in fact they're having one now. So as we're obviously going to need extra storage space anyway, the whole thing should be plain sailing. I'll see if I can have a word with the Chief when he gets back from the palace. He's always in a good mood after a chat with the Amir."

But as William's favourite poet and fellow-countryman had so truly said, "the best laid schemes o' mice an' men gang aft a-gley." Sir Louis had returned unexpectedly late from the palace, and in such a noticeably bad temper that Wally had decided that this was definitely one of those times when junior officers should be seen and not heard.

Normally when Sir Louis paid a social call at the palace, he stayed for about an hour and returned in the best of spirits, particularly on those occasions when, as today, the subject under discussion was the projected tour of the northern provinces, which the Amir had been as enthusiastic about as he himself was. This evening they were to have settled the final details; yet now, with the date of their departure set and endless arrangements already in train, the Amir had suddenly chosen to announce that he could not possibly go—

It was, declared Yakoub Khan, out of the question that he should leave his capital at a time of grave unrest: how could he possibly do so when his regiments in Kabul could not be trusted to behave in an orderly manner? When a number of his provinces were in open revolt, his cousin Abdur Rahman (a protégé of the Russians and living

1074

under their protection) plotting to invade Kandahar and take his throne, and his brother, Ibrahim Khan, intriguing against him with the same object in view? He had no money and little authority, and were he to leave Kabul for so much as a week he was very certain that he would never be able to return again. In the circumstances he was sure that his good friend Sir Louis would fully appreciate the difficulties of his situation, and agree with him that any idea of a tour at this juncture must be abandoned.

One would have thought that Sir Louis (who was equally well aware of those difficulties and had himself reported on them in a number of official telegrams and dispatches during the past few weeks) would have been the first to agree that the tour must be called off: but this was not so. He was seriously upset, for he had visualized this tour as a combination of a Royal Progress under his personal aegis—a public demonstration of the friendship and trust that now existed between Great Britain and Afghanistan—and a subtle reminder that it was the British who had won the recent war. Also, having lavished a great deal of time and thought on plans and arrangements for it, his anger at the Amir's sudden *volte face* was aggravated by an uncomfortable suspicion that he would be made to look foolish when the various officials he had written to, or to whom William had written on his behalf, learned that the tour would not take place after all.

As a result, he had argued with the Amir and done his best to make him change his mind. But nothing he could say had served to make Yakoub Khan budge an inch, and eventually, realizing that if he were not very careful he would lose his temper, he had brought the interview to a close and returned to the Residency in anything but a good mood.

Wally took note of the fact, and wisely recognizing that this was not the moment to start any new hares, decided to say nothing about the possibility of improving the defences of the compound by building storage sheds or a dispensary, and confined himself instead to asking William if he had found out where they could go for fodder.

William had: they could take all that was needed from the *charman,* the uncultivated grazing land that formed a large part of the plain of Kabul, and it had been suggested that a start could be made in the vicinity of the village of Ben-i-Hissar, which was no great distance from the citadel.

"I said we'd be sending our grass-cutters out on the morning of the third. That's the day after tomorrow," said William. "They wanted to know because of sending a guard with them, though they must know we'll be sending one of our own. However, just as well to have them around. We don't want any trouble from villagers claiming afterwards that our chaps trespassed on their fields and damaged their crops, and as long as a squad of Afghan cavalry are keeping an eye on proceedings, that isn't likely to happen."

Wally was in agreement with him, for much as he disliked being followed around by Afghan troopers, their presence on this sort of occasion would ensure that even the most truculent villagers would think twice before flinging a stone at the strangers. All the same he intended to accompany the grass-cutters himself to make certain that they kept well away from any cultivated land; and also to spy out the surrounding country and study the behaviour of the Afghan guard with a view to seeing how easy—or how difficult—it would be to meet and talk to Ash in the course of these forays.

He was inclined to think that it would prove a simple matter once the novelty had worn off and foraging on the *charman* became a routine affair. "No point in his coming out the first day though," decided Wally. "But as our grass-cutters will be out every alternate day the Afghans are going to get bored in next to no time, and after that it will be as easy as falling off a log."

It was only on the following day that it occurred to Wally that there could be no harm if Ash happened to ride past Ben-i-Hissar, say on the morning of the fifth, just to get some idea of the situation and assess the possibilities it offered.

A brief glance at the Munshi's house had already shown him that Ash was at work there, so he strolled across to an itinerant fruit-seller who had set up a stall on the edge of the compound, and bought half-a-dozen oranges, five of which he later placed in a neat row on the window-ledge of his dressing-room before carefully closing the shutters behind them. The room looked out across the roof of the Sikh quarters in the barrack-block towards the stables and the far end of the compound, and the oranges, standing out vividly against the white-painted shutters, could be clearly seen from a considerable distance away.

There was no need to give Ash any directions, for if he did not know already, he would have no difficulty in finding out where Hamilton-Sahib was bound; and if he could manage to get away he would be there. If not, he would certainly come the next time—and as that would be the seventh, there was a reasonable chance that the Afghan guard would not be in attendance. The seventh being a Friday and the Moslem sabbath, with any luck they might be at their devotions in one of the city mosques.

Sir Louis had still been noticeably short-tempered at breakfast, and as the usual succession of callers hoping for preferment or bringing complaints against the Amir or one or other of the ministers had kept him fully occupied until late in the day (after which he had gone off to shoot partridges with one of the local landowners), Wally had no opportunity of bringing up the subject of the sheds: for which he was not altogether sorry. He still considered it a capital scheme, but instinct warned him that his brain-child was likely to receive short shrift from Sir Louis in his present mood, so instead he mentioned it to William, who being a civilian, and at present an exceedingly busy one, was not at all that interested in matters that from the viewpoint of a professional soldier appeared vitally important.

William was well aware of the precarious position of the British Mission, and recognized as clearly as Wally did the alarming insecurity of the accommodation provided for them by the Amir. But then he, like Cavagnari, was convinced that, situated as they were, any defence from a military standpoint was out of the question, and that they must therefore trust to other methods. To diplomacy and the careful and cautious building up of good-will. To the patient breaking-down of suspicion and hostility, and the fostering of friendly relations. Above all, to the preservation of a bold front and a show of complete confidence.

These things might pull them through where tangible defences of brick and plaster could only serve to hold off an armed assault for an hour or two—if that. He was therefore not as enthusiastic about the shed idea as Wally had hoped, though he promised to sound out Sir Louis on

1077

the subject and seemed to think there was a good chance that his reaction would be favourable, because after all, defence or no, they would certainly need to lay in extra fodder against the months when Kabul would be deep in snow. But then there was still plenty of time before that.

William's tepid reception of his "capital scheme" had depressed Wally, but he consoled himself with the reflection that if Sir Louis could be brought to agree and the Amir give his permission, the sheds would not take long to build. And once they were up, he was going to feel a lot easier about the men under his command, whose safety and welfare were his personal responsibility, and who in turn were responsible for the protection of every single person in the Residency compound, from the Envoy down to the humblest sweeper.

Later, strolling back to the Mess House after discussing arrangements for the foraging party with Jemadar Jiwand Singh, he glanced up at the Munshi's house and was pleased to see that the pottery jar with its spray of green leaves was no longer standing dead centre, but had been moved to the right-hand end of the window; which could be translated briefly as "can do"—the left hand signifying the reverse.

Wally returned to the Residency whistling "The Minstrel Boy," and having regained his rooms, removed the five oranges that he had placed on his dressing-room window-sill earlier in the day.

That evening the Envoy had taken his secretary with him when he went off to shoot partridge, and Lieutenant Hamilton and Surgeon-Major Kelly, who had not been invited to the shoot, rode out with an escort of two sowars and the inevitable guard of Afghans along the banks of the Kabul River to the site of the old British cantonments near Sherpur.

The day had been warm and cloudless, and though there had been barely more than a breath of wind, it had been enough to stir up the dust so that the air was faintly hazy, and the sunset, even with that clear sky, was one of the most spectacular that Wally had ever seen.

Having only known Kabul in high summer, he had never been able to understand why Ash thought it such a beautiful place, and could only suppose that because Ash was in love and had been living there with Juli, he saw it through rose-coloured glasses, as thousands of lovers, honeymooning in cheap boarding-houses, see wet seaside towns or foggy industrial cities as gardens of Eden.

The snow peaks were fine enough, but none of them, to Wally's eyes, could rival the heart-stopping loveliness of Nanga Parbat, the "Naked Goddess," as he had first seen her in the dawn from a hillside above Barramulla. Nor would he have dreamed of comparing the flat lands around Kabul with the enchanting valley of Kashmir with its lotus-strewn lakes and winding, willow-shaded streams, its wealth of flowers and trees and Mogul gardens. But now of a sudden it was as though his eyes had been opened and he saw Kabul and its setting for the first time: not as stark and desolate and dun-coloured, but beautiful with a wild, spectacular beauty that took his breath away.

A combination of sunset and dust and the smoke of cooking fires had transformed the valley to a sea of gold, out of which the near hills and the jagged snow-capped ranges behind them rose up in layer after layer of glittering splendour, caught in the bonfire blaze of the dying day and flaming like Sheba's jewels against an opal sky. The soaring pinnacles of the mountains might have been the spires and towers of some fabulous city—Valhalla, perhaps; or the outer ramparts of Paradise . . .

" 'And the city was pure gold, like unto clear glass, and the foundations of the wall of the city were garnished with all manner of precious stones,' " murmured Wally under his breath.

"What did you say?" asked Rosie, turning to look at him.

Wally coloured and said confusedly, "Nothing . . . I mean—it looks like that description of the Holy City, doesn't it. The one in Revelations. The mountains, I mean. All that bit about jasper and topaz and chrysolyte and amethyst . . . and the gates of pearl . . ."

His companion turned back to study the view, and being of a more prosaic turn of mind than Walter, observed that it reminded him more of a transformation scene in a pantomime. "Pretty," approved Rosie, and added that he wouldn't have believed that this god-forsaken corner of the world could ever have looked anything but forbidding.

"Ash used to talk about a mountain called the Dur

Khaima," mused Wally, his gaze still on the jewelled glory of the snow peaks. "The Far Pavilions . . . I never realized . . ." his voice slowed and stopped and Rosie said curiously: "Are you talking about Pandy Martyn, by any chance? He was a friend of yours, wasn't he?"

"Is," corrected Wally briefly. He had not meant to mention Ash's name and was annoyed with himself for having done so, because although Rosie had never actually served with Ash, he must have learned quite a lot from those who had, and might be sufficiently interested to ask awkward questions about Ash's present whereabouts.

"Remarkable fellow, by all accounts," observed Rosie. "The only time I ever met him was in '74, when he turned up in Mardan with a nasty head-wound and I had the job of patching him up. That was the year after I first came to the Guides, I remember. He didn't talk much. But then he wasn't in very good shape at the time, and as soon as he was fit enough he was hustled off to Rawalpindi. But I did hear that he had been to Kabul, so I suppose the mountain he told you about was one of these. Magnificent, aren't they."

Wally nodded agreement and did not contradict the statement about the Dur Khaima, but fell silent, gazing at the enormous panorama of the Hindu Kush and seeing it in astonishing detail so that every last, least fold and spur and gully, and every soaring peak, looked as clear and distinct as though he were seeing it through a powerful telescope—or with the eye of God. And all at once he knew that this was one of those moments that for no particular reason one remembers for ever, and that remain indelibly printed on the mind when many more important ones fade and are lost.

As the light ebbed the valley filled with shadow and the high snow-crests took fire, and it occurred to Wally that he had never realized before what a beautiful place the world was: how full of wonder. Man might be doing his best to mar it, but every bush—and every stone and stick too—was still "afire with God." "Ah, it's good to be alive!" thought Wally with a sudden surge of exultation and a lifting of the heart that made him feel that he would live for ever and ever . . .

A discreet cough from one of the sowars brought him back to earth and reminded him that there were other persons present besides Ambrose Kelly—and also that it was Ramadan and the escort and the Afghan guard must be impatient to be back in their quarters in time to say the customary evening prayers before the setting of the sun allowed them to break the day's fast.

"Come on, Rosie, race you to the river!" He turned away from the ruins of the old cantonment and urging his horse into a gallop, rode back laughing towards the Bala Hissar that stood out blackly against the bright gold of the evening sky.

Ash, leaving the citadel somewhat later than usual, passed him as the small party of Guides rode in through the Shah Shahie Gate. But Wally had not seen him. The sun was still above the horizon, but the Bala Hissar was in shadow, and the air under the dark arch of the gate was so thick with dust and smoke that Ash had walked by unnoticed. He heard Kelly say: "That's a bottle of hock you owe me, young Walter; and faith, it'll be welcome, for it's parched I am." And then they were out of sight.

Ash too was parched, for as "Syed Akbar" he must keep the fast. Besides the day had been a long and tiring one for everyone in the Munshi's employ: one of the regiments stationed within the Bala Hissar, the Ardal Regiment, only recently arrived from Turkestan, had demanded three months' pay, and surprisingly been told that they would receive this on the following morning. The Munshi, among others, had been told to see to this, and Ash and his fellow *likhni wallahs* (writing fellows) had been hard at work all day compiling lists of names and ranks, together with the varying sums due to be paid in cash to each man, and the total sum that would have to be drawn from the Treasury.

Given reasonable notice the task would not have been arduous, but the shortness of time and the fact that it must be done fasting—and for the most part in a small, hot and airless room—made it an exhausting one. The normal mid-day rest had had to be dispensed with, and Ash was both tired and parched with thirst by the time the work was done and he was able to remove the blue and white jar from the window and return to the Sirdar's house and Anjuli. But despite his weariness he was conscious of an enormous sense of relief and a sudden flowering of hope and optimism.

The fact that the Ardal Regiment was to be paid

1081

showed that the Amir and his ministers had at last realized that a starving and mutinous army was far more dangerous to them than no army at all, and despite their protestations of penury, had decided to find the money before another regiment was driven to mutiny. It was a giant stride in the right direction and, to Ash, an excellent omen for the future.

He was pleased too about Wally, whose signal to him proved that their minds had been working on identical lines, which alone was almost as heartening as this Ardal business. It was good to know that they would be meeting soon, and that with the threat of insurrection that had menaced the foreigners in the citadel about to be removed, they would be able to talk of "pleasant things" again.

The news that the regiments were to be paid had blown through Kabul like a fresh breeze, dispersing the tension and the sullen and barely restrained fury that had brooded there for so long, and Ash could sense the difference with every nerve in his body. As he drew back in the shadows under the Shah Shahie Gate to let Wally and Dr. Kelly ride past, and heard Wally laugh in reply to the doctor's words, he caught the infection of the boy's high spirits and his own rose headily. Tiredness and thirst were suddenly forgotten, and walking on with a lighter step along the mud road below the outer wall of the citadel and through the narrow streets of the city, it seemed to him that for the first time in many months the evening air breathed of peace and quiet.

The Envoy and his secretary had returned from the partridge shoot in equally good spirits, the evening's sport having banished Sir Louis' ill-temper and made him forget for the time being his annoyance at the Amir's sudden cancellation of the autumn tour. He was an excellent shot, and the landowner who had organized the shoot had assured him that there would be many more game birds as soon as the weather became cooler. "If that is so," said Sir Louis at dinner that night, "we ought to be able to keep ourselves in duck and teal and roast goose for much of the cold weather."

Turning to Wally, he asked about the foraging party that would be going out on the following morning; and on hearing that Lieutenant Hamilton proposed to accompany them in order to see that they did not go anywhere they shouldn't, was pleased to approve, and suggested that Surgeon-Major Kelly went with him for good measure.

Rosie said that he would be delighted to do so and Wally had no option but to agree, though the suggestion was not a welcome one, because if Rosie were to fall into the habit of accompanying him it was going to be difficult to meet Ash. However he would deal with that later, for at the moment he intended to broach the more important question of winter fodder and the extra sheds that would be needed for storing it. But Sir Louis had begun to talk to Dr. Kelly about the prospects of duck shooting later on in the year, and from there they had passed to discussing hunting in County Down and mutual acquaintances in Ballynahinch. After which the conversation became general, and as Sir Louis retired to his own quarters in the Envoy's House to write his diary as soon as the meal was over, Wally had no further chance to speak of sheds that night.

Even if he had been able to do so, it is doubtful if Sir Louis would have accorded the scheme much sympathy. The good temper engendered by a pleasant evening's sport had been considerably improved by the welcome news, conveyed to him by a trusted agent shortly before dinner, that the Ardal Regiment would parade on the morrow to receive their arrears of pay in full: a piece of information that had much the same effect on Sir Louis' spirits as it had had on Ash's, as it confirmed his belief that the money would and could be found, and that now the rest of the army would shortly be paid its wages and law and order would reign in Kabul. He had immediately instructed William to see that the usual telegram confirming that all was well with the Kabul Residency went off first thing in the morning, and in the circumstances he would not have been particularly interested in a scheme for improving the military defences of the Residency compound by devious and complicated means.

"I'll ask Ash about it, and see what he thinks," decided Wally later that night as he prepared to go to bed. "Ash'll know if it would be any use, and if he thinks it wouldn't and I'm crazy, I'll hold my tongue." On which thought he said his prayers and turned out the lamp, though he did not immediately retire to bed.

The talk at dinner had reminded him of home, and he went to the window, and leaning his arms on the sill, looked out across the dark courtyard below and the flat roof of the Envoy's House towards the horizon, and thought of Inistioge.

Beyond the sheer drop of the outer wall lay the valley, with the pale ribbon of the Kabul River winding across it, and behind and beyond the wrinkled hills, grey in the starlight, rose the immense, shadowy rampart of the Hindu Kush. But the river he saw was the Nore, for he was back in Inistioge . . . There were the dear familiar fields and woods and the blue hills of Kilkenny, and that was not Shah Shahie's tomb, but the little church at Donaghadee, while the far shimmer in the sky was not snow, but white clouds floating high and serenely above the Blackstairs mountains in Carlow . . .

"I wonder," mused Lieutenant Walter Hamilton, v.c., *aetat* twenty-three, "why Generals always seem to choose the name of one of their battles when they are made peers? I shan't—I shall choose Inistioge . . . Field Marshal Lord Hamilton of Inistioge, v.c., k.g., g.c.b., g.c.s.i.—I wonder if I shall be allowed to go Home to bet my medal from the Queen? or if I shall have to wait my turn for Home Leave? . . I wonder if I shall ever get married . . ."

Somehow he did not think that he would: or not unless he found someone exactly like Ash's Juli, which seemed to him unlikely. Ash ought to send her away from Kabul, for by all accounts there was a deal too much cholera in the city. He must speak to him about that on Wednesday. It would be grand to see Ash again, and with any luck . . .

A cavernous yawn interrupted his train of thought and he laughed at himself and went to bed feeling enormously happy.

64

The sun was still well below the horizon when Sir Louis Cavagnari, always an early riser, left for his customary ride on the following morning, attended by his Afridi orderly Amal Din, his syce, four sowars of the Guides and half-a-dozen troopers of the Amir's cavalry.

The dâk-rider had left even earlier, carrying a telegram that would be transmitted from Ali Khel to Simla. And not long afterwards a procession of twenty-five grass-cutters, carrying ropes and sickles, had also left the citadel, shepherded by Kote-Daffadar Fatteh Mohammed and Sowars Akbar Shah and Narain Singh of the Guides, and accompanied by four Afghan troopers.

Wally and Ambrose Kelly had followed some twenty minutes later, just as Ash, who had arrived early that day because of the pay parade, was placing the pottery jar in position on his window-sill. He watched them ride away and wished that he could have gone with them. The air would be sharp and fresh in the open country, whereas it was already stale and warm in here, and would be even warmer in the large open space near the palace where the Ardal Regiment would soon be gathering to receive their pay, as that was not only a sun-trap, but an insalubrious one into the bargain, since all kinds of rubbish was thrown out there, and there were no trees to provide shade.

Ash sighed, envying Wally and his companions riding out to meet the sunrise through the dewy croplands along the river and among the groves of poplars, chenars and walnut trees that hid Ben-i-Hissar and the grassy sweep of the *charman* beyond. The cloudless sky was still pale with the opalescent paleness of dawn, and the land an indeterminate colour between dove-grey and sand, unmarked by shadows. But high above the neutral tinted ridges the hidden sun had already turned the snows to apricot. It was going to be a wonderful day: "a day for singing hymns," as Wally would have said.

Remembering those tuneful mornings in Rawalpindi, Ash smiled to himself and began to hum "All things bright and beautiful," only to check abruptly as he realized, with a queer stab of fear, that he was doing something that was so completely alien to the character of Syed Akbar, scribe, that if anyone had overheard it he would certainly have been betrayed.

For over a year now he had been careful—deadly careful—never to say or do anything that might arouse suspicion, until by now he had imagined that any chance

1085

of his doing so was too remote to be worth considering, and that to all intents and purposes he had become Syed Akbar. Yet now he realized that he had not; and suddenly, with that knowledge, came an intense longing to be rid of pretence and be himself—only himself. But which self? Who was he? Ashton . . .? Ashok . . .? Akbar . . .? Which? Which two could he discard? Or must he always be an amalgam of all three, joined together like . . . "like Siamese triplets," thought Ash wryly.

If so, was there anywhere in the world where he and Juli could live without having to remember and pretend? Where they need not act a part, as both were doing now; forced to be forever on their guard for fear of making some trivial slip that, by exposing them as impostors, could endanger their very lives? The sort of slip he had made just now, when he began to hum an English hymn. It was frightening to realize that he would have done so even if there had been someone else in the room, and that it was only sheer luck that had saved him from being overheard. The knowledge left him profoundly shaken, and when he turned from the window to collect the ledgers that the Munshi would need, he found that his hands were cold and not entirely steady.

The sun was up by the time Wally and his party reached the outskirts of Ben-i-Hissar, and avoiding the village and the croplands surrounding it, selected an area of the uncultivated *charman* where the grass-cutters could collect all they needed without infringing on the rights of the local peasantry.

"By gum, what a day!" breathed Wally, awed by the dazzle of the morning. There had been a heavy dew during the night, and now every leaf and twig and blade of grass was hung with diamonds that flashed and glittered in the early sunlight, while the Bala Hissar, basking in the bright rays, might have been Kubla Khan's palace built on a hill of gold. "Will you look at that now, Rosie. Who would ever believe, seeing it from here, that the place is no more than a rat's nest of tumble-down mud-and-plaster houses and half-ruined walls?"

"Not to mention dirt and smells and sewage," grunted Rosie. "Don't be forgetting that. It's a wonder to me so it is that we aren't all dead from typhoid and cholera. But I grant you it looks very fine from here, and as I'm as empty as a drum and breakfast is calling, I suggest we leave these fellows to their own devices and get back there as soon as possible. Unless you feel we should stay around a bit longer, of course?"

"Good Lord, no. They'll be all right now. Besides, the Chief said he wanted breakfast an hour early this morning—quarter-to-seven at the latest. He has to see some local big-wig at eight, I believe."

Wally turned to the Kote-Daffadar and instructed him to see that the grass-cutters came back before the sun became too hot, and having saluted the escort and the Amir's men, rode off at a gallop, singing "Get thee, watchman, to the ramparts! Gird thee warrior with the sword!"

Ash was usually right about Wally.

"Slow down, you young madman," exhorted Rosie as they raced across the *charman* and their horses, reaching a bank that concealed an irrigation ditch, rose to it as though it had been a bullfinch in distant Kildare and came down on cultivated land once more. Wally reined in reluctantly, and they approached the citadel at a sedate canter and entered the Shah Shahie Gate at a walk; pausing under the arch to exchange salutes with the Afghan sentries and speak to a passing sepoy of the Guides Infantry, one Mohammed Dost, who explained that he was on his way to the Kabul bazaar to arrange for the purchase of flour for the Escort . . .

The fact that he was going there unaccompanied, and plainly had no qualms about doing so, was an indication of how greatly the feeling in the city had changed for the better of late, and both officers realized it, and in consequence returned to the compound buoyed up by a conviction that from now on life in Kabul was going to be far more enjoyable than they had supposed.

Sir Louis, who had returned from his morning ride some time before them, had already bathed and changed and was strolling in the courtyard, and though not normally loquacious before breakfast, today he was full of plans for the cold weather, and in such good spirits that Wally, taking his courage in both hands, at last broached the subject of fodder for the winter months and the extra storage space that would be needed for it; pointing out that the slope of waste ground known as the Kulla-Fi-Arangi would provide ample space for a few sheds, but being careful not to mention the question of defence. Sir Louis agreed that something would have to be done about it, and turned the matter over to William, who made a face at Wally and said blandly that he was sure that the Guides would be able to find room for a haystack or two near the stables.

A few hundred yards away, in a building that overlooked the open ground where the pay parade was due to take place, General Daud Shah, Commander-in-Chief of the Afghan Army, was already seated by an open window from where he could oversee the proceedings, while below him on the ground floor, on a narrow recessed verandah that ran the length of the building, Ash squatted among a number of underlings and watched the Munshi and a number of minor officials fussing with ledgers as the dusty space before them filled up with men.

The prevailing mood was a holiday one, and there was nothing suggestive of smartness or military discipline about the men of the Ardal Regiment as they sauntered up by twos and threes, talking and laughing and making no attempt to form up in ranks. They might have been a crowd of ordinary citizens attending a fair, for they were not in uniform and such weapons as they carried were no more than any subject of the Amir took with him when he walked abroad, a tulwar and an Afghan knife, Daud Shah having prudently ordered that all firearms and ammunition must be handed in and stored in the Arsenal for safe keeping, and even the Herati Regiment on guard there obeying this edict.

By now the sun was well up, but though the time was barely seven o'clock, the day was already warm enough to make Ash grateful for the shade provided by the painted roof and carved wooden arches of the verandah. And even more so for the fact that the matting-covered floor stood a full six feet above the level of the ground, which enabled those who sat there to look down on the crowd and avoid being stifled by that shifting sea of bearded, ill-washed humanity.

It also gave them the opportunity to study the faces of the men who stood below them, and Ash was conscious of a sudden prickle of unease as he recognized one of them: a thin, wizened little man with a hook nose and the eyes of a fanatic, who had no business to be there at all, since he was neither a soldier nor a resident in the

1088

Bala Hissar, but a holy man, the Fakir Buzurg Shah, whom Ash knew to be an agitator who hated all "Kafirs" (unbelievers) with a burning hatred, and worked tirelessly for a Jehad. He wondered what had brought the man here this morning, and whether he hoped to sow the good seed among the soldiers of the Ardal Regiment as he had sowed it among the Heratis? Ash could only hope that this soil would prove less fertile.

He had begun to wonder how long the pay parade would take and if the Munshi would allow him to have the rest of the day off as soon as it was over, when a portly official from the Treasury rose to his feet and took his stand at the top of the central flight of steps that led up to the verandah. Raising a podgy hand he called for silence, and having achieved it, announced that if the men would line up and advance one by one to the foot of the stairs, they would receive their pay; but—here he paused and flapped both hands angrily to quiet the babble of approval—*but* . . . they would have to be content with one month's pay instead of the three that had been promised them, as there was not enough money in the Treasury to cover the sum demanded.

The news had been received with a stunned silence that lasted for what seemed like minutes, but was probably less than twenty seconds. And then pandemonium broke loose as the men of the Ardal Regiment surged forward, pushing and shouting, screaming at the portly gentleman and his companions on the verandah, who screamed back at them that they would be well advised to take what they were offered while they had the chance—the Treasury had already been drained to give them even that one month's pay and there was no more to be had, not so much as one pice. Could they not understand that? The money was not there—they were welcome to come and see for themselves if they did not believe it.

The explosion of rage that greeted this last announcement resembled nothing so much as the snarling roar of a gigantic tiger, hungry, furious and thirsting for prey. And hearing it Ash felt his nerves tighten, and for a brief moment was tempted to run to the Residency and warn them of what had happened. But the narrow verandah was so crowded that it would not be easy to leave without attracting notice; and besides, this was a dispute between the Afghan Government and its soldiers, and no

1089

affair of the British Mission—which would in any case have already been warned by the noise that trouble was afoot, since the uproar must be loud enough to be heard in the city.

It was soon to grow louder.

A bull-voiced man in the forefront of the crowd bellowed *"Dam-i-charya!"*—"pay and food"—and those about him took up the cry. Within seconds half the men were shouting the words in unison, and the thunderous beat of that slogan boomed under arches of the verandah until the whole fabric of the building seemed to vibrate to the sound. *"Dam-i-charya! Dam-i-charya . . . ! Dam-i-charya . . . !"*

Then suddenly stones began to fly as the hungry, cheated troops stooped to snatch up this handy and time-honoured ammunition and hurl it at the upper windows where their Commander-in-Chief sat. One of his Generals and some of the Ardal's officers, who had been standing in a group by the central steps, began to move among the men in an effort to calm them, shouting for silence and exhorting them to remember that they were soldiers and not children or hooligans. But it proved impossible to make themselves heard above the din, and presently one of them fought his way back, and thrusting aside the dismayed officials on the verandah ran into the house to beg the Commander-in-Chief to come down and talk to them himself, as that might quieten them.

Daud Shah had not hesitated. He had suffered many insults of late from the soldiers of the Afghan Army, and only a handful of days ago the departing Herati regiments had booed and jeered him as they marched out. But he was a fearless man, and it was not in his nature to seek safety in inaction. He descended at once and strode to the top of the steps, lifting his arms for silence.

The men of the Ardal Regiment made a concerted rush, and the next moment he was down and fighting for his life as they dragged him from the verandah and fell on him like a pack of wolves on a buck.

In an instant everyone on the verandah leapt to their feet, Ash among them. He was too far to one side to see what was happening, nor could he move forward, for he found himself hemmed in by horror-struck civilians: clerks, chupprassis and minor officials, who pushed and jostled each other as some strove to get a better view and

1090

others struggled to make their escape from the verandah and take refuge in the rooms behind.

Ash himself was in two minds whether to go or stay. But with the troops in their present mood, any civilian intent on escape and trying to force his way through them would probably be beaten up as savagely as they were beating Daud Shah, so it seemed better to stand fast and wait upon events. But for the first time in several days he was glad that he carried a pistol and a knife with him, and regretted that he had not brought his revolver as well, instead of deciding at the last moment that in view of the slackening of tension and the return of a more relaxed and peaceful atmosphere throughout Kabul there was no longer any need to carry such a bulky weapon with him and that it could be safely left in his office, hidden in one of the locked boxes in which he kept the Munshi's files.

That had been a mistake. But then no one had anticipated the present situation—certainly not Daud Shah, who seemed likely to pay for this error of judgement with his life. That he did not do so was due to luck more than anything else, for when the furious Ardalis had beaten and kicked him until he could barely see or speak, one of them plunged a bayonet into the fallen man. The savage act served to sober them, and they drew back and fell silent, staring down at their handiwork and making no attempt to prevent his entourage—who to give them their due had tried to go to his assistance—from carrying him away to his own house.

Ash caught a glimpse of him as they went past, and would have found it hard to believe that this battered object, turbanless and clad now in no more than a few torn and bloodstained rags, could possibly be alive, had it not been for the vigorous stream of profanity that issued from those split and bleeding lips. The indomitable Commander-in-Chief, having recovered his breath, was using it to express his opinion of his assailants: "Filth! Offal! Sons of diseased swine! Spawn of reputationless mothers! Sweepings of hell!" snarled Daud Shah between gasps of pain as he was borne away, dripping blood that left a vivid scarlet trail on the white dust below the verandah.

The Ardal Regiment, deprived of this focus for its rage and realizing that there was nothing to be gained by attacking the hapless array of underlings on the verandah, remembered the Amir, and with shouts and oaths turned to make instead for the palace. But the rulers of Afghanistan had taken good care to fortify the royal residence against just such an eventuality as this, and the palace gates were far too stout to be easily forced, while its battlemented walls were high and massive and well loopholed against attack. Moreover the two regiments on guard were the Kazilbashi Horse and the Artillery Regiment, both loyal to the Amir.

The yelling mutineers found the gates closed against them and the gun-crews standing to their guns, and there was nothing they could do except hurl stones and insults at the Kazilbashis and those who looked down on them from the walls, and renew their demands for pay and food. But after some minutes of this, the shouting gradually began to die down; and taking advantage of the lull, a man on the wall—some say a General of the Afghan Army—shouted at them angrily that if they wanted more money they should go to Cavagnari-Sahib for it—there was plenty of money there.

It is possible that the speaker intended no mischief but was merely exasperated and had put the suggestion sarcastically. But the Ardal Regiment received it with acclaim. Of course!—Cavagnari-Sahib. The very man. Why had they not thought of that before? Everyone knew that the English Raj was rich beyond the dreams of avarice, and was not Cavagnari-Sahib the mouth-piece and representative of that Raj? Why was he here in Kabul, uninvited and far from welcome, if not to buy justice for all and help the Amir out of his difficulties by paying off the arrears due to his troops? Cavagnari-Sahib would right their wrongs. To the Residency, brothers—!

The crowd turned as one, and cheering wildly began to race back the way they had come. And Ash, still on the verandah, saw them coming and heard the shouts of "Cavagnari-Sahib!" and knew where they were headed.

He was not conscious of the process of connected thought. There had been no time for that and his reaction had been purely automatic. There were steps at each end of that long verandah, yet he had not attempted to reach the flight nearest him, but thrusting aside the man in front of him, leapt down from the edge a split second before their panic rush began, to be caught up and swept forward in the van of a tumultuous wave of shouting, cheering men.

It was only then that he knew why he must at all costs reach the Residency compound ahead or at least among the first of the throng.

He had to warn the Mission that this vociferous and apparently menacing crowd was not as yet activated by any hostility towards them, but that their anger was all for their own government, for Daud Shah and the Amir, who having promised them three months' pay had gone back on their word and tried to fob them off with one. Also that they firmly believed that the *Angrezi* Government was not only fabulously rich and well able to pay them, but that its Envoy would be able to obtain justice for them . . .

Running with them, Ash could sense the mood of the crowd as clearly as though he had been one of them. But he knew that the least little thing could change that mood and turn them into a mob, and as he ran he found himself praying that Wally would not let the Guides open fire. They *must* not fire. Provided they kept calm and gave Cavagnari time to talk to the ring-leaders of this shouting horde, all would be well . . . Cavagnari understood these people and could speak their language fluently. He would realize that this was no moment for quibbling and that his only hope was to give them a firm promise to pay them what they were owed, then and there if the money was available, and if it was not, to pledge his word that it would be forthcoming as soon as his government had time to send it . . .

"Dear God, don't let them open fire!" prayed Ash. "Let me get there first . . . If only I can get there first I can warn the sentries that this isn't an attack and that whatever happens they must not lose their heads and do anything silly."

He might even have succeeded, for some of the Guides had known him and would have recognized and obeyed him; but any chance of that was swept away by another and entirely unexpected influx of men from the left. The regiments on duty at the Arsenal had heard the uproar and seen the mutinous Ardalis come pouring down towards the Residency compound, and had raced to join them, and as the two separate streams of excited men, coming from different directions, cannoned into each other, Ash, among others, was sent sprawling.

By the time he was able to roll clear and struggle to his feet, bruised, dazed and choked by dust, the rout had gone past and he was at the back of the crowd; and there was no longer any hope of his being able to get into the compound in time—if at all—for the noisy throng that milled to and fro ahead of him now numbered close on a thousand, and there was no question of his being able to force his way through it.

But he had under-estimated Wally. The youthful commander of the Escort might be an indifferent poet and hold an over-romantic view of life, but he possessed the extreme military virtue of keeping his head in a crisis.

The first inkling that something had gone wrong with the pay parade had dawned on the denizens of the Residency compound when they heard the roar of rage that greeted the disclosure that the Amir's Government was defaulting on its promise. And though that sound and the tumult that followed had been muffled by the houses in between, there were few in the compound who did not hear it, and stop whatever they were doing to stand stock still, listening . . .

They did not hear the suggestion that Cavagnari-Sahib would pay, for that had been a single voice only. But the uproar that had preceded it and the applause with which it was received, above all the cry of *Dam-i-charya* chanted in unison by several hundred voices, had been clearly audible. And when presently they realized that the volume of sound was not only increasing but coming steadily nearer, they knew before they saw the first of the running soldiers where the shouting crowd was heading.

Except for Wally, the Guides were not yet in uniform: the infantry and those who were not on guard duty had been taking their ease in the barracks, and Wally himself had been down at the cavalry pickets beyond the stables, inspecting the horses and talking to the cavalrymen and the syces. A sepoy of the Guides Infantry, Hassan Gul, ran past without seeing him, making for the barracks where the Havildar of B Company stood by the open archway, picking his teeth with a splinter and listen-

1094

ing with detached interest to the hullabaloo being raised by those undisciplined *shaitans* of the Ardal Regiment.

"They are coming here," panted Hassan Gul as he reached the barracks. "I was outside and saw them. Quick, shut the gate!"

It was the makeshift one that Wally had had made and put up only a short while ago, and would not have stood up to any determined battering. But the Havildar closed it while Hassan Gul ran on past the inner door of the deep archway and through the long courtyard, to shut and bolt the far door that faced the entrance to the Residency.

Wally too had been listening to the din of that abortive pay parade as he strolled along the line of picketed horses, pausing to fondle his own charger, Mushki, while he discussed cavalry matters with the sowars. He turned, frowning, to watch the running sepoy, and seeing the door into the barracks being closed, reacted to the situation as swiftly and instinctively as Ash had done:

"You—Miru—go and tell the Havildar to open that gate and keep them open. All three, if they have shut the others. And tell him that whatever happens, no one is to fire unless I give the order. No one!"

Sowar Miru left at a run and Wally turned to the others and snapped: *"No one—*that is an order," and went swiftly back to the Residency by way of the barrack courtyard, where the doors now stood open, to report to Sir Louis.

"You heard what the Sahib said: there will be no firing," said Jemadar Jiwand Singh to his troopers. "Moreover—" But he had no time to say more, for in the next instant a cataract of yelling, leaping Afghans poured into the peaceful compound, shouting for Cavagnari, demanding money, threatening and rollicking, pushing and jostling the Guides with howls of laughter, like a drunken gang of hooligans at a country fair.

A humorist among them called out that if there was no money to be had here either, they could always help themselves to the equipment in the stables, and the suggestion was received and acted upon with enthusiasm, the invaders rushing to get their hands on saddles, bridles, sabres and lances, horse-blankets, buckets and anything else that was movable.

Within minutes the stables were stripped bare and fights had broken out between the looters over the possession of the more highly prized items, such as English saddles. A panting sowar, his clothing torn and his turban awry, fought his way clear of the boisterous mass of looters and managed to get to the Residency to report to his Commanding Officer that the Afghans had stolen everything from the stables and were now stoning and stealing the horses.

"Mushki!" thought Wally with a contraction of the heart, visualizing his beloved charger gashed by stones or in the hands of some Ardali lout. "Oh no, not Mushki . . ."

He would have given anything at that moment to have been able to run to the stables himself, but he knew very well that he would be unable to stand by and see Mushki stolen, and also that even if he did not lift a hand to prevent it, the mood of the crowd could change in a moment and the sight of one of the hated *feringhis* might act on it as a red rag to a bull. There was nothing for it but to order the breathless sowar to return and tell the Guides that they must leave the Cavalry lines and get back into the barracks.

"Tell the Jemadar-Sahib that we need not fear for our horses, because tomorrow the Amir will recover them from these thieves and restore them to us," said Wally. "But we must get our men back into the barracks before one of them starts a fight."

The man saluted and ran back to plunge into the frightening mêlée in the lines where the terrified horses squealed and reared, lashing out at the Afghans, who snatched at them, pulling them this way and that as they quarrelled among themselves for the possession of each animal or cut at them for sheer sport while sowars and syces struggled to save them. But the message was delivered, and because the Afghans were pre-occupied with looting, all but one of the Guides had been able to obey that order and retreat in safety to the barrack block, angry, bitter and dishevelled, but unharmed.

Wally came out to them and ordered twenty-four sepoys of the infantry to take their rifles and go up to the roof to stand behind the high parapet that surrounded it, but to keep their rifles out of sight, and on no account open fire unless they received an order to do so. "Not

1096

even when those reputationless ones come this way, as they will do as soon as they find nothing left to steal in the lines or the stables. See that they find no weapon here. Now up with you—and the rest of you bring your arms and come into the Residency. Quickly."

He had not been a moment too soon. As the last of the twenty-four sepoys disappeared up the steep flight of steps that led to the roof, and the door in the wall of the Residency courtyard closed behind the rest of the Escort, the riotous crowd that had been milling around at the far end of the compound in search of plunder began to break up.

Those who had been lucky enough to gain possession of a horse, or (less enviably) a saddle or a sabre or some such desirable piece of loot, were hastening to leave with their spoils before their less successful comrades succeeded in robbing them of these ill-gotten gains. But the empty-handed, who numbered several hundred, abandoned the deserted lines and ransacked stables, and suddenly recalling the purpose for which they had come, surged in a body across the compound and through and around the barracks, to gather before the Residency and shout once more for money—and for Cavagnari.

A year and more ago Wally, writing to Ash of his latest hero, had said that he did not believe that Cavagnari knew the meaning of fear: an extravagant statement that has been made about many men, and is usually untrue. But in this instance it was no exaggeration. The Envoy had already received a garbled warning from the Amir, who hearing that all was not going well with the pay parade, had hurriedly dispatched a message to Sir Louis urging him not to allow anyone to enter the Mission compound that day. But the message had arrived only minutes before the mob, and far too late to be acted upon, even if there had been any adequate way of keeping them out, which there was not.

The Envoy's first reaction to the tumult in the compound had been anger. It was, he considered, a disgrace that the Afghan authorities should permit the precincts of the British Mission to be invaded in this manner by a horde of undisciplined savages, and he would have to speak sharply about it both to the Amir and Daud Shah. When the looting stopped and the rabble turned their attention to the Residency and began to shout his name,

1097

demanding money with uncouth threats and flinging stones at his windows, his anger merely turned to disgust, and as the chupprassis hurried to close the shutters, he withdrew to his bedroom, where William, running up from his office on the ground floor below, found him donning his Political uniform: not the white of the hot weather, but the blue-black frock-coat usually worn in the cold months, complete with gilt buttons, medals, gold braid and narrow gold sword-belt.

Sir Louis appeared to be completely oblivious of the racket below, and seeing the look of cold and disdainful detachment on his face, William was torn between admiration and an odd feeling of panic that had nothing to do with the howling horde outside or the sound of stones rattling like hail against the wooden shutters. He was not normally given to imaginative flights, but as he watched the Envoy shrug himself into his coat it struck him that so might a noble of Louis XVI's day—an "Aristo"—have looked when hearing the screeching of the *canaille* outside the walls of his château . . .

William cleared his throat, and raising his voice in order to be heard above the din said hesitantly: "Do you mean to . . . are you going to speak to them, sir?"

"Certainly. They are not likely to leave until I do, and we really cannot be expected to put up with this ridiculous form of disturbance any longer."

"But . . . Well, there seem to be an awful lot of them, sir, and—"

"What has that got to do with it?" inquired Sir Louis chillingly.

"Only that we don't know how much they want, and I—I wondered if we'd got enough. Because our own fellows have only just been . . ."

"What on earth are you talking about?" inquired the Envoy, busy adjusting the fastening of his ceremonial sword so that the tassels showed to advantage.

"Money, sir, rupees. It seems to be what they want, and I presume this means that when it came down to brass tacks there wasn't enough to go round this morning, and that is why—"

He was interrupted again. *"Money?"* Sir Louis' head came up with a jerk and he glared at his secretary for a moment and then spoke in tones of ice: "My dear Jenkyns, if you imagine for one moment that I would

1098

even consider allowing myself and the Government I have the honour to represent to be blackmailed—yes, that is the word I mean—*blackmailed,* by a mob of uncivilized hooligans, I can only say that you are very much mistaken. And so are those stone-throwing yahoos outside. My topi, Amal Din—"

His Afridi orderly stepped smartly forward and handed him the white pith helmet topped by a gilt spike that a Political Officer wore with his official uniform, and as he clapped it firmly on his head, adjusted the gilded strap across his chin and moved to the door, William sprang forward saying desperately: "Sir—if you go down there—"

"My dear boy," said Sir Louis impatiently, pausing in the doorway, "I am not really in my dotage. I too realize that if I were to go down to them only those in the forefront of the crowd would see me, while those who could not would continue to shout and make it impossible for me to be heard. I shall of course speak to them from the roof. No, William, I do not require you to come with me. I will take my orderly, and it will be better if the rest of you keep out of sight."

He crooked a finger at Amal Din and the two tall men left the room, Sir Louis striding ahead and the Afridi following a pace behind, hand on sword hilt. William heard their scabbards clash against the side of the narrow stairway to the roof and thought with a mixture of admiration, affection and despair: "He's magnificent. But we aren't in a position to refuse them, even if it does mean giving in to blackmail. Can't he see that? That fellow in Simla was right about him—he's going up there to do just the same sort of thing that French Guards officer did at Fontenoy . . . and the Light Brigade at Balaclava . . . 'C'est manifique, mais ce n'est pas la guerre!' It's suicide—"

Unlike the barracks, there was no parapet surrounding the flat roofs of the two Residency houses, though both were screened from the view of the maze of buildings directly behind them by a man-high wall. The other three sides had a rim of brick no more than a few inches high, and Sir Louis walked to the edge, where all below could see him, and held up a commanding hand for silence.

He did not attempt to make himself heard above the

1099

din but stood waiting, erect and scornful: a tall, black-bearded, imposing figure in the trappings of his official uniform, with the gilt spike on his helmet adding inches to his height. Medals glittered on his coat and the broad gilt stripe that adorned each trouser-leg shone bright in the early sunlight of that brilliant morning, but the cold eyes under the brim of the white pith helmet were hard and unwavering as they stared down contemptuously on the clamouring mob below.

The Envoy's appearance on the roof had been greeted with an ear-splitting yell that might well have made even the bravest man flinch and draw back, but for all the response it drew from Sir Louis it might have been a whisper. He stood there like a rock, waiting until it pleased the crowd to stop shouting, and as they gazed up at him, man after man fell silent, until at last he lowered that imperious hand—it had not even quivered—and demanded in stentorian tones what they had come for and what did they want with him?

Several hundred voices answered him, and once again he raised his hand and waited, and when they fell quiet, asked them to choose a spokesman: "You—you with the scarred cheek"—his lean forefinger pointed unerringly at one of the ring-leaders—"stand forward and speak for your fellows. What is the meaning of this shameful *gurrh-burrh*, and why have you come battering at the doors of one who is the guest of your Amir and under His Highness's protection?"

"The Amir—*ppth!*" The man with the scar spat on the ground, and related how his regiment had been cheated at the pay parade, and that having failed to get any satisfaction from their own Government they had bethought them of Cavagnari-Sahib and come here seeking justice from him. They asked only that he would pay them the money that was their due. "For we know that your Raj is rich and so it will mean little to you. But we here have starved for too long. All we ask for is what we are owed. No more and no less. Give us justice, Sahib!"

Despite the looting and the rowdy, hooligan behaviour of the rebellious troops, it was plain from the speaker's tone that he and his fellows genuinely believed that the British Envoy had it in his power to right their wrongs and give them what their own authorities refused: their arrears of pay. But the expression on the strong, black-bearded face that looked down on them did not change, and the stern, carrying voice that spoke their own language with such admirable fluency remained inflexible:

"I am grieved for you," said Sir Louis Cavagnari. "But what you ask is impossible. I cannot interfere between you and your ruler, or meddle in a matter that is the sole concern of the Amir and his army. I have no power to do so, and it would not become me to attempt it. I am sorry."

And he had stuck to that in the face of howls and shrieks of rage and a growing chorus of threats; repeating again, in pauses in the uproar, that this was a question that they must settle with the Amir or their Commander-in-Chief, and though he sympathized with them he could not interfere. Only when Amal Din, standing behind him, warned him through shut teeth that certain *shaitans* below were gathering stones did he turn and leave the roof. And then only because he realized that to wait any longer left him with the choice of becoming an easy target for the stone-throwers, or else allowing them to suppose that they had driven him to retreat from the roof and take cover below.

"Barbarians," commented Sir Louis unemotionally, divesting himself of his uniform in the safety of his bedroom and replacing it with cooler and more comfortable garb. "I think, William, that I had better send a message to the Amir. It is high time he sent some responsible person to control this rabble. I cannot imagine what Daud Shah is up to. No discipline, that is their trouble."

He strode into his office next door, and was about to sit at his desk to write when a voice that did not come from the lane below, but from the roof of the barrack block on the opposite side where the twenty-four men of the Guides Infantry stood to their arms behind the parapet, bellowed across the narrow gap that fighting had broken out by the stables and that the mutineers had killed a syce and were attacking Sowar Mal Singh . . . That Mal Singh was down . . . That he was wounded . . .

The mob in front of the Residency heard and roared its approval, and while some broke away and began to run back towards the stables, others began to batter on the door leading into the Residency, where Wally, waiting with the Guides in the courtyard behind it, moved among his men, reiterating that no one must fire until ordered to do so, and urging restraint. When the flimsy wood began to splinter and the rusty iron hinges bent and cracked they rushed to put their shoulders to the door, pushing against the weight of the rioters outside; but it was a losing game. As the last hinge snapped the door fell in on them and the crowd burst into the courtyard, and simultaneously, from somewhere outside, a shot rang out.

65

The sharp, staccato sound sliced through the din, silencing it as swiftly and effectively as a slap across the face will silence a fit of hysterics; and Wally thought automatically, "Jezail"—for a modern imported rifle does not make the same noise as the long-barrelled muzzle-loading jezail of India.

The silence lasted less than ten seconds. Then once again pandemonium exploded as the mob, momentarily halted by the sound of the shot, began to fight its way forward into the Residency courtyard, yelling "Kill the *Kafirs!* kill them!—Kill! Kill!" Yet still Wally would not give the order to fire.

Even had he done so it is doubtful if he would have been heard above that frenzied clamour. But suddenly, somewhere in the mêlée, a carbine cracked, and then another—and another . . . And all at once the attackers turned and fled, stumbling and trampling over the bodies of fallen men and the wreckage of the broken door, and shouting now for firearms—for muskets and rifles with which to slay the infidels. *"Topak rawakhlah. Pah makhe! Makhe!"** screamed the mutineers as they ran from the Residency and streamed back across the compound, some making for the Arsenal and the rest for their own cantonments outside the city limits.

Once again the brilliant morning was calm and still . . . and in that stillness the men of the British Mission, left alone, breathed deep and counted the dead. Nine

---

*Go back and get your muskets. On! On!

mutineers and one of their own syces; and Sowar Mal Singh, who was still alive when they found him by the stables, but died as they carried him into the Residency—and whose sabre had accounted for three of the enemy dead, for he had gone to the assistance of the unarmed syce and defended him valiantly against impossible odds. Of the other six, four had been shot and two killed in hand-to-hand fighting, tulwar against sabre. And seven of the escort had been wounded. The Guides looked at each other and knew that this was not the end but only the beginning, and that it would not be long before the enemy returned. And that this time the Afghans would carry more than side-arms.

"Fifteen minutes," thought Wally, "if that. Fifteen minutes at most." And aloud: "Close the gates and give out the ammunition. Block the ends of the lane—no, not with bales of straw, that will burn too easily. Use yak-dans, feed bins, anything—take the bars from the stables. And we will need to cut loopholes in the parapets . . ."

They worked desperately. Officers, servants, syces; soldiers and civilians, toiling together literally for dear life; dragging up baggage-wagons and empty ammunition boxes, flour barrels, firewood, saddle-bags, tents and ground-sheets and anything else that could possibly be pressed into service to reinforce the entrance to the compound and barricade the lane. They piled bales of fodder to form a flimsy wall across the open ground behind the gutted stables, pierced loopholes in the walls of the Residency and the parapet surrounding the barrack roof, and pitched the bodies of the enemy dead into a godown at the far end of the compound, laying their own two on *charpoys* in Amal Din's vacated quarter.

Cavagnari sent an urgent message to the Amir informing him that his troops had made an unprovoked attack upon the Residency, and claiming the protection he owed to his guests; and while awaiting his messenger's return from the palace, turned his hand to helping construct a makeshift parapet out of scratched-up earth, furniture and carpets on the roofs of the two Residency houses. But his messenger did not return.

The man had arrived at the palace only to be put in a side room and told to wait, and an answer had been sent instead by the hand of a palace servant. "As God wills, I am making preparations," wrote His Highness the Amir

Yakoub Khan. But he sent no guards, not even a handful of his loyal Kazilbashis.

Others were also making preparations.

Aided by his lone hospital assistant and a motley group of bearers, *khidmatgars,* cooks and *masalchis* (scullions), Ambrose Kelly was preparing rooms on the lower floor of the Mess House to accommodate casualties and provide an operating theatre, while William Jenkyns and half-a-dozen sepoys raced to and fro removing the contents of the ammunition tent—which, together with a second tent containing an assortment of baggage, had been pitched for greater safety in the Residency courtyard. This they divided between the barracks and an ante-room on the ground floor of the Envoy's House, where it would be less vulnerable to rifle-fire from the rooftops and windows of the many houses that overlooked both the Residency and the Mission's compound—from the nearest of which, though they did not know it, another officer of the Guides was even then looking down on them and watching them as they toiled.

Ash had recognized the futility of forcing his way into the compound in the wake of several hundred disgruntled and undisciplined soldiers, when it was too late to warn or advise. And when no shots greeted the invaders he realized that neither advice nor warning was needed. Wally must already have instructed the Guides not to fire and was in no danger of losing his head and precipitating a battle by reacting too strongly. The boy clearly had his men well in hand, and with a modicum of luck the situation would not get out of control before Cavagnari was able to speak to the Afghan soldiery.

Once let the Envoy talk to them, and their fears would subside. He had only to promise them that he himself would see to it that their grievances were righted and that they would receive the pay they were owed—if not from the Amir then from the British Government—and because to the tribes his name was one to conjure with, they would believe him. They would accept Cavagnari-Sahib's word where they would have accepted no one else's and everything might yet be well.

Ash had turned and gone back to his office in the Munshi's house, and looking down from his window, had witnessed the looting of the stables, the theft of the horses from the cavalry pickets and the subsequent rush to the Residency. He had seen, too, the tall, frock-coated figure in the white helmet come out upon the roof of the Envoy's house and walk calmly to the edge to quell the vociferous crowd below, and had thought, like William, "By God, he's a wonder."

He had never had any great liking for Louis Cavagnari, and had come to detest his policy. But seeing him now he was filled with admiration for the coolness and courage of a man who could walk out, unarmed and alone except for a solitary Afghan orderly, and stand calmly looking down on that threatening, stone-throwing mob without showing the least sign of alarm.

"I'm damned if I could have done that," thought Ash. "Wally is right: he's a great man and he'll get them all out of this jam. He'll pull them through . . . it's going to be all right. It's going to be all right . . ."

The acoustics of that part of the Bala Hissar were peculiar (a fact not fully realized by the dwellers in the Residency compound, though Ash had once warned Wally about it), the reason for this being that the site of the compound made it a natural theatre, in the manner of ancient Greece where the stone seats swept upward in a semi-circle of steeply rising tiers from the stage below, to form a sounding-board that enabled even those in the top-most tiers to hear every word spoken by the actors.

Here, in place of seats there were the solid walls of houses built on rising ground, and therefore producing much the same effect. And though it would be an exaggeration to say that every word spoken in the compound could be heard by the occupants of those houses, shouted orders, raised voices, laughter and snatches of conversation were clearly audible to anyone in the nearer buildings who cared to stand at a window, as Ash was doing, and listen. Particularly when the breeze was blowing from the south, as it was today.

Ash caught every word that the spokesman for the mutineers shouted up to Sir Louis, and every syllable of Sir Louis' reply. And for a full half minute he could not believe that he had heard aright. There must be some mistake . . . he must have heard wrong. Cavagnari could not possibly . . .

But there was no mistaking the full-throated howl of rage that burst from the mob when the Envoy ceased speaking. Or the cries of "Kill the Kafirs!" "Kill! Kill!"

that succeeded it. His ears had not deceived him. Cavagnari had gone mad and now there was no knowing what the mob would do.

He saw the Envoy turn and leave the roof, but his view of the Residency courtyard was restricted by the west wall of the three-storeyed Mess House in which Wally, Jenkyns and Kelly had their quarters, and he could only see the further half by the Envoy's House, and the turbaned heads of the escort who waited there; indistinguishable at that range from the servants, as they were still in undress, having not yet changed into uniform when the compound was invaded. But he could pick out Wally easily enough, for he was hatless.

Ash saw him moving among the Guides and realized from his gestures that he was urging them to remain calm and not on any account to fire. Then suddenly his attention was drawn from the courtyard to the stables by frantic shouts from the sepoys who were stationed on the roof of the barracks . . .

The sepoys were yelling and pointing, and looking in the direction of the outflung arms Ash saw a single man—presumably a sowar, for he was wielding a cavalry sabre—standing astride the huddled body of a syce and surrounded by a ring of Afghans who were attacking him from every side, slashing at him with knives and tulwars and leaping back as he whirled his sabre about him, fighting like a cornered leopard. He had already brought down two of his assailants and wounded others, but he himself had taken terrible punishment: his clothing was ripped in a dozen places and stained with his own blood, and it was only a question of time before he tired sufficiently to allow his attackers to close in. The end came when three men engaged him simultaneously, and as he fought them off, a fourth leapt at him from behind and drove a knife into his back. As he fell the pack closed in, stabbing and hacking, and a yell of rage went up from the watching sepoys on the barrack roof.

Ash saw one of them turn from the parapet and run back along the roof of the Mohammedan quarters to cup his hands about his mouth and bellow the news to the Residency, and heard the mob in the lane below howl their approval as they rushed to attack the door into the Residency courtyard, flinging themselves against it again and again, like a human battering-ram.

He did not see who had fired that first shot, though he too realized that it had been fired from an old-fashioned muzzle-loader and not a rifle, and presumed that one of the men from the Arsenal must have carried a jezail as well as a tulwar, and discharged it to discourage any camp-followers from coming to the rescue of the wounded Sikh. But the momentary silence that followed that shot made the concerted yell that ended it ten times more shocking, and the murderous cries of "Kill! Kill!" told him that any chance there may have been of persuading the mob to leave by peaceful means had been lost.

The pendulum had swung over to violence, and should the mutineers succeed in breaking into the Residency they would loot it as thoroughly as they had looted the stables: only this time there would be no jostling and horseplay. The time for that had gone. The swords and knives were out, and now the Afghans would kill.

The din outside was so great that it was surprising that Ash should have heard the door of his little office creak open. But he had lived too long with danger to be unmindful of small sounds, and he whirled round—to see ex-Risaldar-Major Nakshband Khan, of all people, standing in the doorway.

The Sirdar had never, to his knowledge, visited the Munshi's house before, yet it was not the unexpectedness of his arrival that startled Ash, but the fact that his clothing was torn and dusty and that he was shoeless and breathing heavily, as though he had been running.

"What is it?" demanded Ash sharply. "What are you doing here?"

The Sirdar came in and closed the door behind him, and leaning against it, said jerkily: "I heard that the Ardal Regiment had mutinied and attacked General Daud Shah, and that they were besieging the palace in the hope of getting money from the Amir. But knowing that the Amir has none to give, I ran quickly to warn Cavagnari-Sahib and the young Sahib who commands the Guides to beware of the Ardalis, and to let none of them enter the compound today. But I was too late . . . And when I followed these mutinous dogs and tried to reason with them, they set upon me, calling me traitor, spy and *feringhi*-lover. I was hard put to it to escape them, but having done so I came here to warn you not to leave this room until this *gurrh-burrh* is over, since too many here will know that you dwell as a guest under my roof—and half Kabul knows that I am a pensioner of the Guides, who are now being attacked down there; for which reason I do not dare return to my own house while this trouble lasts. I could be torn to pieces in the streets, so I mean to take refuge with a friend of mine who lives here in the Bala Hissar, close by, and return later when it is safe to do so —which may not be until after dark. Stay you here also until then, and do not venture out until—*Allah! What is that?*"

It was the crack of a carbine, and he ran to join Ash at the window.

The two stood side by side, glaring down at the turmoil below where the Guides in the Residency courtyard, driven back by the sheer weight of numbers, were giving ground before the tulwars and knives of the yelling mob, fighting them off with drawn sabres. But it was clear that the shot had taken effect in more ways than one.

Apart from the fact that fired into the scrimmage it had almost certainly killed or wounded several of the invaders, the impact of the sound in that enclosed space was a sharp reminder that tulwars were useless against bullets. The lesson was driven home by the three shots that followed, and the courtyard cleared like magic; but Ash and the Sirdar, watching the mutineers break and run, knew that they were not seeing a rabble in retreat, but men racing to fetch muskets and rifles—and that it would not be long before they were back.

"May Allah have mercy on them," whispered the Sirdar. "This is the end . . ." And then sharply: "Where are you going?"

"To the palace," said Ash curtly. "The Amir must be told—"

The Sirdar caught his arm and jerked him back. "True. But you are not the man to do it. Not now. You would be set on even as I was—and you they would kill. Besides, Cavagnari-Sahib will send a message at once, if he has not done so already. There is nothing you can do."

"I can go down there and fight with them. They will obey my orders because they know me. They are my own men—it is my own Corps, and if the Amir does not send

1108

help they will have no chance. They will die like rats in a trap—"

"And you with them!" snapped Nakshband Khan, grappling with him.

"Better that than stay here and watch them die. Take your hands off me, Sirdah-Sahib. Let me go."

"And what of your wife?" demanded the Sirdar furiously. "Have you no thought for her? Or of what will become of her if you die?"

"Juli—" thought Ash in horror; and was suddenly still.

He had actually forgotten about her. Unbelievably, in all the turmoil and panic of the last half hour, he had not spared a single thought for her. His mind had been wholly taken up with Wally and the Guides and the terrible danger that menaced them, and he had had no time to think of anyone else. Not even of Anjuli . . .

"She has no kin here, and this is not her own country," said the Sirdar sternly, relieved at having hit upon an argument that appeared to weigh with Ash. "But if you die and your wife, being widowed, wishes to return to her own people, she might find it hard to do so: and harder still to remain here among strangers. Have you made arrangements for her future? Have you thought—?"

Ash pulled the restraining hand from his arm and turning away from the door said harshly: "No, I have thought too much and too long of my friends and my Regiment, and not enough of her. But I am a soldier, Sirdar-Sahib. And she is the wife of a soldier—and the granddaughter of another. She would not have me put my love for her above my duty to my Regiment. Of that I am sure, for her father was a Rajput. If—if I should not return, tell her that I said so . . . and that you and Gul Baz and the Guides will look after her and see that she comes to no harm."

"I will do so," said the Sirdar—and as he spoke reached stealthily for the door, and before Ash had time to turn, snatched it open, whisked through and slammed it shut behind him. The heavy iron key had been on the outside, and even as Ash swung round and leapt forward he heard it turn in the lock.

He was caught and he knew it. The door was far too stout to be broken down and the window-bars were of iron and would not bend. Nevertheless he tugged frantically at the heavy latch and shouted to Nakshband Khan to let him out. But the only answer was the rasp of metal as the key was withdrawn, and then the Sirdar's voice speaking softly through the empty keyhole: "It is better this way, Sahib. I go now to Wali Mohammed's house, where I shall be safe. It is only a stone's throw from here, so I shall reach it long before those *shaitans* return; and when all is quiet again I will come back and release you."

"And what of the Guides?" demanded Ash furiously. "How many of them do you think will be alive by then?"

"That is in God's hands," replied the Sirdar, his voice almost inaudible, "—and there is neither hem nor border nor fringe to the mercy of Allah."

Ash abandoned his assault on the door and fell to pleading, but there was no answer, and presently he realized that Nakshband Khan had gone—taking the key with him.

The room was a narrow oblong with the door at one end, the window at the other, and the entire building, like those on either side of it, was very different from the flimsy Residency houses, for it was of a much earlier date and had once been part of the inner defences. Its outer walls were solidly constructed, and the small square window-frames were of stone in which the bars had been set before the frames were built into the house front. Had Ash possessed a file it might have been possible for him, after hours of labour, to remove two of these (one would not have been enough), but the office equipment did not include that kind of file, and an examination of the lock showed him that nothing short of a considerable charge of gunpowder could blow it in, for it was of a pattern only seen in Europe in a few medieval dungeons; the bolt being formed from a thick rod of iron that when the key was turned, slid home into a deep iron socket embedded in the stone door frame. There was no point in attempting to use his pistol on the thing; the lock was far too strong and too simple for that, and the most that a bullet could do was to damage it so that when Nakshband Khan returned with the key he would be unable to open the door ...

There was no longer any question of attempting to fetch help from the palace or to join Wally and the Guides

1110

in defending the Residency, or of getting back to Juli and the house in the city either. He was as securely trapped as the members of the British Mission to Afghanistan who were making frantic efforts to prepare for the attack that they knew must come at any moment; an attack that they would have to fend off alone unless the Amir sent troops to prevent the return of the mutineers, and closed the gates of the Bala Hissar to the Heratis and others who had made for their cantonments to fetch their rifles.

But the Amir had done nothing.

Yakoub Khan was a weakling, possessing none of the fire and steel of his grandfather the great Dost Mohammed, and few if any of the good qualities (and they were many) of his unfortunate father the late Shere Ali, who might have made an excellent ruler if he had been left to himself instead of being hounded unmercifully by an ambitious Viceroy. Yakoub Khan had ample military resources at his disposal: his Arsenal was crammed with rifles, ammunition and kegs of gunpowder, and quite apart from the mutinous regiments he had close on two thousand loyal troops in the Bala Hissar: the Kazilbashis and the Artillery, and the guard on the Treasury. These, had he given the order, would have closed the citadel against the troops from the cantonments and moved against the men of the Ardal Regiment, who were breaking into the Arsenal to seize rifles and ammunition for themselves, and passing out firearms to the riff-raff from the bazaar and any infidel-hater who would join them.

A mere hundred or so Kazilbashis, or two guns and their crews, sent post-haste to bar the way to the Mission's compound, could have halted the mob and almost certainly have dissuaded them from attacking. But Yakoub Khan was far more concerned for his own safety than that of the guests whom he had sworn to protect, and he would only weep and wring his hands, and bewail his fate.

"My Kismet is bad," wept the Amir to the mullahs and syeds of Kabul, who had hurried to the palace to urge him to take immediate steps to save his guests.

"Your tears will not help them," retorted the head Mullah sternly. "You must send soldiers to guard the approaches to their compound and turn back the mutineers. If you do not, they will all be murdered."

1111

"That will not be *my* fault . . . I never wished it. As God is my witness, it will not be my fault, because I can do nothing—nothing."

"You can close the gates," said the head Mullah.

"Of what use, when there are so many of these evil men already within the citadel?"

"Then give orders for these guns here to be moved where they can fire on the troops when they return from their cantonments, and thus prevent them re-entering."

"How can I do that, when I know that if I did so, the whole city would rise against me and the *budmashes* would force their way in and eat us all up? No, no, there is nothing I can do . . . I tell you, my Kismet is bad. I cannot fight against my fate."

"Then it is better that you should die rather than disgrace Islam," said the Mullah harshly.

But the weeping Amir was lost to all shame, and no argument or pleading—no appeals to him for the sake of honour and in the name of hospitality to protect those who were his guests—could galvanize him into taking any action whatsoever. The wild rioting, and the attack on Daud Shah that had resulted from the pay parade, had so terrified him that he did not dare give any order for fear that it would not be obeyed. For if it were not . . . ? No, no, better anything than that. Oblivious of the scornful eyes of the mullahs, ministers and nobles who stood watching him, he tore his hair and rent his clothes, and bursting into renewed tears, turned from them to stumble away and shut himself up in his private rooms in the palace.

Yet weakling or no, he was still the Amir, and therefore, in name at least, head of the Government and lord and ruler of all Afghanistan. No one else dared give the orders that he himself would not give, and avoiding each others' eyes they followed him into the palace. When the British Envoy's messenger arrived with a letter asking for help and claiming his protection, a senior minister took it in to him, and the reply that was sent back consisted of that single procrastinating sentence: *As God wills, I am making preparations*, which was not even true—unless, of course, he was referring to preparations for the saving of his own skin.

Sir Louis had stared in stunned incredulity at this puerile answer to his urgent appeal for help. " 'Making

1112

preparations . . .' Good God! is *that* all he can say?"
breathed Sir Louis.

His hand clenched on the scrap of paper, crumpling it
up, and lifting his head he gazed blindly out at the far
snows, realizing in that moment that the man of whom he
had written only a day or two ago "I personally believe
he will prove a very good ally" was weak, worthless and
a coward, a broken reed who should never have been
trusted or relied upon; seeing at last and very clearly the
futility of his Mission and the deadly nature of the trap
into which he had led his entourage so proudly. "Her
Britannic Majesty's Mission to the Court of Kabul" had
lasted exactly six weeks—that was all; only forty-two
days . . .

It had all seemed so feasible once—those brave
schemes for establishing a British presence in Afghanistan
as a first step towards planting the Union Jack on the far
side of the Hindu Kush. But now, suddenly, he was not
so sure that that strange fellow Pelham-Martyn—"Akbar,"
who had been a friend of poor Wigram Battye's—had
been so wrong-headed after all when he had argued so
vehemently against the Forward Policy, insisting that the
Afghans were a fiercely proud and courageous people who
would never accept government by any foreign nation for
more than a limited time, a year or two at most—and
had quoted precedents to prove it.

"But we shall be avenged," thought Sir Louis grimly. "Lytton will send an army to occupy Kabul and depose
the Amir. But how long will they be able to stay here? . . .
and how many lives will be lost before . . . before they
have to retreat again? I must write again to the Amir. I
must make him see that it is as much in his interests as
ours to save us, because if we go down he will go down
with us. I must write at once—"

But there was no time. The mutineers who had
broken into the Arsenal were racing back armed with
rifles, muskets and cartridge-belts, the majority heading
for the compound, firing as they ran, while others took up
positions on the rooftops of the surrounding houses, from
where they would be able to fire directly down on to the
beleaguered garrison. And as the first musket ball
whipped across the compound, Sir Louis sloughed off the
politician and the diplomat and became a soldier again.

1113

Flinging away the useless scrap of crumpled paper that bore a coward's reply to his appeal for help, he snatched up a rifle and made for the top of the Mess House where he had lately been helping to erect a make-shift parapet, and lying flat on the sun-baked roof took careful aim at a group of men who had begun to fire at the Residency.

The roof of the Mess House was the highest point in the Mission compound, and from it he had a clear view of the great Arsenal that looked down on the compound from the rising ground beyond the cavalry lines. The range was barely two hundred yards; and there was a man standing in the doorway handing out muskets . . .

Sir Louis fired and saw him throw up his hands and fall, and reloading swiftly, fired again: taking deliberate aim and paying no attention to the hail of bullets that pattered about him as men on the surrounding house-tops began to fire in reply at the roof of the barracks and the Residency. Below him several women of the town, who had been hiding in the servants' quarters where they had no business to be, ran screeching like pea-hens across the compound, herded by a sepoy and one of the *khid-matgars* to the *hammam,* the bath-house, that was built partly underground and where the majority of the servants had already taken refuge. But though Sir Louis heard them, he did not look down.

Had the compound been on higher ground it would have made an excellent defensive position, since it contained a series of courts, each separated from the next by low mud walls that could have been easily loopholed, and the defenders could have held off any number of attackers, inflicting enormous casualties for as long as their ammunition lasted. But its position was precisely that of the arena of a bull-ring to which Wally had compared it on the day of the Mission's arrival, so that the walls that would have provided cover against a frontal attack were useless against an enemy that was able to fire down from above: and by now, on house-tops ahead and along one entire side of the Residency and its compound—in high windows and on the battlements of the Arsenal and even on the roofs of many buildings in the upper Bala Hissar—men clustered thick as flies on a sweetmeat stall, firing as fast as they could load and yelling in triumph whenever a shot told.

1114

Yet for all the notice he took of them, Sir Louis Cavagnari might have been lying peacefully on a rifle-range, engaged in target-practice and intent on marking up a high score. He fired and re-loaded swiftly, calmly, methodically, aiming at the men who swarmed down from the Arsenal, and selecting those in the forefront so that the ones who pressed behind tripped over the bodies as they fell.

He was a superb marksman, and his first nine shots had accounted for nine of the enemy when a spent bullet, ricocheting off the low brick rim of the roof a few inches from his head, struck him on the forehead. His head dropped and his long body jerked once and lay still, while the rifle slid from his nerveless hands and toppled into the lane below.

An exultant yell burst from the enemy on the nearer house-tops, and Ash, who had been watching from the window of his room, drew a harsh breath between his teeth and thought: "Oh God, they've got him"—and in the next moment, "No they haven't!" For the wounded man began to raise himself slowly and painfully, first to his knees and then with an enormous effort to his feet.

Blood was pouring down from the gash in his forehead, blotting out one side of his face and staining his shoulder scarlet, and as he stood there, swaying, a score of muskets cracked and as many puffs of dust exploded all around him from the mud-plastered surface of the roof. But it was as though he bore a charmed life, because not one struck him, and after a moment or two he turned and walked unsteadily to the stairs that led down from the roof and groped his way down and out of sight.

The Mess House was full of servants who had run in from their quarters to take refuge in the Residency, and of Guides who were firing steadily through loopholes cut in the walls and through the wooden shutters, and who did not look round when the wounded Envoy reached the turn of the stairs. Walking unaided into the nearest bedroom, which happened to be Wally's, he told a trembling *masalchi*, whom he found hiding there, to go and fetch the Doctor-Sahib immediately. The youth fled, and a few minutes later Rosie arrived at the double, expecting, from the *masalchi*'s description, to find his Chief dying or dead.

"Only a scratch," said Sir Louis impatiently. "But it's

1115

made my head swim like the very devil. Tie it up like a good fellow and send one of those idiots for William. We've got to get another letter through to the Amir. He's our only hope, and—Oh, there you are, William. No, I'm all right. It's only a flesh wound. Get a pen and paper and write while Kelly patches me up—hurry. Are you ready?"

He began to dictate while William, having snatched pen and paper off the desk in the next room, wrote rapidly, and Rosie cleaned him up and bandaged his head, and stripping off the stained shirt replaced it with one of Wally's.

"Who are we going to get to take it, sir?" asked William, hastily sealing the folded sheet of paper with a wafer. "It isn't going to be easy to send anyone out, now that we're surrounded."

"Ghulam Nabi will take it," said Sir Louis. "Send him up here and I'll talk to him. We shall have to smuggle him out by the back door of the courtyard and pray to God that there is no one out there as yet."

Ghulam Nabi was a native of Kabul and an ex-Guide whose brother was at that time Wordi-Major of the Guides Cavalry in Mardan. He had taken service with the British Mission on their arrival as a chupprassi, and he agreed at once to take Cavagnari-Sahib's letter to the palace. William had accompanied him down to the courtyard and stood by with a revolver while the bolts were withdrawn from a small, unobtrusive and seldom-used door in the back wall of the courtyard, near the tent that housed the baggage.

The wall itself was no thicker than a single mud brick, and behind it lay a narrow street that was part of a network of alleyways and houses, the roofs of the latter already packed with excited spectators, many of whom had armed themselves with ancient jezails and opened fire on the Infidels in the spirit of Jehad. In consequence the street itself was almost deserted, and Ghulam Nabi had slipped through the little door, and crossing to the opposite side where any marksman immediately overhead would find him a difficult target, took to his heels and ran in the direction of the palace in the Upper Bala Hissar.

But even as he vanished round the corner into a connecting alleyway, shouts from behind him and a spatter of shots from above showed that he had been spotted. Feet raced in pursuit, and the door had barely been closed and bolted when fists beat upon it.

Within minutes a crowd had gathered on the far side and were pounding on it with staves and musket butts, and though it was stouter than the main door into the courtyard, there was no knowing how long it would stand up to that sort of treatment. "We shall have to block it off," panted William; and they had done so with everything they could lay their hands on—tables, yakdans, tin-lined boxes full of winter clothing, a sofa and an imported mahogany sideboard, while Ghulam Nabi, having shaken off his pursuers in the maze of alleyways, reached the palace in safety by way of the Shah Bagh, the King's Garden.

But though he had been permitted to deliver Sir Louis' letter, he had not been allowed to return with a reply. Instead, like the previous messenger, he had been ordered to wait in one of the small ante-rooms while the Amir considered what answer he would send. And there he had waited all day.

Out on the plain near Ben-i-Hissar, the grass-cutters and their escort heard the sound of firing, and Kote-Daffadar Fatteh Mohammed, realizing where it came from and well aware of the hatred with which the Herati regiments and the city regarded the foreigners in the Bala Hissar, was uneasily certain that it spelled danger for the British Mission. Hastily rounding up the scattered foragers, he placed all but two of them in the charge of the four Afghan troopers, with instructions to take them at once to the care of the Commander of an Afghan regiment of horse, one Ibrahim Khan who had previously served with the Bengal Cavalry and whose present command was stationed near Ben-i-Hissar. The remaining two, with sowars Akbar Shah and Narain Singh, would return with him to the citadel immediately.

Riding at full gallop it did not take the five men long to come within sight of the south wall of the city and the roofs of the Residency, and the instant they did so any hopes they may have cherished died; for the roof-tops they had been forbidden to appear on for fear of offending the sensibilities of their neighbours were now alive with men, and that sight told them everything. They knew then that it was their own compound that was under attack, and

1117

they spurred towards it hoping to force a passage through the Shah Shahie Gate. But they were too late—the rabble was before them.

Half the city had heard the firing and seen the mutinous regiments running to their cantonments to fetch arms, and the rabble, grasping the situation, had wasted no time. Snatching up any available weapon they had rushed to join the attack on the hated interlopers, and their vanguard was already on the road ahead—racing for the same gate and led by a fakir who waved a green banner and urged them forward with frenzied screams. On their heels came others, many others: the scum of that ancient city, swarming out of every foul-smelling hovel, lane and alleyway, spurred on by the hope of loot and the lust for slaughter, and hastening to be in at the kill.

The Kote-Daffadar reined in savagely, realizing that any attempt to reach the gate first or to cut a path through that murderous horde would be tantamount to committing suicide, and that to seek refuge in the city would be equally fatal. Their best chance—if not their only one—would be to make for the fort commanded by the Amir's father-in-law, Yayhiha Khan; and snapping out a curt order he wrenched his horse round and rode off at a tangent across the plain, his four companions following behind him. But with their goal in sight they were overtaken by the four Afghan troopers, who having placed the grass-cutters in the care of Ibrahim Khan, had followed them with the intention of killing the Sikh sowar, Narain Singh, in which laudable task (for are not the Faithful instructed to slay Unbelievers?) they appeared to think that his four Mussulman comrades would be only too pleased to join. Disillusionment came swiftly . . .

The two grass-cutters were unarmed except for sickles—which can be wicked weapons in a fight—but the three Guides carried cavalry carbines that can be whipped in an instant from the leather buckets that hang from the saddle and levelled with one hand. "Come then, and take him," invited the Kote-Daffadar, the barrel of his weapon aimed at point-blank range at the breast of the spokesman, his finger taut on the trigger.

The Afghans looked at the three carbines and the two knife-edged sickles, and drew back, cursing and scowling, but unwilling to face such daunting odds. They had expected that their fellow-Mussulmans would at least stand aside even if they would not assist in killing the Sikh, and with the odds four to one in their favour would have had no hesitation in attacking a single man armed with a carbine, since he could only fire once and they would have been on him before he could reload. But now they were four against five, and the chances were that if they attempted to rush that group of determined men only one of them would live to get within striking distance, and what chance would that one, armed with a tulwar, have against three sabres and two sickles?

With a final burst of profanity they turned and made for the citadel and the eager hordes that were hurrying to join in the attack upon the Residency, leaving the Kote-Daffadar and his companions to ride on to the fort, where luck had been with them; for a sizable proportion of the garrison were Kazilbashis, men of the Kote-Daffadar and Akbar Shah's own tribe, who had escorted all five to safety in the Murad Khana—their own walled quarter of the city.

Ash, watching from his window, had glimpsed the five tiny figures, dwarfed by distance and trailing a white cloud of dust as they rode back at·a gallop from Ben-i-Hissar, and guessed who they were. But he did not know why they had turned aside until he saw the first of the riff-raff from the city come pouring in from beyond the stables to his right, because the window-bars were set too close to allow him to lean out, so he could not see the Arsenal—or the Kulla-Fi-Arangi either: that empty enclosure on which Wally had hoped to build forage-sheds and servants' quarters so that he could prevent it being used as a way of entering the compound, or in the event of hostilities, occupied by an enemy.

66

Wally had been speaking to the sepoys on the barrack roof when the city *budmarshes* arrived to join the insurgents, and he had seen a number of mutineers, encouraged by these reinforcements, begin to run forward under cover of the fire from the Arsenal towards the Kulla-Fi-Arangi, from where—if they were allowed to occupy it—they would soon be able to make two thirds of the compound untenable. They would have to be dislodged and there was only one way to do it.

Making for the steps that led down in the thickness of the outer wall he pelted down them, raced across the lane into the Residency courtyard, and up to the Envoy's office where he found Cavagnari and William: the Envoy, with his head bandaged, firing through a slit made by breaking out a slat of the shutter, while his orderly acted as loader, taking the empty rifle and handing him a loaded one as fast as he fired, as methodically as though they had been on a duck shoot.

William was kneeling at one of the windows that faced inwards across the courtyard and returning the fire of a group of men on the roof of a house overlooking the barracks, and the room itself was littered with spent shells and full of the reek of black powder.

"Sir," said Wally breathlessly, "they are trying to occupy that Kulla enclosure up on the left, and if they get a foothold there we're done. I believe we could drive them out if we made a charge, only we'll have to do it quickly. If William—"

But Cavagnari had tossed aside the rifle and was already half-way across the room. "Come on, William." He snatched up his sword and revolver and was down the stairs and shouting for Rosie, who was tending a wounded man. "Come on, Kelly, leave that fellow. We've got to chase those bastards out. No, not a rifle, your revolver. And a sword, man—a sword."

Wally, racing ahead of him, collected Jemadar Mehtab Singh and twenty-five men, and explaining the position briefly, watched the sowars stack their carbines and draw their sabres while the sepoys fixed bayonets and two men ran to open the doors in the archway at the far end of the barrack courtyard. "Now we will show those sons of perdition how the Guides fight," said Wally joyously. *"Argi, bhaian. Pah Makhe*—Guides *ki-jai!"**

Ash saw them stream across the lane and into the barracks, where the canvas awnings hid them from his

---

*Forward, brothers. On—Victory to the Guides.

view until they burst out through the archway and into the open, the four Englishmen, Wally leading, running ahead with the Guides racing behind them—the sepoys charging with the bayonet and the sowars with sabre and pistol.

They tore cheering across the bullet-swept compound, the sunlight flashing on their blades; and through all the din and tumult of shouting and rifle fire he could hear Wally singing at the top of his voice: ". . . 'And hearts are brave again and arms are strong. Alleluia!—All-e-lu-ia!' "

"A day for singing hymns," thought Ash, remembering. "Oh God—a day for singing hymns . . ."

Two of the Guides fell before they reached the Cavalry lines, one of them pitching forward on his face as he ran, and recovering almost instantly, rolling aside to avoid being trodden on and limping painfully away to the shelter of the stables; the other checking, to sink slowly to his knees and topple sideways and lie still. The rest swerved to avoid his body and ran on out of Ash's range of view, and he heard the firing stop abruptly and realized that both the enemy and the sepoys on the barracks had been forced to hold their fire for fear of killing their own men.

He did not see the attacking party reach their objective. But Nakshband Khan had done so, for the waste ground of the Kulla-Fi-Arangi lay directly in view of the house where he had taken refuge, and the Sirdar, peering from an upper window of that house, saw them vault over the low mud wall that enclosed it, and charging up the slope, drive the enemy before them: "The Afghans running like sheep before wolves," said the Sirdar, describing it later.

But Ash had seen them come back, walking now, for they brought three wounded men with them, but moving swiftly and confidently like soldiers who have acquitted themselves well and won a victory, though all of them must have known that it could only be a temporary one.

The sowar who had been the first to fall had managed to drag himself back to the barracks with a broken leg, but the second man was dead, and two of his comrades stopped to retrieve his weapon and carry the body into a near-by godown before following the others into the barracks where Wally waited under the arch, his stained sabre in his hand, to see them all safely in before the doors were closed behind them and they returned to the Residency.

The firing that had ceased during the attack on the Kulla-Fi-Arangi broke out again with renewed fury as Kelly hurried back to the wounded, while Cavagnari reeled into the dining-room and called for a glass of water: and when it came remembered that, war or no war, the Mohammedans who had fought with him were keeping the Ramadan fast, and put it down untouched. Jenkyns, the civilian, who had no such scruples, drank thirstily, and wiping his mouth with the back of his hand said hoarsely: "What were our losses, Wally?"

"One dead and four wounded—two of them not too badly. Paras Ram's leg is smashed, but he says that if the Doctor-Sahib will put a splint on it and prop him up at a window, he can still shoot."

"That's the spirit," approved William. "We got off pretty lightly when you think of the damage we must have done. We must have killed at least a dozen, and wounded twice as many more when they were scrambling to get back through the entrance or over the far wall. It was like shooting at a row of haystacks. That ought to hold them for a time."

"With luck, about fifteen minutes," observed Wally.

"Fif—? But Good lord, can't you post a few of your sepoys there to hold it?"

"With around five hundred rifles and muskets able to draw a bead on them from three different directions, and not a shred of cover? Not a chance, I'm afraid."

"Then for God's sake what are we going to do? We can't afford to let them get dug in there."

"As soon as they try it we make another sortie and chase them out again. And when they come back, we do so again—and if necessary, again. It's our only hope, and who knows, if we make it expensive enough for them they may get tired of it before we do."

Wally grinned at him and hurried away, and William said bitterly: "You'd almost think he was enjoying it. Do you suppose he doesn't realize—?"

"He realizes all right," said Cavagnari sombrely, "probably better than any of us. England will lose a first-rate soldier in that boy. Listen to him now—he's cracking jokes with those men out there. Amal Din tells me that the Guides would do anything that Hamilton-Sahib asked of them, because they know that he would never ask them to do anything that he would not do himself. A good boy and a born leader of men. It's a pity . . . Ah well, I'd better get back to my loophole."

He dragged himself from the chair he had slumped into on his return, and stood clutching the back of it, and William said anxiously: "Are you sure you are all right, sir? Oughtn't you to lie down?"

Cavagnari gave a crack of laughter. "My dear boy! At a time like this? If a jawan with a smashed leg is prepared to sit at a window to take pot shots at the enemy provided someone props him up first, I can surely do the same when all I have suffered is a slight crease in my head." He turned away, and followed by William went back up the stairs to take over the positions that had been occupied during their absence by two of the Escort who had been keeping up a steady fire on the mutineers around the Arsenal, and who now moved up to the roof to join a group of the Guides who were firing at the enemy-held house-tops to the north of the compound.

Another and larger group on the roof of the Mess House opposite had turned their attention to the buildings that lay immediately behind the Residency, and Wally, running up to see how they were getting on and to take stock of the situation, saw from that vantage point that his recent estimate of fifteen minutes had erred on the side of generosity. The mutineers were already creeping back again into the Kulla-Fi-Arangi, and there was nothing for it but to launch a second sortie and clear them out again.

Pelting back down the stairs he collected a fresh party of Guides, snatched Rosie away from setting Paras Ram's shattered leg—apologizing in the same breath to the wounded man and assuring him that he would not keep the Doctor-Sahib long—and turned and ran across the courtyard and up the Envoy's staircase to fetch William and Cavagnari. But the sight of the older man's face made him change his mind.

Wally had lost none of his old admiration for his Chief, but he was a soldier first and foremost, and he had no intention of jeopardizing his men unnecessarily. He needed William, but he refused point-blank to allow Cavagnari to accompany them: "No, I'm sorry, sir, but any fool can see you ain't fit and I can't take the risk,"

1123

said Wally brutally. "If you collapsed we'd only have to stop and pick you up, and that could mean throwing away the lives of several valuable men. Besides, it wouldn't do 'em any good to see you fall. Come on, William, we haven't got all day . . ."

Ash and Nakshband Khan, together with several hundred of the enemy, witnessed that second sortie, and seeing that only three of the four Sahibs took part in it, drew their own conclusions. The enemy, being convinced that one of the Sahibs had been slain, were greatly heartened, while Ash and the Sirdar (who had noted the bandage about Cavagnari's head and realized that he had been wounded) were correspondingly dismayed, because they knew that if he were to die it could have a serious effect on the spirits of the beleaguered garrison.

Once again the firing had of necessity slackened off, and once again the waste ground had been cleared. But this time at the cost of two lives and another four men wounded, two of them severely.

"We can't go on like this, Wally," gasped Rosie, wiping the sweat out of his eyes as he directed the stretcher-bearers to carry the injured men into the rooms that he had set aside as hospital wards. "Do you realize that as well as these we've already had over a dozen men killed and God knows how many wounded?"

"I know. But then we've accounted for at least ten of their men to every one of ours—if that's any comfort to you."

"It's none at all—when I'm knowing that those divils out there outnumber us by twenty to one, and that as soon as the lot that left for their cantonments get back here, it'll be nearer fifty or a hundred to one . . . *Accha, Rahman Baksh, mai aunga* (all right, I'm coming)—Look, Wally, isn't it time we tried another letter to that scutt of an Amir? . . . *Accha, accha. Abbi arter* (I'm coming now)."

The doctor hurried away, and Wally handed his sabre to his bearer Pir Buksh, and taking the Havildar with him went over to the barracks to see how things were with the sepoys who were firing from the shelter of the parapets, and if anything could be done to improve the defences of that building against the mass attack that would surely come if the Amir failed to send help. There had still been no reply to the letter that had been taken out by the chuprassi Ghulam Nabi, and now Sir Louis wrote another and sent it by the hand of one of the Mohammedan servants, who volunteered to see if he could not get through by way of the temporarily cleared Kulla-Fi-Arangi, and from there through the King's Garden.

"Keep to the south side of the barracks and seek what cover you can between there and the stables," instructed Sir Louis. "The jawans will distract the enemy with rapid fire until you reach the wall. God be with you."

William sent an orderly to find Wally and tell him what was planned, and to ask for covering fire. And presently the messenger slipped away to the accompaniment of a barrage of shots, and having run the gauntlet of the open stretch of compound between the barracks and the near wall of the Kulla-Fi-Arangi, scrambled over it . . . to be seen no more.

Somewhere between that low mud wall and the palace, the fate that Allah is believed to tie about the neck of all His creatures may have lain in wait for him; or perhaps he had friends or relatives in Kabul or elsewhere in Afghanistan, and decided to take refuge with them in preference to carrying out an appallingly hazardous mission. All that is certain is that his message never reached the palace, and that he himself vanished as completely as though he had been no more than a grain of sand on the autumn wind.

In the barracks Wally and Havildar Hassan, assisted by half-a-dozen sepoys, several syces and some of the Residency servants, had been barricading the doorless stairways that led up in the thickness of the wall on either side of the archway to the long strips of roof that surrounded the canvas-covered central courtyard. This would leave them with only a single staircase—the one at the far end near the door that gave on the Residency lane—but at least, in the event of a mass attack from the front, the men on the roof would not have to worry about the enemy storming up from below when or if Wally's makeshift outer door went down.

Their position was already precarious enough without that, and Rosie had erred in imagining that Wally did not realize the extent of the casualties that the garrison had suffered. Wally not only knew, but had been mentally crossing them off one by one and re-arranging the disposition of his little force, carefully husbanding his resources

1125

and doing everything he could to avoid risking the life of a single man unnecessarily, or allowing their morale to sink. His own was still high, for the sight of a familiar blue and white jar had told him that Ash was somewhere around, and he felt confident that Ash would not be idle.

Ash could be relied on to see that the Amir was informed of the parlous plight of the British Mission, even if every minister and high official in the entire Afghan Government was bent on concealing it. He would manage it somehow, and help would come. It was only a question of holding out long enough and not allowing themselves to be overrun . . . *"Shabash,* Hamzulla! *Ab mazbut hai* . . . That should fox the hosts of Midian," said Wally. "Now if we can—"

He stopped, listening to a new sound: a deep, slowly gathering roar that he had been aware of for the past few minutes as a distant background to the tumult raging beyond the north-western limits of the compound, but that now, unmistakably, was coming nearer. Not *"Dam-i-charya"* this time, but *"Ya-charya"*—the war-cry of the Suni sect of Moslems, rolling towards him with ever-increasing speed and growing louder, nearer and fiercer until even the solid barrack walls seemed to shake to the rhythmic thunder of that rabble-rousing battle cry—

"It is the troops from the cantonments," said Wally. "Bar the doors and get back into the Residency, all of you. Tell Jemadar Jiwand Singh to choose his men and be ready for another sortie. We may have to clear them out of that waste ground again." He turned and made for the stair at the far end of the barrack courtyard, and leaping up it ran forward along the roof above the Mohammedan quarters to the shorter strip of roof above the archway.

Looking over the loopholed parapet and the kneeling sepoys who were firing from behind it, he saw that the high ground by the Arsenal was a solid mass of frenzied humanity that was surging forward, thrust on by the pressure of thousands more behind, towards the flimsy barricades that separated the Mission's compound from the surrounding lanes and houses. The mutinous troops who had run back to their cantonments to fetch arms were back again in force, and not alone—they had brought others with them, the remaining Herati regiments who had been cantoned there, and thousands more *budmarshes* from the city. Even as he watched, they reached the barricades, and trampling them down, overran the cavalry lines and occupied the gutted stables.

In front of them, leading them, ran a wizened figure who waved a green banner and screamed to those behind him to kill the Infidels and show no mercy. Wally did not recognize him, but even at that range Ash did. It was the fakir whom he had seen earlier that day at the pay parade: Buzurg Shah, whom he had also seen on other occasions, calling for a Jehad in the more inflammable sections of the city.

"Destroy them! Root out the Unbelievers. Kill. Kill!" shrieked Fakir Buzurg Shah. "In the name of the Prophet smite and spare not! For the Faith. For the faith. *Maro! Maro*—!*"

"*Ya-charya! Ya-charya!*" yelled his supporters as they fanned out over the compound and began to fire at the heads of the sepoys behind the parapet on the barracks.

Wally saw one of his men fall backwards, shot between the eyes, and a second slump sideways with a bullet through his shoulder, and did not wait for more. It was no longer a question of clearing the waste ground, but of driving the mob out of the compound; and three minutes later Ash saw him lead a third sortie, racing out through the arch of the barracks with William at his side. But this time neither Kelly nor Cavagnari had been with them: Cavagnari because Wally still would not hear of his coming, and Rosie because by now his hands were too full with the care of the wounded to allow him to take part in another charge.,

The fight had been a fiercer one than the two previous sorties into the waste ground, for though once more the marksmen on the rooftops, both inside and outside the compound, were forced to hold their fire for fear of killing their own men, the odds against the garrison had lengthened considerably. The Guides were now outnumbered by fifty to one, and would have been outnumbered by even more if space had permitted, since the forces opposing them included a full three regiments of armed and mutinous soldiers as well as every disaffected, hostile or bloodthirsty citizen in Kabul. But their very numbers

---

*strike; kill.

proved a handicap to the Afghans, for they not only hampered each other, but in the fury and stress of battle no man could be sure that he was not attacking one of his own side, as with the exception of Wally their opponents were not in uniform.

The Guides, on the other hand, knew each other too well to make any such mistake. Moreover, their sepoys carried rifles with fixed bayonets while the two Englishmen and both the Indian officers were armed with service revolvers as well as sabres; and in the murderous hand-to-hand fighting that followed, every revolver shot told, for knowing that there would be no chance to reload, the men of the Escort held their fire until the last possible moment. But the mob had not followed their example, and in the initial rush to reach the Mission compound every Afghan had discharged his musket—many of them into the air—so that now they could only oppose steel to the rifle and revolver bullets of their adversaries.

The Guides had made the best possible use of that tactical error, and followed it up so fiercely with bayonet and sabre that the Afghans gave ground before the fury of their attack. Unable to flee because of the pressure of those at the back, who could not see and urged them forward, hampered by the bodies of the dead and wounded on whom they trod as the fight swayed to and fro, they turned at last and began to attack those behind them; and suddenly panic flared like a fire through dry grass and the mob were turning and clawing at each other in an attempt to escape. Retreat became a rout, and within seconds the compound was clear except for the dead and wounded.

Between them, the little band of Guides had fired exactly thirty-seven shots in the course of that brief engagement, of which no less than four—all heavy bullets fired from Lee-Enfield rifles at a distance of six yards—had smashed straight through the chest of an enemy soldier to kill a second behind him. The remainder had accounted for one man apiece, while a dozen more had been bayonetted and eight cut down by sabres.

The resulting carnage was not pleasant to look upon, for scores of men lay dead on the dusty, blood-spattered ground, while here and there a wounded one strove to drag himself to his knees and crawl like an injured animal towards the kindly shade and out of the glare of the sunlight.

1128

The Guides had exacted a terrible toll and almost evened the odds. But they had paid a high price for that brief victory, one that with their dwindling numbers they could ill afford. Out of the twenty men who had taken part in that third sortie, only fourteen came back; and of these, half-a-dozen were barely able to walk, while none came through entirely unscathed, even though many wounds were no more than superficial.

The sepoys on the barrack roof had covered their return with rifle fire, and others of the Escort waited for them under the archway to bar the doors behind them before following them into the Residency. But this time the victors walked tiredly and there was no elation in their faces, only grimness. The grimness of men who know that the fruits of their hard-won fight cannot be retained, but will have to be fought for again and again—and with ever dwindling resources—or else abandoned to the enemy, which must spell disaster.

They had not been away very long, yet during that brief interval five of the men who had been posted on the roofs of the two Residency houses had been killed and another six wounded; for the makeshift parapets gave them little protection from the marksmen stationed on the higher rooftops of the near-by houses, and the skies seemed to be raining lead. They helped the wounded down to where the desperate Kelly and his solitary Hospital Assistant, Rahman Baksh, were working like men possessed—coatless, and splashed with blood from head to foot like butchers in an abattoir as they tirelessly swabbed, cut and stitched, bandaged, applied tourniquets and administered anaesthetics and opiates in the hopelessly overcrowded rooms where the wounded sat or lay or stood leaning against the walls, their powder-grimed faces drawn with weariness and pain, but making no complaint.

The dead had been treated more cavalierly; there was no time to spare for carrying away corpses, and they had been used instead to reinforce those inadequate parapets. for the Guides were realists. In a crisis such as this they saw no reason why their comrades should not continue to serve their Corps to the end; and the end did not look to be far off, because there were now less than ten men on the two roofs not counting the dead. And the enemy had no shortage of men or ammunition . . .

"Has there been an answer from the Amir yet, sir?"

asked William, stripping off his stained coat as he limped into the office and found his Chief grey-faced from pain, but still firing methodically through the broken shutter.

"No. We must send again. Are you wounded?"

"Only a hack on the shin, sir. Nothing to worry about." William sat down and began to tear his handkerchief into strips and knot them together. "But I'm afraid we lost six men, and several of the others were badly mauled."

"Is young Hamilton all right?" inquired Sir Louis sharply.

"Yes, bar a scratch or two. He's a bonnie fighter, yon laddie. He fought like ten men and sang the whole time. Hymns, of all things. The men seem to like it—I wonder if they've any idea what he's singing about? They probably think it's a war-song . . . which I suppose it is, when you come to think of it: 'The Son of God goes forth to war' and all that—"

"Was that what he was singing?" asked Cavagnari, sighting carefully. He pulled the trigger and gave a grunt of satisfaction: "Got him!"

"No," said William, winding his home-made bandage about a shallow cut on his left hand. "It was something about 'charging for the God of Battle and putting the foe to rout'—" He used his teeth to help him pull the knot tight, and resuming his coat said: "Do you want me to write another letter, sir?"

"Yes. Make it short. And tell that damned scoundrel that if he lets us die he's done for, as the Sirkar will send an army to take over his country and—No, better not say that. Just urge the fellow in the name of hospitality and honour to come to our assistance before we are all murdered. Tell him our case is desperate."

William sat down to write again to the Amir, while Cavagnari sent a servant to inquire if there was anyone with a reasonable knowledge of the Bala Hissar who was prepared to run the risk of trying to take a letter to the palace—other than a soldier, who could not be spared. The risk was a grave one, for, with the back door barricaded, every rooftop within sight occupied by enemy sharpshooters, and the approaches to the compound held by the mob, the chances of anyone being able to win through were negligible. Yet William had barely finished writing when the servant returned with one of the office clerks, an elderly quiet-voiced Hindu with relatives in Kabul, who knew his way about the Bala Hissar, and possessing the Hindu indifference to death, had volunteered to make the attempt.

William went down with him to the courtyard while Wally sent a man over to the barracks and two more up to the roofs of the Residency, to tell the jawans there to do what they could to draw the fire of the enemy while the messenger made his attempt.

The Hindu had been helped over the barricade that blocked the southern end of the lane between the Residency and the barracks, and turning right, hurried forward, hugging the windowless back wall of the Mohammedan quarters, where he was temporarily protected from the enemy on the housetops to the north. But once past the barrack block he had to run the gauntlet of the open ground; and already a number of the enemy had crept back into the compound to take cover in the cavalry lines and behind the low mud walls that enclosed the pickets. A score of these, led by the fakir, rushed out to intercept him before he could reach the Kulla-Fi-Arangi, while others cut off his retreat. And though he held up the letter, calling out to them that he was unarmed and bore a message to their Amir, they fell upon him with knives and tulwars, slashing, stabbing and literally hacking the defenceless man to pieces in full view of the garrison.

The brutal murder did not go unavenged, for the sepoys on the barrack roof leapt to their feet and fired volley after volley at the killers, and Wally, who had watched from the roof of the Mess House, sent Jemadar Jiwand Singh and twenty Guides to drive them out of the compound. It was the fourth sortie that the Guides had launched that morning, and once again they drove the Afghans back and took a terrible revenge for the mangled thing that still clutched in one severed hand a blood-soaked piece of paper that implored the help of the useless craven who sat upon the throne of Afghanistan.

Wally had seen many ugly sights during the past year, and thought himself immune from them. But the savage and barbaric dismembering of the unfortunate Hindu—who as an unarmed messenger carrying a letter to the ruler of Afghanistan should have been protected by his office—had turned his stomach, and he had run down from the roof with the intention of leading that charge himself. But on reaching the courtyard he had been greeted by the news that the enemy in the rear, having failed to break down the small door in the back wall of the Residency courtyard, were now sapping the wall itself and had already broken through in two places.

The threat was too grave to be ignored, so sending the Jemadar to lead the sortie instead, he turned to deal with this new threat. It had been bad enough to have to fend off attacks from their front and their right flank while being harassed by fire from the surrounding housetops; but if the enemy were to break through from the rear and pour in troops at ground level, the garrison might find themselves forced to abandon the Residency, together with their wounded, and retreat to the barracks as the only position left to them. An untenable position at that, as the barracks would be impossible to hold once the Residency was lost, because the enemy would then be able to concentrate their fire on it from a range of a few yards; and once penned inside it there would be no way of seeing across the compound or gaining any idea of what the Afghans were doing.

The rear wall was only too easy to breach as it was woefully thin, and the men who filled the narrow street behind it were hacking at it in perfect safety, for they could not be fired on except from the roofs of the Residency houses—which entailed standing up on the curtain wall of the Envoy's House or the extreme edge of the Mess House, and aiming directly downwards: and since the first three jawans to attempt this were killed instantly by enemy marksmen crouching behind the parapets of rooftops on the opposite side of the street, it was not tried again.

The sappers below had been at work for some time before the danger was spotted, for the continuous crackle of firing, allied to the roar of a mob whose rage against the Infidel and inbred lust for fighting had been inflamed by the long fast of Ramadan, had masked the sounds of pick-axes from the men inside the Residency. The existence of this new and deadly threat had only been realized when a group of servants, crouching in a ground-floor room of the Envoy's House, saw a hole appear near the skirting. One of them had rushed upstairs to give the alarm, and implored the Envoy to leave his office and go over to the other house.

"*Huzoor*, if these *shaitans* break through below, you will be trapped. And then what shall become of us? You are our father and our mother, and if we lose you, we are lost—we are all lost!" yammered the terrified man, beating his head against the floor.

"*Be-wakufi!*" snapped Cavagnari angrily. "Stand up, thou. Weeping will not save your lives, but work may do so. Come on, William—and you others too—they'll need help down there."

He made for the stairs, followed by William and the two jawans who had been firing through loopholes in the shutters, the wailing servant bringing up the rear. But Wally, appraising his Chief's grey face and unfocused eyes and realizing that this time he could not refuse his help, managed to persuade him that he would be far better employed as a sniper on the top floor of the Mess House, firing through a loophole at the mob surrounding the Arsenal to discourage them from invading the compound again.

Cavagnari had not demurred. He was beginning to suffer from the effects of concussion, and he did not suspect that Lieutenant Hamilton's real reason for asking him to man that particular position was that the top floor of the Mess House seemed to Wally a far safer place than the crowded courtyard, and he meant to ensure that his wounded chief ran no unnecessary risks.

As though to prove that his caution was justified, he had no sooner escorted Sir Louis from the courtyard than a musket ball was fired into it from close range and at knee level. The shot had wounded two men, and created considerable confusion among the remainder as it appeared to have come from inside the tent that had contained the ammunition; and it was only when a second and third shot followed that the garrison realized that the enemy's sappers must have broken through the wall behind the empty tent, and were firing at them blindly from the street behind the Residency. The courtyard cleared with magical swiftness, and William detailed Naik Mehr Dil and sepoys Hassan Gul and Udin Singh to block the hole, which could not be reached until the tent came down.

The three jawans had managed to dismantle it and

push the heavy folds of canvas into the breach with the aid of tent poles, after which they had reinforced this inadequate barricade with a large tin-lined box containing their commanding Officer's winter underwear and sheepskin poshteen, and a massive wood and leather screen from the dining-room. But in the process the Naik was shot in the arm, so as soon as the work was finished Hassan Gul took the wounded man into the Mess House to find the Doctor-Sahib, for Mehr Dil's arm hung useless, and blood was pouring from under the waistcloth that he had tied above the wound as a tourniquet in the hope of checking the flow.

They found the ground-floor rooms full of dead, wounded and dying men, but there was no sign of the Doctor-Sahib, and his exhausted hospital assistant, Rahman Baksh, looking up briefly from tying a pad made from a towel over a hole in a sepoy's thigh, said that the Sahib had been called upstairs and that Hassan Gul had better take the Naik up there—there was no room down here for any more wounded.

The two jawans climbed the stairs in search of the doctor, and peering in through an open doorway saw him leaning over Sir Louis, who was lying on a bed with his knees drawn up and one hand to his head. The sight did not dismay them, since everyone knew that the "Burra-Sahib" had been wounded in the head early on in the siege; and supposing him to be suffering from the after-effects of that wound (and being unwilling to call the doctor away from such an exalted patient) they turned back and went below again to wait until he should come down.

But Sir Louis had not collapsed from concussion. He had been hit again: this time in the stomach and by a bullet that had smashed through the wooden shutter into the room in which he had been standing, a bullet fired from one of the English-made rifles that a previous Viceroy, Lord Mayo, had presented to Yakoub Khan's father, Shere Ali, as a good-will gift from the British Government . . .

Sir Louis had managed to reach the bed, and the sowar who had been firing through a loophole to one side of the window had run down to fetch Surgeon-Major Kelly. But there was nothing that Rosie could do beyond giving him water to drink—for he was very thirsty—and something to deaden the pain. And hoping that the end would come quickly.

He could not even stay with him, for there were too many others who needed his help, some of whom could be patched up sufficiently to continue fighting. Nor was there any point in letting it be known that Cavagnari-Sahib was mortally wounded, since such news could only serve to take the heart out of everyone in the garrison, and the assault upon their spirits was already severe enough without that, the rabble in the street and on the house-tops immediately behind it having begun to call upon their fellow-Mussulmans to join them, exhorting them to slay the four Sahibs and help themselves to the treasure in the Residency . . .

"Kill the Unbelievers and join us!" urged the stentorian voices of unseen men who were sapping the flimsy, mud-brick wall. "We have no quarrel with you. You are our brothers and we wish you no harm. Only give up the *Angrezis* to us and you will all go free. Join us—join us!"

"Thank God for young Wally," thought Rosie, listening to that continual stream of exhortations. "If it wasn't for him, some of our fellows might be tempted to do just that and save their own skins." But Wally seemed to know just how to counter those shouted lures and keep up the spirits of the garrison, not only of his own jawans but of the countless non-combatants who had taken refuge in the Residency, both servants and clerical staff. He also appeared to have mastered the art of being in half-a-dozen places at once—one moment on the roof of one or other of the two houses, the next over at the barracks or in the courtyard, and the third in the rooms in which the wounded and dying lay—praising, encouraging, comforting; rallying the faint-hearted, cracking jokes, singing as he raced up the stairs to hearten the dwindling band of Guides who held out on the roof, or over to the barracks to encourage those who knelt firing at the insurgents from behind the inadequate shelter of the parapets.

Rosie looked down at the dying Envoy on the bed, and thought: "When he is gone, the whole responsibility for the defence of this rat-trap is going to fall on young Wally's shoulders . . . it's there now. Well, it couldn't be on better ones." He turned and went out, shutting the door behind him and calling one of the servants to sit in front of it and allow no one in to the room, as the Burra-Sahib's head was paining him and he must be allowed to rest.

The room was an inner one and comparatively cool, but as Rosie left it the heat and stench outside met him like a blow, for by now the sun was overhead and there was little shade to be found in the enclosed courtyard . . . and none at all for the Guides on the rooftops. The freshness of the early morning had vanished long ago, and now the hot air reeked of sulphur and black powder, while from the ground-floor rooms of both houses rose the sickening, all-pervading stench of spilt blood and iodoform—and other, uglier smells that Rosie knew would get worse as the day advanced.

"We shall be out of drugs soon," he thought, "and bandages and lint. And men . . ." He glanced back over his shoulder at the closed door behind him and lifting his hand in a half-unconscious gesture of salute, turned and went back down the stairs to the stifling heat and stench of the rooms below, where buzzing clouds of flies added to the torments of the uncomplaining wounded.

Many of the mutineers had already crept back to the compound to take cover again in the stables, and behind the numerous mud walls in which they were now hacking loopholes so that they could fire at the barracks and the Residency, but Wally no longer had enough men to attempt another sortie against them. Between the enemy in the compound and the ever-increasing numbers on the surrounding house-tops, his inadequate defences were subjected to such a blizzard of fire that it was a wonder to him that anyone in the garrison still survived. Yet survive they did, though their numbers were shrinking rapidly. The fact that the enemy had suffered even more severely gave him no consolation, knowing as he did that they had inexhaustible reserves to draw on, and that however many times the Guides drove them back and however many they killed, a hundred others would spring up like the dragon's teeth to replace them. But there was no replacement for the dead and wounded in the Residency. And still no word from the palace, or any sign of help . . .

He had been organizing counter-measures against the sappers on the far side of the courtyard wall, when a breathless sowar ran down the three flights of stairs from the Mess House roof and panted out that the mob in the street had fetched ladders and were thrusting them out laterally from the houses on the far side, to form bridges across which they were clambering like monkeys. Some had already reached the roof and what were the defenders to do? They could not hold out against the numbers who were getting across.

"Tell them to retreat down the stairs," directed Wally urgently—"but slowly, so that the Afghans will follow." The man fled back, and Wally sent a similar message to the Guides on the roof of the Envoy's House, and calling to Jemadar Mehtab Singh to follow him with every jawan who could be spared, ran for the roof.

The Guides had managed to thrust off the first two ladders and send them hurtling down on the heads of the crowd below. But there had been others—half-a-dozen at least—and though the first Afghans to reach the roof had fallen, shot at point blank range, it had been impossible to stem the tide of those who scrambled across behind them, and the survivors of the little band of Guides retreated to the stairwell and descended, a step at a time.

Wally met them on the top landing with reinforcements at his back, and though he held a loaded revolver he did not fire it, but waved them on downward, issuing terse instructions that were barely audible above the yells of the Afghans, who, seeing them in retreat, tore after them and came leaping down the stairs brandishing their tulwars and jostling each other in their haste. And still the Guides retreated, stumbling ahead of them in apparent disorder and looking back over their shoulders as they went . . .

"Now!" yelled Wally, leaping onto a cane stool that stood outside his bedroom door. *"Maro!"* And as the Guides turned in the narrow hallway and fell upon the leading Afghans, he fired over their heads at those who were crowding down behind them and who could not turn because of the pressure of others treading on their heels.

Even a poor shot would have found it difficult to miss his mark at that range, and Wally was anything but a poor shot. Within six seconds half-a-dozen Afghans on the steep flight of stairs dropped forward with a bullet in their brains, and as many fell headlong over the bodies and came cascading down like a flock of sheep at a bank, to be cut down by the sabres and bayonets of the Guides.

Ambrose Kelly had heard the noise of the fighting, and realizing that the enemy must have broken into the Mess House, he abandoned his scalpel in favour of a revolver and dashed upstairs—only to be swept backwards by a mass of struggling men who stabbed and hacked and wrestled with each other (there was little room for sword-play) or used their carbines and rifles as clubs, there being no time to reload or, for that matter, for anyone in Rosie's position to use a revolver. But Wally, standing head and shoulders above the scrum, caught sight of him, and realizing that he dare not risk a shot into the demented mêlée, took a flying leap from the stool, snatched the weapon from him, and regaining his vantage point, used it himself to excellent effect.

The fusillade of shots, the shambles on the stair and the uproar and confusion of the fight below made the rear ranks of the invaders suddenly aware that disaster had overtaken their leaders. They checked at the top of the stairs and some of them, losing their heads, fired wildly down at the murderous scrimmage below while others scrambled back and made no further attempt to invade the Residency from above. But of their comrades who had rushed so boldly down the steep stairway, not one came back.

"Come on, Rosie," shouted Wally breathlessly, tossing back the empty revolver and hurriedly re-loading his own: "they're bolting. Now's our chance to clear 'em off the roof."

He turned to Hassan Gul, who leant against the wall of the landing panting from his exertions, and told him to call the others together and they would charge up the stairs and clear the roof. But the sepoy only shook his head and said hoarsely: "We cannot do it, Sahib. There are too few of us . . . Jemadar Mehtab Singh is dead, and Havildar Karak Singh also . . . they were killed in the fighting on the stairs . . . And of those who were on the roof, only two remain. I do not know how many there may still be in the other house, but here there are only seven left . . ."

Seven. Only seven left to hold the three floors of that tall, mud and plaster rat-trap that was pock-marked with bullet holes and crammed with wounded men.

"Then we must block off the staircase," said Wally.

"With what?" asked Rosie tiredly. "We've already used almost everything we could lay our hands on to make barricades. Even the doors."

"There's this one—" Wally turned towards it, but the doctor caught his arm and said sharply: "No! Leave it, Wally. Let him be."

"Who? Who is in there? Oh, you mean the Chief. He won't mind. He's only—" He stopped abruptly, staring at Rosie with a sudden horrified comprehension. "Do you mean, it's serious? But—but it was only a head wound. It couldn't . . ."

"He was shot in the stomach not long ago. There wasn't anything I could do except give him as much opium as I could spare and let him die in peace."

"*Peace*," said Wally savagely. "What sort of peace could he possibly die in, unless . . ."

He stopped and his face changed. Then, jerking his arm free, he turned the handle and went into the shadowed room where the only light came through the bullet-splintered slats of the shutters and the rough loopholes that had been hacked through those lath and plaster walls that still bore the scrawled names of the Russians who had been the last—and luckier—guests of an Amir of Afghanistan.

The closed door had kept out the heat that filled the courtyard and beat down upon the whole compound, but it could not keep out the flies that circled and settled in buzzing droves, or the sounds of battle. And here too there was the same choking smell of blood and black powder.

The man on the bed still lay in the same position and, incredibly, he was still alive. He did not move his head, but Rosie, following Wally into the room and shutting the door behind him, saw his eyes turn slowly towards them and thought, "He won't know us. He's too far gone: and too drugged."

The dying man's gaze was blank and it seemed that the movement of those clouded eyes was no more than a reflex action. Then of a sudden intelligence returned to them as with a gigantic effort of will, Louis Cavagnari forced his conscious mind to drag itself back from the darkness that was closing in on it, and summoning the last shred of his strength, spoke in a harsh croak:

1139

"Hullo, Walter. Are we . . . ?"

His breath failed him, but Wally answered the unspoken question:

"Fine, sir. I came to tell you that the Amir has sent two Kazilbashi regiments to our assistance, and the mob are already on the run. I'm thinking it won't be any time now before the place is cleared of them, so you don't have to worry, sir. You can have a rest now, for we've got them licked."

"Good boy," said Sir Louis in a clear, strong voice. A trace of colour returned to his ash-white face and he tried to smile, but a sharp spasm of pain caught him unaware and turned it to a grimace. Once again he fought for breath, and Wally leaned down to catch the words he was struggling to say:

"The . . . Amir," whispered Sir Louis: ". . . glad to know . . . not wrong about him . . . after all. We shall be . . . all right now. Tell William . . . send thanks and . . . telegraph Viceroy. Tell . . . tell my—wife—"

The hunched figure jerked convulsively and was still.

After a moment or two Wally straightened up slowly and became aware once more of the maddening drone of flies and the ceaseless surf-like roar of the mob, which together formed a background for the sharp crackle of musketry and rifle fire and the thwack of bullets striking the walls outside.

"He was a great man," said Rosie quietly.

"A wonderful one. That's why I—we couldn't let him die thinking that he . . ."

"No," said Rosie. "Be easy, Wally, the Lord will forgive you the lie."

"Yes. But *he'll* know by now that it was a lie."

"Where he is, that won't matter."

"No, that's true. I wish—"

A musket ball smashed into one of the shutters and sent a shower of splinters across the floor, and Wally turned and walked quickly out of the room, not seeing where he was going because his eyes were full of tears.

Rosie paused for a moment to cover the quiet face, and following more slowly, found him already at work arranging to block the way to the roof with the only material available: the bodies and the broken weapons—tulwars, muskets and jezails—of the Afghans who had been killed on the stairs.

"We may as well make them useful," said Wally grimly as he helped to pile the corpses one upon the other, wedging them into place with cross-bars made from the long-barrelled jezails, and constructing an effective *chevaux-de-frise* from the razor-sharp blades of tulwars and Afghan knifes from which the hilts had first been removed. "I don't suppose it will hold them up for long, but it's the best we can do; there isn't anything else. I must see William and find out how many of our fellows are over in the other house. Now *suno* (listen), Khairulla"—he turned to one of the sowars—"you and one other remain here and prevent the enemy from removing those bodies. But do not expend more ammunition than you need. A shot or two should be enough."

He left them and went down the stairs to run the gauntlet of the open courtyard and break the news to William that Sir Louis was dead.

"He was always lucky," observed William quietly.

The Secretary's face, like Wally's—like all their faces—was a sweat-streaked mask of blood and dust and black powder. But his eyes were as quiet as his voice, and though he had been firing and fighting without intermission for hours now, he still looked what he was: a civilian and a man of peace. He said: "How much longer do you suppose we can hold out, Wally? They keep tunnelling through like moles, you know. As fast as we block up one hole they make another. It's been fairly easy to deal with, because now we know what they're at, whenever we see a bit of plaster fall out we stand clear and then empty a shot-gun into the hole the minute it gets big enough. They don't fancy that. But it needs a lot of men to watch the whole length of the wall in the courtyard as well as inside both houses. I don't know how many you've got, but there are less than a dozen of your chaps left over here. And not so many more than that in the courtyard, I imagine."

"Fourteen," confirmed Wally briefly. "I've just checked. Abdulla, my bugler, says he thinks there are still between fifteen and twenty over in the barracks, and with seven in the Mess House—"

"Seven!" gasped William. "But I thought—What's happened?"

"Ladders. Didn't you notice? Those bastards behind us got hold of ladders and managed to get onto the roof and drive our fellows off it. They got into the house and gave us a bad few minutes, but we got rid of them. For the time being, anyway."

"I didn't know," said William numbly. "But if they're on the roof that means we're surrounded."

"I'm afraid so. What we've got to do now is to immobilize that gang on the Mess House, by stationing a couple of chaps with shot-guns by the inner windows of the Chief's office to blaze off the moment any scutt up there shows the tip of his nose. They may have chased us off it, but it won't do them any good if they have to huddle on their stomachs in the furthest corner of it. You'd better stay down here and deal with the lot who are trying to dig through the wall, while I—" he stopped, and tilting his chin, sniffed the tainted air and said uneasily: "Can you smell smoke?"

"Yes, it's coming from the street at the back. We've been getting a whiff of it through the holes those rats have been making. I imagine there must be a fire in one of their houses. Not surprising when you think of the number of archaic muzzle-loaders that are being loosed off in every direction."

"As long as it stays on the other side of the wall," said Wally, and was turning to leave when William stopped him.

"Look, Wally, I think we ought to try again to see if we can't get a message through to the Amir. He can't have got any of the others. I won't believe that if he knew how serious things were with us he wouldn't do something to help. We've got to find someone to take another letter."

They had found someone, and this time the messenger had won through, posing as one of the enemy. Dressed in blood-stained garments, with an artistic bandage about his head, he had actually succeeded in delivering William's letter. But the confusion that he found at the palace was far worse than when Ghulam Nabi (who still waited anxiously in an ante-room) had brought that second letter from Sir Louis, hours ago. This latest messenger was also told to wait for a reply: but no reply was ever given him, for by now the Amir had become convinced that when the mobs from the city had dealt with the British Mission, they would turn on him for having permitted the Infidels to come to Kabul, and make him and his family pay for it with their lives:

"They will kill me," wailed the Amir to the persistent mullahs, who had finally been granted another audience. "They will kill us all."

Once again the head Mullah had pleaded with him to save his guests and urged him to order his artillery to fire on the mob. And once again the Amir had refused, insisting hysterically that if he should do so the mob would instantly attack the palace and murder him.

At long last, shamed into action by their reproaches, he summoned his eight-year-old son, Yahya Khan, and setting the little boy on a horse, sent him out accompanied only by a handful of Sirdars and his tutor—the latter carrying a copy of the Koran held high above his head where all could see it—to implore that maddened mob, in the name of God and His Prophet, to sheathe their weapons and return to their homes.

But the mob that had howled so fervently for the blood of the Unbelievers was not to be turned from its savage sport by the mere sight of the Holy Book—or the scared face of a child, heir to Afghanistan or no. The trembling tutor was pulled from his saddle and the Koran wrenched from his hands to be flung on the ground and kicked and trampled upon, while the mob shrieked insults and threats at the hapless ambassadors, jostling and clawing at them until they turned tail and fled back to the palace in fear of their lives.

But there was still one Afghan who did not fear the mob.

The indomitable Commander-in-Chief, Daud Shah, wounded as he was, left his bed, and summoning a few of his faithful troopers, rode out to face the scum of the city with as much courage as he had faced the mutineers of the Ardal Regiment earlier that same day. But the mob cared as little for the authority of the army as it had for the sacred Book of its loudly proclaimed faith. Its interest was concentrated on killing and loot, and it turned on the valiant General like a pack of snarling pariah-dogs attacking a cat; and like a wild cat he fought back with teeth and claws.

For a brief space he and his troopers managed to hold them off, but the odds were too great. He was dragged from his horse, and once on the ground, the mob closed in, kicking and stoning him. Only the intervention of a handful of his soldiers, who had seen him ride out and who now charged to the rescue, laying about them with such fury that they drove the mob back, saved the battered man and his hopelessly outnumbered troopers from death. But they had had no option but to withdraw, and supporting their wounded Commander-in-Chief they limped back to safety.

"We can do no more," said the watching mullahs, and recognizing at last the fruitlessness of human intervention, they left the palace and returned to their mosques to pray instead for Allah's.

67

It seemed to Ash, as he raged to and fro racking his brains for a way of escape, that he had been trapped in this small, stifling cell for a lifetime . . . Could time have moved so slowly for the Guides who had been fighting all through that hot, interminable morning and on into the afternoon without a moment's respite, or were they too hard pressed to take account of it, unaware of its passing because they knew that for them each breath they drew could be the last one, and knowing it lived only for the moment, and that by the grace of God?

There must be *some* way of getting out . . . there *must* be.

Hours ago he had considered the possibility of hacking his way out through the mud ceiling between the joists, until the thud of feet on the hard *mutti* roof overhead warned him that there were men up there, a great many of them judging by the clamour of voices and the vicious crackle of muskets—as many as there were on every house-top and at every window within his range of vision, not to mention those that he could not see.

After that he had turned his attention to the floor. It should be comparatively easy to break through it, since like all the floors in the building it consisted of pine-wood planks supported on heavy crossbeams and plastered over with a mixture of mud and straw; and had it not been only too evident that the room below was already occupied by the enemy, who were firing out of the window immediately under his own, the long Afghan knife he carried with him would have made short work of the dried mud, and enabled him to pry loose a plank so that he could wrench up one or more neighbouring ones. But where the window was concerned the knife was useless.

Ash had spent some time on the window, and had actually made a rope so that he would be able to lower himself from it, using knotted strips torn from the cotton sheeting that covered the platform on which a scribe sat cross-legged at work. But the bars had defeated him. And though the inner walls on either side of him were reasonably thin (in contrast to the one with the door in it) even if he were to break a hole through one or other it would not help him, because the room on his right was a window-less store room crammed to the roof with old files, while the one on the left contained the Munshi's library, and both were always kept locked.

Despite this knowledge, he had wasted a considerable amount of time and energy on burrowing through into the latter, in the hope that either the window-bars or the lock in the library might prove to be flimsier than his own. But when at last he managed to kick and hack and scrape a hole large enough to squeeze through, it was only to discover that the lock was of the same pattern, while the window (besides being as stoutly barred) was even smaller than the one in his own room.

Ash wriggled back again and resumed his vigil, watching and listening, hoping against hope, and praying for a miracle.

He had seen each of the four sorties, and though unlike the Sirdar he had not been able to see the first of the two charges that drove the mutineers out of the waste ground of the Kulla-Fi-Arangi, he had seen the whole of the third engagement. And it was while watching it that he had remembered belatedly that he not only carried a pistol, but had a service revolver and fifty rounds of ammunition hidden away in one of the numerous tin boxes that were stacked against the walls.

If he could not go down and fight with the Guides in the compound below, at least he could still do something to help them, and hastily removing the revolver from its hiding place, he levelled it from the window only to realize afresh why both sides had ceased firing. While the

1145

fight lasted and the protagonists were embroiled in a hand-to-hand struggle, no one could be certain whom a bullet or a musket ball might strike, and he too must hold his fire. Even when the enemy broke and ran, he resisted the temptation to speed them on their way because the range was too great to allow him to be certain of hitting his mark and his supply of ammunition was limited and too valuable to be wasted.

The twenty-three rounds he had subsequently expended during the course of that morning had certainly not been wasted, nor had there been any risk of the shots being traced to his window. There being too much lead flying round for anyone to be certain of such a thing. Five had accounted for as many enemy snipers, who had been firing from other and less closely barred windows lower down and further to the right and been incautious enough to lean well out in order to fire at the sepoys holding the barrack roof. A further fourteen had caused several deaths and considerable damage among the mob who had murdered the Hindu clerk, while the last four had disposed of four mutineers who during the sortie led by Jemadar Jiwand Singh had attempted, under cover of the fighting, to crawl towards the barracks in the lee of the low boundary wall that divided the Munshi's house from the British Mission's compound.

Koda Dad Khan would have approved his pupils' performance, for it had been good shooting. But as the range of a revolver is small, Ash's field of fire was very limited, and he knew that against the enormous numbers that the enemy were throwing against the Residency, any assistance that he could give was at best derisory.

The compound lay stretched out below him like a brightly lit stage seen from the royal box of a theatre, and had he been able to exchange the service revolver for a rifle, or even a shot-gun, he could have helped to reduce the fire that was being directed at the barracks and the Residency from every house-top within a radius of three or four hundred yards. But as it was he could do almost nothing. He could only watch in an agony of fear and frustration as the enemy bored loopholes in the compound wall that enabled them to fire at the garrison in complete security, while members of the mob that had been routed and driven from the compound by that last furious charge began to steal back again, at first by twos and threes, and then, getting bolder, by tens and twenties until at length several hundred had taken cover in the gutted stables and deserted servants' quarters, and behind the maze of crumbling walls.

It was, thought Ash, like watching a spring tide crawling in across mud flats on a windless day, creeping inexorably forward to drown the land; except that the rising of that human tide was not silent, but accompanied by shots and screams and yelling voices that together fused into a continuous roar of sound: a roar that rose and fell as monotonously as storm waves crashing on a pebble beach. *Ya-charya! Ya-charya!* Slay the Infidels. Kill! Kill!—*Maro! Maro!*

Yet gradually, as the day wore on and throats became hoarse from continual shouting and parched with dust and smoke and the choking fumes of black powder, the war cries and the yelling began to die down, and with the voice of the mob reduced to a menacing growl, the sharp crackle of fire-arms became magnified—as did the shrill exhortations of the Fakir Buzurg Shah, who continued to harangue his followers with unflagging zeal; calling upon the Faithful to smite and spare not, and reminding them that Paradise awaited all who died that day.

Ash would have given much to assist the Fakir to achieve this goal himself, and he waited hopefully for the man to come within range. But that fanatical rabble-rouser appeared to be in no hurry to enter Paradise, for he stood well back among the mob on the far side of the stables, safely out of sight of the Guides who manned the parapets of the barracks and the windows of the Residency—and far beyond the reach of Ash's revolver; though not, unfortunately, out of hearing. His high-pitched litany of Hate had the carrying quality of a hunting horn, and his repetitive shrieks of "Kill! Kill! Kill!" rasped at Ash's taut nerves and almost drove him to close the heavy wooden shutters in order to escape from that sound.

He had actually been on the verge of doing so—despite the fact that it meant shutting out the daylight and his view of the compound—when another sound stopped him: one that he was first aware of only as a distant murmur, but that as he listened grew in volume until it was identifiable as cheering . . . The mob were acclaiming someone or something, and as the vociferous applause came steadily nearer and louder until it drowned both the ravings of the Fakir and the din of firing, Ash's heart leapt, for the thought flashed into his mind that the Amir had sent the Kazilbashi Regiments to the relief of the beleaguered British Mission after all.

But the hope was no sooner born than he saw the Fakir and the rabble surrounding him begin to leap and yell and throw up their arms in frenzied welcome, and knew that this was no relieving force that was being hailed, but some form of enemy reinforcements, probably a fresh contingent of mutinous troops from the cantonments, thought Ash.

He did not see the guns that were being man-handled by scores of men through the narrow approaches by the Arsenal until both were well clear of the surrounding buildings and almost level with the cavalry lines. But the Guides on the barrack roof had seen them as they were manoeuvered through a breach in the mud wall and into the compound, and while a sepoy ran to tell Hamilton-Sahib of this new danger, the rest turned their fire on the scores of Afghans who were dragging and pushing the two guns towards the barracks.

The sepoy's news had spread through the Residency with lightning swiftness. But it is one of the advantages of military life that in times of crisis the issues are apt to be clearly defined, and a soldier is often faced with a simple choice: fight or die. No one had needed to wait for orders, and by the time Wally and the men who had been with him on the upper floor of the Envoy's House reached the courtyard, William and every active sepoy and sowar in the Residency had already assembled there.

All that was necessary was to tell the jawan who had brought the news to warn his companions to concentrate their fire on the enemy beyond the perimeter, and to send two men ahead to unbar the far doors that closed off the archway from the barrack courtyard. But even as they ran across the lane, both guns fired almost simultaneously. The men staggered as the ground rocked to the deafening crash of the double explosion, but reeled on, coughing and choking, through an inferno of smoke and flying debris and the reek of saltpetre.

The echoes of that thunderous sound reverberated around the compound and beat against the furthest walls of the Bala Hissar, sending flocks of crows flapping and cawing above the roofs of the palace, and drawing a

1148

howl of triumph from the mob as they saw the shells explode against the corner of the barrack block. But unlike the two buildings in the Residency, the outer walls of the barracks were not lath and plaster but built of mud bricks to a thickness of more than six feet, while the two corners at the western end were further protected by the fact that each contained a stone stairway to the roof.

The shells had therefore done little damage to the men behind the parapets, who, though momentarily blinded by smoke and debris and deafened by the noise, obeyed their orders, and lifting their sights continued to fire at the enemy as Wally and William, with twenty-one Guides, emerged from the archway below them and raced towards the guns.

The fight was a brief one, for the mutineers who had dragged the guns into position and fired them were exhausted by their efforts, while the rabble from the city had no taste for facing trained soldiers at close quarters, and fled at the sight of them. After a fierce ten minutes the mutineers had followed their example, abandoning the guns and leaving behind them more than a score of dead and wounded.

The cost to the Guides had been two men killed and four wounded, yet that by comparison was a far higher figure for a force whose numbers were being whittled down with frightening speed, and though they had captured the guns—and with them the shells that had been brought down from the Arsenal and abandoned when the amateur gunners fled—that too proved to be a hollow victory. For the guns were too heavy and the distance to the barracks too great; and now scores of enemy rifles and muskets were opening fire again . . .

Despite that storm of bullets the Guides had struggled desperately to pull their booty back, harnessing themselves to the ropes and straining to drag the unwieldy things over the dusty, stony ground. But it was soon clear that the task was beyond them: it would take too long, and to persist could only result in the entire party being killed.

They took the shells, though that was small comfort as it was obvious that further supplies would soon be hurried down from the Arsenal; but they could not even put the guns out of action, for in the heat and urgency of the moment one small but vital thing had slipped Wally's mind—the fact that though he alone among his men had

1149

been in uniform when the mutineers from the pay parade had invaded the compound, he had not been wearing his cross-belt, and had not thought to put it on since, or had time to do so. But a cross-belt carries two small items that are not intended for ornament but strictly for use: the "pickers" that can be used, among other things, for spiking guns.

"It's my own fault," said Wally bitterly. "I ought to have thought. If we'd even had a *nail*—anything. I'd clean forgotten we weren't properly dressed. Well, the only thing for it is to concentrate all our fire on those bloody guns and see that no one is able to re-load them again."

The doors inside the archway had been closed and barred again behind them, and the survivors slaked their thirst from chattis of cold water that had been brought up from the hammam: Mussulmans as well as Unbelievers, for the regimental Mulvi had declared this to be a time of war, and at such times it is permissible for soldiers engaged in battle to break the fast of Ramadan.

Having drunk they had returned to the Residency which they had left barely a quarter of an hour ago—only to find it full of smoke, for the enemy behind the wall had not been idle while they were gone. More ladders had been pushed out from house-tops on the far side of the street, and while the Afghans, crawling along these perilous bridges, had reinforced the survivors of the fight on the stairway, their friends in the street below had hacked their way through the flimsy walls and thrust live coals and oil-soaked rags through holes they had made in the foundation.

The Residency and the compound, already hemmed in on three sides, was now being assailed from above and below as well, since besides possessing themselves of the stables and cavalry lines and every house-top in sight, the enemy had established themselves in force on the roof of the Mess House and had broken through its foundations.

The courtyard, the ground-floor rooms and the barrack-block were full of dead and dying men, and of the seventy-seven Guides who had seen the sun rise that morning, only thirty were left. Thirty . . . and the "troops of Midian" who "prowled and howled around" numbered—how many thousands? Four? . . . six? . . . eight thousand men?

For the first time that day Wally's heart sank, and

facing the future squarely and clear-eyed he deliberately abandoned hope. But this was something that William, as a member of the Foreign and Political Department and an apostle of Peace by Negotiation and Compromise, was still not prepared to do.

William had returned from that abortive attack on the guns to exchange the unfamiliar sabre and service revolver for his shot-gun, and hastily filling his pockets with cartridges, he hurried up to the roof of the Envoy's House to fire at the Afghans who were massing on the roof of the higher house on the opposite side of the courtyard. It was only then that he became aware of the volume of smoke that was billowing out from the ground-floor rooms of the Mess House, and realized that if the fire took hold they were lost.

Yet even then he did not give up hope, but once again, lying on the roof among five jawans who were also engaged in discouraging the opposition entrenched on top of the Mess House, scribbled another desperate appeal to the Amir, using a blank page ripped from a small notebook he carried in his pocket. They could not hold out much longer, wrote William, and if His Highness did not come to their aid, their fate—and his own—was sealed. They could not believe that His Highness was prepared to stand aside and do nothing while his guests were murdered . . .

"Take that to Hamilton-Sahib," said William, ripping out the page and handing it to one of the jawans. "Tell him he must find someone among the servants who will deliver it to the Amir."

"They will not go, Sahib," said the man, shaking his head. "They know that four Mussulmans have gone with letters and none have returned, and that the Hindu who went was hacked to pieces in full sight. Nevertheless—"

He tucked it in his belt, and wriggling away in the direction of the stairs, vanished down them in search of his Commanding Officer, whom he found over at the Mess House, firing from a window on the first floor at a group of mutineers who were attempting to reload the guns. Wally took the scrap of paper and dismissing the messenger with a brief nod read it through and wondered with a detached feeling of curiosity why William should think it was worth sending another appeal to the Amir, when the only tangible result of previous appeals had been one evasive reply that could hardly be matched for weakness and hypocrisy. In any case none of the messengers had returned, so it was always possible that all of them had met the same fate as the unfortunate Hindu, and it seemed pointless to Wally to send yet another to his death. But though the entire responsibility for the defence of the Residency had fallen on his shoulders, young Mr. Jenkyns, as the Envoy's Secretary and Political Assistant, still represented the civil authority, and so if William wanted this letter sent, then it must be sent.

"Taimus," called Wally.

"Sahib?" The sowar who had been firing from the other window lowered his carbine and turned to look at his Commanding Officer.

Wally said: "Jenkyns-Sahib has just written another letter to the Amir, asking for help. Do you think that you could reach the palace?"

"I can try," said Taimus. He put his carbine down and came across to take the paper, and folding it small, hid it among his clothing.

Wally smiled and said quietly: *"Shukria, Shahzada* (Prince). *Khuda hafiz!"*

The man grinned at the title, saluted and went out to cross the lane into the barracks and survey the situation from the barrack roof, but a bare half-minute was enough to show him the impossibility of attempting to leave by the compound, for by now the mob were everywhere and not even a lizard could have got through. There was nothing for it but to go back to the Residency and see if he could not find some other way of escape. The back door had been blocked long ago, and since to have opened it again would have been to invite a flood of armed Afghans into the courtyard, he turned in desperation to the Envoy's House and went up to the roof, where one of the jawans who were still holding out there helped him up on to the curtain wall that shielded the roof from the view of the houses behind the Residency.

Standing there, he had been in full sight of the enemy on the roof of the Mess House and in the street below; and as he gazed down on the close-packed crowd of yelling, hate-distorted faces, he was suddenly filled with the same contempt for the mob that Cavagnari had felt much earlier that day. For Sowar Taimus, though serving as a trooper of the Guides, was also a prince of a royal line:

a Shahzada—and an Afghan. His lip curled in disdain as he surveyed those contorted faces, and drawing a deep breath, he deliberately leapt into space, launching himself feet-first into the thick of the press below and landing on heads and shoulders that broke his fall.

The mob, momentarily stunned by shock, recovered itself and set on him with a howl of fury, but he fought his way through them, shouting that he was a prince and an Afghan and that he bore a message to the Amir; which would not have saved him had he not been recognized by a close friend, who rushing to the rescue had managed by dint of blows, high-words and cajolery to extract him from the clutches of the mob—battered and bleeding but alive—and helped him to reach the palace. But once there he had fared no better than anyone else.

The Amir was locked away, weeping, among his women; and though he had eventually agreed to see the Shahzada Taimus and to read the message he carried, he would only bewail his fate and reiterate that his Kismet was bad and that he was not to blame for this and could do nothing—nothing.

He had given orders that the Shahzada was to be detained, and this had been done. But though the Amir's Kismet was undoubtedly bad, Taimus's had proved to be far otherwise, because in the room into which he had been hurriedly thrust by the palace guards lay an Afghan who had been shot in the back during the first attack on the compound. The wounded man had been left to look after himself, and though by now he was in considerable pain, no one had done anything to help him because of the panic that prevailed in the palace. But Taimus had learned something of the treatment of wounds during his service in the Guides, and he had extracted the bullet with his knife, and having washed the wound and managed to staunch the bleeding, had bound it up with the sufferer's waist-cloth.

His grateful patient, who had proved to be a man of some standing, had repaid the debt by smuggling him out of the palace and arranging for his escape from Kabul. And Fate had been doubly kind to him that day, for not five minutes after he had leapt from the roof of the Envoy's House, and while he was still fighting his way forward through the frenzied crowd with his life hanging in the balance, behind him in the Residency the garrison who had been battling equally frantically to dowse the burning foundations of the Mess House were driven back by a sudden uprush of flame that burst through the blinding clouds of smoke, and seconds later the whole lower storey was ablaze.

There had been no question of saving the wounded; the fire had taken hold far too suddenly and violently to allow anyone to attempt it. Those who could do so had run for their lives, and scorched, choked and half blind, had stumbled across the smoke-filled courtyard to take refuge in the Envoy's House.

The Afghans on the roof of the burning building, realizing with what swiftness the flames would destroy that ramshackle wood and plaster structure, had scrambled back across their ladders in haste, and instantly transferred their attentions to the opposite house. Thrusting out other ladders onto the high parapet that Taimus had jumped from, they clambered across and leapt down among the half-dozen men who still held out there: and though their leaders died as they came, falling sideways into the street or pitching head-first on to the roof, those behind them pressed forward, and as William and the jawans reloaded they sprang down to the attack . . .

There had been no hope of holding the roof, even though Wally and every Guide who remained in the Residency had rushed up to try and stem the horde of invaders who came leaping down from the parapet like a band of monkeys swarming on to a melon patch. Their very numbers had made the task impossible and the end a foregone conclusion.

The garrison, closing ranks and using their useless firearms as clubs, retreated towards the stairwell and were driven down it step by step, until the last man down slammed shut the door at the foot of the stairway and dropped the bars into place. But that door, like all the rest in that ancient and dilapidated building, was incapable of withstanding a determined attack, and there was no time —and no materials—to reinforce it.

The house itself would soon be on fire, for if the Afghans sapping from below failed to set it alight, it seemed only too likely that the flames and sparks that were now pouring from every doorway and window of the Mess House would do the job for them; and even if it did not, the garrison could no longer hold out in the Residency, because the enemy, taking advantage of the fighting on the roof and under cover of the smoke, had smashed another breach in the back wall of the courtyard, and widening it unhindered, were streaming in from below.

Wally caught a nightmare glimpse of them through the acrid clouds of smoke, shooting and slashing at a panic-stricken handful of servants who had been driven out of the Mess House by the fire and taken refuge in the lee of a pile of baggage that had been used to barricade the back door, Sir Louis' bearer and his own fat Pir Baksh among them—Pir Baksh defending himself with a knife in one hand and a boot-tree in the other. But there was nothing he could do for them, and he turned away, sickened, and striding to the nearest of the two windows that faced the compound, wrenched back the shutters and sprang up on to the sill.

"Come on!" yelled Wally, waving his companions forward, and in the same breath, leapt out and down across the narrow lane and onto the roof of the barracks.

They had not waited for any further urging, but followed unhesitatingly, leaping as he had done down across the gap to land on the barracks; Jenkyns, Kelly and the jawans who had survived the fight on the roof, and half-a-dozen non-combatants who had been helping to fight the fire and had run up from the floor below.

Even as the last man jumped and landed, the roof of the Mess House fell in with a roar that equalled that of the guns, and they turned and saw a brilliant fountain of sparks, vivid even in the afternoon sunlight, shoot up from the pyre that was consuming the body of Louis Cavagnari—and with it a great number of the soldiers and servants who had accompanied him to Kabul.

"Like a Viking Chieftain going to Valhalla with his warriors and serving-men around him," thought Wally.

He turned from the sight to order his little force off the roof and down into the barracks. For now that the Residency had fallen and the enemy were in possession of the Envoy's House, the Afghans would be able to fire from the windows that he and the other survivors of the garrison had just leapt from—and from an angle that made the scanty cover of the parapets of no account. But down below, the original doors of the block were as stoutly built as its outer walls, while the canvas awnings that shaded the long central courtyard, though no protection against bullets, at least prevented the enemy from seeing what went on there.

"We ought to be able to hold out here for a fair time," said William breathlessly, glancing about him at the solid stone pillars and brick archways that gave on to the cool, windowless cells of the troops' quarters. "Nothing much to set on fire. Except the doors, of course. I don't know why we didn't come here before."

"Because we can't see out of it or shoot out of it, or do a damn thing but stay put and try to prevent those divils breaking the doors down. That's why," snapped Rosie, who had worked like a demon to try and get the wounded into the Residency courtyard, only to desert them in order to defend the Envoy's House: and who now felt that he had abandoned them to be murdered by the Afghans or burned alive in the Mess House.

"Yes. I suppose you're right. I hadn't thought about that. But at least we should be able to stop them breaking in, and providing they don't burn the doors down—"

"Or blow a hole in the wall," said Rosie, "or . . ." He reeled as the guns roared again, and the pillars shuddered to the impact of the force and sound of the shells that struck the front wall of the barracks, missing the archway and burying the stairway to the east of it under a pile of rubble.

It did not need a professional gunner to tell that this second salvo had been fired from a much closer range than the first one, and it was clear to everyone in the barracks that the mob, freed from the sniping of the sepoys who had been harassing them from behind the parapets, had lost no time in reloading the guns and running them forward. And also that the next salvo would probably be fired from directly opposite the archway, which would smash both doors to matchwood and leave the way clear for the enemy to rush in.

Once again the sky rained debris, and the exhausted doctor, who had clutched a pillar and then sat down abruptly, leaning against it, saw Walter Hamilton and Daffadar Hira Singh racing towards the inner door of the archway and pulling it open; and thought dazedly that the shock of the explosions must have unhinged them both, and that they intended to go out and attack the mob before the guns could be reloaded. But they did not touch the new outer door that by now was so spattered with

1156

bullet-holes that it had the appearance of a colander. Instead they turned back to confer briefly with Havildar Hassan and Lance-Naik Janki, and presently Wally nodded briefly, and returning to William and Rosie, said tersely:

"Look, we've got to get those guns. *We've got to!* I don't mean spike them. I mean capture them. If we can only get 'em back here we can blow the Arsenal sky high —and with it most of that mob out there and half the Bala Hissar as well. We've only got to land one shell fair and square on it, and all that ammunition and gunpowder inside is going to go up with a bang that will wreck everything within a radius of several hundred yards."

"Including us," said William wryly.

"What the divil does that matter?" demanded Wally impatiently. "Not that it will, for we're much lower down here, and these walls are far too thick. Ah, I know it sounds a crazy idea, but it's worth a try—anything's worth a try now. If we can get our hands on those guns we've got a fighting chance, but if we don't—well, we can say our prayers now."

William's eyelids flickered and his youthful face whitened under its mask of blood and dust. He said tiredly: "We can't do it, Wally. We've proved that already."

"We hadn't got enough rope last time. Besides, the guns were too far away then. But they aren't now, and I'll bet you anything you like that they are being dragged nearer this minute, because those bastards out there are certain that they've got us beat and we can't do anything about it. My Havildar says that there's a fakir out there who's been egging them on all afternoon, screeching to them to blow in the door so that they can fire straight through the barracks and smash down the back wall to allow their friends in the Residency to rush us from the rear. That's why I had the inner door opened: so that if they smash in the front one, we've still got that to fall back on."

Rosie said shortly: "It's mad you are. What would we be using for ammunition even if we did get a gun? Bullets?"

"The shells we brought back with us last time, of course. We left them here in one of the quarters—twelve of 'em. That's six for each gun. Just think what we could do with that!"

1157

But William remained unconvinced.

"I've no objection to charging the damn things again," said William, "but if we get our hands on them, for God's sake let's spike them this time and be done with it, instead of trying to bring them back with us."

"*No!*" insisted Wally passionately. "If we do that it's all up with us, because they'll have other guns. And they've already got all the ammunition they need, while we're running out of ours; and when we do, and they realize we aren't firing any more, they'll rush this place in force and it will fall inside five minutes. No, there's only one thing for it: we've got to cut off their source of supply, and the only way we can do that is by shelling the Arsenal—and killing as many of them as we can in the process. I tell you we've *got* to get those guns! One of them, anyway. We'll spike the second—I'll get Thakur Singh to do that while the rest of us concentrate on getting the other back. We ought to be able to manage that. Ah sure now, I know it sounds crazy, but it's better than cowering here until they realize that we've run out of ammunition and that all they have to do is get a few ladders and pour in on us over the roof, as they did in the Residency. Is *that* the way you want to die?"

Surgeon-Major Kelly gave a harsh croak of laughter, and coming wearily to his feet, said: "Be easy boy, we're with you. Faith, it's a mad gamble, so it is. But there's no saying it couldn't come off. And if we don't take it we're dead men anyway. Well, if we're going to try it you'd best be telling us what to do and getting us started."

Wally had been right about the guns. While they talked, the mob had been dragging them nearer and nearer until now both were less than seventy yards distant, loaded and facing the wall to the left of the archway; and ready to be fired—

Once again the crash of the double explosion was followed by a wild outburst of cheering. But as the echoes died away the dry-throated mob fell silent, and from his prison high above the compound Ash could hear, cutting through the unceasing rattle of musketry, the muted roar and crackle of burning timber, the hoarse cawing of startled crows and the shrill voice of the Fakir encouraging the mutineers who were pushing the guns towards the barrack archway.

He did not see the barrack doors swing open. But

1158

suddenly Wally came in sight, running with William and Rosie and a dozen Guides at his heels to charge straight into that blizzard of bullets and across the dusty open ground towards the guns.

For the second time that day they drove the crews back, and having done so eight of them swung one of the guns round so that it faced the mob, and with six of them harnessed to the ropes and another two putting their shoulders to the wheels, they began to drag it back towards the barracks while the rest held off the enemy with revolvers and swords, and a solitary jawan flung himself at the other gun with the intention of spiking it. But once again the task had proved beyond them.

The hail of bullets killed two of the men who were harnessed to the gun and the sowar who was attempting to spike the other, and who dropped the spike as he died, letting it fall to be lost in the blood-stained dust below the wheels. Another four were wounded, and Wally shouted to the others to run for it, and sheathing his sabre, hastily reloaded his revolver. William and Rosie followed his example, and as the men freed themselves from the ropes and ran for the barracks, taking their wounded with them, the three Englishmen covered their retreat, walking backwards and firing steadily and with such deadly effect that the Afghans wavered and held back, allowing the little party to reach the shelter of the archway in safety.

At the last moment Wally turned, and looking up at Ash's window, flung up his arm in a Roman salute. But the gesture of farewell went unanswered, for Ash was not there. The despair that had stabbed through him when he saw the guns had served to goad his brain into searching yet again, and for at least the hundredth time that day, for a way of escape; and this time, suddenly, he had remembered something. Something that it had not occurred to him to consider before—the geography of the storey below . . .

He knew which room lay below his own, but he had not thought to visualize those that lay on either side of it; and doing so now he realized that under the Munshi's library lay a small disused room that had once possessed a balcony window. The balcony itself had fallen long ago and the window had subsequently been boarded up; but by now those boards were probably rotten, and once he had broken through the library floor and dropped down

1159

through the cavity, it would not be difficult to wrench them off. After which it would merely be a matter of using the sheet rope to negotiate the twenty-foot drop to the ground below.

Any Afghan seeing him slide down from the window would suppose him to be an ally eager to get to grips with the enemy, and the only danger was that one of the jawans on the barrack roof would spot him, and taking the same view, shoot him before he could reach the ground and the cover of the low wall that separated the line of tall houses from the Residency compound. But that was a risk that would have to be taken, and Ash did not trouble his head over it, but within a matter of seconds was back in the Munshi's library and attacking the floorboards.

William, who had seen that valedictory gesture and jumped to a wrong conclusion, clutched at Wally's arm and said breathlessly: "Who were you waving at? Was someone trying to signal us? Is the Amir . . . are they . . . ?"

"No," gasped Wally, flinging his weight against the door to help close it. "It's—only—Ash . . ."

William stared at him blankly: the name meant nothing to him and the sudden flare of hope that had sprung to life at the sight of that gesture died again. He turned away and sank down to the ground, but Ambrose Kelly looked up from the wounded sepoy he was tending and said sharply: *"Ash?* You can't mean—do you mean Pelham-Martyn?"

"Yes," panted Wally, still busy with the bars of the outer door. "He's up there . . . in one of those . . . houses."

"In—? For Christ's sake! Then why isn't he doing something for us?"

"If he could do anything, he'll have done it. He'll have tried, anyway. And God knows he warned us often enough, but no one would listen—not even the Chief. Get that fellow into one of the quarters, Rosie. We're too near the door and they're bound to blast off again. Get back—all of you."

The mob had only waited until the door was closed before rushing forward to take possession of the guns once more and drag them round and into position in front of the archway, while from every housetop their allies directed a storm of musket-balls onto the stout, windowless walls of the barracks, the unmanned roof and the tattered, bullet-torn canvas awnings.

There was very little light inside the barracks, for the sun had sunk behind the heights of the Shere Dawaza, and by now the whole compound was in shadow. But as the day waned the flames from the burning Residency gathered brightness, and when the guns fired again the flash was no longer dimmed by sunlight, but a vivid glare that dazzled the eyes and gave a fractional warning of the deafening crash that followed.

This time there had been no attempt to fire both guns simultaneously. The first shell had been intended to break in both doors of the archway, and as far as the mutineers were concerned it had done so, for they were unaware that the second one had been left open. They saw the woodwork of the outer one disintegrate in a haze of flying splinters, and when the smoke cleared, the archway gaped on a view of the long central courtyard and the far wall.

Cheering wildly, they touched off the second gun, and the shell streaked through the centre of the barracks to smash a ragged hole that gave access to the lane. Behind that breach lay the courtyard of the Residency—full now of their victorious brothers, who had only to cross the lane and fall upon the infidels from the rear while their exultant allies in the compound rushed them from the front. But though the scheme was an excellent one, it contained two serious flaws, only one of which was immediately apparent: the fact that the inner and far stouter door of the archway had not been destroyed and was now slammed shut.

The other and more serious one, which was known to the garrison but still not realized by the mutineers, was that in setting fire to the Residency the Afghans had made the place untenable for themselves, so that instead of massing there in strength they had looted what they could find and hastily withdrawn out of reach of the flames. The likelihood of an attack from that direction was therefore minimal, and Wally could afford to disregard it and concentrate on one front only since by now there would be no snipers firing on them from the Residency, and the smoke from the burning building would confuse the aim of many of the marksmen on the nearby rooftops.

Secure in this knowledge, his first act after retreating

to the barracks and closing that flimsy outer door had been to order four of his men up the stairway at the far end with instructions to keep down out of sight until the guns fired, and then run forward under cover of the smoke and take up their former positions behind the front parapet above the arch, from where they would open fire on the gun-crews to prevent them reloading.

The rest of his small force had scattered to left and right; neither he nor they having any illusions as to what would happen next. Nor had it been long in happening. The outer door duly went, and the shell that demolished it also damaged one of the stone pillars and brought down a shower of bricks; though without injuring anyone.

They waited tensely for the second, and the instant it came, raced forward to close and bar the heavy inner door, while the four jawans who had been crouching at the top of the far stairs leapt to their feet, and concealed by the smoke, ran forward to take cover behind the parapet overhead and open fire on the cheering gun-crews.

Now the loading and firing of a piece of heavy artillery is no easy task for inexperienced men; and the mutineers were not gunners. Not only should the gun be swabbed out between shots, but the live shell must be thrust into the muzzle and rammed down the barrel, the touchhole primed with gunpowder and lit with a port-fire —or, if necessary, a match. All this takes time, and can be an exceedingly difficult and dangerous task when the crews are being fired on at close range.

Had the walls of the barrack-block possessed proper loopholes that offered protection and a reasonable field of fire, the garrison would have found it a simple matter to prevent the guns being used against them. But as the only place from which they could fire was from behind parapets surrounding a roof that was overlooked by enemy snipers, the guns were strong cards that could not be trumped, and Wally knew it.

He knew too that it was only a matter of time before the four on the roof ran out of ammunition—and that the rest of them had very little left. When that was gone the guns would be loaded without interference and the door would be blown in.

The end was a foregone conclusion, and he realized

now that he must have recognized that long ago, and unconsciously based all his actions upon it.

If they must die, then at least let them die in a manner that would redound to the credit of the Guides and the traditions they upheld. Let them go down fighting, and by doing so add lustre to their Corps and become a legend and an inspiration to future generations of Guides. That was the only thing they could do.

He knew that there was very little time left, and that little was running out fast; but for a brief space he stood silent, staring into space and thinking of many things . . . Of Inistioge and his parents and brothers; of his mother's face as she kissed him goodbye; of Ash and Wigram and all the splendid fellows in the Guides . . . He had had a good life—a wonderful life. Even now he would not have exchanged it for anyone else's.

A host of foolish memories passed in procession before his mind's eye, all of them clear-cut and bright. Birds'-nesting with his brothers on Wimbledon Common. A ball at the Military Academy. The long voyage to Bombay and his first sight of India. The happy days in the bungalow in Rawalpindi and later on in Mardan, and those carefree holidays that he and Ash had spent together . . . The work and the play, the talk and the laughter and the fun. All the pretty girls he had fallen in love with—gay ones, demure ones, shy ones, flirtatious ones . . . their faces merged into one face—Anjuli's, and he smiled at it and thought how lucky he was to have known her.

He would never marry now, and perhaps that was no bad thing; it would have been hard to find anyone who could live up to the ideal she had set: and he would also be spared the sadness of discovering that love does not last and that time, which destroys beauty and youth and strength, can also corrode many things of far greater value. He would never know disillusionment, or failure either, or live to see the gods of his idolatry brought down and shown to have feet of clay . . .

This was the end of the road for him, yet he had no regrets—not even for the loss of that imaginary figure, Field Marshal Lord Hamilton of Inistioge, for had he not won the most coveted award of all, the Victoria Cross? That alone was enough glory to make up for anything: and besides, the Guides would remember him. Perhaps one day, if he could leave an unsullied name, his sword would hang in the Mess at Mardan and men of the Corps yet unborn would finger it and listen to an old story from by-gone history. The story of how once, long ago, seventy-seven men of the Guides under the command of one Walter Hamilton, v.c., had been besieged in the British Residency at Kabul and held it against overwhelming odds for the best part of a day—and died to the last man . . .

"*Stat sua cuique dies, breve tempus—Omnibus est vitae; sed famam extendere factis—Hoc virtutis opus,*" murmured Wally under his breath. It was an odd time to remember a Latin tag from the *Aeneid,* and he thought how Ash would laugh if he knew. But it fitted the occasion: "Everyone has his allotted day. Short and irrecoverable is the lifetime of all; but to extend our fame by deeds, this is the task of greatness."

Today it had been his task to help extend the fame of the Guides, and Ash would understand that. It was good to know that Ash was close by and would see and approve —would realize that he had done his best, and be with him in spirit. He could not have asked for a better friend, and he knew that it was not Ash's fault that help had not come. If he could . . .

The boy collected his wandering thoughts with an effort and looked about him at the tattered, blood-stained, smoke-begrimed scarecrows who were all that were now left of the more than three score and ten whom he could have mustered that morning. He had no idea how long he had been standing there silent and thinking of other things, or what the hour was, for now that the sun had left the compound the barracks were full of shadows. The daylight seemed to be fading, and there was no time to be lost.

Lieutenant Walter Hamilton, v.c., straightened up and drawing a deep breath addressed his men, speaking in Hindustani, which was the lingua-franca of a corps that contained Sikhs, Hindus and Punjabis as well as the Pushtu-speaking Pathans.

They had fought, he said, like heroes, and most splendidly upheld the honour of the Guides. No men could have done more. Now all that remained for them was to die in a like manner, fighting the foe. The alternative was to be killed like rats in a trap. There was no other

1164

choice, and he did not need to ask which they would choose. He therefore proposed that they should make one last effort to capture a gun. But this time they would all harness themselves to it while he alone would hold off the enemy and cover their retreat:

"We will charge the left-hand gun only," said Wally. "And when we reach it you will not look aside even for a moment, but rope yourselves to it and put your shoulders to the wheels, and get it back here. Do not stop for anything—do you understand? You must not turn to look behind you and I will do all I can to cover you. If you get it back, turn it on the Arsenal. If not, no matter if I fall, or how many of us fall, remember that those who are left will still hold the honour of the Guides in their hands. Do not sell it lightly. It is told of a great warrior who conquered this land and half the world many hundreds of years ago—none other than Sikandar Dulkhan (Alexander the Great) of whom all men have heard—that he said "It is a lovely thing to live with courage and to die leaving behind everlasting renown." You have all lived with courage and what you have done this day will bring you everlasting renown; for your deeds will not be forgotten as long as the Guides are remembered. Your children's children will tell their grandchildren the tale and boast of what you have done. Never give in, brothers— never give in. Guides, *ki-jai!*"

The cry was greeted with a shout that echoed under the arches and among the shadowy quarters until it sounded as though the ghosts of all the Guides who had died that day were cheering in unison with the few who still lived. And as the echoes died away, William called out, "Scotland for Ever!—Political Department *ki-jai!*" and the men laughed and took up the sabres and ropes that they had laid down.

Ambrose Kelly came stiffly to his feet and stretched tiredly. He was the oldest of the group by a number of years and, like Gobind, his talents and training had been devoted to saving life and not taking it. But now he loaded and checked his revolver, and buckling on the sword that he had never learned to use, said: "Ah well now, I'm not saying it won't be a relief to get it over with, for it's been a long day and it's dog-tired I am—and as some poet fellow has said, 'how can man die better than facing fearful odds?' Hakim *ki-jai!*"

The Guides laughed again; and their laughter made Wally's heart lift with pride and brought a lump to his throat as he grinned back at them with an admiration and affection that was too deep for words. Yes, life would have been worth living if only to have served and fought with men like these. It had been a privilege to command them—an enormous privilege: and it would be an even greater one to die with them. They were the salt of the earth. They were the Guides. His throat tightened as he looked at them, and he was aware again of a hard lump in it, but his eyes were very bright as he reached for his sabre, and swallowing painfully to clear that constriction, he said almost gaily: "Are we ready? Good. Then open the doors—"

A sepoy sprang forward to lift the heavy iron bar, and as it fell clear, two others swung back the massive wooden leaves. And with a yell of "Guides *ki-jai!*" the little band charged out through the archway and raced towards the left-hand gun, Wally leading, a full six paces ahead.

The sight of them had a curious effect upon the mob: after the failure of the last attack every member of it had been confident that the "foreigners" had shot their bolt and would never be able to mount another, yet here they were, rushing out again and with undiminished ferocity. It was unbelievable—it was uncanny . . . For a moment the mob stared at the ragged scarecrows in almost superstitious awe, and in the next second scattered like dry leaves before the whirlwind force of the attack as Wally fell upon them, his sabre flashing and his revolver spitting death.

As he did so a solitary turbanless Afghan whose hair and clothes were white with plaster and brick dust, raced from the left to join him, and was recognized by two sowars with a yell of "Pelham-Dulkhan! Pelham-Sahib-Bahadur!"

Wally heard that greeting above the clash of battle, and glancing swiftly aside saw Ash fighting beside him—a knife in one hand and a tulwar snatched from a dead Herati in the other: and he laughed triumphantly and cried, "Ash! I knew you'd come. *Now* we'll show 'em—!"

Ash laughed back at him, drunk with the terrible intoxication of battle and the relief of fast, violent action

1166

after the frustrations of that long nerve-wracking day of helpless watching . . . of seeing his comrades die one by one without being able to lift hand or arm to help them. His wild exhilaration communicated itself to Wally, who suddenly lifted out of himself was fighting like one inspired.

Afghans are not small men, but the boy seemed to tower above them, wielding his sabre like a master—or one of Charlemagne's Paladins. And as he fought he sang. It was, as usual, a hymn: the same that Ash himself had sung as he galloped Dagobaz across the plain of Bhithor on the morning of the Rana's funeral. But hearing it now he felt his heart jerk roughly, for this was not a verse that Wally had ever sung before, and listening to it he realized that the boy cherished no false hopes. This was his last fight and he knew it, and his choice of that particular verse was deliberate, a valediction. For calm and rest had never held any appeal for Wally, yet now he sang of both—loudly and joyously so that the words were clearly audible above the clamour of the fight . . .

"The golden evening brightens in the West," sang Wally, plying that deadly sabre: *"Soon, soon, to faithful warriors comes their rest. Sweet is the calm of Paradise the Blest; Alleluia! Al-le-lu—"*

"Look out, Wally!" yelled Ash, and beating aside the blade of an opponent, leapt back to attack an Afghan armed with a long knife who had come up behind them unseen.

But even if Wally had heard, the warning came too late. The knife drove home to the hilt between his shoulder blades, and as Ash's tulwar slashed through his attacker's neck, he staggered, and firing his last round, flung the useless revolver into a bearded face. The man reeled back, tripped and fell, and Wally transferred his sabre to his left hand: but his arm was weakening and he could not lift it. The point dropped and caught on a roughness in the ground, and as he pitched forward, the blade snapped.

In the same moment the butt of a jezail crashed down on Ash's head with stunning force, and for a split second lights seemed to explode inside his skull before he plunged down into blackness. And then the tulwars flashed and the dust fumed up in a blinding cloud as the mob closed in.

A few paces behind them, William had already fallen with a scimitar half buried in his skull and his right arm shattered below the elbow. And Rosie too was dead, his crumpled body lying barely a yard beyond the barrack archway, where he had been struck down by a musket-ball through the temple as he ran out at Wally's heels.

Of the rest, two, like Surgeon-Major Kelly, had died before they reached the gun, and three more had been wounded. But the survivors had obeyed their commander's orders to the letter: they had not looked aside or attempted to fight, but harnessing themselves to the gun had strained every nerve and muscle to drag it back. Yet even as they panted and struggled, others among them dropped; and now the ground was too littered with bodies, fallen weapons and spent bullets, and the dust too sticky with spilt blood, to make the task a possible one for so few men. Those who were left found that they could move the gun no further, and at last they were forced to abandon it and stumble back to the barracks, gasping and exhausted.

They closed and barred the great door behind them, and as it shut, a howl of triumph went up as the mob became aware that all three *feringhis* were dead.

Hundreds began to stream towards the barracks, led by the Fakir, who, leaving the shelter of the stables, ran at their head capering and waving his banner, while the crowds on the house-tops, realizing what had happened, ceased firing to dance and shout and brandish their muskets. But the three remaining jawans of the four whom Wally had sent up to the roof of the barracks continued to fire, though coldly now, for they had very few rounds left.

The mob had forgotten those four. But it remembered when three of its members fell dead and a further two, immediately behind them, were wounded by the same heavy lead bullets that had killed the men in front. As the Afghans checked, the rifles cracked again and a further three died, for the Guides were firing into a solid mass of men at a range of less than fifty yards, and it was not possible for them to miss. And presently a bullet struck the Fakir full in the face, and he threw up his arms and fell backwards, to be trampled under the feet of his followers, who running behind him, could not check in time.

1168

68

There were several factors that contributed to Ash's survival. For one thing, he was wearing Afghan dress and clutching a tulwar; and for another, only those who had been in the forefront of the fighting were aware that a man who appeared to be a citizen of Kabul had for a while fought side by side with the *Angrezi* officer. Then in the subsequent rush to finish off the mortally wounded Sahib, his unconscious body had been spurned aside, so that by the time the dust had settled he was no longer lying where he had fallen, but was some little distance away; not among the fallen Guides, but among half a dozen enemy corpses, his face unrecognizable under a mask of blood and dirt, and his clothing dyed scarlet from the severed jugular of a Herati soldier whose body lay sprawled above his own.

The blow on his head had been a glancing one, and though sufficiently violent to knock him insensible, it had not been severe enough to keep him so for very long; but when he recovered consciousness it was to discover that not one but two corpses lay above him; the second being a heavily built Afghan who had been shot through the head by one of the jawans on the barrack roof less than a minute earlier, and fallen across his legs.

The two inert bodies effectively pinned him to the ground, and finding that he could not move, he lay still for a while, dazed and uncomprehending, and with no idea where he was or what had happened to him. He had a hazy recollection of crawling through a hole—a hole in a wall. After that there was nothing—But as his mind slowly cleared he remembered Wally and strove futilely to move, only to find that the effort was beyond him.

His head throbbed abominably and his whole body felt as though it was one vast bruise and as weak as wet paper; yet gradually, as his wits returned, he realized that in all probability he had received no wound beyond a blow on the head and rough handling at the hands—or more likely the feet—of the mob. In which case there was nothing to prevent him struggling free of this weight that was pinning him down, and returning to the attack the minute he could collect the strength to do so and rid himself of this appalling dizziness: for to get on his feet merely in order to stagger round like a drunken man would be to invite instant death, and be no help to anyone.

The roar of the mob and the continued crackle of muskets and carbines told him that the battle was by no means over, and though his face was bruised and swollen, and his eyelids clogged with a sticky paste of dust and blood that he was unable to remove because he was still too weak to free his arms, he managed by dint of an enormous effort to force open his eyes.

At first it was impossible to focus anything, but after a minute or two his sight, like his brain, began to clear, and he realized that he was lying a yard or two behind the main bulk of the mob, which was being kept at bay by the determined fire of three sepoys above the entrance to the barrack block. But their shots came at longer and longer intervals, and he became dimly aware that they must be running out of ammunition, and presently, as his gaze wandered, that there was some sort of conference going on among the mutineers who stood behind the abandoned guns.

As he watched, one of them—a member of the Ardal Regiment judging from his dress—climbed up onto one of the guns and standing upright brandished a musket to the barrel of which he had tied a strip of white cloth that he waved to and fro as a flag of truce, shouting: *"Sulh. Sulh . . . Kafi. Bus!"** *

The crackle of musketry died and the sepoys kneeling behind the parapet held their fire. And in the silence the man on the gun climbed down, and advancing into the open space before the barracks, called up to the beleaguered garrison that he would have speech with their leaders.

There followed a brief pause in which the sepoys were seen to confer together, and then one of them laid aside his rifle and stood up, and walking to the inner edge of the roof, called down to the survivors in the troops' quarters below.

---

*Please. Enough. Stop!

1170

A few minutes later three more Guides came up to join him, and together they went forward to stand behind the parapet above the archway, erect and unarmed.

"We are here," said the jawan who had been elected spokesman because he was a Pathan and could speak freely to Afghans in their own tongue—and because no one of higher rank was left alive. "What is it that you wish to say to us? Speak."

Ash heard a man who was standing a yard or so away draw in his breath with a hiss and say in an awed whisper: "Are there no more than that? There cannot be only *six* left. Perchance there are others within."

"Six . . ." thought Ash numbly. But the word carried no meaning.

"Your Sahibs are all dead," shouted the mutineer with the flag, "and with you who are left, we have no quarrel. Of what use to continue the fight? If you will throw down your arms we will give you free passage to return to your homes. You have fought honourably. Surrender now, and go free."

One of the Guides laughed, and the grim, battle-grimed faces of his comrades relaxed and they laughed with him, loudly and scornfully, until their listeners scowled and gritted their teeth and began to finger their muskets.

The jawan who was their spokesman had not drunk for many hours and his mouth was dry. But he gathered his spittle and spat deliberately over the edge of the parapet, and raising his voice, demanded loudly: "What manner of men are you, that you can ask us to forfeit our honour and shame our dead? Are we dogs that we should betray those whose salt we have eaten? Our Sahib told us to stand and fight to the last. And that we shall do. You have been answered—*dogs!*"

He spat again and turned on his heel, the rest following; and while the mob yelled its fury the six strode back along the roof and down the far stair into the barrack courtyard. Here they wasted no time, but paused only briefly to line up shoulder to shoulder: Mussulmans, Sikhs and a Hindu—sowars and sepoys of the Queen's Own Corps of Guides. They lifted the bar and threw back the doors, and drawing their swords, marched out under the archway to their deaths as steadily as though they had been on parade.

The Afghan who had spoken before sucked in his breath and said as though the words were wrenched from him: "*Wah-illah!* but these are Men!"

"They are the Guides," thought Ash with a hot surge of pride, and struggled desperately to rise and join them. But even as he fought to free himself, a rush of men from behind trampled him down, driving the breath from his lungs and leaving him writhing helplessly among choking clouds of dust and a forest of *chuppli*-shod feet that trod on him, tripped over him, or spurned him aside as heedlessly as though he had been a bale of straw. He was dimly aware of the clash of steel and the hoarse shouting of men, and, very clearly, of a clarion voice that cried "Guides *ki-jai!*" Then a shod foot struck his temple and once again the world turned black.

This time it had taken him longer to recover his senses, and when at last he swam slowly up out of the darkness it was to find that although he could still hear a clamour of voices from the direction of the Residency the firing had stopped, and except for the dead the part of the compound in which he lay appeared to be deserted.

Nevertheless he made no immediate attempt to move, but lay where he was, conscious only of pain and an enormous weariness, and only after a lapse of many minutes, of the need to think and to act. His brain felt as sluggish and unresponsive as his muscles, and the sheer effort of thinking at all, let alone thinking clearly, seemed too great to make. Yet he knew that he must force himself to it; and presently the cogs of his mind meshed once more and memory returned—and with it the age-old instinct of self-preservation.

At some time during that final massacre the bodies that had lain above him had been displaced, and after a cautious trial he discovered that he could still move, though only just. To stand upright was beyond him but he could crawl, and he did so—as slowly and uncertainly as a wounded beetle: creeping painfully on hands and knees between the sprawled corpses, and making automatically for the nearest shelter, which happened to be the stables.

Others had had the same idea, for the stables were full of dead and wounded Afghans: men from the city and the Bala Hissar as well as soldiers of the Ardal and Herati regiments, huddled together on the reeking straw; and Ash, suffering from a combination of mild concussion, multiple bruises and mental and physical exhaustion, collapsed among them and slept for the best part of an hour, to be aroused at last by a hand that grasped his bruised shoulders and shook him roughly.

The pain of that movement jerked him into consciousness as effectively as though a bucket of snow-water had been dashed onto his face, and he heard a voice say, "By Allah, here is another who lives. Heart up, friend; you are not dead yet, and soon you will be able to break your fast"—and opening his eyes, he found himself staring up at a burly Afghan whose features seemed vaguely familiar to him, though at the moment he could not place him.

"I am attached to the household of the Chief Minister's first secretary," supplied the stranger helpfully, "and you I think are Syed Akbar in the service of Munshi Naim Shah: I have seen you in his office. Come now, up with you—it grows late. Take my arm . . ." The nameless Samaritan helped Ash to his feet and guided him out of the compound and towards the Shah Shahie Gate, talking the while.

The sky ahead was softening to evening and the far snows were already rose-coloured from the sunset; but even here in the smoke-filled alleyways between the houses the corporate voice of the mob was still clearly audible, and Ash checked and said confusedly: "I must go back . . . I thank you for your help, but—but I must go back. I cannot leave . . ."

"You are too late, my friend," said the man softly, "your friends are all dead. But as the mob are now looting the buildings and will be too busy stealing and destroying to trouble themselves with anything else, if we leave quickly we shall do so without being molested."

"Who are you?" demanded Ash in a hoarse whisper, pulling back against the arm that would have urged him forward. "What are you?"

"I am known here as Sobhat Khan, though that is not my name. And like you I am a servant of the Sirkar, who gathers news for the Sahib-log."

Ash opened his mouth to refute the charge and then shut it again without speaking; and seeing this the man grinned and said: "No, I would not have believed you, for an hour ago I spoke with the Sirdar-Bahadur Nakshband

Khan in the house of Wali Mohammed. It was he who gave me a certain key and bade me unlock your door as soon as the fighting was over, which I did—only to find that your room was empty and that there was a hole in one wall large enough for a man to creep through. I went through that hole and saw where the floorboards had been torn up, and looking down, saw also by what means you had escaped. Whereupon I came swiftly to the compound to search for you among the dead, and by good fortune found you living. Now let us leave this place while we can, for once the sun has set the looters will remember their stomachs and hurry home to break the day's fast. Hark to them—"

He cocked his head, listening to the distant sound of shouting and laughter that accompanied the work of destruction, and as he urged Ash forward, said scornfully: "The fools think that because they have slain four *Angrezis* they have rid the land of foreigners. But once the news of this day's doings reaches India the English will come to Kabul, which will spell disaster for them and their Amir. And also for the English—of that we can be sure!"

"How so?" asked Ash incuriously, stumbling obediently forward and discovering with relief that his strength was returning to him and his brain becoming clearer with every step.

"Because they will depose the Amir," replied the spy Sobhat; "and I do not think that they will put his son on the *gadi* in his place. Afghanistan is no country to be ruled by a child. This will leave his brothers, who have no following and would not last long if the English tried to put either on the throne, and his cousin Abdur Rahman; who though a bold man and a good fighter they distrust, because he took refuge with the Russ-log. Therefore I will make you a prophecy. In five years' time, or it may be less, Abdur Rahman will be Amir of Afghanistan, and then this country, upon which the English have twice waged war because (so they said) they feared that it might fall into the hands of the Russ-log and thereby endanger their hold on Hindustan, will be ruled by a man who owes all to those same Russ-log and . . . Ah, it is as I thought; the sentries have left to join in the looting and there is no one to stay us."

He hurried Ash through the unguarded gate and

1174

turned along the dusty road that led past the citadel, in the direction of Nakshband Khan's house. "Wherefore," continued the spy, "all this war and killing will have been in vain, for my countrymen have long memories, and neither Abdur Rahman nor his heirs, or his people who have fought two wars and engaged in countless Border battles with the English, will forget these things. In the years to come they will still remember the English as their enemies—an enemy whom they have defeated. But the Russ-log, whom they have neither fought against nor defeated, they will look upon as their friends and allies. This I told Cavagnari-Sahib when I warned him that the time was not ripe for a British Mission in Kabul, but he would not believe me."

"No," said Ash slowly. "I too . . ."

"Ha, so you also were one of Cavagnari-Sahib's men? I thought as much. He was a great Sirdar, and one who spoke every tongue of this country. But for all his cunning and his great knowledge he did not know the true heart or mind of Afghanistan, else he would not have persisted in coming here. Well, he is dead—as are all whom he brought here with him. It has been a great killing: and soon there will be more . . . much more. This has been a black day for Kabul, an evil day. Do not linger here too long my friend. It is not a safe place for such as you and I. Can you walk alone from here? Good. Then I will leave you, since I have much to do. No, no, do not thank me. *Par makhe da kha.*"

He turned and strode away across country in the direction of the river, and Ash went on alone and reached Nakshband Khan's house without incident.

The Sirdar had returned half an hour earlier, his friend Wali Mohammed having smuggled him out of the Bala Hissar in disguise as soon as the firing stopped. But Ash did not wish to see him.

There was only one person he wanted to see or speak to just then—though even to her he could not bear to talk of what he had seen that day. Nor did he go to her at once, for the horrified expression of the servant who opened the door to him showed him too clearly that his battered face and blood-drenched clothing suggested a mortally wounded man, and even though Juli would have learned by now that he had been securely locked up and

1175

therefore (as far as the Sirdar knew) could have come to no harm, to appear before her in his present state would only add to the terrors that she must have endured during that tragic, interminable day.

Ash sent instead for Gul Baz; who had spent the greater part of the day on guard outside the door leading into the rooms that Nakshband Khan had set aside for the use of his guests, in order to prevent Anjuli-Begum from running through the streets to the Sahib's place of work in the Bala Hissar—which she had attempted to do once it became clear that the Residency was being besieged. In the end reason had prevailed; but Gul Baz was taking no chances, and after that he had remained at his post until the Sirdar returned with the welcome news that he had taken steps to ensure the Sahib's safety. Not that the Sahib's present appearance justified that claim.

But Gul Baz had asked no questions, and done his work so well that by the time Ash went up to see his wife the worst of the damage had been either repaired or hidden, and he was clean again. Nevertheless Anjuli, who had been sitting on a low rush stool by the window and had leapt up joyfully when she heard his step on the stairs, sank back again when she saw his face, her knees weak from shock and her hands at her throat, because it seemed to her that her husband had aged thirty years since he had left her at dawn that morning, and that he had come back to her an old man. So aged and so altered that he might almost have been a stranger . . .

She gave a little wordless cry and stretched out her arms to him, and Ash came to her, walking like a drunken man, and falling on his knees, hid his face in her lap and wept.

The room darkened about them, and outside it lights began to blossom in the windows of the city and on the steep slopes of the Bala Hissar as throughout Kabul men, women and children finished their evening prayers and sat down to break their fast. For though the Residency still burned and hundreds of men had died that day, the evening meal of Ramadan would still have been prepared; and as the spy Sobhat had predicted, the hungry mob had left the ransacked, blood-soaked shambles that only that morning had been a peaceful compound, to hurry home in droves in order to eat and drink with their families and boast of the deeds they had done that day.

And in the same hour, on the other side of the world, a telegram was being handed in to the Foreign Office in London that read: *All well with the Kabul Embassy*.

At long last Ash sighed and lifted his head, and Anjuli took his ravaged face between her cool palms and bent to kiss him, still without speaking. Only when they were seated side by side on the carpet by the window, her hand in his and her hand on his shoulder, did she say quietly: "He is dead, then."

"Yes."

"And the others?"

"They too. They are all dead: and I—I had to stand there and watch them die one by one without being able to do anything to help them. My best friend and close on four score of my own Regiment. And others too—so many others . . ."

Anjuli felt the shudder that racked him and said: "Do you wish to tell me of it?"

"Not now. Some day perhaps. But not now . . ."

There was a cough outside the door and Gul Baz scratched on the panels requesting permission to enter, and when Anjuli had withdrawn to the inner room he came in bearing lamps and accompanied by two of the household servants. The latter carried trays of cooked food, fruit and glasses of snow-cooled sherbet, and brought a message from their master to say that after the exigencies of the day he thought that his guest would prefer to eat alone that night.

Ash was grateful for the thought, as during Ramadan it was the custom of the house for the men-folk to take the evening meal together, the women doing the same in the Zenana Quarters, and he had not been looking forward to the prospect of being forced to listen to a discussion of the harrowing events of the day; or worse still, having to take part in it. But later on, when the meal was over and Gul Baz came to remove the trays, another servant scratched on the door to ask if Syed Akbar could spare the time to see the Sirdar-Sahib, who greatly desired to speak with him; and though Ash would have excused himself, Gul Baz spoke for him, accepting the invitation and saying that his master would be down shortly.

The servant murmured an acknowledgement and left, and as his footsteps retreated Ash said angrily: "Who gave you leave to speak for me? You will now go down yourself to the Sirdar-Sahib and make my apologies to him, because I will see no one tonight: no one, do you hear?"

"I hear," said Gul Baz quietly. "But you will have to see him, for what he has to say is of great import, so—"

"He can say it tomorrow," interrupted Ash brusquely. "Let there be no more talk. You may go."

"We must all go," said Gul Baz grimly. "You and the Memsahib, and myself also. And we must go tonight."

"We . . . ? What talk is this? I do not understand. Who says so?"

"The whole household," said Gul Baz, "the women-folk more loudly than the rest. And because they will put great pressure upon him, the Sirdar-Bahadur may have no remedy but to warn you of it when he sees you tonight. Of that I was sure even before you returned here, for I spoke with certain servants of the Sirdar's friend, Wali Mohammed Khan, with whom he took refuge today when they brought him back to this house. Since then I have listened to much more talk, and learned many things that you as yet do not know. Will you hear them?"

Ash stared at him for a long moment, and then, motioning him to sit, sat down himself on Anjuli's rush stool to listen, while Gul Baz hunkered down on the floor and began to speak. According to Gul Baz, Wali Mohammed Khan had thought along the same lines as the spy Sohbat, and decided that his friend's best chance of leaving the Bala Hissar and reaching his own house in safety lay in going while the mob were engaged in looting the Residency. He had lost no time in arranging it and had, apparently, been only too anxious to get rid of his guest . . .

"Being greatly afraid," said Gul Baz, "that once the killing and looting is done, many who took part in that will turn to searching for fugitives, since it is already being said that two sepoys who were caught up in the fighting and unable to get back to their fellows were saved from death by friends among the mob, and are now in hiding in the city—or perchance in the Bala Hissar itself. There is also another sepoy who is known to have gone into the Great Bazaar to buy *atta* before the fight began, and could not return, as well as the three sowars who rode out with the grass-cutters. This the servants of Wali Mohammed Khan told us when they brought our Sirdar back in disguise after the fighting at the Residency Koti was over.

And hearing it, the folk in this house also became afraid. They fear that tomorrow the mob will turn to searching for these fugitives and attacking anyone whom they suspect of harbouring them or of being a 'Cavagnari-ite.' And that the Sirdar-Bahadur's life may be endangered, because he once served with the Guides. Wherefore they have urged him to leave at once for his house in Aoshar, and remain there until this trouble is past. This he has agreed to do, for he was recognized and sorely mishandled this morning."

"I know. I saw him," said Ash; "and I think he does right to go. But why us?"

"His household insist that he must send you and your Memsahib away now—tonight. For they say that if men should come here asking questions and demanding to search the house, they will become suspicious when they find strangers who cannot give a good account of themselves—such as a man who is not of Kabul and who may well be a spy, and a woman who claims to be Turkish. Foreigners . . ."

"Dear God," whispered Ash. "Even here!"

Gul Baz shrugged and spread out his hands: "Sahib, most men and all women can be hard and cruel when their homes and families are threatened. Also the ignorant everywhere are suspicious of strangers or those who in any way differ from themselves."

"That I have already learned to my cost," retorted Ash bitterly. "But I did not think that the Sirdar-Sahib would do this to me."

"He will not," said Gul Baz. "He has said that the laws of hospitality are sacred, and he will not break them. He has shut his ears and refused to listen to the appeals and arguments of his family and his servants."

"Then why—" began Ash, and stopped. "Yes. Yes, I see. You did right to tell me. The Sirdar-Sahib has been too good a friend to me and mine to be repaid in this fashion. And his people are right: our presence in this house could endanger them all. I will see him now and tell him that I think it best for us to leave at once . . . for our own safety. No need to let him know that you have told me anything."

"So I thought," nodded Gul Baz; and came to his feet: "I will go now and make arrangements." He salaamed and withdrew.

Ash heard the door of the inner room open and turned to see Anjuli standing on the threshold.

"You heard," he said.

It was not a question, but she nodded and came to him, and he rose and took her in his arms, and looking down into her face thought how beautiful she was: more beautiful than ever tonight, for the anxiety and strain that of late he had seen too often in her face had gone, and her candid eyes were serene and unclouded. The lamplight made her skin glow pale gold and the smile on her lovely mouth turned his heart over. He bent his head and kissed it, and after a while he said: "You are not afraid, Larla?"

"To leave Kabul? How could I be? I shall be with you. It has been Kabul and its citadel that I have been afraid of. And after what has taken place today, you are free to go—and must be happy to do so."

"Yes," agreed Ash slowly, "—I had not thought of that . . . I'm free . . . I can go now. But—but what Gul Baz said was true: people everywhere are suspicious of strangers and hostile towards anyone different from themselves, and we two are both strangers, Larla. My people wouldn't accept you because you're both Indian and half-caste, while your people wouldn't accept me because I'm not a Hindu and therefore an outcaste. As for the Mussulmans, to them we are 'Unbelievers' . . . Kafirs—"

"I know, my love. Yet many of different faiths have shown us great kindness."

"Kindness, yes. But they haven't accepted us as one of themselves. Oh dear God, I'm so sick of it all—of intolerance and prejudice and . . . If only there were somewhere we could go where we could just live quietly and be happy, and not be hedged about by rules and trivial, ancient tribal taboos that mustn't be broken. Somewhere where it wouldn't matter who we were or what gods we worshipped or didn't worship, as long as we harmed no one: and were kind, and didn't try to force everyone else into our own mould. There ought to be somewhere like that—somewhere where we can just be ourselves. Where shall we go, Larla?"

"To the valley, where else?" said Anjuli.

"The *valley?*"

"Your mother's valley. The one you used to tell me about, where we were going to build a house and plant fruit trees and keep a goat and a donkey. You cannot have forgotten! I have not."

"But my Heart, that was only a story. Or . . . or I think it may have been. I used to believe it was true and that my mother knew where it was; but afterwards I wasn't so sure: and now I think it was only a tale . . ."

"What does that matter?" asked Juli. "We can make it come true. There must be hundreds of lost valleys among the mountains: thousands. Valleys with streams running through them that would grind our corn, and where we could plant fruit trees and keep goats and build a house. We have only to look, that is all—" and for the first time in several weeks she laughed; that rare, enchanting laugh that Ash had not heard since the day the British Mission came to Kabul. But he did not smile in reply. He said slowly: "That's true, but . . . it would be a hard life. Snow and ice in the winter, and—"

"—and fires of pine-cones and deodar logs, as in all hill villages. Besides, the hill-folk of the Himalayas are a kindly people, soft-spoken, merry, and charitable to all wayfarers. They neither carry arms nor engage in blood-feuds—or make war upon each other. Nor would we need to live in too much isolation, for what is ten *koss* to a hill-man who can walk twice as much in one day? And none would begrudge us a virgin valley that lay too far beyond their home village for their cattle to graze in or their women to collect fodder from. Our hills are not harsh and barren like these of Afghanistan, or in Bhithor, but green with forests and full of streams."

"—and wild animals," said Ash. "Tiger and leopard—and bears. Do not forget that!"

"At least such animals only kill for food. Not for hate or revenge; or because one bows towards Mecca and another burns incense before the gods. Besides, since when has either of us been safe among men? Your foster-mother fled with you to Gulkote to save you from being slain because you, a child, were an *Angrezi;* and later you both fled again because Janoo-Rani would have killed you—as you and I fled from Bhithor fearing death at the hands of the Diwan's men. And now, though we thought ourselves safe in this house we must leave it in haste because our presence here endangers everyone in it and if we stay we may all be slain—you and I for being 'foreigners' and the others for having harboured us. No, Heart's-

1181

dearest, I would rather the wild animals. We shall never lack money, for we have the jewels that were part of my *istri-dhan,* and these we can always sell little by little; a stone at a time as need arises. So let us look for that valley and build our own world."

Ash was silent for a space, and then he said softly: "Our own Kingdom, where all strangers shall be welcome . . . Why not? We could go north, towards Chitral—which will be safer at this time than trying to cross the Border and get back into British India. And from there through Kashmir and Jummu towards the Dur Khaima . . ."

The leaden weight of despair that had fallen on him since he realized that Wally was dead, and that had grown heavier and colder with every word that Gul Baz had spoken, was suddenly lightened, and a measure of the youth and hope that he had lost that day returned to him. Anjuli saw the colour come back to his haggard face and his eyes brighten, and felt his arms tighten about her. He kissed her hard and fiercely, and sweeping her off her feet, carried her into the inner room and sat down on the low bed, holding her close and speaking with his lips buried in her hair . . .

"Once, many years ago, your father's *Mir Akor,* Koda Dad Khan, said something to me that I have never forgotten. I had been complaining that because I was tied to this land by affection and to *Belait* by blood, I must always be two people in one skin; and he replied that one day I might discover in myself a third person—one who was neither Ashok nor Pelham-Sahib, but someone whole and complete: myself. If he was right, then it is time that I found that third person. For Pelham-Sahib is dead: he died today with his friend and the men of his Regiment whom he could not help. As for Ashok and the spy Syed Akbar, those two died many weeks ago—very early one morning on a raft on the Kabul River, near Michni . . . Let us forget all three, and find in their stead a man with an undivided heart: your husband, Larla."

"What are names to me?" whispered Anjuli, her arms tight about his neck. "I will go where you go and live where you live, and pray that the gods will permit me to die before you die, because without you I cannot live. Yet can you be sure that if you turn your back upon your former life you will have no regrets?"

Ash said slowly: "I don't believe that anyone can

1182

have no regrets . . . Perhaps there are times when even God regrets that He created such a thing as man. But one can put them away and not dwell upon them; and I'll have you, Larla . . . that alone is enough happiness for any man."

He kissed her long and lovingly, and then with increasing passion; and after that they did not say anything for a long time, and when at last he spoke again it was to say that he must go down and see the Sirdar at once.

The news that his guests had decided that they were no longer safe in Kabul, but must leave immediately, was more than welcome to the harassed master of the house. But Nakshband Khan was far too polite to betray the fact, and though he agreed that if the mob were to embark on a house-to-house hunt for fugitives or suspected "Cavagnari-ites" they might all find themselves in grave danger, he had insisted that as far as he was concerned, if they wished to stay they were welcome to do so and he would do all he could to protect them. Finding them set on leaving, he had offered to give them any help they might need, and had, in addition, given Ash much good advice.

"I too shall leave the city tonight," confessed the Sirdar. "For until the temper of the mob has cooled, Kabul is no place for one who is known to have served the Sirkar. But I shall not set out until an hour after midnight, by which time all men are asleep—even thieves and cutthroats, who more than any have been too busy today to stay awake this night. I would advise you to do the same, because the moon will not rise until an hour later, and though my road is a short one and easy to follow even on a dark night, yours will not be; and once you are clear of the city you will have need of the moonlight. Where do you go?"

"We go to find our Kingdom, Sirdar-Sahib. Our own Dur Khaima—our far pavilions."

"Your . . . ?"

The Sirdar looked so bewildered that Ash's mouth twitched in the shadow of a smile as he said: "Let me say, rather, that we hope to find it. We go in search of some place where we may live and work in peace, and where men do not kill or persecute each other for sport or at the bidding of Governments—or because others do not think or speak or pray as they do, or have skins of a dif-

1183

ferent colour. I do not know if there is such a place, or, if we find it, whether it will prove too hard to live there, building our own house and growing our own food and raising and teaching our children. Yet others without number have done so in the past. Countless others, since the day that our First Parents were expelled from Eden. And what others have done, we can do."

Nakshband Khan expressed neither surprise nor disapproval. Where a European would have expostulated he merely nodded, and on hearing that Ash's goal was a valley in the Himalayas, agreed that his best plan would be to follow the caravan route to Chitral and from there across the passes into Kashmir. "But you cannot take your own horses," said the Sirdar. "They are not bred for hill work. Also they would attract too much notice. I will give you my four Mongolian ponies in their stead—you will need a spare one. They are small, ill-looking beasts compared with yours, but as strong and hardy as yaks and as sure-footed as mountain goats. You will also need poshteens and Gilgit boots, for as you go further north the nights will become cold."

He had refused to take any payment for his hospitality, saying that the difference in value between Ash's three horses and the sturdy, rough-coated ponies would more than repay him for all. "And now you must sleep," said the Sirdar, "because you have far to ride if you wish to put a safe distance between yourselves and Kabul before the sun rises. I will send a servant to wake you at the half-hour after midnight."

This advice too seemed good, and Ash returned to Juli and told her to take what rest she could, as they would not be leaving the house until one o'clock. He had also spoken to Gul Baz, explaining what he intended to do and asking him to tell Zarin when he returned to Mardan.

"Our ways part here," said Ash. "I have, as you know, made provision for you, and the pension will be paid until you die. That is assured. But no money can repay your care of me and of my wife. For that I can only give you my thanks and my gratitude. I will not forget you."

"Nor I you, Sahib," said Gul Baz. "And were it not that I have a wife and children in Hoti Mardan, and many relatives in the Yusufzai country, I would come with you to look for your kingdom—and maybe live there also. But as it is, I cannot. Nevertheless, we do not part tonight; this is no time for such as the Memsahib to travel through Afghanistan with only one sword to protect her. Two are better and therefore I will go with you as far as Kashmir, and having set you on your way, return from there to Mardan by way of the Murree road to Rawalpindi."

Ash had not argued with him, for apart from the fact that he knew it would be a waste of breath, Gul Baz would be of invaluable help, particularly on the first part of the journey. They talked together for a little while longer before Ash joined his wife in the small inner room, where presently both had fallen asleep, worn out by the terrible strain of that long, agonizing day, and, on Anjuli's part, relieved beyond measure at the prospect of quitting the violent, blood-stained city of Kabul to set out at last for the familiar scenes of her childhood. Those vast forests of fir and deodar, chestnut and rhododendron, where the air smelled sweetly of pine-needles, wild Himalayan roses and maiden-hair fern, and one could hear the sough of the wind in the tree-tops and the sound of running water, and see, high and far away, the serene rampart of the snows and the white wonder of the Dur Khaima.

Thinking of these things she had fallen asleep, happier than she had been for very many days; and Ash too had slept soundly, and woken refreshed.

He left the house half-an-hour earlier than his wife and Gul Baz, for he had an errand to perform that did not call for the presence of any other person. Not even Juli's. He said goodbye to the Sirdar and went away on foot, armed only with the revolver that he carried carefully hidden from sight.

The streets were empty except for the rats that scurried along the gutters and a few lean, prowling cats, and Ash met no one: not even a night watchman. All Kabul seemed to be asleep—and behind barred shutters, for though the night was warm it was noticeable that few if any citizens had cared to leave a single window open, and every house had the appearance of a fortress. Only the gates of the citadel still stood wide and unguarded, the sentries who had been on duty when the Ardal Regiment mutinied having left their posts to join in the attack on the Residency and not returned, and when later ones had followed their example, no one, in the aftermath of the massacre, had thought to post fresh sentries or order the gates to be closed.

There was a lurid glow in the sky above the Bala Hissar, but the houses there, like those in the city, were barred and shuttered; and in darkness—save only for a few lamps in the palace, where the sleepless Amir consulted with his ministers, and the Residency compound where the Mess House still burned with a red glare that rose and fell and flared up again, giving the staring faces of the dead a curious illusion of being alive and aware.

The compound was as silent and deserted as the streets had been, and here too nothing moved except the night wind and the wavering shadows, while the only sound was the steady purr and crackle of the flames, and from somewhere beyond the wall of the citadel, a night-bird crying.

The victorious Afghans had been so occupied with ransacking the buildings and mutilating the bodies of their enemies, that sunset had come upon them before they were aware of it and they had not had time to remove all their own dead. There were still a large number of these lying around the stables and near the entrance to the compound, and it was not too easy to differentiate between them and those jawans who having been Mohammedans, and in many cases Pathans, wore similar clothing. But Wally had been in uniform, and even by that lurid, flickering light it had been easy to pick him out.

He was lying face downward near the gun that he had hoped to capture, his broken sword still in his hand and his head turned a little sideways as though he were asleep. A tall, coltish, brown-haired young man who had celebrated his twenty-third birthday just over two weeks ago . . .

He had been terribly wounded, but unlike William, whose hacked and almost unrecognizable body lay a few yards away, he had not been mutilated after death, and Ash could only suppose that even his enemies had admired the boy's courage and spared him that customary degradation as a tribute to one who had fought a good fight.

Kneeling beside him, Ash turned him over very gently.

Wally's eyes were closed, and *rigor mortis* had not yet stiffened his long body. His face was begrimed by smoke and black powder and smeared with blood and the furrows of sweat, but apart from a shallow cut on the forehead it was unmarked by wounds. And he was smiling . . .

Ash smoothed back the dusty, ruffled hair with a gentle hand, and laying him down, stood up and walked over to the barracks, picking his way between the huddled dead and through the gaping archway.

There was a cistern in the courtyard, and having found it he removed his waist-cloth, tore a strip from it and soaking it in the water, went back to Wally to wash away the blood and grime as gently and carefully as though he were afraid that a rough touch might disturb him. When the young, smiling face was clean again, he brushed the dust from the crumpled tunic, set the sword belt straight above the swathed crimson of the Guides' waist-cloth, and hooked up the open collar.

There was nothing he could do to disguise the gaping swordcuts or the dark, clotted stains that surrounded them. But then they were honourable wounds. When he had set all straight, he took Wally's cold hand in his, and sitting beside him, talked to him as though he were still alive: telling him that what he had done would not be forgotten as long as men remembered the Guides, and that he could sleep quietly, for he had earned his rest—and gone to it as he wished to go, leading his men in battle. Telling him that he, Ash, would remember him always and that if he had a son he would call him Walter "—though I always said it was a terrible name, didn't I, Wally? Never mind, if he turns out half as well as you, we shall have every reason to be proud of him."

He talked too of Juli and the new world they were going to build for themselves—the kingdom where strangers would not be regarded with suspicion and no door would ever be locked against them. And of that future that Wally would have no part in, except as an unfading memory of youth and laughter and unquenchable courage. "We had a lot of good times together, didn't we?" said Ash. "It's good to remember that . . ."

He had taken no account of the passing time and had no idea of how quickly it had gone. He had come to the Residency with the intention of burning or burying Wally's body so that it would not be left to rot in the sun or be torn and disfigured by kites and carrion crows, but now he realized that he could not do this; the ground was too hard for him to dig a grave in it single-handed and the Residency was still burning far too fiercely to make it feasible for him to carry Wally's body into it without being badly burned himself—or possibly overcome by heat and smoke.

Besides, if the body were to disappear, rumours might spread that the Lieutenant-Sahib had not been killed after all but had recovered sufficiently to escape from the compound during the night, and must be hiding somewhere; which would certainly ensure a house-to-house search, and the possible death of a number of innocent people. Anyway, Wally would not know or care what happened to his body now that he had discarded it.

Ash laid down the quiet hand, and getting to his feet, stooped and lifted Wally from the ground, and carrying him to the gun, laid him on it, placing him carefully so that he should not fall. He had led three charges in an effort to take that gun, so it was only right that it should provide him with a bier on which he could lie in state; and when he was found there, those who came would only think that one of their number had placed him there for the same reason that he had been spared mutilation—in recognition of gallantry.

"Goodbye, old fellow," said Ash quietly. "Sleep well!"

He lifted his hand in a gesture of farewell, and it was only as he turned away that he noticed that the stars had begun to pale, and knew that the moon must be rising. He had not realized that so much time had passed since he came into the compound to look for Wally, or that he had stayed far longer than he intended. Juli and Gul Baz would be waiting for him, and wondering if he had come to any harm; and Juli would think—

Ash began to run, and reaching the shadows of the houses around the Arsenal, fled through the network of narrow alleyways and streets to where the Shah Shahie Gate, still unguarded, gaped on a view of the valley and hills of Kabul lying grey in the waning starlight and the first rays of the rising moon.

Anjuli and Gul Baz had been waiting for him in the shelter of a clump of trees by the roadside. But though they had waited there for more than an hour in a growing fever of fear and anxiety, they asked no questions; for which Ash was more grateful than for anything else that either of them could have done for him.

He could not kiss Juli because she was wearing a
1188

bourka, but he put his arms about her and held her close for a brief moment, before turning aside to change quickly into the clothes that Gul Baz had ready for him. It would not do to travel as a scribe, and when he mounted one of the ponies a few minutes later he was to all outward appearances an Afridi, complete with rifle, bandolier and tulwar, and the wicked razor-edged knife that is carried by all men of Afghanistan.

"I am ready," said Ash, "let us go. We have a long way to travel before dawn, and I can smell the morning."

They rode out together from the shadows of the trees, leaving the Bala Hissar and the glowing torch of the burning Residency behind them, and spurred away across the flat lands toward the mountains . . .

And it may even be that they found their Kingdom.

GLOSSARY

1190

Istri-dhan inheritance
Itr scent
Izzat honour

Jawan literally young man; used for soldier
Jehad holy war
Jehanum hell
Jellabies fried sweets made of honey and batter
Jamadar junior Indian officer promoted from the ranks (cavalry or infantry)
Jezail long-barrelled musket
Jheel shallow, marshy lake
Jung-i-lat Sahib Commander-in-Chief

Kola black
Khansamah cook
Khidmatgar waiter at table
Kila fort
Kismet fate
Koss two miles
Kus-kus tatties thick curtains made of woven roots

Larla darling
Lathi long, heavy stick, usually made from bamboo
Lotah small brass water-pot

Machan platform built in a tree for hunting big game
Mahal palace
Mahout elephant driver
Mali gardener
Malik tribal headman
"Maro!" "Strike!"; "Kill!"
"Mubarik!" "Congratulations!" "Well done!"
Mullah Mohammedan priest
Munshi teacher; writer

Narwar coarse webbing
Nauker servant
Nauker-log servants
Nautch-girl dancing girl
Nullah ravine or dry water-course

Ooloo owl

Padishah Empress
Pan betel-nut rolled in a bay leaf and chewed
Panchayat council of five elders
Patarkar small firework
Piara (-i) dear
Pice small coin
Pujah worship
Pulton infantry regiment
Punkah length of matting or heavy material pulled by a rope to make a breeze
Purdah seclusion of women (literally, curtain)
Pushtu the language of the Pathans

Raja King
Rajkumar Prince
Rajkumari Princess
Rakhri pendant worn on the forehead
Rang colour
Rani Queen
Resai quilt
Resaidar junior Indian officer promoted from the ranks (cavalry)
Risaldar senior Indian officer promoted from the ranks (cavalry)
Risaldar-Major the most senior Indian officer promoted from the ranks (cavalry)
Rissala cavalry (regiment)

Sadhu holy man
Sahiba lady
Sahib-log "white-folk"
Saht-bai "seven brothers" small brown birds which go about in groups, usually of seven
Sepoy infantry soldier
Serai caravan hostel
"Shabash!" "Well done!"
Shadi wedding
Shaitan devil
Shamianah large tent
Shikar hunting and shooting
Shikari hunter, finder of game
Shulwa sleeved tunic
Sikunder Dulkhan Alexander the Great
Sirdar Indian officer of high rank
Sirkar the Indian Government
Sowar cavalry trooper
Syce groom

Tálash inquiry
Tamarsha show; festival
Tar telegram (literally, wire)
Tehsildar village headman
Tiffin lunch
Tonga two-wheeled horse-drawn vehicle
Tulwar curved sword

Yakdan leather trunk, made to be carried on mules
Yuveraj heir to the throne

Zenana women's quarter
Zid resentment
Zulum aggression

ABOUT THE AUTHOR

Only M. M. KAYE could have written a book like *The Far Pavilions*. For fifteen years she has devoted herself to writing this novel, and every page bears the indelible stamp of her own experiences in British India as well as her unparalleled knowledge of its tumultuous and varied history, its legends and its people.

M. M. Kaye was born in Simla, the summer residence of the British viceroy and the city to which she returned every summer for the first ten years of her life. At the time, her father was president of the council of an Indian state and she often accompanied him on official visits to other parts of the country. It was during one of these visits that an Indian first told her a story that had been handed down from one generation to the next—a story of a colorful and impressive royal wedding that was complicated by the efforts of the bride's father to substitute another daughter at the last moment. Many years after hearing this tale, M. M. Kaye stumbled across the same story in a diary kept by a young English officer who had figured in the incident. She remembered the version told to her long ago, and decided that here were the makings of the novel she had always wanted to write—and thus was *The Far Pavilions* born.

After her education in England, she returned to India and married Goff Hamilton, an officer in Queen Victoria's Own Corps of Guides. Her husband's military assignments have taken her all over India as well as Egypt, Kenya, Germany, England, Northern Ireland and Scotland. They have two daughters—Carolyn, married to American Tom Bachman, and actress Nichola Hamilton—and two small grandchildren, James and Mollie.

M. M. Kaye is the author of several children's books, eight romantic thrillers and two historical novels—including *Shadow of the Moon*, a sweeping epic of love and war in India during the great mutiny of 1857. First released in an abbreviated version in 1957, *Shadow of the Moon* has been published in its entirety by St. Martin's Press.

M. M. Kaye's most recent novel by Bantam is *Trade Wind*.